The Big Book of

Christmas

MYSTERIES

The Big Book of

Christmas

MYSTERIES

Edited and with an Introduction by

OTTO PENZLER

VINTAGE CRIME/BLACK LIZARD

VINTAGE BOOKS

A DIVISION OF RANDOM HOUSE LLC

NEW YORK

A VINTAGE CRIME/BLACK LIZARD ORIGINAL, OCTOBER 2013

Introductions and compilation copyright © 2013 by Otto Penzler

Owing to limitations of space, permissions to reprint
previously published material appear on pages 651–653.

Library of Congress Cataloging-in-Publication Data
The big book of Christmas mysteries / edited and with an introduction by Otto Penzler.
pages cm
ISBN 978-0-345-80298-9 (trade pbk.)—ISBN 978-0-345-80299-6 (ebook)
1. Christmas stories.   2. Detective and mystery stories.
I. Penzler, Otto, editor of compilation.
PN6071.C6B515 2013
808.8'0334—dc23   2013014764

Book design by Christopher Zucker
Cover design by Joe Montgomery

www.vintagebooks.com

Printed in the United States of America
10 9 8 7 6 5 4 3 2 1

For Bradford Morrow
An original and wonderful writer,
a wise and valued friend

Contents

CONTENTS

Introduction

BY OTTO PENZLER

IT IS NO GREAT profundity to exclaim that Christmas is the happiest time of the year for all but the most churlish, those who claim they can't wait for the season to be over because they hate the forced (to them) cheerfulness, the religious aspects of the celebration of the birth of Jesus Christ (though, of course, there is no biblical or other evidence to suggest that Jesus was born on December 25), or the crass commercialism of the whole thing.

These curmudgeons will like this book.

While most of us are busy shopping for gifts for those we love, or decorating a home and putting up a Christmas tree and hanging mistletoe, and generally enjoying the extra warmth of hellos from friends and shopkeepers, these unsympathetic souls will find solace in the fact that crime, violence, and even murder continue to flourish at what should be a time of peace, joy, and love.

Mystery fiction set during the Christmas season has been with us for a long time, and it is astonishing how many authors have turned their pens and wicked thoughts to this time of year. Perhaps this is because violence seems so out of character, so inappropriate, for this time of year that it takes on extra weight. Think of how often terrible events have been recounted with the sad or angry exclamation, "and at Christmastime!"

It is impossible to think of Christmas stories without first and immediately turning to Charles Dickens, who wrote *A Christmas Carol*, the greatest of all Christmas tales. It enjoyed enormous popularity when it was written in 1843 and it has remained in our hearts ever since, not only as a book but as beloved motion pictures, filmed again and again for each generation to appreciate anew (though none are as good as the version that stars Alastair Sim). It added a word to the English language, as everyone knows what it means to be a "Scrooge," and it changed a holiday tradition. When Ebenezer Scrooge asked a street urchin to fetch the biggest turkey in the window of the poulterer, all of England reconsidered the standard Christmas treat, which had been a roast goose.

As a pure ghost story, *A Christmas Carol* doesn't appear in this collection of crime and mystery tales and, besides, it is readily available in a multitude of editions. Many of the stories in this anthology, on the other hand, are not readily available and, in fact, are almost impossible to find anywhere else. There is a cliché about anthologies (and clichés *become* clichés because they are true) that compares them to a good party, where you see old friends and meet new ones.

Mystery readers will probably be somewhat familiar with the stories by Agatha Christie, Arthur Conan Doyle, and Ellery Queen, even if they haven't read them in a while. But few will have read the more obscure stories by Edgar Wallace, Norvell Page, Mary Roberts Rinehart, or Ethel Lina White.

The variety of subjects and styles may be surprising, ranging from truly chilling to heart-warming to hilarious to puzzling. This is no accident, of course, since genuinely talented authors have their own voices and, like snowflakes, no two are alike (though, to be fair, no one has ever proven that this is true of snowflakes, nor are they likely to do so anytime soon).

Christmas has, for good reasons, been a season for a greater amount of reading than most other times of the year. In times long past, when families and friends gathered, entertainment was more limited than it is nowadays. Wealthier families had musical instruments, and it was common for young ladies especially to enhance their list of accomplishments by playing a pianoforte, harpsichord, or other music-making device. But a group-friendly entertainment that cut across most socioeconomic strata was reading aloud from a book, and there was no better time than when the seemingly endless workday was shuttled aside for a while.

Today, books remain one of the most popular gift items at Christmas, as do electronic readers, so the valued tradition of books and reading remains an integral part of the season. There are tales between these covers that would make especially worthy read-aloud pleasures for groups of neighbors, family, and friends to enjoy together. Go ahead, gather everyone near the Christmas tree, hand out some sweets and the appropriate liquid refreshment, find a comfortable chair, and read aloud Ed McBain's "And All Through the House" or Josephine Bell's "The Carol Singers." It may not be better than watching *A Christmas Carol* or *It's a Wonderful Life* on television, but it will be the kind of evening that will be talked about with fond memories for years to come.

And, if anyone fails to fully appreciate the joys of this gentle, old-fashioned activity, why, then, you can just beat them to death.

—OTTO PENZLER
Christmas 2012
New York

A TRADITIONAL
Little Christmas

THE ADVENTURE OF THE CHRISTMAS PUDDING

Agatha Christie

IT SEEMS FITTING, SOMEHOW, that the "Mistress of Mystery," the "Queen of Crime," set numerous stories in the cozy world of Christmas. The great talent that Dame Agatha brought to her detective stories was the element of surprise, and what could be more surprising than killing someone at what is meant to be the most peaceful, love-filled time of the year? This splendid story was such a favorite of the author that she used it as the title story of her collection *The Adventure of the Christmas Pudding and a Selection of Entrées* (London, Collins, 1960).

The Adventure of the Christmas Pudding

AGATHA CHRISTIE

I

"I REGRET EXCEEDINGLY——" SAID M. Hercule Poirot.

He was interrupted. Not rudely interrupted. The interruption was suave, dexterous, persuasive rather than contradictory.

"Please don't refuse offhand, M. Poirot. There are grave issues of State. Your co-operation will be appreciated in the highest quarters."

"You are too kind," Hercule Poirot waved a hand, "but I really cannot undertake to do as you ask. At this season of the year——"

Again Mr. Jesmond interrupted. "Christmas time," he said, persuasively. "An old-fashioned Christmas in the English countryside."

Hercule Poirot shivered. The thought of the English countryside at this season of the year did not attract him.

"A good old-fashioned Christmas!" Mr. Jesmond stressed it.

"Me—I am not an Englishman," said Hercule Poirot. "In my country, Christmas, it is for the children. The New Year, that is what we celebrate."

"Ah," said Mr. Jesmond, "but Christmas in England is a great institution and I assure you at Kings Lacey you would see it at its best. It's a wonderful old house, you know. Why, one wing of it dates from the fourteenth century."

Again Poirot shivered. The thought of a fourteenth-century English manor house filled him with apprehension. He had suffered too often in the historic country houses of England. He looked round appreciatively at his comfortable modern flat with its radiators and the latest patent devices for excluding any kind of draught.

"In the winter," he said firmly, "I do not leave London."

"I don't think you quite appreciate, M. Poirot, what a very serious matter this is." Mr. Jesmond glanced at his companion and then back at Poirot.

Poirot's second visitor had up to now said nothing but a polite and formal "How do you do." He sat now, gazing down at his well-polished shoes, with an air of the utmost dejection on his coffee-coloured face. He was a young man, not more than twenty-three, and he was clearly in a state of complete misery.

"Yes, yes," said Hercule Poirot. "Of course the matter is serious. I do appreciate that. His Highness has my heartfelt sympathy."

"The position is one of the utmost delicacy," said Mr. Jesmond.

Poirot transferred his gaze from the young man to his older companion. If one wanted to sum up Mr. Jesmond in a word, the word would have been discretion. Everything about Mr. Jesmond was discreet. His well-cut but inconspicuous clothes, his pleasant, well-bred voice which rarely soared out of an agreeable monotone, his

4

light-brown hair just thinning a little at the temples, his pale serious face. It seemed to Hercule Poirot that he had known not one Mr. Jesmond but a dozen Mr. Jesmonds in his time, all using sooner or later the same phrase—"a position of the utmost delicacy."

"The police," said Hercule Poirot, "can be very discreet, you know."

Mr. Jesmond shook his head firmly.

"Not the police," he said. "To recover the—er—what we want to recover will almost inevitably involve taking proceedings in the law courts and we know so little. We *suspect*, but we do not *know*."

"You have my sympathy," said Hercule Poirot again.

If he imagined that his sympathy was going to mean anything to his two visitors, he was wrong. They did not want sympathy, they wanted practical help. Mr. Jesmond began once more to talk about the delights of an English Christmas.

"It's dying out, you know," he said, "the real old-fashioned type of Christmas. People spend it at hotels nowadays. But an English Christmas with all the family gathered round, the children and their stockings, the Christmas tree, the turkey and plum pudding, the crackers. The snowman outside the window——"

In the interests of exactitude, Hercule Poirot intervened.

"To make a snow-man one has to have the snow," he remarked severely. "And one cannot have snow to order, even for an English Christmas."

"I was talking to a friend of mine in the meteorological office only today," said Mr. Jesmond, "and he tells me that it is highly probable there *will* be snow this Christmas."

It was the wrong thing to have said. Hercule Poirot shuddered more forcefully than ever.

"Snow in the country!" he said. "That would be still more abominable. A large, cold, stone manor house."

"Not at all," said Mr. Jesmond. "Things have changed very much in the last ten years or so. Oil-fired central heating."

"They have oil-fired central heating at Kings Lacey?" asked Poirot. For the first time he seemed to waver.

Mr. Jesmond seized his opportunity. "Yes, indeed," he said, "and a splendid hot water system. Radiators in every bedroom. I assure you, my dear M. Poirot, Kings Lacey is comfort itself in the winter time. You might even find the house *too* warm."

"That is most unlikely," said Hercule Poirot.

With practised dexterity Mr. Jesmond shifted his ground a little.

"You can appreciate the terrible dilemma we are in," he said, in a confidential manner.

Hercule Poirot nodded. The problem was, indeed, not a happy one. A young potentate-to-be, the only son of the ruler of a rich and important native state, had arrived in London a few weeks ago. His country had been passing through a period of restlessness and discontent. Though loyal to the father whose way of life had remained persistently Eastern, popular opinion was somewhat dubious of the younger generation. His follies had been Western ones and as such looked upon with disapproval.

Recently, however, his betrothal had been announced. He was to marry a cousin of the same blood, a young woman who, though educated at Cambridge, was careful to display no Western influences in her own country. The wedding day was announced and the young prince had made a journey to England, bringing with him some of the famous jewels of his house to be reset in appropriate modern settings by Cartier. These had included a very famous ruby which had been removed from its cumbersome old-fashioned necklace and had been given a new look by the famous jewellers. So far so good, but after this came the snag. It was not to be supposed that a young man possessed of much wealth and convivial tastes should not commit a few follies of the pleasanter type. As to that there would have been no censure. Young princes were supposed to amuse themselves in this fashion. For the prince to take the girlfriend of the moment for a walk down Bond Street and bestow upon her an emerald bracelet or a diamond clip as a reward for the pleasure she had afforded him would have been regarded as quite natural and suitable, corresponding in fact to the Cadillac cars which his father invariably presented to his favourite dancing girl of the moment.

But the prince had been far more indiscreet than that. Flattered by the lady's interest, he had displayed to her the famous ruby in its new setting, and had finally been so unwise as to accede to her request to be allowed to wear it—just for one evening!

The sequel was short and sad. The lady had retired from their supper-table to powder her nose. Time passed. She did not return. She had left the establishment by another door and since then had disappeared into space. The important and distressing thing was that the ruby in its new setting had disappeared with her.

These were the facts that could not possibly be made public without the most dire consequences. The ruby was something more than a ruby, it was a historical possession of great significance, and the circumstances of its disappearance were such that any undue publicity about them might result in the most serious political consequences.

Mr. Jesmond was not the man to put these facts into simple language. He wrapped them up, as it were, in a great deal of verbiage. Who exactly Mr. Jesmond was, Hercule Poirot did not know. He had met other Mr. Jesmonds in the course of his career. Whether he was connected with the Home Office, the Foreign Office, or some more discreet branch of public service was not specified. He was acting in the interests of the Commonwealth. The ruby must be recovered.

M. Poirot, so Mr. Jesmond delicately insisted, was the man to recover it.

"Perhaps—yes," Hercule Poirot admitted, "but you can tell me so little. Suggestion—suspicion—all that is not very much to go upon."

"Come now, M. Poirot, surely it is not beyond your powers. Ah, come now."

"I do not always succeed."

But this was mock modesty. It was clear enough from Poirot's tone that for him to undertake a mission was almost synonymous with succeeding in it.

"His Highness is very young," Mr. Jesmond said. "It will be sad if his whole life is to be blighted for a mere youthful indiscretion."

Poirot looked kindly at the downcast young man. "It is the time for follies, when one is young," he said encouragingly, "and for the ordinary young man it does not matter so much. The good papa, he pays up; the family lawyer, he helps to disentangle the inconvenience; the young man, he learns by experience and all ends for the best. In a position such as yours, it is hard indeed. Your approaching marriage——"

"That is it. That is it exactly." For the first time words poured from the young man. "You see she is very, very serious. She takes life very seriously. She has acquired at Cambridge many very serious ideas. There is to be education in my country. There are to be schools. There are to be many things. All in the name of progress, you understand, of democracy. It will not be, she says, like it was in my father's time. Naturally she knows that I will have diversions in London, but not the scandal. No! It is the scandal that matters. You see it is very, very famous, this ruby. There is a long trail behind it, a history. Much bloodshed—many deaths!"

"Deaths," said Hercule Poirot thoughtfully. He looked at Mr. Jesmond. "One hopes," he said, "it will not come to that?"

Mr. Jesmond made a peculiar noise rather like a hen who has decided to lay an egg and then thought better of it.

"No, no, indeed," he said, sounding rather prim. "There is no question, I am sure, of anything of *that* kind."

"You cannot be sure," said Hercule Poirot. "Whoever has the ruby now, there may be others who want to gain possession of it, and who will not stick at a trifle, my friend."

"I really don't think," said Mr. Jesmond, sounding more prim than ever, "that we need enter into speculations of that kind. Quite unprofitable."

"Me," said Hercule Poirot, suddenly becoming very foreign, "me, I explore all the avenues, like the politicians."

Mr. Jesmond looked at him doubtfully. Pulling himself together, he said, "Well, I can take it that is settled, M. Poirot? You will go to Kings Lacey?"

"And how do I explain myself there?" asked Hercule Poirot.

Mr. Jesmond smiled with confidence.

"That, I think, can be arranged very easily," he said. "I can assure you that it will all seem quite natural. You will find the Laceys most charming. Delightful people."

"And you do not deceive me about the oil-fired central heating?"

"No, no, indeed." Mr. Jesmond sounded quite pained. "I assure you you will find every comfort."

"*Tout confort moderne,*" murmured Poirot to himself, reminiscently. "*Eh bien,*" he said, "I accept."

II

The temperature in the long drawing-room at Kings Lacey was a comfortable sixty-eight as Hercule Poirot sat talking to Mrs. Lacey by one of the big mullioned windows. Mrs. Lacey was engaged in needlework. She was not doing *petit point* or embroidering flowers upon silk. Instead, she appeared to be engaged in the prosaic task of hemming dishcloths. As she sewed she talked in a soft reflective voice that Poirot found very charming.

"I hope you will enjoy our Christmas party here, M. Poirot. It's only the family, you know. My granddaughter and a grandson and a friend of his and Bridget who's my great-niece, and Diana who's a cousin and David Welwyn who is a very old friend. Just a family party. But Edwina Morecombe said that that's what you really wanted to see. An old-fashioned Christmas. Nothing could be more old-fashioned than we are! My husband, you know, absolutely lives in the past. He likes everything to be just as it was when he was a boy of twelve years old, and used to come here for his holidays." She smiled to herself. "All the same old things, the Christmas tree and the stockings hung up and the oyster soup and the turkey—two turkeys, one boiled and one roast—and the plum pudding with the ring and the bachelor's button and all the rest of it in it. We can't have sixpences nowadays because they're not pure silver any more. But all the old desserts, the Elvas plums and Carlsbad plums and almonds and raisins, and crystallised fruit and ginger. Dear me, I sound like a catalogue from Fortnum and Mason!"

"You arouse my gastronomic juices, madame."

"I expect we'll all have frightful indigestion by tomorrow evening," said Mrs. Lacey. "One isn't used to eating so much nowadays, is one?"

She was interrupted by some loud shouts and whoops of laughter outside the window. She glanced out.

"I don't know what they're doing out there. Playing some game or other, I suppose. I've always been so afraid, you know, that these young people would be bored by our Christmas here. But not at all, it's just the opposite. Now my own son and daughter and their friends, they used to be rather sophisticated about Christmas. Say it was all nonsense and too much fuss and it would be far better to go out to a hotel somewhere and dance. But the younger generation seem to find all this terribly attractive. Besides," added Mrs. Lacey practically, "schoolboys and schoolgirls are always hungry, aren't they? I think they must starve them at these schools. After all, one does know children of that age each eat about as much as three strong men."

Poirot laughed and said, "It is most kind of you and your husband, madame, to include me in this way in your family party."

"Oh, we're both delighted, I'm sure," said Mrs. Lacey. "And if you find Horace a little gruff," she continued, "pay no attention. It's just his manner, you know."

What her husband, Colonel Lacey, had actually said was: "Can't think why you want one of these damned foreigners here cluttering up Christmas! Why can't we have him some other time? Can't stick foreigners! All right, all right, so Edwina Morecombe wished him on us. What's it got to do with *her*, I should like to know? Why doesn't *she* have him for Christmas?"

"Because you know very well," Mrs. Lacey had said, "that Edwina always goes to Claridge's."

Her husband had looked at her piercingly and said, "Not up to something, are you, Em?"

"Up to something?" said Em, opening very blue eyes. "Of course not. Why should I be?"

Old Colonel Lacey laughed, a deep, rumbling laugh. "I wouldn't put it past you, Em," he said. "When you look your most innocent is when you *are* up to something."

Revolving these things in her mind, Mrs. Lacey went on:

"Edwina said she thought perhaps you might help us . . . I'm sure I don't know quite how, but she said that friends of yours had once found you very helpful in—in a case something like ours. I—well, perhaps you don't know what I'm talking about?"

Poirot looked at her encouragingly. Mrs. Lacey was close on seventy, as upright as a ramrod, with snow-white hair, pink cheeks, blue eyes, a ridiculous nose, and a determined chin.

"If there is anything I can do I shall only be too happy to do it," said Poirot. "It is, I understand, a rather unfortunate matter of a young girl's infatuation."

Mrs. Lacey nodded. "Yes. It seems extraordinary that I should—well, want to talk to you about it. After all, you *are* a perfect stranger . . ."

"*And* a foreigner," said Poirot, in an understanding manner.

"Yes," said Mrs. Lacey, "but perhaps that makes it easier, in a way. Anyhow, Edwina seemed to think that you might perhaps know something—how shall I put it—something useful about this young Desmond Lee-Wortley."

Poirot paused a moment to admire the inge-nuity of Mr. Jesmond and the ease with which he had made use of Lady Morecombe to further his own purposes.

"He has not, I understand, a very good reputation, this young man?" he began delicately.

"No, indeed, he hasn't! A very bad reputation! But that's no help so far as Sarah is concerned. It's never any good, is it, telling young girls that men have a bad reputation? It—it just spurs them on!"

"You are so very right," said Poirot.

"In my young day," went on Mrs. Lacey. "(Oh dear, that's a very long time ago!) We used to be warned, you know, against certain young men, and of course it *did* heighten one's interest in them, and if one could possibly manage to dance with them, or to be alone with them in a dark conservatory——" She laughed. "That's why I wouldn't let Horace do any of the things he wanted to do."

"Tell me," said Poirot, "exactly what it is that troubles you?"

"Our son was killed in the War," said Mrs. Lacey. "My daughter-in-law died when Sarah was born so that she has always been with us, and we've brought her up. Perhaps we've brought her up unwisely—I don't know. But we thought we ought always to leave her as free as possible."

"That is desirable, I think," said Poirot. "One cannot go against the spirit of the times."

"No," said Mrs. Lacey, "that's just what I felt about it. And, of course, girls nowadays do do these sort of things."

Poirot looked at her inquiringly.

"I think the way one expresses it," said Mrs. Lacey, "is that Sarah has got in with what they call the coffee-bar set. She won't go to dances or come out properly or be a deb or anything of that kind. Instead she has two rather unpleasant rooms in Chelsea down by the river and wears these funny clothes that they like to wear, and black stockings or bright green ones. Very thick stockings. (So prickly, I always think!) And she goes about without washing or combing her hair."

"*Ça, c'est tout à fait naturel*," said Poirot. "It

is the fashion of the moment. They grow out of it."

"Yes, I know," said Mrs. Lacey. "I wouldn't worry about *that* sort of thing. But you see she's taken up with this Desmond Lee-Wortley and he really has a *very* unsavoury reputation. He lives more or less on well-to-do girls. They seem to go quite mad about him. He very nearly married the Hope girl, but her people got her made a ward in court or something. And of course that's what Horace wants to do. He says he must do it for her protection. But I don't think it's really a good idea, M. Poirot. I mean, they'll just run away together and go to Scotland or Ireland or the Argentine or somewhere and either get married or else live together without getting married. And although it may be contempt of court and all that—well, it isn't really an answer, is it, in the end? Especially if a baby's coming. One has to give in then, and let them get married. And then, nearly always, it seems to me, after a year or two there's a divorce. And then the girl comes home and usually after a year or two she marries someone so nice he's almost dull and settles down. But it's particularly sad, it seems to me, if there is a child, because it's not the same thing, being brought up by a step-father, however nice. No, I think it's much better if we did as we did in my young days. I mean the first young man one fell in love with was *always* someone undesirable. I remember I had a horrible passion for a young man called—now what was his name now?—how strange it is, I can't remember his Christian name at all! Tibbitt, that was his surname. Young Tibbitt. Of course, my father more or less forbade him the house, but he used to get asked to the same dances, and we used to dance together. And sometimes we'd escape and sit out together and occasionally friends would arrange picnics to which we both went. Of course, it was all very exciting and forbidden and one enjoyed it enormously. But one didn't go to the—well, to the *lengths* that girls go nowadays. And so, after a while, the Mr. Tibbitts faded out. And do you know, when I saw him four years later I was surprised what I could *ever* have seen in him! He

seemed to be such a *dull* young man. Flashy, you know. No interesting conversation."

"One always thinks the days of one's own youth are best," said Poirot, somewhat sententiously.

"I know," said Mrs. Lacey. "It's tiresome, isn't it? I mustn't be tiresome. But all the same I *don't* want Sarah, who's a dear girl really, to marry Desmond Lee-Wortley. She and David Welwyn, who is staying here, were always such friends and so fond of each other, and we did hope, Horace and I, that they would grow up and marry. But of course she just finds him dull now, and she's absolutely infatuated with Desmond."

"I do not quite understand, madame," said Poirot. "You have him here now, staying in the house, this Desmond Lee-Wortley?"

"That's *my* doing," said Mrs. Lacey. "Horace was all for forbidding her to see him and all that. Of course, in Horace's day, the father or guardian would have called round at the young man's lodgings with a horse whip! Horace was all for forbidding the fellow the house, and forbidding the girl to see him. I told him that was quite the wrong attitude to take. 'No,' I said. 'Ask him down here. We'll have him down for Christmas with the family party.' Of course, my husband said I was mad! But I said, 'At any rate, dear, let's *try* it. Let her see him in *our* atmosphere and *our* house and we'll be very nice to him and very polite, and perhaps then he'll seem less interesting to her!' "

"I think, as they say, you *have* something there, madame," said Poirot. "I think your point of view is very wise. Wiser than your husband's."

"Well, I hope it is," said Mrs. Lacey doubtfully. "It doesn't seem to be working much yet. But of course he's only been here a couple of days." A sudden dimple showed in her wrinkled cheek. "I'll confess something to you, M. Poirot. I myself can't help liking him. I don't mean I *really* like him, with my *mind*, but I can feel the charm all right. Oh yes, I can see what Sarah sees in him. But I'm an old enough woman and have enough experience to know that he's absolutely no good. Even if I *do* enjoy his company. Though I do think," added Mrs. Lacey, rather wistfully, "he has *some* good points. He asked if he might bring his sister here, you know. She's had an operation and was in hospital. He said it was so sad for her being in a nursing home over Christmas and he wondered if it would be too much trouble if he could bring her with him. He said he'd take all her meals up to her and all that. Well now, I do think that *was* rather nice of him, don't you, M. Poirot?"

"It shows a consideration," said Poirot, thoughtfully, "which seems almost out of character."

"Oh, I don't know. You can have family affections at the same time as wishing to prey on a rich young girl. Sarah will be *very* rich, you know, not only with what we leave her—and of course that won't be very much because most of the money goes with the place to Colin, my grandson. But her mother was a very rich woman and Sarah will inherit all her money when she's twenty-one. She's only twenty now. No, I do think it was nice of Desmond to mind about his sister. And he didn't pretend she was anything very wonderful or that. She's a shorthand typist, I gather—does secretarial work in London. And he's been as good as his word and does carry up trays to her. Not all the time, of course, but quite often. So I think he has some nice points. But all the same," said Mrs. Lacey with great decision, "I don't want Sarah to marry him."

"From all I have heard and been told," said Poirot, "that would indeed be a disaster."

"Do you think it would be possible for you to help us in any way?" asked Mrs. Lacey.

"I think it is possible, yes," said Hercule Poirot, "but I do not wish to promise too much. For the Mr. Desmond Lee-Wortleys of this world are clever, madame. But do not despair. One can, perhaps, do a little something. I shall, at any rate, put forth my best endeavours, if only in gratitude for your kindness in asking me here for this Christmas festivity." He looked round him. "And it cannot be so easy these days to have Christmas festivities."

"No, indeed," Mrs. Lacey sighed. She leaned forward. "Do you know, M. Poirot, what I really dream of—what I would love to have?"

"But tell me, madame."

"I simply long to have a small, modern bungalow. No, perhaps not a bungalow exactly, but a small, modern, easy to run house built somewhere in the park here, and live in it with an absolutely up-to-date kitchen and no long passages. Everything easy and simple."

"It is a very practical idea, madame."

"It's not practical for me," said Mrs. Lacey. "My husband *adores* this place. He *loves* living here. He doesn't mind being slightly uncomfortable, he doesn't mind the inconveniences, and he would hate, simply *hate*, to live in a small modern house in the park!"

"So you sacrifice yourself to his wishes?"

Mrs. Lacey drew herself up. "I do not consider it a sacrifice, M. Poirot," she said. "I married my husband with the wish to make him happy. He has been a good husband to me and made me very happy all these years, and I wish to give happiness to him."

"So you will continue to live here," said Poirot.

"It's not really too uncomfortable," said Mrs. Lacey.

"No, no," said Poirot, hastily. "On the contrary, it is most comfortable. Your central heating and your bath water are perfection."

"We spent a lot of money in making the house comfortable to live in," said Mrs. Lacey. "We were able to sell some land. Ripe for development, I think they call it. Fortunately right out of sight of the house on the other side of the park. Really rather an ugly bit of ground with no nice view, but we got a very good price for it. So that we have been able to have as many improvements as possible."

"But the service, madame?"

"Oh, well, that presents less difficulty than you might think. Of course, one cannot expect to be looked after and waited upon as one used to be. Different people come in from the village. Two women in the morning, another two to cook lunch and wash it up, and different ones again in the evening. There are plenty of people who want to come and work for a few hours a day. Of course for Christmas we are very lucky. My dear Mrs. Ross always comes in every Christmas. She is a wonderful cook, really first-class. She retired about ten years ago, but she comes in to help us in any emergency. Then there is dear Peverell."

"Your butler?"

"Yes. He is pensioned off and lives in the little house near the lodge, but he is so devoted, and he insists on coming to wait on us at Christmas. Really, I'm terrified, M. Poirot, because he's so old and so shaky that I feel certain that if he carries anything heavy he will drop it. It's really an agony to watch him. And his heart is not good and I'm afraid of his doing too much. But it would hurt his feelings dreadfully if I did not let him come. He hems and hahs and makes disapproving noises when he sees the state our silver is in and within three days of being here, it is all wonderful again. Yes. He is a dear faithful friend." She smiled at Poirot. "So you see, we are all set for a happy Christmas. A white Christmas, too," she added as she looked out of the window. "See? It is beginning to snow. Ah, the children are coming in. You must meet them, M. Poirot."

Poirot was introduced with due ceremony. First, to Colin and Michael, the schoolboy grandson and his friend, nice polite lads of fifteen, one dark, one fair. Then to their cousin, Bridget, a black-haired girl of about the same age with enormous vitality.

"And this is my granddaughter, Sarah," said Mrs. Lacey.

Poirot looked with some interest at Sarah, an attractive girl with a mop of red hair; her manner seemed to him nervy and a trifle defiant, but she showed real affection for her grandmother.

"And this is Mr. Lee-Wortley."

Mr. Lee-Wortley wore a fisherman's jersey and tight black jeans; his hair was rather long and it seemed doubtful whether he had shaved that morning. In contrast to him was a young man introduced as David Welwyn, who was solid and quiet, with a pleasant smile, and rather obviously addicted to soap and water. There was one other member of the party, a handsome, rather intense-looking girl who was introduced as Diana Middleton.

Tea was brought in. A hearty meal of scones, crumpets, sandwiches, and three kinds of cake. The younger members of the party appreciated the tea. Colonel Lacey came in last, remarking in a non-committal voice:

"Hey, tea? Oh yes, tea."

He received his cup of tea from his wife's hand, helped himself to two scones, cast a look of aversion at Desmond Lee-Wortley, and sat down as far away from him as he could. He was a big man with bushy eyebrows and a red, weather-beaten face. He might have been taken for a farmer rather than the lord of the manor.

"Started to snow," he said. "It's going to be a white Christmas all right."

After tea the party dispersed.

"I expect they'll go and play with their tape recorders now," said Mrs. Lacey to Poirot. She looked indulgently after her grandson as he left the room. Her tone was that of one who says, "The children are going to play with their toy soldiers."

"They're frightfully technical, of course," she said, "and very grand about it all."

The boys and Bridget, however, decided to go along to the lake and see if the ice on it was likely to make skating possible.

"I thought we could have skated on it this morning," said Colin. "But old Hodgkins said no. He's always so terribly careful."

"Come for a walk, David," said Diana Middleton, softly.

David hesitated for half a moment, his eyes on Sarah's red head. She was standing by Desmond Lee-Wortley, her hand on his arm, looking up into his face.

"All right," said David Welwyn, "yes, let's."

Diana slipped a quick hand through his arm and they turned towards the door into the garden. Sarah said:

"Shall we go, too, Desmond? It's fearfully stuffy in the house."

"Who wants to walk?" said Desmond. "I'll get my car out. We'll go along to the Speckled Boar and have a drink."

Sarah hesitated for a moment before saying:

"Let's go to Market Ledbury to the White Hart. It's much more fun."

Though for all the world she would not have put it into words, Sarah had an instinctive revulsion from going down to the local pub with Desmond. It was, somehow, not in the tradition of Kings Lacey. The women of Kings Lacey had never frequented the bar of the Speckled Boar. She had an obscure feeling that to go there would be to let old Colonel Lacey and his wife down. And why not? Desmond Lee-Wortley would have said. For a moment of exasperation Sarah felt that he ought to know why not! One didn't upset such old darlings as Grandfather and dear old Em unless it was necessary. They'd been very sweet, really, letting her lead her own life, not understanding in the least why she wanted to live in Chelsea in the way she did, but accepting it. That was due to Em of course. Grandfather would have kicked up no end of a row.

Sarah had no illusions about her grandfather's attitude. It was not his doing that Desmond had been asked to stay at Kings Lacey. That was Em, and Em was a darling and always had been.

When Desmond had gone to fetch his car, Sarah popped her head into the drawing-room again.

"We're going over to Market Ledbury," she said. "We thought we'd have a drink there at the White Hart."

There was a slight amount of defiance in her voice, but Mrs. Lacey did not seem to notice it.

"Well, dear," she said, "I'm sure that will be very nice. David and Diana have gone for a walk, I see. I'm so glad. I really think it was a brainwave on my part to ask Diana here. So sad being left a widow so young—only twenty-two—I do hope she marries again *soon*."

Sarah looked at her sharply. "What are you up to, Em?"

"It's my little plan," said Mrs. Lacey gleefully. "I think she's just right for David. Of course I know he was terribly in love with *you*, Sarah dear, but you'd no use for him and I realise that he isn't your type. But I don't want him to go on being unhappy, and I think Diana will really suit him."

"What a matchmaker you are, Em," said Sarah.

"I know," said Mrs. Lacey. "Old women always are. Diana's quite keen on him already, I think. Don't you think she'd be just right for him?"

"I shouldn't say so," said Sarah. "I think Diana's far too—well, too intense, too serious. I should think David would find it terribly boring being married to her."

"Well, we'll see," said Mrs. Lacey. "Anyway, *you* don't want him, do you, dear?"

"No, indeed," said Sarah, very quickly. She added, in a sudden rush, "You *do* like Desmond, don't you, Em?"

"I'm sure he's very nice indeed," said Mrs. Lacey.

"Grandfather doesn't like him," said Sarah.

"Well, you could hardly expect him to, could you?" said Mrs. Lacey reasonably, "but I dare say he'll come round when he gets used to the idea. You mustn't rush him, Sarah dear. Old people are very slow to change their minds and your grandfather *is* rather obstinate."

"I don't care what Grandfather thinks or says," said Sarah. "I shall get married to Desmond whenever I like!"

"I know, dear, I know. But do try and be realistic about it. Your grandfather could cause a lot of trouble, you know. You're not of age yet. In another year you can do as you please. I expect Horace will have come round long before that."

"You're on my side, aren't you, darling?" said Sarah. She flung her arms round her grandmother's neck and gave her an affectionate kiss.

"I want you to be happy," said Mrs. Lacey. "Ah! there's your young man bringing his car round. You know, I like these very tight trousers these young men wear nowadays. They look so smart—only, of course, it does accentuate knock knees."

Yes, Sarah thought, Desmond *had* got knock knees, she had never noticed it before . . .

"Go on, dear, enjoy yourself," said Mrs. Lacey.

She watched her go out to the car, then, remembering her foreign guest, she went along to the library. Looking in, however, she saw that Hercule Poirot was taking a pleasant little nap, and, smiling to herself, she went across the hall and out into the kitchen to have a conference with Mrs. Ross.

"Come on, beautiful," said Desmond. "Your family cutting up rough because you're coming out to a pub? Years behind the times here, aren't they?"

"Of course they're not making a fuss," said Sarah sharply, as she got into the car.

"What's the idea of having that foreign fellow down? He's a detective, isn't he? What needs detecting here?"

"Oh, he's not here professionally," said Sarah. "Edwina Morecombe, my godmother, asked us to have him. I think he's retired from professional work long ago."

"Sounds like a broken-down old cab horse," said Desmond.

"He wanted to see an old-fashioned English Christmas, I believe," said Sarah vaguely.

Desmond laughed scornfully. "Such a lot of tripe, that sort of thing," he said. "How you can stand it I don't know."

Sarah's red hair was tossed back and her aggressive chin shot up.

"I enjoy it!" she said defiantly.

"You can't, baby. Let's cut the whole thing tomorrow. Go over to Scarborough or somewhere."

"I couldn't possibly do that."

"Why not?"

"Oh, it would hurt their feelings."

"Oh, bilge! You know you don't enjoy this childish sentimental bosh."

"Well, not really perhaps, but——" Sarah broke off. She realised with a feeling of guilt

that she was looking forward a good deal to the Christmas celebration. She enjoyed the whole thing, but she was ashamed to admit that to Desmond. It was not the thing to enjoy Christmas and family life. Just for a moment she wished that Desmond had not come down here at Christmas time. In fact, she almost wished that Desmond had not come down here at all. It was much more fun seeing Desmond in London than here at home.

In the meantime the boys and Bridget were walking back from the lake, still discussing earnestly the problems of skating. Flecks of snow had been falling, and looking up at the sky it could be prophesied that before long there was going to be a heavy snowfall.

"It's going to snow all night," said Colin. "Bet you by Christmas morning we have a couple of feet of snow."

The prospect was a pleasurable one.

"Let's make a snow-man," said Michael.

"Good lord," said Colin, "I haven't made a snow-man since—well, since I was about four years old."

"I don't believe it's a bit easy to do," said Bridget. "I mean, you have to know how."

"We might make an effigy of M. Poirot," said Colin. "Give it a big black moustache. There is one in the dressing-up box."

"I don't see, you know," said Michael thoughtfully, "how M. Poirot could ever have been a detective. I don't see how he'd ever be able to disguise himself."

"I know," said Bridget, "and one can't imagine him running about with a microscope and looking for clues or measuring footprints."

"I've got an idea," said Colin. "Let's put on a show for him!"

"What do you mean, a show?" asked Bridget.

"Well, arrange a murder for him."

"What a gorgeous idea," said Bridget. "Do you mean a body in the snow—that sort of thing?"

"Yes. It would make him feel at home, wouldn't it?"

Bridget giggled.

"I don't know that I'd go as far as that."

"If it snows," said Colin, "we'll have the perfect setting. A body and footprints—we'll have to think that out rather carefully and pinch one of Grandfather's daggers and make some blood."

They came to a halt and oblivious to the rapidly falling snow, entered into an excited discussion.

"There's a paintbox in the old schoolroom. We could mix up some blood—crimson-lake, I should think."

"Crimson-lake's a bit too pink, *I* think," said Bridget. "It ought to be a bit browner."

"Who's going to be the body?" asked Michael.

"I'll be the body," said Bridget quickly.

"Oh, look here," said Colin, "*I* thought of it."

"Oh, no, no," said Bridget, "it must be me. It's got to be a girl. It's more exciting. Beautiful girl lying lifeless in the snow."

"Beautiful girl! Ah-ha," said Michael in derision.

"I've got black hair, too," said Bridget.

"What's that got to do with it?"

"Well, it'll show up so well on the snow and I shall wear my red pyjamas."

"If you wear red pyjamas, they won't show the bloodstains," said Michael in a practical manner.

"But they'd look so effective against the snow," said Bridget, "and they've got white facings, you know, so the blood could be on that. Oh, won't it be gorgeous? Do you think he will really be taken in?"

"He will if we do it well enough," said Michael. "We'll have just your footprints in the snow and one other person's going to the body and coming away from it—a man's, of course. He won't want to disturb them, so he won't know that you're not really dead. You don't think," Michael stopped, struck by a sudden idea. The others looked at him. "You don't think he'll be *annoyed* about it?"

"Oh, I shouldn't think so," said Bridget, with facile optimism. "I'm sure he'll understand that we've just done it to entertain him. A sort of Christmas treat."

"I don't think we ought to do it on Christmas Day," said Colin reflectively. "I don't think Grandfather would like that very much."

"Boxing Day then," said Bridget.

"Boxing Day would be just right," said Michael.

"And it'll give us more time, too," pursued Bridget. "After all, there are a lot of things to arrange. Let's go and have a look at all the props."

They hurried into the house.

III

The evening was a busy one. Holly and mistletoe had been brought in in large quantities and a Christmas tree had been set up at one end of the dining-room. Everyone helped to decorate it, to put up the branches of holly behind pictures, and to hang mistletoe in a convenient position in the hall.

"I had no idea anything so archaic still went on," murmured Desmond to Sarah with a sneer.

"We've always done it," said Sarah, defensively.

"What a reason!"

"Oh, don't be tiresome, Desmond. *I* think it's fun."

"Sarah my sweet, you *can't*!"

"Well, not—not really perhaps but—I do in a way."

"Who's going to brave the snow and go to midnight mass?" asked Mrs. Lacey at twenty minutes to twelve.

"Not me," said Desmond. "Come on, Sarah."

With a hand on her arm he guided her into the library and went over to the record case.

"There are limits, darling," said Desmond. "Midnight mass!"

"Yes," said Sarah. "Oh yes."

With a good deal of laughter, donning of coats and stamping of feet, most of the others got off. The two boys, Bridget, David, and Diana set out for the ten minutes' walk to the church through the falling snow. Their laughter died away in the distance.

"Midnight mass!" said Colonel Lacey, snorting. "Never went to midnight mass in my young days. *Mass*, indeed! Popish, that is! Oh, I beg your pardon, M. Poirot."

Poirot waved a hand. "It is quite all right. Do not mind me."

"Matins is good enough for anybody, I should say," said the colonel. "Proper Sunday morning service. 'Hark the herald angels sing,' and all the good old Christmas hymns. And then back to Christmas dinner. That's right, isn't it, Em?"

"Yes, dear," said Mrs. Lacey. "That's what *we* do. But the young ones enjoy the midnight service. And it's nice, really, that they *want* to go."

"Sarah and that fellow don't want to go."

"Well, there, dear, I think you're wrong," said Mrs. Lacey. "Sarah, you know, *did* want to go, but she didn't like to say so."

"Beats me why she cares what that fellow's opinion is."

"She's very young, really," said Mrs. Lacey placidly. "Are you going to bed, M. Poirot? Good-night. I hope you'll sleep well."

"And you, madame? Are you not going to bed yet?"

"Not just yet," said Mrs. Lacey. "I've got the stockings to fill, you see. Oh, I know they're all practically grown up, but they do *like* their stockings. One puts jokes in them! Silly little things. But it all makes for a lot of fun."

"You work very hard to make this a happy house at Christmas time," said Poirot. "I honour you."

He raised her hand to his lips in a courtly fashion.

"Hm," grunted Colonel Lacey, as Poirot departed. "Flowery sort of fellow. Still—he appreciates you."

Mrs. Lacey dimpled up at him. "Have you noticed, Horace, that I'm standing under the mistletoe?" she asked with the demureness of a girl of nineteen.

Hercule Poirot entered his bedroom. It was a large room well provided with radiators. As he went over towards the big four-poster bed he noticed an envelope lying on his pillow. He opened it and drew out a piece of paper. On it was a shakily printed message in capital letters.

DON'T EAT NONE OF THE PLUM PUDDING.
ONE AS WISHES YOU WELL.

Hercule Poirot stared at it. His eyebrows rose. "Cryptic," he murmured, "and most unexpected."

IV

Christmas dinner took place at 2 p.m. and was a feast indeed. Enormous logs crackled merrily in the wide fireplace and above their crackling rose the babel of many tongues talking together. Oyster soup had been consumed, two enormous turkeys had come and gone, mere carcasses of their former selves. Now, the supreme moment, the Christmas pudding was brought in, in state! Old Peverell, his hands and his knees shaking with the weakness of eighty years, permitted no one but himself to bear it in. Mrs. Lacey sat, her hands pressed together in nervous apprehension. One Christmas, she felt sure, Peverell would fall down dead. Having either to take the risk of letting him fall down dead or of hurting his feelings to such an extent that he would probably prefer to be dead than alive, she had so far chosen the former alternative. On a silver dish the Christmas pudding reposed in its glory. A large football of a pudding, a piece of holly stuck in it like a triumphant flag and glorious flames of blue and red rising round it. There was a cheer and cries of "Ooh-ah."

One thing Mrs. Lacey had done: prevailed upon Peverell to place the pudding in front of her so that she could help it rather than hand it in turn round the table. She breathed a sigh of relief as it was deposited safely in front of her.

Rapidly the plates were passed round, flames still licking the portions.

"Wish, M. Poirot," cried Bridget. "Wish before the flame goes. Quick, Gran darling, quick."

Mrs. Lacey leant back with a sigh of satisfaction. Operation Pudding had been a success. In front of everyone was a helping with flames still licking it. There was a momentary silence all round the table as everyone wished hard.

There was nobody to notice the rather curious expression on the face of M. Poirot as he surveyed the portion of pudding on his plate. "DON'T EAT NONE OF THE PLUM PUDDING." What on earth did that sinister warning mean? There could be nothing different about his portion of plum pudding from that of everyone else! Sighing as he admitted himself baffled—and Hercule Poirot never liked to admit himself baffled—he picked up his spoon and fork.

"Hard sauce, M. Poirot?"

Poirot helped himself appreciatively to hard sauce.

"Swiped my best brandy again, eh, Em?" said the colonel good-humouredly from the other end of the table. Mrs. Lacey twinkled at him.

"Mrs. Ross insists on having the best brandy, dear," she said. "She says it makes all the difference."

"Well, well," said Colonel Lacey, "Christmas comes but once a year and Mrs. Ross is a great woman. A great woman and a great cook."

"She is indeed," said Colin. "Smashing plum pudding, this. Mmmm." He filled an appreciative mouth.

Gently, almost gingerly, Hercule Poirot attacked his portion of pudding. He ate a mouthful. It was delicious! He ate another. Something tinkled faintly on his plate. He investigated with a fork. Bridget, on his left, came to his aid.

"You've got something, M. Poirot," she said. "I wonder what it is."

Poirot detached a little silver object from the surrounding raisins that clung to it.

"Oooh," said Bridget, "it's the bachelor's button! M. Poirot's got the bachelor's button!"

Hercule Poirot dipped the small silver button into the finger-glass of water that stood by his plate, and washed it clear of pudding crumbs.

"It is very pretty," he observed.

"That means you're going to be a bachelor, M. Poirot," explained Colin helpfully.

"That is to be expected," said Poirot gravely. "I have been a bachelor for many long years and it is unlikely that I shall change that status now."

"Oh, never say die," said Michael. "I saw in the paper that someone of ninety-five married a girl of twenty-two the other day."

"You encourage me," said Hercule Poirot.

Colonel Lacey uttered a sudden exclamation. His face became purple and his hand went to his mouth.

"Confound it, Emmeline," he roared, "why on earth do you let the cook put glass in the pudding?"

"Glass!" cried Mrs. Lacey, astonished.

Colonel Lacey withdrew the offending substance from his mouth. "Might have broken a tooth," he grumbled. "Or swallowed the damn' thing and had appendicitis."

He dropped the piece of glass into the finger-bowl, rinsed it, and held it up.

"God bless my soul," he ejaculated. "It's a red stone out of one of the cracker brooches." He held it aloft.

"You permit?"

Very deftly M. Poirot stretched across his neighbour, took it from Colonel Lacey's fingers, and examined it attentively. As the squire had said, it was an enormous red stone the colour of a ruby. The light gleamed from its facets as he turned it about. Somewhere around the table a chair was pushed sharply back and then drawn in again.

"Phew!" cried Michael. "How wizard it would be if it was *real*."

"Perhaps it is real," said Bridget hopefully.

"Oh, don't be an ass, Bridget. Why, a ruby of that size would be worth thousands and thousands and thousands of pounds. Wouldn't it, M. Poirot?"

"It would indeed," said Poirot.

"But what *I* can't understand," said Mrs. Lacey, "is how it got into the pudding."

"Oooh," said Colin, diverted by his last mouthful, "I've got the pig. It isn't fair."

Bridget chanted immediately, "Colin's got the pig! Colin's got the pig! Colin is the greedy guzzling *pig*!"

"I've got the ring," said Diana in a clear, high voice.

"Good for you, Diana. You'll be married first, of us all."

"I've got the thimble," wailed Bridget.

"Bridget's going to be an old maid," chanted the two boys. "Yah, Bridget's going to be an old maid."

"Who's got the money?" demanded David. "There's a real ten-shilling piece, gold, in this pudding. I know. Mrs. Ross told me so."

"I think I'm the lucky one," said Desmond Lee-Wortley.

Colonel Lacey's two next-door neighbours heard him mutter, "Yes, you would be."

"*I*'ve got a ring, too," said David. He looked across at Diana. "Quite a coincidence, isn't it?"

The laughter went on. Nobody noticed that M. Poirot carelessly, as though thinking of something else, had dropped the red stone into his pocket.

Mince-pies and Christmas dessert followed the pudding. The older members of the party then retired for a welcome siesta before the tea-time ceremony of the lighting of the Christmas tree. Hercule Poirot, however, did not take a siesta. Instead, he made his way to the enormous old-fashioned kitchen.

"It is permitted," he asked, looking round and beaming, "that I congratulate the cook on this marvellous meal that I have just eaten?"

There was a moment's pause and then Mrs. Ross came forward in a stately manner to meet him. She was a large woman, nobly built with all the dignity of a stage duchess. Two lean grey-haired women were beyond in the scullery washing up and a tow-haired girl was moving to and fro between the scullery and the kitchen. But these were obviously mere myrmidons.

Mrs. Ross was the queen of the kitchen quarters.

"I am glad to hear you enjoyed it, sir," she said graciously.

"Enjoyed it!" cried Hercule Poirot. With an extravagant foreign gesture he raised his hand to his lips, kissed it, and wafted the kiss to the ceiling. "But you are a genius, Mrs. Ross! A genius! *Never* have I tasted such a wonderful meal. The oyster soup"—he made an expressive noise with his lips—"and the stuffing. The chestnut stuffing in the turkey, that was quite unique in my experience."

"Well, it's funny that you should say that, sir," said Mrs. Ross graciously. "It's a very special recipe, that stuffing. It was given me by an Austrian chef that I worked with many years ago. But all the rest," she added, "is just good, plain English cooking."

"And is there anything better?" demanded Hercule Poirot.

"Well, it's nice of you to say so, sir. Of course, you being a foreign gentleman might have preferred the Continental style. Not but what I can't manage Continental dishes, too."

"I am sure, Mrs. Ross, you could manage anything! But you must know that English cooking—*good* English cooking, not the cooking one gets in the second-class hotels or the restaurants—is much appreciated by *gourmets* on the Continent, and I believe I am correct in saying that a special expedition was made to London in the early eighteen hundreds, and a report sent back to France of the wonders of the English puddings. 'We have nothing like that in France,' they wrote. 'It is worth making a journey to London just to taste the varieties and excellencies of the English puddings.' And above all puddings," continued Poirot, well launched now on a kind of rhapsody, "is the Christmas plum pudding, such as we have eaten today. That was a home-made pudding, was it not? Not a bought one?"

"Yes, indeed, sir. Of my own making and my own recipe such as I've made for many, many years. When I came here Mrs. Lacey said that she'd ordered a pudding from a London store to save me the trouble. But no, madam, I said, that may be kind of you but no bought pudding from a store can equal a home-made Christmas one. Mind you," said Mrs. Ross, warming to her subject like the artist she was, "it was made too soon before the day. A good Christmas pudding should be made some weeks before and allowed to wait. The longer they're kept, within reason, the better they are. I mind now that when I was a child and we went to church every Sunday, we'd start listening for the collect that begins 'Stir up O Lord we beseech thee' because that collect was the signal, as it were, that the puddings should be made that week. And so they always were. We had the collect on the Sunday, and that week sure enough my mother would make the Christmas puddings. And so it should have been here this year. As it was, that pudding was only made three days ago, the day before you arrived, sir. However, I kept to the old custom. Everyone in the house had to come out into the kitchen and have a stir and make a wish. That's an old custom, sir, and I've always held to it."

"Most interesting," said Hercule Poirot. "Most interesting. And so everyone came out into the kitchen?"

"Yes, sir. The young gentlemen, Miss Bridget and the London gentleman who's staying here, and his sister and Mr. David and Miss Diana—Mrs. Middleton, I should say—all had a stir, they did."

"How many puddings did you make? Is this the only one?"

"No, sir, I made four. Two large ones and two smaller ones. The other large one I planned to serve on New Year's Day and the smaller ones were for Colonel and Mrs. Lacey when they're alone like and not so many in the family."

"I see, I see," said Poirot.

"As a matter of fact, sir," said Mrs. Lacey, "it was the wrong pudding you had for lunch today."

"The wrong pudding?" Poirot frowned. "How is that?"

"Well, sir, we have a big Christmas mould. A china mould with a pattern of holly and mistletoe on top and we always have the Christmas Day pudding boiled in that. But there was a most unfortunate accident. This morning, when Annie was getting it down from the shelf in the larder, she slipped and dropped it and it broke. Well, sir, naturally I couldn't serve that, could I? There might have been splinters in it. So we had to use the other one—the New Year's Day one, which was in a plain bowl. It makes a nice round but it's not so decorative as the Christmas mould. Really, where we'll get another mould like that I don't know. They don't make things in that size nowadays. All tiddly bits of things. Why, you can't even buy a breakfast dish that'll take a proper eight to ten eggs and bacon. Ah, things aren't what they were."

"No, indeed," said Poirot. "But today that is not so. This Christmas Day has been like the Christmas Days of old, is that not true?"

Mrs. Ross sighed. "Well, I'm glad you say so, sir, but of course I haven't the *help* now that I used to have. Not skilled help, that is. The girls nowadays"—she lowered her voice slightly—"they mean very well and they're very willing but they've not been *trained*, sir, if you understand what I mean."

"Times change, yes," said Hercule Poirot. "I too find it sad sometimes."

"This house, sir," said Mrs. Ross, "it's too large, you know, for the mistress and the colonel. The mistress, she knows that. Living in a corner of it as they do, it's not the same thing at all. It only comes alive, as you might say, at Christmas time when all the family come."

"It is the first time, I think, that Mr. Lee-Wortley and his sister have been here?"

"Yes, sir." A note of slight reserve crept into Mrs. Ross's voice. "A very nice gentleman he is but, well—it seems a funny friend for Miss Sarah to have, according to our ideas. But there—London ways are different! It's sad that his sister's so poorly. Had an operation, she had. She seemed all right the first day she was here, but that very day, after we'd been stirring the puddings, she was took bad again and she's been in bed ever since. Got up too soon after her operation, I expect. Ah, doctors nowadays, they have you out of hospital before you can hardly stand on your feet. Why, my very own nephew's wife . . ." And Mrs. Ross went into a long and spirited tale of hospital treatment as accorded to her relations, comparing it unfavourably with the consideration that had been lavished upon them in older times.

Poirot duly commiserated with her. "It remains," he said, "to thank you for this exquisite and sumptuous meal. You permit a little acknowledgement of my appreciation?" A crisp five-pound note passed from his hand into that of Mrs. Ross, who said perfunctorily:

"You really shouldn't do *that*, sir."

"I insist. I insist."

"Well, it's very kind of you indeed, sir." Mrs. Ross accepted the tribute as no more than her due. "And I wish you, sir, a very happy Christmas and a prosperous New Year."

V

The end of Christmas Day was like the end of most Christmas Days. The tree was lighted, a splendid Christmas cake came in for tea, was greeted with approval but was partaken of only moderately. There was cold supper.

Both Poirot and his host and hostess went to bed early.

"Good-night, M. Poirot," said Mrs. Lacey. "I hope you've enjoyed yourself."

"It has been a wonderful day, madame, wonderful."

"You're looking very thoughtful," said Mrs. Lacey.

"It is the English pudding that I consider."

"You found it a little heavy, perhaps?" asked Mrs. Lacey delicately.

"No, no, I do not speak gastronomically. I consider its significance."

"It's traditional, of course," said Mrs. Lacey. "Well, good-night, M. Poirot, and don't dream too much of Christmas puddings and mince-pies."

"Yes," murmured Poirot to himself as he undressed. "It is a problem certainly, that Christmas plum pudding. There is here something that I do not understand at all." He shook his head in a vexed manner. "Well—we shall see."

After making certain preparations, Poirot went to bed, but not to sleep.

It was some two hours later that his patience was rewarded. The door of his bedroom opened very gently. He smiled to himself. It was as he had thought it would be. His mind went back fleetingly to the cup of coffee so politely handed him by Desmond Lee-Wortley. A little later, when Desmond's back was turned, he had laid the cup down for a few moments on a table. He had then apparently picked it up again and Desmond had had the satisfaction, if satisfaction it was, of seeing him drink the coffee to the last drop. But a little smile lifted Poirot's moustache as he reflected that it was not he but someone else who was sleeping a good sound sleep to-night. "That pleasant young David," said Poirot to himself, "he is worried, unhappy. It will do him no harm to have a night's really sound sleep. And now, let us see what will happen?"

He lay quite still, breathing in an even manner with occasionally a suggestion, but the very faintest suggestion, of a snore.

Someone came up to the bed and bent over him. Then, satisfied, that someone turned away and went to the dressing-table. By the light of a tiny torch the visitor was examining Poirot's belongings neatly arranged on top of the dressing-table. Fingers explored the wallet, gently pulled open the drawers of the dressing-table, then extended the search to the pockets of Poirot's clothes. Finally the visitor approached the bed and with great caution slid his hand under the pillow. Withdrawing his hand, he stood for a moment or two as though uncertain what to do next. He walked round the room looking inside ornaments, went into the adjoining bathroom from whence he presently returned. Then, with a faint exclamation of disgust, he went out of the room.

"Ah," said Poirot, under his breath. "You

have a disappointment. Yes, yes, a serious disappointment. Bah! To imagine, even, that Hercule Poirot would hide something where you could find it!" Then, turning over on his other side, he went peacefully to sleep.

He was aroused next morning by an urgent soft tapping on his door.

"*Qui est là?* Come in, come in."

The door opened. Breathless, red-faced, Colin stood upon the threshold. Behind him stood Michael.

"M. Poirot, M. Poirot."

"But yes?" Poirot sat up in bed. "It is the early tea? But no. It is you, Colin. What has occurred?"

Colin was, for a moment, speechless. He seemed to be under the grip of some strong emotion. In actual fact it was the sight of the nightcap that Hercule Poirot wore that affected for the moment his organs of speech. Presently he controlled himself and spoke.

"I think—M. Poirot, could you help us? Something rather awful has happened."

"Something has happened? But what?"

"It's—it's Bridget. She's out there in the snow. I think—she doesn't move or speak and—oh, you'd better come and look for yourself. I'm terribly afraid—she may be *dead*."

"What?" Poirot cast aside his bed covers. "Mademoiselle Bridget—dead!"

"I think—I think somebody's killed her. There's—there's blood and—oh do come!"

"But certainly. But certainly. I come on the instant."

With great practicality Poirot inserted his feet into his outdoor shoes and pulled a fur-lined overcoat over his pyjamas.

"I come," he said. "I come on the moment. You have aroused the house?"

"No. No, so far I haven't told anyone but you. I thought it would be better. Grandfather and Gran aren't up yet. They're laying breakfast downstairs, but I didn't say anything to Peverell. She—Bridget—she's round the other side of the house, near the terrace and the library window."

"I see. Lead the way. I will follow."

Turning away to hide his delighted grin, Colin led the way downstairs. They went out through the side door. It was a clear morning with the sun not yet high over the horizon. It was not snowing now, but it had snowed heavily during the night and everywhere around was an unbroken carpet of thick snow. The world looked very pure and white and beautiful.

"There!" said Colin breathlessly. "I—it's—*there*!" He pointed dramatically.

The scene was indeed dramatic enough. A few yards away Bridget lay in the snow. She was wearing scarlet pyjamas and a white wool wrap thrown round her shoulders. The white wool wrap was stained with crimson. Her head was turned aside and hidden by the mass of her outspread black hair. One arm was under her body, the other lay flung out, the fingers clenched, and standing up in the centre of the crimson stain was the hilt of a large curved Kurdish knife which Colonel Lacey had shown to his guests only the evening before.

"*Mon Dieu!*" ejaculated M. Poirot. "It is like something on the stage!"

There was a faint choking noise from Michael. Colin thrust himself quickly into the breach.

"I know," he said. "It—it doesn't seem *real* somehow, does it? Do you see those footprints—I suppose we mustn't disturb them?"

"Ah yes, the footprints. No, we must be careful not to disturb those footprints."

"That's what I thought," said Colin. "That's why I wouldn't let anyone go near her until we got you. I thought you'd know what to do."

"All the same," said Hercule Poirot briskly, "first, we must see if she is still alive? Is not that so?"

"Well—yes—of course," said Michael, a little doubtfully, "but you see, we thought—I mean, we didn't like——"

"Ah, you have the prudence! You have read the detective stories. It is most important that nothing should be touched and that the body should be left as it is. But we cannot be sure as yet if it *is* a body, can we? After all, though prudence is admirable, common humanity comes first. We must think of the doctor, must we not, before we think of the police?"

"Oh yes. Of course," said Colin, still a little taken aback.

"We only thought—I mean—we thought we'd better get you before we did anything," said Michael hastily.

"Then you will both remain here," said Poirot. "I will approach from the other side so as not to disturb these footprints. Such excellent footprints, are they not—so very clear? The footprints of a man and a girl going out together to the place where she lies. And then the man's footsteps come back but the girl's—do not."

"They must be the footprints of the murderer," said Colin, with bated breath.

"Exactly," said Poirot. "The footprints of the murderer. A long narrow foot with rather a peculiar type of shoe. Very interesting. Easy, I think, to recognise. Yes, those footprints will be very important."

At that moment Desmond Lee-Wortley came out of the house with Sarah and joined them.

"What on earth are you all doing here?" he demanded in a somewhat theatrical manner. "I saw you from my bedroom window. What's up? Good lord, what's this? It—it looks like——"

"Exactly," said Hercule Poirot. "It looks like murder, does it not?"

Sarah gave a gasp, then shot a quick suspicious glance at the two boys.

"You mean someone's killed the girl—what's-her-name—Bridget?" demanded Desmond. "Who on earth would want to kill her? It's unbelievable!"

"There are many things that are unbelievable," said Poirot. "Especially before breakfast, is it not? That is what one of your classics says. Six impossible things before breakfast." He added: "Please wait here, all of you."

Carefully making a circuit, he approached Bridget and bent for a moment down over the body. Colin and Michael were now both shaking with suppressed laughter. Sarah joined them, murmuring, "What have you two been up to?"

"Good old Bridget," whispered Colin. "Isn't she wonderful? Not a twitch!"

"I've never seen anything look so dead as Bridget does," whispered Michael.

Hercule Poirot straightened up again.

"This is a terrible thing," he said. His voice held an emotion it had not held before.

Overcome by mirth, Michael and Colin both turned away. In a choked voice Michael said:

"What—what must we do?"

"There is only one thing to do," said Poirot. "We must send for the police. Will one of you telephone or would you prefer me to do it?"

"I think," said Colin, "I think—what about it, Michael?"

"Yes," said Michael, "I think the jig's up now." He stepped forward. For the first time he seemed a little unsure of himself. "I'm awfully sorry," he said, "I hope you won't mind too much. It—er—it was a sort of joke for Christmas and all that, you know. We thought we'd—well, lay on a murder for you."

"You thought you would lay on a murder for me? Then this—then this——"

"It's just a show we put on," explained Colin, "to—to make you feel at home, you know."

"Aha," said Hercule Poirot. "I understand. You make of me the April fool, is that it? But today is not April the first, it is December the twenty-sixth."

"I suppose we oughtn't to have done it really," said Colin, "but—but—you don't mind very much, do you, M. Poirot? Come on, Bridget," he called, "get up. You must be half-frozen to death already."

The figure in the snow, however, did not stir.

"It is odd," said Hercule Poirot, "she does not seem to hear you." He looked thoughtfully at them. "It is a joke, you say? You are sure this is a joke?"

"Why, yes." Colin spoke uncomfortably. "We—we didn't mean any harm."

"But why then does Mademoiselle Bridget not get up?"

"I can't imagine," said Colin.

"Come on, Bridget," said Sarah impatiently. "Don't go on lying there playing the fool."

"We really are very sorry, M. Poirot," said Colin apprehensively. "We do really apologise."

"You need not apologise," said Poirot, in a peculiar tone.

"What do you mean?" Colin stared at him. He turned again. "Bridget! Bridget! What's the matter? Why doesn't she get up? Why does she go on lying there?"

Poirot beckoned to Desmond. "*You*, Mr. Lee-Wortley. Come here——"

Desmond joined him.

"Feel her pulse," said Poirot.

Desmond Lee-Wortley bent down. He touched the arm—the wrist.

"There's no pulse . . ." He stared at Poirot. "Her arm's stiff. Good God, she really *is* dead!"

Poirot nodded. "Yes, she is dead," he said. "Someone has turned the comedy into a tragedy."

"Someone—who?"

"There is a set of footprints going and returning. A set of footprints that bears a strong resemblance to the footprints *you* have just made, Mr. Lee-Wortley, coming from the path to this spot."

Desmond Lee-Wortley wheeled round.

"What on earth—— Are you accusing me? *Me*? You're crazy! Why on earth should I want to kill the girl?"

"Ah—why? I wonder . . . Let us see . . ."

He bent down and very gently prised open the stiff fingers of the girl's clenched hand.

Desmond drew a sharp breath. He gazed down unbelievingly. In the palm of the dead girl's hand was what appeared to be a large ruby.

"It's that damn' thing out of the pudding!" he cried.

"Is it?" said Poirot. "Are you sure?"

"Of course it is."

With a swift movement Desmond bent down and plucked the red stone out of Bridget's hand.

"You should not do that," said Poirot reproachfully. "Nothing should have been disturbed."

"I haven't disturbed the body, have I? But this thing might—might get lost and it's evidence. The great thing is to get the police here as soon as possible. I'll go at once and telephone."

He wheeled round and ran sharply towards the house. Sarah came swiftly to Poirot's side.

"I don't understand," she whispered. Her face was dead white. "I don't *understand*." She caught at Poirot's arm. "What did you mean about—about the footprints?"

"Look for yourself, mademoiselle."

The footprints that led to the body and back again were the same as the ones just made accompanying Poirot to the girl's body and back.

"You mean—that it was Desmond? Nonsense!"

Suddenly the noise of a car came through the clear air. They wheeled round. They saw the car clearly enough driving at a furious pace down the drive and Sarah recognised what car it was.

"It's Desmond," she said. "It's Desmond's car. He—he must have gone to fetch the police instead of telephoning."

Diana Middleton came running out of the house to join them.

"What's happened?" she cried in a breathless voice. "Desmond just came rushing into the house. He said something about Bridget being killed and then he rattled the telephone but it was dead. He couldn't get any answer. He said the wires must have been cut. He said the only thing was to take a car and go for the police. Why the police? . . ."

Poirot made a gesture.

"Bridget?" Diana stared at him. "But surely—isn't it a joke of some kind? I heard something—something last night. I thought that they were going to play a joke on you, M. Poirot?"

"Yes," said Poirot, "that was the idea—to play a joke on me. But now come into the house, all of you. We shall catch our deaths of cold here and there is nothing to be done until Mr. Lee-Wortley returns with the police."

"But look here," said Colin, "we can't—we can't leave Bridget here alone."

"You can do her no good by remaining," said Poirot gently. "Come, it is a sad, a very sad tragedy, but there is nothing we can do any more to help Mademoiselle Bridget. So let us come in and get warm and have perhaps a cup of tea or of coffee."

They followed him obediently into the house. Peverell was just about to strike the gong. If he thought it extraordinary for most of the household to be outside and for Poirot to make an appearance in pyjamas and an overcoat, he displayed no sign of it. Peverell in his old age was still the perfect butler. He noticed nothing that he was not asked to notice. They went into the dining-room and sat down. When they all had a cup of coffee in front of them and were sipping it, Poirot spoke.

"I have to recount to you," he said, "a little history. I cannot tell you all the details, no. But I can give you the main outline. It concerns a young princeling who came to this country. He brought with him a famous jewel which he was to have reset for the lady he was going to marry, but unfortunately before that he made friends with a very pretty young lady. This pretty young lady did not care very much for the man, but she did care for his jewel—so much so that one day she disappeared with this historic possession which had belonged to his house for generations. So the poor young man, he is in a quandary, you see. Above all he cannot have a scandal. Impossible to go to the police. Therefore he comes to me, to Hercule Poirot. 'Recover for me,' he says, 'my historic ruby.' *Eh bien*, this young lady, she has a friend and the friend, he has put through several very questionable transactions. He has been concerned with blackmail and he has been concerned with the sale of jewellery abroad. Always he has been very clever. He is suspected, yes, but nothing can be proved. It comes to my knowledge that this very clever gentleman, he is spending Christmas here in this house. It is important that the pretty young lady, once she has acquired the jewel, should disappear for a while from circulation, so that no pressure can be put upon her, no questions can be asked her. It is arranged, therefore, that she comes here to Kings Lacey, ostensibly as the sister of the clever gentleman——"

Sarah drew a sharp breath.

"Oh, no. Oh, no, not *here*! Not with me here!"

"But so it is," said Poirot. "And by a little manipulation I, too, become a guest here for Christmas. This young lady, she is supposed to have just come out of hospital. She is much better when she arrives here. But then comes the news that I, too, arrive, a detective—a well-known detective. At once she has what you call the wind up. She hides the ruby in the first place she can think of, and then very quickly she has a relapse and takes to her bed again. She does not want that I should see her, for doubtless I have a photograph and I shall recognise her. It is very boring for her, yes, but she has to stay in her room and her brother, he brings her up the trays."

"And the ruby?" demanded Michael.

"I think," said Poirot, "that at the moment it is mentioned I arrive, the young lady was in the kitchen with the rest of you, all laughing and talking and stirring the Christmas puddings. The Christmas puddings are put into bowls and the young lady she hides the ruby, pressing it down into one of the pudding bowls. Not the one that we are going to have on Christmas Day. Oh no, that one she knows is in a special mould. She puts it in the other one, the one that is destined to be eaten on New Year's Day. Before then she will be ready to leave, and when she leaves no doubt that Christmas pudding will go with her. But see how fate takes a hand. On the very morning of Christmas Day there is an accident. The Christmas pudding in its fancy mould is dropped on the stone floor and the mould is shattered to pieces. So what can be done? The good Mrs. Ross, she takes the other pudding and sends it in."

"Good lord," said Colin, "do you mean that on Christmas Day when Grandfather was eating his pudding that that was a *real* ruby he'd got in his mouth?"

"Precisely," said Poirot, "and you can imagine the emotions of Mr. Desmond Lee-Wortley when he saw that. *Eh bien*, what happens next? The ruby is passed round. I examine it and I manage unobtrusively to slip it in my pocket. In a careless way as though I were not interested. But one person at least observes what I have done. When I lie in bed that person searches my room. He searches me. He does not find the ruby. Why?"

"Because," said Michael breathlessly, "you had given it to Bridget. That's what you mean. And so that's why—but I don't understand quite—I mean—— Look here, what *did* happen?"

Poirot smiled at him.

"Come now into the library," he said, "and look out of the window and I will show you something that may explain the mystery."

He led the way and they followed him.

"Consider once again," said Poirot, "the scene of the crime."

He pointed out of the window. A simultaneous gasp broke from the lips of all of them. There was no body lying on the snow, no trace of the tragedy seemed to remain except a mass of scuffled snow.

"It wasn't all a dream, was it?" said Colin faintly. "I—has someone taken the body away?"

"Ah," said Poirot. "You see? The Mystery of the Disappearing Body." He nodded his head and his eyes twinkled gently.

"Good lord," cried Michael. "M. Poirot, you are—you haven't—oh, look here, he's been having us on all this time!"

Poirot twinkled more than ever.

"It is true, my children, I also have had my little joke. I knew about your little plot, you see, and so I arranged a counter-plot of my own. Ah, *voilà* Mademoiselle Bridget. None the worse, I hope, for your exposure in the snow? Never should I forgive myself if you attrapped *une fluxion de poitrine*."

Bridget had just come into the room. She was wearing a thick skirt and a woollen sweater. She was laughing.

"I sent a *tisane* to your room," said Poirot severely. "You have drunk it?"

"One sip was enough!" said Bridget. "*I*'m all right. Did I do it well, M. Poirot? Goodness, my arm hurts still after that tourniquet you made me put on it."

"You were splendid, my child," said Poirot. "Splendid. But see, all the others are still in the fog. Last night I went to Mademoiselle Bridget. I told her that I knew about your little *complot* and I asked her if she would act a part for me. She did it very cleverly. She made the footprints with a pair of Mr. Lee-Wortley's shoes."

Sarah said in a harsh voice:

"But what's the point of it all, M. Poirot? What's the point of sending Desmond off to fetch the police? They'll be very angry when they find out it's nothing but a hoax."

Poirot shook his head gently.

"But I do not think for one moment, mademoiselle, that Mr. Lee-Wortley went to fetch the police," he said. "Murder is a thing in which Mr. Lee-Wortley does not want to be mixed up. He lost his nerve badly. All he could see was his chance to get the ruby. He snatched that, he pretended the telephone was out of order, and he rushed off in a car on the pretence of fetching the police. I think myself it is the last you will see of him for some time. He has, I understand, his own ways of getting out of England. He has his own plane, has he not, mademoiselle?"

Sarah nodded. "Yes," she said. "We were thinking of——" She stopped.

"He wanted you to elope with him that way, did he not? *Eh bien*, that is a very good way of smuggling a jewel out of the country. When you are eloping with a girl, and that fact is publicised, then you will not be suspected of also smuggling a historic jewel out of the country. Oh yes, that would have made a very good camouflage."

"I don't believe it," said Sarah. "I don't believe a word of it!"

"Then ask his sister," said Poirot, gently nodding his head over her shoulder. Sarah turned her head sharply.

A platinum blonde stood in the doorway. She

wore a fur coat and was scowling. She was clearly in a furious temper.

"Sister my foot!" she said, with a short unpleasant laugh. "That swine's no brother of mine! So he's beaten it, has he, and left me to carry the can? The whole thing was *his* idea! *He* put me up to it! Said it was money for jam. They'd never prosecute because of the scandal. I could always threaten to say that Ali had *given* me his historic jewel. Des and I were to have shared the swag in Paris—and now the swine runs out on me! I'd like to murder him!" She switched abruptly. "The sooner I get out of here—— Can someone telephone for a taxi?"

"A car is waiting at the front door to take you to the station, mademoiselle," said Poirot.

"Think of everything, don't you?"

"Most things," said Poirot complacently.

But Poirot was not to get off so easily. When he returned to the dining-room after assisting the spurious Miss Lee-Wortley into the waiting car, Colin was waiting for him.

There was a frown on his boyish face.

"But look here, M. Poirot. *What about the ruby?* Do you mean to say you've let him get away with it?"

Poirot's face fell. He twirled his moustache. He seemed ill at ease.

"I shall recover it yet," he said weakly. "There are other ways. I shall still——"

"Well, I do think!" said Michael. "To let that swine get away with the ruby!"

Bridget was sharper.

"He's having us on again," she cried. "You are, aren't you, M. Poirot?"

"Shall we do a final conjuring trick, mademoiselle? Feel in my left-hand pocket."

Bridget thrust her hand in. She drew it out again with a scream of triumph and held aloft a large ruby blinking in crimson splendour.

"You comprehend," explained Poirot, "the one that was clasped in your hand was a paste replica. I brought it from London in case it was possible to make a substitution. You understand? We do not want the scandal. Monsieur Des-

mond will try and dispose of that ruby in Paris or in Belgium or wherever it is that he has his contacts, and then it will be discovered that the stone is not real! What could be more excellent? All finishes happily. The scandal is avoided, my princeling receives his ruby back again, he returns to his country, and makes a sober and we hope a happy marriage. All ends well."

"Except for me," murmured Sarah under her breath.

She spoke so low that no one heard her but Poirot. He shook his head gently.

"You are in error, Mademoiselle Sarah, in what you say there. You have gained experience. All experience is valuable. Ahead of you I prophesy there lies happiness."

"That's what *you* say," said Sarah.

"But look here, M. Poirot," Colin was frowning. "How did you know about the show we were going to put on for you?"

"It is my business to know things," said Hercule Poirot. He twirled his moustache.

"Yes, but I don't see how you could have managed it. Did someone split—did someone come and tell you?"

"No, no, not that."

"Then how? Tell us how?"

They all chorused, "Yes, tell us how."

"But no," Poirot protested. "But no. If I tell you how I deduced that, you will think nothing of it. It is like the conjuror who shows how his tricks are done!"

"Tell us, M. Poirot! Go on. Tell us, tell us!"

"You really wish that I should solve for you this last mystery?"

"Yes, go on. Tell us."

"Ah, I do not think I can. You will be so disappointed."

"Now, come on, M. Poirot, tell us. *How did you know?*"

"Well, you see, I was sitting in the library by the window in a chair after tea the other day and I was reposing myself. I had been asleep and when I awoke you were discussing your plans just outside the window close to me, and the window was open at the top."

"Is that all?" cried Colin, disgusted. "How simple!"

"Is it not?" said Hercule Poirot, smiling. "You see? You *are* disappointed!"

"Oh well," said Michael, "at any rate we know everything now."

"Do we?" murmured Hercule Poirot to himself. "*I* do not. *I*, whose business it is to know things."

He walked out into the hall, shaking his head a little. For perhaps the twentieth time he drew from his pocket a rather dirty piece of paper. "DON'T EAT NONE OF THE PLUM PUDDING. ONE AS WISHES YOU WELL."

Hercule Poirot shook his head reflectively. He who could explain everything could not explain this! Humiliating. Who had written it? *Why* had it been written? Until he found that out he would never know a moment's peace. Suddenly he came out of his reverie to be aware of a peculiar gasping noise. He looked sharply down. On the floor, busy with a dustpan and brush, was a tow-headed creature in a flowered overall. She was staring at the paper in his hand with large round eyes.

"Oh sir," said this apparition. "Oh, *sir. Please,* sir."

"And who may you be, *mon enfant?*" inquired M. Poirot genially.

"Annie Bates, sir, please, sir. I come here to help Mrs. Ross. I didn't mean, sir, I didn't mean to—to do anything what I shouldn't do. I did mean it well, sir. For your good, I mean."

Enlightenment came to Poirot. He held out the dirty piece of paper.

"Did you write that, Annie?"

"I didn't mean any harm, sir. Really I didn't."

"Of course you didn't, Annie." He smiled at her. "But tell me about it. Why did you write this?"

"Well, it was them two, sir. Mr. Lee-Wortley and his sister. Not that she *was* his sister, I'm sure. None of us thought so! And she wasn't ill a bit. We could all tell *that*. We thought—we all thought—something queer was going on. I'll tell you straight, sir. I was in her bathroom taking in the clean towels, and I listened at the door. *He* was in her room and they were talking together. I heard what they said plain as plain. 'This detective,' he was saying. 'This fellow Poirot who's coming here. We've got to do something about it. We've got to get him out of the way as soon as possible.' And then he says to her in a nasty, sinister sort of way, lowering his voice, 'Where did you put it?' And she answered him, '*In the pudding.*' Oh, sir, my heart gave such a leap I thought it would stop beating. I thought they meant to poison you in the Christmas pudding. I didn't know *what* to do! Mrs. Ross, she wouldn't listen to the likes of me. Then the idea came to me as I'd write you a warning. And I did and I put it on your pillow where you'd find it when you went to bed." Annie paused breathlessly.

Poirot surveyed her gravely for some minutes.

"You see too many sensational films, I think, Annie," he said at last, "or perhaps it is the television that affects you? But the important thing is that you have the good heart and a certain amount of ingenuity. When I return to London I will send you a present."

"Oh thank you, sir. Thank you very much, sir."

"What would you like, Annie, as a present?"

"Anything I like, sir? Could I have anything I like?"

"Within reason," said Hercule Poirot prudently, "yes."

"Oh, sir, could I have a vanity box? A real posh slap-up vanity box like the one Mr. Lee-Wortley's sister, wot wasn't his sister, had?"

"Yes," said Poirot, "yes, I think that could be managed.

"It is interesting," he mused. "I was in a museum the other day observing some antiquities from Babylon or one of those places, thousands of years old—and among them were cosmetics boxes. The heart of woman does not change."

"Beg your pardon, sir?" said Annie.

"It is nothing," said Poirot, "I reflect. You shall have your vanity box, child."

"Oh thank you, sir. Oh thank you very much indeed, sir."

Annie departed ecstatically. Poirot looked after her, nodding his head in satisfaction.

"Ah," he said to himself. "And now—I go. There is nothing more to be done here."

A pair of arms slipped round his shoulders unexpectedly. "If you *will* stand just under the mistletoe——" said Bridget.

Hercule Poirot enjoyed it. He enjoyed it very much. He said to himself that he had had a very good Christmas.

GOLD, FRANKINCENSE AND MURDER

Catherine Aird

THE DETECTIVE STORIES OF CATHERINE AIRD are notable for their sense of fair play—that nice, old-fashioned notion that the author should have her detective actually solve mysteries by observation and deduction—not by sheer luck, coincidence, or via confession—and this is proven in the excellent and long-running series featuring her series protagonist, Inspector C. D. Sloan. "Gold, Frankincense and Murder" was first published in Tim Heald's anthology, *A Classic Christmas Crime* (London, Pavilion, 1995).

Gold, Frankincense and Murder

CATHERINE AIRD

"CHRISTMAS!" SAID HENRY TYLER. "Bah!"

"And we're expecting you on Christmas Eve as usual," went on his sister Wendy placidly.

"But . . ." He was speaking down the telephone from London, "but, Wen . . ."

"Now it's no use your pretending to be Ebenezer Scrooge in disguise, Henry."

"Humbug," exclaimed Henry more firmly.

"Nonsense," declared his sister, quite unmoved. "You enjoy Christmas just as much as the children. You know you do."

"Ah, but this year I may just have to stay on in London over the holiday . . ." Henry Tyler spent his working days—and, in these troubled times, quite a lot of his working nights as well—at the Foreign Office in Whitehall.

What he was doing now to his sister would have been immediately recognized in ambassadorial circles as "testing the reaction." In the lower echelons of his department it was known more simply as "flying a kite." Whatever you called it, Henry Tyler was an expert.

"And it's no use your saying there's trouble in the Baltic either," countered Wendy Witherington warmly.

"Actually," said Henry, "it's the Balkans which are giving us a bit of a headache just now."

"The children would never forgive you if you weren't there," said Wendy, playing a trump card; although it wasn't really necessary. She knew that nothing short of an international crisis would keep Henry away from her home in the little market town of Berebury in the heart of rural Calleshire at Christmastime. The trouble was that these days international crises were not nearly so rare as they used to be.

"Ah, the children," said their doting uncle. "And what is it that they want Father Christmas to bring this year?"

"Edward wants a model railway engine for his set."

"Does he indeed?"

"A Hornby LMS red engine called 'Princess Elizabeth,'" said Wendy Witherington readily. "It's a 4—6—2."

Henry made a note, marvelling that his sister, who seemed totally unable to differentiate between the Baltic and the Balkans—and quite probably the Balearics as well—had the details of a child's model train absolutely at her fingertips.

"And Jennifer?" he asked.

Wendy sighed. "The Good Ship Lollipop. Oh, and when you come, Henry, you'd better be able to explain to her how it is that while she could see Shirley Temple at the pictures—we took her last week—Shirley Temple couldn't see her."

Henry, who had devoted a great deal of time in the last ten days trying to explain to a Minister in His Majesty's Government exactly what Monsieur Pierre Laval might have in mind for the best future of France, said he would do his best.

"Who else will be staying, Wen?"

"Our old friends Peter and Dora Watkins—you remember them, don't you?"

"He's something in the bank, isn't he?" said Henry.

"Nearly a manager," replied Wendy. "Then there'll be Tom's old Uncle George."

"I hope," groaned Henry, "that your barometer's up to it. It had a hard time last year." Tom's Uncle George had been a renowned maker of scientific instruments in his day. "He's nearly tapped it to death."

Wendy's mind was still on her house guests. "Oh, and there'll be two refugees."

"Two refugees?" Henry frowned, even though he was alone in his room at the Foreign Office. They were beginning to be very careful about some refugees.

"Yes, the rector has asked us each to invite two refugees from the camp on the Calleford Road to stay for Christmas this year. You remember our Mr. Wallis, don't you, Henry?"

"Long sermons?" hazarded Henry.

"Then you do remember him," said Wendy without irony. "Well, he's arranged it all through some church organization. We've got to be very kind to them because they've lost everything."

"Give them useful presents, you mean," said Henry, decoding this last without difficulty.

"Warm socks and scarves and things," agreed Wendy Witherington vaguely. "And then we've got some people coming to dinner here on Christmas Eve."

"Oh, yes?"

"Our doctor and his wife. Friar's their name. She's a bit heavy in the hand but he's quite good company. And," said Wendy drawing breath, "our new next-door neighbours—they're called Steele—are coming too. He bought the pharmacy in the square last summer. We don't know them very well—I think he married one of his assistants—but it seemed the right thing to invite them at Christmas."

"Quite so," said Henry. "That all?"

"Oh, and little Miss Hooper."

"Sent her measurements, did she?"

"You know what I mean," said his sister, unperturbed. "She always comes then. Besides, I expect she'll know the refugees. She does a lot of church work."

"What sort of refugees are they?" asked Henry cautiously.

But that Wendy did not know.

Henry himself wasn't sure even after he'd first met them, and his brother-in-law was no help.

"Sorry, old man," said that worthy as they foregathered in the drawing-room, awaiting the arrival of the rest of the dinner guests on Christmas Eve. "All I know is that this pair arrived from somewhere in Mitteleuropa last month with only what they stood up in."

"Better out than in," contributed Gordon Friar, the doctor, adding an old medical aphorism, "like laudable pus."

"I understand," said Tom Witherington, "that they only just got out, too. Skin of their teeth and all that."

"As the poet so wisely said," murmured Henry, "'The only certain freedom's in departure.'"

"If you ask me," said old Uncle George, a veteran of the Boer War, "they did well to go while the going was good."

"It's the sort of thing you can leave too late," pronounced Dr. Friar weightily. Leaving things too late was every doctor's nightmare.

"I don't envy 'em being where they are now," said Tom. "That camp they're in is pretty bleak, especially in the winter."

This was immediately confirmed by Mrs. Godiesky the moment she entered the room. She regarded the Witheringtons' glowing fire with deep appreciation. "We 'ave been so cooald, so cooaald," she said as she stared hungrily at the logs stacked by the open fireside. "So very cooald . . ."

Her husband's English was slightly better, although also heavily accented. "If we had not left when we did, then," he opened his hands expressively, "then who knows what would have become of us?"

"Who, indeed?" echoed Henry, who actually

had a very much better idea than anyone else present of what might have become of the Godieskys had they not left their native heath when they did. Reports reaching the Foreign Office were very, very discouraging.

"They closed my university department down overnight," explained Professor Hans Godiesky. "Without any warning at all."

"It was terrrrrible," said Mrs. Godiesky, holding her hands out to the fire as if she could never be warm again.

"What sort of a department was it, sir?" enquired Henry casually of the Professor.

"Chemistry," said the refugee, just as the two Watkins came in and the hanging mistletoe was put to good use. They were followed fairly quickly by Robert and Lorraine Steele from next door. The introductions in their case were more formal. Robert Steele was a good bit older than his wife, who was dressed in a very becoming mixture of red and dark green, though with a skirt that was rather shorter than either Wendy's or Dora's and even more noticeably so than that of Marjorie Friar, who was clearly no dresser.

"We're so glad you could get away in time," exclaimed Wendy, while Tom busied himself with furnishing everyone with sherry. "It must be difficult if there's late dispensing to be done."

"No trouble these days," boomed Robert Steele. "I've got a young assistant now. He's a great help."

Then Miss Hooper, whose skirt was longest of all, was shown in. She was out of breath and full of apology for being so late. "Wendy, dear, I am so very sorry," she fluttered. "I'm afraid the Waits will be here in no time at all . . ."

"And they won't wait," said Henry guilelessly, "will they?"

"If you ask me," opined Tom Witherington, "they won't get past the 'Royal Oak' in a hurry."

"The children are coming down in their dressing-gowns to listen to the carols," said Wendy, rightly ignoring both remarks. "And I don't mind how tired they get tonight."

"Who's playing Father Christmas?" asked Robert Steele jovially. He was a plump fellow, whose gaze rested fondly on his young wife most of the time.

"Not me," said Tom Witherington.

"I am," declared Henry. "For my sins."

"Then, when I am tackled on the matter," said the children's father piously, "I can put my hand on my heart and swear total innocence."

"And how will you get out of giving an honest answer, Henry?" enquired Dora Watkins playfully.

"I shall hope," replied Henry, "to remain true to the traditions of the Foreign Service and give an answer that is at one and the same time absolutely correct and totally meaningless . . ."

At which moment the sound of the dinner gong being struck came from the hall and presently the whole party moved through to the dining-room, Uncle George giving the barometer a surreptitious tap on the way.

Henry Tyler studied the members of the party under cover of a certain amount of merry chat. It was part and parcel of his training that he could at one and the same time discuss Christmas festivities in England with poor Mrs. Godiesky while covertly observing the other guests. Lorraine Steele was clearly the apple of her husband's eye, but he wasn't sure that the same could be said for Marjorie Friar, who emerged as a complainer and sounded—and looked—quite aggrieved with life.

Lorraine Steele though, was anything but dowdy. Henry decided her choice of red and green—Christmas colours—was a sign of a new outfit for yuletide.

He was also listening for useful clues about their homeland in the Professor's conversation, while becoming aware that Tom's old Uncle George really was getting quite senile now and learning that the latest of Mrs. Friar's succession of housemaids had given in her notice.

"And at Christmas, too," she complained. "So inconsiderate."

Peter Watkins was displaying a modest pride in his Christmas present to his wife.

"Well," he said in the measured tones of his profession of banking, "personally, I'm sure that refrigerators are going to be the thing of the future."

"There's nothing wrong with a good old-fashioned larder," said Wendy stoutly, like the good wife she was. There was little chance of Tom Witherington being able to afford a refrigerator for a very long time. "Besides, I don't think Cook would want to change her ways now. She's quite set in them, you know."

"But think of the food we'll save," said Dora. "It'll never go bad now."

"'Use it up, wear it out.'" Something had stirred in old Uncle George's memory.

"'Make it do, do without or we'll send it to Belgium.'"

"And you'll be more likely to avoid food poisoning, too," said Robert Steele earnestly. "Won't they, Dr. Friar?"

"Yes, indeed," the medical man agreed at once. "There's always too much of that about and it can be very dangerous."

The pharmacist looked at both the Watkins and said gallantly, "I can't think of a better present."

"But you did, darling," chipped in Lorraine Steele brightly, "didn't you?"

Henry was aware of an unspoken communication passing between the two Steeles; and then Lorraine Steele allowed her left hand casually to appear above the table. Her fourth finger was adorned with both a broad gold wedding ring and a ring on which was set a beautiful solitaire diamond.

"Robert's present," she said rather complacently, patting her blonde Marcel waved hair and twisting the diamond ring round. "Isn't it lovely?"

"I wanted her to wear it on her right hand," put in Robert Steele, "because she's left-handed, but she won't hear of it."

"I should think not," said Dora Watkins at once. "The gold wedding ring sets it off so nicely."

"That's what I say, too," said Mrs. Steele prettily, lowering her be-ringed hand out of sight again.

"Listen!" cried Wendy suddenly. "It's the Waits. I can hear them now. Come along, everyone . . . it's mince pies and coffee all round in the hall afterwards."

The Berebury carol-singers parked their lanterns outside the front door and crowded round the Christmas tree in the Witheringtons' entrance hall, their sheets of music held at the ready.

"Right," called out their leader, a young man with a rather prominent Adam's apple. He began waving a little baton. "All together now . . ."

The familiar words of "Once in Royal David's City" soon rang out through the house, filling it with joyous sound. Henry caught a glimpse of a tear in Mrs. Godiesky's eye; and noted a look of great nostalgia in little Miss Hooper's earnest expression. There must have been ghosts of Christmases Past in the scene for her, too.

Afterwards, when it became important to re-create the scene in his mind for the police, Henry could only place the Steeles at the back of the entrance hall with Dr. Friar and Uncle George beside them. Peter and Dora Watkins had opted to stand a few steps up the stairs to the first-floor landing, slightly out of the press of people but giving them a good view. Mrs. Friar was standing awkwardly in front of the leader of the choir. Of Professor Hans Godiesky there was no sign whatsoever while the carols were being sung.

Henry remembered noticing suppressed excitement in the faces of his niece and nephew perched at the top of the stairs and hoping it was the music that they had found entrancing and not the piles of mince pies awaiting them among the decorative smilax on the credenza at the back of the hall.

They—and everyone else—fell upon them nonetheless as soon as the last carol had been sung. There was a hot punch, too, carefully mulled to just the right temperature by Tom Witherington, for those old enough to partake of it, and home-made lemonade for the young.

Almost before the last choirboy had scoffed the last mince pie the party at the Witheringtons' broke up.

The pharmacist and his wife were the first to leave. They shook hands all round.

"I know it's early," said Lorraine Steele apologetically, "but I'm afraid Robert's poor old tummy's been playing him up again." Henry, who had been expecting a rather limp paw, was surprised to find how firm her handshake was.

"If you'll forgive us," said Lorraine's husband to Wendy, "I think we'd better be on our way now." Robert Steele essayed a glassy, strained smile, but to Henry's eye he looked more than a little white at the gills. Perhaps he, too, had spotted that the ring that was his Christmas present to his wife had got a nasty stain on the inner side of it.

The pair hurried off together in a flurry of farewells. Then the wispy Miss Hooper declared the evening a great success but said she wanted to check everything at St. Faith's before the midnight service, and she, too, slipped away.

"What I want to know," said Dora Watkins provocatively when the rest of the guests had reassembled in the drawing-room and Edward and Jennifer had been sent back—very unwillingly—to bed, "is whether it's better to be an old man's darling or a young man's slave?"

A frown crossed Wendy's face. "I'm not sure," she said seriously.

"I reckon our Mrs. Steele's got her husband where she wants him, all right," said Peter Watkins, "don't you?"

"Come back, William Wilberforce, there's more work on slavery still to be done," said Tom Witherington lightly. "What about a night-cap, anyone?"

But there were no takers, and in a few moments the Friars, too, had left.

Wendy suddenly said she had decided against going to the Midnight Service after all and would see everyone in the morning. The rest of the household also opted for an early night and in the event Henry Tyler was the only one of the party to attend the Midnight Service at St. Faith's church that night.

The words of the last carol, "We Three Kings of Orient Are . . ." were still ringing in his ears as he crossed the Market Square to the church. Henry wished that the Foreign Office had only kings to deal with: life would be simpler then. Dictators and Presidents—particularly one President not so very many miles from "perfidious Albion"—were much more unpredictable.

He hummed the words of the last verse of the carol as he climbed the church steps:

Myrrh is mine; its bitter perfume
Breathes a life of gathering gloom;
Sorrowing, sighing, bleeding, dying,
Sealed in the stone-cold tomb.

Perhaps, he thought, as he sought a back pew and his nostrils caught the inimical odour of a mixture of burning candles and church flowers, he should have been thinking of frankincense or even—when he saw the burnished candlesticks and altar cross—Melchior's gold . . .

His private orisons were interrupted a few minutes later by a sudden flurry of activity near the front of the church, and he looked up in time to see little Miss Hooper being helped out by the two churchwardens.

"If I might just have a drink of water," he heard her say before she was borne off to the vestry. "I'll be all right in a minute. So sorry to make a fuss. So very sorry . . ."

The rector's sermon was its usual interminable length and he was able to wish his congregation a happy Christmas as they left the church. As Henry walked back across the square he met Dr. Friar coming out of the Steeles' house.

"Chap's collapsed," he murmured. "Severe epigastric pain and vomiting. Mrs. Steele came round to ask me if I would go and see him. There was blood in the vomit and that frightened her."

"It would," said Henry.

"He's pretty ill," said the doctor. "I'm getting him into hospital as soon as possible."

"Could it have been something he ate here?" said Henry, telling him about little Miss Hooper.

"Too soon to tell but quite possible," said the doctor gruffly. "You'd better check how the others are when you get in. I rather think Wendy might be ill, too, from the look of her when we left, and I must say my wife wasn't feeling too grand when I went out. Ring me if you need me."

Henry came back to a very disturbed house indeed, with several bedroom lights on. No one was very ill but Wendy and Mrs. Godiesky were distinctly unwell. Dora Watkins was perfectly all right and was busy ministering to those that weren't.

Happily, there was no sound from the children's room and he crept in there to place a full stocking beside each of their beds. As he came back downstairs to the hall, he thought he heard an ambulance bell next door.

"The position will be clearer in the morning," he said to himself, a Foreign Office man to the end of his fingertips.

It was.

Half the Witherington household had had a severe gastro-intestinal upset during the night, and Robert Steele had died in the Berebury Royal Infirmary at about two o'clock in the morning.

When Henry met his sister on Christmas morning she had a very wan face indeed.

"Oh, Henry," she cried, "isn't it terrible about Robert Steele? And the rector says half the young Waits were ill in the night, too, and poor little Miss Hooper as well!"

"That lets the punch out, doesn't it?" said Henry thoughtfully, "seeing as the youngsters weren't supposed to have any."

"Cook says . . ."

"Is she all right?" enquired Henry curiously.

"She hasn't been ill, if that's what you mean, but she's very upset." Wendy sounded quite nervous. "Cook says nothing like this has ever happened to her before."

"It hasn't happened to her now," pointed out Henry unkindly but Wendy wasn't listening.

"And Edward and Jennifer are all right, thank goodness," said Wendy a little tearfully. "Tom's beginning to feel better but I hear Mrs. Friar's pretty ill still and poor Mrs. Godiesky is feeling terrible. And as for Robert Steele . . . I just

don't know what to think. Oh, Henry, I feel it's all my fault."

"Well, it wasn't the lemonade," deduced Henry. "Both children had lots. I saw them drinking it."

"They had a mince pie each, too," said their mother. "I noticed. But some people who had them have been very ill since . . ."

"Exactly, my dear. Some, but not all."

"But what could it have been, then?" quavered Wendy. "Cook is quite sure she only used the best of everything. And it stands to reason it was something that they ate here." She struggled to put her fears into words. "Here was the only place they all were."

"It stands to reason that it was something they were given here," agreed Henry, whom more than one ambassador had accused of pedantry, "which is not quite the same thing."

She stared at him. "Henry, what do you mean?"

Inspector Milsom knew what he meant.

It was the evening of Boxing Day when he and Constable Bewman came to the Witheringtons' house.

"A number of people would appear to have suffered from the effects of ingesting a small quantity of a dangerous substance at this address," Milsom announced to the company assembled at his behest. "One with fatal results."

Mrs. Godiesky shuddered. "Me, I suffer a lot."

"Me, too," Peter Watkins chimed in.

"But not, I think, sir, your wife?" Inspector Milsom looked interrogatively at Dora Watkins.

"No, Inspector," said Dora. "I was quite all right."

"Just as well," said Tom Witherington. He still looked pale. "We needed her to look after us."

"Quite so," said the Inspector.

"It wasn't food poisoning, then?" said Wendy eagerly. "Cook will be very pleased . . ."

"It would be more accurate, madam," said Inspector Milsom, who didn't have a cook to be in awe of, "to say that there was poison in the food."

Wendy paled. "Oh . . ."

"This dangerous substance of which you speak," enquired Professor Godiesky with interest, "is its nature known?"

"In England," said the Inspector, "we call it corrosive sublimate . . ."

"Mercury? Ah," the refugee nodded sagely, "that would explain everything."

"Not quite everything, sir," said the Inspector mildly. "Now, if we might see you one at a time, please."

"This poison, Inspector," said Henry after he had given his account of the carol-singing to the two policemen, "I take it that it is not easily available?"

"That is correct, sir. But specific groups of people can obtain it."

"Doctors and pharmacists?" hazarded Henry.

"And certain manufacturers . . ."

"Certain . . . Oh, Uncle George?" said Henry. "Of course. There's plenty of mercury in thermometers."

"The old gentleman is definitely a little confused, sir."

"And Professors of Chemistry?" said Henry.

"In his position," said the Inspector judiciously, "I should myself have considered having something with me just in case."

"There being a fate worse than death," agreed Henry swiftly, "such as life in some places in Europe today. Inspector, might I ask what form this poison takes?"

"It's a white crystalline substance."

"Easily confused with sugar?"

"It would seem easily enough," said the policeman drily.

"And what you don't know, Inspector," deduced Henry intelligently, "is whether it was scattered on the mince pies . . . I take it it was on the mince pies?"

"They were the most likely vehicle," conceded the policeman.

"By accident or whether it was meant to make a number of people slightly ill or . . ."

"Or," put in Detective Constable Bewman keenly, "one person very ill indeed?"

"Or," persisted Henry quietly, "both."

"That is so." He gave a dry cough. "As it happens it did both make several people ill and one fatally so."

"Which also might have been intended?" Nobody had ever called Henry slow.

"From all accounts," said Milsom obliquely, "Mr. Steele had a weak tummy before he ingested the corrosive sublimate of mercury."

"Uncle George wasn't ill, was he?"

"No, sir, nor Dr. Friar." He gave his dry cough. "I am told that Dr. Friar never partakes of pastry."

"Mrs. Steele?"

"Slightly ill. She says she just had one mince pie. Mrs. Watkins didn't have any. Nor did the Professor."

"'The one without the parsley,'" quoted Henry, "is the one without the poison."

"Just so, sir. It would appear at first sight from our immediate calculations quite possible that . . ."

"Inspector, if you can hedge your bets as well as that before you say anything, we could find you a job in the Foreign Office."

"Thank you, sir. As I was saying, sir, it is possible that the poison was only in the mince pies furthest from the staircase. Bewman here has done a chart of where the victims took their pies from."

"Which would explain why some people were unaffected," said Henry.

"Which might explain it, sir." The Inspector clearly rivalled Henry in his precision. "The Professor just wasn't there to take one at all. He says he went to his room to finish his wife's Christmas present. He was carving something for her out of a piece of old wood."

"'Needs must when the devil drives,'" responded Henry absently. He was still thinking. "It's a pretty little problem, as they say."

"Means and opportunity would seem to be present," murmured Milsom.

"That leaves motive, doesn't it?" said Henry.

"The old gentleman mightn't have had one, seeing he's as he is, sir, if you take my meaning and of course we don't know anything about the Professor and his wife, do we, sir? Not yet."

"Not a thing."

"That leaves the doctor . . ."

"I'd've murdered Mrs. Friar years ago," announced Henry cheerfully, "if she had been my wife."

"And Mrs. Steele." There was a little pause and then Inspector Milsom said, "I understand the new young assistant at the pharmacy is more what you might call a contemporary of Mrs. Steele."

"Ah, so that's the way the wind's blowing, is it?"

"And then, sir," said the policeman, "after motive there's still what we always call down at the station the fourth dimension of crime . . ."

"And what might that be, Inspector?"

"Proof." He got up to go. "Thank you for your help, sir."

Henry sat quite still after the two policemen had gone, his memory teasing him. Someone he knew had been poisoned with corrosive sublimate of mercury, served to him in tarts. By a tart, too, if history was to be believed.

No, not someone he knew.

Someone he knew of.

Someone they knew about at the Foreign Office because it had been a political murder, a famous political murder set round an eternal triangle . . .

Henry Tyler sought out Professor Godiesky and explained.

"It was recorded by contemporary authors," Henry said, "that when the tarts poisoned with mercury were delivered to the Tower of London for Sir Thomas Overbury, the fingernail of the woman delivering them had accidentally been poked through the pastry . . ."

The professor nodded sapiently. "And it was stained black?"

"That's right," said Henry. History did have some lessons to teach, in spite of what Henry Ford had said. "But it would wash off?"

"Yes," said Hans Godiesky simply.

"So I'm afraid that doesn't get us anywhere, does it?"

The academic leaned forward slightly, as if addressing a tutorial. "There is, however, one substance on which mercury always leaves its mark."

"There is?" said Henry.

"Its—how do you say it in English?—its ineradicable mark."

"That's how we say it," said Henry slowly. "And which substance, sir, would that be?"

"Gold, Mr. Tyler. Mercury stains gold."

"For ever?"

"For ever." He waved a hand. "An amalgam is created."

"And I," Henry gave a faint smile, "I was foolish enough to think it was diamonds that were for ever."

"Pardon?"

"Nothing, Professor. Nothing at all. Forgive me, but I think I may be able to catch the Inspector and tell him to look to the lady. And her gold wedding ring."

"Look to the lady?" The refugee was now totally bewildered. "I do not understand . . ."

"It's a quotation."

"Ach, sir, I fear I am only a scientist."

"There's a better quotation," said Henry, "about looking to science for the righting of wrongs. I rather think Mrs. Steele may have looked to science, too, to—er—improve her lot. And if she carefully scattered the corrosive sublimate over some mince pies and not others it would have been with her left hand . . ."

"Because she was left-handed," said the Professor immediately. "That I remember. And you think one mince pie would have had—I know the English think this important—more than its fair share?"

"I do. Then all she had to do was to give her husband that one and Bob's your uncle. Clever of her to do it in someone else's house."

Hans Godiesky looked totally mystified. "And who was Bob?"

"Don't worry about Bob," said Henry from the door. "Think about Melchior and his gold instead."

BOXING UNCLEVER

Robert Barnard

WHEN SERIAL KILLER NOVELS, police procedurals, and violent crime fiction began to dominate the mystery genre, a handful of British authors maintained the legacy of the traditional detective story, and one of the stars of that challenging subgenre during the last quarter of the twentieth century was Robert Barnard. Born in the deliciously named town of Burnham-on-Crouch, he moved to Australia to teach after his graduation from Oxford University and then taught English at two universities in Norway before settling in Leeds. Many of his humorous and satiric detective novels feature the Scotland Yard inspector Perry Trethowan. "Boxing Unclever" was first published in *A Classic Christmas Crime,* edited by Tim Heald (London, Pavilion, 1995).

Boxing Unclever

ROBERT BARNARD

"THE TRUE SPIRIT OF CHRISTMAS," said Sir Adrian Tremayne, fingering the stem of the small glass of port which was all he was allowed, "is not to be found in the gluttony and ostentation which that charlatan and sentimentalist Charles Dickens encouraged." He looked disparagingly round at the remains of the dinner still encumbering the long table. "Not in turkey and plum pudding, still less in crackers and expensive gifts. No—a thousand times!" His voice was thrilling, but was then lowered to a whisper, and it carried as it once had carried through the theatres of the nation. "The true spirit of Christmas lies of course in reconciliation."

"Reconciliation—very true," said the Reverend Sykes.

"Why else, in the Christmas story, do we find simple shepherds and rich kings worshipping together in the stable?"

"I don't think they actually—" began the Reverend Fortescue, but he was waved aside.

"To show that man is one, of one nature, in the eyes of God. This reconciliation of opposites is the one true heart of the Christmas message. That was the plan that, at every Christmastide, was acted upon by myself and my dear wife Alice, now no longer with us. Or indeed with anyone. Christmas Day we would spend quietly and simply, with just ourselves for company once the children had grown up and made their own lives. On Boxing Day we would invite a lot of people round to Herriton Hall, and in particular people with whom there had been some breech, with whom we needed to be reconciled." He paused, reaching for reserves in that treacle and molasses voice that had thrilled audiences up and down the country.

"That was what we did that memorable Christmas of 1936. Ten . . . years . . . ago."

There were many nods around the table, both from those who had heard the story before, and from those who were hearing it for the first time.

"Christmas Day was quiet—even, it must be confessed, a little dull," Sir Adrian resumed. "We listened to the new King's broadcast, and wondered at his conquest of his unfortunate speech impediment. It is always good to reflect on those who do not have one's own natural advantages. I confess the day was for me mainly notable for a sense of anticipation. I thought with joy of the beautiful work of reconciliation that was to be undertaken on the next day. And of the other work . . ."

There was a regrettable snigger from one or two quarters of the table.

"Reconciliation has its limits," suggested Martin Lovejoy.

"Regrettably it does," acknowledged Sir Adrian, with a courteous bow in Martin's direction. "We are but human, after all. I could only hope that the Christian work of reconciliation in all cases but one would plead for me at the Judgement Seat against that one where . . . Ah well, who knows? Does not the Bible speak of there being only one unforgivable sin?"

The three reverend gentlemen present all seemed to want to talk at once, which enabled Sir Adrian to sweep ahead with his story. "The first to arrive that Boxing morning was Angela Montfort, closely followed by Daniel West, the critic. Indeed, I think it probable that they in fact arrived *together,* because there was no sign of transport for Angela. West's reviews of her recent performances had made me wonder—so mindlessly enthusiastic were they—whether Something was Going On. Something usually was, with Angela, and the idea that the English critic is incorruptible is pure stardust. My quarrel with Angela, however, had nothing to do with Sex. It was her ludicrous and constant upstaging of me during the national tour of *Private Lives,* for which I had taken over the Coward role, and gave a performance which many thought—but, no matter. Old triumphs, old triumphs."

It was given a weary intonation worthy of Prospero's farewell to his Art.

"And West's offence?" asked Martin Lovejoy innocently. He was the most theatrically sophisticated of them, and he knew.

"A review in his provincial newspaper of my Malvolio," said Sir Adrian shortly, "which was hurtful in the extreme."

"Was that the one which spoke of your 'shrunken shanks'?" asked Peter Carbury, who was the only person present who read the *Manchester Guardian.*

"A deliberate effect of costuming!" said Sir Adrian fiercely. "A very clever design by my dear friend Binkie Mather. Typical of a critic's ignorance and malice that he could not see that."

He took a sip of port to restore his equanimity, and while he did so Peter winked at Martin and Martin winked at Peter.

"Angela gushed, of course," resumed Sir Adrian, "as I led her into the drawing-room. 'So wonderful to be back at dear old Herriton again'—that kind of thing. West looked around with a cynical expression on his face. He had been there before, when I had been under the il-

lusion that he was one of the more perceptive of the up-and-coming critics, and I knew he coveted the house, with its magnificent views over the Sussex Downs. I suspected that he found the idea of the gentleman actor rather ridiculous, but the idea of the gentleman critic not ridiculous at all. The gentleman's code allows dabbling. West had a large independent income, which is no guarantee of sound judgement. His cynical expression was assumed, but I was relentlessly courteous to them both, and it was while I was mixing them cocktails that Alice—dear Alice—led in Frank Mandeville."

"Her lover," said Peter Carbury.

"My dear boy, do not show your provinciality and vulgarity," said Sir Adrian severely. "In the theatre we take such things in our stride. Let us say merely that in the past he had been her *cavalier servente.*"

"Her *what?*" demanded Stephen Coates in an aggrieved voice. He had an oft-proclaimed and very British hatred of pretension.

"An Italian term," explained Sir Adrian kindly, "for a man who serves a lady as a sort of additional husband. There is a long tradition of such people in Italy."

"They are usually a lot younger," said Peter Carbury. "As in this case."

"Younger," conceded Sir Adrian. "Though hardly a *lot* younger. Frank Mandeville had been playing juvenile leads for so long he could have taken a Ph.D. in juvenility. Alice's . . . patronage of him was short and long over, and when she led him in it was clear to me from the expression on her face that she was mystified as to what had once attracted her. When I saw his hair, slicked back with so much oil that it must have felt like being pleasured by a garage mechanic, I felt similarly mystified."

"It must have been a jolly party," commented Stephen Coates. Sir Adrian smiled at him, to signify to all that Stephen was not the sort of young man who could be expected to understand the ways of polite, still less theatrical, society.

"I must confess that when Frank bounced in

Angela did say, 'What is this?' and looked suspiciously from Alice to me and back. But we had taken—*I* had taken—the precaution of inviting a number of local nonentities—the headmaster of a good school, an impoverished squire and his dreary wife, at least two vicars, and other such good people—and as they now began arriving they, so to speak, defused suspicion."

"Suspicion?" asked Mike, who had never heard the story before and was far from bright. Sir Adrian waved his hand with an airy grandness gained playing aristocrats of the old school.

"It was not until things were well under way that Richard Mallatrat and his wife arrived."

"The greatest Hamlet of his generation," put in Peter Carbury, with malicious intent.

"I cannot think of fainter praise," responded Sir Adrian loftily. "The art of Shakespearean acting is dead. If the newspapers are to be believed the Theatre today is dominated by young Olivier, who can no more speak the Bard than he can underplay a role."

"You and Mallatrat were rivals for the part, weren't you?" Carbury asked. Sir Adrian, after a pause, allowed the point.

"At the Old Vic. No money to speak of, but a great deal of prestige. I certainly wanted the part badly."

"To revive your career?" suggested the Reverend Sykes. He received a look of concentrated hatred.

"My career has never needed revival! To show the younger generation how it should be done! To set standards for people who had lost the true art of acting. Instead of which Mallatrat was given the role and had in it a showy success, lacking totally the quality of *thought,* which is essential to the role, and quite without too the *music* which . . . another more experienced actor would have brought to it." He bent forward malevolently, eyes glinting. *"And I was offered the role of Polonius."*

"It's a good role," said the Reverend Fortescue, probably to rub salt in the wound. He was ignored.

"That was his malice, of course. He orga-

nized that, put the management up to it, then told the story to all his friends. I never played the Old Vic again. I had to disappoint my legion of fans, but there are some insults not to be brooked."

"You did try to get even through his wife, didn't you?" asked Martin Lovejoy, who was all too well informed in that sort of area.

"A mere newspaper story. Gloria Davere was not then his wife, though as good as, and she was not the trumpery Hollywood 'star' she has since become. Certainly we had—what is this new film called?—a brief encounter. I have told you the morality of the theatre is not the morality of Leamington Spa or Catford. We happened to meet on Crewe Station one Saturday night, after theatre engagements elsewhere. I confess—sordid though it may sound—that for me it was no more than a means of passing the time, stranded as we were by the vagaries of the London, Midland, and Scottish Railway. But the thought did occur to me that I would be teaching this gauche young thing more gracious ways—introducing her to the lovemaking of an earlier generation, when romance still reigned, and a lady was treated with chivalry and respect."

"I believe she told the *News of the World* it was like fucking Old Father Time," said Carbury to Martin Lovejoy, but so *sotto* was his *voce* that Sir Adrian was able to roll on regardless.

"She later, of course, talked, and spitefully, but the idea that our encounter had anything in it of revenge on my part is sheer moonshine. On her part, perhaps, in view of the talk she put around, but as to myself, I plead innocent of any such sordid emotion."

"So that was the cast-list assembled, was it?" asked the Reverend Sykes.

"Nearly, nearly," said Sir Adrian, with the unhurried stance of the habitual narrator, which in the case of this story he certainly was. "Thus far the party seemed to be going well. The attractions of Richard Mallatrat and his flashy wife to the nonentities was something I had anticipated: they crowded around them, larding them with gushing compliments and expressions of admiration for this or that trumpery performance on stage or screen. Everyone, it seemed, had seen a Gloria Davere talkie or Richard Mallatrat as Hamlet, or Romeo, or Richard II. I knew it would be nauseating, and nauseating it was. Angela Montfort, for one, was immensely put out, with no knot of admirers to feed her self-love. She contented herself with swapping barbs with Frank Mandeville, who was of course enraged by the attention paid to Richard Mallatrat."

"Hardly a Shakespearean actor, though, this Frank Mandeville," commented Peter Carbury.

"Hardly an actor at all," amended Sir Adrian. "But logic does not come into theatrical feuds and jealousies. Mandeville playing Hamlet would hardly have passed muster on a wet Tuesday in Bolton, but that did not stop him grinding his teeth at the popularity of Richard Mallatrat."

"He wasn't the only one," whispered Stephen Coates.

"And so it was time for a second round of drinks. I decided on that as I saw toiling up the drive the figure of my dear old dresser Jack Roden. My once-dear old dresser. I poured out a variety of drinks including some already-mixed cocktails, two kinds of sherry, some gins and tonic, and two glasses of neat whisky. There was only one person in the room with the appalling taste to drink neat whisky before luncheon. Pouring two glasses gave that person a fifty-fifty chance of survival. Depending on how the tray was presented. With my back to the guests I dropped the hyoscine into one of the whisky glasses."

"Who was the whisky-drinker?" asked Roland, knowing the question would not be answered.

"The one with the worst taste," said Sir Adrian dismissively. "Then I went off to open the front door. Jack shuffled in, muttering something about the dreadful train and bus service you got over Christmas. He was a pathetic sight. The man who had been seduced away from me by Richard Mallatrat, and then dumped because he was not up to the contemporary demands of the job, could hardly any longer keep himself clean and neat, let alone anyone else. I threw the bottle of hyoscine as far as I could manage into the shrubbery, then ushered him with conspicuous kindness in to the drawing-room, solicitously introducing him to people he didn't know and people he did. 'But you two are old friends,' I remember saying when I led him up the scoundrel Mallatrat. Even that bounder had the grace to smile a mite queasily. Out of the corner of my eye I was pleased to see that some of the guests had already helped themselves from the tray."

"Why were you pleased?"

"It meant that others than myself had been up the tray. And it would obviously be theatrical people—the nonentities wouldn't dare."

"It doesn't sound the happiest of parties," commented Lovejoy.

"Doesn't it? Oh, but theatre people can relax anywhere, particularly if there are admirers present. Once some of the nonentities felt they should tear themselves away from the star duo of Mallatrat and Davere, then Angela got her share of attention, and Alice as hostess had her little knot—she had left the stage long before, of course, though she was still by nature a stage person. No, it was far from an unhappy party."

"Until the fatality," suggested the Reverend Fortescue.

"Until the fatality," agreed Sir Adrian. "Though even that . . ."

"Did not dampen spirits?"

"Not entirely. Poison is slow, of course. You can have a quick, dramatic effect with cyanide—even I have acted on occasion in thrillers, and know that—but most of them take their time. People thought at first it was an upset tummy. Alice said she hoped that was all it was. She of course was not in on my plans. I've never found women entirely reliable, have you?"

He looked around the table. None of his listeners had found women entirely reliable.

"So it wasn't she who took the tray round?" asked Simon. "Was it one of your servants?"

"No, indeed. The servants had been set to preparing lunch, and that was *all* they did. As a gentleman I had an instinctive aversion to involving faithful retainers in . . . a matter of this kind."

"I assume you didn't take it round yourself, though?"

"I did not. I tapped poor old Jack Roden on the shoulder—he was deep in rambling reminiscence with Daniel West (viewpoints from well away from the footlights)—and I asked him if he could help by taking round fresh drinks. That had always been my plan, though I confess that when I saw how doddering and uncertain he had become I very nearly changed it, fearing he would drop everything on the floor. But I placed the tray in his hands exactly as I wanted it, so that the poisoned whisky would be closest to hand when he got to the victim."

"And—to state the obvious—the victim took it," suggested the Reverend Fortescue.

"He took it. That was the signal for the toast. I cleared my throat and all fell silent. I flatter myself I know how to enforce silence. I had thought hard about the toast, and even today I think it rather beautiful. 'My friends,' I said. 'To friends old and new, to renewal and reconciliation, to the true spirit of Christmas.' There was much warm assent to my words, and glasses were raised. We all drank to Christmas, and the victim drank his down."

"He wasn't a sipper?" enquired Stephen.

"No. The victim was the sort who drank down and then had an interval before the next. I rather think myself that sipping is more social."

"How long was it before the effects were felt?"

"Oh, twenty minutes or more," said Sir Adrian, his face set in a reminiscent smile. "First just the look of queasiness, then some time later confessions of feeling ill. Alice was all solicitude. She took the victim to my study, plied him with glasses of water, nostrums from our medicine cupboard. He was sweating badly, and his vision was impaired. Finally she came in and suggested that I ring Dr. Cameron from the village. He was *not* happy at being fetched out on Boxing Day, particularly as he had not been invited to the party."

"Because he might have spotted what was wrong with him and saved him in time?"

"Precisely. Fortunately Dr. Cameron was the old-fashioned type of doctor, now rare, who went everywhere on foot. By the time he arrived, all Scottish tetchiness and wounded self-esteem, there was nothing to be done. Then it was questions, suspicions, and eventually demands that the police be called in. It made for an exciting if somewhat uneasy atmosphere—not a Boxing Day, I fancy, that anyone present will forget."

"And the police were quick to fix the blame, were they?" asked Mike. Sir Adrian sighed a Chekhovian sigh.

"Faster, I confess, than even I could have feared. The village bobby was an unknown quantity to me, being new to the district. I had counted on a thick-headed rural flatfoot of the usual kind, but even my first impression told me that he was unusually bright. He telephoned at once for a superior from Mordwick, the nearest town, but before he arrived with the usual team so familiar to us from detective fiction, the local man had established the main sequence of events, and could set out clearly for the investigating inspector's benefit all the relevant facts."

"But those facts would have left many people open to suspicion," suggested Peter Carbury.

"Oh, of course. Practically all the theatre people had been near the tray, except the victim, and all of them might be thought to bear malice to the victim. It was, alas, my wife Alice who narrowed things down so disastrously—quite inadvertently, of course." Sir Adrian was unaware that the foot of the Reverend Sykes touched the foot of the Reverend Fortescue at this point. They knew a thing or two about human nature, those clerics. And not just their own sins of the flesh. "Yes, Alice was apparently already on friendly terms with our new constable." The feet touched again. "And when she was chatting to him quite informally after a somewhat fraught lunch, she happened to mention at some point that she had been standing near the window and imagined she saw something flying through the air."

"The bottle?"

"The bottle. That did it. The grounds were searched, the bottle was found, and its content analysed. Then there could be no doubt."

"No doubt?" asked Mike, not the brightest person there.

"Because the hyoscine had been put in the second round of drinks, and the only person who had left the room to go to the door had been myself—to let in Jack Roden. Roden could not have done it because the bottle was empty and thrown away by the time he got into the drawing-room. It could only be me. I was arrested and charged, and Theatre was the poorer."

They all shook their heads, conscious they had reached the penultimate point in Sir Adrian's narrative.

"Come along all," said Archie by the door, on cue and jangling his keys. "Time you were making a move. We've got Christmas dinner to go to as well, you know."

"But tell us," said Mike who, apart from being stupid, hadn't heard the story before, "who the victim was."

Sir Adrian turned and surveyed them, standing around the table and the debris of their meal. He was now well into the run of this particular performance: there had been ten Christmases since a concerted chorus of Thespians had persuaded the new King not to celebrate his coronation with a theatrical knight on the scaffold. His head came forward and his stance came to resemble his long-ago performance as Richard III.

"You have to ask?" he rasped. "Who else could it be but the *critic*?" How he spat it out! "Who else could it be but the man who had libelled my legs?"

As he turned and led the shuffle back to the cells all eyes were fixed on the shrunken thighs and calves of one who had once been to tights what Betty Grable now was to silk stockings.

THE PROOF OF THE PUDDING

Peter Lovesey

ALL THE BOOKS PETER LOVESEY WROTE in the early part of his career were set in the past, including the Victorian-era adventures of Sergeant Cribb and Constable Thackeray, who made their debut in *Wobble to Death* (1970) and went on to become the basis for a popular television series on the PBS *Mystery!* program. He later wrote a series featuring Albert Edward, Prince of Wales, better known as Bertie—later King Edward VII. His more recent novels, notably those featuring the irascible Bath detective Peter Diamond, have been set in contemporary times. "The Proof of the Pudding" was first published in *A Classic Christmas Crime,* edited by Tim Heald (London, Pavilion, 1995).

The Proof of the Pudding

PETER LOVESEY

FRANK MORRIS STRODE INTO THE kitchen and slammed a cold, white turkey on the kitchen table. "Seventeen pounds plucked. Satisfied?"

His wife Wendy was at the sink, washing the last few breakfast bowls. Her shoulders had tensed. "What's that, Frank?"

"You're not even bloody looking, woman."

She took that as a command and wheeled around, rubbing her wet hands on the apron. "A turkey! That's a fine bird. It really is."

"Fine?" Frank erupted. "It's nineteen forty-six, for Christ's sake! It's a bloody miracle. Most of them round here will be sitting down to joints of pork and mutton—if they're lucky. I bring a bloody great turkey in on Christmas morning, and all you say is 'fine'?"

"I just wasn't prepared for it."

"You really get my goat, you do."

Wendy said tentatively, "Where did it come from, Frank?"

Her huge husband stepped towards her and for a moment she thought he would strike her. He lowered his face until it was inches from hers. Not even nine in the morning and she could smell sweet whisky on his breath. "I won it, didn't I?" he said, daring her to disbelieve. "A meat raffle in the Valiant Trooper last night."

Wendy nodded, pretending to be taken in. It didn't do to challenge Frank's statements. Black eyes and beatings had taught her well. She knew Frank's rule of fist had probably won him

the turkey, too. Frank didn't lose at anything. If he could punch his way to another man's prize, then he considered it fair game.

"Just stuff the thing and stick it in the oven," he ordered. "Where's the boy?"

"I think he's upstairs," Wendy replied warily. Norman had fled at the sound of Frank's key in the front door.

"Upstairs?" Frank ranted. "On bloody Christmas Day?"

"I'll call him." Wendy was grateful for the excuse to move away from Frank to the darkened hallway. "Norman," she gently called. "Your father's home. Come and wish him a Happy Christmas."

A pale, solemn young boy came cautiously downstairs, pausing at the bottom to hug his mother. Unlike most children of his age—he was nine—Norman was sorry that the war had ended in 1945. He had pinned his faith in the enemy putting up a stiff fight and extending it indefinitely. He still remembered the VE Day street party, sitting at a long wooden bench surrounded by laughing neighbours. He and his mother had found little to celebrate in the news that "the boys will soon be home."

Wendy smoothed down his hair, whispered something, and led him gently into the kitchen.

"Happy Christmas, Dad," he said, then added unprompted, "Did you come home last night?"

Wendy said quickly, "Never you mind about

45

that, Norman." She didn't want her son provoking Frank on this of all days.

Frank didn't appear to have heard. He was reaching up to the top shelf of a cupboard, a place where he usually kept his old army belt. Wendy pushed her arm protectively in front of the boy.

But instead of the belt, Frank took down a brown paper parcel. "Here you are, son," he said, beckoning to Norman. "You'll be the envy of the street in this. I saved it for you, specially."

Norman stepped forward. He unwrapped his present, egged on by his grinning father.

He now owned an old steel helmet. "Thanks, Dad," he said politely, turning it in his hands.

"I got it off a dead Jerry," Frank said with gusto. "The bastard who shot your Uncle Ted. Sniper, he was. Holed up in a bombed-out building in Potsdam, outside Berlin. He got Ted with a freak shot. Twelve of us stormed the building and took him out."

"Outside?"

"Topped him, Norman. See the hole round the back? That's from a Lee Enfield .303. Mine." Frank levelled an imaginary rifle to Wendy's head and squeezed the trigger, miming both the recoil and report. "There wasn't a lot left of Fritz after we'd finished. But I brought back the helmet for you, son. Wear it with pride. It's what your Uncle Ted would have wanted." He took the helmet and rammed it on the boy's head.

Norman grimaced. He felt he was about to be sick.

"Frank dear, perhaps we should put it away until he's a bit older," Wendy tried her tact. "We wouldn't want such a special thing to get damaged, would we? You know what young boys are like."

Frank was unimpressed. "What are you talking about—'special thing'? It's a bloody helmet, not a thirty-piece tea service. Look at the lad. He's totally stunned. He loves it. Why don't you get on and stuff that ruddy great turkey, like I told you?"

"Yes, Frank."

Norman raised his hand, his small head an absurd sight in the large helmet. "May I go now?"

Frank beamed. "Of course, son. Want to show it off to all your friends, do you?"

Norman nodded, causing the helmet to slip over his eyes. He lifted it off his head. Smiling weakly at his father, he left the kitchen and dashed upstairs. The first thing he would do was wash his hair.

Wendy began to wash and prepare the bird, listening to Frank.

"I know just how the kid feels. I still remember my old Dad giving me a bayonet he brought back from Flanders. Said he ran six men through with it. I used to look for specks of blood, and he'd tell me how he stuck them like pigs. It was the best Christmas present I ever had."

"I've got you a little something for Christmas. It's behind the clock," said Wendy, indicating a small package wrapped in newspaper and string.

"A present?" Frank snatched it up and tore the wrapping away. "Socks?" he said in disgust. "Is that it? Our first Christmas together in three bloody years, and all you can give your husband is a miserable pair of socks."

"I don't have much money, Frank," Wendy reminded him, and instantly wished she had not.

Frank seized her by the shoulders, practically tipping the turkey off the kitchen table. "Are you saying that's my fault?"

"No, love."

"I'm not earning enough—is that what you're trying to tell me?"

Wendy tried to pacify him, at the same time bracing herself for the violent shaking that would surely follow. Frank tightened his grip, forced her away from the table, and pushed her hard against the cupboard door, punctuating each word with a thump.

"That helmet cost me nothing," he ranted. "Don't you understand, woman? It's the thought that counts. You don't need money to show affection. You just need some savvy, some intelligence. Bloody socks—an insult!"

He shoved her savagely towards the table

again. "Now get back to your work. This is Christmas Day. I'm a reasonable man. I'm prepared to overlook your stupidity. Stop snivelling, will you, and get that beautiful bird in the oven. Mum will be here at ten. I want the place smelling of turkey. I'm not having you ruining my Christmas."

He strode out, heavy boots clumping on the wooden floor of the hallway. "I'm going round to Polly's," he shouted. "She knows how to treat a hero. Look at this dump. No decorations, no holly over the pictures. You haven't even bought any beer, that I've seen. Sort something out before I get back."

Wendy was still reeling from the shaking, but she knew she must speak before he left. If she didn't remind him now, there would be hell to pay later. "Polly said she would bring the Christmas pudding, Frank. Would you make sure she doesn't forget? Please, Frank."

He stood grim-faced in the doorway, silhouetted against the drab terraced houses opposite. "Don't tell me what to do, Wendy," he said threateningly. "You're the one due for a damned good reminding of what to do round here."

The door shook in its frame. Wendy stood at the foot of the stairs, her heart pounding. She knew what Frank meant by a damned good reminding. The belt wasn't used only on the boy.

"Is he gone, Mum?" Norman called from the top stair.

Wendy nodded, readjusting the pins in her thin, blonde hair, and drying her eyes. "Yes, love. You can come downstairs now."

At the foot of the stairs, he told her, "I don't want the helmet. It frightens me."

"I know, dear."

"I think there's blood on it. I don't want it. If it belonged to one of our soldiers, or one of the Yankees, I'd want it, but this is a dead man's helmet."

Wendy hugged her son. The base of her spine throbbed. A sob was building at the back of her throat.

"Where's he gone?" Norman asked from the folds of her apron.

"To collect your Aunt Polly. She's bringing a Christmas pudding, you know. We'd better make custard. I'm going to need your help.

"Was he there last night?" Norman asked innocently. "With Aunt Polly? Is it because she doesn't have Uncle Ted any more?"

"I don't know, Norman." In truth, she didn't want to know. Her widowed sister-in-law was welcome to Frank. Polly didn't know the relief Wendy felt to be rid of him sometimes. Any humiliation was quite secondary to the fact that Frank stopped out all night, bringing respite from the tension and the brutality. The local gossips had been quick to suspect the truth, but she could do nothing to stop them.

Norman, sensing the direction her thoughts had taken, said, "Billy Slater says Dad and Aunt Polly are doing it."

"That's enough, Norman."

"He says she's got no elastic in her drawers. What does he mean, Mum?"

"Billy Slater is a disgusting little boy. Now let's hear no more of this. We'll make the custard."

Norman spent the next hour helping his mother in the kitchen. The turkey barely fitted in the oven, and Norman became concerned that it wouldn't be ready in time. Wendy knew better. There was ample time for the cooking. They couldn't start until Frank and Polly rolled home from the Valiant Trooper. With last orders at a quarter to three, it gave the bird five hours to roast.

A gentle knock at the front door sent Norman hurrying to open it.

"Mum, it's Grandma Morris!" he called out excitedly as he led the plump old woman into the kitchen. Maud Morris had been a marvellous support through the war years. She knew exactly when help was wanted.

"I've brought you some veggies," Maud said to Wendy, dumping a bag of muddy cabbage and carrots on the table and removing her coat and hat. "Where's that good-for-nothing son of mine? Need I ask?"

"He went to fetch Polly," Wendy calmly replied.

"Did he, indeed?"

Norman said, "About an hour ago. I expect they'll go to the pub."

The old lady went into the hall to hang up her things. When she returned, she said to Wendy, "You know what people are saying, don't you?"

Wendy ignored the question. "He brought in a seventeen-pound turkey this morning."

"Have you got a knife?" her mother-in-law asked.

"A knife?"

"For the cabbage." Maud turned to look at her grandson. "Have you had some good presents?"

Norman stared down at his shoe-laces.

Wendy said, "Grandma asked you a question, dear."

"Did you get everything you asked for?"

"I don't know."

"Did you write to Saint Nick?" Maud asked with a sideward glance at Wendy.

Norman rolled his eyes upwards. "I don't believe in that stuff anymore."

"That's a shame."

"Dad gave me a dead German's helmet. He says it belonged to the one who shot Uncle Ted. I hate it."

Wendy gathered the carrots from the table and put them in the sink. "I'm sure he was only doing what he thought was best, Norman."

"It's got a bullet hole."

"Didn't he give you anything else?" his grandmother asked.

Norman shook his head. "Mum gave me some chocolate and the *Dandy Annual*."

"But your dad didn't give you a thing apart from the helmet?"

Wendy said, "Please don't say anything. You know what it's like."

Maud Morris nodded. It was pointless to admonish her son. He'd only take it out on Wendy. She knew from personal experience the dilemma of the battered wife. To protest was to invite more violence. The knowledge that her second son had turned out such a bully shamed and angered her. Ted, her dear first-born Ted, would never have harmed a woman. Yet Ted had

been taken from her. She took an apron from the back of the door and started shredding the cabbage. Norman was sent to lay the table in the front room.

Four hours later, when the King was speaking to the nation, they heard a key being tried at the front door. Wendy switched off the wireless. The door took at least three attempts to open before Frank and Polly stumbled in to the hallway. Frank stood swaying, a bottle in his hand and a paper hat cocked ridiculously on the side of his head. His sister-in-law clung to his coat, convulsed in laughter, a pair of ankle-strap shoes dangling from her right hand.

"Happy Christmas!" Frank roared. "Peace on earth and goodwill to all men except the Jerries and the lot next door."

Polly doubled up in uncontrollable giggling.

"Let me take your coat, Polly," Wendy offered. "Did you remember the pudding? I want to get it on right away."

Polly turned to Frank. "The pudding. What did you do with the pudding, Frank?"

"What pudding?" said Frank.

Maud had come into the hall behind Wendy. "I know she's made one. Don't mess about, Frank. Where is it?"

Frank pointed vaguely over his shoulder.

Wendy said despairingly, "Back at Polly's house? Oh no!"

"Stupid cow. What are you talking about?" said Frank. "It's on our own bloody doorstep. I had to put it down to open the door, didn't I?"

Wendy squeezed past them and retrieved the white basin covered with a grease-proof paper top. She carried it quickly through to the kitchen and lowered it into the waiting saucepan of simmering water. "It looks a nice big one."

This generous remark caused another gale of laughter from Polly. Finally, slurring her words, she announced, "You'll have to make allowances. Your old man's a very naughty boy. He's took me out and got me tiddly."

Maud said, "It beats me where he gets the money from."

"Beats Wendy, too, I expect," said Polly. She

leaned closer to her sister-in-law, a lock of brown hair swaying across her face. "From what I've heard, you know a bit about beating, don't you, Wen?" The remark was not made in sympathy. It was triumphant.

Wendy felt the shame redden her face. Polly smirked and swung around, causing her black skirt to swirl as she left the room. The thick pencil lines she had drawn up the back of her legs to imitate stocking seams were badly smudged higher up. Wendy preferred not to think why.

She took the well-cooked bird from the oven, transferred it to a platter, and carried it into the front room. Maud and Norman brought in the vegetables.

"Would you like to carve, Frank?"

"Hold your horses, woman. We haven't said the grace."

Wendy started to say, "But we never . . ."

Frank had already intoned the words, "Dear Lord God Almighty."

Everyone dipped their heads.

"Thanks for what we are about to receive," Frank went on, "and for seeing to it that a skinny little half-pint won the meat raffle and decided to donate it to the Morris family."

Maud clicked her tongue in disapproval.

Polly began to giggle.

"I can't begin to understand the workings of your mysterious ways," Frank insisted on going on, "because if there really is someone up there he should have made damned sure my brother Ted was sitting at this table today."

Maud said, "That's enough, Frank! Sit down."

Frank said, "Amen. Where's the carving knife?"

Wendy handed it to him, and he attended to the task, cutting thick slices and heaping them on the plates held by his mother. "That's for Polly. She likes it steaming hot."

Polly giggled again.

The plates were distributed around the table.

Not to be outdone in convivial wit, Polly said, "You've gone overboard on the breast, Frankie dear. I thought you were a leg man."

Maud said tersely, "You should know."

"Careful, Mum," Frank cautioned, wagging the knife. "Goodwill to all men."

Polly said, "Only if they behave themselves."

A voice piped up, "Bill Slater says that—"

"Be quiet, Norman!" Wendy ordered.

They ate in heavy silence, save for Frank's animalistic chewing and swallowing. The first to finish, he quickly filled his glass with more beer.

"Dad?"

"Yes, son."

"Would we have won the war without the Americans?"

"The Yanks?" Frank scoffed. "Bunch of part-timers, son. They only came into it after men like me and your Uncle Ted had done all the real fighting. Just like the other war, the one my old Dad won. They waited till 1917. Isn't that a fact, Mum? Americans? Where were they at Dunkirk? Where were they in Africa? I'll tell you where they were—sitting on their fat backsides a couple of thousand miles away."

"From what I remember, Frank," Maud interjected. "You were sitting on yours in the snug-bar of the Valiant Trooper."

"That was different!" Frank protested angrily. "Ted and I didn't get called up until 1943. And when we were, we did our share. We chased Jerry all the way across Europe, right back to the bunker. Ted and me, brothers in arms, fighting for King and country. Ready to make the ultimate sacrifice. If Dad could have heard what you said just then, Mum, he'd turn in his grave."

Maud said icily, "That would be difficult, seeing that he's in a pot on my mantelpiece."

Polly burst into helpless laughter and almost choked on a roast potato. It was injudicious of her.

"Belt up, will you?" Frank demanded. "We're talking about the sacred memory of your dead husband. My brother."

"Sorry, Frank." Polly covered her mouth with her hands. "I don't know what came over me. Honest."

"You have no idea, you women," Frank went on. "God knows what you got up to, while we were winning the war."

"Anyway," said Norman, "Americans have chewing gum. And jeeps."

Fortunately, at this moment Frank was being distracted.

Wendy whispered in Norman's ear and they both began clearing the table, but Maud put her hand over Wendy's. She said, "Why don't you sit down? You've done more than enough. I'll fetch the pudding and custard. I'd like to get up for a while. It's beginning to get a little warm in here."

Polly offered to help. "It is my pudding, after all." But she didn't mean to get up because, unseen by the others, she had her hand on Frank's thigh.

Maud said, "I'll manage."

Norman asked, "Is it a proper pudding?"

"I don't know what you mean by proper," said Polly. "It used up most of my rations when I made it. They have to mature, do puddings. This one is two years old. It should be delicious. There was only one drawback. In 1944, I didn't have a man at home to help me stir the ingredients." She gave Frank a coy smile.

Ignoring it, Wendy said, "When Norman asked if it was a proper pudding, I think he wanted to know if he might find a lucky sixpence inside."

With a simper, Polly said, "He might, if he's a good boy, like his dad. Of *course* it's a proper pudding."

Frank quipped, "What about the other sort? Do you ever make an improper pudding?"

Before anyone could stop him, Norman said, "You should know, Dad." His reflexes were too quick for his drunken father's, and the swinging blow missed him completely.

"You'll pay for that remark, my son," Frank shouted. "You'll wash your mouth out with soap and water and then I'll beat your backside raw."

Wendy said quickly, "The boy doesn't know what he's saying, Frank. It's Christmas. Let's forgive and forget, shall we?"

He turned his anger on her. "And I know very well who puts these ideas in the boy's head. And spreads the filthy rumours all over town. You

can have your Christmas Day, Wendy. Make the most of it, because tomorrow I'm going to teach you why they call it Boxing Day."

Maud entered the suddenly silent front room carrying the dark, upturned pudding decorated with a sprig of holly. "Be an angel and fetch the custard, Norman."

The boy was thankful to run out to the kitchen.

Frank glanced at the pudding and then at Polly and then grinned. "What a magnificent sight!" He was staring at her cleavage.

Polly beamed at him, fully herself again, her morale restored by the humiliation her sister-in-law had just suffered. "The proof of the pudding . . ." she murmured.

"We'll see if 1944 was a vintage year," said Frank.

Maud sliced and served the pudding, giving Norman an extra large helping. The pudding was a delicious one, as Polly had promised, and there were complimentary sounds all round the table.

Norman sifted the rich, fruity mass with his spoon, hoping for one of those coveted silver sixpenny pieces. But Frank was the first to find one.

"You can have a wish. Whatever you like, lucky man," said Polly in a husky, suggestive tone.

Frank's thoughts were in another direction. "I wish," he said sadly, holding the small coin between finger and thumb, "I wish God's peace to my brother Ted, rest his soul. And I wish a Happy Christmas to all the blokes who fought with us and survived. And God rot all our enemies. And the bloody Yanks, come to that."

"That's about four wishes," Polly said, "and it won't come true if you tell everyone."

Wendy felt the sharp edge of a sixpence in her mouth, and removed it unnoticed by the others. She wished him out of her life, with all her heart.

Norman finally found his piece of the pudding's buried treasure. He spat the coin onto his plate and then examined it closely. "Look at this!" he said in surprise. "It isn't a sixpence. It doesn't have the King's head."

"Give it here." Frank picked up the silver coin. "Jesus Christ! He's right. It's a dime. An American dime. How the hell did that get in the pudding?"

All eyes turned to Polly for an explanation. She stared wide-eyed at Frank. She was speechless.

Frank was not. He had reached his own conclusion. "I'll tell you exactly how it got in there," he said, thrusting it under Polly's nose. "You've been stirring it up with a Yank. There was a GI base down the road, wasn't there? When did you say you made the pudding? 1944?"

He rose from the table, spittle flying as he ranted. Norman slid from his chair and hid under the table, clinging in fear to his mother's legs. He saw his father's heavy boots turned towards Polly, whose legs braced. The hem of her dress was quivering.

Frank's voice boomed around the small room. "Ted and I were fighting like bloody heroes while you were having it off with Americans. Whore!"

Norman saw a flash of his father's hand as it reached into the fireplace and picked up a poker. He heard the women scream, then a sickening thump.

The poker fell to the floor. Polly's legs jerked once and then appeared to relax. One of her arms flopped down and remained quite still. A drop of blood fell from the table edge. Presently there was another. Then it became a trickle. A crimson pool formed on the wooden floor.

Norman ran out of the room. Out of the house. Out into the cold afternoon, leaving the screams behind. He ran across the street and beat on a neighbour's door with his fists. His frantic cries of "Help, murder!" filled the street. Within a short time an interested crowd in party hats had surrounded him. He pointed in horror to his own front door as his blood-stained father charged out and lurched towards him.

It took three men to hold Frank Morris

down, and five policemen to take him away. The last of the policemen didn't leave the house until long after Norman should have gone to bed. His mother and his grandmother sat silent for some time in the kitchen, unable to stay in the front room, even though Polly's body had been taken away.

"He's not going to come back, is he, Mum?"

Wendy shook her head. She was only beginning to think about what happened next. There would be a trial, of course, and she would try to shield Norman from the publicity. He was so impressionable.

"Will they hang him?"

"I think it's time for your bed, young man," Maud said. "You've got to be strong. Your mum will need your support more than ever now."

The boy asked, "How did the dime get in the pudding, Grandma Morris?"

Wendy snapped out of her thoughts of what was to come and stared at her mother-in-law.

Maud went to the door, and for a moment it appeared as if she was reaching to put on her coat prior to leaving, but she had already promised to stay the night. Actually she was taking something from one of the pockets.

It was a Christmas card, a little bent at the edges now. Maud handed it to Wendy. "It was marked 'private and confidential' but it had my name, you see. I opened it thinking it was for me. It came last week. The address was wrong. They made a mistake over the house number. The postman delivered it to the wrong Mrs. Morris."

Wendy took the card and opened it.

"The saddest thing is," Maud continued to speak as Wendy read the message inside, "he is the only son I have left, but I really can't say I'm sorry it turned out this way. I know what he did to you, Wendy. His father did the same to me for nearly forty years. I had to break the cycle. I read the card, love. I had no idea. I couldn't let this chance pass by. For your sake, and the boy's."

A tear rolled down Wendy's cheek. Norman watched as the two women hugged. The card drifted from Wendy's lap and he pounced on it immediately. His eager eyes scanned every word.

My Darling Wendy,

Since returning home, my thoughts are filled with you, and the brief time we shared together. It's kind of strange to admit, but I sometimes catch myself wishing the Germans made you a widow. I can't stand to think of you with any other guy.

My heart aches for news of you. Not a day goes by when I don't dream of being back in your arms. My home, and my heart, will always be open for you.

Take care and keep safe,
Nick

Nick Saint, (Ex-33rd US Reserve)
221C Plover Avenue
Mountain Home
Idaho

P.S. The dime is a tiny Christmas present for Norman to remember me by.

Norman looked up at his grandmother and understood what she had done, and why. He didn't speak. He could keep a secret as well as a grown-up. He was the man of the house now, at least until they got to America.

THE ADVENTURE OF THE DAUPHIN'S DOLL
Ellery Queen

IN A BRILLIANT MARKETING DECISION, the cousins who collaborated under the pseudonym Ellery Queen (Frederic Dannay and Manfred B. Lee) also named their detective Ellery Queen. They reasoned that if readers forgot the name of the author or the name of the character, they might remember the other. It worked, as Ellery Queen is counted among the handful of best-known names in the history of mystery fiction. More than a dozen movies, as well as several radio and television shows, were based on Queen books. "The Adventure of the Dauphin's Doll" was first published in the December 1948 issue of *Ellery Queen's Mystery Magazine*.

The Adventure of the Dauphin's Doll

ELLERY QUEEN

THERE IS A LAW AMONG STORY-tellers, originally passed by Editors at the cries (they say) of their constituents, which states that stories about Christmas shall have children in them. This Christmas story is no exception; indeed, misopedists will complain that we have overdone it. And we confess in advance that this is also a story about Dolls, and that Santa Claus comes into it, and even a Thief; though as to this last, whoever he was—and that was one of the questions—he was certainly not Barabbas, even parabolically.

Another section of the statute governing Christmas stories provides that they shall incline towards Sweetness and Light. The first arises, of course, from the orphans and the never-souring savor of the annual Miracle; as for Light, it will be provided at the end, as usual, by that luminous prodigy, Ellery Queen. The reader of gloomier temper will also find a large measure of Darkness, in the person and works of one who, at least in Inspector Queen's harassed view, was surely the winged Prince of that region. His name, by the way, was not Satan, it was Comus; and this is paradox enow, since the original Comus, as everyone knows, was the god of festive joy and mirth, emotions not commonly associated with the Underworld. As Ellery struggled to embrace his phantom foe, he puzzled over this *non sequitur* in vain; in vain, that is, until Nikki Porter, no scorner of the obvious, suggested that he *might* seek the answer where any ordinary mortal would go at once. And there, to the great man's mortification, it was indeed to be found: On page 262b of Volume 6, *Coleb to Damasci*, of the 175th Anniversary edition of the *Encyclopaedia Britannica*. A French conjuror of that name—Comus—performing in London in the year 1789 caused his wife to vanish from the top of a table—the very first time, it appeared, that this feat, uxorial or otherwise, had been accomplished without the aid of mirrors. To track his dark adversary's *nom de nuit* to its historic lair gave Ellery his only glint of satisfaction until that blessed moment when light burst all around him and exorcised the darkness, Prince and all.

But this is chaos.

Our story properly begins not with our invisible character but with our dead one.

Miss Ypson had not always been dead; *au contraire*. She had lived for seventy-eight years, for most of them breathing hard. As her father used to remark, "She was a very active little verb." Miss Ypson's father was a professor of Greek at a small Midwestern university. He had conjugated his daughter with the rather bewildered assistance of one of his brawnier students, an Iowa poultry heiress.

Professor Ypson was a man of distinction. Unlike most professors of Greek, he was a Greek professor of Greek, having been born Gerasymos Aghamos Ypsilonomon in Polykhnitos, on the island of Mytilini, "where," he was fond of recalling on certain occasions, "burning Sappho loved and sung"—a quotation he found unfailingly useful in his extracurricular activities; and, the Hellenic ideal notwithstanding, Professor Ypson believed wholeheartedly in immoderation in all things. This hereditary and cultural background explains the professor's interest in fatherhood—to his wife's chagrin, for Mrs. Ypson's own breeding prowess was confined to the barnyards on which her income was based—a fact of which her husband sympathetically reminded her whenever he happened to sire another wayward chick; he held their daughter to be nothing less than a biological miracle.

The professor's mental processes also tended to confuse Mrs. Ypson. She never ceased to wonder why instead of shortening his name to Ypson, her husband had not sensibly changed it to Jones. "My dear," the professor once replied, "you are an Iowa snob." "But nobody," Mrs. Ypson cried, "can spell it or pronounce it!" "This is a cross," murmured Professor Ypson, "which we must bear with Ypsilanti." "Oh," said Mrs. Ypson.

There was invariably something Sibylline about his conversation. His favorite adjective for his wife was "ypsiliform," a term, he explained, which referred to the germinal spot at one of the fecundation stages in a ripening egg and which was, therefore, exquisitely *à propos*. Mrs. Ypson continued to look bewildered; she died at an early age.

And the professor ran off with a Kansas City variety girl of considerable talent, leaving his baptized chick to be reared by an eggish relative of her mother's, a Presbyterian named Jukes.

The only time Miss Ypson heard from her father—except when he wrote charming and erudite little notes requesting, as he termed it, *lucrum*—was in the fourth decade of his odyssey, when he sent her a handsome addition to her collection, a terra cotta play doll of Greek origin over three thousand years old which, unhappily, Miss Ypson felt duty-bound to return to the Brooklyn museum from which it had unaccountably vanished. The note accompanying her father's gift had said, whimsically: "*Timeo Danaos et dona ferentes.*"

There was poetry behind Miss Ypson's dolls. At her birth the professor, ever harmonious, signalized his devotion to fecundity by naming her Cytherea. This proved the Olympian irony. For, it turned out, her father's philo-progenitiveness throbbed frustrate in her mother's stony womb; even though Miss Ypson interred five husbands of quite adequate vigor, she remained infertile to the end of her days. Hence it is classically tragic to find her, when all passion was spent, a sweet little old lady with a vague if eager smile who, under the name of her father, pattered about a vast and echoing New York apartment playing enthusiastically with dolls.

In the beginning they were dolls of common clay: a Billiken, a kewpie, a Kathe Kruse, a Patsy, a Foxy Grandpa, and so forth. But then, as her need increased, Miss Ypson began her fierce sack of the past.

Down into the land of Pharaoh she went for two pieces of thin desiccated board, carved and painted and with hair of strung beads, and legless—so that they might not run away—which any connoisseur will tell you are the most superb specimens of ancient Egyptian paddle doll extant, far superior to those in the British Museum, although this fact will be denied in certain quarters.

Miss Ypson unearthed a foremother of "Letitia Penn," until her discovery held to be the oldest doll in America, having been brought to Philadelphia from England in 1699 by William Penn as a gift for a playmate of his small daughter's. Miss Ypson's find was a wooden-hearted "little lady" in brocade and velvet which had been sent by Sir Walter Raleigh to the first English child born in the New World. Since Virginia Dare had been born in 1587, not even the Smithsonian dared impugn Miss Ypson's triumph.

On the old lady's racks, in her plate-glass cases, might be seen the wealth of a thousand childhoods, and some riches—for such is the genetics of dolls—possessed by children grown. Here could be found "fashion babies" from fourteenth century France, sacred dolls of the Orange

Free State Fingo tribe, Satsuma paper dolls and court dolls from old Japan, beady-eyed "Kalifa" dolls of the Egyptian Sudan, Swedish birch-bark dolls, "Katcina" dolls of the Hopis, mammoth-tooth dolls of the Eskimos, feather dolls of the Chippewa, tumble dolls of the ancient Chinese, Coptic bone dolls, Roman dolls dedicated to Diana, *pantin* dolls which had been the street toys of Parisian exquisites before Madame Guillotine swept the boulevards, early Christian dolls in their *crèches* representing the Holy Family—to specify the merest handful of Miss Ypson's Briarean collection. She possessed dolls of pasteboard, dolls of animal skin, spool dolls, crab-claw dolls, eggshell dolls, cornhusk dolls, rag dolls, pine-cone dolls with moss hair, stocking dolls, dolls of *bisque*, dolls of palm leaf, dolls of *papier-mâché*, even dolls made of seed pods. There were dolls forty inches tall, and there were dolls so little Miss Ypson could hide them in her gold thimble.

Cytherea Ypson's collection bestrode the centuries and took tribute of history. There was no greater—not the fabled playthings of Montezuma, or Victoria's, or Eugene Field's; not the collection at the Metropolitan, or the South Kensington, or the royal palace in old Bucharest, or anywhere outside the enchantment of little girls' dreams.

It was made of Iowan eggs and the Attic shore, corn-fed and myrtle-clothed; and it brings us at last to Attorney John Somerset Bondling and his visit to the Queen residence one December twenty-third not so very long ago.

December the twenty-third is ordinarily not a good time to seek the Queens. Inspector Richard Queen likes his Christmas old-fashioned; his turkey stuffing, for instance, calls for twenty-two hours of over-all preparation and some of its ingredients are not readily found at the corner grocer's. And Ellery is a frustrated gift-wrapper. For a month before Christmas he turns his sleuthing genius to tracking down unusual wrapping papers, fine ribbons, and artistic stickers; and he spends the last two days creating beauty.

So it was that when Attorney John S. Bondling called, Inspector Queen was in his kitchen, swathed in a barbecue apron, up to his elbows in *fines herbes*, while Ellery, behind the locked door of his study, composed a secret symphony in glittering fuchsia metallic paper, forest-green moiré ribbon, and pine cones.

"It's almost useless," shrugged Nikki, studying Attorney Bondling's card, which was as crackly-looking as Attorney Bondling. "You say you know the Inspector, Mr. Bondling?"

"Just tell him Bondling the estate lawyer," said Bondling neurotically. "Park Row. He'll know."

"Don't blame me," said Nikki, "if you wind up in his stuffing. Goodness knows he's used everything else." And she went for Inspector Queen.

While she was gone, the study door opened noiselessly for one inch. A suspicious eye reconnoitered from the crack.

"Don't be alarmed," said the owner of the eye, slipping through the crack and locking the door hastily behind him. "Can't trust them, you know. Children, just children."

"Children!" Attorney Bondling snarled. "You're Ellery Queen, aren't you?"

"Yes?"

"Interested in youth, are you? Christmas? Orphans, dolls, that sort of thing?" Mr. Bondling went on in a remarkably nasty way.

"I suppose so."

"The more fool you. Ah, here's your father. Inspector Queen—!"

"Oh, that Bondling," said the old gentleman absently, shaking his visitor's hand. "My office called to say someone was coming up. Here, use my handkerchief; that's a bit of turkey liver. Know my son? His secretary, Miss Porter? What's on your mind, Mr. Bondling?"

"Inspector, I'm handling the Cytherea Ypson estate, and—"

"Nice meeting you, Mr. Bondling," said Ellery. "Nikki, the door is locked, so don't pretend you forgot the way to the bathroom . . ."

"Cytherea Ypson," frowned the Inspector. "Oh, yes. She died only recently."

"Leaving me with the headache," said Mr.

Bondling bitterly, "of disposing of her Dollection."

"Her what?" asked Ellery, looking up from the key.

"Dolls—collection. Dollection. She coined the word."

Ellery put the key back in his pocket and strolled over to his armchair.

"Do I take this down?" sighed Nikki.

"Dollection," said Ellery.

"Spent about thirty years at it. Dolls!"

"Yes, Nikki, take it down."

"Well, well, Mr. Bondling," said Inspector Queen. "What's the problem? Christmas comes but once a year, you know."

"Will provides the Dollection be sold at auction," grated the attorney, "and the proceeds used to set up a fund for orphan children. I'm holding the public sale right after New Year's."

"Dolls and orphans, eh?" said the Inspector, thinking of Javanese black pepper and Country Gentleman Seasoning Salt.

"That's *nice*," beamed Nikki.

"Oh, is it?" said Mr. Bondling softly. "Apparently, young woman, you've never tried to satisfy a Surrogate. I've administered estates for nine years without a whisper against me, but let an estate involve the interests of just one little ba— little fatherless child, and you'd think from the Surrogate's attitude I was Bill Sykes himself!"

"My stuffing," began the Inspector.

"I've had those dolls catalogued. The result is frightening! Did you know there's no set market for the damnable things? And aside from a few personal possessions, the Dollection constitutes the old lady's entire estate. Sank every nickel she had in it."

"But it should be worth a fortune," protested Ellery.

"To whom, Mr. Queen? Museums always want such things as free and unencumbered gifts. I tell you, except for one item, those hypothetical orphans won't realize enough from that sale to keep them in—in bubble gum for two days!"

"Which item would that be, Mr. Bondling?"

"Number Eight-seventy-four," snapped the lawyer. "This one."

"Number Eight-seventy-four," read Inspector Queen from the fat catalogue Bondling had fished out of a large greatcoat pocket. "The Dauphin's Doll. Unique. Ivory figure of a boy Prince eight inches tall, clad in court dress, genuine ermine, brocade, velvet. Court sword in gold strapped to waist. Gold circlet crown surmounted by single blue brilliant diamond of finest water, weight approximately 49 carats—"

"How many carats?" exclaimed Nikki.

"Larger than the *Hope* and the *Star of South Africa*," said Ellery, with a certain excitement.

"—appraised," continued his father, "at one hundred and ten thousand dollars."

"Expensive dollie."

"Indecent!" said Nikki.

"This indecent—I mean exquisite royal doll," the Inspector read on, "was a birthday gift from King Louis XVI of France to Louis Charles, his second son, who became dauphin at the death of his elder brother in 1789. The little dauphin was proclaimed Louis XVII by the royalists during the French Revolution while in custody of the *sans-culottes*. His fate is shrouded in mystery. Romantic, historic item."

"*Le prince perdu*. I'll say," muttered Ellery. "Mr. Bondling, is this on the level?"

"I'm an attorney, not an antiquarian," snapped their visitor. "There are documents attached, one of them a sworn statement— holograph—by Lady Charlotte Atkyns, the English actress-friend of the Capet family— she was in France during the Revolution—or purporting to be in Lady Charlotte's hand. It doesn't matter, Mr. Queen. Even if the history is bad, the diamond's good!"

"I take it this hundred-and-ten-thousand-dollar dollie constitutes the bone, as it were, or that therein lies the rub?"

"You said it!" cried Mr. Bondling, cracking his knuckles in a sort of agony. "For my money the Dauphin's Doll is the only negotiable asset of that collection. And what's the old lady do? She provides by will that on the day preceding

Christmas the Cytherea Ypson Dollection is to be publicly displayed . . . on the main floor of Nash's Department Store! *The day before Christmas, gentlemen!* Think of it!"

"But why?" asked Nikki, puzzled.

"Why? Who knows why? For the entertainment of New York's army of little beggars, I suppose! Have you any notion how many peasants pass through Nash's on the day before Christmas? My cook tells me—she's a very religious woman—it's like Armageddon."

"Day before Christmas," frowned Ellery. "That's tomorrow."

"It does sound chancy," said Nikki anxiously. Then she brightened. "Oh, well, maybe Nash's won't co-operate, Mr. Bondling."

"Oh, won't they!" howled Mr. Bondling. "Why, old lady Ypson had this stunt cooked up with that gang of peasant-purveyors for years! They've been snapping at my heels ever since the day she was put away!"

"It'll draw every crook in New York," said the Inspector, his gaze on the kitchen door.

"Orphans," said Nikki. "The orphans' interests *must* be protected." She looked at her employer accusingly.

"Special measures, Dad," said Ellery.

"Sure, sure," said the Inspector, rising. "Don't you worry about this, Mr. Bondling. Now if you'll be kind enough to excu—"

"Inspector Queen," hissed Mr. Bondling, leaning forward tensely, "that is not all."

"Ah." Ellery briskly lit a cigaret. "There's a specific villain in this piece, Mr. Bondling, and you know who he is."

"I do," said the lawyer hollowly, "and then again I don't. I mean, it's Comus."

"*Comus!*" the Inspector screamed.

"Comus?" said Ellery slowly.

"Comus?" said Nikki. "Who dat?"

"Comus," nodded Mr. Bondling. "First thing this morning. Marched right into my office, bold as day—must have followed me; I hadn't got my coat off, my secretary wasn't even in. Marched in and tossed this card on my desk."

Ellery seized it. "The usual, Dad."

"His trademark," growled the Inspector, his lips working.

"But the card just says 'Comus,'" complained Nikki. "Who—?"

"Go on, Mr. Bondling!" thundered the Inspector.

"And he calmly announced to me," said Bondling, blotting his cheeks with an exhausted handkerchief, "that he's going to steal the Dauphin's Doll tomorrow, in Nash's."

"Oh, a maniac," said Nikki.

"Mr. Bondling," said the old gentleman in a terrible voice, "just what did this fellow look like?"

"Foreigner—black beard—spoke with a thick accent of some sort. To tell you the truth, I was so thunderstruck I didn't notice details. Didn't even chase him till it was too late."

The Queens shrugged at each other, Gallically.

"The old story," said the Inspector; the corners of his nostrils were greenish. "The brass of the colonel's monkey and when he does show himself nobody remembers anything but beards and foreign accents. Well, Mr. Bondling, with Comus in the game it's serious business. Where's the collection right now?"

"In the vaults of the Life Bank & Trust, Forty-third Street branch."

"What time are you to move it over to Nash's?"

"They wanted it this evening. I said nothing doing. I've made special arrangements with the bank, and the collection's to be moved at seven-thirty tomorrow morning."

"Won't be much time to set up," said Ellery thoughtfully, "before the store opens its doors." He glanced at his father.

"You leave Operation Dollie to us, Mr. Bondling," said the Inspector grimly. "Better give me a buzz this afternoon."

"I can't tell you, Inspector, how relieved I am—"

"Are you?" said the old gentleman sourly. "What makes you think he won't get it?"

When Attorney Bondling had left, the

Queens put their heads together, Ellery doing most of the talking, as usual. Finally, the Inspector went into the bedroom for a session with his direct line to Headquarters.

"Anybody would think," sniffed Nikki, "you two were planning the defense of the Bastille. Who is this Comus, anyway?"

"We don't know, Nikki," said Ellery slowly. "Might be anybody. Began his criminal career about five years ago. He's in the grand tradition of Lupin—a saucy, highly intelligent rascal who's made stealing an art. He seems to take a special delight in stealing valuable things under virtually impossible conditions. Master of make-up—he's appeared in a dozen different disguises. And he's an uncanny mimic. Never been caught, photographed, or fingerprinted. Imaginative, daring—I'd say he's the most dangerous thief operating in the United States."

"If he's never been caught," said Nikki skeptically, "how do you know he commits these crimes?"

"You mean and not someone else?" Ellery smiled pallidly. "The techniques mark the thefts as his work. And then, like Arsène, he leaves a card—with the name 'Comus' on it—on the scene of each visit."

"Does he usually announce in advance that he's going to swipe the crown jewels?"

"No." Ellery frowned. "To my knowledge, this is the first such instance. Since he's never done anything without a reason, that visit to Bondling's office this morning must be part of his greater plan. I wonder if—"

The telephone in the living room rang clear and loud.

Nikki looked at Ellery. Ellery looked at the telephone.

"Do you suppose—?" began Nikki. But then she said, "Oh, it's too absurd!"

"Where Comus is involved," said Ellery wildly, "nothing is too absurd!" and he leaped for the phone. "Hello!"

"A call from an old friend," announced a deep and hollowish male voice. "Comus."

"Well," said Ellery. "Hello again."

"Did Mr. Bondling," asked the voice jovially, "persuade you to 'prevent' me from stealing the Dauphin's Doll in Nash's tomorrow?"

"So you know Bondling's been here."

"No miracle involved, Queen. I followed him. Are you taking the case?"

"See here, Comus," said Ellery. "Under ordinary circumstances I'd welcome the sporting chance to put you where you belong. But these circumstances are not ordinary. That doll represents the major asset of a future fund for orphaned children. I'd rather we didn't play catch with it. Comus, what do you say we call this one off?"

"Shall we say," asked the voice gently, "Nash's Department Store—tomorrow?"

Thus the early morning of December twenty-fourth finds Messrs. Queen and Bondling, and Nikki Porter, huddled on the iron sidewalk of Forty-third Street before the holly-decked windows of the Life Bank & Trust Company, just outside a double line of armed guards. The guards form a channel between the bank entrance and an armored truck, down which Cytherea Ypson's Dollection flows swiftly. And all about gapes New York, stamping callously on the aged, icy face of the street against the uncharitable Christmas wind.

Now is the winter of his discontent, and Mr. Queen curses.

"I don't know what you're beefing about," moans Miss Porter. "You and Mr. Bondling are bundled up like Yukon prospectors. Look at *me*."

"It's that rat-hearted public relations tripe from Nash's," said Mr. Queen murderously. "They all swore themselves to secrecy, Brother Rat included. Honor! Spirit of Christmas!"

"It was all over the radio last night," whimpers Mr. Bondling. "And in this morning's papers."

"I'll cut his creep's heart out. Here! Velie, keep those people away!"

Sergeant Velie says good-naturedly from the doorway of the bank, "You jerks stand back."

Little does the Sergeant know the fate in store for him.

"Armored trucks," says Miss Porter bluishly. "Shotguns."

"Nikki, Comus made a point of informing us in advance that he meant to steal the Dauphin's Doll in Nash's Department Store. It would be just like him to have said that in order to make it easier to steal the doll en route."

"Why don't they hurry?" shivers Mr. Bondling. "Ah!"

Inspector Queen appears suddenly in the doorway. His hands clasp treasure.

"Oh!" cries Nikki.

New York whistles.

It is magnificence, an affront to democracy. But street mobs, like children, are royalists at heart.

New York whistles, and Sergeant Thomas Velie steps menacingly before Inspector Queen, Police Positive drawn, and Inspector Queen dashes across the sidewalk between the bristling lines of guards with the Dauphin's Doll in his embrace.

Queen the Younger vanishes, to materialize an instant later at the door of the armored truck.

"It's just immorally, hideously beautiful, Mr. Bondling," breathes Miss Porter, sparkly-eyed.

Mr. Bondling cranes, thinly.

ENTER *Santa Claus, with bell.*

Santa. Oyez, oyez. Peace, good will. Is that the dollie the radio's been yappin' about, folks?

Mr. B. Scram.

Miss P. Why, Mr. Bondling.

Mr. B. Well, he's got no business here. Stand back, er, Santa. Back!

Santa. What eateth you, my lean and angry friend? Have you no compassion at this season of the year?

Mr. B. Oh . . . Here! *(Clink.)* Now will you *kindly* . . . ?

Santa. Mighty pretty dollie. Where they takin' it, girlie?

Miss P. Over to Nash's, Santa.

Mr. B. You asked for it. Officer!!!

Santa (hurriedly). Little present for you, girlie. Compliments of Santy. Merry, merry.

Miss P. For *me*? (EXIT *Santa, rapidly, with bell.*) Really, Mr. Bondling, was it necessary to . . . ?

Mr. B. Opium for the masses! What did that flatulent faker hand you, Miss Porter? What's in that unmentionable envelope?

Miss P. I'm sure I don't know, but isn't it the most touching idea? Why, it's addressed to *Ellery*. Oh! Elleryyyyyy!

Mr. B (EXIT *excitedly*). Where is he? You—! Officer! Where did that baby-deceiver disappear to? A Santa Claus . . . !

Mr. Q (entering on the run). Yes? Nikki, what is it? What's happened?

Miss P. A man dressed as Santa Claus just handed me this envelope. It's addressed to you.

Mr. Q. Note? *(He snatches it, withdraws a miserable slice of paper from it on which is block-lettered in pencil a message which he reads aloud with considerable expression.)* "Dear Ellery, Don't you trust me? I said I'd steal the Dauphin in Nash's emporium today and that's exactly where I'm going to do it. Yours—" Signed . . .

Miss P (craning). "Comus." That Santa?

Mr. Q. (Sets his manly lips. An icy wind blows.)

Even the master had to acknowledge that their defenses against Comus were ingenious.

From the Display Department of Nash's they had requisitioned four miter-jointed counters of uniform length. These they had fitted together, and in the center of the hollow square thus formed they had erected a platform six feet high. On the counters, in plastic tiers, stretched the long lines of Miss Ypson's babies. Atop the platform, dominant, stood a great chair of hand-carved oak, filched from the Swedish Modern section of the Fine Furniture Department; and on this Valhalla-like throne, a huge and rosy rotundity, sat Sergeant Thomas Velie of Police Headquarters, morosely grateful for the anonymity endowed by the scarlet suit and the jolly mask and whiskers of his appointed role.

Nor was this all. At a distance of six feet outside the counters shimmered a surrounding rampart of plate glass, borrowed in its various elements from *The Glass Home of the Future* display on the sixth floor rear, and assembled to shape an eight foot wall quoined with chrome, its glistening surfaces flawless except at one point, where a thick glass door had been installed. But the edges fitted intimately and there was a formidable lock in the door, the key to which lay buried in Mr. Queen's right trouser pocket.

It was 8:54 a.m. The Queens, Nikki Porter, and Attorney Bondling stood among store officials and an army of plainclothesmen on Nash's main floor surveying the product of their labors.

"I think that about does it," muttered Inspector Queen at last. "Men! Positions around the glass partition."

Twenty-four assorted gendarmes in mufti jostled one another. They took marked places about the wall, facing it and grinning up at Sergeant Velie. Sergeant Velie, from his throne, glared back.

"Hagstrom and Piggott—the door."

Two detectives detached themselves from a group of reserves. As they marched to the glass door, Mr. Bondling plucked at the Inspector's overcoat sleeve. "Can all these men be trusted, Inspector Queen?" he whispered. "I mean, this fellow Comus—"

"Mr. Bondling," replied the old gentleman coldly, "you do your job and let me do mine."

"But—"

"Picked men, Mr. Bondling! I picked 'em myself."

"Yes, yes, Inspector. I merely thought I'd—"

"Lieutenant Farber."

A little man with watery eyes stepped forward.

"Mr. Bondling, this is Lieutenant Geronimo Farber, Headquarters jewelry expert. Ellery?"

Ellery took the Dauphin's Doll from his greatcoat pocket, but he said, "If you don't mind, Dad, I'll keep holding on to it."

Somebody said, "Wow," and then there was silence.

"Lieutenant, this doll in my son's hand is the famous Dauphin's Doll with the diamond crown that—"

"Don't touch it, Lieutenant, please," said Ellery. "I'd rather nobody touched it."

"The doll," continued the Inspector, "has just been brought here from a bank vault which it ought never to have left, and Mr. Bondling, who's handling the Ypson estate, claims it's the genuine article. Lieutenant, examine the diamond and give us your opinion."

Lieutenant Farber produced a *loupe*. Ellery held the dauphin securely, and Farber did not touch it.

Finally, the expert said: "I can't pass an opinion about the doll itself, of course, but the diamond's a beauty. Easily worth a hundred thousand dollars at the present state of the market—maybe more. Looks like a very strong setting, by the way."

"Thanks, Lieutenant. Okay, son," said the Inspector. "Go into your waltz."

Clutching the dauphin, Ellery strode over to the glass gate and unlocked it.

"This fellow Farber," whispered Attorney Bondling in the Inspector's hairy ear. "Inspector, are you absolutely sure he's—?"

"He's really Lieutenant Farber?" The Inspector controlled himself. "Mr. Bondling, I've known Gerry Farber for eighteen years. Calm yourself."

Ellery was crawling perilously over the nearest counter. Then, bearing the dauphin aloft, he hurried across the floor of the enclosure to the platform.

Sergeant Velie whined, "Maestro, how in hell am I going to sit here all day without washin' my hands?"

But Mr. Queen merely stooped and lifted from the floor a heavy little structure faced with black velvet consisting of a floor and a backdrop, with a two-armed chromium support. This object he placed on the platform directly between Sergeant Velie's massive legs.

Carefully, he stood the Dauphin's Doll in the velvet niche. Then he clambered back across the counter, went through the glass door, locked it with the key, and turned to examine his handiwork.

Proudly the prince's plaything stood, the jewel in his little golden crown darting "on pale electric streams" under the concentrated tide of a dozen of the most powerful floodlights in the possession of the great store.

"Velie," said Inspector Queen, "you're not to touch that doll. Don't lay a finger on it."

The Sergeant said, "Gaaaaa."

"You men on duty. Don't worry about the crowds. Your job is to keep watching that doll. You're not to take your eyes off it all day. Mr. Bondling, are you satisfied?" Mr. Bondling seemed about to say something, but then he hastily nodded. "Ellery?"

The great man smiled. "The only way he can get that bawbie," he said, "is by well-directed mortar fire or spells and incantations. Raise the portcullis!"

Then began the interminable day, *dies irae*, the last shopping day before Christmas. This is traditionally the day of the inert, the procrastinating, the undecided, and the forgetful, sucked at last into the mercantile machine by the perpetual pump of Time. If there is peace upon earth, it descends only afterward; and at no time, on the part of anyone embroiled, is there good will toward men. As Miss Porter expresses it, a cat fight in a bird cage would be more Christian.

But on this December twenty-fourth, in Nash's, the normal bedlam was augmented by the vast shrilling of thousands of children. It may be, as the Psalmist insists, that happy is the man that hath his quiver full of them; but no bowmen surrounded Miss Ypson's darlings this day, only detectives carrying revolvers, not a few of whom forbore to use same only by the most heroic self-discipline. In the black floods of humanity overflowing the main floor little folks darted about like electrically charged min-

nows, pursued by exasperated maternal shrieks and the imprecations of those whose shins and rumps and toes were at the mercy of hot, happy little limbs; indeed, nothing was sacred, and Attorney Bondling was seen to quail and wrap his greatcoat defensively about him against the savage innocence of childhood. But the guardians of the law, having been ordered to simulate store employees, possessed no such armor; and many a man earned his citation that day for unique cause. They stood in the millrace of the tide; it churned about them, shouting, "Dollies! *Dollies!*" until the very word lost its familiar meaning and became the insensate scream of a thousand Loreleis beckoning strong men to destruction below the eye-level of their diamond Light.

But they stood fast.

And Comus was thwarted. Oh, he tried. At 11:18 a.m. a tottering old man holding to the hand of a small boy tried to wheedle Detective Hagstrom into unlocking the glass door "so my grandson here—he's terrible nearsighted—can get a closer look at the pretty dollies." Detective Hagstrom roared, "Rube!" and the old gentleman dropped the little boy's hand violently and with remarkable agility lost himself in the crowd. A spot investigation revealed that, coming upon the boy, who had been crying for his mommy, the old gentleman had promised to find her. The little boy, whose name—he said—was Lance Morganstern, was removed to the Lost and Found Department; and everyone was satisfied that the great thief had finally launched his attack. Everyone, that is, but Ellery Queen. He seemed puzzled. When Nikki asked him why, he merely said: "Stupidity, Nikki. It's not in character."

At 1:46 p.m., Sergeant Velie sent up a distress signal. He had, it seemed, to wash his hands. Inspector Queen signaled back: "O.K. Fifteen minutes." Sergeant Santa C. Velie scrambled off his perch, clawed his way over the counter, and pounded urgently on the inner side of the glass door. Ellery let him out, relocking the door immediately, and the Sergeant's red-clad figure disappeared on the double in the general direction of the main-floor gentlemen's relief station, leaving the dauphin in solitary possession of the dais.

During the Sergeant's recess, Inspector Queen circulated among his men repeating the order of the day.

The episode of Velie's response to the summons of Nature caused a temporary crisis. For at the end of the specified fifteen minutes he had not returned. Nor was there a sign of him at the end of a half hour. An aide dispatched to the relief station reported back that the Sergeant was not there. Fears of foul play were voiced at an emergency staff conference held then and there and counter-measures were being planned even as, at 2:35 p.m., the familiar Santa-clad bulk of the Sergeant was observed battling through the lines, pawing at his mask.

"Velie," snarled Inspector Queen, "where have you been?"

"Eating my lunch," growled the Sergeant's voice, defensively. "I been taking my punishment like a good soldier all this damn day, Inspector, but I draw the line at starvin' to death even in the line of duty."

"Velie—!" choked the Inspector; but then he waved his hand feebly and said, "Ellery, let him back in there."

And that was very nearly all. The only other incident of note occurred at 4:22 p.m. A well-upholstered woman with a red face yelled, "Stop! Thief! He grabbed my pocketbook! Police!" about fifty feet from the Ypson exhibit. Ellery instantly shouted, "*It's a trick! Men, don't take your eyes off that doll!*" "It's Comus disguised as a woman," exclaimed Attorney Bondling, as Inspector Queen and Detective Hesse wrestled the female figure through the mob. She was now a wonderful shade of magenta. "What are you *doing*?" she screamed. "Don't arrest *me!*—catch that crook who stole my pocketbook!" "No dice, Comus," said the Inspector. "Wipe off that makeup." "McComas?" said the woman loudly. "My name is Rafferty, and all these folks saw it. He was a fat man with a mustache." "Inspec-

tor," said Nikki Porter, making a surreptitious scientific test. "This is a female. Believe me." And so, indeed it proved. All agreed that the mustachioed fat man had been Comus, creating a diversion in the desperate hope that the resulting confusion would give him an opportunity to steal the little dauphin.

"Stupid, stupid," muttered Ellery, gnawing his fingernails.

"Sure," grinned the Inspector. "We've got him nibbling his tail, Ellery. This was his do-or-die pitch. He's through."

"Frankly," sniffed Nikki, "I'm a little disappointed."

"Worried," said Ellery, "would be the word for me."

Inspector Queen was too case-hardened a sinner's nemesis to lower his guard at his most vulnerable moment. When the 5:30 bells bonged and the crowds began struggling toward the exits, he barked: "Men, stay at your posts. Keep watching that doll!" So all hands were on the *qui vive* even as the store emptied. The reserves kept hustling people out. Ellery, standing on an Information booth, spotted bottlenecks and waved his arms.

At 5:50 p.m. the main floor was declared out of the battle zone. All stragglers had been herded out. The only persons visible were the refugees trapped by the closing bell on the upper floors, and these were pouring out of elevators and funneled by a solid line of detectives and accredited store personnel to the doors. By 6:05 they were a trickle; by 6:10 even the trickle had dried up. And the personnel itself began to disperse.

"No, men!" called Ellery sharply from his observation post. "Stay where you are till all the store employees are out!" The counter clerks had long since disappeared.

Sergeant Velie's plaintive voice called from the other side of the glass door. "I got to get home and decorate my tree. Maestro, make with the key."

Ellery jumped down and hurried over to release him. Detective Piggott jeered, "Going to play Santa to your kids tomorrow morning, Velie?" at which the Sergeant managed even through his mask to project a four-letter word distinctly, forgetful of Miss Porter's presence, and stamped off toward the gentlemen's relief station.

"Where you going, Velie?" asked the Inspector, smiling.

"I got to get out of these x-and-dash Santy clothes somewheres, don't I?" came back the Sergeant's mask-muffled tones, and he vanished in a thunder-clap of his fellow-officers' laughter.

"Still worried, Mr. Queen?" chuckled the Inspector.

"I don't understand it." Ellery shook his head. "Well, Mr. Bondling, there's your dauphin, untouched by human hands."

"Yes. Well!" Attorney Bondling wiped his forehead happily. "I don't profess to understand it, either, Mr. Queen. Unless it's simply another case of an inflated reputation . . ." He clutched the Inspector suddenly. "Those men!" he whispered. *"Who are they?"*

"Relax, Mr. Bondling," said the Inspector good-naturedly. "It's just the men to move the dolls back to the bank. Wait a minute, you men! Perhaps, Mr. Bondling, we'd better see the dauphin back to the vaults ourselves."

"Keep those fellows back," said Ellery to the Headquarters men, quietly, and he followed the Inspector and Mr. Bondling into the enclosure. They pulled two of the counters apart at one corner and strolled over to the platform. The dauphin was winking at them in a friendly way. They stood looking at him.

"Cute little devil," said the Inspector.

"Seems silly now," beamed Attorney Bondling. "Being so worried all day."

"Comus must have had *some* plan," mumbled Ellery.

"Sure," said the Inspector. "That old man disguise. And that purse-snatching act."

"No, no, Dad. Something clever. He's always pulled something clever."

"Well, there's the diamond," said the lawyer comfortably. "He didn't."

"Disguise . . ." muttered Ellery. "It's always been a disguise. Santa Claus costume—he used that once—this morning in front of the bank . . . Did we see a Santa Claus around here today?"

"Just Velie," said the Inspector, grinning. "And I hardly think—"

"Wait a moment, please," said Attorney Bondling in a very odd voice. He was staring at the Dauphin's Doll.

"Wait for what, Mr. Bondling?"

"What's the matter?" said Ellery, also in a very odd voice.

"But . . . not possible . . ." stammered Bondling. He snatched the doll from its black velvet repository. *"No!"* he howled. *"This isn't the dauphin! It's a fake—a copy!"*

Something happened in Mr. Queen's head—a little *click!* like the turn of a switch. And there was light.

"Some of you men!" he roared. *"After Santa Claus!"*

"Who, Mr. Queen?"

"What's he talkin' about?"

"After who, Ellery?" gasped Inspector Queen.

"What's the matter?"

"I dunno!"

"Don't stand here! *Get him!"* screamed Ellery, dancing up and down. "The man I just let out of here! The Santa who made for the men's room!"

Detectives started running, wildly.

"But, Ellery," said a small voice, and Nikki found that it was her own, "that was Sergeant Velie."

"It was *not* Velie, Nikki! When Velie ducked out just before two o'clock to relieve himself, *Comus waylaid him!* It was Comus who came back in Velie's Santa Claus rig, wearing Velie's whiskers and mask! *Comus has been on this platform all afternoon!*" He tore the dauphin from Attorney Bondling's grasp. "Copy . . . ! Somehow he did it, he did it."

"But, Mr. Queen," whispered Attorney Bondling, "his voice. He spoke to us . . . in Sergeant Velie's voice."

"Yes, Ellery," Nikki heard herself saying.

"I told you yesterday Comus is a great mimic, Nikki. Lieutenant Farber! Is Farber still here?"

The jewelry expert, who had been gaping from a distance, shook his head as if to clear it and shuffled into the enclosure.

"Lieutenant," said Ellery in a strangled voice. "Examine this diamond . . . I mean, *is* it a diamond?"

Inspector Queen removed his hands from his face and said froggily, "Well, Gerry?"

Lieutenant Farber squinted once through his *loupe.* "The hell you say. It's strass—"

"It's what?" said the Inspector piteously.

"Strass, Dick—lead glass—paste. Beautiful job of imitation—as nice as I've ever seen."

"Lead me to that Santa Claus," whispered Inspector Queen.

But Santa Claus was being led to him. Struggling in the grip of a dozen detectives, his red coat ripped off, his red pants around his ankles, but his whiskery mask still on his face, came a large shouting man.

"But I tell you," he was roaring, "I'm Sergeant Tom Velie! Just take the mask off—that's all!"

"It's a pleasure," growled Detective Hagstrom, trying to break their prisoner's arm, "we're reservin' for the Inspector."

"Hold him, boys," whispered the Inspector. He struck like a cobra. His hand came away with Santa's face.

And there, indeed, was Sergeant Velie.

"Why it's Velie," said the Inspector wonderingly.

"I only told you that a thousand times," said the Sergeant, folding his great hairy arms across his great hairy chest. "Now who's the so-and-so who tried to bust my arm?" Then he said, "My pants!" and, as Miss Porter turned delicately away, Detective Hagstrom humbly stooped and raised Sergeant Velie's pants.

"Never mind that," said a cold, remote voice. It was the master, himself.

"Yeah?" said Sergeant Velie, hostilely.

"Velie, weren't you attacked when you went to the men's room just before two?"

"Do I look like the attackable type?"

"You did go to lunch?—in person?"

"And a lousy lunch it was."

"It was *you* up here among the dolls all afternoon?"

"Nobody else, Maestro. Now, my friends, I want action. Fast patter. What's this all about? Before," said Sergeant Velie softly, "I lose my temper."

While divers Headquarters orators delivered impromptu periods before the silent Sergeant, Inspector Richard Queen spoke.

"Ellery. Son. How in the name of the second sin did he do it?"

"Pa," replied the master, "you got me."

Deck the hall with boughs of holly, but not if your name is Queen on the evening of a certain December twenty-fourth. If your name is Queen on that lamentable evening you are seated in the living room of a New York apartment uttering no falalas but staring miserably into a somber fire. And you have company. The guest list is short, but select. It numbers two, a Miss Porter and a Sergeant Velie, and they are no comfort.

No, no ancient Yuletide carol is being trolled; only the silence sings.

Wail in your crypt, Cytherea Ypson; all was for nought; your little dauphin's treasure lies not in the empty coffers of the orphans but in the hot clutch of one who took his evil inspiration from a long-crumbled specialist in vanishments.

Speech was spent. Should a wise man utter vain knowledge and fill his belly with the east wind? He who talks too much commits a sin, says the Talmud. He also wastes his breath; and they had now reached the point of conservation, having exhausted the available supply.

Item: Lieutenant Geronimo Farber of Police Headquarters had examined the diamond in the genuine dauphin's crown a matter of seconds before it was conveyed to its sanctuary in the enclosure. Lieutenant Farber had pronounced the diamond a diamond, and not merely a diamond, but a diamond worth in his opinion over one hundred thousand dollars.

Question: Had Lieutenant Farber lied?

Answer: Lieutenant Farber was (a) a man of probity, tested in a thousand fires, and (b) he was incorruptible. To (a) and (b) Inspector Richard Queen attested violently, swearing by the beard of his personal Prophet.

Question: Had Lieutenant Farber been mistaken?

Answer: Lieutenant Farber was a nationally famous police expert in the field of precious stones. It must be presumed that he knew a real diamond from a piece of lapidified glass.

Question: Had it *been* Lieutenant Farber?

Answer: By the same beard of the identical Prophet, it had been Lieutenant Farber and no facsimile.

Conclusion: The diamond Lieutenant Farber had examined immediately preceding the opening of Nash's doors that morning had been the veritable diamond of the dauphin, the doll had been the veritable Dauphin's Doll, and it was this genuine article which Ellery with his own hands had carried into the glass-enclosed fortress and deposited between the authenticated Sergeant Velie's verified feet.

Item: All day—specifically, between the moment the dauphin had been deposited in his niche until the moment he was discovered to be a fraud; that is, during the total period in which a theft-and-substitution was even theoretically possible—no person whatsoever, male or female, adult or child, had set foot within the enclosure except Sergeant Thomas Velie, alias Santa Claus.

Question: Had Sergeant Velie switched dolls, carrying the genuine dauphin concealed in his Santa Claus suit, to be cached for future retrieval or turned over to Comus or a confederate of Comus's, during one of his two departures from the enclosure?

Answer (by Sergeant Velie): *

Confirmation: Some dozens of persons with police training and specific instructions, not to mention the Queens themselves, Miss Porter,

* Deleted. —*Editor.*

and Attorney Bondling, testified unqualifiedly that Sergeant Velie had not touched the doll, at any time, all day.

Conclusion: Sergeant Velie could not have stolen, and therefore he did not steal, the Dauphin's Doll.

Item: All those deputized to watch the doll swore that they had done so without lapse or hindrance the everlasting day; moreover, that at no time had anything touched the doll—human or mechanical—either from inside or outside the enclosure.

Question: The human vessel being frail, could those so swearing have been in error? Could their attention have wandered through weariness, boredom, *et cetera*?

Answer: Yes; but not all at the same time, by the laws of probability. And during the only two diversions of the danger period, Ellery himself testified that he had kept his eyes on the dauphin and that nothing whatsoever had approached or threatened it.

Item: Despite all of the foregoing, at the end of the day they had found the real dauphin gone and a worthless copy in its place.

"It's brilliantly, unthinkably clever," said Ellery at last. "A master illusion. For, of course, it *was* an illusion . . ."

"Witchcraft," groaned the Inspector.

"Mass mesmerism," suggested Nikki Porter.

"Mass bird gravel," growled the Sergeant.

Two hours later Ellery spoke again.

"So Comus had a worthless copy of the dauphin all ready for the switch," he muttered. "It's a world-famous dollie, been illustrated countless times, minutely described, photographed . . . All ready for the switch, but how did he make it? How? How?"

"You said that," said the Sergeant, "once or forty-two times."

"The bells are tolling," sighed Nikki, "but for whom? Not for us." And indeed, while they slumped there, Time, which Seneca named father of truth, had crossed the threshold of Christmas; and Nikki looked alarmed, for as that glorious song of old came upon the midnight clear, a great light spread from Ellery's eyes and beatified the whole contorted countenance, so that peace sat there, the peace that approximateth understanding; and he threw back that noble head and laughed with the merriment of an innocent child.

"Hey," said Sergeant Velie, staring.

"Son," began Inspector Queen, half-rising from his armchair; when the telephone rang.

"Beautiful!" roared Ellery. "Oh, exquisite! How did Comus make the switch, eh? Nikki—"

"From somewhere," said Nikki, handing him the telephone receiver, "a voice is calling, and if you ask me it's saying 'Comus.' Why not ask him?"

"Comus," whispered the Inspector, shrinking.

"Comus," echoed the Sergeant, baffled.

"Comus?" said Ellery heartily. "How nice. Hello there! Congratulations."

"Why, thank you," said the familiar deep and hollow voice. "I called to express my appreciation for a wonderful day's sport and to wish you the merriest kind of Yuletide."

"You anticipate a rather merry Christmas yourself, I take it."

"*Laeti triumphantes*," said Comus jovially.

"And the orphans?"

"They have my best wishes. But I won't detain you, Ellery. If you'll look at the doormat outside your apartment door, you'll find on it—in the spirit of the season—a little gift, with the compliments of Comus. Will you remember me to Inspector Queen and Attorney Bondling?"

Ellery hung up, smiling.

On the doormat he found the true Dauphin's Doll, intact except for a contemptible detail. The jewel in the little golden crown was missing.

"It was," said Ellery later, over pastrami sandwiches, "a fundamentally simple problem. All great illusions are. A valuable object is placed in full view in the heart of an impenetrable enclosure, it is watched hawkishly by dozens of thoroughly screened and reliable trained persons, it is never out of their view, it is not once touched by human hand or any other agency, and yet, at the expiration of the danger period, it is gone—exchanged for a worthless copy. Wonderful. Amazing. It defies the imagination. Actually, it's susceptible—like all magical hocus-pocus—to immediate solution if only one is able—as I was not—to ignore the wonder and stick to the fact. But then, the wonder is there for precisely that purpose: to stand in the way of the fact.

"What is the fact?" continued Ellery, helping himself to a dill pickle. "The fact is that between the time the doll was placed on the exhibit platform and the time the theft was discovered no one and no thing touched it. Therefore between the time the doll was placed on the platform and the time the theft was discovered *the dauphin could not have been stolen*. It follows, simply and inevitably, that the dauphin must have been stolen *outside that period*.

"Before the period began? No. I placed the authentic dauphin inside the enclosure with my own hands; at or about the beginning of the period, then, no hand but mine had touched the doll—not even, you'll recall, Lieutenant Farber's.

"Then the dauphin must have been stolen after the period closed."

Ellery brandished half the pickle. "And who," he demanded solemnly, "is the only one besides myself who handled that doll after the period closed and before Lieutenant Farber pronounced the diamond to be paste? The only one?"

The Inspector and the Sergeant exchanged puzzled glances, and Nikki looked blank.

"Why, Mr. Bondling," said Nikki, "and he doesn't count."

"He counts very much, Nikki," said Ellery, reaching for the mustard, "because the facts say Bondling stole the dauphin at that time."

"Bondling!" The Inspector paled.

"I don't get it," complained Sergeant Velie.

"Ellery, you must be wrong," said Nikki. "At the time Mr. Bondling grabbed the doll off the platform, the theft had already taken place. It was the worthless copy he picked up."

"That," said Ellery, reaching for another sandwich, "was the focal point of his illusion. How do we know it was the worthless copy he picked up? Why, he said so. Simple, eh? He said so, and like the dumb bunnies we were, we took his unsupported word as gospel."

"That's right!" mumbled his father. "We didn't actually examine the doll till quite a few seconds later."

"Exactly," said Ellery in a munchy voice. "There was a short period of beautiful confusion, as Bondling knew there would be. I yelled to the boys to follow and grab Santa Claus—I mean, the Sergeant here. The detectives were momentarily demoralized. You, Dad, were stunned. Nikki looked as if the roof had fallen in. I essayed an excited explanation. Some detectives ran; others milled around. And while all this was happening—during those few moments when nobody was watching the genuine doll in Bondling's hand because everyone thought it was a fake—Bondling calmly slipped it into one of his greatcoat pockets and from the other produced the worthless copy which he'd been carrying there all day. When I did turn back to him, it was the copy I grabbed from his hand. And his illusion was complete.

"I know," said Ellery dryly. "It's rather on the let-down side. That's why illusionists guard their professional secrets so closely; knowledge is disenchantment. No doubt the incredulous amazement aroused in his periwigged London audience by Comus the French conjuror's dematerialization of his wife from the top of a table would have suffered the same fate if he'd revealed the trap door through which she had dropped. A good trick, like a good woman, is best in the dark. Sergeant, have another pastrami."

"Seems like funny chow to be eating early Christmas morning," said the Sergeant, reaching. Then he stopped. Then he said, "Bondling," and shook his head.

"Now that we know it was Bondling," said the Inspector, who had recovered a little, "it's a cinch to get that diamond back. He hasn't had

time to dispose of it yet. I'll just give downtown a buzz—"

"Wait, Dad," said Ellery.

"Wait for what?"

"Whom are you going to sic the dogs on?"

"What?"

"You're going to call Headquarters, get a warrant, and so on. Who's your man?"

The Inspector felt his head. "Why . . . Bondling, didn't you say?"

"It might be wise," said Ellery, thoughtfully searching with his tongue for a pickle seed, "to specify his alias."

"Alias?" said Nikki. "Does he have one?"

"What alias, son?"

"Comus."

"*Comus!*"

"*Comus?*"

"Comus."

"Oh, come off it," said Nikki, pouring herself a shot of coffee, straight, for she was in training for the Inspector's Christmas dinner. "How could Bondling be Comus when Bondling was with us all day?—and Comus kept making disguised appearances all over the place . . . that Santa who gave me the note in front of the bank—the old man who kidnapped Lance Morganstern—the fat man with the mustache who snatched Mrs. Rafferty's purse."

"Yeah," said the Sergeant. "How?"

"These illusions die hard," said Ellery. "Wasn't it Comus who phoned a few minutes ago to rag me about the theft? Wasn't it Comus who said he'd left the stolen dauphin—minus the diamond—on our doorstep? Therefore Comus is Bondling.

"I told you Comus never does anything without a good reason," said Ellery. "Why did 'Comus' announce to 'Bondling' that he was *going* to steal the Dauphin's Doll? Bondling told us that—putting the finger on his *alter ego*—because he wanted us to believe he and Comus were separate individuals. He wanted us to watch for *Comus* and take *Bondling* for granted. In tactical execution of this strategy, Bondling provided us with three 'Comus'-appearances during the day—obviously, confederates.

"Yes," said Ellery, "I think, Dad, you'll find on backtracking that the great thief you've been trying to catch for five years has been a respectable estate attorney on Park Row all the time, shedding his quiddities and his quillets at night in favor of the soft shoe and the dark lantern. And now he'll have to exchange them all for a number and a grilled door. Well, well, it couldn't have happened at a more appropriate season; there's an old English proverb that says the Devil makes his Christmas pie of lawyers' tongues. Nikki, pass the pastrami."

MORSE'S GREATEST MYSTERY

Colin Dexter

IN THE TRADITION OF DOROTHY L. SAYERS and Michael Innes, Colin Dexter's mysteries combine scholarly erudition, well-constructed plots, and humor. His series character, Inspector Morse, appears in all of his novels and inspired an enormously successful British television series, the eponymous *Inspector Morse,* in which Dexter made a cameo appearance (much as Alfred Hitchcock did) in almost every episode. It may be interesting to note that Dexter is one of the world's most accomplished solvers of crossword puzzles, winning its top competitions on several occasions. "Morse's Greatest Mystery" was first collected in *Morse's Greatest Mystery and Other Stories* (London, Macmillan, 1993).

Morse's Greatest Mystery

COLIN DEXTER

"Hallo!" growled Scrooge, in his accustomed voice as near as he could feign it. "What do you mean by coming here at this time of day?"

Dickens, *A Christmas Carol*

HE HAD KNOCKED DIFFIDENTLY AT Morse's North Oxford flat. Few had been invited into those book-lined, Wagner-haunted rooms: and even he—Sergeant Lewis—had never felt himself an over-welcome guest. Even at Christmastime. Not that it sounded much like the season of goodwill as Morse waved Lewis inside and concluded his ill-tempered conversation with the bank manager.

"Look! If I keep a couple of hundred in my current account, that's *my* look-out. I'm not even asking for any interest on it. All I *am* asking is that you don't stick these bloody bank charges on when I go—what? once, twice a year?—into the red. It's not that I'm mean with money"—Lewis's eyebrows ascended a centimetre—"but if you charge me again I want you to ring and tell me *why*!"

Morse banged down the receiver and sat silent.

"You don't sound as if you've caught much of the Christmas spirit," ventured Lewis.

"I don't like Christmas—never have."

"You staying in Oxford, sir?"

"I'm going to decorate."

"What—decorate the Christmas cake?"

"Decorate the kitchen. I don't like Christmas cake—never did."

"You sound more like Scrooge every minute, sir."

"*And* I shall read a Dickens novel. I always do over Christmas. *Re*-read, rather."

"If I were just *starting* on Dickens, which one——?"

"I'd put *Bleak House* first, *Little Dorrit* second——"

The phone rang and Morse's secretary at HQ informed him that he'd won a £50 gift-token in the Police Charity Raffle, and this time Morse cradled the receiver with considerably better grace.

"'Scrooge,' did you say, Lewis? I'll have you know I bought five tickets—a quid apiece!—in that Charity Raffle."

"I bought five tickets myself, sir."

Morse smiled complacently. "Let's be more charitable, Lewis! It's *supporting* these causes that's important, not *winning*."

"I'll be in the car, sir," said Lewis quietly. In truth, he was beginning to feel irritated. Morse's irascibility he could stomach; but he couldn't stick hearing much more about Morse's selfless generosity!

Morse's old Jaguar was in dock again ("Too mean to buy a new one!" his colleagues claimed) and it was Lewis's job that day to ferry the chief inspector around; doubtless, too (if things went to form), to treat him to the odd pint or two. Which indeed appeared a fair probability, since Morse had so managed things on that Tuesday morning that their arrival at the George would coincide with opening time. As they drove out past the railway station, Lewis told Morse what he'd managed to discover about the previous day's events . . .

The patrons of the George had amassed £400 in aid of the Littlemore Charity for Mentally Handicapped Children, and this splendid total was to be presented to the Charity's Secretary at the end of the week, with a photographer promised from *The Oxford Times* to record the grand occasion. Mrs. Michaels, the landlady, had been dropped off at the bank in Carfax by her husband at about 10:30 a.m., and had there exchanged a motley assemblage of coins and notes for forty brand-new tenners. After this she had bought several items (including grapes for a daughter just admitted to hospital) before catching a minibus back home, where she had arrived just after midday. The money, in a long white envelope, was in her shopping bag, together with her morning's purchases. Her husband had not yet returned from the Cash and Carry Stores, and on re-entering the George via the saloon bar, Mrs. Michaels had heard the telephone ringing. Thinking that it was probably the hospital (it was) she had dumped her bag on the bar counter and rushed to answer it. On her return, the envelope was gone.

At the time of the theft, there had been about thirty people in the saloon bar, including the regular OAPs, the usual cohort of pool-playing unemployables, and a pre-Christmas party from a local firm. And—yes!—from the very beginning Lewis had known that the chances of recovering the money were virtually nil. Even so, the three perfunctory interviews that Morse conducted appeared to Lewis to be sadly unsatisfactory.

After listening a while to the landlord's unilluminating testimony, Morse asked him why it had taken him so long to conduct his business at the Cash and Carry; and although the explanation given seemed perfectly adequate, Morse's dismissal of this first witness had seemed almost offensively abrupt. And no man could have been more quickly or more effectively antagonised than the temporary barman (on duty the previous morning) who refused to answer Morse's brusque enquiry about the present state of his overdraft. What then of the attractive, auburn-haired Mrs. Michaels? After a rather lopsided smile had introduced Morse to her regular if slightly nicotine-stained teeth, that distressed lady had been unable to fight back her tears as she sought to explain to Morse why she'd insisted on some genuine notes for the publicity photographer instead of a phonily magnified cheque.

But wait! Something dramatic had just happened to Morse, Lewis could see that: as if the light had suddenly shined upon a man that hitherto had sat in darkness. He (Morse) now asked—amazingly!—whether by any chance the good lady possessed a pair of bright green, high-heeled leather shoes; and when she replied that, yes, she did, Morse smiled serenely, as though he had solved the secret of the universe, and promptly summoned into the lounge bar not only the three he'd just interviewed but all those now in the George who had been drinking there the previous morning.

As they waited, Morse asked for the serial numbers of the stolen notes, and Lewis passed over a scrap of paper on which some figures had been hastily scribbled in blotchy Biro. "For Christ's sake, man!" hissed Morse. "Didn't they teach you to write at school?"

Lewis breathed heavily, counted to five, and then painstakingly rewrote the numbers on a virginal piece of paper: 773741–773780. At which numbers Morse glanced cursorily before sticking the paper in his pocket, and proceeding to address the George's regulars.

He was *virtually* certain (he said) of who had stolen the money. What he was *absolutely* sure about was exactly where that money was *at that very moment*. He had the serial numbers of the notes—but that was of no importance what-soever now. The thief might well have been tempted to spend the money earlier—but not any more! And why not? Because at this Christ-mas time that person *no longer had the power to resist his better self.*

In that bar, stilled now and silent as the grave itself, the faces of Morse's audience seemed mesmerised—and remained so as Morse gave his instructions that the notes should be re-placed in their original envelope and returned (he cared not by what means) to Sergeant Lew-is's office at Thames Valley Police HQ *within the next twenty-four hours.*

As they drove back, Lewis could restrain his curiosity no longer. "You really *are* confident that——?"

"Of course!"

"I never seem to be able to put the clues to-gether myself, sir."

"Clues? What clues, Lewis? I didn't know we had any."

"Well, those shoes, for example. How do they fit in?"

"Who said they fitted in anywhere? It's just that I used to know an auburn-haired beauty who had six—*six,* Lewis!—pairs of bright green shoes. They suited her, she said."

"So . . . they've got nothing to do with the case at all?"

"Not so far as I know," muttered Morse.

The next morning a white envelope was deliv-ered to Lewis's office, though no one at recep-tion could recall when or whence it had arrived. Lewis immediately rang Morse to congratulate him on the happy outcome of the case.

"There's just one thing, sir. I'd kept that scrappy bit of paper with the serial numbers on it, and these are brand-new notes all right—but they're not the same ones!"

"Really?" Morse sounded supremely uncon-cerned.

"You're not worried about it?"

"Good Lord, no! You just get that money back to ginger-knob at the George, and tell her to settle for a jumbo cheque next time! Oh, and one other thing, Lewis. I'm on *leave.* So no in-terruptions from anybody—understand?"

"Yes, sir. And, er . . . Happy Christmas, sir!"

"And to you, old friend!" replied Morse qui-etly.

The bank manager rang just before lunch that same day. "It's about the four hundred pounds you withdrew yesterday, Inspector. I did promise to ring about any further bank charges——"

"I explained to the girl," protested Morse. "I needed the money quickly."

"Oh, it's perfectly all right. But you did say you'd call in this morning to transfer——"

"Tomorrow! I'm up a ladder with a paint brush at the moment."

Morse put down the receiver and again sank back in the armchair with the crossword. But his mind was far away, and some of the words he himself had spoken kept echoing around his brain: something about one's better self . . . And he smiled, for he knew that this would be a Christmas he might enjoy almost as much as the children up at Littlemore, perhaps. He had solved so many mysteries in his life. Was he now, he wondered, beginning to glimpse the solution to the greatest mystery of them all?

MORE THAN FLESH AND BLOOD

Susan Moody

SUSAN MOODY HAS CREATED several memorable characters for her mystery fiction, notably the jet-setting Penny Wanawake, who is tall, gorgeous, and "black and shiny as a licorice-stick." Her lover is a jewel thief whose loot is fenced, the proceeds sent to the poor in Africa by Penny. She is a powerful crime-fighter, though she does not regard stealing from the rich as a crime. Moody's other series detective is the somewhat more traditional Cassandra Swann, a businesswoman and bridge instructor. "More Than Flesh and Blood" was first published in *A Classic Christmas Crime,* edited by Tim Heald (London, Pavilion, 1995).

More Than Flesh and Blood

SUSAN MOODY

LOOKING BACK, HE WAS ALWAYS TO remember the place as like a honeycomb, full of golden light. The walls of the houses, made of some yellowish local stone, were glazed with it. Roofs, covered in ochre-edged rings of lichen, dripped it back into the single narrow street, where the front doors opened straight into what would once have been called the parlour.

After the long journey through the barren hills, the village welcomed him. Driving across the humped stone bridge, he knew at once that he'd found what he was looking for. He stopped the car and got out. There were no shops, no pub, no one to ask the way. At the far end of the street there were cows, creamy-gold in the fierce light of the starting-to-set sun, sauntering towards an open farm gate. Beyond it, stone buildings, mud and hay, metal churns, indicated a dairy. He followed them.

A woman was already clamping the first cow to the nozzles of an electric milking-machine. She looked up at him without straightening, her face strong from confronting the weather unprotected for fifty or sixty years.

"I'm trying to find this house," he said, city-diffident in the presence of elemental sources. He showed her the photograph, thumb and fourth finger grasping the edges of the thick cardboard.

"Aye," she said.

"Beckwith House, I believe it's called."

"Aye."

"Is it here? In the village?"

"Noo." Her voice was soft, rounded as the cows she tended. "Noo, it's not."

That shook him a little. He had been so sure it would be here, friendly with other houses, neighboured.

"Where then?"

"It's up t'dale a way." She nodded towards the road behind him and the deep hills into which it led. Already, shadows were tumbling down the slopes, only the higher crests fully daylit, though he could still see the outlines of the dry-stone walls which criss-crossed the lower slopes, and the occasional brooding bulk of a barn.

"How far?"

"Two, three miles. Mebbe four. It's right on t'road."

"Thank you."

As she moved back towards the gate, she called after him: "Does she know you're coming?"

He stopped. "Does who know I'm coming?"

"The missus."

He smiled and shook his head. "No," he said. "She doesn't."

Back in the open again, after the temporary closing in of the village, he could feel wind sweeping down from the high fells, gusting the car towards the edge of the black road. Now that he was close to where he had been heading for most of his life, he felt none of the excitement he had anticipated, merely a sense of a waiting void about to be filled.

"... *somewhere*..." she used to say, cruelly. But where? Until today, he had not known. Now, the place, the time, the night edging down on him from above, fitted round him as though tailor-made.

The road began to wind. In the bend of a turn, he saw stone gateposts, iron gates twice as tall as he was, laurels massed behind walls. He parked on the verge, tucking the car in close. Behind the gates was a short drive curving towards a house, square and two-storied. Though he had never been here before, he knew precisely how the path led round behind the house, past deep-silled windows to a porched side door. He knew it would come out on to a flag-stoned terrace looking over an enclosed garden. He knew the view from the windows at the rear of the house, and where the plums and apples would stand on either side of the wrought-iron gate set in the garden wall, through which, like a photograph, could be seen a segment of landscape. There would be a pond, too, beside the terrace, and a rockery full of alpines, little crawling plants that overflowed and spilled down the edges of white stones. On one of the gateposts there was a round slate plaque. Beckwith House. He traced the two meniscal curves of the B with his finger. He turned the handle of the right-hand gate. It whimpered metallically. The iron bars resisted as he pushed, then opened, following a deep groove in the gravelled earth behind it.

"... *somewhere*..."

Here. He'd found it at last, been drawn to it, almost, though perhaps that was a trifle fanciful. He had had so little to go on, just the whispered, half-heard word—"Garthway..." Garthway? The more he tried to re-run the sequence in his head, the dying eyes filming even as they looked at him, the huge body heaving, the lips puckering as they tried to form the word while one hand twitched slowly on the turndown of the linen sheet with the border of drawn-thread work, the less he could remember what exactly had been said.

His feet made no sound on the earth. The gravel had long since sunk into the soil and now lay embedded in it like the eyes of drowning men below the surface of the water. Neglect entombed the house. He walked between the leaves of dark unpruned laurels. There was a faint light in one of the windows, its dirt-streaked panes almost hidden by creeper long left untended.

There was a glow, too, from the ornate fanlight above the front door. He banged the knocker and felt the house pause, listening, questioning. Footsteps came along the passage towards him, brisk, almost eager.

The woman who opened the door stared at him for a time. Later he could not have said for how long. Two or three seconds? Or had they been minutes? Her mouth moved towards a welcoming smile, then let it be. She brushed her hand against the side of her head, even though her hair was neatly tidy.

"Martin," she said. Not a question.

"Yes."

"I knew you'd come."

"Yes."

"It's taken you long enough."

"I wasn't sure where to look." Even with the help of the police computers, it had taken weeks of work to pinpoint this place, this woman.

She nodded, as if she knew what the difficulties in tracing her had been.

"You'd best come in, then." She stood aside, flat against the wall of the narrow hall to let him pass in front of her.

"Straight through. I'm in the kitchen."

The kitchen was warm, pined, full of good smells. They were part of the things which had been denied him. He saw that the room had been redecorated: the wallpaper had been changed and there was shelving that had not been there before.

In the fuller light, he was able to see her properly. She was younger than he had expected. And much less sad. It seemed to him that she ought to have been sad.

"What are you now?" she said. "Thirty-two?"

"Next birthday," he said.

"Early June, isn't it?"

He nodded, not minding that she had forgotten the precise date; though they had not met for over thirty years, she knew the month, just as he knew that behind the door to the left of the range was the larder, that although there were only five brass dish-covers hanging above it, there had once been seven. She leaned back against the warm curves of the Aga and shook her head. "I'd have known you anywhere," she said.

"Yes." Of course she would.

She frowned. "You're with the police, aren't you?" she said.

"Am I?"

She frowned. "That's what she said, last time I heard. That you were with the police."

Was he? Sometimes, he could scarcely remember who he was or where he came from. Sometimes he could scarcely remember that he didn't really know the answer to the question. Which was why he was here now.

He reached into the pocket of his coat and pulled out a package. He spread the contents on the shiny oilcloth which covered the kitchen table. And as he did so, the voices which never seemed to be far away, came back.

"... somewhere ..."

"Where?"

"Somewhere."

"Where, Gran?"

"Up north."

"Where up north?"

"That would be telling, wouldn't it now?"

"Tell me, Gran. Tell me." Because even then, a child, six, seven, ten years old, he had known it was important. If she would just pinpoint the place for him, just give it space, meaning, then he himself would finally be rooted.

"What happened, Gran?"

She would start again. "It was Christmas Eve." Then stop, laughing at him, the heavy rolls of her flesh shaking up and down her body. She was all too aware of the depth of the desire to know that filled him. Only to know.

"Christmas Day, Gran." It was part of the cruel ritual that the beginning must never vary.

"Oh yes. You're a knowing little monkey, aren't you?" A nod of the head, a stare over the tops of her glasses, a small not-quite-pleasant smile. "It was Christmas Day, and there was champagne in a silver bucket ..."

Ah, that champagne. For years he hadn't really known what it was. "Wine, dear, with a sparkle," she'd told him. "It made you feel good. Or bad, depending on your viewpoint." And she had giggled, an old woman scratching at memories.

When he was older, of course, he'd seen real, not imagined champagne, seen the big bottles, the shiny tops, the labels, special, rich, different from other labels on other bottles. Later still, drunk it, felt the bubbles at the top of his mouth. The sparkle of it was entwined in his earliest memories: that Christmas, that champagne.

"Yes, Gran. The champagne."

"There was champagne in a silver bucket, and then your mother ..."

And she would stop. Always. Her fingers would float above the photographs, her hands small and delicate against the grossness of her bulk, and he would see the past in her eyes, the something terrible that she would never tell him. He knew it was terrible by her silence. And always, briefly, her face would register again the shock of whatever it was had happened that Christmas Day, before she turned off into a story of Santa Claus or mince pies or some other yuletide banality which he knew had nothing to do with the one which lurked behind her eyes.

"Then what, Gran? What?" But there would be no force in his voice now. She wasn't going to tell him. Not then. Not ever.

Now, the woman came forward, stood beside him, stirred the photographs on the table with her finger.

"Still got all the snaps, then?" she said.

"Yes."

"I suppose she's dead."

"Yes."

"About time. How did she die?"

Slowly, he wanted to say, but did not.

"Because I hope it hurt her to let go of life,"

the woman said. "I hope she fought against it, knowing she would lose."

That was exactly how it had been. He said nothing.

"I hope it was . . . violent." Her voice shook. "Like his." She sifted through the photographs and picked one out. "Like his."

He was young. Dark. Hair falling over his forehead. A military cap held under one arm.

The woman moved her head from side to side. "He was so beautiful," she said, lifeless. "So . . . *beautiful*."

"My father."

"Yes. What did she tell you about him?"

"She told me nothing. Except that he was dead."

"I don't imagine she told you why."

"No. Not even that this was his picture. At least—not until very recently." He'd managed to choke that from her, squeezing and relaxing the soft flesh of her throat, alternately giving her hope, then removing it. *"And my mother,"* he'd said. *"Tell me where she is, where she is."* And almost left it too late. *"Garthway,"* she had managed. That was all.

Outside the window, at the edge of the garden, he could see how the last of the sun caught the green hill through the iron gate which led out on to the moors. It shone like a transparency between the shadowed walls on either side.

"And now you've come back to see for yourself where it all happened, have you?" The woman filled a kettle at the tap and set it on top of the red Aga.

"She never told me what exactly . . ." He picked two photographs out of the pile on the table. ". . . but I knew something must have."

Somewhere in his mind he heard the echo of the hateful voice: *"It was Christmas Day, somewhere up north . . ."*

Two photographs. Christmas dinner, every detail clear: the turkey, the sausages, the roast potatoes and steaming sprouts, a cut glass dish of cranberry sauce, a china gravy boat. Beside the table, a silver bucket. The people leaned towards each other, smiling, holding up glasses,

about to celebrate. At the head of the table was a woman of maybe forty, big-boned, fair-haired, her dress cut low over prominent breasts. She was handsome, ripe. His workmates at the police station would have whistled if he'd shown them the photo, would have nudged each other, said she was pleading for it, they wouldn't have minded a bit of that themselves. She was leaning towards the young girl sitting at her right, saying something.

"That's you, isn't it?" he said, his finger brushing across the girl's face.

"It is. It was."

And the same scene, seconds later. Glasses still in the air, but the smiles gone as they stared towards something out of frame, their faces full of horror and shock. The girl was gone. The woman at the head of the table looked straight ahead at the camera, smiling a small not-quite-pleasant smile.

"What happened?" he said. "I have to know." Because the body down in Wandsworth would never tell now. The swollen protruding tongue was silent at last. Had been for weeks. The small white hands would never again turn and turn through the photographs, reliving a past that a cataclysm had destroyed.

The woman lifted her shoulder and released a sighing breath. "You have a right, if anybody does," she said. "I didn't know Bobby was taking photographs then."

"Bobby?"

"My youngest brother. He was camera mad. He took all of these, photographed everything. 'It'll be a record for posterity,' he'd say.

"It's been that, all right."

Staring down at the photographs, the woman said softly: "She hated me, of course."

"Who did?"

"My mother." She indicated the woman at the head of the table. "It must have been some kind of madness, some pathological obsession. Or maybe she was just jealous because Dad loved me more than he loved her. They'd have a word for it today, I suppose. Perhaps they did then, but I never knew what it was, just that she was dangerous. My brothers tried to protect me, even little Bobby. So did Dad, while he was alive. I think she would have killed me, if she could." A silence. "She did the next best thing."

"Tell me."

Again the shuddering sigh. "Edward. Your father. He lived further up the dale. His family was rich, owned a lot of land. Edward was ten years older than I was, but it never mattered. Right from the beginning there was never anyone else for either of us." She turned her gaze on him. "We *loved* one another." On the Aga the kettle began to fizz, water drops skittering like ants across the surface of the hot plate. The woman got up, found a teapot, cups, saucers. "Do you understand that?"

"Yes," he said, though he knew nothing of love.

"I was sent away to school, to keep me from my mother, but the first day of the holidays, Edward would be there, outside the garden gate, and then it was like summer, like fireworks, like roses shooting out of the ground and birds singing." She smiled, looking back. Her voice was without emotion.

"What happened?"

"On my sixteenth birthday, in the middle of September, Edward wrote to me at school—he was in the Army by then—and said he was being posted overseas after Christmas and wanted me to come with him. He said I was old enough, he'd ask my mother if we could get married, since Dad had died the year before."

"What did she say?"

"That it was out of the question, that I was far too young. I wrote and said I didn't need her consent, I was legally able to get married and I was going to, soon as I came home at Christmas, so I could go abroad with Edward. She was furious."

He nodded. He knew Gran's furies. The violence, the hatred, flowing out of her like champagne from a shaken bottle.

"Edward said he thought my brothers could persuade her. And in the end, she gave in. She invited Edward to have Christmas dinner with us." She checked, touched her forehead, closed her eyes. "I really thought that she . . ."

Softly, he said: "It was Christmas Day, somewhere up north."

Equally softly, she said: "It was snowing that day and Edward was so late that we were about to start without him. Then he suddenly appeared at the door of the dining-room. He stood there, looking at me. Just—looking. Not smiling. And then my mother leaned over to me and said . . . she said . . ."

"What?" All these years, and he could feel the inner emptiness begin to fill at last with what should always have been there.

"She must have planned it, decided exactly when she would tell me, right down to the second. Normally I would never have sat next to her at the table but that day she made me. So nobody but me heard her say that she and Edward . . . that they were lovers. That she'd seduced him, that it had been easy, that it was not me he loved but her."

"Did you believe her?"

"No. Not all of it. Not . . . everything."

"What then?"

"Edward knew what she was doing. He called my name. He said he loved me, that in spite of everything, I was to remember he loved me. Then he—suddenly, he was gone, out through the front door. We heard a shot."

"My God."

"I ran and ran across the grass, in my new shoes. I could see him lying on the ground with his gun beside him, and I knelt in the snow and held him while he died. His blood was so red against the white. She put her arm round me for the first time in her life. She said they would have married. That Edward had no choice, not in the circumstances."

"Did you believe her?" he said again.

"Not at first." She sighed. "Later, I went into a . . . hospital for a while."

"Of course. If you were carrying . . . I suppose in those days . . . more of a stigma . . . unmarried . . ." His voice died away.

"When I came out, Bobby had died in a car

crash and my elder brothers had both gone out to Australia. She'd gone, too. She took you away with her, down south. You were all that was left of my Edward."

"You poor thing."

"Because of course, she and Edward *had* . . . not that I ever blamed him. It was all her fault."

"Poor darling Mother." He covered her hand. They would be friends, she and he. They would make up for all the years that the evil old woman, Gran, had taken from them both. He thought swiftly about Gran's dying, wished it had taken her longer, that she had suffered more, that he had been, perhaps, more brutal at the beginning. "Why didn't you come looking for me?"

She moved from under his hand. "Why would I? It would only have brought it back. The trauma. Besides, eventually I got over the shock of it all."

He wished she did not sound so indifferent. "I didn't," he said.

"Jim and I started courting, we got married, had the children . . ." She shrugged. "You know how it is."

"But, Mother . . ." The word hung in his mouth, succulent, unaccustomed.

She stared at him for a moment. "I'm not your mother," she said, giving the word a hard emphasis.

"What?" He did not take in what she was saying.

She smiled a small, familiar, not-quite-pleasant smile. "Not me, Martin. Your father and I didn't . . . hadn't . . . I was a virgin when I wed Jim."

"Then . . . who?"

She didn't answer.

"*Gran?*" he said.

"If that's what you called her."

"She told me my parents were dead," he said. Tears filled his eyes. Hatred, raw and red-edged, filled him. Was Gran, that blowsy, disgusting old woman, was she the mother, the flesh and blood, it had taken him so long to find?

The woman looked at him. "In a way, she was right, wasn't she?"

"No! Don't say that!" His hands were around her neck. He could feel the bone at the base of her skull and the convulsive movements of her throat. He shook his head. "She can't be . . . not Gran," he said.

He squeezed harder, trying to force the right words from her mouth, while her white fingers tore at his hands and her face darkened. "Tell me it wasn't Gran," he screamed, but she did not answer.

When he let her drop back in her chair her eyes, so like his own, had grown dull. In one of her small hands she still held the photograph of that long-past never-finished luncheon, and the champagne in a silver bucket, on Christmas Day.

THE BUTLER'S CHRISTMAS EVE
Mary Roberts Rinehart

THE FIRST MYSTERY NOVEL to appear on the bestseller list in America was *The Man in Lower Ten* by Mary Roberts Rinehart in 1909. She had written it as a serial for the first pulp magazine, *Munsey's Magazine,* which also serialized her novel *The Circular Staircase* (1908), which was released in book form before *The Man in Lower Ten,* probably her most successful work. She and Avery Hopwood adapted it for the stage as *The Bat* in 1920, by which time she had become the highest-paid writer in America. As the creator of the now frequently parodied "Had-I-But-Known" school, Rinehart regularly had her plucky heroines put themselves in situations from which they needed to be rescued. "The Butler's Christmas Eve" was first published in her short story collection *Alibi for Isabel* (New York, Farrar & Rinehart, 1944).

The Butler's Christmas Eve

MARY ROBERTS RINEHART

WILLIAM STOOD IN THE RAIN WAITING for the bus. In the fading daylight he looked rather like a freshly washed eighty-year-old and beardless Santa Claus, and underneath his raincoat he clutched a parcel which contained a much-worn nightshirt, an extra pair of socks, a fresh shirt, and a brand-new celluloid collar. It also contained a pint flask of the best Scotch whisky.

Not that William drank, or at least not to speak of. The whisky was a gift, and in more than one way it was definitely contraband. It was whisky which had caused his trouble.

The Christmas Eve crowd around him was wet but amiable.

"Look, mama, what have you done with the suitcase?"

"What do you think you're sitting on? A bird cage?"

The crowd laughed. The rain poured down. The excited children were restless. They darted about, were lost and found again. Women scolded.

"You stand right here, Johnny. Keep under this umbrella. That's your new suit."

When the bus came along one of them knocked William's package into the gutter, and he found himself shaking with anxiety. But the bottle was all right. He could feel it, still intact. The Old Man would have it, all right, Miss Sally or no Miss Sally; the Old Man, left sitting in a wheelchair with one side of his big body dead and nothing warm in his stomach to comfort

him. Just a year ago tonight on Christmas Eve William had slipped him a small drink to help him sleep, and Miss Sally had caught him at it.

She had not said anything. She had kissed her grandfather good-night and walked out of the room. But the next morning she had come into the pantry where William was fixing the Old Man's breakfast tray and dismissed him, after fifty years.

"I'm sorry, William. But you know he is forbidden liquor."

William put down the Old Man's heated egg cup and looked at her.

"It was only because it was Christmas Eve, Miss Sally. He was kind of low, with Mr. Tony gone and everything."

She went white at that, but her voice was even.

"I am trying to be fair," she said. "But even without this— You have worked a long time, and grandfather is too heavy for you to handle. I need a younger man, now that—"

She did not finish. She did not say that her young husband had enlisted in the Navy after Pearl Harbor, and that she had fought tooth and nail against it. Or that she suspected both her grandfather and William of supporting him.

William gazed at her incredulously.

"I've handled him, one way and another, for fifty years, Miss Sally."

"I know all that. But I've talked to the doctor. He agrees with me."

He stood very still. She couldn't do this to him, this girl he had raised, and her father before her. She couldn't send him out at his age to make a life for himself, after living a vicarious one in this house for half a century. But he saw helplessly that she could and that she meant to.

"When am I to go?" he asked.

"It would be kinder not to see him again, wouldn't it?"

"You can't manage alone, Miss Sally," he said stubbornly. But she merely made a little gesture with her hands.

"I'm sorry, William. I've already arranged for someone else."

He took the breakfast tray to the Old Man's door and gave it to the nurse. Then he went upstairs to his room and standing inside looked around him. This had been his room for most of his life. On the dresser was the faded snapshot of the Old Man as a Major in the Rough Riders during the Spanish War. There was a picture of Miss Sally's father, his only son, who had not come home from France in 1918. There was a very new one of Mr. Tony, young and good-looking and slightly defiant, taken in his new Navy uniform. And of course there were pictures of Miss Sally herself, ranging from her baby days to the one of her, smiling and lovely, in her wedding dress.

William had helped to rear her. Standing there he remembered the day when she was born. The Major—he was Major Bennett then, not the Old Man—had sent for him when he heard the baby's mother was dead.

"Well," he said heavily, "it looks as though we've got a child to raise. A girl at that! Think we can do it?"

"We've done harder things, sir," said William.

"All right," said the Major. "But get this, William, I want no spoiled brat around the place. If I find you spoiling her, by the Lord Harry I'll fire you."

"I won't spoil her," William had said sturdily. "But she'll probably be as stubborn as a mule."

"Now why the hell do you say that?" the Major had roared.

But William had only smiled.

So she had grown up. She was lovable, but she was wild as a March wind and as stubborn as the Bennetts had always been. Then—it seemed almost no time to William—she met Mr. Tony, and one day she was walking down a church aisle on her grandfather's arm, looking beautiful and sedate, and when she walked out again she was a married woman.

The old house had been gay after that. It was filled with youth and laughter. Then one day Miss Sally had gone to the hospital to have her baby, and her grandfather, gray of face, had waited for the news. William had tried to comfort him.

"I understand it's a perfectly normal process, sir," he said. "They are born every day. Millions of them."

"Get your smug face out of here," roared the Major. "You and your millions! What the hell do I care about them? It's my girl who's in trouble."

He was all right then. He was even all right when the message came that it was over, and Miss Sally and Mr. Tony had a ten-minute-old son. But going out of the hospital he had staggered and fallen, and he had never walked again. That was when the household began to call him the Old Man. Behind his back, of course.

It was tragic, because Miss Sally had had no trouble at all. She wakened at the hospital to learn that she had borne a man-child, asked if he had the proper number of fingers and toes, stated flatly that she had no intention of raising him for purposes of war, and then asked for a cigarette.

That had been two years ago, and she had come home on Christmas Eve. Mr. Tony had a little tree for the baby in the Old Man's bedroom, with Miss Sally's battered wax angel on the top, and the Old Man lay in his bed and looked at it.

"I suppose this kind of thing will save us, in the end," he said to William. "Damn it, man, people will go on having babies, and the babies will have Christmas trees, long after Hitler is dead and rotted."

The baby of course had not noticed the tree, and there was nothing to indicate that a year later William would be about to be dismissed, or that Mr. Tony, feverishly shaking a rattle before his sleeping offspring, would be in his country's uniform and somewhere on the high seas.

It was a bad year, in a way. It had told on Miss Sally, William thought. Her grandfather had taken his stroke badly. He would lie for hours, willing that stubborn will of his to move an arm, a leg, even a finger, on the stricken side. Nothing happened, of course, and at last he had accepted it, wheelchair and all. William had helped to care for him, turning his big body when the nurse changed the sheets, bathing him when he roared that he would be eternally damned if he would allow any woman to wash him. And during the long hours of the night it had been William who sat with him while he could not sleep.

Yet Miss Sally had taken it bravely.

"He cared for me all my life," she said. "Now I can care for him. William and I."

She had done it, too. William had to grant her that. She had turned a wing of the ground floor over to him, with a porch where he could sit and look out at the sea. She gave him time and devotion. Until Pearl Harbor, that is, and the night when Mr. Tony had slipped into the Old Man's room while William was playing chess with him, and put his problem up to them.

"You know Sally," he said. "I can't even talk to her about this war. But she's safe here, and the boy too. And—well, somebody's got to fight."

The Old Man had looked down at that swollen helpless hand of his, lying in his lap.

"I see," he said. "You want to go, of course?"

"It isn't a question of wanting, is it?"

"It is, damn it," said the Old Man fiercely. "I wanted to go to Cuba. Her father couldn't get to France fast enough. I wouldn't give a tinker's curse for the fellow who doesn't want to go. But"—his voice softened—"it will hurt Sally like hell, son. She's had enough of war."

It had hurt her. She had fought it tooth and nail. But Tony had enlisted in the Navy almost at once, and he had gone a few days before

Christmas. She did not cry when she saw him off, but she had the bleak look in her face which had never since entirely left it.

"I hope you enjoy it," she said.

"I don't expect to enjoy it, darling."

She was smiling, a strange stiff smile.

"Then why are you going?" she asked. "There are plenty of men who don't have to leave a wife to look after a baby and a helpless old man. Two old men," she said, and looked at William, standing by with the bags.

She was still not crying when after he had gone she had walked to the Old Man's room. William was there. She stood in the doorway looking at them.

"I hope you're both satisfied," she said, her voice frozen. "You can sit here, safe and sound, and beat the drums all you like. But I warn you, don't beat them where I can hear them. I won't have it."

Her grandfather eyed her.

"I raised you," he said. "William and I raised you. I guess we went wrong somewhere. You're spoiled after all. And I'll beat the drums all I damn please. So will William."

Only William knew that she had not gone to bed at all that night. Some time toward morning he had seen her down on the beach in the cold, staring out at the sea.

He had trimmed the boy's tree for him that Christmas Eve. And when it was finished, with the same ancient wax angel on the top, the Old Man had suddenly asked for a drink.

"To hell with the doctors," he said. "I'll drink to Tony if it's the last thing I ever do."

As it happened, it was practically the last thing William had to do for him. For of course he had just got the liquor down when Miss Sally walked in.

She dismissed William the next morning. He had gone upstairs and packed, leaving his livery but taking the photographs with him in his battered old suitcase. When he came down the stairs Miss Sally was waiting for him. He thought she had been crying, but the bleak look was in her face again.

"I'm sorry it has to be like this, William," she said stiffly. "I have your check here, and of course if you ever need any help—"

"I've saved my money," he told her stiffly. "I can manage. If it's all right I'd like to see the baby before I go."

She nodded, and he left her and went outside. The baby toddled to him, and William picked him up and held him close.

"You be a good boy," he said. "Be a good boy and eat your cereal every day."

"Dood boy," said the child.

William stood for a minute, looking out at the winter ocean where perhaps even now Mr. Tony might be. Then he put the child down.

"Look after him, Miss Jones," he told the nurse huskily. "He's about all his great-grandfather has left."

He found he was shaking when he got into the station wagon. Paul, the chauffeur, had to lift his suitcase. Evidently he knew. He looked concerned.

"This'll be hard as hell on the Old Man," he said. "What happened, anyhow?"

"Miss Sally's upset," said William evenly. "Mr. Tony going, and all that. She has no reason to like war."

"Who does?" said Paul glumly. "What do you bet they'll get me next?"

As they left a taxi was turning in at the gate. There was a tall swarthy man inside, and William disliked him instantly. Paul grunted.

"If that's the new fellow the Old Man will have him on his backside in a week," he said.

But so far as William knew the man was still there, and now he himself was on his way back, after a year, on some mysterious business he did not understand.

The bus rattled and roared along. The crowd was still amiable. It called Merry Christmas to each other, and strangers talked across the aisle. It was as though for this one night in the year one common bond united them. William, clutching his parcel, felt some of its warmth infecting him.

He had been very lonely. He had taken a room in the city, but most of the people he knew had died or moved away. He took out a card to the public library, and read a good bit. And when the weather was good he sat in the park at the edge of the river, watching the ships on their way up to the Sound to join their convoys. They traveled one after the other, great grayish black monsters, like elephants in a circus holding each others' tails. Sometimes they were battleships, sometimes freighters, laden to their Plimsoll marks, their decks covered with tanks and huge crates. So close were they that once on the bridge of a destroyer he thought he saw Mr. Tony. He stood up and waved his old hat, and the young officer saluted. But it was not Tony.

When the sinkings began he watched the newspapers, his heart beating fast. Then one day he saw Tony's picture. His ship had helped to rescue a crew at sea, and Tony was smiling. He looked tired and older, however. William had cut it out and sent it to the Old Man. But the only acknowledgment had been a post card. It had been duly censored for the United States Mail, and so all it said was: "Come back, you blankety blank fool."

However, if the Old Man had his pride, so did William. He had not gone back.

Then, just a week before, he had received a telegram. It too had evidently been censored, this time for the benefit of the telegraph company. So it read: DRAT YOUR STIFF–NECKED PRIDE. COME AND SEE ME. LETTER FOLLOWS.

As the bus rattled along he got out the letter. The crowd had settled down by that time. One by one the tired children had dropped off to sleep, and even the adults looked weary, as though having worked themselves into a fine pitch of excitement they had now relapsed into patient waiting. He got out his spectacles and reread the letter.

It was a very odd sort of letter, written as it was in the Old Man's cramped hand. It was almost as though he had expected someone else to read it. If there was anything wrong it did not say so. In fact, it alluded only to a Christmas surprise for the baby. Nevertheless the directions were puzzling. William was to arrive quietly and after dark. He was to leave his taxi at the gate, walk in, and rap on the Old Man's bedroom window. It added that the writer would get rid of the nurse if he had to drown her in the bathtub, and it closed with what sounded like an appeal. "Don't be a damn fool. I need you."

He was still thinking about it when the bus reached its destination. The rain had continued, and the crowd got out to an opening of umbrellas and another search for missing parcels. William was stiff from the long ride, and the town surprised him. It was almost completely blacked out and his taxi, when he found one, had some sort of black material over all but a narrow strip on its headlights.

"Good thing too," said the driver companionably. "We're right on the coast. Too many ships getting sunk these days. One sunk off here only a week ago. If you ask me them Germans has fellows at work right in this place. Where'd you say to go?"

"The Bennett place. Out on the beach."

The driver grinned.

"Used to drive the Major now and then," he said. "Kind of a violent talker, ain't he?"

"He's had quite a bit of trouble," said William.

"Well, his granddaughter's a fine girl," said the driver. "Know where she is tonight? Trimming a tree out at the camp. I seen her there myself."

"She always was a fine girl," said William sturdily.

The driver protested when he got out at the gate.

"Better let me take you in. It's raining cats and dogs."

But William shook his head.

"I want to surprise them. I know the way."

The cab drove off to an exchange of Christmas greetings, and William started for the house. There were no lights showing as he trudged along the driveway, but he could hear ahead of him the steady boom of the waves as the Atlantic rolled in, the soft hiss of the water as it rolled up the beach. Just so for fifty years had he heard it.

Only now it meant something new and different. It meant danger, men in ships watching against death; Mr. Tony perhaps somewhere out there in the dark, and the Old Man knowing it and listening, as he was listening.

He was relieved when he saw the garage doors open and no cars inside. He made his way cautiously around the house to the Old Man's wing, and stood listening under the bedroom window. There was no sound inside, however, and he wondered what to do. If he was asleep— Suddenly he sneezed, and he almost jumped out of his skin when a familiar voice spoke, almost at his ear.

"Come in, damn it," said the voice irritably. "What the hell are you waiting for? Want to catch your death of pneumonia?"

Suddenly William felt warm and comfortable again. This was what he had needed, to be sworn at and shouted at, to see the Old Man again, to hear him roar, or to be near him in contented silence. He crawled through the window, smiling happily.

"Nothing wrong with your voice, anyhow," he said. "Well, here I am, sir."

"And about time," said the Old Man. "Turn up the light and let me look at you. Shut the window and draw those curtains. Hah! You're flabby!"

"I've gained a little weight," William admitted.

"A little! Got a tummy like a bowl of jelly."

These amenities over they grinned at each other, and the Old Man held out his good hand.

"God," he said, "I'm glad to see you. We're going straight to the devil here. Well, a Merry Christmas to you anyhow."

"The same to you, sir."

They shook hands, and William surveyed the Old Man, sitting bolt upright in his wheelchair. He looked as truculent as ever, but some of the life had gone out of his face.

"So you ran out on me!" he said. "Why the devil didn't you turn Sally over your knee and spank her? I've seen you do it."

"I'm not as strong as I used to be," said William apologetically. The Old Man chuckled.

"She's a Bennett," he said. "Always was, always will be. But she's learning. Maybe it's the hard way, but she's learning." He eyed William. "Take off that coat, man," he said. "You're dripping all over the place. What's that package? Anything in it but your nightshirt?"

"I've got a pint of Scotch," William admitted.

"Then what are we waiting for?" shouted the Old Man. "Sally's out. The nurse is out. Jarvis is out—that's the butler, if he is a butler and if that's his name. And the rest have gone to bed. Let's have it. It's Christmas Eve, man!"

"They oughtn't to leave you like that," William said reprovingly.

"Each of them thinks somebody else is looking after me." The Old Man chuckled. "Get some glasses. I guess you know your way. And take a look around when you get there."

William went back to the familiar rear of the house. His feet were wet and a small trickle of water had escaped his celluloid collar and gone down his back; but he walked almost jauntily. Until he saw his pantry, that is.

He did not like what he saw. The place even smelled unclean, and the silver was only half polished, the glasses he held to the light were smeared, and the floor felt sticky under his feet.

Resentfully he washed two glasses, dried them on a not too clean dish towel, and went back. The Old Man watched him from under his heavy eyebrows.

"Well, what do you think of it?" he inquired. "Is the fellow a butler?"

"He's not a good one, sir."

But the Old Man said nothing more. He took his glass and waited until William had poured his own drink. Then he lifted the glass.

"To Tony," he said. "A safe Christmas to him, and to all the other men with the guts to fight this war."

It was like a prayer. It probably was a prayer, and William echoed it.

"To Mr. Tony," he said, "and all the rest."

Then at last the Old Man explained his letter. He didn't trust the man Jarvis. Never had. Too smooth. Sally, of course, did not suspect him, although he was damned inefficient. Anyhow what could she do, with every able-bodied man in service or making armament?

"But there's something queer about him," he said. "And you may not know it, but we had a ship torpedoed out here last week. Some of the men landed on the beach. Some never landed anywhere, poor devils."

"I heard about it," said William. "What do you want me to do?"

"How the hell do I know?" said the Old Man. "Look around. See if there's anything suspicious. And if there isn't, get rid of him anyhow. I don't like him."

A thin flush rose to William's wrinkled face.

"You mean I'm to stay?" he inquired.

"Why the devil do you suppose I brought you back?" shouted the Old Man. "Don't stand there staring. Get busy. We haven't got all night."

William's strictly amateur activities, however, yielded him nothing. His old room—now belonging to Jarvis—surprised him by its neatness, but unless that in itself was suspicious, there was nothing more. No flashlight for signaling, no code book, which William would certainly not have recognized anyhow, not even a radio.

"Tidy, is it?" said the Old Man when he reported back. "Well, I suppose that's that. I'd hoped to hand the FBI a Christmas gift, but— All right, no spy. I've got another job for you, one you'll like better." He leaned back in his chair and eyed William quizzically. "Sally's not having a tree this year for the boy. I don't blame her. For months she's worked her fool head off. Army, Navy, and what have you. She's tired. Maybe she's breaking her heart. Sometimes I think she is. But by the Lord Harry he's having a tree just the same."

William looked at his watch.

"It's pretty late to buy one," he said. "But of course I can try."

The Old Man grinned, showing a perfect set of his own teeth, only slightly yellowed.

"Think I'm getting old, don't you?" he scoffed. "Always did think you were smarter than I was, didn't you? Well, I'm not in my dotage yet. The tree's on the porch. Had it delivered tonight. Unless," he added unkindly, "you're too feeble to drag it in!"

William also grinned, showing a perfect set of teeth, certainly not his own, except by purchase.

"I suppose you wouldn't care to take a bet on it, sir?" he said happily.

Ten minutes later the tree was in place in a corner of the Old Man's sitting room. William was perspiring but triumphant. The Old Man himself was exhilarated with one small drink and an enormous pride. Indeed, both were eminently cheerful until, without warning, they heard the sound of a car outside.

It was Sally, and before she had put up her car and got back to the house, William was hidden in the darkened sitting room, and her grandfather was sedately reading in his chair beside a lamp. From where he stood William could see her plainly. She had changed, he thought. She looked older. But she looked gentler, too, as though at last she had learned some of the lessons of life. Her eyes were no longer bleak, but they were sunken in her head. Nevertheless William felt a thrill of pride. She was their girl, his and the Old Man's, and now she was a woman. A lovely woman, too. Even William, no connoisseur, could see that.

"Good gracious, why aren't you in bed?" she said, slipping off her fur coat. "And where's the nurse?"

"It's Christmas Eve, my dear. I sent her off for a while. She'll be back."

But Sally was not listening. Even William could see that. She sat down on the edge of a chair and twisted her fingers in her lap.

"There wasn't any mail, was there?"

"I'm afraid not. Of course we don't know where he is. It may be difficult for him to send any."

Suddenly she burst out.

"Why don't you say it?" she demanded. "You always say what you think. I sent Tony off wrong. I can't forgive myself for that. I was wrong about William, too. You miss him, don't you?"

"Miss him?" said the Old Man, deliberately raising his voice. "Why would I miss the old rascal? Always pottering around and doing nothing! I get along fine without him."

"I think you're lying to make me feel better," she said, and got up. "I was wrong about him, and tonight I realized I'd been wrong about the baby's tree. When I saw the men around the one we'd fixed for them— I've made a mess of everything, haven't I?"

"Most of us do, my dear," said her grandfather. "But we learn. We learn."

She went out then, closing the door quietly behind her. When William went into the bedroom he found the Old Man staring somberly at the fire.

"Damn war anyhow," he said violently. "Damn the blasted lunatics who wished it on the earth. All I need now is for some idiots to come around and sing 'Peace on earth, good will to men!'"

As though it might have been a signal, from beyond the window suddenly came a chorus of young voices, and William gingerly raised the shade. Outside, holding umbrellas in one hand and clutching their blowing cassocks around them with the other, the choir boys from the nearby church were singing, their small scrubbed faces earnest and intent. They sang about peace, and the King of peace who had been born to save the world, and the Old Man listened. When they had gone he grinned sheepishly.

"Well, maybe they're right at that," he said. "Sooner or later peace has to come. How about a small drink to the idea, anyhow?"

They drank it together and in silence, and once more they were back where they had been a year ago. No longer master and man, but two friends of long standing, content merely to be together.

"So you've been doing fine without me, sir?" said William, putting down his glass.

"Hell, did you hear that?" said the Old Man innocently.

They chuckled as at some ancient joke.

It was after eleven when William in his socks made his way to the attic where the trimmings for the tree were stored. Sally was still awake. He could hear her stirring in her room. For a moment he stood outside and listened, and it seemed no time at all since he had done the same thing when she was a child, and had been punished and sent to bed. He would stand at her door and tap, and she would open it and throw herself sobbing into his arms.

"I've been a bad girl, William."

He would hold her and pat her thin little back.

"Now, now," he would say. "Take it easy, Sally. Maybe William can fix it for you."

But of course there was nothing he could fix now. He felt rather chilly as he climbed the attic stairs.

To his relief the attic was orderly. He turned on the light and moving cautiously went to the corner where the Christmas tree trimmings, neatly boxed and covered, had always stood. They were still there. He lifted them, one by one, and placed them behind him. Then he stiffened and stood staring.

Neatly installed behind where they had been was a small radio transmitter.

He knew it at once for what it was, and a slow flush of fury suffused his face as he knelt down to examine it.

"The spy!" he muttered thickly, "the dirty devil of a spy!"

So this was how it was done. This was how ships were being sunk at sea; the convoys assembling, the ships passing along the horizon, and men like Jarvis watching, ready to unleash the waiting submarine wolves upon them.

He was trying to tear it out with his bare hands when he heard a voice behind him.

"Stay where you are, or I'll shoot."

But it was not Jarvis. It was Sally, white and terrified, in a dressing gown over her nightdress and clutching a revolver in her hand. William got up slowly and turned, and she gasped and dropped the gun.

"Why, William!" she said. "What are you doing here?"

He stood still, concealing the transmitter behind his stocky body.

"Your grandfather sent for me," he said, with dignity. "He was planning a little surprise for you and the boy, in the morning."

She looked at him, at his dependable old face, at the familiar celluloid collar gleaming in the light, at his independent sturdy figure, and suddenly her chin quivered.

"Oh, William," she said. "I've been such a dreadful person."

All at once she was in his arms, crying bitterly.

"Everything's so awful," she sobbed. "I'm so frightened, William. I can't help it."

And once more he was holding her and saying:

"It will be all right, Sally girl. Don't you worry. It will be all right."

She quieted, and at last he got her back to her room. He found that he was shaking, but he went methodically to work. He did what he could to put the transmitter out of business. Then he piled up the boxes of trimmings and carried them down the stairs. There was still no sign of Jarvis, and the Old Man was dozing in his chair. William hesitated. Then he shut himself in the sitting room and cautiously called the chief of the local police.

"This is William," he said. "The butler at Major Bennett's. I—"

"So you're back, you old buzzard, are you?" said the chief. "Well, Merry Christmas and welcome home."

But he sobered when William told him what he had discovered. He promised to round up some men, and not—at William's request—to come as if they were going to a fire.

"We'll get him all right," he said. "We'll get all these dirty polecats sooner or later. All right. No siren. We'll ring the doorbell."

William felt steadier after that. He was in the basement getting a ladder for trimming the tree when he heard Jarvis come back. But he went directly up the back stairs to his room, and William, listening below, felt that he would not visit the attic that night.

He was singularly calm now. The Old Man

was sound asleep by that time, and snoring as violently as he did everything else. William placed the ladder and hung the wax angel on the top of the tree. Then he stood precariously and surveyed it.

"Well, we're back," he said. "We're kind of old and battered, but we're still here, thank God."

Which in its way was a prayer too, like the Old Man's earlier in the evening.

He got down, his legs rather stiff, and going into the other room touched the sleeper lightly on the shoulder. He jerked awake.

"What the hell did you do that for?" he roared. "Can't a man take a nap without your infernal interfering?"

"The tree's ready to trim," said William quietly.

Fifteen minutes later the nurse came back. The bedroom was empty, and in the sitting room before a half-trimmed tree the Old Man was holding a small—a very small—drink in his hand. He waved his glass at her outraged face.

"Merry Christmas," he said, a slight—a very

slight—thickness in his voice. "And get me that telegram that came for Sally today."

She looked disapprovingly at William, a William on whom the full impact of the situation—plus a very small drink—had suddenly descended like the impact of a pile-driver. Her austere face softened.

"You look tired," she said. "You'd better sit down."

"Tired? Him?" scoffed the Old Man. "You don't know him. And where the hell's that telegram?"

She brought it, and he put on his spectacles to read it.

"Sally doesn't know about it," he explained. "Held it out on her. Do her good." Then he read it aloud. "Home for breakfast tomorrow. Well. Love. Merry Christmas. Tony."

He folded it and looked around, beaming.

"How's that for a surprise?" he demanded. "Merry Christmas! Hell, it will be a real Christmas for everybody."

William stood still. He wanted to say something, but his voice stuck in his throat. Then he stiffened. Back in the pantry the doorbell was ringing.

THE TRINITY CAT

Ellis Peters

FEW CHARACTERS HAVE ENJOYED such a depth of affection among mystery aficionados as Brother Cadfael, the medieval herbalist in a Benedictine abbey in Shropshire. He was created in 1977 by Ellis Peters in *A Morbid Taste for Bones*, and nineteen additional novels and a short story collection followed. Even though Edith Pargeter (Ellis Peters's real name) wrote scores of other books, the wise and gentle monk was a fan favorite for thirty years. In addition to being an outstanding detective, often helping the deputy sheriff bring transgressors to justice, Cadfael, who had been a man of the world before entering the abbey, was also frequently instrumental in helping young lovers find happiness. The author won the Edgar for Best Novel in 1963 for *Death and the Joyful Woman* and was presented with the Diamond Dagger for lifetime achievement by the (British) Crime Writers' Association in 1993. "The Trinity Cat" was first published in *Winter's Crimes #8* (London, Macmillan, 1976); it was first collected in the author's collection *A Rare Benedictine* (London, Headline, 1988).

The Trinity Cat

ELLIS PETERS

HE WAS SITTING ON TOP OF ONE of the rear gate-posts of the churchyard when I walked through on Christmas Eve, grooming in his lordly style, with one back leg wrapped round his neck, and his bitten ear at an angle of forty-five degrees, as usual. I reckon one of the toms he'd tangled with in his nomad days had ripped the starched bit out of that one, the other stood up sharply enough. There was snow on the ground, a thin veiling, just beginning to crackle in promise of frost before evening, but he had at least three warm refuges around the place whenever he felt like holing up, besides his two houses, which he used only for visiting and cadging. He'd been a known character around our village for three years then, ever since he walked in from nowhere and made himself agreeable to the vicar and the verger, and finding the billet comfortable and the pickings good, constituted himself resident cat to Holy Trinity church, and took over all the jobs around the place that humans were too slow to tackle, like rat-catching, and chasing off invading dogs.

Nobody knows how old he is, but I think he could only have been about two when he settled here, a scrawny, chewed-up black bandit as lean as wire. After three years of being fed by Joel Woodward at Trinity Cottage, which was the verger's house by tradition, and flanked the lych-gate on one side, and pampered and petted by Miss Patience Thomson at Church Cottage on the other side, he was double his old

size, and sleek as velvet, but still had one lop ear and a kink two inches from the end of his tail. He still looked like a brigand, but a highly prosperous brigand. Nobody ever gave him a name, he wasn't the sort to get called anything fluffy or familiar. Only Miss Patience ever dared coo at him, and he was very gracious about that, she being elderly and innocent and very free with little perks like raw liver, on which he doted. One way and another, he had it made. He lived mostly outdoors, never staying in either house overnight. In winter he had his own little ground-level hatch into the furnace-room of the church, sharing his lodgings matily with a hedgehog that had qualified as assistant vermin-destructor around the churchyard, and preferred sitting out the winter among the coke to hibernating like common hedgehogs. These individualists keep turning up in our valley, for some reason.

All I'd gone to the church for that afternoon was to fix up with the vicar about the Christmas peal, having been roped into the bell-ringing team. Resident police in remote areas like ours get dragged into all sorts of activities, and when the area's changing, and new problems cropping up, if they have any sense they don't need too much dragging, but go willingly. I've put my finger on many an astonished yobbo who thought he'd got clean away with his little breaking-and-entering, just by keeping my ears open during a darts match, or choir practice.

When I came back through the churchyard, around half-past two, Miss Patience was just coming out of her gate, with a shopping bag on her wrist, and heading towards the street, and we walked along together a bit of the way. She was getting on for seventy, and hardly bigger than a bird, but very independent. Never having married or left the valley, and having looked after a mother who lived to be nearly ninety, she'd never had time to catch up with new ideas in the style of dress suitable for elderly ladies. Everything had always been done mother's way, and fashion, music, and morals had stuck at the period when mother was a carefully-brought-up girl learning domestic skills, and preparing for a chaste marriage. There's a lot to be said for it! But it had turned Miss Patience into a frail little lady in long-skirted black or grey or navy blue, who still felt undressed without hat and gloves, at an age when Mrs. Newcombe, for instance, up at the pub, favoured shocking pink trouser suits and red-gold hair-pieces. A pretty little old lady Miss Patience was, though, very straight and neat. It was a pleasure to watch her walk. Which is more than I could say for Mrs. Newcombe in her trouser suit, especially from the back!

"A happy Christmas, Sergeant Moon!" she chirped at me on sight. And I wished her the same, and slowed up to her pace.

"It's going to be slippery by twilight," I said. "You be careful how you go."

"Oh, I'm only going to be an hour or so," she said serenely. "I shall be home long before the frost sets in. I'm only doing the last bit of Christmas shopping. There's a cardigan I have to collect for Mrs. Downs." That was her cleaning-lady, who went in three mornings a week. "I ordered it long ago, but deliveries are so slow nowadays. They've promised it for today. And a gramophone record for my little errand-boy." Tommy Fowler that was, one of the church trebles, as pink and wholesome-looking as they usually contrive to be, and just as artful. "And one mustn't forget our dumb friends, either, must one?" said Miss Patience cheerfully. "They're all important, too."

I took this to mean a couple of packets of some new product to lure wild birds to her garden. The Church Cottage thrushes were so fat they could hardly fly, and when it was frosty she put out fresh water three and four times a day.

We came to our brief street of shops, and off she went, with her big jet-and-gold brooch gleaming in her scarf. She had quite a few pieces of Victorian and Edwardian jewellery her mother'd left behind, and almost always wore one piece, being used to the belief that a lady dresses meticulously every day, not just on Sundays. And I went for a brisk walk round to see what was going on, and then went home to Molly and high tea, and took my boots off thankfully.

That was Christmas Eve. Christmas Day little Miss Thomson didn't turn up for eight o'clock Communion, which was unheard-of. The vicar said he'd call in after matins and see that she was all right, and hadn't taken cold trotting about in the snow. But somebody else beat us both to it. Tommy Fowler! He was anxious about that pop record of his. But even he had no chance until after service, for in our village it's the custom for the choir to go and sing the vicar an aubade in the shape of "Christians, Awake!" before the main service, ignoring the fact that he's then been up four hours, and conducted two Communions. And Tommy Fowler had a solo in the anthem, too. It was a quarter-past twelve when he got away, and shot up the garden path to the door of Church Cottage.

He shot back even faster a minute later. I was heading for home when he came rocketing out of the gate and ran slam into me, with his eyes sticking out on stalks and his mouth wide open, making a sort of muted keening sound with shock. He clutched hold of me and pointed back towards Miss Thomson's front door, left half-open when he fled, and tried three times before he could croak out:

"Miss Patience . . . She's there on the floor— she's bad!"

I went in on the run, thinking she'd had a heart attack all alone there, and was lying helpless. The front door led through a diminutive hall, and through another glazed door into the living-room, and that door was open, too, and there was Miss Patience face-down on the carpet, still in her coat and gloves, and with her shopping-bag lying beside her. An occasional table had been knocked over in her fall, spilling a vase and a book. Her hat was askew over one ear, and caved in like a trodden mushroom, and her neat grey bun of hair had come undone and trailed on her shoulder, and it was no longer grey but soiled, brownish black. She was dead and stiff. The room was so cold, you could tell those doors had been ajar all night.

The kid had followed me in, hanging on to my sleeve, his teeth chattering. "I didn't open the door—it was open! I didn't touch her, or anything. I only came to see if she was all right, and get my record."

It was there, lying unbroken, half out of the shopping-bag by her arm. She'd meant it for him, and I told him he should have it, but not yet, because it might be evidence, and we mustn't move anything. And I got him out of there quick, and gave him to the vicar to cope with, and went back to Miss Patience as soon as I'd telephoned for the outfit. Because we had a murder on our hands.

So that was the end of one gentle, harmless old woman, one of very many these days, battered to death because she walked in on an intruder who panicked. Walked in on him, I judged, not much more than an hour after I left her in the street. Everything about her looked the same as then, the shopping-bag, the coat, the hat, the gloves. The only difference, that she was dead. No, one more thing! No handbag, unless it was under the body, and later, when we were able to move her, I wasn't surprised to see that it wasn't there. Handbags are where old ladies carry their money. The sneak-thief who panicked and lashed out at her had still had greed and presence of mind enough to grab the bag as he fled. Nobody'd have to describe that bag to me, I knew it well, soft black leather with an old-fashioned gilt clasp and a short handle,

a small thing, not like the holdalls they carry nowadays.

She was lying facing the opposite door, also open, which led to the stairs. On the writing-desk by that door stood one of a pair of heavy brass candlesticks. Its fellow was on the floor beside Miss Thomson's body, and though the bun of hair and the felt hat had prevented any great spattering of blood, there was blood enough on the square base to label the weapon. Whoever had hit her had been just sneaking down the stairs, ready to leave. She'd come home barely five minutes too soon.

Upstairs, in her bedroom, her bits of jewellery hadn't taken much finding. She'd never thought of herself as having valuables, or of other people as coveting them. Her gold and turquoise and funereal jet and true-lover's-knots in gold and opals, and mother's engagement and wedding rings, and her little Edwardian pendant watch set with seed pearls, had simply lived in the small top drawer of her dressing-table. She belonged to an honest epoch, and it was gone, and now she was gone after it. She didn't even lock her door when she went shopping. There wouldn't have been so much as the warning of a key grating in the lock, just the door opening.

Ten years ago not a soul in this valley behaved differently from Miss Patience. Nobody locked doors, sometimes not even overnight. Some of us went on a fortnight's holiday and left the doors unlocked. Now we can't even put out the milk money until the milkman knocks at the door in person. If this generation likes to pride itself on its progress, let it! As for me, I thought suddenly that maybe the innocent was well out of it.

We did the usual things, photographed the body and the scene of the crime, the doctor examined her and authorised her removal, and confirmed what I'd supposed about the approximate time of her death. And the forensic boys lifted a lot of smudgy latents that weren't going to be of any use to anybody, because they weren't going to be on record, barring a million to one chance. The whole thing stank of the amateur. There wouldn't be any easy matching up of prints, even if they got beauties. One more thing we did for Miss Patience. We tolled the dead-bell for her on Christmas night, six heavy, muffled strokes. She was a virgin. Nobody had to vouch for it, we all knew. And let me point out, it is a title of honour, to be respected accordingly.

We'd hardly got the poor soul out of the house when the Trinity cat strolled in, taking advantage of the minute or two while the door was open. He got as far as the place on the carpet where she'd lain, and his fur and whiskers stood on end, and even his lop ear jerked up straight. He put his nose down to the pile of the Wilton, about where her shopping bag and handbag must have lain, and started going round in interested circles, snuffing the floor and making little throaty noises that might have been distress, but sounded like pleasure. Excitement, anyhow. The chaps from the C.I.D. were still busy, and didn't want him under their feet, so I picked him up and took him with me when I went across to Trinity Cottage to talk to the verger. The cat never liked being picked up, after a minute he started clawing and cursing, and I put him down. He stalked away again at once, past the corner where people shot their dead flowers, out at the lych-gate, and straight back to sit on Miss Thomson's doorstep. Well, after all, he used to get fed there, he might well be uneasy at all these queer comings and goings. And they don't say "as curious as a cat" for nothing, either.

I didn't need telling that Joel Woodward had had no hand in what had happened, he'd been nearest neighbour and good friend to Miss Patience for years, but he might have seen or heard something out of the ordinary. He was a little, wiry fellow, gnarled like a tree-root, the kind that goes on spry and active into his nineties, and then decides that's enough, and leaves overnight. His wife was dead long ago, and his daughter had come back to keep house for him after her husband deserted her, until she died, too, in a bus accident. There was just old Joel now, and the grandson she'd left with him, young Joel Barnett, nineteen, and a bit of a tearaway by his

grandad's standards, but so far pretty innocuous by mine. He was a sulky, graceless sort, but he did work, and he stuck with the old man when many another would have lit out elsewhere.

"A bad business," said old Joel, shaking his head. "I only wish I could help you lay hands on whoever did it. But I only saw her yesterday morning about ten, when she took in the milk. I was round at the church hall all afternoon, getting things ready for the youth social they had last night, it was dark before I got back. I never saw or heard anything out of place. You can't see her living-room light from here, so there was no call to wonder. But the lad was here all afternoon. They only work till one, Christmas Eve. Then they all went boozing together for an hour or so, I expect, so I don't know exactly what time he got in, but he was here and had the tea on when I came home. Drop round in an hour or so and he should be here, he's gone round to collect this girl he's mashing. There's a party somewhere tonight."

I dropped round accordingly, and young Joel was there, sure enough, shoulder-length hair, frilled shirt, outsize lapels and all, got up to kill, all for the benefit of the girl his grandad had mentioned. And it turned out to be Connie Dymond, from the comparatively respectable branch of the family, along the canal-side. There were three sets of Dymond cousins, boys, no great harm in 'em but worth watching, but only this one girl in Connie's family. A good-looker, or at least most of the lads seemed to think so, she had a dozen or so on her string before she took up with young Joel. Big girl, too, with a lot of mauve eye-shadow and a mother-of-pearl mouth, in huge platform shoes and the fashionable drab granny-coat. But she was acting very prim and proper with old Joel around.

"Half-past two when I got home," said young Joel. "Grandad was round at the hall, and I'd have gone round to help him, only I'd had a pint or two, and after I'd had me dinner I went to sleep, so it wasn't worth it by the time I woke up. Around four, that'd be. From then on I was here watching the telly, and I never saw nor heard a thing. But there was nobody else here, so I could be spinning you the yarn, if you want to look at it that way."

He had a way of going looking for trouble before anybody else suggested it, there was nothing new about that. Still, there it was. One young fellow on the spot, and minus any alibi. There'd be plenty of others in the same case.

In the evening he'd been at the church social. Miss Patience wouldn't be expected there, it was mainly for the young, and anyhow, she very seldom went out in the evenings.

"*I* was there with Joel," said Connie Dymond. "He called for me at seven, I was with him all the evening. We went home to our place after the social finished, and he didn't leave till nearly midnight."

Very firm about it she was, doing her best for him. She could hardly know that his movements in the evening didn't interest us, since Miss Patience had then been dead for some hours.

When I opened the door to leave the Trinity cat walked in, stalking past me with a purposeful stride. He had a look round us all, and then made for the girl, reached up his front paws to her knees, and was on her lap before she could fend him off, though she didn't look as if she welcomed his attentions. Very civil he was, purring and rubbing himself against her coat sleeve, and poking his whiskery face into hers. Unusual for him to be effusive, but when he did decide on it, it was always with someone who couldn't stand cats. You'll have noticed it's a way they have.

"Shove him off," said young Joel, seeing she didn't at all care for being singled out. "He only does it to annoy people."

And she did, but he only jumped on again, I noticed as I closed the door on them and left. It was a Dymond party they were going to, the senior lot, up at the filling station. Not much point in trying to check up on all her cousins and swains when they were gathered for a booze-up. Coming out of a hangover, tomorrow, they might be easy meat. Not that I had any special reason to look their way, they were an extrovert

lot, more given to grievous bodily harm in street punch-ups than anything secretive. But it was wide open.

Well, we summed up. None of the lifted prints was on record, all we could do in that line was exclude all those that were Miss Thomson's. This kind of sordid little opportunist break-in had come into local experience only fairly recently, and though it was no novelty now, it had never before led to a death. No motive but the impulse of greed, so no traces leading up to the act, and none leading away. Everyone connected with the church, and most of the village besides, knew about the bits of jewellery she had, but never before had anyone considered them as desirable loot. Victoriana now carry inflated values, and are in demand, but this still didn't look calculated, just wanton. A kid's crime, a teenager's crime. Or the crime of a permanent teenager. They start at twelve years old now, but there are also the shiftless louts who never get beyond twelve years old, even in their forties.

We checked all the obvious people, her part-time gardener—but he was demonstrably elsewhere at the time—and his drifter of a son, whose alibi was non-existent but voluble, the window-cleaner, a sidelong soul who played up his ailments and did rather well out of her, all the delivery men. Several there who were clear, one or two who could have been around, but had no particular reason to be. Then we went after all the youngsters who, on their records, were possibles. There were three with breaking-and-entering convictions, but if they'd been there they'd been gloved. Several others with petty theft against them were also without alibis. By the end of a pretty exhaustive survey the field was wide, and none of the runners seemed to be ahead of the rest, and we were still looking. None of the stolen property had so far showed up.

Not, that is, until the Saturday. I was coming from Church Cottage through the graveyard again, and as I came near the corner where the dead flowers were shot, I noticed a glaring black patch making an irregular hole in the veil of frozen snow that still covered the ground.

You couldn't miss it, it showed up like a black eye. And part of it was the soil and rotting leaves showing through, and part, the blackest part, was the Trinity cat, head down and back arched, digging industriously like a terrier after a rat. The bent end of his tail lashed steadily, while the remaining eight inches stood erect. If he knew I was standing watching him, he didn't care. Nothing was going to deflect him from what he was doing. And in a minute or two he heaved his prize clear, and clawed out to the light a little black leather handbag with a gilt clasp. No mistaking it, all stuck over as it was with dirt and rotting leaves. And he loved it, he was patting it and playing with it and rubbing his head against it, and purring like a steam-engine. He cursed, though, when I took it off him, and walked round and round me, pawing and swearing, telling me and the world he'd found it, and it was his.

It hadn't been there long. I'd been along that path often enough to know that the snow hadn't been disturbed the day before. Also, the mess of humus fell off it pretty quick and clean, and left it hardly stained at all. I held it in my handkerchief and snapped the catch, and the inside was clean and empty, the lining slightly frayed from long use. The Trinity cat stood upright on his hind legs and protested loudly, and he had a voice that could outshout a Siamese.

Somebody behind me said curiously: "Whatever've you got there?" And there was young Joel standing open-mouthed, staring, with Connie Dymond hanging on to his arm and gaping at the cat's find in horrified recognition.

"Oh, no! My gawd, that's Miss Thomson's bag, isn't it? I've seen her carrying it hundreds of times."

"Did *he* dig it up?" said Joel, incredulous. "You reckon the chap who—you know, *him*!—he buried it there? It could be anybody, everybody uses this way through."

"My gawd!" said Connie, shrinking in fascinated horror against his side. "Look at that cat! You'd think he *knows* . . . He gives me the shivers! What's got into him?"

What, indeed? After I'd got rid of them and taken the bag away with me I was still wondering. I walked away with his prize and he followed me as far as the road, howling and swearing, and once I put the bag down, open, to see what he'd do, and he pounced on it and started his fun and games again until I took it from him. For the life of me I couldn't see what there was about it to delight him, but he was in no doubt. I was beginning to feel right superstitious about this avenging detective cat, and to wonder what he was going to unearth next.

I know I ought to have delivered the bag to the forensic lab, but somehow I hung on to it overnight. There was something fermenting at the back of my mind that I couldn't yet grasp.

Next morning we had two more at morning service besides the regulars. Young Joel hardly ever went to church, and I doubt if anybody'd ever seen Connie Dymond there before, but there they both were, large as life and solemn as death, in a middle pew, the boy sulky and scowling as if he'd been press-ganged into it, as he certainly had, Connie very subdued and big-eyed, with almost no make-up and an unusually grave and thoughtful face. Sudden death brings people up against daunting possibilities, and creates penitents. Young Joel felt silly there, but he was daft about her, plainly enough, she could get him to do what she wanted, and she'd wanted to make this gesture. She went through all the movements of devotion, he just sat, stood and kneeled awkwardly as required, and went on scowling.

There was a bitter east wind when we came out. On the steps of the porch everybody dug out gloves and turned up collars against it, and so did young Joel, and as he hauled his gloves out of his coat pocket, out with them came a little bright thing that rolled down the steps in front of us all and came to rest in a crack between the flagstones of the path. A gleam of pale blue and gold. A dozen people must have recognised it. Mrs. Downs gave tongue in a shriek that informed even those who hadn't.

"That's Miss Thomson's! It's one of her turquoise ear-rings! *How did you get hold of that, Joel Barnett?*"

How, indeed? Everybody stood staring at the tiny thing, and then at young Joel, and he was gazing at the flagstones, struck white and dumb. And all in a moment Connie Dymond had pulled her arm free of his and recoiled from him until her back was against the wall, and was edging away from him like somebody trying to get out of range of flood or fire, and her face a sight to be seen, blind and stiff with horror.

"You!" she said in a whisper. "It was you! Oh, my God, *you* did it—*you* killed her! And me keeping company—how could I? How could *you*!"

She let out a screech and burst into sobs, and before anybody could stop her she turned and took to her heels, running for home like a mad thing.

I let her go. She'd keep. And I got young Joel and that single ear-ring away from the Sunday congregation and into Trinity Cottage before half the people there knew what was happening, and shut the world out, all but old Joel who came panting and shaking after us a few minutes later.

The boy was a long time getting his voice back, and when he did he had nothing to say but, hopelessly, over and over: "I didn't! I never touched her, I wouldn't. I don't know how that thing got into my pocket. I didn't do it. I never . . ."

Human beings are not all that inventive. Given a similar set of circumstances they tend to come out with the same formula. And in any case, "deny everything and say nothing else" is a very good rule when cornered.

They thought I'd gone round the bend when I said: "Where's the cat? See if you can get him in."

Old Joel was past wondering. He went out and rattled a saucer on the steps, and pretty soon the Trinity cat strolled in. Not at all excited, not wanting anything, fed and lazy, just curious enough to come and see why he was wanted. I turned him loose on young Joel's overcoat, and he couldn't have cared less. The pocket that had

held the ear-ring held very little interest for him. He didn't care about any of the clothes in the wardrobe, or on the pegs in the little hall. As far as he was concerned, this new find was a non-event.

I sent for a constable and a car, and took young Joel in with me to the station, and all the village, you may be sure, either saw us pass or heard about it very shortly after. But I didn't stop to take any statement from him, just left him there, and took the car up to Mary Melton's place, where she breeds Siamese, and borrowed a cat-basket from her, the sort she uses to carry her queens to the vet. She asked what on earth I wanted it for, and I said to take the Trinity cat for a ride. She laughed her head off.

"Well, *he's* no queen," she said, "and no king, either. Not even a jack! And you'll never get that wild thing into a basket."

"Oh, yes, I will," I said. "And if he isn't any of the other picture cards, he's probably going to turn out to be the joker."

A very neat basket it was, not too obviously meant for a cat. And it was no trick getting the Trinity cat into it, all I did was drop in Miss Thomson's handbag, and he was in after it in a moment. He growled when he found himself shut in, but it was too late to complain then.

At the house by the canal Connie Dymond's mother let me in, but was none too happy about letting me see Connie, until I explained that I needed a statement from her before I could fit together young Joel's movements all through those Christmas days. Naturally I understood that the girl was terribly upset, but she'd had a lucky escape, and the sooner everything was cleared up, the better for her. And it wouldn't take long.

It didn't take long. Connie came down the stairs readily enough when her mother called her. She was all stained and pale and tearful, but had perked up somewhat with a sort of shivering pride in her own prominence. I've seen them like that before, getting the juice out of being the centre of attention even while they wish they were elsewhere. You could even say she hurried down, and she left the door of her bedroom open behind her, by the light coming through at the head of the stairs.

"Oh, Sergeant Moon!" she quavered at me from three steps up. "Isn't it *awful*? I still can't believe it! *Can* there be some mistake? Is there any chance it *wasn't* . . . ?"

I said soothingly, yes, there was always a chance. And I slipped the latch of the cat-basket with one hand, so that the flap fell open, and the Trinity cat was out of there and up those stairs like a black flash, startling her so much she nearly fell down the last step, and steadied herself against the wall with a small shriek. And I blurted apologies for accidentally loosing him, and went up the stairs three at a time ahead of her, before she could recover her balance.

He was up on his hind legs in her dolly little room, full of pop posters and frills and garish colours, pawing at the second drawer of her dressing-table, and singing a loud, joyous, impatient song. When I came plunging in, he even looked over his shoulder at me and stood down, as though he knew I'd open the drawer for him. And I did, and he was up among her fancy undies like a shot, and digging with his front paws.

He found what he wanted just as she came in at the door. He yanked it out from among her bras and slips, and tossed it into the air, and in seconds he was on the floor with it, rolling and wrestling it, juggling it on his four paws like a circus turn, and purring fit to kill, a cat in ecstasy. A comic little thing it was, a muslin mouse with a plaited green nylon string for a tail, yellow beads for eyes, and nylon threads for whiskers, that rustled and sent out wafts of strong scent as he batted it around and sang to it. A catmint mouse, old Miss Thomson's last-minute purchase from the pet shop for her dumb friend. If you could ever call the Trinity cat dumb! The only thing she bought that day small enough to be slipped into her handbag instead of the shopping bag.

Connie let out a screech, and was across that room so fast I only just beat her to the open drawer. They were all there, the little pendant watch, the locket, the brooches, the true-lover's-knot, the purse, even the other ear-ring. A mistake, she should have ditched both while she was about it, but she was too greedy. They were for pierced ears, anyhow, no good to Connie.

I held them out in the palm of my hand—such a large haul they made—and let her see what she'd robbed and killed for.

If she'd kept her head she might have made a fight of it even then, claimed he'd made her hide them for him, and she'd been afraid to tell on him directly, and could only think of staging that public act at church, to get him safely in custody before she came clean. But she went wild. She did the one deadly thing, turned and kicked out in a screaming fury at the Trinity cat. He was spinning like a humming-top, and all she touched was the kink in his tail. He whipped round and clawed a red streak down her leg through the nylon. And then she screamed again, and began to babble through hysterical sobs that she never meant to hurt the poor old sod, that it wasn't her fault! Ever since she'd been going with young Joel she'd been seeing that little old bag going in and out, draped with her bits of gold. What in hell did an old witch like her want with jewellery? She had no *right*! At her age!

"But I never meant to hurt her! She came in too soon," lamented Connie, still and for ever the aggrieved. "What was I supposed to do? I had to get away, didn't I? *She was between me and the door!*"

She was half her size, too, and nearly four times her age! Ah well! What the courts would do with Connie, thank God, was none of my business. I just took her in and charged her, and got her statement. Once we had her dabs it was all over, because she'd left a bunch of them sweaty and clear on that brass candlestick. But if it hadn't been for the Trinity cat and his single-minded pursuit, scaring her into that ill-judged attempt to hand us young Joel as a scapegoat, she might, she just might, have got clean away with it. At least the boy could go home now, and count his blessings.

Not that she was very bright, of course. Who but a stupid harpy, soaked in cheap perfume and gimcrack dreams, would have hung on even to the catmint mouse, mistaking it for an herbal sachet to put among her smalls?

I saw the Trinity cat only this morning, sitting grooming in the church porch. He's getting very self-important, as if he knows he's a celebrity, though throughout he was only looking after the interests of Number One, like all cats. He's lost interest in his mouse already, now most of the scent's gone.

A FUNNY
Little Christmas

THE BURGLAR AND THE WHATSIT

Donald E. Westlake

I MEAN NO OFFENSE TO ANYONE, but there can be little dispute that the funniest mystery writer who ever lived was Donald E. Westlake. He showed his versatility by also writing a very hard-boiled series about the tough professional thief Parker, using the pen name Richard Stark, and the poignant series about Mitch Tobin, under the pseudonym Tucker Coe. It is for his complex and hilarious caper novels, mainly about the unlucky criminal genius John Dortmunder, for whom every perfectly planned burglary goes woefully wrong, that Westlake has been most honored, notably by the Mystery Writers of America, which named him a Grand Master for lifetime achievement in 1993. "The Burglar and the Whatsit" was first published in *Playboy* in 1996; it was first collected in *A Good Story and Other Stories* (Unity, ME, Five Star, 1999).

The Burglar and the Whatsit

DONALD E. WESTLAKE

"HEY, SANITY CLAUSE," SHOUTED the drunk from up the hall. "Wait up. C'mere."

The man in the red Santa Claus suit, with the big white beard on his face and the big heavy red sack on his shoulder, did not wait up, and did not come here, but instead continued to plod on down the hall in this high floor of a Manhattan apartment building in the middle of a cold evening in the middle of December.

"Hey, Sanity! Wait *up*, will ya?"

The man in the Santa Claus suit did not at all want to wait up, but on the other hand he also did not at all want a lot of shouting in this hall here, because in fact he was not your normal Santa Claus but was something else entirely, which was a burglar, named Jack. This Jack was a burglar who had learned some time ago that if he were to enter apartment buildings costumed like the sort of person who in the normal course of events would carry on himself some sort of large bag or box or reticule or sack, he could probably fill that sack or whatever with any number of valuable items without much risk of his being challenged, questioned, or—in the worst case—arrested.

Often, therefore, this Jack would roam the corridors of the cliff dwellers garbed as, for instance, a mailman or other parcel delivery person, or as a supermarket clerk pushing a cart full of grocery bags (paper, because you can see through plastic, and plastic bags don't stand up). Just once he'd been a doctor, with a stethoscope and a doctor's black bag, but that time he'd been snagged at once, for everybody knows doctors don't make house calls. A master of disguise, Jack even occasionally appeared as a Chinese restaurant delivery guy. The bicycle clip around his right ankle, to protect his pants leg from the putative bicycle's supposed chain, was the masterstroke of that particular impersonation.

But the best was Santa Claus. First of all, the disguise was so complete, with the false stomach and the beard and the hat and the gloves. Also, the Santa sack was more capacious than almost anything else he could carry. And finally, people *liked* Santa Claus, and it made the situation more humane, somehow, gentler and nicer, to be smiled upon by the people he'd just robbed.

The downside of Santa was that his season was so short. There was only about a three-week period in December when the appearance of a Santa Claus in an apartment building's public areas would not raise more questions than it would answer. But those three weeks were the peak of the year for Jack, when he could move in warmth and safety and utter anonymity, his sack full of gifts—not for the nearby residents but from them. And all in peace and quiet, because people leave Santa Claus alone, when they see him they know he's on his way somewhere, to a party or a chimney or something.

So they leave Santa *alone*. Except for this drunk here, shouting in the hallway. Jack the burglar didn't need a lot of shouting in the hallway, and he didn't want a lot of shouting in the hall-way, so with some reluctance he turned around at last and waited up, gazing at the approaching drunk from eyes that were the one false in the costume: They definitely did not twinkle.

The drunk reeled closer and stared at the burglar out of his own awful eyes, like blue eggs sunny-side up. "You're just the guy I need," he announced, inaccurately, for clearly what he most urgently needed was both a 12-step pro-gram and a whole lot of large, humorless people to enforce it.

The burglar waited, and the drunk leaned against the wall to keep the building from fall-ing over. "If anybody can get the goddamn thing to work," he said, "it's Sanity Clause. But don't talk to me about batteries. Batteries not included is *not* the problem here."

"Good," the burglar said, and then expanded on that: "Goodbye."

"Wait!" the drunk shouted as the burglar turned away.

The burglar turned back. "Don't shout," he said.

"Well, don't keep going away," the drunk told him. "I got a real problem here."

The burglar sighed through his thick white beard. One of the reasons he'd taken up this line of work in the first place was that you could do it alone. "All right," he said, hoping this would be short, at least. "What's the problem?"

"Come on, I'll show you." Risking all, the drunk pushed off from the wall and tottered away down the hall. The burglar followed him, and the drunk touched his palm to an apart-ment door, which clicked and swung open—*that* was cute—and they went inside. The door swung shut, and the burglar stopped dead and stared.

Jack the burglar had seen a lot of living rooms in his business, but this one was definitely the strangest. Nothing in it looked right. All the furniture, if that's what it was, consisted of hard and soft shapes from geometry class, in a variety of pastel colors. Tall narrow things that looked like metal plants might have been lamps. Short

wide things that crouched could have been chairs. Some of the stuff didn't seem to be any-thing in particular at all.

The drunk tottered through this abstract landscape to an inner doorway, then said, "Be right back," and disappeared.

The burglar made a circuit of the room, and to his surprise found items of interest. A small pale pyramid turned out to be a clock; into his sack it went. Also, this avocado with ears seemed to be a CD player; pop, in it went.

In a far corner, in amazing contrast to every-thing else, stood a Christmas tree, fat and richly green and hung with a million ornaments, the only normal object in sight. Or, wait a minute. The burglar stared and frowned, and the Christ-mas tree shimmered over there as though it were about to be beamed up to the starship *Enterprise*. What was wrong with that tree?

The drunk returned, aglow with happy pride. Waving at the wavering Christmas tree, he said, "Whaddya think?"

"What *is* it, that's what I think."

"A hologram," the drunk said. "You can walk all around it, see all the sides, and you never have to water it, and it never drops a needle and you can use it next year. Pretty good, huh?"

"It isn't traditional," the burglar said. He had his own sense of the fitness of things.

"Tra-*dish*-unal!" The drunk almost knocked himself over, he rocketed that word out so hard. "I don't need tradition, I'm an *inventor*!" Point-ing at a whatsit that was just now following him into the room, he said, "See?"

The burglar saw. This whatsit was a metal box, pebbly gray, about four feet tall and a foot square, scattered all over with dials and switches and antennas, plus a smooth dome on the top and little wheels on the bottom that hummed as the thing came straight across the bare gray floor to stop in front of the burglar and go, "Chick-chick, chillick, chillick."

The burglar didn't like this artifact at all. He said. "Well what's this supposed to be?"

"That's just it," the drunk said and collapsed backward onto a trapezoid that just possibly could have been a sofa. "I don't know *what* the heck it is."

"I don't like it," the burglar said. The thing buzzed and chicked as though it were a supermarket scanner and Jack the burglar were equipped with a bar code. "It's making me nervous."

"It makes *me* nervous," the drunk said. "I invented the darn thing, and I don't know what it's for. Whyn't you sit down?"

The burglar looked around. "On what?"

"Oh, anything. You want an eggnog?"

Revolted, the burglar said, "Eggnog? No!" And he sat on a nearby rhomboid, which fortunately was more comfortable than it looked.

"I just thought, you know, the uniform," the drunk said, and sat up straighter on his trapezoid and began to applaud.

What's he got to applaud about? But here came another whatsit, this one with skinny metal arms and a head shaped like a tray. The drunk told it, "I'll have the usual." To the burglar he said, "And what for you?"

"Nothing," said the burglar. "Not, uh, on duty."

"OK. Give him a seltzer with a slice of lime," he told the tray-headed whatsit, and the thing wheeled about and left as the drunk explained, "I don't like to see anybody without a glass."

"So you got a lot of these, uh, things, huh? Invented them all?"

"Used to have a lot more," the drunk said, getting mad, "but a bunch got stolen. Goddamn it, goddamn it!"

"Oh, yeah?"

"If I could get my hands on those burglars!" The drunk tried to demonstrate a pretend choke in midair, but his fingers got all tangled together, and in trying to untangle them he fell over on his side. Lying there on the trapezoid, one eye visible, he glared at the domed whatsit hovering near the burglar and snarled, "I wish they'd steal *that* thing."

The burglar said, "How can you invent it and not know what it is?"

"Easy." The drunk, with a lot of arm and leg movements, pushed himself back to a seated po-

sition as the bartender whatsit came rolling back into the room with two drinks on its head/tray. It zipped past the drunk, who grabbed his glass from it on the fly, then paused in front of the burglar on the rhomboid, who accepted the glass of seltzer and suppressed the urge to say "Thanks."

Tray-head wheeled around the enigmatic whatsit and left. The drunk frowned at the whatsit and said, "Half the things I invent I don't remember. I just do them. I do the drawing and fax it to my construction people, and then I go think about other things. And after a while, dingdong, United Parcel, and there it is, according to specifikah—speci—plan."

"Then how do you find out what anything's for?

"I leave myself a note in the computer when I invent it. When the package shows up, I check back and the screen says, 'We now have a perfect vacuum cleaner.' Or, 'We now have a perfect pocket calculator.' "

"How come you didn't do that this time?"

"I did!" A growl escaped the drunk's throat and his face reddened with remembered rage. "Somebody stole the computer!"

"Ah," said the burglar.

"So, here I am," the drunk went on, pointing with his free hand at himself and the whatsit and his drink and the Christmas tree and various other things, "here I am, I got this thing— for all I know it's some sorta boon to mankind, a perfect Christmas present to humanity—and I don't know what it is!"

"But what do you want from me?" the burglar asked, shifting on his rhomboid. "I don't know about inventions."

"You know about *things*," the drunk told him. "You know about *stuff*. Nobody in the world knows *stuff* like Sanity Clause. Electric pencil sharpeners. Jigsaw puzzles. *Stuff*."

"Yeah? And? So?"

"So tell me stuff," the drunk said. "Any kinda stuff that you can think of, and I'll tell you if I did one yet, and when it's something I never did we'll try out some commands on Junior here and see what happens."

"I don't know," the burglar said, as the whatsit at last wheeled away from him and out into the middle of the room. It stopped, as though poised there. "You mean, just say *products* to you?"

"S'only thing I can think off," the drunk explained, "that might help." Then he sat up even more and gaped at the whatsit. "Looka that!"

The whatsit was extruding more aerials. Little lights ran around its square body. A buzzing sound came from within. The burglar said, "It isn't gonna explode, is it?"

"I don't think so," the drunk said. "It looks like it's broadcasting. Suppose I invented something to look for intelligence on other planets?"

"Would you want something like that?"

The drunk considered, then shook his head. "No. You're right, it isn't that." Perking up, he said, "But you got the idea, right? Try me, come on, tell me stuff. We gotta get moving here. I gotta figure out what this thing's supposed to do before it starts doing it all on its own. Come on, come on."

The burglar thought. He wasn't actually Santa Claus, of course, but he was certainly familiar with stuff. "A fax machine," he said, there being three of them at the moment in his sack on the floor beside the rhomboid.

"Did one," the drunk said. "Recycles newspapers, prints on it."

"Coffee maker."

"Part of my breakfast maker."

"Rock polisher."

"Don't want one."

"Air purifier."

"I manufacture my own air in here."

They went on like that, the burglar pausing to think of more things, trying them out, bouncing them off the drunk, but none of them right, while the whatsit entertained itself with its chirruping and buzzing in the middle of the room, until at last the burglar's mind had become drained of artifacts, of ideas, of things, of *stuff*. "I'm sorry, pal," the burglar said, after their final silence. Shaking his head, he got up from the rhomboid, picked up his sack, and said, "I'd like to help. But I gotta get on with my life, you know?"

"I appreciate all you done," the drunk said, trying but failing to stand. Then, getting mad all over again, he clenched his fists and shouted, "If only they didn't steal my computer!" He pointed an angry fist toward a keypad beside the front door. "You see that pad? That's the building's so-called burglar alarm! Ha! Burglars laugh at it!"

They did. Jack himself had laughed at several of them just tonight. "Hard to find a really good burglar al—" he said, and stopped.

They both stared at the whatsit, still buzzing away at itself like a drum machine with the mute on. "By golly," breathed the drunk, "you got it."

The burglar frowned. "It's a burglar alarm? That thing?"

"It's the perfect burglar alarm," the drunk said, and bounced around with new confidence on his trapezoid. "You know what's wrong with regular burglar alarms?" he demanded.

"They aren't very good," the burglar said.

"They trap the innocent," the drunk told him, "and they're too stupid to catch the guilty."

"That's pretty much true," the burglar agreed.

"A *perfect* burglar alarm would sense burglars, know them by a thousand tiny indications, too subtle for you and me, and call the cops before they could pull the job!"

Behind his big white Santa Claus beard, Jack the burglar's chin felt itchy all of a sudden. The big round fake stomach beneath his red costume was heavier than before. Giving the whatsit a sickly smile, he said, "A machine that can *sense* burglars? Impossible."

"No, sir," said the drunk. "Heavier-than-air flight is impossible. Sensing guilt is a snap, for the right machine." Contemplating his invention, frowning in thought, the drunk said, "But it was broadcasting. Practicing, do you suppose? Telling me it's ready to go to work?"

"Me, too," the burglar said, moving toward the door.

"Go to work. Nice to—"

The doorbell rang. "Huh," the drunk said. "Who do you suppose that is at this hour?"

DANCING DAN'S CHRISTMAS

Damon Runyon

BOOKIES, CON MEN, ROBBERS, bootleggers, prostitutes, and murderers populate the stories of Damon Runyon, but they are generally presented as having hearts of gold. Runyon always will be associated with New York's Broadway and the colorful characters whose humorous slang enlivened his prose. Shady characters and members of the underworld are usually involved in his stories, most famously *Guys and Dolls*, which was adapted as a popular musical and a motion picture. He eventually went to Hollywood to write movies, producing the Shirley Temple vehicle *Little Miss Marker*, based on his short story about bookies. "Dancing Dan's Christmas" was first published in the December 21, 1932, issue of *Collier's Weekly*; it was collected in *Blue Plate Special* (New York, Stokes, 1934).

Dancing Dan's Christmas

DAMON RUNYON

NOW ONE TIME IT COMES ON CHRIST-
mas, and in fact it is the evening before Christmas, and I am in Good Time Charley Bern-
stein's little speakeasy in West Forty-seventh
Street, wishing Charley a Merry Christmas and
having a few hot Tom and Jerrys with him.

This hot Tom and Jerry is an old time drink
that is once used by one and all in this country to
celebrate Christmas with, and in fact it is once
so popular that many people think Christmas is
invented only to furnish an excuse for hot Tom
and Jerry, although of course this is by no means
true.

But anybody will tell you that there is nothing that brings out the true holiday spirit like hot
Tom and Jerry, and I hear that since Tom and
Jerry goes out of style in the United States, the
holiday spirit is never quite the same.

Well, as Good Time Charley and I are ex-
pressing our holiday sentiments to each other
over our hot Tom and Jerry, and I am trying
to think up the poem about the night before
Christmas and all through the house, which I
know will interest Charley no little, all of a sudden there is a big knock at the front door, and
when Charley opens the door, who comes in carrying a large package under one arm but a guy
by the name of Dancing Dan.

This Dancing Dan is a good-looking young
guy, who always seems well-dressed, and he is
called by the name of Dancing Dan because he
is a great hand for dancing around and about

with dolls in night clubs, and other spots where
there is any dancing. In fact, Dan never seems to
be doing anything else, although I hear rumors
that when he is not dancing he is carrying on in
a most illegal manner at one thing and another.
But of course you can always hear rumors in this
town about anybody, and personally I am rather
fond of Dancing Dan as he always seems to be
getting a great belt out of life.

Anybody in town will tell you that Dancing Dan is a guy with no Barnaby whatever in
him, and in fact he has about as much gizzard as
anybody around, although I wish to say I always
question his judgment in dancing so much with
Miss Muriel O'Neill, who works in the Half
Moon night club. And the reason I question
his judgment in this respect is because everybody knows that Miss Muriel O'Neill is a doll
who is very well thought of by Heine Schmitz,
and Heine Schmitz is not such a guy as will take
kindly to anybody dancing more than once and a
half with a doll that he thinks well of.

Well, anyway, as Dancing Dan comes in, he
weighs up the joint in one quick peek, and then
he tosses the package he is carrying into a corner where it goes plunk, as if there is something
very heavy in it, and then he steps up to the bar
alongside of Charley and me and wishes to know
what we are drinking.

Naturally we start boosting hot Tom and
Jerry to Dancing Dan, and he says he will take a
crack at it with us, and after one crack, Dancing

Dan says he will have another crack, and Merry Christmas to us with it, and the first thing anybody knows it is a couple of hours later and we still are still having cracks at the hot Tom and Jerry with Dancing Dan, and Dan says he never drinks anything so soothing in his life. In fact, Dancing Dan says he will recommend Tom and Jerry to everybody he knows, only he does not know anybody good enough for Tom and Jerry, except maybe Miss Muriel O'Neill, and she does not drink anything with drugstore rye in it.

Well, several times while we are drinking this Tom and Jerry, customers come to the door of Good Time Charley's little speakeasy and knock, but by now Charley is commencing to be afraid they will wish Tom and Jerry, too, and he does not feel we will have enough for ourselves, so he hangs out a sign which says "Closed on Account of Christmas," and the only one he will let in is a guy by the name of Ooky, who is nothing but an old rumdum, and who is going around all week dressed like Santa Claus and carrying a sign advertising Moe Lewinsky's clothing joint around in Sixth Avenue.

This Ooky is still wearing his Santa Claus outfit when Charley lets him in, and the reason Charley permits such a character as Ooky in his joint is because Ooky does the porter work for Charley when he is not Santa Claus for Moe Lewinsky, such as sweeping out, and washing the glasses, and one thing and another.

Well, it is about nine-thirty when Ooky comes in, and his puppies are aching, and he is all petered out generally from walking up and down and here and there with his sign, for any time a guy is Santa Claus for Moe Lewinsky he must earn his dough. In fact, Ooky is so fatigued, and his puppies hurt him so much that Dancing Dan and Good Time Charley and I all feel very sorry for him, and invite him to have a few mugs of hot Tom and Jerry with us, and wish him plenty of Merry Christmas.

But old Ooky is not accustomed to Tom and Jerry and after about the fifth mug he folds up in a chair, and goes right to sleep on us. He is wearing a pretty good Santa Claus makeup, what with a nice red suit trimmed with white cotton, and a wig, and false nose, and long white whiskers, and a big sack stuffed with excelsior on his back, and if I do not know Santa Claus is not apt to be such a guy as will snore loud enough to rattle the windows, I will think Ooky is Santa Claus sure enough.

Well, we forget Ooky and let him sleep, and go on with our hot Tom and Jerry, and in the meantime we try to think up a few songs appropriate to Christmas, and Dancing Dan finally renders "My Dad's Dinner Pail" in a nice baritone and very loud, while I do first rate with "Will You Love Me in December As You Do in May?"

About midnight Dancing Dan wishes to see how he looks as Santa Claus.

So Good Time Charley and I help Dancing Dan pull off Ooky's outfit and put it on Dan, and this is easy as Ooky only has this Santa Claus outfit on over his ordinary clothes, and he does not even wake up when we are undressing him of the Santa Claus uniform.

Well, I wish to say I see many a Santa Claus in my time, but I never see a better-looking Santa Claus than Dancing Dan, especially after he gets the wig and white whiskers fixed just right, and we put a sofa pillow that Good Time Charley happens to have around the joint for the cat to sleep on down his pants to give Dancing Dan a nice fat stomach such as Santa Claus is bound to have.

"Well," Charley finally says, "it is a great pity we do not know where there are some stockings hung up somewhere, because then," he says, "you can go around and stuff things in these stockings, as I always hear this is the main idea of a Santa Claus. But," Charley says, "I do not suppose anybody in this section has any stockings hung up, or if they have," he says, "the chances are they are so full of holes they will not hold anything. Anyway," Charley says, "even if there are any stockings hung up we do not have anything to stuff in them, although personally," he says, "I will gladly donate a few pints of Scotch."

Well, I am pointing out that we have no reindeer and that a Santa Claus is bound to look like a terrible sap if he goes around without any reindeer, but Charley's remarks seem to give Dancing Dan an idea, for all of a sudden he speaks as follows:

"Why," Dancing Dan says, "I know where a stocking is hung up. It is hung up at Miss Muriel O'Neill's flat over here in West Forty-ninth Street. This stocking is hung up by nobody but a party by the name of Gammer O'Neill, who is Miss Muriel O'Neill's grandmamma," Dancing Dan says. "Gammer O'Neill is going on ninety-odd," he says, "and Miss Muriel O'Neill tells me she cannot hold out much longer, what with one thing and another, including being a little childish in spots.

"Now," Dancing Dan says, "I remember Miss Muriel O'Neill is telling me just the other night how Gammer O'Neill hangs up her stocking on Christmas Eve all her life, and," he says, "I judge from what Miss Muriel O'Neill says that the old doll always believes Santa Claus will come along some Christmas and fill the stocking full of beautiful gifts. But," Dancing Dan says, "Miss Muriel O'Neill tells me Santa Claus never does this, although Miss Muriel O'Neill personally always takes a few gifts home and pops them into the stocking to make Gammer O'Neill feel better.

"But, of course," Dancing Dan says, "these gifts are nothing much because Miss Muriel O'Neill is very poor, and proud, and also good, and will not take a dime off of anybody and I can lick the guy who says she will.

"Now," Dancing Dan goes on, "it seems that while Gammer O'Neill is very happy to get whatever she finds in her stocking on Christmas morning, she does not understand why Santa Claus is not more liberal, and," he says, "Miss Muriel O'Neill is saying to me that she only wishes she can give Gammer O'Neill one real big Christmas before the old doll puts her checks back in the rack.

"So," Dancing Dan states, "here is a job for us. Miss Muriel O'Neill and her grandmamma

live all alone in this flat over in West Forty-ninth Street, and," he says, "at such an hour as this Miss Muriel O'Neill is bound to be working, and the chances are Gammer O'Neill is sound asleep, and we will just hop over there and Santa Claus will fill up her stocking with beautiful gifts."

Well, I say, I do not see where we are going to get any beautiful gifts at this time of night, what with all the stores being closed, unless we dash into an all-night drug store and buy a few bottles of perfume and a bum toilet set as guys always do when they forget about their ever-loving wives until after store hours on Christmas Eve, but Dancing Dan says never mind about this, but let us have a few more Tom and Jerrys first.

So we have a few more Tom and Jerrys and then Dancing Dan picks up the package he heaves into the corner, and dumps most of the excelsior out of Ooky's Santa Claus sack, and puts the bundle in, and Good Time Charley turns out all the lights, but one, and leaves a bottle of Scotch on the table in front of Ooky for a Christmas gift, and away we go.

Personally, I regret very much leaving the hot Tom and Jerry, but then I am also very enthusiastic about going along to help Dancing Dan play Santa Claus, while Good Time Charley is practically overjoyed, as it is the first time in his life Charley is ever mixed up in so much holiday spirit.

As we go up Broadway, headed for Forty-ninth Street, Charley and I see many citizens we know and give them a large hello, and wish them Merry Christmas, and some of these citizens shake hands with Santa Claus, not knowing he is nobody but Dancing Dan, although later I understand there is some gossip among these citizens because they claim a Santa Claus with such a breath on him as our Santa Claus has is a little out of line.

And once we are somewhat embarrassed when a lot of little kids going home with their parents from a late Christmas party somewhere gather about Santa Claus with shouts of childish glee, and some of them wish to climb up Santa

Claus' legs. Naturally, Santa Claus gets a little peevish, and calls them a few names, and one of the parents comes up and wishes to know what is the idea of Santa Claus using such language, and Santa Claus takes a punch at the parent, all of which is no doubt astonishing to the little kids who have an idea of Santa Claus as a very kindly old guy.

Well, finally we arrive in front of the place where Dancing Dan says Miss Muriel O'Neill and her grandmamma live, and it is nothing but a tenement house not far back of Madison Square Garden, and furthermore it is a walk-up, and at this time there are no lights burning in the joint except a gas jet in the main hall, and by the light of this jet we look at the names on the letter boxes, such as you always find in the hall of these joints, and we see that Miss Muriel O'Neill and her grandmamma live on the fifth floor.

This is the top floor, and personally I do not like the idea of walking up five flights of stairs, and I am willing to let Dancing Dan and Good Time Charley go, but Dancing Dan insists we must all go, and finally I agree with him because Charley is commencing to argue that the right way for us to do is to get on the roof and let Santa Claus go down a chimney, and is making so much noise I am afraid he will wake somebody up.

So up the stairs we climb and finally we come to a door on the top floor that has a little card in a slot that says O'Neill, so we know we reach our destination. Dancing Dan first tries the knob, and right away the door opens, and we are in a little two- or three-room flat, with not much furniture in it, and what furniture there is, is very poor. One single gas jet is burning near a bed in a room just off the one the door opens into, and by this light we see a very old doll is sleeping on the bed, so we judge this is nobody but Gammer O'Neill.

On her face is a large smile, as if she is dreaming of something very pleasant. On a chair at the head of the bed is hung a long black stocking, and it seems to be such a stocking as is often patched and mended, so I can see that what Miss Muriel O'Neill tells Dancing Dan about her grandmamma hanging up her stocking is really true, although up to this time I have my doubts.

Finally Dancing Dan unslings the sack on his back, and takes out his package, and unties this package, and all of a sudden out pops a raft of big diamond bracelets, and diamond rings, and diamond brooches, and diamond necklaces, and I do not know what else in the way of diamonds, and Dancing Dan and I begin stuffing these diamonds into the stocking and Good Time Charley pitches in and helps us.

There are enough diamonds to fill the stocking to the muzzle, and it is no small stocking, at that, and I judge that Gammer O'Neill has a pretty fair set of bunting sticks when she is young. In fact, there are so many diamonds that we have enough left over to make a nice little pile on the chair after we fill the stocking plumb up, leaving a nice diamond-studded vanity case sticking out the top where we figure it will hit Gammer O'Neill's eye when she wakes up.

And it is not until I get out in the fresh air again that all of a sudden I remember seeing large headlines in the afternoon papers about a five-hundred-G's stickup in the afternoon of one of the biggest diamond merchants in Maiden Lane while he is sitting in his office, and I also recall once hearing rumors that Dancing Dan is one of the best lone-hand git-'em-up guys in the world.

Naturally, I commence to wonder if I am in the proper company when I am with Dancing Dan, even if he is Santa Claus. So I leave him on the next corner arguing with Good Time Charley about whether they ought to go and find some more presents somewhere, and look for other stockings to stuff, and I hasten on home and go to bed.

The next day I find I have such a noggin that I do not care to stir around, and in fact I do not stir around much for a couple of weeks.

Then one night I drop around to Good Time Charley's little speakeasy, and ask Charley what is doing.

"Well," Charley says, "many things are doing, and personally," he says, "I'm greatly surprised

I do not see you at Gammer O'Neill's wake. You know Gammer O'Neill leaves this wicked old world a couple of days after Christmas," Good Time Charley says, "and," he says, "Miss Muriel O'Neill states that Doc Moggs claims it is at least a day after she is entitled to go, but she is sustained," Charley says, "by great happiness in finding her stocking filled with beautiful gifts on Christmas morning.

"According to Miss Muriel O'Neill," Charley says, "Gammer O'Neill dies practically convinced that there is a Santa Claus, although of course," he says, "Miss Muriel O'Neill does not tell her the real owner of the gifts, an all-right guy by the name of Shapiro leaves the gifts with her after Miss Muriel O'Neill notifies him of finding of same.

"It seems," Charley says, "this Shapiro is a tender-hearted guy, who is willing to help keep Gammer O'Neill with us a little longer when Doc Moggs says leaving the gifts with her will do it.

"So," Charley says, "everything is quite all right, as the coppers cannot figure anything except that maybe the rascal who takes the gifts from Shapiro gets conscience-stricken, and leaves them the first place he can, and Miss Muriel O'Neill receives a ten-G's reward for finding the gifts and returning them. And," Charley says, "I hear Dancing Dan is in San Francisco and is figuring on reforming and becoming a dancing teacher, so he can marry Miss Muriel O'Neill, and of course," he says, "we all hope and trust she never learns any details of Dancing Dan's career."

Well, it is Christmas Eve a year later that I run into a guy by the name of Shotgun Sam, who is mobbed up with Heine Schmitz in Harlem, and who is a very, very obnoxious character indeed.

"Well, well, well," Shotgun says, "the last time I see you is another Christmas Eve like this, and you are coming out of Good Time Charley's joint, and," he says, "you certainly have your pots on."

"Well, Shotgun," I says, "I am sorry you get such a wrong impression of me, but the truth is," I say, "on the occasion you speak of, I am suffering from a dizzy feeling in my head."

"It is all right with me," Shotgun says. "I have a tip this guy Dancing Dan is in Good Time Charley's the night I see you, and Mockie Morgan, and Gunner Jack and me are casing the joint, because," he says, "Heine Schmitz is all sored up at Dan over some doll, although of course," Shotgun says, "it is all right now, as Heine has another doll.

"Anyway," he says, "we never get to see Dancing Dan. We watch the joint from six-thirty in the evening until daylight Christmas morning, and nobody goes in all night but old Ooky the Santa Claus guy in his Santa Claus makeup, and," Shotgun says, "nobody comes out except you and Good Time Charley and Ooky.

"Well," Shotgun says, "it is a great break for Dancing Dan he never goes in or comes out of Good Time Charley's, at that, because," he says, "we are waiting for him on the second-floor front of the building across the way with some nice little sawed-offs, and are under orders from Heine not to miss."

"Well, Shotgun," I say, "Merry Christmas."

"Well, all right," Shotgun says, "Merry Christmas."

A VISIT FROM ST. NICHOLAS

Ron Goulart

IT IS NO SMALL THING to be able to blend three genres into good, readable stories, but Ron Goulart has proven to be a master at this juggling act, combining mystery, science fiction, and humor to produce scores of books with this rich stew, one of which, *After Things Fell Apart* (1970), was nominated for an Edgar Award. Many of his private eye stories are set in the future, a time and place with which he was comfortable enough to mentor William Shatner when the popular actor began to write a series of *Star Trek* novels. "A Visit from St. Nicholas" was first published in *Santa Clues*, edited by Martin H. Greenberg and Carol-Lynn Rossel Waugh (New York, Signet, 1993).

A Visit from St. Nicholas

RON GOULART

THE MEDIA, AS USUAL, GOT IT completely wrong. The corpse in the Santa Claus suit hadn't been the victim of a mugging and therefore wasn't an all too obvious symbol of what's wrong with our decaying society.

Actually Harry Wilkie had gotten dressed up as St. Nicholas to commit grand larceny. Things obviously went quite wrong, which is why he ended up, decked out in a scarlet costume and snowy white whiskers, sprawled on that midnight beach in Southport, Connecticut.

It snowed on what was to be Harry's final birthday. That was December 20th last year and the snowfall was fitful and halfhearted, not a traditional New England Christmas-card snow at all. And a foot or so of good snow would have improved the view through the narrow window of the living room of the condo where he'd been living in exile since his last divorce almost two years ago.

Harry was sitting there, phone in his lap, looking out at his carport, his two blue plastic garbage cans, and a bleak patch of dead lawn.

"Didn't I warn you?" his brother Roy was asking from his mansion way out in Oregon someplace. "You take up residence in something named Yankee Woodlands Village, you're obviously going to have problems. There probably aren't any woodlands within miles, are there?"

"Six trees. The point, Roy, is—"

"What kind of trees?"

"Elms. The point, Roy, is that it's been over four months since I was let go at Forman & McCay. You may not have heard, but the economy is—"

"You really had talent once. I still remember those great caricatures you did of Mr. Washburn."

"Who?"

"Our high school math teacher. Washburn, the one with the nose shaped like—"

"My high school math teachers were Miss Dillingham and Mr. Ribera. The point is, Roy, that I'm running short of cash and—"

"To go from really brilliant caricatures to the worst kind of commercial art is sad and—"

"Forman & McCay is the second largest ad agency in Manhattan, Roy. I work on the Kubla Kola account, which annually bills—"

"*Worked.* Past tense."

"And the Cyclops Security System account and—"

"Okay, how much?"

"Do I need, you mean?"

"I can't let you have more than $5000. Abigail wants to go for her MA degree next sem—"

"You don't have a daughter named Abigail."

"Mistress. Will $5000 help?"

"Sure, yes. I've got a lead on a new art director job and right after the first of the—"

"Another job in the Apple?"

"No, it's just over in Norwalk. Near Wilton

here. A small, aggressive young agency that specializes in health food and herbal remedy accounts."

"Have you considered trying one of those career counselors? It's probably not too late, even at your age, to start fresh and—"

"*My* age? I'm two years, Roy, younger than you are."

"Well, I'm nearly fifty."

"You're nearly fifty-one. I'm forty-nine. And I'll tell you something else—having a damned birthday so close to Christmas is not that great. This year especially, since I'm not married or seeing anybody seriously, I got hardly any presents or even—"

"You maybe shouldn't become serious about another woman, Harry. Not right yet anyway," advised his brother. "Four marriages gone flooey is enough for now."

"*Three* marriages gone flooey."

"Was there one that didn't go flooey?"

"There were only three marriages all told, Roy."

"You sure?"

"Yeah, I've kept track."

"Only three, huh? Let's see . . . there was the fat one. Was that Alexandra?"

"That was Alice, who was *plump* and not fat."

"Hereabouts we judge a woman who tips the scale at two-fifty plus as fat."

"At her peak she weighed one seventy-five."

"That's still pretty close to fat, Harry. And then there was that crazy skinny one. What was her name? Some kind of flower."

"Pearl."

"That's the one. Loony as a fruitbar."

"Nutty as a fruitcake."

"Exactly."

"No, I wasn't agreeing, I was just correcting your cliché. Pearl was a mite eccentric, yes, though certainly not crazy."

Out in Oregon his brother made a grunting sound. "The first one wasn't too terrible. The best of the lot, in fact. Was her name Amy?"

"Yep."

"She was halfway good-looking, too."

Harry asked, "Could you, Roy, FedEx me the check?"

"Things that bad?"

"The condo payment is a mite past due. And—" His phone signaled that he had another call. "Hold on, Roy, I have another call." He pushed a button. "Hello?"

"Gee, you sound awful. Are you sick?"

"No," he said tentatively.

The woman continued, "You sound absolutely rotten. I bet it's another of those frequent bouts of bronchitis you were always having."

"I've had bronchitis exactly *twice* in my entire life, Amy."

"Most people never have it at all," said his first wife. "Listen, can I talk to you?"

"Hold on a minute. I'm on the other line with Roy."

"Roy?"

"My brother. The best man at our wedding."

"Was his name Roy? That all seems like a hundred years ago and I try not to clutter my memory with all that old junk. Give him my best, though."

He pushed a button and said to his brother, "I've got to take this other call. Send the money and—"

"It's a woman, isn't it? I can tell by the furtive tone of your voice."

"Do I also sound like I have bronchitis?"

"Is this some new lady? You really, Harry, in your present state shouldn't even consider—"

"It's only my ex-wife. It's Amy. She sends you her best wishes, by the way."

"She wasn't half bad, especially compared to what came later. Merry Christmas—and, oh, happy birthday."

"Thanks, Roy. . . . Hello, Amy, what is it?"

And that's when he first heard about what was up in the attic of the Southport mansion she and her latest husband had recently moved into.

The Southport mansion was less than a block from the Sound. A century-old Victorian, it rose up three stories and was encrusted with intricacies of gingerbread and wrought iron.

Harry arrived there at a quarter past one the day after his former wife's call. Standing on the wide front porch, he noted that they had a new Cyclops alarm system.

"Late as usual," Amy observed as she admitted him to the large hallway. The house was filled with the scents of fresh paint, new carpeting, furniture polish, and cut flowers.

"It took longer to drive over here from Wilton, probably because of the wind and sleet. And then, too, I—"

"You never were very good at planning anything, even a simple visit from one town to another." She helped him out of his overcoat, holding it gingerly and then rushing it into a large closet. "Isn't this the same shabby overcoat?"

"Same as what?"

"It certainly resembles the shabby old overcoat you insisted on wearing back when we were . . . um . . . together."

"Married. We were married." Harry thrust his hands into his trouser pockets and glanced around. There were several small abstract paintings on the walls, bright and in silvery metal frames. He couldn't identify the artist.

"Yes, they're Businos." She smiled thinly and nodded at the nearest painting, which was mostly red.

"Oh, right, Busino." He had no idea who the hell Busino was.

"What happened to your hair?"

He reached up and touched his head. "Still there, Amy."

"Not very much of it," she observed. "You used to have a great deal much more hair back when we were . . . um . . . cohabiting."

He asked, "What about the paintings you wanted me to look at?"

"My husband . . . have you ever met Tops?"

"Tops? Your husband's first name is Tops? No, I'd remember if I'd ever encountered somebody who was named Tops. What's it short for?"

"Nothing. It's a nickname. Obviously."

"Is he home?"

"No, he's with his parents over on Long Island. I'll be joining them Christmas Eve day. I find two days with Mommy Nayland is all I can safely tolerate."

"What do they call Tops's father?"

"Jared."

Harry nodded. "About the pictures?"

"I was trying to say that Tops has a full head of wavy hair."

"I once did myself."

She sighed briefly. "Follow me," Amy invited. "We left them up in the attic after we found them last month. You see, as I mentioned to you over the telephone yesterday, many years ago an art director from some New York advertising concern lived in this house. A coincidence, isn't it, since you're an art director, too? His name was . . . um . . . Hoganbanger."

"I doubt it."

"Something like that. Perhaps Bangerhagen." She started up the ornate staircase. "Tops and I think they may be from the 1950s or possibly earlier. Left behind by the art director. It's old artwork by various artists, stuff he must have brought home. This Hagenfarmer seems to—"

"Do you mean Faberhagen? Eric Faberhagen?"

"That sounds about right. Have you ever heard of him?"

"Sure, he was a famous art director in the 1930s and 1940s. He still gets written up in advertising graphics magazines now and then," Harry answered. "He worked for the agency that, back then, had the Kubla Kola account."

"Yes, some of these awful paintings have cola bottles in them."

Harry felt a sudden tightening across his chest. He let out an inadvertent gasp, took hold of the bannister. "Really?" he managed to say.

"Have you had a physical exam lately? Climbing a few flights of stairs shouldn't—"

"It's the bronchitis, that's all."

"With all the weight you seem to have put on, you have to think seriously about your heart."

"I weigh exactly what I did while we were . . . um . . . married."

"C'mon, Harry." She laughed. "You used to be quite slim."

"I was never slim, no."

"Well, certainly slimmer than you are now," she insisted. "Two more flights to go. Can you make it?"

"Yes, ma'am."

"I understand you're not married just now."

"I'm not."

"I've been meaning to call you before this. Ever since Tops and I bought this place five months ago and I quit working with Thigpen Reality," his former wife told him as they began another flight. "The thing is, Tops isn't that keen on my seeing old beaus . . . or old husbands. But when we came across these old advertising paintings, it occurred to me you were the perfect person to tell us what they're worth. I got Tops to see it my way. And, really, there's no reason why you and I can't be friends again—in a distant way at least."

"When you moved out you implied you never wanted to see me again. Let's see . . . the exact words were 'I never want to look at that awful pudgy face of yours as long as we both shall live.'"

"Well, then I guess you were overweight back then, too," she said, nodding slowly. "As I told you, I weed out my memories fairly often. I have no recollection what I might have said to you eleven years ago. Did my remarks hurt you?"

"Not as much as the bricks."

"Oh, my. Did I throw a brick at you, Harry?"

"Bricks, plural. Three."

"I have no recollection. Wherever did I get bricks?"

"The bookcase in my den was constructed from boards and bricks."

"Oh, that ugly thing. Yes, I remember that," she said. "Tops and I got to talking, after we discovered this small cache of old advertising art that had been mouldering in the attic for untold years, and I suggested that it might be worth something. Tops simply wants to donate it to St. Norby."

"Another nickname?"

"St. Norbert's Holy Denominational Church. You must've driven past it on your way here."

"Big building with a cross on top?"

"That's dear old St. Norby, yes." She started up another flight. "But before we donate this stuff to their fair next month, I thought I ought to get an expert opinion. And, after some debate, Tops gave in and allowed me to ask you over. Maybe this crap is worth something after all."

When they reached the large, chill attic and he saw the seven canvases, it took Harry almost a minute to get himself to where he could speak. He had to sit down on a highly polished hump-back trunk and cough a few times.

Six of the unframed canvases were, indeed, crap. But the seventh, as he'd hoped ever since he'd heard the old art director's name, was a large oil painting of Santa Claus in his shirt-sleeves sitting in front of a roaring fireplace after a long night of delivering toys. He was relaxing by drinking Kubla Kola straight from the bottle. It was, beyond doubt, an authentic Maxwell Van Gelder.

Although most people knew nothing about the long-dead commercial artist, who'd been a favorite of the equally long dead Faberhagen, his Kubla Kola Santa paintings were highly prized by certain collectors. He'd done fifteen during his lifetime, but only five had surfaced thus far. The last one that had been sold, over three years ago, had been purchased by a Kubla executive for nearly $400,000. This one, which was much handsomer, ought to bring at least $500,000.

Harry was finally able, after another cough, to inform his ex-wife, "They're not worth anything, Amy."

"Nothing, not anything?"

"Not exactly nothing, no. There are people who collect old advertising art. I'd say you could get probably a hundred dollars or so for each of these," he said. "That Santa, since it has a Christmas theme, might bring as much as two or three hundred."

Amy looked disappointed for a few seconds, then smiled. "Tops was right this time," she said, starting for the attic door.

"Wait a minute." He rose off the trunk. "I collect this sort of stuff myself."

"I didn't realize that. Although you did tend to clutter up the house with all sorts of silly—"

"How about a thousand dollars for the lot? I'd like to hang that Santa in my den, to remind me of my days with Kubla."

"That seems a fair price, and this stuff is only gathering dust up here."

His brother's check ought to get here tomorrow. He could write Amy a check for a thousand and still cover his condo payment and some of the other bills. And if he could sell the Van Gelder, very quietly, for even $450,000—hell, he could live on that for years. Sure, if you invested that wisely, you could even live well here in Fairfield County.

"I'll take them with me, Amy, and send you a check first thing—"

"Oh, I'll have to talk it over with Tops first."

"Sure, of course. Can you phone him over in Long Island? Now, I mean."

"Well, he's off at lunch somewhere, I'm not exactly sure where, with Mommy Nayland and Dr. Boopsy and—"

"Dr. Boopsy?"

"His real name is Bublitzky. When Tops was little, he couldn't pronounce that and his cute way of—"

"You can get in touch with him tonight, though?"

"Or tomorrow morning, yes."

"I could take them along now, save me another trip and you more bother. He's likely to say okay and—"

"I'd better not, Harry. I don't want to annoy Tops by making a household decision without consulting him first. Unlike the days when you and I were . . . um . . . living in the same house, Tops and I have a very democratic marriage."

"So did we, Amy, until you declared yourself fuhrer and . . . But that's, as you say, all lost in the dim past." He forced himself to smile. "Do call me as soon as you talk it over with your husband. And be sure to wish Tops a joyous Noel."

* * *

Harry waited until noon the next day before phoning Amy. He didn't want to convey undue eagerness, which might make his erstwhile wife suspicious.

He let the phone ring eleven times.

After pacing his living room for what seemed a half hour but was actually only thirteen minutes, he tried the Southport mansion again. This time he got their answering tape.

While Chopin music played softly in the background, a thin, nasal male voice said, "Well, hi, this is, as you no doubt expected, the Nayland residence. But, as you may not have expected, neither Tops nor Amy can come to the phone just now. You know the drill, so wait for the beep, won't you?"

Not waiting for the beep, Harry hung up, muttering, "What an asshole."

A chill, heavy rain was falling outside and it made his narrow view even bleaker. Harry sat there, phone waiting in his lap, watching the view for another twenty-six minutes.

Then he punched out Amy's number again.

She answered, sounding impatient and out of breath, on the sixth ring. "Yes, what?"

"This is Harry and—"

"Oh, you picked a rotten time to call, dear heart. I've got Mr. Sanhammel in the parlor in his shorts and—"

"Beg pardon?"

"It's because of the Santa Claus Choraleers," she explained. "I'll be right back, Mr. Sanhammel. He's going on eighty, poor dear man."

"But why is he in your parlor in his underwear?"

"That should be obvious. As people grow older, they tend to put on weight, as you well know. His Santa Claus suit doesn't fit him anymore and has to be let out, quite a bit in fact, especially around the middle. But poor old Mrs. Sanhammel happens to be in intensive care at the Norwalk Hospital because of her—"

"What are the Santa Claus Choraleers?"

"A Southport tradition."

"Oh, so?"

"Every Christmas Eve they roam the streets and byways of our town, every man jack of them dressed as St. Nicholas, stopping at various spots to sing carols and unoffensive hymns."

"That's fascinating, Amy. Now about—"

"You don't think it's fascinating at all. I can tell by that familiar patronizing tone in—"

"Actually I was wondering if you'd talked to your husband about those second-rate old ad paintings. I'm going to be over your way this—"

"Yes, I did. Tops feels that if they're really only worth one thousand dollars, why we'll donate them to St. Norby."

"I'll go up to twelve hundred. I'll donate the money to St. Norby and save them the trouble of—"

"Let me be absolutely candid with you, Harry," she cut in. "Tops says he'd rather toss the paintings on the landfill than sell them to an odious toad such as yourself."

"What gave him the notion I was an odious toad?"

After a few silent seconds she answered, "Well, I may have exagerated my accounts of some of the low points of our wretched marriage, Harry."

He said, "Fifteen hundred dollars."

"It's no use. He won't sell them to you. But, hey, you can go to the fair at the church next month. I'll have Father Boody send you an invitation."

That was too risky. If the Van Gelder got out in public, somebody else might recognize it. "Wouldn't it be much easier if—"

"Poor Mr. Sanhammel is getting all covered with gooseflesh. I really have to go. Merry Christmas and maybe I'll see you at the church fair next month."

"Yeah, Merry Christmas."

The most difficult part was finding a Santa Claus suit. Harry didn't come up with his plan until the afternoon of Christmas Eve and by then the few costume shops in his part of Connecticut had long since sold or rented what they'd had in stock.

He persisted, however, and finally located a used-clothing outlet over in Westchester County that had one threadbare Santa costume for sale. They wanted two hundred dollars for the damn thing, but since the check from his brother had come in, he was able to rush over into New York State with the cash to buy it. The beard was in bad shape, stringy and a dirty yellow color. When he got it home, Harry used some ivory spray paint on the whiskers and livened them up considerably.

The rest of that gray afternoon and into the evening he sat at his drawing board, studying all the material he'd saved about the Cyclops Security System from the days when he worked on the account. It seemed to him definitely possible, just by using the tools he had on hand, to outfox the type of alarm setup they were using at Amy's mansion.

His plan was a simple one. There'd be a dozen costumed Santas—he'd found out how many choraleers there were from the back files of the Southport weekly at the library—roaming the streets of the town from nine until midnight. Nobody was likely to pay much attention to a thirteenth. Especially not on Christmas Eve. Amy and Tops were now over in Long Island and their house sat empty.

The Van Gelder Santa painting was resting quietly up in the attic. All Harry had to do was disarm the alarm system, enter the house, and gather up the picture. To throw suspicion off himself, he'd also swipe whatever silver and jewelry he could find. And he'd take all those awful Busino paintings that decorated the hall. The police would assume that the thief had stolen the advertising art under the assumption that it, too, was valuable.

Then, after a safe interval, he'd sell the painting and live on the $500,000. There wouldn't be any more job interviews with art directors who were ten or twenty years younger. No more loans or lectures from Roy.

To explain his income, he'd pretend he was doing gallery painting. As a matter of fact, he'd been a damn good painter once and he might really give that a try again.

His plan wasn't a bad one. But what Harry hadn't anticipated was the fourteenth Santa Claus.

A strong wind came up at nightfall and the rain grew heavier. When Harry went running out to his carport, shortly after ten p.m., the rain hit at him hard.

He was carrying the Santa costume in a large, cloth laundry bag. Later, after he'd changed into the outfit, he was going to use the sack to carry off the Van Gelder and the rest of the loot. No one would pay much attention to a Santa Claus with what looked like a bulging sack of toys.

The Southport library sat less than a block from Amy's mansion. The building was dark and there were only two other cars in the unlit parking lot. Harry parked there and opened the sack. He took out the jacket to the Santa suit.

After glancing around at the rainswept lot, he started getting into the jacket. The sleeves had several moth holes in them. Next he struggled into the pants, which were tough to tug on over his jeans. He heard a ripping sound, but when he felt at the trousers he couldn't locate a rip.

The rain was drumming on the car roof, the wind rattled the tree branches overhead.

"Oh, shit," he said aloud. "Where's the beard? Where's the damn beard?"

He thrust his hand deep into the sack again. "Ow! Damn it."

He'd stuck his forefinger with one of the screwdrivers he'd brought along for working on the alarm system.

"Ah, here it is." He yanked out what felt like the false whiskers. It turned out, however, to be his Santa hat.

"I had the beard. I know I put it in the sack."

Then he noticed something white on the floor of the car, over on the passenger side. He grabbed up the beard and attached it with the wire ear loops. Stretching up, he attempted to get a look at himself in the rearview mirror. The thing was all steamed and there wasn't enough light anyway.

Harry started to open the door. "Half-wit," he reminded himself. "Gloves! You almost forgot the damn gloves."

They were in the laundry bag someplace, too. "Ow!" He found them and slipped them on.

Nodding to himself, Harry gathered up the big laundry bag and left the car.

Wind and rain struck at him, shoving him off in the wrong direction. He fought, gasping, and managed to get himself aimed right. The wind caught at the beard, and unhooked it from one ear.

Harry rescued it, got the whiskers back in place. As he stood on the sidewalk watching Amy's dark mansion across the way, a Mercedes drove by on the wet street.

The driver honked and someone yelled, "Merry Christmas, Mr. Sanhammel!" out a briefly lowered window.

Harry waved. Maybe he *was* putting on weight.

After the car had been swallowed up by darkness, he ran across the street. He sloshed swiftly across the lawn, circled around to the backside of the Victorian house.

He intended to enter by the back door, which couldn't be seen from the street and was sheltered by a stand of maples. Down across the back acre of lawn was a narrow stretch of beach. The water on the Sound was dark and foamy.

"This is typical of Amy," he muttered when he reached the rear door. "She was always going off and leaving things wide open."

The door stood an inch open. Gingerly Harry reached out with his gloved right hand and pushed at the door. Creaking faintly, it swung open inward.

After listening for a half minute, he crossed the threshold and started along the back hall.

The house smelled exactly as it had the other day.

In the front hall, he stopped and frowned. Even in this dim light he noticed that the Busino paintings weren't hanging on the walls anymore.

Then he spotted them, stacked and leaning against the bottom steps of the staircase.

That was just ten seconds before he became aware that somebody was coming down the stairs.

"Well, sir, hi there," said Harry, affecting what he hoped was an older man's voice. "I'm Mr. Sanhammel from—"

"You walked in at the wrong time, friend." The man approaching him had a suitcase in his right hand and a .38 revolver in his left. Tucked under his arm was a lighted flash.

He was also wearing a Santa Claus suit and a handsome beard.

"Damn! Somebody else with the same idea." Harry pivoted and made ready to run.

The other Santa came diving down the stairs. He dropped the suitcase and it hit the floor with a metallic rattle. He grabbed Harry by the arm, swung him around, and hit him hard across the temple with the butt of his gun.

That wasn't what killed Harry, though. It was falling to the floor and cracking his head against the frame of the topmost Busino.

What the burglar did next was to gather up the loot he'd left downstairs, add it to the loot he'd gathered upstairs, and stash it all in his suitcase along with Harry's laundry bag. Leaving it behind for a few moments, he carried the obviously dead Harry out of the house and down across the back acre. He left him lying at the edge of the water.

Returning to the house, he collected his things, took his leave, and reset the alarm system. When they found Harry's body down on the beach, it probably wouldn't occur to them that a burglary had been committed. Not immediately anyway.

None of the advertising art in the attic was stolen. In January, Amy and Tops did donate the paintings to the St. Norbert fair.

A young commercial artist from Westport picked up the Van Gelder for $225. Harry, by the way, overestimated the value of the Santa painting. It brought only $260,000 when it was auctioned at a Manhattan gallery last month.

THE THIEVES WHO COULDN'T HELP SNEEZING

Thomas Hardy

NO, THIS IS NOT THE USUAL TALE of gloom and doom that is so closely associated with the work of the Victorian novelist Thomas Hardy. The title alone suggests a sense of lightness and in that expectation you will not be disappointed. In 1896, by contrast, disturbed by the public uproar over the unconventional subjects of two of his greatest novels, *Tess of the D'Urbervilles* (1891) and *Jude the Obscure* (1895), Hardy announced that he would never write fiction again. A bishop solemnly burned the books, "probably in his despair at not being able to burn me," Hardy noted. "The Thieves Who Couldn't Help Sneezing" was first published in the December 1877 issue of *Father Christmas*.

The Thieves Who Couldn't Help Sneezing

THOMAS HARDY

MANY YEARS AGO, WHEN OAK-TREES now past their prime were about as large as elderly gentlemen's walking-sticks, there lived in Wessex a yeoman's son, whose name was Hubert. He was about fourteen years of age, and was as remarkable for his candor and lightness of heart as for his physical courage, of which, indeed, he was a little vain.

One cold Christmas Eve his father, having no other help at hand, sent him on an important errand to a small town several miles from home. He travelled on horseback, and was detained by the business till a late hour the evening. At last, however, it was completed; he returned to the inn, the horse was saddled, and he started on his way. His journey homeward lay through the Vale of Blackmore, a fertile but somewhat lonely district, with heavy clay roads and crooked lanes. In those days, too, a great part of it was thickly wooded.

It must have been about nine o'clock when, riding along amid the over-hanging trees upon his stout-legged cob, Jerry, and singing a Christmas carol, to be in harmony with the season, Hubert fancied that he heard a noise among the boughs. This recalled to his mind that the spot he was traversing bore an evil name. Men had been waylaid there. He looked at Jerry, and wished he had been of any other color than light gray; for on this account the docile animal's form was visible even here in the dense shade. "What do I care?" he said aloud, after a few min-

utes of reflection. "Jerry's legs are too nimble to allow any highwayman to come near me."

"Ha! ha! indeed," was said in a deep voice; and the next moment a man darted from the thicket on his right hand, another man from the thicket on his left hand, and another from a tree-trunk a few yards ahead. Hubert's bridle was seized, he was pulled from his horse, and although he struck out with all his might, as a brave boy would naturally do, he was overpowered. His arms were tied behind him, his legs bound tightly together, and he was thrown into the ditch. The robbers, whose faces he could now dimly perceive to be artificially blackened, at once departed, leading off the horse.

As soon as Hubert had a little recovered himself, he found that by great exertion he was able to extricate his legs from the cord; but, in spite of every endeavor, his arms remained bound as fast as before. All, therefore, that he could do was to rise to his feet and proceed on his way with his arms behind him, and trust to chance for getting them unfastened. He knew that it would be impossible to reach home on foot that night, and in such a condition; but he walked on. Owing to the confusion which this attack caused in his brain, he lost his way, and would have been inclined to lie down and rest till morning among the dead leaves had he not known the danger of sleeping without wrappers in a frost so severe. So he wandered further onwards, his arms wrung and numbed by the cord which pinioned him, and his heart aching for the loss of poor Jerry, who never had been known to kick, or bite, or show a single vicious habit. He was not a little glad when he discerned through the trees a distant light. Towards this he made his way, and presently found himself in front of a large mansion with flanking wings, gables, and towers, the battlements and chimneys showing their shapes against the stars.

All was silent; but the door stood wide open, it being from this door that the light shone which had attracted him. On entering he found himself in a vast apartment arranged as a dining-hall, and brilliantly illuminated. The walls were covered with a great deal of dark wainscoting, formed into moulded panels, carvings, closet-doors, and the usual fittings of a house of that kind. But what drew his attention most was the large table in the midst of the hall, upon which was spread a sumptuous supper, as yet untouched. Chairs were placed around, and it appeared as if something had occurred to interrupt the meal just at the time when all were ready to begin.

Even had Hubert been so inclined, he could not have eaten in his helpless state, unless by dipping his mouth into the dishes, like a pig or cow. He wished first to obtain assistance; and was about to penetrate further into the house for that purpose when he heard hasty footsteps in the porch and the words, "Be quick!" uttered in the deep voice which had reached him when he was dragged from the horse. There was only just time for him to dart under the table before three men entered the dining-hall. Peeping from beneath the hanging edges of the tablecloth, he perceived that their faces, too, were blackened, which at once removed any remaining doubts he may have felt that these were the same thieves.

"Now, then," said the first—the man with the deep voice—"let us hide ourselves. They will all be back again in a minute. That was a good trick to get them out of the house—eh?"

"Yes. You well imitated the cries of a man in distress," said the second.

"Excellently," said the third.

"But they will soon find out that it was a false alarm. Come, where shall we hide? It must be some place we can stay in for two or three hours, till all are in bed and asleep. Ah! I have it. Come this way! I have learnt that the further closet is not opened once in a twelve-month; it will serve our purpose exactly."

The speaker advanced into a corridor which led from the hall. Creeping a little farther forward, Hubert could discern that the closet stood at the end, facing the dining-hall. The thieves entered it, and closed the door. Hardly breathing, Hubert glided forward, to learn a little more of their intention, if possible; and, coming close, he could hear the robbers whispering about the different rooms where the jewels, plate, and other valuables of the house were kept, which they plainly meant to steal.

They had not been long in hiding when a gay chattering of ladies and gentlemen was audible on the terrace without. Hubert felt that it would not do to be caught prowling about the house, unless he wished to be taken for a robber himself; and he slipped softly back to the hall, out the door, and stood in a dark corner of the porch, where he could see everything without being himself seen. In a moment or two a whole troop of personages came gliding past him into the house. There were an elderly gentleman and lady, eight or nine young ladies, as many young men, besides half-a-dozen men-servants and maids. The mansion had apparently been quite emptied of its occupants.

"Now, children and young people, we will resume our meal," said the old gentleman. "What the noise could have been I cannot understand. I never felt so certain in my life that there was a person being murdered outside my door."

Then the ladies began saying how frightened they had been, and how they had expected an adventure, and how it had ended in nothing at all.

"Wait a while," said Hubert to himself. "You'll have adventure enough by-and-by, ladies."

It appeared that the young men and women

were married sons and daughters of the old couple, who had come that day to spend Christmas with their parents.

The door was then closed, Hubert being left outside in the porch. He thought this a proper moment for asking their assistance; and, since he was unable to knock with his hands, began boldly to kick the door.

"Hullo! What disturbance are you making here?" said a footman who opened it; and, seizing Hubert by the shoulder, he pulled him into the dining-hall. "Here's a strange boy I have found making a noise in the porch, Sir Simon."

Everybody turned.

"Bring him forward," said Sir Simon, the old gentleman before mentioned. "What were you doing there, my boy?"

"Why, his arms are tied!" said one of the ladies.

"Poor fellow!" said another.

Hubert at once began to explain that he had been waylaid on his journey home, robbed of his horse, and mercilessly left in this condition by the thieves.

"Only to think of it!" exclaimed Sir Simon.

"That's a likely story," said one of the gentlemen-guests, incredulously.

"Doubtful, hey?" asked Sir Simon.

"Perhaps he's a robber himself," suggested a lady.

"There is a curiously wild, wicked look about him, certainly, now that I examine him closely," said the old mother.

Hubert blushed with shame; and, instead of continuing his story, and relating that robbers were concealed in the house, he doggedly held his tongue, and half resolved to let them find out their danger for themselves.

"Well, untie him," said Sir Simon. "Come, since it is Christmas Eve, we'll treat him well. Here, my lad; sit down in that empty seat at the bottom of the table, and make as good a meal as you can. When you have had your fill we will listen to more particulars of your story."

The feast then proceeded; and Hubert, now at liberty, was not at all sorry to join in. The more they ate and drank the merrier did the company become; the wine flowed freely, the logs flared up the chimney, the ladies laughed at the gentlemen's stories; in short, all went as noisily and as happily as a Christmas gathering in old times possibly could do.

Hubert, in spite of his hurt feelings at their doubts of his honesty, could not help being warmed both in mind and in body by the good cheer, the scene, and the example of hilarity set by his neighbors. At last he laughed as heartily at their stories and repartees as the old Baronet, Sir Simon, himself. When the meal was almost over one of the sons, who had drunk a little too much wine, after the manner of men in that century, said to Hubert, "Well, my boy, how are you? Can you take a pinch of snuff?" He held out one of the snuff-boxes which were then becoming common among young and old throughout the country.

"Thank you," said Hubert, accepting a pinch.

"Tell the ladies who you are, what you are made of, and what you can do," the young man continued, slapping Hubert upon the shoulder.

"Certainly," said our hero, drawing himself up, and thinking it best to put a bold face on the matter. "I am a traveling magician."

"Indeed!"

"What shall we hear next?"

"Can you call up spirits from the vasty deep, young wizard?"

"I can conjure up a tempest in a cupboard," Hubert replied.

"Ha-ha!" said the old Baronet, pleasantly rubbing his hands. "We must see this performance. Girls, don't go away: here's something to be seen."

"Not dangerous, I hope?" said the old lady.

Hubert rose from the table. "Hand me your snuff-box, please," he said to the young man who had made free with him. "And now," he continued, "without the least noise, follow me. If any of you speak it will break the spell."

They promised obedience. He entered the corridor, and, taking off his shoes, went on tiptoe to the closet door, the guests advancing in a silent group at a little distance behind him. Hubert next placed a stool in front of the door, and, by standing upon it, was tall enough to reach to the top. He then, just as noiselessly, poured all the snuff from the box along the upper edge of the door, and, with a few short puffs of breath, blew the snuff through the chink into the interior of the closet. He held up his finger to the assembly, that they might be silent.

"Dear me, what's that?" said the old lady, after a minute or two had elapsed.

A suppressed sneeze had come from inside the closet.

Hubert held up his finger again.

"How very singular," whispered Sir Simon. "This is most interesting."

Hubert took advantage of the moment to gently slide the bolt of the closet door into its place. "More snuff," he said, calmly.

"More snuff," said Sir Simon. Two or three gentlemen passed their boxes, and the contents were blown in at the top of the closet. Another sneeze, not quite so well suppressed as the first, was heard: then another, which seemed to say that it would not be suppressed under any circumstances whatever. At length there arose a perfect storm of sneezes.

"Excellent, excellent for one so young!" said Sir Simon. "I am much interested in this trick of throwing the voice—called, I believe, ventriloquism."

"More snuff," said Hubert.

"More snuff," said Sir Simon. Sir Simon's man brought a large jar of the best scented Scotch.

Hubert once more charged the upper chink of the closet, and blew the snuff into the interior, as before. Again he charged, and again, emptying the whole contents of the jar. The tumult of sneezes became really extraordinary to listen to—there was no cessation. It was like wind, rain, and sea battling in a hurricane.

"I believe there are men inside, and that it is

no trick at all!" exclaimed Sir Simon, the truth flashing on him.

"There are," said Hubert. "They are come to rob the house; and they are the same who stole my horse."

The sneezes changed to spasmodic groans. One of the thieves, hearing Hubert's voice, cried, "Oh! mercy! mercy! let us out of this!"

"Where's my horse?" said Hubert.

"Tied to the tree in the hollow behind Short's Gibbet. Mercy! mercy! let us out, or we shall die of suffocation!"

All the Christmas guests now perceived that this was no longer sport, but serious earnest. Guns and cudgels were procured; all the men-servants were called in, and arranged in position outside the closet. At a signal Hubert withdrew the bolt, and stood on the defensive. But the three robbers, far from attacking them, were found crouching in the corner, gasping for breath. They made no resistance; and, being pinioned, were placed in an outhouse till the morning.

Hubert now gave the remainder of his story to the assembled company, and was profusely thanked for the services he had rendered. Sir Simon pressed him to stay over the night, and accept the use of the best bedroom the house afforded, which had been occupied by Queen Elizabeth and King Charles successively when on their visits to this part of the country. But Hubert declined, being anxious to find his horse Jerry, and to test the truth of the robbers' statements concerning him.

Several of the guests accompanied Hubert to the spot behind the gibbet, alluded to by the thieves as where Jerry was hidden. When they reached the knoll and looked over, behold! there the horse stood, uninjured, and quite unconcerned. At sight of Hubert he neighed joyfully; and nothing could exceed Hubert's gladness at finding him. He mounted, wished his friends "Good-night!" and cantered off in the direction they pointed out, reaching home safely about four o'clock in the morning.

RUMPOLE AND THE SPIRIT OF CHRISTMAS

John Mortimer

IN AN UNUSUAL REVERSAL OF CUSTOM, John Mortimer's famous character, the irascible barrister Horace Rumpole, was created for television and the scripts were novelized for books by Mortimer himself—and very nicely, too. The iconoclastic, poetry-quoting, cheap wine–drinking lawyer was based on Mortimer's father, and the character was so perfectly portrayed by Leo McKern in the long-running Thames and PBS series, *Rumpole of the Bailey*, that Mortimer once stated that he would continue writing the series only as long as McKern was willing to portray him. "Rumpole and the Spirit of Christmas" was first published in *Murder Under the Mistletoe*, edited by Cynthia Manson (New York, Signet, 1992).

Rumpole and the Spirit of Christmas

JOHN MORTIMER

I REALIZED THAT CHRISTMAS WAS upon us when I saw a sprig of holly over the list of prisoners hung on the wall of the cells under the Old Bailey.

I pulled out a new box of small cigars and found its opening obstructed by a tinseled band on which a scarlet-faced Santa was seen hurrying a sleigh full of carcinoma-packed goodies to the Rejoicing World. I lit one as the lethargic screw, with a complexion the color of faded Bronco, regretfully left his doorstep sandwich and mug of sweet tea to unlock the gate.

"Good morning, Mr. Rumpole. Come to visit a customer?"

"Happy Christmas, officer," I said as cheerfully as possible. "Is Mr. Timson at home?"

"Well, I don't believe he's slipped down to his little place in the country."

Such were the pleasantries that were exchanged between us legal hacks and discontented screws; jokes that no doubt have changed little since the turnkeys unlocked the door at Newgate to let in a pessimistic advocate, or the cells under the Coliseum were opened to admit the unwelcome news of the Imperial thumbs-down.

"My mum wants me home for Christmas."

Which Christmas? It would have been an unreasonable remark and I refrained from it. Instead, I said, "All things are possible."

As I sat in the interviewing room, an Old Bailey hack of some considerable experience, looking through my brief and inadvertently using my waistcoat as an ashtray, I hoped I wasn't on another loser. I had had a run of bad luck during that autumn season, and young Edward Timson was part of that huge south London family whose criminal activities provided such welcome grist to the Rumpole mill. The charge in the seventeen-year-old Eddie's case was nothing less than wilful murder.

"We're in with a chance, though, Mr. Rumpole, ain't we?"

Like all his family, young Timson was a confirmed optimist. And yet, of course, the merest outsider in the Grand National, the hundred-to-one shot, is in with a chance, and nothing is more like going round the course at Aintree than living through a murder trial. In this particular case, a fanatical prosecutor named Wrigglesworth, known to me as the Mad Monk, as to represent Beechers, and Mr. Justice Vosper, a bright but wintry-hearted judge who always felt it his duty to lead for the prosecution, was to play the part of a particularly menacing fence at the Canal Turn.

"A chance. Well, yes, of course you've got a chance, if they can't establish common purpose, and no one knows which of you bright lads had the weapon."

No doubt the time had come for a brief glance at the prosecution case, not an entirely cheering prospect. Eddie, also known as "Turpin" Timson, lived in a kind of decaying barracks, a sort of highrise Lubianka, known as Keir Hardie Court, somewhere in south London, together with his parents, his various brothers, and his thirteen-year-old sister, Noreen. This particular branch of the Timson family lived on the thirteenth floor. Below them, on the twelfth, lived the large clan of the O'Dowds. The war between the Timsons and the O'Dowds began, it seems, with the casting of the Nativity play at the local comprehensive school.

Christmas comes earlier each year and the school show was planned about September. When Bridget O'Dowd was chosen to play the lead in the face of strong competition from Noreen Timson, an incident occurred comparable in historical importance to the assassination of an obscure Austrian archduke at Sarejevo. Noreen Timson announced in the playground that Bridget O'Dowd was a spotty little tart unsuited to play any role of which the most notable characteristic was virginity.

Hearing this, Bridget O'Dowd kicked Noreen Timson behind the anthracite bunkers. Within a few days, war was declared between the Timson and O'Dowd children, and a present of lit fireworks was posted through the O'Dowd front door. On what is known as the "night in question," reinforcements of O'Dowds and Timsons arrived in old bangers from a number of south London addresses and battle was joined on the stone staircase, a bleak terrain of peeling walls scrawled with graffiti, blowing empty Coca-Cola tins and torn newspapers. The weapons seemed to have been articles in general domestic use, such as bread knives, carving knives, broom handles, and a heavy screwdriver. At the end of the day it appeared that the upstairs flat had repelled the invaders, and Kevin O'Dowd lay on the stairs. Having been stabbed with a slender and pointed blade, he was in a condition to become known as "the deceased" in the case of the Queen against Edward Timson. I made an application for bail for my client which was refused, but a speedy trial was ordered.

So even as Bridget O'Dowd was giving her Virgin Mary at the comprehensive, the rest of the family was waiting to give evidence against Eddie Timson in that home of British drama, Number One Court at the Old Bailey.

"I never had no cutter, Mr. Rumpole. Straight up, I never had one," the defendant told me in the cells. He was an appealing-looking lad with soft brown eyes, who had already won the heart of the highly susceptible lady who wrote his social inquiry report. ("Although the charge is a serious one, this is a young man who might respond well to a period of probation." I could imagine the steely contempt in Mr. Justice Vosper's eye when he read that.)

"Well, tell me, Edward. Who had?"

"I never seen no cutters on no one, honest I didn't. We wasn't none of us tooled up, Mr. Rumpole."

"Come on, Eddie. Someone must have been. They say even young Noreen was brandishing a potato peeler."

"Not me, honest."

"What about your sword?"

There was one part of the prosecution evidence that I found particularly distasteful. It was agreed that on the previous Sunday morning, Eddie "Turpin" Timson had appeared on the stairs of Keir Hardie Court and flourished what appeared to be an antique cavalry saber at the assembled O'Dowds, who were just popping out to Mass.

"Me sword I bought up the Portobello? I didn't have that there, honest."

"The prosecution can't introduce evidence about the sword. It was an entirely different occasion." Mr. Barnard, my instructing solicitor who fancied himself as an infallible lawyer, spoke with a confidence which I couldn't feel. He, after all, wouldn't have to stand up on his hind legs and argue the legal toss with Mr. Justice Vosper.

"It rather depends on who's prosecuting us. I mean, if it's some fairly reasonable fellow—"

"I think," Mr. Barnard reminded me, shattering my faint optimism and ensuring that we were all in for a very rough Christmas indeed,

"I think it's Mr. Wrigglesworth. Will he try to introduce the sword?"

I looked at "Turpin" Timson with a kind of pity. "If it is the Mad Monk, he undoubtedly will."

When I went into Court, Basil Wrigglesworth was standing with his shoulders hunched up round his large, red ears, his gown dropped to his elbows, his bony wrists protruding from the sleeves of his frayed jacket, his wig pushed back, and his huge hands joined on his lectern in what seemed to be an attitude of devoted prayer. A lump of cotton wool clung to his chin where he had cut himself shaving. Although well into his sixties, he preserved a look of boyish clumsiness. He appeared, as he always did when about to prosecute on a charge carrying a major punishment, radiantly happy.

"Ah, Rumpole," he said, lifting his eyes from the police verbals as though they were his breviary. "Are you defending *as usual*?"

"Yes, Wrigglesworth. And you're prosecuting *as usual*?" It wasn't much of a riposte but it was all I could think of at the time.

"Of course, I don't defend. One doesn't like to call witnesses who may not be telling the truth."

"You must have a few unhappy moments then, calling certain members of the Constabulary."

"I can honestly tell you, Rumpole—" his curiously innocent blue eyes looked at me with a sort of pain, as though I had questioned the doctrine of the immaculate conception "—I have never called a dishonest policeman."

"Yours must be a singularly simple faith, Wrigglesworth."

"As for the Detective Inspector in this case," counsel for the prosecution went on, "I've known Wainwright for years. In fact, this is his last trial before he retires. He could no more invent a verbal against a defendant than fly."

Any more on that tack, I thought, and we should soon be debating how many angels could dance on the point of a pin.

"Look here, Wrigglesworth. That evidence about my client having a sword: it's quite irrelevent. I'm sure you'd agree."

"Why is it irrelevant?" Wrigglesworth frowned.

"Because the murder clearly wasn't done with an antique cavalry saber. It was done with a small, thin blade."

"If he's a man who carries weapons, why isn't that relevant?"

"A man? Why do you call him a man? He's a child. A boy of seventeen!"

"Man enough to commit a serious crime."

"*If* he did."

"If he didn't, he'd hardly be in the dock."

"That's the difference between us, Wrigglesworth," I told him. "I believe in the presumption of innocence. You believe in original sin. Look here, old darling." I tried to give the Mad Monk a smile of friendship and became conscious of the fact that it looked, no doubt, like an ingratiating sneer. "Give us a chance. You won't introduce the evidence of the sword, will you?"

"Why ever not?"

"Well," I told him, "the Timsons are an industrious family of criminals. They work hard, they never go on strike. If it weren't for people like the Timsons, you and I would be out of a job."

"They sound in great need of prosecution and punishment. Why shouldn't I tell the jury about your client's sword? Can you give me one good reason?"

"Yes," I said, as convincingly as possible.

"What is it?" He peered at me, I thought, unfairly.

"Well, after all," I said, doing my best, "it is Christmas."

It would be idle to pretend that the first day in Court went well, although Wrigglesworth restrained himself from mentioning the sword in his opening speech, and told me that he was considering whether or not to call evidence about it the next day. I cross-examined a few members of the clan O'Dowd on the presence of lethal articles in the hands of the attacking force. The evidence about this varied, and weapons came and went in the hands of the inhabitants of Number Twelve as the witnesses were blown hither and thither in the winds of Rumpole's cross-examination. An interested observer from one of the other flats spoke of having seen a machete.

"Could that terrible weapon have been in the hands of Mr. Kevin O'Dowd, the deceased in this case?"

"I don't think so."

"But can you rule out the possibility?"

"No, I can't rule it out," the witness admitted, to my temporary delight.

"You can never rule out the possibility of anything in this world, Mr. Rumpole. But he doesn't think so. You have your answer."

Mr. Justice Vosper, in a voice like a splintering iceberg, gave me this unwelcome Christmas present. The case wasn't going well, but at least, by the end of the first day, the Mad Monk had kept out all mention of the swords. The next day he was to call young Bridget O'Dowd, fresh from her triumph in the Nativity play.

"I say, Rumpole, I'd be *so* grateful for a little help."

I was in Pommeroy's Wine Bar, drowning the sorrows of the day in my usual bottle of the cheapest Chateau Fleet Street (made from grapes which, judging from the bouquet, might have been not so much trodden as kicked to death by sturdy peasants in gum boots) when I looked up to see Wrigglesworth, dressed in an old mackintosh, doing business with Jack Pommeroy at the sales counter. When I crossed to him, he was not buying the jumbo-sized bottle of ginger beer which I imagined might be his celebratory Christmas tipple, but a tempting and respectably aged bottle of Chateau Pichon Longueville.

"What can I do for you, Wrigglesworth?"

"Well, as you know, Rumpole, I live in Croydon."

"Happiness is given to few of us on this earth," I said piously.

"And the Anglican Sisters of St. Agnes, Croydon, are anxious to buy a present for their Bishop," Wrigglesworth explained. "A dozen bottles for Christmas. They've asked my advice, Rumpole. I know so little about wine. You wouldn't care to try this for me? I mean, if you're not especially busy."

"I should be hurrying home to dinner." My wife, Hilda (She Who Must Be Obeyed), was laying on rissoles and frozen peas, washed down by my last bottle of Pommeroy's extremely ordinary. "However, as it's Christmas, I don't mind helping you out, Wrigglesworth."

The Mad Monk was clearly quite unused to wine. As we sampled the claret together, I saw the chance of getting him to commit himself on the vital question of the evidence of the sword, as well as absorbing an unusually decent bottle. After the Pichon Longueville I was kind enough to help him by sampling a Boyd-Cantenac and then I said, "Excellent, this. But of course the Bishop might be a burgundy man. The nuns might care to invest in a decent Macon."

"Shall we try a bottle?" Wrigglesworth suggested. "I'd be grateful for your advice."

"I'll do my best to help you, my old darling. And while we're on the subject, that ridiculous bit of evidence about young Timson and the sword—"

"I remember you saying I shouldn't bring that out because it's Christmas."

"Exactly." Jack Pommeroy had uncorked the Macon and it was mingling with the claret to produce a feeling of peace and goodwill towards men. Wrigglesworth frowned, as though trying to absorb an obscure point of theology.

"I don't quite see the relevance of Christmas to the question of your man Timson threatening his neighbors with a sword."

"Surely, Wrigglesworth—" I knew my prosecutor well "—you're of a religious disposition?" The Mad Monk was the product of some bleak northern Catholic boarding school. He lived alone, and no doubt wore a hair shirt under his black waistcoat and was vowed to celibacy. The fact that he had his nose deep into a glass of burgundy at the moment was due to the benign influence of Rumpole.

"I'm a Christian, yes."

"Then practice a little Christian tolerance."

"Tolerance towards evil?"

"Evil?" I asked. "What do you mean, evil?"

"Couldn't that be your trouble, Rumpole? That you really don't recognize evil when you see it."

"I suppose," I said, "evil might be locking up a seventeen-year-old during Her Majesty's pleasure, when Her Majesty may very probably forget all about him, banging him up with a couple of hard and violent cases and their own chamber-pots for twenty-two hours a day, so he won't come out till he's a real, genuine, middle-aged murderer."

"I did hear the Reverend Mother say—" Wrigglesworth was gazing vacantly at the empty Macon bottle "—that the Bishop likes his glass of port."

"Then in the spirit of Christmas tolerance I'll help you to sample some of Pommeroy's Light and Tawny."

A little later, Wrigglesworth held up his port glass in a reverent sort of fashion.

"You're suggesting, are you, that I should make some special concession in this case because it's Christmastime?"

"Look here, old darling." I absorbed half my glass, relishing the gentle fruitiness and the slight tang of wood. "If you spent your whole life in that highrise hell-hole called Keir Hardie Court, if you had no fat prosecutions to occupy your attention and no prospect of any job at all, if you had no sort of occupation except war with the O'Dowds—"

"My own flat isn't particularly comfortable. I don't know a great deal about *your* home life, Rumpole, but you don't seem to be in a tearing hurry to experience it."

"Touché, Wrigglesworth, my old darling." I ordered us a couple of refills of Pommeroy's port to further postpone the encounter with She Who Must Be Obeyed and her rissoles.

"But we don't have to fight to the death on the staircase," Wrigglesworth pointed out.

"We don't have to fight at all, Wrigglesworth."

"As your client did."

"As my client *may* have done. Remember the presumption of innocence."

"This is rather funny, this is." The prosecutor pulled back his lips to reveal strong, yellowish teeth and laughed appreciatively. "You know why your man Timson is called 'Turpin'?"

"No." I drank port uneasily, fearing an unwelcome revelation.

"Because he's always fighting with that sword of his. He's called after Dick Turpin, you see, who's always dueling on television. Do you watch television, Rumpole?"

"Hardly at all."

"I watch a great deal of television, as I'm alone rather a lot." Wrigglesworth referred to the box as though it were a sort of penance, like fasting or flagellation. "Detective Inspector Wainwright told me about your client. Rather amusing, I thought it was. He's retiring this Christmas."

"My client?"

"No. D. I. Wainwright. Do you think we should settle on this port for the Bishop? Or would you like to try a glass of something else?"

"Christmas," I told Wrigglesworth severely as we sampled the Cockburn, "is not just a material, pagan celebration. It's not just an occasion for absorbing superior vintages, old darling. It must be a time when you try to do good, spiritual good to our enemies."

"To your client, you mean?"

"And to me."

"To you, Rumpole?"

"For God's sake, Wrigglesworth!" I was conscious of the fact that my appeal was growing desperate. "I've had six losers in a row down the Old Bailey. Can't I be included in any Christmas spirit that's going around?"

"You mean, at Christmas especially it is more blessed to give than to receive?"

"I mean exactly that." I was glad that he seemed, at last, to be following my drift.

"And you think I might give this case to someone, like a Christmas present?"

"If you care to put it that way, yes."

"I do not care to put it in *exactly* that way." He turned his pale-blue eyes on me with what I thought was genuine sympathy. "But I shall try and do the case of R. *v.* Timson in the way most appropriate to the greatest feast of the Christian year. It is a time, I quite agree, for the giving of presents."

When they finally threw us out of Pommeroy's, and after we had considered the possibility of buying the Bishop brandy in the Cock Tavern, and even beer in the Devereux, I let my instinct, like an aged horse, carry me on to the Underground and home to Gloucester Road, and there discovered the rissoles, like some traces of a vanished civilization, fossilized in the oven. She Who Must Be Obeyed was already in bed, feigning sleep. When I climbed in beside her, she opened a hostile eye.

"You're drunk, Rumpole!" she said. "What on earth have you been doing?"

"I've been having a legal discussion," I told her, "on the subject of the admissibility of certain evidence. Vital, from my client's point of view. And, just for a change, Hilda, I think I've won."

"Well, you'd better try and get some sleep." And she added with a sort of satisfaction, "I'm sure you'll be feeling quite terrible in the morning."

As with all the grimmer predictions of She Who Must Be Obeyed, this one turned out to be true. I sat in the Court the next day with the wig feeling like a lead weight on the brain and the stiff collar sawing the neck like a blunt execution. My mouth tasted of matured birdcage and from a long way off I heard Wrigglesworth say to Bridget O'Dowd, who stood looking particularly saintly and virginal in the witness box, "About a week before this, did you see the defendant, Ed-

ward Timson, on your staircase flourishing any sort of weapon?"

It is no exaggeration to say that I felt deeply shocked and considerably betrayed. After his promise to me, Wrigglesworth had turned his back on the spirit of the great Christmas festival. He came not to bring peace but a sword.

I clambered with some difficulty to my feet. After my forensic efforts of the evening before, I was scarcely in the mood for a legal argument. Mr. Justice Vosper looked up in surprise and greeted me in his usual chilly fashion.

"Yes, Mr. Rumpole. Do you object to this evidence?"

Of course I object, I wanted to say. It's inhuman, unnecessary, unmerciful, and likely to lead to my losing another case. Also, it's clearly contrary to a solemn and binding contract entered into after a number of glasses of the Bishop's putative port. All I seemed to manage was a strangled, "Yes."

"I suppose Mr. Wrigglesworth would say—" Vosper, J., was, as ever, anxious to supply any argument that might not yet have occurred to the prosecution "—that it is evidence of 'system.' "

"System?" I heard my voice faintly and from a long way off. "It may be, I suppose. But the Court has a discretion to omit evidence which may be irrelevant and purely prejudicial."

"I feel sure Mr. Wrigglesworth has considered the matter most carefully and that he would not lead this evidence unless he considered it entirely relevant."

I looked at the Mad Monk on the seat beside me. He was smiling at me with a mixture of hearty cheerfulness and supreme pity, as though I were sinking rapidly and he had come to administer supreme unction. I made a few ill-chosen remarks to the Court, but I was in no condition, that morning, to enter into a complicated legal argument on the admissibility of evidence.

It wasn't long before Bridget O'Dowd had told a deeply disapproving jury all about Eddie "Turpin" Timson's sword. "A man," the judge said later in his summing up about young Edward, "clearly prepared to attack with cold steel whenever it suited him."

When the trial was over, I called in for refreshment at my favorite watering hole and there, to my surprise, was my opponent Wrigglesworth, sharing an expensive-looking bottle with Detective Inspector Wainwright, the officer in charge of the case. I stood at the bar, absorbing a consoling glass of Pommeroy's ordinary, when the D. I. came up to the bar for cigarettes. He gave me a friendly and maddeningly sympathetic smile.

"Sorry about that, sir. Still, win a few, lose a few. Isn't that it?"

"In my case lately, it's been win a few, lose a lot!"

"You couldn't have this one, sir. You see, Mr. Wrigglesworth had promised it to me."

"He had *what*?"

"Well, I'm retiring, as you know. And Mr. Wrigglesworth promised me faithfully that my last case would be a win. He promised me that, in a manner of speaking, as a Christmas present. Great man is our Mr. Wrigglesworth, sir, for the spirit of Christmas."

I looked across at the Mad Monk and a terrible suspicion entered my head. What was all that about a present for the Bishop? I searched my memory and I could find no trace of our having, in fact, bought wine for any sort of cleric. And was Wrigglesworth as inexperienced as he would have had me believe in the art of selecting claret?

As I watched him pour and sniff a glass from his superior bottle and hold it critically to the light, a horrible suspicion crossed my mind. Had the whole evening's events been nothing but a deception, a sinister attempt to nobble Rumpole, to present him with such a stupendous hangover that he would stumble in his legal argument? Was it all in aid of D. I. Wainwright's Christmas present?

I looked at Wrigglesworth, and it would be no exaggeration to say the mind boggled. He was, of course, perfectly right about me. I just didn't recognize evil when I saw it.

Meredith Nicholson

ALONG WITH BOOTH TARKINGTON, George Ade, and the poet James Whitcomb Riley, Meredith Nicholson was part of what was regarded as the Golden Age of literature in Indiana in the first quarter of the twentieth century. Although not an author whose works have stood the test of time well, he was a bestseller in his day whose fiction was governed by the invariable triumph of true love and by insistence on the virtues of wholesome, bourgeois life, always told with good-natured humor. "A Reversible Santa Claus" was first published as a slim, illustrated book of that title (Boston, Houghton Mifflin, 1917).

A Reversible Santa Claus

MEREDITH NICHOLSON

I

MR. WILLIAM B. AIKINS, *ALIAS* "Softy" Hubbard, *alias* Billy The Hopper, paused for breath behind a hedge that bordered a quiet lane and peered out into the highway at a roadster whose tail light advertised its presence to his felonious gaze. It was Christmas Eve, and after a day of unseasonable warmth a slow, drizzling rain was whimsically changing to snow.

The Hopper was blowing from two hours' hard travel over rough country. He had stumbled through woodlands, flattened himself in fence corners to avoid the eyes of curious motorists speeding homeward or flying about distributing Christmas gifts, and he was now bent upon committing himself to an inter-urban trolley line that would afford comfortable transportation for the remainder of his journey. Twenty miles, he estimated, still lay between him and his domicile.

The rain had penetrated his clothing and vigorous exercise had not greatly diminished the chill in his blood. His heart knocked violently against his ribs and he was dismayed by his shortness of wind. The Hopper was not so young as in the days when his agility and genius for effecting a quick "get-away" had earned for him his sobriquet. The last time his Bertillon measurements were checked (he was subjected to this humiliating experience in Omaha during the Ak-Sar-Ben carnival three years earlier), of-

ficial note was taken of the fact that The Hopper's hair, long carried in the records as black, was rapidly whitening.

At forty-eight a crook—even so resourceful and versatile a member of the fraternity as The Hopper—begins to mistrust himself. For the greater part of his life, when not in durance vile, The Hopper had been in hiding, and the state or condition of being a fugitive, hunted by keen-eyed agents of justice, is not, from all accounts, an enviable one. His latest experience of involuntary servitude had been under the auspices of the State of Oregon, for a trifling indiscretion in the way of safe-blowing. Having served his sentence, he skillfully effaced himself by a year's siesta on a pine-apple plantation in Hawaii. The island climate was not wholly pleasing to The Hopper, and when pine-apples palled he took passage from Honolulu as a stoker, reached San Francisco (not greatly chastened in spirit), and by a series of characteristic hops, skips, and jumps across the continent landed in Maine by way of the Canadian provinces.

The Hopper needed money. He was not without a certain crude philosophy, and it had been his dream to acquire by some brilliant *coup* a sufficient fortune upon which to retire and live as a decent, law-abiding citizen for the remainder of his days. This ambition, or at least the means to its fulfillment, can hardly be defended as praiseworthy, but The Hopper was a singular character and we must take him as we find him.

Many prison chaplains and jail visitors bearing tracts had striven with little success to implant moral ideals in the mind and soul of The Hopper, but he was still to be catalogued among the impenitent; and as he moved southward through the Commonwealth of Maine he was so oppressed by his poverty, as contrasted with the world's abundance, that he lifted forty thousand dollars in a neat bundle from an express car which Providence had sidetracked, apparently for his personal enrichment, on the upper waters of the Penobscot. Whereupon he began perforce playing his old game of artful dodging, exercising his best powers as a hopper and skipper. Forty thousand dollars is no inconsiderable sum of money, and the success of this master stroke of his career was not to be jeopardized by careless moves. By craftily hiding in the big woods and making himself agreeable to isolated lumberjacks who rarely saw newspapers, he arrived in due course on Manhattan Island, where with shrewd judgment he avoided the haunts of his kind while planning a future commensurate with his new dignity as a capitalist.

He spent a year as a diligent and faithful employee of a garage which served a fashionable quarter of the metropolis; then, animated by a worthy desire to continue to lead an honest life, he purchased a chicken farm fifteen miles as the crow flies from Center Church, New Haven, and boldly opened a bank account in that academic center in his newly adopted name of Charles S. Stevens, of Happy Hill Farm. Feeling the need of companionship, he married a lady somewhat his junior, a shoplifter of the second class, whom he had known before the vigilance of the metropolitan police necessitated his removal to the Far West. Mrs. Stevens's inferior talents as a petty larcenist had led her into many difficulties, and she gratefully availed herself of The Hopper's offer of his heart and hand.

They had added to their establishment a retired yegg who had lost an eye by the premature popping of the "soup" (i.e., nitro-glycerin) poured into the crevices of a country post-office in Missouri. In offering shelter to Mr. James Whitesides, *alias* "Humpy" Thompson, The Hopper's motives had not been wholly unselfish, as Humpy had been entrusted with the herding of poultry in several penitentiaries and was familiar with the most advanced scientific thought on chicken culture.

The roadster was headed toward his home and The Hopper contemplated it in the deepening dusk with greedy eyes. His labors in the New York garage had familiarized him with automobiles, and while he was not ignorant of the pains and penalties inflicted upon lawless persons who appropriate motors illegally, he was the victim of an irresistible temptation to jump into the machine thus left in the highway, drive as near home as he dared, and then abandon it. The owner of the roadster was presumably eating his evening meal in peace in the snug little cottage behind the shrubbery, and The Hopper was aware of no sound reason why he should not seize the vehicle and further widen the distance between himself and a suspicious-looking gentleman he had observed on the New Haven local.

The Hopper's conscience was not altogether at ease, as he had, that afternoon, possessed himself of a bill-book that was protruding from the breast-pocket of a dignified citizen whose strap he had shared in a crowded subway train. Having foresworn crime as a means of livelihood, The Hopper was chagrined that he had suffered himself to be beguiled into stealing by the mere propinquity of a piece of red leather. He was angry at the world as well as himself. People should not go about with bill-books sticking out of their pockets; it was unfair and unjust to those weak members of the human race who yield readily to temptation.

He had agreed with Mary when she married him and the chicken farm that they would respect the Ten Commandments and all statutory laws, State and Federal, and he was painfully conscious that when he confessed his sin she would deal severely with him. Even Humpy, now enjoying a peace that he had rarely known outside the walls of prison, even Humpy would be bitter. The thought that he was again among the hunted would depress Mary and Humpy, and he knew that their harshness would be intensified because of his violation of the unwritten law of the underworld in resorting to purse-lifting, an infringement upon a branch of felony despicable and greatly inferior in dignity to safe-blowing.

These reflections spurred The Hopper to action, for the sooner he reached home the more quickly he could explain his protracted stay in New York (to which metropolis he had repaired in the hope of making a better price for eggs with the commission merchants who handled his products), submit himself to Mary's chastisement, and promise to sin no more. By returning on Christmas Eve, of all times, again a fugitive, he knew that he would merit the unsparing condemnation that Mary and Humpy would visit upon him. It was possible, it was even quite likely, that the short, stocky gentleman he had seen on the New Haven local was not a "bull"—not really a detective who had observed the little transaction in the subway; but the very uncertainty annoyed The Hopper. In his happy and profitable year at Happy Hill Farm he had learned to prize his personal comfort, and he was humiliated to find that he had been frightened into leaving the train at Bansford to continue his journey afoot, and merely because a man had looked at him a little queerly.

Any Christmas spirit that had taken root in The Hopper's soul had been disturbed, not to say seriously threatened with extinction, by the untoward occurrences of the afternoon.

II

The Hopper waited for a limousine to pass and then crawled out of his hiding-place, jumped into the roadster, and was at once in motion. He glanced back, fearing that the owner might have heard his departure, and then, satisfied of his immediate security, negotiated a difficult turn in the road and settled himself with a feeling of relief to careful but expeditious flight. It was at this moment, when he had urged the car to its highest speed, that a noise startled him—an amazing little chirrupy sound which corresponded to none of the familiar forewarnings of engine trouble. With his eyes to the front he listened for a repetition of the sound. It rose again—it was like a perplexing cheep and chirrup, changing to a chortle of glee.

"Goo-goo! Goo-goo-goo!"

The car was skimming a dark stretch of road and a superstitious awe fell upon The Hopper. Murder, he gratefully remembered, had never been among his crimes, though he had once winged a too-inquisitive policeman in Kansas City. He glanced over his shoulder, but saw no pursuing ghost in the snowy highway; then, looking down apprehensively, he detected on the seat beside him what appeared to be an animate bundle, and, prompted by a louder "goo-goo," he put out his hand. His fingers touched something warm and soft and were promptly seized and held by Something.

The Hopper snatched his hand free of the tentacles of the unknown and shook it violently. The nature of the Something troubled him. He renewed his experiments, steering with his left hand and exposing the right to what now seemed to be the grasp of two very small mittened hands.

"Goo-goo! Goody; teep wunnin'!"

"A kid!" The Hopper gasped.

That he had eloped with a child was the blackest of the day's calamities. He experienced a strange sinking feeling in the stomach. In moments of apprehension a crook's thoughts run naturally into periods of penal servitude, and the punishment for kidnaping, The Hopper recalled, was severe. He stopped the car and inspected his unwelcome fellow passenger by the light of matches. Two big blue eyes stared at him from a hood and two mittens were poked into his face. Two small feet, wrapped tightly in a blanket, kicked at him energetically.

"Detup! Mate um skedaddle!"

Obedient to this command The Hopper made the car skedaddle, but superstitious dread settled upon him more heavily. He was satisfied now that from the moment he transferred the strap-hanger's bill-book to his own pocket he had been hoodooed. Only a jinx of the most malevolent type could have prompted his hurried exit from a train to dodge an imaginary "bull." Only the blackest of evil spirits could be responsible for this involuntary kidnaping!

"Mate um wun! Mate um 'ippity stip!"

The mittened hands reached for the wheel at this juncture and an unlooked-for "jippity skip" precipitated the young passenger into The Hopper's lap.

This mishap was attended with the jolliest baby laughter. Gently but with much firmness The Hopper restored the youngster to an upright position and supported him until sure he was able to sustain himself.

"Ye better set still, little feller," he admonished.

The little feller seemed in no wise astonished to find himself abroad with a perfect stranger and his courage and good cheer were not lost upon The Hopper. He wanted to be severe, to vent his rage for the day's calamities upon the only human being within range, but in spite of himself he felt no animosity toward the friendly little bundle of humanity beside him. Still, he had stolen a baby and it was incumbent upon him to free himself at once of the appalling burden; but a baby is not so easily disposed of. He could not, without seriously imperiling his liberty, return to the cottage. It was the rule of house-breakers, he recalled, to avoid babies. He had heard it said by burglars of wide experience and unquestioned wisdom that babies were the most dangerous of all burglar alarms. All things considered, kidnaping and automobile theft were not a happy combination with which to appear before a criminal court. The Hopper was vexed because the child did not cry; if he had shown a bad disposition The Hopper might have abandoned him; but the youngster was the cheeriest and most agreeable of traveling companions. Indeed, The Hopper's spirits rose under his continued "goo-gooing" and chirruping.

"Nice little Shaver!" he said, patting the child's knees.

Little Shaver was so pleased by this friendly demonstration that he threw up his arms in an effort to embrace The Hopper.

"Bil-lee," he gurgled delightedly.

The Hopper was so astonished at being addressed in his own lawful name by a strange baby that he barely averted a collision with a passing motor truck. It was unbelievable that the baby really knew his name, but perhaps it was a good omen that he had hit upon it. The Hopper's resentment against the dark fate that seemed to pursue him vanished. Even though he had stolen a baby, it was a merry, brave little baby who didn't mind at all being run away with! He dismissed the thought of planting the little shaver at a door, ringing the bell, and running away; this was no way to treat a friendly child that had done him no injury, and The Hopper highly resolved to do the square thing by the youngster even at personal inconvenience and risk.

The snow was now falling in generous Christmasy flakes, and the high speed the car had again attained was evidently deeply gratifying to the young person, whose reckless tumbling about made it necessary for The Hopper to keep a hand on him.

"Steady, little un; steady!" The Hopper kept mumbling.

His wits were busy trying to devise some means of getting rid of the youngster without exposing himself to the danger of arrest. By this time some one was undoubtedly busily engaged in searching for both baby and car; the police far and near would be notified, and would be on the lookout for a smart roadster containing a stolen child.

"Merry Christmas!" a boy shouted from a farm gate.

"M'y Kwismus!" piped Shaver.

The Hopper decided to run the machine home and there ponder the disposition of his blithe companion with the care the unusual circumstances demanded.

"'Urry up; me's goin' 'ome to me's gwanpa's Kwismus t'ee!"

"Right ye be, little un; right ye be!" affirmed The Hopper.

The youngster was evidently blessed with a sanguine and confiding nature. His reference to his grandfather's Christmas tree impinged sharply upon The Hopper's conscience. Christmas had never figured very prominently in his scheme of life. About the only Christmases that he recalled with any pleasure were those that he had spent in prison, and those were marked only by Christmas dinners varying with the generosity of a series of wardens.

But Shaver was entitled to all the joys of Christmas, and The Hopper had no desire to deprive him of them.

"Keep a-larfin', Shaver, keep a-larfin'," said the Hopper. "Ole Hop ain't a-goin' to hurt ye!"

The Hopper, feeling his way cautiously round the fringes of New Haven, arrived presently at Happy Hill Farm, where he ran the car in among the chicken sheds behind the cottage and carefully extinguished the lights.

"Now, Shaver, out ye come!"

Whereupon Shaver obediently jumped into his arms.

III

The Hopper knocked twice at the back door, waited an instant, and knocked again. As he completed the signal the door was opened guardedly. A man and woman surveyed him in hostile silence as he pushed past them, kicked the door shut, and deposited the blinking child on the kitchen table. Humpy, the one-eyed, jumped to the windows and jammed the green shades close into the frames. The woman scowlingly waited for the head of the house to explain himself, and this, with the perversity of one who knows the dramatic value of suspense, he was in no haste to do.

"Well," Mary questioned sharply. "What ye got there, Bill?"

The Hopper was regarding Shaver with a grin of benevolent satisfaction. The youngster had seized a bottle of catsup and was making heroic efforts to raise it to his mouth, and the Hopper was intensely tickled by Shaver's efforts to swallow the bottle. Mrs. Stevens, *alias* Weeping Mary, was not amused, and her husband's enjoyment of the child's antics irritated her.

"Come out with ut, Bill!" she commanded, seizing the bottle. "What ye been doin'?"

Shaver's big blue eyes expressed surprise and displeasure at being deprived of his plaything, but he recovered quickly and reached for a plate with which he began thumping the table.

"Out with ut, Hop!" snapped Humpy nervously. "Nothin' wuz said about kidnapin', an' I don't stand for ut!"

"When I heard the machine comin' in the yard I knowed somethin' was wrong an' I guess it couldn't be no worse," added Mary, beginning to cry. "You hadn't no right to do ut, Bill. Hookin' a buzz-buzz an' a kid an' when we wuz playin' the white card! You ought t' 'a' told me, Bill, what ye went to town fer, an' it bein' Christmas, an' all."

That he should have chosen for his fall the Christmas season of all times was reprehensible, a fact which Mary and Humpy impressed upon him in the strongest terms. The Hopper was fully aware of the inopportuneness of his transgressions, but not to the point of encouraging his wife to abuse him.

As he clumsily tried to unfasten Shaver's hood, Mary pushed him aside and with shaking fingers removed the child's wraps. Shaver's cheeks were rosy from his drive through the cold; he was a plump, healthy little shaver and The Hopper viewed him with intense pride. Mary held the hood and coat to the light and inspected them with a sophisticated eye. They were of excellent quality and workmanship, and she shook her head and sighed deeply as she placed them carefully on a chair.

"It ain't on the square, Hop," protested Humpy, whose lone eye expressed the most poignant sorrow at The Hopper's derelictions.

Humpy was tall and lean, with a thin, many-lined face. He was an ill-favored person at best, and his habit of turning his head constantly as though to compel his single eye to perform double service gave one an impression of restless watchfulness.

"Cute little Shaver, ain't 'e? Give Shaver somethin' to eat, Mary. I guess milk'll be the right ticket considerin' th' size of 'im. How ole you make 'im? Not more'n three, I reckon?"

"Two. He ain't more'n two, that kid."

"A nice little feller; you're a cute un, ain't ye, Shaver?"

Shaver nodded his head solemnly. Having wearied of playing with the plate he gravely inspected the trio; found something amusing in Humpy's bizarre countenance and laughed merrily. Finding no response to his friendly overtures he appealed to Mary.

"Me wants me's paw-widge," he announced.

"Porridge," interpreted Humpy with the air of one whose superior breeding makes him the proper arbiter of the speech of children of high social station. Whereupon Shaver appreciatively poked his forefinger into Humpy's surviving optic.

"I'll see what I got," muttered Mary. "What ye used t' eatin' for supper, honey?"

The "honey" was a concession, and The Hopper, who was giving Shaver his watch to play with, bent a commendatory glance upon his spouse.

"Go on an' tell us what ye done," said Mary, doggedly busying herself about the stove.

The Hopper drew a chair to the table to be within reach of Shaver and related succinctly his day's adventures.

"A dip!" moaned Mary as he described the seizure of the purse in the subway.

"You hadn't no right to do ut, Hop!" bleated Humpy, who had tipped his chair against the wall and was sucking a cold pipe. And then, professional curiosity overmastering his shocked conscience, he added: "What'd she measure, Hop?"

The Hopper grinned.

"Flubbed! Nothin' but papers," he confessed ruefully.

Mary and Humpy expressed their indignation and contempt in unequivocal terms, which they repeated after he told of the suspected "bull" whose presence on the local had so alarmed him. A frank description of his flight and of his seizure of the roadster only added to their bitterness.

Humpy rose and paced the floor with the quick, short stride of men habituated to narrow spaces. The Hopper watched the telltale step so disagreeably reminiscent of evil times and shrugged his shoulders impatiently.

"Set down, Hump; ye make me nervous. I got thinkin' to do."

"Ye'd better be quick about doin' ut!" Humpy snorted with an oath.

"Cut the cussin'!" The Hopper admonished sharply. Since his retirement to private life he had sought diligently to free his speech of profanity and thieves' slang, as not only unbecoming in a respectable chicken farmer, but likely to arouse suspicions as to his origin and previous condition of servitude. "Can't ye see Shaver ain't use to ut? Shaver's a little gent; he's a reg'ler little juke; that's wot Shaver is."

"The more 'way up he is the worse fer us," whimpered Humpy. "It's kidnapin', that's wot ut is!"

"That's wot it *ain't*," declared The Hopper, averting a calamity to his watch, which Shaver was swinging by its chain. "He was took by accident I tell ye! I'm goin' to take Shaver back to his ma—ain't I, Shaver?"

"Take 'im back!" echoed Mary.

Humpy crumpled up in his chair at this new evidence of The Hopper's insanity.

"I'm goin' to make a Chris'mas present o' Shaver to his ma," reaffirmed The Hopper, pinching the nearer ruddy cheek of the merry, contented guest.

Shaver kicked The Hopper in the stomach and emitted a chortle expressive of unshakable confidence in The Hopper's ability to restore him to his lawful owners. This confidence was not, however, manifested toward Mary, who had prepared with care the only cereal her pantry afforded, and now approached Shaver, bowl and spoon in hand. Shaver, taken by surprise, inspected his supper with disdain and spurned it with a vigor that sent the spoon rattling across the floor.

"Me wants me's paw-widge bowl! Me wants me's *own* paw-widge bowl!" he screamed.

Mary expostulated; Humpy offered advice as to the best manner of dealing with the refractory Shaver, who gave further expression to his resentment by throwing The Hopper's watch with violence against the wall. That the table-service of The Hopper's establishment was not to Shaver's liking was manifested in repeated rejections of the plain white bowl in which Mary offered the porridge. He demanded his very own porridge bowl with the increasing vehemence of one who is willing to starve rather than accept so palpable a substitute. He threw himself back on the table and lay there kicking and crying. Other needs now occurred to Shaver: he wanted his papa; he wanted his mamma; he wanted to go to his gwan'pa's. He clamored for Santa Claus and numerous Christmas trees which, it seemed, had been promised him at the houses of his kinsfolk. It was amazing and bewildering that the heart of one so young could desire so many things that were not immediately attainable. He had begun to suspect that he was among strangers who were not of his way of life, and this was fraught with the gravest danger.

"They'll hear 'im hollerin' in China," wailed the pessimistic Humpy, running about the room and examining the fastenings of doors and windows. "Folks goin' along the road'll hear 'im, an' it's terms fer the whole bunch!"

The Hopper began pacing the floor with Shaver, while Humpy and Mary denounced the child for unreasonableness and lack of discipline, not overlooking the stupidity and criminal carelessness of The Hopper in projecting so lawless a youngster into their domestic circle.

"Twenty years, that's wot ut is!" mourned Humpy.

"Ye kin get the chair fer kidnapin'," Mary added dolefully. "Ye gotta get 'im out o' here, Bill."

Pleasant predictions of a long prison term with capital punishment as the happy alternative failed to disturb The Hopper. To their surprise and somewhat to their shame he won the Shaver to a tractable humor. There was nothing in The Hopper's known past to justify any expectation that he could quiet a crying baby, and yet Shaver with a child's unerring instinct realized that The Hopper meant to be kind. He patted The Hopper's face with one fat little paw, chokingly declaring that he was hungry.

"'Course Shaver's hungry; an' Shaver's goin' to eat nice porridge Aunt Mary made fer 'im. Shaver's goin' to have 'is own porridge bowl to-morry—yes, sir-ee, oo is, little Shaver!"

Restored to the table, Shaver opened his mouth in obedience to The Hopper's patient pleading and swallowed a spoonful of the mush, Humpy holding the bowl out of sight in tactful deference to the child's delicate æsthetic sensibilities. A tumbler of milk was sipped with grateful gasps.

The Hopper grinned, proud of his success, while Mary and Humpy viewed his efforts with somewhat grudging admiration, and waited patiently until The Hopper took the wholly surfeited Shaver in his arms and began pacing the floor, humming softly. In normal circumstances The Hopper was not musical, and Humpy and Mary exchanged looks which, when interpreted, pointed to nothing less than a belief that the owner of Happy Hill Farm was bereft of his senses. There was some question as to whether Shaver should be undressed. Mary discouraged the idea and Humpy took a like view.

"Ye gotta chuck 'im quick; that's what ye gotta do," said Mary hoarsely. "We don't want 'im sleepin' here."

Whereupon The Hopper demonstrated his entire independence by carrying the Shaver to Humpy's bed and partially undressing him. While this was in progress, Shaver suddenly opened his eyes wide and raising one foot until it approximated the perpendicular, reached for it with his chubby hands.

"Sant' Claus comin'; m'y Kwismus!"

"Jes' listen to Shaver!" chuckled The Hopper. "'Course Santy is comin,' an' we're goin' to hang up Shaver's stockin', ain't we, Shaver?"

He pinned both stockings to the footboard of Humpy's bed. By the time this was accomplished under the hostile eyes of Mary and Humpy, Shaver slept the sleep of the innocent.

IV

They watched the child in silence for a few minutes and then Mary detached a gold locket from his neck and bore it to the kitchen for examination.

"Ye gotta move quick, Hop," Humpy urged. "The white card's what we wuz all goin' to play. We wuz fixed nice here, an' things goin' easy; an' the yard full o' br'ilers. I don't want to do no more time. I'm an ole man, Hop."

"Cut ut!" ordered The Hopper, taking the locket from Mary and weighing it critically in his hand. They bent over him as he scrutinized the face on which was inscribed:—

Roger Livingston Talbot
June 13, 1913

"Lemme see; he's two an' a harf. Ye purty nigh guessed 'im right, Mary."

The sight of the gold trinket, the probability that the Shaver belonged to a family of wealth, proved disturbing to Humpy's late protestations of virtue.

"They'd be a heap o' kale in ut, Hop. His folks is rich, I reckon. Ef we wuzn't playin' the white card—"

Ignoring this shocking evidence of Humpy's moral instability, The Hopper became lost in reverie, meditatively drawing at his pipe.

"We ain't never goin' to quit playin' ut square," he announced, to Mary's manifest relief. "I hadn't ought t' 'a' done th' dippin'. It

were a mistake. My ole head wuzn't workin' right er I wouldn't 'a' slipped. But ye needn't jump on me no more."

"Wot ye goin' to do with that kid? Ye tell me that!" demanded Mary, unwilling too readily to accept The Hopper's repentance at face value.

"I'm goin' to take 'im to 'is folks, that's wot I'm goin' to do with 'im," announced The Hopper.

"Yer crazy—yer plum' crazy!" cried Humpy, slapping his knees excitedly. "Ye kin take 'im to an orphant asylum an' tell um ye found 'im in that machine ye lifted. And mebbe ye'll git by with ut an' mebbe ye won't, but ye gotta keep me out of ut!"

"I found the machine in th' road, right here by th' house; an' th' kid was in ut all by hisself. An' bein' humin an' respectible I brought 'im in to keep 'im from freezin' t' death," said The Hopper, as though repeating lines he was committing to memory. "They ain't nobody can say as I didn't. Ef I git pinched, that's my spiel to th' cops. It ain't kidnapin'; it's life-savin', that's wot ut is! I'm a-goin' back an' have a look at that place where I got 'im. Kind o' queer they left the kid out there in the buzz-wagon; *mighty* queer, now's I think of ut. Little house back from the road; lots o' trees an' bushes in front. Didn't seem to be no lights. He keeps talkin' about Chris'mas at his grandpa's. Folks must 'a' been goin' to take th' kid somewheres fer Chris'mas. I guess it'll throw a skeer into 'em to find him up an' gone."

"They's rich, an' all the big bulls'll be lookin' fer 'im; ye'd better 'phone the New Haven cops ye've picked 'im up. Then they'll come out, an' yer spiel about findin' 'im'll sound easy an' sensible like."

The Hopper, puffing his pipe philosophically, paid no heed to Humpy's suggestion even when supported warmly by Mary.

"I gotta find some way o' puttin' th' kid back without seein' no cops. I'll jes' take a sneak back an' have a look at th' place," said The Hopper. "I ain't goin' to turn Shaver over to no cops. Ye can't take no chances with 'em. They don't know nothin' about us bein' here, but they ain't fools, an' I ain't goin' to give none o' 'em a squint at me!"

He defended his plan against a joint attack by Mary and Humpy, who saw in it only further proof of his tottering reason. He was obliged to tell them in harsh terms to be quiet, and he added to their rage by the deliberation with which he made his preparations to leave.

He opened the door of a clock and drew out a revolver which he examined carefully and thrust into his pocket. Mary groaned; Humpy beat the air in impotent despair. The Hopper possessed himself also of a jimmy and an electric lamp. The latter he flashed upon the face of the sleeping Shaver, who turned restlessly for a moment and then lay still again. He smoothed the coverlet over the tiny form, while Mary and Humpy huddled in the doorway. Mary wept; Humpy was awed into silence by his old friend's perversity. For years he had admired The Hopper's cleverness, his genius for extricating himself from difficulties; he was deeply shaken to think that one who had stood so high in one of the most exacting of professions should have fallen so low. As The Hopper imperturbably buttoned his coat and walked toward the door, Humpy set his back against it in a last attempt to save his friend from his own foolhardiness.

"Ef anybody turns up here an' asks for th' kid, ye kin tell 'em wot I said. We finds 'im in th' road right here by the farm when we're doin' th' night chores an' takes 'im in t' keep 'im from freezin'. Ye'll have th' machine an' kid here to show 'em. An' as fer me, I'm off lookin' fer his folks."

Mary buried her face in her apron and wept despairingly. The Hopper, noting for the first time that Humpy was guarding the door, roughly pushed him aside and stood for a moment with his hand on the knob.

"They's things wot is," he remarked with a last attempt to justify his course, "an' things wot ain't. I reckon I'll take a peek at that place an' see wot's th' best way t' shake th' kid. Ye can't jes' run up to a house in a machine with his folks all settin' round cryin' an' cops askin' questions. Ye got to do some plannin' an' thinkin'. I'm goin' t' clean ut all up before daylight, an' ye need n't worry none about ut. Hop ain't worryin'; jes' leave ut t' Hop!"

There was no alternative but to leave it to Hop, and they stood mute as he went out and softly closed the door.

V

The snow had ceased and the stars shone brightly on a white world as The Hopper made his way by various trolley lines to the house from which he had snatched Shaver. On a New Haven car he debated the prospects of more snow with a policeman who seemed oblivious to the fact that a child had been stolen—shamelessly carried off by a man with a long police record. Merry Christmas passed from lip to lip as if all creation were attuned to the note of love and peace, and crime were an undreamed-of thing.

For two years The Hopper had led an exemplary life and he was keenly alive now to the joy of adventure. His lapses of the day were unfortunate; he thought of them with regret and misgivings, but he was zestful for whatever the unknown held in store for him. Abroad again with a pistol in his pocket, he was a lawless being, but with the difference that he was intent now upon making restitution, though in such manner as would give him something akin to the old thrill that he experienced when he enjoyed the reputation of being one of the most skillful yeggs in the country. The successful thief is of necessity an imaginative person; he must be able to visualize the unseen and to deal with a thousand hidden contingencies. At best the chances are against him; with all his ingenuity the broad, heavy hand of the law is likely at any moment to close upon him from some unexpected quarter. The Hopper knew this, and knew, too, that in yielding to the exhilaration of the hour he was likely to come to grief. Justice has a long memory, and if he again made himself the object of police scrutiny that little forty-thousand-dollar affair in Maine might still be fixed upon him.

When he reached the house from whose gate he had removed the roadster with Shaver attached, he studied it with the eye of an experienced strategist. No gleam anywhere published the presence of frantic parents bewailing the loss of a baby. The cottage lay snugly behind its barrier of elms and shrubbery as though its young heir had not vanished into the void. The Hopper was a deliberating being and he gave careful weight to these circumstances as he crept round the walk, in which the snow lay undisturbed, and investigated the rear of the premises. The lattice door of the summer kitchen opened readily, and, after satisfying himself that no one was stirring in the lower part of the house, he pried up the sash of a window and stepped in. The larder was well stocked, as though in preparation for a Christmas feast, and he passed on to the dining-room, whose appointments spoke for good taste and a degree of prosperity in the householder.

Cautious flashes of his lamp disclosed on the table a hamper, in which were packed a silver cup, plate, and bowl which at once awoke the Hopper's interest. Here indubitably was proof that this was the home of Shaver, now sleeping sweetly in Humpy's bed, and this was the porridge bowl for which Shaver's soul had yearned. If Shaver did not belong to the house, he had at least been a visitor there, and it struck The Hopper as a reasonable assumption that Shaver had been deposited in the roadster while his lawful guardians returned to the cottage for the hamper preparatory to an excursion of some sort. But The Hopper groped in the dark for an explanation of the calmness with which the householders accepted the loss of the child. It was not in human nature for the parents of a youngster so handsome and in every way so delightful as Shaver to permit him to be stolen from under their very noses without making an outcry. The Hopper examined the silver pieces and found them engraved with the name borne by the locket. He crept through a living-room and came to a Christmas tree—the smallest of

Christmas trees. Beside it lay a number of packages designed clearly for none other than young Roger Livingston Talbot.

Housebreaking is a very different business from the forcible entry of country post-offices, and The Hopper was nervous. This particular house seemed utterly deserted. He stole upstairs and found doors open and a disorder indicative of the occupants' hasty departure. His attention was arrested by a small room finished in white, with a white enameled bed, and other furniture to match. A generous litter of toys was the last proof needed to establish the house as Shaver's true domicile. Indeed, there was every indication that Shaver was the central figure of this home of whose charm and atmosphere The Hopper was vaguely sensible. A frieze of dancing children and water-color sketches of Shaver's head, dabbed here and there in the most unlooked-for places, hinted at an artistic household. This impression was strengthened when The Hopper, bewildered and baffled, returned to the lower floor and found a studio opening off the living-room. The Hopper had never visited a studio before, and, satisfied now that he was the sole occupant of the house, he passed about shooting his light upon unfinished canvases, pausing finally before an easel supporting a portrait of Shaver—newly finished, he discovered, by poking his finger into the wet paint. Something fell to the floor and he picked up a large sheet of drawing-paper on which this message was written in charcoal:—

Six-thirty.

Dear Sweetheart:—

This is a fine trick you have played on me, you dear girl! I've been expecting you back all afternoon. At six I decided that you were going to spend the night with your infuriated parent and thought I'd try my luck with mine! I put Billie into the roadster and, leaving him there, ran over to the Flemings' to say Merry Christmas and tell 'em we were off for the night. They kept me just a min-

ute to look at those new Jap prints Jim's so crazy about, and while I was gone you came along and skipped with Billie and the car! I suppose this means that you've been making headway with your dad and want to try the effect of Billie's blandishments. Good luck! But you might have stopped long enough to tell me about it! How fine it would be if everything could be straightened out for Christmas! Do you remember the first time I kissed you—it was on Christmas Eve four years ago at the Billings's dance! I'm just trolleying out to father's to see what an evening session will do. I'll be back early in the morning.

Love always,
Roger.

Billie was undoubtedly Shaver's nickname. This delighted The Hopper. That they should possess the same name appeared to create a strong bond of comradeship. The writer of the note was presumably the child's father and the "Dear Sweetheart" the youngster's mother. The Hopper was not reassured by these disclosures. The return of Shaver to his parents was far from being the pleasant little Christmas Eve adventure he had imagined. He had only the lowest opinion of a father who would, on a winter evening, carelessly leave his baby in a motor-car while he looked at pictures, and who, finding both motor and baby gone, would take it for granted that the baby's mother had run off with them. But these people were artists, and artists, The Hopper had heard, were a queer breed, sadly lacking in common sense. He tore the note into strips which he stuffed into his pocket.

Depressed by the impenetrable wall of mystery along which he was groping, he returned to the living-room, raised one of the windows, and unbolted the front door to make sure of an exit in case these strange, foolish Talbots should unexpectedly return. The shades were up and he shielded his light carefully with his cap as he passed rapidly about the room. It began to

look very much as though Shaver would spend Christmas at Happy Hill Farm—a possibility that had not figured in The Hopper's calculations.

Flashing his lamp for a last survey a letter propped against a lamp on the table arrested his eye. He dropped to the floor and crawled into a corner where he turned his light upon the note and read, not without difficulty, the following:—

Seven o'clock.

Dear Roger:—

I've just got back from father's where I spent the last three hours talking over our troubles. I didn't tell you I was going, knowing you would think it foolish, but it seemed best, dear, and I hope you'll forgive me. And now I find that you've gone off with Billie, and I'm guessing that you've gone to your father's to see what you can do. I'm taking the trolley into New Haven to ask Mamie Palmer about that cook she thought we might get, and if possible I'll bring the girl home with me. Don't trouble about me, as I'll be perfectly safe, and, as you know, I rather enjoy prowling around at night. You'll certainly get back before I do, but if I'm not here don't be alarmed.

We are so happy in each other, dear, and if only we could get our foolish fathers to stop hating each other, how beautiful everything would be! And we could all have such a merry, merry Christmas!

Muriel.

The Hopper's acquaintance with the epistolary art was the slightest, but even to a mind unfamiliar with this branch of literature it was plain that Shaver's parents were involved in some difficulty that was attributable, not to any lessening of affection between them, but to a row of some sort between their respective fathers. Muriel, running into the house to write her note, had failed to see Roger's letter in the studio, and this was very fortunate for The Hopper; but Muriel might return at any moment, and it would add nothing to the plausibility of the story he meant to tell if he were found in the house.

VI

Anxious and dejected at the increasing difficulties that confronted him, he was moving toward the door when a light, buoyant step sounded on the veranda. In a moment the living-room lights were switched on from the entry and a woman called out sharply:—

"Stop right where you are or I'll shoot!"

The authoritative voice of the speaker, the quickness with which she had grasped the situation and leveled her revolver, brought The Hopper to an abrupt halt in the middle of the room, where he fell with a discordant crash across the keyboard of a grand piano. He turned, cowering, to confront a tall, young woman in a long ulster who advanced toward him slowly, but with every mark of determination upon her face. The Hopper stared beyond the gun, held in a very steady hand, into a pair of fearless dark eyes. In all his experiences he had never been cornered by a woman, and he stood gaping at his captor in astonishment. She was a very pretty young woman, with cheeks that still had the curve of youth, but with a chin that spoke for much firmness of character. A fur toque perched a little to one side gave her a boyish air.

This undoubtedly was Shaver's mother who had caught him prowling in her house, and all The Hopper's plans for explaining her son's disappearance and returning him in a manner to win praise and gratitude went glimmering. There was nothing in the appearance of this Muriel to encourage a hope that she was either embarrassed or alarmed by his presence. He had been captured many times, but the trick had never been turned by any one so cool as this young woman. She seemed to be pondering with the greatest calmness what disposition she should make of him. In the intentness of her

thought the revolver wavered for an instant, and The Hopper, without taking his eyes from her, made a cat-like spring that brought him to the window he had raised against just such an emergency.

"None of that!" she cried, walking slowly toward him without lowering the pistol. "If you attempt to jump from that window I'll shoot! But it's cold in here and you may lower it."

The Hopper, weighing the chances, decided that the odds were heavily against escape, and lowered the window.

"Now," said Muriel, "step into that corner and keep your hands up where I can watch them."

The Hopper obeyed her instructions strictly. There was a telephone on the table near her and he expected her to summon help; but to his surprise she calmly seated herself, resting her right elbow on the arm of the chair, her head slightly tilted to one side, as she inspected him with greater attention along the blue-black barrel of her automatic. Unless he made a dash for liberty this extraordinary woman would, at her leisure, turn him over to the police as a house-breaker and his peaceful life as a chicken farmer would be at an end. Her prolonged silence troubled The Hopper. He had not been more nervous when waiting for the report of the juries which at times had passed upon his conduct, or for judges to fix his term of imprisonment.

"Yes'm," he muttered, with a view to ending a silence that had become intolerable.

Her eyes danced to the accompaniment of her thoughts, but in no way did she betray the slightest perturbation.

"I ain't done nothin'; hones' to God, I ain't!" he protested brokenly.

"I saw you through the window when you entered this room and I was watching while you read that note," said his captor. "I thought it funny that you should do that instead of packing up the silver. Do you mind telling me just why you read that note?"

"Well, miss, I jes' thought it kind o' funny there wuzn't nobody round an' the letter was

148

layin' there all open, an' I didn't see no harm in lookin'."

"It was awfully clever of you to crawl into the corner so nobody could see your light from the windows," she said with a tinge of admiration. "I suppose you thought you might find out how long the people of the house were likely to be gone and how much time you could spend here. Was that it?"

"I reckon ut wuz somethin' like that," he agreed.

This was received with the noncommittal "Um" of a person whose thoughts are elsewhere. Then, as though she were eliciting from an artist or man of letters a frank opinion as to his own ideas of his attainments and professional standing, she asked, with a meditative air that puzzled him as much as her question:—

"Just how good a burglar are you? Can you do a job neatly and safely?"

The Hopper, staggered by her inquiry and overcome by modesty, shrugged his shoulders and twisted about uncomfortably.

"I reckon as how you've pinched me I ain't much good," he replied, and was rewarded with a smile followed by a light little laugh. He was beginning to feel pleased that she manifested no fear of him. In fact, he had decided that Shaver's mother was the most remarkable woman he had ever encountered, and by all odds the handsomest. He began to take heart. Perhaps after all he might hit upon some way of restoring Shaver to his proper place in the house of Talbot without making himself liable to a long term for kidnaping.

"If you're really a successful burglar—one who doesn't just poke around in empty houses as you were doing here, but clever and brave enough to break into houses where people are living and steal things without making a mess of it; and if you can play fair about it—then I think—I think—maybe—we can come to terms!"

"Yes'm!" faltered The Hopper, beginning to wonder if Mary and Humpy had been right in saying that he had lost his mind. He was so astonished that his arms wavered, but she was instantly on her feet and the little automatic was again on a level with his eyes.

"Excuse me, miss, I didn't mean to drop 'em. I weren't goin' to do nothin'. Hones' I wuzn't!" he pleaded with real contrition. "It jes' seemed kind o' funny what ye said."

He grinned sheepishly. If she knew that her Billie, *alias* Shaver, was not with her husband at his father's house, she would not be dallying in this fashion. And if the young father, who painted pictures, and left notes in his studio in a blind faith that his wife would find them,—if that trusting soul knew that Billie was asleep in a house all of whose inmates had done penance behind prison bars, he would very quickly become a man of action. The Hopper had never heard of such careless parenthood! These people were children! His heart warmed to them in pity and admiration, as it had to little Billie.

"I forgot to ask you whether you are armed," she remarked, with just as much composure as though she were asking him whether he took two lumps of sugar in his tea; and then she added, "I suppose I ought to have asked you that in the first place."

"I gotta gun in my coat—right side," he confessed. "An' that's all I got," he added, batting his eyes under the spell of her bewildering smile.

With her left hand she cautiously extracted his revolver and backed away with it to the table.

"If you'd lied to me I should have killed you; do you understand?"

"Yes'm," murmured The Hopper meekly.

She had spoken as though homicide were a common incident of her life, but a gleam of humor in the eyes she was watching vigilantly abated her severity.

"You may sit down—there, please!"

She pointed to a much bepillowed davenport and The Hopper sank down on it, still with his hands up. To his deepening mystification she backed to the windows and lowered the shades, and this done she sat down with the table between them, remarking,—

"You may put your hands down now, Mr.——?"

He hesitated, decided that it was unwise to give any of his names; and respecting his scruples she said with great magnanimity:—

"Of course you wouldn't want to tell me your name, so don't trouble about that."

She sat, wholly tranquil, her arms upon the table, both hands caressing the small automatic, while his own revolver, of different pattern and larger caliber, lay close by. His status was now established as that of a gentleman making a social call upon a lady who, in the pleasantest manner imaginable and yet with undeniable resoluteness, kept a deadly weapon pointed in the general direction of his person.

A clock on the mantel struck eleven with a low, silvery note. Muriel waited for the last stroke and then spoke crisply and directly.

"We were speaking of that letter I left lying here on the table. You didn't understand it, of course; you couldn't—not really. So I will explain it to you. My husband and I married against our fathers' wishes; both of them were opposed to it."

She waited for this to sink into his perturbed consciousness. The Hopper frowned and leaned forward to express his sympathetic interest in this confidential disclosure.

"My father," she resumed, "is just as stupid as my father-in-law and they have both continued to make us just as uncomfortable as possible. The cause of the trouble is ridiculous. There's nothing against my husband or me, you understand; it's simply a bitter jealousy between the two men due to the fact that they are rival collectors."

The Hopper stared blankly. The only collectors with whom he had enjoyed any acquaintance were persons who presented bills for payment.

"They are collectors," Muriel hastened to explain, "of ceramics—precious porcelains and that sort of thing."

"Yes'm," assented The Hopper, who hadn't the faintest notion of what she meant.

"For years, whenever there have been important sales of these things, which men fight for and are willing to die for—whenever there has been something specially fine in the market, my father-in-law—he's Mr. Talbot—and Mr. Wilton—he's my father—have bid for them. There are auctions, you know, and people come from all over the world looking for a chance to buy the rarest pieces. They've explored China and Japan hunting for prizes and they are experts—men of rare taste and judgment—what you call connoisseurs."

The Hopper nodded gravely at the unfamiliar word, convinced that not only were Muriel and her husband quite insane, but that they had inherited the infirmity.

"The trouble has been," Muriel continued, "that Mr. Talbot and my father both like the same kind of thing; and when one has got something the other wanted, of course it has added to the ill-feeling. This has been going on for years and recently they have grown more bitter. When Roger and I ran off and got married, that didn't help matters any; but just within a few days something has happened to make things much worse than ever."

The Hopper's complete absorption in this novel recital was so manifest that she put down the revolver with which she had been idling and folded her hands.

"Thank ye, miss," mumbled The Hopper.

"Only last week," Muriel continued, "my father-in-law bought one of those pottery treasures—a plum-blossom vase made in China hundreds of years ago and very, very valuable. It belonged to a Philadelphia collector who died not long ago and Mr. Talbot bought it from the executor of the estate, who happened to be an old friend of his. Father was very angry, for he had been led to believe that this vase was going to be offered at auction and he'd have a chance to bid on it. And just before that father had got hold of a jar—a perfectly wonderful piece of red Lang-Yao—that collectors everywhere have coveted for years. This made Mr. Talbot furious at father. My husband is at his father's now trying to make him see the folly of all this, and I visited *my* father to-day to try to persuade him to stop being so foolish. You see I wanted us all to be happy for Christmas! Of course, Christmas ought to be a time of gladness for everybody. Even people in your—er—profession must feel that Christmas is one day in the year when all hard feelings should be forgotten and everybody should try to make others happy."

"I guess yer right, miss. Ut sure seems foolish fer folks t' git mad about jugs like you says. Wuz they empty, miss?"

"Empty!" repeated Muriel wonderingly, not understanding at once that her visitor was unaware that the "jugs" men fought over were valued as art treasures and not for their possible contents. Then she laughed merrily, as only the mother of Shaver could laugh.

"Oh! Of course they're *empty*! That does seem to make it sillier, doesn't it? But they're like famous pictures, you know, or any beautiful work of art that only happens occasionally. Perhaps it seems odd to you that men can be so crazy about such things, but I suppose sometimes *you* have wanted things very, very much, and—oh!"

She paused, plainly confused by her tactlessness in suggesting to a member of his profession the extremities to which one may be led by covetousness.

"Yes, miss," he remarked hastily; and he rubbed his nose with the back of his hand, and grinned indulgently as he realized the cause of her embarrassment. It crossed his mind that she might be playing a trick of some kind; that her story, which seemed to him wholly fantastic and not at all like a chronicle of the acts of veritable human beings, was merely a device for detaining him until help arrived. But he dismissed this immediately as unworthy of one so pleasing, so beautiful, so perfectly qualified to be the mother of Shaver!

"Well, just before luncheon, without telling my husband where I was going, I ran away to papa's, hoping to persuade him to end this silly feud. I spent the afternoon there and he was very unreasonable. He feels that Mr. Talbot wasn't fair about that Philadelphia purchase, and I gave it up and came home. I got here a little after dark and found my husband had taken Billie—that's

our little boy—and gone. I knew, of course, that he had gone to *his* father's hoping to bring him round, for both our fathers are simply crazy about Billie. But you see I never go to Mr. Talbot's and my husband never goes—Dear me!" she broke off suddenly. "I suppose I ought to telephone and see if Billie is all right."

The Hopper, greatly alarmed, thrust his head forward as she pondered this. If she telephoned to her father-in-law's to ask about Billie, the jig would be up! He drew his hand across his face and fell back with relief as she went on, a little absently:—

"Mr. Talbot hates telephoning, and it might be that my husband is just getting him to the point of making concessions, and I shouldn't want to interrupt. It's so late now that of course Roger and Billie will spend the night there. And Billie and Christmas ought to be a combination that would soften the hardest heart! You ought to see—you just ought to see Billie! He's the cunningest, dearest baby in the world!"

The Hopper sat pigeon-toed, beset by countless conflicting emotions. His ingenuity was taxed to its utmost by the demands of this complex situation. But for his returning suspicion that Muriel was leading up to something; that she was detaining him for some purpose not yet apparent, he would have told her of her husband's note and confessed that the adored Billie was at that moment enjoying the reluctant hospitality of Happy Hill Farm. He resolved to continue his policy of silence as to the young heir's whereabouts until Muriel had shown her hand. She had not wholly abandoned the thought of telephoning to her father-in-law's, he found, from her next remark.

"You think it's all right, don't you? It's strange Roger didn't leave me a note of some kind. Our cook left a week ago and there was no one here when he left."

"I reckon as how yer kid's all right, miss," he answered consolingly.

Her voluble confidences had enthralled him, and her reference of this matter to his judgment was enormously flattering. On the rough edges of society where he had spent most of his life, fellow craftsmen had frequently solicited his advice, chiefly as to the disposition of their ill-gotten gains or regarding safe harbors of refuge, but to be taken into counsel by the only gentle-woman he had ever met roused his self-respect, touched a chivalry that never before had been wakened in The Hopper's soul. She was so like a child in her guilelessness, and so brave amid her perplexities!

"Oh, I know Roger will take beautiful care of Billie. And now," she smiled radiantly, "you're probably wondering what I've been driving at all this time. Maybe"—she added softly—"maybe it's providential, your turning up here in this way!"

She uttered this happily, with a little note of triumph and another of her smiles that seemed to illuminate the universe. The Hopper had been called many names in his varied career, but never before had he been invested with the at-tributes of an agent of Providence.

"They's things wot is an' they's things wot ain't, miss; I reckon I ain't as bad as some. I mean to be on the square, miss."

"I believe that," she said. "I've always heard there's honor among thieves, and"—she lowered her voice to a whisper—"it's possible I might be-come one myself!"

The Hopper's eyes opened wide and he crossed and uncrossed his legs nervously in his agitation.

"If—if'"—she began slowly, bending for-ward with a grave, earnest look in her eyes and clasping her fingers tightly—"if we could only get hold of father's Lang-Yao jar and that plum-blossom vase Mr. Talbot has—if we could only do that!"

The Hopper swallowed hard. This fearless, pretty young woman was calmly suggesting that he commit two felonies, little knowing that his score for the day already aggregated three—purse-snatching, the theft of an automobile from her own door, and what might very readily be construed as the kidnaping of her own child!

"I don't know, miss," he said feebly, calculat-ing that the sum total of even minimum penal-ties for the five crimes would outrun his natural life and consume an eternity of reincarnations.

"Of course it wouldn't be stealing in the or-dinary sense," she explained. "What I want you to do is to play the part of what we will call a reversible Santa Claus, who takes things away from stupid people who don't enjoy them any-how. And maybe if they lost these things they'd behave themselves. I could explain afterward that it was all my fault, and of course I wouldn't let any harm come to *you*. I'd be responsible, and of course I'd see you safely out of it; you would have to rely on me for that. I'm trusting *you* and you'd have to trust *me!*"

"Oh, I'd trust ye, miss! An' ef I was to get pinched I wouldn't never squeal on ye. We don't never blab on a pal, miss!"

He was afraid she might resent being called a "pal," but his use of the term apparently pleased her.

"We understand each other, then. It really won't be very difficult, for papa's place is over on the Sound and Mr. Talbot's is right next to it, so you wouldn't have far to go."

Her utter failure to comprehend the enor-mity of the thing she was proposing affected him queerly. Even among hardened criminals in the underworld such undertakings are suggested cautiously; but Muriel was ordering a burglary as though it were a pound of butter or a dozen eggs!

"Father keeps his most valuable glazes in a safe in the pantry," she resumed after a mo-ment's reflection, "but I can give you the combi-nation. That will make it a lot easier."

The Hopper assented, with a pontifical nod, to this sanguine view of the matter.

"Mr. Talbot keeps his finest pieces in a cabi-net built into the bookshelves in his library. It's on the left side as you stand in the drawing-room door, and you look for the works of Thomas Car-lyle. There's a dozen or so volumes of Carlyle, only they're not books—not really—but just the backs of books painted on the steel of a safe. And if you press a spring in the upper right-hand corner of the shelf just over these books the whole section swings out. I suppose you've seen that sort of hiding-place for valuables?"

"Well, not exactly, miss. But havin' a tip helps, an' ef there ain't no soup to pour—"

"Soup?" inquired Muriel, wrinkling her pretty brows.

"That's the juice we pour into the cracks of a safe to blow out the lid with," The Hopper elucidated. "Ut's a lot handier ef you've got the combination. Ut usually ain't jes' layin' around."

"I should hope not!" exclaimed Muriel.

She took a sheet of paper from the leathern stationery rack and fell to scribbling, while he furtively eyed the window and again put from him the thought of flight.

"There! That's the combination of papa's safe." She turned her wrist and glanced at her watch. "It's half-past eleven and you can catch a trolley in ten minutes that will take you right past papa's house. The butler's an old man who forgets to lock the windows half the time, and there's one in the conservatory with a broken catch. I noticed it to-day when I was thinking about stealing the jar myself!"

They were established on so firm a basis of mutual confidence that when he rose and walked to the table she didn't lift her eyes from the paper on which she was drawing a diagram of her father's house. He stood watching her nimble fingers, fascinated by the boldness of her plan for restoring amity between Shaver's grandfathers, and filled with admiration for her resourcefulness.

He asked a few questions as to exits and entrances and fixed in his mind a very accurate picture of the home of her father. She then proceeded to enlighten him as to the ways and means of entering the home of her father-in-law, which she sketched with equal facility.

"There's a French window—a narrow glass door—on the veranda. I think you might get in *there*!" She made a jab with the pencil. "Of course I should hate awfully to have you get caught! But you must have had a lot of experience, and with all the help I'm giving you—!"

A sudden lifting of her head gave him the full benefit of her eyes and he averted his gaze reverently.

"There's always a chance o' bein' nabbed, miss," he suggested with feeling.

Shaver's mother wielded the same hypnotic power, highly intensified, that he had felt in Shaver. He knew that he was going to attempt what she asked; that he was committed to the project of robbing two houses merely to please a pretty young woman who invited his coöperation at the point of a revolver!

"Papa's always a sound sleeper," she was saying. "When I was a little girl a burglar went all through our house and carried off his clothes and he never knew it until the next morning. But you'll have to be careful at Mr. Talbot's, for he suffers horribly from insomnia."

"They got any o' them fancy burglar alarms?" asked The Hopper as he concluded his examination of her sketches.

"Oh, I forgot to tell you about that!" she cried contritely. "There's nothing of the kind at Mr. Talbot's, but at papa's there's a switch in the living-room, right back of a bust—a white marble thing on a pedestal. You turn it off *there*. Half the time papa forgets to switch it on before he goes to bed. And another thing—be careful about stumbling over that bearskin rug in the hall. People are always sticking their feet into its jaws."

"I'll look out for ut, miss."

Burglar alarms and the jaws of wild beasts were not inviting hazards. The programme she outlined so light-heartedly was full of complexities. It was almost pathetic that any one could so cheerfully and irresponsibly suggest the perpetration of a crime. The terms she used in describing the loot he was to filch were much stranger to him than Chinese, but it was fairly clear that at the Talbot house he was to steal a blue-and-white thing and at the Wilton's a red one. The form and size of these articles she illustrated with graceful gestures.

"If I thought you were likely to make a mistake I'd—I'd go with you!" she declared.

"Oh, no, miss; ye couldn't do that! I guess I can do ut fer ye. Ut's jes' a *leetle* ticklish. I reckon ef yer pa wuz to nab me ut'd go hard with me."

"I wouldn't let him be hard on you," she replied earnestly. "And now I haven't said anything about a—a—about what we will call a *reward* for bringing me these porcelains. I shall expect to pay you; I couldn't think of taking up your time, you know, for nothing!"

"Lor', miss, I couldn't take nothin' at all fer doin' ut! Ye see ut wuz sort of accidental our meetin', and besides, I ain't no housebreaker—not, as ye may say, reg'ler. I'll be glad to do ut fer ye, miss, an' ye can rely on me doin' my best fer ye. Ye've treated me right, miss, an' I ain't a-goin' t' fergit ut!"

The Hopper spoke with feeling. Shaver's mother had, albeit at the pistol point, confided her most intimate domestic affairs to him. He realized, without finding just these words for it, that she had in effect decorated him with the symbol of her order of knighthood and he had every honorable—or dishonorable!—intention of proving himself worthy of her confidence.

"If ye please, miss," he said, pointing toward his confiscated revolver.

"Certainly; you may take it. But of course you won't *kill* anybody?"

"No, miss; only I'm sort o' lonesome without ut when I'm on a job."

"And you do understand," she said, following him to the door and noting in the distance the headlight of an approaching trolley, "that I'm only doing this in the hope that good may come of it. It isn't really criminal, you know; if you succeed, it may mean the happiest Christmas of my life!"

"Yes, miss. I won't come back till mornin', but don't you worry none. We gotta play safe, miss, an' ef I land th' jugs I'll find cover till I kin deliver 'em safe."

"Thank you; oh, thank you ever so much! And good luck!"

She put out her hand; he held it gingerly for a moment in his rough fingers and ran for the car.

VII

The Hopper, in his rôle of the Reversible Santa Claus, dropped off the car at the crossing Muriel had carefully described, waited for the car to vanish, and warily entered the Wilton estate through a gate set in the stone wall. The clouds of the early evening had passed and the stars marched through the heavens resplendently, proclaiming peace on earth and good-will toward men. They were almost oppressively brilliant, seen through the clear, cold atmosphere, and as The Hopper slipped from one big tree to another on his tangential course to the house, he fortified his courage by muttering, "They's things wot is an' things wot ain't!"—finding much comfort and stimulus in the phrase.

Arriving at the conservatory in due course, he found that Muriel's averments as to the vulnerability of that corner of her father's house were correct in every particular. He entered with ease, sniffed the warm, moist air, and, leaving the door slightly ajar, sought the pantry, lowered the shades, and, helping himself to a candle from a silver candelabrum, readily found the safe hidden away in one of the cupboards. He was surprised to find himself more nervous with the combination in his hand than on memorable occasions in the old days when he had broken into country post-offices and assaulted safes by force. In his haste he twice failed to give the proper turns, but the third time the knob caught, and in a moment the door swung open disclosing shelves filled with vases, bottles, bowls, and plates in bewildering variety. A chest of silver appealed to him distractingly as a much more tangible asset than the pottery, and he dizzily contemplated a jewel-case containing a diamond necklace with a pearl pendant. The moment was a critical one in The Hopper's eventful career. This dazzling prize was his for the taking, and he knew the operator of a fence in Chicago who would dispose of the necklace and make him a fair return. But visions of Muriel, the beautiful, the confiding, and of her little Shaver asleep on Humpy's bed, rose before him. He steeled his heart against temptation, drew his candle along the shelf, and scrutinized the glazes. There could be no mistaking the red Lang-Yao whose brilliant tints kindled in the candle-glow. He lifted it tenderly, verifying the various points of Muriel's description, set it down on the floor, and locked the safe.

He was retracing his steps toward the conservatory and had reached the main hall when the creaking of the stairsteps brought him up with a start. Some one was descending, slowly and cautiously. For a second time and with grateful appreciation of Muriel's forethought, he carefully avoided the ferocious jaws of the bear, noiselessly continued on to the conservatory, crept through the door, closed it, and then, crouching on the steps, awaited developments. The caution exercised by the person descending the stairway was not that of a householder who has been roused from slumber by a disquieting noise. The Hopper was keenly interested in this fact.

With his face against the glass he watched the actions of a tall, elderly man with a short, grayish beard, who wore a golf-cap pulled low on his head—points noted by The Hopper in the flashes of an electric lamp with which the gentleman was guiding himself. His face was clearly the original of a photograph The Hopper had seen on the table at Muriel's cottage—Mr. Wilton, Muriel's father, The Hopper surmised; but just why the owner of the establishment should be prowling about in this fashion taxed his speculative powers to the utmost. Warned by steps on the cement floor of the conservatory, he left the door in haste and flattened himself against the wall of the house some distance away and again awaited developments.

Wilton's figure was a blur in the starlight as he stepped out into the walk and started furtively across the grounds. His conduct greatly displeased The Hopper, as likely to interfere with the further carrying out of Muriel's instructions. The Lang-Yao jar was much too large to go into his pocket and not big enough to fit snugly under his arm, and as the walk was slippery he was beset by the fear that he might fall

and smash this absurd thing that had caused so bitter an enmity between Shaver's grandfathers. The soft snow on the lawn gave him a surer footing and he crept after Wilton, who was carefully pursuing his way toward a house whose gables were faintly limned against the sky. This, according to Muriel's diagram, was the Talbot place. The Hopper greatly mistrusted conditions he didn't understand, and he was at a loss to account for Wilton's strange actions.

He lost sight of him for several minutes, then the faint click of a latch marked the prowler's proximity to a hedge that separated the two estates. The Hopper crept forward, found a gate through which Wilton had entered his neighbor's property, and stole after him. Wilton had been swallowed up by the deep shadow of the house, but The Hopper was aware, from an occasional scraping of feet, that he was still moving forward. He crawled over the snow until he reached a large tree whose boughs, sharply limned against the stars, brushed the eaves of the house.

The Hopper was aroused, tremendously aroused, by the unaccountable actions of Muriel's father. It flashed upon him that Wilton, in his deep hatred of his rival collector, was about to set fire to Talbot's house, and incendiarism was a crime which The Hopper, with all his moral obliquity, greatly abhorred.

Several minutes passed, a period of anxious waiting, and then a sound reached him which, to his keen professional sense, seemed singularly like the forcing of a window. The Hopper knew just how much pressure is necessary to the successful snapping back of a window catch, and Wilton had done the trick neatly and with a minimum amount of noise. The window thus assaulted was not, he now determined, the French window suggested by Muriel, but one opening on a terrace which ran along the front of the house. The Hopper heard the sash moving slowly in the frame. He reached the steps, deposited the jar in a pile of snow, and was soon peering into a room where Wilton's presence was advertised by the fitful flashing of his lamp in a far corner.

"He's beat me to ut!" muttered The Hopper, realizing that Muriel's father was indeed on burglary bent, his obvious purpose being to purloin, extract, and remove from its secret hiding-place the coveted plum-blossom vase. Muriel, in her longing for a Christmas of peace and happiness, had not reckoned with her father's passionate desire to possess the porcelain treasure—a desire which could hardly fail to cause scandal, if it did not land him behind prison bars.

This had not been in the programme, and The Hopper weighed judicially his further duty in the matter. Often as he had been the chief actor in daring robberies, he had never before enjoyed the high privilege of watching a rival's labors with complete detachment. Wilton must have known of the concealed cupboard whose panel fraudulently represented the works of Thomas Carlyle, the intent spectator reflected, just as Muriel had known, for though he used his lamp sparingly Wilton had found his way to it without difficulty.

The Hopper had no intention of permitting this monstrous larceny to be committed in contravention of his own rights in the premises, and he was considering the best method of wresting the vase from the hands of the insolent Wilton when events began to multiply with startling rapidity. The panel swung open and the thief's lamp flashed upon shelves of pottery.

At that moment a shout rose from somewhere in the house, and the library lights were thrown on, revealing Wilton before the shelves and their precious contents. A short, stout gentleman with a gleaming bald pate, clad in pajamas, dashed across the room, and with a yell of rage flung himself upon the intruder with a violence that bore them both to the floor.

"Roger! Roger!" bawled the smaller man, as he struggled with his adversary, who wriggled from under and rolled over upon Talbot, whose arms were clasped tightly about his neck. This embrace seemed likely to continue for some time, so tenaciously had the little man gripped his neighbor. The fat legs of the infuriated householder pawed the air as he hugged Wilton, who was now trying to free his head and gain a position of greater dignity. Occasionally, as opportunity offered, the little man yelled vociferously, and from remote recesses of the house came answering cries demanding information as to the nature and whereabouts of the disturbance.

The contestants addressed themselves vigorously to a spirited rough-and-tumble fight. Talbot, who was the more easily observed by reason of his shining pate and the pink stripes of his pajamas, appeared to be revolving about the person of his neighbor. Wilton, though taller, lacked the rotund Talbot's liveliness of attack.

An authoritative voice, which The Hopper attributed to Shaver's father, anxiously demanding what was the matter, terminated The Hopper's enjoyment of the struggle. Enough was the matter to satisfy The Hopper that a prolonged stay in the neighborhood might be highly detrimental to his future liberty. The combatants had rolled a considerable distance away from the shelves and were near a door leading into a room beyond. A young man in a bath-wrapper dashed upon the scene, and in his precipitate arrival upon the battle-field fell sprawling across the prone figures. The Hopper, suddenly inspired to deeds of prowess, crawled through the window, sprang past the three men, seized the blue-and-white vase which Wilton had separated from the rest of Talbot's treasures, and then with one hop gained the window. As he turned for a last look, a pistol cracked and he landed upon the terrace amid a shower of glass from a shattered pane.

A woman of unmistakable Celtic origin screamed murder from a third-story window. The thought of murder was disagreeable to The Hopper. Shaver's father had missed him by only the matter of a foot or two, and as he had no intention of offering himself again as a target he stood not upon the order of his going.

He effected a running pick-up of the Lang-Yao, and with this art treasure under one arm and the plum-blossom vase under the other, he sprinted for the highway, stumbling over shrubbery, bumping into a stone bench that all but caused disaster, and finally reached the road on which he continued his flight toward New Haven, followed by cries in many keys and a fusillade of pistol shots.

Arriving presently at a hamlet, where he paused for breath in the rear of a country store, he found a basket and a quantity of paper in which he carefully packed his loot. Over the top he spread some faded lettuce leaves and discarded carnations which communicated something of a blithe holiday air to his encumbrance. Elsewhere he found a bicycle under a shed, and while cycling over a snowy road in the dark, hampered by a basket containing pottery representative of the highest genius of the Orient, was not without its difficulties and dangers, The Hopper made rapid progress.

Halfway through New Haven he approached two policemen and slowed down to allay suspicion.

"Merry Chris'mas!" he called as he passed them and increased his weight upon the pedals.

The officers of the law, cheered as by a greeting from Santa Claus himself, responded with an equally hearty Merry Christmas.

VIII

At three o'clock The Hopper reached Happy Hill Farm, knocked as before at the kitchen door, and was admitted by Humpy.

"Wot ye got now?" snarled the reformed yeggman.

"He's gone and done ut ag'in!" wailed Mary, as she spied the basket.

"I sure done ut, all right," admitted The Hopper good-naturedly, as he set the basket on the table where a few hours earlier he had deposited Shaver. "How's the kid?"

Grudging assurances that Shaver was asleep and hostile glances directed at the mysterious basket did not disturb his equanimity.

Humpy was thwarted in an attempt to pry into the contents of the basket by a tart reprimand from The Hopper, who with maddening deliberation drew forth the two glazes, found that they had come through the night's vicissitudes unscathed, and held them at arm's length, turning them about in leisurely fashion as though lost in admiration of their loveliness. Then he lighted his pipe, seated himself in Mary's rocker, and told his story.

It was no easy matter to communicate to his irritable and contumelious auditors the sense of Muriel's charm, or the reasonableness of her request that he commit burglary merely to assist her in settling a family row. Mary could not understand it; Humpy paced the room nervously, shaking his head and muttering. It was their judgment, stated with much frankness, that if he had been a fool in the first place to steal the child, his character was now blackened beyond any hope by his later crimes. Mary wept copiously; Humpy most annoyingly kept counting upon his fingers as he reckoned the "time" that was in store for all of them.

"I guess I got into ut an' I guess I'll git out," remarked The Hopper serenely. He was disposed to treat them with high condescension, as incapable of appreciating the lofty philosophy of life by which he was sustained. Meanwhile, he gloated over the loot of the night.

"Them things is wurt' mints; they's more valible than di'mon's, them things is! Only eddicated folks knows about 'em. They's fer emp'rors and kings t' set up in their palaces, an' men goes nutty jes' hankerin' fer 'em. The pigtails made 'em thousand o' years back, an' th' secret died with 'em. They ain't never goin' to be no more jugs like them settin' right there. An' them two ole sports give up their business jes' t' chase things like them. They's some folks goes loony about chickens, an' hosses, an' fancy dogs, but this here kind o' collectin' 's only fer millionaires. They's more difficult t' pick than a lucky race-hoss. They's barrels o' that stuff in them houses, that looked jes' as good as them there, but nowheres as valible."

An informal lecture on Chinese ceramics before daylight on Christmas morning was not to the liking of the anxious and nerve-torn Mary and Humpy. They brought The Hopper down from his lofty heights to practical questions touching his plans, for the disposal of Shaver in the first instance, and the ceramics in the second. The Hopper was singularly unmoved by their forebodings.

"I guess th' lady got me to do ut!" he retorted finally. "Ef I do time fer ut I reckon's how she's in fer ut, too! An' I seen her pap breakin' into a house an' I guess I'd be a state's witness fer that! I reckon they ain't goin' t' put nothin' over on Hop! I guess they won't peep much about kidnapin' with th' kid safe an' us pickin' 'im up out o' th' road an' shelterin' 'im. Them folks is goin' to be awful nice to Hop fer all he done fer 'em." And then, finding that they were impressed by his defense, thus elaborated, he magnanimously referred to the bill-book which had started him on his downward course.

"That were a mistake; I grant ye ut were a mistake o' jedgment. I'm goin' to keep to th' white card. But ut's kind o' funny about that poke—queerest thing that ever happened."

He drew out the book and eyed the name on the flap. Humpy tried to grab it, but The Hopper, frustrating the attempt, read his colleague a sharp lesson in good manners. He restored it to his pocket and glanced at the clock.

"We gotta do somethin' about Shaver's stockin's. Ut ain't fair fer a kid to wake up an' think Santy missed 'im. Ye got some candy, Mary; we kin put candy into 'em; that's reg'ler."

Humpy brought in Shaver's stockings and they were stuffed with the candy and popcorn Mary had provided to adorn their Christmas feast. Humpy inventoried his belongings, but could think of nothing but a revolver that seemed a suitable gift for Shaver. This Mary scornfully rejected as improper for one so young. Whereupon Humpy produced a Mexican silver dollar, a treasured pocket-piece preserved through many tribulations, and dropped it reverently into one of the stockings. Two brass buttons of unknown history, a mouth-organ Mary had bought for a neighbor boy who assisted at

times in the poultry yard, and a silver spectacle case of uncertain antecedents were added.

"We ought t' 'a' colored eggs fer 'im!" said The Hopper with sudden inspiration, after the stockings had been restored to Shaver's bed. "Some yaller an' pink eggs would 'a' been the right ticket."

Mary scoffed at the idea. Eggs wasn't proper fer Christmas; eggs was fer Easter. Humpy added the weight of his personal experience of Christian holidays to this statement. While a trusty in the Missouri penitentiary with the chicken yard in his keeping, he remembered distinctly that eggs were in demand for purposes of decoration by the warden's children sometime in the spring; mebbe it was Easter, mebbe it was Decoration Day; Humpy was not sure of anything except that it wasn't Christmas.

The Hopper was meek under correction. It having been settled that colored eggs would not be appropriate for Christmas he yielded to their demand that he show some enthusiasm for disposing of his ill-gotten treasures before the police arrived to take the matter out of his hands.

"I guess that Muriel'll be glad to see me," he remarked. "I guess me and her understands each other. They's things wot is an' things wot ain't; an' I guess Hop ain't goin' to spend no Chris'mas in jail. It's the white card an' poultry an' eggs fer us; an' we're goin' t' put in a couple more incubators right away. I'm thinkin' some o' rentin' that acre across th' brook back yonder an' raisin' turkeys. They's mints in turks, ef ye kin keep 'em from gettin' their feet wet an' dyin' o' pneumonia, which wipes out thousands o' them birds. I reckon ye might make some coffee, Mary."

The Christmas dawn found them at the table, where they were renewing a pledge to play "the white card" when a cry from Shaver brought them to their feet.

Shaver was highly pleased with his Christmas stockings, but his pleasure was nothing to that of The Hopper, Mary, and Humpy, as they stood about the bed and watched him. Mary and Humpy were so relieved by The Hopper's promises to lead a better life that they were now disposed to treat their guest with the most distinguished consideration. Humpy, absenting himself to perform his morning tasks in the poultry-houses, returned bringing a basket containing six newly hatched chicks. These cheeped and ran over Shaver's fat legs and performed exactly as though they knew they were a part of his Christmas entertainment. Humpy, proud of having thought of the chicks, demanded the privilege of serving Shaver's breakfast. Shaver ate his porridge without a murmur, so happy was he over his new playthings.

Mary bathed and dressed him with care. As the candy had stuck to the stockings in spots, it was decided after a family conference that Shaver would have to wear them wrong side out as there was no time to be wasted in washing them. By eight o'clock The Hopper announced that it was time for Shaver to go home. Shaver expressed alarm at the thought of leaving his chicks; whereupon Humpy conferred two of them upon him in the best imitation of baby talk that he could muster.

"Me's tate um to me's gwanpas," said Shaver; "chickee for me's two gwanpas,"—a remark which caused The Hopper to shake for a moment with mirth as he recalled his last view of Shaver's "gwanpas" in a death grip upon the floor of "Gwanpa" Talbot's house.

IX

When The Hopper rolled away from Happy Hill Farm in the stolen machine, accompanied by one stolen child and forty thousand dollars' worth of stolen pottery, Mary wept, whether because of the parting with Shaver, or because she feared that The Hopper would never return, was not clear.

Humpy, too, showed signs of tears, but concealed his weakness by performing a grotesque dance, dancing grotesquely by the side of the car, much to Shaver's joy—a joy enhanced just as the car reached the gate, where, as a farewell attention, Humpy fell down and rolled over and over in the snow.

The Hopper's wits were alert as he bore Shaver homeward. By this time it was likely that the confiding young Talbots had conferred over the telephone and knew that their offspring had disappeared. Doubtless the New Haven police had been notified, and he chose his route with discretion to avoid unpleasant encounters. Shaver, his spirits keyed to holiday pitch, babbled ceaselessly, and The Hopper, highly elated, babbled back at him.

They arrived presently at the rear of the young Talbots' premises, and The Hopper, with Shaver trotting at his side, advanced cautiously upon the house bearing the two baskets, one containing Shaver's chicks, the other the precious porcelains. In his survey of the landscape he noted with trepidation the presence of two big limousines in the highway in front of the cottage and decided that if possible he must see Muriel alone and make his report to her.

The moment he entered the kitchen he heard the clash of voices in angry dispute in the living-room. Even Shaver was startled by the violence of the conversation in progress within, and clutched tightly a fold of The Hopper's trousers.

"I tell you it's John Wilton who has stolen Billie!" a man cried tempestuously. "Anybody who would enter a neighbor's house in the dead of night and try to rob him—rob him, yes, and *murder* him in the most brutal fashion—would not scruple to steal his own grandchild!"

"Me's gwanpa," whispered Shaver, gripping The Hopper's hand, "an' 'im's mad."

That Mr. Talbot was very angry indeed was established beyond cavil. However, Mr. Wilton was apparently quite capable of taking care of himself in the dispute.

"You talk about my stealing when you robbed me of my Lang-Yao—bribed my servants to plunder my safe! I want you to understand once for all, Roger Talbot, that if that jar isn't returned within one hour,—within one hour, sir,—I shall turn you over to the police!"

"Liar!" bellowed Talbot, who possessed a voice of great resonance. "You can't mitigate your foul crime by charging me with another! I never saw your jar; I never wanted it! I wouldn't have the thing on my place!"

Muriel's voice, full of tears, was lifted in expostulation.

"How can you talk of your silly vases when Billie's lost! Billie's been stolen—and you two men can think of nothing but pot-ter-ree!"

Shaver lifted a startled face to The Hopper.

"Mamma's cwyin'; gwanpa's hurted mamma!"

The strategic moment had arrived when Shaver must be thrust forward as an interruption to the exchange of disagreeable epithets by his grandfathers.

"You trot right in there t' yer ma, Shaver. Ole Hop ain't goin' t' let 'em hurt ye!"

He led the child through the dining-room to the living-room door and pushed him gently on the scene of strife. Talbot, senior, was pacing the floor with angry strides, declaiming upon his wrongs,—indeed, his theme might have been the misery of the whole human race from the vigor of his lamentations. His son was keeping step with him, vainly attempting to persuade him to sit down. Wilton, with a patch over his right eye, was trying to disengage himself from his daughter's arms with the obvious intention of doing violence to his neighbor.

"I'm sure papa never meant to hurt you; it was all a dreadful mistake," she moaned.

"He had an accomplice," Talbot thundered, "and while he was trying to kill me there in my own house the plum-blossom vase was carried off; and if Roger hadn't pushed him out of the window after his hireling—I'd—I'd—"

A shriek from Muriel happily prevented the completion of a sentence that gave every promise of intensifying the prevailing hard feeling.

"Look!" Muriel cried. "It's Billie come back! Oh, Billie!"

She sprang toward the door and clasped the frightened child to her heart. The three men gathered round them, staring dully. The Hopper from behind the door waited for Muriel's joy over Billie's return to communicate itself to his father and the two grandfathers.

"Me's dot two chick-ees for Kwis-mus," announced Billie, wriggling in his mother's arms.

Muriel, having satisfied herself that Billie was intact,—that he even bore the marks of maternal care,—was in the act of transferring him to his bewildered father, when, turning a tear-stained face toward the door, she saw The Hopper awkwardly twisting the derby which he had donned as proper for a morning call of ceremony. She walked toward him with quick, eager step.

"You—you came back!" she faltered, stifling a sob.

"Yes'm," responded The Hopper, rubbing his hand across his nose. His appearance roused Billie's father to a sense of his parental responsibility.

"You brought the boy back! You are the kidnaper!"

"Roger," cried Muriel protestingly, "don't speak like that! I'm sure this gentleman can explain how he came to bring Billie."

The quickness with which she regained her composure, the ease with which she adjusted herself to the unforeseen situation, pleased The Hopper greatly. He had not misjudged Muriel; she was an admirable ally, an ideal confederate. She gave him a quick little nod, as much as to say, "Go on, sir; we understand each other perfectly,"—though, of course, she did not understand, nor was she enlightened until some time later, as to just how The Hopper became possessed of Billie.

Billie's father declared his purpose to invoke the law upon his son's kidnapers no matter where they might be found.

"I reckon as mebbe ut wuz a kidnapin' an' I reckon as mebbe ut wuz n't," The Hopper began unhurriedly. "I live over Shell Road way; poultry and eggs is my line; Happy Hill Farm. Stevens's the name—Charles S. Stevens. An' I found Shaver—'scuse me, but ut seemed sort o' nat'ral name fer 'im—I found 'im a settin' up in th' machine over there by my place, chipper's ye please. I takes 'im into my house an' Mary—that's th' missus—she gives 'im supper and puts 'im t' sleep. An' we thinks mebbe somebody'd come along askin' fer 'im. An' then this mornin' I calls th' New Haven police, an' they tole me about you folks, an' me and Shaver comes right over."

This was entirely plausible and his hearers, The Hopper noted with relief, accepted it at face value.

"How dear of you!" cried Muriel. "Won't you have this chair, Mr. Stevens!"

"Most remarkable!" exclaimed Wilton. "Some scoundrelly tramp picked up the car and finding there was a baby inside left it at the roadside like the brute he was!"

Billie had addressed himself promptly to the Christmas tree, to his very own Christmas tree that was laden with gifts that had been assembled by the family for his delectation. Efforts of Grandfather Wilton to extract from the child some account of the man who had run away with him were unavailing. Billie was busy, very busy, indeed. After much patient effort he stopped sorting the animals in a bright new Noah's Ark to point his finger at The Hopper and remark:—

"'Ims nice mans; 'ims let Bil-lee play wif 'ims watch!"

As Billie had broken the watch his acknowledgment of The Hopper's courtesy in letting him play with it brought a grin to The Hopper's face.

Now that Billie had been returned and his absence satisfactorily accounted for, the two connoisseurs showed signs of renewing their quarrel. Responsive to a demand from Billie, The Hopper got down on the floor to assist in the proper mating of Noah's animals. Billie's father was scrutinizing him fixedly and The Hopper wondered whether Muriel's handsome young husband had recognized him as the person who had vanished through the window of the Talbot home bearing the plum-blossom vase. The thought was disquieting; but feigning deep interest in the Ark he listened attentively to a violent tirade upon which the senior Talbot was launched.

"My God!" he cried bitterly, planting himself before Wilton in a belligerent attitude, "every infernal thing that can happen to a man happened to me yesterday. It wasn't enough that you robbed me and tried to murder me—yes, you did, sir!—but when I was in the city I was robbed in the subway by a pick-pocket. A thief took my bill-book containing invaluable data I had just received from my agent in China giving me a clue to porcelains, sir, such as you never dreamed of! Some more of your work—Don't you contradict me! You don't contradict me! Roger, he doesn't contradict me!"

Wilton, choking with indignation at this new onslaught, was unable to contradict him.

Pained by the situation, The Hopper rose from the floor and coughed timidly.

"Shaver, go fetch yer chickies. Bring yer chickies in an' put 'em on th' boat."

Billie obediently trotted off toward the kitchen and The Hopper turned his back upon the Christmas tree, drew out the pocket-book, and faced the company.

"I beg yer pardon, gents, but mebbe this is th' book yer fightin' about. Kind o' funny like! I picked ut up on th' local yistiddy afternoon. I wuz goin' t' turn ut int' th' agint, but I clean fergot ut. I guess them papers may be valible. I never touched none of 'em."

Talbot snatched the bill-book and hastily examined the contents. His brow relaxed and he was grumbling something about a reward when Billie reappeared, laboriously dragging two baskets.

"Bil-lee's dot chick-ees! Bil-lee's dot pitty dishes. Bil-lee make dishes go 'ippity!"

Before he could make the two jars go 'ippity, The Hopper leaped across the room and seized the basket. He tore off the towel with which he had carefully covered the stolen pottery and disclosed the contents for inspection.

"'Scuse me, gents; no crowdin'," he warned as the connoisseurs sprang toward him. He placed the porcelains carefully on the floor under the Christmas tree. "Now ye kin listen t' me, gents. I reckon I'm goin' t' have somethin' t' say about this here crockery. I stole 'em—I stole 'em fer th' lady there, she thinkin' ef ye didn't have 'em no more ye'd stop rowin' about 'em. Ye kin call th' bulls an' turn me over ef ye likes; but I ain't goin' t' have ye fussin' an' causin' th' lady trouble no more. I ain't goin' to stand fer ut!"

"Robber!" shouted Talbot. "You entered my house at the instance of this man; it was you—"

"I never saw the gent before," declared The Hopper hotly. "I ain't never had nothin' to do with neither o' ye."

"He's telling the truth!" protested Muriel, laughing hysterically. "I did it—I got him to take them!"

The two collectors were not interested in explanations; they were hungrily eyeing their property. Wilton attempted to pass The Hopper and reach the Christmas tree under whose protecting boughs the two vases were looking their loveliest.

"Stand back," commanded The Hopper, "an' stop callin' names! I guess ef I'm yanked fer this I ain't th' only one that's goin' t' do time fer house breakin'."

This statement, made with considerable vigor, had a sobering effect upon Wilton, but Talbot began dancing round the tree looking for a chance to pounce upon the porcelains.

"Ef ye don't set down—the whole caboodle o' ye—I'll smash 'em—I'll smash 'em both! I'll bust 'em—sure as shootin'!" shouted The Hopper.

They cowered before him; Muriel wept softly; Billie played with his chickies, disdainful of the world's woe. The Hopper, holding the two angry men at bay, was enjoying his command of the situation.

"You gents ain't got no business to be fussin' an' causin' yer childern trouble. An' ye ain't goin' to have these pretty jugs to fuss about no more. I'm goin' t' give 'em away; I'm goin' to make a Chris'mas present of 'em to Shaver. They're goin' to be little Shaver's right here, all orderly

an' peace'ble, or I'll tromp on 'em! Looky here, Shaver, wot Santy Claus brought ye!"

"Nice dood Sant' Claus!" cried Billie, diving under the davenport in quest of the wandering chicks.

Silence held the grown-ups. The Hopper stood patiently by the Christmas tree, awaiting the result of his diplomacy.

Then suddenly Wilton laughed—a loud laugh expressive of relief. He turned to Talbot and put out his hand.

"It looks as though Muriel and her friend here had cornered us! The idea of pooling our trophies and giving them as a Christmas present to Billie appeals to me strongly. And, besides we've got to prepare somebody to love these things after we're gone. We can work together and train Billie to be the greatest collector in America!"

"Please, father," urged Roger as Talbot frowned and shook his head impatiently.

Billie, struck with the happy thought of hanging one of his chickies on the Christmas tree, caused them all to laugh at this moment. It was difficult to refuse to be generous on Christmas morning in the presence of the happy child!

"Well," said Talbot, a reluctant smile crossing his face, "I guess it's all in the family anyway."

The Hopper, feeling that his work as the Reversible Santa Claus was finished, was rapidly retreating through the dining-room when Muriel and Roger ran after him.

"We're going to take you home," cried Muriel, beaming.

"Yer car's at the back gate, all right-side-up," said The Hopper, "but I kin go on the trolley."

"Indeed you won't! Roger will take you home. Oh, don't be alarmed! My husband knows everything about our conspiracy. And we want you to come back this afternoon. You know I owe you an apology for thinking—for thinking you were—you were—a—"

"They's things wot is an' things wot ain't, miss. Circumstantial evidence sends lots o' men to th' chair. Ut's a heap more happy like," The

Hopper continued in his best philosophical vein, "t' play th' white card, helpin' widders an' orfants an' settlin' fusses. When ye ast me t' steal them jugs I hadn't th' heart t' refuse ye, miss. I wuz scared to tell ye I had yer baby an' ye seemed so sort o' trustin' like. An' ut bein' Chris'mus an' all."

When he steadfastly refused to promise to return, Muriel announced that they would visit The Hopper late in the afternoon and bring Billie along to express their thanks more formally.

"I'll be glad to see ye," replied The Hopper, though a little doubtfully and shame-facedly. "But ye mustn't git me into no more house-breakin' scrapes," he added with a grin. "It's mighty dangerous, miss, fer amachures, like me an' yer pa!"

X

Mary was not wholly pleased at the prospect of visitors, but she fell to work with Humpy to put the house in order. At five o'clock not one, but three automobiles drove into the yard, filling Humpy with alarm lest at last The Hopper's sins had overtaken him and they were all about to be hauled away to spend the rest of their lives in prison. It was not the police, but the young Talbots, with Billie and his grandfathers, on their way to a family celebration at the house of an aunt of Muriel's.

The grandfathers were restored to perfect amity, and were deeply curious now about The Hopper, whom the peace-loving Muriel had cajoled into robbing their houses.

"And you're only an honest chicken farmer, after all!" exclaimed Talbot, senior, when they were all sitting in a semicircle about the fireplace in Mary's parlor. "I hoped you were really a burglar; I always wanted to know a burglar."

Humpy had chopped down a small fir that had adorned the front yard and had set it up as a Christmas tree—an attention that was not lost upon Billie. The Hopper had brought some mechanical toys from town and Humpy essayed the agreeable task of teaching the youngster how to operate them. Mary produced coffee and pound cake for the guests; The Hopper assumed the rôle of lord of the manor with a benevolent air that was intended as much to impress Mary and Humpy as the guests.

"Of course," said Mr. Wilton, whose appearance was the least bit comical by reason of his bandaged head,—"of course it was very foolish for a man of your sterling character to allow a young woman like my daughter to bully you into robbing houses for her. Why, when Roger fired at you as you were jumping out of the window, he didn't miss you more than a foot! It would have been ghastly for all of us if he had killed you!"

"Well, o' course it all begun from my goin' into th' little house lookin' fer Shaver's folks," replied The Hopper.

"But you haven't told us how you came to find our house," said Roger, suggesting a perfectly natural line of inquiries that caused Humpy to become deeply preoccupied with a pump he was operating in a basin of water for Billie's benefit.

"Well, ut jes' looked like a house that Shaver would belong to, cute an' comfortable like," said The Hopper; "I jes' suspicioned it wuz th' place as I wuz passin' along."

"I don't think we'd better begin trying to establish alibis," remarked Muriel, very gently, "for we might get into terrible scrapes. Why, if Mr. Stevens hadn't been so splendid about *everything* and wasn't just the kindest man in the world, he could make it very ugly for *me*."

"I shudder to think of what he might do to me," said Wilton, glancing guardedly at his neighbor.

"The main thing," said Talbot,—"the main thing is that Mr. Stevens has done for us all what nobody else could ever have done. He's made us see how foolish it is to quarrel about mere baubles. He's settled all our troubles for us, and for my part I'll say his solution is entirely satisfactory."

"Quite right," ejaculated Wilton. "If I ever have any delicate business negotiations that are beyond my powers I'm going to engage Mr. Stevens to handle them."

"My business's hens an' eggs," said The Hopper modestly; "an' we're doin' purty well."

When they rose to go (a move that evoked strident protests from Billie, who was enjoying himself hugely with Humpy) they were all in the jolliest humor.

"We must be neighborly," said Muriel, shaking hands with Mary, who was at the point of tears so great was her emotion at the success of The Hopper's party. "And we're going to buy all our chickens and eggs from you. We never have any luck raising our own."

Whereupon The Hopper imperturbably pressed upon each of the visitors a neat card stating his name (his latest and let us hope his last!) with the proper rural route designation of Happy Hill Farm.

The Hopper carried Billie out to his Grandfather Wilton's car, while Humpy walked beside him bearing the gifts from the Happy Hill Farm Christmas tree. From the door Mary watched them depart amid a chorus of merry Christmases, out of which Billie's little pipe rang cheerily.

When The Hopper and Humpy returned to the house, they abandoned the parlor for the greater coziness of the kitchen and there took account of the events of the momentous twenty-four hours.

"Them's what I call nice folks," said Humpy. "They jes' put us on an' wore us like we wuz a pair o' ole slippers."

"They wuzn't uppish—not to speak of," Mary agreed. "I guess that girl's got more gumption than any of 'em. She's got 'em straightened up now and I guess she'll take care they don't cut up no more monkey-shines about that Chinese stuff. Her husban' seemed sort o' gentle like."

"Artists is that way," volunteered The Hopper, as though from deep experience of art and life. "I jes' been thinkin' that knowin' folks like

that an' findin' 'em humin, makin' mistakes like th' rest of us, kind o' makes ut seem easier fer us all t' play th' game straight. Ut's goin' to be th' white card fer me—jes' chickens an' eggs, an' here's hopin' the bulls don't ever find out we're settled here."

Humpy, having gone into the parlor to tend the fire, returned with two envelopes he had found on the mantel. There was a check for a thousand dollars in each, one from Wilton, the other from Talbot, with "Merry Christmas" written across the visiting-cards of those gentlemen. The Hopper permitted Mary and Humpy to examine them and then laid them on the kitchen table, while he deliberated. His meditations were so prolonged that they grew nervous.

"I reckon they could spare ut, after all ye done fer 'em, Hop," remarked Humpy.

"They's millionaires, an' money ain't nothin' to 'em," said The Hopper.

"We can buy a motor-truck," suggested Mary, "to haul our stuff to town; an' mebbe we can build a new shed to keep ut in."

The Hopper set the catsup bottle on the checks and rubbed his cheek, squinting at the ceiling in the manner of one who means to be careful of his speech.

"They's things wot is an' things wot ain't," he began. "We ain't none o' us ever got nowheres bein' crooked. I been figurin' that I still got about twenty thousan' o' that bunch o' green I pulled out o' that express car, planted in places where 'taint doin' nobody no good. I guess ef I do ut careful I kin send ut back to the company, a little at a time, an' they'd never know where ut come from."

Mary wept; Humpy stared, his mouth open, his one eye rolling queerly.

"I guess we kin put a little chunk away every year," The Hopper went on. "We'd be comfortabler doin' ut. We could square up ef we lived long enough, which we don't need t' worry about, that bein' the Lord's business. You an' me's cracked a good many safes, Hump, but we never made no money at ut, takin' out th' time we done."

"He's got religion; that's wot he's got!" moaned Humpy, as though this marked the ultimate tragedy of The Hopper's life.

"Mebbe ut's religion an' mebbe ut's jes' sense," pursued The Hopper, unshaken by Humpy's charge. "They wuz a chaplin in th' Minnesoty pen as used t' say ef we're all square with our own selves ut's goin' to be all right with God. I guess I got a good deal o' squarin' t' do, but I'm goin' t' begin ut. An' all these things happenin' along o' Chris'mus, an' little Shaver an' his ma bein' so friendly like, an' her gittin' me t' help straighten out them ole gents, an' doin' all I done an' not gittin' pinched seems more 'n jes' luck; it's providential's wot ut is!"

This, uttered in a challenging tone, evoked a sob from Humpy, who announced that he "felt like" he was going to die.

"It's th' Chris'mus time, I reckon," said Mary, watching The Hopper deposit the two checks in the clock. "It's the only decent Chris'mus I ever knowed!"

A SHERLOCKIAN

Little Christmas

A SCANDAL IN WINTER

Gillian Linscott

GILLIAN LINSCOTT IS A PROFESSIONAL WRITER who began as a journalist for *The Guardian* and the BBC before becoming a full-time author of mystery fiction. In that genre, she has shown range, with her major books being about the suffragette detective Nell Bray, for which she has won the (British) Crime Writers' Association Ellis Peters Historical Dagger. She has also written stories set in ancient Egypt and is an aficionado of Sherlock Holmes, having written stories for such anthologies as *Murder in Baker Street* (New York, Carroll & Graf, 2001) and *Sherlock Holmes in America* (New York, Skyhorse, 2009). "A Scandal in Winter" was first published in another Holmes collection, *Holmes for the Holidays*, edited by Martin H. Greenberg, Jon L. Lellenberg, and Carol-Lynn Waugh (New York, Berkley, 1996).

A Scandal in Winter

GILLIAN LINSCOTT

AT FIRST SILVER STICK AND HIS Square Bear were no more to us than incidental diversions at the Hotel Edelweiss. The Edelweiss at Christmas and the new year was like a sparkling white desert island, or a very luxurious ocean liner sailing through snow instead of sea. There we were, a hundred people or so, cut off from the rest of the world, even from the rest of Switzerland, with only each other for entertainment and company. It was one of the only possible hotels to stay at in 1910 for this new fad of winter sporting. The smaller Berghaus across the way was not one of the possible hotels, so its dozen or so visitors hardly counted. As for the villagers in their wooden chalets with the cows living downstairs, they didn't count at all. Occasionally, on walks, Amanda and I would see them carrying in logs from neatly stacked woodpiles or carrying out forkfuls of warm soiled straw that sent columns of white steam into the blue air. They were part of the valley like the rocks and pine trees but they didn't ski or skate, so they had no place in our world—apart from the sleighs. There were two of those in the village. One, a sober affair drawn by a stolid bay cob with a few token bells on the harness, brought guests and their luggage from the nearest railway station. The other, the one that mattered to Amanda and me, was a streak of black and scarlet, swift as the mountain wind, clamourous with silver bells, drawn by a sleek little honey-coloured Haflinger with a silvery mane and tail

that matched the bells. A pleasure sleigh, with no purpose in life beyond amusing the guests at the Edelweiss. We'd see it drawn up in the trampled snow outside, the handsome young owner with his long whip and blonde moustache waiting patiently. Sometimes we'd be allowed to linger and watch as he helped in a lady and gentleman and adjusted the white fur rug over their laps. Then away they'd go, hissing and jingling through the snow, into the track through the pine forest. Amanda and I had been promised that, as a treat on New Year's Day, we would be taken for a ride in it. We looked forward to it more eagerly than Christmas.

But that was ten days away and until then we had to amuse ourselves. We skated on the rink behind the hotel. We waved good-bye to our father when he went off in the mornings with his skis and his guide. We sat on the hotel terrace drinking hot chocolate with blobs of cream on top while Mother wrote and read letters. When we thought Mother wasn't watching, Amanda and I would compete to see if we could drink all the chocolate so that the blob of cream stayed marooned at the bottom of the cup, to be eaten in luscious and impolite spoonfuls. If she glanced up and caught us, Mother would tell us not to be so childish, which, since Amanda was eleven and I was nearly thirteen, was fair enough, but we had to get what entertainment we could out of the chocolate. The truth was that we were all of us, most of the time, bored out of our wits. Which was why we turned our attention to the affairs of the other guests and Amanda and I had our ears permanently tuned to the small dramas of the adults' conversation.

"I still can't believe she will."

"Well, that's what the headwaiter said, and he should know. She's reserved the table in the corner overlooking the terrace and said they should be sure to have the Tokay."

"The same table as last year."

"The same wine, too."

Our parents looked at each other over the croissants, carefully not noticing the maid as she poured our coffee. ("One doesn't notice the servants, dear, it only makes them awkward.")

"I'm sure it's not true. Any woman with any feeling . . ."

"What makes you think she has any?"

Silence, as eye signals went on over our heads. I knew what was being signalled, just as I'd known what was being discussed in an overheard scrap of conversation between our parents at bedtime the night we arrived. ". . . effect it might have on Jessica."

My name. I came rapidly out of drowsiness, kept my eyes closed but listened.

"I don't think we need worry about that. Jessica's tougher than you think." My mother's voice. She needed us to be tough so that she didn't have to waste time worrying about us.

"All the same, she must remember it. It is only a year ago. That sort of experience can mark a child for life."

"Darling, they don't react like we do. They're much more callous at that age."

Even with eyes closed I could tell from the quality of my father's silence that he wasn't convinced, but it was no use arguing with Mother's certainties. They switched the light off and closed the door. For a minute or two I lay awake in the dark wondering whether I was marked for life by what I'd seen and how it would show, then I wondered instead whether I'd ever be able to do pirouettes on the ice like the girl from Paris,

and fell asleep in a wistful dream of bells and the hiss of skates.

The conversation between our parents that breakfast time over what she would or wouldn't do was interrupted by the little stir of two other guests being shown to their table. Amanda caught my eye.

"Silver Stick and his Square Bear are going ski-ing."

Both gentlemen—elderly gentlemen as it seemed to us, but they were probably no older than their late fifties—were wearing heavy wool jumpers, tweed breeches, and thick socks, just as Father was. He nodded to them across the tables, wished them good morning and received nods and good-mornings back. Even the heavy sports clothing couldn't take away the oddity and distinction from the tall man. He was, I think, the thinnest person I'd ever seen. He didn't stoop as so many tall older people did but walked upright and lightly. His face with its eagle's beak of a nose was deeply tanned, like some of the older inhabitants of the village, but unlike them it was without wrinkles apart from two deep folds from the nose to the corners of his mouth. His hair was what had struck us most. It clung smoothly to his head in a cap of pure and polished silver, like the knob on an expensive walking stick. His companion, large and square shouldered in any case, looked more so in his ski-ing clothes. He shambled and tended to trip over chairs. He had a round, amiable face with pale, rather watery eyes, a clipped grey moustache but no more than a fringe of hair left on his gleaming pate. He always smiled at us when we met on the terrace or in corridors and appeared kindly. We'd noticed that he was always doing things for Silver Stick, pouring his coffee, posting his letters. For this reason we'd got it into our heads that Square Bear was Silver Stick's keeper. Amanda said Silver Stick probably went mad at the full moon and Square Bear had to lock him up and sing loudly so that people wouldn't hear his howling. She kept asking people when the next full moon would be, but so far nobody knew. I thought he'd probably come to Switzerland because he was dying of consumption, which explained the thinness, and Square Bear was his doctor. I listened for a coughing fit to confirm this, but so far there'd been not a sign of one. As they settled to their breakfast we watched as much as we could without being rebuked for staring. Square Bear opened the paper that had been lying beside his plate and read things out to Silver Stick, who gave the occasional little nod over his coffee, as if he'd known whatever it was all the time. It was the *Times* of London and must have been at least two days old because it had to come up from the station in the sleigh.

Amanda whispered: "He eats."

The waiter had brought a rack of toast and a stone jar of Oxford marmalade to their table instead of croissants. Silver Stick was eating toast like any normal person.

Father asked: "Who eats?"

We indicated with our eyes.

"Well, why shouldn't he eat? You need a lot of energy for ski-ing."

Mother, taking an interest for once, said they seemed old for ski-ing.

"You'd be surprised. Dr. Watson's not bad, but as for the other one—well, he went past me like a bird in places so steep that even the guide didn't want to try it. And stayed standing up at the end of it when most of us would have been just a big hole in the snow. The man's so rational he's completely without fear. It's fear that wrecks you when you're ski-ing. You come to a steep place, you think you're going to fall and nine times out of ten, you do fall. Holmes comes to the same steep place, doesn't see any reason why he can't do it—so he does it."

My mother said that anybody really rational would have the sense not to go ski-ing in the first place. My ear had been caught by one word.

"Square Bear's a doctor? Is Silver Stick ill?"

"Not that I know. Is there any more coffee in that pot?"

And there we left it for the while. You might say that Amanda and I should have known at once who they were, and I suppose nine out of ten children in Europe would have known. But we'd led an unusual life, mainly on account of Mother, and although we knew many things unknown to most girls of our age, we were ignorant of a lot of others that were common currency.

We waved off Father and his guide as they went wallowing up in the deep snow through the pine trees, skis on their shoulders, then turned back for our skates. We stopped at the driveway to let the sober black sleigh go past, the one that went down the valley to the railway. There was nobody in the back, but the rugs were ready and neatly folded.

"Somebody new coming," Amanda said.

I knew Mother was looking at me, but she said nothing. Amanda and I were indoors doing our holiday reading when the sleigh came back, so we didn't see who was in it, but when we went downstairs later there was a humming tension about the hotel, like the feeling you get when a violinist is holding his bow just above the string and the tingle of the note runs up and down your spine before you hear it. It was only mid-afternoon but dusk was already settling on the valley. We were allowed a last walk outside before it got dark, and made as usual for the skating rink. Coloured electric lights were throwing patches of yellow, red, and blue on the dark surface. The lame man with the accordion was playing a Strauss waltz and a few couples were skating to it, though not very well. More were clustered round the charcoal brazier at the edge of the rink where a waiter poured small glasses of mulled wine. Perhaps the man with the accordion knew the dancers were getting tired or wanted to go home himself, because when the waltz ended he changed to something wild and gypsy sounding, harder to dance to. The couples on the ice tried it for a few steps, then gave up, laughing, to join the others round the brazier. For a while the ice was empty and the lame man played on to the dusk and the dark mountains.

Then a figure came gliding onto the ice. There was a decisiveness about the way she did it that marked her out at once from the other skaters. They'd come on staggering or swaggering, depending on whether they were beginners or thought themselves expert, but staggerers and swaggerers alike had a self-conscious air, knowing that this was not their natural habitat. She took to the ice like a swan to the water or a swallow to the air. The laughter died away, the drinking stopped and we watched as she swooped and dipped and circled all alone to the gypsy music. There were no showy pirouettes like the girl from Paris, no folding of the arms and look-at-me smiles. It's quite likely that she was not a particularly expert skater, that what was so remarkable about it was her willingness to take the rink, the music, the attention as hers by right. She wasn't even dressed for skating. The black skirt coming to within a few inches of the instep of her skate boots, the black mink jacket, the matching cap, were probably what she'd been wearing on the journey up from the station. But she'd been ready for this, had planned to announce her return exactly this way.

Her return. At first, absorbed by the performance, I hadn't recognised her. I'd registered that she was not a young woman and that she was elegant. It was when a little of my attention came back to my mother that I knew. She was standing there as stiff and prickly as one of the pine trees, staring at the figure on the ice like everybody else, but it wasn't admiration on her face, more a kind of horror. They were all looking like that, all the adults, as if she were the messenger of something dangerous. Then a woman's voice, not my mother's, said, "How could she? Really, how could she?"

There was a murmuring of agreement and I could feel the horror changing to something more commonplace—social disapproval. Once the first words had been said, others followed and there was a rustling of sharp little phrases like a sledge runner grating on gravel.

"Only a year . . . to come here again . . . no respect . . . lucky not to be . . . after what happened."

My mother put a firm hand on each of our shoulders. "Time for your tea."

Normally we'd have protested, begged for another few minutes, but we knew that this was serious. To get into the hotel from the ice rink you go up some steps to the back terrace and in at the big glass doors to the breakfast room. There were two men standing on the terrace. From there you could see the rink and they were staring down at what was happening. Silver Stick and Square Bear. I saw the thin man's eyes in the light from the breakfast room. They were harder and more intent than anything I'd ever seen, harder than the ice itself. Normally, being properly brought up, we'd have said good evening to them as we went past, but Mother propelled us inside without speaking. As soon as she'd got us settled at the table she went to find Father, who'd be back from ski-ing by then. I knew they'd be talking about me and felt important, but concerned that I couldn't live up to that importance. After all, what I'd seen had lasted only a few seconds and I hadn't felt any of the things I was supposed to feel. I'd never known him before it happened, apart from seeing him across the dining room a few times and I hadn't even known he was dead until they told me afterwards.

What happened at dinner that evening was like the ice rink, only without gypsy music. That holiday Amanda and I were allowed to come down to dinner with our parents for the soup course. After the soup we were supposed to say good night politely and go up and put ourselves to bed. People who'd been skating and ski-ing all day were hungry by evening so usually attention was concentrated discreetly on the swing doors to the kitchen and the procession of waiters with the silver tureens. That night was different. The focus of attention was one small table in the corner of the room beside the window. A table laid like the rest of them with white linen, silver cutlery, gold-bordered plates, and a little array of crystal glasses. A table for one. An empty table.

My father said: "Looks as if she's funked it. Can't say I blame her."

My mother gave him one of her "be quiet" looks, announced that this was our evening for speaking French and asked me in that language to pass her some bread, if I pleased.

I had my back to the door and my hand on the breadbasket. All I knew was that the room went quiet.

"Don't turn round," my mother hissed in English.

I turned round and there she was, in black velvet and diamonds. Her hair, with more streaks of grey than I remembered from the year before, was swept up and secured with a pearl-and-diamond comb. The previous year, before the thing happened, my mother had remarked that she was surprisingly slim for a retired opera singer. This year she was thin, cheekbones and collarbones above the black velvet bodice sharp enough to cut paper. She was inclining her elegant head towards the headwaiter, probably listening to words of welcome. He was smiling, but then he smiled at everybody. Nobody else smiled as she followed him to the table in the far, the very far, corner. You could hear the creak of necks screwing themselves away from her. No entrance she ever made in her stage career could have been as nerve racking as that long walk across the hotel floor. In spite of the silent commands now radiating from my mother, I could no more have turned away from her than from Blondin crossing Niagara Falls. My disobedience was rewarded, as disobedience so often is, because I saw it happen. In the middle of that silent dining room, amid a hundred or so people pretending not to notice her, I saw Silver Stick get to his feet. Among all those seated people he looked even taller than before, his burnished silver head gleaming like snow on the Matterhorn above that rock ridge of a nose, below it the glacial white and black of his evening clothes. Square Bear hesitated for a moment, then followed his example. As in her lonely walk she came alongside their table, Silver Stick bowed with the dignity of a man who did not have to bow very often, and again Square Bear copied him, less elegantly. Square Bear's face was red

and flustered, but the other man's hadn't altered. She paused for a moment, gravely returned their bows with a bend of her white neck, then walked on. The silence through the room lasted until the headwaiter pulled out her chair and she sat down at her table, then, as if on cue, the waiters with their tureens came marching through the swinging doors and the babble and the clash of cutlery sounded as loud as war starting.

At breakfast I asked Mother: "Why did they bow to her?" I knew it was a banned subject, but I knew too that I was in an obscurely privileged position, because of the effect all this was supposed to be having me. I wondered when it would come out, like secret writing on a laurel leaf you keep close to your chest to warm it. When I was fourteen, eighteen?

"Don't ask silly questions. And you don't need two lumps of sugar in your café au lait."

Father suggested a trip to the town down the valley after lunch, to buy Christmas presents. It was meant as a distraction and it worked to an extent, but I still couldn't get her out of my mind. Later that morning, when I was supposed to be having a healthy snowball fight with boring children, I wandered away to the back terrace overlooking the ice rink. I hoped that I might find her again, but it was occupied by noisy beginners, slithering and screeching. I despised them for their ordinariness.

I'd turned away and was looking at the back of the hotel, thinking no particular thoughts, when I heard footsteps behind me and a voice said: "Was that where you were standing when it happened?"

It was the first time I'd heard Silver Stick's voice at close quarters. It was a pleasant voice, deep but clear, like the sea in a cave. He was standing there in his rough tweed jacket and cap with earflaps only a few yards away from me. Square Bear stood behind him, looking anxious, neck muffled in a woollen scarf. I considered, looked up at the roof again and down to my feet.

"Yes, it must have been about here."

"Holmes, don't you think we should ask this little girl's mother? She might . . ."

"My mother wasn't there. I was."

Perhaps I'd learnt something already about taking the centre of the stage. The thought came to me that it would be a great thing if he bowed to me, as he'd bowed to her.

"Quite so."

He didn't bow, but he seemed pleased.

"You see, Watson, Miss Jessica isn't in the least hysterical about it, are you?"

I saw that he meant that as a compliment, so I gave him the little inclination of the head that I'd been practising in front of the mirror when Amanda wasn't looking. He smiled, and there was more warmth in the smile than seemed likely from the height and sharpness of him.

"I take it that you have no objection to talking about what you saw."

I said graciously: "Not in the very least." Then honesty compelled me to spoil it by adding, "Only I didn't see very much."

"It's not how much you saw, but how clearly you saw it. I wonder if you'd kindly tell Dr. Watson and me exactly what you saw, in as much detail as you can remember."

The voice was gentle, but there was no gentleness in the dark eyes fixed on me. I don't mean they were hard or cruel, simply that emotion of any sort had no more part in them than in the lens of a camera or telescope. They gave me an odd feeling, not fear exactly, but as if I'd become real in a way I hadn't quite been before. I knew that being clear about what I'd seen that day a year ago mattered more than anything I'd ever done. I closed my eyes and thought hard.

"I was standing just here. I was waiting for Mother and Amanda because we were going out for a walk and Amanda had lost one of her fur gloves as usual. I saw him falling, then he hit the roof over the dining room and came sliding down it. The snow started moving as well, so he came down with the snow. He landed just over there, where that chair is, and all the rest of the snow came down on top of him, so you could only see his arm sticking out. The arm

wasn't moving, but I didn't know he was dead. A lot of people came running and started pushing the snow away from him, then somebody said I shouldn't be there so they took me away to find Mother, so I wasn't there when they got the snow off him."

I stopped, short of breath. Square Bear was looking ill at ease and pitying but Silver Stick's eyes hadn't changed.

"When you were waiting for your mother and sister, which way were you facing?"

"The rink. I was watching the skaters."

"Quite so. That meant you were facing away from the hotel."

"Yes."

"And yet you saw the man falling?"

"Yes."

"What made you turn round?"

I'd no doubt about that. It was the part of my story that everybody had been most concerned with at the time.

"He shouted."

"Shouted what?"

"Shouted 'No.'"

"When did he shout it?"

I hesitated. Nobody had asked me that before because the answer was obvious.

"When he fell."

"Of course, but at what point during his fall? I take it that it was before he landed on the roof over the dining room or you wouldn't have turned round in time to see it."

"Yes."

"And you turned round in time to see him in the air and falling?"

"Holmes, I don't think you should . . ."

"Oh, do be quiet, Watson. Well, Miss Jessica?"

"Yes, he was in the air and falling."

"And he'd already screamed by then. So at what point did he scream?"

I wanted to be clever and grown up, to make him think well of me.

"I suppose it was when she pushed him out of the window."

It was Square Bear's face that showed most

emotion. He screwed up his eyes, went red, and made little imploring signs with his fur-mittened hands, causing him to look more bear-like than ever. This time the protest was not at his friend, but at me. Silver Stick put up a hand to stop him saying anything, but his face had changed too, with a sharp V on the forehead. The voice was a shade less gentle.

"When who pushed him out of the window?"

"His wife, Mrs. McEvoy."

I wondered whether to add, "The woman you bowed to last night," but decided against it.

"Did you see her push him?"

"No."

"Did you see Mrs. McEvoy at the window?"

"No."

"And yet you tell me that Mrs. McEvoy pushed her husband out of the window. Why?"

"Everybody knows she did."

I knew from the expression on Square Bear's face that I'd gone badly wrong, but couldn't see where. He, kindly man, must have guessed that because he started trying to explain to me.

"You see, my dear, after many years with my good friend Mr. Holmes . . ."

Yet again he was waved into silence.

"Miss Jessica, Dr. Watson means well but I hope he will permit me to speak for myself. It's a fallacy to believe that age in itself brings wisdom, but one thing it infallibly brings is experience. Will you permit me, from my experience if not from my wisdom, to offer you a little advice?"

I nodded, not gracious now, just awed.

"Then my advice is this: always remember that what everybody knows, nobody knows."

He used that voice like a skater uses his weight on the blade to skim or turn.

"You say everybody knows that Mrs. McEvoy pushed her husband out of the window. As far as I know you are the only person in the world who saw Mr. McEvoy fall. And yet, as you've told me, you did not see Mrs. McEvoy push him. So who is this 'everybody' who can claim such certainty about an event which, as far as we know, nobody witnessed?"

It's miserable not knowing answers. What is nineteen times three? What is the past participle of the verb *faire*? I wanted to live up to him, but unwittingly he'd pressed the button that brought on the panic of the schoolroom. I blurted out: "He was very rich and she didn't love him, and now she's very rich and can do what she likes."

Again the bear's fur mitts went up, scrabbling the air. Again he was disregarded.

"So Mrs. McEvoy is rich and can do what she likes? Does it strike you that she's happy?"

"Holmes, how can a child know . . . ?"

I thought of the gypsy music, the gleaming dark fur, the pearls in her hair. I found myself shaking my head.

"No. And yet she comes here again, exactly a year after her husband died, the very place in the world that you'd expect her to avoid at all costs. She comes here knowing what people are saying about her, making sure everybody has a chance to see her, holding her head high. Have you any idea what that must do to a woman?"

This time Square Bear really did protest and went on protesting. How could he expect a child to know about the feelings of a mature woman? How could I be blamed for repeating the gossip of my elders? Really, Holmes, it was too much. This time too Silver Stick seemed to agree with him. He smoothed out the V shape in his forehead and apologised.

"Let us, if we may, return to the surer ground of what you actually saw. I take it that the hotel has not been rebuilt in any way since last year."

I turned again to look at the back of the hotel. As far as I could see, it was just as it had been, the glass doors leading from the dining room and breakfast room onto the terrace, a tiled sloping roof above them. Then, joined onto the roof, the three main guest floors of the hotel. The top two floors were the ones that most people took because they had wrought-iron balconies where, on sunny days, you could stand to look at the mountains. Below them were the smaller rooms. They were less popular because, being directly above the kitchen and dining room, they suffered from noise and cooking smells and had no balconies.

Silver Stick said to Square Bear: "That was the room they had last year, top floor, second from the right. So if he were pushed, he'd have to be pushed over the balcony as well as out of the window. That would take quite a lot of strength, wouldn't you say?"

The next question was to me. He asked if I'd seen Mr. McEvoy before he fell out of the window and I said yes, a few times.

"Was he a small man?"

"No, quite big."

"The same size as Dr. Watson here, for instance?"

Square Bear straightened his broad shoulders, as if for military inspection.

"He was fatter."

"Younger or older?"

"Quite old. As old as you are."

Square Bear made a chuffing sound and his shoulders slumped a little.

"So we have a man about the same age as our friend Watson and heavier. Difficult, wouldn't you say, for any woman to push him anywhere against his will?"

"Perhaps she took him by surprise, told him to lean out and look at something, then swept his legs off the floor."

That wasn't my own theory. The event had naturally been analysed in all its aspects the year before and all the parental care in the world couldn't have kept it from me.

"A touching picture. Shall we come back to things we know for certain? What about the snow? Was there as much snow as this last year?"

"I think so. It came up above my knees last year. It doesn't quite this year, but then I've grown."

Square Bear murmured: "They'll keep records of that sort of thing."

"Just so, but we're also grateful for Miss Jessica's calibrations. May we trouble you with just one more question?"

I said yes rather warily.

"You've told us that just before you turned round and saw him falling you heard him shout 'No.' What sort of 'No' was it?"

I was puzzled. Nobody had asked me that before.

"Was it an angry 'No'? A protesting 'No'? The kind of 'No' you'd shout if somebody were pushing you over a balcony?"

The other man looked as if he wanted to protest again but kept quiet. The intensity in Silver Stick's eyes would have frozen a brook in mid-babble. When I didn't answer at once he visibly made himself relax and his voice went softer.

"It's hard for you to remember, isn't it? Everybody was so sure that it was one particular sort of 'No' that they've fixed their version in your mind. I want you to do something for me, if you would be so kind. I want you to forget that Dr. Watson and I are here and stand and look down at the ice rink just as you were doing last year. I want you to clear your mind of everything else and think that it really is last year and you're hearing that shout for the first time. Will you do that?"

I faced away from them. First I looked at this year's skaters then I closed my eyes and tried to remember how it had been. I felt the green itchy scarf round my neck, the cold getting to my toes and fingers as I waited. I heard the cry and it was all I could do not to turn round and see the body tumbling again. When I opened my eyes and looked at them they were still waiting patiently.

"I think I've remembered."

"And what sort of 'No' was it?"

It was clear in my mind but hard to put into words.

"It . . . it was as if he'd been going to say something else if he'd had time. Not just no. No something."

"No something what?"

More silence while I thought about it, then a prompt from Square Bear.

"Could it have been a name, my dear?"

"Don't put any more ideas into her head. You thought he was going to say something after the no, but you don't know what, is that it?"

"Yes, like no running, or no cakes today, only that wasn't it. Something you couldn't do."

"Or something not there, like the cakes?"

"Yes, something like that. Only it couldn't have been, could it?"

"Couldn't? If something happened in a particular way, then it happened, and there's no could or couldn't about it."

It was the kind of thing governesses said, but he was smiling now and I had the idea that something I'd said had pleased him.

"I see your mother and sister coming, so I'm afraid we must end this very useful conversation. I am much obliged to you for your powers of observation. Will you permit me to ask you some more questions if any more occur to me?"

I nodded.

"Is it a secret?"

"Do you want it to be?"

"Holmes, I don't think you should encourage this young lady . . ."

"My dear Watson, in my observation there's nothing more precious you can give a child to keep than a secret."

My mother came across the terrace with Amanda. Silver Stick and Square Bear touched their hats to her and hoped we enjoyed our walk. When she asked me later what we'd been talking about I said they'd asked whether the snow was as deep last year and hugged the secret of my partnership. I became in my imagination eyes and ears for him. At the children's party at teatime on Christmas Eve the parents talked in low tones, believing that we were absorbed in the present giving round the hotel tree. But it would have taken more than the porter in red robe and white whiskers or his largesse of three wooden geese on a string to distract me from my work. I listened and stored up every scrap against the time when he'd ask me questions again. And I watched Mrs. McEvoy as she went round the hotel through Christmas Eve and Christmas Day, pale and upright in her black and her jewels, trailing silence after her like the long train of a dress.

My call came on Boxing Day. There was another snowball fight in the hotel grounds, for parents as well this time. I stood back from it all and waited by a little clump of bare birches and,

sure enough, Silver Stick and Square Bear came walking over to me.

"I've found out a lot about her," I said.

"Have you indeed?"

"He was her second husband. She had another one she loved more, but he died of a fever. It was when they were visiting Egypt a long time ago."

"Ten years ago."

Silver Stick's voice was remote. He wasn't even looking at me.

"She got married to Mr. McEvoy three years ago. Most people said it was for his money, but there was an American lady at the party and she said Mr. McEvoy seemed quite nice when you first knew him and he was interested in music and singers, so perhaps it was one of those marriages where people quite like each other without being in love, you know?"

I thought I'd managed that rather well. I'd tried to make it like my mother talking to her friends and it sounded convincing in my ears. I was disappointed at the lack of reaction, so brought out my big guns.

"Only she didn't stay liking him because after they got married she found out about his eye."

"His eye?"

A reaction at last, but from Square Bear, not Silver Stick. I grabbed for the right word and clung to it.

"Roving. It was a roving eye. He kept looking at other ladies and she didn't like it."

I hoped they'd understand that it meant looking in a special way. I didn't know myself exactly what special way, but the adults talking among themselves at the party had certainly understood. But it seemed I'd over-estimated these two because they were just standing there staring at me. Perhaps Silver Stick wasn't as clever as I'd thought. I threw in my last little oddment of information, something anybody could understand.

"I found out her first name. It's Irene."

Square Bear cleared his throat. Silver Stick said nothing. He was looking over my head at the snowball fight.

"Holmes, I really think we should leave Jessica to play with her little friends."

"Not yet. There's something I wanted to ask her. Do you remember the staff at the hotel last Christmas?"

Here was a dreadful comedown. I'd brought him a head richly crammed with love, money, and marriages and he was asking about the domestics. Perhaps the disappointment on my face looked like stupidity because his voice became impatient.

"The people who looked after you, the porters and the waiters and the maids, especially the maids."

"They're the same . . . I think." I was running them through my head. There was Petra with her thick plaits who brought us our cups of chocolate, fat Renata who made our beds, grey-haired Ulrike with her limp.

"None left?"

"I don't think so."

Then the memory came to me of blonde curls escaping from a maid's uniform cap and a clear voice singing as she swept the corridors, blithe as a bird.

"There was Eva, but she got married."

"Who did she marry?"

"Franz, the man who's got the sleigh."

It was flying down the drive as I spoke, silver bells jangling, the little horse gold in the sunshine.

"A good marriage for a hotel maid."

"Oh, he didn't have the sleigh last year. He was only the under porter."

"Indeed. Watson, I think we must have a ride in this sleigh. Will you see the head porter about booking it?"

I hoped he might invite me to go with them but he said nothing about that. Still, he seemed to be in a good temper again—although I couldn't see that it was from anything I'd told him.

"Miss Jessica, again I'm obliged to you. I may have yet another favour to ask, but all in good time."

I went reluctantly to join the snowballers as the two of them walked through the snow back to the hotel.

That afternoon, on our walk, they went past us on their way down the drive in Franz's sleigh. It didn't look like a pleasure trip. Franz's handsome face was serious and Holmes was staring straight ahead. Instead of turning up towards the forest at the end of the hotel drive they turned left for the village. Our walk also took us to the village because Father wanted to see an old man about getting a stick carved. When we walked down the little main street we saw the sleigh and horse standing outside a neat chalet with green shutters next to the church. I knew it was Franz's own house and wondered what had become of his passengers. About half an hour later, when we'd seen about Father's stick, we walked back up the street and there were Holmes and Watson standing on the balcony outside the chalet with Eva, the maid from last year. Her fair hair was as curly as ever but her head was bent. She seemed to be listening intently to something that Holmes was saying and the droop of her shoulders told me she wasn't happy.

"Why is Silver Stick talking to her?"

Amanda, very properly, was rebuked for staring and asking questions about things that didn't concern her. Being older and wiser, I said nothing but kept my secret coiled in my heart. Was it Eva who pushed him? Would they lock her up in prison? A little guilt stirred along with the pleasure, because he wouldn't have known about Eva if I hadn't told him, but not enough to spoil it. Later I watched from our window hoping to see the sleigh coming back, but it didn't that day. Instead, just before it got dark, Holmes and Watson came back on foot up the drive, walking fast, saying nothing.

Next morning, Square Bear came up to Mother at coffee time. "I wonder if you would permit Miss Jessica to take a short walk with me on the terrace."

Mother hesitated, but Square Bear was so

obviously respectable, and anyway you could see the terrace from the coffee room. I put on my hat, cape, and gloves and walked with him out of the glass doors into the cold air. We stood looking down at the rink, in exactly the same place as I'd been standing when they first spoke to me. I knew that was no accident. Square Bear's fussiness, the tension in his voice that he was so unsuccessful in hiding, left no doubt of it. There was something odd about the terrace, too—far more people on it than would normally be the case on a cold morning. There must have been two dozen or so standing round in stiff little groups, talking to each other, waiting.

"Where's Mr. Holmes?"

Square Bear looked at me, eyes watering from the cold.

"The truth is, my dear, I don't know where he is or what he's doing. He gave me my instructions at breakfast and I haven't seen him since."

"Instructions about me?"

Before he could answer, the scream came. It was a man's scream, tearing through the air like a saw blade, and there was a word in it. The word was "No." I turned with the breath choking in my throat and, just as there'd been last year, there was a dark thing in the air, its clothes flapping out round it. A collective gasp from the people on the terrace, then a soft thump as the thing hit the deep snow on the restaurant roof and began sliding. I heard "No" again and this time it was my own voice, because I knew from last year what was coming next—the slide down the steep roof gathering snow as it came, the flop onto the terrace only a few yards from where I was standing, the arm sticking out.

At first the memory was so strong that I thought that was what I was seeing, and it took a few seconds for me to realise that it wasn't happening that way. The thing had fallen a little to the side and instead of sliding straight down the roof it was being carried to a little ornamental railing at the edge of it, where the main hotel joined onto the annex, driving a wedge of snow in front of it. Then somebody said, unbelievingly: "He's stopped." And the thing had

stopped. Instead of plunging over the roof to the terrace it had been swept up against the railing, bundled in snow like a cylindrical snowball, and stopped within a yard of the edge. Then it sat up, clinging with one hand to the railing, covered from waist down in snow. If he'd been wearing a hat when he came out of the window he'd lost it in the fall because his damp hair was gleaming silver above his smiling brown face. It was an inward kind of smile, as if only he could appreciate the thing that he'd done.

Then the chattering started. Some people were yelling to get a ladder, others running. The rest were asking each other what had happened until somebody spotted the window wide open three floors above us.

"Her window. Mrs. McEvoy's window."

"He fell off Mrs. McEvoy's balcony, just like last year."

"But he didn't . . ."

At some point Square Bear had put a hand on my shoulder. Now he bent down beside me, looking anxiously into my face, saying we should go in and find Mother. I wished he'd get out of my way because I wanted to see Silver Stick on the roof. Then Mother arrived, wafting clouds of scent and drama. I had to go inside, of course, but not before I'd seen the ladder arrive and Silver Stick coming down it, a little stiffly but dignified. And one more thing. Just as he stepped off the ladder the glass doors to the terrace opened and out she came. She hadn't been there when it happened but now in her black fur jacket, she stepped through the people as if they weren't there, and gave him her hand and thanked him.

At dinner that night she dined alone at her table, as on the other nights, but it took her longer to get to it. Her long walk across the dining room was made longer by all the people who wanted to speak to her, to inquire after her health, to tell her how pleased they were to see her again. It was as if she'd just arrived that afternoon, instead of being there for five days already. There were several posies of flowers on her table that must have been sent up especially from the town, and champagne in a silver bucket beside it. Silver Stick and Square Bear bowed to her as she went past their table, but ordinary polite little nods, not like that first night. The smile she gave them was like the sun coming up.

We were sent off to bed as soon as we'd had our soup as usual. Amanda went to sleep at once but I lay awake, resenting my exile from what mattered. Our parents' sitting room was next to our bedroom and I heard them come in, excited still. Then, soon afterwards, a knock on the door of our suite, the murmur of voices, and my father, a little taken aback, saying yes come in by all means. Then their voices, Square Bear's first, fussing with apologies about it being so late, then Silver Stick's cutting through him: "The fact is, you're owed an explanation, or rather your daughter is. Dr. Watson suggested that we should give it to you so that some time in the future when Jessica's old enough, you may decide to tell her."

If I'd owned a chest of gold and had watched somebody throwing it away in a crowded street I couldn't have been more furious than hearing my secret about to be squandered. My first thought was to rush through to the other room in my nightdress and bare feet and demand that he should speak to me, not to them. Then caution took over, and although I did get out of bed, I went just as far as the door, opened it a crack so that I could hear better, and padded back to bed. There were sounds of chairs being rearranged, people settling into them, then Silver Stick's voice.

"I should say at the start, for reasons we need not go into, that Dr. Watson and I were convinced that Irene McEvoy had not pushed her husband to his death. The question was how to prove it, and in that regard your daughter's evidence was indispensable. She alone saw Mr. McEvoy fall and she alone heard what he shouted. The accurate ear of childhood—once certain adult nonsenses had been discarded—recorded that shout as precisely as a phonograph and knew that strictly speaking it was only half a shout, that Mr. McEvoy, if he'd had time, would have added something else to it."

A pause. I sat up in bed with the counterpane round my neck, straining not to miss a word of his quiet, clear voice.

"No—something. The question was, no what? Mr. McEvoy had expected something to be there and his last thought on earth was surprise at the lack of it, surprise so acute that he was trying to shout it with his last breath. The question was, what that thing could have been."

Silence, waiting for an answer, but nobody said anything.

"If you look up at the back of the hotel from the terrace you will notice one obvious thing. The third and fourth floors have balconies. The second floor does not. The room inhabited by Mr. and Mrs. McEvoy had a balcony. A person staying in the suite would be aware of that. He would not necessarily be aware, unless he were a particularly observant man, that the second-floor rooms had no balconies. Until it was too late. I formed the theory that Mr. McEvoy had not in fact fallen from the window of his own room but from a lower room belonging to somebody else, which accounted for his attempted last words: "No . . . balcony.""

My mother gasped. My father said: "By Jove . . ."

"Once I'd arrived at that conclusion, the question was what Mr. McEvoy was doing in somebody else's room. The possibility of thieving could be ruled out since he was a very rich man. Then he was seeing somebody. The next question was who. And here your daughter was incidentally helpful in a way she is too young to understand. She confided to us in all innocence an overheard piece of adult gossip to the effect that the late Mr. McEvoy had a roving eye."

My father began to laugh, then stifled it. My mother said "Well" in a way that boded trouble for me later.

"Once my attention was directed that way, the answer became obvious. Mr. McEvoy was in somebody else's hotel room for what one might describe as an episode of *galanterie*. But the accident happened in the middle of the morning. Did ever a lady in the history of the world make a romantic assignation for that hour of the day? Therefore it wasn't a lady. So I asked myself what group of people are most likely to be encountered in hotel rooms in mid-morning and the answer was . . ."

"Good heavens, the chambermaid!"

My mother's voice, and Holmes was clearly none too pleased at being interrupted.

"Quite so. Mr. McEvoy had gone to meet a chambermaid. I asked some questions to establish whether any young and attractive chambermaid had left the hotel since last Christmas. There was such a one, named Eva. She'd married the under porter and brought him as a dowry enough money to buy that elegant little sleigh. Now a prudent chambermaid may amass a modest dowry by saving tips, but one look at that sleigh will tell you that Eva's dowry might best be described as, well . . . immodest."

Another laugh from my father, cut off by a look from my mother I could well imagine.

"Dr. Watson and I went to see Eva. I told her what I'd deduced and she, poor girl, confirmed it with some details—the sound of the housekeeper's voice outside, Mr. McEvoy's well-practised but ill-advised tactic of taking refuge on the balcony. You may say that the girl Eva should have confessed at once what had happened . . ."

"I do indeed."

"But bear in mind her position. Not only her post at the hotel but her engagement to the handsome Franz would be forfeited. And, after all, there was no question of anybody being tried in court. The fashionable world was perfectly happy to connive at the story that Mr. McEvoy had fallen accidentally from his window—while inwardly convicting an innocent woman of his murder."

My mother said, sounding quite subdued for once: "But Mrs. McEvoy must have known. Why didn't she say something?"

"Ah, to answer that one needs to know something about Mrs. McEvoy's history, and it so happens that Dr. Watson and I are in that position. A long time ago, before her first happy marriage, Mrs. McEvoy was loved by a prince. He was not, I must admit, a particularly admirable prince, but prince he was. Can you imagine how it felt for a woman to come from that to being deceived with a hotel chambermaid by a man who made his fortune from bathroom furnishings? Can you conceive that a proud woman might choose to be thought a murderess rather than submit to that indignity?"

Another silence, then my mother breathed: "Yes. Yes, I think I can." Then, "Poor woman."

"It was not pity that Irene McEvoy ever needed." Then, in a different tone of voice: "So there you have it. And it is your decision how much, if anything, you decide to pass on to Jessica in due course."

There were sounds of people getting up from chairs, then my father said: "And your, um, demonstration this morning?"

"Oh, that little drama. I knew what had happened, but for Mrs. McEvoy's sake it was necessary to prove to the world she was innocent. I couldn't call Eva as witness because I'd given her my word. I'd studied the pitch of the roof and the depth of the snow and I was scientifically convinced that a man falling from Mrs. McEvoy's balcony would not have landed on the terrace. You know the result."

Good-nights were said, rather subdued, and they were shown out. Through the crack in the door I glimpsed them. As they came level with the crack, Silver Stick, usually so precise in his movements, dropped his pipe and had to kneel to pick it up. As he knelt, his bright eyes met mine through the crack and he smiled, an odd, quick smile unseen by anybody else. He'd known I'd been listening all the time.

When they'd gone Mother and Father sat for a long time in silence.

At last Father said: "If he'd got it wrong, he'd have killed himself."

"Like the ski-ing."

"He must have loved her very much."

"It's his own logic he loves."

But then, my mother always was the unromantic one.

THE CHRISTMAS CLIENT

Edward D. Hoch

WHILE SUCH MASTERS OF THE FORM as Edgar Allan Poe and
O. Henry became famous having written only short stories, and Arthur Conan
Doyle had little success with Sherlock Holmes until he produced short stories, it
has been virtually impossible for an author to earn a living as a short story writer
during the last half century or more, but Edward D. Hoch was a rare exception.
He produced more than nine hundred stories in his career, his most famous being "The Oblong Room" (1967), for which he won the Edgar Award, and "The
Long Way Down" (1965), in which a man goes out the window of a skyscraper
but doesn't land until hours later; it was the basis for a two-hour episode of the
television series *McMillan and Wife*. "The Christmas Client" was first published
in *Holmes for the Holidays*, edited by Martin H. Greenberg, Jon L. Lellenberg,
and Carol-Lynn Waugh (New York, Berkley, 1996).

The Christmas Client

EDWARD D. HOCH

IT WAS ON CHRISTMAS DAY OF THE year 1888, when I was in residence with Mr. Sherlock Holmes at his Baker Street lodgings, that our restful holiday was interrupted by the arrival of a most unusual client. Mrs. Hudson had already invited us to partake of her goose later in the day, and when we heard her on the stair I assumed she was coming to inform us of the time for dinner. Instead, she brought a surprising announcement.

"A gentleman to see Mr. Holmes."

"On Christmas Day?" I was aghast at such a thoughtless interruption, and immediately put down my copy of the *Christmas Annual* I'd been perusing. Holmes, seated in his chair by the fireplace, seemed more curious than irritated.

"My dear Watson, if someone seeks our help on Christmas Day it must be a matter of extreme urgency—either that, or the poor soul is so lonely this day he has no one else to turn to. Please send him up, Mrs. Hudson."

Our visitor proved to be a handsome man with a somewhat youthful face, though his long white hair and the lines of his neck told me he was most likely in his mid-fifties. He was a little under six feet tall, but slight of build, with his fresh face giving the impression of extreme cleanliness. Holmes greeted him with a gentle handshake. "Our Christmas greetings to you, sir. I am Sherlock Holmes and this is my dear friend Dr. Watson."

The man shook my hand too and spoke in a soft voice. "Charles Lutwidge Dodgson. I am pleased to meet you, sir, and I-I thank you for taking the time to see me on this most festive of days."

As he spoke I detected a slight stammer that trembled his upper lip as he spoke. "Please be seated," Holmes said, and he chose the armchair between the two of us. "Now tell us what brought you out on Christmas Day. Certainly it must be a matter of extreme urgency to keep you from conducting the Christmas service at Christ Church up in Oxford."

Our slender visitor seemed taken aback by his words. "Do you know me, sir? Has my infamy spread this far?"

Sherlock Holmes smiled. "I know nothing about you, Mr. Dodgson, other than that you are a minister and most likely a mathematician at Oxford's Christ Church College, that you are a writer, that you are unmarried, and that you have had an unpleasant experience since arriving in London earlier today."

"Are you a wizard?" Dodgson asked, his composure shaken. I had seen Holmes astonish visitors many times, but I still enjoyed the sight of it.

Holmes, for his part, casually reached for his pipe and tobacco. "Only a close observer of my fellow man, sir. Extending from your waistcoat pocket I can see a small pamphlet on which the author's name is given as Reverend Charles Dodgson, Christ Church. Along with it is a return ticket to Oxford. Surely if you had come down to London before today the ticket would not still be carried in such a haphazard manner. Also on the front of your pamphlet I note certain advanced mathematical equations jotted down in pencil, no doubt during the train journey from Oxford. It is not the usual manner of passing time unless one is interested in mathematics as a profession. Since you have only one return ticket, I presume you came alone, and what married man would dare to leave his wife on Christmas Day?"

"What about the unpleasant experience?" I reminded Holmes.

"You will note, Watson, that the knees of our visitor's pants are scraped and dirty. He would certainly have noticed them on the train ride and brushed them off. Therefore it appears he fell or was thrown to his knees since his arrival in London."

"You're correct in virtually everything, Mr. Holmes," Charles Dodgson told him. "I left the mathematics faculty at Oxford seven years ago but I-I continue to reside at Christ Church College, my alma mater."

"And what brought you to London this day?"

Dodgson took a deep breath. "You must understand that I tell you this in the utmost confidence. What I am about to say is highly embarrassing to me, though I swear to you I am innocent of an-any moral wrong."

"Go on," Holmes urged, lighting his pipe.

"I am being blackmailed." He paused for a moment after speaking the words, as if he expected some shocked reaction from Holmes or myself. When he got none he continued. "Some years ago, when the art was just beginning, I took up photography. I was especially fond of camera portraits, of adults and children. I-I liked to pose young girls in various costumes. With the permission of their parents I sometimes did nude studies." His voice had dropped to barely a whisper now, and I noticed that his frozen smile was slightly askew.

"My God, Dodgson!" I exclaimed before I could help myself.

He seemed not to hear me, since he was turned toward Holmes. I wondered if his hearing might be impaired. Holmes, puffing on his pipe as if he'd just been presented with a vexing puzzle, asked, "Was this after you had taken holy orders?"

"I sometimes use 'Reverend' before my name but I am only a deacon. I nev-never went on to holy orders because my speech defect makes it difficult for me to preach. Some-sometimes it's worse than this. I also have some deafness in one ear."

"Tell me about the pictures. How old were the girls?"

"They were usually prepubescent. I took the photographs in all innocence, you—you must realize that. I photographed adults, too, people like Ellen Terry and Tennyson and Rossetti."

"With their clothes on, I trust," said Holmes with a slight smile.

"I know what I did was viewed with distaste by many of my acquaintances," our white-haired visitor said. "For that reason I abandoned photography some eight years ago."

"Then what is the reason for this blackmail?"

"I must go back to 1879, when I published my mathematical treatise *Euclid and His Modern Rivals*. Although the general public paid it little heed, I was pleased that it caused something of a stir in mathematical circles. One of the men who contacted me at the time was a professor who held the mathematical chair at one of our smaller universities. We became casual friends and he learned of my photographic interests. Later, af-after I'd ceased my photography, he apparently did some picture taking of his own. I was at the beach in Brighton this past summer when I met a lovely little girl. We chatted for a time and I asked if she wouldn't like to go wading in the surf. I carried some safety pins with me and I used them to pin up her skirt so she co-could wade without getting it wet."

I could restrain myself no longer. "This is perversion you speak of! These innocent children—"

"I swear to you I did nothing wrong!" he

insisted. "But somehow this former friend arranged to have me photographed in the very act of pinning up the little girl's skirt. Now he is using these pictures to blackmail me."

"What brought you to London today," Holmes asked, "and what unpleasantness brought you here to seek my help?"

"The professor contacted me some months ago with his threats and blackmail. He demanded a large sum of money in return for those pictures taken at the beach."

"And what made him believe that a retired mathematics instructor, even at Oxford, would have a large sum of money?"

"I have ha-had some success with my writing. It has not made me wealthy, but I live comfortably."

"Was your Euclid treatise that successful?" Holmes chided.

"Certain of my other writings . . ." He seemed reluctant to continue.

"What happened today?"

"The professor demanded that I meet him here at Paddington Station, with one hundred quid. I came down from Oxford on the noon train as instructed, but he was not at the station to meet me. Instead I was assaulted by a beggar, who pushed me down in the street after handing me an odd message of some sort."

"Did you report this to the police?"

"How could I? My rep-reputation—"

"So you came here?"

"I was at my wit's end. I knew of your reputation and I hoped you could help me. This man has me in his clutches. He will drain me of my money and destroy my reputation as well."

"Pray tell me the name of this blackmailer," Holmes said, picking up a pencil.

"It is Moriarty—Professor James Moriarty."

Sherlock Holmes put down his pencil and smiled slightly. "I think I will be able to help you, Reverend Dodgson."

It was then that Mrs. Hudson interrupted us with word that the Christmas goose would be served in thirty minutes. We were welcome to come down earlier if we liked, to partake of some holiday sherry. Holmes introduced her to Dodgson and then a remarkable event occurred. She stared at him through her spectacles and repeated his name to be sure she'd heard it correctly. "Reverend Charles Dodgson?"

"That's correct."

"It would be a pleasure if you joined us, too. There is enough food for four."

Holmes and I exchanged glances. Mrs. Hudson had never even conversed with a visitor before, to say nothing of inviting one to dinner. Still, it was Christmas Day and perhaps she was only being hospitable.

While she escorted Dodgson downstairs, I whispered to Holmes, "What's this about Moriarty? You spoke of him earlier this year in connection with the Valley of Fear affair."

"I did indeed, Watson. If he is Dodgson's blackmailer, I welcome the opportunity to challenge him once again."

We said nothing of our visitor's problems during dinner. Mrs. Hudson entertained him with accounts of her young nieces and their occasional visits to Baker Street. "I read to them often," she said, gesturing toward a small shelf of children's books she maintained for such occasions. "All children should be exposed to good books."

"I couldn't agree more," Dodgson replied.

As we were finishing our mince pie and Mrs. Hudson was busy clearing the table, Holmes returned to the subject that had brought Dodgson to us. "If you and Professor Moriarty were casual friends, what caused this recent enmity between you?"

"It was the book, I suppose. Moriarty's most celebrated volume of pure mathematics is *The Dynamics of an Asteroid*. When I followed it with my own somewhat humorous effort, *The Dynamics of a Particle*, he believed the satire was aimed at him. I tried to explain that it dealt with an Oxford subject, a contest between Gladstone and Gathorne Hardy, but he would have none of it. From then on, he seemed to be seeking ways to destroy me."

Holmes finished the last of his pie. "Excellent, Mrs. Hudson, excellent! Your cooking is a delight!"

"Thank you, Mr. Holmes." She retreated to the kitchen while he took out his pipe but did not light it.

"Tell me about this cryptic message you alluded to earlier."

"I can do better than that." He reached into his pocket and produced a folded piece of paper. "This is what the beggar gave me. When I tried to stop him he knocked me down and escaped."

Holmes read the message twice before passing the paper to me:

On Benjamin Caunt's day,
Beneath his lofty face,
A ransom you must pay,
To cancel your disgrace.

Come by there at one,
On Mad Hatter's clock.
The Old Lady's done,
And gone 'neath the block.

"It makes no sense, Holmes" was my initial reaction. "It's just some childish verse, and not a very good one."

"I can make nothing of it," Dodgson admitted. "Who is Benjamin Ca-Caunt?"

"He was a prizefighter," Holmes remarked. "I remember hearing my father speak of him." He puzzled over the message. "From what I know of Moriarty, it would be in character for him to reveal everything in this verse, and challenge us to decipher it."

"What of Caunt's lofty face?" I asked.

"It could be a statue or a portrait in a high place. His day could be the day of his birth, or of some special triumph, or perhaps the day of his death? I have nothing about the man in my files upstairs, and it will be two days before the libraries are open."

"And what is this about the Mad Hatter?" I inquired.

Mrs. Hudson had returned from the kitchen at that moment and heard my question. "My niece prefers the March Hare, Mr. Dodgson," she told him. "But then little girls usually like soft, furry animals." She walked over to the little bookshelf and took out a slender volume. "See? Here is my copy of your book. I have the other one, too."

She held a copy of *Alice in Wonderland.*

Holmes put a hand to his forehead, as if pained by his failure. "My mind must be elsewhere today. Of course! You are the author of *Alice* and *Through the Looking Glass* under the pseudonym of Lewis Carroll!"

Charles Dodgson smiled slightly. "It seems to be an open secret, though it is something I neither confirm nor deny."

"This puts a whole new light on the affair," said Holmes, laying down his pipe and turning to Mrs. Hudson. "Thank you for refreshing my memory." He looked again at the message.

I puzzled over it myself before turning once again to our client. "Moriarty must know of your writing, since he makes reference to the Mad Hatter."

"Of course he knows. But what does the message mean?"

"I believe you should remain in the city overnight," Holmes told him. "All may come clear tomorrow."

"Why is that?"

"The message speaks of Benjamin Caunt's Day, and he was a prizefighter—a boxer. Tomorrow, of course, is Boxing Day."

Charles Dodgson shook his head in amazement. "That is something worthy of the Mad Hatter himself!"

Mrs. Hudson found an unoccupied room in which Dodgson spent the night. In the morning I knocked at his door and invited him to join us for breakfast. Holmes had spent much of the night awake in his chair, poring over his books and files, studying maps of the city and lists of various sorts. Dodgson immediately asked if he had discovered anything, but my friend's answer was bleak. "Not a thing, sir! I can find no statue in all of London erected to the boxer Benjamin Caunt, nor is there any special portrait of him. Certainly there is none in a lofty position as the verse implies."

"Then what am I to do?"

"The entire matter seems most odd. You have the blackmail money on your person. Why did not this beggar simply take it, instead of giving you a further message?"

"It's Moriarty's doing," Dodgson insisted. "He wants to humiliate me."

"From my limited knowledge of the good professor, he is more interested in financial gain than in humiliation." Holmes reached for another of his several guidebooks to the city and began paging through it.

"Have you ever met Moriarty?" our visitor asked.

"Not yet," Holmes responded. "But someday—Hello, what's this?" His eyes had fallen upon something in the book he'd been skimming.

"A portrait of Caunt?"

"Better than that. This guidebook states that our best-known tower bell, Big Ben, may have been named after Benjamin Caunt, who was a famous boxer in 1858, when the bell was cast at the Whitechapel Foundry. Other books attribute the name Big Ben to Sir Benjamin Hall, chief commissioner of the works. The truth is of no matter. What does matter is that Big Ben, the clock, certainly does have a lofty face looking out over Parliament and the Thames."

"Then he is to meet Moriarty at one o'clock today—Boxing Day—beneath Big Ben," I said. At last it was becoming clear to me.

But Charles Dodgson was not so certain. "The Mad Hatter's clock, meaning the watch he carried in his pocket, told the day of the month but not the time."

Sherlock Holmes smiled. "I bow to your superior knowledge of *Alice in Wonderland*."

"But where does that leave us?" I asked, pouring myself another cup of breakfast tea. "The number one in the message must refer to a time rather than a date. Surely you are not to wait until New Year's Day to pay this blackmail when the first line speaks of Benjamin Caunt's day. It has to be Boxing Day!"

"Agreed," Holmes said. "I suggest we three travel to Big Ben and see what awaits us at one o'clock."

The day was pleasant enough, with even a few traces of sunshine breaking through the familiar winter clouds. A bit of snow the previous week had long since melted, and the day's temperature was hovering in the low forties. We took a cab to Westminster Abbey, just across the street from our destination, and joined the holiday strollers out enjoying the good weather.

"There's no sign of anyone waiting," I observed as we walked toward Westminster Bridge.

Holmes's eyes were like a hawk's as he scanned the passersby. "It is only five to the hour, Watson. But I suggest, Mr. Dodgson, that you walk a bit ahead of us. If no one attempts to intercept you by the time you reach the bridge, pause for a moment and then walk back this way."

"Do you have a description of Moriarty?" I asked as Dodgson walked ahead of us as instructed.

"He will not come himself. It will be one of his hirelings, and all the more dangerous for that."

"What should we look for?"

He seemed to remember the poem. "An old lady, Watson."

But there was no old lady alone, no one who paused as if waiting for someone or attempted to approach Charles Dodgson. He had reached the bridge and started back along the sidewalk, stepping around a small boy who was chalking a rough design on the sidewalk.

It was Holmes whose curiosity was aroused. As the boy finished his drawing and ran off, he paused to study it. "What do you make of this, Watson?"

I saw nothing but a crude circle drawn in chalk, with clocklike numbers running around the inner rim from one to thirty-one. An arrow seemed pointed at the number twenty-six, the day's date.

"Surely no more than a child's drawing," I said.

Dodgson had returned to join us and when he saw the chalked design he gave a start of surprise. "It's the Mad Hatter's watch, with dates instead of the time. Who drew this?"

"A young lad," said Holmes. "No doubt paid and instructed by Moriarty. He'll be blocks away by now."

"But what does it mean?" Dodgson asked.

"'Come by there at one, on Mad Hatter's clock,'" Holmes quoted from memory. "There is no time on the clock, only dates. The phrase 'on Mad Hatter's clock' must be taken literally. You must stand on the chalk drawing of the clock."

Dodgson did as he was told, attracting the puzzled glances of passersby. "Now what?"

It was I who noticed the box about the size of my medical bag, carefully wrapped and resting against the wall to the east of the Big Ben tower. "What's this?" I asked, stooping to pick it up. "Perhaps they're your pictures."

"Watson!"

It was Holmes who shouted as I began to unwrap the box. He was at my side in a flash, yanking it from my grasp just as I was about to open it. "What is it, Holmes?"

"One o'clock!" he yelled as the great bell above our heads tolled the hour. He ran several steps and hurled the box with all his strength toward the river. He had a strong arm, but his throw was a good deal short of the water when the box exploded in a blinding flash and a roar like a cannon.

Two strollers near Westminster Bridge had been slightly injured by the blast and all of us were shaken. Within minutes police were everywhere, and somehow I was not even surprised when our old friend Inspector Lestrade of Scotland Yard arrived on the scene about fifteen minutes later.

"Ah, Mr. Holmes, they said you were in-

volved in this. I was hoping for a peaceful holiday."

"The Christmas box held an infernal machine," Holmes told him, having recovered his composure. "I glimpsed a clock and some sticks of dynamite before I hurled it away. It was set to go off at one o'clock, exactly the time that Mr. Dodgson here had been lured to Big Ben."

Lestrade, lean and ferretlike as always, stepped forward to brush a speck of dirt from my coat. "And, Dr. Watson, I trust you weren't injured in this business."

"I'm all right," I answered gruffly. "Mr. Dodgson here was the target of the attack, or so we believe."

People were clustered around, and it was obvious Lestrade was anxious to get us away from there. "Come, come, here is a police carriage. Let us adjourn to my office at Scotland Yard and get to the bottom of this matter."

I was concerned for Charles Dodgson, who seemed to have been in a state of shock since the explosion. "Why should he want to kill me?" he kept asking. "I was willing to pay him his hundred quid."

"Professor Moriarty is after bigger game than a hundred quid," Holmes assured him.

"But what?"

The police carriage was pulling away as Lestrade shouted instructions to the driver. Holmes peered at the vast number of bobbies and horse-drawn police vehicles attracted by the explosion. "You have a great many men out here on a holiday."

"It's Big Ben, Mr. Holmes—one of London's sacred institutions! We don't take this lightly. It could be some revolutionary group behind it."

"I doubt that," Holmes responded with a smile.

He said no more until we had reached the dingy offices at Scotland Yard. "Our new building will be ready soon," Lestrade informed us a bit apologetically. "Now let us get down to business."

Charles Dodgson told his story somewhat haltingly, explaining how he'd come to Holmes on Christmas Day after being roughed up at Paddington Station. He tried to treat the episodes with the young girls with some delicacy, but Lestrade gnawed away at the story until he grasped the full picture. "You are being blackmailed!" he said with a start. "This should have been reported to the Oxford police at once."

"More easily said than done," the white-haired man responded. "A hundred is not a bad price to save my reputation and my honor."

It was here that Sherlock Holmes interrupted. "Surely, Lestrade, you must see that the plot against Mr. Dodgson is merely a diversion, a red herring. And if it is a diversion, why cannot the bomb at Big Ben also be a diversion?"

"What are you saying?"

"We must return to Moriarty's cryptic message. All has been explained except the final two lines: 'The Old Lady's done / And gone 'neath the block.'"

"A nonsense rhyme," Dodgson insisted. "Nothing more."

"But your own nonsense rhymes usually have a meaning," Holmes pointed out. "I admit to a sparse knowledge of your work, but I know a great deal about London crime. I ask you, Lestrade, which Old Lady could the verse refer to?"

"I have no idea, Holmes."

"Robbing an old lady would be akin to blackmailing a retired Oxford professor. Unless it was a particular old lady."

Lestrade's face drained of blood. "You can't mean"—his voice dropped to a whisper—"Queen Victoria!"

"No, no, I refer to the playwright Sheridan's quaint phrase, *The Old Lady of Threadneedle Street.*"

Lestrade and I spoke the words in the same breath. "The Bank of England!"

"Quite so," Holmes said. "The Big Ben bombing brought out virtually all the police on duty today. The financial district, closed for the holiday in any event, is virtually unguarded. I would guess that at this very moment Moriarty's men are looting the Bank of England and escaping back through their tunnel *'neath the block.*"

"My God!" Dodgson exclaimed. "Is such a thing possible?"

"Not only possible, but probable for Professor Moriarty. Lestrade, if you will bring me a large-scale map of the area, I will show you exactly where to find this tunnel."

"If you do that," said Dodgson, "you are truly a wizard."

"Hardly," Holmes said with a smile. "If you are tunneling under a street between buildings, you naturally would choose the shortest route."

Less than an hour later, while I watched with Holmes and Dodgson from a safe distance, Lestrade's men took the tunneling bank robbers without a struggle. Moriarty, unfortunately, was not among them.

"One day, Watson," Holmes said with confidence. "One day we will meet. In any event, Mr. Dodgson, I believe your troubles are over. All this blackmail business was a sham, and now that you have made a clean slate of it to the authorities there is nothing to be gained by blackmail."

"I cannot thank you enough, sir," the white-haired author said. "What do I owe you for your services?"

"Consider it a Christmas gift," Holmes announced with a wave of his hand. "Now, if I am not mistaken, you have just time to catch the next train back to Oxford. Let us escort you to Paddington Station and wish you an uneventful journey home."

THE SECRET IN THE PUDDING BAG & HERLOCK SHOLMES'S CHRISTMAS CASE

Peter Todd

ONE OF ENGLAND'S most prolific and popular authors (especially in the first half of the twentieth century), Charles Hamilton is largely unknown in the United States. He used more than twenty-five pseudonyms to produce more than seventy million words (the equivalent of nearly a thousand novels). His most popular creation was Billy Bunter, who appeared under the Frank Richards byline in more than fourteen hundred novellas. He used the Peter Todd pseudonym for his one hundred Herlock Sholmes stories, the first Sherlock Holmes parody cycle. "The Secret in the Pudding Bag" was first published in the December 27, 1924, issue of *Penny Popular;* "Herlock Sholmes's Christmas Case" was first published in the December 3, 1916, edition of *The Magnet.*

The Secret in the Pudding Bag & Herlock Sholmes's Christmas Case

PETER TODD

BEFORE REVEALING THE AMAZING Secret of the Pudding Bag, I, Herlock Sholmes, detective of Shaker Street, London, desire to explain my action to my readers.

For years my faithful friend, Dr. Jotson, who assists me to pay Mrs. Spudson's exorbitant rent, had acted as the official recorder of my cases. Never was there a better man. Although a general practitioner, he is an expert on disordered brains. As I have told him many a time, he should be in a mental asylum—as house-surgeon, of course. Yet his great talents have not been wasted altogether in Shaker Street.

But his very devotion to me has one drawback. He refuses to record any but my astounding successes. And the case of the Pudding Bag can hardly be classified as one. But because of its Christmas flavour the Editor desired it greatly—the story, not the pudding bag.

One day just after I had successfully solved the mystery of the Poisoned Doughnut, in Tooting Bec, I found the Great Man in our consulting-room at Shaker Street, begging Jotson to narrate the tale for the benefit of his readers. Jotson refused. Therefore, I insisted on recording this amazing case myself.*

For long Dr. Jotson had been run-down and depressed. Ever since that day when he left his best

*And on pocketing the fee usually awarded to poor Jotson. —Ed.

pair of silver-plated scissors inside the patient upon whom he had operated for liver trouble, he had not been himself.

For some time I must admit it did not occur to me that there was anything else wrong with poor Jotson save worry for the loss of his patient and the scissors. But shortly before Christmas it was borne on me that something else was amiss.

One night as I sat in my armchair playing Schnoffenstein's Five-Finger Exercise in B Flat on my violin, curious rumbling noises assailed my ear. At first I thought the G string wanted tightening; then it occurred to me that the strange, deep sounds were proceeding from the next room.

I ceased playing. Creeping stealthily towards the bed-room door, my fiddle grasped in my right hand ready for any emergency, I stooped down with the skilled grace of long practice, and applied my ear to the keyhole.

Now I could hear the rumbling clearly. Dr. Jotson was talking to himself. Throwing open the door, I stood a tall and, I hope, dignified figure in my purple dressing-gown with the little green birds on the holly branches round the hem.

"Jotson!" I cried. "You are distraught."

My old friend Jotson, who had been pacing the bed-room, stopped, his hands behind him. There was a startled look on his face, his sandy, walrus moustache drooping guiltily.

"Sholmes," he said, "you have been listening. What have you heard?"

"Aah," I said. "What! Well might I ask you a question. What are you concealing from me, Jotson? What have you behind your back?"

"He, he, he! Only a couple of patches," replied Jotson, faintly laughing at his own feeble joke. "Now pray go and resume your amateur vivisection on my guinea pigs!"

Candidly, I felt offended, and I left the room. But I resolved to keep my eye on my old and faithful friend for any further symptoms before formally notifying Colney Hatch.

Gradually, as the days sped by, I became more convinced that Jotson was ailing mentally. Several times I heard him mumbling behind closed doors. Occasionally, too, he left the house in the evenings on some pretext or another. But I felt that when Jotson needed my help he would tell me. So I snuffed my cocaine, played my violin, and solved a couple of dozen poison mysteries which had baffled Scotland Yard and the Continental police, and temporarily left Jotson to look after himself.

On Christmas Eve Dr. Jotson made one more of his mysterious disappearances. For long I sat before the fire in the consulting-room, casually perusing the evening paper as I smoked my pipe. Outside the snow snowed and the waits waited—I was hard up that Christmas.

Suddenly a paragraph on an inner news page riveted my attention. It was headed: "Proposed River Trip for Crown Prince," and read: "The Crown Prince of Schlacca-Splittzen, who arrived this afternoon in London from Paris, has expressed a desire to see the London County Council Hall from the river. He remarked to reporters that his view of this magnificent structure from the railway reminded him of the municipal Torture House in Tchmnomzyte, the capital of his own state of Schlacca-Splittzen, which lies to the south of Russia. The Crown Prince is being carefully guarded by Inspector Pinkeye and three other well-known detectives from Scotland Yard. These precautions are being taken because it is rumoured that the

Schlacca-Splittzen Co-operative Society of Anarchists have threatened to drop a bomb into his porridge if he visited Britain's shores."

As I read this little paragraph a dark suspicion entered my mind, and there I determined that Jotson must be watched.

It was eleven o'clock on Christmas Eve. Mrs. Spudson, her hair in curl-papers, had retired to rest. I damped down the fire, covered the canary's cage, turned the consulting-room lights out, chained up the dog, put out the cat, and left the key under the front doormat for Jotson. Then I went to my room.

I was about to doff my dressing-gown when I heard Jotson enter the house. Slowly he came upstairs, and I heard him switch on the consulting-room light. Leaving my room, I crept along the passage and quickly opened the door of the consulting-room.

As I did so Jotson leaped from the hearth as though stung.

"Great porous plasters!" he gasped. "What a fright you gave me! For a moment I thought you were the ghost of Old Man Scrooge. You see, I've been attending the recital of the 'Christmas Carol.' He, he, he!"

The halting words of my old friend and his musical cackle told me he was not speaking the truth.

"Jotson," I said sternly, "you've no more been to any recital to-night than I've been to the tax-collector to pay next year's income-tax in advance. Now, tell me. Where have you been?"

As I spoke, my trained eye swept the fire grate. From the flames and ashes which I saw there I deduced that Jotson had been burning something. Quickly I averted my gaze so that he should not know I knew.

My old friend tugged nervously at his moustache.

"It's nothing, really, my dear Sholmes," he said nervously. "If I told you, you would only laugh at me. And I hate being laughed at!"

"Nonsense, Jotson!" I said heartily. "Everyone laughs at you—er—except your patients, of course. And they usually don't last long enough to laugh long."

This I said in a gentle, bantering tone to cheer Jotson up. To my surprise, it seemed to have the opposite effect, and he stumped out of the room in a huff.

That was the opportunity I wanted. In a moment my nose was in the fender. Quickly I peered about. Before you could say "force-meat stuffing" I had found a narrow strip of torn paper bearing some typewritten words. Hearing Jotson's footsteps returning I hastily crammed it in my pocket, and was innocently cracking Brazil nuts with my teeth when he entered the consulting-room to apologise for his former rudeness.

I said nothing about my discovery, but in my bedroom I examined the find carefully. To my stupefaction the typewritten words, which were in English, read as follows:

". . . this honour. You have been chosen, comrade. See you fail not."

Ding, dong! Clatter Bang! Ding dong!

The merry Christmas bells were chiming as Jotson and I met at breakfast on the following morning and exchanged greetings.

My eagle eye was quick to notice that Dr. Jotson was not himself at breakfast. Quite absent-mindedly he helped me to the larger half of the breakfast kipper, and then gave me the first cup from the coffee-pot, instead of the usual dregs. All my old fears for my poor friend's condition returned with renewed force.

Sitting in my chair, daintily flicking the kipper-bones from the lapel of my mauve dressing-gown, I watched Jotson as he went to the window and tried to entice the friendship of a robin redbreast by means of a fish-head.

"What do you say to a walk round Marylebone Station or the Waxworks, to get an appetite for our Christmas dinner, Jotson!" I remarked casually.

Jotson's walrus moustache gave a perceptible quiver.

"Er—I'm afraid you will have to excuse me, my dear Sholmes!" he stammered. "A new patient of mine, a dear old lady who is suffering from a temporary attack of suspended vibration of the right bozookum, and wishes me to test her high tension battery to enable her to get 2LO for the Christmas glee singers. I'm afraid—"

"Tut, tut!" I said. "I'll come with you, Jotson."

"No, my dear Sholmes," said Jotson very firmly. "I shouldn't think of taking you to a case like this on Christmas Day. Why don't you take the bus up to the Zoological Gardens, or, if you prefer it, remain in front of the fire cracking a few monkey-nuts yourself?"

I said no more, but I thought a lot. For a time I sat myself in the armchair.

Speedily it became apparent that Jotson was up to some game. It seemed almost impossible to keep track of his movements. He was as slippery as an eel in an old pail. But at last I heard him stealthily take his hat and coat from the peg in the hall and leave the house.

Within a minute I was tracking my old friend down Shaker Street. Dr. Jotson had a large brown paper parcel under his right arm. The parcel looked innocent enough. What did that parcel contain? That I was determined to find out.

Poor Jotson was worried. I deduced that from the absent-minded way that he pushed the face of a little boy who asked him for a cigarette-card. Stopping at the corner outside the Goat and Gooseberry Bush, he hesitated a moment, and then leaped on a passing bus. I waited until he had gone inside with his parcel; then I swung myself on the step and darted aloft.

Peering from the bus top, I saw Jotson alight at Charing Cross. I waited a few moments until the bus had started to move again, and then I ran nimbly down the steps. As I did so, with consummate cunning I knocked off the conductor's hat and leaped into the road. As he prepared to stop the bus I swiftly tossed him my own cap, and retrieved his fallen property. Then replacing the peaked, blue cap on my head and gumming a false black moustache to my upper lip, I followed in the track of my old friend.

Once Jotson stopped and looked back. All he saw, apparently, was an attenuated bus-conductor about to turn into a near by chop-house.

Waiting in the shelter of the doorway a minute, I emerged and followed him again. As I watched his stocky form stumping down White-hall towards the Houses of Parliament, a gust of wind blew the paper from under his arm. A white, earthenware pudding basin was revealed, with a cloth over the top of it.

After a vain attempt to retrieve the paper Jotson went on his way, looking uncommonly foolish walking down Whitehall holding that pudding-cloth, with the basin swinging at his side.

At first the sight of that pudding-basin brought a sense of relief to me. Then a horrible thought occurred to me. This was no pudding-basin. It was a bomb! Rapidly I reviewed in my mind the events leading up to this Christmas morning walk. I remembered Jotson's curious mumblings. I remembered the paragraph about the Crown Prince of Schlacca-Splittzen. I called to mind the mysterious message on the scrap of paper I had taken from the fire-grate. With a bomb in that innocent-looking bag, Jotson was on his way to the river to fulfill his dread mission.

My friend strode firmly to the Thames Embankment.

Quite a crowd was lining the parapet.

"What's the excitement?" I heard him ask a low-looking ruffian.

"It's that there Crown Prince of Slaccy-Splittem," replied the fellow. "He's just about to land at the jetty."

Jotson pushed his way through the crowd to the parapet. I kept close at his heels, my heart hammering against my ribs.

With a gasp of dismay I saw Jotson hoist the pudding-basin on to the parapet and give it a gentle shove.

"Stop!" I cried, and thrust my hand forward.

I must have diverted Jotson's aim, for the basin struck against a jutting ledge of the Embankment. There was no time to duck, for I feared the next moment there would be an explosion that would bring about the end of all things as far as we were concerned. To my surprise, however, the basin broke, and out shot a great plum-pudding. It struck a boatman standing on the jetty waiting for the prince's launch right on the back of the neck and burst into fragments, while the onlookers gasped with astonishment. Then when they realised what had happened, a great shout of laughter burst forth. The boatman was annoyed—very! He looked aloft, with a great piece of pudding crowning his head, and passed a few remarks totally unconnected with that "peace on earth and good will to men" which one associates with the Yuletide season. Then, as the fellow turned to help with the mooring of the prince's launch, I grasped Jotson by the hand and dragged him away.

"You thundering idiot!" I said. "What do you mean by it all?"

"Sholmes!" cried Jotson. There was both surprise and disappointment in his tone.

And then bit by bit I dragged the story out of Jotson. He knew that Mrs. Spudson had made a Christmas pudding and that she would insist on him and me partaking of it at the Christmas dinner.

"Knowing your good nature, Sholmes," he said, "I knew that you would have eaten some of it to avoid offending our landlady. You did last year, and what was the consequence? For two days you groaned on the couch with the colly-wobbles. This year I determined at all costs I would get rid of the Christmas pudding. As a medical man I knew it was positively dangerous, but I didn't want to drag you into the matter, nor did I wish to offend Mrs. Spudson. And so I quietly lifted the basin containing the pudding, intending to dispose of it in the first possible way that presented itself. As you know, in desperation I finally toppled it over into the river."

Then I told him how his rumblings had roused my suspicions, and the finding of the torn piece of typewritten paper had corroborated them.

Now it was Jotson's turn to laugh.

"'Pon my word, Sholmes!" he chuckled. "I didn't know you were so worried about me! You see, a fortnight ago I joined the Marylebone Dramatic Society, and was offered the role of Koffituppe in the play, "Crown Jewels in Pawn," by Msmooji, the famous Russian dramatist. Afraid you would laugh at me, I would retire to my bed-room to study my role. Finally, in disgust at my inability to learn the part, I tore it up and threw it on the fire. The typewritten piece of paper you found was a portion of the play."

"But why on earth didn't you tell me all this before, my dear fellow?" I cried.

"Because," answered Jotson, "I should have had to acknowledge failure, and, as you know, no man likes to do that."

"Ah, well," I laughed, "the mystery is solved! And we can safely return to Shaker Street to pull the wish-bone of a turkey without the fear of having to partake of any of the amazing stodgy concoction which Mrs. Spudson calls Christmas pudding!"

I

"CHRISTMAS TOMORROW!" HERLOCK Sholmes remarked thoughtfully.

I started.

"My dear Sholmes!" I murmured.

Herlock Sholmes smiled.

"You are surprised, Jotson, to hear me make that statement with such positiveness," he remarked. "Yet, I assure you that such is the case."

"I acknowledge, Sholmes, that I ought no longer to be surprised at anything you may say or do. But from what grounds do you infer——"

"Quite simple, my dear Jotson. Look from the window upon the slushy streets and the hurrying crowds, all indicative of the approach of Christmas!"

"True! But why tomorrow precisely?"

"Ah, there we go a little deeper, Jotson. I deduce that Christmas occurs tomorrow from a study of the calendar!"

"The calendar!" I exclaimed, in astonishment.

"Exactly!"

"As you know, Sholmes, I have endeavoured to study your methods, in my humbler way, yet I confess that I do not see the connection——"

"Probably not, Jotson. But to the trained, professional mind it presents no difficulties. Christmas, you are aware, falls upon the twenty-fifth day of the month!"

"True!"

"Look at the calendar, Jotson!"

I obeyed.

"It tells you nothing?"

"Nothing!" I confessed.

Sholmes smiled again, a somewhat bored smile.

"My dear fellow, the calendar indicates that today is the twenty-fourth!"

"Quite so. But——"

"And as Christmas falls upon the twenty-fifth, it follows—to an acute mind accustomed to rapid deductions—that tomorrow is Christmas!"

I could only gaze at my amazing friend in silent admiration.

"But there will be no holiday for us tomorrow, my dear Jotson," resumed Herlock Sholmes. "I have received a wire from the Duke of Hookey-walker, who—— Ah, his Grace has arrived!"

Even as Sholmes spoke, the Duke of Hookey-walker was shown into our sitting-room.

Herlock Sholmes removed his feet from the mantelpiece with the graceful courtesy so natural to him.

"Pray be seated," said Sholmes. "You may speak quite freely before my friend, Dr. Jotson!"

"Mr. Sholmes, I have sustained a terrible loss!"

Sholmes smiled.

"Your Grace has lost the pawnticket?" he inquired.

"Mr. Sholmes, you must be a wizard! How did you guess——"

"I never guess," said Herlock Sholmes quietly. "My business is to deal with facts. Pray let me have some details."

"It is true, Mr. Sholmes, that the pawnticket is missing," said the duke in an agitated voice. "You are aware that the house of Hookeywalker has a great reputation for hospitality, which must be kept up even in these days of stress. It was necessary for me to give a large Christmas party at Hookey Castle, and, to obtain the necessary funds, the family jewels were pledged with Mr. Ikey Solomons, of Houndsditch. The ticket was in my own keeping—it never left me. I kept it in my own card-case. The card-case never left my person. Yet now, Mr. Sholmes, the ticket is missing!"

"And the card-case?"

"Still in my pocket!"

"When were the Hookeywalker jewels placed with Mr. Solomons?"

"Yesterday morning!"

"And the ticket was missing——"

"Last night," faltered the duke. "I looked in my card-case to make sure that it was still safe, and it was gone. How it had been purloined, Mr. Sholmes, is a mystery—an unfathomable mystery!"

"No mystery is unfathomable to a trained mind," said Sholmes calmly. "I have every hope of recovering the missing pawnticket."

"Mr. Sholmes, you give me new life. But how——"

Sholmes interrupted.

"After leaving Mr. Solomons's establishment, where did your Grace go?"

"I had to make a call at the Chinwag Department of the War Office, and from there I returned to Hookey Castle."

"You made no other call?"

"None."

"It is scarcely possible that a skilled pickpocket is to be found in the Chinwag Department," said Sholmes thoughtfully.

"Impossible, Mr. Sholmes! Every official of that great Department is far above suspicion of being skilled in any manner whatsoever!"

"True!"

"There is no clue!" said the duke in despairing tones. "But unless the missing ticket is recovered, Mr. Sholmes, the famous Hookeywalker jewels are lost!"

"You may leave the case in my hands," said Herlock Sholmes carelessly. "I may call at Hookey Castle with news for you tomorrow."

"Bless you, Mr. Sholmes!"

And the duke took his leave.

Herlock Sholmes lighted a couple of pipes, a habit of his when a particularly knotty problem required great concentration of thought. I did not venture to interrupt the meditations of that mighty intellect.

Sholmes spoke at last, with a smile.

"A very interesting little problem, Jotson. I can see that you are puzzled by my deduction that the pawnticket was lost before his Grace had mentioned it."

"I am astounded, Sholmes."

"Yet it was simple. I had heard of the great social gathering at Hookey Castle," explained Sholmes. "I deduced that his Grace could only meet the bills by hypothecating the family jewels. His hurried visit to me and his agitation could have had but one meaning—I deduced that the pawnticket was lost or stolen. Quite elementary, my dear Jotson! But the recovery of the missing ticket——"

"That will not be so simple, Sholmes."

"Who knows, Jotson?" Sholmes rose to his feet and drew his celebrated dressing-gown about him. "I must leave you for a short time, Jotson. You may go and see your patients, my dear fellow."

"One question, Sholmes. You are going——"

"To the Chinwag Department."

"But——"

But Herlock Sholmes was gone.

II

I confess that Sholmes's behaviour perplexed me. He had declared that the pickpocket could not be found in the Chinwag Department, yet he had gone there to commence his investigations. When he returned to Shaker Street, he made no remark upon the case, and I did not venture to question him. The next morning he greeted me with a smile as I came down into the sitting-room.

"You are ready for a little run this morning, Jotson?" he asked.

"I am always at your service, Sholmes."

"Good! Then call a taxi."

A few minutes later a taxicab was bearing us away. Sholmes had given the direction to the driver—"Hookey Castle."

"We are going to see the duke, Sholmes?" I asked.

He nodded.

"But the missing pawnticket?"

"Wait and see!"

This reply, worthy of a great statesman, was all I could elicit from Sholmes on the journey.

The taxi drove up the stately approach to Hookey Castle. A gorgeous footman admitted us to the great mansion, and we were shown into the presence of the duke.

His Grace had left his guests to see us. There was a slight impatience in his manner.

"My dear Mr. Sholmes," he said, "I supposed I had given you the fullest particulars yesterday. You have called me away from a shove-ha'penny party."

"I am sorry," said Sholmes calmly. "Return to the shove-ha'penny party, by all means your Grace, and I will call another time with the pawnticket."

The duke bounded to his feet.

"Mr. Sholmes! You have recovered it?"

Sholmes smiled. He delighted in these dramatic surprises.

The duke gazed with startled eyes at the slip of pasteboard my amazing friend presented to him.

"The missing pawnticket!" he ejaculated.

"The same!" said Sholmes.

"Sholmes!" I murmured. I could say no more.

The Duke of Hookeywalker took the ticket with trembling fingers.

"Mr. Sholmes" he said in tones of deep emotion, "you have saved the honour of the name of Hookeywalker! You will stay to dinner, Mr. Sholmes. Come, I insist—there will be tripe and onions!" he added.

"I cannot resist the tripe and onions," said Sholmes, with a smile.

And we stayed.

III

It was not till the taxi was whirling us homeward to Shaker Street that Herlock Sholmes relieved my curiosity.

"Sholmes!" I exclaimed as the taxi rolled out of the stately gates of Hookey Castle. "How, in the name of wonder——"

Sholmes laughed.

"You are astounded, as usual, Jotson?"

"As usual, Sholmes."

"Yet it is very simple. The duke carried the pawnticket in his card-case," said Sholmes. "He called only at the Chinwag Department of the War Office before returning home. Only a particularly clever pickpocket could have extracted the ticket without the cardcase, and, as his Grace himself remarked, it was useless to assume the existence of any particularly clever individual in a Government department. That theory, therefore, was excluded—the ticket had not been taken."

"Sholmes!"

"It had not been taken, Jotson," said Sholmes calmly. "Yet it had left the duke's possession. The question was—how?"

"I confess it is quite dark to me, Sholmes."

"Naturally," said Sholmes drily. "But my mental powers, my dear Jotson, are of quite a different calibre."

"Most true."

"As the ticket had not been taken from the duke, I deduced that he had parted with it un-intentionally."

"But is that possible, Sholmes?"

"Quite! Consider, my dear Jotson. His Grace kept the pawnticket, for safety, in his card-case. On calling at the Chinwag Department he sent in his card, naturally. By accident, Jotson, he handed over the pawnticket instead of his own card——"

"Sholmes!"

"And that ticket, Jotson, was taken in in-stead. That was the only theory to be deduced from the known facts. I proceeded to the Chin-wag Department, and interviewed the official upon whom the duke called. There was a little difficulty in obtaining an interview; but he was awakened at last, and I questioned him. As I had deduced, the missing pawnticket was discovered on the salver, where it had lain unnoticed since the duke's call."

"Wonderful!" I exclaimed.

Sholmes smiled in a bored way.

"Elementary, my dear Jotson. But here we are at Shaker Street."

CHRISTMAS EVE
S. C. Roberts

IN ADDITION TO BEING A NOTED EXPERT in eighteenth century English literature, especially the life and works of Dr. Samuel Johnson, S. C. Roberts (Sydney Castle Roberts) was also a scholar and aficionado of Sherlock Holmes. He wrote analytical works on the subject, such as *Holmes and Watson: A Miscellany* and *Doctor Watson: Prolegomena to the Study of a Biographical Problem,* as well as contributing regularly to Holmesian magazines and anthologies. He also wrote parodies and pastiches about Holmes and Watson, including this short play and *The Strange Case of the Megatherium Thefts.* "Christmas Eve" was first published as a chapbook limited to 100 copies (Cambridge, privately printed, 1936).

Christmas Eve

S. C. ROBERTS

(SHERLOCK HOLMES, *disguised as a loafer, is discovered probing in a sideboard cupboard for something to eat and drink.*)

HOLMES: Where in the world is that decanter? I'm sure I—

(*Enter* DR. WATSON, *who sees only the back of* HOLMES'S *stooping figure*)

WATSON: (*Turning quickly and whispering hoarsely offstage*) Mrs. Hudson! Mrs. Hudson! My revolver, quick. There's a burglar in Mr. Holmes's room. (WATSON *exits*)

HOLMES: Ah, there's the decanter at last. But first of all I may as well discard some of my properties. (*Takes off cap, coat, beard, etc., and puts on dressing gown*) My word, I'm hungry. (*Begins to eat sandwich*) But, bless me, I've forgotten the siphon! (*Stoops at cupboard in same attitude as before*)

(*Enter* WATSON, *followed by* MRS. HUDSON)

WATSON: (*Sternly*) Now, my man, put those hands up.

HOLMES: (*Turning round*) My dear Watson, why this sudden passion for melodrama?

WATSON: Holmes!

HOLMES: Really, Watson, to be the victim of a murderous attack at your hands, of all people's—and on Christmas Eve, too.

WATSON: But a minute ago, Holmes, there was a villainous-looking scoundrel trying to wrench open that cupboard—a really criminal type. I caught a glimpse of his face.

HOLMES: Well, well, my dear Watson, I suppose I ought to be grateful for the compliment to my make-up. The fact is that I have spent the day loafing at the corner of a narrow street leading out of the Waterloo Road. They were all quite friendly to me there. . . . Yes, I obtained the last little piece of evidence that I wanted to clear up that case of the Kentish Town safe robbery—you remember? Quite an interesting case, but all over now.

MRS. HUDSON: Lor', Mr. 'Olmes, how you do go on. Still, I'm learnin' never to be surprised at anything now.

HOLMES: Capital, Mrs. Hudson. That's what every criminal investigator has to learn, isn't it, Watson? (MRS. HUDSON *leaves*)

WATSON: Well, I suppose so, Holmes. But you must feel very pleased to think you've got that Kentish Town case off your mind before Christmas.

HOLMES: On the contrary, my dear Watson, I'm miserable. I like having things on my mind—it's the only thing that makes life tolerable. A mind empty of problems is worse even than a stomach empty of food. (*Eats sandwich*) But Christmas is commonly a slack season. I suppose even criminals' hearts are softened. The result is that I have nothing to do but to look

out of the window and watch other people being busy. That little pawnbroker at the corner,
for instance, you know the one, Watson?

WATSON: Yes, of course.

HOLMES: One of the many shops you have often
seen, but never observed, my dear Watson.
If you had watched that pawnbroker's front
door as carefully as I have during the last
ten days, you would have noted a striking increase in his trade; you might have observed
also some remarkably well-to-do people going
into the shop. There's one well–set-up young
woman whom I have seen at least four times.
Curious to think what her business may have
been. . . . But it's a shame to depress your
Christmas spirit, Watson. I see that you are
particularly cheerful this evening.

WATSON: Well, yes, I don't mind admitting that
I am feeling quite pleased with things today.

HOLMES: So "Rio Tintos" have paid a good dividend, have they?

WATSON: My dear Holmes, how on earth do you
know that?

HOLMES: Elementary, my dear Watson. You told
me years ago that "Rio Tintos" was the one
dividend which was paid in through your
bank and not direct to yourself. You come
into my room with an envelope of a peculiar shade of green sticking out of your coat
pocket. That particular shade is used by your
bank—Cox's—and by no other, so far as I am
aware. Clearly, then, you have just obtained
your pass-book from the bank and your
cheerfulness must proceed from the good
news which it contains. *Ex hypothesi,* that
news must relate to "Rio Tintos."

WATSON: Perfectly correct, Holmes; and on the
strength of the good dividend, I have deposited ten good, crisp, five-pound notes in the
drawer of my dressing table just in case we
should feel like a little jaunt after Christmas.

HOLMES: That was charming of you, Watson.
But in my present state of inertia I should
be a poor holiday companion. Now if only—
(*Knock at door*) Come in.

MRS. HUDSON: Please sir, there's a young lady to
see you.

HOLMES: What sort of young lady, Mrs. Hudson? Another of these young women wanting
half a crown towards some Christmas charity? If so, Dr. Watson's your man, Mrs. Hudson. He's bursting with bank-notes today.

MRS. HUDSON: I'm sure I'm very pleased to 'ear
it, sir; but this lady ain't that kind at all, sir.
She's sort of agitated, like . . . very anxious
to see you and quite scared of meeting you at
the same time, if you take my meaning, sir.

HOLMES: Perfectly, Mrs. Hudson. Well, Watson,
what are we to do? Are we to interview this
somewhat unbalanced young lady?

WATSON: If the poor girl is in trouble, Holmes,
I think you might at least hear what she has
to say.

HOLMES: Chivalrous as ever, my dear Watson—
bring the lady up, Mrs. Hudson.

MRS. HUDSON: Very good, sir. (*To the lady outside*) This way, Miss.

(*Enter* MISS VIOLET DE VINNE, *an elegant
but distracted girl of about twenty-two*)

HOLMES: (*Bowing slightly*) You wish to consult
me?

MISS DE VINNE: (*Nervously*) Are you Mr. Sherlock Holmes?

HOLMES: I am—and this is my friend and colleague, Dr. Watson.

WATSON: (*Coming forward and holding out hand*)
Charmed, I am sure, Miss—

HOLMES: (*To* MISS DE VINNE) You have come
here, I presume, because you have a story to
tell me. May I ask you to be as concise as possible?

MISS DE VINNE: I will try, Mr. Holmes. My name is
de Vinne. My mother and I live together in Bayswater. We are not very well off but my father
was . . . well . . . a gentleman. The Countess of
Barton is one of our oldest friends—

HOLMES: (*Interrupting*) And the owner of a very
wonderful pearl necklace.

MISS DE VINNE: (*Startled*) How do you know that, Mr. Holmes?

HOLMES: I am afraid it is my business to know quite a lot about other people's affairs. But I'm sorry. I interrupted. Go on.

MISS DE VINNE: Two or three times a week I spend the day with Lady Barton and act as her secretary in a casual, friendly way. I write letters for her and arrange her dinner-tables when she has a party and do other little odd jobs.

HOLMES: Lady Barton is fortunate, eh, Watson?

WATSON: Yes, indeed, Holmes.

MISS DE VINNE: This afternoon a terrible thing happened. I was arranging some flowers when Lady Barton came in looking deathly white. "Violet," she said, "the pearls are gone." "Heavens." I cried, "what do you mean?" "Well," she said, "having quite unexpectedly had an invitation to a reception on January 5th, I thought I would make sure that the clasp was all right. When I opened the case (you know the special place where I keep it) it was empty—that's all." She looked as if she was going to faint, and I felt much the same.

HOLMES: (*Quickly*) And did you faint?

MISS DE VINNE: No, Mr. Holmes, we pulled ourselves together somehow and I asked her whether she was going to send for the police, but she wouldn't hear of it. She said Jim (that's her husband) hated publicity and would be furious if the pearls became "copy" for journalists. But of course she agreed that something had to be done and so she sent me to you.

HOLMES: Oh, Lady Barton sent you?

MISS DE VINNE: Well, not exactly. You see, when she refused to send for the police, I remembered your name and implored her to write you . . . and . . . well . . . here I am and here's the letter. That's all, Mr. Holmes.

HOLMES: I see. (*Begins to read letter*) Well, my dear lady, neither you nor Lady Barton has given me much material on which to work at present.

MISS DE VINNE: I am willing to answer any questions, Mr. Holmes.

HOLMES: You live in Bayswater, Miss Winnie?

WATSON: (*Whispering*) "De Vinne," Holmes.

HOLMES: (*Ignoring* WATSON) You said Bayswater, I think, Miss Winnie?

MISS DE VINNE: Quite right, Mr. Holmes, but—forgive me, my name is de Vinne.

HOLMES: I'm sorry, Miss Dwinney—

MISS DE VINNE: De Vinne, Mr. Holmes, D . . . E . . . V . . .

HOLMES: How stupid of me. I think the chill I caught last week must have left a little deafness behind it. But to save further stupidity on my part, just write your name and address for me, will you? (*Hands her pen and paper, on which* MISS DE VINNE *writes*) That's better. Now, tell me, Miss de Vinne, how do you find Bayswater for shopping?

MISS DE VINNE: (*Surprised*) Oh, I don't know. Mr. Holmes, I hardly—

HOLMES: You don't care for Whiteley's, for instance?

MISS DE VINNE: Well, not very much. But I can't see . . .

HOLMES: I entirely agree with you, Miss de Vinne. Yet Watson, you know, is devoted to that place—spends hours there . . .

WATSON: Holmes, what nonsense are you—

HOLMES: But I think you are quite right, Miss de Vinne. Harrod's is a great deal better in my opinion.

MISS DE VINNE: But I never go to Harrod's, Mr. Holmes, in fact I hardly ever go to any big store, except for one or two things. But what has this got to do—

HOLMES: Well, in principle, I don't care for them much either, but they're convenient sometimes.

MISS DE VINNE: Yes, I find the Army and Navy stores useful now and then, but why on earth are we talking about shops and stores when the thing that matters is Lady Barton's necklace?

HOLMES: Ah, yes, I was coming to that. (*Pauses*)

I'm sorry, Miss de Vinne, but I'm afraid I can't take up this case.

MISS DE VINNE: You refuse, Mr. Holmes?

HOLMES: I am afraid I am obliged to do so. It is a case that would inevitably take some time. I am in sore need of a holiday and only to-day my devoted friend Watson has made all arrangements to take me on a Mediterranean cruise immediately after Christmas.

WATSON: Holmes, this is absurd. You know that I merely—

MISS DE VINNE: Dr. Watson, if Mr. Holmes can't help me, won't you? You don't know how terrible all this is for me as well as for Lady Barton.

WATSON: My dear lady, I have some knowledge of my friend's methods and they often seem incomprehensible. Holmes, you can't mean this?

HOLMES: Certainly I do, my dear Watson. But I am unwilling that any lady should leave this house in a state of distress. (*Goes to door*) Mrs. Hudson!

MRS. HUDSON: Coming, sir. (MRS. HUDSON *enters*)

HOLMES: Mrs. Hudson, be good enough to conduct this lady to Dr. Watson's dressing room. She is tired and a little upset. Let her rest on the sofa there while Dr. Watson and I have a few minutes' quiet talk.

MRS. HUDSON: Very good, sir.

(*Exeunt* MRS. HUDSON *and* MISS DE VINNE, *the latter looking appealingly at* DR. WATSON)

HOLMES: (*Lighting cherry-wood pipe*) Well, Watson?

WATSON: Well, Holmes, in all my experience I don't think I have ever seen you so unaccountably ungracious to a charming girl.

HOLMES: Oh, yes, she has charm, Watson—they always have. What do you make of her story?

WATSON: Not very much, I confess. It seemed fairly clear as far as it went, but you wouldn't let her tell us any detail. Instead, you began a perfectly ridiculous conversation about the comparative merits of various department stores. I've seldom heard you so inept.

HOLMES: Then you accept her story?

WATSON: Why not?

HOLMES: Why not, my dear Watson? Because the whole thing is a parcel of lies.

WATSON: But, Holmes, this is unreasoning prejudice.

HOLMES: Unreasoning, you say? Listen, Watson. This letter purports to have come from the Countess of Barton. I don't know her Ladyship's handwriting, but I was struck at once by its labored character, as exhibited in this note. It occurred to me, further, that it might be useful to obtain a specimen of Miss de Vinne's to put alongside it—hence my tiresome inability to catch her name. Now, my dear Watson, I call your particular attention to the capital B's which happen to occur in both specimens.

WATSON: They're quite different, Holmes, but—yes, they've both got a peculiar curl where the letter finishes.

HOLMES: Point No. 1, my dear Watson, but an isolated one. Now, although I could not recognize the handwriting, I knew this note-paper as soon as I saw and felt it. Look at the watermark, Watson, and tell me what you find.

WATSON: (*Holding the paper to the light*) A. and N. (*After a pause*) Army and Navy . . . Why, Holmes, d'you mean that—

HOLMES: I mean that this letter was written by your charming friend in the name of the Countess of Barton.

WATSON: And what follows?

HOLMES: Ah, that is what we are left to conjecture. What will follow immediately is another interview with the young woman who calls herself Violet de Vinne. By the way, Watson, after you had finished threatening me with that nasty-looking revolver a little while ago, what did you do with the instrument?

WATSON: It's here, Holmes, in my pocket.

HOLMES: Then, having left my own in my bedroom, I think I'll borrow it, if you don't mind.

WATSON: But surely, Holmes, you don't suggest that—

HOLMES: My dear Watson, I suggest nothing—except that we may possibly find ourselves in rather deeper waters than Miss de Vinne's charm and innocence have hitherto led you to expect. (*Goes to door*) Mrs. Hudson, ask the lady to be good enough to rejoin us.

MRS. HUDSON: (*Off*) Very good, sir.

(*Enter* MISS DE VINNE)

HOLMES: (*Amiably*) Well, Miss de Vinne, are you rested?

MISS DE VINNE: Well, a little perhaps, but as you can do nothing for me, hadn't I better go?

HOLMES: You look a little flushed, Miss de Vinne; do you feel the room rather too warm?

MISS DE VINNE: No, Mr. Holmes, thank you, I—

HOLMES: Anyhow, won't you slip your coat off and—

MISS DE VINNE: Oh no, really. (*Gathers coat round her*)

HOLMES: (*Threateningly*) Then, if you won't take your coat off, d'you mind showing me what is in the right-hand pocket of it? (*A look of terror comes on* MISS DE VINNE'S *face*) The game's up, Violet de Vinne. (*Points revolver, at which* MISS DE VINNE *screams and throws up her hands*) Watson, oblige me by removing whatever you may discover in the right-hand pocket of Miss de Vinne's coat.

WATSON: (*Taking out note-case*) My own note-case, Holmes, with the ten five-pound notes in it!

HOLMES: Ah!

MISS DE VINNE: (*Distractedly*) Let me speak, let me speak. I'll explain everything.

HOLMES: Silence! Watson, was there anything else in the drawer of your dressing table besides your note-case?

WATSON: I'm not sure, Holmes.

HOLMES: Then I think we had better have some verification.

MISS DE VINNE: No, no. Let me—

HOLMES: Mrs. Hudson!

MRS. HUDSON: (*Off*) Coming, sir.

HOLMES: (*To* MRS. HUDSON *off*) Kindly open the right-hand drawer of Dr. Watson's dressing table and bring us anything that you may find in it.

MISS DE VINNE: Mr. Holmes, you are torturing me. Let me tell you everything.

HOLMES: Your opportunity will come in due course, but in all probability before a different tribunal. I am a private detective, not a Criminal Court judge. (MISS DE VINNE *weeps*)

(*Enter* MRS. HUDSON *with jewel case*)

MRS. HUDSON: I found this, sir. But it must be something new that the doctor's been buying. I've never seen it before. (MRS. HUDSON *leaves*)

HOLMES: Ah, Watson, more surprises! (*Opens case and holds up a string of pearls*) The famous pearls belonging to the Countess of Barton, if I'm not mistaken.

MISS DE VINNE: For pity's sake, Mr. Holmes, let me speak. Even the lowest criminal has that right left him. And this time I will tell you the truth.

HOLMES: (*Sceptically*) The truth? Well?

MISS DE VINNE: Mr. Holmes, I have an only brother. He's a dear—I love him better than anyone in the world—but, God forgive him, he's a scamp . . . always in trouble, always in debt. Three days ago he wrote to me that he was in an even deeper hole than usual. If he couldn't raise fifty pounds in the course of a week, he would be done for and, worse than that, dishonored and disgraced forever. I couldn't bear it. I'd no money. I daren't tell my mother. I swore to myself that I'd get that fifty pounds if I had to steal it. That same day at Lady Barton's, I was looking, as I'd often looked, at the famous pearls. An idea suddenly came to me. They were worn only once or twice a year on special occasions. Why shouldn't I pawn them for a month or so? I could surely get fifty pounds for them and then somehow I would scrape together the money to redeem them. It was almost certain that Lady Barton wouldn't want them for six months. Oh, I know I was mad, but I did it. I found a fairly obscure little pawnbroker quite near here, but to my horror he wouldn't take the pearls—looked at me very suspiciously and wouldn't budge, though I went to him two or three times. Then, this afternoon, the crash came. When Lady Barton discovered that the pearls were missing I rushed out of the house, saying that I would tell the police. But actually I went home and tried to think. I remembered your name. A wild scheme came into my head. If I could pretend to consult you and somehow leave the pearls in your house, then you could pretend that you had recovered them and return them to Lady Barton. Oh, I know you'll laugh, but you don't know how distraught I was. Then, when you sent me into that dressing room, I prowled about like a caged animal. I saw those banknotes and they seemed like a gift from Heaven. Why shouldn't I leave the necklace in their place? You would get much more than fifty pounds for recovering them from Lady Barton and I should save my brother. There, that's all . . . and now, I suppose, I exchange Dr. Watson's dressing room for a cell at the police station!

HOLMES: Well, Watson?

WATSON: What an extraordinary story, Holmes!

HOLMES: Yes, indeed. (*Turning to* MISS DE VINNE) Miss de Vinne, you told us in the first instance a plausible story of which I did not believe a single word; now you have given us a version which in many particulars seems absurd and incredible. Yet I believe it to be the truth. Watson, haven't I always told you that fact is immeasurably stranger than fiction?

WATSON: Certainly, Holmes. But what are you going to do?

HOLMES: Going to do? Why—er—I'm going to send for Mrs. Hudson. (*Calling offstage*) Mrs. Hudson!

MRS. HUDSON: (*Off*) Coming, sir. (*Enters*) Yes, sir.

HOLMES: Oh, Mrs. Hudson, what are your views about Christmas?

WATSON: Really, Holmes.

HOLMES: My dear Watson, please don't interrupt. As I was saying, Mrs. Hudson, I should be very much interested to know how you feel about Christmas.

MRS. HUDSON: Lor', Mr. 'Olmes, what questions you do ask. I don't hardly know exactly how to answer but . . . well . . . I suppose Christmas is the season of good will towards men—and women too, sir, if I may say so.

HOLMES: (*Slowly*) "And women too." You observe that, Watson.

WATSON: Yes, Holmes, and I agree.

HOLMES: (*To* MISS DE VINNE) My dear young lady, you will observe that the jury are agreed upon their verdict.

MISS DE VINNE: Oh, Mr. Holmes, how can I ever thank you?

HOLMES: Not a word. You must thank the members of the jury . . . Mrs. Hudson!

MRS. HUDSON: Yes, sir.

HOLMES: Take Miss de Vinne, not into Dr. Watson's room this time, but into your own comfortable kitchen and give her a cup of your famous tea.

MRS. HUDSON: How do the young lady take it, sir? Rather stronglike, with a bit of a tang to it?

HOLMES: You must ask her that yourself. Anyhow Mrs. Hudson, give her a cup that cheers.

(*Exeunt* MRS. HUDSON *and*
MISS DE VINNE)

WATSON: (*In the highest spirits*) Half a minute, Mrs. Hudson. I'm coming to see that Miss de Vinne has her tea as she likes it. And I tell you what, Holmes (*Looking towards* MISS DE VINNE *and holding up note-case*), you are not going to get your Mediterranean cruise.

(*As* WATSON *goes out, carol-singers are
heard in the distance singing "Good King
Wenceslas."*)

HOLMES: (*Relighting his pipe and smiling meditatively*) Christmas Eve!

CURTAIN

THE ADVENTURE OF THE BLUE CARBUNCLE

Arthur Conan Doyle

ALTHOUGH WRITTEN IN THE VICTORIAN ERA, the Sherlock Holmes stories lack the overwrought verbosity so prevalent in the prose of that era and remain as readable and fresh as anything produced in recent times. Having created the greatest character in the history of English literature, it is astonishing that Arthur Conan Doyle believed his most important works of fiction were such historical novels and short story collections as *Micah Clarke* (1889), *The White Company* (1891), and *Sir Nigel* (1906). He was further convinced that his most significant nonfiction work was in the spiritualism field, to which he devoted the last twenty years of his life, a considerable portion of his fortune, and prodigious energy. "The Adventure of the Blue Carbuncle" was first published in the January 1892 issue of *The Strand Magazine;* it was first collected in *The Adventures of Sherlock Holmes* (London, Newnes, 1892).

The Adventure of the Blue Carbuncle

ARTHUR CONAN DOYLE

I HAD CALLED UPON MY FRIEND Sherlock Holmes upon the second morning after Christmas, with the intention of wishing him the compliments of the season. He was lounging upon the sofa in a purple dressing-gown, a pipe-rack within his reach upon the right, and a pile of crumpled morning papers, evidently newly studied, near at hand. Beside the couch was a wooden chair, and on the angle of the back hung a very seedy and disreputable hard felt hat, much the worse for wear, and cracked in several places. A lens and a forceps lying upon the seat of the chair suggested that the hat had been suspended in this manner for the purpose of examination.

"You are engaged," said I; "perhaps I interrupt you."

"Not at all. I am glad to have a friend with whom I can discuss my results. The matter is a perfectly trivial one," (he jerked his thumb in the direction of the old hat) "but there are points in connection with it which are not entirely devoid of interest and even of instruction."

I seated myself in his armchair and warmed my hands before his crackling fire, for a sharp frost had set in, and the windows were thick with the ice crystals. "I suppose," I remarked, "that, homely as it looks, this thing has some deadly story linked on to it—that it is the clue which will guide you in the solution of some mystery and the punishment of some crime."

"No, no. No crime," said Sherlock Holmes, laughing. "Only one of those whimsical little incidents which will happen when you have four million human beings all jostling each other within the space of a few square miles. Amid the action and reaction of so dense a swarm of humanity, every possible combination of events may be expected to take place, and many a little problem will be presented which may be striking and bizarre without being criminal. We have already had experience of such."

"So much so," I remarked, "that of the last six cases which I have added to my notes, three have been entirely free of any legal crime."

"Precisely. You allude to my attempt to recover the Irene Adler papers, to the singular case of Miss Mary Sutherland, and to the adventure of the man with the twisted lip. Well, I have no doubt that this small matter will fall into the same innocent category. You know Peterson, the commissionaire?"

"Yes."

"It is to him that this trophy belongs."

"It is his hat."

"No, no; he found it. Its owner is unknown. I beg that you will look upon it not as a battered billycock but as an intellectual problem. And, first, as to how it came here. It arrived upon Christmas morning, in company with a good fat goose, which is, I have no doubt, roasting at this moment in front of Peterson's fire. The facts are these. About four o'clock on Christmas morning, Peterson, who, as you know, is a very honest fellow, was returning from some small jollification and was making his way homeward down Tottenham Court Road. In front of him he saw, in the gaslight, a tallish man, walking with a slight stagger and carrying a white goose slung over his shoulder. As he reached the corner of Goodge Street, a row broke out between this stranger and a little knot of roughs. One of the latter knocked off the man's hat, on which he raised his stick to defend himself and, swinging it over his head, smashed the shop window behind him. Peterson had rushed forward to protect the stranger from his assailants; but the man, shocked at having broken the window, and seeing an official-looking person in uniform rushing towards him, dropped his goose, took to his heels, and vanished amid the labyrinth of small streets which lie at the back of Tottenham Court Road. The roughs had also fled at the appearance of Peterson, so that he was left in possession of the field of battle, and also of the spoils of victory in the shape of this battered hat and a most unimpeachable Christmas goose."

"Which surely he restored to their owner?"

"My dear fellow, there lies the problem. It is true that 'For Mrs. Henry Baker' was printed upon a small card which was tied to the bird's left leg, and it is also true that the initials 'H. B.' are legible upon the lining of this hat; but as there are some thousands of Bakers, and some hundreds of Henry Bakers in this city of ours, it is not easy to restore lost property to any one of them."

"What, then, did Peterson do?"

"He brought round both hat and goose to me on Christmas morning, knowing that even the smallest problems are of interest to me. The goose we retained until this morning, when there were signs that, in spite of the slight frost, it would be well that it should be eaten without unnecessary delay. Its finder has carried it off, therefore, to fulfil the ultimate destiny of a goose, while I continue to retain the hat of the unknown gentleman who lost his Christmas dinner."

"Did he not advertise?"

"No."

"Then, what clue could you have as to his identity?"

"Only as much as we can deduce."

"From his hat?"

"Precisely."

"But you are joking. What can you gather from this old battered felt?"

"Here is my lens. You know my methods. What can you gather yourself as to the individuality of the man who has worn this article?"

I took the tattered object in my hands and turned it over rather ruefully. It was a very ordinary black hat of the usual round shape, hard and much the worse for wear. The lining had been of red silk, but was a good deal discoloured. There was no maker's name; but, as Holmes had remarked, the initials "H. B." were scrawled upon one side. It was pierced in the brim for a hat-securer, but the elastic was missing. For the rest, it was cracked, exceedingly dusty, and spotted in several places, although there seemed to have been some attempt to hide the discoloured patches by smearing them with ink.

"I can see nothing," said I, handing it back to my friend.

"On the contrary, Watson, you can see everything. You fail, however, to reason from what you see. You are too timid in drawing your inferences."

"Then, pray tell me, what it is that you can infer from this hat?"

He picked it up and gazed at it in the peculiar introspective fashion which was characteristic of him. "It is perhaps less suggestive than it might have been," he remarked, "and yet there are a few inferences which are very distinct, and a few others which represent at least a strong balance of probability. That the man was highly intellectual is of course obvious upon the face of it, and also that he was fairly well-to-do within the last three years, although he has now fallen upon evil days. He had foresight, but has less now than formerly, pointing to a moral retrogression, which, when taken with the decline of his fortunes, seems to indicate some evil influence, probably drink, at work upon him. This may account also for the obvious fact that his wife has ceased to love him."

"My dear Holmes!"

"He has, however, retained some degree of self-respect," he continued, disregarding my remonstrance. "He is a man who leads a sedentary life, goes out little, is out of training entirely, is middle-aged, has grizzled hair which he has had cut within the last few days, and which he anoints with lime-cream. These are the more patent facts which are to be deduced from his hat. Also, by the way, that it is extremely improbable that he has gas laid on in his house."

"You are certainly joking, Holmes."

"Not in the least. Is it possible that even now, when I give you these results, you are unable to see how they are attained?"

"I have no doubt that I am very stupid, but I must confess that I am unable to follow you. For example, how did you deduce that this man was intellectual?"

For answer Holmes clapped the hat upon his head. It came right over the forehead and settled upon the bridge of his nose. "It is a question of cubic capacity," said he; "a man with so large a brain must have something in it."

"The decline of his fortunes, then?"

"This hat is three years old. These flat brims curled at the edge came in then. It is a hat of the very best quality. Look at the band of ribbed silk and the excellent lining. If this man could afford to buy so expensive a hat three years ago, and has had no hat since, then he has assuredly gone down in the world."

"Well, that is clear enough, certainly. But how about the foresight and the moral retrogression?"

Sherlock Holmes laughed. "Here is the foresight," said he, putting his finger upon the little disc and loop of the hat-securer. "They are never sold upon hats. If this man ordered one, it is a sign of a certain amount of foresight, since he went out of his way to take this precaution against the wind. But since we see that he has broken the elastic and has not troubled to re-

place it, it is obvious that he has less foresight now than formerly, which is a distinct proof of a weakening nature. On the other hand, he has endeavoured to conceal some of these stains upon the felt by daubing them with ink, which is a sign that he has not entirely lost his self-respect."

"Your reasoning is certainly plausible."

"The further points, that he is middle-aged, that his hair is grizzled, that it has been recently cut, and that he uses lime-cream, are all to be gathered from a close examination of the lower part of the lining. The lens discloses a large number of hair-ends, clean cut by the scissors of the barber. They all appear to be adhesive, and there is a distinct odour of lime-cream. This dust, you will observe, is not the gritty, gray dust of the street but the fluffy brown dust of the house, showing that it has been hung up indoors most of the time; while the marks of moisture upon the inside are proof positive that the wearer perspired very freely, and could, therefore, hardly be in the best of training."

"But his wife—you said that she had ceased to love him."

"This hat has not been brushed for weeks. When I see you, my dear Watson, with a week's accumulation of dust upon your hat, and when your wife allows you to go out in such a state, I shall fear that you also have been unfortunate enough to lose your wife's affection."

"But he might be a bachelor."

"Nay, he was bringing home the goose as a peace-offering to his wife. Remember the card upon the bird's leg."

"You have an answer to everything. But how on earth do you deduce that the gas is not laid on in his house?"

"One tallow stain, or even two, might come by chance; but when I see no less than five, I think that there can be little doubt that the individual must be brought into frequent contact with burning tallow—walks upstairs at night probably with his hat in one hand and a guttering candle in the other. Anyhow, he never got tallow-stains from a gas-jet. Are you satisfied?"

"Well, it is very ingenious," said I, laughing; "but since, as you said just now, there has been no crime committed, and no harm done save the loss of a goose, all this seems to be rather a waste of energy."

Sherlock Holmes had opened his mouth to reply, when the door flew open, and Peterson, the commissionaire, rushed into the apartment with flushed cheeks and the face of a man who is dazed with astonishment.

"The goose, Mr. Holmes! The goose, sir!" he gasped.

"Eh? What of it, then? Has it returned to life and flapped off through the kitchen window?" Holmes twisted himself round upon the sofa to get a fairer view of the man's excited face.

"See here, sir! See what my wife found in its crop!" He held out his hand and displayed upon the centre of the palm a brilliantly scintillating blue stone, rather smaller than a bean in size, but of such purity and radiance that it twinkled like an electric point in the dark hollow of his hand.

Sherlock Holmes sat up with a whistle. "By Jove, Peterson!" said he, "this is treasure trove indeed. I suppose you know what you have got?"

"A diamond, sir? A precious stone. It cuts into glass as though it were putty."

"It's more than a precious stone. It is *the* precious stone."

"Not the Countess of Morcar's blue carbuncle!" I ejaculated.

"Precisely so. I ought to know its size and shape, seeing that I have read the advertisement about it in *The Times* every day lately. It is absolutely unique, and its value can only be conjectured, but the reward offered of a thousand pounds is certainly not within a twentieth part of the market price."

"A thousand pounds! Great Lord of Mercy!" The commissionaire plumped down into a chair and stared from one to the other of us.

"That is the reward, and I have reason to know that there are sentimental considerations in the background which would induce the Countess to part with half her fortune if she could but recover the gem."

"It was lost, if I remembered aright, at the Hotel Cosmopolitan," I remarked.

"Precisely so, on the twenty-second of December, just five days ago. John Horner, a plumber, was accused of having abstracted it from the lady's jewel-case. The evidence against him was so strong that the case has been referred to the Assizes. I have some account of the matter here, I believe." He rummaged amid his newspapers, glancing over the dates, until at last he smoothed one out, doubled it over, and read the following paragraph:

"Hotel Cosmopolitan Jewel Robbery. John Horner, 26, plumber, was brought up upon the charge of having upon the 22nd inst., abstracted from the jewel-case of the Countess of Morcar the valuable gem known as the blue carbuncle. James Ryder, upper-attendant at the hotel, gave his evidence to the effect that he had shown Horner up to the dressing-room of the Countess of Morcar upon the day of the robbery in order that he might solder the second bar of the grate, which was loose. He had remained with Horner some little time, but had finally been called away. On returning, he found that Horner had disappeared, that the bureau had been forced open, and that the small morocco casket in which, as it afterwards transpired, the Countess was accustomed to keep her jewel, was lying empty upon the dressing-table. Ryder instantly gave the alarm, and Horner was arrested the same evening; but the stone could not be found either upon his person or in his rooms. Catherine Cusack, maid to the Countess, deposed to having heard Ryder's cry of dismay on discovering the robbery, and to having rushed into the room, where she found matters as described by the last witness. Inspector Bradstreet, B division, gave evidence as to the arrest of Horner, who struggled frantically, and protested his innocence in the strongest terms. Evidence of a previous conviction for robbery having been given against the prisoner, the magistrate refused to deal summarily with the offence, but referred it to the Assizes. Horner, who had shown signs of intense emotion during the proceedings, fainted away at the conclusion and was carried out of court.

"Hum! So much for the police-court," said Holmes thoughtfully, tossing aside the paper. "The question for us now to solve is the sequence of events leading from a rifled jewel-case at one end to the crop of a goose in Tottenham Court Road at the other. You see, Watson, our little deductions have suddenly assumed a much more important and less innocent aspect. Here is the stone; the stone came from the goose, and the goose came from Mr. Henry Baker, the gentleman with the bad hat and all the other characteristics with which I have bored you. So now we must set ourselves very seriously to finding this gentleman and ascertaining what part he has played in this little mystery. To do this, we must try the simplest means first, and these lie undoubtedly in an advertisement in all the evening papers. If this fails, I shall have recourse to other methods."

"What will you say?"

"Give me a pencil and that slip of paper. Now, then:

"Found at the corner of Goodge Street, a goose and a black felt hat. Mr. Henry Baker can have the same by applying at 6:30 this evening at 221B Baker Street.

That is clear and concise."

"Very. But will he see it?"

"Well, he is sure to keep an eye on the papers, since, to a poor man, the loss was a heavy one. He was clearly so scared by his mischance in breaking the window and by the approach of Peterson that he thought of nothing but flight, but since then he must have bitterly regretted the impulse which caused him to drop his bird.

Then, again, the introduction of his name will cause him to see it, for everyone who knows him will direct his attention to it. Here you are, Peterson, run down to the advertising agency and have this put in the evening papers."

"In which, sir?"

"Oh, in the *Globe, Star, Pall Mall, St. James's Gazette, Evening News, Standard, Echo,* and any others that occur to you."

"Very well, sir. And this stone?"

"Ah, yes, I shall keep the stone. Thank you. And, I say, Peterson, just buy a goose on your way back and leave it here with me, for we must have one to give to this gentleman in place of the one which your family is now devouring."

When the commissionaire had gone, Holmes took up the stone and held it against the light. "It's a bonny thing," said he. "Just see how it glints and sparkles. Of course it is a nucleus and focus of crime. Every good stone is. They are the devil's pet baits. In the larger and older jewels every facet may stand for a bloody deed. This stone is not yet twenty years old. It was found in the banks of the Amoy River in southern China and is remarkable in having every characteristic of the carbuncle, save that it is blue in shade instead of ruby red. In spite of its youth, it has already a sinister history. There have been two murders, a vitriol-throwing, a suicide, and several robberies brought about for the sake of this forty-grain weight of crystallized charcoal. Who would think that so pretty a toy would be a purveyor to the gallows and the prison? I'll lock it up in my strong box now and drop a line to the Countess to say that we have it."

"Do you think that this man Horner is innocent?"

"I cannot tell."

"Well, then, do you imagine that this other one, Henry Baker, had anything to do with the matter?"

"It is, I think, much more likely that Henry Baker is an absolutely innocent man, who had no idea that the bird which he was carrying was of considerably more value than if it were made of solid gold. That, however, I shall determine by a very simple test if we have an answer to our advertisement."

"And you can do nothing until then?"

"Nothing."

"In that case I shall continue my professional round. But I shall come back in the evening at the hour you have mentioned, for I should like to see the solution of so tangled a business."

"Very glad to see you. I dine at seven. There is a woodcock, I believe. By the way, in view of recent occurrences, perhaps I ought to ask Mrs. Hudson to examine its crop."

I had been delayed at a case, and it was a little after half-past six when I found myself in Baker Street once more. As I approached the house I saw a tall man in a Scotch bonnet with a coat which was buttoned up to his chin waiting outside in the bright semicircle which was thrown from the fanlight. Just as I arrived the door was opened, and we were shown up together to Holmes's room.

"Mr. Henry Baker, I believe," said he, rising from his armchair and greeting his visitor with the easy air of geniality which he could so readily assume. "Pray take this chair by the fire, Mr. Baker. It is a cold night, and I observe that your circulation is more adapted for summer than for winter. Ah, Watson, you have just come at the right time. Is that your hat, Mr. Baker?"

"Yes, sir, that is undoubtedly my hat."

He was a large man with rounded shoulders, a massive head, and a broad, intelligent face, sloping down to a pointed beard of grizzled brown. A touch of red in nose and cheeks, with a slight tremor of his extended hand, recalled Holmes's surmise as to his habits. His rusty black frock-coat was buttoned right up in front, with the collar turned up, and his lank wrists protruded from his sleeves without a sign of cuff or shirt. He spoke in a low staccato fashion, choosing his words with care, and gave the impression generally of a man of learning and letters who had had ill-usage at the hands of fortune.

"We have retained these things for some days," said Holmes, "because we expected to see an advertisement from you giving your address.

I am at a loss to know now why you did not advertise."

Our visitor gave a rather shamefaced laugh. "Shillings have not been so plentiful with me as they once were," he remarked. "I had no doubt that the gang of roughs who assaulted me had carried off both my hat and the bird. I did not care to spend more money in a hopeless attempt at recovering them."

"Very naturally. By the way, about the bird, we were compelled to eat it."

"To eat it!" Our visitor half rose from his chair in his excitement.

"Yes, it would have been of no use to anyone had we not done so. But I presume that this other goose upon the sideboard, which is about the same weight and perfectly fresh, will answer your purpose equally well?"

"Oh, certainly, certainly," answered Mr. Baker with a sigh of relief.

"Of course, we still have the feathers, legs, crop, and so on of your own bird, so if you wish——"

The man burst into a hearty laugh. "They might be useful to me as relics of my adventure," said he, "but beyond that I can hardly see what use the *disjecta membra* of my late acquaintance are going to be to me. No, sir, I think that, with your permission, I will confine my attentions to the excellent bird which I perceive upon the sideboard."

Sherlock Holmes glanced sharply across at me with a slight shrug of his shoulders.

"There is your hat, then, and there your bird," said he. "By the way, would it bore you to tell me where you got the other one from? I am somewhat of a fowl fancier, and I have seldom seen a better grown goose."

"Certainly, sir," said Baker, who had risen and tucked his newly gained property under his arm. "There are a few of us who frequent the Alpha Inn, near the Museum—we are to be found in the Museum itself during the day, you understand. This year our good host, Windigate by name, instituted a goose club, by which, on consideration of some few pence every week, we were each to receive a bird at Christmas. My pence were duly paid, and the rest is familiar to you. I am much indebted to you, sir, for a Scotch bonnet is fitted neither to my years nor my gravity." With a comical pomposity of manner he bowed solemnly to both of us and strode off upon his way.

"So much for Mr. Henry Baker," said Holmes when he had closed the door behind him. "It is quite certain that he knows nothing whatever about the matter. Are you hungry, Watson?"

"Not particularly."

"Then I suggest that we turn our dinner into a supper and follow up this clue while it is still hot."

"By all means."

It was a bitter night, so we drew on our ulsters and wrapped cravats about our throats. Outside, the stars were shining coldly in a cloudless sky, and the breath of the passers-by blew out into smoke like so many pistol shots. Our footfalls rang out crisply and loudly as we swung through the doctors' quarter, Wimpole Street, Harley Street, and so through Wigmore Street into Oxford Street. In a quarter of an hour we were in Bloomsbury at the Alpha Inn, which is a small public-house at the corner of one of the streets which runs down into Holborn. Holmes pushed open the door of the private bar and ordered two glasses of beer from the ruddy-faced, white-aproned landlord.

"Your beer should be excellent if it is as good as your geese," said he.

"My geese!" The man seemed surprised.

"Yes. I was speaking only half an hour ago to Mr. Henry Baker, who was a member of your goose club."

"Ah! yes, I see. But you see, sir, them's not *our* geese."

"Indeed! Whose, then?"

"Well, I got the two dozen from a salesman in Covent Garden."

"Indeed? I know some of them. Which was it?"

"Breckinridge is his name."

"Ah! I don't know him. Well, here's your good health, landlord, and prosperity to your house. Good-night.

"Now for Mr. Breckinridge," he continued, buttoning up his coat as we came out into the frosty air. "Remember, Watson, that though we have so homely a thing as a goose at one end of this chain, we have at the other a man who will certainly get seven years' penal servitude unless we can establish his innocence. It is possible that our inquiry may but confirm his guilt; but, in any case, we have a line of investigation which has been missed by the police, and which a singular chance has placed in our hands. Let us follow it out to the bitter end. Faces to the south, then, and quick march!"

We passed across Holborn, down Endell Street, and so through a zigzag of slums to Covent Garden Market. One of the largest stalls bore the name of Breckinridge upon it, and the proprietor, a horsy-looking man, with a sharp face and trim side-whiskers, was helping a boy to put up the shutters.

"Good-evening. It's a cold night," said Holmes.

The salesman nodded and shot a questioning glance at my companion.

"Sold out of geese, I see," continued Holmes, pointing at the bare slabs of marble.

"Let you have five hundred to-morrow morning."

"That's no good."

"Well, there are some on the stall with the gas-flare."

"Ah, but I was recommended to you."

"Who by?"

"The landlord of the Alpha."

"Oh, yes; I sent him a couple of dozen."

"Fine birds they were, too. Now where did you get them from?"

To my surprise the question provoked a burst of anger from the salesman.

"Now, then, mister," said he, with his head cocked and his arms akimbo, "what are you driving at? Let's have it straight, now."

"It is straight enough. I should like to know who sold you the geese which you supplied to the Alpha."

"Well, then, I shan't tell you. So now!"

"Oh, it is a matter of no importance; but I don't know why you should be so warm over such a trifle."

"Warm! You'd be as warm, maybe, if you were as pestered as I am. When I pay good money for a good article there should be an end of the business; but it's 'Where are the geese?' and 'Who did you sell the geese to?' and 'What will you take for the geese?' One would think they were the only geese in the world, to hear the fuss that is made over them."

"Well, I have no connection with any other people who have been making inquiries," said Holmes carelessly. "If you won't tell us the bet is off, that is all. But I'm always ready to back my opinion on a matter of fowls, and I have a fiver on it that the bird I ate is country bred."

"Well, then, you've lost your fiver, for it's town bred," snapped the salesman.

"It's nothing of the kind."

"I say it is."

"I don't believe it."

"D'you think you know more about fowls than I, who have handled them ever since I was a nipper? I tell you, all those birds that went to the Alpha were town bred."

"You'll never persuade me to believe that."

"Will you bet, then?"

"It's merely taking your money, for I know that I am right. But I'll have a sovereign on with you, just to teach you not to be obstinate."

The salesman chuckled grimly. "Bring me the books, Bill," said he.

The small boy brought round a small thin volume and a great greasy-backed one, laying them out together beneath the hanging lamp.

"Now then, Mr. Cocksure," said the salesman, "I thought that I was out of geese, but before I finish you'll find that there is still one left in my shop. You see this little book?"

"Well?"

"That's the list of the folk from whom I buy. D'you see? Well, then, here on this page are the country folk, and the numbers after their names are where their accounts are in the big ledger. Now, then! You see this other page in red ink? Well, that is a list of my town suppliers. Now, look at that third name. Just read it out to me."

"Mrs. Oakshott, 117 Brixton Road—249," read Holmes.

"Quite so. Now turn that up in the ledger."

Holmes turned to the page indicated. "Here you are, 'Mrs. Oakshott, 117 Brixton Road, egg and poultry supplier."

"Now, then, what's the last entry?"

"'December 22d. Twenty-four geese at 7s. 6d.'"

"Quite so. There you are. And underneath?"

"'Sold to Mr. Windigate of the Alpha, at 12s.'"

"What have you to say now?"

Sherlock Holmes looked deeply chagrined. He drew a sovereign from his pocket and threw it down upon the slab, turning away with the air of a man whose disgust is too deep for words. A few yards off he stopped under a lamp-post and laughed in the hearty, noiseless fashion which was peculiar to him.

"When you see a man with whiskers of that cut and the 'Pink 'un' protruding out of his pocket, you can always draw him by a bet," said he. "I daresay that if I had put a hundred pounds down in front of him, that man would not have given me such complete information as was drawn from him by the idea that he was doing me on a wager. Well, Watson, we are, I fancy, nearing the end of our quest, and the only point which remains to be determined is whether we should go on to this Mrs. Oakshott to-night, or whether we should reserve it for tomorrow. It is clear from what that surly fellow said that there are others besides ourselves who are anxious about the matter, and I should——"

His remarks were suddenly cut short by a loud hubbub which broke out from the stall which we had just left. Turning round we saw a little rat-faced fellow standing in the centre of the circle of yellow light which was thrown by the swinging lamp, while Breckinridge, the salesman, framed in the door of his stall, was shaking his fists fiercely at the cringing figure.

"I've had enough of you and your geese," he shouted. "I wish you were all at the devil together. If you come pestering me any more with your silly talk I'll set the dog at you. You bring Mrs. Oakshott here and I'll answer her, but what have you to do with it? Did I buy the geese off you?"

"No; but one of them was mine all the same," whined the little man.

"Well, then, ask Mrs. Oakshott for it."

"She told me to ask you."

"Well, you can ask the King of Proosia, for all I care. I've had enough of it. Get out of this!" He rushed fiercely forward, and the inquirer flitted away into the darkness.

"Ha! this may save us a visit to Brixton Road," whispered Holmes. "Come with me, and we will see what is to be made of this fellow." Striding through the scattered knots of people who lounged round the flaring stalls, my companion speedily overtook the little man and touched him upon the shoulder. He sprang round, and I could see in the gaslight that every vestige of colour had been driven from his face.

"Who are you, then? What do you want?" he asked in a quavering voice.

"You will excuse me," said Holmes blandly, "but I could not help overhearing the questions which you put to the salesman just now. I think that I could be of assistance to you."

"You? Who are you? How could you know anything of the matter?"

"My name is Sherlock Holmes. It is my business to know what other people don't know."

"But you can know nothing of this?"

"Excuse me, I know everything of it. You are endeavouring to trace some geese which were sold by Mrs. Oakshott, of Brixton Road, to a salesman named Breckinridge, by him in turn to Mr. Windigate, of the Alpha, and by him to his club, of which Mr. Henry Baker is a member."

"Oh, sir, you are the very man whom I have longed to meet," cried the little fellow with outstretched hands and quivering fingers. "I can hardly explain to you how interested I am in this matter."

Sherlock Holmes hailed a four-wheeler which was passing. "In that case we had better discuss it in a cosy room rather than in this windswept market-place," said he. "But pray tell me, before we go further, who it is that I have the pleasure of assisting."

The man hesitated for an instant. "My name is John Robinson," he answered with a sidelong glance.

"No, no; the real name," said Holmes sweetly. "It is always awkward doing business with an alias."

A flush sprang to the white cheeks of the stranger. "Well, then," said he, "my real name is James Ryder."

"Precisely so. Head attendant at the Hotel Cosmopolitan. Pray step into the cab, and I shall soon be able to tell you everything which you would wish to know."

The little man stood glancing from one to the other of us with half-frightened, half-hopeful eyes, as one who is not sure whether he is on the verge of a windfall or of a catastrophe. Then he stepped into the cab, and in half an hour we were back in the sitting-room at Baker Street. Nothing had been said during our drive, but the high, thin breathing of our new companion, and the claspings and unclaspings of his hands, spoke of the nervous tension within him.

"Here we are!" said Holmes cheerily as we filed into the room. "The fire looks very seasonable in this weather. You look cold, Mr. Ryder. Pray take the basket-chair. I will just put on my slippers before we settle this little matter of yours. Now, then! You want to know what became of those geese?"

"Yes, sir."

"Or rather, I fancy, of that goose. It was one bird, I imagine, in which you were interested—white, with a black bar across the tail."

Ryder quivered with emotion. "Oh, sir," he cried, "can you tell me where it went to?"

"It came here."

"Here?"

"Yes, and a most remarkable bird it proved. I don't wonder that you should take an interest in it. It laid an egg after it was dead—the bonniest, brightest little blue egg that ever was seen. I have it here in my museum."

Our visitor staggered to his feet and clutched the mantelpiece with his right hand. Holmes unlocked his strong-box and held up the blue carbuncle, which shone out like a star, with a cold, brilliant, many-pointed radiance. Ryder stood glaring with a drawn face, uncertain whether to claim or to disown it.

"The game's up, Ryder," said Holmes quietly. "Hold up, man, or you'll be into the fire! Give him an arm back into his chair, Watson. He's not got blood enough to go in for felony with impunity. Give him a dash of brandy. So! Now he looks a little more human. What a shrimp it is, to be sure!"

For a moment he had staggered and nearly fallen, but the brandy brought a tinge of colour into his cheeks, and he sat staring with frightened eyes at his accuser.

"I have almost every link in my hands, and all the proofs which I could possibly need, so there is little which you need tell me. Still, that little may as well be cleared up to make the case complete. You had heard, Ryder, of this blue stone of the Countess of Morcar's?"

"It was Catherine Cusack who told me of it," said he in a crackling voice.

"I see—her ladyship's waiting-maid. Well, the temptation of sudden wealth so easily acquired was too much for you, as it has been for better men before you; but you were not very scrupulous in the means you used. It seems to me, Ryder, that there is the making of a very pretty villain in you. You knew that this man Horner, the plumber, had been concerned in some such matter before, and that suspicion would rest the more readily upon him. What did you do, then? You made some small job in my lady's room—you and your confederate Cusack—and you managed that he should be the man sent for. Then, when he had left, you rifled the jewel-case, raised the alarm, and had this unfortunate man arrested. You then——"

Ryder threw himself down suddenly upon the rug and clutched at my companion's knees. "For God's sake, have mercy!" he shrieked. "Think of my father! of my mother! It would break their hearts. I never went wrong before! I never will again. I swear it. I'll swear it on a Bible. Oh, don't bring it into court! For Christ's sake, don't!"

"Get back into your chair!" said Holmes sternly. "It is very well to cringe and crawl now, but you thought little enough of this poor Horner in the dock for a crime of which he knew nothing."

"I will fly, Mr. Holmes. I will leave the country, sir. Then the charge against him will break down."

"Hum! We will talk about that. And now let us hear a true account of the next act. How came the stone into the goose, and how came the goose into the open market? Tell us the truth, for there lies your only hope of safety."

Ryder passed his tongue over his parched lips. "I will tell you it just as it happened, sir," said he. "When Horner had been arrested, it seemed to me that it would be best for me to get away with the stone at once, for I did not know at what moment the police might not take it into their heads to search me and my room. There was no place about the hotel where it would be safe. I went out, as if on some commission, and I made for my sister's house. She had married a man named Oakshott, and lived in Brixton Road, where she fattened fowls for the market. All the way there every man I met seemed to me to be a policeman or a detective; and, for all that it was a cold night, the sweat was pouring down my face before I came to the Brixton Road. My sister asked me what was the matter, and why I was so pale; but I told her that I had been upset by the jewel robbery at the hotel. Then I went into the back yard and smoked a pipe, and wondered what it would be best to do.

"I had a friend once called Maudsley, who

went to the bad, and has just been serving his time in Pentonville. One day he had met me, and fell into talk about the ways of thieves, and how they could get rid of what they stole. I knew that he would be true to me, for I knew one or two things about him; so I made up my mind to go right on to Kilburn, where he lived, and take him into my confidence. He would show me how to turn the stone into money. But how to get to him in safety? I thought of the agonies I had gone through in coming from the hotel. I might at any moment be seized and searched, and there would be the stone in my waistcoat pocket. I was leaning against the wall at the time and looking at the geese which were waddling about round my feet, and suddenly an idea came into my head which showed me how I could beat the best detective that ever lived.

"My sister had told me some weeks before that I might have the pick of her geese for a Christmas present, and I knew that she was always as good as her word. I would take my goose now, and in it I would carry my stone to Kilburn. There was a little shed in the yard, and behind this I drove one of the birds—a fine big one, white, with a barred tail. I caught it, and prising its bill open, I thrust the stone down its throat as far as my finger could reach. The bird gave a gulp, and I felt the stone pass along its gullet and down into its crop. But the creature flapped and struggled, and out came my sister to know what was the matter. As I turned to speak to her the brute broke loose and fluttered off among the others.

"'Whatever were you doing with that bird, Jem?' says she.

"'Well,' said I, 'you said you'd give me one for Christmas, and I was feeling which was the fattest.'

"'Oh,' says she, 'we've set yours aside for you—Jem's bird, we call it. It's the big white one over yonder. There's twenty-six of them, which makes one for you, and one for us, and two dozen for the market.'

"'Thank you, Maggie,' says I; 'but if it is all the same to you, I'd rather have that one I was handling just now.'

"'The other is a good three pound heavier,' said she, 'and we fattened it expressly for you.'

"'Never mind. I'll have the other, and I'll take it now,' said I.

"'Oh, just as you like,' said she, a little huffed. 'Which is it you want, then?'

"'That white one with the barred tail, right in the middle of the flock.'

"'Oh, very well. Kill it and take it with you.'

"Well, I did what she said, Mr. Holmes, and I carried the bird all the way to Kilburn. I told my pal what I had done, for he was a man that it was easy to tell a thing like that to. He laughed until he choked, and we got a knife and opened the goose. My heart turned to water, for there was no sign of the stone, and I knew that some terrible mistake had occurred. I left the bird, rushed back to my sister's, and hurried into the back yard. There was not a bird to be seen there.

"'Where are they all, Maggie?' I cried.

"'Gone to the dealer's, Jem.'

"'Which dealer's?'

"'Breckinridge, of Covent Garden.'

"'But was there another with a barred tail?' I asked. 'The same as the one I chose.'

"'Yes, Jem; there were two barred-tailed ones, and I could never tell them apart.'

"Well, then, of course I saw it all, and I ran off as hard as my feet would carry me to this man Breckinridge; but he had sold the lot at once, and not a word would he tell me as to where they had gone. You heard him yourselves to-night. Well, he has always answered me like that. My sister thinks I am going mad. Sometimes I think that I am myself. And now—and now I am myself a branded thief, without ever having touched the wealth for which I sold my character. God help me! God help me!" He burst into convulsive sobbing, with his face buried in his hands.

There was a long silence, broken only by his heavy breathing, and by the measured tapping of Sherlock Holmes's finger-tips upon the edge of the table. Then my friend rose and threw open the door.

"Get out!" said he.

"What, sir! Oh, Heaven bless you!"

"No more words. Get out!"

And no more words were needed. There was a rush, a clatter upon the stairs, the bang of a door, and the crisp rattle of running footfalls from the street.

"After all, Watson," said Holmes, reaching up his hand for his clay pipe, "I am not retained by the police to supply their deficiences. If Horner were in danger it would be another thing; but this fellow will not appear against him, and the case must collapse. I suppose that I am commiting a felony, but it is just possible that I am saving a soul. This fellow will not go wrong again; he is too terribly frightened. Send him to gaol now, and you make him a gaolbird for life. Besides, it is the season of forgiveness. Chance has put in our way a most singular and whimsical problem, and its solution is its own reward. If you will have the goodness to touch the bell, Doctor, we will begin another investigation, in which, also, a bird will be the chief feature."

A PULPY
Little Christmas

DEAD ON CHRISTMAS STREET

John D. MacDonald

JOHN D. MACDONALD'S MOST FAMOUS CHARACTER, Travis McGee, lived on a houseboat named "The Busted Flush," which he won in a poker game. One of the great characters of mystery fiction, McGee is a combined private detective and thief who makes his living by recovering stolen property and, while operating outside the law, victimizes only criminals. MacDonald's outstanding suspense novel, *The Executioners*, was filmed twice as *Cape Fear* (in 1962, with Gregory Peck, Robert Mitchum, and Polly Bergen, and in 1991, with Nick Nolte, Robert De Niro, Jessica Lange, and Juliette Lewis). "Dead on Christmas Street" was first published in the December 20, 1952, issue of *Collier's*.

Dead on Christmas Street

JOHN D. MACDONALD

THE POLICE IN THE FIRST PROWL car on the scene got out a tarpaulin. A traffic policeman threw it over the body and herded the crowd back. They moved uneasily in the gray slush. Some of them looked up from time to time.

In the newspaper picture the window would be marked with a bold X. A dotted line would descend from the X to the spot where the covered body now lay. Some of the spectators, laden with tinsel- and evergreen-decorated packages, turned away, suppressing a nameless guilt.

But the curious stayed on. Across the street, in the window of a department store, a vast mechanical Santa rocked back and forth, slapping a mechanical hand against a padded thigh, roaring forever, "Whaw haw ho ho ho. Whaw haw ho ho ho." The slapping hand had worn the red plush from the padded thigh.

The ambulance arrived, with a brisk intern to make out the DOA. Sawdust was shoveled onto the sidewalk, then pushed off into the sewer drain. Wet snow fell into the city. And there was nothing else to see. The corner Santa, a leathery man with a pinched, blue nose, began to ring his hand bell again.

Daniel Fowler, one of the young Assistant District Attorneys, was at his desk when the call came through from Lieutenant Shinn of the Detective Squad. "Dan? This is Gil. You heard about the Garrity girl yet?"

For a moment the name meant nothing, and then suddenly he remembered: Loreen Garrity was the witness in the Sheridan City Loan Company case. She had made positive identification of two of the three kids who had tried to pull that holdup, and the case was on the calendar for February. Provided the kids didn't confess before it came up, Dan was going to prosecute. He had the Garrity girl's statement, and her promise to appear.

"What about her, Gil?" he asked.

"She took a high dive out of her office window—about an hour ago. Seventeen stories, and right into the Christmas rush. How come she didn't land on somebody, we'll never know. Connie Wyant is handling it. He remembered she figured in the loan-company deal, and he told me. Look, Dan. She was a big girl, and she tried hard not to go out that window. She was shoved. That's how come Connie has it. Nice Christmas present for him."

"Nice Christmas present for the lads who pushed over the loan company, too," Dan said grimly. "Without her, there's no case. Tell Connie that. It ought to give him the right line."

Dan Fowler set aside the brief he was working on and walked down the hall. The District Attorney's secretary was at her desk. "Boss busy, Jane?"

She was a small girl with wide, gray eyes, a mass of dark hair, a soft mouth. She raised one eyebrow and looked at him speculatively. "I could be bribed, you know."

He looked around with exaggerated caution, went around her desk on tiptoe, bent and kissed her upraised lips. He smiled down at her. "People are beginning to talk," he whispered, not getting it as light as he meant it to be.

She tilted her head to one side, frowned, and said, "What is it, Dan?"

He sat on the corner of her desk and took her hands in his, and he told her about the big, dark-haired, swaggering woman who had gone out the window. He knew Jane would want to know. He had regretted bringing Jane in on the case, but he had had the unhappy hunch that Garrity might sell out, if the offer was high enough. And so he had enlisted Jane, depending on her intuition. He had taken the two of them to lunch, and had invented an excuse to duck out and leave them alone.

Afterward, Jane had said, "I guess I don't really like her, Dan. She was suspicious of me, of course, and she's a terribly vital sort of person. But I would say that she'll be willing to testify. And I don't think she'll sell out."

Now as he told her about the girl, he saw the sudden tears of sympathy in her gray eyes. "Oh, Dan! How dreadful! You'd better tell the boss right away. That Vince Servius must have hired somebody to do it."

"Easy, lady," he said softly.

He touched her dark hair with his fingertips, smiled at her, and crossed to the door of the inner office, opened it, and went in.

Jim Heglon, the District Attorney, was a narrow-faced man with glasses that had heavy frames. He had a professional look, a dry wit, and a driving energy.

"Every time I see you, Dan, I have to conceal my annoyance," Heglon said. "You're going to cart away the best secretary I ever had."

"Maybe I'll keep her working for awhile. Keep her out of trouble."

"Excellent! And speaking of trouble—"

"Does it show, Jim?" Dan sat on the arm of a heavy leather chair which faced Heglon's desk. "I do have some. Remember the Sheridan City Loan case?"

"Vaguely. Give me an outline."

"October. Five o'clock one afternoon, just as the loan office was closing. Three punks tried to knock it over. Two of them, Castrella and Kelly, are eighteen. The leader, Johnny Servius, is nineteen. Johnny is Vince Servius's kid brother.

"They went into the loan company wearing masks and waving guns. The manager had more guts than sense. He was loading the safe. He saw them and slammed the door and spun the knob. They beat on him, but he convinced them it was a time lock, which it wasn't. They took fifteen dollars out of his pants, and four dollars off the girl behind the counter and took off.

"Right across the hall is the office of an accountant named Thomas Kistner. He'd already left. His secretary, Loreen Garrity, was closing up the office. She had the door open a crack. She saw the three kids come out of the loan company, taking their masks off. Fortunately, they didn't see her.

"She went into headquarters and looked at the gallery, and picked out Servius and Castrella. They were picked up. Kelly was with them, so they took him in, too. In the lineup, the Garrity girl made a positive identification of Servius and Castrella again. The manager thought he could recognize Kelly's voice.

"Bail was set high, because we expected Vince Servius would get them out. Much to everybody's surprise, he's left them in there. The only thing he did was line up George Terrafierro to defend them, which makes it tough from our point of view, but not too tough—if we could put the Garrity girl on the stand. She was the type to make a good witness. Very positive sort of girl."

"Was? Past tense?"

"This afternoon she was pushed out the window of the office where she works. Seventeen stories above the sidewalk. Gil Shinn tells me that Connie Wyant has it definitely tagged as homicide."

"If Connie says it is, then it is. What would conviction have meant to the three lads?"

"Servius had one previous conviction—car

theft; Castrella had one conviction for assault with a deadly weapon. Kelly is clean, Jim."

Heglon frowned. "Odd, isn't it? In this state, armed robbery has a mandatory sentence of seven to fifteen years for a first offense in that category. With the weight Vince can swing, his kid brother would do about five years. Murder seems a little extreme as a way of avoiding a five-year sentence."

"Perhaps, Jim, the answer is in the relationship between Vince and the kid. There's quite a difference in ages. Vince must be nearly forty. He was in the big time early enough to give Johnny all the breaks. The kid has been thrown out of three good schools I know of. According to Vince, Johnny can do no wrong. Maybe that's why he left those three in jail awaiting trial—to keep them in the clear on this killing."

"It could be, Dan," Heglon said. "Go ahead with your investigation. And let me know."

Dan Fowler found out at the desk that Lieutenant Connie Wyant and Sergeant Levandowski were in the Interrogation Room. Dan sat down and waited.

After a few moments Connie waddled through the doorway and came over to him. He had bulging blue eyes and a dull expression.

Dan stood up, towering over the squat lieutenant. "Well, what's the picture, Connie?"

"No case against the kids, Gil says. Me, I wish it was just somebody thought it would be nice to jump out a window. But she grabbed the casing so hard, she broke her fingernails down to the quick.

"Marks you can see, in oak as hard as iron. Banged her head on the sill and left black hair on the rough edge of the casing. Lab matched it up. And one shoe up there, under the radiator. The radiator sits right in front of the window. Come listen to Kistner."

Dan followed him back to the Interrogation Room. Thomas Kistner sat at one side of the long table. A cigar lay dead on the glass ashtray near his elbow. As they opened the door, he glanced up quickly. He was a big, bloated man with an unhealthy grayish complexion and an important manner.

He said, "I was just telling the sergeant the tribulations of an accountant."

"We all got troubles," Connie said. "This is Mr. Fowler from the D. A.'s office, Kistner."

Mr. Kistner got up laboriously. "Happy to meet you, sir," he said. "Sorry that it has to be such an unpleasant occasion, however."

Connie sat down heavily. "Kistner, I want you to go through your story again. If it makes it easier, tell it to Mr. Fowler instead of me. He hasn't heard it before."

"I'll do anything in my power to help, Lieutenant," Kistner said firmly. He turned toward Dan. "I am out of my office a great deal. I do accounting on a contract basis for thirty-three small retail establishments. I visit them frequently.

"When Loreen came in this morning, she seemed nervous. I asked her what the trouble was, and she said that she felt quite sure somebody had been following her for the past week.

"She described him to me. Slim, middle height, pearl-gray felt hat, tan raglan topcoat, swarthy complexion. I told her that because she was the witness in a trial coming up, she should maybe report it to the police and ask for protection. She said she didn't like the idea of yelling for help. She was a very—ah—independent sort of girl."

"I got that impression," Dan said.

"I went out then and didn't think anything more about what she'd said. I spent most of the morning at Finch Pharmacy, on the north side. I had a sandwich there and then drove back to the office, later than usual. Nearly two.

"I came up to the seventeenth floor. Going down the corridor, I pass the Men's Room before I get to my office. I unlocked the door with my key and went in. I was in there maybe three minutes. I came out and a man brushed by me in the corridor. He had his collar up, and was pulling down on his hatbrim and walking fast. At the moment, you understand, it meant nothing to me.

"I went into the office. The window was wide open, and the snow was blowing in. No Loreen. I couldn't figure it. I thought she'd gone to the Ladies' Room and had left the window open for some crazy reason. I started to shut it, and then I heard all the screaming down in the street.

"I leaned out. I saw her, right under me, sprawled on the sidewalk. I recognized the cocoa-colored suit. A new suit, I think. I stood in a state of shock, I guess, and then suddenly I remembered about the man following her, and I remembered the man in the hall—he had a gray hat and a tan topcoat, and I had the impression he was swarthy-faced.

"The first thing I did was call the police, naturally. While they were on the way, I called my wife. It just about broke her up. We were both fond of Loreen."

The big man smiled sadly. "And it seems to me I've been telling the story over and over again ever since. Oh, I don't mind, you understand. But it's a dreadful thing. The way I see it, when a person witnesses a crime, they ought to be given police protection until the trial is all over."

"We don't have that many cops," Connie said glumly. "How big was the man you saw in the corridor?"

"Medium size. A little on the thin side."

"How old?"

"I don't know. Twenty-five, forty-five. I couldn't see his face, and you understand I wasn't looking closely."

Connie turned toward Dan. "Nothing from the elevator boys about this guy. He probably took the stairs. The lobby is too busy for anybody to notice him coming through by way of the fire door. Did the Garrity girl ever lock herself in the office, Kistner?"

"I never knew of her doing that, Lieutenant."

Connie said, "Okay, so the guy could breeze in and clip her one. Then, from the way the rug was pulled up, he lugged her across to the window. She came to as he was trying to work her out the window, and she put up a battle. People

in the office three stories underneath say she was screaming as she went by."

"How about the offices across the way?" Dan asked.

"It's a wide street, Dan, and they couldn't see through the snow. It started snowing hard about fifteen minutes before she was pushed out the window. I think the killer waited for that snow. It gave him a curtain to hide behind."

"Any chance that she marked the killer, Connie?" Dan asked.

"Doubt it. From the marks of her fingernails, he lifted her up and slid her feet out first, so her back was to him. She grabbed the sill on each side. Her head hit the window sash. All he had to do was hold her shoulders, and bang her in the small of the back with his knee. Once her fanny slid off the sill, she couldn't hold on with her hands any longer. And from the looks of the doorknobs, he wore gloves."

Dan turned to Kistner. "What was her home situation? I tried to question her. She was pretty evasive."

Kistner shrugged. "Big family. She didn't get along with them. Seven girls, I think, and she was next to oldest. She moved out when she got her first job. She lived alone in a one-room apartment on Leeds Avenue, near the bridge."

"You know of any boy friend?" Connie asked.

"Nobody special. She used to go out a lot, but nobody special."

Connie rapped his knuckles on the edge of the table. "You ever make a pass at her, Kistner?"

The room was silent. Kistner stared at his dead cigar. "I don't want to lie to you, but I don't want any trouble at home, either. I got a boy in the Army, and I got a girl in her last year of high school. But you work in a small office alone with a girl like Loreen, and it can get you.

"About six months ago I had to go to the state Capitol on a tax thing. I asked her to come along. She did. It was a damn fool thing to do. And it—didn't work out so good. We agreed to forget it ever happened.

"We were awkward around the office for a couple of weeks, and then I guess we sort of forgot. She was a good worker, and I was paying her well, so it was to both our advantages to be practical and not get emotional. I didn't have to tell you men this, but, like I said, I don't see any point in lying to the police. Hell, you might have found out some way, and that might make it look like I killed her or something."

"Thanks for leveling," Connie said expressionlessly. "We'll call you if we need you."

Kistner ceremoniously shook hands all around and left with obvious relief.

As soon as the door shut behind him, Connie said, "I'll buy it. A long time ago I learned you can't jail a guy for being a jerk. Funny how many honest people I meet I don't like at all, and how many thieves make good guys to knock over a beer with. How's your girl?"

Dan looked at his watch. "Dressing for dinner, and I should be, too," he said. "How are the steaks out at the Cat and Fiddle?"

Connie half closed his eyes. After a time he sighed. "Okay. That might be a good way to go at the guy. Phone me and give me the reaction if he does talk. If not, don't bother."

Jane was in a holiday mood until Dan told her where they were headed. She said tartly, "I admit freely that I am a working girl. But do I get overtime for this?"

Dan said slowly, carefully, "Darling, you better understand, if you don't already, that there's one part of me I can't change. I can't shut the office door and forget the cases piled up in there. I have a nasty habit of carrying them around with me. So we go someplace else and I try like blazes to be gay, or we go to the Cat and Fiddle and get something off my mind."

She moved closer to him. "Dull old work horse," she said.

"Guilty."

"All right, now I'll confess," Jane said. "I was going to suggest we go out there later. I just got sore when you beat me to the draw."

He laughed, and at the next stop light he kissed her hurriedly.

The Cat and Fiddle was eight miles beyond the city line. At last Dan saw the green-and-blue neon sign, and he turned into the asphalt parking area. There were about forty other cars there.

They went from the check room into the low-ceilinged bar and lounge. The only sign of Christmas was a small silver tree on the bar; a tiny blue spot was focused on it.

They sat at the bar and ordered drinks. Several other couples were at the tables, talking in low voices. A pianist played softly in the dining room.

Dan took out a business card and wrote on it: *Only if you happen to have an opinion.*

He called the nearest bartender over. "Would you please see that Vince gets this?"

The man glanced at the name. "I'll see if Mr. Servius is in." He said something to the other bartender and left through a paneled door at the rear of the bar. He was back in less than a minute, smiling politely.

"Please go up the stairs. Mr. Servius is in his office—the second door on the right."

"I'll wait here, Dan," Jane said.

"If you are Miss Raymer, Mr. Servius would like to have you join him, too," the bartender said.

Jane looked at Dan. He nodded and she slid off the stool.

As they went up the stairs, Jane said, "I seem to be known here."

"Notorious female. I suspect he wants a witness."

Vincent Servius was standing at a small corner bar mixing himself a drink when they entered. He turned and smiled. "Fowler, Miss Raymer. Nice of you to stop by. Can I mix you something?"

Dan refused politely, and they sat down.

Vince was a compact man with cropped, prematurely white hair, a sunlamp tan, and beautifully cut clothes. He had not been directly concerned with violence in many years. In that time he had eliminated most of the traces of the hoodlum.

The over-all impression he gave was that of

the up-and-coming clubman. Golf lessons, voice lessons, plastic surgery, and a good tailor—these had all helped; but nothing had been able to destroy a certain aura of alertness, ruthlessness. He was a man you would never joke with. He had made his own laws, and he carried the awareness of his own ultimate authority around with him, as unmistakable as a loaded gun.

Vince went over to the fieldstone fireplace, drink in hand, and turned, resting his elbow on the mantel.

"Very clever, Fowler. 'Only if you happen to have an opinion.' I have an opinion. The kid is no good. That's my opinion. He's a cheap punk. I didn't admit that to myself until he tried to put the hook on that loan company. He was working for me at the time. I was trying to break him in here—buying foods.

"But now I'm through, Fowler. You can tell Jim Heglon that for me. Terrafierro will back it up. Ask him what I told him. I said, 'Defend the kid. Get him off if you can and no hard feelings if you can't. If you get him off, I'm having him run out of town, out of the state. I don't want him around.' I told George that.

"Now there's this Garrity thing. It looks like I went out on a limb for the kid. Going out on limbs was yesterday, Fowler. Not today and not tomorrow. I was a sucker long enough."

He took out a crisp handkerchief and mopped his forehead. "I go right up in the air," he said. "I talk too loud."

"You can see how Heglon is thinking," Dan said quietly. "And the police, too."

"That's the hell of it. I swear I had nothing to do with it." He half smiled. "It would have helped if I'd had a tape recorder up here last month when the Garrity girl came to see what she could sell me."

Dan leaned forward. "She came here?"

"With bells on. Nothing coy about that kid. Pay off, Mr. Servius, and I'll change my identification of your brother."

"What part of last month?"

"Let me think. The tenth it was. Monday the tenth."

Jane said softly, "That's why I got the impression she wouldn't sell out, Dan. I had lunch with her later that same week. She had tried to and couldn't."

Vince took a sip of his drink. "She started with big money and worked her way down. I let her go ahead. Finally, after I'd had my laughs, I told her even one dollar was too much. I told her I wanted the kid sent up.

"She blew her top. For a couple of minutes I thought I might have to clip her to shut her up. But after a couple of drinks she quieted down. That gave me a chance to find out something that had been bothering me. It seemed too pat, kind of."

"What do you mean, Servius?" Dan asked.

"The setup was too neat, the way the door *happened* to be open a crack, and the way she *happened* to be working late, and the way she *happened* to see the kids come out.

"I couldn't get her to admit anything at first, because she was making a little play for me, but when I convinced her I wasn't having any, she let me in on what really happened. She was hanging around waiting for the manager of that loan outfit to quit work.

"They had a system. She'd wait in the accountant's office with the light out, watching his door. Then, when the manager left, she'd wait about five minutes and leave herself. That would give him time to get his car out of the parking lot. He'd pick her up at the corner. She said he was the super-cautious, married type. They just dated once in a while. I wasn't having any of that. Too rough for me, Fowler."

There was a long silence. Dan asked, "How about friends of your brother, Servius, or friends of Kelly and Castrella?"

Vince walked over and sat down, facing them. "One—Johnny didn't have a friend who'd bring a bucket of water if he was on fire. And two—I sent the word out."

"What does that mean?"

"I like things quiet in this end of the state. I didn't want anyone helping those three punks. Everybody got the word. So who would do anything? Now both of you please tell Heglon exactly what I said. Tell him to check with Terrafierro. Tell him to have the cops check their pigeons. Ask the kid himself. I paid him a little visit. Now, if you don't mind, I've got another appointment."

They had finished their steaks before Dan was able to get any line on Connie Wyant. On the third telephone call, he was given a message. Lieutenant Wyant was waiting for Mr. Fowler at 311 Leeds Street, Apartment 6A, and would Mr. Fowler please bring Miss Raymer with him.

They drove back to the city. A department car was parked in front of the building. Sergeant Levandowski was half asleep behind the wheel. "Go right in. Ground floor in the back. 6A."

Connie greeted them gravely and listened without question to Dan's report of the conversation with Vince Servius. After Dan had finished, Connie nodded casually, as though it was of little importance, and said, "Miss Raymer, I'm not so good at this, so I thought maybe you could help. There's the Garrity girl's closet. Go through it and give me an estimate on the cost."

Jane went to the open closet. She began to examine the clothes. "Hey!" she exclaimed.

"What do you think?" Connie asked.

"If this suit cost a nickel under two hundred, I'll eat it. And look at this coat. Four hundred, anyway." She bent over and picked up a shoe. "For ages I've dreamed of owning a pair of these. Thirty-seven fifty, at least."

"Care to make an estimate on the total?" Connie asked her.

"Gosh, thousands. I don't know. There are nine dresses in there that must have cost at least a hundred apiece. Do you have to have it accurate?"

"That's close enough, thanks." He took a small blue bankbook out of his pocket and flipped it to Dan. Dan caught it and looked inside. Loreen Garrity had more than eleven hundred dollars on hand. There had been large deposits and large withdrawals—nothing small.

Connie said, "I've been to see her family.

They're good people. They didn't want to talk mean about the dead, so it took a little time. But I found out our Loreen was one for the angles—a chiseler—no conscience and less morals. A rough, tough cookie to get tied up with.

"From there, I went to see the Kistners. Every time the old lady would try to answer a question, Kistner'd jump in with all four feet. I finally had to have Levandowski take him downtown just to get him out of the way. Then the old lady talked.

"She had a lot to say about how lousy business is. How they're scrimping and scraping along, and how the girl couldn't have a new formal for the Christmas dance tomorrow night at the high school gym.

"Then I called up an accountant friend after I left her. I asked him how Kistner had been doing. He cussed out Kistner and said he'd been doing fine; in fact, he had stolen some nice retail accounts out from under the other boys in the same racket. So I came over here and it looked like this was where the profit was going. So I waited for you so I could make sure."

"What can you do about it?" Dan demanded, anger in his voice, anger at the big puffy man who hadn't wanted to lie to the police.

"I've been thinking. It's eleven o'clock. He's been sitting down there sweating. I've got to get my Christmas shopping done tomorrow, and the only way I'll ever get around to it is to break him fast."

Jane had been listening, wide-eyed. "They always forget some little thing, don't they?" she asked. "Or there is something they don't know about. Like a clock that is five minutes slow, or something. I mean, in the stories . . ." Her voice trailed off uncertainly.

"Give her a badge, Connie," Dan said with amusement.

Connie rubbed his chin. "I might do that, Dan. I just might do that. Miss Raymer, you got a strong stomach? If so, maybe you get to watch your idea in operation."

* * *

It was nearly midnight, and Connie had left Dan and Jane alone in a small office at headquarters for nearly a half hour. He opened the door and stuck his head in. "Come on, people. Just don't say a word."

They went to the Interrogation Room. Kistner jumped up the moment they came in. Levandowski sat at the long table, looking bored.

Kistner said heatedly, "As you know, Lieutenant, I was perfectly willing to cooperate. But you are being high-handed. I demand to know why I was brought down here. I want to know why I can't phone a lawyer. You are exceeding your authority, and I—"

"Siddown!" Connie roared with all the power of his lungs.

Kistner's mouth worked silently. He sat down, shocked by the unexpected roar. A tired young man slouched in, sat at the table, flipped open a notebook, and placed three sharp pencils within easy reach.

Connie motioned Dan and Jane over toward chairs in a shadowed corner of the room. They sat side by side, and Jane held Dan's wrist, her nails sharp against his skin.

"Kistner, tell us again about how you came back to the office," Connie said.

Kistner replied in a tone of excruciating patience, as though talking to children, "I parked my car in my parking space in the lot behind the building. I used the back way into the lobby. I went up—"

"You went to the cigar counter."

"So I did! I had forgotten that. I went to the cigar counter. I bought three cigars and chatted with Barney. Then I took an elevator up."

"And talked to the elevator boy."

"I usually do. Is there a law?"

"No law, Kistner. Go on."

"And then I opened the Men's Room door with my key, and I was in there perhaps three minutes. And then when I came out, the man I described brushed by me. I went to the office and found the window open. I was shutting it and I heard—"

"All this was at two o'clock, give or take a couple of minutes?"

"That's right, Lieutenant." Talking had restored Kistner's self-assurance.

Connie nodded to Levandowski. The sergeant got up lazily, walked to the door, and opened it. A burly, diffident young man came in. He wore khaki pants and a leather jacket.

"Sit down," Connie said casually. "What's your name?"

"Paul Hilbert, officer."

The tired young man was taking notes.

"What's your occupation?"

"I'm a plumber, officer. Central Plumbing, Incorporated."

"Did you get a call today from the Associated Bank Building?"

"Well, I didn't get the call, but I was sent out on the job. I talked to the super, and he sent me up to the seventeenth floor. Sink drain clogged in the Men's Room."

"What time did you get there?"

"That's on my report, officer. Quarter after one."

"How long did it take you to finish the job?"

"About three o'clock."

"Did you leave the Men's Room at any time during that period?"

"No, I didn't."

"I suppose people tried to come in there?"

"Three or four. But I had all the water connections turned off, so I told them to go down to sixteen. The super had the door unlocked down there."

"Did you get a look at everybody who came in?"

"Sure, officer."

"You said three or four. Is one of them at this table?"

The shy young man looked around. He shook his head. "No, sir."

"Thanks, Hilbert. Wait outside. We'll want you to sign the statement when it's typed up."

Hilbert's footsteps sounded loud as he walked to the door. Everyone was watching Kistner. His face was still, and he seemed to be looking into a remote and alien future, as cold as the back of the moon.

Kistner said in a husky, barely audible voice, "A bad break. A stupid thing. Ten seconds it would have taken me to look in there. I had to establish the time. I talked to Barney. And to the elevator boy. They'd know when she fell. But I had to be some place else. Not in the office.

"You don't know how it was. She kept wanting more money. She wouldn't have anything to do with me, except when there was money. And I didn't have any more, finally.

"I guess I was crazy. I started to milk the accounts. That wasn't hard; the clients trust me. Take a little here and a little there. She found out. She wanted more and more. And that gave her a new angle. Give me more, or I'll tell.

"I thought it over. I kept thinking about her being a witness. All I had to do was make it look like she was killed to keep her from testifying. I don't care what you do to me. Now it's over, and I feel glad."

He gave Connie a long, wondering look. "Is that crazy? To feel glad it's over? Do other people feel that way?"

Connie asked Dan and Jane to wait in the small office. He came in ten minutes later; he looked tired. The plumber came in with him.

Connie said, "Me, I hate this business. I'm after him, and I bust him, and then I start bleeding for him. What the hell? Anyway, you get your badge, Miss Raymer."

"But wouldn't you have found out about the plumber anyway?" Jane asked.

Connie grinned ruefully at her. He jerked a thumb toward the plumber. "Meet Patrolman Hilbert. Doesn't know a pipe wrench from a faucet. We just took the chance that Kistner was too eager to toss the girl out the window—so eager he didn't make a quick check of the Men's Room. If he had, he could have laughed us under the table. As it is, I can get my Christmas shopping done tomorrow. Or is it today?"

Dan and Jane left headquarters. They walked down the street, arm in arm. There was holly, and a big tree in front of the courthouse, and a car went by with a lot of people in it singing about We Three Kings of Orient Are. Kistner was a stain, fading slowly.

They walked until it was entirely Christmas Eve, and they were entirely alone in the snow that began to fall again, making tiny, perfect stars of lace that lingered in her dark hair.

CRIME'S CHRISTMAS CAROL
Norvell Page

ALREADY A PROLIFIC WRITER for such pulp magazines as *Black Mask*, *Dime Mystery*, and others, Norvell Page began to write novels for the hero pulp *The Spider*, under the house name Grant Stockbridge, in 1933. Created to compete with *The Shadow*, the first two issues of the magazine were written by R. T. M. Scott, then turned over to the twenty-nine-year-old Page, who gave the ruthless and fearless vigilante a mask and a disguise (as a fang-toothed hunchback named Richard Wentworth). A series of horrific villains were hunted down and killed by Wentworth, who then branded his prey on the forehead with a seal of a spider. At his most prolific, Page wrote more than one hundred thousand words a month, half for the Spider novels and the rest for a wide range of fiction. "Crime's Christmas Carol" was first published in the May 1939 issue of *Detective Tales*.

Crime's Christmas Carol

NORVELL PAGE

ANNA HELPED TOM PUT ON HIS COAT and, as always, the thread-bare lightness of it twisted something inside of her. The wind rattling the windows had such a hungry, thin sound. It surged in around the loose frames in spite of all the newspaper stuffing; it made the little red bows she had pinned up in place of Christmas wreaths whirl and dance.

"Don't do anything I wouldn't do, Mr. Mann," Anna said.

Tom twisted his young thin face around and winked. "And what wouldn't you do, Mrs. Mann, seeing as how it's Christmas Eve?"

"Well," Anna made it cheerful, "I wouldn't rob a bank. I don't think I would."

"Sure?"

"Certain sure, Mr. Mann. Why, we're practically rolling in money. I've got ninety-seven cents!"

"Let me see all this wealth, woman." Tom stared down at the handful of silver and coppers, poked doubtfully at a slick-faced nickel. "I might be able to use that in a subway turnstile—if I went through a subway turnstile."

Anna said firmly, "Mr. Osterschmidt is going to take that lead nickel back. He gave it to me."

Tom stared at her and made his eyes open wide. "Don't tell me that we're going to have meat for Christmas, Mrs. Mann!"

Anna tried to keep her smile. Tom's lips were stretched tight; maybe they were smiling. He began to swear in a thin, faltering voice. He turned sharply away and slammed out of the room. Anna ran after him into the drafty hall.

"Tom," she cried. "Tom, you didn't kiss me good-bye!"

That would always stop him. But this time . . . he didn't stop. His feet kept thumping down the three flights of rickety stairs, getting fainter and fainter. The front door banged. It made empty echoes clatter through the cold ancient house.

"Oh, Tom," Anna whispered. "Tom, don't do anything . . . anything *foolish*. Please, God, he mustn't!" She took a deep breath then, and smiled a little to herself. Of course, Tom wouldn't. He was just trying for a job, any job now that the shop where he'd been working part-time was closed down. It would open again, maybe, in February. . . . Anna's hand knotted about her ninety-seven cents. . . .

Anna scoured their little room and closet kitchenette until the shabby furniture shone, and three hours were gone. She spent an hour stuffing more paper around those rattling windows. And there wasn't another thing to do—except think. Anna stared about her with frightened eyes. Hours before she could expect Tom home again; hours . . .

At last she dragged on her thin coat and ran down the steps. The bitter wind of the street was welcome. Tom was out in this somewhere, wasn't he? Why should anybody be warm and comfortable when Tom was cold? People had such silly smiles on their faces, arms full of packages, yelling at one another, "Merry Christmas!"

The cold pavements, the slush of the streets came through the thinness of Anna's soles. She had forgotten to line them with newspaper. Thinking of that, her eyes brightened. She could lose some time doing that; maybe as much as a half hour! She turned toward home, loitering. After that . . . but she would not think of their troubles; or think of anything else.

Anna knew now that she and Tom had been foolish in their careless bravery, marrying in the face of times like these, in defiance of what her father had said.

"You can come home whenever you're ready, Anna," she could hear the sharp practical accents of his voice so clearly. "But I'm not prepared to support an indigent son-in-law. You're a couple of inexperienced fools."

Tom had been so earnest, so . . . *young.* "You see, sir, we love each other, and I'm not afraid of work. It may be tough—but not so tough a man can't provide for his wife, sir!"

Anna could even remember how his voice had softened when he said "wife." It was so new to her ears, so sweet. . . . Maybe Tom was already home! Maybe he had the promise of some work after Christmas! Anna began to run along the wind-gutted streets, a tiny thing whose dark eyes seemed too big for the thinness of her face. . . .

Tom wasn't home, and after she had lined her shoes, it didn't seem worthwhile going out again. Anna sat by the window with her hands limp in her lap and watched the grey day gather into dusk, watched the silly people hurrying along with their silly smiles. . . .

"Please, Tom," she whispered. "Not anything foolish . . ."

It was after dark when Anna realized she was shivering with cold—and she couldn't see the street any more except where lights made swaying, cold white puddles on the walk. She had to do her shopping. She had already calculated every penny of her purchases. Hamburger was twenty-three cents a pound, so that in buying only a half-pound, you had to pay that extra half cent. Clever, weren't they, getting that extra half cent! She'd fool them this time. She . . . she would buy a whole pound of hamburger for Christmas dinner! Anna's cheeks flushed a little. She held her money tightly in her hand and went down the steps rapidly—before she should change her mind.

The wind made her cheeks ache, gnawed at her knees. It was colder, and the slush was frozen again into rough hummocks of ice. If she fell and hurt herself, would her father relent, she wondered? A broken leg . . . Tom would notify her father to make sure she received proper care. He had been urging her to go home. . . .

"Why should you put up with a failure like me?" he pleaded sometimes when the money just wouldn't stretch; when he couldn't find a job. "Why should you suffer . . ."

Anna wondered if a broken leg hurt much. She ran recklessly across the icy street and a car skittered to a halt just in time.

"Look out, kid," the driver shouted. "It won't be a Merry Christmas in the hospital."

Anna ran on. She was glad now she hadn't been hit. Tom would only blame himself, and . . . and she might be hurt even worse. She might be killed! Tom would be left alone. . . . There were tears stinging her eyes. She whispered, "Oh, thank you, God. I—I didn't really mean it!"

She turned the corner with her head down and somebody bumped into her and muttered, " 'Scuse me, lady." It was a delivery boy with a box of groceries on his shoulder, and there at the curb was the delivery truck from Osterschmidt's, heaped up with piles of food. Big boxes safely tucked away behind a locked iron grill. They might at least have solid doors, so people couldn't see. . . .

Anna moved closer. Just inside the grating was the biggest box of all, the biggest turkey . . . The wind snatched at Anna's coat, blundered against the truck and, with a rasping creak, the iron grating swung open. Why, it wasn't locked at all! The boy must have forgotten. . . . The biggest turkey of all, and the gate open so invitingly . . .

There was a weary drag to the way Tom Mann moved in his polished, shabby shoes. His shoulders ached from consciously bracing them all day long as he went futilely from shop to shop hunting even a promise of work. The Christmas rush was over and the proprietors only shrugged, "Maybe by February . . . ." How in hell did they expect a man and his wife to live until then? How . . . for all his efforts. Tom's shoulders sagged. It was not other peoples' responsibility. It was his . . . and he had failed.

Tom slipped, stepping down from a curb, and caught himself frantically. Now, that would be a swell Christmas present for Anne, wouldn't it, breaking a leg! Or maybe it would be the best present of all! She'd have to go home to her father then. Tom stood on the curb and stared out across the icy street and his young, thin face was suddenly old-looking. . . . Reluctantly, he turned toward home. The sole of his right shoe had come loose a little, and his feet made small scuffing sounds that kept time to his thoughts. Failure, failure, failure . . .

Ahead of him, Tom saw a mail-man, bowed under a heavily loaded bag, turn up the steps of a house. Tom's eyes clung in fascination to the grey-uniformed man. Lucky people, getting Christmas presents; maybe even money! Yes, it was money, a registered letter. They were signing for it at the door.

"Merry Christmas," the lucky woman said, and closed the door.

Tom smothered a laugh that was bitter in his throat. If he had any guts, he'd *make* this a Merry Christmas for Anna! There was money within reach, a dozen registered letters in the postman's hand as he stumped down the steps—and it was dark here between the street lights. . . . Tom shook his head. Anna wouldn't want it that way.

"Merry Christmas," he called to the descending postman.

The man grinned. "Nuts to you. I still got five hours' work."

Tom thought, "But you've *got* work." He didn't say it, and the postman stepped down to the pavement . . . and slipped. His arms flew wide in an effort to catch his balance. Letters scattered from his hands—and Tom caught him just as he was falling. The wrench almost yanked Tom off his feet. He hadn't realized he was so weak.

He said, panting, "You almost got out of that five hours' work."

The postman swore and began to pick up letters. "Thanks, buddy," he said. "Now I got an extra hour re-sorting this damned stuff. . . ."

Tom began to pick up letters and hand them to the postman. It was an accident that he noticed the extra postage and "Registered" stamp on a letter half-hidden in the shadow beside the steps. It was almost an accident that he covered it with his foot. . . .

Tom stood there until he saw the postman turn into a lunch-room to re-sort the mail. The carrier would miss this registered letter in a few moments, probably, and the law would be after Tom at once. He was a fool to think he could get away with this. By tomorrow morning they'd trace him. Christmas morning. Better to take the letter to the postman and explain he had found it later in the dark. Tom picked it up, and the envelope was thick between his cold fingers. It made a faint, crackling sound. . . . Tom's hands trembled.

What the hell difference did it make if the police came for him in the morning? He and Anna would have had a happy evening together: a big dinner, presents. And tomorrow? Why, let the police come! With him in jail, Anna would have to go home where she could be taken care of. Her father would see that Anna divorced him. God, he couldn't lose Anna. He . . . But he had already lost her, because he was a failure. Grimly, he ripped open the envelope before he lost courage, felt a thick sheaf of money. He ducked around the corner. He had to get rid of the envelope. It was evidence, wasn't it? Tom laughed shakily, stuffed the money in his pocket and, as he walked rapidly on, dropped the letter to the sidewalk.

"Hey!" A man's voice boomed out behind him. "Hey, there! Wait a minute!"

Out of the corner of his eye, Tom saw a man in a policeman's blue uniform hurrying toward him. Good God! Were they after him so soon? Tom pretended he hadn't heard and ducked around the corner. Anna had to have this one night. . . . Tom broke into a run, ducked into an alley before the policeman turned the corner. Tom was panting, his whole body shaking with the effort. He hurried on.

First, he went to Osterschmidt's for the biggest turkey he had. Then some presents for Anna. There was a feverish light in Tom's eyes as he thumbed through the money. *Fifty-sixty-seventy* . . . He didn't dare count any farther. He hadn't held so much money at one time since . . . since . . . oh, God, did it matter? One happy evening with Anna!

There was a perky, thick coat that he had seen Anna eye longingly, when she thought he didn't see, and in the same shop window a hood of soft, red wool and mittens. Warm . . . He'd make Anna take a walk tonight just for the fun of seeing her warm for once. She wouldn't go back home looking like a beggar. Or would they take the things from her when they came in the morning? The thought stopped Tom in front of a florist window. Red roses . . . great, long-stemmed, red roses. There was something they couldn't take from her! Crazy laughter was on his lips as he staggered into the shop.

Afterward, he almost ran along the street. Only three blocks to home; no, only two . . . How Anna's eyes would light up when she saw him coming! The groceries were already there, probably, and the big turkey. She would know fortune had smiled on them. Or maybe, the groceries would be delayed in the rush. That would be better still! Anna would clap her hands and

laugh again; laugh without that queer, tight look of worry in her eyes.

One more block. He turned the corner—and stopped. There in front of the lodging house, looking up at the door, was a policeman! Tom's shoulders sagged. Couldn't they have even their one night together? He was willing to pay. . . . Tom stumbled back around the corner, walking slowly, heavily. . . .

Back on wind-swept Fenton Street, the policeman rang the doorbell long and insistently, but presently went away and when he had gone, a girl popped around the other corner of the block. She was staggering under a weight of groceries. Her face was white and her eyes were huge, but she ran . . . she ran with a dogged little trot while her arms strained around that great box of food. Her lips were tight, and sobs kept pushing at them.

"Oh, please," she whispered. "Please, let me make it! Don't let them find me yet!"

She had her key in her hand and somehow she got the door open; made the long climb up the stairs and into their one little room. She stood against the door to listen, shivering. Presently she drew in a quavering breath of relief. Not yet. How she flew about the room! She had set the table hours ago and now she ran, stowing away the food on the kitchen shelves where Tom could see. She had her story all set. Mr. Osterschmidt had been so nice. When she had told him about the lead nickel and he had understood how much it meant to her, he had insisted on her taking a great load of groceries and a turkey.

That was what she would say when Tom came . . . when Tom came. Anna realized suddenly how late it was. Why didn't Tom come? Anna was abruptly standing very still. Dear God, let nothing happen to Tom! Not because of what she had done! That wouldn't be fair. It wouldn't . . . oh, if any one must pay, let it be herself! That was fair, wasn't it? Please, God, that was fair. . . .

Fear drew her white hands twisting together.

Perhaps that policeman hadn't been after her. Perhaps Tom had done something foolish, and they were after him. Or—or maybe he had been hurt. That was the way they notified you when you didn't have a telephone. They sent around a policeman. . . .

Anna rushed to the window and peered down into the dark windy canyon of Fenton Street. Nobody down there now. Anna's hands ached with twisting. There mustn't be anything like that. Please, let Tom come home. Please . . . She'd take all the food back. She could wrap it back up just like it came from the store.

Anna ran to the door and listened, painfully. Yes, there were footsteps on the stairs, a heavy portentous tread. It sounded a little like Tom when he was very tired, but so heavy, heavy.

The police? Anna leaned over the stairwell and peered down. No, not a policeman. She saw somebody's grey sleeve and a lot of bundles, moving upward. Probably Mr. Sacco on the second floor. No, the man was coming on past. Then it would be Mr. France or Mr. Getty on the third floor. . . . But the man was walking toward the flight that led to the fourth floor. Oh . . .

"Tom," Anna cried. "Oh, *Tom!*"

She stood staring down at him in the dim-lit hall, at his face smiling over a great armload of bundles. Tom . . .

"Merry Christmas, Mrs. Mann," he called.

Anna tried to smile. She was grateful, very grateful, God, but . . . all those packages! He hadn't . . . he *couldn't* have done anything *foolish*. Anna was running down the steps.

"Oh, Tom, you foolish boy," she panted. "What have you done?"

Tom grinned at her, "Is that any way to greet Santa Claus?"

"Tom," she cried. "You're teasing. Here, let me—" She took some of the bundles and ran ahead of him. Her feet made little dancing steps on the rickety stairs and Tom followed, making himself laugh. What the hell? He had this moment anyhow. . . . In the room, he gravely told her about a kind man whose wallet he had found

and returned. It must have been *loaded* with money!

"He had white hair exactly like Santa Claus," Tom told her, "and a big fur collar on his coat, and his belly shook just exactly like a bowl full of jelly. . . . 'By Gadfrey,' he said, 'an honest man, and on Christmas Eve, too! Here, buy yourself a Christmas present!' And he handed me . . . *a hundred-dollar bill!*"

"He never did," Anna cried. "Oh the good, wonderful man. And, darling, Mr. Osterschmidt was playing Santa Claus today, too. Look—look at all these wonderful things he gave us. A big turkey . . ."

Tom threw himself into the rickety old chair by the window. "You've got a surprise coming to you, young lady," he cried. "We're going to have *two* turkeys for Christmas. I went by Osterschmidt's and ordered the biggest bird in the shop. It should be here any minute now, I guess."

Anna said slowly, "Oh—oh, two turkeys. How wonderful!" She turned toward the tiny little kitchen. So she had stolen when there was no need at all! And now, when they came after her . . . Oh, what would Tom do? Frantically, she caught up the big box of roses Tom had brought her. "Roses! Oh, Tom, you dear foolish boy . . . I've got to kiss you for that!"

Tom pushed out a laugh, but it wasn't coming off. Damn it, their one night . . . and it wasn't coming off. Anna knew he was lying, and she was trying gallantly. To hell with it. This was their night. He picked up the box with the red hood and the mittens and . . . he couldn't help it . . . he stole a glance down at the street. The policeman was walking toward the house again!

Tom's hands shook as he drew the red hood snugly down over Anna's black curls, kissed her smiling lips . . . and Anna sobbed, and put her arms around his neck and clung.

"Oh, Tom," she cried. "I can't keep it up! I can't lie to you. I . . . I *stole* the groceries! The wagon gate was unlocked and the wind blew it open, like it was asking me in. And there was this big turkey, the biggest one Mr. Osterschmidt ever had. And . . ."

The bell made its sharp, whirring clatter, and Anna whipped out of Tom's arms and faced the door. "Oh," she whispered. "Oh, they're coming for me!"

Tom said, "Nonsense." His voice sounded strained. "The biggest bird Osterschmidt had . . . Darling, did you look to see whose groceries they were? Did you?"

"Oh," Anna gasped. "Oh, you mean—"

She was on her knees in an instant, searching among all that mess of paper off the packages, brushing it aside, hunting furiously with that red hood so snug about her head. Then she whirled toward Tom with a slip trembling in her hand. She swallowed hard, twice, before she got out words.

"Oh, Tommy, you're right. I—*I stole our own groceries!* Oh, now everything is all right. Oh, I've never been so happy. I'll never do a foolish thing like that again. It isn't worth it, is it, Tommy?"

Tom said dryly, "No, Mrs. Mann, it isn't worth it." But he was gazing into the glisten of her dark eyes and drinking in the smile on her lips . . . and he thought that what he had done was worth it. . . . The doorbell whirred again.

Tom said hurriedly, "That's probably the delivery boy checking up to see if the stuff reached you all right. And I want some cigarettes, haven't had any in a long time. I'll just run down and see the boy and get the cigarettes. I'll be back in a little while." He was straining his ears, listening. Somebody must have opened the front door because there were voices in the hall; a man's deep voice, and afterward feet climbing the stairs steadily. Tom moved sharply toward the door. He couldn't let Anna know yet. Let her be happy, waiting for him to come back—for a little while. . . .

Anna stopped him at the door . . . Anna with tears trembling on her lashes, and a small smile on her lips. She said, so low he could hardly hear her, "It's the police, isn't it, Tommy?"

Tom tried to think of a lie, and he couldn't.

He stood and looked at Anna and, presently, he put his arms about her and hugged her tight, tight. . . . Tight enough to last forever. It would have to. The footsteps were on the second floor now.

"I knew who it was," Anna said rapidly. "I saw the policeman waiting outside the door just before I came in with the groceries. And now I know that he wasn't coming after me. Why—why, Tom, even good kind men don't hand out hundred-dollar rewards."

Tom said slowly, because he couldn't make the words clear any other way, "It's all right, kid. And you're right. I—I stole a registered letter a postman dropped. You go to your father and just forget . . . forget about me. It's best this way. I haven't been exactly . . . exactly the husband I had planned to be, Mrs. Mann."

Anna said violently, "You darned old fool, you're just exactly the only husband in the world that's worth a damn! You—I won't let you go. I'll tell them that I—"

And a man's fist knocked at the door. Tom's smile got a little twisted. He braced his shoulders. Well, this was something he could face like a man. He opened the door and the policeman was standing there.

"Mrs. Thomas Mann?" he said.

Tom sucked in a breath. So someone had seen Anna steal the groceries!

"You mean me, Thomas Mann," he said fiercely.

The cop shook his head and took off his cap, pulled out a letter. "Nope, this letter is addressed to Mrs. Thomas Mann. I saw a guy drop it and called, but he didn't hear me. See, it's registered. I figured it might be important. Mrs. Thomas Mann . . ."

Tom stared down at the letter. It was the same, the one he had stolen. There couldn't be any doubt of it at all. He remembered the way the stamps were on it and there was even the mark of his foot on the envelope.

"Thank you, officer," he said slowly. "That's just about the most important letter in the world, I guess."

"Oh," Anna whispered. "From father. It's from father."

The cop looked a little puzzled. "Sure . . . Well, Merry Christmas to you both."

"Oh, such a Merry Christmas," Anna whispered, and threw both arms around the policeman's neck. . . .

The door was closed again and Anna was in Tom's arms. "It couldn't happen," he said slowly, "but it has. I stole your father's letter to you, and it was the gift money I spent. Darling, we'll stop being such stiff-necked fools. You'll go home until I can take care of you properly."

There was real, ringing happiness in Anna's laughter. "Oh, it won't be necessary," she said.

"Father says that if we're such young idiots that we'll starve together rather than separate, we'd better come on home! He's got a job lined up for you, and—Tom, you won't refuse?"

Tom said, quietly, "Mrs. Mann, I only *look* like a damned fool! If you'll get on your bonnet and shawl, Mrs. Mann, we'll go out and do a little telephoning . . . and take your dad up on that before he forgets it! Just incidentally, of course, we might tell him Merry Christmas. . . ."

The smiles on people's faces weren't silly at all. Even the streetlights seemed to have smiling haloes around them. But perhaps that was because there was something in Anna's eyes that made them blur a little now and then. . . .

SERENADE TO A KILLER

Joseph Commings

JOSEPH COMMINGS WAS ONE OF THE MASTERS of the locked room mystery—that demanding form in which crimes appear to be impossible—and the present story is no exception. Commings's writing career began when he made up stories to entertain his fellow soldiers during World War II. With some rewriting after the war, he found a ready market for them in the pulps. Although the pulps were dying in the late 1940s, new digest-sized magazines came to life and Commings sold stories to *Mystery Digest, The Saint Mystery Magazine,* and *Mike Shayne Mystery Magazine.* Although he wrote several full-length mystery novels, none ever was published, in spite of the encouragement of his friend John Dickson Carr. "Serenade to a Killer" was first published in the July 1957 issue of *Mystery Digest.*

Serenade to a Killer

JOSEPH COMMINGS

MURDER AND CHRISTMAS ARE usually poles apart. But this Yuletide Senator Brooks U. Banner had the crazy killing at Falconridge dumped into his over-sized elastic stocking.

At the Cobleskill Orphanage, he stood among the re-painted toys like a clean-shaven Kris Kringle. He was telling the kids how he'd begun his career as a parentless tyke—just as they—with a loaf of Bohemian rye under one arm and six bits in his patched jeans. He followed that revelation with a fruity true crime story about a lonely hearts blonde who killed six mail-order husbands and how he'd helped the police to catch her. The two old maids who ran the orphanage paused to listen and were scandalized, but the kids loved him. He was six feet three inches tall and weighed 280 pounds, and he looked so quaint in his greasy black string tie, dusty frock-coat, baggy grey britches, and the huge storm rubbers with the red ridged soles.

Presenting the toys, he made little comic speeches and ruffled up the kids' hair. While this was going on a young man came in and stood in the bare, draughty dining-hall with its shrivelled brown holly wreaths. He was sallow-skinned and slight, with a faint moustache and large lustrous eyes.

He waited impatiently until Banner was done, then he approached.

"Senator, my name is Verl Griffon. I'm a reporter for my father who owns the local paper, *The Griffon*."

Banner beamed. "And you wanna interview me!" He stabbed a fresh corona cigar in his mouth. "Yass, yass! Wal, my lad, if you'd come in a li'l earlier, you'd've heard me telling the young-timers that—"

"No, this isn't merely an interview, Senator." Verl's luminous eyes zigzagged nervously. "Where can I see you privately?"

Frowning, Banner led the way into a gloomy office that had a cold radiator and a two-dimensional red-cardboard Christmas bell on the window. They looked dubiously at the rickety ladder-backed chairs and remained standing.

Verl chewed his knuckles. "Senator, I've read a lot about the way you handle things. Things like murders. And I was at the trial of Jack Horner in New York."

Banner grunted from his top pants-button. "Izzat so? Then you saw how I made that poisoner holler uncle."

"Indeed I did. Now I need your help. You've heard of Caspar Woolfolk, the famous pianist, haven't you?"

Banner grinned. "Lad, when it comes to music, I lissen to a jook-box every Saturday night."

Verl plunged on regardless. "Early this morning Woolfolk was murdered!"

"No!"

"And a woman I know very well says she killed him—but the facts are all against it!" His eyes, peering into the middle distance, were stunned with bewilderment.

Banner shifted ponderously. "Tell it to me from A to Izzard. Pin the donkey on the tail."

Verl talked rapidly, gravely. "Woolfolk owned Falconridge, a manor outside town. On the grounds is a little octagonal house he called the Music Box. He kept his piano and music library there. This morning I found him in there dead. He was killed and no one knows how the murderer could have done it . . . You see, I went to the manor after breakfast to wish everybody a happy holiday. Ora met me at the door. She had the jitters."

"Who's Ora?"

"Ora Spires. That's the woman I referred to. She's governess to little Beryl, Woolfolk's ten-year-old daughter. Woolfolk was a widower. Ora, as I said, greeted me with a look of panic. All she could tell me was that something terrible must have happened to Woolfolk inside the Music Box. She hadn't dared go look for herself . . . It snowed during the night. There's over an inch of it on the ground. The snow on the lawns hadn't been disturbed, save where Woolfolk had walked out in it toward the Music Box. I could see by the single line of clear-cut footprints that Woolfolk hadn't come back. I walked alongside his tracks. The door opened to my touch. This morning was so gloomy that I switched on the light. Woolfolk was at the grand piano, sitting on the bench, the upper part of his body lying across the music. He was stone cold dead—shot through the centre of the forehead."

Cold as the room was, Banner could see a sheen of sweat on Verl's puckered forehead.

"Remembering that I'd seen only Woolfolk's tracks," continued Verl, "the first thought that struck me was: *If he's been murdered, the murderer is still here!* I searched the place. There was no one else there. Even the weapon that'd killed Woolfolk was missing—proving beyond a doubt that it wasn't suicide. How can a thing like that be.

It stopped snowing around midnight. Woolfolk walked out there after that time. Then somebody killed him. And whoever it was got away *without leaving a trace anywhere in the snow!*"

"How far from the main house is the Music Box?"

"A good hundred yards."

"A sharpshooter might've plugged Woolfolk through an open window while standing a hundred yards or more away."

"No," said Verl. "The doors and windows were closed. Woolfolk was shot at close range. The murderer stood on the other side of the piano."

Ruminating, Banner finally said: "Wal, sir. You can take your pick of three possible answers."

"Three!" said Verl with a bounce of surprise.

Banner held up a thick blunt thumb. "One. The murderer went out there *before* it'd stopped snowing. The snow that fell after he walked through it covered up his tracks. When Woolfolk came later, he killed Woolfolk and managed to conceal himself so cleverly in the Music Box that you failed to see him."

Verl looked annoyed—and disappointed. "That's out of the question. No one was there, I tell you."

Banner, undismayed, stuck up his forefinger. "Two. Both the murderer *and* Woolfolk went out there before it'd stopped snowing. *Both* their tracks were covered up by the falling snow. After killing Woolfolk, the murderer put on Woolfolk's shoes and walked backwards toward the main house."

Verl shook his head sourly. "Woolfolk was wearing his own shoes when I found him. The police, who came later, went over all that. There's absolutely no trickery about the footprints. They were made by a man walking forward. Made by Woolfolk. That's certain!"

Banner lifted his middle finger. He stared at it thoughtfully and with hesitation. "Three. Again, the murderer got out there before Woolfolk did—"

He paused so long that Verl said: "And how did he get back?"

"He knows a way of crossing a hundred yards of snow without leaving a mark on it!"

Verl's mouth dropped open. He snapped it shut again. "Ora Spires," he said, jittery, "has part of an answer. She thinks she killed Woolfolk. She keeps saying that." He paused. "But she doesn't know how she got out there and back."

Quizzically Banner raised his black furry eyebrows. "Right now," he said, reaching for the doorknob, "I'm so fulla curiosity that Ora has more lure for me than a sarong gal."

Verl took a step toward the held-open door and then he said: "Something else, Senator. She walks in her sleep."

The great Spanish shawl that covered the whole top of the grand piano in the Music Box was clotted with blood. Woolfolk's body had been removed. Banner walked behind the piano bench. On the piano-rack was the sheet music for Bellini's *La Somnambula*.

"Was this electric lamp tipped over when you found him?" asked Banner.

Verl nodded.

Ten paces beyond the piano stood a grandfather's clock. The wall shelves were stuffed with music albums.

Verl said: "Doesn't that music on the piano strike you as being particularly significant, Senator? *La Somnambula*. The Sleep Walker!"

"Uh-huh." Banner bobbed his grizzled mop of hair.

Verl rattled on as if he couldn't restrain himself. "Woolfolk was a funny one. Peculiar. His talk wasn't all music. He was full of weird theories about the power of suggestion, mind over matter, that sort of thing. He sometimes mentioned a lot of grotesque characters and objects, like: Abbé Faria, Carl Saxtus's zinc button, Baron du Potet's magic mirror, and Father Hell's magnet. He thought all that esoteric knowledge would help him to rule women. But I don't think it helped very much. Women," he

added regretfully, "know intuitively how to get the best of men."

Banner didn't answer. He lumbered to both windows. He opened each. Thirty feet to the east of the small house stood a pole with insulated cross-arms. Nowhere was the snow on the ground disturbed. There was no snow on either of the window-sills. The over-hanging eaves had sheltered them. He looked up at the eaves.

Verl said in a tired voice: "The snow on the roof hasn't been disturbed either."

Banner closed the windows and they both trudged across the white lawn to the manor house.

Ora Spires was a thirty-one-year-old spinster. She wore horn-rimmed eyeglasses and her hair was drawn back from a worried brow and knotted into a tight black bun. Her slack dress left you guessing about her figure. Her mouth had a pinched-in look as if she were trying to cork up all her feelings with her lips. Yet with some attention to her features she wouldn't have been half bad-looking. Banner wondered if she deliberately made herself unattractive or if she didn't know any better.

"The police have gone," she said in a cracked whisper to Verl. "They've taken him to Hostetler's." She looked at Verl as if he had just come in to have her try on the glass slipper.

Verl said to Banner: "Ora means Woolfolk's body. Hostetler is the town undertaker . . . Ora, you haven't told the police what you told—"

"Oh no," she said.

Banner got impatient. "I'm Senator Banner. Verl thinks I can help you."

"Oh, yes," she said quickly. "I voted for you once."

"Mighty fine. Tickled to meetcha." He pumped her limp hand. "Come sit down. We'll iron this out."

When they sat down in the parlor she said fretfully: "This morning I thought I'd dreamed I'd killed Mr. Woolfolk, but the whole nightmare has turned out to be real."

Banner was deep in the waffle-back armchair. "Tell me everything."

Her eyes were cloudy behind the glasses. She would tell him everything. Banner was the kind of man you told your troubles to. "I've lived in Cobleskill all my life. My parents are dead and my sister Caroline helped bring me up. She's four years older than I am. About three years ago I came to work for Mr. Woolfolk taking care of his little daughter. Have you told him much about Beryl, Verl?"

Verl shuffled his feet on the bird-of-paradise pattern rug. "Only just mentioned her."

Ora smiled sadly. "Beryl's ten now, she's very hard to manage."

"That's putting it mildly," groaned Verl.

"But I stuck it out, Senator. Mr. Woolfolk was always going away on concert tours, leaving me alone with Beryl." She was thatching her long, white, sensitive fingers nervously. "I keep a diary. It's locked up secretly in my bureau drawer and I wear the key around my neck. One night, about two weeks ago, I took it out of the drawer to make my day's entry. I was stunned to see that the last words I had written were: *I hate Mr. Woolfolk*!" She stiffened. "I never remember writing those words!"

"Clever forgery?" suggested Banner.

She shook her head. "How could it be? It was positively my handwriting. Besides, how could the forger have gotten to where I hide my diary? The lock on the bureau drawer wasn't forced . . . All that night I lay sleepless thinking about it. I realized there were a lot of things I didn't like about Mr. Woolfolk, things that could make me hate him. Things that had never entered my conscious mind before."

"What were they?" said Banner when she paused to draw a shuddery breath.

"Why, little habits I detested. The way he dressed—one shoe always used to squeak when he walked. The way he put extra spoonfuls of sugar on his morning cereal. The way he coughed irritatingly after he'd smoked a cigarette too many. The—the thin whistle of the breath in his nose whenever he breathed too near me. And the way he would drop little hints to me about what a devil he was with the ladies, trying to get it across to me that—Yes, all that night an inner voice kept saying to me: *I hate Mr. Woolfolk*!

"During this last week he got on my nerves more than I can say. Yesterday was Christmas Eve. After supper he left for town to visit my sister Caroline. She's been deathly sick lately. I tried to amuse Beryl, but she was extra unruly and I finally had to pack her off to bed as punishment. Mr. Woolfolk returned about ten o'clock. There was snow on his coat. He said, 'It's snowing out.' And I thought that was perfectly hateful. I *knew* it was snowing. I could see it on him. It was a perfectly exasperating remark and I hated his false teeth when he grinned at me. He hung his coat up and came over to me. He reached out and felt my hand. It was the first time he'd ever touched me like that. Inwardly I squirmed. I tried to draw my hand back without offending him. He said suggestively, 'I'm going out to the Music Box afterwards. Come out where you hear me playing.'

"I answered with as much sarcasm as I dared. 'Christmas carols?' He was still grinning. 'No,' he said. 'Not exactly Christmas carols.' I didn't answer him. I walked away from him." She paused to straighten her eyeglasses primly on her narrow nose. "Oh, I knew what he meant. But he didn't press me about it. I worked on the Christmas tree and spread presents around it until I noticed the clock striking in the hall. It was twelve midnight. I felt he was down here in the parlor and went up the stairs. On the first landing I stopped for a moment and looked out the window. The snow had stopped falling. The moon was out. Everything was beautiful and white. I hurried up the rest of the stairs to my bedroom. I locked the door. I felt too tired to open my diary last night, but something kept drawing me to it. At last I decided: A few words. When I opened it and saw what was in it, it fell out of my hands. The last words written in it were: *Tonight I'm going to kill Mr. Woolfolk*."

She swallowed painfully. "I thought I must have gone insane. Why should I have written such a terrible thing? It couldn't have been me.

Yet it was in my own handwriting. I flung the book back into the drawer and crawled into bed, trembling, sick at my thoughts. It was as if some evil thing had come into the house and taken possession of me during the past two weeks. I knew I walked in my sleep. Beryl told me that she'd seen me. Once I found some silverware in my room where I'd hidden it while I was asleep. I was afraid I'd do something horrible when I had no conscious control of myself. I didn't want to go to sleep, ever. I lay awake, fighting it, for as long a time as I could. I kept listening. The house was still. But I couldn't keep awake. I couldn't. I did fall asleep—and I dreamed . . ."

Her face was the color of ashes. "Somewhere in a dim corner of my mind I remembered Mr. Woolfolk saying, 'Come where you hear me playing.' My actions were all of a dreamlike floating quality. In the distance I could hear Mr. Woolfolk playing a part of *La Somnambula* score. I don't know how I got there, but I was eventually facing him across the Spanish shawl on the piano. The music had stopped. He was rising to his feet, grinning. I hated him more than I ever did. There was a gun in my hand. I don't know how it got there. He kept repeating, 'Shoot me! Go ahead! Shoot me! If you hate me so much, why don't you shoot?' I heard the shots stabbing into my brain. Then it all faded out again.

"When I woke up it was morning and I was in bed. I thought: Thank God, it's all been a horrible dream. I dressed, woke Beryl up, and went down to make breakfast. Mr. Woolfolk wasn't anywhere in the house and when I looked outside for him I saw those footprints that led to the Music Box. That's where he was. He wouldn't have stayed out here all night, unless—I *knew* what had happened, but I was too terrified to go and look. And then Verl came . . ."

Banner frowned. "When did Woolfolk die?"

Verl answered: "The police say about four o'clock in the morning—four hours after it'd stopped snowing."

"And the weapon used?"

"The old horse pistol that was kept in the stable."

"Have they found it?"

"They searched the house from top to bottom first, before they did find it. The murderer had laid a stick across the chimney stack and the gun was hanging halfway down on the inside tied to a string."

Banner heard a thin voice pipe up behind his chair. "You should see the dog now. I painted him blue."

Banner swiveled his big head. The child was staring at him with blank green eyes as if they were painted on a wooden face. Two rat-tails of carroty hair hung down over her scrawny shoulders. The pale-skinned arms had freckles sprinkled on them and her bloodless lips were chapped.

Ora had reached the limit of her endurance. She lifted her voice shrilly. "Beryl! I told you to stay in bed!"

"I won't. I tore up the bed. You'll have to make it over." She stared steadily at Banner. "I don't like you. You're fat and filthy and you can't play the piano."

Banner said sweetly to Ora: "Does Snookums know about Daddy?"

"Yes, we told her," said Ora.

"She doesn't seem very grieved," said Verl.

"Let her stay up if she wants to." Banner plowed his hand into one of the roomy kangaroo pockets of his coat and took out a paper-wrapped candy bar. He held it up. "Butterscotch," he said. "It melts in your mouth. I would've given it to you, tadpole, if you'd wiggled off to bed. But since you'd rather stay up—" He gave a titanic shrug.

She watched sullenly while he returned the butterscotch to his pocket. Then she sat on a footstool and appeared to be reconsidering the situation.

Verl's mind was tinkering with something. He said: "Ora, has the radio aerial been fixed yet?"

"No," said Ora listlessly.

"What happened to it?" said Banner.

Beryl squirmed on the footstool. "I broke it yesterday," she confessed.

"*You* broke it!" said Banner.

Beryl shrugged her thin shoulders. "Sure. I was up on the roof, breaking off shingles, when I thought I'd climb the aerial. Is it any business of yours?"

Banner scowled. "Yep. I investigate that under the head of monkey business."

Ora was sitting looking wide-eyed at Verl. "How did you know the aerial was broken? I never told—"

"Yes, you did. You told me about it when you saw me yesterday in town."

"I never saw you yesterday!" she said strongly.

"Why, Ora, you most certainly did. You dropped into *The Griffon* editorial office and asked me if I wanted to go with you to the all-Tschaikovsky afternoon concert at the school hall. And we went. And you liked the *Nutcracker Suite.*"

"Verl! Stop ragging me! I was right here all afternoon. I stayed in and cleaned the house."

"See here, Ora. You spent at least two full hours with me."

"That's a lie!"

Verl checked an angry retort. "Ora," he said tightly, "I can prove it. Several other people saw you too, my father among them. Why should we all lie about it?"

She was near frantic tears. "But, Verl, I never left the house. I remember what I did all afternoon. I never went out!"

"Someone was masquerading as you, I suppose?" Verl shook his head. "No, it was you. We've grown up together. Nobody could pull off a deception like that."

Beryl perked up accusingly. "You walk in your sleep."

"People don't act that wide-awake in their sleep," argued Verl. "I tell you, Ora, you were awake and you were with me."

"I won't listen to any more." Ora stood up. "Beryl, for the last time, are you going to lie down?"

Beryl looked questioningly at Banner's pocket. "I might go if—"

Banner chuckled. "Hunky-dory." He put the butterscotch in her hand. "Off to blanket class."

Beryl, pacified, left with Ora.

Banner said sternly: "What snicklefritz needs is to get the tar whaled outta her."

Verl flung out his arms and snapped: "Why should she deny being with me? I know I'm not lying."

"Mebbe she ain't either," said Banner cryptically. "Does anybody like Beryl?"

"Her father did. God knows why. She's a heller. She spies on people and tells nothing but lies. Breaking the aerial was just another one of those things. She takes showers with all her clothes on. She rings the dinner bell before time. She lets all the horses out of the stable. She floods the garden. She puts heavy books in her pillow-slip when she wants a pillow fight. She says Ora is loony."

Verl broke off suddenly.

Banner glanced sideways at a slight sound and saw a strange woman standing in the doorway. It was Caroline Spires. Caroline was totally different from her dowdy sister. The figure was thickening (fat with sin, as Banner liked to put it), but it was dressed in the latest of fashions. She had strawy blonde hair, fresh from a cold perm-wave and a little too much pancake makeup on. Banner had a feeling that in spite of her placid exterior she could be a vixen when aroused.

"Hello, Caroline," said Verl, with some surprise. "I want you to meet Senator Banner."

Caroline teetered in on very high heels and used the properly sorrowful smile for the occasion as she shook his hand. "How do you do?" she enunciated.

"Meetcha," said Banner.

"Seeing you standing there, Caroline," went on Verl, "gave me a turn. Ora said that last night you weren't able to lift a finger. You've made a very rapid recovery."

A crease of annoyance came and went between her penciled brows. "Oh, no matter how I felt, I couldn't stay away at a time like this." She took a package wrapped in holiday tissue from her handbag. "I know that Caspar would have wanted me to bring this." She let her lower lip tremble. "Who knows? In another few weeks I might have been Mrs. Woolfolk."

Banner thought: *Nice acting, baby.*

He said: "You felt that Beryl needed you for a mother."

"I should say not," said Caroline forcefully. "She's ungovernable. I wouldn't feel safe living in the same house with that brat. I wanted her sent away to a school. I told him so. I wouldn't marry him under any other condition."

"Woolfolk visited you at your sick-bed last night. He left near ten. Didja get up any time after that?"

She smiled archly. "I hardly dared. My nurse looked in every half hour to see if I was asleep. Surely you don't think *I* did it. I'm not one that's likely to kill a goose with golden eggs." She twisted the wrapped gift over in her manicured hands. "Excuse me. I want to put this under the tree." Before she turned away she added: "What a horrible Christmas!"

They listened to her heels tap away in the hall.

Verl said: "If she'd had her way with Woolfolk, she'd be mistress of Falconridge now. Lately she's been afraid that Woolfolk might get too interested in Ora. There's a rivalry between those two sisters, but it doesn't show on the surface. I don't think she was sick for one minute. This sudden recovery proves it. She did it to keep Woolfolk at her bedside morning and night. Finally he would have married her out of sheer sympathy."

Banner studied him with his shrewd baby-blue eyes. "Are you in love with Ora? Or vice versa?"

Verl looked genuinely surprised, then he grinned. "That's funny. I never thought of that before." He shook his head. "I'm afraid not, Senator. We've known each other all our lives. We're good friends. But I doubt that Ora will ever marry anyone. She's a born and bred spinster. Since she was a tot, Caroline put the fear of men in her." He paused. "There's that interesting sidelight on Woolfolk that I was telling you about. Come into the library. I'll show you."

Banner followed him in.

Three of the room's four walls were banked with heavy books.

Verl waved his hand at them. "Abnormal psychology—every last one of them." He handled a volume. "Most of these subjects are old familiars with me. I majored in psych at Holy Cross."

Banner ran his eye over the titles: *Paranoia. Mania. Melancholy. Hallucination. Hypochondria. Sadism. Masochism. Lycanthropy.*

There was a volume lying closed on a square table. Banner leafed through it and stopped at a chapter headed *Schizophrenia*. There was a marginal note in a fine masculine hand: *There's no doubt she has a split personality.*

Banner snapped the book shut. To whom had Woolfolk referred? Ora? Beryl? Caroline? Or someone else?

Banner trotted across the library and laid the book on a victrola top. "What kinda gun did the police find hanging down the chimney?"

"I told you. The old horse pistol. A single loader."

"When the police searched the house, they didn't find another gun?"

"Another one? No. Why should they? It was the horse pistol that killed Woolfolk."

Without answering, Banner galumphed across the carpet and out of the library. He went into the dining room. Verl followed.

The Christmas fir was there. The gifts underneath its tinseled boughs were undisturbed. Beryl, the little brat, had hung some of her soiled underwear on the tree. Caroline was nowhere in sight.

Banner plumped down on his well-padded knees and sorted out all the packages meant for Woolfolk. He ripped open the smaller ones like a ghoulish vandal. It wasn't until he reached the fifth package. When he tore it open a small black automatic fell out and clattered on the parquet floor.

"The devil!" cried Verl. "How'd that get there?"

Banner's head shot around, his eyes probing. "You've seen it before?"

"Yes. It's Woolfolk's."

"Tell Ora and Caroline to come to the library."

"But, Senator, what's the gun doing there?"

"That's where Ora hid it and that's the one place the police neglected to look."

"Ora!"

"Find her and Caroline! Skeedaddle!"

Verl ran upstairs.

Banner stuck a pencil into the pistol-barrel and picked it up. He pranced into the library and looked thoughtfully at the victrola. Then he opened the records cabinet and hunted. Finally he held up a record to the dull light from the window. He chuckled. The label said: *Selections from La Somnambula. Pianist, Caspar Woolfolk.*

He heard the other three coming.

"Ora," he said to her in his bullfrog voice as she came faltering in, "your story didn't fuse. If you'd walked out to the li'l house on the lawn in your sleep, you'd've left tracks in the snow. And when you told me how you killed Woolfolk you used the word *shots.*"

"I did," she said frantically. "I kept shooting over and over. I don't know how many times."

"Woolfolk was shot only once. He was killed with a single loader. You can't fire the horse pistol more than once without jamming in another round."

Ora stared. "You mean *I* didn't shoot—"

Banner held up the black automatic. "This's the gun you shot at him with."

"Then I killed him after all," she cried in bewildered despair.

Banner chuckled. "With *blanks!*"

"Blanks!" exploded Verl. "What kind of games were they playing last night?"

"Mighty deep ones," said Banner seriously. "Woolfolk was hipped on psychology. What started him off we'll go into later. Woolfolk tried an ignoble experiment on Ora. Would she—hypnotized—be compelled to commit murder!"

"Hypnotism!" Verl snapped his fingers with elation.

"Sure," said Banner. "Woolfolk babbled about the magic mirror, Carl Saxtus's zinc but-ton, and Father Hell's magnet. It's all hypnotism!"

"I was hypnotized?" said Ora dully. "Oh no. No. Mr. Woolfolk never hypnotized me. He couldn't do that against my will. Nobody can."

"You walk in your sleep, duck," said Banner. "Somnambulism's the nearest thing to a hypnotic trance. Woolfolk would meet you and gently suggest—"

"He saw me—he saw me in my night clothes!" She was mortified. This was worse than being accused of murder.

Banner grinned and continued: "Bug doctors call it post-hypnotic suggestion. You tell a person to do something the next day and to forget they've done it."

"That's why she didn't remember being with me in town yesterday afternoon," said Verl.

"Yass. At his suggestion, Ora, you put notations in your diary. He was experimenting with you, as I said. He was conditioning your mind for a pseudo murder. He wanted to see how far a gentle-natured woman, like yourself, would go. And he'd selected himself as the victim. Finally Woolfolk was ready for the experiment. He told you to come where you could hear him playing."

"I remember that," she said.

Caroline Spires, in the background, was drinking it all in greedily, not making a sound.

Banner said: "Last night, Ora, you woke up about 3:30, under post-hypnotic compulsion. The little black automatic, loaded with blanks, had been laid on your night table by your bed by Woolfolk himself. You couldn't help but see it when you woke. You took the gun in your hand and started downstairs. You could hear Woolfolk's arrangement of *La Somnambula.* But the music wasn't coming from outside the house. It came from right here in the library. Woolfolk had considered the cold and the snow and your scanty nightdress. So he duplicated the Music Box here in the library. All he needed was piano music and a piano. He built up this square table with books and threw the large Spanish shawl over all of it. You *thought* it was the piano, cuz the shawl always covered the piano. The music you heard was from one of Woolfolk's own recordings being played on the victrola." He jabbed a dynamic forefinger at it. "He turned it off when he heard you coming. He rose up, then goaded you till you fired the harmless automatic at him. That's how you *murdered* Woolfolk."

She sobbed with relief.

"But somebody *did* kill Woolfolk in the Music Box!" cried Verl.

"I'm coming to that. After Ora fled back to her room, he put the record and books away—probably with mixed emotions over what'd just occurred—and threw the Spanish shawl over his arm. He went to the door. It was nearly four o'clock. It'd stopped snowing some time before. Carrying the shawl, he walked across the snow to the Music Box, leaving the only tracks."

The others were breathlessly silent.

"The murderer was waiting in the little house—had been waiting there for hours . . ."

"Ah," said Verl. It was as soft as a prayer.

Caroline cleared her throat raspingly. "How did the murderer know that Caspar was going out there at all?"

"Cuz," said Banner, "the murderer overheard Woolfolk telling Ora *to come where he would be playing*. And where else would that be but the Music Box where the piano is?" There was a light dawning in Verl's eyes, but Banner went on evenly: "Woolfolk came in and arranged the shawl and sheet music on the piano, putting everything back in its proper place, y'see. The murderer was hiding behind the grandfather's clock, the horse pistol cocked, the fingers that held it stiff from waiting. As Woolfolk sat down on the bench to run his fingers over the keys, the murderer stepped out into view and fired. Woolfolk, a bullet in his skull, fell forward onto the piano."

"My God," breathed Ora, her hand fluttering at her white throat.

Verl was excited. "But now you've got the murderer trapped out there!"

"For the moment. To walk back across the snow would leave distinctive, incriminating footprints. There had to be another way." Banner looked into Verl's luminous eyes. "You told

me the answer at the orphanage, in your first recital of your discovery of the crime. There's only one way out."

"*I?*" said Verl incredulously. "*I* know?"

Banner nodded grimly. "You said that when you came into the little house the day was so gloomy that you had to switch on the light. Later I also called attention to the tipped-over table lamp. That means *electricity*!"

"No, I can't—" puzzled Verl.

"And electricity means *wires*!"

"Oh," said Verl, like a deflated balloon.

"The insulated wire runs at a long slant up from under the eaves to the cross-armed pole thirty feet away. You can reach the wire from one of the windows. It ain't slippy. It hasn't been cold enough for ice. More poles carry the wire across the snow to the trampled road, where all footprints're lost." Banner shrugged. "That's all there is to know."

Caroline whispered: "Then the murderer is someone who would have no trouble climbing. Like a little monkey."

"Yass," said Banner gloomily. "Someone who can climb things like radio aerials. That should've given you an idea. A tomboy—"

Ora had her hands up to her mouth in shocked horror.

Someone screamed in the hall and dashed in furiously to spit and tear at Banner.

"He was going to send me away!" Beryl screeched at him. "I heard him tell Caroline! He wanted to marry her and send me away! And he liked Ora even better than me!"

Ora sat horrified listening to a child's confession of murder.

Later a psychiatrist said to Banner: "So Woolfolk took up psychology to study his own child's case. His layman's diagnosis was correct. She is schizophrenic."

Another psychiatrist interrupted: "I think, in this particular case, that dementia praecox is the more precise term."

Banner waggled his big speckled hand at both of them and grunted: "Gentlemen, she was just plain nuts."

AN UNCANNY

Little Christmas

THE HAUNTED CRESCENT

Peter Lovesey

FEW CONTEMPORARY MYSTERY WRITERS have been as be-
loved by their fans as Peter Lovesey, and fewer still have received a similar degree of the accolades of reviewers and his peers. His first book, *Wobble to Death*
(1970), won the first prize in a contest sponsored by Macmillan for a best first
mystery. The wonderfully funny novel *The False Inspector Dew* (1982) won the
(British) Crime Writers' Association Gold Dagger. *Rough Cider* (1986) and *The
Summons* (1995) were nominated for Edgars. *Waxwork* (1978), *The Summons*,
and *Bloodhounds* (1996) all won CWA Silver Daggers, and Lovesey was given the
CWA's Carter Diamond Dagger for lifetime achievement in 2000. There have
been many other awards from all around the world, but you get the idea. "The
Haunted Crescent" was first published in *Mistletoe Mysteries*, edited by Char-
lotte MacLeod (New York, Mysterious Press, 1989).

The Haunted Crescent

PETER LOVESEY

A GHOST WAS SEEN LAST CHRIST-mas in a certain house in the Royal Crescent. Believe me, this is true. I speak from personal experience, as a resident of the City of Bath and something of an authority on psychic phenomena. I readily admit that ninety-nine percent of so-called hauntings turn out to have been hallucinations of one sort or another, but this is the exception, a genuine haunted house. Out of consideration for the present owners (who for obvious reasons wish to preserve their privacy), I shall not disclose the exact address, but if you doubt me, read what happened to me on Christmas Eve, 1988.

The couple who own the house had gone to Norfolk for the festive season, leaving on Friday, December twenty-third. Good planning. The ghost was reputed to walk on Christmas Eve. Knowing of my interest, they had generously placed their house at my disposal. I am an ex-policeman, by the way, and it takes a lot to frighten me.

For those who like a ghost story with all the trimmings—deep snow and howling winds outside—I am sorry. I must disappoint you. Christmas, 1988, was not a white one in Bath. It was unseasonably warm. There wasn't even any fog. All I can offer in the way of atmospheric effects are a full moon that night and an owl that hooted periodically in the trees at the far side of the sloping lawn that fronts the Crescent. It has to be admitted that this was not a spooky-looking

barn owl, but a tawny owl, which on this night was making more of a high-pitched "kee-wik" call than a hoot, quite cheery, in fact. Do not despair, however. The things that happened in the house that night more than compensated for the absence of werewolves and banshees outside.

It is vital to the story that you are sufficiently informed about the building in which the events occurred. Whether you realize it or not, you have probably seen the Royal Crescent, if not as a resident, or a tourist, then in one of the numerous films in which it has appeared as a backdrop to the action. It is in a quiet location northwest of the city and comprises thirty houses in a semielliptical terrace completed in 1774 to the specification of John Wood the Younger. It stands comparison with any domestic building in Europe. I defy anyone not to respond to its uncomplicated grandeur, the majestic panorama of 114 Ionic columns topped by a portico and balustrade; and the roadway at the front where Jane Austen and Charles Dickens trod the cobbles. But you want me to come to the ghost.

My first intimation of something unaccountable came at about twenty past eleven that Christmas Eve. I was in the drawing room on the first floor. I had stationed myself there a couple of hours before. The door was ajar and the house was in darkness. No, that isn't quite accurate. I should have said simply that none of the lights were switched on; actually the moonlight gave a certain amount of illumination, silver-blue rectangles projected across the carpet and over the base of the Christmas tree, producing an effect infinitely prettier than fairy lights. The furniture was easily visible, too, armchairs, table, and grand piano. One's eyes adjust. It didn't strike me as eerie to be alone in that unlit house. Anyone knows that a spirit of the departed is unlikely to manifest itself in electric light.

No house is totally silent, certainly no centrally heated house. The sounds produced by expanding floorboards in so-called haunted houses up and down the land must have fooled ghost-hunters by the hundred. In this case, as a precaution against a sudden freeze, the owners had left the system switched on. It was timed to turn off at eleven, so the knocks and creaks I was hearing now ought to have been the last of the night.

As events turned out, it wasn't a sound that alerted me first. It was a sudden draft against my face and a flutter of white across the room. I tensed. The house had gone silent. I crossed the room to investigate.

The disturbance had been caused by a Christmas card falling off the mantelpiece into the grate. Nothing more alarming than that. Cards are always falling down. That's why some people prefer to suspend them on strings. I stooped, picked up the card, and replaced it, smiling at my overactive imagination.

Yet I had definitely noticed a draft. The house was supposed to be free of drafts. All the doors and windows were closed and meticulously sealed against the elements. Strange. I listened, holding my breath. The drawing room where I was standing was well placed for picking up any unexplained sound in the house. It was at the center of the building. Below me were the ground floor and the cellar, above me the second floor and the attic.

Hearing nothing, I decided to venture out to the landing and listen there. I was mystified, yet unwilling at this stage to countenance a supernatural explanation. I was inclined to wonder whether the cut-off of the central heating had resulted in some trick of convection that gave the impression or the reality of a disturbance in the air. The falling card was not significant in itself. The draft required an explanation. My state of mind, you see, was calm and analytical.

Ten or fifteen seconds passed. I leaned over the banisters and looked down the stairwell to make sure that the front door was firmly shut, and so it proved to be. Then I heard a rustle from the room where I had been. I knew what it was—the card falling into the grate again—for another distinct movement of air had stirred the curtain on the landing window, causing a shift in the moonlight across the stairs. I was in no doubt anymore that this was worth investigating. My only uncertainty was whether to start with the floors above me, or below.

I chose the latter, reasoning that if, as I suspected, someone had opened a window, it was likely to be at the ground or basement levels. My assumption was wrong. I shall not draw out the suspense. I merely wish to record that I checked the cellar, kitchen, scullery, dining room, and study and found every window and external door secure and bolted from inside. No one could have entered after me.

So I began to work my way upstairs again, methodically visiting each room. And on the staircase to the second floor, I heard a sigh.

Occasionally in Victorian novels a character would "heave" a sigh. Somehow the phrase had always irritated me. In real life I never heard a sigh so weighty that it seemed to involve muscular effort—until this moment. This was a sound hauled up from the depths of somebody's inner being, or so I deduced. Whether it really originated with somebody or some *thing* was open to speculation.

The sound had definitely come from above me. Unable by now to suppress my excitement, I moved up to the second-floor landing, where I found three doors, all closed. I moved from one to the other, opening them rapidly and glancing briefly inside. Two bedrooms and a bathroom. I hesitated. A bathroom. Had the "sigh," I wondered, been caused by some aberration of the plumbing? Air locks are endemic in the complicated systems installed in these old Georgian buildings. The houses were not built with valves and cisterns. The efficiency of the pipework depended on the variable skill of generations of plumbers.

The sound must have been caused by trapped air.

Rationality reasserted itself. I would finish my inspection and prove to my total satisfaction that what I had heard was neither human nor spectral in origin. I closed the bathroom door behind me and crossed the landing to the last flight of stairs, more narrow than those I had used so far. In times past they had been the means of access to the servants' quarters in the attic. I glanced up at the white-painted door at the head of these stairs and observed that it was slightly ajar.

My foot was on the first stair and my hand on the rail when I stiffened. That door moved.

It was being drawn inward. The movement was slow and deliberate. As the gap increased, a faint glow of moonlight was cast from the interior onto the paneling to my right. I stared up and watched the figure of a woman appear in the doorway.

She was in a white gown or robe that reached to her feet. Her hair hung loose to the level of her chest—fine, gently shifting hair so pale in color that it appeared to merge with the dress. Her skin, too, appeared bloodless. The eyes were flint black, however. They widened as they took me in. Her right hand crept to her throat and I heard her give a gasp.

The sensations I experienced in that moment of confrontation are difficult to convey. I was convinced that nothing of flesh and blood had entered that house in the hours I had been there. All the entrances were bolted—I had checked. I could not account for the phenomenon, or whatever it was, that had manifested itself, yet I refused to be convinced. I was unwilling to accept what my eyes were seeing and my rational faculties could not explain. She could not be a ghost.

I said, "Who are you?"

The figure swayed back as if startled. For a moment I thought she was going to close the attic door, but she remained staring at me, her hand still pressed to her throat. It was the face and form of a young woman, not more than twenty.

I asked, "Can you speak?"

She appeared to nod.

I said, "What are you doing here?"

She caught her breath. In a strange, half-whispered utterance she said, as if echoing my words, "Who are you?"

I took a step upward toward her. It evidently frightened her, for she backed away and became almost invisible in the shadowy interior of the attic room. I tried to dredge up some reassuring words. "It's all right. Believe me, it's all right."

Then I twitched in surprise. Downstairs, the doorbell chimed. After eleven on Christmas Eve!

I said, "What on earth . . . ?"

The woman in white whimpered something I couldn't hear.

I tried to make light of it. "Santa, I expect."

She didn't react.

The bell rang a second time.

"He ought to be using the chimney," I said. I had already decided to ignore the visitor, whoever it was. One unexpected caller was all I could cope with.

The young woman spoke up, and the words sprang clearly from her. "For God's sake, send him away!"

"You know who it is?"

"Please! I beg you."

"If you know who it is," I said reasonably, "wouldn't you like to answer it?"

"I can't."

The chimes rang out again.

I said, "Is it someone you know?"

"Please. Tell him to go away. If you answer the door he'll go away."

I was letting myself be persuaded. I needed her cooperation. I wanted to know about her. "All right," I relented. "But will you be here when I come back?"

"I won't leave."

Instinctively I trusted her. I turned and descended the two flights of stairs to the hall. The bell rang again. Even though the house was in darkness, the caller had no intention of giving up.

I drew back the bolts, opened the front door a fraction, and looked out. A man was on the doorstep, leaning on the iron railing. A young man in a leather jacket glittering with studs and chains. His head was shaven. He, at any rate, looked like flesh and blood. He said, "What kept you?"

I said, "What do you want?"

He glared. "For crying out loud—who the hell are you?" His eyes slid sideways, checking the number on the wall.

I said with frigid courtesy, "I think you must have made a mistake."

"No," he said. "This is the house all right. What's your game, mate? What are you doing here with the lights off?"

I told him that I was an observer of psychic phenomena.

"Come again?"

"Ghosts," I said. "This house has the reputation of being haunted. The owners have kindly allowed me to keep watch tonight."

"Oh, yes?" he said with heavy skepticism. "Spooks, is it? I'll have a gander at them myself." With that, he gave the door a shove. There was no security chain and I was unable to resist the pressure. He stepped across the threshold. "Ghost-buster, are you, mate? You wouldn't, by any chance, be lifting the family silver at the same time? Anyone else in here?"

I said, "I take exception to that. You've no right to force your way in here."

"No more right than you," he said, stepping past me. "Were you upstairs when I rang?"

I said, "I'm going to call the police."

He flapped his hand dismissively. "Be my guest. I'm going upstairs, right?"

Sheer panic inspired me to say, "If you do, you'll be on film."

"What?"

"The cameras are ready to roll," I lied. "The place is riddled with mikes and tripwires."

He said, "I don't believe you," but the tone of his voice said the opposite.

"This ghost is supposed to walk on Christmas Eve," I told him. "I want to capture it on film." I gave a special resonance to the word "capture."

He said, "You're round the twist." And with as much dignity as he could muster he sidled back toward the door, which still stood open. Apparently he was leaving. "You ought to be locked up. You're a nutcase."

As he stepped out of the door I said, "Shall I tell the owners you called? What name shall I give?"

He swore and turned away. I closed the door and slid the bolts back into place. I was shaking. It had been an ugly, potentially dangerous incident. I'm not so capable of tackling an intruder as I once was and I was thankful that my powers of invention had served me so well.

I started up the stairs again and as I reached the top of the first flight, the young woman in white was waiting for me. She must have come down two floors to overhear what was being said. This area of the house was better illuminated than the attic stairs, so I got a better look at her. She appeared less ethereal now. Her dress was silk or satin, I observed. It was an evening gown. Her makeup was as pale as a mime artist's, except for the black liner around her eyes.

She said, "How can I thank you enough?"

I answered flatly, "What I want from you, young lady, is an explanation."

She crossed her arms, rubbing at her sleeves. "I feel shivery here. Do you mind if we go in there?"

As we moved into the drawing room I noticed that she made no attempt to switch on the light. She pointed to some cigarettes on the table. "Do you mind?"

I found some matches by the fireplace and gave her a light. "Who was that at the door?"

She inhaled hard. "Some guy I met at a party. I was supposed to be with someone else, but we got separated. You know how it is. Next thing I knew, this bloke in the leather jacket was chatting me up. He was all right at first. I didn't know he was going to come on so strong. I mean I didn't encourage him. I was trying to cool it. He offered me these tablets, but I refused. He said they would make me relax. By then I was really scared. I moved off fast. The stupid thing was that I moved upstairs. There were plenty of people about, and it seemed the easiest way to go. The bloke followed. He kept on following. I went right to the top of the house and shut myself in a room. I pushed a cupboard against the door. He was beating his fist on the door, saying what he was going to do to me. I was scared out of my skull. All I could think of doing was get through the window, so I did. I climbed out and found myself up there behind the little stone wall."

"Of this building? The balustrade at the top?"

"Didn't I make that clear? The party was in a house a couple of doors away from you. I ran along this narrow passageway between the roof and the wall, trying all the windows. The one upstairs was the first one I could shift."

"The attic window. Now I understand." The sudden draft was explained, and the gasp as she had caught her breath after the effort.

She said, "I'm really grateful."

"Grateful?"

"Grateful to you for getting rid of him."

I said, "It would be sensible now to call a taxi. Where do you live?"

"Not far. I can walk."

"It wouldn't be advisable, would it, after what happened? He's persistent. He may be waiting."

"I didn't think." She stubbed the cigarette into an ashtray. After a moment's reflection she said, "All right. Where's the phone?"

There was one in the study. While she was occupied, I gave some thought to what she had said. I didn't believe a word of it, but I had something vastly more important on my mind.

She came back into the room. "Ten minutes, they reckon. Was it true what you said downstairs, about this house being haunted?"

"Mm?" I was still preoccupied.

"The spook. All that stuff about hidden cameras. Did you mean it?"

"There aren't any cameras. I'm useless with machinery of any sort. I reckoned he'd think twice about coming in if he knew he was going to be on film. It was just a bluff."

"And the bit about the ghost?"

"That was true."

"Would you mind telling me about it?"

"Aren't you afraid of the supernatural?"

"It's scary, yes. Not so scary as what happened already. I want to know the story. Christmas Eve is a great night for a ghost story."

I said, "It's more than just a story."

"Please."

"On one condition. Before you get into that taxi, you tell me the truth about yourself—why you really came into this house tonight."

She hesitated.

I said, "It needn't go any further."

"All right. Tell me about the ghost." She reached for another cigarette and perched on the arm of a chair.

I crossed to the window and looked away over the lawn toward the trees silhouetted against the city lights. "It can be traced back, as all ghost stories can, to a story of death and an unquiet spirit. About a hundred and fifty years ago this house was owned by an army officer, a retired colonel by the name of Davenport. He had a daughter called Rosamund, and it was believed in the city that he doted on her. She was dressed fashionably and given a good education, which in those days was beyond the expectation of most young women. Rosamund was a lively, intelligent, and attractive girl. Her hair when she wore it long was very like yours, fine and extremely fair. Not surprisingly, she had admirers. The one she favored most was a young man from Bristol, Luke Robertson, who at that time was an architect. In the conventions of the time they formed an attachment which amounted to little more than a few chaperoned meetings, some letters, poems, and so on. They were lovers in a very old-fashioned sense that you may find difficult to credit. In physical terms it amounted to no more than a few stolen kisses, if that. Somewhere in this house there is supposed to be carved into woodwork the letters *L* and *R* linked. I can't show you. I haven't found it."

Outside, a taxi trundled over the cobbles. I watched it draw up at a house some doors down. Two couples came out of the building, laughing, and climbed into the cab. It was obvious that they were leaving a party. The heavy beat of music carried up to me.

I said, "I wonder if it's turned midnight. It might be Christmas Day already."

She said, "Please go on with the story."

"Colonel Davenport—the father of this girl—was a lonely man. His wife had died some years before. Lately he had become friendly with a neighbor, another resident of the Crescent, a widow approaching fifty years of age by the name of Mrs. Crandley, who lived in one of the houses at the far end of the building. She was a musician, a pianist, and she gave lessons. One of her pupils was Rosamund. So far as one can tell, Mrs. Crandley was a good teacher and the girl a promising pupil. Do you play?"

"What?"

I turned to face her. "I said, do you play the piano?"

"Oh. Just a bit," said the girl.

"You didn't tell me your name."

"I'd rather not, if you don't mind. What happened between the colonel and Mrs. Crandley?"

"Their friendship blossomed. He wanted her to marry him. Mrs. Crandley was not unwilling. In fact, she agreed, subject to one condition. She had a son of twenty-seven called Justinian."

"What was that?"

"Justinian. There was a vogue for calling your children after emperors. This Justinian was a dull fellow without much to recommend him. He was lazy and overweight. He rarely ventured out of the house. Mrs. Crandley despaired of him."

"She wanted him off her hands?"

"That is what it amounted to. She wanted him married and she saw the perfect partner for him in Rosamund. Surely such a charming, talented girl would bring out some positive qualities in her lumpish son. Mrs. Crandley applied herself diligently to the plan, insisting that Jus-

tinian answer the doorbell each time Rosamund came for her music lesson. Then he would be told to sit in the room and listen to her playing. Everything Mrs. Crandley could do to promote the match was done. For his part, Justinian was content to go along with the plan. He was promised that if he married the girl he would be given his mother's house, so the pattern of his life would alter little, except that a pretty wife would keep him company rather than a discontented, nagging mother. He began to eye Rosamund with increasing favor. So when the colonel proposed marriage to Mrs. Crandley, she assented on the understanding that Justinian would be married to Rosamund at the same time."

"How about Rosamund? Was she given any choice?"

"You have to be aware that marriages were commonly arranged by the parents in those days."

"But you said she already had a lover. He was perfectly respectable, wasn't he?"

I nodded. "Absolutely. But Luke Robertson didn't feature in Mrs. Crandley's plan. He was ignored. Rosamund bowed under the pressure and became engaged to Justinian in the autumn of 1838. The double marriage was to take place in the Abbey on Christmas Eve."

"Oh, dear—I think I can guess the rest of the story."

"It may not be quite as you expect. As the day of the wedding approached, Rosamund began to dread the prospect. She pleaded with her father to allow her to break off the engagement. He wouldn't hear of it. He loved Mrs. Crandley and his thoughts were all of her. In despair, Rosamund sent the maidservant with a message to Luke, asking him to meet her secretly on the basement steps. She had a romantic notion that Luke would elope with her."

My listener was enthralled. "And did he come?"

"He came. Rosamund poured out her story. Luke listened with sympathy, but he was cautious. He didn't see elopement as the solution. Rather bravely, he volunteered to speak to the colonel and appeal to him to allow Rosamund to marry the man of her choice. If that failed, he would remind the colonel that Rosamund could not be forced to take the sacred vows. Her consent had to be freely given in church, and she was entitled to withhold it. So this uncomfortable interview took place a day or two later. The colonel, naturally, was outraged. Luke was banished from the house and forbidden to speak to Rosamund again. The unfortunate girl was summoned by her father and accused of wickedly consorting with her former lover when she was promised to another. The story of the secret note and the meeting on the stairs was dragged from her. She was told that she wished to destroy her father's marriage. She was said to be selfish and disloyal. Worse, she might be taken to court by Justinian for breach of promise."

"Poor little soul! Did it break her?"

"No. Amazingly, she stood her ground. Luke's support had given her courage. She would not marry Justinian. It was the colonel who backed down. He went to see Mrs. Crandley. When he returned, it was to tell Rosamund that his marriage would not, after all, take place. Mrs. Crandley had insisted on a double wedding, or nothing."

"I wouldn't have been in Rosamund's shoes for a million pounds."

"She was told by her father that she had behaved no better than a servant, secretly meeting her lover on the basement steps and trifling with another man's affections, so in future he would treat her as a servant. And he did. He dismissed the housemaid. He ordered Rosamund to move her things to the maid's room in the attic, and he gave her a list of duties that kept her busy from five-thirty each morning until late at night."

"Cruel."

"All his bitterness was heaped on her."

"Did she kill herself?"

"No," I said with only the slightest pause. "She was murdered."

"*Murdered?*"

"On Christmas Eve, the day that the weddings would have taken place, she was suffocated in her bed."

"Horrible!"

"A pillow was held against her face until she ceased to breathe. She was found dead in bed by the cook on Christmas morning after she failed to report for duty. The colonel was informed and the police were sent for."

"Who killed her?"

"The inspector on the case, a local man without much experience of violent crimes, was in no doubt that Colonel Davenport was the murderer. He had a powerful motive. The animus he felt toward his daughter had been demonstrated by the way he treated her. It seemed that his anger had only increased as the days passed. On the date he was due to have married, it became insupportable."

"Was it true? Did he confess to killing her?"

"He refused to make any statement. But the evidence against him was overwhelming. Three inches of snow fell on Christmas Eve. It stopped about eight-thirty that evening. The time of death was estimated at about eleven p.m. When the inspector and his men arrived next morning no footsteps were visible on the path leading to the front door except those of the cook, who had gone for the police. The only other person in the house was Colonel Davenport. So he was charged with murdering his own daughter. The trial was short, for he refused to plead. He remained silent to the end. He was found guilty and hanged at Bristol in February 1839."

She put out the cigarette. "Grim."

"Yes."

"There's more to the story, isn't there? The ghost. You said something about an unquiet spirit."

I said, "There was a feeling of unease about the fact that the colonel wouldn't admit to the crime. After he was convicted and condemned, they tried to persuade him to confess, to lay his sins before his Maker. A murderer often would confess in the last days remaining to him, even after protesting innocence all through the trial. They all did their utmost to persuade him—the prison governor, the warders, the priest, and the hangman himself. Those people had harrowing duties to perform. It would have helped them to know that the man going to the gallows was truly guilty of the crime. Not one word would that proud old man speak."

"You sound almost sorry for him. There wasn't really any doubt, was there?"

I said, "There's a continuous history of supernatural happenings in this house for a century and a half. Think about it. Suppose, for example, someone else committed the murder."

"But who else could have?"

"Justinian Crandley."

"That's impossible. He didn't live here. His footprints would have shown up in the snow."

"Not if he entered the house as you did tonight—along the roof and through the attic window. He could have murdered Rosamund and returned to his own house by the same route."

"It's possible, I suppose, but why—what was his motive?"

"Revenge. He would have been master in his own house if the marriage had not been called off. Instead, he faced an indefinite future with his domineering and now embittered mother. He blamed Rosamund. He decided that if he was not to have her as his wife, no one else should."

"Is that what you believe?"

"It is now," said I.

"Why didn't the colonel tell them he was innocent?"

"He blamed himself. He felt a deep sense of guilt for the way he had treated his own daughter. But for his selfishness the murder would never have taken place."

"Do you think he knew the truth?"

"He must have worked it out. He loved Mrs. Crandley too much to cause her further unhappiness."

There was an interval of silence, broken finally by the sound of car tires on the cobbles below.

She stood up. "Tonight when you saw me at the attic door you thought I was Rosamund's ghost."

I said, "No. Rosamund doesn't haunt this place. Her spirit is at rest. I didn't take you for a real ghost any more than I believed your story of escaping from the fellow in the leather jacket."

She walked to the window. "It is my taxi."

I wasn't going to let her leave without admitting the truth. "You went to the party two doors along with the idea of breaking into this house. You climbed out onto the roof and forced your way in upstairs, meaning to let your friend in by the front door. You were going to burgle the place."

She gasped and swung around. "How did you know that?"

"When I opened the door he was expecting you. He said 'What kept you?' He knew which house to call at, so it must have been planned. If your story had been true, he wouldn't have known where to come."

She stared down at the waiting cab.

I said, "Until I suggested the taxi, you were quite prepared to go out into the street where this man who had allegedly threatened you was waiting."

"I'm leaving."

"And I noticed that you didn't want the lights turned on."

Her tone altered. "You're not one of the fuzz, are you? You wouldn't turn me in? Give me a break, will you? It's the first time. I'll never try it again."

"How can I know that?"

"I'll give you my name and address, if you want. Then you can check."

It is sufficient to state here that she supplied the information. I shall keep it to myself. I'm no longer in the business of exposing petty criminals. I saw her to her taxi. She promised to stop seeing her boyfriend. Perhaps you think I let her off too lightly. Her misdemeanor was minor compared with the discovery I had made—and I owed that discovery to her.

It released me from my obligation, you see. I told you I was once a policeman. An inspector, actually. I made a fatal mistake. I have had a hundred and fifty years to search for the truth and now that I found it I can rest. The haunting of the Royal Crescent is at an end.

A CHRISTMAS IN CAMP

Edmund Cox

WHILE WE ARE ACCUSTOMED to think of Christmas as a Dickensian event in Victorian England, or in a romantic little clapboard house in snowy Connecticut, it is a holiday celebrated in all parts of the world—snowy or not. This story is by Sir Edmund Charles Cox, who served for many years as a member of the Indian Imperial Police and wrote several factual books about that country. He also wrote three rare short story collections: *John Carruthers, Indian Policeman* (1905), *The Achievements of John Carruthers* (1911), and *The Exploits of Kesho Naik, Dacoit* (1912). In the books about his British policeman, Carruthers is at the center of all the stories, but each is narrated by different officers under his command. "A Christmas in Camp" was first published in *The Achievements of John Carruthers* (London, Constable, 1911).

A Christmas in Camp

EDMUND COX

Told by William Trench, District Superintendent of Police

MR. CARRUTHERS WAS FURIOUSLY angry. I had seldom seen him angry at all, and never anything approaching this. He glared at me until I felt as if his glance would wither me away.

"You indescribable idiot," he thundered. "You hopeless fool! You have ruined yourself for life. I did think that we had one decent young policeman. After all that I have done for you too. Good heavens, it is too monstrous. Ruined utterly! Never a stroke of honest work to be got out of you again! Talk of brains, intellect, enthusiasm, keenness! And all for what? Endless trouble, worry, and annoyance! Damn it, man, it is too intolerable!"

And what was the cause of all this outburst? Merely this, that I had asked him to congratulate me on my going to be married. I had hoped that he would be pleased, especially when I told him that she was the dearest girl in the world. But this only seemed to add fuel to the flames.

"The dearest girl in the world!" he snorted. "The fools always say that. They learn in good time what there is dear about it when they have to pay for their idiotcy."

I felt unspeakably hurt and indignant. What crime had I committed? I was now twenty-six, and old enough to judge for myself, I thought; and many men married at that age and seemed to be as happy as possible. I had been home on three month's privilege leave and had become engaged to—well, to the dearest girl in the world, without any possible exception. It was now August, and she was to come out in November, and we were to be married in the Bombay cathedral. I had the greatest regard for Mr. Carruthers, and I was looking forward to his congratulations on my good luck. And now to be treated like this! I felt exceedingly disconcerted. We both stood silent for a while. He had not even offered me a chair.

"Forgive me if I have been violent, Trench," he said at last, holding out his hand, which I took. "I was quite upset at this sudden announcement. Why didn't you have some consideration for me, and let me have a little preliminary warning by letter?"

"Well, you see, sir," I replied, "I wanted to give you a surprise and have your congratulations personally."

"By the prophets," he said, "you certainly achieved your object in giving me a surprise; but this sort of surprise is not good for one—not for me at any rate. And as for my congratulations, well, my dear boy, as you have asked for them I am afraid you must have them. This is the prospect on which I have to congratulate you. A very pretty but evanescent glimpse of fairy land to begin with; then incessant thinking of every rupee, anna, and pie; worries about health;

complaints about being in a wretched dull station, a transfer about every two years at ruinous expense, for double first-class fare doesn't go far with a family; no money to go home on leave when leave is due; instead of investigating a crime at length, as you ought to, scheming how soon you can get back to the mem-sahib; and to pass on for a bit, in fifteen years' time, when you are forty-one and a generous Government is giving you possibly eight hundred depreciated rupees a month, there will be three youngsters being educated at home and the wife there to look after them. You will be sending the family five hundred rupees a month; you will be in debt for their steamer passages, and paying this off at the rate of fifty rupees a month, leaving you two hundred and fifty to live on, the same as you had when you started life, a nice income on which to keep up the position of Head of the Police in a district; you will be all alone and fagged and worried and unable to do justice to your work; but there will be no going home for you, my boy, unless some old aunt leaves you a legacy; and long before your pension is due, though still comparatively young in years, you will be a despondent, worn-out, useless old man. You asked me for my congratulations and, by the Lord, you have had them."

Here was food for reflection. I could have cried. I felt so miserable at this crushing summary of my future circumstances. For I knew that though it was one-sided, and did not say anything about the companionship of married life, and so on, yet truth compelled me to admit that I had seen something of the same kind in other cases. However, if every one, at all events in India, was going to look so far ahead as that, very few people would be married at all; and I cheered up at this reflection, and took a brighter view of the future. In fact, when I thought of the girl who was coming out to be my wife in a few months, and how delightful it would be to be in camp together, and ride together, and dine together in the tents, and breakfast together under the trees, how could I feel anything but overjoyed with life? And Mr. Carruthers, having scolded me to his heart's content, to my unspeakable satisfaction wished me all the joy in the world, and said that if she was anything like the photograph I was indeed a lucky fellow. He was my best man at the wedding, and he gave us as a present on that occasion, a splendid district tonga, with a pair of fourteen-one ponies that went in saddle as well as in harness.

The good ship "Arabia" arrived in Bombay harbour one morning late in November, bringing a certain Ellen Bramwell, as well as a few hundred other passengers who did not count at all. We were married within a few hours. She looked perfection in her wedding gown of soft white satin, and a Limerick lace veil that had been worn by her mother; and I was, of course, in full uniform. After the ceremony there was a very pleasant little meeting of a few old friends, and Mr. Carruthers made a most neat and humorous speech, wishing good luck to the happy pair. Then we changed into travelling costume, and went up for a ten days' honeymoon to the delightful hill station of Matheran—a few hours in the train and then a seven miles' ride up the hill on hired ponies. I shall never forget what a delightful time we had there. But I must restrain my pen or it will fly away evolving sheets and sheets about the joys of Matheran. I must not omit to mention one very welcome wedding present; and that was an announcement in the "Government Gazette," on the day of our wedding, which appointed me to act in a long vacancy as D.S.P. of Tarapur, the next district to Somapur, where Mr. Carruthers was again stationed.

"This is excellent news, Trench," said he. "I will have a Christmas camp at Loni, just in my district, and on the borders of yours. You must both spend the holidays with me; and we will see what Mrs. Trench can do with a gun or a rifle."

Of course we accepted, and looked forward greatly to this merry meeting. Things that are looked forward to sometimes fail to realise expectations; but this certainly didn't. We enjoyed it immensely, and none the less for a mysterious and exciting incident that occurred. But I must not anticipate. It was exceptionally good cold weather. By this I mean it was colder than usual, and Ellen was glad of her winter wraps. There was just a touch of frost in the early morning, and a bite in the air, and everything looked heavenly in the brilliant sunshine, which was not too strong to prevent us from being out all day long. Late in the afternoon of Christmas Eve we arrived at the camp, after a twenty-four-mile drive in our wedding present tonga, the ponies as fresh as could be, and ready for a good many miles more. Mr. Carruthers was standing in front of his tent, and gave us the warmest of welcomes. I was surprised to see how extensive the camp was. There were half a dozen large tents, apart from those provided for servants' and sepoys' accommodation. They were all pitched under a beautiful mango tope. Everything was in perfect order; and rows of wild plantains had been planted in the ground to mark out the roads leading from tent to tent. Strings of yellow marigolds hung along the lines thus formed; and Ellen said that she had never seen anything so like fairyland.

"By the by, Trench," said Mr. Carruthers, after we had exchanged greetings, "I have a little surprise for you. Who do you think are coming? Do you remember your visit to me at Indapur when the Collector was stolen away, one Fleming by name? Well, he and the mem-sahib and the two children will be here. I expect them any minute. She was rather pretty, if you recollect. Some one described her as looking like a dream, and having the most wonderful eyes and hair. But I don't suppose you would have noticed such things."

It was mean of Mr. Carruthers to indulge in this little pleasantry; but there was not a twinkle on his countenance, and Ellen seemed entirely unsuspicious that he was amusing himself at my expense. However, I lit a cigarette as quick as I could to cover my confusion. The Flemings arrived in due course. He seemed far brighter and livelier than he used to be; and though there was no denying that she was a pretty woman, when I saw her alongside Ellen I wondered how I could have admired her so much at Indapur. She and the wife were soon the best of friends, and a very merry party we all were. After dinner we put on warm coats and wraps and sat over a roaring bonfire a little way from the tents, and we roasted chestnuts and made jokes and told stories, and drank milk punch, and Ellen got out her guitar and sang to us, and Mr. Carruthers was the life and soul of the whole thing; and the whole thing was delightful. I forgot to mention that the two little Flemings, Jack and Dolly, were allowed to sit up as a great treat, and they enjoyed it all as much as their elders. Great excitement there was at bedtime as to whether "Christmas Father," as they called him, would be able to find his way to the camp to fill their stockings; but Mr. Carruthers told them that Christmas Father was very clever and was sure not to disappoint them. Certainly by the result he would appear to have visited the tents in the night; for the stockings were full to overflowing the next morning. But I have a story to tell, and at this rate I shall never begin. But it is difficult to pass over such a jolly time without trying to write something about it. It would seem positively ungrateful not to do so.

Christmas Day was, indeed, a day to remember. Our host had provided seasonable presents for every one; and all the servants and orderlies were called up and presented with a rupee or two according to their respective rank and deserts, in recognition of which they respectfully salaamed to the Sahib-logue for their kindness in remembering the humble ones on Natal-ka-din, or Christmas Day. The natives always speak of Christmas as Natal. I suppose the word was introduced by the Portuguese. Well, after a substantial chota hazri we all started out for the day. We drove six or seven miles in various conveyances, and we found breakfast arranged for us in a forest glade. We had a little shooting, and made a small bag of quail and black partridge. Mr. Carruthers initiated Ellen into the mysteries of loading and firing a gun, and aiming nowhere in particular and yet bringing down the bird. After a glorious day in the jungle we went back to the camp for dinner, and when that thoroughly enjoyable meal with its regulation puddings and mince pies was over, there was a wonderful surprise for us all.

"I want you to come out and see something that may interest you," said our host. "Put on warm coats and come along."

Out we went in obedience to instructions; and, lo and behold, where there had been a canvas enclosure to which I had given no particular attention there stood a gleaming, scintillating, dazzling Christmas tree, a mass of pretty things resting on its branches. There were no bounds to the delight of Jack and Dolly at the sight, and all of us felt a thrill of excitement at the sudden replica of the festivities that were being celebrated in thousands of homes in dear old England. Ellen could hardly contain herself, and she simply waltzed round and round the tree again and again. Jack and Dolly were laden with presents, and there was something for all of us; but this did not complete the proceedings. There was an enormous crowd of natives whose attendance had been invited. Every one in the place who had any children seemed to be there, including all the police who were blessed with youthful progeny. The natives had never seen such a sight before. They were immensely impressed, and there was a chorus of "Wah, wah," "Arhe Bapre," and similar ejaculations. For every child there was something, whether a handful of sweets or some glittering toy, and I think it will be a long time before that Natal-ka-din of Carruthers Sahib will pass out of remembrance at Loni. There are days in one's life which stand out for ever in one's memory, and I am sure this was one of them for all of us English people. As for the natives the Christmas tree was a foretaste of Bihisht or Paradise. Nevertheless it appeared to me that there was some kind of apprehension in the air. Mothers hung on to their children very persistently, never for a moment letting go of their hands, and anxious looks were distinctly noticeable. However, no one said anything, and neither Mr. Carruthers nor I were going to spoil the day's enjoyment by

asking if anything was wrong, and thus inviting a flow of eloquence on some possible or impossible subject. So the whole crowd went away quietly, after giving three cheers in English fashion for Carruthers Sahib.

The next morning when we had assembled and were doing justice to our chota hazri Ellen suddenly told us of a curious dream that she had had in the night.

"At least I suppose it must have been a dream," she said, "though it did not in the least seem like a dream at the time. But, of course, on thinking over it, it could have been nothing else. Perhaps it was the result of the mince pies. I woke up with a feeling that some strange person was in the tent. There was not a sound to be heard, and at first I could not see anything. But I had a most vivid impression that someone, or something, was present. After a brief space of time, what do you think I saw? A tall figure passed along the foot of the bed, and its head was a horrible skull with red lights gleaming through the openings where its eyes had once been. Wasn't it terrifying? I could have shrieked aloud, but I was positively afraid to, and something seemed to withhold me from uttering a sound. The figure disappeared as silently as it had come, and I don't know how it left the tent. I soon went to sleep again; and now, of course, I know it must have been a dream. But it was ghastly, wasn't it?"

Mr. Carruthers looked very attentive and concerned as he listened to this recital.

"What an extraordinary coincidence!" he exclaimed. "You know that I am an early riser; and for the last hour I have been listening to a deputation of the inhabitants of Loni, who want me to lay a ghost for them. A policeman's duties in this country are of a very multifarious nature. By the by, Mrs. Trench, can you give me any further description of your ghostly visitor?"

Ellen reflected for a moment or so and then said:

"Yes; there was a dim light burning in the tent, you know, and I could see that the apparition, or whatever it was, was above middle height. He, or it—what am I to call it?—wore ordinary native costume with the exception of a red waistcoat with brass buttons."

"This is indeed remarkable," said Mr. Carruthers. "Now I will tell you the story that has been related to me to-day. The whole village is in a state of consternation; and it is all caused by a gentleman who exactly answers to the description you have given of what you saw in the night. The curious thing is that when I was in these parts a few years ago I personally knew this individual, who seems to have returned from the astral plane, or whatever it was that he went to after his departure from Loni. His name was Maruti."

"Then why should it not be Maruti in the flesh, playing a practical joke?" asked the matter-of-fact Ellen.

"Because," replied Mr. Carruthers, "Maruti is dead and buried, or rather burnt. He was a somewhat reckless kind of man, fond of spending more money than he earned. He was, as I remember him, very popular in the neighbourhood. He and his wife Chandra Bai resided in a small cottage on the outskirts of the village. With them lived Maruti's brother Dhondi, whose intelligence was of the most limited order. However, he was able to do his work, which consisted in helping to cultivate a couple of fields. Chandra Bai was not a bad-looking woman, but was a terrible scold; and my friend Maruti was invariably worsted when there was a war of words. She, like her husband, was very extravagant, and was fond of new saris and ornaments. Maruti was willing enough to gratify her, but this resulted in his becoming more and more involved in debt to the village money-lender named Kashiram, and at last his fields were hopelessly mortgaged. I have mentioned his two fields, and as a matter of fact there were only two that were of any use. But there was a third one, a wretched barren piece of land, to which he attached greater value, from sentimental reasons, than to his really fertile fields, for its possession had been a matter of dispute from time immemorial between his own progenitors and those of one Tatya, a neighbour of Maruti's. This Tatya, who now claimed the land, was an over-bearing, hectoring man; and there was bitter enmity between him and Maruti. Each had been heard to threaten that he would take the other's life unless he gave up his claim to the disputed field. I must mention, Mrs. Trench, that Maruti, who was intensely conceited, used to wear a considerably larger puggree than his station in life entitled him to, and he was very proud of a ridiculous red waistcoat with brass buttons. Now you have all the dramatis personæ. As time went on Maruti's financial position grew worse and worse. Chandra Bai upbraided him for not giving her more money to buy clothes and ornaments to deck herself out with; Kashiram refused to advance him a pice over and above what he had already had, and Tatya's enmity became more bitter than ever. Suddenly one night Maruti disappeared. That was a little more than two years ago, when I was in this district. Inquiries were made in every direction, but not the faintest trace was found of Maruti or his red waistcoat. This seemed to sober Chandra Bai, and she and Dhondi managed to cultivate the two fields, pay the interest on the mortgage, and keep a roof over their heads for some time. But Tatya seized the disputed piece of land. As the last harvest was a bad one the interest on the mortgage was not available, and Kashiram has taken proceedings in the civil court to foreclose. Well, this morning early, as I have told you, a deputation came to me. They had, with the most unusual consideration for a Sahib's feelings, refrained from saying anything before, lest they should spoil our Christmas Day; but they could keep silence no longer. This is their story. Four days ago, the day before I came to this camp, some coolies were engaged on making a new local fund road, about half a mile away, and they had to remove a large heap of stones. Beneath the stones what do you think they found? The body, or rather the skeleton, of Maruti, for the flesh, of course, was gone; but the identity was unmistakable from the red waistcoat, brass buttons, and exceptional pug-gree, which, though more or less stained, were perfectly recognisable. Instead of informing the police and having an inquest on the remains, they burnt them, red waistcoat, brass buttons, and all that very night, with the usual ceremonies. Then there was trouble. Maruti had slept peacefully under his stones ever since his disappearance; but his spirit was evidently displeased at the unwarrantable interference with his resting-place, and his ghost proceeded to worry his former relations and acquaintances. The ghost was not satisfied with the appurtenances that he had worn in this life. There were the original red waistcoat, brass buttons, and large puggree; but his face was a skull with fire gleaming in the sockets where his eyes had been, just as you describe it, Mrs. Trench. First he went to his own house, where Dhondi and Chandra Bai were having their meal. In a hoarse whisper he uttered 'Beware!' Chandra Bai went off into a swoon, while Dhondi ran shrieking down the village streets, with his extraordinary tale. Next the ghost visited Kashiram, the money-lender, and said, 'Give me my mortgage bond, or you die!' Terribly frightened and hardly knowing if he was in his senses or not the sowar produced the document, threw it at the feet of his unearthly visitor, and fled for his life. He next appeared to his old antagonist Tatya, and said, 'Your turn has come!' Tatya has behaved like a madman ever since. The ghost has been seen by various other people, and the whole village is, as I say, in a state of consternation."

"Good heavens! How amazing! How extraordinary!" were a few of the exclamations that we listeners made on hearing this narrative.

"Wait a minute," continued Mr. Carruthers; "I have not finished yet. It appears that last night, after they had all gone away from the Christmas tree, they went through the most elaborate ritual, which was warranted to lay any ghost in creation. This seems to have been the gist of the proceedings. All the caste-fellows of Maruti, together with Chandra Bai, went off to the place where Maruti's body had been found.

They took with them one Mahdu, a gondhali, or master of occult ceremonies, and Govind, a bhagat, or medium, a kind of go-between who carries communications between mortals and the unseen world. The assembled persons sat down in a circle round these two agents of the supernatural. For some time Mahdu and Govind sat wrapped in deep thought, and then Mahdu commenced a strange wailing chant, in which he called upon the spirit of Maruti to remain peaceably in the under world, and to cease from troubling the inhabitants of Loni. Next Govind took a copper pot and asked all present to contribute a small coin, which should be expended on such comforts and luxuries as the deceased Maruti might require in his present abode. The collection was duly made, and so anxious were the people to appease the ghost that many of them promised other things in addition, such as an umbrella, a brass lota for drinking from, or a pair of shoes; and Tatya, who had been dragged most unwillingly to the conclave, offered to give a red waistcoat with brass buttons similar to that which Maruti used to wear on earth. At the mention of each item Govind said, 'Receive this gift, Maruti, for thy needs in thy new home.' Next Mahdu took out from a bag in which it had been brought, a black cock, and proceeded to cut its throat while reciting some weird incantations, and then sprinkled its blood upon the place where the corpse had been found and even upon the bystanders."

"How horrible!" exclaimed Ellen. "Whatever was that for?"

"It was evidently an important part of the ritual necessary for the laying of a ghost," answered Mr. Carruthers. "To continue, when this was done, the whole assembly at the direction of Mahdu, shouted three times, 'O Shiva, receive his spirit,' and with a general feeling of satisfaction and confidence that their efforts would be crowned with success they were on the point of returning to their homes when, to their horror, the ghost of Maruti appeared with his dreadful skull and the lights in his eyes, and pointing his hand towards Tatya he said, 'Your turn has come!' With wild screams of terror the assembly scattered to the winds, leaving the spectre in possession of the field. And now, finding that their gods have failed them, they have come to me to get them out of their difficulty. It is rather out of my line of business, and I confess I do not exactly see my way. I should have been inclined to think that the whole thing was the result of imagination were it not for Mrs. Trench's narrative."

"I am quite sure it was not any imagination on my part," said Ellen. "It was either a dream or some sort of visitation. Why should I imagine or dream exactly the same thing which all those people think that they have seen, especially as I had never heard anything about it before?"

"Precisely, Mrs. Trench. Now as you are the only one of us who has seen the apparition, I wonder what you think about it, after hearing all the story. Have you any theory to suggest, or any advice to offer me as to clearing up the mystery?"

"I am very complimented at your asking my advice," she said; "but I am half afraid you are making fun of me. I can't suggest any explanation, much less any means of solving the conundrum. It is too dreadfully puzzling. The strange thing is that the ghost of Maruti kept perfectly quiet till they found the poor man's body. What was the coincidence that made it walk from that time onward? Then the ghost evidently knew all about his mundane affairs, as he promptly visited the money-lender and the other man. I can't manage the curious names yet. And the skull and the lights in the eyes. It is all most incomprehensible. And why should he have come to me? I'll tell you one thing that I think, Mr. Carruthers, and that is, that the people who performed that elaborate ritual and incantation did not give or promise half enough to the poor ghost. In fact, they were very mean. Fancy an umbrella and a pair of shoes! Now if the rival were to give up his claim to the field, and the money-lender allowed his mortgage to go on without foreclosing, the ghost might be satisfied and keep quiet."

"By Jove, splendid! Mrs. Trench," said Mr. Carruthers, "that is a very concise summing up. There is nothing like getting the facts into order.

That is the first business of a policeman. You will be a credit to the force yet. This matter needs thinking out; but we will begin on your suggestion. I will send for these people and have a talk to them. Every one can listen to the conversation."

In due course they all arrived. There was Mahdu, the gondhali, and Govind, the medium; there was Chandra Bai, who in spite of the mortgage was wearing some fine gold ornaments; Dhondi, the brother of the ghost; Kashiram, the money-lender; and Tatya, the claimant of the disputed field.

"Look here," said Mr. Carruthers, when they were all seated, "I have been thinking much over this matter; and I have taken the opinion of this lady, who knows much more about ghosts than I do, and who has actually seen the spirit of Maruti, exactly as you all describe him. He entered the lady's tent last night, after he had given you that fright at the place where the body was found. This proves that your story is quite true. Now, as I have told you, this is a very wise lady and learned on the subject of ghosts. And this is what she says. When Maruti was alive you gave him great trouble. After his death he was content to do nothing and remain quiet. But you disturbed his body, and he has become displeased. You have tried to pacify him by raising for his benefit a collection of small coins, and promising an umbrella and a pair of shoes, and so on; and Tatya, who has seized the land which Maruti believed to be his, has promised a red waistcoat and some buttons. Is not this foolish? Is this not contemptible? You have raised the enmity of a ghost, who can cause you all inconceivable trouble, and you think that you can pacify him by petty gifts such as you have told me of. This wise lady says that this is no ordinary ghost. The wearing of a skull with lights instead of eyes shows that it is a very extraordinary ghost, and therefore extraordinary means are required to avert his displeasure. Now if you want to be relieved of your terror you must all give that which you really value. Do you agree?"

There was a murmur signifying that they all concurred in the suggestion.

"Very well, then. Now in the first place, you, Chandra Bai, were very wrong, considering that your husband was a poor man and at the same time a generous, open-handed man, in being so extravagant and indulging in expensive clothes and ornaments which he could not possibly afford to give you, also in constantly scolding him and making his life unpleasant. You still wear valuable ornaments although your land is likely to be lost to you. What you will give to the ghost of your dead husband is all your ornaments, and a written statement that you regret your bad treatment of him. Will you do this, or will you be plagued by his ghost for the rest of your life? Yes, I thought you would agree. Next, Kashiram, I want a statement of your account with Maruti and his family. I can send for your books, so it is no use telling me any lies. Yes, I thought it would be something of the sort. Advanced altogether from time to time, six hundred rupees. Interest paid on loan, nine hundred rupees. Interest still due, four hundred rupees. Total due for interest and capital, one thousand rupees. And then you sowars wonder that you have your noses cut off now and then! Well, what you will give is this, a statement that nothing whatever remains due to you on account of either interest or principal. Do you agree or will you rather be plagued for the remainder of your life by the ghost of Maruti? Yes, I thought so. You, Tatya, will sign a paper that you renounce all claims to the disputed field. It is a bitter blow to you, but preferable to having your life ruined by the ghost. Next, Mahdu and Govind. You ought to know your business better. Fancy trying to put off a really superior ghost like this with such trumpery presents! Now this is my order. You will again meet to-night where you met last night, and make these new gifts to the ghost. You can have any ceremonies and incantations that you like, except that no cock is to be killed. This lady will be present, and she says that there is to be no cock-killing, as ghosts do not really like it, and she knows all about ghosts. Now you have permission to go."

I explained to Ellen all that Mr. Carruthers had been saying in the vernacular, and she took him to task as severely as she could for putting the whole responsibility on her. But I don't think she was seriously annoyed. Anyhow, she was quite pleased at the prospect of seeing the ceremony in the night, although not a little frightened at the idea. But the Flemings promised to come too, and that restored her courage. We were very excited about the ghost during the day, and we made all kinds of guesses regarding the strange mystery. Opinions were divided as to whether the proposed remedy would have any effect or not. Mr. Carruthers would not pronounce any theory. He insisted that the case was in the charge of Mrs. Trench, and that he was merely carrying out her suggestions. It was she, and she alone of our party, who had seen the ghost, and that was a clear sign that she was intended to have charge of the whole inquiry. She had begun so well that he had every confidence in her skill and intelligence, and her ability to unravel the mystery. Ellen laughed at this, and while disclaiming any powers such as she was credited with, promised to do her best. We had a delightful day. In the afternoon we drove to see the ruins of a really beautiful Hindoo temple, four or five miles off, and had our tea there beside a running stream. Mr. Carruthers had begged us to excuse him from making one of the party on the grounds that he had urgent work to dispose of. But we laughed him to scorn and insisted on his coming. He was quite unable to resist the united argument and entreaties of Ellen and Mrs. Fleming and Jack and Dolly, whatever he might have done if only Mr. Fleming and I were concerned. Mrs. Fleming said that if he were not with us to look after him her husband might be spirited away again, perhaps by the ghost this time, and there was no homing pigeon in his pocket to put a rescuer on the track. So we thoroughly enjoyed the outing, and forgot all about the spectre, and came back to dress for dinner. Mr. Carruthers was always very punctilious about regulation dinner costume in camp just as much as anywhere else. He said it made all the difference between feeding and dining. At dinner the conversation was, of course, mainly on the coming event, and after pulling some crackers and drinking to the health of absent friends we put on our warmest wraps and proceeded to the scene of the incantation. There was no road, so we had to walk, and it was pitch dark; but with the aid of some lanterns we managed to find our way without any particular difficulty. There was a tremendous crowd when we arrived at the place, and we found a row of chairs placed in position for the Sahib-logue. At Mr. Carruthers' direction our lanterns were turned down.

"There is only one thing that I have to say before Mahdu and Govind begin," said Mr. Carruthers. "You all know why we are here, to make proper and liberal offerings to the ghost of Maruti. Govind will recite the offerings to the departed spirit, and we may be sure that he will accept them and not trouble you again. But it is only reasonable to suppose that he will be present to accept the offerings; so it is my order that if he comes you are not to be frightened and run away, but just stay where you are. Now Mahdu and Govind, you can commence."

It was a weird sight, if, indeed, you could have called it a sight. As our eyes got accustomed to the darkness we could just make out an enormous ring of people huddled closely together, while in the centre sat the two mystics, Mahdu the master of the ceremonies, and Govind the medium. Mahdu called for silence; and I must say a feeling of awe and of something supernatural crept over us all during the prolonged period of absolute stillness which succeeded. We could just make out the master of occult lore going through some strange ritual. At length Govind stood up and commenced a long-drawn piteous wail, which seemed to emanate from the depths of the earth, and ought to have been enough to lay every ghost in creation. Gradually the chant wove itself into intelligible words, and we could make out an invocation to Shiva to receive into rest the soul of the departed Maruti, for whose benefit they had now made the most complete offerings. Then the medium addressed his supplications to the departed.

"Spirit of Maruti," he cried, "be pleased

with our offerings. There has come to us a lady, young in years but old in wisdom, having full knowledge of the unseen world, who has taught us that what we promised was insufficient. Now we offer thee these things. Tatya gives up his claim to the disputed field; Kashiram remits the debts due to him; Chandra Bai gives all her ornaments, and offers amends for her harsh words. And Carruthers Sahib is witness. Be pleased, O Spirit of Maruti, to manifest thy acceptance and trouble us no more."

A sudden stir in the part of the circle opposite to us attracted our attention. People edged away and made an opening. There were cries and shrieks; and men prostrated themselves and women swooned. For there, advancing through the opening, was a tall figure with two lights for its eyes; and, yes, we could make it out now, a skull for its head. There was a general movement, indicating that all were about to flee for their lives.

"Silence!" shouted Mr. Carruthers, jumping up. "Be still. There is nothing to fear. I told you to expect the spirit of Maruti. The wise lady says that you are to listen to him. Govind, repeat the offers that have been made."

The medium's teeth appeared to be chattering as he did what he was told; but he completed his task, much as he would obviously have preferred to be anywhere but where he was.

"Now, spirit of Maruti," said Mr. Carruthers, "the wise lady bids you speak. Do you accept these offers and will your spirit cease from troubling the people of Loni?"

"The wise lady has spoken, and so shall it be," replied the spirit, in a singularly human voice. "My spirit is satisfied." And as a sign of agreement out went the lights in the eyes of the skull.

Mr. Carruthers leapt forward and stood beside the apparition.

"Now, my good people, you can go," he said to the assembled throng. "You have heard the word, and you may be sure that you will be troubled no more."

There was not much reluctance manifested

in obeying the order to go. Off they all rushed as fast as their legs would carry them.

"What awful fun!" said Jack; but Dolly held on to her mother.

"Now we require a little explanation on one or two points," said Mr. Carruthers, as he came back to our chairs leading with him a tall figure. "But first I want to see one thing. Now, Maruti, switch on those lights of yours."

Instantly the lights gleamed in the sockets of the skull. They gave sufficient illumination for us to make out the figure of a man with a red waistcoat and brass buttons and a peculiarly big puggree. A close inspection showed us that the skull did not exactly cover the real face, but was rather above it, so giving an additional appearance of height. The skull was cleverly fixed on to the puggree, but in the dark, and of course the apparition would only manifest itself when it was dark or there was only a very dim light such as there generally is in native houses, this would not be noticed. Then Mr. Carruthers directed the orderlies to turn up the lanterns that we had brought with us, and irresistibly funny was the sight of the spirit of Maruti under the collective glare of our lamps.

"How do you do the trick?" asked the Chief.

"Sahib, yih lictric lait hai" was the reply, or, *Anglicé, it is electric light.* "It is nearly used up," the speaker continued, "but it has frightened those fools here. A Sahib gave me the apparatus when I was on the sugar plantation at Mauritius; and I thought of this tamasha."

The spectre laughed. It was not at all weird or uncanny; but a good, hearty, soul-filling laugh. We all joined in and laughed to our hearts' content.

"Now, Mrs. Trench," said the Chief, "we will have the ghost's explanation in a minute or so. Meanwhile tell me this? You knew it was the real Maruti all along, didn't you?"

"I was certain of it," said Ellen, "in spite of the difficulties and improbabilities. Why he should have appeared from the exact time that the corpse was discovered and burnt, I do not know. But that didn't very much matter. I don't

believe in ghosts, and so I was sure that it must have been a man. He knew too much about Maruti's private affairs for it to be any one else but Maruti. As for the corpse, it might have been anybody's, red waistcoat or no red waistcoat. The supply of red waistcoats in the world, even with brass buttons attached to them, is not necessarily limited to one."

"*Shabash:* well done!" said the Chief; "you will be a great policeman some day. And then your advice about the offerings?"

"Well, I thought that Maruti had been rather roughly treated; and I wanted to do something for him. So far as I can make out, now he has everything that he desired."

"Splendid," said Mr. Carruthers. "Now, Maruti, you can tell us your story. What were the circumstances of your leaving Loni?"

"Sahib, I will tell you the truth. Fate was against me. I need not repeat what is known to the Sahib. There was Kashiram and Tatya, and there was Chandra Bai. I said to myself that I would go away secretly and not return until I had a thousand rupees. Sahib, I have brought more than a thousand—my wages on the sugar plantations. Yes, I went away with five rupees in my pocket and said not a word. I meant to begin life afresh. I gave up my name Maruti and have called myself Sakharam. As luck would have it, when I left the village after nightfall I met a beggar who asked me for alms. I offered him a rupee if he would exchange his rags for my red waistcoat and big puggree. He was very pleased to do so. I thought no more of him. I went to Mauritius and had good wages and saved them. I came back a few days ago. I had bought a waistcoat and puggree like I used to wear before. But I did not want to be known at first. I wished to see what had happened in my absence, so I hid my good clothes in the jungle outside the village and put on poor garments and disguised my face. Sahib, to my amazement I at once came upon a funeral party that was about to burn a corpse wearing my old waistcoat and puggree. I thought then of the beggar who had exchanged his clothes for mine. The people were all saying that it was the corpse of Maruti; and it was a strange thing that a man should witness his own funeral ceremony. And I heard about Tatya and the field, and Kashiram and the foreclosing of the mortgage. And I laughed and I swore to be revenged. And there was Chandra Bai. Her tongue is sharp, and she deserved a frightening; but I was greatly wishing to see her. And now by the favour of the Sahib and of the wise lady my destiny is made happy."

"A very interesting story, Maruti," said Mr. Carruthers. "But what were you doing in the wise lady's tent?"

"In truth, Sahib, you had known me before, and had been kind to me, and an inclination came to me to see the Sahib in his tent, and when I entered the tent and found that it was not the tent of the Sahib, I was ashamed and went and hid in the jungle again."

"Well, Maruti, the best thing you can do is to come to my camp to-morrow morning and there let me introduce you to your family and friends, so that further trouble may be avoided. There is some one else whom I have to see in the morn-ing, and that is Tatya. There is the matter of the beggar who was killed when he was wearing clothes that gave him the appearance of Maruti. There was a talk of putting Maruti to death. Krishna," he said to the head constable of the party, "let it be known that Tatya is to come to me the first thing to-morrow."

I may here remark, parenthetically, that Tatya did not come in the morning, for he disappeared and was never seen again. Of course, proof would have been practically impossible; but there was no moral doubt that he had killed the beggar thinking that he was Maruti, and had hidden the body beneath the stones.

We walked back to the tents and a bottle of champagne was opened and consumed, and, I think, a pint in addition; and much talk and laughter we had over the day's adventures. Mr. Carruthers said that Ellen was a born detective and the most promising member of the Force, and he quite forgave me for having been married.

Altogether this is quite the finest Christmas party that I can remember.

THE CHRISTMAS BOGEY

Pat Frank

HARRY HART FRANK, who wrote books and stories under the pseudonym Pat Frank, was an author, journalist, and government consultant. After service in World War II, he returned to work as a journalist but also began writing
nonfiction books in which he took on the Washington bureaucracy, challenging
many assumptions about how well the government functioned. Hart's most en-
duringly popular work is the novel *Alas, Babylon* (1959), which tells the story of
ordinary Americans in an isolated Florida community coping with survival following a Soviet-American nuclear war. "The Christmas Bogey" was first collected
in *This Week's Stories of Mystery and Suspense* (New York, Random House, 1957).

The Christmas Bogey

PAT FRANK

WHEN THE AIR FORCE PRIVATELY evaluated the affair later, delay in reporting the original sighting received much of the blame. This delay was the fault of Airman 2/c Warren Pitts, but the cause of Pitts's lapse never was committed to paper, for it would sound so emotional and unmilitary. The truth is that Warren Pitts was only eighteen, and he was homesick, and weeping at his post.

Pitts was the youngest of five technicians assigned, that morning, to 48-hour duty in the Early Warning Radar shack atop a wind-scoured hill overlooking the sprawling Thule base in northern Greenland.

It was Tail End Charley duty. Down on the base everybody was celebrating. There was a USO troupe, including dancers from Hollywood, at the theater. Pitts had not seen a woman in three months. There was a Christmas tree, flown from Maine in a B-36 bomb bay, in the gymnasium. It was the only tree in a thousand miles. There were parties in the clubs and day rooms, and turkey dinners in the mess halls, and a mountain of still undistributed mail and packages. Pitts hadn't received the Christmas box his folks had promised.

Even in the radar shack there was a celebration of a sort. In the other room the older men had concocted an eggnog from evaporated milk, powdered eggs, vanilla extract, and medicinal alcohol. Since Pitts didn't drink, he had drawn the six to midnight watch.

The other room was bright, and warm, and they were listening to Christmas music on the radio, and Sergeant Hake was telling almost believable stories about girls he had known Stateside.

There was no light in the viewing room, so that vision would be sharper. Pitts sat lonely in darkness and watched a thin white sliver revolve in hypnotic circles on the screen.

He wasn't thinking of himself as the guardian of a continent. He was thinking of Tucson's hot sun. He hadn't seen the sun in weeks, and wouldn't see it for weeks more. He said, aloud, "Oh, God, I want to go home."

When at last he looked up there was a fat, green blip winking evilly at him from the upper right-hand quadrant of the screen. How long it had been there he could not guess. It could have come across the Pole, or it might have entered from the east. The radar had a range of perhaps 300 miles. When he first saw the blip, it was closing on the 150-mile circle.

Had Pitts instantly reported this sighting, successful interception would have been possible at Thule, but he didn't. He told the blip to go away. He begged it to go away. On occasion, Russian weather planes crossed the Pole, but always they turned around and went back and he wished this blip would do the same, so he would not have to explain to Sergeant Hake. The blip kept on coming, skirting the edge of the 150-mile circle, as if making a careful detour.

Pitts rose from his canvas chair and shouted, "I've got a bogey!"

Except for Sinatra singing "White Christmas," there was silence in the other room, and then suddenly they were all in with him. Hake watched the blip for three revolutions, and said: "How long you been asleep, kid?"

"I haven't been asleep. Honest I haven't."

The sergeant noted the boy's reddened eyes and the tear channels down his pinched white face. He turned back to the scope.

"What do you think it is?" Pitts asked, fearfully.

"It could be a large flying saucer," said Hake, "or it could be Santa Claus and eight tiny reindeer, or it could be an enemy jet bomber." He reached for the telephone and called Central Radar Control.

That night Lieutenant Preble, a serious young man, had the duty. Ranged along the wall inside Control were many types of radar, including a repeater set from the early warning installation on the hill. Lieutenant Preble switched on this set. As it heated, the blip appeared. He estimated the bogey at 140 miles from Thule, bearing 80 degrees, speed 400 knots, and headed due south.

It could be a Scandinavian airliner bound for Canada and Chicago. And, it could be a jet tanker, on a training flight from Prestwick, Scotland, which had failed to report its position in the last hour.

Or it could be an enemy jet bomber sneaking around Thule.

Whatever it was, Radar Control had a standing order to scramble fighters and alert the batteries if a bogey could not be identified within 60 seconds. That would certainly have been done, except for several human factors.

Lieutenant Preble often played chess with a Captain Canova, an F-94 fighter pilot, and at this moment Captain Canova and his radar observer were in the ready room. In an alert, they would be scrambled—the first ones to face that icy air.

On a base like Thule you will find many poker, bridge, and gin rummy players, but few devoted to chess. So Lieutenant Preble and Captain Canova were firm friends, and Preble knew that this was probably Canova's last duty at Thule.

In the morning, Canova would pack up and board the air tanker coming in from Scotland. Canova's wife was ill and Canova had been given compassionate leave. The tanker's base was Westover Field, Massachusetts, and Canova lived in Boston. He should be with his wife Christmas night—barring accident.

Outside, the temperature was 42 below, and the wind an erratic Phase Three—above 50 knots. If the bogey continued its course and speed, it would be an extreme long-range interception, outside the protective cloak of his radar. So there could very well be an accident.

Preble turned to his communicator and said, "Let's try to raise this bogey. Call the tanker again."

The tanker didn't respond. Preble wasn't worried about the tanker. There had been no distress calls, and near the magnetic pole on top of the world radio frequently went haywire.

They tried the commercial channels. No answer.

Preble took a good hold on the edge of his desk. The blip had closed to 120 miles, but it was now due east of Thule, and moving fast to the south. Each second, now, was taking it away. Unless he scrambled Canova immediately, there would be no chance for an intercept.

He looked at the clock. The big second hand was sweeping down like a guillotine.

Even if Canova shot down the bogey, it might turn out to be a transport loaded with people racing home for Christmas.

But whatever the bogey was, an alarm would stop the USO show in the theatre, and empty the clubs, and send some thousands of troops and gunners and airmen to their posts in the frightful cold, and wreck Christmas. If Canova shot down a friendly plane, there would be no more room for Lieutenant Preble at Thule, or perhaps anywhere.

Preble slammed his hand on the red alarm button, and spoke into the microphone: "Scramble, Lightning Blue! Ready, Lightning Red!"

He looked at the clock, and marked the hour, minute, and second. Canova would be airborne in under three minutes, requesting instructions. But the chase would be long, and would carry beyond the fringe area and guidance of his radar. In his heart, he knew he was too late. Outside, he heard the sirens screaming.

At 6:24 p.m., EST, Christmas Eve, the priority message from Thule reached the enormous plotting room of the Eastern Defense Command, Newburgh, New York. A bogey had slipped past Thule. Interception had been unsuccessful, and the pilot had returned to base. The bogey was headed for Labrador or Newfoundland at better than 400 miles an hour, estimated altitude 30,000 feet.

Upon the shoulders of Major Hayden, an ace in two wars but the youngest and least experienced officer on the senior staff, rested the awful responsibility for the safety and security of the vital third of the United States, from Chicago east to the Atlantic. This was normal, on Christmas Eve, for alone among the Master Controllers Major Hayden was a bachelor.

Major Hayden was not alarmed at this first report. The day's intelligence forecasts showed that the world, this season, was comparatively peaceful. Also, it was only one plane, and Major Hayden did not believe an attack would be launched by one plane, or even so small a number as one hundred.

Besides, the bogey could be reasonably explained. One of his plotting boards showed every aircraft, military and commercial, aloft on the approaches to the Eastern states. The bogey could be a British Comet which had announced it was going far north to seek the jet stream. It could be a Scandinavian airliner looking for Goose Bay. It could be most anything.

Major Hayden ordered a miniature plane set upon the plotting board at the spot this bogey ought to be, according to its projected course and speed. A red flag, showing it was unidentified, topped this plane. He would keep his eyes on it.

He didn't want to bother the General, although the General had visited the plotting room, at six, to look things over. The General always seemed anxious. This may have been because on December 7, 1941, when Major Hayden was a sophomore in college, the General was a major commanding a bomber squadron at Hickam Field, Hawaii, and all his planes had been bombed and shot up on the ground. The last thing the General had said was, "I'm going over to my daughter's, at the Point, for dinner. You know the number. If anything happens call me."

Major Hayden didn't believe that anything, really, had happened yet. Besides, he knew that every Christmas Eve the General trimmed the tree for his grandchildren. He didn't want to break that up.

Major Hayden did call the Royal Canadian Air Force liaison officer, and he did alert the outlying bases, and the border radar sites. Then he waited.

An hour later, reports began to come in. The jet tanker from Prestwick turned up at Thule, its radio out. The Comet landed at Gander after a record crossing. It had not been near Thule. The Scandinavian, it developed, was grounded in Iceland.

Major Hayden fretted. Every fifteen minutes, one of his girls inched the red-flagged bogey closer to his air space. The bogey became the only thing he could see on the board. He alerted all fighter bases north of Washington, and the anti-aircraft people, and the Ground Observer Corps. The GOC was apologetic. It doubted that many of its posts were manned. The GOC would do what it could, but he would have to remember that they were volunteers, and this was Christmas Eve.

When the second sighting came, there could be no doubt of the menace. The Limestone, Maine, radar picked up an unidentified blip moving at 600 knots and at 40,000 feet. It came out of an unguarded Canadian sector. Instead of moving down the coast toward the heavily populated areas, it had headed out to sea, dived steeply, and vanished. It had appeared so swiftly, and left the radar screen so suddenly, that interception had not been possible. Limestone's best night-fighter pilots were older men, and away on Christmas leave.

Major Hayden knew what had happened, and what to expect. The intruder had shrewdly avoided the picket ships, and airfields, near the shore. Then it had crossed the danger zone at tremendous speed.

Once at sea, it had dropped below 4,000 feet—safe from the eyes of radar. Now it would come in at its target, very low, and achieve tactical surprise. Major Hayden called the General.

When the phone rang in the Smith home at West Point, the General, a spare man with iron-gray hair, was balanced atop a ladder, putting the angel on top of the tree, while his grandchildren shrilled their advice and admonitions. Tracy Smith, his daughter, answered the phone, and said, "It's for you, Dad."

The General said, "Tell 'em I'm busy. Tell 'em to wait a minute."

It took the General three minutes to place the angel exactly as he wanted, and exactly straight and upright. "Well," he said, climbing down, "there's the angel that stands guard over this house." At that moment, three minutes may have been the critical factor.

The General picked up the phone. He listened without speaking, and then said, "All right, red alert. Order SCAT. SCAT's all that will save us now. I'm coming."

When he put down the phone the General looked ten years older. His daughter said, "What's up?"

"An unidentified plane," he said, putting on his coat, "off the coast. I believe an enemy."

"Just one?" said Tracy Smith.

"One plane, one bomb, one city," said the General. "Maybe New York."

And he was gone.

Major Hayden flashed the SCAT order to every airfield in his zone. SCAT meant Security Control of Air Traffic. Under SCAT, every plane, military and commercial—except fighters on tactical missions—was to land at the nearest field immediately. In thirty minutes the air must be cleared of everything except the enemy, and our fighters, to give the anti-aircraft batteries and the Nike rocket battalions a chance to work in congested areas.

Very shortly, Major Hayden discovered that on this particular night—of all nights—SCAT couldn't operate properly. In all the big cities, holiday travel was setting records. Planes were stacked in layers up to 20,000 feet over Idlewild, La Guardia, and Newark. Boston, Philadelphia-Camden, and Washington National were the same. And the airways between cities were jammed. He didn't know how long it would be before the Nike rockets could be used. A Nike is a smart rocket, but it cannot tell a transport loaded with 80 people from a jet bomber.

The General came into the plotting room just as the report came in from a lonely spotter at East Moriches, Long Island. A huge jet had come in from the sea at a speed he refused to estimate. It had swept wings, and its four engines were housed in these wings, close to the fuselage. It was bigger than a B-47. It had come in at 2,000 feet, and he swore it was marked with a red star.

The General knew, then, that it was too late, unless he ordered everything shot out of the air. This he could not do—not at Christmas.

A few minutes later a strange plane joined the traffic pattern circling Idlewild, easing itself between two Constellations. It was a jet. One of the Constellations came in for a landing, and then the jet turned on its wing lights and landed. It taxied up to the Administration Building, as if it owned the place, and the blue and red flames of its engines were snuffed out, one by one. Three men got out. They wore strange uniforms.

The Air Force liaison officer at Idlewild called in the news to the General. "Two of them are Poles," he said, "and the other a Czech.

"The plane is this new type Russian 428 that

they showed last May Day over Moscow, only this one is fitted out as a weather ship. These three guys said they had been planning this for almost a year. One of them used to live in Hamtramck, and another has an uncle in Pittsburgh, and they all speak English."

"It's wonderful!" the General said. "But it's a miracle they got here. By rights, they should long ago have been shot down."

"Well," said the liaison officer, "they said they had it all figured out. They said nothing means so much to Americans as Christmas."

"Yes," said the General. "They're three smart men. Real wise."

THE KILLER CHRISTIAN
Andrew Klavan

ANDREW KLAVAN HAS ENJOYED both popular and critical success as a mystery writer, with numerous Edgar nominations, two of which were winners: *Mrs. White* (1987), co-authored with his brother Laurence under the pseudonym Margaret Tracy, the basis for *White of the Eye*, a film released in 1987 starring David Keith and Cathy Moriarty, and *The Rain* (1988), under the pseudonym Keith Peterson. In 1992, he was nominated for Best Novel for *Don't Say a Word*, released as a film in 2001 starring Michael Douglas. His 1995 novel *True Crime* was released as a film in 1999 with Clint Eastwood as the director and the star. While still producing acclaimed crime fiction, he is also an active writer and blogger with libertarian conservative views. "The Killer Christian" was first published as a chapbook and given to customers of the Mysterious Bookshop as a Christmas gift in 2007.

The Killer Christian

ANDREW KLAVAN

A CERTAIN PORTION OF MY MIS-spent youth was misspent in the profession of journalism. I'm not proud of it, but a man has to make a living and there it is. And, in fact, I learned a great many things working as a reporter. Most importantly, I learned how to be painstakingly honest and lie at the same time. That's how the news business works. It's not that anyone goes around making up facts or anything—not on a regular basis anyway. No, most of the time, newspeople simply learn how to pick and choose which facts to tell, which will heighten your sense that their gormless opinions are reality or at least delay your discovery that everything they believe is provably false. If ever you see a man put his fingers in his ears and whistle Dixie to keep from hearing the truth, you may assume he's a fool, but if he puts his fingers in *your* ears and starts whistling, then you know you are dealing with a journalist.

As an example of what I mean, consider the famous shootout above the Mysterious Bookshop in the downtown section of Manhattan known as Tribeca. Because of the drama of the violence, the personalities involved, and the high level arrests that followed, the newspaper and television coverage of the incident ran for weeks on end. Every crime expert in the country seems to have had his moment on the talk shows. Two separate nonfiction books were written about it, not to mention the one novel. And along with several movies and TV shows featur-

ing gunfights reminiscent of the actual event, there was a docu-drama scripted by a Pulitzer Prize–winning newspaperman who covered the story, though it was never released theatrically and went straight to DVD.

There was all that—and no one got the story right. Oh, they got some of the facts down well enough, but the truth? So help me, they did not come nigh it. Why? Because they were journalists—and because the truth offended their sensibilities and contradicted their notions of what the world is like.

So they talked about how La Cosa Nostra had been hobbled by the trials of the '80s and '90s and how new gangs were moving in to divide the spoils left behind. They focused on what they called Sarkesian's "betrayal" of Picarone and speculated about the underworld's realigning loyalties and racial tensions. They even unearthed some evidence for a sort of professional rivalry between Sarkesian and the man known as "The Death."

But the truth is, from the very start, this was really a story about faith and redemption—quite a mysterious story too, by the end of it. And that was too much for them—the journalists. They could not—they would not—see it that way. And because they couldn't see it, they put forward the facts in such a fashion as to insure that you would fail to see it too.

It falls upon me, then, to tell it as it actually happened.

Sarkesian, to begin with, was a Christian, a Catholic, very devout. He took communion as often as he could, daily when he could, and went to confession no less frequently than once a week. What he said in those confessions of course I wouldn't know, but it must've been pretty interesting because, along with being a Christian, Sarkesian was also an enforcer—a killer when he had to be—for Raymond Picarone. How Sarkesian reconciled these two facets of his life can be explained simply enough: he was stupid. Some people just are—a lot of people are, if you ask me—and he was one of them: dumb as dirt.

So on a given day, Sarkesian might kneel before the Prince of Peace asking that he be forgiven as he himself forgave; he might listen attentively to a sermon about charity and compassion; lift his eyes with childlike expectation to the priest who handed him the body of his Lord—and then toodle off to smash his knuckles into the mouth of one of Picarone's debtors until the man's teeth went pitter-pattering across the floor like a handful of pebbles. Virtually every journalist who reported the story discounted the sincerity of Sarkesian's beliefs because of the nature of his actions, but they were mistaken in this. Indeed, if it seems strange to you that a man might hold his faith in one part of his mind and his deeds in another and never fully examine the latter in the light of the former . . . well, congratulations, you may be qualified to become a journalist yourself.

No. Sarkesian prayed with a committed heart and did his job with a committed heart and that his job included murder everyone who knew him knew. That he did that murder efficiently and without apparent compunction made him much feared by his employer's enemies. It also made him much appreciated by his employer.

"Sarkesian," Raymond Picarone used to say with an approving smile, "is not the sharpest razor at the barber shop, but when you tell him you need the thing done, it gets done."

Now it happened one day that the thing Picarone needed done was the killing of a young man named Steven Bean. Bean was a minor functionary in Picarone's organization and a sleazy weasel of a boy even for that company. For the third time in six months, Picarone had caught Bean skimming from his profits. He had decided to make an example of him.

So he summoned Sarkesian to his gentlemen's club on West 45th Street by the river and he said to him, "Sarkesian . . . Stevie B . . . it's no good . . . we have to make, you know, a new arrangement." Picarone had taken to talking in this elliptical fashion in order to baffle any law enforcement personnel who might be eavesdropping electronically on his conversations.

Unfortunately Sarkesian, being not very intelligent as I said, was frequently also baffled. "Arrangement," he said slowly, chewing on the word as if it were a solid mass and blinking his heavily lidded eyes.

"Yeah," said Picarone impatiently. "Bean and us . . . I think we're done . . . you see what I'm saying? It's no good . . . we've come to a parting of the ways."

Sarkesian blinked again and licked his thick lips uncertainly.

"Kill him!" said Picarone. "Would you just kill him? Christ, what an idiot."

Sarkesian brightened, delighted to understand what was expected of him, and set off on his way.

It was mid-December and the city was done up for Christmas. The great snowflake was hung over Fifth Avenue and 57th Street and the great tree was sparkling by the skating rink just downtown. Gigantic ribbons decorated the sides of some buildings. Sprays of colored lights bedecked the fronts of others. And early flurries of snow had been blowing in from the north all week, enough to give the streets a festive wintry air but not so much as to be a pain in the neck and tie up traffic.

So when Steven Bean awoke one early evening in his cramped studio apartment on the Upper West Side, he staggered to the window and looked out at a cheery Yuletide scene. There was snow in the air and lights in the windows of the brownstones across the way. There were green wreaths on the doors and the sound of a tinkling bell drifting from where Santa Claus was standing on the corner.

Unfortunately, there was also Sarkesian, trudging over the sidewalk on his way to kill him.

Steven had full awareness of his guilt, as do we all, though he'd managed to push that awareness to one side of his consciousness, as likewise do we all. But seeing Sarkesian plodding along with his great shoulders hunched and his big, murdering hands stuffed deep into the pockets of his overcoat, the guilt awareness snapped back front and center and Steven understood exactly what the killer was here for.

He leapt off the sofa and jammed his scrawny legs into his jeans, his scrawny feet into his sneakers. He already had a sweatshirt on and was pulling a blue ski jacket over it as he rushed out of the apartment. He could hear the front door closing three floors below as he raced up the stairs. He could hear Sarkesian's heavy footsteps rising toward him as he reached the next landing. There was a ladder there leading up to a trapdoor. Steven climbed quickly and pushed through the trap and up to the roof.

Here, the white sky opened above him and the swirling flakes fell cold upon his face. Steven dashed through the chill air, across the shadow of the water tower. He reached the parapet at the roof's edge and leapt over it, flying across a narrow airshaft to land on the roof of the building next door. From there, he found his way to another trap, down another ladder, to the stairs of the neighboring building. In moments, he was on the street, running along the damp-darkened pavement, dodging the homecoming pedestrians. The streetlamps were just coming on above him as he passed, making the falling snow glisten against the night.

At first, as he ran, he asked himself where he would go, but it was really a rhetorical question. There was only one place he could go: to the downtown theater where he knew he would find his younger sister.

Hailey Bean was in her mid-twenties, and was just beginning to realize she was not going to be a successful actress. She was a sweet girl, kind and gentle and loving; practical, down-to-earth, and sane. Which is to say she was completely unsuited for a life in show business.

At the moment, however, she was rehearsing a very small part in a once-popular drama that was to be revived off-off—not to mention off—Broadway. Hailey's role was that of an angel. At the end of the first act, she was to be lowered toward the stage in a harness-and-wire contraption. Hanging in mid-air, she would then deliver words of prophecy as the first act curtain fell. It was only a 45-second scene—with another scene about the same length in the second act—but it was pivotal. An elaborately beautiful costume— a white robe with gold trimming and two enormous feathery wings—had been designed to make Hailey's attractive but not very imposing figure more impressive, and electronic enhancements and echoes were going to be added to her pleasing but less than awe-inspiring voice.

She was in the back of the small theater discussing these embellishments with the stage manager when Steven Bean burst through a rear door. Trying to keep a low profile, he planted himself in a dark corner—where he proceeded to make himself ridiculously conspicuous by gaping and whispering and waving frantically in an attempt to get his sister's attention.

The differences in character between Hailey and her brother can probably be at least partially explained by the fact that they were, in fact, only half-siblings. Steven had endured his parents' vituperative divorce, whereas Hailey had grown up in their mother's second, more stable, and loving household. Hailey was aware of her advantages and she felt compassion for her brother. But she also knew he was corrupt and reckless and dangerous, incapable of feeling anything more for her than a sort of puling, hissing envy and a fear of her decency which could shade over into hatred whenever she refused to give him whatever it was he was trying to get out of her at the time.

Still, he was family. So, as soon as she politely could, she excused herself to the stage manager and went over to see what he wanted now.

"He's after me" were the first words he gasped at her.

"Calm down." Hailey touched his arm gently. "Who's after you?"

"Sarkesian. He's coming to kill me."

The sister caught her breath and straightened. She didn't bother with any expressions of disbelief. She believed him well enough. "What do you want me to do?"

"Hide me!" Steven whined.

"Steven, where can I hide you? My apartment is the first place he'll look."

"You must have friends!"

"Oh, Steven, I can't send you to my friends with some thug coming after you."

"Well, give me some money at least so I can get away!"

"I don't have any more money."

"I'm your brother and I'm going to be murdered in cold blood and everything's fine for you and you won't do anything for me," Steven said.

Hailey sighed. She knew he was just trying to make her feel guilty but it didn't matter that she knew: she felt guilty anyway. Especially because, as she was forced to admit to herself, she wasn't being completely honest with him about the money.

Hailey was a clerk during the day at the Mysterious Bookshop, a store specializing in crime fiction located on Warren Street downtown. Because Hailey was pretty and efficient and meltingly feminine, she had become a favorite of the avuncular gentleman who ran the place. Sympathetic to her situation, he'd supplied her with an apartment in the brownstone over the shop and so her rent and expenses were fairly cheap. Thus, while it was true that Steven had all but cleaned out her savings six months ago when he'd gotten himself in trouble with Picarone's bookies, Hailey, by working overtime and scrimping on luxuries, had actually managed to save up a little more since then. The trouble was, she had a strong feeling she was going to need that money

pretty soon. In a sort of semi-subconscious way, she had begun making plans to give up her acting career and go back to school.

She hesitated another few seconds, but she couldn't stand up to Steven's terrified eyes and his accusatory wheedling and her own guilt. Finally she said, "All right. I can't leave now. But come back at nine when the rehearsal is over and we'll go to the bank and I'll give you whatever I have."

Steven whined and pleaded a little more, hoping to convince her to go with him right away or even to let him use her bank card, but she stood firm and at last he slunk back out into the snow.

On some other evening, he might well have persuaded her to come with him. But as it happened, this was the night of a special technical rehearsal dedicated almost entirely to her character. An hour after their conversation, Hailey was dressed in her winged robe of white and gold, trussed up in her harness and dangling in mid-air about ten feet off the stage.

She was alone. The other actors had gone home for the night. Only the director and the stage manager were left and they were shut away in the booth at the back of the balcony. They had finished perfecting the echo effect for Hailey's voice and were now discussing their various lighting options, but where Hailey was, their conversation was inaudible. The theater was silent around her. For long periods, it was dark as well. Then, every so often, a spotlight would appear and catch Hailey dangling there in her magnificent winged costume. It would hold her in its glow for a moment as the director judged the effectiveness of the light's color and intensity. Then it would go off again as he and the technician fell to discussing their options once more.

For Hailey, it was a boring process. And since the harness dug into the flesh under her arms, it was kind of uncomfortable too. To distract herself, she tried going over her part in her mind but as she only had four lines, her thoughts soon began to wander. She thought about Steven, of course, about the danger he was in and the troubles he had had as a child and the sad mess he had made of his adulthood. She thought about the money she was going to give him and how hard she had worked to save it and how long it would take her to save some more. She fretted that she would never find a way to improve her life. Ironically, if she could have peered only a little more than a decade into the future, she would have seen herself the mistress of a large house in the northwestern corner of Connecticut, the cheerful mother of no less than five children, and the wife of a man who felt more love and gratitude to her than I can rightly say. But for the present, all this lay obscured within the mists of time, and she hung in the darkness anxious and troubled.

Then, as she hung, she saw a pale slanting beam of light fall at the head of one of the theater's aisles. Someone—a man—had opened the door from the foyer. Now his enormous shadow fell into the light and now he himself was there. He came forward a few steps, but as the foyer door swung shut behind him, the theater was plunged into a nearly impenetrable blackness, and he paused uncertainly.

Hailey felt her pulse speed up. She had caught a glimpse of the man as he entered and there was no doubt in her mind who he was. A hoodlum that size with a face that low—surely, this was the very Sarkesian her brother had told her about, the one who was coming to kill him.

Hailey dangled in the air and watched as the man began slowly advancing again down the aisle, hunting, no doubt, for Steven. She held her breath. Her heart pounded against her chest. The killer came nearly to the foot of the stage. He stopped almost directly beneath her. Sarkesian took a long slow look from one side of the proscenium to the other. Hailey shuddered with fear that he would now lift his eyes and see her.

And then the spotlight came on.

Suddenly, to Hailey's horror, she was fully exposed, hanging there helpless and ridiculous in her white and golden robe with the feathery wings outstretched on either side of her.

Sarkesian looked up—and Hailey was surprised to see he seemed even more horrified than she was. He cried out. He threw his scaly ham-sized hands up beside his face. He leaned back as if afraid Hailey would strike him down on the spot. Frozen there, trembling, he stared up at her with a mixture of terror and awe.

Hailey understood at once what had happened—understood what Sarkesian must've thought she was, and understood too the incredible piety and even more incredible stupidity of a man capable of believing such a thing. Acting almost as quickly as she thought, she stretched out her arm and pointed her finger at him sternly.

"Sarkesian!" she thundered—and the echo effect, which the director had left on for further testing, magnified her voice so that it vibrated from floor to rafters. "Sarkesian—repent!"

At that, as if the timing had been arranged by a power higher even than the director, the spotlight went out again.

Hailey couldn't see what happened next. The light had temporarily blinded her. But she heard Sarkesian send up a high-pitched wail—and the next instant, she could hear his enormous body fumbling and bumping into seats as he made his panicked way back up the aisle.

The door at the rear of the theater flew open. Sarkesian's massive silhouette filled the lighted frame. Then he was gone. There was the light alone. The door swung shut. There was darkness.

Sarkesian didn't look back. He didn't even look to left or right. He ran out of the theater and into the street and was nearly struck down by an oncoming taxi. He found himself bent over the cab's hood, both hands braced against the wet metal as he gaped through the windshield at the frightened driver. Waving his arm wildly to make the cabbie stay, he rushed around to the car's side door and tumbled into the back seat. He gasped out his address to the driver. He sat huddled in a corner, shivering and whimpering, all the way home.

Now, all right, you may laugh at Sarkesian. But even outside of journalism, truth and fiction are sometimes impossibly intertwined. A figment of imagination, a myth, even a fraud may lead us to powerful revelations. Come to think of it, do we ever find revelations in any other way? If Sarkesian was fooled by Hailey's quick-witted improvisation, if it caused him to stagger into his apartment and fall to his knees, if it made him pray and weep in the searing realization that he had lived a life of wretched wickedness in complete contravention to the commandments of his God—was that realization any less true for the way it came to him?

In any case, the fact is: he remained on his knees all night long. And when the gray day dawned, he knew exactly what he had to do.

He went to see Picarone. He found his boss eating breakfast with his wife on the terrace of their penthouse. The presence of the glamorous and somewhat regal Mrs. P. cowed Sarkesian and he spoke with his chin on his chest, gazing down at his own titanic feet.

"I can't do that thing we talked about," he said in his slow, dull voice. "I can't do any of that anymore. The bad stuff. I gotta do, I don't know, good stuff now, from now on. Like the Bible says."

"O-o-oh," said Picarone, lifting his chin. "Yeah. The Bible. Sure. Sure, Sarkesian, I get it. We'll only give you the good stuff from now on. Like the Bible says, sure."

It was touching, Mrs. Picarone later told her friends, to see Sarkesian's great, granite face wreathed in childlike smiles as he floated dreamily out of the room.

When he was gone, Picarone picked up the phone. "Hey," he said, "I need you to take care of a little weasel named Steven Bean for me. And while you're at it, you can do me Sarkesian too."

The call had gone out to a man named Billy Shine. He was known to all who feared him as "The Death." There was no one who didn't fear him. He was a lean, sinewy man with a long rat-like face. He moved like smoke and half the terror he inspired was due to the way he could appear beside you suddenly, as if out of thin air. He could find anyone anywhere and reach them

no matter what. And when he did find them, when he did reach them, they were shortly thereafter dead.

Sarkesian would never have seen him coming. But he was tipped off—warned that The Death was on his trail. Mrs. Picarone had been sincere when she told her friends she'd been moved by Sarkesian's simple faith. She was, in fact, a regular church-goer herself. Sometimes, she lay awake in a cold sweat, painfully aware of the contrast between the dictates of her religion and the source of her wealth. Normally, a quarter of an hour spent running her fingers over the contents of her jewelry box soothed her until she could sleep again. But that night, somehow, this was not enough. Exhausted, she made a stealthy phone call to a manicurist with whom Sarkesian sometimes shared a bed.

Steven Bean, meanwhile, was sleeping just fine, curled up on the sofa in his apartment. I know: you'd think he'd be just about anywhere else *doing* anything else. But after scrounging money from his sister to fund his escape, he had hit on the brilliant idea of increasing the stash by joining a 24-hour poker game he knew of. By the time he wandered out into the streets the next evening, he was all but broke again—and so tired that he convinced himself it would surely be safe at his apartment by now. Sarkesian had probably only been sent to scare him anyway. He might even have been in the neighborhood to see someone else. Maybe it was Steven's own guilty conscience that had made him jump to conclusions and panic when he saw the killer approaching. What he really needed, he thought, was to be home and snug on his own little sofa. And so that's where he went and, after a few more drinks and a joint or two, he was out like a light.

It's amazing people do these things but they do. It's amazing what little distance there needs to be between our actions and their consequences before the consequences seem to us to disappear entirely. One a.m. rolled around and there was Steven, snoring away with his hands tucked under his head, so deeply unconscious that even the entry buzzer couldn't wake him.

But the door woke him when it crashed open, when its wooden frame splintered and fragments of it went flying across the room. That made him sit bolt upright, his jaw dangling, his eyes spiraling crazily. Before he could speak—before he could even think—someone grabbed him by the shirtfront.

It was Sarkesian.

"The Death is coming," the big man said. "Get up. Let's go."

What had happened: Sarkesian had become a new man since his encounter with the "Angel of the Lord" and he was determined to stay that way. After getting the warning call from the manicurist, he understood that it was not enough to just save himself. Knowing that The Death would come after Steven first, he saw he was responsible for protecting him as well. A sterner moralist than I am might wonder why he didn't call the police. But others had called the police in an attempt to avoid The Death and they were dead. No, Sarkesian knew Steven's safety was in his own hands. So here he was, shaking him awake

At the first mention of The Death's terrible name, whatever was left of Steven's drunken complacency vanished like an ace of spades at a magician's fingersnap. He didn't know why Sarkesian had come to help him. At the moment, he hardly knew where he was. But he did understand that he had to run—and that there was nowhere to run from the likes of Billy Shine.

Sarkesian didn't wait for him to figure this out, or for anything else. He grabbed him by the arm, got him dressed, and dragged him out the door. They were halfway down the second flight of stairs, Sarkesian in the lead, before he spoke again.

"Where can you go?" he asked Steven over his shoulder.

And Steven, still stupid with sleep, gave the only answer he could think of. "Tribeca. Above the bookshop. My sister's there."

They took three cabs to avoid being followed. They traveled the last few blocks on foot. Soon they were running together through the severe, slanting shadows falling across the downtown boulevard from the line of brownstone buildings to their right. Tinsel and colored Christmas lights hung from the windows above them. And snow fell, a thin layer of it muffling their footsteps as they ran.

As they approached the Mysterious Bookshop itself, they saw warm yellow light spilling through its storefront to lay in an oblong pool on the snowy sidewalk. Shadows moved behind the storefront's display of brightly jacketed books. Murmuring voices and laughter trailed out from within and a Christmas carol was playing—"O Holy Night."

With a silent curse, Sarkesian understood: there was a Christmas party going on inside.

A moment later, the voices and music grew louder. The bookshop door was coming open. A man and woman were leaving the party, waving over their shoulders as they stepped laughing into the night.

Suddenly Steven found himself shoved hard into an alcove, Sarkesian's massive body pressed against him, pinning him, hiding him. They huddled there together, still, as the couple walked away from them toward West Broadway.

When Sarkesian's body relaxed, Steven was able to move his arm, to lift his finger to point out his sister's name above a mailbox in the alcove. Sarkesian nodded. But Steven didn't press the buzzer button below Hailey's name. He was afraid she would turn them away. Instead, he went to work on the lock of the outside door. His fingers were trembling with cold and fear, but it wasn't much of a lock to speak of. In a second or two, he had worked it and they were inside.

The talk and music from the bookshop came through the walls inside. "O, Little Town of Bethlehem" followed them up the stairway as Sarkesian and Steven raced to the fourth-floor landing. They made their way down the long hallway to the last door. Steven pounded on it with his fist. He shouted, "Hailey! It's me! Open up!"

There was a pause. Steven was gripped by the fear that Hailey herself might be at the party in the bookshop downstairs. But then, her sleepy voice came muffled from within, "Steven?"

"Hailey, please! It's life or death!"

There was the sound of a chain sliding back. The door started to open . . .

And at that moment, Sarkesian, waiting at Steven's side, felt a chill on his neck and looked to his left.

There was The Death standing at the other end of the hall.

He had materialized there in his trademark fashion, without warning, silent as smoke. Now, like smoke, he began drifting toward them.

Sarkesian reacted quickly. With one hand, he shoved Steven in the back, pushing him through Hailey's door. With the other, he drew his gun.

The Death also had a gun. He was lifting it, pointing it at Sarkesian.

"Don't you do it, Billy Shine!" Sarkesian shouted.

He heard a loud *clap:* the terrified Steven had shut Hailey's door, hoping Sarkesian would kill The Death while he cowered inside. But that changed nothing for Sarkesian. He was already moving down the hall toward Shine.

The two killers walked toward each other, their guns upraised. They were fifty yards apart, then forty, then thirty-five. Sarkesian called out again: "Don't do it!" The Death answered him with a gunshot. Sarkesian fired back. The men began pulling the triggers of their guns again and again in rapid succession. One blast blended with another, deafening in the narrow corridor. The two kept firing and walking toward each other as steadily as if hot metal were not ripping into them, were not tearing their insides apart.

At last, their bullets were exhausted. Each heard the snap of an empty chamber. They stopped where they were, not ten yards between them. Shine lowered his arm and Sarkesian lowered his. Shine smiled. Then he pitched forward to the floor and The Death lay dead at Sarkesian's feet.

Sarkesian barely looked at him. He simply started walking again, stepping over the body

without a pause. He let the gun slip from his fingers. It fell with a thud to the hall carpet. Only when he reached the stairway did he stagger for a moment. He held onto the banister until he was steady again. Then he started down the stairs.

All this time, no one on the fourth floor had ventured out of his apartment. People heard the gunfire. They guessed what it was. They called the police and just hunkered down. But on the floors below there were doors opening, faces peeking out. The sound of choral music from the bookshop grew louder. "Silent Night."

As the moments passed with no more shots, people on the fourth floor looked out too. Hailey looked out and Steven peeked over her shoulder, hiding behind her.

"Yes!" he said, pumping his fist when he saw that The Death had fallen.

But Hailey said, "What happened to Sarkesian?"

Steven had told her in a single sentence about his rescue. She had guessed the rest, guessed what had happened to Sarkesian as a result of their encounter in the theater. Tender soul that she was, she felt bad for the thug. She felt any injuries he might have suffered were in part her responsibility.

She came out of her apartment into the hall.

"Sis! Sis!" Steven hissed after her, frantically waving her back.

But she kept moving forward cautiously until she reached the stairway. She saw the trail of blood on the risers. With a soft cry of distress, she started down the stairs.

She found Sarkesian lying on his back in front of the building, his blood running out into the snow. The partygoers in the Mysterious Bookshop had poured out of the store to investigate the noise and now stood gathered around him. The sound of sirens was growing louder as the police drew near. The bookshop door was propped open so that "Silent Night" drifted through the window into the air.

No one came near Sarkesian. He lay alone

in the center of the crowd. He blinked up at the falling snow, his breathing labored.

Then Hailey came toward him, her long white flannel nightgown trailing behind her. Many people saw and heard what happened next. Many of them talked about it to the journalists who soon flooded the scene. And yet it was never reported in a single newspaper, never mentioned on radio or television even once. This is the first time it's ever been told.

Hailey knelt down in the snow beside Sarkesian. She leaned over him. He stirred, turning his eyes toward her. He tried to speak. He couldn't. He licked his lips and tried again.

"I see . . ." he whispered hoarsely. "I see an angel."

"Oh, Sarkesian," said Hailey miserably. "I'm really not."

Sarkesian blinked slowly and shook his head. "No," he whispered. "There." And with a terrible effort, he lifted his enormous hand and pointed over her shoulder at the sky.

Then his hand dropped back into the snow and he was dead.

THE GHOST'S TOUCH
Fergus Hume

ALTHOUGH CHARLES DICKENS AND WILKIE COLLINS wrote mystery fiction, their books were not identified as being part of the genre, either by publishers, booksellers, or reviewers. It then falls to Fergus Hume to have the honor of writing the bestselling mystery novel, so described, of the nineteenth century, *The Mystery of a Hansom Cab* (1886). He paid to have it published but it quickly became successful and he sold all rights to a group of English investors for fifty pounds sterling. It went on to sell more than a half-million copies. Hume wrote an additional one hundred thirty novels—all of which have been completely forgotten. "The Ghost's Touch" was first published in the author's short story collection, *The Dancer in Red* (London, Digby, 1906).

The Ghost's Touch

FERGUS HUME

I SHALL NEVER FORGET THE TER-rible Christmas I spent at Ringshaw Grange in the year '93. As an army doctor I have met with strange adventures in far lands, and have seen some gruesome sights in the little wars which are constantly being waged on the frontiers of our empire; but it was reserved for an old country house in Hants to be the scene of the most noteworthy episode in my life. The experience was a painful one, and I hope it may never be repeated; but indeed so ghastly an event is not likely to occur again. If my story reads more like fiction than truth, I can only quote the well-worn saying, of the latter being stranger than the former. Many a time in my wandering life have I proved the truth of this proverb.

The whole affair rose out of the invitation which Frank Ringan sent me to spend Christmas with himself and his cousin Percy at the family seat near Christchurch. At that time I was home on leave from India; and shortly after my arrival I chanced to meet with Percy Ringan in Picca-dilly. He was an Australian with whom I had been intimate some years before in Melbourne: a dapper little man with sleek fair hair and a transparent complexion, looking as fragile as a Dresden china image, yet with plenty of pluck and spirits. He suffered from heart disease, and was liable to faint on occasions; yet he fought against his mortal weakness with silent courage, and with certain precautions against over-excitement, he managed to enjoy life fairly well.

Notwithstanding his pronounced effeminacy, and somewhat truckling subserviency to rank and high birth, I liked the little man very well for his many good qualities. On the present occasion I was glad to see him, and expressed my pleasure.

"Although I did not expect to see you in England," said I, after the first greetings had passed.

"I have been in London these nine months, my dear Lascelles," he said, in his usual mincing way, "partly by way of a change and partly to see my cousin Frank—who indeed invited me to come over from Australia."

"Is that the rich cousin you were always speaking about in Melbourne?"

"Yes. But Frank is not rich. I am the wealthy Ringan, but he is the head of the family. You see, Doctor," continued Percy, taking my arm and pursuing the subject in a conversational manner, "my father, being a younger son, emigrated to Melbourne in the gold-digging days, and made his fortune out there. His brother remained at home on the estates, with very little money to keep up the dignity of the family; so my father helped the head of his house from time to time. Five years ago both my uncle and father died, leaving Frank and me as heirs, the one to the family estate, the other to the Australian wealth. So—"

"So you assist your cousin to keep up the dignity of the family as your father did before you."

"Well, yes, I do," admitted Percy, frankly. "You see, we Ringans think a great deal of our birth and position. So much so, that we have made our wills in one another's favour."

"How do you mean?"

"Well, if I die Frank inherits my money; and if he dies, I become heir to the Ringan estates. It seems strange that I should tell you all this, Lascelles; but you were so intimate with me in the old days that you can understand my apparent rashness."

I could not forbear a chuckle at the reason assigned by Percy for his confidence, especially as it was such a weak one. The little man had a tongue like a town-crier, and could no more keep his private affairs to himself than a woman could guard a secret. Besides, I saw very well that with his inherent snobbishness he desired to impress me with the position and antiquity of his family, and with the fact—undoubtedly true—that it ranked amongst the landed gentry of the kingdom.

However, the weakness, though in bad taste, was harmless enough, and I had no scorn for the confession of it. Still, I felt a trifle bored, as I took little interest in the chronicling of such small beer, and shortly parted from Percy after promising to dine with him the following week.

At this dinner, which took place at the Athenian Club, I met with the head of the Ringan family; or, to put it plainer, with Percy's cousin Frank. Like the Australian he was small and neat, but enjoyed much better health and lacked the effeminacy of the other. Yet on the whole I liked Percy the best, as there was a sly cast about Frank's countenance which I did not relish; and he patronized his colonial cousin in rather an offensive manner.

The latter looked up to his English kinsman with all deference, and would, I am sure, have willingly given his gold to regild the somewhat tarnished escutcheon of the Ringans. Outwardly, the two cousins were so alike as to remind one of Tweedledum and Tweedledee; but after due consideration I decided that Percy was the better-natured and more honourable of the two.

For some reason Frank Ringan seemed desirous of cultivating my acquaintance; and in one way and another I saw a good deal of him during my stay in London. Finally, when I was departing on a visit to some relatives in Norfolk he invited me to spend Christmas at Ringshaw Grange—not, as it afterwards appeared, without an ulterior motive.

"I can take no refusal," said he, with a heartiness which sat ill on him. "Percy, as an old friend of yours, has set his heart on my having you down; and—if I may say so—I have set my heart on the same thing."

"Oh, you really must come, Lascelles," cried Percy, eagerly. "We are going to keep Christmas in the real old English fashion. Washington Irving's style, you know: holly, wassail-bowl, games, and mistletoe."

"And perhaps a ghost or so," finished Frank, laughing, yet with a side glance at his eager little cousin.

"Ah," said I. "So your Grange is haunted."

"I should think so," said Percy, before his cousin could speak, "and with a good old Queen Anne ghost. Come down, Doctor, and Frank shall put you in the haunted chamber."

"No!" cried Frank, with a sharpness which rather surprised me, "I'll put no one in the Blue Room; the consequences might be fatal. You smile, Lascelles, but I assure you our ghost has been proved to exist!"

"That's a paradox; a ghost can't exist. But the story of your ghost—"

"Is too long to tell now," said Frank, laughing. "Come down to the Grange and you'll hear it."

"Very good," I replied, rather attracted by the idea of a haunted house, "you can count upon me for Christmas. But I warn you, Ringan, that I don't believe in spirits. Ghosts went out with gas."

"Then they must have come in again with electric light," retorted Frank Ringan, "for Lady Joan undoubtedly haunts the Grange. I don't mind as it adds distinction to the house."

"All old families have a ghost," said Percy,

importantly. "It is very natural when one has ancestors."

There was no more said on the subject for the time being, but the upshot of this conversation was that I presented myself at Ringshaw Grange two or three days before Christmas. To speak the truth, I came more on Percy's account than my own, as I knew the little man suffered from heart disease, and a sudden shock might prove fatal. If, in the unhealthy atmosphere of an old house, the inmates got talking of ghosts and goblins, it might be that the consequences would be dangerous to so highly strung and delicate a man as Percy Ringan.

For this reason, joined to a sneaking desire to see the ghost, I found myself a guest at Ringshaw Grange. In one way I regret the visit; yet in another I regard it as providential that I was on the spot. Had I been absent the catastrophe might have been greater, although it could scarcely have been more terrible.

Ringshaw Grange was a quaint Elizabethan house, all gables and diamond casements, and oriel windows, and quaint terraces, looking like an illustration out of an old Christmas number. It was embowered in a large park, the trees of which came up almost to the doors, and when I saw it first in the moonlight—for it was by a late train that I came from London—it struck me as the very place for a ghost.

Here was a haunted house of the right quality if ever there was one, and I only hoped when I crossed the threshold that the local spectre would be worthy of its environment. In such an interesting house I did not think to pass a dull Christmas; but—God help me—I did not anticipate so tragic a Yuletide as I spent.

As our host was a bachelor and had no female relative to do the honours of his house the guests were all of the masculine gender. It is true that there was a housekeeper—a distant cousin, I understood—who was rather elderly but very juvenile as to dress and manner. She went by the name of Miss Laura, but no one saw much of her as, otherwise than attending to her duties, she remained mostly in her own rooms.

So our party was composed of young men—none save myself being over the age of thirty, and few being gifted with much intelligence. The talk was mostly of sport, of horse-racing, big game shooting, and yacht-sailing: so that I grew tired at times of these subjects and retired to the library to read and write. The day after I arrived Frank showed me over the house.

It was a wonderful old barrack of a place, with broad passages, twisting interminably like the labyrinth of Daedalus; small bedrooms furnished in an old-fashioned manner; and vast reception apartments with polished floors and painted ceilings. Also there were the customary number of family portraits frowning from the walls; suits of tarnished armour; and ancient tapestries embroidered with grim and ghastly legends of the past.

The old house was crammed with treasures, rare enough to drive an antiquarian crazy; and filled with the flotsam and jetsam of many centuries, mellowed by time into one soft hue, which put them all in keeping with one another. I must say that I was charmed with Ringshaw Grange, and no longer wondered at the pride taken by Percy Ringan in his family and their past glories.

"That's all very well," said Frank, to whom I remarked as much; "Percy is rich, and had he this place could keep it up in proper style; but I am as poor as a rat, and unless I can make a rich marriage, or inherit a comfortable legacy, house and furniture, park and timber may all come to the hammer."

He looked gloomy as he spoke; and, feeling that I had touched on a somewhat delicate matter, I hastened to change the subject, by asking to be shown the famous Blue Chamber, which was said to be haunted. This was the true Mecca of my pilgrimage into Hants.

"It is along this passage," said Frank, leading the way, "and not very far from your own quarters. There is nothing in its looks likely to hint at the ghost—at all events by day—but it is haunted for all that."

Thus speaking he led me into a large room with a low ceiling, and a broad casement looking out onto the untrimmed park, where the woodland was most sylvan. The walls were hung with blue cloth embroidered with grotesque figures in black braid or thread, I know not which. There was a large old-fashioned bed with tester and figured curtains and a quantity of cumbersome furniture of the early Georgian epoch. Not having been inhabited for many years the room had a desolate and silent look—if one may use such an expression—and to my mind looked gruesome enough to conjure up a battalion of ghosts, let alone one.

"I don't agree with you!" said I, in reply to my host's remark. "To my mind this is the very model of a haunted chamber. What is the legend?"

"I'll tell it to you on Christmas Eve," replied Ringan, as we left the room. "It is rather a blood-curdling tale."

"Do you believe it?" said I, struck by the solemn air of the speaker.

"I have had evidence to make me credulous," he replied dryly, and closed the subject for the time being.

It was renewed on Christmas Eve when all our company were gathered round a huge wood fire in the library. Outside, the snow lay thick on the ground, and the gaunt trees stood up black and leafless out of the white expanse. The sky was of a frosty blue with sharply twinkling stars, and a hard-looking moon. On the snow the shadows of interlacing boughs were traced blackly as in Indian ink, and the cold was of Arctic severity.

But seated in the holly-decked apartment before a noble fire which roared bravely up the wide chimney we cared nothing for the frozen world out of doors. We laughed and talked, sang songs and recalled adventures, until somewhere about ten o'clock we fell into a ghostly vein quite in keeping with the goblin-haunted season. It was then that Frank Ringan was called upon to chill our blood with his local legend. This he did without much pressing.

"In the reign of the good Queen Anne," said he, with a gravity befitting the subject, "my ancestor Hugh Ringan was the owner of this house. He was a silent misanthropic man, having been soured early in life by the treachery of a woman. Mistrusting the sex he refused to marry for many years; and it was not until he was fifty years of age that he was beguiled by the arts of a pretty girl into the toils of matrimony. The lady was Joan Challoner, the daughter of the Earl of Branscourt; and she was esteemed one of the beauties of Queen Anne's court.

"It was in London that Hugh met her, and thinking from her innocent and child-like appearance that she would make him a true-hearted wife, he married her after a six months' courtship and brought her with all honour to Ringshaw Grange. After his marriage he became more cheerful and less distrustful of his fellow-creatures. Lady Joan was all to him that a wife could be, and seemed devoted to her husband and child—for she early became a mother—when one Christmas Eve all this happiness came to an end."

"Oh!" said I, rather cynically. "So Lady Joan proved to be no better than the rest of her sex."

"So Hugh Ringan thought, Doctor; but he was as mistaken as you are. Lady Joan occupied the Blue Room, which I showed you the other day; and on Christmas Eve, when riding home late, Hugh saw a man descend from the window. Thunderstruck by the sight, he galloped after the man and caught him before he could mount a horse which was waiting for him. The cavalier was a handsome young fellow of twenty-five, who refused to answer Hugh's questions. Thinking, naturally enough, that he had to do with a lover of his wife's, Hugh fought a duel with the stranger and killed him after a hard fight.

"Leaving him dead on the snow he rode back to the Grange, and burst in on his wife to accuse her of perfidy. It was in vain that Lady Joan tried to defend herself by stating that the visitor was her brother, who was engaged in plots for the restoration of James II, and on that account wished to keep secret the fact of his presence in England. Hugh did not believe her, and told her plainly that he had killed her lover; whereupon Lady Joan burst out into a volley of reproaches and cursed her husband. Furious at what he deemed was her boldness Hugh at first attempted to kill her, but not thinking the punishment sufficient, he cut off her right hand."

"Why?" asked everyone, quite unprepared for this information.

"Because in the first place Lady Joan was very proud of her beautiful white hands, and in the second Hugh had seen the stranger kiss her hand—her right hand—before he descended from the window. For these reasons he mutilated her thus terribly."

"And she died."

"Yes, a week after her hand was cut off. And she swore that she would come back to touch all those in the Blue Room—that is who slept in it—who were foredoomed to death. She kept her promise, for many people who have slept in that fatal room have been touched by the dead hand of Lady Joan, and have subsequently died."

"Did Hugh find out that his wife was innocent?"

"He did," replied Ringan, "and within a month after her death. The stranger was really her brother, plotting for James II, as she had stated. Hugh was not punished by man for his crime, but within a year he slept in the Blue Chamber and was found dead next morning with the mark of three fingers on his right wrist. It was thought that in his remorse he had courted death by sleeping in the room cursed by his wife."

"And there was a mark on him?"

"On his right wrist red marks like a burn; the impression of three fingers. Since that time the room has been haunted."

"Does everyone who sleeps in it die?" I asked.

"No. Many people have risen well and hearty in the morning. Only those who are doomed to an early death are thus touched!"

"When did the last case occur?"

"Three years ago" was Frank's unexpected reply. "A friend of mine called Herbert Spencer would sleep in that room. He saw the ghost and was touched. He showed me the marks next morning—three red finger marks."

"Did the omen hold good?"

"Yes. Spencer died three months afterwards. He was thrown from his horse."

I was about to put further questions in a sceptical vein, when we heard shouts outside, and we all sprang to our feet as the door was thrown open to admit Miss Laura in a state of excitement.

"Fire! Fire!" she cried, almost distracted. "Oh! Mr. Ringan," addressing herself to Percy, "your room is on fire! I—"

We waited to hear no more, but in a body rushed up to Percy's room. Volumes of smoke were rolling out of the door, and flames were flashing within. Frank Ringan, however, was prompt and cool-headed. He had the alarm bell rung, summoned the servants, grooms, and stable hands, and in twenty minutes the fire was extinguished.

On asking how the fire had started, Miss Laura, with much hysterical sobbing, stated that she had gone into Percy's room to see that all was ready and comfortable for the night. Unfortunately the wind wafted one of the bed-curtains towards the candle she was carrying, and in a moment the room was in a blaze. After pacifying Miss Laura, who could not help the accident, Frank turned to his cousin. By this time we were back again in the library.

"My dear fellow," he said, "your room is swimming in water, and is charred with fire. I'm afraid you can't stay there tonight; but I don't know where to put you unless you take the Blue Room."

"The Blue Room!" we all cried. "What! The haunted chamber?"

"Yes; all the other rooms are full. Still, if Percy is afraid—"

"Afraid!" cried Percy indignantly. "I'm not afraid at all. I'll sleep in the Blue Room with the greatest of pleasure."

"But the ghost—"

"I don't care for the ghost," interrupted the Australian, with a nervous laugh. "We have no ghosts in our part of the world, and as I have not seen one, I do not believe there is such a thing."

We all tried to dissuade him from sleeping in the haunted room, and several of us offered to give up our apartments for the night—Frank among the number. But Percy's dignity was touched, and he was resolute to keep his word. He had plenty of pluck, as I said before, and the fancy that we might think him a coward spurred him on to resist our entreaties.

The end of it was that shortly before midnight he went off to the Blue Room, and declared his intention of sleeping in it. There was nothing more to be said in the face of such obstinacy, so one by one we retired, quite unaware of the events to happen before the morning. So on that Christmas Eve the Blue Room had an unexpected tenant.

On going to my bedroom I could not sleep. The tale told by Frank Ringan haunted my fancy, and the idea of Percy sleeping in that ill-omened room made me nervous. I did not believe in ghosts myself, nor, so far as I knew, did Percy, but the little man suffered from heart disease—he was strung up to a high nervous pitch by our ghost stories—and if anything out of the common—even from natural causes—happened in that room, the shock might be fatal to its occupant.

I knew well enough that Percy, out of pride, would refuse to give up the room, yet I was determined that he should not sleep in it; so, failing persuasion, I employed stratagem. I had my medicine chest with me, and taking it from my portmanteau I prepared a powerful narcotic. I left this on the table and went along to the Blue Room, which, as I have said before, was not very far from mine.

A knock brought Percy to the door, clothed in pyjamas, and at a glance I could see that the ghostly atmosphere of the place was already telling on his nerves. He looked pale and disturbed, but his mouth was firmly set with an obstinate expression likely to resist my proposals. However, out of diplomacy, I made none, but blandly stated my errand, with more roughness, indeed, than was necessary.

"Come to my room, Percy," I said, when he appeared, "and let me give you something to calm your nerves."

"I'm not afraid!" he said, defiantly.

"Who said you were?" I rejoined, tartly. "You believe in ghosts no more than I do, so why should you be afraid? But after the alarm of fire your nerves are upset, and I want to give you something to put them right. Otherwise, you'll get no sleep."

"I shouldn't mind a composing draught, certainly," said the little man. "Have you it here?"

"No, it's in my room, a few yards off. Come along."

Quite deluded by my speech and manner, Percy followed me into my bedroom, and obediently enough swallowed the medicine. Then I made him sit down in a comfortable armchair, on the plea that he must not walk immediately after the draught. The result of my experiment was justified, for in less than ten minutes the poor little man was fast asleep under the influence of the narcotic. When thus helpless, I placed him on my bed, quite satisfied that he would not awaken until late the next day. My task accomplished, I extinguished the light, and went off myself to the Blue Room, intending to remain there for the night.

It may be asked why I did so, as I could easily have taken my rest on the sofa in my own room; but the fact is, I was anxious to sleep in a haunted chamber. I did not believe in ghosts, as I had never seen one, but as there was a chance of meeting here with an authentic phantom I did not wish to lose the opportunity.

Therefore when I saw that Percy was safe for the night, I took up my quarters in the ghostly territory, with much curiosity, but—as I can safely aver—no fear. All the same, in case of practical jokes on the part of the feather-headed young men in the house, I took my revolver with me. Thus prepared, I locked the door of the Blue Room and slipped into bed, leaving the light burning. The revolver I kept under my pillow ready to my hand in case of necessity.

"Now," said I grimly, as I made myself comfortable, "I'm ready for ghosts, or goblins, or practical jokers."

I lay awake for a long time, staring at the queer figures on the blue draperies of the apartment. In the pale flame of the candle they looked ghostly enough to disturb the nerves of anyone: and when the draught fluttered the tapestries the figures seemed to move as though alive. For this sight alone I was glad that Percy had not slept in that room. I could fancy the poor man lying in that vast bed with blanched face and beating heart, listening to every creak, and watching the fantastic embroideries waving on the walls. Brave as he was, I am sure the sounds and sights of that room would have shaken his nerves. I did not feel very comfortable myself, sceptic as I was.

When the candle had burned down pretty low I fell asleep. How long I slumbered I know not: but I woke up with the impression that something or someone was in the room. The candle had wasted nearly to the socket and the flame was flickering and leaping fitfully, so as to display the room one moment and leave it almost in darkness the next. I heard a soft step crossing the room, and as it drew near a sudden spurt of flame from the candle showed me a little woman standing by the side of the bed. She was dressed in a gown of flowered brocade, and wore the towering head dress of the Queen Anne epoch. Her face I could scarcely see, as the flash of flame was only momentary: but I felt what the Scotch call a deadly grue as I realized that this was the veritable phantom of Lady Joan.

For the moment the natural dread of the supernatural quite overpowered me, and with my hands and arms lying outside the counterpane I rested inert and chilled with fear. This sensation of helplessness in the presence of evil was like what one experiences in a nightmare of the worst kind.

When again the flame of the expiring candle shot up, I beheld the ghost close at hand, and—as I felt rather than saw—knew that it was bending over me. A faint odour of musk was in the air, and I heard the soft rustle of the brocaded skirts echo through the semi-darkness. The next moment I felt my right wrist gripped in a burning grasp, and the sudden pain roused my nerves from their paralysis.

With a yell I rolled over, away from the ghost, wrenching my wrist from that horrible clasp, and, almost mad with pain I groped with my left hand for the revolver. As I seized it the candle flared up for the last time, and I saw the ghost gliding back towards the tapestries. In a second I raised the revolver and fired. The next moment there was a wild cry of terror and agony, the fall of a heavy body on the floor, and almost before I knew where I was I found myself outside the door of the haunted room. To attract attention I fired another shot from my revolver, while the Thing on the floor moaned in the darkness most horribly.

In a few moments guests and servants, all in various stages of undress, came rushing along the passage bearing lights. A babel of voices arose, and I managed to babble some incoherent explanation, and led the way into the room. There on the floor lay the ghost, and we lowered the candles to look at its face. I sprang up with a cry on recognizing who it was.

"Frank Ringan!"

It was indeed Frank Ringan disguised as a woman in wig and brocades. He looked at me with a ghostly face, his mouth working nervously. With an effort he raised himself on his hands and tried to speak—whether in confession or exculpation, I know not. But the attempt was too much for him, a choking cry escaped his lips, a jet of blood burst from his mouth, and he fell back dead.

Over the rest of the events of that terrible night I draw a veil. There are some things it is as well not to speak of. Only I may state that all through the horror and confusion Percy Ringan, thanks to my strong sleeping draught, slumbered as peacefully as a child, thereby saving his life.

With the morning's light came discoveries and explanations. We found one of the panels behind the tapestry of the Blue Room open, and it gave admittance into a passage which on examination proved to lead into Frank Ringan's bedroom. On the floor we discovered a delicate hand formed of steel, and which bore marks of having been in the fire. On my right wrist were three distinct burns, which I have no hesitation in declaring were caused by the mechanical hand which we picked up near the dead man. And the explanation of these things came from Miss Laura, who was wild with terror at the death of her master, and said in her first outburst of grief and fear, what I am sure she regretted in her calmer moments.

"It's all Frank's fault," she wept. "He was poor and wished to be rich. He got Percy to make his will in his favour, and wanted to kill him by a shock. He knew that Percy had heart disease and that a shock might prove fatal; so he contrived that his cousin should sleep in the Blue Room on Christmas Eve; and he himself played the ghost of Lady Joan with the burning hand. It was a steel hand, which he heated in his own room so as to mark with a scar those it touched."

"Whose idea was this?" I asked, horrified by the devilish ingenuity of the scheme.

"Frank's!" said Miss Laura, candidly. "He promised to marry me if I helped him to get the money by Percy's death. We found that there was a secret passage leading to the Blue Room; so some years ago we invented the story that it was haunted."

"Why, in God's name?"

"Because Frank was always poor. He knew that his cousin in Australia had heart disease, and invited him home to kill him with fright. To make things safe he was always talking about the haunted room and telling the story so that everything should be ready for Percy on his arrival. Our plans were all carried out. Percy arrived and Frank got him to make the will in his favour. Then he was told the story of Lady Joan and her hand, and by setting fire to Percy's room last night I got him to sleep in the Blue Chamber without any suspicion being aroused."

"You wicked woman!" I cried. "Did you fire Percy's room on purpose?"

"Yes. Frank promised to marry me if I helped him. We had to get Percy to sleep in the Blue Chamber, and I managed it by setting fire to his bedroom. He would have died with fright when Frank, as Lady Joan, touched him with the steel hand, and no one would have been the wiser. Your sleeping in that haunted room saved Percy's life, Dr. Lascelles, yet Frank invited you down as part of his scheme, that you might examine the body and declare the death to be a natural one."

"Was it Frank who burnt the wrist of Herbert Spencer some years ago?" I asked.

"Yes!" replied Miss Laura, wiping her red eyes. "We thought if the ghost appeared to a few other people, that Percy's death might seem more natural. It was a mere coincidence that Mr. Spencer died three months after the ghost touched him."

"Do you know you are a very wicked woman, Miss Laura?"

"I am a very unhappy one," she retorted. "I have lost the only man I ever loved; and his miserable cousin survives to step into his shoes as the master of Ringshaw Grange."

That was the sole conversation I had with the wretched woman, for shortly afterwards she disappeared, and I fancy must have gone abroad, as she was never more heard of. At the inquest held on the body of Frank the whole strange story came out, and was reported at full length by the London press to the dismay of ghost-seers: for the fame of Ringshaw Grange as a haunted mansion had been great in the land.

I was afraid lest the jury should bring in a verdict of manslaughter against me, but the peculiar features of the case being taken into consideration I was acquitted of blame, and shortly afterwards returned to India with an unblemished character. Percy Ringan was terribly distressed on hearing of his cousin's death, and shocked by the discovery of his treachery. However, he was consoled by becoming the head of the family, and as he lives a quiet life at Ringshaw Grange there is not much chance of his early death from heart disease—at all events from a ghostly point of view.

The Blue Chamber is shut up, for it is haunted now by a worse spectre than that of Lady Joan, whose legend (purely fictitious) was so ingeniously set forth by Frank. It is haunted by the ghost of the cold-blooded scoundrel who fell into his own trap; and who met with his death in the very moment he was contriving that of another man. As to myself, I have given up ghost-hunting and sleeping in haunted rooms. Nothing will ever tempt me to experiment in that way again. One adventure of that sort is enough to last me a lifetime.

A WREATH FOR MARLEY
Max Allan Collins

THE VERSATILE AND PROLIFIC MAX ALLAN COLLINS
has written dozens of novels, including some about Nolan, a hit man; Mallory,
a mystery writer who solves real-life crimes; Eliot Ness, who gained fame as the
leader of the Untouchables; and Nathan Heller, a Chicago P. I. who becomes involved in well-known crimes of the era, meeting up with such famous characters
as Orson Welles and Sally Rand, the fan-dancer. He also wrote the Dick Tracy
comic strip, some *Batman* comic books, and created the comic book private eye
Ms. Tree. His graphic novel, *Road to Perdition,* became the basis of the Academy
Award–winning Tom Hanks film. "A Wreath for Marley" was first published in
Dante's Disciples, edited by Peter Crowther and Edward E. Kramer (Clarkston,
GA, White Wolf, 1995).

A Wreath for Marley

MAX ALLAN COLLINS

PRIVATE DETECTIVE RICHARD STONE wasn't much for celebrations, or holidays—or holiday celebrations, for that matter.

Nonetheless, this Christmas Eve, in the year of our Lord 1942, he decided to throw a little holiday party in the modest two-room suite of offices on Wabash that he had once shared with his late partner, Jake Marley.

Present for the festivities were his sandy-tressed cutie-pie secretary, Katie Crockett, and his fresh-faced young partner, Joey Ernest. Last to arrive was his best pal (at least since Jake died), burly homicide dick Sgt. Hank Ross.

Katie had strung up some tinsel and decorated a little tree by her reception desk. Right now the little group was having a Yuletide toast with heavily rum-spiked egg nog. The darkly handsome Stone's spirits were good—just this morning, he'd been declared 4-F, thanks to his flat feet.

"Every flatfoot should have 'em!" he laughed.

"What'd you do?" Ross asked. "Bribe the draft-board doc?"

"What's it to you?" Stone grinned. "You cops get automatic deferments!"

And the two men clinked cups.

Actually, bribing the draft-board doctor was exactly what Stone had done; but he saw no need to mention it.

"Hell," Joey said—and the word was quite a curse coming from this kid—"I wish I *could* go. If it wasn't for this damn perforated eardrum . . ."

"You and Sinatra," Stone laughed.

Katie said nothing; her eyes were on the framed picture on her desk—her young brother Ben, who was spending Christmas in the Pacific somewhere.

"I got presents for all of you," Stone said, handing envelopes around.

"What's this?" Joey asked, confused, opening his envelope to see a slip of paper with a name and address on the South Side.

"Best black market butcher in the city," Stone said. "You and the missus and the brood can start the next year out with a coupla sirloins, on me."

"I'd feel funny about that . . . it's not legal. . . ."

"Jesus! How can you be such a square and still work for me? You're lucky there's a manpower shortage, kid."

Ross, envelope open, was thumbing through five twenty-dollar bills. "You always know just what to get me, Stoney."

"Cops are so easy to shop for," Stone said.

Katie, seeming embarrassed, whispered her thanks into Stone's ear.

"Think nothin' of it, baby," he said. "It's as much for me as for you."

He'd given her a fifty-dollar gift certificate at the lingerie counter at Marshall Field's. Not every boss would be so generous.

They all had gifts for him, too: Joey gave him a ten-dollar war bond, Katie a hand-tooled leather shoulder holster, and Hank the latest *Esquire* "Varga" calendar.

"To give this rat-trap some class," the cop said.

Joey raised his cup. "Here's to Mr. Marley," he said.

"To Mr. Marley," Katie said, her eyes suddenly moist. "Rest his soul."

"Yeah," Ross said, lifting his cup, "here's to Jake—dead a year to the day."

"To the night, actually," Stone said, and hoisted his cup. "What the hell—to my partner Jake. You were a miserable bastard, but Merry Christmas, anyway."

"You shouldn't talk that way!" Katie said.

"Even if it's the truth?" Stone asked with a smirk.

Suddenly it got quiet.

Then Ross asked, "Doesn't it bother you, Stoney? You're a detective and your partner's murder goes unsolved? Ain't it bad for business?"

"Naw. Not when you do mostly divorce work."

Ross grinned, shook his head. "Stoney, you're an example to us all," he said, waved, and ambled out.

Katie had a heartsick expression. "Doesn't Mr. Marley's death mean *anything* to you? He was your best friend!"

Stone patted his .38 under his shoulder. "Sadie here's my best friend. And, sure, Marley's death means something to me: full ownership of the business, and the only name on the door is mine."

She shook her head, slowly, sadly. "I'm so disappointed in you, Richard. . . ."

He took her gently aside. "Then I'm not welcome at your apartment anymore?" he whispered.

"Of course you're welcome. I'm still hoping you'll come have Christmas dinner with my family and me, tomorrow."

"I'm not much for family gatherings. Ain't it enough I got you the black-market turkey?"

"Richard!" She shushed him. "Joey will hear. . . ."

"What, and find out you're no Saint Kate?" He gave her a smack of a kiss on the forehead, then patted her fanny. "See you the day after . . . we'll give that new casino on Rush Street a try."

She sighed, said, "Merry Christmas, Richard," gathered her coat and purse, and went out.

Now it was just Joey and Stone. The younger man said, "You know, Katie's starting to get suspicious."

"About what?"

"About what. About you and Mrs. Marley!"

Stone snorted. "Katie just thinks I'm bein' nice to my late partner's widow."

"You being 'nice' is part of why it seems so suspicious. While you were out today, Mrs. Marley called about five times."

"The hell! Katie didn't say so."

"See what I mean?" Joey plucked his topcoat off the coat tree. "Mr. Stone—please don't expect me to keep covering for you. It makes me feel . . . dirty."

"Are you *sure* you were born in Chicago, kid?" Stone opened the door for him. "Go home! Have yourself a merry the hell little Christmas! Tell your kids Santa's comin', send 'em up to bed, and make the missus under the mistletoe one time for me."

"Thanks for the sentiment, Mr. Stone," he said, and was gone.

Stone—alone, now—decided to skip the egg nog and head straight for the rum. He was downing a cup when a knock called him to the door.

Two representatives of the Salvation Army stepped into his outer office, in uniform—a white-haired old gent, with a charity bucket, and a pretty shapely thing, her innocent face devoid of make-up under the Salvation Army bonnet.

"We're stopping by some of the offices to—" the old man began.

"Make a touch," Stone finished. "Sure thing. Help yourself to the egg nog, pops." Then he cast a warm smile on the young woman. "Honey, step inside my private office . . . that's where I keep the cash."

He shut himself and the little dame inside his office and got a twenty-dollar bill out of his cashbox from a desk drawer, then tucked the bill inside the swell of the girl's blouse.

Her eyes widened. "Please!"

"Baby, you don't have to say 'please.'" Stone put his hands on her waist and brought her to him. "Come on . . . give Santa a kiss."

Her slap sounded like a gunshot, and stung like hell. He whisked the bill back out of her blouse.

"Some Christmas spirit *you* got," he said, and opened the door and pushed her into the outer office.

"What's the meaning of this?" the old man sputtered, and Stone wadded up the twenty, tossed it in the bucket, and shoved them both out the door.

"Squares," he muttered, returning to his rum.

Before long, the door opened and a woman in black appeared there, like a curvaceous wraith. Her hair was icy blonde, her thin lips blood-red, like cuts in her angular white Joan Crawford-ish face. It had been a while since she'd seen forty, but she was better preserved than your grandma's strawberry jam.

She fell immediately into his arms. "Merry Christmas, darling!"

"In a rat's ass," he said coldly, pushing her away.

"Darling . . . what's wrong . . . ?"

"You been calling the office again! I told you not to do that. People are gonna get the wrong idea."

He'd been through this with her a million times: they were perfect suspects for Jake Marley's murder; neither of them had an alibi for the time of the killing—Stone was in his apartment, alone, and Maggie claimed she'd been alone at home, too.

But to cover for each other, they had lied to the cops about being together at Marley's penthouse, waiting for his return for a Christmas Eve supper.

"If people think we're an item," Stone told her, "we'll be prime suspects!"

"It's been a year. . . ."

"That's not long enough."

She threw her head back and her blonde hair shimmered, and so did her diamond earrings. "I want to get out of black, and be on your arm, unashamed. . . ."

"Since when were you ever ashamed of anything?" He shuddered, wishing he'd never met Maggie Marley, let alone climbed in bed with her; now, he was in bed with her, for God knew how long, and in every sense of the word. . . .

She touched his face with a gloved hand. "Are we spending Christmas Eve together, Richard?"

"Can't, baby. Gotta spend it with relatives."

"Who, your uncle and aunt?" She smirked in disbelief. "I can't believe you're going back to *farm* country, to see them. . . . You *hate* it there!"

"Hey, wouldn't be right not seein' 'em. Christmas and all."

Her gaze seemed troubled. "I'd hoped we could talk. Richard . . . we may have a problem . . ."

"Such as?"

". . . Eddie's trying to blackmail me."

"Eddie? What does that slimy little bastard want?"

Eddie was Jake Marley's brother.

"He's in over his head with the Outfit," she said.

"What, gambling losses again? He'll never learn . . ."

"He's trying to squeeze me for dough," she said urgently. "He's got photos of us, together . . . at that resort!"

"So what?" He shrugged.

"Photos of us in *our* room at that resort . . . and he's got the guest register."

Stone frowned. "That was just a week after Jake was killed."

"I know. You were . . . consoling me."

Who was she trying to kid?

Stone said, "I'll talk to him."

She moved close to him again. "He's waiting for me now, at the Blue Spot Bar . . . would you keep the appointment for me, Richard?"

And she kissed him. Nobody kissed hotter than this dame. Or colder. . . .

Half an hour later, Stone entered the smoky Rush Street saloon, where a thrush in a gown cut to her toenails was embracing the microphone, singing "White Christmas" off-key.

He found mustached weasel Eddie Marley sitting at the bar working on a Scotch—a bald little man in a bow tie and a plaid zoot suit.

"Hey, Dickie . . . nice to see ya. Buy ya a snort?"

"Don't call me 'Dickie.' "

"Stoney, then."

"Grab your topcoat and let's talk in my office," Stone said, nodding toward the alley door.

A cat chasing a rat made garbage cans clatter as the two men came out into the alley. A cold Christmas rain was falling, puddling on the frozen remains of a snow and ice storm from a week before. Ducking into the recession of a doorway, Eddie got out a cigarette and Stone, a statue standing out in the rain, leaned in with a Zippo to light it for him.

For a moment, the world wasn't pitch dark. But only for a moment.

"I don't *like* to stick it to ya, Stoney . . . but if I don't cough up five gees to the Outfit, I won't live to see '43! My brother left me high and dry, ya know."

"I'm all choked up, Eddie."

Eddie was shrugging. "Jake's life insurance paid off big—double indemnity. So Maggie's sittin' pretty. And the agency partnership reverted to you—so you're in the gravy. Where's that leave Eddie?"

Stone picked him up by the throat. The little man's eyes opened wide and his cigarette tumbled from his lips and sizzled in a puddle.

"It leaves you on your ass, Eddie."

And the detective hurled the little man into the alley, onto the pavement, where he bounced up against some garbage cans.

"Ya shouldn'ta done that, ya bastid! I got the goods on ya!"

Stone's footsteps splashed toward the little man. "You got nothin', Eddie."

"I got photos! I got your handwritin' on a motel register!"

"Don't try to tell *me* the bedroom-dick business. You bring me the negatives and the register page, and I'll give you five C's. First and last payment."

The weasel's eyes went very wide. "Five C's?!? I need five *G*'s by tomorrow—they'll break my knees if I don't pay up! Have a heart— have some Christmas charity, fer chrissakes!"

Stone pulled his trenchcoat collar up around his face. "I gave at the office, Eddie. Five C's is all you get."

"What are ya—Scrooge? Maggie's rich! And you're rolling in your own dough!"

Stone kicked Eddie in the side and the little man howled.

"The negatives and the register page, Eddie. Hit me up again and you'll take a permanent swim in the Chicago river. Agreed?"

"Agreed! Don't hurt me anymore! *Agreed!*"

"Merry X-mas, moron," Stone said, and exited the alley, pausing near the street to light up his own cigarette. Christmas carols were being piped through department-store loud speakers: *"Joy to the world!"*

"In a rat's ass," he muttered, and hailed a taxi. In the back seat, he sipped rum from a flask. The cabbie made holiday small talk and Stone said, "Make you a deal—skip the chatter and maybe you'll get a tip for Christmas."

Inside his Gold Coast apartment building, Stone was waiting for the elevator when he caught a strange reflection in a lobby mirror. He saw—or *thought* he saw—an imposing trenchcoated figure in a fedora standing behind him.

His late partner—Jake Marley!

Stone whirled, but . . . no one was there.

He blew out air, glanced at the mirror again, seeing only himself. "No more rum for you, pal."

On the seventh floor, Stone unlocked 714 and slipped inside his apartment. The *art moderne* furnishings reflected his financial success; the divorce racket had made him damn near wealthy. He tossed his jacket on a half-circle white couch, loosened his tie and headed to his well-appointed bar, already changing his mind about more rum.

He'd been lying, of course, about going to see his uncle and aunt. Christmas out in the sticks—*that* was a laugh! That had just been an excuse, so he didn't have to spend the night with that blood-sucking Maggie.

From the ice box he built a salami and swiss cheese on rye, smearing on hot mustard. Drifting back into the living room, where only one small lamp was on, he switched on his console radio, searching for sports or swing music or even war news, anything other than damn Christmas carols. But that maudlin muck was all he could find, and he switched it off in disgust.

Settling in a comfy overstuffed chair, still in his shoulder holster, he sat and ate and drank. Boredom crept in on him like ground fog.

Katie was busy with family tonight, and even most of the hookers he knew were taking the night off.

What the hell, he thought. *I'll just enjoy my own good company. . . .*

Without realizing it, he drifted off to sleep; a noise woke him, and Sadie—his trusty .38— was in his hand before his eyes had opened all the way.

"Who's there?" he said, and stood. Somebody had switched off the lamp! *Who in hell? The room was in near darkness. . . .*

"Sorry, keed," a familiar voice said. "The light hurts my peepers."

Standing by the window was his late partner—Jake Marley.

"I must be dreamin'," Stone said ratio-nally, after just the briefest flinch of a reaction, "'cause, pal—you're dead as a doornail."

"I'm dead, all right," Marley said. "Been dead a whole year." Red neon, from the window behind him, pulsed in on the tall, trenchcoated fedora-sporting figure—a hawkishly handsome man with a grooved face and thin mustache. "But, keed—you ain't dreamin'."

"What sorta gag *is* this . . . ?"

Stone walked over to Marley and took a close look: no make-up, no mask—it was no masquer-ade. And the trenchcoat had four scorched holes stitched across the front.

Bullet holes.

He put a hand on Marley's shoulder—and it passed right through.

"Jesus!" Stone stepped back. "You're not dead—I'm dead *drunk*." He turned away. "Havin' the heebie-jeebies or somethin'. When I wake up, you better be gone, or I'm callin' Ri-pley. . . ."

Marley smiled a little. "Nobody can see me but you, keed. Talk about it, and they'll toss ya in the laughin' academy, and toss away the key. Mind if I siddown? Feet are killin' me."

"Your eyes hurt, your feet hurt—what kinda goddamn ghost *are* you, anyway?"

"'Zactly what you said, keed," Marley said, and he slowly moved toward the sofa, dragging himself along, to the sound of metallic scraping. "The God-*damned* kind . . . and I'll stay that way if you don't come through for me."

Below the trenchcoat, Marley's feet were heavily shackled, like a chain-gang prisoner.

"You think *mine's* heavy," Marley said, "wait'll ya see what the boys in the metal shop are cookin' up for you."

The ghost sat heavily, his shackles clanking. Stone kept his distance.

"What do ya want from me, Jake?"

"The near-impossible, keed—I want ya to do the right thing."

"The right thing?"

"Find my murderer, ya chowderhead! Jesus!"

At that last exclamation, Marley cowered,

glanced upward, muttering, "No offense, Boss," and continued: "You're a detective, Stoney—when a detective's partner's killed, he's supposed to do somethin' about it. That's the code."

"That's the bunk," Stone said. "I left it to the cops. They mucked it up." He shrugged. "End of story."

"Nooooo!" Marley moaned, sounding like a ghost for the first time, and making the hair stand up on Stone's neck. "I was your partner, I was your only friend . . . your *mentor* . . . and you let me die an unsolved murder while you took over my business—*and* my wife."

Stone flinched again; lighted up a Lucky. "You know about that, huh? Maggie, I mean."

"Of course I know!" Marley waved a dismissive hand. "Oh, her I don't care two cents about . . . she always was a witch, with a capital 'b.' Having her in your life is punishment enough for *any* crime. But, keed—you and me, we're *tied* to each other! Chained for eternity . . ."

Convinced he was dreaming, Stone snorted. "Really, Jake? How come?"

Marley leaned forward and his shackles clanked. "My best pal—a detective—didn't think I was worth a measly murder investigation. Where I come from, a man who can't inspire any more loyalty than *that* outta his best pal is one lost soul."

Stone shrugged. "It was nothin' personal."

"Oh, I take gettin' murdered *real* personal! And you didn't give a rat's ass *who* killed me! And that's why *you're* as good as damned."

"Baloney!" Stone touched his stomach. ". . . or maybe salami . . ."

Marley shifted in his seat and his shackles rattled. "You *knew* I always looked after my little brother, Eddie—he's a louse and weakling, but he was the only brother I had . . . and what have you done for Eddie? Tossed him in some garbage cans! Left 'im for the Boys to measure for cement overshoes!"

"He's a weasel."

"He's your dead best pal's brother! Cut him some slack!"

"I did cut him some slack! I didn't kill him when he tried to blackmail me."

"Over you sleeping with his dead brother's wife, you mean?"

Stone batted the air dismissively. "The hell with you, Marley! You're not real! You're some meat that went bad. Some mustard that didn't agree with me. I'm goin' to bed."

"You were right the first time," Marley said. "You're goin' to hell . . . or anyway, hell's waitin' room. Like me." Marley's voice softened into a plea. "Stoney—help me outa this, pal. Help yourself."

"How?"

"Solve my murder."

Stone blew a smoke ring. "Is that all?"

Marley stood and a howling wind seemed to blow through the apartment, drapes waving like ghosts. *"It means something to me!"*

Now Stone was sweating; this *was* happening.

"One year ago," Marley said in a deep rumbling voice, "they found me in the alley behind the Bismarck Hotel, my back to the wall, one bullet in the pump, two in the stomach, and one in between . . . *remember?*"

And Marley removed the bullet-scorched trenchcoat to reveal the four wounds—beams of red neon light from the window behind him cut through Marley like swords through a magician's box.

"Remember?"

Stone was backing up, patting the air with his palms. "Okay, okay . . . why don't you just *tell* me who bumped you off, and I'll settle up for you. Then we'll be square."

"It's not that easy . . . I'm not . . . *allowed* to tell you."

"Who *made* these goddamn rules?"

Marley raised an eyebrow, lifted a finger, pointed up. "Right again. To save us both, you gotta act like a detective . . . you gotta look for clues . . . and you must do this *yourself* . . . though you *will* be aided."

"How?"

"You're gonna have three more visitors."

"Swell! Who's first? Karloff, or Lugosi?"

Marley moved away from the couch, toward the door, shackles clanking. "Don't blow it for the both of us, keed," he said, and left through the door—*through* the door.

Stone stood staring at where his late partner had literally disappeared, and shook his head. Then he went to the bar and poured himself a drink. Soon he was questioning the reality of what had just happened; and, a drink later, he stumbled into his bedroom and flopped onto his bed, fully clothed.

He was sleeping the sound sleep of the dead-drunk when his bed got jostled.

Somebody was kicking it.

Waking to semi-darkness, Stone said, "Who in hell . . ."

Looming over him was a roughly handsome, Clark Gable–mustached figure in a straw hat and a white double-breasted seersucker.

Stone dove for Sadie, his .38 in its shoulder holster slung over his nightstand, but then, in an eyeblink, the guy was gone.

"Over here, boyo."

Stone turned and the guy in the jauntily cocked straw hat was standing there, picking his teeth with a toothpick.

"Save yourself the ammo," the guy said. "They already got me."

And he unbuttoned his jacket and displayed several ugly gaping exit wounds.

"In the back," the guy said, "the bastards."

The guy looked oddly familiar. "Who the hell are you?"

"Let's put it this way. If a bunch of trigger-happy feds are chasin' ya, don't duck down that alley by the Biograph—it's a dead-end, brother."

"John Dillinger!"

"Right—only it's a hard 'g,' like in gun: Dil-lin-*ger*. Okay, sonny? Pet peeve o' mine." Dillinger was buttoning up his jacket.

"You . . . you must not have been killed wearing *that* suit."

"Naw—it's new. Christmas present from the Boss. I got a pretty good racket goin' here—helpin' chumps like you make good. Another five hundred years, and I get sprung."

"How exactly is a cheap crook like you gonna help *me* make good?"

Dillinger grabbed Stone by the shirt front. Stone took a swing at the ghost, but his hand only passed through.

"There ain't nothin' cheap about John Dillinger! I didn't rob nobody but banks, and times was hard, then, *banks* was the bad guys . . . and I never shot nobody. Otherwise, I'da got the big heat."

"The big heat?"

Dillinger raised an eyebrow and angled a thumb, downward. "Which is where you're headed, sonny, if you don't get your lousy head screwed on right. Come with me."

"Where are we goin'?"

"Into your past. Maybe that's why *I* got picked for this caper—see, I was a Midwest farm kid like you. Come on! Don't make me drag ya . . ."

Reluctantly, Stone followed the spirit into the next room . . .

. . . where Stone found himself not in the living room of his apartment, but in the snowy yard out in front of a small farmhouse. Snowflakes fell lazily upon an idyllic rural winter landscape; an eight-year-old boy was building a snowman.

"I know this place," Stone said.

"You know the *kid,* too," Dillinger said. "It's you. You live in that house."

"Why aren't I cold? It's gotta be freezing, but I feel like I'm still in my apartment."

"You're a shadow here, just like me," Dillinger said.

"Dickie!" a voice called from the porch. "Come inside—you'll catch your death!"

"Ma!" Stone said, and moved toward her. He studied her serene, beautiful face in the doorway. "Ma . . ."

He tried to touch her and his hand passed through.

Behind him, Dillinger said, "I told ya, boyo—you're a shadow. Just lean back and watch . . . maybe you'll learn somethin'."

Then eight-year-old Dickie Stone ran right

through the shadow of his future self, and inside the house, closing the door behind him, leaving Stone and Dillinger on the porch.

"Now what?" Stone asked.

"Since when were you shy about breaking and entering?" Dillinger said.

And walked *through* the door. . . .

"Look who's talking," Stone said. He took a breath and followed.

Stone found himself in the cozy farmhouse, warmed by a wood-burning stove, which, surprisingly, he could feel. In one corner of the modestly furnished living room stood a pine tree, almost too tall for the room to contain, decorated with tinsel and a star, wrapped gifts scattered under it. A spinet piano hugged a wall. Stone watched his eight-year-old self strip out of an aviator cap and woolen coat and boots and sit at a little table where he began working on a puzzle.

"Five hundred pieces," Stone said. "It's a picture of Tom Mix and his horse what's-his-name."

"Tony," said Dillinger.

"God, will ya smell that pine tree! And my mother's cooking! If I'm a shadow, how come I can smell her cooking?"

"Hey, pal—don't ask me. I'm just the tour guide. Maybe somebody upstairs wants your memory jogged."

Stone moved into the kitchen, where his mother was at the stove, stirring gravy.

"God, that gravy smells good . . . can you smell it?"

"No," said Dillinger.

"She's baking mincemeat pie, too . . . you're *lucky* you can't smell that. Garbage! But Pa always liked it. . . ."

"My ma made a mean plum pudding at Christmas," Dillinger said.

"Mine, too! It's bubbling on the stove! Can't you smell it?"

"No! This is *your* past, pal, not mine. . . ."

The back door opened and a man in a blue denim coat and woolen knit cap entered, stomping the snow off his workboots.

"That mincemeat pie must be what heaven smells like," the man said. Sky-blue eyes were an incongruously gentle presence in his hard, weathered face.

"Pa," Stone said.

Taking off his jacket, the man walked right through the shadow of his grown son. "Roads are still snowed in," his father told his mother.

"Oh dear! I was so counting on Bob and Helen for Christmas supper!"

"That's my uncle and aunt," Stone told Dillinger. "Bob was mom's brother."

"They'll be here," Pa Stone said, with a thin smile. "Davey took the horse and buggy into town after them."

"My brother Davey," Stone explained to Dillinger.

"Oh dear," his mother was saying. "He's so frail . . . oh how could you . . ."

"Send a boy to do a man's job? Sarah, Davey's sixteen. Proud as I am of the boy for his school marks, he's got to learn to be a man. Anyway, he *wanted* to do it. He *likes* to help."

Stone's ma could only say, "Oh dear," again and again.

"Now, Sarah—I'll *not* have these boys babied!"

"Well, the old S. O. B. sure didn't baby *me*," Stone said to Dillinger.

"Davey just doesn't have Dickie's spirit," said Pa. "Dickie's always getting in scrapes, and he sure don't make the grades Davey does, but the boy's got gumption and guts."

Stone had never known his pa felt that way about him.

"Then why are you so hard on the child, Jess?" his mother was asking. "Last time he got caught playing hookey from school, you gave him the waling of his life."

"How else is the boy to learn? That's how my pa taught *me* the straight and narrow path."

"Straight and narrow razor strap's more like it," Stone said.

Ma was stroking Pa's rough face. "You love both your boys. It's Christmas, Jess. Why don't you tell 'em how you feel?"

"They know," he said gruffly.

Emotions churned in Stone, and he didn't like it. "Tour guide—I've had about all of this I can take. . . ."

"Not just yet," Dillinger said. "Let's go in the other room."

They did, but it was suddenly later, after dark, the living room filled with family members sitting on sofas and chairs and even the floor, having cider after a supper that everybody was raving about.

A pudgy, good-natured man in his forties was saying to eight-year-old Dickie, "How do you like your gift, young man?"

The boy was wearing a policeman's cap and a little tin badge; he also had a miniature nightstick, a pair of handcuffs, and a traffic whistle. "It's the cat's meow, Uncle Bob!"

"Where does he get those vulgar expressions?" his mother asked disapprovingly, but not sternly.

"*Cap'n Billy's Whiz Bang,*" Stone whispered to Dillinger.

"Never missed an issue myself," Dillinger said.

The boy started blowing the whistle shrilly and there was laughter, but the boy's father said, "Enough!"

And the boy obeyed.

The door opened. A boy of sixteen, but skinny and not much taller than Dickie, came in; bundled in winter clothes, he was bringing in a pile of firewood for the wood-burning stove.

"Davey," Stone said.

"Did you like your older brother?" Dillinger asked.

"He was a great guy. You could always depend on him for a smile or a helpin' hand. . . . But what did it get him?"

Out of his winter jacket, firewood deposited, Davey went over to his younger brother and ruffled his hair. "Gonna get the bad guys, little brother?"

"I'm gonna bop 'em," Dickie said, "then slap the cuffs on!"

"On Christmas?" Davey asked. "Even crooks got a right to celebrate the Savior's birth, don't ya think?"

"Yeah. Well, okay . . . day *after,* then."

Everybody was laughing as little Dickie swung his nightstick at imaginary felons.

"Dickie, my lad," said Uncle Bob, "someday I'll hire you on at the station."

Stone explained to Dillinger: "He was police chief, over at DeKalb."

"Peachy," said Dillinger.

Davey said, "Ma—how about sitting down at the piano, and helping put us all in the Yuletide spirit?"

"Yeah, Ma!" said little Dickie. "Tickle the ol' ivories!"

Soon the group was singing carols, Davey leading them: "*God Rest Ye Merry Gentlemen. . . .*"

"Seen enough?" Dillinger said.

"Just a second," Stone said. "Let me hear a little more . . . this is the last decent Christmas I can remember. . . ."

After a while, the gaily singing people began to fade, but the room remained, and suddenly Stone saw the figure of his father, kneeling at the window, a rifle in his hands, face contorted savagely. There was no Christmas tree, although Stone knew at once that this was indeed a later Christmas Day in his family's history. His mother cowered by the piano; she seemed frightened and on the verge of tears. A fourteen-year-old Dickie was crouched beside his father near the window.

"God," said Stone. "Not *this* Christmas . . ."

"Son," his pa was saying to the teenage Stone, "I want you and your mother to go on out."

"No, Pa! I want to stay beside you! Ma should go, but . . ."

"You're not too big to get your hide tanned, boy."

"Pa . . ."

A voice through a megaphone outside called: "Jess! It's Bob! Let me come in and at least talk!"

"When hell freezes over!" Pa shouted. "Now get off my property, or so help me, I'll shoot you where you stand!"

"Jess, that's my *brother*," Ma said, tears brimming. "And it's . . . it's not *our* property, anymore. . . ."

"Whose is it, then? The bank's? Did the bankers work this ground for twenty years? Did the bankers put blood and sweat and years into this land?"

Dillinger elbowed Stone. "*That's* why this country *needed* guys like me. Say—where's your older brother, anyway?"

"Dead," Stone said. "He caught pneumonia the winter of '28 . . . stayed outside for hours and hours, helping get some family's flivver out of a ditch in the wind and cold. All my folks' dreams died with him."

"Let Bob come in," Ma was saying. "Hear him out."

Pa thought it over; he looked so much older, now. Not years older—decades. Finally he said, "All right. For you, Sarah. Just 'cause he's kin of yours."

When the door opened, and Bob came in, he was in full police-chief array, under a fur-lined jacket; the badge on his cap gleamed.

"Jess," he said solemnly, "you're at the end of your string. I wish I could help you, but the bank's foreclosed, and the law's the law."

"Why's the law on *their* side?" teenage Stone asked. "Isn't the law supposed to help everybody equal?"

"People with money get treated a hell of a lot more equal, son," his father said bitterly.

"I worked out a deal," Bob said. "You can keep your furniture. I can come over with the paddy wagon and load 'er up with your things; we'll store 'em in my garage. There'll be no charges brought. Helen and I have room for you and Sarah and Dick—you can stay with us till you find something."

The rifle was still in Pa's hands. "*This* is my home, Robert."

"No, Jess—it's a house the bank owns. Your home is your family, and you take them with you. Let me ask you this—what would Davey want you to do?"

Stone looked away; he knew what was coming: one of two times he ever saw his father cry—the other was the night Davey died.

A single tear running down his cheek, Pa said, "How am I supposed to support my family?"

Bob's voice was gentle: "I got friends at the barb-wire factory. Already talked to 'em about you. They'll take you on. Having a job in times like these is a blessing."

Pa nodded. He sighed, handed his rifle over. "Thank you, Robert."

"Yeah, Uncle Bob," teenage Stone said sarcastically. "Merry Christmas! In a rat's ass . . ."

"Richard!" his ma said.

His father slapped him.

"You ever do that to me again, old man," teenage Stone said, pointing a hard finger at his father, "I'll knock your damn block off!"

And as his teenage self rushed out, Stone shook his head. "Jesus! Did I have to say that to him, right then? Poor bastard hits rock bottom, and I find a way to push him down lower . . ."

Pa was standing rigidly, looking downward, as Ma clung to him in a desperate embrace. Uncle Bob, looking ashamed of himself, trudged out.

"You were just a kid," Dillinger said. "What did you know?"

"Why are you puttin' me through this hell?" Stone demanded. "I can't change the past! What does any of this have to do with finding out who killed Jake Marley?!"

"Don't ask me!" Dillinger flared. "I'm just the damn help!"

The bank robber's ghost stalked out, and Stone—not eager to be left in this part of his past—quickly followed.

Stone now found himself, and his ghostly companion, in the reception area of a small-town police station where officers milled and a reception desk loomed. Dillinger led Stone to a partitioned-off office where a Christmas wreath hung on a frosted glass door, which they went through without opening.

Jake Marley, Deputy Chief of Police of Dekalb, Illinois, sat leaned back in his chair, at his desk, smiling as he opened Christmas cards;

as he did, cool green cash dropped out of each card.

"Lot of people remembered Jake at Christmas," Stone said.

"Lot of people remember a *lot* of cops at Christmas," Dillinger sneered.

A knock at the door prompted Marley to sweep the cash into a desk drawer. "Yeah?" he called gruffly. "What?"

The uniformed police officer who peeked in was a young Dick Stone. "Deputy Chief Marley? I had word you wanted me to drop by . . . ?"

"Come on in, keed, come on in!" The slick mustached deputy chief gestured magnanimously to the chair opposite his desk. "Take a load off. . . ."

Young Stone sat while his future self and the ghost of a public enemy eavesdropped nearby.

Marley's smile tried a little too hard. "Yesterday was your first day on, I understand."

"Yes, sir."

"Well, I just wanted you to know I don't hold it against you, none—you gettin' this job through patronage."

"What's that supposed to mean?"

Marley shrugged. "Nothin'. A guy does what he has to, to get ahead. It's unusual, your Uncle Bob playin' that kinda game, though. He's a real straight arrow."

"Uncle Bob's kind of a square john, but he's family and I stand by him."

"Swell! Admirable, keed. Admirable. But there's things go on around here that he don't know about . . . and I'd like to keep it that way."

Young Stone frowned. "Such as?"

"Let me put it this way—if you got a fifty-dollar bill every month, for just lookin' the other way . . . if it was for something truly harmless . . . could you sleep at night?"

"Lookin' the other way, how?"

Marley explained that he was from Chicago—in '26, a local congressman greased the wheels for him to land this rural deputy chief slot, so he could do some favors for the Outfit.

"Not so much goin' on now," said Marley, "not like back in dry days, when the Boys had stills out here. Couple roadhouses where people like to have some extra-legal fun . . ."

"Gambling and girls, you mean."

"Right. And there's a farmhouse the Boys use, when things get hot in the city, and a field where they like to do some . . . planting . . . now and then."

"I don't think I could sleep at night, knowing that's going on."

Marley's eyebrows shot up. "Oh?"

"Not for fifty a month." The young officer grinned. "Seventy-five, maybe. A C-note, and I'd be asleep when my head hit the pillow."

Marley stuck his hand across his desk. "I think this is gonna be the start of a beautiful friendship."

They shook hands, but when young Stone brought his hand back, there was a C-note in it.

"Merry Christmas, Mr. Marley."

"Make it 'Jake.' Many happy returns, keed."

Dillinger tugged Stone's arm and they walked through the office wall and were suddenly in another office: the outer office of MARLEY AND STONE: CONFIDENTIAL INVESTIGATIONS. Katie was watering the base of a Christmas tree in the corner.

"This is, what?" Dillinger asked Stone. "Five years ago?"

"Right. Christmas Eve, '37, I think. . . ."

Marley was whispering to a five-years' younger Stone. "Nice-lookin' twist you hired."

"She'll class up the front office. And remember, Jake—I saw her first."

Marley grinned. "What do I need with a kid like her, when I got a woman like Maggie? Ah! Speak of the devil. . . ."

Maggie was entering the outer office on the arm of a blond, boyishly handsome man in a crisp business suit.

"Stoney," Marley said, "meet our biggest client: this is Larry Turner . . . he's the V. P. with Consolidated who's tossing all that investigating our way."

"Couldn't do this without you, Mr. Turner," Stone said.

"Make it 'Larry,'" he said. "Pleasure to do business with such a well-connected firm."

Dillinger said, "What's *this* boy scout's angle?"

Stone said, "We been kicking that boy scout back twenty percent of what his firm pays us since day one. I don't know how Jake knew him, but Consolidated was the account that let us leave DeKalb and set up shop in the Loop."

"How'd your Uncle Bob feel about you leaving the force?"

"He damn near cried . . . he always figured I'd step in and fill his shoes someday. Poor yokel . . . just didn't have a clue—all that corruption going on right under his nose."

"By his deputy chief and his nephew, you mean."

Stone said nothing, but the five-years-ago him was saying to Marley, "Look—this insurance racket is swell. But the real dough is in divorce work."

"You're right, keed. I'm ahead of you . . . we get the incriminating photos of the cheating spouse, then sell 'em to the highest bidder."

"Sweet! That's what they get for not love, honor, and obeyin'."

The private eyes shared a big horse laugh. Katie looked their way and smiled, glad to see her bosses enjoying themselves on Christmas Eve.

"Come on," Dillinger said, summoning Stone with a crooked finger.

And the late bank robber walked Stone through a wall into the alley where Jake Marley lay crumpled against a brick wall, between two garbage cans, holes shot in the front of him, eyes wide and empty and staring.

Sgt. Hank Ross was showing the body to Stone. "Thought you better see this, pal. Poor slob never even got his gun out. Still tucked away under his buttoned-up topcoat. Shooter musta been somebody who knew him, don't ya figure?"

Stone shrugged. "You're the homicide dick."

"Now, Stoney . . . I don't want you looking into this. I know he was your partner, and your friend, but . . ."

"You talked me out of it." Stone lighted up a Lucky. "I'll take care of informin' the widow."

Ross just looked at him. Then he said, "Merry goddamn Christmas, Stoney."

"In a rat's ass," he said, turning away from his dead partner.

"Jeez!" Dillinger said. "That's cold! Couldn't ya squeeze out just one tear for your old pal?"

Stone said nothing. His year-ago self walked right through him.

"You want the truth, Dillin-*ger*? All I was thinkin' was, with all the people he jacked around, Jake was lucky to've lived *this* long. And how our partnership agreement spelled out that the business was mine, now."

"Hell! I thought *Gillis* was cold."

"Gillis?"

"Lester Gillis. Baby Face Nelson to you. Come on, sonny. You and me reached the end of the line."

And Dillinger shoved Stone, hard—right through the brick wall; and when the detective blinked again, he was alone on his bed, in his apartment.

He sat up; rubbed his eyes, scratched his head. "Meat shortage or not, that salami gets pitched. . . ."

He flopped back on the bed, still fully dressed, and stared at the ceiling; the dream was hanging with him—thoughts, images, of his mother, father, brother, even Marley, floated in front of him, speaking to him. . . .

Out in the other room, the doorbell rang, startling him. He checked the round bakelite clock on his nightstand: two a.m. Who in hell would be calling on him at this hour?

On the other hand, he thought as he stumbled out to his door, *talking to somebody with a* pulse *would be nice for a change. . . .*

And there on his doorstep was a crisply uniformed soldier, a freshly scrubbed young man with his overseas cap tugged down onto his forehead.

"Mr. Stone?"

"Ben? Is that *you*? Ben Crockett!" Stone's grin split his face. "Katie's little brother, back from the wars—is *she* gonna be tickled!"

The boy seemed somewhat dazed as he stepped inside.

"Uh, Ben . . . if you're lookin' for Katie, she's at her place tonight."

"I'm here to see *you*, Mr. Stone."

"Well, that's swell, kid . . . but why?"

"I'm not really sure," the boy said. "May I sit down?"

"Sure, kid, sure! You want something to drink?"

"No thanks. You'll have to excuse me, sir— I'm kinda confused. The briefing I got . . . it was pretty screwy."

"Briefing?"

"Yeah. This is a temporary assignment. But they said I was 'uniquely qualified' for this mission."

"What do they want you to do, kid? Haul me down for another physical?"

"That reminds me!" Private Crockett dug into a pocket and found a scrap of paper. "Does this mean anything to you? 'Tell the 4-F Mr. Stone he really *does* have flat feet and the doctor he paid off was scamming *him*.'"

Stone's mouth dropped open, then he laughed. "Well, that's a Chicago doc for ya. So, is that the extent of your 'mission'?"

The boy tucked the scrap of paper away. "No. There's more . . . and it's *weird*. I'm supposed to tell you to go look in the mirror."

"Look in the mirror?"

"Yeah—that one over there, I guess."

"Kid . . ."

"Please, Mr. Stone. I don't think I get to go home for Christmas till I get this done."

Stone sighed, said okay, and shuffled over to the mirror near his console radio; he saw his now unshaven, slightly bleary-eyed reflection, and the boy in his trim overseas cap looking gravely over his shoulder. "Now what, kid?"

"You're supposed to look in there, is all. I was told you're gonna see tomorrow . . . or, actually, it's after midnight already, ain't it? Anyway, Christmas Day, 1942 . . ."

And the mirror before Stone became a window.

Through the window, he saw Maggie Marley and Larry Turner, the insurance company V. P., toasting cocktail glasses—Maggie in a negligee, Turner in a silk smoking jacket; they were snuggled on a couch in her fancy apartment.

"What the hell's this?" Stone asked. "Maggie and that snake Turner . . . since when are *they* an item?"

"How much longer," Maggie was saying to Turner, "do I have to put up with him?"

"You *need* Stone," Turner said, nuzzling her neck. "He's your alibi, baby."

"But I didn't *kill* Jake!"

"Sure you didn't. Sure you didn't . . . anyway, string him along a little way, then let him down easy. . . . Right now you still need him in your pocket. He helped you get Eddie off your tail, didn't he?"

Maggie frowned. "Well . . . you're right about that. But his touch . . . it makes my skin crawl. . . ."

"Why you little . . ." Stone began.

But the images in the mirror blurred, and were replaced with another image: Eddie Marley, in his sleazy little apartment, not answering his door, cowering as somebody out there was banging with a fist.

"Let us in, Eddie! We got a Christmas present for ya!"

Eddie, sweating, shaking like crazy, looked at a framed photo of his late brother Jake.

"How could you do this to me, Jake?" he whispered. "You promised you'd take care of me. . . ."

The door splintered open and two Outfit thugs—huge hulking faceless creatures in topcoats and fedoras—cornered him quickly.

"Gimme another week, fellas! I can get ya five C's today, to tide us over till then!"

"Too late, Eddie," one ominous goon said. "You kept the Outfit waitin' just one time too many. . . ."

A hand filled itself with a .45 automatic that erupted once, twice, three times. Eddie crumpled to the floor, bleeding. Dying.

"Jake . . . Jake . . . you let me down . . . you promised. . . ."

The mirror blurred again. Stone looked at Private Crockett. "Is that a done deal, kid? If that's gonna happen Christmas Day, can't I still bail that little weasel out . . . ?"

"I don't know, Mr. Stone. They didn't tell me that."

A new image began to form in the mirror: Stone's young employee, Joey Ernest, seated in his living room, by a fireplace, looking glum—in fact, he seemed on the verge of tears. Nearby, his little boy of six and his little girl of four were playing with some nice new toys under a tree bright with Christmas lights.

Joey's wife Linda, a pretty blonde in a red Christmas dress, came over and slipped an arm around him.

"Why are you so blue, darling?"

"I can't help it . . . I know I should be happy. It's been a great Christmas . . . but I feel so . . . so ashamed. . . ."

"Darling . . ."

"Other guys my age, they're fighting on bloody beaches to preserve the honor and glory of God and country. Me, I crawl around under beds and hide in hotel closets and take dirty pictures of adulterers."

"Joey! The children!"

"I know! The children . . . I want to give them a good life . . . but do I have to do it like this? Covering up for my philandering boss, among a million other indignities? I'm quitting! I swear, I'm quitting Monday!"

She kissed his cheek. "Then I'll stand right beside you."

He gave her a hangdog look. "I shouldn't have got us so far in over our heads with all these time payments. . . . How are we gonna make it, Linda?"

"I'm going to take that job at the defense plant. Mom can look after the kids, when one of us isn't here. It's going to be fine."

"Aw, Linda. I love you so much. Merry Christmas, baby."

"Merry Christmas, darling."

They were embracing as the image blurred.

Now the mirror filled with a tableau of home-less men in a soup kitchen. They were standing in line, receiving soup and bread and a hot meal. Serving them was the pretty young Salvation Army worker Stone made a pass at, at the office. In the background, voices of men at the mission were singing a carol: "God Rest Ye Merry Gentlemen."

"We used to sing that song at home," Stone told the soldier. "My ma would play the piano. Christ! What a heel."

"Who, Mr. Stone?"

But the image on the mirror was different again: Katie Crockett and a plump older woman and a frail-looking older man . . .

"Hey, kid," Stone said, "it's your sister!"

"And my folks," he said quietly.

. . . sitting around the Christmas tree in Katie's little apartment, opening presents and chatting happily. The doorbell rang, and Katie bounced up to answer it.

But she didn't come bouncing back.

"It's . . . it's a telegram from the war department," Katie said.

"Oh no!" her mother said. "Not . . ."

"It's Ben, isn't it?" her father said.

They huddled together and read the telegram and tears streamed down their faces.

"Well, that's wrong, kid," Stone said to Private Crockett. "You gotta go there tomorrow, and straighten that out. It's breaking their hearts—they think you're dead!"

"Mr. Stone," the boy said, removing his overseas cap, revealing the bullet hole in the center of his forehead, "I'm afraid they're right."

"God . . ."

"I have to go home now," he said. "Tell sis I love her, would you, Mr. Stone? And the folks, too?"

The young soldier, like another image blurring in the mirror, faded away.

Alone in his bedroom again, Stone held his throbbing head in his hands. "Did somebody slip me a mickey or something?" Exhausted, he stumbled back to his bed, falling face first, and sleep, mercifully, descended.

I'll have a blue Christmas without you. . . .

Stone's eyes popped open; his bedroom was still dark. Someone was singing, a sort of hillbilly Bing Crosby, a strange voice, an earthy unearthly voice . . .

. . . *blue Christmas, that's certain* . . .

The little round clock said 4 a.m.

. . . *decorations of white.* . . .

"What the hell is that racket? The radio?"

"It's me, sir," the same voice said. Mellow, baritone, slurry.

Stone hauled himself off the bed and beheld the strangest apparition of all: the man standing before him wore a white leather outfit with a cape, glittering with rhinestones. The (slightly overweight) man had longish jet black hair, an insolently handsome if puffy face, and heavy-lidded eyes.

"Who the hell are you?"

"Ah don't mean to soun' immodest, sir," he said huskily, "but where ah come from they call me 'the King.'"

"Don't tell me *you're* Jesus Christ!" Stone said, eyes popping.

"Not hardly, sir. Ah'm just a poor country boy. Right now, ah'd be about seven years old, sir."

"If you're seven years old, I'd cut down on the Baby Ruths, if I was you."

The apparition in white moved toward him, a leather ghost; his shoes were strange, too—rhinestone-studded white cowboy boots. "Ah'm afraid you don't understand, sir—ah'm the ghost of somebody who hasn't grown up and lived yet, in your day . . . let alone died."

"You haven't died yet, but you're a ghost? A ghost in a white-leather zoot suit! This is the best one yet. This is my favorite so far. . . ."

"See, ah was a very famous person, or ah'm goin' to be. Ah really don't mean to brag, but ah was bigger than the Beatles."

"You're the biggest bug I ever saw, period, pal."

"Sir, ah abused my talent, and my body, so ah'm payin' some dues. That's how come ah got this gig."

"'Gig'?"

"Ah'm here to show you a little preview of comin' attractions, sir. Somethin' that's gonna go down 'long about next Christmas . . . Christmas of '43. . . ."

The apparition struck a strange pose, as if turning his entire body into a pointing arrow, and suddenly both the King and Stone were in a small chapel, bedecked rather garishly with Christmas decorations that seemed un-church-like, somehow.

"Where *are* we?"

"Welcome to *my* world, sir. We're a few years early to appreciate it, but someday, this is gonna be a real bright light city."

"What are you *talkin'* about?"

The King grinned sideways. "We're in Vegas, man!"

Up at the front of the chapel, a man and woman faced a minister. Canned organ music was filtering in. A wedding ceremony was under way.

Stone walked up to have a look.

"I'll be damned," Stone said.

"That's what we're tryin' to prevent, sir."

"It's Maggie and that creep Larry Turner! Getting hitched! Well, good riddance to both of 'em. . . ."

"Maybe you oughta see how *you're* spendin' next Christmas . . ."

And now Stone and the rhinestone ghost were in a jail cell. So was a haggard-looking, next year's Stone—in white-and-black prison garb, seated on his cot, looking desperate. On a stool across from him was Sgt. Hank Ross.

"Hank, you *know* I'm innocent!"

"I believe you, Stoney. But the jury didn't. That eye witness held up . . ."

"He was bought and paid for!"

". . . and your gun turning out to be the murder weapon, well . . ."

"You get an anonymous phone tip to match the slugs that killed Jake with my gun, a *year* later, and you don't think that's suspicious?"

"The ballistics tests were positive."

"Some crooked cop must've switched the real bullets with some phonies shot from my gun! I told you, Hank, when I went to Miami on vacation, I left the gun in my desk drawer. Anybody coulda . . ."

"Old news, Stoney."

"You gotta believe me. . . ."

"I do. But with your appeal turned down . . ."

"What about the governor?"

"The papers want your ass, and the governor wants votes. You know how it works."

"Yeah, Hank. I know how it works, all right. . . ."

"Stoney, better put things right between you and your maker." Ross sighed, heavily. "'Cause tomorrow about now . . . you're gonna be meetin' him."

Ross patted his friend on the shoulder, called for the guard, and was soon gone. Stone stood and clung onto the bars of his cell as a forlorn harmonica played "Come All Ye Faithful."

"Death row?" Stone said to the King. "Next Christmas, I'm on death row?"

"Sir, ah'm afraid that's right. And ah think we're gonna have to be movin' on. . . ."

And they were back in the apartment.

"I have no idea who the hell you are," Stone said, "but I owe you. Of all the visions I've seen tonight, yours are the ones that brought it all home to me."

"Thank you vurry much," the King said.

Stone glanced away, but when he turned back, his visitor had left the building.

Almost dizzy, Stone fell back onto the bed, head whirling; sleep descended. . . .

When he awakened, it was almost noon. He felt re-born. He showered and shaved, whistling "Joy to the World." As he got dressed, he slung on his shoulder-holstered revolver, removing the gun and checking its cylinder.

"Jeez, Sadie," Stone said. "What kinda girl *are* you? Loaded on Christmas . . ."

Chuckling, he tucked the gun in its holster, then frowned and had a closer look at the .38, studying its handle.

"I'll be damned," he said to himself. Then he smiled knowingly. ". . . Or maybe not."

He slipped the gun back in its hand-tooled shoulder holster, tossed on his topcoat. Then, as an afterthought, he went to his wall safe and counted out five thousand dollars in C notes, and folded the wad in his pocket.

When Stone knocked at Eddie's apartment, there was no answer. Was he too late? He yelled: "Eddie—it's Stone! I got your cash. All five grand of it!"

Finally Eddie peeked out; he was a little bruised up from the rough handling Stone had given him last night. "What is this—a gag?"

"No. Lemme in."

In the little apartment—strewn with old issues of *Racing News*, dirty clothes, and take-out dinner cartons—Stone counted the cash out to a stunned Eddie.

"What is this?"

"It's a Christmas present, you little weasel."

"Why . . . ?"

"You're my partner's brother. I had a responsibility to help you out. But this is *it* . . . this'll bail you out today, and don't ask me for no more bail-outs in the future, got it? When the goons come, pay 'em off. And if you wanna lose your gambling habit, I might find some legwork for you to do, at the office. But otherwise, you're on your own."

"I don't get it. Why help me, after I tried to blackmail you . . . ?"

"Oh, well, I'll break your arms if you try *that* again."

"Now, that sounds like the old Stoney."

"No—the old Stoney woulda killed you. Eddie—you said your brother promised to 'take care of' you, if anything happened to him. You seemed real sure of that. . . ."

Eddie nodded emphatically. "He told me I was on his insurance policy—fifty percent was supposed to go to me, but somehow that witch wound up with *all* of it!"

Before long, Stone was knocking at the penthouse apartment door of the widow Marley.

Maggie tried not to betray her discomfort at seeing Stone. "Why, Richard," she said, raising her voice, "what a lovely Christmas surpri—"

But he pushed past her, before Larry Turner

could find a hiding place. Turner was caught by the fireplace, where no stockings were hung.

"Merry Christmas, Larry," Stone said. "I got a present for ya . . ."

Stone pulled the .38 out from under his shoulder and pointed it at the trembling Turner, who wore the silk smoking jacket Stone had seen in the vision in the mirror last night.

"Actually, it's a present *you* gave *me*," Stone said. "My best friend—my best girl—is Sadie. My gun. Kind of a sad commentary, ain't it?"

"I don't know what's gotten into you, Stone . . . just don't point that thing at me. . . ."

"Funny thing is, this isn't Sadie. Imagine—me goin' around with the wrong dame for over a year, and not knowin' it!"

Maggie said, "Richard, please put that gun away—"

"Sweetheart, would you mind standin' over there by your boy friend? I honestly don't think you were in on this, but I'm not takin' any chances."

She started to say something, and Stone said, "Move!" and, with the .38, waved her over by Turner.

Stone continued: "Sometime last year, Larry . . . I don't know when exactly, just that it had to be before Christmas Eve . . . you stole my Sadie, and substituted a similar gun. Trouble is, Sadie has a little chip out of the handle . . . tiny, but it's there, only it's *not* there on *this* gun."

"Why in hell would I do that?" Turner asked.

"Because you wanted to use *my* gun to kill Jake with. Which you did."

"Kill Jake! Why would I . . ."

"Because you and Maggie are an item. A secret item, but an item. You fixed her insurance policy so that *all* those double-indemnity dollars went to her, even though Jake intended his no-good brother get half. Jake considered you a friend—that's why his hands were in his pockets, and his gun under his coat, when you got up close to him and sent him those thirty-eight caliber Christmas greetings."

"With *your* gun? If any of this were true, I'd have given that gun to the police, long ago."

"Not necessarily. You're an insurance man . . . using my gun was like takin' out a policy. Any time it looked like suspicion was headed your way, or even Maggie's, you could switch guns again and make a nice little anonymous call."

Maggie was watching Turner, eyes wide, horror growing. "Is this true? Did you kill Jake?"

"It's nonsense," Turner told her dismissively.

"Well, then," she said bitterly, "what was that gun you had me put in my wall safe? For my 'protection,' you said!"

"Shut up," he said.

"Now I know what *I* want for Christmas," Stone said. "Maggie, open the safe."

She went to an oil painting of herself, removed it, and revealed the round safe, which she opened.

"Stand aside, sweetheart," Stone said, "and let *him* get the gun out."

Turner, sweating, licked his lips and reached in and grabbed the gun, wheeled, fired, dove behind the nearby couch. When Turner peeked around to fire again at Stone, the detective had already dropped to the floor. Stone returned fire, his slug piercing a plump couch cushion. Turner popped up again, and Stone nailed him through the shoulder.

Turner yelped and fell, his dropped gun spinning away harmlessly on the marble floor.

Stone stood over Turner, who looked up in anger and anguish, holding onto his shot-up shoulder. "You *wanted* me to try to shoot it out with you!"

"That's right."

"Why?"

" 'Cause it was all theory till you tried to shoot me. Now it'll hold up with the cops and in court."

"You bastard, Stone . . . why don't you just do it? Why don't you just shoot me and be the hell done with it?"

"I don't think so. First of all, I like the idea of you spendin' next Christmas on death row. Second, you're not worth goin' to hell over."

Stone phoned Sgt. Ross. "Yeah, I know

you're at home, Hank—but I got another present for ya—all gift-wrapped. . . ."

He hung up, then found himself facing a slyly smiling Maggie.

"No hard feelings?" she asked.

"Naw. We were both louses. Both running around on each other."

Maggie was looking at him seductively; running a finger up and down his arm. "You were so *sexy* shooting it out like that . . . I don't think I was ever more attracted to you. . . ."

He just laughed, shook his head, pushed her gently aside.

"I would rather go to hell," he said.

Later, with Turner turned over to Ross, Stone stopped at Joey Ernest's house out in the north suburbs.

"Mr. Stone—what are you . . . ?"

"I just wanted to wish you a Merry Christmas, kid. And tell you my New Year's resolution is to dump the divorce racket."

"Really?"

"Really. There's some retail credit action we can get . . . it won't pay the big bucks, but we'll be able to look at ourselves in the mirror."

Joey's face lighted up. "You don't know what this means to me, Mr. Stone!"

"I think maybe I do. Incidentally, Mrs. Marley and me are kaput. No more covering up for your dirty boss."

"Mr. Stone . . . come in and say hello to the family. We haven't sat down to dinner yet. Please join us!"

"I'd love to say hi, but I can't stay long. I have another engagement."

Finally, he knocked at the door of Katie's little apartment.

"Why . . . Richard!" Her beaming face told him that certain news hadn't yet reached her.

"Can a guy change his mind? And his ways? I'd love to have Christmas with you and your folks."

She slipped her arm in his and ushered him in. "Oh, they'll be so thrilled to meet you! You've made me so happy, Richard . . ."

"I just wanted to be with you today," he said, "and maybe sometime, before New Year's, we could drive over to DeKalb and see my Uncle Bob and Aunt Helen."

"That would be lovely!" she said, as she walked him into the living room with its sparkling Christmas tree. Her mother and father rose from the couch with smiles.

It would be a blue Christmas for this family, when the doorbell rang, as it would all too soon; but when it did, Stone at least wanted to be with them.

With Katie.

And when they would eventually go to the young soldier's grave, to say a prayer and lay a wreath, Stone would do the same for his late friend and partner.

A SCARY

Little Christmas

THE CAROL SINGERS

Josephine Bell

ONE OF THE FOUNDERS OF THE (BRITISH) CRIME WRITERS' Association and its chairwoman from 1959 to 1960, Doris Bell Collier Ball took the pseudonym Josephine Bell largely because of Sherlock Holmes. It has been widely reported that Arthur Conan Doyle based many of the characteristics of his great detective on his teacher at the University of Edinburgh, Dr. Joseph Bell. Since the author was also a physician, she particularly liked the symmetry of using Dr. Bell's name as the inspiration for the one that would appear on forty-five of her own works. "The Carol Singers" was first published in *Murder Under the Mistletoe*, edited by Cynthia Manson (New York, Signet, 1992).

The Carol Singers

JOSEPHINE BELL

OLD MRS. FAIRLANDS STEPPED carefully off the low chair she had pulled close to the fireplace. She was very conscious of her eighty-one years every time she performed these mild acrobatics. Conscious of them and determined to have no humiliating, potentially dangerous mishap. But obstinate, in her persistent routine of dusting her own mantelpiece, where a great many, too many photographs and small ornaments daily gathered a film of greasy London dust.

Mrs. Fairlands lived in the ground floor flat of a converted house in a once fashionable row of early Victorian family homes. The house had been in her family for three generations before her, and she herself had been born and brought up there. In those faroff days of her childhood, the whole house was filled with a busy throng of people, from the top floor where the nurseries housed the noisiest and liveliest group, through the dignified, low-voiced activities of her parents and resident aunt on the first and ground floors, to the basement haunts of the domestic staff, the kitchens and the cellars.

Too many young men of the family had died in two world wars and too many young women had married and left the house to make its original use in the late 1940's any longer possible. Mrs. Fairlands, long a widow, had inherited the property when the last of her brothers died. She had let it for a while, but even that failed. A conversion was the obvious answer. She was a vigor-

ous seventy at the time, fully determined, since her only child, a married daughter, lived in the to her barbarous wastes of the Devon moors, to continue to live alone with her much-loved familiar possessions about her.

The conversion was a great success and was made without very much structural alteration to the house. The basement, which had an entrance by the former back door, was shut off and was let to a businessman who spent only three days a week in London and preferred not to use an hotel. The original hall remained as a common entrance to the other three flats. The ground floor provided Mrs. Fairlands with three large rooms, one of which was divided into a kitchen and bathroom. Her own front door was the original dining room door from the hall. It led now into a narrow passage, also chopped off from the room that made the bathroom and kitchen. At the end of the passage two new doors led into the former morning room, her drawing room as she liked to call it, and her bedroom, which had been the study.

This drawing room of hers was at the front of the house, overlooking the road. It had a square bay window that gave her a good view of the main front door and the steps leading up to it, the narrow front garden, now a paved forecourt, and from the opposite window of the bay, the front door and steps of the house next door, divided from her by a low wall.

Mrs. Fairlands, with characteristic obstinacy,

strength of character, integrity, or whatever other description her forceful personality drew from those about her, had lived in her flat for eleven years, telling everyone that it suited her perfectly and feeling, as the years went by, progressively more lonely, more deeply bored, and more consciously apprehensive. Her daily came for four hours three times a week. It was enough to keep the place in good order. On those days the admirable woman cooked Mrs. Fairlands a good solid English dinner, which she shared, and also constructed several more main meals that could be eaten cold or warmed up. But three half days of cleaning and cooking left four whole days in each week when Mrs. Fairlands must provide for herself or go out to the High Street to a restaurant. After her eightieth birthday she became more and more reluctant to make the effort. But every week she wrote to her daughter Dorothy to say how well she felt and how much she would detest leaving London, where she had lived all her life except when she was evacuated to Wiltshire in the second war.

She was sincere in writing thus. The letters were true as far as they went, but they did not go the whole distance. They did not say that it took Mrs. Fairlands nearly an hour to wash and dress in the morning. They did not say she was sometimes too tired to bother with supper and then had to get up in the night, feeling faint and thirsty, to heat herself some milk. They did not say that although she stuck to her routine of dusting the whole flat every morning, she never mounted her low chair without a secret terror that she might fall and break her hip and perhaps be unable to reach the heavy stick she kept beside her armchair to use as a signal to the flat above.

On this particular occasion, soon after her eighty-first birthday, she had deferred the dusting until late in the day, because it was Christmas Eve and in addition to cleaning the mantelpiece she had arranged on it a pile of Christmas cards from her few remaining friends and her many younger relations.

This year, she thought sadly, there was not really much point in making the display. Dorothy and Hugh and the children could not come to her as usual, nor could she go to them. The tiresome creatures had chicken pox, in their late teens, too, except for Bobbie, the afterthought, who was only ten. They should all have had it years ago, when they first went to school. So the visit was canceled, and though she offered to go to Devon instead, they told her she might get shingles from the same infection and refused to expose her to the risk. Apart altogether from the danger to her of traveling at that particular time of the year, the weather and the holiday crowds combined, Dorothy had written.

Mrs. Fairlands turned sadly from the fireplace and walked slowly to the window. A black Christmas this year, the wireless report had promised. As black as the prospect of two whole days of isolation at a time when the whole western world was celebrating its midwinter festival and Christians were remembering the birth of their faith.

She turned from the bleak prospect outside her window, a little chilled by the downdraft seeping through its closed edges. Near the fire she had felt almost too hot, but then she needed to keep it well stocked up for such a large room. In the old days there had been logs, but she could no longer lift or carry logs. Everyone told her she ought to have a cosy stove or even do away with solid fuel altogether, install central heating and perhaps an electric fire to make a pleasant glow. But Mrs. Fairlands considered these suggestions defeatist, an almost insulting reference to her age. Secretly she now thought of her life as a gamble with time. She was prepared to take risks for the sake of defeating them. There were few pleasures left to her. Defiance was one of them.

When she left the window, she moved to the far corner of the room, near the fireplace. Here a small table, usually covered, like the mantelpiece, with a multitude of objects, had been cleared to make room for a Christmas tree. It was mounted in a large bowl reserved for this annual purpose. The daily had set it up for her and wrapped the bowl round with crinkly red paper, fastened with safety pins. But the tree was not yet decorated.

Mrs. Fairlands got to work upon it. She knew that it would be more difficult by artificial light to tie the knots in the black cotton she used for the dangling glass balls. Dorothy had provided her with some newfangled strips of pliable metal that needed only to be threaded through the rings on the glass balls and wrapped round the branches of the tree. But she had tried these strips only once. The metal had slipped from her hands and the ball had fallen and shattered. She went back to her long practiced method with black cotton, leaving the strips in the box for her grandchildren to use, which they always did with ferocious speed and efficiency.

She sighed as she worked. It was not much fun decorating the tree by herself. No one would see it until the day after Boxing Day when the daily would be back. If only her tenants had not gone away she could have invited them in for some small celebration. But the basement man was in his own home in Essex, and the first floor couple always went to an hotel for Christmas, allowing her to use their flat for Dorothy and Hugh and the children. And this year the top floor, three girl students, had joined a college group to go skiing. So the house was quite empty. There was no one left to invite, except perhaps her next-door neighbors. But that would be impossible. They had detestable children, rude, destructive, uncontrolled brats. She had already complained about broken glass and dirty sweet papers thrown into her forecourt. She could not possibly ask them to enjoy her Christmas tree with her. They might damage it. Perhaps she ought to have agreed to go to May, or let her come to her. She was one of the last of her friends, but never an intimate one. And such a chatterer. Nonstop, as Hugh would say.

By the time Mrs. Fairlands had fastened the last golden ball and draped the last glittering piece of tinsel and tied the crowning piece, the six-pronged shining silver star, to the topmost twig and fixed the candles upright in their socket

clips, dusk had fallen. She had been obliged to turn on all her lights some time before she had done. Now she moved again to her windows, drew the curtains, turned off all the wall lights, and with one reading lamp beside her chair sat down near the glowing fire.

It was nearly an hour after her usual teatime, she noticed. But she was tired. Pleasantly tired, satisfied with her work, shining quietly in its dark corner, bringing back so many memories of her childhood in this house, of her brief marriage, cut off by the battle of the Marne, of Dorothy, her only child, brought up here, too, since there was nowhere for them to live except with the parents she had so recently left. Mrs. Fairlands decided to skip tea and have an early supper with a boiled egg and cake.

She dozed, snoring gently, her ancient, wrinkled hand twitching from time to time as her head lolled on and off the cushion behind it.

She woke with a start, confused, trembling. There was a ringing in her head that resolved, as full consciousness returned to her, into a ringing of bells, not only her own, just inside her front door, but those of the other two flats, shrilling and buzzing in the background.

Still trembling, her mouth dry with fright and open-mouthed sleep, she sat up, trying to think. What time was it? The clock on the mantelpiece told her it was nearly seven. Could she really have slept for two whole hours? There was silence now. Could it really have been the bell, all the bells, that had woken her? If so, it was a very good thing. She had no business to be asleep in the afternoon, in a chair of all places.

Mrs. Fairlands got to her feet, shakily. Whoever it was at the door must have given up and gone away. Standing still, she began to tremble again. For she remembered things Dorothy and Hugh and her very few remaining friends said to her from time to time. "Aren't you afraid of burglars?" "I wouldn't have the nerve to live alone!" "They ring you up, and if there is no answer, they know you're out, so they come and break in."

Well, there had been no answer to this bell ringing, so whoever it was, if ill-intentioned, might even now be forcing the door or prowling round the house, looking for an open window.

While she stood there in the middle of her drawing room, trying to build up enough courage to go round her flat pulling the rest of the curtains, fastening the other windows, Mrs. Fairlands heard sounds that instantly explained the situation. She heard, raggedly begun, out of tune, but reassuringly familiar, the strains of "Once in Royal David's City."

Carol singers! Of course. Why had she not thought of them instead of frightening herself to death with gruesome suspicions?

Mrs. Fairlands, always remembering her age, her gamble, went to the side window of the bay and, pulling back the edge of the curtain, looked out. A darkclad group stood there, six young people, four girls with scarves on their heads, two boys with woolly caps. They had a single electric torch directed onto a sheet of paper held by the central figure of the group.

Mrs. Fairlands watched them for a few seconds. Of course they had seen the light in her room, so they knew someone was in. How stupid of her to think of burglars. The light would have driven a burglar away if he was out looking for an empty house to break into. All her fears about the unanswered bell were nonsense.

In her immense relief, and seeing the group straighten up as they finished the hymn, she tapped at the glass. They turned quickly, shining the torch in her face. Though she was a little startled by this, she smiled and nodded, trying to convey the fact that she enjoyed their performance.

"Want another, missis?" one boy shouted.

She nodded again, let the curtain slip into place, and made her way to her bureau, where she kept her handbag. Her purse in the handbag held very little silver, but she found the half crown she was looking for and took it in her hand. "The Holly and the Ivy" was in full swing outside. Mrs. Fairlands decided that these

children must have been well taught in school. It was not usual for small parties to sing real carols. Two lines of "Come, All Ye Faithful," followed by loud knocking, was much more likely.

As she moved to the door with the half crown in one hand, Mrs. Fairlands put the other to her throat to pull together the folds of her cardigan before leaving her warm room for the cold passage and the outer hall door. She felt her brooch, and instantly misgiving struck her. It was a diamond brooch, a very valuable article, left to her by her mother. It would perhaps be a mistake to appear at the door offering half a crown and flaunting several hundred pounds. They might have seen it already, in the light of the torch they had shone on her.

Mrs. Fairlands slipped the half crown into her cardigan pocket, unfastened the brooch, and, moving quickly to the little Christmas tree on its table, reached up to the top and pinned the brooch to the very center of the silver tinsel star. Then, chuckling at her own cleverness, her quick wit, she went out to the front door just as the bell rang again in her flat. She opened it on a group of fresh young faces and sturdy young bodies standing on her steps.

"I'm sorry I was so slow," she said. "You must forgive me, but I am not very young."

"I'll say," remarked the younger boy, staring. He thought he had never seen anything as old as this old geyser.

"You shut up," said the girl next to him, and the tallest one said, "Don't be rude."

"You sing very nicely," said Mrs. Fairlands. "Very well indeed. Did you learn at school?"

"Mostly at the club," said the older boy, whose voice went up and down, on the verge of breaking, Mrs. Fairlands thought, remembering her brothers.

She held out the half crown. The tallest of the four girls, the one who had the piece of paper with the words of the carols on it, took the coin and smiled.

"I hope I haven't kept you too long," Mrs. Fairlands said. "You can't stay long at each house, can you, or you would never get any money worth having."

"They mostly don't give anything," one of the other girls said.

"Tell us to get the 'ell out," said the irrepressible younger boy.

"We don't do it mostly for the money," said the tallest girl. "Not for ourselves, I mean."

"Give it to the club. Oxfam collection and that," said the tall boy.

"Don't you want it for yourselves?" Mrs. Fairlands was astonished. "Do you have enough pocket money without?"

They nodded gravely.

"I got a paper round," said the older boy.

"I do babysitting now and then," the tallest girl added.

"Well, thank you for coming," Mrs. Fairlands said. She was beginning to feel cold, standing there at the open door. "I must go back into my warm room. And you must keep moving, too, or you might catch colds."

"Thank you," they said in chorus. "Thanks a lot. Bye!"

She shut and locked the door as they turned, clattered down the steps, slammed the gate of the forecourt behind them. She went back to her drawing room. She watched from the window as they piled up the steps of the next house. And again she heard, more faintly because they were farther away, "Once in Royal David's City." There were tears in her old eyes as she left the window and stood for a few minutes staring down at the dull coals of her diminishing fire.

But very soon she rallied, took up the poker, mended her fire, went to her kitchen, and put on the kettle. Coming back to wait for it to boil, she looked again at her Christmas tree. The diamond brooch certainly gave an added distinction to the star, she thought. Amused once more by her originality, she went into her bedroom and from her jewel box on the dressing table took her two other valuable pieces, a pearl necklace and a diamond bracelet. The latter she had not worn for years. She wound each with a tinsel string and hung them among the branches of the tree.

She had just finished preparing her combined tea and supper when the front doorbell rang again. Leaving the tray in the kitchen, she went to her own front door and opened it. Once again a carol floated to her, "Hark, the Herald Angels Sing" this time. There seemed to be only one voice singing. A lone child, she wondered, making the rounds by himself.

She hurried to the window of her drawing room, drew back the curtain, peeped out. No, not alone, but singing a solo. The pure, high boy's voice was louder here. The child, muffled up to the ears, had his head turned away from her towards three companions, whose small figures and pale faces were intent upon the door. They did not seem to notice her at the window as the other group had done, for they did not turn in her direction. They were smaller, evidently younger, very serious. Mrs. Fairlands, touched, willing again to defeat her loneliness in a few minutes' talk, took another half crown from her purse and went out to the main hall and the big door.

"Thank you, children," she said as she opened it. "That was very—"

Her intended praise died in her throat. She gasped, tried to back away. The children now wore black stockings over their faces. Their eyes glittered through slits; there were holes for their noses and mouths.

"That's a very silly joke," said Mrs. Fairlands in a high voice. "I shall not give you the money I brought for you. Go home. Go away."

She backed inside the door, catching at the knob to close it. But the small figures advanced upon her. One of them held the door while two others pushed her away from it. She saw the fourth, the singer, hesitate, then turn and run out into the street.

"Stop this!" Mrs. Fairlands said in a voice that had once been commanding but now broke as she repeated the order. Silently, remorselessly, the three figures forced her back; they shut and locked the main door, they pushed her, stumbling now, terrified, bewildered, through her own front door and into her drawing room.

It was an outrage, an appalling, unheard-of challenge. Mrs. Fairlands had always met a challenge with vigor. She did so now. She tore herself from the grasp of one pair of small hands to box the ears of another short figure. She swept round at the third, pulling the stocking halfway up his face, pushing him violently against the wall so his face met it with a satisfactory smack.

"Stop it!" she panted. "Stop it or I'll call the police!"

At that they all leaped at her, pushing, punching, dragging her to an upright chair. She struggled for a few seconds, but her breath was going. When they had her sitting down, she was incapable of movement. They tied her hands and ankles to the chair and stood back. They began to talk, all at once to start with, but at a gesture from one, the other two became silent.

When Mrs. Fairlands heard the voices, she became rigid with shock and horror. Such words, such phrases, such tones, such evil loose in the world, in her house, in her quiet room. Her face grew cold, she thought she would faint. And still the persistent demand went on.

"We want the money. Where d'you keep it? Come on. Give. Where d'you keep it?"

"At my bank," she gasped.

"That's no answer. Where?"

She directed them to the bureau, where they found and rifled her handbag, taking the three pound notes and five shillings' worth of small change that was all the currency she had in the flat.

Clearly they were astonished at the small amount. They threatened, standing round her, muttering threats and curses.

"I'm *not* rich," she kept repeating. "I live chiefly on the rents of the flats and a very small private income. It's all paid into my bank. I cash a check each week, a small check to cover my food and the wages of my daily help."

"Jewelry," one of them said. "You got jewelry. Rich old cows dolled up—we seen 'em. That's why we come. You got it. Give."

She rallied a little, told them where to find her poor trinkets. Across the room her diamond brooch winked discreetly in the firelight. They were too stupid, too savage, too—horrible to think of searching the room carefully. Let them take the beads, the dress jewelry, the amber pendant. She leaned her aching head against the hard back of the chair and closed her eyes.

After what seemed a long time they came back. Their tempers were not improved. They grumbled among themselves—almost quarreling—in loud harsh tones.

"Radio's worth nil. Prehistoric. No transistor. No record player. Might lift that old clock."

"Money stashed away. Mean old bitch."

"Best get going."

Mrs. Fairlands, eyes still closed, heard a faint sound outside the window. Her doorbell rang once. More carol singers? If they knew, they could save her. If they knew—

She began to scream. She meant to scream loudly, but the noise that came from her was a feeble croak. In her own head it was a scream. To her tormentors it was derisory, but still a challenge. They refused to be challenged.

They gagged her with a strip of sticking plaster, they pulled out the flex of her telephone. They bundled the few valuables they had collected into the large pockets of their overcoats and left the flat, pulling shut the two front doors as they went. Mrs. Fairlands was alone again, but gagged and bound and quite unable to free herself.

At first she felt a profound relief in the silence, the emptiness of the room. The horror had gone, and though she was uncomfortable, she was not yet in pain. They had left the light on—all the lights, she decided. She could see through the open door of the room the lighted passage and, beyond, a streak of light from her bedroom. Had they been in the kitchen? Taken her Christmas dinner, perhaps, the chicken her daily had cooked for her? She remembered her supper and realized fully, for the first time, that she could not open her mouth and that she could not free her hands.

Even now she refused to give way to panic.

She decided to rest until her strength came back and she could, by exercising it, loosen her bonds. But her strength did not come back. It ebbed as the night advanced and the fire died and the room grew cold and colder. For the first time she regretted not accepting May's suggestion that she should spend Christmas with her, occupying the flat above in place of Dorothy. Between them they could have defeated those little monsters. Or she could herself have gone to Leatherhead. She was insured for burglary.

She regretted those things that might have saved her, but she did not regret the gamble of refusing them. She recognized now that the gamble was lost. It had to be lost in the end, but she would have chosen a more dignified finish than this would be.

She cried a little in her weakness and the pain she now suffered in her wrists and ankles and back. But the tears ran down her nose and blocked it, which stopped her breathing and made her choke. She stopped crying, resigned herself, prayed a little, considered one or two sins she had never forgotten but on whose account she had never felt remorse until now. Later on she lapsed into semiconsciousness, a half-dream world of past scenes and present cares, of her mother, resplendent in low-cut green chiffon and diamonds, the diamond brooch and bracelet now decorating the tree across the room. Of Bobbie, in a fever, plagued by itching spots, of Dorothy as a little girl, blotched with measles.

Towards morning, unable any longer to breathe properly, exhausted by pain, hunger, and cold, Mrs. Fairlands died.

The milkman came along the road early on Christmas morning, anxious to finish his round and get back to his family. At Mrs. Fairlands's door he stopped. There were no milk bottles standing outside and no notice. He had seen her in person the day before when she had explained that her daughter and family were not coming this year so she would only need her usual pint that day.

"But I'll put out the bottles and the ticket for tomorrow as usual," she had said.

"You wouldn't like to order now, madam?" he had asked, thinking it would save her trouble.

"No, thank you," she had answered. "I prefer to decide in the evening, when I see what milk I have left."

But there were no bottles and no ticket and she was a very, very old lady and had had this disappointment over her family not coming.

The milkman looked at the door and then at the windows. It was still dark, and the light shone clearly behind the closed curtains. He had seen it when he went in through the gate but had thought nothing of it, being intent on his job. Besides, there were lights on in a good many houses and the squeals of delighted children finding Christmas stockings bulging on the posts of their beds. But here, he reminded himself, there were no children.

He tapped on the window and listened. There was no movement in the house. Perhaps she'd forgotten, being practically senile. He left a pint bottle on the doorstep. But passing a constable on a scooter at the end of the road, he stopped to signal to him and told him about Mrs. Fairlands. "Know 'oo I mean?" he asked.

The constable nodded and thanked the milkman. No harm in making sure. He was pretty well browned off—nothing doing—empty streets—not a hooligan in sight—layabouts mostly drunk in the cells after last night's parties—villains all at the holiday resorts, casing jobs.

He left the scooter at the curb and tried to rouse Mrs. Fairlands. He did not succeed, so his anxiety grew. All the lights were on in the flat, front and back as far as he could make out. All her lights. The other flats were in total darkness. People away. She must have had a stroke or actually croaked, he thought. He rode on to the nearest telephone box.

The local police station sent a sergeant and another constable to join the man on the beat. Together they managed to open the kitchen window at the back, and when they saw the tray with a meal prepared but untouched, one of them climbed in. He found Mrs. Fairlands as the thieves had left her. There was no doubt at all what had happened.

"Ambulance," said the sergeant briefly. "Get the super first, though. We'll be wanting the whole works."

"The phone's gone," the constable said. "Pulled out."

"Bastard! Leave her like this when she couldn't phone anyway and wouldn't be up to leaving the house till he'd had plenty time to make six getaways. Bloody bastard!"

"Wonder how much he got?"

"Damn all, I should think. They don't keep their savings in the mattress up this way."

The constable on the scooter rode off to report, and before long, routine investigations were well under way. The doctor discovered no outward injuries and decided that death was probably due to shock, cold, and exhaustion, taking into account the victim's obviously advanced age. Detective-Inspector Brooks of the divisional CID found plenty of papers in the bureau to give him all the information he needed about Mrs. Fairlands's financial position, her recent activities, and her nearest relations. Leaving the sergeant in charge at the flat while the experts in the various branches were at work, he went back to the local station to get in touch with Mrs. Fairlands's daughter, Dorothy Evans.

In Devonshire the news was received with horror, indignation, and remorse. In trying to do the best for her mother by not exposing her to possible infection, Mrs. Evans felt she had brought about her death.

"You can't think of it like that," her husband Hugh protested, trying to stem the bitter tears. "If she'd come down, she might have had an accident on the way or got pneumonia or something. Quite apart from shingles."

"But she was all alone! That's what's so frightful!"

"And it wasn't your fault. She could have had what's-her-name—Miss Bolton, the old girl who lives at Leatherhead."

"I thought May Bolton was going to have *her*.

But you couldn't make Mother do a thing she hadn't thought of herself."

"Again, that wasn't your fault, was it?"

It occurred to him that his wife had inherited to some extent this characteristic of his mother-in-law, but this was no time to remind her of it.

"You'll go up at once, I suppose?" he said when she was a little calmer.

"How can I?" The tears began to fall again. "Christmas Day and Bobbie's temperature still up and his spots itching like mad. Could *you* cope with all that?"

"I'd try," he said. "You know I'd do anything."

"Of course you would, darling." She was genuinely grateful for the happiness of her married life and at this moment of self-reproach prepared to give him most of the credit for it. "Honestly, I don't think I could face it. There'd be identification, wouldn't there? And hearing detail—" She shuddered, covering her face.

"Okay. I'll go up," Hugh told her. He really preferred this arrangement. "I'll take the car in to Exeter and get the first through train there is. It's very early. Apparently her milkman made the discovery."

So Hugh Evans reached the flat in the early afternoon to find a constable on duty at the door and the house locked up. He was directed to the police station, where Inspector Brooks was waiting for him.

"My wife was too upset to come alone," he explained, "and we couldn't leave the family on their own. They've all got chicken pox; the youngest's quite bad with it today."

He went on to explain all the reasons why Mrs. Fairlands had been alone in the flat.

"Quite," said Brooks, who had a difficult mother-in-law himself and was inclined to be sympathetic. "Quite. Nothing to stop her going to an hotel here in London over the holiday, was there?"

"Nothing at all. She could easily afford it. She isn't—wasn't—what you call rich, but she'd reached the age when she really *couldn't* spend much."

This led to a full description of Mrs. Fairlands's circumstances, which finished with Hugh pulling out a list, hastily written by Dorothy before he left home, of all the valuables she could remember that were still in Mrs. Fairlands's possession.

"Jewelry," said the inspector thoughtfully. "Now where would she keep that?"

"Doesn't it say? In her bedroom, I believe."

"Oh, yes. A jewel box, containing—yes. Well, Mr. Evans, there was no jewel box in the flat when we searched it."

"Obviously the thief took it, then. About the only thing worth taking. She wouldn't have much cash there. She took it from the bank in weekly amounts. I know that."

There was very little more help he could give, so Inspector Brooks took him to the mortuary where Mrs. Fairlands now lay. And after the identification, which Hugh found pitiable but not otherwise distressing, they went together to the flat.

"In case you can help us to note any more objects of value you find are missing," Brooks explained.

The rooms were in the same state in which they had been found. Hugh found this more shocking, more disturbing, than the colorless, peaceful face of the very old woman who had never been close to him, who had never shown a warm affection for any of them, though with her unusual vitality she must in her youth have been capable of passion.

He went from room to room and back again. He stopped beside the bureau. "I was thinking, on the way up," he said diffidently. "Her solicitor—that sort of thing. Insurances. I ought— can I have a look through this lot?"

"Of course, sir," Inspector Brooks answered politely. "I've had a look myself. You see, we aren't quite clear about motive."

"Not— But wasn't it a burglar? A brutal, thieving thug?"

"There is no sign whatever of breaking and entering. It appears that Mrs. Fairlands let the murderer in herself."

"But that's impossible."

"Is it? An old lady, feeling lonely perhaps. The doorbell rings. She thinks a friend has called to visit her. She goes and opens it. It's always happening."

"Yes. Yes, of course. It could have happened that way. Or a tramp asking for money—Christmas—"

"Tramps don't usually leave it as late as Christmas Eve. Generally smash a window and get put inside a day or two earlier."

"What worries you, then?"

"Just in case she had someone after her. Poor relation. Anyone who had it in for her, if she knew something damaging about him. Faked the burglary."

"But he seems to have taken her jewel box, and according to my wife, it was worth taking."

"Quite. We shall want a full description of the pieces, sir."

"She'll make it out for you. Or it may have been insured separately."

"I'm afraid not. Go ahead, though, Mr. Evans. I'll send my sergeant in, and he'll bring you back to the station with any essential papers you need for Mrs. Fairlands's solicitor."

Hugh worked at the papers for half an hour and then decided he had all the information he wanted. No steps of any kind need, or indeed could, be taken until the day after tomorrow, he knew. The solicitor could not begin to wind up Mrs. Fairlands's affairs for some time. Even the date of the inquest had not been fixed and would probably have to be adjourned.

Before leaving the flat, Hugh looked round the rooms once more, taking the sergeant with him. They paused before the mantelpiece, untouched by the thieves, a poignant reminder of the life so abruptly ended. Hugh looked at the cards and then glanced at the Christmas tree.

"Poor old thing!" he said. "We never thought she'd go like this. We ought all to have been here today. She always decorated a tree for us—" He broke off, genuinely moved for the first time.

"So I understand," the sergeant said gruffly, sharing the wave of sentiment.

"My wife—I wonder— D'you think it'd be in order to get rid of it?"

"The tree, sir?"

"Yes. Put it out at the back somewhere. Less upsetting—Mrs. Evans will be coming up the day after tomorrow. By that time the dustmen may have called."

"I understand. I don't see any harm—"

"Right."

Hurrying, in case the sergeant should change his mind, Hugh took up the bowl, and turning his face away to spare it from being pricked by the pine needles, he carried it out to the back of the house where he stood it beside the row of three dustbins. At any rate, he thought, going back to join the sergeant, Dorothy would be spared the feelings that overcame him so unexpectedly.

He was not altogether right in this. Mrs. Evans traveled to London on the day after Boxing Day. The inquest opened on this day, with a jury. Evidence was given of the finding of the body. Medical evidence gave the cause of death as cold and exhaustion and bronchial edema from partial suffocation by a plaster gag. The verdict was murder by a person or persons unknown.

After the inquest, Mrs. Fairlands's solicitor, who had supported Mrs. Evans during the ordeal in court, went with her to the flat. They arrived just as the municipal dust cart was beginning to move away. One of the older dustmen came up to them.

"You for the old lady they did Christmas Eve?" he asked, with some hesitation.

"I'm her daughter," Dorothy said, her eyes filling again, as they still did all too readily.

"What d'you want?" asked the solicitor, who was anxious to get back to his office.

"No offense," said the man, ignoring him and keeping his eyes on Dorothy's face. "It's like this 'ere, see. They put a Christmas tree outside, by the bins, see. Decorated. We didn't like to take it, seeing it's not exactly rubbish and her gone and that. Nobody about we could ask—"

Dorothy understood. The Christmas tree. Hugh's doing, obviously. Sweet of him.

"Of course you must have it, if it's any use to you now, so late. Have you got children?"

"Three, ma'am. Two younguns. I arsked the other chaps. They don't want it. They said to leave it."

"No, you take it," Dorothy told him. "I don't want to see it. I don't want to be reminded—"

"Thanks a lot, dear," the dustman said, gravely sympathetic, walking back round the house.

The solicitor took the door key from Dorothy and let her in, so she did not see the tree as the dustman emerged with it held carefully before him.

In his home that evening the tree was greeted with a mixture of joy and derision.

"As if I 'adn't enough to clear up yesterday and the day before," his wife complained, half angry, half laughing. "Where'd you get it, anyway?"

When he had finished telling her, the two children, who had listened, crept away to play with the new glittering toy. And before long Mavis, the youngest, found the brooch pinned to the star. She unfastened it carefully and held it in her hand, turning it this way and that to catch the light.

But not for long. Her brother Ernie, two years older, soon snatched it. Mavis went for him, and he ran, making for the front door to escape into the street where Mavis was forbidden to play. Though she seldom obeyed the rule, on this occasion she used it to make loud protest, setting up a howl that brought her mother to the door of the kitchen.

But Ernie had not escaped with his prize. His elder brother Ron was on the point of entering, and when Ernie flung wide the door, Ron pushed in, shoving his little brother back.

"'E's nicked my star," Mavis wailed. "Make 'im give me back, Ron. It's mine. Off the tree."

Ron took Ernie by the back of his collar and swung him round.

"Give!" he said firmly. Ernie clenched his

right fist, betraying himself. Ron took his arm, bent his hand over forwards, and, as the brooch fell to the floor, stooped to pick it up. Ernie was now in tears.

"Where'd 'e get it?" Ron asked over the child's doubled-up, weeping form.

"The tree," Mavis repeated. "*I* found it. On the star—on the tree."

"Wot the 'ell d'she mean?" Ron asked, exasperated.

"Shut up, the lot of you!" their mother cried fiercely from the kitchen where she had retreated. "Ron, come on in to your tea. Late as usual. Why you never—"

"Okay, Mum," the boy said, unrepentant. "I never—"

He sat down, looking at the sparkling object in his hand.

"What'd Mavis mean about a tree?"

"Christmas tree. Dad brought it in. I've a good mind to put it on the fire. Nothing but argument since 'e fetched it."

"It's pretty," Ron said, meaning the brooch in his hand. "Dress jewelry, they calls it." He slipped it into his pocket.

"That's mine," Mavis insisted. "I found it pinned on that star on the tree. You give it back, Ron."

"Leave 'im alone," their mother said, smacking away the reaching hands. "Go and play with your blasted tree. Dad didn't ought t'ave brought it. Ought t'ave 'ad more sense—"

Ron sat quietly, eating his kipper and drinking his tea. When he had finished, he stacked his crockery in the sink, went upstairs, changed his shirt, put a pair of shiny dancing shoes in the pockets of his mackintosh, and went off to the club where his current girlfriend, Sally, fifteen like himself, attending the same comprehensive school, was waiting for him.

"You're late," she said over her shoulder, not leaving the group of her girlfriends.

"I've 'eard that before tonight. Mum was creating. Not my fault if Mr. Pope wants to see me about exam papers."

"You're never taking G.C.E.?"

"Why not?"

"Coo! 'Oo started that lark?"

"Mr. Pope. I just told you. D'you want to dance or don't you?"

She did and she knew Ron was not one to wait indefinitely. So she joined him, and together they went to the main hall where dancing was in progress, with a band formed by club members.

"'Alf a mo!" Ron said as they reached the door. "I got something you'll like."

He produced the brooch.

Sally was delighted. This was no cheap store piece. It was slap-up dress jewelry, like the things you saw in the West End, in Bond Street, in the Burlington Arcade, even. She told him she'd wear it just below her left shoulder near the neck edge of her dress. When they moved on to the dance floor she was holding her head higher and swinging her hips more than ever before. She and Ron danced well together. That night many couples stood still to watch them.

About an hour later the dancing came to a sudden end with a sound of breaking glass and shouting that grew in volume and ferocity.

"Raid!" yelled the boys on the dance floor, deserting their partners and crowding to the door. "Those bloody Wingers again."

The sounds of battle led them, running swiftly, to the table tennis and billiards room, where a shambles confronted them. Overturned tables, ripped cloth, broken glass were everywhere. Tall youths and younger lads were fighting indiscriminately. Above the din the club warden and the three voluntary workers, two of them women, raised their voices in appeal and admonishment, equally ignored. The young barrister who attended once a week to give legal advice free, as a form of social service, to those who asked for it plunged into the battle, only to be flung out again nursing a twisted arm. It was the club caretaker, old and experienced in gang warfare, who summoned the police. They arrived silently, snatched ringleaders with expert knowledge or recognition, hemmed in their captives while the battle melted, and waited while their colleagues, posted at the doors of the club, turned back all would-be escapers.

Before long complete order was restored. In the dance hall the line of prisoners stood below the platform where the band had played. They included club members as well as strangers. The rest, cowed, bunched together near the door, also included a few strangers. Murmurings against these soon added them to the row of captives.

"Now," said the sergeant, who had arrived in answer to the call, "Mr. Smith will tell me who belongs here and who doesn't."

The goats were quickly separated from the rather black sheep.

"Next, who was playing table tennis when the raid commenced?"

Six hands shot up from the line. Some disheveled girls near the door also held up their hands.

"The rest were in here dancing," the warden said. "The boys left the girls when they heard the row, I think."

"That's right," Ron said boldly. "We 'eard glass going, and we guessed it was them buggers. They been 'ere before."

"They don't learn," said the sergeant with a baleful glance at the goats, who shuffled their feet and looked sulky.

"You'll be charged at the station," the sergeant went on, "and I'll want statements from some of your lads," he told the warden. "Also from you and your assistants. These other kids can all go home. Quietly, mind," he said, raising his voice. "Show us there's some of you can behave like reasonable adults and not childish savages."

Sally ran forward to Ron as he left the row under the platform. He took her hand as they walked towards the door. But the sergeant had seen something that surprised him. He made a signal over their heads. At the door they were stopped.

"I think you're wanted. Stand aside for a minute," the constable told them.

The sergeant was the one who had been at the flat in the first part of the Fairlands case. He had been there when a second detailed examination of the flat was made in case the missing jewelry had been hidden away and had therefore escaped the thief. He had formed a very clear picture in his mind of what he was looking for from Mrs. Evans's description. As Sally passed him on her way to the door with Ron, part of the picture presented itself to his astonished eyes.

He turned to the warden.

"That pair. Can I have a word with them somewhere private?"

"Who? Ron Sharp and Sally Biggs? Two of our very nicest—"

The two were within earshot. They exchanged a look of amusement instantly damped by the sergeant, who ordered them briefly to follow him. In the warden's office, with the door shut, he said to Sally, "Where did you get that brooch you're wearing?"

The girl flushed. Ron said angrily, "I give it 'er. So what?"

"So where did you come by it?"

Ron hesitated. He didn't want to let himself down in Sally's eyes. He wanted her to think he'd bought it specially for her. He said, aggressively, "That's my business."

"I don't think so." Turning to Sally, the sergeant said, "Would you mind letting me have a look at it, miss?"

The girl was becoming frightened. Surely Ron hadn't done anything silly? He was looking upset. Perhaps—

"All right," she said, undoing the brooch and handing it over. "Poor eyesight, I suppose."

It was feeble defiance, and the sergeant ignored it. He said, "I'll have to ask you two to come down to the station. I'm not an expert, but we shall have to know a great deal more about this article, and Inspector Brooks will be particularly interested to know where it came from."

Ron remaining obstinately silent in spite of Sally's entreaty, the two found themselves presently sitting opposite Inspector Brooks, with the brooch lying on a piece of white paper before them.

"This brooch," said the inspector sternly,

"is one piece of jewelry listed as missing from the flat of a Mrs. Fairlands, who was robbed and murdered on Christmas Eve or early Christmas Day."

"*Never!*" whispered Sally, aghast.

Ron said nothing. He was not a stupid boy, and he realized at once that he must now speak, whatever Sally thought of him. Also that he had a good case if he didn't say too much. So, after careful thought, he told Brooks exactly how and when he had come by the brooch and advised him to check this with his father and mother. The old lady's son had stuck the tree out by the dustbins, his mother had said, and her daughter had told his father he could have it to take home.

Inspector Brooks found the tale too fantastic to be untrue. Taking the brooch and the two subdued youngsters with him, he went to Ron's home, where more surprises awaited him. After listening to Mr. Sharp's account of the Christmas tree, which exactly tallied with Ron's, he went into the next room where the younger children were playing and Mrs. Sharp was placidly watching television.

"Which of you two found the brooch?" Brooks asked. The little girl was persuaded to agree that she had done so.

"But I got these," the boy said. He dived into his pocket and dragged out the pearl necklace and the diamond bracelet.

"'Struth!" said the inspector, overcome. "She must've been balmy."

"No, she wasn't," Sally broke in. "She was nice. She give us two and a tanner."

"She *what*?"

Sally explained the carol singing expedition. They had been up four roads in that part, she said, and only two nicker the lot.

"Mostly it was nil," she said. "Then there was some give a bob and this old gentleman and the woman with 'im ten bob each. We packed it in after that."

"This means you actually went to Mrs. Fairlands's house?" Brooks said sternly to Ron.

"With the others—yes."

"Did you go inside?"

"No."

"No." Sally supported him. "She come out."

"Was she wearing the brooch?"

"No," said Ron.

"Not when she come out, she wasn't," Sally corrected him.

Ron kicked her ankle gently. The inspector noticed this.

"When did you see it?" he asked Sally.

"When she looked through the window at us. We shone the torch on 'er. It didn't 'alf shine."

"But you didn't recognize it when Ron gave it to you?"

"Why should I? I never saw it close. It was pinned on 'er dress at the neck. I didn't think of it till you said."

Brooks nodded. This seemed fair enough. He turned to face Ron.

"So you went back alone later to get it? Right?"

"I never! It's a damned lie!" the boy cried fiercely.

Mr. Sharp took a step forward. His wife bundled the younger children out of the room. Sally began to cry.

"'Oo are you accusing?" Mr. Sharp said heavily. "You 'eard 'ow I come by the tree. My mates was there. The things was on it. I got witnesses. If Ron did that job, would 'e leave the only things worth 'aving? It says in the paper nothing of value, don't it?"

Brooks realized the force of this argument, however badly put. He'd been carried away a little. Unusual for him; he was surprised at himself. But the murder had been a particularly revolting one, and until these jewels turned up, he'd had no idea where to look. Carol singers. It might be a line and then again it mightn't.

He took careful statements from Ron, Sally, Ron's father, and the two younger children. He took the other pieces of jewelry and the Christmas tree. Carol singers. Mrs. Fairlands had opened the door to Ron's lot, having taken off her brooch if the story was true. Having hidden it very cleverly. He and his men had missed it completely. A Christmas tree decorated with flashy bits and pieces as usual. Standing back against a wall. They'd ignored it. Seen nothing but tinsel and glitter for weeks past. Of course they hadn't noticed it. The real thief or thieves hadn't noticed it, either.

Back at the station he locked away the jewels, labeled, in the safe and rang up Hugh Evans. He did not tell him where the pieces had been found.

Afterwards he had to deal with some of the hooligans who had now been charged with breaking, entering, willful damage, and making an affray. He wished he could pin Mrs. Fairlands's murder on their ringleader, a most degenerate and evil youth. Unfortunately, the whole gang had been in trouble in the West End that night; most of them had spent what remained of it in Bow Street police station. So they were out. But routine investigations now had a definite aim. To collect a list of all those who had sung carols at the houses on Mrs. Fairlands's road on Christmas Eve, to question the singers about the times they had appeared there and about the houses they had visited.

It was not easy. Carol singers came from many social groups and often traveled far from their own homes. The youth clubs in the district were helpful; so were the various student bodies and hostels in the neighborhood. Brooks's manor was wide and very variously populated. In four days he had made no headway at all.

A radio message went out, appealing to carol singers to report at the police station if they were near Mrs. Fairlands's house at any time on Christmas Eve. The press took up the quest, dwelling on the pathetic aspects of the old woman's tragic death at a time of traditional peace on earth and goodwill towards men. All right-minded citizens must want to help the law over this revolting crime.

But the citizens maintained their attitude of apathy or caution.

Except for one, a freelance journalist, Tom Meadows, who had an easy manner with young people because he liked them. He became interested because the case seemed to involve young people. It was just up his street. So he went first to the Sharp family, gained their complete confidence, and had a long talk with Ron.

The boy was willing to help. After he had got over his indignation with the law for daring to suspect him, he had had sense enough to see how this had been inevitable. His anger was directed more truly at the unknown thugs responsible. He remembered Mrs. Fairlands with respect and pity. He was ready to do anything Tom Meadows suggested.

The journalist was convinced that the criminal or criminals must be local, with local knowledge. It was unlikely they would wander from house to house, taking a chance on finding one that might be profitable. It was far more likely that they knew already that Mrs. Fairlands lived alone, would be quite alone over Christmas and therefore defenseless. But their information had been incomplete. They had not known how little money she kept at the flat. No one had known this except her family. Or had they?

Meadows, patient and amiable, worked his way from the Sharps to the postman, the milkman, and through the latter to the daily.

"Well, of course I mentioned 'er being alone for the 'oliday. I told that detective so. In the way of conversation, I told 'im. Why shouldn't I?"

"Why indeed? But who did you tell, exactly?"

"I disremember. Anyone, I suppose. If we was comparing. I'm on me own now meself, but I go up to me brother's at the 'olidays."

"Where would that be?"

"Notting 'Ill way. 'E's on the railway. Paddington."

Bit by bit Meadows extracted a list of her friends and relations, those with whom she had talked most often during the week before Christmas. Among her various nephews and nieces was a girl who went to the same comprehensive school as Ron and his girlfriend Sally.

Ron listened to the assignment Meadows gave him.

"Sally won't like it," he said candidly.

"Bring her into it, then. Pretend it's all your own idea."

Ron grinned.

"Shirl won't like that," he said.

Tom Meadows laughed.

"Fix it any way you like," he said. "But I think this girl Shirley was with a group and did go to sing carols for Mrs. Fairlands. I know she isn't on the official list, so she hasn't reported it. I want to know why."

"I'm not shopping anymore," Ron said warily.

"I'm not asking you to. I don't imagine Shirley or her friends did Mrs. Fairlands. But it's just possible she knows or saw something and is afraid to speak up for fear of reprisals."

"Cor!" said Ron. It was like a page of his favorite magazine working out in real life. He confided in Sally, and they went to work.

The upshot was interesting. Shirley did have something to say, and she said it to Tom Meadows in her own home with her disapproving mother sitting beside her.

"I never did like the idea of Shirl going out after dark, begging at house doors. That's all it really is, isn't it? My children have very good pocket money. They've nothing to complain of."

"I'm sure they haven't," Meadows said mildly. "But there's a lot more to carol singing than asking for money. Isn't there, Shirley?"

"I'll say," the girl answered. "Mum don't understand."

"You can't stop her," the mother complained. "Self-willed. Stubborn. I don't know, I'm sure. Out after dark. My dad'd've taken his belt to me for less."

"There were four of us," Shirley protested. "It wasn't late. Not above seven or eight."

The time was right, Meadows noted, if she was speaking of her visit to Mrs. Fairlands's road. She was. Encouraged to describe everything, she agreed that her group was working towards the house especially to entertain the old lady who was going to be alone for Christmas. She'd got that from her aunt, who worked for Mrs. Fairlands. They began at the far end of the road on the same side as the old lady. When they were about six houses away, they saw an-

other group go up to it or to one near it. Then they were singing themselves. The next time she looked round, she saw one child running away up the road. She did not know where he had come from. She did not see the others.

"You did not see them go on?"

"No. They weren't in the road then, but they might have gone right on while we were singing. There's a turning off, isn't there?"

"Yes. Go on."

"Well, we went up to Mrs. Fairlands's and rang the bell. I thought I'd tell her she knew my aunt and we'd come special."

"Yes. What happened?"

"Nothing. At least—"

"Go on. Don't be frightened."

Shirley's face had gone very pale.

"There were men's voices inside. Arguing like. Nasty. We scarpered."

Tom Meadows nodded gravely.

"That would be upsetting. *Men's* voices? Or big boys?"

"Could be either, couldn't it? Well, perhaps more like sixth form boys, at that."

"You thought it was boys, didn't you? Boys from your school."

Shirley was silent.

"You thought they'd know and have it in for you if you told. Didn't you? I won't let you down, Shirley. Didn't you?"

She whispered, "Yes," and added, "Some of our boys got knives. I seen them."

Meadows went to Inspector Brooks. He explained how Ron had helped him to get in touch with Shirley and the result of that interview. The inspector, who had worked as a routine matter on all Mrs. Fairlands's contacts with the outer world, was too interested to feel annoyed at the other's success.

"Men's voices?" Brooks said incredulously.

"Most probably older lads," Meadows answered. "She agreed that was what frightened her group. They might have looked out and recognized them as they ran away."

"There'd been no attempt at intimidations?"

"They're not all *that* stupid."

"No."

Brooks considered.

"This mustn't break in the papers yet, you understand?"

"Perfectly. But I shall stay around."

Inspector Brooks nodded, and Tom went away. Brooks took his sergeant and drove to Mrs. Fairlands's house. They still had the key of the flat, and they still had the house under observation.

The new information was disturbing, Brooks felt. Men's voices, raised in anger. Against poor Mrs. Fairlands, of course. But there were no adult fingerprints in the flat except those of the old lady herself and of her daily. Gloves had been worn, then. A professional job. But no signs whatever of breaking and entering. Therefore, Mrs. Fairlands had let them in. Why? She had peeped out at Ron's lot, to check who they were, obviously. She had not done so for Shirley's. Because she was in the power of the "men" whose voices had driven this other group away in terror.

But there had been two distinct small footprints in the dust of the outer hall and a palmprint on the outer door had been small, childsize.

Perhaps the child that Shirley had seen running down the road had been a decoy. The whole group she had noticed at Mrs. Fairlands's door might have been employed for that purpose and the men or older boys were lurking at the corner of the house, to pounce when the door opened. Possible, but not very likely. Far too risky, even on a dark evening. Shirley could not have seen distinctly. The streetlamps were at longish intervals in that road. But there were always a few passersby. Even on Christmas Eve no professional group of villains would take such a risk.

Standing in the cold drawing room, now covered with a grey film of dust, Inspector Brooks decided to make another careful search for clues. He had missed the jewels. Though he felt justified in making it, his mistake was a distinct blot on his copybook. It was up to him now to retrieve his reputation. He sent the sergeant to take another look at the bedroom, with particular attention to the dressing table. He himself began to go over the drawing room with the greatest possible care.

Shirley's evidence suggested there had been more than one thief. The girl had said "voices." That meant at least two, which probably accounted for the fact, apart from her age, that neither Mrs. Fairlands nor her clothes gave any indication of a struggle. She had been overpowered immediately, it seemed. She had not been strong enough or agile enough to tear, scratch, pull off any fragment from her attackers' clothes or persons. There had been no trace of any useful material under her fingernails or elsewhere.

Brooks began methodically with the chair to which Mrs. Fairlands had been bound and worked his way outwards from that center. After the furniture, the carpet and curtains. After that the walls.

Near the door, opposite the fireplace, he found on the wall—two feet, three inches up from the floor—a small, round, brownish, greasy smear. He had not seen it before. In artificial light, he checked, it was nearly invisible. On this morning, with the first sunshine of the New Year coming into the room, the little patch was entirely obvious, slightly shiny where the light from the window caught it.

Inspector Brooks took a wooden spatula from his case of aids and carefully scraped off the substance into a small plastic box, sniffing at it as he did so.

"May I, too?" asked Tom Meadows behind him.

The inspector wheeled round with an angry exclamation.

"How did you get in?" he asked.

"Told the copper in your car I wanted to speak to you."

"What about?"

"Well, about how you were getting on, really," Tom said disarmingly. "I see you are. Please let me have one sniff."

Inspector Brooks was annoyed, both by the intrusion and the fact that he had not heard it, being so concentrated on his work. So he closed his box, shut it into his black bag, and called to the sergeant in the next room.

Meadows got down on his knees, leaned towards the wall, and sniffed. It was faint, since most of it had been scraped off, but he knew the smell. His freelancing had not been confined to journalism.

He was getting to his feet as the sergeant joined Inspector Brooks. The sergeant raised his eyebrows at the interloper.

"You can't keep the press's noses out of anything," said Brooks morosely.

The other two grinned. It was very apt.

"I'm just off," Tom said. "Good luck with your specimen, Inspector. I know where to go now. So will you."

"Come back!" called Brooks. The young man was a menace. He would have to be controlled.

But Meadows was away, striding down the road until he was out of sight of the police car, then running to the nearest tube station, where he knew he would find the latest newspaper editions. He bought one, opened it at the entertainments column, and read down the list.

He was a certain six hours ahead of Brooks, he felt sure, possibly more. Probably he had until tomorrow morning. He skipped his lunch and set to work.

Inspector Brooks got the report from the lab that evening, and the answer to his problem came to him as completely as it had done to Tom Meadows in Mrs. Fairlands's drawing room. His first action was to ring up Olympia. This proving fruitless, he sighed. Too late now to contact the big stores; they would all be closed and the employees of every kind gone home.

But in the morning some very extensive telephone calls to managers told him where he must go. He organized his forces to cover all the exits of a big store not very far from Mrs. Fairlands's house. With his sergeant he entered modestly by way of the men's department.

They took a lift from there to the third floor, emerging among the toys. It was the tenth day of Christmas, with the school holidays in full swing and eager children, flush with Christmas money, choosing long-coveted treasures. A Father Christmas, white-bearded, in the usual red, hooded gown, rather too short for him, was moving about trying to promote a visit to the first of that day's performances of "Snowdrop and the Seven Dwarfs." As his insistence seeped into the minds of the abstracted young, they turned their heads to look at the attractive cardboard entrance of the little "theater" at the far end of the department. A gentle flow towards it began and gathered momentum. Inspector Brooks and the sergeant joined the stream.

Inside the theater there were small chairs in rows for the children. The grownups stood at the back. A gramophone played the Disney film music.

The early scenes were brief, mere tableaux with a line thrown in here and there for Snowdrop. The queen spoke the famous doggerel to her mirror.

The curtain fell and rose again on Snowdrop, surrounded by the Seven Dwarfs. Two of them had beards, real beards. Dopey rose to his feet and began to sing.

"Okay," whispered Brooks to the sergeant. "The child who sang and ran away."

The sergeant nodded. Brooks whispered again. "I'm going round the back. Get the audience here out quietly if the balloon goes up before they finish."

He tiptoed quietly away. He intended to catch the dwarfs in their dressing room immediately after the show, arrest the lot, and sort them out at the police station.

But the guilty ones had seen him move. Or rather Dopey, more guilt-laden and fearful than the rest, had noticed the two men who seemed to have no children with them, had seen their heads close together, had seen one move silently away. As Brooks disappeared, the midget's nerve broke. His song ended in a scream; he fled from the stage.

In the uproar that followed, the dwarf's scream was echoed by the frightened children. The lights went up in the theater, the shop assistants and the sergeant went into action to subdue their panic and get them out.

Inspector Brooks found himself in a maze of lathe and plaster backstage arrangements. He found three bewildered small figures, with anxious, wizened faces, trying to restrain Dopey, who was still in the grip of his hysteria. A few sharp questions proved that the three had no idea what was happening.

The queen and Snowdrop appeared, highly indignant. Brooks, now holding Dopey firmly by the collar, demanded the other three dwarfs. The two girls, subdued and totally bewildered, pointed to their dressing room. It was empty, but a tumbled heap of costumes on the floor showed what they had done. The sergeant appeared, breathless.

"Take this chap," Brooks said, thrusting the now fainting Dopey at him. "Take him down. I'm shopping him. Get on to the management to warn all departments for the others."

He was gone, darting into the crowded toy department, where children and parents stood amazed or hurried towards the lifts, where a dense crowd stood huddled, anxious to leave the frightening trouble spot.

Brooks bawled an order.

The crowd at the lift melted away from it, leaving three small figures in overcoats and felt hats, trying in vain to push once more under cover.

They bolted, bunched together, but they did not get far. Round the corner of a piled table of soft toys Father Christmas was waiting. He leaped forward, tripped up one, snatched another, hit the third as he passed and grabbed him, too, as he fell.

The tripped one struggled up and on as Brooks appeared.

"I'll hold these two," panted Tom Meadows

through his white beard, which had fallen sideways.

The chase was brief. Brooks gained on the dwarf. The latter knew it was hopeless. He snatched up a mallet lying beside a display of camping equipment and, rushing to the side of the store, leaped on a counter, from there clambered up a tier of shelves, beat a hole in the window behind them, and dived through. Horrified people and police on the pavement below saw the small body turning over and over like a leaf as it fell.

"All yours," said Tom Meadows, handing his captives, too limp now to struggle, to Inspector Brooks and tearing off his Father Christmas costume. "See you later."

He was gone, to shut himself in a telephone booth on the ground floor of the store and hand his favorite editor the scoop. It had paid off, taking over from the old boy, an ex-actor like himself, who was quite willing for a fiver to write a note pleading illness and sending a substitute. "Your reporter, Tom Meadows, dressed as Father Christmas, today captured and handed over to the police two of the three murderers of Mrs. Fairlands—"

Inspector Brooks, with three frantic midgets demanding legal aid, scrabbling at the doors of their cells, took a lengthy statement from the fourth, the one with the treble voice whose nerve had broken on the fatal night, as it had again that day. Greasepaint had betrayed the little fiends, Brooks told him, privately regretting that Meadows had been a jump ahead of him there. Greasepaint left on in the rush to get at their prey. One of the brutes must have fallen against the wall, pushed by the old woman herself perhaps. He hoped so. He hoped it was her own action that had brought these squalid killers to justice.

WAXWORKS
Ethel Lina White

IT IS AN UNFORTUNATE FACT THAT ETHEL LINA WHITE'S
seventeen books are seldom read today, though two motion pictures inspired by
her extremely suspenseful novels are in constant rerun on classic movie channels. *The Spiral Staircase*, directed by Robert Siodmak and starring Dorothy
McGuire and Ethel Barrymore, was released in 1945; it was based on White's
1934 novel *Some Must Watch*. Even more successful was *The Lady Vanishes*,
directed by Alfred Hitchcock and starring Margaret Lockwood, Michael Red-
grave, and Dame May Whitty. Released in 1938, it was inspired by White's 1936
novel *The Wheel Spins*. "Waxworks" was first published in the December 1930
issue of *Pearson's Magazine*.

Waxworks

ETHEL LINA WHITE

SONIA MADE HER FIRST ENTRY IN her notebook:

> Eleven o'clock. The lights are out. The porter has just locked the door. I can hear his footsteps echoing down the corridor. They grow fainter. Now there is silence. I am alone.

She stopped writing to glance at her company. Seen in the light from the streetlamp, which streamed in through the high window, the room seemed to be full of people. Their faces were those of men and women of character and intelligence. They stood in groups, as though in conversation, or sat apart, in solitary reverie.

But they neither moved nor spoke.

When Sonia had last seen them in the glare of the electric globes, they had been a collection of ordinary waxworks, some of which were the worse for wear. The black velvet which lined the walls of the Gallery was alike tawdry and filmed with dust.

The side opposite to the window was built into alcoves, which held highly moral tableaux, depicting contrasting scenes in the career of Vice and Virtue. Sonia had slipped into one of these recesses, just before closing-time, in order to hide for her vigil.

It had been a simple affair. The porter had merely rung his bell, and the few courting-couples who represented the Public had taken his hint and hurried towards the exit.

No one was likely to risk being locked in, for the Waxwork Collection of Oldhampton had lately acquired a sinister reputation. The foundation for this lay in the fate of a stranger to the town—a commercial traveller—who had cut his throat in the Hall of Horrors.

Since then, two persons had, separately, spent the night in the Gallery and, in the morning, each had been found dead.

In both cases the verdict had been "Natural death, due to heart failure." The first victim—a local alderman—had been addicted to alcohol, and was in very bad shape. The second—his great friend—was a delicate little man, a martyr to asthma, and slightly unhinged through unwise absorption in spiritualism.

While the coincidence of the tragedies stirred up a considerable amount of local superstition, the general belief was that both deaths were due to the power of suggestion, in conjunction with macabre surroundings. The victims had let themselves be frightened to death by the Waxworks.

Sonia was there, in the Gallery, to test its truth.

She was the latest addition to the staff of the *Oldhampton Gazette*. Bubbling with enthusiasm, she made no secret of her literary ambitions, and it was difficult to feed her with enough work.

Her colleagues listened to her with mingled amusement and boredom, but they liked her as a refreshing novelty. As for her fine future, they looked to young Wells—the Sporting Editor—to effect her speedy and painless removal from the sphere of journalism.

On Christmas Eve, Sonia took them all into her confidence over her intention to spend a night in the Waxworks, on the last night of the old year.

"Copy there," she declared. "I'm not timid and I have fairly sensitive perceptions, so I ought to be able to write up the effect of imagination on the nervous system. I mean to record my impressions, every hour, while they're piping-hot."

Looking up suddenly, she had surprised a green glare in the eyes of Hubert Poke.

When Sonia came to work on the *Gazette,* she had a secret fear of unwelcome amorous attentions, since she was the only woman on the staff. But the first passion she awoke was hatred.

Poke hated her impersonally, as the representative of a Force, numerically superior to his own sex, which was on the opposing side in the battle for existence. He feared her, too, because she was the unknown element, and possessed the unfair weapon of charm.

Before she came, he had been the star turn on the *Gazette.* His own position on the staff gratified his vanity and entirely satisfied his narrow ambition. But Sonia had stolen some of his thunder. On more than one occasion she had written up a story he had failed to cover, and he had to admit that her success was due to a quicker wit.

For some time past he had been playing with the idea of spending a night in the Waxworks, but was deterred by the knowledge that his brain was not sufficiently temperate for the experiment. Lately he had been subject to sudden red rages, when he had felt a thick hot taste in his throat, as though of blood. He knew that his jealousy of Sonia was accountable. It had almost reached the stage of mania, and trembled on the brink of homicidal urge.

While his brain was still creaking with the idea of first-hand experience in the ill-omened Gallery, Sonia had nipped in with her ready-made plan.

Controlling himself with an effort, he listened while the sub-editor issued a warning to Sonia.

"Bon idea, young woman, but you will find the experience a bit raw. You've no notion how uncanny these big deserted buildings can be."

"That's so," nodded young Wells. "I once spent a night in a haunted house."

Sonia looked at him with her habitual interest. He was short and thick-set, with a three-cornered smile which appealed to her.

"Did you see anything?" she asked.

"No, I cleared out before the show came on. Windy. After a bit, one can imagine *anything.*"

It was then that Poke introduced a new note into the discussion by his own theory of the mystery deaths.

Sitting alone in the deserted Gallery, Sonia preferred to forget his words. She resolutely drove them from her mind while she began to settle down for the night.

Her first action was to cross to the figure of Cardinal Wolsey and unceremoniously raise his heavy scarlet robe. From under its voluminous folds, she drew out her cushion and attaché-case, which she had hidden earlier in the evening.

Mindful of the fact that it would grow chilly at dawn, she carried on her arm her thick white tennis-coat. Slipping it on, she placed her cushion in the angle of the wall, and sat down to await developments.

The Gallery was far more mysterious now that the lights were out. At either end, it seemed to stretch away into impenetrable black tunnels. But there was nothing uncanny about it, or about the figures, which were a tame and conventional collection of historical personages. Even the adjoining Hall of Horrors contained no horrors, only a selection of respectable-looking poisoners.

Sonia grinned cheerfully at the row of waxworks which were visible in the lamplight from the street.

"So you are the villains of the piece," she

murmured. "Later on, if the office is right, you will assume unpleasant mannerisms to try to cheat me into believing you are alive. I warn you, old sports, you'll have your work cut out for you . . . And now I think I'll get better acquainted with you. Familiarity breeds contempt."

She went the round of the figures, greeting each with flippancy or criticism. Presently she returned to her corner and opened her note-book ready to record her impressions.

Twelve o'clock. The first hour has passed almost too quickly. I've drawn a complete blank. Not a blessed thing to record. Not a vestige of reaction. The waxworks seem a commonplace lot, without a scrap of hyp-notic force. In fact, they're altogether too matey.

Sonia had left her corner, to write her entry in the light which streamed through the window. Smoking was prohibited in the building, and, lest she should yield to temptation, she had left both her cigarettes and matches behind her, on the office table.

At this stage she regretted the matches. A little extra light would be a boon. It was true she carried an electric torch, but she was saving it, in case of emergency.

It was a loan from young Wells. As they were leaving the office together, he spoke to her con-fidentially.

"Did you notice how Poke glared at you? Don't get up against him. He's a nasty piece of work. He's so mean he'd sell his mother's shroud for old rags. And he's a cruel little devil, too. He turned out his miserable pup, to starve in the streets, rather than cough up for the license."

Sonia grew hot with indignation.

"What he needs to cure his complaint is a strong dose of rat-poison," she declared. "What became of the poor little dog?"

"Oh, he's all right. He was a matey chap, and he soon chummed up with a mongrel of his own class."

"You?" asked Sonia, her eyes suddenly soft.

"A mongrel, am I?" grinned Wells. "Well, anyway, the pup will get a better Christmas than his first, when Poke went away and left him on the chain . . . We're both of us going to over-eat and over-drink. You're on your own, too. Won't you join us?"

"I'd love to."

Although the evening was warm and muggy the invitation suffused Sonia with the spirit of Christmas. The shade of Dickens seemed to be hovering over the parade of the streets. A red-nosed Santa Claus presided over a spangled Christmas-tree outside a toy-shop. Windows were hung with tinselled balls and coloured paper festoons. Pedestrians, laden with parcels, called out seasonable greetings.

"Merry Christmas."

Young Wells's three-cornered smile was his tribute to the joyous feeling of festival. His eyes were eager as he turned to Sonia.

"I've an idea. Don't wait until after the holi-days to write up the Waxworks. Make it a Christ-mas stunt, and go there tonight."

"I will," declared Sonia.

It was then that he slipped the torch into her hand.

"I know you belong to the stronger sex," he said. "But even your nerve might crash. If it does, just flash this torch under the window. Stretch out your arm above your head, and the light will be seen from the street."

"And what will happen then?" asked Sonia.

"I shall knock up the miserable porter and let you out."

"But how will *you* see the light?"

"I shall be in the street."

"All night?"

"Yes; I sleep there." Young Wells grinned. "Understand," he added loftily, "that this is a matter of principle. I could not let any woman—even one so aged and unattractive as yourself—feel beyond the reach of help."

He cut into her thanks as he turned away with a parting warning.

"Don't use the torch for light, or the juice may give out. It's about due for a new battery."

As Sonia looked at the torch, lying by her side, it seemed a link with young Wells. At this moment he was patrolling the street, a sturdy figure in an old tweed overcoat, with his cap pulled down over his eyes.

As she tried to pick out his footsteps from among those of the other passers-by, it struck her that there was plenty of traffic, considering that it was past twelve o'clock.

"The witching hour of midnight is another lost illusion," she reflected. "Killed by night-clubs, I suppose."

It was cheerful to know that so many citizens were abroad, to keep her company. Some optimists were still singing carols. She faintly heard the strains of "Good King Wenceslas." It was in a tranquil frame of mind that she unpacked her sandwiches and thermos.

"It's Christmas Day," she thought, as she drank hot coffee. "And I'm spending it with Don and the pup."

At that moment her career grew misty, and the flame of her literary ambition dipped as the future glowed with the warm firelight of home. In sudden elation, she held up her flask and toasted the waxworks.

"Merry Christmas to you all! And many of them."

The faces of the illuminated figures remained stolid, but she could almost swear that a low murmur of acknowledgment seemed to swell from the rest of her company—invisible in the darkness.

She spun out her meal to its limit, stifling her craving for a cigarette. Then, growing bored, she counted the visible waxworks, and tried to memorise them.

"Twenty-one, twenty-two . . . Wolsey. Queen Elizabeth, Guy Fawkes, Napoléon ought to go on a diet. Ever heard of eighteen days, Nap? Poor old Julius Caesar looks as though he'd been

sun-bathing on the Lido. He's about due for the melting-pot."

In her eyes they were a second-rate set of dummies. The local theory that they could terrorise a human being to death or madness seemed a fantastic notion.

"No," concluded Sonia. "There's really more in Poke's bright idea."

Again she saw the sun-smitten office—for the big unshielded window faced south—with its blistered paint, faded wall-paper, ink-stained desks, typewriters, telephones, and a huge fire in the untidy grate. Young Wells smoked his big pipe, while the sub-editor—a ginger, pig-headed young man—laid down the law about the mystery deaths.

And then she heard Poke's toneless dead-man's voice.

"You may be right about the spiritualist. He died of fright—but not of the waxworks. My belief is that he established contact with the spirit of his dead friend, the alderman, and so learned his real fate."

"What fate?" snapped the sub-editor.

"I believe that the alderman was murdered," replied Poke.

He clung to his point like a limpet in the face of all counter-arguments.

"The alderman had enemies," he said. "Nothing would be easier than for one of them to lie in wait for him. In the present circumstances, *I* could commit a murder in the Waxworks, and get away with it."

"How?" demanded young Wells.

"How? To begin with, the Gallery is a one-man show and the porter's a bonehead. Anyone could enter, and leave, the Gallery without his being wise to it."

"And the murder?" plugged young Wells.

With a shudder Sonia remembered how Poke had glanced at his long, knotted fingers.

"If I could not achieve my object by fright, which is the foolproof way," he replied, "I should try a little artistic strangulation."

"And leave your marks?"

"Not necessarily. Every expert knows that there are methods which show no trace."

Sonia fumbled in her bag for the cigarettes which were not there.

"Why did I let myself think of that, just now?" she thought. "Really too stupid."

As she reproached herself for her morbidity, she broke off to stare at the door which led to the Hall of Horrors.

When she had last looked at it, she could have sworn that it was tightly closed . . . But now it gaped open by an inch.

She looked at the black cavity, recognizing the first test of her nerves. Later on, there would be others. She realized the fact that, within her cool, practical self, she carried a hysterical, neurotic passenger, who would doubtless give her a lot of trouble through officious suggestions and uncomfortable reminders.

She resolved to give her second self a taste of her quality, and so quell her at the start.

"That door was merely closed," she remarked as, with a firm step, she crossed to the Hall of Horrors and shut the door.

One o'clock. I begin to realize that there is more in this than I thought. Perhaps I'm missing my sleep. But I'm keyed up and horribly expectant. Of what? I don't know. But I seem to be waiting for—something. I find myself listening—listening. The place is full of mysterious noises. I know they're my fancy . . . And things appear to move. I can distinguish footsteps and whispers, as though those waxworks which I cannot see in the darkness are beginning to stir to life.

Sonia dropped her pencil at the sound of a low chuckle. It seemed to come from the end of the Gallery which was blacked out by shadows.

As her imagination galloped away with her, she reproached herself sharply.

"Steady, don't be a fool. There must be a cloak-room here. That chuckle is the air escaping in a pipe—or something. I'm betrayed by my own ignorance of hydraulics."

In spite of her brave words, she returned rather quickly to her corner.

With her back against the wall she felt less apprehensive. But she recognized her cowardice as an ominous sign.

She was desperately afraid of someone—or something—creeping up behind her and touching her.

"I've struck the bad patch," she told herself. "It will be worse at three o'clock and work up to a climax. But when I make my entry, at three, I shall have reached the peak. After that every minute will be bringing the dawn nearer."

But of one fact she was ignorant. There would be no recorded impression at three o'clock.

Happily unconscious, she began to think of her copy. When she returned to the office—sunken-eyed, and looking like nothing on earth—she would then rejoice over every symptom of groundless fear.

"It's a story all right," she gloated, looking at Hamlet. His gnarled, pallid features and dark, smouldering eyes were strangely familiar to her.

Suddenly she realized that he reminded her of Hubert Poke.

Against her will, her thoughts again turned to him. She told herself that he was exactly like a waxwork. His yellow face—symptomatic of heart-trouble—had the same cheesy hue, and his eyes were like dull black glass. He wore a denture which was too large for him, and which forced his lips apart in a mirthless grin.

He always seemed to smile—even over the episode of the lift—which had been no joke.

It happened two days before. Sonia had rushed into the office in a state of molten excitement because she had extracted an interview from a Personage who had just received the Freedom of the City. This distinguished freeman had the reputation of shunning newspaper publicity, and Poke had tried his luck, only to be sent away with a flea in his ear.

At the back of her mind, Sonia knew that she had not fought level, for she was conscious of the effect of violet-blue eyes and a dimple upon a reserved but very human gentleman. But in her elation she had been rather blatant about her score.

She transcribed her notes, rattling away at her typewriter in a tremendous hurry, because she had a dinner-engagement. In the same breathless speed she had rushed towards the automatic lift.

She was just about to step into it when young Wells had leaped the length of the passage and dragged her back.

"Look, where you're going!" he shouted.

Sonia looked—and saw only the well of the shaft. The lift was not waiting in its accustomed place.

"Out of order," explained Wells before he turned to blast Hubert Poke, who stood by.

"You almighty chump, why didn't you grab Miss Fraser, instead of standing by like a stuck pig?"

At the time Sonia had vaguely remarked how Poke had stammered and sweated, and she accepted the fact that he had been petrified by shock and had lost his head.

For the first time, she realized that his inaction had been deliberate. She remembered the flame of terrible excitement in his eyes and his stretched ghastly grin.

"He *hates* me," she thought. "It's my fault. I've been tactless and cocksure."

Then a flood of horror swept over her.

"But he wanted to see me crash. It's almost *murder*."

As she began to tremble, the jumpy passenger she carried reminded her of Poke's remark about the alderman.

"He had enemies."

Sonia shook away the suggestion angrily.

"My memory's uncanny," she thought. "I'm stimulated and all strung up. It must be the atmosphere . . . Perhaps there's some gas in the air that accounts for these brainstorms. It's hopeless to be so utterly unscientific. Poke would have made a better job of this."

She was back again to Hubert Poke. He had become an obsession.

Her head began to throb and a tiny gong started to beat in her temples. This time, she recognized the signs without any mental ferment.

"Atmospherics. A storm's coming up. It might make things rather thrilling. I must concentrate on my story. Really, my luck's in."

She sat for some time, forcing herself to think of pleasant subjects—of arguments with young Wells and the Tennis Tournament. But there was always a point when her thoughts gave a twist and led her back to Poke.

Presently she grew cramped and got up to pace the illuminated aisle in front of the window. She tried again to talk to the waxworks, but, this time, it was not a success.

They seemed to have grown remote and secretive, as though they were removed to another plane, where they possessed a hidden life.

Suddenly she gave a faint scream. Someone—or something—had crept up behind her, for she felt the touch of cold fingers upon her arm.

Two o'clock. They're only wax. They shall not frighten me. But they're trying to. One by one they're coming to life . . . Charles the Second no longer looks sour dough. He is beginning to leer at me. His eyes remind me of Hubert Poke.

Sonia stopped writing, to glance uneasily at the image of the Stuart monarch. His black velveteen suit appeared to have a richer pile. The swart curls which fell over his lace collar looked less like horse-hair. There really seemed a gleam of amorous interest lurking at the back of his glass optics.

Absurdly, Sonia spoke to him, in order to reassure herself.

"Did *you* touch me? At the first hint of a liberty, Charles Stuart, I'll smack your face. You'll learn a modern journalist has not the manners of an orange-girl."

Instantly the satyr reverted to a dummy in a moth-eaten historical costume.

Sonia stood, listening for young Wells's footsteps. But she could not hear them, although the street now was perfectly still. She tried to picture him, propping up the opposite building, solid and immovable as the Rock of Gibraltar.

But it was no good. Doubts began to obtrude.

"I don't believe he's there. After all, why should he stay? He only pretended, just to give me confidence. He's gone."

She shrank back to her corner, drawing her tennis-coat closer, for warmth. It was growing colder, causing her to think of tempting things— of a hot-water bottle and a steaming tea-pot.

Presently she realized that she was growing drowsy. Her lids felt as though weighted with lead, so that it required an effort to keep them open.

This was a complication which she had not foreseen. Although she longed to drop off to sleep, she sternly resisted the temptation.

"No. It's not fair. I've set myself the job of recording a night spent in the Waxworks. It *must* be the genuine thing."

She blinked more vigorously, staring across to where Byron drooped like a sooty flamingo.

"Mercy, how he yearns! He reminds me of—— No, I won't think of *him* . . . I must keep awake . . . Bed . . . blankets, pillows . . . No."

Her head fell forward, and for a minute she dozed. In that space of time, she had a vivid dream.

She thought that she was still in her corner in the Gallery, watching the dead alderman as he paced to and fro, before the window. She had never seen him, so he conformed to her own idea of an alderman—stout, pompous, and wearing the dark-blue, fur-trimmed robe of his office.

"He's got a face like a sleepy pear," she decided. "Nice old thing, but brainless."

And then, suddenly, her tolerant derision turned to acute apprehension on his account, as she saw that he was being followed. A shape was stalking him as a cat stalks a bird.

Sonia tried to warn him of his peril, but, after the fashion of nightmares, she found herself voiceless. Even as she struggled to scream, a grotesquely long arm shot out and monstrous fingers gripped the alderman's throat.

In the same moment, she saw the face of the killer. It was Hubert Poke.

She awoke with a start, glad to find that it was but a dream. As she looked around her with dazed eyes, she saw a faint flicker of light. The mutter of very faint thunder, together with a patter of rain, told her that the storm had broken.

It was still a long way off, for Oldhampton seemed to be having merely a reflection and an echo.

"It'll clear the air," thought Sonia.

Then her heart gave a violent leap. One of the waxworks had come to life. She distinctly saw it move, before it disappeared into the darkness at the end of the Gallery.

She kept her head, realizing that it was time to give up.

"My nerve's crashed," she thought. "That figure was only my fancy. I'm just like the others. Defeated by wax."

Instinctively, she paid the figures her homage. It was the cumulative effect of their grim company, with their simulated life and sinister associations, that had rushed her defences.

Although it was bitter to fail, she comforted herself with the reminder that she had enough copy for her article. She could even make capital out of her own capitulation to the force of suggestion.

With a slight grimace, she picked up her notebook. There would be no more on-the-spot impressions. But young Wells, if he was still there, would be grateful for the end of his vigil, whatever the state of mind of the porter.

She groped in the darkness for her signal-lamp. But her fingers only scraped bare polished boards.

The torch had disappeared.

In a panic, she dropped down on her knees, and searched for yards around the spot where she was positive it had lain.

It was the instinct of self-preservation which caused her to give up her vain search.

"I'm in danger," she thought. "And I've no one to help me now. I must see this through myself."

She pushed back her hair from a brow which had grown damp.

"There's a brain working against mine. When I was asleep, someone—or something—stole my torch."

Something? The waxworks became instinct with terrible possibility as she stared at them. Some were merely blurred shapes—their faces opaque oblongs or ovals. But others—illuminated from the street—were beginning to reveal themselves in a new guise.

Queen Elizabeth, with peaked chin and fiery hair, seemed to regard her with intelligent malice. The countenance of Napoléon was heavy with brooding power, as though he were willing her to submit. Cardinal Wolsey held her with a glittering eye.

Sonia realized that she was letting herself be hypnotised by creatures of wax—so many pounds of candles moulded to human form.

"This is what happened to those others," she thought. "*Nothing happened.* But I'm afraid of them. I'm terribly afraid . . . There's only one thing to do. I must count them again."

She knew that she must find out whether her torch had been stolen through human agency; but she shrank from the experiment, not knowing which she feared more—a tangible enemy or the unknown.

As she began to count, the chilly air inside the building seemed to throb with each thud of her heart.

"Seventeen, eighteen." She was scarcely conscious of the numerals she murmured. "Twenty-two, twenty-three."

She stopped. Twenty-three? If her tally were correct, there was an extra waxwork in the Gallery.

On the shock of the discovery came a blinding flash of light, which veined the sky with fire. It seemed to run down the figure of Joan of Arc like a flaming torch. By a freak of atmospherics, the storm, which had been a starved, whimpering affair of flicker and murmur, culminated, and ended, in what was apparently a thunderbolt.

The explosion which followed was stunning; but Sonia scarcely noticed it, in her terror.

The unearthly violet glare had revealed to her a figure which she had previously overlooked.

It was seated in a chair, its hand supporting its peaked chin, and its pallid, clean-shaven features nearly hidden by a familiar broad-brimmed felt hat, which—together with the black cape—gave her the clue to its identity.

It was Hubert Poke.

Three o'clock.

Sonia heard it strike, as her memory began to reproduce, with horrible fidelity, every word of Poke's conversation on murder.

"Artistic strangulation." She pictured the cruel agony of life leaking—bubble by bubble, gasp by gasp. It would be slow—for he had boasted of a method which left no tell-tale marks.

"Another death," she thought dully. "If it happens everyone will say that the Waxworks have killed me. What a story . . . Only, I shall not write it up."

The tramp of feet rang out on the pavement below. It might have been the policeman on his beat; but Sonia wanted to feel that young Wells was still faithful to his post.

She looked up at the window, set high in the wall, and, for a moment, was tempted to shout.

But the idea was too desperate. If she failed to attract outside attention, she would seal her own fate, for Poke would be prompted to hasten her extinction.

"Awful to feel he's so near, and yet I cannot reach him," she thought. "It makes it so much worse."

She crouched there, starting and sweating at every faint sound in the darkness. The rain, which still pattered on the sky-light, mimicked footsteps and whispers. She remembered her dream and the nightmare spring and clutch.

It was an omen. At any moment it would come . . .

Her fear jolted her brain. For the first time she had a glimmer of hope.

"I didn't see him before the flash, because he looked exactly like one of the waxworks. Could I hide among them, too?" she wondered.

She knew that her white coat alone revealed her position to him. Holding her breath, she wriggled out of it, and hung it on the effigy of Charles II. In her black coat, with her handkerchief-scarf tied over her face, burglar fashion, she hoped that she was invisible against the sable-draped walls.

Her knees shook as she crept from her shelter. When she had stolen a few yards, she stopped to listen . . . In the darkness, someone was astir. She heard a soft padding of feet, moving with the certainty of one who sees his goal.

Her coat glimmered in her deserted corner.

In a sudden panic, she increased her pace, straining her ears for other sounds. She had reached the far end of the Gallery where no gleam from the window penetrated the gloom. Blindfolded and muffled, she groped her way towards the alcoves which held the tableaux.

Suddenly she stopped, every nerve in her body quivering. She had heard a thud, like rubbered soles alighting after a spring.

"He knows now." Swift on the trail of her thought flashed another. "He will look for me. Oh, *quick*!"

She tried to move, but her muscles were bound, and she stood as though rooted to the spot, listening. It was impossible to locate the footsteps. They seemed to come from every quarter of the Gallery. Sometimes they sounded remote, but, whenever she drew a freer breath, a sudden creak of the boards close to where she stood made her heart leap.

At last she reached the limit of endurance. Unable to bear the suspense of waiting, she moved on.

Her pursuer followed her at a distance. He gained on her, but still withheld his spring. She had the feeling that he held her at the end of an invisible string.

"He's playing with me, like a cat with a mouse," she thought.

If he had seen her, he let her creep forward until the darkness was no longer absolute. There were gradations in its density, so that she was able to recognize the first alcove. Straining her eyes, she could distinguish the outlines of the bed where the Virtuous Man made his triumphant exit from life, surrounded by a flock of his sorrowing family and their progeny.

Slipping inside the circle, she added one more mourner to the tableau.

The minutes passed, but nothing happened. There seemed no sound save the tiny gong beating inside her temples. Even the raindrops had ceased to patter on the sky-light.

Sonia began to find the silence more deadly than noise. It was like the lull before the storm. Question after question came rolling into her mind.

"Where is he? What will he do next? Why doesn't he strike a light?"

As though someone were listening-in to her thoughts, she suddenly heard a faint splutter as of an ignited match. Or it might have been the click of an exhausted electric torch.

With her back turned to the room, she could see no light. She heard the half-hour strike, with a faint wonder that she was still alive.

"What will have happened before the next quarter?" she asked.

Presently she began to feel the strain of her pose, which she held as rigidly as any artist's model. For the time—if her presence were not already detected—her life depended on her immobility.

As an overpowering weariness began to steal over her a whisper stirred in her brain:

"The alderman was found dead on a bed."

The newspaper account had not specified which especial tableau had been the scene of the tragedy, but she could not remember another alcove which held a bed. As she stared at the white dimness of the quilt she seemed to see it blotched with a dark, sprawling form, writhing under the grip of long fingers.

To shut out the suggestion of her fancy, she closed her eyes. The cold, dead air in the alcove was sapping her exhausted vitality, so that once again she began to nod. She dozed as she stood, rocking to and fro on her feet.

Her surroundings grew shadowy. Sometimes she knew that she was in the alcove, but at others she strayed momentarily over strange borders . . . She was back in the summer, walking in a garden with young Wells. Roses and sunshine . . .

She awoke with a start at the sound of heavy breathing. It sounded close to her—almost by her side. The figure of a mourner kneeling by the bed seemed to change its posture slightly.

Instantly maddened thoughts began to flock and flutter wildly inside her brain.

"Who was it? Was it Hubert Poke? Would history be repeated? Was she doomed also to be strangled inside the alcove? Had Fate led her there?"

She waited, but nothing happened. Again she had the sensation of being played with by a master mind—dangled at the end of his invisible string.

Presently she was emboldened to steal from the alcove, to seek another shelter. But though she held on to the last flicker of her will, she had reached the limit of endurance. Worn out with the violence of her emotions and physically spent from the strain of long periods of standing, she staggered as she walked.

She blundered round the Gallery, without any sense of direction, colliding blindly with the groups of waxwork figures. When she reached the window her knees shook under her and she sank to the ground—dropping immediately into a sleep of utter exhaustion.

She awoke with a start as the first grey gleam of dawn was stealing into the Gallery. It fell on the row of waxworks, imparting a sickly hue to their features, as though they were creatures stricken with plague.

It seemed to Sonia that they were waiting for her to wake. Their peaked faces were intelligent and their eyes held interest, as though they were keeping some secret.

She pushed back her hair, her brain still thick with clouded memories. Disconnected thoughts began to stir, to slide about . . . Then suddenly her mind cleared, and she sprang up—staring at a figure wearing a familiar black cape.

Hubert Poke was also waiting for her to wake.

He sat in the same chair, and in the same posture, as when she had first seen him, in the flash of lightning. He looked as though he had never moved from his place—as though he could not move. His face had not the appearance of flesh.

As Sonia stared at him, with the feeling of a bird hypnotised by a snake, a doubt began to gather in her mind. Growing bolder, she crept closer to the figure.

It was a waxwork—a libellous representation of the actor—Kean.

Her laugh rang joyously through the Gallery as she realized that she had passed a night of baseless terrors, cheated by the power of imagination. In her relief she turned impulsively to the waxworks.

"My congratulations," she said. "You are my masters."

They did not seem entirely satisfied by her homage, for they continued to watch her with an expression half-benevolent and half-sinister.

Wait! they seemed to say.

Sonia turned from them and opened her bag to get out her mirror and comb. There, among a jumble of notes, letters, lipsticks, and powder-compresses, she saw the electric torch.

"Of course!" she cried. "I remember now, I put it there. I was too windy to think properly . . . Well, I have my story. I'd better get my coat."

The Gallery seemed smaller in the returning light. As she approached Charles Stuart, who looked like an umpire in her white coat, she glanced down the far end of the room, where she had groped in its shadows before the pursuit of imaginary footsteps.

A waxwork was lying prone on the floor. For the second time she stood and gazed down upon a familiar black cape—a broad-brimmed conspirator's hat. Then she nerved herself to turn the figure so that its face was visible.

She gave a scream. There was no mistaking the glazed eyes and ghastly grin. She was looking down on the face of a dead man.

It was Hubert Poke.

The shock was too much for Sonia. She heard a singing in her ears, while a black mist gathered before her eyes. For the first time in her life she fainted.

When she recovered consciousness she forced herself to kneel beside the body and cover it with its black cape. The pallid face resembled a death-mask, which revealed only too plainly the lines of egotism and cruelty in which it had been moulded by a gross spirit.

Yet Sonia felt no repulsion—only pity. It was Christmas morning, and he was dead, while her own portion was life triumphant. Closing her eyes, she whispered a prayer of supplication for his warped soul.

Presently, as she grew calmer, her mind began to work on the problem of his presence. His motive seemed obvious. Not knowing that she had changed her plan, he had concealed himself in the Gallery, in order to poach her story.

"He was in the Hall of Horrors at first," she thought, remembering the opened door. "When he came out he hid at this end. We never saw each other, because of the waxworks between us; but we heard each other."

She realized that the sounds which had terrified her had not all been due to imagination, while it was her agency which had converted the room into a whispering gallery of strange murmurs and voices. The clue to the cause of death was revealed by his wrist-watch, which had smashed when he fell. Its hands had stopped at three minutes to three, proving that the flash and explosion of the thunderbolt had been too much for his diseased heart—already overstrained by superstitious fears.

Sonia shuddered at a mental vision of his face, distraught with terror and pulped by raw primal impulses, after a night spent in a madman's world of phantasy.

She turned to look at the waxworks. At last she understood what they seemed to say.

"But for Us, you should have met—at dawn."

"Your share shall be acknowledged, I promise you," she said, as she opened her notebook.

Eight o'clock. The Christmas bells are ringing and it is wonderful just to be alive. I'm through the night, and none the worse for the experience, although I cracked badly after three o'clock. A colleague who, unknown to me, was also concealed in the Gallery has met with a tragic fate, caused, I am sure, by the force of suggestion. Although his death is due to heart-failure, the superstitious will certainly claim it is another victory for the Waxworks.

CAMBRIC TEA

Marjorie Bowen

GABRIELLE MARGARET VERE LONG used at least six pseudonyms for her prodigious output of more than one hundred fifty novels and countless short stories, the most famous bylines being Marjorie Bowen and Joseph Shearing. To help support her sister and profligate, unstable mother after her father left the family, she began to write and had her first novel published when she was only sixteen, immediately becoming the prime supporter of her small family. Her dark and unhappy early years led her to produce a plethora of fictional works with Gothic overtones. While many were hastily written potboilers, she often wrote finely crafted tales that remain highly readable and popular today. "Cambric Tea" was first collected in *The World's 100 Best Detective Stories*, edited by Eugene Thwing (New York & London, Funk & Wagnalls, 1929).

Cambric Tea

MARJORIE BOWEN

THE SITUATION WAS BIZARRE; THE accurately trained mind of Bevis Holroyd was impressed foremost by this; that the opening of a door would turn it into tragedy.

"I am afraid I can't stay," he had said pleasantly, humouring a sick man; he was too young and had not been long enough completely successful to have a professional manner but a certain balanced tolerance just showed in his attitude to this prostrate creature.

"I've got a good many claims on my time," he added, "and I'm afraid it would be impossible. And it isn't the least necessary, you know. You're quite all right. I'll come back after Christmas if you really think it worth while."

The patient opened one eye; he was lying flat on his back in a deep, wide-fashioned bed hung with a thick, dark, silk-lined tapestry; the room was dark for there were thick curtains of the same material drawn half across the windows, rigidly excluding all save a moiety of the pallid winter light; to make his examination Dr. Holroyd had had to snap on the electric light that stood on the bedside table; he thought it a dreary unhealthy room, but had hardly found it worthwhile to say as much.

The patient opened one eye; the other lid remained fluttering feebly over an immobile orb.

He said in a voice both hoarse and feeble:

"But, doctor, I'm being poisoned."

Professional curiosity and interest masked by genial incredulity instantly quickened the doctor's attention.

"My dear sir," he smiled, "poisoned by this nasty bout of 'flu you mean, I suppose—"

"No," said the patient, faintly and wearily dropping both lids over his blank eyes, "by my wife."

"That's an ugly sort of fancy for you to get hold of," replied the doctor instantly. "Acute depression—we must see what we can do for you—"

The sick man opened both eyes now; he even slightly raised his head as he replied, not without dignity:

"I fetched you from London, Dr. Holroyd, that you might deal with my case impartially— from the local man there is no hope of that, he is entirely impressed by my wife."

Dr. Holroyd made a movement as if to protest but a trembling sign from the patient made him quickly subsist.

"Please let me speak. *She* will come in soon and I shall have no chance. I sent for you secretly, she knows nothing about that. I had heard you very well spoken of—as an authority on this sort of thing. You made a name over the Pluntre murder case as witness for the Crown."

"I don't specialize in murder," said Dr. Holroyd, but his keen handsome face was alight with interest. "And I don't care much for this kind of case—Sir Harry."

"But you've taken it on," murmured the sick man. "You couldn't abandon me now."

"I'll get you into a nursing home," said the doctor cheerfully, "and there you'll dispel all these ideas."

"And when the nursing home has cured me I'm to come back to my wife for her to begin again?"

Dr. Holroyd bent suddenly and sharply over the sombre bed. With his right hand he deftly turned on the electric lamp and tipped back the coral silk shade so that the bleached acid light fell full over the patient lying on his back on the big fat pillows.

"Look here," said the doctor, "what you say is pretty serious."

And the two men stared at each other, the patient examining his physician as acutely as his physician examined him.

Bevis Holroyd was still a young man with a look of peculiar energy and austere intelligence that heightened by contrast purely physical dark good looks that many men would have found sufficient passport to success; resolution, dignity, and a certain masculine sweetness, serene and strong, different from feminine sweetness, marked his demeanour which was further softened by a quick humour and a sensitive judgment.

The patient, on the other hand, was a man of well past middle age, light, flabby and obese with a flaccid, fallen look about his large face which was blurred and dimmed by the colours of ill health, being one pasty livid hue that threw into unpleasant relief the grey speckled red of his scant hair.

Altogether an unpleasing man, but of a certain fame and importance that had induced the rising young doctor to come at once when hastily summoned to Strangeways Manor House; a man of a fine, renowned family, a man of repute as a scholar, an essayist who had once been a politician who was rather above politics; a man whom Dr. Holroyd only knew vaguely by reputation, but who seemed to him symbolical of all that was staid, respectable, and stolid.

And this man blinked up at him and whimpered:

"My wife is poisoning me."

Dr. Holroyd sat back and snapped off the electric light.

"What makes you think so?" he asked sharply.

"To tell you that," came the laboured voice of the sick man, "I should have to tell you my story."

"Well, if you want me to take this up—"

"I sent for you to do that, doctor."

"Well, how do you think you are being poisoned?"

"Arsenic, of course."

"Oh? And how administered?"

Again the patient looked up with one eye, seeming too fatigued to open the other.

"Cambric tea," he replied.

And Dr. Holroyd echoed:

"Cambric tea!" with a soft amazement and interest.

Cambric tea had been used as the medium for arsenic in the Pluntre case and the expression had become famous; it was Bevis Holroyd who had discovered the doses in the cambric tea and who had put his finger on this pale beverage as the means of murder.

"Very possibly," continued Sir Harry, "the Pluntre case made her think of it."

"For God's sake, don't," said Dr. Holroyd; for in that hideous affair the murderer had been a woman; and to see a woman on trial for her life, to see a woman sentenced to death, was not an experience he wished to repeat.

"Lady Strangeways," continued the sick man, "is much younger than I—I over persuaded her to marry me, she was at that time very much attracted by a man of her own age, but he was in a poor position and she was ambitious."

He paused, wiped his quivering lips on a silk handkerchief, and added faintly:

"Lately our marriage has been extremely unhappy. The man she preferred is now prosperous, successful, and unmarried—she wishes to dispose of me that she may marry her first choice."

"Have you proof of any of this?"

"Yes. I know she buys arsenic. I know she reads books on poisons. I know she is eating her heart out for this other man."

"Forgive me, Sir Harry," replied the doctor, "but have you no near friend nor relation to whom you can confide your—suspicions?"

"No one," said the sick man impatiently. "I have lately come from the East and am out of touch with people. Besides I want a doctor, a doctor with skill in this sort of thing. I thought from the first of the Pluntre case and of you."

Bevis Holroyd sat back quietly; it was then that he thought of the situation as bizarre; the queerness of the whole thing was vividly before him, like a twisted figure on a gem—a carving at once writhing and immobile.

"Perhaps," continued Sir Harry wearily, "you are married, doctor?"

"No." Dr. Holroyd slightly smiled; his story was something like the sick man's story but taken from another angle; when he was very poor and unknown he had loved a girl who had preferred a wealthy man; she had gone out to India, ten years ago, and he had never seen her since; he remembered this, with sharp distinctness, and in the same breath he remembered that he still loved this girl; it was, after all, a commonplace story.

Then his mind swung to the severe professional aspect of the case; he had thought that his patient, an unhealthy type of man, was struggling with a bad attack of influenza and the resultant depression and weakness, but then he had never thought, of course, of poison, nor looked nor tested for poison.

The man might be lunatic, he might be deceived, he might be speaking the truth; the fact that he was a mean, unpleasant beast ought not to weigh in the matter; Dr. Holroyd had some enjoyable Christmas holidays in prospect and now he was beginning to feel that he ought to give these up to stay and investigate this case; for he could readily see that it was one in which the local doctor would be quite useless.

"You must have a nurse," he said, rising.

But the sick man shook his head.

"I don't wish to expose my wife more than need be," he grumbled. "Can't you manage the affair yourself?"

As this was the first hint of decent feeling he had shown, Bevis Holroyd forgave him his brusque rudeness.

"Well, I'll stay the night anyhow," he conceded.

And then the situation changed, with the opening of a door, from the bizarre to the tragic.

This door opened in the far end of the room and admitted a bloom of bluish winter light from some uncurtained, high-windowed corridor; the chill impression was as if invisible snow had entered the shaded, dun, close apartment.

And against this background appeared a woman in a smoke-coloured dress with some long lace about the shoulders and a high comb; she held a little tray carrying jugs and a glass of crystal in which the cold light splintered.

Dr. Holroyd stood in his usual attitude of attentive courtesy, and then, as the patient, feebly twisting his gross head from the fat pillow, said:

"My wife—doctor—" he recognized in Lady Strangeways the girl to whom he had once been engaged in marriage, the woman he still loved.

"This is Doctor Holroyd," added Sir Harry. "Is that cambric tea you have there?"

She inclined her head to the stranger by her husband's bed as if she had never seen him before, and he, taking his cue, and for many other reasons, was silent.

"Yes, this is your cambric tea," she said to her husband. "You like it just now, don't you? How do you find Sir Harry, Dr. Holroyd?"

There were two jugs on the tray; one of crystal half full of cold milk, and one of white porcelain full of hot water; Lady Strangeways proceeded to mix these fluids in equal proportions and gave the resultant drink to her husband, helping him first to sit up in bed.

"I think that Sir Harry has a nasty turn of influenza," answered the doctor mechanically. "He wants me to stay. I've promised till the morning, anyhow."

"That will be a pleasure and a relief," said Lady Strangeways gravely. "My husband has been ill some time and seems so much worse than he need—for influenza."

The patient, feebly sipping his cambric tea, grinned queerly at the doctor.

"So much worse—you see, doctor!" he muttered.

"It is good of you to stay," continued Lady Strangeways equally. "I will see about your room, you must be as comfortable as possible."

She left as she had come, a shadow-coloured figure retreating to a chill light.

The sick man held up his glass as if he gave a toast.

"You see! Cambric tea!"

And Bevis Holroyd was thinking: does she not want to know me? Does he know what we once were to each other? How comes she to be married to this man—her husband's name was Custiss—and the horror of the situation shook the calm that was his both from character and training; he went to the window and looked out on the bleached park; light, slow snow was falling, a dreary dance over the frozen grass and before the grey corpses that paled, one behind the other, to the distance shrouded in colourless mist.

The thin voice of Harry Strangeways recalled him to the bed.

"Would you like to take a look at this, doctor?" He held out the half drunk glass of milk and water.

"I've no means of making a test here," said Dr. Holroyd, troubled. "I brought a few things, nothing like that."

"You are not so far from Harley Street," said Sir Harry. "My car can fetch everything you want by this afternoon—or perhaps you would like to go yourself?"

"Yes," replied Bevis Holroyd sternly. "I would rather go myself."

His trained mind had been rapidly covering the main aspects of his problem and he had instantly seen that it was better for Lady Strange-

ways to have this case in his hands. He was sure there was some hideous, fantastic hallucination on the part of Sir Harry, but it was better for Lady Strangeways to leave the matter in the hands of one who was friendly towards her. He rapidly found and washed a medicine bottle from among the sick room paraphernalia and poured it full of the cambric tea, casting away the remainder.

"Why did you drink any?" he asked sharply.

"I don't want her to think that I guess," whispered Sir Harry. "Do you know, doctor, I have a lot of her love letters—written by—"

Dr. Holroyd cut him short.

"I couldn't listen to this sort of thing behind Lady Strangeways's back," he said quickly. "That is between you and her. My job is to get you well. I'll try and do that."

And he considered, with a faint disgust, how repulsive this man looked sitting up with pendant jowl and drooping cheeks and discoloured, pouchy eyes sunk in pads of unhealthy flesh and above the spiky crown of Judas-coloured hair.

Perhaps a woman, chained to this man, living with him, blocked and thwarted by him, might be wrought upon to—

Dr. Holroyd shuddered inwardly and refused to continue his reflection.

As he was leaving the gaunt sombre house about which there was something definitely blank and unfriendly, a shrine in which the sacred flames had flickered out so long ago that the lamps were blank and cold, he met Lady Strangeways.

She was in the wide entrance hall standing by the wood fire that but faintly dispersed the gloom of the winter morning and left untouched the shadows in the rafters of the open roof.

Now he would not, whether she wished or no, deny her; he stopped before her, blocking out her poor remnant of light.

"Mollie," he said gently, "I don't quite understand—you married a man named Custiss in India."

"Yes. Harry had to take this name when he

inherited this place. We've been home three years from the East, but lived so quietly here that I don't suppose anyone has heard of us."

She stood between him and the firelight, a shadow among the shadows; she was much changed; in her thinness and pallor, in her restless eyes and nervous mouth he could read signs of discontent, even of unhappiness.

"I never heard of you," said Dr. Holroyd truthfully. "I didn't want to. I liked to keep my dreams."

Her hair was yet the lovely cedar wood hue, silver, soft, and gracious; her figure had those fluid lines of grace that he believed he had never seen equalled.

"Tell me," she added abruptly, "what is the matter with my husband? He has been ailing like this for a year or so."

With a horrid lurch of his heart that was usually so steady, Dr. Holroyd remembered the bottle of milk and water in his pocket.

"Why do you give him that cambric tea?" he counter questioned.

"He will have it—he insists that I make it for him—"

"Mollie," said Dr. Holroyd quickly, "you decided against me, ten years ago, but that is no reason why we should not be friends now—tell me, frankly, are you happy with this man?"

"You have seen him," she replied slowly. "He seemed different ten years ago. I honestly was attracted by his scholarship and his learning as well as—other things."

Bevis Holroyd needed to ask no more; she was wretched, imprisoned in a mistake as a fly in amber; and those love letters? Was there another man?

As he stood silent, with a dark reflective look on her weary brooding face, she spoke again:

"You are staying?"

"Oh yes," he said, he was staying, there was nothing else for him to do.

"It is Christmas week," she reminded him wistfully. "It will be very dull, perhaps painful, for you."

"I think I ought to stay."

Sir Harry's car was announced; Bevis Holroyd, gliding over frozen roads to London, was absorbed with this sudden problem that, like a mountain out of a plain, had suddenly risen to confront him out of his level life.

The sight of Mollie (he could not think of her by that sick man's name) had roused in him tender memories and poignant emotions and the position in which he found her and his own juxtaposition to her and her husband had the same devastating effect on him as a mine sprung beneath the feet of an unwary traveller.

London was deep in the whirl of a snow storm and the light that penetrated over the grey roof tops to the ugly slip of a laboratory at the back of his consulting rooms was chill and forbidding.

Bevis Holroyd put the bottle of milk on a marble slab and sat back in the easy chair watching that dreary chase of snow flakes across the dingy London pane.

He was thinking of past springs, of violets long dead, of roses long since dust, of hours that had slipped away like lengths of golden silk rolled up, of the long ago when he had loved Mollie and Mollie had seemed to love him; then he thought of that man in the big bed who had said:

"My wife is poisoning me."

Late that afternoon Dr. Holroyd, with his suit case and a professional bag, returned to Strangeways Manor House in Sir Harry's car; the bottle of cambric tea had gone to a friend, a noted analyst; somehow Doctor Holroyd had not felt able to do this task himself; he was very fortunate, he felt, in securing this old solitary and his promise to do the work before Christmas.

As he arrived at Strangeways Manor House which stood isolated and well away from a public high road where a lonely spur of the weald of Kent drove into the Sussex marshes, it was in a blizzard of snow that effaced the landscape and gave the murky outlines of the house an air of unreality, and Bevis Holroyd experienced that sensation he had so often heard of and read about, but which so far his cool mind had dismissed as a fiction.

He did really feel as if he was in an evil dream; as the snow changed the values of the scene, altering distances and shapes, so this meeting with Mollie, under these circumstances, had suddenly changed the life of Bevis Holroyd.

He had so resolutely and so definitely put this woman out of his life and mind, deliberately refusing to make enquiries about her, letting all knowledge of her cease with the letter in which she had written from India and announced her marriage.

And now, after ten years, she had crossed his path in this ghastly manner, as a woman her husband accused of attempted murder.

The sick man's words of a former lover disturbed him profoundly; was it himself who was referred to? Yet the love letters must be from another man for he had not corresponded with Mollie since her marriage, not for ten years.

He had never felt any bitterness towards Mollie for her desertion of a poor, struggling doctor, and he had always believed in the integral nobility of her character under the timidity of conventionality; but the fact remained that she had played him false—what if that *had* been "the little rift within the lute" that had now indeed silenced the music!

With a sense of bitter depression he entered the gloomy old house; how different was this from the pleasant ordinary Christmas he had been rather looking forward to, the jolly homely atmosphere of good fare, dancing, and friends!

When he had telephoned to these friends excusing himself his regret had been genuine and the cordial "bad luck!" had had a poignant echo in his own heart; bad luck indeed, bad luck—

She was waiting for him in the hall that a pale young man was decorating with boughs of prickly stiff holly that stuck stiffly behind the dark heavy pictures.

He was introduced as the secretary and said gloomily:

"Sir Harry wished everything to go on as usual, though I am afraid he is very ill indeed."

Yes, the patient had been seized by another violent attack of illness during Dr. Holroyd's absence; the young man went at once upstairs and found Sir Harry in a deep sleep and a rather nervous local doctor in attendance.

An exhaustive discussion of the case with this doctor threw no light on anything, and Dr. Holroyd, leaving in charge an extremely sensible-looking housekeeper who was Sir Harry's preferred nurse, returned, worried and irritated, to the hall where Lady Strangeways now sat alone before the big fire.

She offered him a belated but fresh cup of tea.

"Why did you come?" she asked as if she roused herself from deep reverie.

"Why? Because your husband sent for me."

"He says you offered to come; he has told everyone in the house that."

"But I never heard of the man before today."

"You had heard of me. He seems to think that you came here to help me."

"He cannot be saying that," returned Dr. Holroyd sternly, and he wondered desperately if Mollie was lying, if she had invented this to drive him out of the house.

"Do you want me here?" he demanded.

"I don't know," she replied dully and confirmed his suspicions; probably there was another man and she wished him out of the way; but he could not go, out of pity towards her he could not go.

"Does he know we once knew each other?" he asked.

"No," she replied faintly, "therefore it seems such a curious chance that he should have sent for you, of all men!"

"It would have been more curious," he responded grimly, "if I had heard that you were here with a sick husband and had thrust myself in to doctor him! Strangeways must be crazy to spread such a tale and if he doesn't know we are old friends it becomes nonsense!"

"I often think that Harry is crazy," said Lady Strangeways wearily; she took a rose silk-lined work basket, full of pretty trifles, on her knee, and began winding a skein of rose-coloured silk; she looked so frail, so sad, so lifeless that the heart of Bevis Holroyd was torn with bitter pity.

"Now I am here I want to help you," he said earnestly. "I am staying for that, to help you—"

She looked up at him with a wistful appeal in her fair face.

"I'm worried," she said simply. "I've lost some letters I valued very much—I think they have been stolen."

Dr. Holroyd drew back; the love letters; the letters the husband had found, that were causing all his ugly suspicions.

"My poor Mollie!" he exclaimed impulsively. "What sort of a coil have you got yourself into!"

As if this note of pity was unendurable, she rose impulsively, scattering the contents of her work basket, dropping the skein of silk, and hastened away down the dark hall.

Bevis Holroyd stooped mechanically to pick up the hurled objects and saw among them a small white packet, folded, but opened at one end; this packet seemed to have fallen out of a needle case of gold silk.

Bevis Holroyd had pounced on it and thrust it in his pocket just as the pale secretary returned with his thin arms most incongruously full of mistletoe.

"This will be a dreary Christmas for you, Dr. Holroyd," he said with the air of one who forces himself to make conversation. "No doubt you had some pleasant plans in view—we are all so pleased that Lady Strangeways had a friend to come and look after Sir Harry during the holidays."

"Who told you I was a friend?" asked Dr. Holroyd brusquely. "I certainly knew Lady Strangeways before she was married—"

The pale young man cut in crisply:

"Oh, Lady Strangeways told me so herself."

Bevis Holroyd was bewildered; why did she tell the secretary what she did not tell her husband?—both the indiscretion and the reserve seemed equally foolish.

Languidly hanging up his sprays and bunches

of mistletoe the pallid young man, whose name was Garth Deane, continued his aimless remarks.

"This is really not a very cheerful house, Dr. Holroyd—I'm interested in Sir Harry's oriental work or I should not remain. Such a very unhappy marriage! I often think," he added regardless of Bevis Holroyd's darkling glance, "that it would be very unpleasant indeed for Lady Strangeways if anything happened to Sir Harry."

"Whatever do you mean, sir?" asked the doctor angrily.

The secretary was not at all discomposed.

"Well, one lives in the house, one has nothing much to do—and one notices."

Perhaps, thought the young man in anguish, the sick husband had been talking to this creature, perhaps the creature *had* really noticed something.

"I'll go up to my patient," said Bevis Holroyd briefly, not daring to anger one who might be an important witness in this mystery that was at present so unfathomable.

Mr. Deane gave a sickly grin over the lovely pale leaves and berries he was holding.

"I'm afraid he is very bad, doctor."

As Bevis Holroyd left the room he passed Lady Strangeways; she looked blurred, like a pastel drawing that has been shaken; the fingers she kept locked on her bosom; she had flung a silver fur over her shoulders that accentuated her ethereal look of blonde, pearl, and amber hues.

"I've come back for my work basket," she said. "Will you go up to my husband? He is ill again—"

"Have you been giving him anything?" asked Dr. Holroyd as quietly as he could.

"Only some cambric tea, he insisted on that."

"Don't give him anything—leave him alone. He is in my charge now, do you understand?"

She gazed up at him with frightened eyes that had been newly washed by tears.

"Why are you so unkind to me?" she quivered.

She looked so ready to fall that he could not resist the temptation to put his hand protectingly on her arm, so that, as she stood in the low doorway leading to the stairs, he appeared to be supporting her drooping weight.

"Have I not said that I am here to help you, Mollie?"

The secretary slipped out from the shadows behind them, his arms still full of winter evergreens.

"There is too much foliage," he smiled, and the smile told that he had seen and heard.

Bevis Holroyd went angrily upstairs; he felt as if an invisible net was being dragged closely round him, something which, from being a cobweb, would become a cable; this air of mystery, of horror in the big house, this sly secretary, these watchful-looking servants, the nervous village doctor ready to credit anything, the lovely agitated woman who was the woman he had long so romantically loved, and the sinister sick man with his diabolic accusations, a man Bevis Holroyd had, from the first moment, hated—all these people in these dark surroundings affected the young man with a miasma of apprehension, gloom, and dread.

After a few hours of it he was nearer to losing his nerve than he had ever been; that must be because of Mollie, poor darling Mollie caught into all this nightmare.

And outside the bells were ringing across the snow, practising for Christmas Day; the sound of them was to Bevis Holroyd what the sounds of the real world are when breaking into a sleeper's thick dreams.

The patient sat up in bed, fondling the glass of odious cambric tea.

"Why do you take the stuff?" demanded the doctor angrily.

"She won't let me off, she thrusts it on me," whispered Sir Harry.

Bevis Holroyd noticed, not for the first time since he had come into the fell atmosphere of this dark house that enclosed the piteous figure of the woman he loved, that husband and wife were telling different tales; on one side lay a burden of careful lying.

"Did she—" continued the sick man, "speak to you of her lost letters?"

The young doctor looked at him sternly.

"Why should Lady Strangeways make a confidante of me?" he asked. "Do you know that she was a friend of mine ten years ago before she married you?"

"Was she? How curious! But you met like strangers."

"The light in this room is very dim—"

"Well, never mind about that, whether you knew her or not—" Sir Harry gasped out in a sudden snarl. "The woman is a murderess, and you'll have to bear witness to it—I've got her letters, here under my pillow, and Garth Deane is watching her—"

"Ah, a spy! I'll have no part in this, Sir Harry. You'll call another doctor—"

"No, it's your case, you'll make the best of it— My God, I'm dying, I think—"

He fell back in such a convulsion of pain that Bevis Holroyd forgot everything in administering to him. The rest of that day and all that night the young doctor was shut up with his patient, assisted by the secretary and the housekeeper.

And when, in the pallid light of Christmas Eve morning, he went downstairs to find Lady Strangeways, he knew that the sick man was suffering from arsenic poison, that the packet taken from Mollie's work box was arsenic, and it was only an added horror when he was called to the telephone to learn that a stiff dose of the poison had been found in the specimen of cambric tea.

He believed that he could save the husband and thereby the wife also, but he did not think he could close the sick man's mouth; the deadly hatred of Sir Harry was leading up to an accusation of attempted murder; of that he was sure, and there was the man Deane to back him up.

He sent for Mollie, who had not been near her husband all night, and when she came, pale, distracted, huddled in her white fur, he said grimly:

"Look here, Mollie, I promised that I'd help you and I mean to, though it isn't going to be as easy as I thought, but you have got to be frank with me."

"But I have nothing to conceal—"

"The name of the other man—"

"The other man?"

"The man who wrote those letters your husband has under his pillow."

"Oh, Harry has them!" she cried in pain. "That man Deane stole them then! Bevis, they are your letters of the olden days that I have always cherished."

"*My* letters!"

"Yes, do you think that there has ever been anyone else?"

"But he says—Mollie, there is a trap or trick here, someone is lying furiously. Your husband is being poisoned."

"Poisoned?"

"By arsenic given in that cambric tea. And he knows it. And he accuses you."

She stared at him in blank incredulity, then she slipped forward in her chair and clutched the big arm.

"Oh, God," she muttered in panic terror. "He always swore that he'd be revenged on me—because he knew that I never cared for him—"

But Bevis Holroyd recoiled; he did not dare listen, he did not dare believe.

"I've warned you," he said, "for the sake of the old days, Mollie—"

A light step behind them and they were aware of the secretary creeping out of the embrowning shadows.

"A cold Christmas," he said, rubbing his hands together. "A really cold, seasonable Christmas. We are almost snowed in—and Sir Harry would like to see you, Dr. Holroyd."

"I have only just left him—"

Bevis Holroyd looked at the despairing figure of the woman, crouching in her chair; he was distracted, overwrought, near to losing his nerve.

"He wants particularly to see you," cringed the secretary.

Mollie looked back at Bevis Holroyd, her lips moved twice in vain before she could say: "Go to him."

The doctor went slowly upstairs and the secretary followed.

Sir Harry was now flat on his back, staring at the dark tapestry curtains of his bed.

"I'm dying," he announced as the doctor bent over him.

"Nonsense. I am not going to allow you to die."

"You won't be able to help yourself. I've brought you here to see me die."

"What do you mean?"

"I've a surprise for you too, a Christmas present. These letters now, these love letters of my wife's—what name do you think is on them?"

"Your mind is giving way, Sir Harry."

"Not at all—come nearer, Deane—the name is Bevis Holroyd."

"Then they are letters ten years old. Letters written before your wife met you."

The sick man grinned with infinite malice.

"Maybe. But there are no dates on them and the envelopes are all destroyed. And I, as a dying man, shall swear to their recent date—I, as a foully murdered man."

"You are wandering in your mind," said Bevis Holroyd quietly. "I refuse to listen to you any further."

"You shall listen to me. I brought you here to listen to me. I've got you. Here's my will, Deane's got that, in which I denounced you both, there are your letters, every one thinks that *she* put you in charge of the case, every one knows that you know all about arsenic in cambric tea through the Pluntre case, and every one will know that I died of arsenic poisoning."

The doctor allowed him to talk himself out; indeed it would have been difficult to check the ferocity of his malicious energy.

The plot was ingenious, the invention of a slightly insane, jealous recluse who hated his wife and hated the man she had never ceased to love; Bevis Holroyd could see the nets very skillfully drawn round him; but the main issue of the mystery remained untouched; who *was* administering the arsenic?

The young man glanced across the sombre bed to the dark figure of the secretary.

"What is your place in all this farrago, Mr. Deane?" he asked sternly.

"I'm Sir Harry's friend," answered the other stubbornly, "and I'll bring witness any time against Lady Strangeways. I've tried to circumvent her—"

"Stop," cried the doctor. "You think that Lady Strangeways is poisoning her husband and that I am her accomplice?"

The sick man, who had been looking with bitter malice from one to another, whispered hoarsely:

"That is what you think, isn't it, Deane?"

"I'll say what I think at the proper time," said the secretary obstinately.

"No doubt you are being well paid for your share in this."

"I've remembered his services in my will," smiled Sir Harry grimly. "You can adjust your differences then, Dr. Holroyd, when I'm dead, *poisoned, murdered*. It will be a pretty story, a nice scandal, you and she in the house together, the letters, the cambric tea!"

An expression of ferocity dominated him, then he made an effort to dominate this and to speak in his usual suave stilted manner.

"You must admit that we shall all have a very Happy Christmas, doctor."

Bevis Holroyd was looking at the secretary, who stood at the other side of the bed, cringing, yet somehow in the attitude of a man ready to pounce; Dr. Holroyd wondered if this was the murderer.

"Why," he asked quietly to gain time, "did you hatch this plan to ruin a man you had never seen before?"

"I always hated you," replied the sick man faintly. "Mollie never forgot you, you see, and she never allowed *me* to forget that she never for-

got you. And then I found those letters she had cherished."

"You are a very wicked man," said the doctor dryly, "but it will all come to nothing, for I am not going to allow you to die."

"You won't be able to help yourself," replied the patient. "I'm dying, I tell you. I shall die on Christmas Day."

He turned his head towards the secretary and added:

"Send my wife up to me."

"No," interrupted Dr. Holroyd strongly. "She shall not come near you again."

Sir Harry Strangeways ignored this.

"Send her up," he repeated.

"I will bring her, sir."

The secretary left, with a movement suggestive of flight, and Bevis Holroyd stood rigid, waiting, thinking, looking at the ugly man who now had closed his eyes and lay as if insensible. He was certainly very ill, dying perhaps, and he certainly had been poisoned by arsenic given in cambric tea, and, as certainly, a terrible scandal and a terrible danger would threaten with his death; the letters were *not* dated, the marriage was notoriously unhappy, and he, Bevis Holroyd, was associated in every one's mind with a murder case in which this form of poison, given in this manner, had been used.

Drops of moisture stood out on the doctor's forehead; sure that if he could clear himself it would be very difficult for Mollie to do so; how could even he himself in his soul swear to her innocence!

Of course he must get the woman out of the house at once, he must have another doctor from town, nurses—but could this be done in time; if the patient died on his hands would he not be only bringing witnesses to his own discomfiture? And the right people, his own friends, were difficult to get hold of now, at Christmas time.

He longed to go in search of Mollie—she must at least be got away, but how, without a scandal, without a suspicion?

He longed to have the matter out with this

odious secretary, but he dared not leave his patient.

Lady Strangeways returned with Garth Deane and seated herself, mute, shadowy, with eyes full of panic, on the other side of the sombre bed.

"Is he going to live?" she presently whispered as she watched Bevis Holroyd ministering to her unconscious husband.

"We must see that he does," he answered grimly.

All through that Christmas Eve and the bitter night to the stark dawn when the church bells broke ghastly on their wan senses did they tend the sick man who only came to his senses to grin at them in malice.

Once Bevis Holroyd asked the pallid woman:

"What was that white packet you had in your work box?"

And she replied:

"I never had such a packet."

And he:

"I must believe you."

But he did not send for the other doctors and nurses, he did not dare.

The Christmas bells seemed to rouse the sick man from his deadly swoon.

"You can't save me," he said with indescribable malice. "I shall die and put you both in the dock—"

Mollie Strangeways sank down beside the bed and began to cry, and Garth Deane, who by his master's express desire had been in and out of the room all night, stopped and looked at her with a peculiar expression. Sir Harry looked at her also.

"Don't cry," he gasped, "this is Christmas Day. We ought all to be happy—bring me my cambric tea—do you hear?"

She rose mechanically and left the room to take in the tray with the fresh milk and water that the housekeeper had placed softly on the table outside the door; for all through the nightmare vigil, the sick man's cry had been for "cambric tea."

As he sat up in bed feebly sipping the vapid and odious drink the tortured woman's nerves slipped her control.

"I can't endure those bells, I wish they would stop those bells!" she cried and ran out of the room.

Bevis Holroyd instantly followed her; and now as suddenly as it had sprung on him, the fell little drama disappeared, fled like a poison cloud out of the compass of his life.

Mollie was leaning against the closed window, her sick head resting against the mullions; through the casement showed, surprisingly, sunlight on the pure snow and blue sky behind the withered trees.

"Listen, Mollie," said the young man resolutely. "I'm sure he'll live if you are careful—you mustn't lose heart—"

The sick room door opened and the secretary slipped out.

He nervously approached the two in the window place.

"I can't stand this any longer," he said through dry lips. "I didn't know he meant to go so far, he is doing it himself, you know; he's got the stuff hidden in his bed, he puts it into the cambric tea, he's willing to die to spite you two, but I can't stand it any longer."

"You've been abetting this!" cried the doctor.

"Not abetting," smiled the secretary wanly. "Just standing by. I found out by chance—and then he forced me to be silent—I had his will, you know, and I've destroyed it."

With this the strange creature glided downstairs.

The doctor sprang at once to Sir Harry's room; the sick man was sitting up in the sombre bed and with a last effort was scattering a grain of powder into the glass of cambric tea.

With a look of baffled horror he saw Bevis Holroyd but the drink had already slipped down his throat; he fell back and hid his face, baulked at the last of his diabolic revenge.

When Bevis Holroyd left the dead man's chamber he found Mollie still leaning in the window; she was free, the sun was shining, it was Christmas Day.

THE 74TH TALE

Jonathan Santlofer

THE AUTHOR OF FIVE DETECTIVE NOVELS, JONATHAN SANTLOFER is even better known as an artist who has works in the permanent collections of such prestigious institutions as the Art Institute of Chicago and the Norton Simon Museum, among many others, and has been reviewed by every major publication devoted to contemporary art, including *Art in America*, *ArtForum*, and the *New York Times*. His crime novels feature Kate McKinnon, a Queens cop and art historian, and Nate Rodriguez, a New York City forensic sketch artist; the author includes his own original sketches in this series. "The 74th Tale" was first published as a chapbook, given to customers of the Mysterious Bookshop as a Christmas gift in 2008.

The 74th Tale

JONATHAN SANTLOFER

I SWEAR IT WOULDN'T HAVE HAP-pened if it were not for the book. Really, I didn't plan it. It's just that I'm impressionable you know, sensitive to others and to suggestion. It's the way I'm made, the way my brain works and I've come to accept that.

The book was a gift to myself. For Christmas. I knew I wasn't going to get any and was feeling a little bad, like I deserved something, you know, at least one, and it was just a paperback, no big deal, though you could say it changed my life; two lives, really.

I got it at this place called the Mysterious Bookshop. Woo, woo, right? Like it should have been Halloween, not Christmas. What lured me in were the books in the window, all those titles with death and murder and blood, which is not something I think about all the time, just on oc-casion like most people. Someone had tied black and red ribbons around some of the books which is what got me thinking about a present, plus the little lights, black and orange ones, again more Halloween than Christmas, and funny.

Inside, the store was old and new at the same time, lots of wood and stuff but airy and nice, with books everywhere, floor-to-ceiling, on ta-bles, stacked on the floor; I'd never seen so many in one space. There was even one of those lad-ders you have to climb to get at the books on the top rows which I couldn't do for "insurance rea-sons" I was told by this woman, from England I think, with a fancy accent, who smiled when she told me I couldn't use the ladder, that she'd get the higher-up books for me. I said I'd make do with the ones I could reach which was more than enough.

They were in alphabetical order, which ap-pealed to my mind. I may not have leadership qualities but I'm organized and methodical, just as important, if you ask me, and why I was so good in my job at the post office.

I spent a long time going from A to Z but of course there were big gaps, like I missed half of D and more of H and other letters as they were in the top rows, but it didn't matter because I was just choosing books with titles that appealed to me. I wasn't looking for anything special. That's always the way, isn't it, the important things just sort of coming to you when you least expect it?

After a while my eyes were starting to blur from all the books and the English lady came over and asked if she could help me. I told her I was okay and then this white-haired guy came out of a back room and the English lady went and talked to him and I could see they were eying me and then he came over and asked exactly what the English lady had asked: if he could help me, which was annoying because I could tell they thought I was going to shoplift, which I'd never do, I'm not that kind of guy.

I told him I was making up my mind and he said that was fine but they were closing in a few minutes so I had to hurry, which sort of annoyed me, I mean the pressure of making a decision like that when I could buy only one book and I had pulled out about twenty. Like I said I was feeling bad because I knew I wasn't going to get any Christmas presents, not from my mother who I hadn't spoken to in like five years and my father was long dead and my brother, hell, he hated me because I'd mouthed off to his wife last time I saw him which was at Thanksgiving two years ago, a holiday I haven't celebrated since, but she deserved it and to be honest I don't miss my brother or his wife or his two bratty kids or their stupid split-level house out in Levittown or wherever. He, my brother, is six years older than me and never really gave a crap about me and told me I was crazy, like I'm crazy and he isn't? and I'm not going to patch it up unless he calls me and makes like a huge apology and I don't see that happening because I read in the newspaper that some reporter called him and he said I have nothing to say, which proves he never really cared about me, right? I mean, wouldn't you say something nice about your brother at a time like this?

The white-haired guy was going around the store adjusting books but keeping an eye on me which made me want to leave but I wasn't ready to go back to my one room above the Korean deli because the thought of seeing the owner with his creepy bent finger and the way he was always looking at me, squinting, was just too much, too much, so I went through the twenty books and decided to buy the one that had seventy-three stories, which seemed like the best deal, all those stories for the price of one book. It was a paperback, like I said, but really fat with poems in it too, which I didn't think I'd read but it was still a good deal.

The white-haired guy came over while I was looking through it and said it was a classic and how I'd made the right choice and that made me feel good and he smiled and patted me on the arm and called me son, which was nice even though I'm not crazy about being touched and he said, You'll learn a lot from that book.

I asked him what he meant and he said I'd have to read the book to find out, which was pretty cagey, like he was pressing me to buy it

and that's when I saw it was fifteen dollars so I said no way I could afford it being out of work and all and he asked how much I could spend and I told him I had seven bucks on me, a lie, I had twenty-two but wasn't going to admit that. He sort of rocked back on his heels and tilted his head with his face screwed up like he was making a decision and finally said, Okay, it's yours for seven dollars, Merry Christmas, which kind of blew me away.

If I'd known then that the book was going to change everything I wouldn't have felt so good, but when someone does something nice like that you just want to believe in the goodness of people, don't you?

Funny thing is I hadn't planned to buy a book. I'm not much of reader; I haven't read much my whole life except for comic books, lately *Bloody Skull* and *Blade* and *Hack/Slash,* before that *X-Men* and *Fantastic Four* which are more for kids but when I turned twenty-one my brother—this was before we had our fight—said I needed to improve my mind which sort of irritated me but my friend Larry who worked with me at the Post Office before I got laid off said the same thing when he saw me reading *Fantastic Four* and he meant it as a good thing because he knows how smart I am and he's the one who turned me on to horror comics, so I figured I could learn a lot from a book with seventy-three stories and that was true, though some people don't agree it was such a good thing.

By the time I left the store it was dark and drizzling with little icy puddles that looked like frozen lemonade because of the yellow light cast from streetlamps, no one around and I was glad. I liked the feeling that I was alone in the world, which I guess I am but don't start feeling sorry for me because I could have lots of friends and a girlfriend if I wanted one. I've had plenty, and most girls say I'm good-looking which doesn't mean anything to me though I wouldn't say it's a bad thing. My last girlfriend who I met in a bar and went home to her apartment in Murray Hill decorated all modern with girly touches like a ruffled bedspread and such said my mouth was pouty. I wasn't totally sure what she meant but didn't want to ask and appear uneducated so I looked it up in her dictionary. It said: To protrude the lips in an expression of displeasure or sulkiness. That didn't sound so good to me though I was pretty sure Loretta, that was her name, meant it as a good thing since she liked running her finger over my lips, but we didn't last too long so it didn't matter if my lips were pouty or not.

I live only five blocks from the bookstore so it was weird that I'd never seen it. I guess you could say it was fate or evil forces, as they say in *X-Men*, that drew me to it.

When I got to my apartment building I stopped into the deli downstairs and bought a six-pack of beer and a family-size bag of potato chips and a Snickers bar. I tried not to look at the owner's bent finger. I carefully laid my money on the counter so I wouldn't have to touch him, but when he gave me the change he made a point of rubbing his finger against my hand and I know it was on purpose because he's done it before, and I swear a chill went through my entire body.

As soon as I got inside my apartment I gulped down a beer then started another, tore open the chips and sunk onto my couch, which I got from the street, leather and really nice except for a few stains and a tear on one of the back pillows and on one arm which I fixed with Scotch Magic Tape and you can hardly see it now, I'm handy that way. Then I skimmed through my new book and read all the titles making sure I was not moving my lips even though no one was around because one of my girlfriends, Susie, I think her name was, made fun of me for doing that.

I was sorry I hadn't asked the white-haired guy or the English lady which were the best tales, as they were called, because there were so many, so I just went by the titles like I do the names of the horses when I put a few dollars down at OTB, though I usually don't win.

The first tale I chose was about a gold bug that bites a guy, I think, I wasn't sure because it was really hard to read with too many words and sentences that went on so long that I had

to reread them and I finally stopped and might have given up and been really annoyed that I'd wasted seven dollars if I hadn't started another tale which grabbed me right away about a nervous guy who gets pretty crazy as the story goes on because this old guy's eye is driving him nuts. It was pretty funny and got me thinking about the guy in the deli downstairs and his pinky, which is arched up away from his hand as if it's been yanked out of the socket and put back in all wrong with no nail at the end, just a stump. I always end up staring at it, you know how that is, and then it stays in my mind. Sometimes I avoid going into the store for weeks so I won't have to see it but when I need something quick it just makes sense to go there and then I see it again and it's all I can think about for days.

I didn't want to think about the finger so I read another tale about some guy named Roderick and his friend who bury Roderick's twin sister, only she isn't dead, which reminded me of the time I found an injured bird on the sidewalk outside my apartment building when I was a kid. I think it flew into the side of the building; it was alive but couldn't fly. I put it in a shoe box and fed it birdseed and gave it water with an eyedropper but it just got weaker and I knew it was going to die—which is exactly what Roderick and his friend thought about Roderick's sister—but I couldn't kill it outright so I buried the box in an empty lot on the corner and marked the spot with a brick. A week later I dug it up but it was gone and I was never sure if someone else dug it up or if the brick got moved or what happened so I tried again with a mouse that I caught in one of those glue traps.

I didn't wait so long this time, just a day, but when I dug the mouse up he was dead. Mice are easy to catch, so I used more, burying one for like a half day or so—dead when I dug him up—another for like a third of a day, also dead, so I decided I had to make it more methodical. Like I said my mind works best when I'm methodical which is why I was good in the post office and would still have that job if I hadn't gotten into that fight, which wasn't my fault.

I buried the next mouse for exactly eight hours, dead, then one for seven, also dead, and so on subtracting an hour until one finally lived. Two mice lived for five hours after being buried alive. It was awesome, you know, to open the box and see this little creature panting for breath but alive. But then I had to see if they could live for six hours and they both died.

I did that, buried animals and such, on and off for the next few years till we moved away from the corner lot and I sort of stopped thinking about it; well not really but I hadn't thought about actually doing it again until I read the story because Roderick's sister who doesn't die but comes back at the end, like a zombie, and falls onto her brother and they both die and the friend races out—I couldn't blame him for that—and when he looks back the house is cracking apart and crashing down and my heart was beating like the heart under the floorboard in the first tale but I kept reading and the next tale was about the same thing—like the writer was speaking just to me—all about being buried alive, and worse because the guy who told this tale had this like sick fear of being buried alive and in the end he wakes up and he is buried alive, at least he thinks so, really he's in a boat or something, which was a cheat, but it got me all caught up again in the idea of being buried alive, well not me, but something, someone.

I couldn't get the idea out of my mind. It was all I thought about for days while everyone else was thinking about Christmas.

Now they're saying it was premeditated, and it's true I thought about it, a lot, I even dreamed about it, but I still say, and I told this to my court-appointed lawyer—a woman who looks at me with a blank stare and wears the same suit every time I see her—gray stripes with a different blouse so she thinks it looks different but it doesn't—that it was the book, the tales that were the premeditation part, not me. You see what I'm saying? But she says that's no defense, which makes me think she's a lousy lawyer.

I've been here for seven months now and have read all seventy-three tales, some more

than once, and a lot of the poems, which were okay, and they inspired me to write my own tale especially since there have been lots of stories written about me, one by a reporter who came to interview me but still got it wrong, so I decided to write my story, my own tale of what really happened and why. It was the hardest thing I ever did.

I let my lawyer read it and she says I should destroy it because it will seal my fate, but like I said I don't think she's a very good lawyer because I think I did a really good job of explaining my feelings and my motive, if you want to call it that, but you be the judge.

The Tale of the Man & the Construction Site

First of all I am not nervous. I am sensitive. Very, very, dredfully sensitive, but not so dredful that it is a bad thing. I eschew that people are saying I am crazy—mad as they use to say in the olden days but I am not. How could I be mad and get away with what I did and I would have gotten away with it I could have if I wanted to. That is the unequivocal point!

I was careful and filled with dissimulation for days before I did it and I was methodical which is how my mind works and a little melancholy main-ley because I live alone and there is a veil of gloom draping over my apartment and I was all-absorbed with this fancy of being buried alive which is like the shadow between life and death and I had to know where one ended and the other begins.

It vexed me for days but methought I could not do it I mean you cannot exactly bury yourself and even if I could get someone to help me like Larry who laboured beside me at the post office how could I keep track of the time and unearth the grave and see if I lived right? Impossible!

So I needed a volunteer! I wasn't sure who but once I had the idea I was inflamed with intense excitement and bought the trunk which was not made well just a mockery of cardbord painted to look like lether which I could scrap off with my fingernail but

I thought it would work singularly well for my endeavor!

There was a construction site right next to my apartment and I went thereupon at night feeling torrents of blood beating in my heart and dug the grave way in the back where they were not building yet. It took me 3 nights but fineally I was ready and with slight quivering I went down to the deli and there he was! Giving me the evil eye like always and I looked upon that hideous bent finger of his and my blood ran cold and I had a bottel of chloroform and a rag with me but there was a customer a woman buying laundery detergent so I went into the back near the frozen food and my nerves were very unstrung and I waited and he could not see me but I could see him and his finger!

I waited a customary duration for the woman to leave then I seezed upon a package of Oreos and delivered them to the counter and I could see the guy was vexed to see me because he made a little grunt which I heard because my hearing is acute and like I told you I am sensitive. For a moment I did not think I would be able to do it but then his hideous finger brushed against my hand and I shivered all the way to my soul and I got the rag over his nose and he fought me but he was not very strong and even when he made a low mowning cry I had an impetuous fury that kept me going and I did not stop until he grew tremulous and slumped down and fell on the floor.

I felt intense paroxysms and went back upstairs in haste to bring the trunk down and closed the deli door behind me and put the closed sign in the window and endeavored to get the guy into the trunk. Not easy! I had to be careful not to touch that gruesome hideous finger! It took like an eternal period but I fineally got him in and then the top would not close! I was vexed and inflamed but found some duck tape which worked to keep it shut tight in case he tried to get out.

It was all blackness and absolute night when I dragged the trunk outside and my heart was vacillating and no doubt I grew very pale but I had made solem promises to do what I was doing so I dragged the trunk around the corner and into the construction sight and back to the grave I had dug

and pushed the trunk in vehemently and piled dirt over it so it was very entombed. Then I found formidable rocks and put them on top the whole time sweating and my heart pounding but it was thrilling!

After that I went back to the deli and my limbs were trembeling but I fetched two bags of potato chips and a six-pack of beer and another Snickers and went upstairs to my apartment where I was consumed by a burning thirst and drank the beer and devoured the chips and Snickers and my heart stopped pounding and I was feeling less vexed and I counted off the hours because I needed to know how long the guy was entombed. My plan was to keep him buried over night. I did not wish him any ill harm! I wanted him to live! I had good intentions! It was not a crime! It was an experament!

But then I realized with trepidation that I could not unentomb him in the morning because there would be a throng of construction workers and all my cunning and resolve would be ruined!

The next thing I knew it had dawned morning. I had fallen into a deep slumber from the beer and hard work and I was feeling unwell because all I had eaten was the 2 bags of chips and the Snickers bar but when I pictured the guy encoffined in the trunk and how by now the chloroform must be worn off and he could be awake and filled with a terrible dread I felt better and I read my favourite story again the one that inspired me to such fancy and I made a methodical decizion to wait another day and night because one night was not much of a test for a premature burial and so I resolved that he should stay buried for 2 nights!

I was again filed with a hunger so I went down to the deli which still had the closed sign in the window to keep people out and got some Kraft American cheese and Wonder bread and mayo and a giant-size bag of chips and 2 bottels of Yoo-Hoo and went back upstairs and made cheese sanwiches and watched TV til I fell asleep and the next day dawned. Then I watched DVDs of old movies to pass the duration even though I could hardly sit still thinking about the man and what must be going thru his mind in that underground box and that kept me stirring until I started thinking that if my experament worked and the guy lived it would be no good if I was the only one who knew about it and I got tumultuous and started pacing and I did not know how many hours passed but it was starting to darken again and then it came to me who I could tell and it made perfect sense so I raced downstairs in haste and ran 5 blocks feeling like I was in a gossamer dream and went right in and saw all the books and decorations that reminded me it was Xmas and the English lady was there and she looked surprized and discordant to see me and I asked if the white-haired guy was around and she said you must mean Otto and I said yes if that is his name and she went to fetch him and he came out of the back room and I told them both how they must hasten to come with me that I had something awesome to show them and I guess they could see how aroused I was because Otto told the young guy with all the tatoos who was at the desk near the door to watch the store and then they followed me into the gloomy night.

Otto kept telling me to calm down but I could not and when we got to the construction site Otto said to the English lady Sally to wait on the street but I said no she had to come to see what I had done and she said ok and Otto held her hand because the ground had much irregularity and depression from all the construction.

Then we were there and my heart was thumping in my chest and I took the rocks off and started scrapping the dirt away with my shaking hands and Otto asked what are you doing? but I just kept going and then you could see the trunk and I got really aroused and had to rip the tape asunder to get it off but once I did I stopped because it was a rapturous moment and I remembered the line I had memorized and bespoke it—

Arise! Did I not bid they arise?

Otto and Sally stared at me with discordant looks and then I did it! I took the top off! and there

was the wretched guy! Groaning and filed with agony! and whiter than the sheet of paper upon which I write these words but alive!

Otto and Sally looked truly vexed and impetuous but Otto helped the Korean man out of the box. He was trembeling and pitiful looking and Otto tried to calm him down and I saw Sally was getting her cel phone out but it was ok because I had made a discovery! A man could be entombed for 2 nights and live so the world should know and praize my endeavor and when the police came I did not put up a fight I just went into the car with them.

The End

I sent my story to the one person I was sure would like it, the white-haired guy Otto and he wrote back asking if he could publish it in this book he did every year about true crime. He said he was going to use the magazine article written by the guy who interviewed me and would publish my story along with it, which was awesome because that way people would get to hear my side. Otto said there would be about twenty stories in the book and I'd have my name on mine but he couldn't pay me because it was illegal to make money from a crime, though I still say it wasn't like a real crime but that was okay because the idea of having my tale in a book with twenty others was awesome and Otto promised I could have ten copies to give my friends though the only person I could think of was Larry and maybe the man from the deli so that he would understand what I was trying to do. It gets pretty boring in here so I'm looking forward to the book and reading my tale and the others too. I hope there will be some good ones that will appeal to my sensitive nature and maybe even inspire me.

THE UNINNOCENT

Bradford Morrow

AS A MAJOR FIGURE IN THE WORLD OF LITERARY FICTION, Bradford Morrow has received an Academy Award from the American Academy of Arts and Letters, a Guggenheim Fellowship, and many other honors. He is the founding editor of the prestigious literary journal *Conjunctions* and the author of many acclaimed works of fiction, including *The Diviner's Tale* (2011), *Giovanni's Gift* (1997), and *Trinity Fields* (1995). "The Uninnocent" was first published in *The Village Voice Literary Supplement* and was collected in *The Uninnocent* (New York, Pegasus, 2011).

The Uninnocent

BRADFORD MORROW

IN OUR INNOCENCE, WE BURNED candles. We got them from a nearby church, and because my sister believed what we were doing was holy, she said it was fair to take them. Churches, Sister said, were not in the business of making money off children. "Alms for the poor," said she. "Suffer the little ones to come before me and unto them I shall make many gifts." My sister enjoyed creating scripture. She had an impressive collection of hymnals, though neither of us could sing. And, as I say, many candles. I worried about her logic and thefts sometimes, but made it a point never to contradict her. She was older than I, and anyway, what was a hymnal but paper and ink? What was a candle but so much wax and string?

The yellow tongues at the ends of their tapers would flutter when the wind flowed off the lake, and we'd look at each other, down there in the old boathouse, our eyes wide, our mouths agape. And yes, when the flames made shadows all over the rustic wooden walls, where the canoes lay on their shelves and oars were lined up like rifles in a gun case, we would know that *he* was there. We weren't, to say the least, objective in these exercises, these private séances. It didn't occur to either my sister or me that the flickering of the candle flames might have been caused by our own expectant breath. The wind, we knew, could have nothing to do with it. No, it was him. He had come back. He never failed us. After all, he was our Christmas brother.

He never spoke. Our task was to decide what his signs meant. Everything had deep meaning. If the smoke of the candles drifted in a certain direction, it was up to us to deduce what such a thing portended. If a bat flew out of the boathouse, if a flock of chorusing birds lit in a tree overhead, if a mouse danced along the length of the wall, by our reckoning there were valuable ramifications. We took it upon ourselves to determine what the signs were, and interpret. This must, I know, sound indiscriminate and childish.

An instance. Down by the lake. Blind old dear Bob Coconut, the dog, stiffened in the legs, lying in the long grass. The air blue. Autumn. The water was cold, and red and brown leaves clotted the surface of the lake near the shore, like an oil slick. Angela and I had a sign that day. We'd found a dead ovenbird that'd flown into the kitchen window, and we knew what that meant. Out in the boat, we got our friend Butter calmed down enough so that he would let us tie him up like we always liked to do, and tickled him, and warned him if he laughed we would throw him overboard. The blue air was turning toward purple as the sun moved down into the trees and evening was on us. We'd been so hard at our game we hadn't noticed how quickly the hours passed.

Butter wasn't having a very good time. Nice boy with his round face and wide-open pale-gray eyes. He couldn't complain, of course, because those were the rules, and because my sister had wrapped her muffler around his mouth. "Don't worry, little guy," Angela told him. "We're taking you home now." And he squirmed a bit before falling back into the bottom of the boat to breathe. "Don't you cry," she finished, "or Angie will have to hurt."

I was slowly rowing us in. Butter's parents would soon be worried. The evening star was up, a tiny eye of foil, winking. And then I saw him, our brother. He was standing on the lake. He was a milky swirl. His feet were in the mist that had come up out of the water into the warm and cool atmosphere. My sister put her palms over Butter's eyes so that he couldn't see. She thought he had been through enough, and she didn't want him to be so scared that he'd never come out to play with us again. Moreover, she felt that nobody deserved to see our brother but us. Butter sobbed in the bottom of the boat. Angela and I cried too, while the evening star got brighter and brighter.

Butter was drawn into all this because one of the candles went out at just the moment he walked into the boathouse when we were praying for the ovenbird's soul. Too bad for Butter, my sister told me later. And true, it was too bad, because from that moment on, all Butter's problems became a matter of fate. Nothing we did, said Angela, was because we decided to do it. Our Christmas brother—who was one with fate— told us what to do and we did as we were told.

Looking back, I must admit to some surprise at how unparented we were. My father's persistent absences were difficult to fathom, and what I've since been able to fathom is difficult to articulate, for the shame of what I think I understand. He worked hard to support us. He had a long daily commute from our rural home into the city. He was a tall, meek, square-headed, decent sort of man. And I've become unshakable in my conviction that he was a dedicated philanderer. I have no proof, and I never confronted him. My deduction is the nasty product of all those days and nights of fatherlessness coupled with my sure memory of his wandering, unprincipled eyes.

As for Mother, she was transformed into a cipher, a drifting and listless creature, by the Christmas brother's death. We never knew her any other way, though Father told us she used to be a happy girl. She took it all to be her fault. She was the one who slipped on the ice. No one pushed her. The miscarriage that followed her accident was quite probably the end of her life, too, along with that of the blackened holiday fetus. Angela and I—who came along later— were unexpected, were not even afterthoughts. Mother carried us, birthed us, but gave us to understand we would never be our brother. Nothing would ever replace him. Much as I loved him, sometimes he made me want to do bad things.

In our innocence, sometimes we were compelled to go to extremes to get our brother to come to us. We felt forced to do things we weren't proud of, yet never lost our faith in him even when, in our mad desire to tempt him home, we hurt things that didn't deserve hurt.

We always feared Christmas. We couldn't understand that other world, that parallel world where he resided, we couldn't see why Christmas made him so reluctant a guest. Here, we thought, was the one time of year when families should celebrate together, reunite and rejoice.

Angela was the one who decided to hurt Bob Coconut. I didn't make the connection between the dog and our brother, but Angela told me to trust her and I did. This was during Christmas, of course. My father and I had brought in the tree we'd sawed down at the tree farm. A prickly, nasty blue spruce. Ornaments, twinkling lights, cookies, the train set, cards hung over pendant string from end to end on the mantel. Bob Coconut lay on a rug before the fire, and twitched pleasantly under the influence of his dreams.

"You think Coco remembers when he could see?" Angela asked me.

I didn't know, but I thought so.

"Coco?" she whispered in his old ear. "Oh, Co-co."

"Let him sleep," I said.

"I bet Coco could see him if he wanted to.

Dogs have those abilities, you know. They can hear things we can't hear. And they can smell better than we can. I bet he can see right into that other world, can't you, Coco dear?"

"Doubt it," I said.

"Hey, I've got an idea," she said.

I don't want to write down what my sister did to him. I wasn't surprised, though, that it failed to work. Our brother was farther away from us than ever, after that. From then on, I decided to trust nothing my sister said or did. Instead, I began to observe her.

Two Angela stories.

First Angela story. There was a period when she thought she was our brother, after he stopped appearing to us. "He's in me now," she announced one night. She liked possessing him, liked being possessed. On occasion, she allowed me to pose questions. "What is it like being dead?" I asked. "You'll know soon enough," he answered through his medium. "Do you love me?" I asked. "I love you fine, but I love Angela better," she said, her eyelids closing to narrow slits, the corners of her mouth lifted into a satisfied smile.

Then she found out one day that she wasn't our brother. Something mysterious happened to her, and Mother told her she was a woman. And so it was time for her to start wearing dresses. I got to shave her legs. My sister even photographed me while I shaved them, telling me it was good for both of us, a sacrifice. She wouldn't let me shave the hair under her arms, though. She said this was because she couldn't take a picture of me doing it. I would be too close to her. That is what she said. The real reason she wouldn't let me do it, I think, was that part of her still believed she was our brother. She could walk around with her glistening and smooth white legs in the sun beneath the pleat of her billowy skirt, a young woman with strong calves and hard thighs, and we could admire her lush femininity, but we could never release her from her masculine possessiveness.

Second Angela story. Once there was a parade in the little upstate town where we lived. I don't

remember what holiday it was. There were a couple of makeshift floats. There were marching bands from county schools. I remember because it was the day my sister ran away from home. She was eighteen. She managed to vanish—"like a ghost," said our mother—and was not heard from for many years. She was a missing person. Some people thought she was dead. I knew better; I knew she was truly missing.

In our innocence, we grew up. Tonight is his birthday, or would have been. He'll always seem older than me, no matter how many years I keep on going. Angela is married and lives in New Hampshire now, her personal cold complementing its heavy winters. She has been married twice. She's been around, as she likes to phrase it. She has three children—she may be cold, but she's not frigid—and mentioned in a recent letter that she wants another.

I never understood this marrying business, and I can't imagine what it must be like to raise children. The dog I own here in the city reminds me of old Bob Coconut. He's far too lively and large for this apartment, but he is an amiable companion. When he curls up by the fireplace—the landlord won't let me burn a fire in the hearth, so I make do with a gouache painting of flames I made on cardboard—I think of those times, of the complexities and strangeness of a child's world. We were isolated. We didn't know what we were doing; we didn't realize how splendidly we were able to do what we wanted. All that is gone now. Is it schizophrenic of me to say that I regret the loss and couldn't care less?

Here is Christmas night again. Christmas Eve I spent with my friends. We ate dinner down in Chinatown. It was a noisy evening there, the streets teeming with revelers. Tonight, it is silent. I've thought about phoning Mother, even considered giving Angela a call. Not fond of Mother's new husband, and knowing Angela to be a chore, I have decided against communication. Were Bob Coconut here, I might light a candle for old times' sake. There is a cathedral around the corner, where I could snag one. I miss my ghost; he'd have made a decent brother, despite how our mother would have raised him, smothering him with a flood of feeling, drinking his love like a vampire. Yes, I miss my Christmas brother. He would have been a felicity in my olding life. He'd have been able to tell me why I'm all alone.

Outside the window, snow is making a feeble attempt to fall. The streetlights that form halos of its transient passage are cheery. A whole world tries its best to rise to the dignity and joy of the occasion. I wish the world happiness, and everyone in it peace. I do. I'll always regret what happened to Butter. We were uninnocent, but the very isolation that in some ways damned us has also acted as our benefactor and protector. I suppose I'm grateful no one has ever found out how it happened, or will.

BLUE CHRISTMAS
Peter Robinson

DETECTIVE CHIEF INSPECTOR BANKS works in a fictional town in Yorkshire, where Peter Robinson was born and lived until he moved to Canada in 1974. The cop who appears in virtually all of the author's books is tough enough to do his job but, as in the present story, has a giant heart, helping to make his adventures among the most popular crime fiction being written today, with regular appearances on the bestseller lists in Canada, the United States, and Great Britain, numerous awards on both sides of the Atlantic, and frequent recognition among the notable books of the year by various publications. "Blue Christmas" was first published as a chapbook limited to three hundred fifty-five copies (Norfolk, VA, Crippen & Landru, 2005).

Blue Christmas

PETER ROBINSON

A THREE-DAY HOLIDAY. BANKS SAT down at the breakfast table and made some notes on a lined pad. If he was doomed to spend Christmas alone this year, he was going to do it in style. For Christmas Eve, Alastair Sim's *Scrooge*, the black and white version, of course. For Christmas Day, *Love, Actually*. Mostly it was a load of crap, no doubt about that, but it was worth the silliness for Bill Nighy's Billy Mack, and Keira Knightley was always worth watching. For Boxing Day, *David Copperfield*, the one with the Harry Potter actor in it, because it had helped him through a nasty hangover one Boxing Day a few years ago, and thus are traditions born.

Music was more problematic. Bach's *Christmas Oratorio* and Handel's *Messiah,* naturally. Both were on his iPod and could be played through his main sound system. But some years ago, he had made a Christmas compilation tape of all his favourite songs, from Bing's "White Christmas" to Elvis's "Santa Claus Is Back in Town" and "Blue Christmas," The Pretenders' "2000 Miles" and Roland Kirk's "We Free Kings." Unfortunately, that had gone up in flames along with the rest of his music collection. Which meant a quick trip to HMV in Eastvale that afternoon to pick up a few seasonal CDs so he could make a playlist. He had to go to Marks and Spencer, anyway, for his turkey dinner, so he might as well drop in at HMV while he was in the Swainsdale Centre. As for wine, he still had a more than decent selection from his brother's cellar—including some fine Amarone, Chianti Classico, Clarets, and Burgundies—which would certainly get him through the next three days without any pain. Luckily, he had bought and given out all his Christmas presents earlier—what few there were: money for Tracy, a Fairport Convention box-set for Brian, chocolates and magazine subscriptions for his parents, and a silver and jet bracelet for Annie Cabbot.

Banks put his writing pad aside and reached for his coffee mug. Beside it sat a pristine copy of Kate Atkinson's *Behind the Scenes at the Museum,* which he fully intended to read over the holidays. There should be plenty of peace and quiet. Brian was with his band in Europe and wouldn't be able to get up to Gratly until late on Boxing Day. Tracy was spending Christmas with her mother Sandra, stepdad Sean, and baby Sinead, and Annie was heading home to the artists' colony in St. Ives, where they would all no doubt be having a good weep over *The Junky's Christmas*, which, Annie had told him, was a Christmas staple among her father's crowd. He had seen it once, himself, and he had to admit that it wasn't bad, but it hadn't become a tradition with him.

All in all, then, this Christmas was beginning to feel like something to be got through with liberal doses of wine and music. Even the weather was refusing to cooperate. The white Christmas that everyone had been hoping for since a tentative sprinkle of snow in late November had not materialized, though the optimists at the meteorological centre were keeping their options open. At the moment, though, it was uniformly grey and wet in Yorkshire. The only good thing that could be said for it was that it wasn't cold. Far from it. Down south people were sitting outside at Soho cafes and playing golf in the suburbs. Banks wondered if he should have gone away, taken a holiday. Paris. Rome. Madrid. A stranger in a strange city. Even London would have been better than this. Maybe he could still catch a last-minute flight.

But he knew he wasn't going anywhere. He sipped some strong coffee and told himself not to be so maudlin. Christmas was a notoriously dangerous time of year. It was when people got depressed and gave in to their deepest fears, when all their failures, regrets, and disappointments came back to haunt them. Was he going to let himself give in to that, become a statistic?

He decided to go into town now and get his last-minute shopping over with before it got really busy. Just before he left, though, his phone rang. Banks picked up the receiver.

"Sir? It's DC Jackman."

"Yes, Winsome. What's the problem?"

"I'm really sorry to disturb you at home, sir, but we've got a bit of a problem."

"What is it?" Banks asked. Despite having to spend Christmas alone, he had been looking forward to a few days away from the Western Area Headquarters, if only to relax and unwind after a particularly difficult year. But perhaps that wasn't to be.

"Missing person, sir."

"Can't someone else handle it?"

"It needs someone senior, sir, and DI Cabbot's already on her way to Cornwall."

"Who's missing?"

"A woman by the name of Brenda Mercer. Forty-two years old."

"How long?"

"Overnight."

"Any reason to think there's been foul play?"

"Not really."

"Who reported her missing?"

"The husband."

"Why did he leave it until this morning?"

"He didn't. He reported it at 6 p.m. yesterday evening. We've been looking into it. But you know how it is with missing persons, sir, unless it's a kid. It was very early days. Usually they turn up, or you find a simple explanation quickly enough."

"But not in this case?"

"No, sir. Not a sign. The husband's getting frantic. Difficult. Demanding to see someone higher up. And he's got the daughter and her husband in tow now. They're not making life any easier. I've only just managed to get rid of them by promising I'd get someone in authority to come and talk to them."

"All right," Banks said, with a sigh. "Hang on. I'll be right in."

Major Crimes and CID personnel were thin on the ground at Western Area Headquarters that Christmas Eve, and DC Winsome Jackman was one who had drawn the short straw. She didn't mind, though. She couldn't afford to visit her parents in Jamaica, and she had politely passed up a Christmas dinner invitation from a fellow member of the potholing club, who had been pursuing her for some time now, so she had no real plans for the holidays. She hadn't expected it to be particularly busy in Major Crimes. Most Christmas incidents were domestic and, as such, they were dealt with by the officers on patrol. Even criminals, it seemed, took a bit of time off for turkey and Christmas pud. But a missing person case could turn nasty very quickly, especially if it was a woman.

While she was waiting for Banks, Winsome went through the paperwork again. There wasn't much other than the husband's report and statement, but that gave her the basics.

When David Mercer got home from work on 23rd December at around 6 p.m., he was surprised to find his wife not home. Surprised because she was always home and always had his dinner waiting for him. He worked in the administration offices of the Swainsdale Shopping Centre, and his hours were regular. A neighbour had seen Mrs. Mercer walking down the street where she lived on the Leaview Estate at about a quarter past four that afternoon. She was alone and was wearing a beige overcoat and carrying a scuffed brown leather bag, the kind with a shoulder-strap. She was heading in the direction of the main road, and the neighbour assumed she was going to catch a bus. She knew that Mrs. Mercer didn't drive. She said hello, but said that Mrs. Mercer hadn't seemed to hear her, had seemed a bit "lost in her own world."

Police had questioned the bus-drivers on the route, but none of them recalled seeing anyone matching the description. Uniformed officers also questioned taxi drivers and got the same response. All Mrs. Mercer's relatives had been contacted, and none had any idea where she was. Winsome was beginning to think it was possible, then, that someone had picked Mrs. Mercer up on the main road, possibly by arrangement, and that she didn't want to be found. The alternative, that she had been somehow abducted, didn't bear thinking about, at least not until all other possible avenues had been exhausted.

Winsome had not been especially impressed by David Mercer—he was the sort of pushy, aggressive alpha white male she had seen far too much of over the past few years, puffed up with self-importance, acting as if everyone else were a mere lackey to meet his demands, especially if she happened to be black and female. But she tried not to let personal impressions interfere with her reasoning. Even so, there was something about Mercer's tone, something that didn't quite ring true. She made a note to mention it to Banks.

The house was a modern Georgian-style semi with a bay window, stone cladding, and neatly kept garden, and when Banks rang the doorbell, Winsome beside him, David Mercer opened it so quickly he might have been standing right behind it. He led Banks and Winsome into a cluttered but clean front room, where a young woman sat on the sofa wringing her hands, and a whippet-thin man in an expensive, out-of-date suit paced the floor. A tall Christmas tree stood in one corner, covered with ornaments and lights. On the floor were a number of brightly wrapped presents and one ornament, a tiny pair of ice skates, which seemed to have fallen off the tree. The radio was playing Christmas music faintly in the background. Fa-la-la-la-lah.

"Have you heard anything?" David Mercer asked.

"Nothing yet," Banks answered. "But, if I may, I'd like to ask you a few more questions."

"We've already told everything to her," he said, gesturing in Winsome's direction.

"I know," said Banks. "And DC Jackman has discussed it with me. But I still have a few questions."

"Don't you think you should be out there on the streets searching for her," said the whippet-thin man, who was also turning prematurely bald.

Banks turned to face him slowly. "And you are?"

He puffed out what little chest he had. "Claude Mainwaring, Solicitor." He pronounced it "Mannering," like the Arthur Lowe character on *Dad's Army*. "I'm David's son-in-law."

"Well, Mr. Mainwaring," said Banks, "it's not normally my job, as a detective chief inspector, to get out on the streets looking for people. In fact, it's not even my job to pay house calls asking questions, but as it's nearly Christmas, and as Mr. Mercer here is worried about his wife, I thought I might bend the rules just a little. And believe me, there are already more than enough people out there trying to find Mrs. Mercer."

Mainwaring grunted as if he were unsatisfied with the answer, then he sat down next to his wife. Banks turned to David Mercer, who finally bade him and Winsome to sit, too. "Mr. Mercer," Banks asked, thinking of the doubts that Winsome had voiced on their way over, "can you think of anywhere your wife might have gone?"

"Nowhere," said Mercer. "That's why I called you lot."

"Was there any reason why your wife might have gone away?"

"None at all," said Mercer, just a beat too quickly for Banks's liking.

"She wasn't unhappy about anything?"

"Not that I know of, no."

"Everything was fine between the two of you?"

"Now, look here!" Mainwaring got to his feet.

"Sit down and be quiet, Mr. Mainwaring," Banks said as gently as he could. "You're not in court now, and you're not helping. I'll get to you later." He turned back to Mercer and ignored the slighted solicitor. "Had you noticed any difference in her behaviour before she left, any changes of mood or anything?"

"No," said Mercer. "Like I said, everything was quite normal. May I ask what you're getting at?"

"I'm not getting at anything," Banks said. "These are all questions that have to be asked in cases such as these."

"Cases such as these?"

"Missing persons."

"Oh God," cried the daughter. "I can't believe it. Mother a missing person."

She used the same tone as she might have used to say "homeless person," Banks thought, as if she were somehow embarrassed by her mother's going missing. He quickly chided himself for being so uncharitable. It was Christmas, after all, and no matter how self-important and self-obsessed these people seemed to be, they *were* worried about Brenda Mercer. He could only do his best to help them. He just wished they would stop getting in his way.

"Has she ever done anything like this before?" Banks asked.

"Never," said David Mercer. "Brenda is one of the most stable and reliable people you could ever wish to meet."

"Does she have any close friends?"

"The family means everything to her."

"Might she have met someone? Someone she could confide in?"

Mercer seemed puzzled. "I don't know what you mean. Met? Confide? What would Brenda have to confide? And if she did, why would she confide in someone else rather than in me? No, it doesn't make sense."

"People do, you know, sometimes. A girlfriend, perhaps?"

"Not Brenda."

This was going nowhere fast, Banks thought, seeing what Winsome had meant. "Do you have any theories about where she might have gone?"

"Something's happened to her. Someone's abducted her, obviously. I can't see any other explanation."

"Why do you say that?"

"It stands to reason, doesn't it? She'd never do anything so irresponsible and selfish as to mess up all our Christmas plans and cause us so much fuss and worry."

"But these things, abductions and the like, are much rarer than you imagine," said Banks. "In most cases, missing persons are found healthy and safe."

Mainwaring snorted in the background. "And the longer you take to find her, the less likely she is to be healthy and safe," he said.

Banks ignored him and carried on talking to David Mercer. "Did you and your wife have any arguments recently?" he asked.

"Arguments? No, not really."

"Not really?"

"I mean nothing significant, nothing that would cause her to do something like this. We had our minor disagreements from time to time, of course, just like any married couple."

"But nothing that might upset her, make her want to disappear."

"No, of course not."

"Do you know if she has any male friends?" Banks knew he was treading on dangerous ground now, but he had to ask.

"If you're insinuating that she's run off with someone," Mercer said, "then you're barking up the wrong tree. Brenda would never do that to me. Or to Janet," he added, glancing over at the daughter. "Besides, she's . . ."

"She's what?"

"I was simply going to say that Brenda's not exactly a Playboy centrefold, if you catch my drift. Not the sort of woman men would chase after or fantasize about."

Nice one, Banks thought. He had never expected his wife Sandra to run off with another man, either—and not because he didn't think she was attractive to men—but she had done. No sense in labouring the point, though. If anything like that had happened, the Mercers would be the last people to admit it, assuming that they even knew themselves. But if Brenda had no close friends or relatives, then there was no-one else he could question who might be able to tell him more about her. All in all, it was beginning to seem like a tougher job than he had imagined.

"We'll keep you posted," he said, then he and Winsome headed back to the station.

Unfortunately, most people were far too absorbed in their Christmas plans—meals, family visits, last-minute shopping, church events, and what have you—to pay as much attention to local news stories as they did the rest of the year, and even that wasn't much. As Banks and Winsome whiled away the afternoon at Western Area Headquarters, uniformed police officers went from house to house asking questions and searched the wintry Dales landscape in an ever-widening circle, but nothing came to light.

Banks remembered, just before the shops closed, that he had things to buy, so he dashed over to the Swainsdale Centre. Of course, by closing time on Christmas Eve it was bedlam, and everyone was impatient and bad-tempered. He queued fifteen minutes to pay for his turkey dinner because he would have had nothing else to eat otherwise, but just one glance at the crowds in HMV made him decide to forgo the

Christmas music for this year, relying on what he had already, and what he could catch on the radio.

By six o'clock he was back at home, and the men and women on duty at the police station had strict instructions to ring him if anything concerning Brenda Mercer came up.

But nothing did.

Banks warmed his leftover lamb curry and washed it down with a bottle of Black Sheep. After he'd finished the dishes, he made a start on *Behind the Scenes at the Museum*, then he opened a bottle of decent claret and took it with him into the TV room. There, he slid the shiny DVD of *Scrooge* into the player, poured himself a healthy glass and settled back. He always enjoyed spotting the bit where you could see the cameraman reflected in the mirror when Scrooge examines himself on Christmas morning, and he found Alastair Sims's over-the-top excitement at seeing the world anew as infectious and uplifting as ever. Even so, as he took himself up to bed around midnight, he still had a thought to spare for Brenda Mercer, and it kept him awake far longer than he would have liked.

The first possible lead came early on Christmas morning, when Banks was eating a soft-boiled egg for breakfast and listening to a King's College Choir concert on the radio. Winsome rang to tell him that someone had seen a woman resembling Mrs. Mercer in a rather dazed state wandering through the village of Swainshead shortly after dawn. The description matched, down to the coat and shoulder-bag, so Banks finished his breakfast and headed out.

The sky was still like iron, but the temperature had dropped overnight, and Banks thought he sniffed a hint of snow in the air. As he drove down the dale, he glanced at the hillsides, all in shades of grey, their peaks obscured by low-lying cloud. Here and there a silver stream meandered down the slope, glittering in the weak light. Whatever was wrong with Brenda Mercer,

Banks thought, she must be freezing if she had been sleeping rough for two nights now.

Before he got to Swainshead, he received another call on his mobile, again from Winsome. This time she told him that a local train driver had seen a woman walking aimlessly along the tracks over the Swainshead Viaduct. When Banks arrived there, Winsome was already waiting on the western side along with a couple of uniformed officers in their patrol cars, engines running so they could stay warm. The huge viaduct stretched for about a quarter of a mile across the broad valley, carrying the main line up to Carlisle and beyond, into Scotland, and its twenty or more great arches framed picture-postcard views of the hills beyond.

"She's up there, sir," said Winsome, pointing as Banks got out of the car. Way above him, more than a hundred feet up, a tiny figure in brown perched on the edge of the viaduct wall.

"Jesus Christ," said Banks. "Has anyone called to stop the trains? Anything roaring by her right now could give her the fright of her life, and it's a long way down."

"It's been done," said Winsome.

"Right," said Banks. "At the risk of stating the obvious, I think we'd better get someone who knows about these things to go up there and talk to her."

"It'll be difficult to get a professional, sir, on Christmas Day."

"Well, what do you . . . ? No. I can read your expression, Winsome. Don't look at me like that. The answer's no. I'm not a trained psychologist or a counsellor. We need someone like Jenny Fuller."

"But she's away, and you know you're the best person for the job, sir. You're good with people. You listen to them. They trust you."

"But I wouldn't know where to begin."

"I don't think there are any set rules."

"I'm hardly the sort to convince someone that life is full of the joys of spring."

"I don't really think that's what's called for."

"But what if she jumps?"

Winsome shrugged. "She'll either jump or fall if someone doesn't go up there soon and find out what's going on."

Banks glanced up again and swallowed. He thought he felt the soft, chill touch of a snowflake melt on his eyeball. Winsome was right. He couldn't send up one of the uniformed lads—they were far too inexperienced for this sort of thing—and time was of the essence.

"Look," he said, turning to Winsome, "see if you can raise some sort of counsellor or negotiator, will you? In the meantime, I'll go up and see what I can do. Just temporary, you understand?"

"Right you are, sir." Winsome smiled. Banks got back in his car. The quickest way to reach the woman was drive up to Swainshead station, just before the viaduct, and walk along the tracks. At least that way he wouldn't have to climb any hills. The thought didn't comfort him much, though, when he looked up again and saw the woman's legs dangling over the side of the wall.

"Stop right there," she said. "Who are you?"

Banks stopped. He was about four or five yards away from her. The wind was howling more than he had expected, whistling around his ears, making it difficult to hear properly, and it seemed much colder up there, too. He wished he were wearing something warmer than his leather jacket. The hills stretched away to the west, some still streaked with November's snow. In the distance, Banks thought he could make out the huge rounded mountains of the Lake District.

"My name's Banks," he said. "I'm a policeman."

"I thought you'd find me eventually," she said. "It's too late, though."

From where Banks was standing, he could only see her in profile. The ground was a long way below. Banks had no particular fear of heights, but even so, her precarious position on the wall unnerved him. "Are you sure you don't want to come back from the edge and talk?" he said.

"I'm sure. Do you think it was easy getting here in the first place?"

"It's a long walk from Eastvale."

She cast him a sidelong glance. "I didn't mean that."

"Sorry. It just looks a bit dangerous there. You could slip and fall off."

"What makes you think that wouldn't be a blessing?"

"Whatever it is," said Banks, "it can't be worth this. Come on, Brenda, you've got a husband who loves you, a daughter who needs—"

"My husband doesn't love me, and my daughter doesn't need me. Do you think I don't know? David's been shagging his secretary for two years. Can you imagine such a cliché? He thinks I don't know. And as for my daughter, I'm just an embarrassment to her and that awful husband of hers. I'm the shop-girl who married up, and now I'm just a skivvy for the lot of them. That's all I've been for years."

"But things can change."

She stared at him with pity and shook her head. "No they can't," she said, and gazed off into the distance. "Do you know why I'm here? I mean, do you know what set me off? I've put up with it all for years, the coldness, the infidelity, just for the sake of order, not rocking the boat, not causing a scene. But do you know what it was, the straw that finally broke the camel's back?"

"No," said Banks, anxious to keep her talking. "I don't know. Tell me." He edged a little closer so he could hear her voice above the wind. She didn't tell him to stop. Snowflakes started to swirl around them.

"People say it's smell that sparks memory the most, but it wasn't, not this time. It was a Christmas ornament. I was putting a few last-minute decorations on the tree before Janet and Claude arrived, and I found myself holding these tiny, perfect ice skates I hadn't seen for years. They sent me right back to a particular day, when I was a child. It's funny because it didn't seem like just a memory. I felt as if I was *really* there. My father took me skating on a pond somewhere in the country. I don't remember where. But it was just getting dark and there were red

and green and white Christmas lights and music playing—carols like "Silent Night" and "Away in a Manger"—and someone was roasting chestnuts on a brazier. The air was full of the smell. I'll never forget that smell. I was . . . My father died last year." She paused and brushed tears and melted snowflakes from her eyes with the back of her hand. "I kept falling down. It must have been my first time on ice. But my father would just pick me up, tell me I was doing fine, and set me going again. I don't know what it was about that day, but I was so happy, the happiest I can ever remember. Everything seemed perfect and I felt I could do anything. I wished it would never end. I didn't even feel the cold. I was just all warm inside and full of love. Did you ever feel like that?"

Banks couldn't remember, but he was sure he must have. Best to agree, anyway. Stay on her wavelength. "Yes," he said. "I know just what you mean." It wasn't exactly a lie.

"And it made me feel worthless," she said. "The memory made me feel that my whole life was a sham, a complete waste of time, of any potential I once might have had. And it just seemed that there was no point in carrying on." She shifted on the wall.

"Don't!" Banks cried, moving forward.

She looked at him. He thought he could make out a faint smile. She appeared tired and drawn, but her face was a pretty one, he noticed. A slightly pointed chin and small mouth, but beautiful hazel eyes. Obviously this was something her husband didn't notice. "It's all right," she said. "I was just changing position. My bum's gone numb. The wall's hard and cold. I just wanted to get more comfortable."

She was concerned about comfort. Banks took that as a good sign. He was within two yards of her now, but he still wasn't close enough to make a grab. At least she didn't tell him to move back. "Just be careful," he said. "It's dangerous. You might slip."

"You seem to be forgetting that's what I'm here for."

"The memory," said Banks. "That day at the

pond. It's something to cherish, surely, to live for?"

"No. It just suddenly made me feel that my life's all wrong. Worthless. Has been for years. I don't feel like *me* any more. I don't feel anything. Do you know what I mean?"

"I know," said Banks. "But this isn't the answer."

"I don't know," Brenda said, shaking her head, then looking down into the swirling white of the chasm below. "I just feel so sad and so lost."

"So do I sometimes," said Banks, edging a little closer. "Every Christmas since my wife left me for someone else and the kids grew up and moved away from home. But it doesn't mean that you don't feel anything. You said before that you felt nothing, but you do, even if it is only sadness."

"So how do you cope?"

"Me? With what?"

"Being alone. Being abandoned and betrayed."

"I don't know," said Banks. He was desperate for a cigarette, but remembered that he had stopped smoking ages ago. He put his hands in his pockets. The snow was really falling now, obscuring the view. He couldn't even see the ground.

"Did you love her?" Brenda asked.

The question surprised Banks. He had been quizzing her, but all of a sudden she was asking about him. He took that as another good sign. "Yes."

"What happened?"

"I suppose I neglected her," said Banks. "My job . . . the hours . . . I don't know. She's a pretty independent person. I thought things were OK, but they weren't. It took me by surprise."

"I'm sure David thinks everything is fine as long as no-one ruffles the surface of his comfortable little world. And I know he doesn't think I'm attractive. Were you unfaithful?"

"No. But my wife was. I don't suppose I blame her now. I did at the time. When she had a baby with him, that really hurt. It seemed . . . I don't know . . . the ultimate betrayal, the final gesture."

"She had a baby with another man?"

"Yes. I mean, we were divorced and they got married and everything. My daughter's spending Christmas with them."

"And you?"

Was she starting to feel sorry for him? If she did, then perhaps it would help to make her see that she wasn't the only one suffering, that suffering was a part of life and you just had to put up with it and get on with things. "By myself," he said. "My son's abroad. He's in a rock group. The Blue Lamps. They're doing really well. You might even have heard of them."

"David doesn't like pop music."

"Well . . . they're really good."

"The proud father. My daughter's a stuck-up, social-climbing bitch who's ashamed of her mother."

Banks remembered Janet Mainwaring's reaction to the description of her mother as missing: an embarrassment. "People can be cruel," he said. "They don't always mean what they say."

"But how do you cope?"

Banks found that he had edged closer to her now, within a yard or so. It was almost grabbing range. That was a last resort, though. If he wasn't quick enough, she might flinch and fall off as he reached for her. Or she might simply slip out of his hands. "I don't know," he said. "Christmas is a difficult time for all sorts of people. On the surface, it's all peace and happiness and giving and family and love, but underneath . . . You see it a lot in my job. People reach a breaking point. There's so much stress."

"But how do *you* cope with it alone? Surely it must all come back and make you feel terrible?"

"It does, sometimes. I suppose I seek distractions. Music. *Scrooge. Love, Actually*—for Bill Nighy and Keira Knightley—and *David Copperfield*, the one with the Harry Potter actor. I probably drink too much as well."

"Daniel Radcliffe. That's his name. The Harry Potter actor."

"Yes."

"And I'd watch *Love, Actually* for Colin Firth." She shook her head. "But I don't know if it would work for me."

"I suppose it's all just a pointless sort of ritual," said Banks, "but I'd still recommend it. The perfect antidote to spending Christmas alone and miserable."

"But I wouldn't be alone and miserable, would I? That's the problem. I'd be with my family and I'd still be bloody miserable."

"You don't have to be."

"What are you suggesting?"

"I told you. Things can change. You can change things." Banks leaned his hip against the wall. He was so close to her now that he could have put his arms around her and pulled her back, but he didn't think he was going to need to. "Do it for yourself," he said. "Not for them. If you think your husband doesn't love you, leave him and live for yourself."

"Leave David? But where would I go? How would I manage? David has been my life. David and Janet."

"There's always a choice," Banks went on. "There are people who can help you. People who know about these things. Counsellors, social services. Other people have been where you are now. You can get a job, a flat. A new life. I did."

"But where would I go?"

"You'd find somewhere. There are plenty of flats available in Eastvale, for a start."

"I don't know if I can do that. I'm not as strong as you." Banks noticed that she managed a tight smile. "And I think if I did, I would have to go far away."

"That's possible, too." Banks reached out his hand. "For crying out loud, you can come and have Christmas dinner with *me* if you want. Just let me help you." The snow was coming down heavily now, and the area had become very slippery. She looked at his hand, shaking her head and biting her lip.

"*Scrooge?*" she said.

"Yes. Alastair Sim."

"I always preferred James Stewart in *It's a Wonderful Life.*"

Banks laughed. "That'll do nicely, too. I've got the DVD."

"I couldn't . . . you know . . . If I . . . well, I'd have to go home and face the music."

"I know that. But after, there's help. There are choices."

She hesitated for a moment, then she took hold of his hand, and he felt her grip tightening as she climbed off the wall and stood up. "Be careful now," he said. "The ground's quite treacherous."

"Isn't it just," she said, and moved towards him.

A SURPRISING
Little Christmas

NOEL, NOEL

Barry Perowne

THE GREATEST CRIMINAL CHARACTER in literature is A. J. Raffles, the gentleman jewel thief created by E. W. Hornung at the end of the Victorian era. A few years after the author's death in 1921, the popularity of the character remained so high that the British magazine *The Thriller* asked Philip Atkey (using the pseudonym Barry Perowne) to continue the rogue's adventures, and he produced more stories about Raffles than the creator had. Over a fifty-year career, Atkey wrote hundreds of stories and more than twenty novels, many featuring the suave safecracker and his sidekick, Bunny Manders. "Noel, Noel" was first collected in *Murder Under the Mistletoe*, edited by Cynthia Manson (New York, Signet, 1992).

Noel, Noel

BARRY PEROWNE

IT WAS ON A GRAY DECEMBER MORNING, under a sky threatening snow, that I called by request at the Colonial Office (Pacific Section) in the matter of my brother, recently deceased. As his only relative surviving in England, I was handed a letter written by the Resident Commissioner of the remote archipelago where my brother's life had come to an end. The letter was accompanied by a photograph of his grave, and I was given also a small box or chest, carved with strange island designs, which had been found in his palm-thatched house and contained, I was told, a manuscript he had left, of an autobiographical nature.

The official who interview me was a young-old individual, impeccably dressed in a black jacket and striped trousers, and of great urbanity. When I took my leave, he helped me into my tweed overcoat, handed me my gray bowler hat and my cane. No doubt in deference to my frailty and my silver hair, he insisted on carrying the chest out to the waiting taxi.

The snow had set in by now, in earnest.

"Christmas in a few days," said my official, as we shook hands through the taxi window. "It'll be a white one."

He gave me a rather odd look, and I had no doubt, as the taxi set off for Victoria Station, that he was thinking about my brother, who had been born on a Christmas Day and named, accordingly, Noel.

I lived in the country, and returning home in the train, I had a first-class compartment to myself. Prior to opening the chest on the seat beside me, I studied again the photograph of my brother's far-off memorial. A small obelisk of what look like white coral, it bore the curious epitaph "1°.58' N., 157°.27' W.," together with two sets of initials, my brother's and, I had been told, those of the woman to whom he had been for a great many years (though today was the first I had heard of it) most happily married.

Touching those years, the terms used by the Resident Commissioner to describe them, filled me with astonishment as I glanced over his letter again: "Beloved by this small community of forty-two souls—a source of comfort—sage in council—kind, courageous, selfless—"

With the best will in the world, I could not recognize in this picture my brother as I had known him. I turned for enlightenment to the chest on the seat beside me. I studied the carving for a moment—designs of outrigged canoes, paddles, coconut palms, turtles, and land crabs, and when, with an uncomfortable sense of intrusion, I lifted the lid, there came from the chest a subtle aroma that suggested to my imagination palm fibre and sea shells, sunshine and coral grottoes, baked breadfruit and petals of frangipani. I breathed again, it seemed to me—in that train rocking through the December snowfall—the trade winds which had blown from the pages of my boyhood reading, which was as near as I had ever got to the Pacific.

I took from the chest my brother's manuscript book, ran my fingers over its frayed binding, turned the yellowed leaves at random. They were covered with faded writing in a hand which, even after all the long years, I recognized as my brother's. And at the opening sentence, simple and conventional—*My earliest memory is Christmas in the year 1880*—I nodded to myself, remembering that and many another Christmas at home.

I was five years older than Noel. We were a large family, living in a rambling country house, and our father, an awesome man normally, was always rollicking and jovial at Christmastime. For us, his eight children, it was always, outstandingly, the happiest time of the year. Especially was it so, in boyhood and adolescence, for Noel, the youngest of us, being his birthday as well as the season for which he was named. For Noel it was a time of pure magic. His eyes shone with excitement. He was a handsome boy, sensitive and imaginative, not a bit like the rest of us, who were rather homely-looking and stodgy. Yes, at Yuletide my Noel, as a boy, was always at his best—though later, in young manhood, by a kind of reaction to a most unfortunate circumstance, he was to be always at his disastrous worst.

My sister Emily once remarked, "I suppose it's natural that Christmas should mean even more to Noel than to the rest of us, but, you know, I wonder at times if his excitement is quite healthy. His anxiety that we should all be here together, his intense preoccupation with whether it will snow at just the right time, the utter extravagance with which he'd reward the waits if we didn't restrain him—it all makes me wonder if there's not perhaps a slight instability in him somewhere. Really, I tremble at times to think of his future."

She had good reason. At sixteen he began to get into scrapes. At eighteen his behavior gave rise to a deeper disquiet. At twenty, while articled to an estate agent in Shropshire, he kicked over the traces so seriously that my father told him never to show his face at home again.

Poor Noel. Christmas was not the same for him without us—or for us without him. Some of us were married by then, but we always foregathered in the old home in deference to our father. Our natural stodginess, lacking the inspiration of Noel's presence, was quite stupefying.

As for Noel, the very next Christmas season after he had been cast out, he was brought before a London magistrate and charged with drunkenness and insulting behavior. We heard about it later. Asked if he had anything to say, he blamed his misdemeanor on the need he had felt to drown the memory of past joyous Christmases in the home from which his own folly had barred him forever.

"Young man," said the magistrate, "your trouble is less unique than you fancy. We are all prone to self-pity at this season. We all have memories and regrets. We are all sensitive at Christmastime, but it is a sign of immaturity in you that you have allowed such a universal feeling to become, in your case, morbidly developed. Case dismissed, but don't leave the court. I haven't finished with you."

What followed was surprising. The magistrate, moved perhaps by Noel's good looks and charm of manner, and by a certain pathos in his aberration, invited him into his own home as a guest over Christmas. The visit grew extended. Long after the holly had been taken down, my brother continued to loll in the magistrate's house. Instead of resenting this, the magistrate and his good lady felt a growing affection for him. In a sense, they adopted him; but, not liking to see him idle, they found him a sound position in a South Coast town.

The following Christmas found Noel in trouble again. It was so serious that, instead of returning "home" to the magistrate's house, where he was expected on Christmas Eve, he sent the unfortunate man a telegram announcing his intention of throwing himself from Beachy Head at midnight.

The harassed magistrate caused police to be rushed to the spot. Noel, however, having sent his telegram, had succumbed to drink and was later found insensible in a snow-covered beach shelter. The magistrate, though furious, yielded to his wife's insistence that he smooth over the trouble Noel was in; but he told my brother from thenceforth he could go to the devil in his own way.

The magistrate and his wife, on the other hand, went to Aix-les-Bains to recuperate from their undeserved anxieties. One morning, as they were walking from their hotel to the curative baths, in the pleasant winter sunshine, a man darted out from behind a date palm and planted himself squarely in their path.

It was my brother Noel, handsome as ever, but much disheveled and in that state of excitement, peculiar to himself, which my sister Emily had once described as "unhealthy."

"Go to the devil, may I?" he shouted at the magistrate. "In my own way? All right, watch me! *This* is my way!"

His hand flashed to his mouth. A cloaked gendarme came running towards the scene, blowing his whistle. My brother Noel lurched heavily to the left. He lurched heavily to the right. His knees buckled. The magistrate's good lady screamed. My brother Noel fell contorted at her feet with a white froth on his lips.

It was proved afterward that he had eaten soap.

His object had been to frighten the couple into taking him back into their good graces. The extraordinary thing was that the magistrate did not have him jailed. He was eager to do so, but his good lady took the view that it was no good sending Noel to prison, since he would be out in a month or two, and free to plague them again. She would be terrified to put a foot outside her house, she said, for fear he might spring at her from the shrubbery and open his veins with a razor before her very eyes. He must be sent, she insisted, somewhere very far away.

The magistrate provided funds for Noel's emigration to Australia.

At home, we of his family heard of all this later. Our father passed away in the interim— our sister Emily too—and those of us who were still living in the family home had resolved to let bygones be bygones and to make Noel welcome among us, should he ever show up.

But we heard nothing from him, and it was only now as I sat in the train reading his manuscript that I came to that part of it which dealt with adventures of which I had had no previous inkling.

I laid down the book on my knees for a moment. The lights had come on in the compartment. Outside, the snow was falling thickly, and the woods and fields glimmered under their mantle of white as the December evening drew in.

Poor Noel, I thought again; he had been worthless through and through when he had left England. I marveled again at the letter, so full of praise of my brother, which I had been handed at the Colonial Office. What experience had befallen him, I wondered, to have changed him so greatly?

I picked up the book again, to read of a continuing succession of disasters and infamies. Within a year, he had made Australia too hot to hold him. He was compelled to leave clandestinely aboard a trading schooner, the *Ellis P. Harkness,* skippered by a toothless Cockney named Larkin, as incorrigible a scoundrel as my brother.

The third member of the schooner's company was a slim, brown, silent, smiling boy, a native of Tokelau called Rahpi. He was far too good for the precious party he sailed with, but through months of their huckstering and rogueries among the archipelagos he served them loyally, and for my brother the boy conceived an inexplicable devotion.

One day, as the two men were drinking morosely in the cabin, an excited hail from Rahpi, at the wheel, sent them staggering up the companionway. The boy pointed off to starboard. Far across the shining water, under the blue Pacific sky, was an open boat. The prevailing easterly blew light and fitful; the boat's sail trembled. It was clear there was no hand at the helm.

By mid-afternoon the schooner came up

with the boat. There lay in it the sun-blackened body of a man. My brother Noel dropped down into the boat to examine the corpse. Clutched in its brittle fingers was a wash-leather bag. Noel loosed it from the dead man's grip and shook the contents onto his palm. His heart gave a great thud.

Pearls!

He felt the boat rock as Larkin leaped down into it.

"Halves, mate!" Larkin said. "How about it, mate?"

Noel looked at him. Larkin's eyes narrowed, his tongue moved round over his toothless gums, his right hand rested tensely on the bulge of the revolver in the pocket of his tattered ducks.

My brother smiled. "Halves it is," he said.

Larkin looked with sly gloating at the pearls on my brother Noel's palm. "What a Christmas present, mate!" Larkin said. "Eh, mate?"

The bright day seemed to my brother Noel suddenly, strangely to darken. He said slowly, "Christmas present?"

Larkin flared up. It was as though, all at once, he were anxious to find cause for offense, an excuse for a fight.

"Why, you lowdown, busted boozer," he shouted, "ain't you got a spark of decency left in you? Ain't you got a family back home to bow your head in shame to think of at a time like this? Don't you know tomorrow's Christmas Eve?"

The pearls spilled unheeded from my brother's hand to the bottom of the boat. Larkin plunged to his knees, pouring curses on the corpse as he shoved it aside to get at the boat's bilges. Noel swung himself back to the schooner's deck. He thrust past the staring Rahpi and went below. He flung his broken-peaked cap across the cabin and reached for a bottle.

That night, swaying on his feet as he stood his trick at the wheel, he brooded alcoholically, heedless of the star-bright sky. More acutely than ever before, the memory of long-lost happy Yuletides returned to plague him. He could neither relive them nor forget them. That nostalgia known to all men—but developed in my brother Noel to a destructive morbidity—made him as desperate as a trapped animal. He had a blind urge to flight, which in his befuddled mind shaped itself into a plan to seize the schooner and the pearls and *be rid of Larkin—*

Suddenly, leaving the wheel spokes spinning aimlessly, he lurched down the companion into the cabin. The lamp there, swaying in gimbals, cast an oily yellow gleam that made the shadows move. Larkin lay on his back in his bunk, snoring, his toothless mouth agape, his gums glistening pink in a tangle of beard.

My brother, holding his breath, slid a hand under the man's pillow. He felt the wash-leather bag, the butt of the revolver. He drew them out cautiously. He raised the revolver to Larkin's head, but then the thought of the boy Rahpi flashed into his mind. The Tokelau boy was asleep in the forepeak. He would hear a shot. My brother stood biting his lips. His rage flamed up again. Kill one, kill both! Rahpi must go, too. He must be hounded out and ruthlessly shot down.

Again my brother raised the revolver to Larkin's head. But now the schooner, to a sudden freshening of the wind, and with the wheel spinning free, broached-to with a jerk that sent Noel staggering. Before he could recover himself, the squall struck—one of those Pacific squalls which an alert wheelsman could see coming from afar in good time to reef down and make all snug. But there was no wheelsman, and with a rush and hiss of rain and screaming wind, the squall was on them. Larkin woke with a shout as the schooner was lifted high on the top of the rollers, then dropped dizzily into its trough. Glass crashed as the lamp blacked out.

The two men were flung together, struggling, fighting with each other to be first up the companion. Finally both gained the deck and clung where they could as a wave swept over them. Through the tumult about them sounded a deeper, more distant note, a rumbling note like thunder.

"Breakers!" Larkin yelled.

After that, according to the account in the manuscript, my brother Noel had no clear idea of what happened, no recollection of clawing a handhold on the reef as the schooner struck. He did not know how many hours passed before he regained consciousness. His whole body stung from the cruel abrasions of the coral. His head seemed to weigh a ton as he raised it.

He struggled to his knees. The vast sky of morning was sheened over with radiant tints of pearl. The passing of the squall had left the sea shining and level to the horizon, though here and there along the curve of the reef spray leaped with a white flash against the blue. At some distance from him, two figures were picking their way along the reef, slowly and painfully, sometimes stumbling.

Noel watched them, conscious of the heavy, measured thumping in his chest. Larkin and Rahpi! Alive! With a creeping horror he remembered how a few hours before, in his madness, he had stood at the very brink of murder. Mere change had plucked him back from that awful precipice. They were alive, and he drew in his breath, deeply, in relief and gratitude.

A shout reached him, not from the men on the reef, but from the lagoon within its shelter. Noel got to his feet with difficulty, his salt-soaked body smarting, and turned. The lagoon lay tranquil, edged in the distanced by a white beach and leaning palms. A canoe, driven swiftly by paddles that flashed as they rose and fell, was coming towards him. There were two people in it, a young man and a girl. The *pareus* they wore were gaily colored, and the girl's shining dark hair streamed over her brown shoulders.

"Hello?" the young man called to Noel. "All right, there? Hello?"

My brother lifted a hand slowly in reply. He wondered where he was. The young man had spoken in English. Nearing the reef, the couple, obviously brother and sister, and Tahitian in appearance, backed with their paddles, and beached the canoe.

The girl looked up at my brother with dark, gentle eyes that seemed to hold a puzzled look. She was very beautiful. My brother had a strange feeling that this meeting between them had been inevitable—that he had come to the one place in the world where he could find peace—that before him, here, lay the beginning of his real life.

There had been nobody here to greet Captain Cook when he had discovered the island on December 24, 1777, at precisely $1°.58'$ N., $157°.27'$ W. But for my brother Noel there was this girl, and she smiled at him gravely, yet with a kind of wonder in her eyes, as though she had been waiting for him for a long time and could not quite believe that he had come, at last.

"Welcome," she said, "to Christmas Island."

DEATH ON CHRISTMAS EVE
Stanley Ellin

THE THREE-TIME EDGAR AWARD WINNER and the Mystery
Writers of America's Grand Master honoree in 1981, Stanley Ellin was one of
America's greatest short story writers of the twentieth century. His first story,
"The Specialty of the House" (1948), went on to become a relentlessly antholo-
gized classic of crime fiction and was adapted for an episode of the television
series *Alfred Hitchcock Presents*. Many more of his stories were adapted for TV
by Hitchcock and other series, and six of his stories were nominated for Edgars,
two of which won; his superb novel, *The Eighth Circle* (1958), also won an Edgar.
Each of his stories is a perfectly polished gem, as you will see when you read this
masterpiece. "Death on Christmas Eve" was first published in the January 1950
issue of *Ellery Queen's Mystery Magazine;* it was first collected in *Mystery Stories* (New York, Simon & Schuster, 1956).

Death on Christmas Eve

STANLEY ELLIN

AS A CHILD I HAD BEEN VASTLY impressed by the Boerum house. It was fairly new then, and glossy; a gigantic pile of Victorian rickrack, fretwork, and stained glass, flung together in such chaotic profusion that it was hard to encompass in one glance. Standing before it this early Christmas Eve, however, I could find no echo of that youthful impression. The gloss was long since gone; woodwork, glass, metal, all were merged to a dreary gray, and the shades behind the windows were drawn completely so that the house seemed to present a dozen blindly staring eyes to the passerby.

When I rapped my stick sharply on the door, Celia opened it.

"There is a doorbell right at hand," she said. She was still wearing the long outmoded and badly wrinkled black dress she must have dragged from her mother's trunk, and she looked, more than ever, the image of old Katrin in her later years: the scrawny body, the tightly compressed lips, the colorless hair drawn back hard enough to pull every wrinkle out of her forehead. She reminded me of a steel trap ready to snap down on anyone who touched her incautiously.

I said, "I am aware that the doorbell has been disconnected, Celia," and walked past her into the hallway. Without turning my head, I knew that she was glaring at me; then she sniffed once, hard and dry, and flung the door shut. Instantly we were in a murky dimness that made the smell of dry rot about me stick in my throat. I fumbled for the wall switch, but Celia said sharply, "No! This is not the time for lights."

I turned to the white blur of her face, which was all I could see of her. "Celia," I said, "spare me the dramatics."

"There has been a death in this house. You know that."

"I have good reason to," I said, "but your performance now does not impress me."

"She was my own brother's wife. She was very dear to me."

I took a step toward her in the murk and rested my stick on her shoulder. "Celia," I said, "as your family's lawyer, let me give you a word of advice. The inquest is over and done with, and you've been cleared. But nobody believed a word of your precious sentiments then, and nobody ever will. Keep that in mind, Celia."

She jerked away so sharply that the stick almost fell from my hand. "Is that what you have come to tell me?" she said.

I said, "I came because I knew your brother would want to see me today. And if you don't mind my saying so, I suggest that you keep to yourself while I talk to him. I don't want any scenes."

"Then keep away from him yourself!" she cried. "He was at the inquest. He saw them clear my name. In a little while he will forget the evil he thinks of me. Keep away from him so that he can forget."

She was at her infuriating worst, and to break the spell I started up the dark stairway, one hand warily on the balustrade. But I heard her follow eagerly behind, and in some eerie way it seemed as if she were not addressing me, but answering the groaning of the stairs under our feet.

"When he comes to me," she said, "I will forgive him. At first I was not sure, but now I know. I prayed for guidance, and I was told that life is too short for hatred. So when he comes to me I will forgive him."

I reached the head of the stairway and almost went sprawling. I swore in annoyance as I righted myself. "If you're not going to use lights, Celia, you should, at least, keep the way clear. Why don't you get that stuff out of here?"

"Ah," she said, "those are all poor Jessie's belongings. It hurts Charlie to see anything of hers, I knew this would be the best thing to do—to throw all her things out."

Then a note of alarm entered her voice. "But you won't tell Charlie, will you? You won't tell him?" she said, and kept repeating it on a higher and higher note as I moved away from her, so that when I entered Charlie's room and closed the door behind me it almost sounded as if I had left a bat chittering behind me.

As in the rest of the house, the shades in Charlie's room were drawn to their full length. But a single bulb in the chandelier overhead dazzled me momentarily, and I had to look twice before I saw Charlie sprawled out on his bed with an arm flung over his eyes. Then he slowly came to his feet and peered at me.

"Well," he said at last, nodding toward the door, "she didn't give you any light to come up, did she?"

"No," I said, "but I know the way."

"She's like a mole," he said. "Gets around better in the dark than I do in the light. She'd rather have it that way too. Otherwise she might look into a mirror and be scared of what she sees there."

"Yes," I said, "she seems to be taking it very hard."

He laughed short and sharp as a sea-lion barking. "That's because she's still got the fear in her. All you get out of her now is how she loved Jessie, and how sorry she is. Maybe she figures if she says it enough, people might get to believe it. But give her a little time and she'll be the same old Celia again."

I dropped my hat and stick on the bed and laid my overcoat beside them. Then I drew out a cigar and waited until he fumbled for a match and helped me to a light. His hand shook so violently that he had hard going for a moment and muttered angrily at himself. Then I slowly exhaled a cloud of smoke toward the ceiling, and waited.

Charlie was Celia's junior by five years, but seeing him then it struck me that he looked a dozen years older. His hair was the same pale blond, almost colorless so that it was hard to tell if it was graying or not. But his cheeks wore a fine, silvery stubble, and there were huge blue-black pouches under his eyes. And where Celia was braced against a rigid and uncompromising backbone, Charlie sagged, standing or sitting, as if he were on the verge of falling forward. He stared at me and tugged uncertainly at the limp mustache that dropped past the corners of his mouth.

"You know what I wanted to see you about, don't you?" he said.

"I can imagine," I said, "but I'd rather have you tell me."

"I'll put it to you straight," he said. "It's Celia. I want to see her get what's coming to her. Not jail. I want the law to take her and kill her, and I want to be there to watch it."

A large ash dropped to the floor, and I ground it carefully into the rug with my foot. I said, "You were at the inquest, Charlie; you saw what happened. Celia's cleared, and unless additional evidence can be produced, she stays cleared."

"Evidence! My God, what more evidence does anyone need! They were arguing hammer and tongs at the top of the stairs. Celia just grabbed Jessie and threw her down to the bottom and killed her. That's murder, isn't it? Just the same as if she used a gun or poison or whatever she would have used if the stairs weren't handy?"

I sat down wearily in the old leather-bound armchair there and studied the new ash that was forming on my cigar. "Let me show it to you from the legal angle," I said, and the monotone of my voice must have made it sound like a well-memorized formula. "First, there were no witnesses."

"I heard Jessie scream and I heard her fall," he said doggedly, "and when I ran out and found her there, I heard Celia slam her door shut right then. She pushed Jessie and then scuttered like a rat to be out of the way."

"But you didn't *see* anything. And since Celia claims that she wasn't on the scene, there were no witnesses. In other words, Celia's story cancels out your story, and since you weren't an eyewitness you can't very well make a murder out of what might have been an accident."

He slowly shook his head.

"You don't believe that," he said. "You don't really believe that. Because if you do, you can get out now and never come near me again."

"It doesn't matter what I believe; I'm showing you the legal aspects of the case. What about motivation? What did Celia have to gain from Jessie's death? Certainly there's no money or property involved; she's as financially independent as you are."

Charlie sat down on the edge of his bed and leaned toward me with his hands resting on his knees. "No," he whispered, "there's no money or property in it."

I spread my arms helplessly. "You see?"

"But you know what it is," he said. "It's me. First, it was the old lady with her heart trouble any time I tried to call my soul my own. Then when she died and I thought I was free, it was Celia. From the time I got up in the morning until I went to bed at night, it was Celia every step of the way. She never had a husband or a baby—but she had me!"

I said quietly, "She's your sister, Charlie. She loves you," and he laughed that same unpleasant, short laugh.

"She loves me like ivy loves a tree. When I think back now, I still can't see how she did it, but she would just look at me a certain way and all the strength would go out of me. And it was like that until I met Jessie . . . I remember the day I brought Jessie home, and told Celia we were married. She swallowed it, but that look was in her eyes the same as it must have been when she pushed Jessie down those stairs."

I said, "But you admitted at the inquest that you never saw her threaten Jessie or do anything to hurt her."

"Of course I never *saw*! But when Jessie would go around sick to her heart every day and not say a word, or cry in bed every night and not tell me why, I knew damn well what was going on. You know what Jessie was like. She wasn't so smart or pretty, but she was good-hearted as the day was long, and she was crazy about me. And when she started losing all that sparkle in her after only a month, I knew why. I talked to her and I talked to Celia, and both of them just shook their heads. All I could do was go around in circles, but when it happened, when I saw Jessie lying there, it didn't surprise me. Maybe that sounds queer, but it didn't surprise me at all."

"I don't think it surprised anyone who knows Celia," I said, "but you can't make a case out of that."

He beat his fist against his knee and rocked from side to side. "What can I do?" he said. "That's what I need you for—to tell me what to do. All my life I never got around to doing anything because of her. That's what she's banking on now—that I won't do anything, and that she'll get away with it. Then after a while, things'll settle down, and we'll be right back where we started from."

I said, "Charlie, you're getting yourself all worked up to no end."

He stood up and stared at the door, and then at me. "But I can do something," he whispered. "Do you know what?"

He waited with bright expectancy of one who has asked a clever riddle that he knows will stump the listener. I stood up facing him, and shook my head slowly. "No," I said. "Whatever you're thinking, put it out of your mind."

"Don't mix me up," he said. "You know you can get away with murder if you're as smart as Celia. Don't you think I'm as smart as Celia?"

I caught his shoulders tightly. "For God's sake, Charlie," I said, "don't start talking like that."

He pulled out of my hands and went staggering back against the wall. His eyes were bright, and his teeth showed behind his drawn lips. "What should I do?" he cried. "Forget everything now that Jessie is dead and buried? Sit here until Celia gets tired of being afraid of me and kills me too?"

My years and girth had betrayed me in that little tussle with him, and I found myself short of dignity and breath. "I'll tell you one thing," I said. "You haven't been out of this house since the inquest. It's about time you got out, if only to walk the streets and look around you."

"And have everybody laugh at me as I go!"

"Try it," I said, "and see. Al Sharp said that some of your friends would be at his bar and grill tonight, and he'd like to see you there. That's my advice—for whatever it's worth."

"It's not worth anything," said Celia. The door had been opened, and she stood there rigid, her eyes narrowed against the light in the room. Charlie turned toward her, the muscles of his jaw knotting and unknotting.

"Celia," he said, "I told you never to come into this room!"

Her face remained impassive. "I'm not *in* it. I came to tell you that your dinner is ready."

He took a menacing step toward her. "Did you have your ear at that door long enough to hear everything I said? Or should I repeat it for you?"

"I heard an ungodly and filthy thing," she said quietly, "an invitation to drink and roister while this house is in mourning. I think I have every right to object to that."

He looked at her incredulously and had to struggle for words. "Celia," he said, "tell me

you don't mean that! Only the blackest hypocrite alive or someone insane could say what you've just said, and mean it."

That struck a spark in her. "Insane!" she cried. "*You* dare use that word? Locked in your room, talking to yourself, thinking heaven knows what!" She turned to me suddenly. "You've talked to him. You ought to know. Is it possible that—"

"He is as sane as you, Celia," I said heavily.

"Then he should know that one doesn't drink in saloons at a time like this. How could you ask him to do it?"

She flung the question at me with such an air of malicious triumph that I completely forgot myself. "If you weren't preparing to throw out Jessie's belongings, Celia, I would take that question seriously!"

It was a reckless thing to say, and I had instant cause to regret it. Before I could move, Charlie was past me and had Celia's arms pinned in a paralyzing grip.

"Did you dare go into her room?" he raged, shaking her savagely. "Tell me!" And then, getting an immediate answer from the panic in her face, he dropped her arms as if they were red hot, and stood there sagging with his head bowed.

Celia reached out a placating hand toward him. "Charlie," she whimpered, "don't you see? Having her things around bothers you. I only wanted to help you."

"Where are her things?"

"By the stairs, Charlie. Everything is there."

He started down the hallway, and with the sound of his uncertain footsteps moving away I could feel my heartbeat slowing down to its normal tempo. Celia turned to look at me, and there was such a raging hatred in her face that I knew only a desperate need to get out of that house at once. I took my things from the bed and started past her, but she barred the door.

"Do you see what you've done?" she whispered hoarsely. "Now I will have to pack them all over again. It tires me, but I will have to pack them all over again—just because of you."

"That is entirely up to you, Celia," I said coldly.

"You," she said. "You old fool. It should have been you along with her when I—"

I dropped my stick sharply on her shoulder and could feel her wince under it. "As your lawyer, Celia," I said, "I advise you to exercise your tongue only during your sleep, when you can't be held accountable for what you say."

She said no more, but I made sure she stayed safely in front of me until I was out in the street again.

From the Boerum house to Al Sharp's Bar and Grill was only a few minutes' walk, and I made it in good time, grateful for the sting of the clear winter air in my face. Al was alone behind the bar, busily polishing glasses, and when he saw me enter he greeted me cheerfully. "Merry Christmas, counsellor," he said.

"Same to you," I said, and watched him place a comfortable-looking bottle and a pair of glasses on the bar.

"You're regular as the seasons, counsellor," said Al, pouring out two stiff ones. "I was expecting you along right about now."

We drank to each other and Al leaned confidingly on the bar. "Just come from there?"

"Yes," I said.

"See Charlie?"

"And Celia," I said.

"Well," said Al, "that's nothing exceptional. I've seen her too when she comes by to do some shopping. Runs along with her head down and that black shawl over it like she was being chased by something. I guess she is at that."

"I guess she is," I said.

"But Charlie, he's the one. Never see him around at all. Did you tell him I'd like to see him some time?"

"Yes," I said. "I told him."

"What did he say?"

"Nothing. Celia said it was wrong for him to come here while he was in mourning."

Al whistled softly and expressively, and twirled a forefinger at his forehead. "Tell me," he said, "do you think it's safe for them to be alone together like they are? I mean, the way things stand, and the way Charlie feels, there could be another case of trouble there."

"It looked like it for a while tonight," I said. "But it blew over."

"Until next time," said Al.

"I'll be there," I said.

Al looked at me and shook his head. "Nothing changes in that house," he said. "Nothing at all. That's why you can figure out all the answers in advance. That's how I knew you'd be standing here right about now talking to me about it."

I could still smell the dry rot of the house in my nostrils, and I knew it would take days before I could get it out of my clothes.

"This is one day I'd like to cut out of the calendar permanently," I said.

"And leave them alone to their troubles. It would serve them right."

"They're not alone," I said. "Jessie is with them. Jessie will always be with them until that house and everything in it is gone."

Al frowned. "It's the queerest thing that ever happened in this town, all right. The house all black, her running through the streets like something hunted, him lying there in that room with only the walls to look at, for—when was it Jessie took that fall, counsellor?"

By shifting my eyes a little I could see in the mirror behind Al the reflection of my own face: ruddy, deep jowled, a little incredulous.

"Twenty years ago," I heard myself saying. "Just twenty years ago tonight."

THE CHINESE APPLE

Joseph Shearing

MOST OF THE BOOKS WRITTEN UNDER GABRIELLE MARGARET Vere Long's Joseph Shearing pseudonym are historical novels, usually based on real-life criminal cases. While the other nom de plumes of the prolific author have faded into obscurity, the Marjorie Bowen and Shearing names endure. Among Shearing's best known crime novels are *Moss Rose* (1934), the basis for the 1947 film of the same name; *Blanche Fury* (1939), a film released in 1948; and the psychological thriller *So Evil My Love* (1947), the basis for the film starring Ann Todd, Ray Milland, and Geraldine Fitzgerald, set in England in 1876. (In England the film was also titled *So Evil My Love;* it was released in the United States as *The Obsessed.*) "The Chinese Apple" was first published in the April 1949 issue of *Ellery Queen's Mystery Magazine.*

The Chinese Apple

JOSEPH SHEARING

ISABELLE CROSLAND FELT VERY depressed when the boat train drew into the vast London station. The gas lamps set at intervals down the platform did little more than reveal filth, fog, and figures huddled in wraps and shawls. It was a mistake to arrive on Christmas Eve, a matter of missed trains, of indecision and reluctance about the entire journey. The truth was she had not wanted to come to London at all. She had lived in Italy too long to be comfortable in England. In Florence she had friends, admirers; she had what is termed "private means" and she was an expert in music. She performed a little on the harpsichord and she wrote a great deal about ancient musical instruments and ancient music. She had been married and widowed some years before and was a childless woman who had come to good terms with life. But with life in Florence, not London. Mrs. Crosland really rather resented the fact that she was performing a duty. She liked things to be taken lightly, even with a touch of malice, of heartlessness, and here she was in this gloomy, cold station, having left the pleasant south behind, just because she ought to be there.

"How," she thought, as she watched the porter sorting out her baggage, "I dislike doing the right thing; it is never becoming, at least to me."

A widowed sister she scarcely remembered had died: there was a child, quite alone. She, this Lucy Bayward, had written; so had her solicitors. Mrs. Crosland was her only relation.

Money was not needed, companionship was. At last it had been arranged, the child was coming up from Wiltshire, Mrs. Crosland was to meet her in London and take her back to Florence.

It would really be, Isabelle Crosland reflected, a flat sort of Christmas. She wished that she could shift her responsibility, and, as the four-wheeled cab took her along the dingy streets, she wondered if it might not be possible for her to evade taking Lucy back to Italy.

London was oppressive. The gutters were full of dirty snow, overhead was a yellow fog.

"I was a fool," thought Mrs. Crosland, "ever to have left Florence. The whole matter could have been settled by letter."

She did not care for the meeting-place. It was the old house in Islington where she and her sister had been born and had passed their childhood. It was her own property and her tenant had lately left, so it was empty. Convenient, too, and suitable. Only Isabelle Crosland did not very much want to return to those sombre rooms. She had not liked her own childhood, nor her own youth. Martha had married, though a poor sort of man, and got away early. Isabelle had stayed on, too long, then married desperately, only saving herself by Italy and music. The south had saved her in another way, too. Her husband, who was a dull, retired half-pay officer, had died of malaria.

Now she was going back. On Christmas Eve, nothing would be much altered; she had always let the house furnished. Why had she not sold, long ago, those heavy pieces of Jamaica mahogany? Probably out of cowardice, because she did not wish to face up to writing, or hearing anything about them. There it was, just as she remembered it, Roscoe Square, with the church and graveyard in the centre, and the houses, each like one another as peas in a pod, with the decorous areas and railings and the semicircular fanlights over the doors with heavy knockers.

The streetlamps were lit. It was really quite late at night. "No wonder," Mrs. Crosland thought, "that I am feeling exhausted." The sight of the Square chilled her: it was as if she had been lured back there by some malign power. A group of people were gathered round the house in the corner, directly facing her own that was number twelve. "Carols," she thought, "or a large party." But there seemed to be no children and the crowd was very silent.

There were lights in her own house. She noticed that bright façade with relief. Alike in the parlour and in the bedrooms above, the gas flared. Lucy had arrived then. That part of the arrangements had gone off well. The lawyers must have sent the keys, as Isabelle Crosland had instructed them to do, and the girl had had the good sense to get up to London before the arrival of the boat train.

Yet Mrs. Crosland felt unreasonably depressed. She would, after all, have liked a few hours by herself in the hateful house.

Her own keys were ready in her purse. She opened the front door and shuddered. It was as if she had become a child again and dreaded the strong voice of a parent.

There should have been a maid. Careful in everything that concerned her comfort, Mrs. Crosland had written to a woman long since in her employment to be in attendance. The woman had replied, promising compliance. But now she cried: "Mrs. Jocelyn! Mrs. Jocelyn!" in vain, through the gas-lit house.

The cabby would not leave his horse and his rugs, but her moment of hesitancy was soon filled. One of the mongrel idlers who, more fre-

quently than formerly, lounged about the streets, came forward. Mrs. Crosland's trunks and bags were placed in the hall, and she had paid her dues with the English money carefully acquired at Dover.

The cab drove away, soon lost in the fog. But the scrawny youth lingered. He pointed to the crowd on the other side of the Square, a deeper patch amid the surrounding gloom.

"Something has happened there, Mum," he whispered.

"Something horrible, you mean?" Mrs. Crossland was annoyed she had said this, and added: "No, of course not; it is a gathering for Christmas." With this she closed her front door on the darkness and stood in the lamp-lit passage.

She went into the parlour, so well remembered, so justly hated.

The last tenant, selected prudently, had left everything in even too good a state of preservation. Save for some pale patches on the walls where pictures had been altered, everything was as it had been.

Glowering round, Mrs. Crosland thought what a fool she had been to stay there so long.

A fire was burning and a dish of cakes and wine stood on the deep red mahogany table.

With a gesture of bravado, Mrs. Crosland returned to the passage, trying to throw friendliness into her voice as she called out: "Lucy, Lucy, my dear, it is I, your aunt Isabelle Crosland."

She was vexed with herself that the words did not have a more genial sound. "I am ruined," she thought, "for all family relationship."

A tall girl appeared on the first landing.

"I have been waiting," she said, "quite a long time."

In the same second Mrs. Crosland was relieved that this was no insipid bore, and resentful of the other's self-contained demeanour.

"Well," she said, turning it off with a smile. "It doesn't look as if I need have hurried to your assistance."

Lucy Bayward descended the stairs.

"Indeed, I assure you, I am extremely glad to see you," she said gravely.

The two women seated themselves in the parlour. Mrs. Crosland found Lucy looked older than her eighteen years and was also, in her dark, rather flashing way, beautiful. Was she what one might have expected Martha's girl to be? Well, why not?

"I was expecting Mrs. Jocelyn, Lucy."

"Oh, she was here; she got everything ready, as you see—then I sent her home because it is Christmas Eve."

Mrs. Crosland regretted this; she was used to ample service. "We shall not be able to travel until after Christmas," she complained.

"But we can be very comfortable here," said Lucy, smiling.

"No," replied Mrs. Crosland, the words almost forced out of her. "I don't think I can—be comfortable here—I think we had better go to an hotel."

"But you arranged this meeting."

"I was careless. You can have no idea—you have not travelled?"

"No."

"Well, then, you can have no idea how different things seem in Florence, with the sun and one's friends about—"

"I hope we shall be friends."

"Oh, I hope so. I did not mean that, only the Square and the house. You see, I spent my childhood here."

Lucy slightly shrugged her shoulders. She poured herself out a glass of wine. What a false impression those school-girlish letters had given! Mrs. Crosland was vexed, mostly at herself.

"You—since we have used the word—have friends of your own?" she asked.

Lucy bowed her dark head.

"Really," added Mrs. Crosland, "I fussed too much. I need not have undertaken all that tiresome travelling at Christmas, too."

"I am sorry that you did—on my account; but please believe that you are being of the greatest help to me."

Mrs. Crosland apologised at once.

"I am over-tired. I should not be talking like this. I, too, will have a glass of wine. We ought to get to know each other."

They drank, considering one another carefully.

Lucy was a continuing surprise to Mrs. Crosland. She was not even in mourning, but wore a rather ill-fitting stone-coloured satin, her sleek hair had recently been twisted into ringlets, and there was no doubt that she was slightly rouged.

"Do you want to come to Italy? Have you any plans for yourself?"

"Yes—and they include a trip abroad. Don't be afraid that I shall be a burden on you."

"This independence could have been expressed by letter," smiled Mrs. Crosland. "I have my own interests—that Martha's death interrupted—"

"Death always interrupts—some one or some thing, does it not?"

"Yes, and my way of putting it was harsh. I mean you do not seem a rustic miss, eager for sympathy."

"It must be agreeable in Florence," said Lucy. "I dislike London very much."

"But you have not been here more than a few hours—"

"Long enough to dislike it—"

"And your own home, also?"

"You did not like your own youth, either, did you?" asked Lucy, staring.

"No, no, I understand. Poor Martha would be dull, and it is long since your father died. I see, a narrow existence."

"You might call it that. I was denied everything. I had not the liberty, the pocket-money given to the kitchenmaid."

"It was true of me also," said Mrs. Crosland, shocked at her own admission.

"One is left alone, to struggle with dark things," smiled Lucy. "It is not a place that I dislike, but a condition—that of being young, vulnerable, defenceless."

"As I was," agreed Mrs. Crosland. "I got away and now I have music."

"I shall have other things." Lucy sipped her wine.

"Well, one must talk of it: you are not what I expected to find. You are younger than I was when I got away," remarked Mrs. Crosland.

"Still too old to endure what I endured."

Mrs. Crosland shivered. "I never expected to hear this," she declared. "I thought you would be a rather flimsy little creature."

"And I am not?"

"No, indeed, you seem to me quite determined."

"Well, I shall take your small cases upstairs. Mrs. Jocelyn will be here in the morning."

"There's a good child." Mrs. Crosland tried to sound friendly. She felt that she ought to manage the situation better. It was one that she had ordained herself, and now it was getting out of hand.

"Be careful with the smallest case in red leather: it has some English gold in it, and a necklace of Roman pearls that I bought as a Christmas present for you—"

Mrs. Crosland felt that the last part of this sentence fell flat. ". . . pearl beads, they are really very pretty."

"So are these." Lucy put her hand to her ill-fitting tucker and pulled out a string of pearls.

"The real thing," said Mrs. Crosland soberly. "I did not know that Martha—"

Lucy unclasped the necklace and laid it on the table; the sight of this treasure loosened Mrs. Crosland's constant habit of control. She thought of beauty, of sea-water, of tears, and of her own youth, spilled and wasted away, like water running into sand.

"I wish I had never come back to this house," she said passionately.

Lucy went upstairs. Mrs. Crosland heard her moving about overhead. How well she knew that room. The best bedroom, where her parents had slept, the huge wardrobe, the huge dressing-table, the line engravings, the solemn air of tedium, the hours that seemed to have no end. What had gone wrong with life anyway? Mrs. Crosland asked herself this question fiercely, daunted, almost frightened by the house.

The fire was sinking down and with cold hands she piled on the logs.

How stupid to return. Even though it was such a reasonable thing to do. One must be careful of these reasonable things. She ought to have done the unreasonable, the reckless thing, forgotten this old house in Islington, and taken Lucy to some cheerful hotel.

The steps were advancing, retreating, overhead. Mrs. Crosland recalled old stories of haunted houses. How footsteps would sound in an upper storey and then, on investigation, the room be found empty.

Supposing she were to go upstairs now and find the great bedroom forlorn and Lucy vanished! Instead, Lucy entered the parlour.

"I have had the warming-pan in the bed for over two hours, the fire burns briskly and your things are set out—"

Mrs. Crosland was grateful in rather, she felt, an apathetic manner.

This journey had upset a painfully acquired serenity. She was really fatigued, the motion of the ship, the clatter of the train still made her senses swim.

"Thank you, Lucy, dear," she said, in quite a humble way, then leaning her head in her hand and her elbow on the table, she began to weep.

Lucy regarded her quietly and drank another glass of wine.

"It is the house," whimpered Mrs. Crosland, "coming back to it—and those pearls—I never had a necklace like that—"

She thought of her friends, of her so-called successful life, and of how little she had really had.

She envied this young woman who had escaped in time.

"Perhaps you had an accomplice?" she asked cunningly.

"Oh, yes, I could have done nothing without that."

Mrs. Crosland was interested, slightly confused by the wine and the fatigue. Probably, she thought, Lucy meant that she was engaged to some young man who had not been approved by Martha. But what did either of them mean by the word "accomplice"?

"I suppose Charles Crosland helped me," admitted his widow. "He married me and we went to Italy. I should never have had the courage to do that alone. And by the time he died, I had found out about music, and how I understood it and could make money out of it—" "Perhaps," she thought to herself, "Lucy will not want, after all, to come with me to Italy—what a relief if she marries someone. I don't really care if she has found a ruffian, for I don't like her—no, nor the duty, the strain and drag of it."

She was sure that it was the house making her feel like that. Because in this house she had done what she ought to have done so often. Such wretched meals, such miserable silences, such violences of speech. Such suppression of all one liked or wanted. Lucy said:

"I see that you must have suffered, Mrs. Crosland. I don't feel I can be less formal than that—we are strangers. I will tell you in the morning what my plans are—"

"I hardly came from Italy in the Christmas season to hear your plans," replied Mrs. Crosland with a petulance of which she was ashamed. "I imagined you as quite dependent and needing my care."

"I have told you that you are the greatest possible service to me," Lucy assured her, at the same time taking up the pearls and hiding them in her bosom. "I wear mourning when I go abroad, but in the house I feel it to be a farce," she added.

"I never wore black for my parents," explained Mrs. Crosland. "They died quite soon, one after the other; with nothing to torment, their existence became insupportable."

Lucy sat with her profile towards the fire. She was thin, with slanting eyebrows and a hollow at the base of her throat.

"I wish you would have that dress altered to fit you," remarked Mrs. Crosland. "You could never travel in it, either, a grey satin—"

"Oh, no, I have some furs and a warm pelisse of a dark rose colour."

"Then certainly you were never kept down as I was—"

"Perhaps I helped myself, afterwards—is not that the sensible thing to do?"

"You mean you bought these clothes since Martha's death? I don't see how you had the time or the money." And Mrs. Crosland made a mental note to consult the lawyers as to just how Lucy's affairs stood.

"Perhaps you have greater means than I thought," she remarked. "I always thought Martha had very little."

"I have not very much," said Lucy. "But I shall know how to spend it. And how to make more."

Mrs. Crosland rose. The massive pieces of furniture seemed closing in on her, as if they challenged her very right to exist.

Indeed, in this house she had no existence, she was merely the wraith of the child, of the girl who had suffered so much in this place, in this house, in this Square with the church and the graveyard in the centre, and from which she had escaped only just in time. Lucy also got to her feet.

"It is surprising," she sighed, "the amount of tedium there is in life. When I think of all the dull Christmases—"

"I also," said Mrs. Crosland, almost in terror. "It was always so much worse when other people seemed to be rejoicing." She glanced round her with apprehension. "When I think of all the affectations of good will, of pleasure—"

"Don't think of it," urged the younger woman. "Go upstairs, where I have put everything in readiness for you."

"I dread the bedroom."

The iron bell clanged in the empty kitchen below.

"The waits," added Mrs. Crosland. "I remember when we used to give them sixpence, nothing more. But I heard no singing."

"There was no singing. I am afraid those people at the corner house have returned."

Mrs. Crosland remembered vaguely the crowd she had seen from the cab window, a blot of dark in the darkness. "You mean someone has been here before?" she asked. "What about?"

"There has been an accident, I think. Someone was hurt—"

"But what could that have to do with us?"

"Nothing, of course. But they said they might return—"

"Who is 'they'?"

Mrs. Crosland spoke confusedly and the bell rang again.

"Oh, do go, like a good child," she added. She was rather glad of the distraction. She tried to think of the name of the people who had lived in the house on the opposite corner. Inglis—was not that it? And one of the family had been a nun, a very cheerful, smiling nun, or had she recalled it all wrongly?

She sat shivering over the fire, thinking of those past musty Christmas Days, when the beauty and magic of the season had seemed far away, as if behind a dense wall of small bricks. That had always been the worst of it, that somewhere, probably close at hand, people had really been enjoying themselves.

She heard Lucy talking with a man in the passage. The accomplice, perhaps? She was inclined to be jealous, hostile.

But the middle-aged and sober-looking person who followed Lucy into the parlour could not have any romantic complications.

He wore a pepper-and-salt-pattern suit and carried a bowler hat. He seemed quite sure of himself, yet not to expect any friendliness.

"I am sorry to disturb you again," he said.

"I am sorry that you should," agreed Mrs. Crosland. "But on the other hand, my memories of this house are by no means pleasant."

"Name of Teale, Henry Teale," said the stranger.

"Pray be seated," said Mrs. Crosland.

The stranger, this Mr. Teale, took the edge of the seat, as if very diffident. Mrs. Crosland was soon fascinated by what he had to say.

He was a policeman in private clothes. Mrs.

Crosland meditated on the word "private"— "private life," "private means." He had come about the Inglis affair, at the corner house.

"Oh, yes, I recall that was the name, but we never knew anyone—who are they now—the Inglis family?"

"I've already told Miss Bayward here—it was an old lady, for several years just an old lady living with a companion—"

"And found dead, you told me, Mr. Teale," remarked Lucy.

"Murdered, is what the surgeon says and what was suspected from the first."

"I forgot that you said that, Mr. Teale. At her age it does not seem to matter very much—you said she was over eighty years of age, did you not?" asked Lucy, pouring the detective a glass of wine.

"Very old, nearly ninety years of age, I understand, Miss Bayward. But murder is murder."

Mrs. Crosland felt this affair to be an added weariness. Murder in Roscoe Square on Christmas Eve. She felt that she ought to apologise to Lucy. "I suppose that was what the crowd had gathered for," she remarked.

"Yes, such news soon gets about, Ma'am. A nephew called to tea and found her—gone."

Mr. Teale went over, as if it were a duty, the circumstances of the crime. The house had been ransacked and suspicion had fallen on the companion, who had disappeared. Old Mrs. Inglis had lived so much like a recluse that no one knew what she possessed. There had been a good deal of loose money in the house, the nephew, Mr. Clinton, thought. A good deal of cash had been drawn every month from the Inglis bank account, and very little of it spent. The companion was a stranger to Islington. Veiled and modest, she had flitted about doing the meagre shopping for the old eccentric, only for the last few weeks.

The woman she had replaced had left in tears and temper some months ago. No one knew where this creature had come from—probably an orphanage; she must have been quite friendless and forlorn to have taken such a post.

"You told me all this," protested Lucy.

"Yes, Miss, but I did say that I would have to see Mrs. Crosland when she arrived—"

"Well, you are seeing her," remarked that lady. "And I cannot help you at all. One is even disinterested. I lived, Mr. Teale, so cloistered a life when I was here, that I knew nothing of what was going on—even in the Square."

"So I heard from Miss Bayward here, but I thought you might have seen someone; I'm not speaking of the past, but of the present—"

"Seen someone here—on Christmas Eve—?"

Mr. Teale sighed, as if, indeed, he had been expecting too much. "We've combed the neighbourhood, but can't find any trace of her—"

"Why should you? Of course, she has fled a long way off—"

"Difficult, with the railway stations and then the ports all watched."

"You may search again through the cellars if you wish," said Lucy. "I am sure that my aunt won't object—"

Mrs. Crosland put no difficulties in the way of the detective, but she felt the whole situation was grotesque.

"I hope she escapes," Mrs. Crosland, increasingly tired and confused by the wine she had drunk without eating, spoke without her own volition. "Poor thing—shut up—caged—"

"It was a very brutal murder," said Mr. Teale indifferently.

"Was it? An over-draught of some sleeping potion, I suppose?"

"No, Ma'am, David and Goliath, the surgeon said. A rare kind of murder. A great round stone in a sling, as it might be a lady's scarf, and pretty easy to get in the dusk round the river ways."

Mrs. Crosland laughed. The picture of this miserable companion, at the end of a dismal day lurking round the dubious dockland streets to find a target for her skill with sling and stone, seemed absurd.

"I know what you are laughing at," said Mr. Teale without feeling. "But she found her target—it was the shining skull of Mrs. Inglis, nodding in her chair—"

"One might understand the temptation," agreed Mrs. Crosland. "But I doubt the skill."

"There is a lovely walled garden," suggested the detective. "And, as I said, these little by-way streets. Anyway, there was her head smashed in, neatly; no suffering, you understand."

"Oh, very great suffering, for such a thing to be possible," broke out Mrs. Crosland. "On the part of the murderess, I mean—"

"I think so, too," said Lucy soberly.

"That is not for me to say," remarked the detective. "I am to find her if I can. There is a fog and all the confusion of Christmas Eve parties, and waits, and late services at all the churches."

Mrs. Crosland impulsively drew back the curtains. Yes, there was the church, lit up, exactly as she recalled it, light streaming from the windows over the graveyard, altar tombs, and headstones, sliding into oblivion.

"Where would a woman like that go?" asked Lucy, glancing over Mrs. Crosland's shoulder at the churchyard.

"That is what we have to find out," said Mr. Teale cautiously. "I'll be on my way again, ladies, just cautioning you against any stranger who might come here, on some pretext. One never knows."

"What was David's stone? A polished pebble? I have forgotten." Mrs. Crosland dropped the curtains over the view of the church and the dull fog twilight of evening in the gas-lit Square.

"The surgeon says it must have been a heavy stone, well aimed, and such is missing. Mr. Clinton, the nephew, her only visitor and not in her confidence, remarked on such a weapon, always on each of his visits on the old lady's table."

"How is that possible?" asked Mrs. Crosland.

Mr. Teale said that the object was known as the Chinese apple. It was of white jade, dented like the fruit, with a leaf attached, all carved in one and beautifully polished. The old lady was very fond of it, and it was a most suitable weapon.

"But this dreadful companion," said Mrs. Crosland, now perversely revolted by the crime, "could not have had time to practise with this—suitable weapon—she had not been with Mrs. Inglis long enough."

"Ah," smiled Mr. Teale. "We don't know where she was before, Ma'am. She might have had a deal of practice in some lonely place—birds, Ma'am, and rabbits. Watching in the woods, like boys do."

Mrs. Crosland did not like this picture of a woman lurking in coverts with a sling. She bade the detective "Good-evening" and Lucy showed him to the door.

In the moment that she was alone, Mrs. Crosland poured herself another glass of wine. When Lucy returned, she spoke impulsively.

"Oh, Lucy, that is what results when people are driven too far—they kill and escape with the spoils, greedily. I do wish this had not happened. What sort of woman do you suppose this may have been? Harsh, of course, and elderly—"

"Mr. Teale, when he came before, said she might be in almost any disguise."

"Almost any disguise," repeated Mrs. Crosland, thinking of the many disguises she had herself worn until she had found herself in the lovely blue of Italy, still disguised, but pleasantly enough. She hoped that this mask was not now about to be torn from her; the old house was very oppressive, it had been foolish to return. A relief, of course, that Lucy seemed to have her own plans. But the house was what really mattered: the returning here and finding everything the same, and the memories of that dreadful childhood.

Lucy had suffered also, it seemed. Odd that she did not like Lucy, did not feel any sympathy with her or her schemes.

At last she found her way upstairs and faced the too-familiar bedroom. Her own was at the back of the house; that is, it had been. She must not think like this: her own room was in the charming house of the villa in Fiesole, this place had nothing to do with her at all.

But it had, and the knowledge was like a lead cloak over her. Of course it had. She had

returned to meet not Lucy, but her own childhood.

Old Mrs. Inglis—how did she fit in?

Probably she had always been there, even when the woman who was now Isabelle Crosland had been a child. Always there, obscure, eccentric, wearing out a succession of companions until one of them brained her with the Chinese apple, the jade fruit, slung from a lady's scarf.

"Oh, dear," murmured Mrs. Crosland, "what has that old, that very old woman got to do with me?"

Her cases were by her bedside. She was too tired to examine them. Lucy had been scrupulous in putting out her toilet articles. She began to undress. There was nothing to do but to rest; what was it to her that a murderess was being hunted round Islington—what had Mr. Teale said? The stations, the docks . . . She was half-undressed and had pulled out her wrapper when the front-door bell rang.

Hastily covering herself up, she was out on the landing. At least this was an excuse not to get into the big, formal bed where her parents had died, even if this was only Mr. Teale returned. Lucy was already in the hall, speaking to someone. The gas-light in the passage illuminated the girl in the stone-coloured satin and the man on the threshold to whom she spoke.

It was not Mr. Teale.

Isabelle Crosland, half-way down the stairs, had a glance of a sharp face, vividly lit. A young man, with his collar turned up and a look of expectation in his brilliant eyes. He said something that Isabelle Crosland could not hear, and then Lucy closed the heavy front door.

Glancing up at her aunt, she said:

"Now we are shut in for the night."

"Who was that?" asked Mrs. Crosland, vexed that Lucy had discerned her presence.

"Only a neighbour; only a curiosity-monger."

Lucy's tone was reassuring. She advised her aunt to go to bed.

"Really, it is getting very late. The church is dark again. All the people have gone home."

"Which room have you, Lucy, dear?"

"That which you had, I suppose; the large room at the back of the house."

"Oh, yes—that—"

"Well, do not concern yourself—it has been rather a disagreeable evening, but it is over now."

Lucy, dark and pale, stood in the doorway, hesitant for a second. Mrs. Crosland decided, unreasonably, not to kiss her and bade her a quick good-night of a forced cheerfulness.

Alone, she pulled the chain of the gas-ring and was at once in darkness. Only wheels of light across the ceiling showed the passing of a lonely hansom cab.

Perhaps Mr. Teale going home.

Mrs. Inglis, too, would have gone home by now; the corner house opposite would be empty.

Isabelle Crosland could not bring herself to sleep on the bed after all. Wrapped in travelling rugs, snatched up in the dark, she huddled on the couch. Presently she slept, but with no agreeable dreams. Oppressive fancies lay heavily on her and several times she woke, crying out.

It was with a dismal sense of disappointment that she realised each time that she was not in Florence.

With the dawn she was downstairs. Christmas morning; how ridiculous!

No sign of Lucy, and the cold, dismal house was like a trap, a prison.

Almost crying with vexation, Mrs. Crosland was forced to look into the room that once had been her own. The bed had not been slept in. On the white honeycomb coverlet was a package and a note.

This, a single sheet of paper, covered an opened letter. Mrs. Crosland stared at this that was signed "Lucy Bayward." It was a childish sort of scrawl, the writer excused herself from reaching London until after the holidays.

The note was in a different hand:

I promised to let you know my plans. I am away down the river with my accomplice. Taking refuge in your empty house I found this note. The whole arrangement was entirely useful to me. I left the Roman pearls for Lucy, as I had those of my late employer, but I took the gold. No one will ever find us. I leave you a Christmas present.

Mrs. Crosland's cold fingers undid the package. In the ghastly half-light she saw the Chinese apple.

A MODERN

Little Christmas

AND ALL THROUGH THE HOUSE
Ed McBain

EVAN HUNTER, UNDER THE PSEUDONYM OF ED MCBAIN, created the iconic 87th Precinct series, the best and most famous series of police procedurals ever written, with a unique concept: The entire squad room was intended to be the hero, rather than a single police officer, though Steve Carella took center stage more often than not. Fifty-four novels succeeded *Cop Hater* (1956), the first book in the series. Under his own name, Hunter wrote *The Blackboard Jungle* (1954), the first significant book to deal with juvenile delinquents and gang violence in New York. "And All Through the House" was first published in *Playboy,* then issued as a chapbook for members of the Mystery Guild in 1984.

And All Through the House

ED MCBAIN

DETECTIVE STEVE CARELLA WAS alone in the squad room. It was very quiet for a Christmas Eve.

Normally, all hell broke loose the moment the stores closed. But tonight the squad room and the entire station house seemed unusually still. No phones ringing. No typewriters clacking away. No patrolmen popping upstairs to ask if any coffee was brewing in the clerical office down the hall. Just Carella, sitting at his desk and re-reading the D. D. report he'd just typed, checking it for errors. He'd misspelled the "armed" in "armed robbery." It had come out "aimed robbery." He overscored the I with a ballpoint pen, giving the felony its true title. Armed robbery. Little liquor store on Culver Avenue. Guy walked in with a .357 Magnum and an empty potato sack. The owner hit a silent alarm and the two uniforms riding Boy One apprehended the thief as he was leaving the store.

Carella separated the carbons and the triplicate pages—white one in the uppermost basket, pink one in the basket marked for Miscolo in clerical, yellow one for the lieutenant. He looked up at the clock. Ten-thirty. The graveyard shift would be relieving at a quarter to twelve, maybe a bit earlier, since it was Christmas Eve.

God, it was quiet around here.

He got up from his desk and walked around the bank of high cabinets that partitioned the rest of the squad room from a small sink in the corner opposite the detention cage. Quiet night like this one, you could fall asleep on the job. He opened the faucet, filled his cupped hands with water and splashed it onto his face. He was a tall man and the mirror over the sink was set just a little too low to accommodate his height. The top of his head was missing. The mirror caught him just at his eyes, a shade darker than his brown hair and slanted slightly downward to give him a faintly Oriental appearance. He dried his face and hands with a paper towel, tossed the towel into the wastebasket under the sink, and then yawned and looked at the clock again, unsurprised to discover that only two minutes had passed since the last time he'd looked at it. The silent nights got to you. He much preferred it when things were really jumping.

He walked to the windows on the far side of the squad room and looked down at the street. Things looked as quiet down there as they were up here. Not many cars moving, hardly a pedestrian in sight. Well, sure, they were all home already, putting the finishing touches on their Christmas trees. The forecasters had promised snow, but so far there wasn't so much as a flurry in the air. He was turning from the window when all of a sudden everything got bloody.

The first thing he saw was the blood streaming down the side of Cotton Hawes's face. Hawes was shoving two white men through the gate in the slatted rail divider that separated the squad room from the corridor outside. The men were cuffed at the wrist with a single pair of cuffs, right wrist to left wrist, and one of them was complaining that Hawes had made the cuff too tight.

"I'll give you tight," Hawes said and shoved again at both men. One of them went sprawling almost headlong into the squad room, dragging the other one with him. They were both considerably smaller than Hawes, who towered over them like a redheaded fury, his anger somehow pictorially exaggerated by the streak of white in the hair over his right temple, where a burglar had cut him and the hair had grown back white. The white was streaked with blood now from an open cut on his forehead. The cut streamed blood down the right side of his face. It seemed not to console Hawes at all that the two men with him were also bleeding.

"What the hell happened?" Carella asked.

He was already coming across the squad room as if someone had called in an assist officer, even though Hawes seemed to have the situation well in hand and this was, after all, a police station and not the big, bad streets outside. The two men Hawes had brought in were looking over the place as if deciding whether or not this was really where they wanted to spend Christmas Eve. The empty detention cage in the corner of the room did not look too terribly inviting to them. One of them kept glancing over his shoulder to see if Hawes was about to shove them again. Hawes looked as if he might throttle both of them at any moment.

"Sit down!" he yelled and then went to the mirror over the sink and looked at his face. He tore a paper towel loose from the holder, wet it, and dabbed at the open cut on his forehead. The cut kept bleeding.

"I'd better phone for a meat wagon," Carella said.

"No, I don't need one," Hawes said.

"*We* need one," one of the two men said.

He was bleeding from a cut on his left cheek. The man handcuffed to him was bleeding from a cut just below his jaw line. His shirt was stained with blood, too, where it was slashed open over his rib cage.

Hawes turned suddenly from the sink. "What'd I do with that bag?" he said to Carella. "You see me come in here with a bag?"

"No," Carella said. "What happened?"

"I must've left it downstairs at the desk," Hawes said and went immediately to the phone. He picked up the receiver, dialed three numbers, and then said, "Dave, this is Cotton. Did I leave a shopping bag down there at the desk?" He listened and then said, "Would you send one of the blues up with it, please? Thanks a lot." He put the receiver back on the cradle. "Trouble I went through to make this bust," he said, "I don't want to lose the goddamn evidence."

"You ain't got no evidence," the man bleeding from the cheek said.

"I thought I told you to shut up," Hawes said, going to him. "What's your name?"

"I'm supposed to shut up, how can I give you my name?" the man said.

"How would you like to give me your name through a mouthful of broken teeth?" Hawes said. Carella had never seen him this angry. The blood kept pouring down his cheek, as if in visible support of his anger. "What's your goddamn name?" he shouted.

"I'm calling an ambulance," Carella said.

"Good," the man bleeding from under his jaw line said.

"Who wants this?" a uniformed cop at the railing said.

"Bring it in here and put it on my desk," Hawes said. "What's your name?"

"Henry," the cop at the railing said.

"Not you," Hawes said.

"Which desk is yours?" the cop asked.

"Over there," Hawes said and gestured vaguely.

"What happened up here?" the cop asked, carrying the shopping bag in and putting it on the desk he assumed Hawes had indicated. The shopping bag was from one of the city's larger department stores. A green wreath and a red bow were printed on it. Carella, already on the phone, glanced at the shopping bag as he dialed Mercy General.

"Your name," Hawes said to the man bleeding from the cheek.

"I don't tell you nothing till you read me my rights," the man said.

"My name is Jimmy," the other man said.

"Jimmy what?"

"You dope, don't tell him nothin' till he reads you Miranda."

"You shut up," Hawes said. "Jimmy what?"

"Knowles. James Nelson Knowles."

"Now you done it," the man bleeding from the cheek said.

"It don't mean nothin' he's got my name," Knowles said.

"You gonna be anonymous all night?" Hawes said to the other man.

Into the phone, Carella said, "I'm telling you we've got three people bleeding up here."

"I don't need an ambulance," Hawes said.

"Well, make it as fast as you can, will you?" Carella said and hung up. "They're backed up till Easter, be a while before they can get here. Where's that first-aid kit?" he said and went to the filing cabinets. "Don't we have a first-aid kit up here?"

"This cut gets infected," the anonymous man said, "I'm gonna sue the city. I die in a police station, there's gonna be hell to pay. You better believe it."

"What name should we put on the death certificate?" Hawes asked.

"Who the hell filed this in the missing-persons drawer?" Carella said.

"Tell him your name already, willya?" Knowles said.

"Thomas Carmody, OK?" the other man said. He said it to Knowles, as if he would not allow himself the indignity of discussing it with a cop.

Carella handed the kit to Hawes. "Put a bandage on that, willya?" he said. "You look like hell."

"How about the *citizens*?" Carmody said. "You see that?" he said to Knowles. "They always take care of their own first."

"On your feet," Carella said.

"Here comes the rubber hose," Carmody said.

Hawes carried the first-aid kit to the mirror. Carella led Carmody and Knowles to the detention cage. He threw back both bolts on the door, took the cuffs off them and said, "Inside, boys." Carmody and Knowles went into the cage. Carella double-bolted the door again. Both men looked around the cage as if deciding whether or not the accommodations suited their taste. There were bars on the cage and protective steel mesh. There was no place to sit inside the cage. The two men walked around it, checking out the graffiti scribbled on the walls. Carella went to where Hawes was dabbing at his cut with a swab of cotton.

"Better put some peroxide on that," he said. "What happened?"

"Where's that shopping bag?" Hawes asked.

"On the desk there. What happened?"

"I was checking out a ten-twenty on Culver and Twelfth, guy went in and stole a television set this guy had wrapped up in his closet, he was giving it to his wife for Christmas, you know? They were next door with their friends, having a drink, burglar must've got in through the fire-escape window; anyway, the TV's gone. So I take down all the information—fat chance of ever getting it back—and then I go downstairs, and I'm heading for the car when there's this yelling and screaming up the street, so I go see what's the matter, and these two jerks are arguing over the shopping bag there on the desk."

"It was all your fault," Carmody said to Knowles.

"You're the one started it," Knowles said.

"Anyway, it ain't our shopping bag," Carmody said.

"I figure it's just two guys had too much to drink," Hawes said, putting a patch over the cut, "so I go over to tell them to cool it, go home and sleep it off, this is Christmas Eve, right? All of a sudden, there's a knife on the scene. One of them's got a knife in his hand."

"Not me," Carmody said from the detention cage.

"Not me, either," Knowles said.

"I don't know who started cutting who first," Hawes said, "but I'm looking at a lot of blood. Then the other guy gets hold of the knife some way, and *he* starts swinging away with it, and next thing I know, I'm in the middle of it, and *I'm* cut, too. What it turns out to be——"

"What knife?" Carmody said. "He's dreaming."

"Yeah, what knife?" Knowles said.

"The knife you threw down the sewer on the corner of Culver and Eleventh," Hawes said, "which the blues are out searching in the muck for right this minute. I need this on Christmas Eve," he said, studying the adhesive patch on his forehead. "I really need it."

Carella went to the detention cage, unbolted the door and handed the first-aid kit to Carmody. "Here," he said. "Use it."

"I'm waiting for the ambulance to come," Carmody said. "I want real medical treatment."

"Suit yourself," Carella said. "How about you?"

"If he wants to wait for the ambulance, then I want to wait for the ambulance, too," Knowles said.

Carella bolted the cage again and went back to where Hawes was wiping blood from his hair with a wet towel. "What were they arguing about?" he asked.

"Nobody was arguing," Carmody said.

"We're good friends," Knowles said.

"The stuff in the bag there," Hawes said.

"I never saw that bag in my life," Carmody said.

"Me, either," Knowles said.

"What's in the bag?" Carella asked.

"What do you think?" Hawes said.

"Frankincense," Carmody said.

"Myrrh," Knowles said, and both men burst out laughing.

"My ass," Hawes said. "There's enough pot in that bag to keep the whole city happy through New Year's Day."

"OK, let's go," a voice said from the railing. Both detectives turned to see Meyer Meyer lead a kid through the gate in the railing. The kid looked about fourteen years old, and he had a sheep on a leash. The sheep's wool was dirty and matted. The kid looked equally dirty and matted. Meyer, wearing a heavy overcoat and no hat, looked pristinely bald and sartorial by contrast.

"I got us a shepherd," he said. His blue eyes were twinkling; his cheeks were ruddy from the cold outside. "Beginning to snow out there," he said.

"I ain't no shepherd," the kid said.

"No, what you are is a thief, is what you are," Meyer said, taking off his overcoat and hanging it on the rack to the left of the railing. "Sit down over there. Give your sheep a seat, too."

"Sheeps carry all kinds of diseases," Carmody said from the detention cage.

"Who asked you?" Meyer said.

"I catch some kind of disease from that animal, I'll sue the city," Carmody said.

In response, the sheep shit on the floor.

"Terrific," Meyer said. "Whyn't you steal something clean, like a snake, you dummy?"

"My sister wanted a sheep for Christmas," the kid said.

"Steals a goddamn sheep from the farm in the zoo, can you believe it?" Meyer said. "You know what you can get for stealing a sheep? They can send you to jail for twenty years, you steal a sheep."

"*Fifty* years," Hawes said.

"My sister wanted a sheep," the kid said and shrugged.

"His sister is Little Bopeep," Meyer said. "What happened to your head?"

"I ran into a big-time dope operation," Hawes said.

"That ain't our dope in that bag there," Carmody said.

"That ain't even our bag there," Knowles said.

"When do we get a lawyer here?" Carmody said.

"Shut up," Hawes said.

"Don't tell them nothin' till they read you your rights, kid," Carmody said.

"Who's gonna clean up this sheep dip on the floor?" Carella asked.

"Anybody want coffee?" Miscolo said from outside the railing. "I got a fresh pot brewing in the office." He was wearing a blue sweater over regulation blue trousers, and there was a smile on his face until he saw the sheep. His eyes opened wide. "What's that?" he asked. "A deer?"

"It's Rudolph," Carmody said from the detention cage.

"No kidding, is that a *deer* in here?" Miscolo asked.

"It's a raccoon," Knowles said.

"It's my sister's Christmas present," the kid said.

"I'm pretty sure that's against regulations, a deer up here in the squad room," Miscolo said. "Who wants coffee?"

"I wouldn't mind a cup," Carmody said.

"I'd advise against it," Meyer said.

"Even on Christmas Eve, I have to take crap about my coffee," Miscolo said, shaking his head. "You want some, it's down the hall."

"I already told you I want some," Carmody said.

"You ain't in jail yet," Miscolo said. "This ain't a free soup kitchen."

"Christmas Eve," Carmody said, "he won't give us a cup of coffee."

"You better get that animal out of here," Miscolo said to no one and went off down the corridor.

"Why won't you let me take the sheep to my sister?" the kid asked.

"'Cause it ain't your sheep," Meyer said. "It belongs to the zoo. You stole it from the zoo."

"The zoo belongs to everybody in this city," the kid said.

"Tell 'im," Carmody said.

"What's this I hear?" Bert Kling said from the railing. "Inside, mister." His blond hair was wet with snow. He was carrying a huge valise in one hand, and his free hand was on the shoulder of a tall black man whose wrists were handcuffed behind his back. The black man was wearing a red-plaid Mackinaw, its shoulders wet. Snow-

flakes still glistened in his curly black hair. Kling looked at the sheep. "Miscolo told me it was a deer," he said.

"Miscolo's a city boy," Carella said.

"So am I," Kling said, "but I know a sheep from a deer." He looked down. "Who made on the floor?" he asked.

"The sheep," Meyer said.

"My sister's present," the kid said.

Kling put down the heavy valise and led the black man to the detention cage. "OK, back away," he said to Carmody and Knowles and waited for them to move away from the door. He unbolted the door, took the cuffs off his prisoner and said, "Make yourself at home." He bolted the door again. "Snowing up a storm out there," he said and went to the coatrack. "Any coffee brewing?"

"In the clerical office," Carella said.

"I meant *real* coffee," Kling said, taking off his coat and hanging it up.

"What's in the valise?" Hawes asked. "Looks like a steamer trunk you got there."

"Silver and gold," Kling said. "My friend there in the cage ripped off a pawnshop on The Stem. Guy was just about to close, he walks in with a sawed-off shotgun, wants everything in the store. I got a guitar downstairs in the car. You play guitar?" he asked the black man in the cage.

The black man said nothing.

"Enough jewelry in here to make the queen of England happy," Kling said.

"Where's the shotgun?" Meyer asked.

"In the car," Kling said. "I only got two hands." He looked at Hawes. "What happened to your head?" he asked.

"I'm getting tired of telling people what happened to my head," Hawes said.

"When's that ambulance coming?" Carmody asked. "I'm bleeding to death here."

"So use the kit," Carella said.

"And jeopardize my case against the city?" Carmody said. "No way."

Hawes walked to the windows.

"Really coming down out there," he said.

"Think the shift'll have trouble getting in?" Meyer said.

"Maybe. Three inches out there already, looks like."

Hawes turned to look at the clock.

Meyer looked at the clock, too.

All at once, everyone in the squad room was looking at the clock.

The detectives were thinking the heavy snow would delay the graveyard shift and cause them to get home later than they were hoping. The men in the detention cage were thinking the snow might somehow delay the process of criminal justice. The kid sitting at Meyer's desk was thinking it was only half an hour before Christmas and his sister wasn't going to get the sheep she wanted. The squad room was almost as silent as when Carella had been alone in it.

And then Andy Parker arrived with his prisoners.

"Move it," he said and opened the gate in the railing.

Parker was wearing a leather jacket that made him look like a biker. Under the jacket, he was wearing a plaid-woolen shirt and a red muffler. The blue-woolen watch cap on his head was covered with snow. His blue-corduroy trousers were covered with snow. Even the three-day beard stubble on his face had snowflakes clinging to it. His prisoners looked equally white, their faces pale and frightened.

The young man was wearing a rumpled black suit, sprinkled with snow that was rapidly melting as he stood uncertainly in the opening to the squad room. Under the suit, he wore only a shirt open at the collar, no tie. Carella guessed he was twenty years old. The young woman with him—*girl*, more accurately—couldn't have been older than sixteen. She was wearing a lightweight spring coat open over what Carella's mother used to call a house dress, a printed-cotton thing with buttons at the throat. Her long black hair was dusted with snow. Her brown eyes were wide in her face. She stood shivering just inside the railing, looking more terrified than any human being Carella had ever seen.

She also looked enormously pregnant.

As Carella watched her, she suddenly clutched her belly and grimaced in pain. He realized all at once that she was already in labor.

"I said *move* it," Parker said, and it seemed to Carella that he actually would *push* the pregnant girl into the squad room. Instead, he shoved past the couple and went directly to the coatrack. "Sit down over there," he said, taking off his jacket and hat. "What the hell is that, a sheep?"

"That's my sister's Christmas present," the kid said, though Parker hadn't been addressing him.

"Lucky her," Parker said.

There was only one chair alongside his desk. The young man in the soggy black suit held it out for the girl, and she sat in it. He stood alongside her as Parker took a seat behind the desk and rolled a sheaf of D. D. forms into the typewriter.

"I hope you all got chains on your cars," he said to no one and then turned to the girl. "What's your name, sister?" he asked.

"Maria Garcia Lopez," the girl said and winced again in pain.

"She's in labor," Carella said and went quickly to the telephone.

"You're a doctor all of a sudden?" Parker said and turned to the girl again. "How old are you, Maria?" he asked.

"Sixteen."

"Where do you live, Maria?"

"Well, thass the pro'lem," the young man said.

"Who's talking to you?" Parker said.

"You were assin' Maria——"

"Listen, you understand English?" Parker said. "When I'm talkin' to this girl here, I don't need no help from——"

"You wann' to know where we live——"

"I want an address for this *girl* here, is what I——"

"You wann' the address where we s'pose' to be livin'?" the young man said.

"All right, what's *your* name, wise guy?" Parker said.

"José Lopez."

"The famous bullfighter?" Parker said and turned to look at Carella, hoping for a laugh.

Carella was on the telephone. Into the receiver, he said, "I *know* I already called you, but now we've got a pregnant woman up here. Can you send that ambulance in a hurry?"

"I ain' no bullfighter," José said to Parker.

"What are you, then?"

"I wass cut sugar cane in Puerto Rico, but now I don' have no job. Thass why my wife an' me we come here this city, to fine a job. Before d' baby comes."

"So what were you doing in that abandoned building?" Parker said and turned to Carella again. "I found them in an abandoned building on South Sixth, huddled around this fire they built."

Carella had just hung up the phone. "Nothing's moving out there," he said. "They don't know *when* the ambulance'll be here."

"You know it's against the law to take up residence in a building owned by the city?" Parker said. "That's called squatting, José, you know what squatting is? You also know it's against the law to set fires inside buildings? That's called arson, José, you know what arson is?"

"We wass cold," José said.

"Ahhh, the poor kids were cold," Parker said.

"Ease off," Carella said softly. "It's Christmas Eve."

"So what? That's supposed to mean you can break the law, it's Christmas Eve?"

"The girl's in labor," Carella said. "She may have the baby any damn minute. Ease off."

Parker stared at him for a moment and then turned back to José. "OK," he said, "you came up here from Puerto Rico looking for a job——"

"*Sí, señor.*"

"Talk English. And don't interrupt me. You came up here lookin' for a job; you think jobs grow on trees here?"

"My cousin says he hass a job for me. D' factory where he works, he says there's a job there. He says come up."

"Oh, now there's a cousin," Parker said to

Hawes, hoping for a more receptive audience than he'd found in Carella. "What's your cousin's name?" he asked José.

"Cirilo Lopez."

"Another bullfighter?" Parker said and winked at Hawes. Hawes did not wink back.

"Whyn't you leave him alone?" Carmody said from the cage.

Parker swiveled his chair around to face the cage. "Who said that?" he asked and looked at the black man. "You the one who said that?"

The black man did not answer.

"I'm the one said it," Carmody admitted.

"What are you in that cage for?"

"Holding frankincense and myrrh," Carmody said and laughed. Knowles laughed with him. The black man in the cage did not crack a smile.

"How about you?" Parker asked, looking directly at him.

"He's mine," Kling said. "That big valise there is full of hot goods."

"Nice little crowd we get here," Parker said and swiveled his chair back to the desk. "I'm still waitin' for an address from you two," he said. "A *legal* address."

"We wass s'pose' to stay with my cousin," José said. "He says he hass a room for us."

"Where's that?" Parker asked.

"Eleven twenny-four Mason Avenue, apar'men' thirty-two."

"But there's no room for us," Maria said. "Cirilo, he's——" She caught her breath. Her face contorted in pain again.

José took her hand. She looked up at him. "D' lady lives ness door," he said to Parker, "she tells us Cirilo hass move away."

"When's the last time you heard from him?"

"Lass' month."

"So you don't think to check, huh? You come all the way up from Puerto Rico without checkin' to see your cousin's still here or not? Brilliant. You hear this, Bert?" he said to Kling. "Jet-set travelers we got here; they come to the city in their summer clothes in December, they end up in an abandoned building."

"They thought the cousin was still here, that's all," Kling said, watching the girl, whose hands were now spread wide on her belly.

"OK, what's the big emergency here?" someone said from the railing.

The man standing there was carrying a small black satchel. He was wearing a heavy black overcoat over white trousers and tunic. The snow on the shoulders of the coat and dusted onto his bare head was as white as the tunic and pants. "Mercy General at your service," he said. "Sorry to be so late; it's been a busy night. Not to mention two feet of snow out there. Where's the patient?"

"You'd better take a look at the girl," Carella said. "She's in——"

"Right here," Carmody said from the cage.

"Me, too," Knowles said.

"Somebody want to let them out?" the intern said. "One at a time, please."

Hawes went to the cage and threw back the bolts on the door.

"Who's first?" the intern said.

Carella started to say, "The girl over there is in la——"

"Free at last," Carmody interrupted, coming out of the cage.

"Don't hold your breath," Hawes said and bolted the door again.

The intern was passing Parker's desk when Maria suddenly gasped.

"You OK, miss?" he said at once.

Maria clutched her belly.

"Miss?" he said.

Maria gasped again and sucked in a deep breath of air.

Meyer rolled his eyes. He and Miscolo had delivered a baby right here in the squad room not too long ago, and he was grateful for the intern's presence.

"This woman is in *labor!*" the intern said.

"Comes the dawn," Carella said, sighing.

"Iss it d' baby comin'?" José asked.

"Looks that way, mister," the intern said. "Somebody get a blanket or something. You got any blankets up here?"

Kling was already on his way out of the squad room.

"Just take it easy, miss," the intern said. "Everything's gonna be fine." He looked at Meyer and said, "This is my first baby."

Terrific, Meyer thought, but he said nothing.

"You need some hot water?" Hawes asked.

"That's for the movies," the intern said.

"Get some hot water," Carmody said.

"I don't need hot water," the intern said. "I just need someplace for her to lie down." He thought about this for a moment. "Maybe I *do* need hot water," he said.

Hawes ran out of the squad room, almost colliding with Kling, who was on his way back with a pair of blankets he'd found in the clerical office. Miscolo was right behind him.

"Another baby coming?" he asked Meyer. He seemed eager to deliver it.

"We got a professional here," Meyer said.

"You need any help," Miscolo said to the intern, "just ask, OK?"

"I won't need any help," the intern said, somewhat snottily, Miscolo thought. "Put those blankets down someplace. You OK, miss?" He suddenly looked very nervous.

Maria nodded and then gasped again and clutched her belly and stifled a scream. Kling was spreading one of the blankets on the floor to the left of the detention cage, near the hissing radiator. Knowles and the black man moved to the side of the cage nearest the radiator.

"Give her some privacy," Carella said softly. "Over there, Bert. Behind the filing cabinets."

Kling spread the blanket behind the cabinets.

"She's gonna have her baby right here," Knowles said.

The black man said nothing.

"I never experienced nothin' like this in my life," Knowles said, shaking his head.

The black man still said nothing.

"Maria?" José said.

Maria nodded and then screamed.

"Try to keep it down, willya?" Parker said. He looked as nervous as the intern did.

"Just come with me, miss," the intern said, easing Maria out of the chair, taking her elbow and guiding her to where Kling had spread the blanket behind the cabinets. "Easy, now," he said. "Everything's gonna be fine."

Hawes was back with a kettle of hot water. "Where do you want——" he started to say, just as Maria and the intern disappeared from view behind the bank of high cabinets.

It was three minutes to midnight, three minutes to Christmas Day.

From behind the filing cabinets, there came only the sounds of Maria's labored breathing and the intern's gentle assurances that everything was going to be all right. The kid kept staring at the clock as it threw the minutes before Christmas into the room. Behind the filing cabinets, a sixteen-year-old girl and an inexperienced intern struggled to bring a life into the world.

There was a sudden sharp cry from behind the cabinets.

The hands of the clock stood straight up.

It was Christmas Day.

"Is it OK?" Parker asked. There was something like concern in his voice.

"Fine baby boy," the intern said, as if repeating a line he'd heard in a movie. "Where's that water? Get me some towels. You've got a fine, healthy boy, miss," he said to Maria and covered her with the second blanket.

Hawes carried the kettle of hot water to him.

Carella brought him paper towels from the rack over the sink.

"Just going to wash him off a little, miss," the intern said.

"You got a fine baby boy," Meyer said to José, smiling.

José nodded.

"What're you gonna name him?" Kling asked.

The black man, who'd been silent since he'd entered the squad room, suddenly said in a deep and sonorous voice, "'Behold, a virgin shall conceive and bear a son, and his name shall be called Emmanuel.'"

"Amen," Knowles said.

The detectives were gathered in a knot around the bank of filing cabinets now, their backs to Carmody. Carmody could have made a run for it, but he didn't. Instead, he picked up first the shopping bag of pot he and Knowles had been busted for and then the valise containing the loot Kling had recovered when he'd collared the black man. He carried them to where Maria lay behind the cabinets, the baby on her breast. He knelt at her feet. He dipped his hand into the bag, grabbed a handful of pot and sprinkled it onto the blanket. He opened the valise. There were golden rings and silver plates in the valise, bracelets and necklaces, rubies and diamonds and sapphires that glittered in the pale, snow-reflected light that streamed through the corner windows.

"*Gracias*," Maria said softly. "*Muchas gracias.*"

Carella, standing closest to the windows, looked up at the sky, where the snow still swirled furiously.

"That's not a bad name," Meyer said to José. "Emmanuel."

"I will name him Carlos," José said. "After my father."

Carella turned from the windows.

"What'd you expect to see out there?" Parker asked. "A star in the East?"

Doug Allyn

LIKE THE NEW YORK YANKEES DURING THE MICKEY MANTLE era and the Boston Celtics when Bill Russell and John Havlicek played, Doug Allyn has had a stranglehold on the prestigious Reader's Award given annually by *Ellery Queen's Mystery Magazine.* It is a poll voted on by readers of the magazine for their favorite story of the year, and ten of his stories have come in first, and over twenty have been in the top three. "An Early Christmas" was selected as the favorite story of the year in 2009; it was published in the January issue.

An Early Christmas

DOUG ALLYN

JARED SNAPPED AWAKE TO THE sound of laughter. On the bedside TV, Jay Leno was yukking it up with a ditzy blonde celeb. Jared sat up slowly, dazed and groggy from too much brandy, too much sex. Fumbling around, he found the remote control, and killed the tinny TV cackling, then looked around slowly, trying to get his bearings.

A bedroom. Not his own. Sunny Lockhart was sprawled beside him, nude, snoring softly with her mouth open, her platinum hair a tousled shambles. At fifty-one, Sunny had crow's feet and smile lines, but her breasts were D-cup and she made love like a teenybopper. Better, in fact.

Gratitude sex. The best kept secret in the legal profession. After settling cases involving serious money, clients were often elated, horny, and very, *very* grateful to the guy who made it happen.

Thanks to Jared's legal expertise, Sunny Lockhart was financially set for life, a free and independent woman of means. Unfortunately, she was also crowding fifty. Too old for Jared by a dozen years. And he had to be in the office to meet with a client at nine sharp.

Damn. Time to go.

Stifling a groan, Jared slid silently out of Sunny's rumpled bed and began gathering up his clothes.

* * *

Roaring down the shore road in his Mercedes SL500 through a gentle snowfall, Jared set his radio on scan, listening to the momentary snippets of songs flashing past. Mostly Christmas carols or country. Finally caught a tune he liked. *Back in Black,* AC/DC. Cranking the volume, he slapped the wheel on the back beat, getting an energy surge from the music.

Couldn't stop grinning. Wondering if he could arrange a weekend getaway with Sunny. Getting hot and bothered again just thinking about it.

He paid no attention to the rust-bucket pickup truck rumbling down the side road to his left. Until he realized the truck wasn't slowing for the stop sign! The crazy bastard was speeding up, heading straight for him!

Stomping his brakes, Jared swerved over onto the shoulder, trying to avoid a crash. Knowing it was already too late!

Blowing through the intersection at eighty, the pickup came howling across the centerline, sheering off at the last second to slam broadside into Jared's roadster, smashing him off the road.

Airbags and the windshield exploded together, smothering Jared in a world of white as the Benz plowed into the massive snowdrift piled along the highway, then blew through it, hurtling headlong down the steep embankment.

Fighting free of the airbag's embrace, Jared wrestled the wheel, struggling to control the roadster in its downhill skid. He managed to avoid one tree, then glanced off another. For a split second he thought he might actually make it—but his rear fender clipped a towering pine, snapping the car around, sending it tumbling end over end down the slope.

Bouncing off tree trunks like a pinball, the Benz was being hammered into scrap metal. The side windows shattered inward, spraying Jared with glass fragments. For a heart-freezing instant, he felt the car go totally airborne, then it slammed down nose-first into the bottom of the gorge with stunning force.

A lightning strike of white-hot agony flashed up Jared's spine, driving his breath out in a shriek. Freezing him in place. He was afraid to breathe, or even blink, for fear of triggering the godawful pain again.

Christ. He couldn't feel his legs. Didn't know what was wrong with them, but knew it was serious. Total numbness meant his back might be broken or—

"Mister?" A voice broke through Jared's terrified daze. "Can you hear me down there?"

"Yes!" Jared gasped.

"Hey, I saw what happened. That crazy bastard never even slowed down. Are you okay?"

"I—can't move," Jared managed. "I think my back may be broken. Call 911."

"Already did that. Hang on, I've got a first-aid kit in my car."

Unable to risk turning his head, Jared could only catch glimpses in his shattered rearview mirror, a dark figure working his way down the steep, snowy slope, carrying a red plastic case. Twice, the man stumbled in the roadster's torn tracks, but managed to regain his balance and press on.

As he drew closer, the mirror shards broke the image into distorted fragments, monstrous and alien . . . Then he vanished altogether.

"Are you there?" Jared gasped, gritting his teeth. Every word triggered a raw wave of pain.

"Almost. Stay still." The voice came from somewhere behind the wreck. Jared couldn't see him at all.

"You're Jared Bannan, the real estate lawyer, right?"

"Do I know you?"

No answer. Then Jared glimpsed the twisted figure in the mirror again. Climbing back up the track the way he'd come.

"Wh—where are you going? I need help!"

"Can't risk it." The figure continued on without turning. "Your gas tank ruptured. Can't you smell it? Your car could go off like a bomb any second."

"But—" Jared coughed. My god. The guy was right! The raw stench of gasoline was filling his nostrils, making it hard to breathe.

"Wait! Come back, you sonofabitch! Don't leave me! I have money! I'll pay you!"

At the mention of money, the climber stopped and turned around. But in the tree shadows, Jared still couldn't make out his face.

"That's more like it," Jared said. "I'll give you ten thousand dollars. Cash. Just get me out of this car and—"

"Ten grand? Is that what you're worth?"

"No! I mean, look, I'll give you any amount you want . . ." A flash of light revealed the climber's face for a split second. *Definitely familiar.* Someone Jared had met or . . . His mind suddenly locked up, freezing with soul-numbing horror.

The flash was a flame. The climber had lit a cigarette. "Oh, Jesus," Jared murmured softly, licking his lips. "What are you doing? Wait. Please."

"Jesus?" the climber mimicked, taking a long drag. "Wait? Please? Is that the best you can do? I thought shyster lawyers were supposed to be sweet talkers."

Jared didn't answer. Couldn't. He watched in growing terror as the smoker tapped the ashes off, bringing the tip to a cherry glow. Then he flipped the cigarette high in the air, sending it arcing through the darkness, trailing sparks as it fell.

Jared's shriek triggered another bolt of agony from his shattered spine, but he was beyond caring. He couldn't stop screaming any more than he could stop the cigarette's fiery fall.

* * *

Leaving his unmarked patrol car at the side of the highway, Doyle Stark trotted the last hundred yards along the shoulder to the accident scene. A serious one, by north country standards. A Valhalla County fire truck was parked crossways across one lane of the highway, blocking it. Two uniformed sheriff's deputies, Hurst and Van Duzen, were directing traffic around the truck on the far shoulder. Van flipped him a quick salute and Doyle shot him with a fingertip.

Yellow police line tapes stretched from both bumpers of the fire truck to stakes planted in the roadside snowdrifts. The tapes outlined a savage gap in the snowy embankment, over the top and on down out of sight.

Detective Zina Redfern was squatting at the rear of the fire truck, warming her mittened hands in the heat of its exhaust pipe. She was dressed in her usual Johnny Cash black, black nylon POLICE parka over a turtleneck and jeans, a black watch cap pulled down around her ears. The woman took the term "plainclothes officer" literally.

Even her combat boots were the real deal, LawPro Pursuits with steel toes. With a Fairbairn blade clipped to her right ankle.

"Sergeant Stark," she nodded, straightening up to her full, squared-off five foot five, one forty. "Whoa, what happened to your eye?"

Six foot and compactly built, with sandy hair and gray eyes, Doyle was sporting a white bandage over his left brow.

"Reffing a Peewee pickup game," Doyle said. "Ten-year-olds watch way too much hockey on TV. What happened here?"

"A car crashed through the embankment, tumbled all the way to the bottom, then blew up and burned down to the frame. What's left of the driver is still inside. Beyond that, I'm not sayin' squat. I need you to see this with fresh eyes."

"Fair enough," Doyle nodded, picking up the edge in her tone. Zina had worked in Flint four years before transferring north to the Valhalla force. She was an experienced investigator, and if something was bothering her about this . . .

He swiveled slowly, taking in the accident scene as a steady stream of traffic crawled past on the far shoulder. Wide-eyed gawkers, wondering what was up. Doyle knew the feeling.

Two sets of broad black skid marks met in the center of the lane, then followed an impossible angle to the torn snowbanks at the side of the road. "Who called this in?"

"A long-haul trucker spotted the wreckage as he crested the hill, around ten this morning. We caught a real break. The wreck's not visible from the roadside. If we'd gotten a little more snow during the night, the poor bastard might have stayed buried till spring. I marked off a separate trail away from the skid track," she said, leading him to a rough footpath up and over the berm. "There are footprints that . . . well, take a look for yourself."

Clambering to the top of the drift, Doyle stopped, scanning the scene below. A ragged trail of torn snow and shattered trees led down the slope to a charred obscenity crouched at the bottom of the gorge. A burned-out hulk that had once been an expensive piece of German automotive engineering.

The charred Mercedes Benz was encircled by a blackened ring of torn earth and melted slush, its savagery already softening beneath a gentle gauze of lightly falling snow.

Joni Javitz, the Joint Investigative Unit's only tech, was hunched over the car, dutifully photographing the corpse. Even at this distance, Doyle could see the gaping mouth and bared teeth of the Silent Scream, a burn victim's final rictus. A few patches of skull were showing through the blackened flesh . . .

Damn. He hated burn scenes. The ugly finality and the vile stench that clung to your clothing for days. In Detroit, cops called them Crispy Critters. But here in the north, no one in Doyle's unit joked about them. There's nothing funny about a death by fire. Ever.

Working his way warily down the slope, Doyle noted the uneven footprints in the snow of the roadster's trail. "Did the trucker climb down to the car?"

"The trucker didn't stop," Zina said. "He

spotted the wreck and a little smoke. Wasn't sure what it was, but thought somebody should take a look."

"It was still smoking at ten o'clock? Any idea when this happened, Joni?"

"My best guess would be around midnight, boss, give or take an hour," Javitz said without turning. Tall and slender as a whip, she had to fold herself into a question mark to shoot the wreck's interior. "The car and the body are both cool to the touch now, but they're still ten degrees warmer than the ambient temperature. The State Police Crime Scene Team is already en route from Gaylord. They should be here anytime."

"Okay . . ." Doyle said, swiveling slowly, taking in the scene. "We've got a hot shot in a Benz roadster who runs off the road at midnight, crashes and burns. Tough break for him. Or her?"

"Him, definitely," Joni said.

"Fine. Him then. And why exactly am I here on my day off?"

Wordlessly, Joni stepped away from the car, revealing the charred corpse, and the deep crease in the driver's-side door.

"Wow," Doyle said softly, lowering himself to his haunches, studying the dent more closely. "Metal on metal. Red paint traces. No tree did this. Which explains the second set of skid marks on the highway. Somebody ran this poor bastard off the road . . ." He broke off, eyeing a small circle of dark red droplets, scattered like a spray of blood near the trunk.

"Plastic pellets?" Doyle said. "Any chance they're from the taillights?"

"Nope, the taillight lenses are Lexan," Joni said. "These pellets are definitely polypropylene, probably from a plastic gas container. A small one, a gallon or two. Like you'd use for a chain saw or a lawn mower. The can was definitely on the ground outside the vehicle. I've already bagged up some residue to test for accelerants."

"I didn't see any skid marks from the other vehicle until the last second, just before it struck the Benz," Doyle mused. "From the depth of these dents, both cars must have been traveling at one hell of a clip. So car number two runs the stop sign at high speed, nails the Benz dead center, hard enough to drive it through the snowdrifts . . ."

"He's damned lucky he isn't down here too," Zina said.

"Maybe it wasn't luck," Doyle said, staring up the incline toward the highway. "If he hadn't hit the Benz, he definitely would have blown through the berm himself. And there's not much traffic out here at night. So, either he ran that stop sign, drunk, asleep, whatever, and the Benz had the million to one bad luck to get in his way or . . . ?"

"He wasn't out of control at all," Zina nodded, following Doyle's gaze up the hillside. "You think he drilled him deliberately?"

"Tell you what, Detective, why don't you hoof it back up the hill and check out that side road for tire tracks or exhaust stains in the snow. See if car number two was sitting up there, waiting for the Benz to show."

"Jesus," Joni said softly. "You mean somebody rammed this poor bastard on purpose? Then climbed down with a gas can and lit him up?"

"I don't like it either, but it works," Doyle agreed grimly. "Have you identified him yet?"

"The car's registered jointly to Jared and Lauren Bannan, Valhalla address."

"Jared Bannan?" Doyle echoed, surprised. "Damn. I know this guy. I've played racquetball against him."

"A friend?"

"No, just a guy. He's an attorney, a transplant from downstate, works mostly in real estate."

"A yuppie lawyer?" Zina said. "Whoa! Want me to cancel the Crime Scene team?"

The door to the classroom was ajar. Doyle raised his fist to knock, then hesitated, surprised at the utter silence from within. Curious, he peered around the doorjamb. A tall, trim woman with boyishly short dark hair, was addressing the class. Soundlessly. Her lips were moving, the fingers of both hands flickering, mediating an animated discussion with a dozen rapt teenagers, who were answering with equally adept sign language, their lips miming speech, but with no sound at all.

It was like watching an Olympic fencing match, silvery signals flashing too quickly for the eye to follow.

The woman glanced up, frowning. "Can I help you?"

"Sorry to intrude, ma'am. If you're Doctor Lauren Bannan, I need a few minutes of your time."

"I'm in the middle of a class."

"This really can't wait, ma'am."

"My god," Lauren said softly, "are you absolutely sure it's Jared?"

"The identification isn't final, but he was carrying your husband's identification and driving his car."

"Jared wore a U of M class ring on his right hand," she offered. "Did the driver . . . ?"

Doyle nodded. They were in Doctor Bannan's office, a Spartan ten by ten box at Blair Center, the county magnet school for special-needs students. Floor to ceiling bookshelves on three sides, Doctor Bannan's diplomas and teaching awards neatly displayed on the fourth wall. No photographs, Doyle noted.

"I didn't see a wedding ring," Zina said. "Did he normally wear one?"

"We're separated," Lauren said. "God. I can't believe this."

"Are you all right, Mrs. Bannan?" Doyle asked. "Can I get you a glass of water or something?"

"No, I'm . . . just a bit shaken. Do you have any idea what happened?"

"Your husband was apparently sideswiped on the shore road a few miles outside of town. Hit and run. His car went over a steep embankment, probably late last night. Midnight, maybe. He

was pronounced dead at the scene. We're very sorry for your loss."

Lauren's mouth narrowed as she visibly brought her emotions under control. An elegant woman, Doyle thought. Slender as a willow with dark hair, a complexion as exquisite as a porcelain doll.

But not fragile. She took the news of her husband's death like a prizefighter rocked by a stiff punch. Drawing within herself to camouflage the damage.

After a moment, she took a deep breath, and carefully straightened her jacket.

"You said someone ran Jared off the road. What happened to the other driver?"

"We don't know yet, ma'am. Do you know why your husband might have been on that road last night?"

"No idea. Jared and I separated last year. Except for conferences with our attorney, I rarely see him. Why?"

Zina glanced the question at Doyle, who nodded.

"Judging from the skid marks, the collision may not have been accidental, Doctor Bannan," Zina said. "Do you know why anyone would want to harm your husband?"

"Whoa, back up a moment," Lauren said, raising her hand. "Are you saying someone deliberately rammed Jared's car?"

"We aren't certain yet, ma'am," Doyle said. "But the evidence does lean that way. At this point we're treating it as a possible homicide."

"For the record, would you mind telling us your whereabouts last night?" Zina asked.

Lauren glanced up at her sharply. "I was at home all evening. Alone. What are you implying?"

"Nothing, ma'am," Doyle put in. "It's strictly routine. We're not the enemy."

Lauren looked away a moment. "All right then. If you have questions, let's clear them up now."

"You said you separated last year?" Zina asked. "Have you filed for divorce?"

"We filed right after we separated. Last spring. March, I think."

"Do you have children?"

Lauren hesitated. "No. No children."

"Then help me out here, Mrs. Bannan. Without children involved, you can get a no-fault divorce in sixty days, and I'm speaking from experience. Was your husband contesting the divorce?"

"Only the property settlement. Jared earns considerably more than I do, so he felt he was entitled to a larger share. He kept coming up with new demands."

"Michigan's a community property state," Doyle put in. "A wife's entitled to half, no matter who earns what."

"My husband is an attorney, Sergeant, though most of his work is in real estate. Fighting him in court wouldn't be cost effective. We had our final meeting last Tuesday. He made an offer and I took it."

"But you weren't happy about it?" Zina said.

"Divorce seldom makes anyone happy."

"You're newcomers to the area, right?" Doyle asked. "When did you move north?"

"A little over two years ago."

"Why was that? The move, I mean?"

"Why?" Lauren blinked. But didn't answer.

That was a hit, Zina thought. Though she had no idea what it meant.

"I knew your husband in passing," Doyle offered, easing the silence. "I played racquetball against him a few times."

"And?" Lauren said, with an odd smile.

"And what? Why the smile?"

"Jared was the most competitive man I've ever known. Did he beat you, Sergeant?"

"As a matter of fact, he did. Twice."

"And did he cheat?"

"He didn't have to. He was quicker than I am. Why do you ask that?"

"Jared could be a very sore loser. I beat him at tennis once and he smashed his racquet to splinters in front of a hundred spectators. I filed for divorce a week later."

"Over a tennis match?" Zina asked, arching an eyebrow.

"It was such a childish display that I realized that Jared was never going to grow up. And I was tired of waiting. I wanted out."

"And now you are," Zina said. "Will the accident affect your financial settlement?"

"I have no idea. Money always mattered more to Jared than to me."

"Money doesn't matter?" Zina echoed.

"I was buying my freedom, Detective. How much is that worth? Can we wrap this up? I have a class in five minutes."

"You might want to make other arrangements, Doctor," Doyle suggested. "Give yourself a break."

"Working with handicapped kids is a two-way street, Sergeant. It keeps your problems in perspective. The last thing I need is to sit around brooding."

"You're not exactly brooding, ma'am," Zina noted. "If you don't mind my saying, you're taking this pretty calmly."

"I deal with problems every day, Detective. Kids who will never hear music or their mother's voices, kids with abusive parents. Last week I had to tell an eight-year-old her chemotherapy regimen had failed and she probably won't see Christmas. So this is very hard news, but . . ." Lauren gave a barely perceptible shrug.

"A thing like that would be a lot harder," Zina conceded, impressed in spite of herself.

"And yet the sun also rises," Lauren said firmly. "Every morning, ready or not. Are we done?"

"Just a few final questions," Doyle said quickly. "Your husband had a string of traffic citations, mostly for speeding. Was he a reckless driver?"

"Jared never hit anyone, he had great reflexes. But every trip was Le Mans for him. I hated that damned car."

"Was he ever involved in conflicts with other drivers?"

"Road rage, you mean? His driving often

ticked people off, but he never stopped to argue. It was more fun to leave them in the dust."

"Which brings us full circle to question number one," Doyle said. "Can you think of *anybody* who might wish to harm your husband?"

Lauren hesitated a split second. *Another hit,* Zina thought, though not as strong as the first.

"No one," Lauren said carefully. "Jared was a charming man, as long as you weren't playing tennis against him or facing him in court. If he was having trouble with a client, his office staff would know more than I do. He's with Lehman and Greene, downtown."

"How about you, ma'am?" Doyle asked. "The Benz is jointly owned, so it's at least possible your husband wasn't the intended victim. Have you had any problems? Threats, a stalker, anything like that?"

"No."

"What about your students?" Zina asked. "Your schedule includes mentally challenged students as well as hearing impaired. Are any of them violent? Maybe overly affectionate? Seems like there's a lot of teacher-student hanky-panky in the papers."

Lauren met Zina's eyes a moment, tapping on the desk with a single fingernail.

"You two are really good," she said abruptly. "Usually the male plays the aggressive 'bad cop,' while the female plays the sympathetic sister. Reversing the roles is very effective."

"Thanks, I think," Zina said. "But you didn't answer the question."

"As I'm sure you're aware, Detective Redfern, some of my students have behavioral problems that keep them out of mainstream schools. But none of them would have any reason to harm Jared. Or me. Now if you don't mind, I'd like a minute alone before my next class. Please."

"Of course, ma'am," Doyle said, rising. "I apologize for the tone of our questions. We're sorry for your loss, Doctor Bannan." He handed her his card. "If you think of anything, please call, day or night."

Zina hesitated in the doorway.

Lauren raised an eyebrow. "Something else, Detective?"

"That kid you mentioned? What did she say when you told her the cancer had come back?"

"She . . . asked her father if they could celebrate an early Christmas. So she could re-gift her toys to her friends."

"Good god," Zina said softly. "How do you handle it? Telling a child a thing like that?"

"Some days are like triage on the *Titanic,* Detective," Lauren admitted, releasing a deep breath. "You protect the children as best you can. And the battered women. And at five o'clock, you go home, pour a stiff brandy and curl up with a good book."

"And tomorrow, the sun also rises," Zina finished.

"Every single day. Ready or not."

In the hallway, Doyle glanced at Zina. "What?"

"I hate having to tell the wives. The tears, the wailing. Rips your freakin' heart out."

"The lady's used to dealing with bad news."

"She's also pretty good at dodgeball. She echoed half of our questions to buy time before she answered. Or didn't answer at all."

"She's got degrees in psych and special ed. She's probably better at this than we are. Anything else?"

"Yeah. Her clothes were expensive but not very stylish. She's a good-looking woman, but she dresses like a schoolmarm."

"She is a schoolmarm. What are we, the fashion police now?"

"Nope, we're the damn-straight real poleece, Sarge. I'm just saying a few things about that lady don't add up. If a toasted husband can't crack your cool, what would it take?"

"You think she might be involved in her husband's death?"

"Let me get back to you on that. Who's next?"

"She said Bannan's office staff would know about any threats."

"Argh, more lawyers," Zina groaned. "I'd rather floss with freakin' barbed wire."

The offices of Lehman, Barksdale, and Greene, Attorneys at Law, occupied the top floor of the old Montgomery Wards building in downtown Valhalla. Old town, it's called now. The historic heart of the village.

The new big box stores, Walmart, Home Depot, and the rest, are outside the city limits, sprawling along the Lake Michigan shore like a frontier boomtown, fueled by new money, new people. High tech émigrés from Detroit or Seattle, flocking to the north country to get away from it all. And bringing most of it with them.

But Old Town remains much as it was before the second war, brick streets and sidewalks, quaint, globular streetlamps. Nineteenth-century buildings artfully restored to their Victorian roots, cast-iron facades, shop windows sparkling with holiday displays, tinny carols swirling in the wintry air. Christmas in Valhalla.

Harbor Drive offers a marvelous view of the boat basin and the Great Lake beyond it, white ice calves drifting in the dark water all the way to the horizon, to infinity, really.

Few of the locals give it a glance, but the two cops paused a moment, taking it in. They'd both worked the concrete canyons of southern Michigan, Detroit for Doyle, Flint for Zee, before returning home to the north. Beauty shouldn't be taken for granted.

Totally rehabbed during the recent real estate push, the offices of Lehman and Greene were top drawer now, an ultra-modern hive of glass cubicles framed in oak with ecru carpeting. Scandinavian furniture in the reception area, original art on the walls.

Doyle badged the receptionist, who buzzed Martin Lehman Jr. to the front desk. Mid thirties, with fine blonde hair worn long, thinning prematurely. Casually dressed. Shirtsleeves and slacks, loafers with no socks. No tie either. New age corporate chic.

"How can I help you, Officer?"

"It's Sergeant, actually. I understand Jared Bannan works here?"

"He's one of the partners, yes. He missed a deposition this morning, though. Is there a problem?"

"Maybe we'd better talk in your office, Mr. Lehman. Wait here, Redfern. I'll call you if we need anything."

"Hurry up and wait," Zina sighed, leaning on the reception counter as Doyle and Lehman disappeared down the hallway. "Is there a coffee machine somewhere?"

"Over in the corner, I'll get—"

"Don't get up," Zina said. "You're on the job, I'm just hanging around. Can I get you a cup?"

"If you wouldn't mind," the receptionist said.

"My treat," Zina winked. "Working girls should look out for each other, don't you think?"

"Jared dead? Good lord," Marty Lehman said, sinking into the *Enterprise* chair behind his antique desk. "We played golf last Saturday, I can't—"

He caught Doyle's look.

"We flew down to Flint, there's an indoor course there," Lehman said absently. "It doesn't seem possible. Jared had so much energy . . . Had he been drinking?"

"Did he drink a lot?"

"Not really. He loved to party, though, and . . . look, I'm just trying to make sense of this."

"Join the club, Mr. Lehman. Your partner was apparently the victim of a hit and run that may have been deliberate. What kind of work did Mr. Bannan do here?"

"Real estate cases, mostly. He was a fixer. He brokered deals, arranged financing, resolved legal problems. One of the best in the state. We were lucky to land him."

"But since at least one party's unhappy in most business deals—"

"You know that I can't discuss Jared's cases with you, Sergeant. Attorney/client privilege applies."

"I'm not asking for specifics."

"Even so, our firm's reputation for discretion—"

"*Listen up, Mr. Lehman!* Somebody rammed your buddy's car off the freaking road, into a ravine. Where he *burned* to death! Do you get the picture yet?"

"My god," Lehman murmured, massaging his eyes with his fingertips.

"I'm not asking you to violate privilege, but we could use a heads-up about any problem cases or clients that could have triggered this thing."

"That's not so easy. Jared specialized in difficult cases."

"Define difficult."

"Property cases where the parties are in conflict, foreclosures, or the disposal of assets during a divorce. Jared loved confrontations. He'd needle the opposition until they blew, then he'd file a restraining order or sue for damages, generally make their lives miserable until they settled."

"So he was what? A hatchet man?"

"The best I ever saw," Lehman admitted. "The slogan on his office wall says *Refuse to Lose.* He rarely did."

"That kind of attitude might make him a few enemies."

"It also made a lot of money. Real estate law is a tough game, and Jared's a guy you'd want on your team. Even if down deep, he scared you a little."

"Were you afraid of him?"

"I had no reason to be, we were colleagues. But in court or in negotiations, he was a ferocious opponent. No quarter asked or given."

"I get the picture," Doyle nodded. "Can you give me a quick rundown of any seriously unhappy customers?"

"Butch Lockhart would top the list," Lehman said, bridging his fingertips.

"The Cadillac dealer? Used to play linebacker for the Lions?"

"That's Butch. Jared represented Butch's ex wife, Sunny, in a suit over their divorce settlement. He got their pre-nuptial agreement voided on a technicality and Sunny wound up with half of everything. Fourteen million for a six-year marriage."

"Wow. I'm guessing Butch is unhappy?"

"He threatened, and I quote, to 'tear Jared's head off and cram it up his ass' during a deposition. Looked angry enough to do it too. Naturally, Jared got the blowup on video. Butch's lawyers settled the same day. But there's more. Jared and Sunny Lockhart . . ."

"Have been celebrating?"

"Banging his clients was almost a ritual with Jared," Lehman sighed. "And Sunny lives in Brookside. Jared may have been coming from her place last night."

"Is Butch Lockhart aware of their relationship?"

"I would assume so. Jared and Sunny haven't been subtle about it."

"Noted," Doyle nodded. "Who else?"

"He recently brokered a deal for the Ferguson family. The three sons wanted to sell the family farm, the father didn't. Jared managed to get the old man declared incompetent. Mr. Ferguson threatened to kill him in open court, which pretty much clinched the case. Personally, I think the old man was dead serious."

"We'll look into that. Any others?"

Lehman hesitated, thinking. "Jared had a divorce case slated for final hearings next week. Emil and Rosie Reiser. They own the Lone Pine Boatworks on Point Lucien."

"What's the problem?"

"There's some . . . friction over the timing of the closing. Emil Reiser bought the boat yard ten years ago, built it up, married a local girl. They're splitting up and cashing out, but their daughter is very ill. Emil wanted to put everything on hold, but Jared has a buyer lined up who won't wait. The wife wants out immediately. Jared promised to make it happen."

"How?"

"I'm sorry, but that definitely falls under attorney/client privilege."

"Are you trying to tell me something, counselor?"

"We both know the rules, Sergeant. I've already said more than I should."

"Fair enough. Lockhart, Ferguson, and Reiser are on the list. Who else?"

"Those are the top three. I'll scan through Jared's files, and flag any others that seem problematic."

"What about Bannan's wife? She said they're divorcing. Amicably?"

"No divorce is amicable, but they're both professional people. The discussions were *very* chilly, but civil. I'm handling—was handling—the paperwork for them."

"For both parties?" Doyle asked, surprised. "Isn't that unusual?"

"The only dispute was the terms of the settlement, and they hammered those out in meetings that I refereed. We wrapped it up last week."

"To everyone's satisfaction?"

"Jared was certainly satisfied. Lauren's harder to read. Jared and I have been friends since college. I could tell you the juicy details on every girlfriend he ever had, up to and including Sunny Lockhart. But I can't tell you a thing about his wife. He never talked about her. I do know that a few years ago, they had . . . a serious problem."

"What kind of problem?"

"That I truly don't know. But Jared had a *very* successful practice downstate, and we didn't recruit him, he called me up out of the blue. Said he wanted to make a fresh start."

"Trying to save his marriage?"

"Jared never took marriage all that seriously."

"How seriously did his wife take it? Should we be looking at her? Or a boyfriend?"

"Can't help you there, Sergeant. As I said, I simply don't know the lady well. I was surprised when I met her. She's a handsome woman but not Jared's type at all. He liked them hot, blonde, and bubbly and Lauren's the opposite. Cool, intelligent, and very private. I've seen more of her during the settlement conferences than I did the whole time they . . . sweet Jesus."

"What?"

"Their settlement isn't finalized," Lehman frowned. "We ironed out the details but nothing's been signed or witnessed."

"So? What's the problem?"

"It's void. All of it, even Jared's new will. As things stand, Lauren's still his wife and sole heir. She gets everything."

"How much are we talking about?"

"I really shouldn't—"

"Just a ballpark figure. Please."

"Very well. Property and investments would be . . . roughly two and a half mil. And Jared had a substantial life insurance policy. I'd put the total estate in the neighborhood of five million."

"Nice neighborhood," Doyle whistled.

"I'm afraid that's really all I can tell you for the moment," Lehman said, rising. "I'll fax you the information on any problem clients by the end of business today."

"I'd appreciate it, counselor. About Bannan's death being a possible homicide? That stays between us."

"God. I don't even like to think about it, let alone tell anyone else."

"Thanks for your time, Mr. Lehman. I'm sorry about your partner."

"So am I, Sergeant," Lehman said, shaking his head glumly. "So am I."

Zina was waiting for Doyle on the sidewalk. "What'd you get?" she asked, falling into step as they headed for the SUV.

"A lot. Bannan was having an affair with Sunny Lockhart and half of his other clients, his life's been threatened at least twice recently, and his widow stands to inherit five million. How'd you make out with the receptionist?"

"Same basic story. Bannan wasn't doing her but he certainly could have. He was a killer negotiator who loved ticking off the opposition. He also got into a major shouting match with his partner last week."

"With Lehman? About what?"

"The receptionist wasn't sure, those flashy glass offices may look wide open but they're soundproof. The Reisers had just left, and Mrs. Bannan was waiting in reception. The argument could have been about either of them."

"Or something else altogether."

"Whatever it was, she said Bannan and Lehman were shouting loud enough to rattle the glass."

"Too bad they didn't break it. What else?"

"Bannan's clients loved him, in every sense of the word, especially the ladies. I'm feeling a little wistful that he never gave me a call."

"You hate lawyers."

"Only defense lawyers. What's next?"

"Let's take the Lockharts separately, before they have time to cross-check their stories. I'll charm Sunny, you dazzle Butch."

"Can't I just beat it out of him?" Zina said. "The Lions sucked when Lockhart played for 'em."

"You're kidding?" Butch Lockhart grinned hugely, not bothering to conceal his delight. "That mouthy sumbitch is dead? For sure?"

"I'm afraid so," Zina said, eyeing him curiously. They were in Lockhart's office, a glass cubicle five steps up from the showroom floor that overlooked a gleaming row of Cadillacs that stretched the length of a football field. Lockhart loomed even larger than his playing days, fifty pounds heavier now, a behemoth in a tailored silk suit, tinted glasses, tinted dark hair. A smile too perfect to be real.

"What kind of a car was he driving?" Lockhart asked.

"A Mercedes roadster."

"Better and better. A smart-ass yuppie buys it in his Kraut car. If he'd been driving a Caddy, he could've survived the accident."

"Actually, we don't think it *was* an accident," Mr. Lockhart. He was clipped by a hit and run driver. Would you mind telling me your whereabouts between ten and midnight, last night?"

Lockhart stared at her, blinking, as the ques-tion penetrated his bullet skull. "Whoa, wait a minute, Shorty. Why ask me? What the hell, you think *I* killed him?"

"You did threaten to tear Mr. Bannan's head off in front of witnesses—"

"Maybe I would have, if I'd run into him in a bar after I'd had a few. But I didn't. And if I wanted him dead, I wouldn't need a car to do it. It's bad enough I had to take crap from that punk while he was alive, I'll be damned if I'll take any more now that he's toast. Especially from some backwoods taco bender. Get the hell out of my office."

"Actually, I'm not Latin, sir, I'm Native American," Zina said, rising. "Anishnabeg. And you're not required to answer questions without an attorney. No problem, I'll be happy to clear your name another way. How many red Cadillacs do you have in stock."

"Red? What are you talking about?"

"The vehicle that struck Mr. Bannan's car left red paint scrapes on his door. I can just scrape paint samples from every red vehicle on your lot, then ship 'em to Lansing to see if any of them match. I'm sure your body shop can touch up the scratches, good as new."

"Touch 'em up?" Butch echoed, standing up, towering over her. "Look, you little beaner—" He broke off, staring at the gleaming blade of the boot knife Zina slid out of her ankle sheath.

"I see two red Caddies out on your showroom floor," she continued calmly. "I'll just scrape some paint samples on my way out. Unless you'd like to be the sweet guy I know you really are, and tell me where the hell you were last night. Mr. Lockhart. Sir."

"He was banging his new girlfriend," Zina sighed, dropping into the chair at her desk. "A high school cheerleader, no less." They were in the Mackie Law Enforcement Center, a brown brick blockhouse just outside Valhalla, named for a trooper killed by a psycho survivalist dur-ing a routine traffic stop.

Covering a five-county area, "the House" is

shared by Valhalla P.D., the Sheriff's Department, and the Joint Investigative Unit. Amicably, for the most part.

"How old is the girl?"

"Eighteen. Street legal but just barely. She confirmed Lockhart's story. I politely suggested she might want to try dating guys her own age. She told me to stick my advice in the trunk of her brand-new Escalade. Paid-up lease, thirty-six months."

"She's eighteen and he's what? Forty?"

"Men are pond scum. I may have to switch to girls. What'd you get from Lockhart's ex?"

"Bannan was with her last night. They ate a late dinner, then thoroughly enjoyed each other's company. She fell asleep afterward. Her best guess is, he bailed out sometime after eleven. She has no alibi, but no motive either. He made her rich and she was in love with the guy."

"Or in heat," Zee said. "Scratch both Lockharts then, who does that leave?"

"Old man Ferguson can't be too happy about being declared incompetent. And the Reisers, who have some kind of a beef over their scheduling. Plus pretty much everybody Jared Bannan ever met. The guy loved ticking people off."

"You're forgetting the widow. Five mil's a helluva motive, Doyle, and she definitely ducked some of our questions."

"Lehman said their relationship was pretty chilly. What did you make of her?"

"Same as you. She's smart, has great legs, and she's about to have five mil in the bank. Hey, maybe I will switch to girls. You want me to re-interview her while you run down Ferguson?"

"No, let's try the Reisers first. If we hurry, we can get there before the boatworks closes for the day."

The Lone Pine Boat Yard was on the tip of Point Lucien, an isolated peninsula jutting into Grand Traverse Bay. A narrow, two-lane blacktop is the only access.

"Not much development out here," Zina noted. "Can't be many private shoreline sites left."

"Which should make the Reisers a bundle when they sell," Doyle said, wheeling the cruiser into the small parking lot. Switching off the engine, they sat a moment, listening to the lonely lapping of the waves and the cries of the gulls.

The yard wasn't much to look at. The only buildings were a cabin, a curing shed stacked with drying lumber, and the boatworks itself, a long warehouse surrounded by a deck that extended out over the water, built of rough-hewn timbers culled from the surrounding forest.

A young girl was huddled in a lawn chair at the end of the dock, fishing with a cane pole, an ancient Labrador retriever at her feet. The dog raised its head, growling a warning as the two officers approached.

"Shush, Smokey," the girl said. "Daaa-ad! The police are here. Have you been bad again?" Her impish grin faded into a spate of coughing. She was muffled in a heavy parka, though the temp on the point was a full ten degrees warmer than the inland hills. Lake effect. Her head was swathed in a turban against the cold, and to cover her baldness.

"Something I can do for you folks?" Emil Reiser asked, stepping out to meet them. He was a bear of a man, dressed for blue-collar work, red and black checked flannel shirt, jeans, and cork boots. He needed a shave and his wild salt and pepper mane hung loosely to his shoulders. Two fingertips on his left hand were missing.

"Don't mind the dog, he's harmless, mostly. Is this business or pleasure?"

"It's business, Mr. Reiser."

"Yeah? Buying a boat, are you? Cause that's the only business I'm in."

"Actually, it's about your wife's attorney, Jared Bannan?"

"Hell, what does that bastard—" Reiser broke off, glancing at his daughter, who was watching them intently. He flashed her a quick command in sign language and the girl turned away.

"She's hearing impaired?" Doyle asked.

"Among other things," Reiser sighed. "We'd

better talk inside. That kid can eavesdrop at fifty yards."

Reiser's workshop was like stepping back in time. The long room had four wooden hulls on trestles, in various states of completion. The air was redolent of sawdust, wood shavings, and shellac. Not a power tool in sight. But for the bare bulbs dangling from the ceiling beams, the works could have time-traveled from the last century. Or the one before that.

Zina wandered between the boats, running her hand over the hulls.

"Beautiful," she murmured. She paused in front of a rifle rack that held a dozen long guns, scoped Springfields and Remingtons, plus a pair of '94 Winchester lever action carbines.

"Expecting a war, Mr. Reiser?"

"They're hunting guns, miss."

"What do you hunt?"

"I don't, anymore. I build boats. And don't be wanderin' around back there. Workshops can be dangerous."

"Is that how you lost your fingertips?" Zina asked, rejoining them.

"My fingers?" Reiser glanced at them, as if he was surprised they were missing. "Yeah. Bandsaw, couple of years ago."

"Looks like it hurt," Doyle said.

"Compared to what?" Reiser snapped. "Your eye don't look so hot either, sport. Can we get on with this? I got work to do."

"I understand you had a beef with Jared Bannan?" Doyle said.

"My wife and I are breaking up. God knows, we've had enough trouble the past few years to wreck anybody. I got no beef with Rosie taking half of everything, though she's been doing more drinkin' than workin' lately. When this is over, I'll probably get drunk for a month myself."

"When what's over?"

"Our daughter is dying," Reiser said bluntly. "Cancer. You'd think being born deaf would be enough grief for any child, but . . ." He trailed off, swallowing hard.

"I'm sorry," Doyle said. "Truly."

"It can't be helped," Reiser said grimly. "All I asked from Bannan was a few extra months, so Jeanie could be at home until . . . her time. Rosie was okay with it, but Bannan said he had a big-bucks buyer lined up who wouldn't wait. Then Rosie's drunk-ass boyfriend put in his two cents. If Marty Lehman hadn't broken things up I swear I would've pounded 'em both to dog meat. But I never laid a hand on either of 'em. If Bannan claims I did, he's lying."

"Mr. Bannan isn't claiming anything," Doyle said mildly, watching Reiser's face. "He's dead. His car was run off the road last night."

"Jesus," Reiser said, combing his thick mane back out of his face with his shortened fingertips. "Look, I had no use for the guy, but I had no cause to harm him."

"Not even to get the extra time you wanted?" Zina asked.

"We already worked that out. My wife'll tell you."

"Where is she?"

"Stayin' at the Lakefront Inn, in town. On my dime. With her speed freak boyfriend, Mal La Roche."

"We know Mal," Doyle nodded. "Would you mind telling us where you were last night?"

"Here with Jeanie, where else? You can ask her if you want, just don't upset her, okay? She's got enough to deal with."

"We'll take your word for it, Mr. Reiser. No need to bother the girl. Thanks for your time. And we're very sorry for your trouble."

Zina craned around to take a long look back as they pulled out of the boatyard. Reiser was at the water's edge, standing beside his daughter, his hand on her shoulder. Talking intently on a cell phone.

"We'll take your word for it?" she echoed, swiveling in her seat to face Doyle.

"As sick as that kid is, she probably goes to bed early, and she's hearing impaired. How would she know whether Reiser went out? What did you make of him?"

"An edgy guy with a world of trouble. Given his state of mind, I wouldn't want to get cross-ways of him right now. You think his daughter's the kid Doctor Bannan mentioned? The one who wanted an early Christmas?"

"She's deaf and the Blair Center is the only school for special-needs students. Check with the school when we get back to the House. Meantime, we'll talk to Reiser's wife, confirm his story."

"Or not," Zina said.

"Rosie don't want to talk to you," Mal La Roche said, blocking the motel room doorway, his massive arms folded. Shaggy and unshaven, Mal was a poster boy for the cedar savages, backwoodsmen who still live off the land, though nowadays they're more likely to be growing reefer or cooking crank than running trap lines.

Mal has two brothers and a dozen cousins rougher than he is. Every cop north of Midland knows them by their first names.

"This isn't a roust, Mal, it's a murder case," Doyle explained. "We need to ask the lady a few questions, then we're gone."

"Or we can pat you down for speed," Zina added. "You look jumpy to me, Mal. Been tootin' your own product again?"

"I ain't—"

"It's all right, Mal, I'll talk to them." Rosie Reiser edged past Mal. Bottle blonde and blowsy, in a faded bathrobe, she looked exhausted, defeated. And half in the bag. "We'll talk out here, things are a mess inside. Is this about Mr. Bannan?"

"Your husband called you?" Doyle asked.

"He said you might be by," she nodded.

"Did he also tell you what to say?"

"I don't need him for that!" Rosie said resentfully. "I'm here ain't I?"

"So you are," Zina said, glancing pointedly around at the rundown motel cabin, "though I can't imagine why. Your daughter—"

"Is where she needs to be! With her father, by the damn lake. His little princess. It's always

about her! Has been since she was born. Never about me."

"Okay, what about you?" Zina said coolly. "Is this dump where you should be?"

"Just ask your questions and git!" Mal put in. We don't need no lectures."

"What was the beef between your husband and Jared Bannan?" Doyle asked.

"It's over and done with."

"I didn't ask if it was settled. I asked what it was about."

"It . . ." Rosie blinked rapidly, trying to focus through a whiskey haze. "I don't know. Something about . . . Emil wanted to wait until after Jeanie . . . you know."

"Dies?" Zina prompted coldly. "And Bannan had a problem with that?"

"He had some big-shot buyer lined up, but they wanted to break ground right away," Mal put in. "It's taken care of now, though. Jared and Emil worked it out."

"How?" Doyle asked.

"I don't know the details."

"Who was the buyer?"

"We don't *know*!" Rosie snapped. "I just know it's settled."

"Because your husband said so?"

"Screw this, I don't have to talk to you. You want to arrest me, go ahead."

"Why would we arrest you?" Doyle asked, puzzled.

"That's what you do, ain't it? So get to it or take a hike." She thrust out her wrists, waiting for the cuffs.

"We're sorry for your trouble, ma'am," Doyle sighed. "Have a nice day."

Zina started to follow him to the car, then turned back.

"Mrs. Reiser? It's none of my business, but losing a child must be incredibly difficult. You might want to wait a bit before you throw away your marriage for the likes of Mal La Roche."

"Hey," Mal began, "you can't—"

"Shut up, Mal, or I'll kick your ass into next week. Mrs. Reiser—"

"Butt out, Pocahontas," Rosie said, clutching

La Roche's arm protectively. "At least Mal can show me a good time. Just because Emil's got no life don't mean *I* gotta live like a damn hermit."

"No, I guess not," Zee shrugged. "You're right, ma'am. You're exactly where you belong."

"It's the same kid," Zina said, hanging up her phone. "Jeanie Reiser is enrolled at Blair Center. Or was. A special-needs student, hearing impaired. She was taken out of school a few weeks ago, because of health issues."

They were in their office at the House.

"Which means Doctor Bannan knows Emil Reiser," Zee continued. "Interesting."

"Interesting how?" Doyle snorted. "Like *Strangers on a Train*? He kills her husband and . . . Who does she kill? Mal La Roche? Besides, neither one of 'em has an alibi."

"Maybe they aren't as tricky as the guys in the movie."

"Yep, that sounds like the doc all right. Dumb as a box of rocks."

"That's not what I—"

"Glad I caught you two," Captain Kazmarek interrupted, poking his head in the door. Fifty and fit, "Cash" Kazmarek bossed the Investigations unit. An affable politician, he was also a rock-solid cop, twenty-five years on the Tri County Force. "I got a call from the sheriff's department at Gaylord. They have your truck. Red Ford pickup, passenger's-side front fender damaged, reported stolen yesterday. Found it an hour ago, abandoned in a Walmart parking lot. What the hell happened to your eye, Doyle?"

"Hockey game," Doyle said. "Did the security cameras catch anything?"

"Nope. The driver dumped it behind a delivery van to avoid the cameras. No prints either. Wiped clean, looks like."

"A professional?" Zina asked.

"Could be," Kazmarek said, dropping into the chair beside Doyle's desk. "Or maybe some buzzed-up teenager with more luck than brains. Where are you on this thing?"

"We've got suspects, but it's a fairly long list," Doyle said. "Bannan majored in making enemies. Why?"

"Actually, a matter of overlapping jurisdictions has come up. I want you to drop a name to the bottom of your list."

"Let me guess," Zina said. "Doctor Lauren Bannan?"

"Lauren?" Kazmarek asked, surprised. "Is she a suspect?"

"The wife's always a suspect. Why, do you know her?"

"We've met. She's done some counseling for the department."

"No kidding? Who'd she shrink?" Zee asked.

"None of your business, Detective. And Lauren's not the name we need to move anyway. According to my sources, Emil Reiser has an ironclad alibi for that night."

"What alibi?" Doyle asked. "He claimed he was home alone with his sick kid. There's no way to verify that."

"Consider it verified," Cash said, rising briskly. "As far as we're concerned, Mr. Reiser was at the policeman's ball, waltzing with J. Edgar Hoover in a red dress."

"Hoover?" Zina echoed. "Are you saying the Feds want us to lay off Reiser?"

"I didn't mention the Feds, because a snotty FBI agent in Lansing asked me not to," Cash said mildly. "That crack about Hoover must have been a Freudian thing. Forget you heard it. Clear?"

"Crystal. Does this mean Reiser is totally off limits, Captain?"

"Not at all, this is a murder case, not a traffic stop. Just make sure you exhaust *all* other avenues of investigation before you lean on Reiser. And if you come up with solid evidence against him, I'll want to see it before you go public. Any questions?"

"You're the boss," Doyle said. "What about Mrs. Bannan?"

"I'd be surprised if Lauren's involved," Kazmarek said, pausing in the doorway. "But I'm obviously a lousy judge of character. I hired you two, didn't I?"

Zina and Doyle eyed each other a moment after Cash had gone.

"Federal," Doyle said at last.

"There's no way Reiser can be a confidential informant," Zina said positively. "That boatyard's in the middle of nowhere and he's been out there for years."

"Which leaves WITSEC," Doyle agreed. "Witness protection."

"So Reiser gets a free pass just because he testified for the Feds once upon a time?"

"No way, in fact it makes him a lot more interesting. But since he's officially at the bottom of our list, let's see how fast we can work our way back down to him. Ferguson's the only suspect we haven't interviewed. We might want to look at Mal La Roche too, just on general principles—"

"That's the second time you've done that," Zina said.

"Done what?"

"Skipped over the foxy doc. She's got five million reasons to want her husband dead, Doyle, she's connected to Reiser, and she definitely ducked some of our questions. Or maybe you didn't notice? Because you're a guy and the doc definitely isn't."

"That's a load!" Doyle snapped. "I'm not . . ." He broke off, meeting Zee's level gaze. Realizing there might just be a kernel of truth in what she said. As usual.

"Okay," he nodded. "Straight up, do you seriously think she killed her husband? Or had it done?"

"I don't know. Neither do you. But she was definitely holding something back. Maybe it's connected to her husband's death, maybe not, but if we're crossing names off our list, I think I should question her again. Alone, this time. Girl talk. Unless you've got some objection? Sergeant?"

Doyle scanned her face for irony. He'd been partnered with Zina Redfern since she transferred north. Nearly two years now. And he still had no idea how her mind worked. Nor any other woman's mind, for that matter.

"Hell, go for it, Zee. Seeing a shrink might do you some good. Just be careful she doesn't have you committed."

"Screw that. I'm more worried about getting torched in my car."

Lauren Bannan delayed making the phone call as long as she could. She meant to make it after lunch, but wound up working at her desk well into the afternoon.

So she swore to make it the last call of the business day. Then forgot again. Sort of.

But when she stepped into the kitchen of the small lakefront cottage she'd leased after her separation, she knew she couldn't delay any longer. And like most tasks we dread, it wasn't as difficult as she'd feared.

Nearly eighty now, Jared Bannan's mother had been in a rest home in Miami for years. She was used to receiving bad news. In the home, it came on a daily basis.

"Don't make a big fuss over the funeral, Lauren," she quavered. "Jared never cared a fig for religion and I won't be coming. I'm sorry, but I'm simply not up to it. Hold whatever service you feel is appropriate, then send his ashes to me. He can be on the mantle, beside his father. I'll be seeing them both before long. How are you holding up, my dear?"

And Lauren started to cry. Tears streaming silently as she listened to words of comfort from an elderly lady she hardly knew. And would never see again.

"I'm all right, Mother Bannan," she lied. "I'll be fine."

Afterward, she washed her face, made herself a stiff cup of Irish coffee, then sat down at her kitchen table to scan the Yellow Pages listings for funeral homes.

The doorbell rang.

Padding barefoot to her front door, Lauren checked the peephole, half expecting Marty Lehman. He'd been hinting about offering her a shoulder to cry on—

But it wasn't.

"Detective Redfern," Lauren said, opening the door wide. "What can I do for Valhalla's finest?"

"Sorry to bother you at home, Doctor Bannan, but a few things have come up. Can you spare me a minute?"

"Actually, your timing's perfect, Detective. I have to choose a funeral home for Jared's service. Can you recommend one?"

"McGuinn's downtown handles the department funerals." Zina followed Lauren through the living room to the kitchen, glancing around the small apartment. It was practically barren. She'd seen abandoned homes that looked friendlier. "Love what you've done with the place."

"I'm still living out of boxes in the garage," Lauren admitted. "I took the place for the lakefront. The back deck overlooks the big lake. The view will break your heart. Sit down, please. I'm having Irish coffee. Would you like some?"

"Coffee's fine, but hold the Irish, please." Zina took a chair at the kitchen table. "This isn't a social call."

"Good," Lauren said, placing a steaming mug in front of Zina, sitting directly across from her. "I wouldn't know how to deal with a social call. Our friends were mostly Jared's business buddies. What do you need, Detective?"

"You sure you're up for this? You seem a bit . . . distracted."

"This hasn't been a day to relive in my golden years, but I'm not a china doll either. Cut to the chase, please."

"Fair enough. We've got an ugly murder on our hands, and you're screwing up our case."

"In what way?"

"By lying to us or withholding information."

"Holy crap," Lauren said, sipping her coffee. "That's pretty direct."

"You're not a china doll."

"No I'm not," Lauren said, taking a deep breath. "I'm a special ed teacher and counselor, licensed by the state and prohibited by federal law from divulging information obtained in my work. To anyone."

"Are you trying to tell me you know who killed your husband?"

"No. Absolutely not."

"But you know something?"

"Nothing that directly relates to Jared's death. And nothing I can discuss with you in any case."

"Reality check, Doc. A fair amount of evidence points directly at you. Shut us out and you could end up in a jackpot that can wreck your life, guilty or not."

"I'll help you in any way I can."

Leaning back in her chair, Zee sipped her coffee, reading Lauren's face openly. "All right. Let's hit the high spots. In our first interview, Doyle asked why you moved north. You ducked that question. Why was that?"

Lauren glanced away a moment, then met Zina's eyes, straight on. "Jared and I needed a fresh start after the death of our son," she said flatly. "Jared Junior was born with a congenital heart defect. He lived five months. We hoped a new place might help. It didn't."

"I'm sorry."

"It was four years ago. I didn't become a counselor because I'm a good person who wanted to help others, Detective. I was only trying to save myself."

"How's it going?"

"A day at a time. Next question?"

"The big one. When Doyle asked who might have cause to hurt your husband, you hesitated."

"Did I?"

"You just did again. Are you protecting someone?"

"I'm sorry," Lauren said, shaking her head slowly. "I can't."

"You *can't*? *I* can't believe you'd protect a killer over some damned technicality. Give me a name! Hell, give me his initials!"

"I just told you, I can't!"

"Jesus H. Christ!" Zina said, rising from her chair, leaning across the table. "In Flint I worked gangland, lady. The east side. I've known some hardcore bangers, but I've never met a colder case than you. The guy may have killed your husband!"

"You'd better go, Detective."

"Damn right I'd better, before I slap the crap out of you. But I'm warning you, Doc, if anybody else gets hurt because you held out on us? I'll burn you down, swear to God!"

Doyle was at his desk when Zina stormed in.

"She definitely knows something, but won't give it up," Zina said, dropping into her seat, still seething. "What did you get?"

"More than I wanted to," Doyle said absently.

"About who? Ferguson?"

"The old man's been in the county psych ward for a week, for evaluation. Twenty-four observation. He's totally clear. So I ran Reiser through the Law Enforcement Information Net."

"Cash told us to lay off him."

"I didn't run his name, just his general description and those missing fingertips. Got a dozen possibilities, but only one serious hit. A case I actually remembered, from twelve years ago in Ohio. I was a rookie on the Detroit force then. A Toledo hit man called the Jap, rolled on the Volchek crime family, busted up a major drug ring. They wiped out his wife and kids as a payback."

"Nobody in our case is Japanese."

"Neither was the hit man. He got that nickname because he had some fingertips missing. Japanese Yakuza gangsters whack off their fingertips over matters of honor."

"Hell, Doyle, half my backwoods relatives are missing fingers or toes because they swing chain saws for a living. That doesn't make 'em hit men."

"There's more. After the trial, the Jap disappeared. No mention of prison time, no updates on his whereabouts. Zip, zilch, nada."

"You think the Feds put him in the witness protection program?"

"Probably," Doyle agreed. "Let's say you've got a witness with a contract out on him. You can give him a new identity, maybe even plastic surgery. But you can't grow his fingers back . . ."

"They stashed him in chain saw country," Zina finished, "where nobody notices missing fingers. You think Reiser's this Jap?"

"I can't think of any other reason a backwoods boat builder would be waltzing with J. Edgar Hoover."

"And this hit man's daughter is in Mrs. Bannan's school, so they almost certainly know each other. Do you think she knows who he really is?"

"I know they've been talking a lot," Doyle said. "I pulled her telephone L.U.D.s. She calls the parents of her students on a monthly basis, probably to discuss problems or progress. But over the past few months she's been talking to Emil Reiser several times a week."

"His daughter's dying."

"And as her teacher, the Doc would naturally be concerned," Doyle nodded. "But they usually talk during business hours. She calls his shop or he calls the school. Except for last Tuesday. She called him at ten p.m. And two days later . . ."

"Somebody greased her husband," Zina whistled. "Wow. But can we move on this? Cash told us to lay off Rieser unless we had rock-solid evidence. All we've got is a possible connection between the Doc and a possible hit man. And I guarantee she won't give anything up. That's one tough broad."

"Cash ordered us to give Emil Reiser a pass. He didn't say anything about *Mrs.* Reiser."

"Rosie was already half in the bag this afternoon," Zina agreed. "By now she's probably sloshed and looking for a shoulder to cry on."

But Rosie Reiser wasn't at the Lakefront Inn. Her boyfriend told them she'd been called to the hospital. An ambulance had brought princess Jeanie to the emergency room an hour earlier.

D.O.A.

They found Rosie Reiser in the E.R. waiting room, alone and dazed, her hair a shambles, cheeks streaked with mascara like a mime's tears. Her eyes were vacant as an abandoned building.

"Mrs. Reiser," Zina said, kneeling beside Rosie's chair. "We're very sorry for your loss. Can you tell us what happened?"

"Emil called. Said Jeanie was gone. She was fishin' off the end of the dock, that kid loved bein' outdoors . . . But she dropped her pole. And when Emil checked, she was . . ." Rosie took an unsteady breath. "He called the ambulance, they brought her here. They let me see her before they took her downstairs."

"Where's your husband now?" Doyle asked.

"He split. He knew when Jeanie died, the Doc would give him up. Figured you'd come for him."

"You mean Doctor Bannan knows who he is?"

"Hell, she was the one that warned him. That bitch almost got me killed!"

"Warned him about what, Mrs. Reiser? What happened?"

"Our final hearing was coming up, Jared had a buyer lined up for the business, we could cash out and be gone. But Emil kept stalling, wanted to wait because of Jeanie. Him and Jared had a big blowout about it. After Emil stormed out, I told Jared about Emil being in witness protection, hiding out up here. Jared planned to out him in court, make Emil run for his damn life. That way I'd get everything, not just half."

"Clever plan," Zina said, her tone neutral.

"Marty Lehman didn't think so. He argued with Jared about it. Claimed Jared was an officer of the court, shouldn't give Emil up. Jared told him to screw himself. I thought we'd won. Then the Doc tipped Emil what was up and he took Jared out. Told me if I opened my mouth, he'd do me and Mal the same way."

"How did Doctor Bannan find out about Emil?" Doyle asked. "Are they involved?"

"Involved?" Rosie echoed, puzzled.

"Are they lovers, Mrs. Reiser? Are they friends?"

"Hell, Emil's got no friends. We had to live like goddamn hermits out there." And she began to sob, great gasping yawps of self-pity.

"Mrs. Reiser, do you know where your husband might have gone?" Zina pressed.

"He went with Jeanie when they took her down. He didn't want her to be alone in that place."

"What place—whoa, you mean the morgue? Doyle, the morgue's in the basement. Reiser's still here!"

But he wasn't. They found the morgue attendant sitting on the floor, in a daze, his skull bloodied. He said Reiser clipped him with a gun butt. He was gone. And he'd taken his daughter's body.

Lights and sirens, flying through town pedal to the metal, Doyle driving, Zina hanging on to the dashboard crash bar.

Turning onto the Point Lucien road, he switched off the sirens without slowing. Not that it mattered. Reiser would be expecting them.

"Eavesdropping," Zina said suddenly.

"What?"

"When we were out here before, the girl was fishing. Emil signed for her to turn her back. He said she could eavesdrop at fifty yards. But she was deaf."

"He meant she could read lips."

"That's right. And where would a kid learn to do that?"

Doyle risked a quick sidelong glance, then refocused on the road. "In school," he nodded. "Doctor Bannan teaches hearing impaired kids and she was in the anteroom when her husband and Lehman were arguing about outing Reiser."

"In an office with glass walls," Zee finished. "The secretary couldn't hear them, but the Doc could have picked up the gist of their argument. And warned Reiser."

"And Reiser killed her husband to—Sweet Jesus!" Doyle broke off. "What the hell is all that?"

Ahead of them, the sky was glowing red, dancing shadows flickering through the trees as Doyle whipped the patrol car around, skidding broadside into the Lone Pine parking lot.

The boatworks was engulfed in flame, a seething, crackling inferno fueled by the stacks of dried wood. Black smoke and sparks roiling upward into the winter night. Backlit by the blaze, Emil Rieser was calmly watching the fire consume years of his work. And his daughter. His whole life.

As Doyle and Zina stepped out of the car, Reiser turned to face them, his work clothes blackened with soot, his shaggy mane wild. Holding a hunting rifle cradled in his arms.

Doyle carefully drew his own weapon, keeping it at his side.

"Mr. Reiser, we'd appreciate it if you'd put that gun down, and step away from it."

"Not a chance, Stark. Just give me a few minutes. Jeanie wanted her ashes scattered out here, this is my last chance to do for her. Let the fire go a bit longer, then we'll get to it."

"To what?" Zina asked.

"You know who I am, don't you? And what I've done."

"You killed Jared Bannan?" Doyle asked.

"I did the world a favor with that one. I only wanted another month or so. Less, as it turned out. He was gonna wreck the little time Jeanie had left just to squeeze a few more dollars out of the deal. If anybody ever had it comin', that sonofabitch did."

"Was Bannan's wife a part of it?"

"Part of what?" Reiser asked, glancing absently at the fire, gauging its progress.

"Did she know you were going to kill her husband?" Doyle pressed.

"She phoned me, warned me he was going to blow my cover. Tell her I said thanks."

"You can tell her yourself."

"No," Reiser said. "It's too late for that. Fire's about done. Let's get to the rest of it."

"Please don't do anything crazy, Mr. Reiser," Zina pleaded quietly. "Do you think your daughter would want this?"

"All Jeanie ever asked for was an early Christmas. She didn't even get that. Maybe it's an early Christmas where she is now. Hell, maybe it's Christmas every damn day. We'll see."

Zina and Doyle exchanged a lightning glance, reading the vacancy in Reiser's eyes. Knowing what it meant.

"Hold on, Mr. Reiser," Zee said, drawing her automatic. "Please, don't do this."

"Funny, that's what Bannan said. Don't. Please. Something like that. It didn't work for him either." Reiser jacked a shell into the chamber of his rifle. "It's on you two now, lady. You can send me over. Or come along for the ride."

And he raised the rifle.

Doyle fired first, spinning Reiser halfway around, then all three of them were desperately exchanging fire as the boatyard blazed madly in the background, flames and smoke coiling upward, smothering the stars of the winter night. A funeral pyre worthy of a princess.

"Do you think he was really trying to kill us?" Zina asked, fingering the rip in the shoulder of her black nylon POLICE jacket, the only damage from the fatal shootout.

"I don't think he cared. He sure as hell didn't leave us any choice." They were in the car, roaring back through town, lights and sirens. Leaving the smoldering boatyard to the firemen and the crime scene team. And the coroner.

"What's your hurry?" Though she already knew.

"Like the man said, it's time to settle up. Any problem with that?"

"Nope. I told the Doc if anyone else died, we'd be along."

"All right then."

It was past midnight when they skidded into Lauren Bannan's driveway. Doyle left the strobes flashing. Wanting the neighbors to know. He hammered on the door. No answer.

"I'm out here," Lauren called.

They circled the house to the rear deck. Lauren was standing by the rail, in black slacks and a turtleneck, looking out over the lake. Slivers of early ice floating ghostly in the dark waters, as far as the eye could see.

"Reiser's dead," Doyle said bluntly. "His daughter too."

Lauren nodded, absorbing it, showing nothing. "Did Jeanie go easily?"

"I . . . suppose so," he said, surprised by the question. "She died in her chair, on the dock."

"That's good. It can be far worse, with that type of cancer. What's the rest of it?"

"Emil Reiser killed your husband, Mrs. Bannan. He admitted it. Before we had to kill him."

"I'm sorry it came to that."

"It didn't have to! You could have stopped it! Warned us. The way you warned him. You knew what he'd do."

"No. I didn't know that. I thought—he'd bring pressure on Jared, that he'd contact the marshals or—"

"But you damn sure knew what happened after the fact! And you still didn't tell us."

"I couldn't."

"Because of some damned health regulation?"

"No. Not because of the law. I would have broken the law. Perhaps I should have. But my obligation wasn't to you, Sergeant, or even to my husband."

"Triage," Zina said quietly, getting it. "You told us the first day. It was too late to save your husband. Or Reiser. You were protecting the child."

"Jeanie's mother is a hopeless alcoholic, drowning in self-pity, with a violent boyfriend. If I'd warned you about her father, she would have spent her last days in foster care with strangers or even in court. She had so little time left and she was already dealing with so much. I simply couldn't do that to her."

"But you knew Reiser was a murderer!" Doyle raged.

"Actually, I didn't, not to a certainty. But it wouldn't have mattered. You saw them together. She worshiped him. And he treated her like . . ."

"A princess," Zina finished.

"What?" Doyle said, whirling on her. "You can't be buying into this crock?"

Zina didn't answer. Didn't have to.

"Are you here to arrest me?" Lauren asked.

Doyle eyed his partner, then Lauren, then back again.

"It's your call," Zina said.

"No," he said slowly. "Not tonight, anyway. But you're not clear of this, lady. You'll be answering a lot more questions before it's done."

"I'm terribly sorry about the way this played out, Sergeant. About what you were forced to do. I hope you can believe that."

"I don't know what I believe," Doyle said, releasing a ragged breath. "Let's go, Zee."

In the car, he sat behind the wheel without starting it, staring into the snowy darkness.

"I know what's bugging you," Zina said quietly.

"What's that?"

"It's one helluva coincidence. That warning Reiser, for the sake of his daughter, just happened to make the doc a very rich woman."

"You think she's capable of that?"

"I think she's awfully bright, Doyle. She has the degrees to prove it and she's one very cool customer. So is it at least possible? Damn straight. But given her choices? I don't know what I would have done."

"Nor do I," he admitted. "I just wish . . ."

"What?"

"I wish that kid had gotten her early Christmas, that's all."

"Hell, maybe she did," Zee said. "Maybe her father was right. Maybe where she is now, it's Christmas every day. Start the damn car, Doyle, before we freeze to death."

Doyle nodded, firing up the Ford, dropping it into gear. But as he pulled out, he realized Zina was still eyeing him. Smiling. "Now what?"

"My grandfather Gesh once told me he'd killed many a deer with one perfect shot," she said. "Right through the heart. But sometimes a buck will keep on running, a hundred yards or more. He doesn't realize he's been hit, you see. Right through the heart."

"I don't follow you," Doyle said.

"I know," Zina grinned, shaking her head. "I'm just sayin'."

THE LIVE TREE

John Lutz

WITH MORE THAN FORTY NOVELS AND TWO HUNDRED short stories to his credit, John Lutz has demonstrated both the ingenuity and work ethic of early pulp writers who turned out readable, entertaining prose year after year. His most commercially successful book is probably *SWF Seeks Same* (1990), a suspense thriller that served as the basis for the 1992 movie *Single White Female* starring Bridget Fonda and Jennifer Jason Leigh. Lutz has served as the president of the Mystery Writers of America and has been nominated for four Edgar Awards, winning in 1986 for best short story. "The Live Tree" was first published in *Mistletoe Mysteries*, edited by Charlotte MacLeod (New York, Mysterious Press, 1989).

The Live Tree

JOHN LUTZ

CLAYTON BLAKE WAS TIRED OF Christmas, and it was still five days away. His four-year-old son, Andy, was curled on the sofa pouting, making Clayton feel about as small as one of Santa's elves. But damn it, he was *right* about this.

His wife, Blair, said, "You're wrong about this, Clay. What would it hurt to buy one more real Christmas tree? It's a big thing to Andy, and he's still so young. He doesn't understand how you feel about Christmas."

Clayton's argument with Blair and Andy had left his nerves ragged. But he was still determined to buy a small artificial tree this year, keep god-awful Christmas fuss to a minimum. "How Andy feels doesn't change what Christmas really is," he said. "Nothing but a major marketing blitz that starts sometime in October. You know the retail stores make half their profits during the Christmas season?" He peaked his eyebrows in indignation. "*Half!* I mean, it's reached the point where how well they can con us at Christmas determines how the entire economy's gonna go. The *world* economy! Goddamn governments rise or fall on it."

Andy said, "Wanna weal tree." It came out as a pitiful bleat.

Blair looked as if she were suffering physical pain. Then she shook her head, her long blond hair swaying. A beautiful woman still in her thirties. Slightly myopic blue eyes. Bedroom eyes. "Tell Andy about the economy," she said. "He'll understand your position once the two of you have talked about gross national product and the trade imbalance."

There was a clatter on the porch. Stomping footsteps. The mail being delivered. Clayton was grateful for the interruption.

He and Blair both strode to the front door to get the mail. When she saw what was happening she stopped and let Clayton step out onto the porch to collect it. As he pushed outside, the winter wind seemed to slice to his bones like icy razor blades.

He was still cold after he came back in. Just those few seconds outside had chilled him to the quick. Temperature must be near zero. He really hated not only Christmas, but this time of year in general. Gray skies and gloom.

"Twee," Andy insisted.

Clayton hardened his heart and ignored his son. Said with disappointment, "Looks like nothing but Christmas cards." He dropped the stack of mail on the table in the foyer. Laughed without humor at the one envelope he was still holding. It was a longer envelope than the others, and he recognized the return address. The state penitentiary. This would be the yearly Christmas card from his brother, Willy, who was serving time for mail fraud. Clayton said, "The usual card from Willy," and tossed the envelope in with the unpaid bills piling up from Christmas shopping. *'Tis the season to be indebted.*

Blair said, "Even in prison, Willy's got the Christmas spirit."

"Even in prison, Willy's got you conned," Clayton said. "Willy can con anybody he wants to, and from any distance."

"He might be a con man," Blair said petulantly, "but he's also a decent person." Left hanging heavy in the air was the implication that Clayton was *not* a decent sort; he was the kind of miser who wouldn't even let his family have a genuine Christmas tree. That irritated him. Wasn't he an excellent provider? A faithful and sober husband? A good father to their son, if perhaps a stricter one than Blair would have liked? And how was Willy—a convicted criminal—a decent person? Wasn't that just what a con artist needed you to believe—that he was basically decent?

Blair began opening the Christmas cards, using a long red fingernail to pry beneath envelope flaps. "Well, when are you going to buy this *artificial* tree?" she asked resignedly, without meeting his gaze.

"In a little while."

Still not looking up, she said, "Andy was looking forward to picking out a real one with us over at the lot on Elm Avenue."

Clayton didn't answer. He actually didn't even want to go to the trouble of buying and setting up even an artificial tree. Some of them were complicated and the branches didn't fit right. What he really wanted was a window shade with a picture of a tree on it. He could pull it down during the holidays, then roll it up sometime around the new year. Better not tell Blair about that idea, though.

Andy said, "Pweese, Daddy!" from the sofa.

"You can get up now, son," Clayton said just as the doorbell rang. "But behave. No more temper tantrums."

He took two steps to the door and opened it. Stood with his mouth hanging open, breathing in cold air.

His brother, Willy, was standing on the porch.

"Willy, how'd you—"

"I'm let out on a good behavior program till after Christmas," Willy said. "They're doing that now for trusties convicted of nonviolent crimes." He grinned. "Nobody'll skip. Not this time of year. That's why they call us trusties."

Clayton didn't know what to say. He wasn't actually all that glad to see his brother. They'd never gotten along well.

"Willy!" Blair said behind Clayton. "For God's sake, come on in!"

"Yeah!" Clayton said, pulling out of his shock. "Get in here, Willy. Cold out there."

Willy the master criminal smiled. He was a shorter, bulkier version of Clayton, but with a face that perpetually beamed and a nose red from hanging over too many highball glasses. While Clayton's features were lean and intense, giving him the look of a concerned headmaster, Willy resembled a life-coarsened department store Santa out of uniform and on his way to a bar. Clayton wondered if Willy had been drinking before coming here. *Did Santa's reindeer have antlers?*

Willy hadn't moved. He said, "I got something with me." Reached off to his left and tugged at an obviously heavy and resisting object.

A Christmas tree came into view.

Not only a tree, but a large one. Almost six feet tall and also big around.

Not only a large tree, but a live one. Its roots still surrounded by a massive clump of earth that was wrapped in burlap tied with twine.

What was going on here? Clayton wondered. Had Willy conned a tree from a nursery in the spirit of Christmas? He was capable of it, and that was sure how it appeared.

Blair almost screamed, "A *real* tree!"

"Weal twee!" Andy scampered across the living room and bounced off Clayton's leg.

Clayton cleared his throat and said, "This is your uncle Willy, son."

Andy said, "Wi-wee."

Willy was beaming down at Andy with an expression so tender it surprised Clayton. He'd been in prison since before Andy's birth. "Finally get to see you, little buddy."

Clayton said, "Leave the tree on the porch for now and come inside, Willy. You're so cold you're white." *Except for the drinker's nose.*

As Willy leaned the tree against the house and stepped through the door, Blair said, "You sure you're feeling okay, Willy? You *are* kind of pale."

"Oh, yeah. Pri—where I been does that to the complexion. You know me, always healthy. Never even a cold."

Germs slain by alcohol, Clayton thought, but he kept the opinion to himself.

Willy peeled off his coat. He was wearing a cheap blue suit. Scuffed black shoes. Prison issue.

Willy handed his coat to Clayton and glanced around. "Good. I was hoping you hadn't bought a tree yet. Wanted to surprise you. We gotta get it in a washtub with some water in it pretty soon. Then, after Christmas, you can plant it someplace in your yard. It'll grow tall and strong right along with Andy, here."

Clayton wasn't surprised to see that Andy, like all things warm-blooded, had taken an immediate liking to Willy. He was standing close and gazing up at him as if Willy were a life-size G.I. Joe. War toys, Clayton thought. At least Willy hadn't brought Andy war toys.

Blair bustled off to get Willy a cup of hot chocolate. Willy settled down on the sofa with Andy next to him. Old pals already.

Clayton said, "Where you staying, Willy?"

Willy waited until Blair had returned. He said, "Well, I thought maybe here. I gotta report back in right after Christmas."

Clayton had barely opened his mouth when Blair said, "Great, Willy. We've got a guest room."

Andy said, "Back in where, Uncle Wi-wee?"

"Uncle Willy meant he had to go back home," Clayton said quickly. "Soon as Christmas is over."

Willy sat back in the softness of the sofa and looked around. "Great place, Clayt. Great family. Great cup of chocolate. You know how lucky you are?"

Clayton said he knew.

* * *

They went out for supper at a family-style restaurant that served fried chicken and was decorated with holly and pine rope and red bows. Willy was his usual mesmerizing self and Andy behaved beautifully. Clayton was surprised to be enjoying himself. Actually glad to see Willy, the older brother of whom he'd always been so jealous. In high school Willy had stolen from Clayton the affections of Janet Gerinski, a cheerleader whose good looks transcended even the glinting metal orthodontic braces of the era. Janet had interested Willy for about two passionate weeks, and was now married to an insurance man and living in an even more expensive part of town than the Blakes.

Clayton knew he'd never really forgiven Willy, who, after dropping Janet, left school and hitchhiked to California. There Willy's intended career in rock music had quickly fallen through. That was when Willy began plying his charm in pursuit of illegal profits. From the record industry to telephone boiler rooms to plush hotel suites in Reno, Willy had bilked thousands of dollars from unsuspecting admirers and business associates.

Odd, Clayton thought, how nobody liked what Willy had done, but everybody seemed to like Willy. It was something Clayton had never understood.

The next morning was Saturday, and the three adults, with Andy's help, stood the live pine tree more or less straight in a washtub and decorated it. Clayton felt good watching Andy. Thought for the first time that maybe it hadn't been such a good idea to deprive the boy of a real Christmas tree at only four years old.

"Hey, Clayt!" Willy said that evening after Blair's home-cooked dinner. "Let's all drive downtown and show Andy the display windows. They got a train about a mile long in one of the department stores." He grinned over at Andy. "You sat on Santa's lap yet, buddy?"

"Not since he was a year old," Blair said, shooting a glance at Clayton Scrooge.

Willy shoved his chair back and stood up. "Well, we can fix that tonight. Stores are open late. C'mon, folks. I got some shopping to do anyway."

Clayton was surprised. "Where would you get money in—"

Blair raised a hand palm out to silence Clayton.

"Aw, you know me, Clayt," Willy said. "How I always been able to play cards."

Cheat at cards, Clayton thought. But again he kept his silence.

After Willy helped Blair load the dishwasher, they set off in the station wagon for the highway leading downtown. Willy suggested they sing. Clayton objected only briefly before being overruled. By the time they got downtown he was actually enjoying belting out Christmas carols, listening to Andy sing with lisping soprano gusto. Blair was smiling and looking—well, angelic.

Willy winked at Clayton in the rearview mirror. "Holiday spirit, Clayt."

Clayt. Clayton had always hated that nickname. And now only Willy called him that.

Andy was enthralled by the colorful display windows. Sat beaming on Santa's lap and asked for a model plane. Which amazed Clayton; he and Blair were giving Andy a simple plastic model plane for Christmas.

An hour before the stores were due to close, Willy told the rest of the family to drive home without him. He wanted to do some shopping and then he'd take a cab back to the house.

Clayton agreed, and they said good-bye and went outside to walk the short, cold two blocks to the parking lot.

No one said anything. Even Clayton thought the drive home was comparatively dull.

And during the drive he began to think. Why was Willy laying on the charm? Was he trying to work some kind of con? Clayton couldn't be sure, but he was determined to be careful.

Christmas morning was a delight. Clayton felt a warmth he hadn't thought possible watching

Andy open the many presents placed under the tree by his uncle Willy. With the warmth was an unexpected melancholy yearning for Christmas mornings years ago when he and Willy had been held in check at the top of the stairs and then allowed to race downstairs and examine their own presents. He remembered the pungent scent of the real Christmas tree, the same scent that was now Andy's to remember. The years at home with Willy might not have been as bad as Clayton usually recalled them. Besides, shouldn't there be a time limit, a statute of limitations on ancient injuries?

It had snowed that morning, as if the weather knew one of Willy's gifts to Andy would be a sled. That afternoon, after a meal of ham and sweet potatoes, with apple pie for dessert, Willy suggested they all go to a hill in a nearby park and test the sled. Clayton was reluctant at first, but he went along and had a marvelous time even though he suspected three or four fingers might be frostbitten. He even soloed downhill with the sled, something he hadn't done since he was twelve. "Got carried away," he explained to a grinning Blair when he'd clomped uphill, snow-speckled and trailing the sled on its rope.

As they were trudging through the snow back to the car, Clayton and Andy fell behind Willy and Blair. Andy looked up at Clayton, his reddened face curious beneath his ski cap. "How come Uncle Wi-wee don't get cold?"

"He does get cold, I'm sure."

"Don't act cold."

Which was true, Clayton realized. Maybe Willy was fortified with alcohol, he thought, and then immediately felt guilty. As far as he knew, Willy hadn't touched anything alcoholic since he'd arrived for his Christmas visit.

That night, after an exhausted Andy had fallen asleep on the sofa next to Willy and then been carried upstairs to bed, Blair made some eggnog and the three adults sat around talking.

"I always envied you, Clayt," Willy said, wiping eggnog from his upper lip.

Clayton was surprised.

"Still do. The roots you put down early. You

oughta take stock of what's yours in this world and appreciate it. I mean, nothing lasts forever, and you got this time with Blair and Andy . . ."

Now Clayton was astonished. For a moment it appeared that Willy might actually break down and weep. *Willy a family man?*

Then Willy sat up straighter and asked for a refill on the eggnog. The familiar Willy; there was alcohol in eggnog. He was again the charming con man who'd bilked thousands from people who strangely wouldn't count him among their enemies.

After Willy had gone to bed, Blair said, "He knows he's getting older, and he has to go back to prison tomorrow. I feel terrible about that, don't you? Clay?"

For the first time in years, Clayton said without reservation, "I pity him."

The morning after Christmas, Willy was gone.

They hadn't heard him depart.

He'd left no note.

His bed was made and there was no sign that he'd even visited them. When Andy woke up and asked about him, Clayton told him his uncle Willy had gone back to where he worked in another country. Peru, Clayton had finally said, when pressed. Andy didn't like it. Cried for a while. Then accepted this explanation and got interested in the array of toys he'd received yesterday.

Two days later Clayton was reading the morning paper when Blair said, "Clay!" Something in her voice alarmed him. He put down the paper and saw her standing by the table in the foyer, where she'd been sorting through the mail. Her face was pale and puzzled. "I found this still unopened," she said, and held out a white envelope and the letter that had been inside.

Clayton stood up and walked over to her. Saw she was holding the envelope that had come from the state prison. "Willy's Christmas card," he said.

He'd never before seen such a look in her

blue, blue eyes. "But it's not a card. It's . . ." As he gently took the letter from her hand she said, ". . . a death notice."

Clayton stood paralyzed and read. Blair was right. The state penitentiary had written to inform Clayton as Willy's next of kin that one Willard Blake had died of pneumonia. They were awaiting word concerning the disposition of the body.

Clayton stood with his arms limp, the hand holding the letter and envelope dangling at his side.

"Look at the postmark," Blair said in a hoarse whisper, crossing her arms and cupping her elbows in her palms, as if she were cold. "Look at the date on the letter. It's three days before Willy's visit."

Something with a thousand tiny legs seemed to crawl up the back of Clayton's neck. He drew a deep breath. Exhaled. "A mistake, that's all. Some kind of mistake at the prison."

He looked again at the letterhead. Found a phone number. Strode into the kitchen and called the prison.

It hadn't been a mistake, the woman he talked to said. She told him she was sorry about his brother. Said, "About the remains . . ."

Clayton slowly replaced the receiver and sat staring at the phone. Blair walked into the kitchen and saw the expression on his face. Slumped down opposite him.

They stared at each other.

Andy helped Clayton plant the live tree in the backyard. Every Christmas they lovingly decorated it with strings of outdoor colored lights.

There was something—something he knew was absurd—that Clayton couldn't shake from his mind. In a place beyond lies, Willy had come face to face either with St. Peter or with the devil. Could Willy—even the magnificent faker Willy—con either of *those* two? Maybe.

Only maybe.

Which was what nagged unreasonably at

Clayton. If Willy hadn't worked a con to buy his extra time on earth, had he worked a trade?

Even after Andy had grown up and left home for college, Clayton continued to decorate the stately pine tree every Christmas. And in the summer he'd unreel the garden hose and stand patiently in the glaring sun, watering the ground around its thick trunk. He'd thoroughly soak the earth beneath the carpet of brown dried needles.

It was impossible to know how deep the roots of such a tree might reach.

Sara Paretsky

ONE OF THE PIONEERS OF THE HARD-BOILED FEMALE
private eye school of crime writing in the early 1980s, Sara Paretsky was one of
the co-founders of Sisters in Crime, an organization created to increase awareness for women mystery writers. In V. I. Warshawski, she created one of the most
significant tough female PIs in literature, unafraid to use a gun or martial arts
to whip her opponents into shape—or kill them. The character inspired the
dreadful 1991 motion picture *V. I. Warshawski,* which starred Kathleen Turner;
it was not based on any of Paretsky's novels. The author was honored as a Grand
Master by the Mystery Writers of America for lifetime achievement in 2011.
"Three-Dot Po" was first published in *The Eyes Have It,* edited by Robert J.
Randisi (New York, Mysterious Press, 1984).

Three-Dot Po

SARA PARETSKY

CINDA GOODRICH AND I WERE jogging acquaintances. A professional photographer, she kept the same erratic hours as a private investigator; we often met along Belmont Harbor in the late mornings. By then we had the lakefront to ourselves; the hip young professionals run early so they can make their important eight o'clock meetings.

Cinda occasionally ran with her boyfriend, Jonathan Michaels, and always with her golden retriever, Three-Dot Po, or Po. The dog's name meant something private to her and Jonathan; they only laughed and shook their heads when I asked about it.

Jonathan played the piano, often at late-night private parties. He was seldom up before noon and usually left exercise to Cinda and Po. Cinda was a diligent runner, even on the hottest days of summer and the coldest of winter. I do twenty-five miles a week in a grudging fight against age and calories, but Cinda made a ten-mile circuit every morning with religious enthusiasm.

One December I didn't see her out for a week and wondered vaguely if she might be sick. The following Saturday, however, we met on the small promontory abutting Belmont Harbor— she returning from her jaunt three miles farther north, and I just getting ready to turn around for home. As we jogged together, she explained that Eli Burton, the fancy North Michigan Avenue department store, had hired her to photograph children talking to Santa. She made a face. "Not the way Eric Lieberman got his start, but it'll finance January in the Bahamas for Jonathan and me." She called to Po, who was inspecting a dead bird on the rocks by the water, and moved on ahead of me.

The week before Christmas the temperature dropped suddenly and left us with the bitterest December on record. My living room was so cold I couldn't bear to use it; I handled all my business bundled in bed, even moving the television into the bedroom. I didn't go out at all on Christmas Eve.

Christmas Day I was supposed to visit friends in one of the northern suburbs. I wrapped myself in a blanket and went to the living room to scrape a patch of ice on a window. I wanted to see how badly snowed over Halsted Street was, assuming my poor little Omega would even start.

I hadn't run for five days, since the temperature first fell. I was feeling flabby, knew I should force myself outside, but felt too lazy to face the weather. I was about to go back to the bedroom and wrap some presents when I caught sight of a golden retriever moving smartly down the street. It was Po; behind her came Cinda, warm in an orange down vest, face covered with a ski mask.

"Ah, nuts," I muttered. If she could do it, I could do it. Layering on thermal underwear, two pairs of wool socks, sweatshirts, and a down vest, I told myself encouragingly, "Quitters never win and winners never quit," and "It's not the size of the dog in the fight that counts but the size of the fight in the dog."

The slogans got me out the door, but they didn't prepare me for the shock of cold. The wind sucked the air out of my lungs and left me gasping. I staggered back into the entryway and tied a scarf around my face, adjusted earmuffs and a wool cap, and put on sunglasses to protect my eyes.

Even so, it was bitter going. After the first mile the blood was flowing well and my arms and legs were warm, but my feet were cold, and even heavy muffling couldn't keep the wind from scraping the skin on my cheeks. Few cars were on the streets, and no other people. It was like running through a wasteland. This is what it would be like after a nuclear war: no people, freezing cold, snow blowing across in fine pelting particles like a desert sandstorm.

The lake made an even eerier landscape. Steam rose from it as from a giant cauldron. The water was invisible beneath the heavy veils of mist. I paused for a moment in awe, but the wind quickly cut through the layers of clothes.

The lake path curved around as it led to the promontory so that you could only see a few yards ahead of you. I kept expecting to meet Cinda and Po on their way back, but the only person who passed me was a solitary male jogger, anonymous in a blue ski mask and khaki down jacket.

At the far point of the promontory the wind blew unblocked across the lake. It swept snow and frozen mist pellets with it, blowing in a high persistent whine. I was about to turn and go home when I heard a dog barking above the keening wind. I hesitated to go down to the water, but what if it was Po, separated from her mistress?

The rocks leading down to the lake were covered with ice. I slipped and slid down, trying desperately for hand- and toe-holds—even if someone were around to rescue me I wouldn't survive a bath in subzero water.

I found Po on a flat slab of rock. She was standing where its edge hung over the mist-covered water, barking furiously. I called to her. She turned her head briefly but wouldn't come.

By now I had a premonition of what would meet me when I'd picked my way across the slab. I lay flat on the icy rock, gripping my feet around one end, and leaned over it through the mist to peer in the water. As soon as I showed up, Po stopped barking and began an uneasy pacing and whining.

Cinda's body was just visible beneath the surface. It was a four-foot drop to the water from where I lay. I couldn't reach her and I didn't dare get down in the water. I thought furiously and finally unwound a long muffler from around my neck. Tying it to a jagged spur near me I wrapped the other end around my waist and prayed. Leaning over from the waist gave me the length I needed to reach into the water. I took a deep breath and plunged my arms in. The shock of the water was almost more than I could bear; I concentrated on Cinda, on the dog, thought of Christmas in the northern suburbs, of everything possible but the cold which made my arms almost useless. "You only have one chance, Vic. Don't blow it."

The weight of her body nearly dragged me in on top of Cinda. I slithered across the icy rock, scissoring my feet wildly until they caught on the spur where my muffler was tied. Po was no help, either. She planted herself next to me, whimpering with anxiety as I pulled her mistress from the water. With water soaked in every garment, Cinda must have weighed two hundred pounds. I almost lost her several times, almost lost myself, but I got her up. I tried desperately to revive her, Po anxiously licking her face, but there was no hope. I finally realized I was going to die of exposure myself if I didn't get away from there. I tried calling Po to come with me, but she wouldn't leave Cinda. I ran as hard as I could back to the harbor, where I flagged down a car. My teeth were chattering so hard I almost couldn't speak, but I got the strangers to realize there was a dead woman back on the promontory point. They drove me to the Town Hall police station.

I spent most of Christmas Day in bed, layered in blankets, drinking hot soup prepared by my friend Dr. Lotty Herschel. I had some frostbite in two of my fingers, but she thought they would recover. Lotty left at seven to eat dinner with her nurse, Carol Alvarado, and her family.

The police had taken Cinda away, and Jonathan had persuaded Po to go home with him. I guess it had been a fairly tragic scene—Jonathan crying, the dog unwilling to let Cinda's body out of her sight. I hadn't been there myself, but one of my newspaper friends told me about it.

It was only eight o'clock when the phone next to my bed began ringing, but I was deep in sleep, buried in blankets. It must have rung nine or ten times before I even woke up, and another several before I could bring myself to stick one of my sore arms out to answer it.

"Hello?" I said groggily.

"Vic. Vic, I hate to bother you, but I need help."

"Who is this?" I started coming to.

"Jonathan Michaels. They've arrested me for killing Cinda. I only get the one phone call." He was trying to speak jauntily, but his voice cracked.

"Killing Cinda?" I echoed. "I thought she slipped and fell."

"Apparently someone strangled her and pushed her in after she was dead. Don't ask me how they know. Don't ask me why they thought I did it. The problem is—the problem is—Po. I don't have anyone to leave her with."

"Where are you now?" I swung my legs over the bed and began pulling on longjohns. He was at their apartment, four buildings up the street from me, on his way downtown for booking and then to Cook County jail. The arresting officer, not inhuman on Christmas Day, would let him wait for me if I could get there fast.

I was half dressed by the time I hung up and quickly finished pulling on jeans, boots, and a heavy sweater. Jonathan and two policemen were standing in the entryway of his building when I ran up. He handed me his apartment keys. In the distance I could hear Po's muffled barking.

"Do you have a lawyer?" I demanded.

Ordinarily a cheerful, bearded young man with long golden hair, Jonathan now looked rather bedraggled. He shook his head dismally.

"You need one. I can find someone for you, or I can represent you myself until we come up with someone better. I don't practice anymore, so you need someone who's active, but I can get you through the formalities."

He accepted gratefully, and I followed him into the waiting police car. The arresting officers wouldn't answer any of my questions. When we got down to the Eleventh Street police headquarters, I insisted on seeing the officer in charge, and was taken in to Sergeant John McGonnigal.

McGonnigal and I had met frequently. He was a stocky young man, very able, and I had a lot of respect for him. I'm not sure he reciprocated it. "Merry Christmas, Sergeant. It's a terrible day to be working, isn't it?"

"Merry Christmas, Miss Warshawski. What are you doing here?"

"I represent Jonathan Michaels. Seems someone got a little confused and thinks he pushed Ms. Goodrich into Lake Michigan this morning."

"We're not confused. She was strangled and pushed into the lake. She was dead before she went into the water. He has no alibi for the relevant time."

"No alibi! Who in this city does have an alibi?"

There was more to it than that, he explained stiffly. Michaels and Cinda had been heard quarreling late at night by their neighbors across the hall and underneath. They had resumed their fight in the morning. Cinda had finally slammed out of the house with the dog around nine-thirty.

"He didn't follow her, Sergeant."

"How do you know?"

I explained that I had watched Cinda from my living room. "And I didn't run into Mr. Michaels out on the point. I only met one person."

He pounced on that. How could I be sure it wasn't Jonathan? Finally agreeing to get a description of his clothes to see if he owned a navy ski mask or a khaki jacket, McGonnigal also pointed out that there were two ways to leave the lakefront—Jonathan could have gone north instead of south.

"Maybe. But you're spinning a very thin thread, Sergeant. It's not going to hold up. Now I need some time alone with my client."

He was most unhappy to let me represent Jonathan, but there wasn't much he could do about it. He left us alone in a small interrogation room.

"I'm taking it on faith that you didn't kill Cinda," I said briskly. "But, for the record, did you?"

He shook his head. "No way. Even if I had stopped loving her, which I hadn't, I don't solve my problems that way." He ran a hand through his long hair. "I can't believe this. I can't even really believe Cinda is dead. It's all happened too fast. And now they're arresting me." His hands were beautiful, with long strong fingers. Strong enough to strangle someone, certainly.

"What were you fighting about this morning?"

"Fighting?"

"Don't play dumb with me, Jonathan: I'm the only help you've got. Your neighbors heard you—that's why the police arrested you."

He smiled a little foolishly. "It all seems so stupid now. I keep thinking, if I hadn't gotten her mad, she wouldn't have gone out there. She'd be alive now."

"Maybe. Maybe not. What were you fighting about?"

He hesitated. "Those damned Santa Claus pictures she took. I never wanted her to do it, anyway. She's too good—she was too good a photographer to be wasting her time on that kind of stuff. Then she got mad and started accusing me of being Lawrence Welk, and who was I to talk. It all started because someone phoned her at one this morning. I'd just gotten back from a gig"— he grinned suddenly, painfully—"a Lawrence Welk gig, and this call came in. Someone who had been in one of her Santa shots. Said he was

very shy, and wanted to make sure he wasn't in the picture with his kid, so would she bring him the negatives?"

"She had the negatives? Not Burton's?"

"Yeah. Stupid idiot. She was developing the film herself. Apparently this guy called Burton's first. Anyway, to make a long story short, she agreed to meet him today and give him the negatives, and I was furious. First of all, why should she go out on Christmas to satisfy some moron's whim? And why was she taking those dumb-assed pictures anyway?"

Suddenly his face cracked and he started sobbing. "She was so beautiful and I loved her so much. Why did I have to fight with her?"

I patted his shoulder and held his hand until the tears stopped. "You know, if that was her caller she was going to meet, that's probably the person who killed her."

"I thought of that. And that's what I told the police. But they say it's the kind of thing I'd be bound to make up under the circumstances."

I pushed him through another half-hour of questions. What had she said about her caller? Had he given his name? She didn't know his name. Then how had she known which negatives were his? She didn't—just the day and the time he'd been there, so she was taking over the negatives for that morning. That's all he knew; she'd been too angry to tell him what she was taking with her. Yes, she had taken negatives with her.

He gave me detailed instructions on how to look after Po. Just dry dog food. No table scraps. As many walks as I felt like giving her—she was an outdoor dog and loved snow and water. She was very well trained; they never walked her with a leash. Before I left, I talked to McGonnigal. He told me he was going to follow up on the story about the man in the photograph at Burton's the next day but he wasn't taking it too seriously. He told me they hadn't found any film on Cinda's body, but that was because she hadn't taken any with her—Jonathan was making up that, too. He did agree, though, to hold Jonathan at Eleventh Street overnight. He could get a bail hearing in the morning and maybe not have to put his life at risk among the gang members who run Cook County jail disguised as prisoners.

I took a taxi back to the north side. The streets were clear and we moved quickly. Every mile or so we passed a car abandoned on the roadside, making the Arctic landscape appear more desolate than ever.

Once at Jonathan's apartment it took a major effort of will to get back outside with the dog. Po went with me eagerly enough, but kept turning around, looking at me searchingly as though hoping I might be transformed into Cinda.

Back in the apartment, I had no strength left to go home. I found the bedroom, let my clothes drop where they would on the floor and tumbled into bed.

Holy Innocents' Day, lavishly celebrated by my Polish Catholic relatives, was well advanced before I woke up again. I found Po staring at me with reproachful brown eyes, panting slightly. "All right, all right," I grumbled, pulling the covers back and staggering to my feet.

I'd been too tired the night before even to locate the bathroom. Now I found it, part of a large darkroom. Cinda apparently had knocked down a wall connecting it to the dining room; she had a sink and built-in shelves all in one handy location. Prints were strung around the room, and chemicals and lingerie jostled one another incongruously. I borrowed a toothbrush, cautiously smelling the toothpaste to make sure it really held Crest, not developing chemicals.

I put my clothes back on and took Po around the block. The weather had moderated considerably; a bank thermometer on the corner stood at 9 degrees. Po wanted to run to the lake, but I didn't feel up to going that far this morning, and called her back with difficulty. After lunch, if I could get my car started, we might see whether any clues lay hidden in the snow.

I called Lotty from Cinda's apartment, explaining where I was and why. She told me I was an idiot to have gotten out of bed the night before, but if I wasn't dead of exposure by now I would probably survive until someone shot me. Somehow that didn't cheer me up.

While I helped myself to coffee and toast in Cinda's kitchen I started calling various attorneys to see if I could find someone to represent Jonathan. Tim Oldham, who'd gone to law school with me, handled a good-sized criminal practice. He wasn't too enthusiastic about taking a client without much money, but I put on some not very subtle pressure about a lady I'd seen him with on the Gold Coast a few weeks ago who bore little resemblance to his wife. He promised me Jonathan would be home by supper time, called me some unflattering names, and hung up.

Besides the kitchen, bedroom, and darkroom, the apartment had one other room, mostly filled by a grand piano. Stacks of music stood on the floor—Jonathan either couldn't afford shelves or didn't think he needed them. The walls were hung with poster-sized photographs of Jonathan playing, taken by Cinda. They were very good.

I went back into the darkroom and poked around at the pictures. Cinda had put all her Santa Claus photographs in neatly marked envelopes. She'd carefully written the name of each child next to the number of the exposure on that roll of film. I switched on a light table and started looking at them. She'd taken pictures every day for three weeks, which amounted to thousands of shots. It looked like a needle-in-the-haystack type task. But most of the pictures were of children. The only others were ones Cinda had taken for her own amusement, panning the crowd, or artsy shots through glass at reflecting lights. Presumably her caller was one of the adults in the crowd.

After lunch I took Po down to my car. She had no hesitation about going with me and leaped eagerly into the backseat. "You have too trusting a nature," I told her. She grinned at me and panted heavily. The Omega started, after a few grumbling moments, and I drove north to Bryn Mawr and back to get the battery well charged before turning into the lot at Belmont Harbor. Po was almost beside herself with excitement, banging her tail against the rear window until I got the door open and let her out. She raced ahead of me on the lake path. I didn't try to call her back; I figured I'd find her at Cinda's rock.

I moved slowly, carefully scanning the ground for traces of—what? Film? A business card? The wind was so much calmer today and the air enough warmer that visibility was good, but I didn't see anything.

At the lake the mist had cleared away, leaving the water steely gray, moving uneasily under its iron bands of cold. Po stood as I expected, on the rock where I'd found her yesterday. She was the picture of dejection. She clearly had expected to find her mistress there.

I combed the area carefully and at last found one of those gray plastic tubes that film comes in. It was empty. I pocketed it, deciding I could at least show it to McGonnigal and hope he would think it important. Po left the rocks with utmost reluctance. Back on the lake path, she kept turning around to look for Cinda. I had to lift her into the car. During the drive to police headquarters, she kept turning restlessly in the back of the car, a trying maneuver since she was bigger than the seat.

McGonnigal didn't seem too impressed with the tube I'd found, but he took it and sent it to the forensics department. I asked him what he'd learned from Burton's. They didn't have copies of the photographs. Cinda had all those. If someone ordered one, they sent the name to Cinda and she supplied the picture. They gave McGonnigal a copy of the list of the seven hundred people requesting pictures and he had someone going through to see if any of them were known criminals, but he obviously believed it was a waste of time. If it weren't for the fact that his boss, Lieutenant Robert Mallory, had been a friend of my father's, he probably wouldn't even have made this much of an effort.

I stopped to see Jonathan, who seemed to be in fairly good spirits. He told me Tim Oldham had been by. "He thinks I'm a hippy and not very interesting compared to some of the mob figures he represents, but I can tell he's doing his best." He was working out the fingering to a Schubert score, using the side of the bed as a keyboard. I told him Po was well, but waiting for me in the car outside, so I'd best be on my way.

I spent the rest of the afternoon going through Cinda's Santa photographs. I'd finished about a third of them at five when Tim Oldham phoned to say that Jonathan would have to spend another night in jail: because of the Christmas holidays he hadn't been able to arrange for bail.

"You owe me, Vic; this has been one of the more thankless ways I've spent a holiday."

"You're serving justice, Tim," I said brightly. "What more could you ask for? Think of the oath you swore when you became a member of the bar."

"I'm thinking of the oaths I'd like to swear at you," he grumbled.

I laughed and hung up. I took Po for one last walk, gave her her evening food and drink and prepared to leave for my own place. As soon as the dog saw me putting my coat back on, she abandoned her dinner and started dancing around my feet, wagging her tail, to show that she was always ready to play. I kept yelling "No" to her with no effect. She grinned happily at me as if to say this was a game she often played—she knew humans liked to pretend they didn't want her along, but they always took her in the end.

She was very upset when I shoved her back into the apartment behind me. As I locked the door, she began barking. Retrievers are quiet dogs; they seldom bark and never whine. But their voices are deep and full-bodied, coming straight from their huge chests. Good diaphragm support, the kind singers seldom achieve.

Cinda's apartment was on the second floor. When I got to the ground floor, I could still hear Po from the entryway. She was clearly audible outside the front door. "Ah, nuts!" I muttered. How long could she keep this up? Were dogs like babies? Did you just ignore them for a while and discipline them into going to sleep? Did that really work with babies? After standing five minutes in the icy wind I could still hear Po. I swore under my breath and let myself back into the building.

She was totally ecstatic at seeing me, jumping up on my chest and licking my face to show there were no hard feelings. "You're shameless and a fraud," I told her severely. She wagged her tail with delight. "Still, you're an orphan; I can't treat you too harshly."

She agreed and followed me down the stairs and back to my apartment with unabated eagerness. I took a bath and changed my clothes, made dinner and took care of my mail, then walked Po around the block to a little park, and back up the street to her own quarters. I brought my own toothbrush with me this time; there didn't seem much point in trying to leave the dog until Jonathan got out of jail.

Cinda and Jonathan had few furnishings, but they owned a magnificent stereo system and a large record collection. I put some Britten quartets on, found a novel buried in the stack of technical books next to Cinda's side of the bed, and purloined a bottle of burgundy. I curled up on a beanbag chair with the book and the wine. Po lay at my feet, panting happily. Altogether a delightful domestic scene. Maybe I should get a dog.

I finished the book and the bottle of wine a little after midnight and went to bed. Po padded into the bedroom after me and curled up on a rug next to the bed. I went to sleep quickly.

A single sharp bark from the dog woke me about two hours later. "What is it, girl? Nightmares?" I started to turn over to go back to sleep when she barked again. "Quiet, now!" I commanded.

I heard her get to her feet and start toward the door. And then I heard the sound that her sharper ears had caught first. Someone was trying to get into the apartment. It couldn't be Jonathan; I had his keys, and this was someone fumbling, trying different keys, trying to pick the lock. In about thirty seconds I pulled on jeans, boots, and a sweatshirt, ignoring underwear. My intruder had managed the lower lock and was starting on the upper.

Po was standing in front of the door, hackles raised on her back. Obedient to my whispered command she wasn't barking. She followed me reluctantly into the darkroom-bathroom. I took her into the shower stall and pulled the curtain across as quietly as I could.

We waited there in the dark while our intruder finished with locks. It was an unnerving business listening to the rattling, knowing someone would be on us momentarily. I wondered if I'd made the right choice; maybe I should have dashed down the back stairs with the dog and gotten the police. It was too late now, however; we could hear a pair of boots moving heavily across the living room. Po gave a deep, mean growl in the back of her throat.

"Doggy? Doggy? Are you in here, Doggy?" The man knew about Po, but not whether she was here. He must not have heard her two short barks earlier. He had a high tenor voice with a trace of a Spanish accent.

Po continued to growl, very softly. At last the far door to the darkroom opened and the intruder came in. He had a flashlight which he shone around the room; through the curtain I could see its point of light bobbing.

Satisfied that no one was there, he turned on the overhead switch. This was connected to a ventilating fan, whose noise was loud enough to mask Po's continued soft growling.

I couldn't see him, but apparently he was looking through Cinda's photograph collection. He flipped on the switch at the light table and then spent a long time going through the negatives. I was pleased with Po; I wouldn't have expected such patience from a dog. The intruder must have sat for an hour while my muscles cramped and water dripped on my head, and she stayed next to me quietly the whole time.

At last he apparently found what he needed. He got up and I heard more paper rustling, then the light went out.

"Now!" I shouted at Po. She raced out of the room and found the intruder as he was on his way out the far door. Blue light flashed; a gun barked. Po yelped and stopped momentarily. By that time I was across the room, too. The intruder was on his way out the apartment door.

I pulled my parka from the chair where I'd

left it and took off after him. Po was bleeding slightly from her left shoulder, but the bullet must only have grazed her because she ran strongly. We tumbled down the stairs together and out the front door into the icy December night. As we went outside, I grabbed the dog and rolled over with her. I heard the gun go off a few times but we were moving quickly, too quickly to make a good target.

Streetlamps showed our man running away from us down Halsted to Belmont. He wore the navy ski mask and khaki parka of the solitary runner I'd seen at the harbor the day before yesterday.

Hearing Po and me behind him he put on a burst of speed and made it to a car waiting at the corner. We were near the Omega now; I bundled the dog into the backseat, sent up a prayer to the patron saint of Delco batteries, and turned on the engine.

The streets were deserted. I caught up with the car, a dark Lincoln, where Sheridan Road crossed Lake Shore Drive at Belmont. Instead of turning onto the drive, the Lincoln cut straight across to the harbor.

"This is it, girl," I told Po. "You catch this boy, then we take you in and get that shoulder stitched up. And then you get your favorite dinner—even if it's a whole cow."

The dog was leaning over the front seat, panting, her eyes gleaming. She was a retriever, after all. The Lincoln stopped at the end of the harbor parking lot. I halted the Omega some fifty yards away and got out with the dog. Using a row of parked cars as cover, we ran across the lot, stopping near the Lincoln in the shelter of a van. At that point, Po began her deep, insistent barking.

This was a sound which would attract attention, possibly even the police, so I made no effort to stop her. The man in the Lincoln reached the same conclusion; a window opened and he began firing at us. This was just a waste of ammunition, since we were sheltered behind the van.

The shooting only increased Po's vocal efforts. It also attracted attention from Lake Shore Drive; out of the corner of my eye I saw the flashing blue lights which herald the arrival of Chicago's finest.

Our attacker saw them, too. A door opened and the man in the ski mask slid out. He took off along the lake path, away from the harbor entrance, out toward the promontory. I clapped my hands at Po and started running after him. She was much faster than me; I lost sight of her in the dark as I picked my way more cautiously along the icy path, shivering in the bitter wind, shivering at the thought of the dark freezing water to my right. I could hear it slapping ominously against the ice-covered rocks, could hear the man pounding ahead of me. No noise from Po. Her tough pads picked their way sure and silent across the frozen gravel.

As I rounded the curve toward the promontory I could hear the man yelling in Spanish at Po, heard a gun go off, heard a loud splash in the water. Rage at him for shooting the dog gave me a last burst of speed. I rounded the end of the point. Saw his dark shape outlined against the rocks and jumped on top of him.

He was completely unprepared for me. We fell heavily, rolling down the rocks. The gun slipped from his hand, banged loudly as it bounced against the ice and fell into the water. We were a foot away from the water, fighting recklessly—the first person to lose a grip would be shoved in to die.

Our parkas weighted our arms and hampered our swings. He lunged clumsily at my throat. I pulled away, grabbed hold of his ski mask and hit his head against the rocks. He grunted and drew back, trying to kick me. As I moved away from his foot I lost my hold on him and slid backwards across the ice. He followed through quickly, giving a mighty shove which pushed me over the edge of the rock. My feet landed in the water. I swung them up with an effort, two icy lumps, and tried to back away.

As I scrabbled for a purchase, a dark shape came out of the water and climbed onto the rock next to me. Po. Not killed after all. She shook herself, spraying water over me and over my assailant. The sudden bath took him by surprise. He stopped long enough for me to get well away and gain my breath and a better position.

The dog, shivering violently, stayed close to me. I ran a hand through her wet fur. "Soon, kid. We'll get you home and dry soon."

Just as the attacker launched himself at us, a searchlight went on overhead. "This is the police," a loudspeaker boomed. "Drop your guns and come up."

The dark shape hit me, knocked me over. Po let out a yelp and sunk her teeth into his leg. His yelling brought the police to our sides.

They carried strong flashlights. I could see a sodden mass of paper, a small manila envelope with teethmarks in it. Po wagged her tail and picked it up again.

"Give me that!" our attacker yelled in his high voice. He fought with the police to try to reach the envelope. "I threw that in the water. How can this be? How did she get it?"

"She's a retriever," I said.

Later, at the police station, we looked at the negatives in the envelope Po had retrieved from the water. They showed a picture of the man in the ski mask looking on with intense, brooding eyes while Santa Claus talked to his little boy. No wonder Cinda found him worth photographing.

"He's a cocaine dealer," Sergeant McGonnigal explained to me. "He jumped a ten-million-dollar bail. No wonder he didn't want any photographs of him circulating around. We're holding him for murder this time."

A uniformed man brought Jonathan into McGonnigal's office. The sergeant cleared his throat uncomfortably. "Looks like your dog saved your hide, Mr. Michaels."

Po, who had been lying at my feet, wrapped in a police horse blanket, gave a bark of pleasure. She staggered to her feet, trailing the blanket, and walked stiffly over to Jonathan, tail wagging.

I explained our adventure to him, and what a heroine the dog had been. "What about that empty film container I gave you this afternoon, Sergeant?"

Apparently Cinda had brought that with her to her rendezvous, not knowing how dangerous her customer was. When he realized it was empty, he'd flung it aside and attacked Cinda. "We got a complete confession," McGonnigal said. "He was so rattled by the sight of the dog with the envelope full of negatives in her mouth that he completely lost his nerve. I know he's got good lawyers—one of them's your friend Oldham—but I hope we have enough to convince a judge not to set bail."

Jonathan was on his knees fondling the dog and talking to her. He looked over his shoulder at McGonnigal. "I'm sure Oldham's relieved that you caught the right man—a murderer who can afford to jump a ten-million-dollar bail is a much better client than one who can hardly keep a retriever in dog food." He turned back to the dog. "But we'll blow our savings on a steak; you get the steak and I'll eat Butcher's Blend tonight, Miss Three-Dot Po of Blackstone, People's Heroine, and winner of the Croix de Chien for valor." Po panted happily and licked his face.

MAD DOG
Dick Lochte

DICK LOCHTE'S FIRST NOVEL, *SLEEPING DOG* (1985), recounts the adventures of a precocious fourteen-year-old girl and a worn-out Los Angeles private detective as they search for the girl's mother across most of California. It was nominated for the Edgar, Shamus, and Anthony awards and won the Nero Wolfe Award. It also was selected by the *New York Times* as a "Notable Book of the Year." The Independent Mystery Booksellers of America named it one of the 100 Most Popular Mystery Novels of the Century. More recently, he has been co-writing books with Christopher Darden and Al Roker. "Mad Dog" was first published in *Santa Clues*, edited by Martin H. Greenberg and Carol-Lynn Rossell Waugh (New York, Signet, 1993).

Mad Dog

DICK LOCHTE

THE GUY WHO SAID APRIL WAS THE cruelest month must not have spent much time alone in Hollywood during the Christmas season. There's all that smog-filtered sun shining down. Neon trees. Elves with tans. Reindeer with chrome sidewalls. And the street decorations are flat-out cheesy—sprigs of wilted holly with greetings that are so busy being nondenominational they might as well be serving some other purpose, like telling you to keep off the grass. If there was any grass.

As you might guess from the foregoing, I was fairly depressed that night before Christmas Eve. My few friends were scattered to the winds and the holidays loomed so bleak that I was at the end of my tether. So I agreed to appear on *The Mad Dog Show*.

Mad Dog, last name unknown if it wasn't "Dog," was the latest thing in radio talk hosts. He was rumored to be young, irreverent, glib to the max, and funny on occasion, usually at the expense of someone else. As I discovered by listening to his show the night before my scheduled appearance, he was also brash and self-opinionated and he had an annoying habit of pausing from time to time to let loose with a baying noise. But his coast-to-coast audience was not only charmed by such behavior, it was large and loyal. And, as my publisher's publicity agent informed me, Mad Dog actually read books and was able to sell them.

Even stranger, much to the agent's surprise, the self-described "howling hound of America's airways" specifically requested that I appear on his pre-Christmas Eve show to talk about my latest novel.

His station, KPLA-FM, was in a no-man's-land just off the San Diego freeway, nestled between a large lumberyard, apparently closed for the holidays, and a bland apartment complex that looked newer than the suit I was wearing, if not more substantial. The station would have resembled a little white clapboard cottage except for the rooftop antenna that went up for nearly three stories. It was situated in the middle of a shell-coated compound surrounded by a chain fence.

Security was a big thing at KPLA-FM, apparently. A lighted metal gate blocked the only road in that I could find. I aimed my car at it, braked, and waited for a little watchman camera to spin on its axis until its lens was pointed at my windshield.

"Hello," an electronically neutered voice said, "have you an appointment?"

"I'm Leo Bloodworth," I replied, sticking my head out of the side window. "I'm guesting on the . . ."

"Of course," the voice interrupted me. "Mad Dog's expecting you. Please enter and park in the visitor section."

There weren't many cars. I pulled in between a black sedan and a sports convertible, got out without dinging either, and strolled to the brightly lit front door, my current novel under my arm.

The door was locked.

I couldn't find a bell, so I knocked.

A little peephole broke the surface of the door, through which an interior light glowed. A shadow covered the light and the door was opened by a pleasant woman in her senior years, rather plump and motherly. There was something familiar about her intelligent, cobalt-blue eyes. Had she been an actress on one of those TV shows my family used to watch? Aunt Somebody who was always baking cookies and dispensing comfort and advice?

"I'm Sylvia Redfern, the assistant station manager," she said. "I'm not usually here this late, but we're very short-staffed because of the holidays. Come, I'll show you to what passes for our greenroom."

She led me to a small, pale blue and white, windowless space furnished with thrift-sale sofas and chairs, a large soft-drink machine, and a loudspeaker against a far wall, from which emanated music that sounded vaguely classical.

There were two people in the room. The man was a reedy type whose lined face and sparse white hair made me place his age as somewhere in his mid-sixties, at least a decade older than me. The woman, tall and handsome with good cheekbones and short black hair, I figured for being at least twenty years my junior.

"Another fellow guest," Sylvia Redfern announced cheerily. "Ms. Landy Thorp and Dr. Eldon Varney, this is Officer Leo Bloodworth."

"Just Leo Bloodworth," I corrected, nodding to them both.

Sylvia Redfern looked chagrined. "Oh, my," she said, "I thought you were with the police."

"Not for twenty years or so. I hope our host isn't expecting me to . . ."

"I'm sure his information is more up to date than mine," she replied, embarrassed. "Please make yourself comfortable. I'd better go back front and see to the other guests when they arrive."

Dr. Varney's tired eyes took in the jacket of my book. He gave me a brief, condescending smile and returned to his chair. Landy Thorp said, "You're the one who writes with that little girl."

It was true. Through a series of circumstances too painful to discuss, my writing career had been linked to that of a bright and difficult teenager named Serendipity Dahlquist. Two moderately successful books, *Sleeping Dog* and *Laughing Dog,* had carried both our names. This was the newest in the series, *Devil Dog.*

"May I?" Landy Thorp asked and I handed her the novel.

She looked at the back cover where Serendipity and I were posed in my office. "She's darling," Landy Thorp said. "Is she going to be on the show, too?"

"No. She's in New England with her grandmother." And having a real Christmas, I thought. "So I'm here to flog the book. What brings *you* to *The Mad Dog Show,* Miss Thorp?"

She frowned and returned *Devil Dog* as she replied, "I'm not sure I know." Then the frown disappeared and she added, "But please call me Landy."

"Landy and Leo it will be," I said. "You don't know why you're here?"

"Somebody from the show called the magazine where I work and asked for them to send a representative and here I am."

"What magazine?" I asked.

"Los Angeles Today."

"Los Angeles Today?" Dr. Varney asked with a sneer twisting his wrinkled face. "That monument to shoddy journalism?"

Landy stared at him.

"The magazine ruffle your feathers, Doc?" I asked.

"I gather they're in the midst of interring some very old bones better left undisturbed."

Landy shrugged. "Beats me," she said. "I've only been there for a year. What's the story?"

"Nothing I care to discuss," Dr. Varney said. "Which is precisely what I told the research person who phoned me."

I strolled to the drink machine and was studying its complex instructions when the background music was replaced by an unmistakable "Ahooooooo, ruff-ruff, ahoooooooooo. It's near the nine o'clock hour and this is your pal, Mad Dog, inviting you to step into the doghouse with my special guest, businessman Gabriel Warren. Mr. Warren has currently curtailed his activities as CEO of Altadine Industries, to head up Project Rebuild, a task force that hopes to revitalize business in the riot-torn South Central area of our city. With him are his associates in the project, Norman Daken, a member of the board at Altadine and Charles 'Red' Rafferty, formerly a commander in the LAPD, ahooooo, ahoooooo, and now Altadine's head of security.

"Also taking part in tonight's discussion are Victor Newgate of the legal firm of Axminster and Newgate, mystery novelist slash private detective, Leo Bloodworth, journalist Landy Thorp, and Dr. Clayton Varney, shrink to the stars."

Varney scowled at his billing. I was doing a little scowling, myself. Red Rafferty had been the guy who'd asked for and accepted my badge and gun when I was booted off the LAPD. I suppose he'd had reason. It all took place back in the Vietnam days. Two kids had broken into a branch of the Golden Pacific Bank one night as a protest. The manager had been there and tried to shoot them and me and so I wound up subduing *him* and letting the kids go. The banker pushed it and Rafferty did what he thought he had to. But I never exactly loved him for it. And I was not pleased at the prospect of spending an hour with him in the doghouse.

A commercial for a holiday bloodbath movie resonated from the speaker. Dr. Varney stood suddenly and headed for the door. Before he got there, it was opened by a meek little guy carrying a clipboard. He looked like he could still be in college, with his blond crew cut and glasses. "Hi," he said, "I'm Mad Dog's engineer, Greg. This way to the studio."

"First, I demand a clarification," Dr. Varney told him. "I want to know precisely what we're going to be discussing tonight."

Greg seemed a bit taken aback by the doctor.

He blinked and consulted his clipboard. "Crime in the inner city. What's causing the current rash of bank robberies. The working of the criminal mind. Like that."

"Contemporary issues," Dr. Varney said.

"Oh, absolutely," Greg replied. "Mad Dog's a very happening-now dude."

Somewhat mollified, Dr. Varney dragged along behind us as the little guy led us down a short hall and into a low-ceilinged, egg-carton-lined, claustrophobic room with one large picture window which exposed an even smaller room with two empty chairs facing a soundboard.

The men in the room looked up at us. They occupied five of the nine chairs. In front of each chair was a microphone. Mad Dog stood to welcome us. He was a heavyset young guy, with a faceful of long black hair that looked fake, and a forelock that looked real bothering his forehead and nearly covering one of his baby blues. He was in shirtsleeves and black slacks and he waved us to the empty seats with a wide, hairy grin.

Since I was locking eyes with Red Rafferty while I located a chair across from him, I didn't spot the animal until I was seated. It was a weird-looking mutt nestled on a dirty, brown cushion in a far corner.

"That's Dougie Dog, the show's mascot, Mr. Bloodworth," Mad Dog explained. "We use him for the Wet Veggie spots. He's not very active. Kinda O-L-D. But we love him."

"Is this for him?" I asked, indicating the empty chair next to me.

"No." Mad Dog smiled and settled into his chair. "The D-Dog prefers his cushion. That's for . . . someone falling by later."

"Sir?" Dr. Varney, who was hovering beside the table, addressed our host.

"Please, Doctor. It's Mad Dog."

"Mad Dog, then." Dr. Varney's lips curled on the nickname as if he'd bitten into a bad plum. "Before I participate in tonight's program, I want your assurances that we will be discussing issues of current concern."

"Tonight's topic is crime, Doctor. As current as today's newspaper. Or, in Ms. Thorp's case, today's magazine."

"Sit here, Clayton," the dapper, fifty-something Gabriel Warren said, pulling out a chair next to him for the doctor. "Good seeing you again." He looked like the complete CEO with his hand-tailored pinstripe, his no-nonsense hundred dollar razor cut, his gleaming white shirt, and red-striped power tie. His voice was clear and confident, just the sort of voice you need if you're planning on running for the Senate in the near future, which everyone seemed to think he was. "You know Norman, don't you?" he asked Varney.

"Of course." The doc nodded to the plump, middle-aged man in a rumpled tweed suit at Warren's left hand, Norman Daken.

"What are you doin' here, Bloodworth?" my old chief asked unpleasantly. Never a thin man, he'd added about six inches around the middle and one more chin, bringing his total to three.

"Pushing my novel," I said, pointing to the book on the table.

He glanced at it. "Beats workin', I guess," he said.

"It takes a little more effort than having somebody stick a fifty-dollar bill in your pocket," I said. That brought a nice shade of purple to his face. There'd been rumors that he'd made considerably more money as a cop than had been in his bimonthly paycheck, especially in his early days.

"Aaoooo, aaoooo," Mad Dog bayed. "Gentlemen, lady, I think Greg would like to get levels on all of us."

While each of us, in turn, babbled nonsense into our respective mikes to Greg's satisfaction, the woman who'd greeted me at the door, Sylvia Redfern, entered the engineer's cubicle and positioned the chair beside him—the better to observe us through the window.

Mad Dog asked innocently, "Any questions before we start? We've got one minute."

There was something about his manner, the edge to his voice, that made me wonder if we weren't going to be in for a few surprises before the show was over. The empty chair at our table was added intimidation. I think the feeling was shared by the others. They asked no questions, but they looked edgy, even lawyer Newgate whom I had observed in the past staying as cool as a polar bear under tremendous courtroom pressure.

Seated at his console behind the glass window, Greg stared at the clock on the wall and raised his hand, the index finger pointed out like the barrel of a gun. Then he aimed it at Mad Dog, who emitted one of his loud trademark moans. As it faded out, Greg faded in the show's theme (a rather regal-sounding melody that Landy later identified for me as Noel Coward's "Mad Dogs and Englishmen").

Then our host was telling his radio audience that they were in for a special show, one that people would be talking about through the holiday season.

Dr. Varney's frown deepened and even the smooth Gabriel Warren seemed peeved as Mad Dog blithely continued his opening comments. "Thirty years ago tonight, before I was even a little Mad Puppy, a terrible crime was committed in this city." Gabriel Warren leaned back in his chair. Norman Daken edged forward in his. Rafferty scowled. "Two crimes, really," Mad Dog corrected. "But the one people know about was the lesser of the two. The one people know about concerned the grisly death of a man of importance in this city, the father of one of our guests tonight, Theodore Daken."

Norman Daken's face turned white and his mouth dropped open in surprise. He had a red birthmark on his right cheek the size and shape of a teardrop and it seemed to glow from the sudden tension in his body. Mad Dog rolled right along. "Theodore Daken was then president of Altadine Industries, which in the early 1960s had developed one of this country's first successful experimental communications satellites, Altastar."

"Excuse me," Gabriel Warren interjected sharply. "I understood we were here to discuss urban violence."

"If Theodore Daken's death doesn't qualify," our host replied, "then I don't know the meaning of 'urban violence.'"

"Please," Norman Daken said shakily. "I don't really feel I want . . ."

"Bear with me, Mr. Daken. I'm just trying to acquaint the listeners with the events surrounding that evening. Both you and Mr. Warren were young executives at Altadine at the time, weren't you?"

"Yes, but . . ."

"You were the company's treasurer and Mr. Warren was executive vice president, sort of your father's protege. Is that right?"

"I suppose so." The birthmark looked like a drop of blood. "I handled the books and Dad was grooming Gabe to assume major responsibilities."

"Yes," Mad Dog said. His blue eyes danced merrily. "Anyway, on that night you two and other executives—and their secretaries, that's what they called 'em then, not assistants—had your own little holiday party in a large suite at the Hotel Brentwood. A good party, Mr. Warren?"

"As a matter of fact, Norman and I both had to leave early. Theo, Mr. Daken, was expecting an important telex from overseas that needed an immediate reply. It concerned an acquisition that we knew would involve a rather sizable investment on our part and Norman was there to advise me how far we could extend ourselves."

"And you didn't return to the party?" Mad Dog asked.

"The telex didn't arrive until rather late," Warren said. "I assumed the party must have ended."

"Not quite," Mad Dog said. "You missed what sounded like, for the most part, a very jolly affair. Lots of food and drink. Altastar had gone into space and it had taken your company's stock with it. Each guest at the party was presented with a commemorative Christmas present—a model of the satellite and a hefty bonus check. And everyone was happy.

"Daken, very much in the spirit of things, presented the gifts wearing a Santa Claus suit.

He didn't need a pillow. He was a man of appetite. For food and for women."

"Please," Norman Daken said, "this is so unnecessary."

"Forgive me if I seem insensitive," Mad Dog said. "But it *was* thirty years ago."

"And he *was* my father," Norman Daken countered.

"True," Mad Dog acknowledged. "I apologize. But the fact is that he did set his sights on one of the ladies that night. Isn't that true, Mr. Newgate?"

"I'm not sure what point you're trying to make," lawyer Newgate said.

"Simple enough," Mad Dog replied. "On that night of nights, after all the food had been consumed, the booze drunk, and the presents dispersed, everyone left the party. Except for Daken and his new office manager. While they were alone together . . . something happened. Perhaps you can enlighten us on that, Mr. Rafferty."

Red Rafferty was living up to his nickname. He looked apopletic. "Sure. What happened is that the woman went crazy and bashed . . . did away with poor Mr. Daken. Then she dragged his body down to her car and tried to get rid of it in a dumpster off Wilshire."

Mad Dog's lips formed a thin line as he said, "The woman's name was Victoria Douglas and because the story about her and Theodore Daken was all anybody talked about that holiday season, she became known as 'The Woman Who Killed Christmas.' She was tried and eventually placed into a hospital for the criminally insane. And, after a while, she escaped.

"She was at large for several years. Then fate caught up with her and she was discovered driving her car on an Arizona road, tripped up by a faulty brake light. She was put back into another facility and again she escaped. Five times over the past three decades did Victoria Douglas escape. She was found and brought back four times. And yes, my math is correct. The last time she escaped from a hospital, eleven years ago, she remained free.

"But The Woman Who Killed Christmas has never been forgotten. Even now, thirty years after the fact, her 'crime' remains one of the most infamous in this nation's history. And, all of you dog lovers out in radioland, here's something to chew on during the next commercial: It's entirely possible that the worst crime that took place that night wasn't the one committed by Victoria Douglas. Of that greater crime, *she* was the helpless victim."

Mad Dog leaned back in his chair, let loose a howl, and surrendered the airways to a commercial for soybean turkey stuffing.

Gabriel Warren stood up and turned to his associates. "Our host seems to have made a mistake inviting us here tonight. I suggest we leave him to contemplate it."

Red Rafferty knocked over his chair in his hurry to stand. Victor Newgate was a bit smoother, but no less anxious. The same was true of Dr. Varney. Norman Daken stood also. He said to Mad Dog, "I can't imagine why you're doing this terrible thing."

"How can you call it 'terrible' until you know what I'm doing?" Mad Dog asked. He turned to me. "You going, too, Bloodworth?"

"To tell the truth, I never was certain justice triumphed in the Daken case. So I'll stick around to see what's on your mind."

"Good," he said.

Since he didn't bother to ask Landy if she was staying, I figured she was in on his game, whatever it was.

The others were having trouble with the door, which wouldn't budge. Warren was losing his composure. "Open this goddamn door, son, if you know what's good for you."

"You'll be free to leave when the show is over in a little under an hour," Mad Dog informed them. "In twenty seconds we'll be back on the air. Whatever you have to say to me will be heard by nearly a million listeners. They love controversy. So feel free to voice whatever's on your mind. It can only boost my ratings."

Red Rafferty lifted his foot and smashed it against the door where the lock went into the clasp. The door didn't give and Rafferty grabbed his hip with a groan of pain.

"Not as easy as they make it seem in the police manuals, is it, Rafferty?" I asked.

"You son—" Rafferty began.

He was cut off by Mad Dog's howl. "We're back in the doghouse where some of my guests are milling about. Something on your minds, gentlemen?"

The others looked to Warren for guidance. He glared at Mad Dog and slowly walked back to his seat. The others followed. In the engineer's booth, Sylvia Redfern was viewing the proceedings with a rather startled expression on her face. In truth, I was a little startled myself at the way Mad Dog was carrying on.

"O.K., Mr. Bloodworth," he said, "why don't you tell us what you know about the eve of Christmas Eve, three decades ago?"

"Sure." And I dug into my memory bank. "I was barely in my twenties, the new cop on the beat in West L.A. My partner, John Gilfoyle, and I were cruising down Santa Monica Boulevard when we got a Code Two—that's urgent response, no siren or light. Somebody had reported a woman in distress in an alley off Wilshire.

"We arrived on the scene within minutes and found a tan Ford sedan parked in the alley with its engine going. The subject of the call was moving slowly down the alley, away from the car, a small woman in her mid to late thirties. She was in a dazed condition with abrasions on her face and arms. Her party dress was rumpled and torn.

"She didn't seem to understand who we were at first. I thought she might have been stoned, but it was more like shock. Then she seemed to get the drift and said, 'I'm the one you want, officers. I killed Theo Daken.'

"Around that time, John Gilfoyle poked his nose into her car. He shouted something to me about a big Santa Claus dummy on the backseat. Then he took a better look and saw the blood. He ran back to our car to call in the troops."

"Did Victoria Douglas make any effort to escape?" Mad Dog asked.

"No. She was too far out of it. I don't know how she was able to drive the car."

"Did she say anything?"

"Nothing," I answered. "I had to get her name from the identification cards in her purse."

"What happened then?"

"Gilfoyle and I were helping her to our vehicle when the newspaper guys showed up. I don't know how the heck they got there that fast. I put Miss Douglas in the back of our vehicle and helped Gilfoyle pull the photographers away from the body. But they got their pictures. And the people of Los Angeles got their dead Santa for Christmas."

Norman Daken opened his mouth, but decided against whatever he was going to say. I remembered what he was like back then, sitting in the courtroom, in obvious pain. Thinner, more hair. Women might even have found him handsome. Not now. Unlike Warren, to whom the years had been more than kind, Daken resembled an over-the-hill Pillsbury Doughboy.

Mad Dog turned to Rafferty. "You took charge of the Daken case personally, Mr. Rafferty. Care to say why?"

"Because it was a . . ." he began, shouting. Then, realizing that his voice was being carried on an open radio line, he started again, considerably more constrained. "Because it was a circus. There was this crazy woman who'd used a blunt instrument on Santa Claus. Not just any Santa, but a Santa who was an old pal of the governor's. And a damn fine man." This last was said with a glance at Norman Daken. "And my chief wanted action. That's why I took charge."

"Even though there was this tremendous pressure, you feel that the police did all that they could in investigating the murder?"

"Absolutely. It was handled by the book."

"Mr. Bloodworth." Mad Dog shifted back to me. "According to an account printed at the time of Victoria Douglas's trial, you felt that

maybe the detectives on the case had missed a few bets."

"Bloodworth was a cop on the beat," Rafferty squealed. "His opinion is worth bupkis."

"It wasn't just my opinion," I said. "Ferd Loomis, one of the investigating officers, agreed with me."

"Ferd Loomis was a soak," Rafferty growled. "That's why he took early retirement and why he wound up eating his Colt."

"I wouldn't know about that," I said. "All I know is what he told me. He said that the officers sent to secure the crime scene were greener than I was and they let reporters in before the lab boys got there. Not only that, a hotel bellboy was collecting tips to sneak curious guests into the room.

"All the evidence—the glass statue that was the supposed murder weapon, wiped clean of fingerprints, the dead man's clothes, the bloody pillow—was polluted by a stream of gawkers wandering through."

"But the evidence was allowed, wasn't it?" Mad Dog asked with the assurance of a man who'd read the trial transcripts. He wanted to lay it out clearly for the radio audience. When no one replied, he specified, "Mr. Newgate, you were Miss Douglas's lawyer."

"Judge Fogle allowed the evidence," Newgate said flatly. "I objected and was overruled. It was highly irregular. I don't know what made Fogle rule the way he did. Since he's been senile for nearly fifteen years, I don't suppose I ever will."

"What was the motive for the murder?" Mad Dog asked, like a man who already knew the answer.

Rafferty didn't mind responding. "According to our investigation, Victoria Douglas had been having an affair with Daken. We figured he broke it off that night."

"Sort of a 'Merry Christmas, Honey, Get Lost' approach?" I asked.

"Yeah. Why not? He dumped her. And then made the big mistake of falling asleep on the bed. She picked up one of those satellite statues and beaned him with it. Then she hit him a few more times to be sure and lugged him down to her car."

"Without one witness seeing her," I said.

Rafferty shook his head as if I were the biggest dufus in the world. "She took the freight elevator or the stairs. My God, Bloodworth. The suite was only on the third floor."

Mad Dog was vastly amused by our interchange. The others were expressionless. Landy Thorpe winked at me.

I realized that I probably wasn't going to be plugging my book that night. But maybe this was better. As I said, I'd never felt right about the trial. And even if nothing came of this re-examination, it was getting under Rafferty's hide.

I said, "When we found Victoria Douglas, she looked like she'd been roughed up. But that wasn't mentioned at the trial."

"You can muss yourself up pretty bad swinging a heavy statue fifteen or twenty times with all your might," Rafferty explained.

"Then there's her size. She weighed about one hundred twenty-five pounds. Daken weighed twice that. How'd she get him down the stairs?"

"Maybe she rolled him down." Rafferty's little eyes flickered toward Norman Daken, ready to apologize for his crudeness. But Daken seemed to have adapted a posture of disbelief that the discussion had anything to do with him. He stared at his microphone as if he were waiting for it to suddenly dance a jig. The fingers of his right hand idly brushed his cheek where the birthmark was.

"Anyways," Rafferty said, "crazy people sometimes have the strength of ten."

"Which brings us to you, Dr. Varney," Mad Dog announced, getting back into the act. "The defense used your testimony to legitimize its insanity plea. But was Miss Douglas truly insane?"

"That was my opinion," Dr. Varney said, huffily.

"You came to this conclusion because of tests?"

"She refused to take part in tests," Dr. Varney said.

"Then it was her answers to questions?" Mad Dog inquired.

"She wouldn't answer questions. She wouldn't talk at all, except to repeat what she'd said to the police, that she'd killed Daken."

"Then how could you form a definite conclusion?"

"My God, man! All one had to do was see pictures of the corpse. It was determined that she'd hit him at least twenty times, most of the blows after he was dead."

Norman Daken closed his eyes tight.

"Ah," Mad Dog said, not noticing Norman, or choosing to ignore him. "But suppose she'd hit him only once? One fatal blow?"

Dr. Varney frowned. "I decline to speculate on what might have been. I was faced with what really did happen."

"So now we've come to the beauty part of the story," Mad Dog said, blue eyes sparkling. "What really *did* happen?" He lowered his hand to the floor and snapped his fingers. The ancient cur, Dougie Dog, rose up on creaky bones and padded toward him. "But first, a word from Mad Dog's own mutt about Wet Veggies."

Mad Dog lowered the mike and Dougie Dog gave out with a very laid-back but musical bark. Greg, the engineer, followed the bark with a taped commercial for a dog food that consisted of vegetables "simmering in savory meat sauce." I was getting a little peckish, myself.

Gabriel Warren tapped Victor Newgate on the arm and asked, "How many laws is our friend Mad Dog breaking by keeping us here against our will?"

"Enough to keep him off the radio for quite a few years, I'd think," Newgate replied.

"C'mon, guys," Mad Dog told them. "Aren't you even the least bit interested in where we're headed?"

Norman Daken's eyes moved to the picture window where Greg was staring at the clock and Sylvia Redfern was looking at us with concern. His fingers continued their nervous brushing of his cheek near the birthmark. "Where *are* we headed?" he asked, so softly I could barely hear him.

"Thirty years ago, I would have been interested," Warren said dryly. "Today, I couldn't care less. It's old news."

Dougie Dog put his paws on his master's leg and made a little begging sound. Mad Dog reached into his jacket pocket and found a biscuit that he placed in the animal's open mouth. "Good old boy," he said.

"Family dog?" I asked.

Mad Dog smiled at me and his clear blue eyes didn't blink. "Yes," he said. "Fact is, he was given to me by my mother when I moved out on my own."

"You can sit there and talk about dogs all you want," Dr. Varney said. "But I am definitely not going to let you get by with . . ."

"Awoooo, awoooo," Mad Dog interrupted. "We're back again, discussing the thirty-year-old murder of industrialist Theodore Daken. You were saying, Dr. Varney?"

"Nothing, actually."

"We were getting to a description of what *really* happened in the murder room that night."

"What happened is public record," Rafferty said. "The verdict was in three decades ago. Case closed. Some of you guys like to play around with stuff like this, but you can't change history."

"Things do happen to make us doubt the accuracy of history books, however. Look at all the fuss over Columbus. Or the crusades. Or maybe a murder case that wasn't murder at all."

"What the devil's that mean?" Rafferty asked.

"This really is quite absurd," Gabriel Warren said flatly. "Why Victoria Douglas killed Theo Daken three decades ago is an intriguing question, but its answer will solve none of today's problems. We should be discussing the murders that take place every seven hours in this city, or the bank robberies that take place on an average of one every other day."

"That's what I thought we were here to talk about," Victor Newgate added.

"We can discuss crime in L.A. for the next year and not come up with any concrete answers," Mad Dog said. "But tonight, it's possible that we will actually be able to conclude what really happened to Theodore Daken. Isn't that worth an hour of your time?"

"You're going to solve the Daken murder?" Rafferty asked sneeringly.

"Actually, I was hoping to leave the solving to Mr. Bloodworth."

"Huh?" I replied. "Thanks for the vote of confidence, Mad Dog. But I'm not exactly Sherlock Holmes. I'm just a guy who plods from one point to another."

"Plod away, then."

"The world turns over a few times in thirty years, and its secrets get buried deeper and deeper. Too deep to uncover in an hour."

"Suppose we make it a little easier?" Mad Dog said.

I thought I knew where he was headed. I pointed at the empty chair at the table. "If Victoria Douglas were to come out of hiding and join us, that might make it easier."

The others didn't think much of that idea. They eyed the chair suspiciously. "She's still a wanted woman," Rafferty said. "And it'd be my duty to perform a citizen's arrest and send her back where she belongs."

"Don't worry," Mad Dog said. "The chair's not for her. Is it, Miss Thorp?"

We all turned to Landy expectantly. "Victoria Douglas is dead," she stated flatly. It was the first sentence she'd spoken since we all sat down and it more than made up for her silence. "She died of a heart attack nearly six months ago in the Northern California town of Yreka, where her neighbors knew her as Violet Dunn. Knew and loved her, I should add."

The others seemed to relax. Then Landy added, "But before she died, we had many long talks together."

"What kind of talks?" Gabriel Warren asked.

"Talks that I'm using in an article on Victoria Douglas for my magazine."

Dr. Varney exclaimed, "I told you about it, Gabriel. Someone phoned my office."

"N-nobody called me," Norman Daken said.

"You're on my list," Landy told him. "We're just starting the major research. I'll be calling each of you."

Warren stared at her appraisingly. Rafferty seemed amused. "So, honey, on these long talks you supposedly had," he asked, "did she happen to mention anything about the murder?"

Landy stared at him. "She told me that she killed Theodore Daken in self-defense. It was she who fell asleep that night. She was not used to alcohol and had had too much champagne. When she awoke, Daken was beside her on the bed in his underwear, trying to remove her clothes.

"She called out, but everyone else had gone. She tried to push him away and he slapped her across the face. Struggle seemed useless. He was a big, powerful man. Her hand found the statue somehow and she brought it down against his skull. Then she blacked out. She doesn't remember hitting him more than once."

"Doesn't remember? That's damn convenient," Rafferty said. "No wonder she didn't try that yarn on us at the time."

"She might have," Mad Dog informed us, "if she'd taken the stand at her trial."

Newgate waved a dismissive hand. "She would have hurt her case immensely. It was my feeling that, in light of the grisly aspects of the situation, she was better off with an insanity plea. She could only have hurt that defense by taking the stand."

"She told me she did mention self-defense at her first parole hearing," Landy said.

"And, alas, as I feared, they didn't believe her," Newgate said. "I suppose that's what pushed her into making her initial escape."

"How did you come to be her lawyer, Newgate?" I asked.

He stared at me as if he didn't feel he had to waste his time responding. But we were on radio, so he replied, "I'd met her socially."

"You mean you'd dated her?" I asked.

"No. But, from time to time, I had lunch with her and . . . other employees of Altadine. The firm I was working for did quite a lot of business with the company."

"Did Daken sit in on these lunches?" I asked.

"The old man? Hardly," Newgate replied with a smile. "He was the CEO. We were a few rungs down."

"Who else would be there?" Mad Dog wondered.

Newgate brushed the question away with an angry hand. "I don't really know. An assortment of people."

"Mr. Warren?" I asked.

"I was part of the crowd," Warren said. "Eager young execs and pretty women who worked for the company. Victoria Douglas included. There was nothing sinister about it. Nothing particularly significant, either."

"According to testimony from a woman named Joan Lapeer," Mad Dog said, "Miss Douglas had been Theodore Daken's girlfriend. Did she confirm that, Miss Thorp?"

"Victoria told me that Joan Lapeer had been Altadine's office manager before her. Theodore Daken fired the woman and hired Victoria. Joan Lapeer was so bitter that she spread the word that Daken had wanted to hire his girlfriend."

"Then there was no truth to it?"

"None," Landy said. "Victoria told me she'd only met Daken once or twice before she went to work for Altadine."

"Met him where?" I asked.

"Joan Lapeer was a very lazy, very incompetent worker," Gabriel Warren suddenly announced. Norman Daken looked up from the table at him, without expression.

"So she lied about Victoria Douglas's involvement with Theodore Daken," Mad Dog said.

"Miss Douglas said he asked her out a few times," Landy told us. "But she always refused."

"Because he was her boss?" Mad Dog asked. "Or a fat slob, or . . . ?"

"Because she was involved with someone else," Landy said.

"Who?"

Landy shook her head. "She wouldn't name him. She said it was the one oath she would never break."

"She used the word, 'oath'?" I asked.

"Precisely."

"Is he our mystery guest?" I asked Mad Dog, indicating the empty chair.

"No," he said, turning toward Greg in the booth. "But this might be a good time to cut to a commercial." He nodded, let out one of his wails and Greg responded to the cue with a spot announcement for a holiday lawn fertilizer, "The perfect gift for the gardener around your home."

"How much longer are you going to hold us here against our will?" Warren demanded.

"The old clock on the wall says another nineteen minutes."

"This is going to turn into a very expensive hour," Warren said.

"Why don't you just make your point," lawyer Newgate said to our host, "and be done with it? Why must we put up with all this cat-and-mouse routine?"

"That's how radio works," Mad Dog replied. "We have to build to a conclusion." He leaned toward me. "Are you willing to give us a wrap-up, Mr. Bloodworth, of what you think happened that night?"

"I wouldn't want to go on record with any heavy speculation. You don't seem to care about these litigious bozos, but I personally would just as soon stay clear of courtrooms."

"No need to mention any names," he said. "Just give us . . ."

He paused, some sixth sense informing him that the commercial had ended and he was about to go back on the air. He let out a howl and said, "Welcome back to the doghouse. Private Detective Leo Bloodworth is about to give us his version of what happened back at that hotel thirty years ago."

"Well," I said. "I'll take Victoria Douglas's word for it that she acted in self-defense. That would explain her battered condition. But if the guy attacked her and she repelled him, why wouldn't she just stay there and call the cops?"

"Because she panicked?" Landy speculated.

"When you panic, you run away. But Rafferty and his detectives tell us she didn't do that. Their scenario has her hanging around the suite and finally taking the body with her when she left. Why would she do that?"

"The dame was *crazy*." Rafferty was almost beside himself.

I replied, "She's just killed a man. She's confused. She decides to take the dead guy with her? Nobody's that crazy. Wouldn't it have been much more natural for her to just run away? Probably down the service stairs?"

"That's your trouble, Bloodworth," Rafferty said. "You refuse to believe what your eyes tell you. You saw her with the stiff . . . ah, the poor guy's body."

"That was later. What I think is that she ran away to the one person she trusted—the guy she was in love with. She told him what had happened in the hotel suite. He told her he'd help her, but she had to promise to keep him out of it, no matter what.

"They went back to the hotel in her car, parking it near the service exit. Maybe they went up together. Maybe he told her to stay in the car. He, or the both of 'em got Daken's body down in the service elevator. They put it in the back of Victoria Douglas's car. By then, she was in no condition to drive. So the boyfriend drove to the alley off Wilshire. And here's where it gets a little foggy. For some reason the boyfriend ran out on her and left her to face the music all alone. And true to her promise, her 'oath,' she refused to name him. Even though it made her look like a crazy woman."

"Wait a minute, Bloodworth," Rafferty blustered. "If it didn't make sense for *her* to move the body, why did *he* decide to do it?"

"Because there would be less scandal if Daken were found beaten to death in an alley wearing a Santa Claus suit than if he turned up dead in a hotel room in his skivvies."

"You're saying that Theodore Daken was moved to salvage his reputation?" Mad Dog asked.

"And that of his company's," I said. "I assume Douglas's boyfriend was an executive at Altadine . . ."

"Why?" Mad Dog asked.

"That's one way Victoria Douglas would have met Daken once or twice before he hired her. It's also how she would have known about the job opening. For all we know, the boyfriend could have closed the deal with Daken for her to come aboard. Anyway, he was the one who was trying to downplay any scandal."

"Only it didn't work," Mad Dog said.

"And I bet the guy next in line to the presidency, Gabriel Warren, had quite a job on his hands keeping Altadine's investors high on the company." I looked at him.

"You're right about one thing," he said. "It would have been quite a lot easier if Theo's death had been minus the sordid details. But as bad as it got, I managed."

"I'll bet you did," I said.

"Wait a minute!" Landy interrupted. "This was a company Christmas party. If Victoria's lover had been an Altadine exec, would he have just gone off, leaving his girlfriend passed out and easy prey for Daken?"

"I think the guy left the party early, before she was in any danger," I said, looking at Warren.

"Would you care to take a guess at the name of Victoria Douglas's lover, Mr. Bloodworth?" Mad Dog asked.

I continued staring at Gabriel Warren. "Like I said, somebody who left the party early. Somebody who wanted to squelch the scandal. But when that didn't happen, he was shrewd enough to know when to cut and run. Somebody smooth and savvy and well-connected enough to know how to push enough buttons, once Victoria Douglas was on the spot, to keep himself clear of the fallout."

"How would he do that?" Mad Dog asked. Warren glared at me.

"By pressuring a high-ranking police officer to disregard a few facts that didn't jibe with the official story of how Daken died. By getting a defense lawyer to plead his client insane and keep her off the stand, just to make sure his name didn't come up in testimony. By convincing a judge to bend a few rules. All to keep one of America's great corporations flying high. Because, surely, if one more guy at the top of Altadine had got caught by that tar baby, the company might never have recovered."

"You're not going to name him?" Mad Dog asked.

"He knows who he is," I said, nodding at Warren.

I was hoping to get the guy to do something. Like snarl. Or show his fangs. When he didn't, I said, "It just occurred to me that maybe Victoria Douglas didn't really kill Theodore Daken at all. She told Miss Thorp that she didn't remember hitting him more than once. Suppose that wasn't enough to do the job, though she thought it was. Suppose the boyfriend went up to that hotel room, saw Daken on the bed sleeping off that nonfatal whack and picked up the statue and finished the job, wiping the weapon clean. Then he had an even stronger reason for wanting Victoria Douglas to keep quiet about his participation in the removal of the body. What do you think, Warren?"

"You're making a big mistake," he hissed.

I shrugged.

"This may be the perfect time to bring in our mystery guest," Mad Dog said. And almost at once, the door opened and a wizened old man entered. He looked like he was a hundred-and-one, his khaki pants flapping against his legs, his bright red windbreaker hanging on his bony frame. A plaid cap with a pom-pom covered his bald pate at a jaunty angle.

The door slammed behind him and he turned and looked at it for a second.

"We've just been joined by Mr. Samuel J. Kleinmetz," Mad Dog informed his listening audience, which included me. "Mr. Kleinmetz, would you please take this chair?"

As the old duffer shuffled to the chair, Mad Dog said, "Mr. Kleinmetz was working that night before Christmas Eve, thirty years ago. What was your occupation, sir?"

The old man was easing himself onto the chair. "Eh?"

"Occupation."

"Nothing," he said, louder than necessary, sending Greg jumping for his dials. "Been retired for fifteen years. Used to drive a cab, though. Beverly Hills Cab. Drove a Mercedes. Leather seats. Wonderful radio. Worked all the best hotels . . ."

"Good enough," Mad Dog said, stemming the man's flow. "You were working the night . . ."

"The night the woman killed Christmas?" the old man finished. "Sure. I worked six days a week, fifty-two weeks a year. I was working that night, absolutely."

"In the Wilshire district?"

"That's where I used to park and wait," the old man said. He squinted his eyes in delight, staring at the microphone. "This is working?" he asked.

"I hope it is," Mad Dog told him. "On that night, you picked up a passenger not far from where they later found the body of Theodore Daken?"

"The guy in the Santa Claus suit, yeah. I guess it was minutes before. The paper said they found the guy at about ten-thirty. I picked up my fare at maybe ten-twenty . . ."

"How the devil can he remember that?" Gabriel Warren snapped. "It was thirty years ago."

"There are days you remember," the old man said. "I can remember the morning I woke up to hear the Japs bombed Pearl Harbor. I can tell you everything that happened that day. And the day that great young president John Fitzgerald Kennedy was assassinated by that Oswald creep. And the night the woman killed Christmas."

"We showed Mr. Steinmetz photographs of the members of the executive board of Altadine taken that year," Mad Dog said. "He identified his passenger. We then showed him a photograph of that same man today. Would you tell us if he's in this room tonight?"

"Sure." Sam Steinmetz looked across the table in the direction of Gabriel Warren, and I could feel a smug grin forming on my face. "That's him right there."

My smug grin froze. Steinmetz was pointing a bony finger at Norman Daken. "You didn't have to show me all those pictures. He's changed a lot, but I'd have known him right away, as soon as I saw that red dot on his face. Never seen one quite like it before or since."

Daken looked more relaxed than he had all evening. "So many years ago," he said, almost wistfully. "I'd almost forgotten. As if anyone could."

"Don't say a word, Norman," Gabriel Warren cautioned.

"No more, Gabe. I don't want to hold it in any longer. My father and I . . . we had our disagreements. He thought I was weak. I suppose I am. I loved Victoria."

I looked from him to the engineer booth. Both Greg and Sylvia Redfern were totally caught up in the tableau in the studio. Her expression was impossible to read, but her blue eyes looked kind and sympathetic.

"I think that's why he felt he had to have her," Norman continued. "Because I loved her. And he ruined it all for us. I never blamed her. It wasn't her fault, poor woman. She fought him and knocked him unconscious. She didn't hate him, you see. Not like I did."

Warren was scowling at him. "What the devil are . . ."

"Bloodworth was right. I killed him, Gabe. I thought you knew that."

"You thought I . . . How could . . . ?" Warren was having trouble articulating.

Norman Daken gave him a pitying smile. "He wanted you to be his son. I guess you felt that way, too."

"I would never have . . ."

"That's what was so beautiful about it, Gabe. You fixed it so that I stayed clear of it."

"I was trying to save the company," Warren said. "But if I'd known . . ."

"Well, now you do," Norman Daken told him. "You did everything you could to keep Altadine going. I, on the other hand . . ."

He didn't finish his sentence. I said, "I always wondered who reported Victoria Douglas to the police that night. And who called the reporters. That was you, wasn't it, Norman? You left that poor woman in the alley and went off to call the cops."

"I'm sorry I hurt Vicki so," he said. "I told her that she would never go to prison and I lived up to that. Thanks to Gabe's influence."

"But she wasn't exactly free," I said.

"No," Norman agreed. "But I had to make that sacrifice, if my father's reputation was to be thoroughly destroyed." He looked at Mad Dog hopefully. "Maybe now, thanks to you, he'll be dragged through the mud again."

Station KPLA-FM went off the air early that night, even though the police made short work of their task. They came, they saw, they escorted Norman off to be booked. As they explained, there was no statute of limitations on murder, not that he really wanted one.

As for the crimes Warren and his associates may have committed, the police were less certain of their footing. So that foursome left on their own recognizance. Even if it turned out to be too late to nail them for railroading Victoria Douglas, they probably wouldn't be suing Mad Dog or myself. And I doubted I'd be seeing Warren's name on any ballots in the near future.

When they'd all departed, leaving only Mad Dog, Landy, Dougie Dog, and myself in the main studio, I asked, "Are you both her children?"

"Just me," Mad Dog admitted, grinning. "What tipped you?"

"Dougie Dog, for one," I said, looking at the drooping mongrel. "The family hound, you said. Dougie. Douglas. And then, there's your nickname. Mad Dog. Madison Douglas?"

"Nope. Just Charlie Douglas. The 'mad' is, well, they said she was mad and what happened to her made me pretty angry. My dad worked at the hospital where Mom spent her first three years. He helped her escape. When she was sent back, I was raised by my paternal grandparents."

"And you kept her name?"

"It's mine, too. They never married officially. How could they? Anyway, figuring out that I was her son, that was good detecting."

"It's the least I could do after picking the wrong murderer," I said.

"We didn't know about the murder," Landy said. "Poor Victoria always thought she'd killed Daken."

"Who are you?" I asked. "Just a friend of the family?"

"As I said, I'm a journalist. I happened to rent a house next door to Victoria's a few years ago. We became friends and eventually she opened up to me about who she was. I think she hoped Charlie and I might get together."

"And you did."

They both smiled.

The dog rose to its feet, yawning, and dragged itself to the door and out of the studio.

"And you two decided to clear Victoria's name," I said.

"Right again," Charlie "Mad Dog" Douglas said. "Thanks for the help."

I stood up and picked my book from the table. "I didn't sell many of these tonight," I said.

"Come on back," he offered.

"It's too bad your mother passed away without ever learning the truth about that night. But I guess it's just as well that she won't have to go through the ordeal of Norman's trial."

They both nodded solemnly.

I left them and wandered out into the corridor. A light was on in the greenroom. As I passed, I saw Sylvia Redfern sitting on the couch, reading a book. Dougie Dog was curled up at her feet, sleeping peacefully. Her eyes, blue as a lagoon, blue as Mad Dog's, suddenly looked up and caught me staring at her. She smiled.

"Goodnight, Mr. Bloodworth," she said. "Thanks for everything."

I told her it was my pleasure and wished her a very merry Christmas.

"It will be," she replied, "the merriest in years."

A PUZZLING

Little Christmas

SISTER BESSIE

Cyril Hare

BORN ALFRED ALEXANDER GORDON CLARK, the author was bound by family tradition to become a lawyer, which he did, beginning his practice in 1924. He worked in Hare Court and had a residence in Cyril Mansions, providing him with the names he used for his nom de plume. After writing some comic sketches for *Punch*, he produced *Tenant for Death*, his first detective novel, in 1937, and wrote two others before creating his most popular series character, barrister Francis Pettigrew, in *Tragedy at Law* (1942). He was not prolific, partly due to the fact that he never learned to use a typewriter and so wrote in longhand, but mainly due to what he described as his "constitutional and incurable indolence." "Sister Bessie" was first published in the December 23, 1948, issue of *The Weekly Standard*.

Sister Bessie

CYRIL HARE

At Christmas-time we gladly greet
Each old familiar face.
At Christmas-time we hope to meet
At th' old familiar place.
Five hundred loving greetings, dear,
From you to me
To welcome in the glad New Year
I look to see!

HILDA TRENT TURNED THE CHRIST-mas card over with her carefully manicured fingers as she read the idiotic lines aloud.

"Did you ever hear anything so completely palsied?" she asked her husband. "I wonder who on earth they can get to write the stuff. Timothy, do you know anybody called Leech?"

"Leech?"

"Yes—that's what it says: 'From your old Leech.' Must be a friend of yours. The only Leach I ever knew spelt her name with an a and this one has two e's." She looked at the envelope. "Yes, it was addressed to you. Who is the old Leech?" She flicked the card across the breakfast-table.

Timothy stared hard at the rhyme and the scrawled message beneath it.

"I haven't the least idea," he said slowly.

As he spoke he was taking in, with a sense of cold misery, the fact that the printed message on the card had been neatly altered by hand. The word "Five" was in ink. The original, poet no doubt, had been content with "A hundred loving greetings."

"Put it on the mantelpiece with the others," said his wife. "There's a nice paunchy robin on the outside."

"Damn it, no!" In a sudden access of rage he tore the card in two and flung the pieces into the fire.

It was silly of him, he reflected as he travelled up to the City half an hour later, to break out in that way in front of Hilda; but she would put it down to the nervous strain about which she was always pestering him to take medical advice. Not for all the gold in the Bank of England could he have stood the sight of that damnable jingle on his dining-room mantelpiece. The insolence of it! The cool, calculated devilry! All the way to London the train wheels beat out the maddening rhythm:

At Christmas-time we gladly greet . . .

And he had thought that the last payment had seen the end of it. He had returned from James's funeral triumphant in the certain belief that he had attended the burial of the blood-sucker who called himself "Leech." But he was wrong, it seemed.

Five hundred loving greetings, dear . . .

Five hundred! Last year it had been three, and that had been bad enough. It had meant selling out some holdings at an awkward moment. And now five hundred, with the market in its present state! How in the name of all that was horrible was he going to raise the money?

He would raise it, of course. He would have to. The sickening, familiar routine would be gone through again. The cash in Treasury notes would be packed in an unobstrusive parcel and left in the cloakroom at Waterloo. Next day he would park his car as usual in the railway yard at his local station. Beneath the windscreen wiper—"the old familiar place"—would be tucked the cloakroom ticket. When he came down again from work in the evening the ticket would be gone. And that would be that—till next time. It was the way that Leech preferred it and he had no option but to comply.

The one certain thing that Trent knew about the identity of his blackmailer was that he—or could it be she?—was a member of his family. His family! Thank heaven, they were no true kindred of his. So far as he knew he had no blood relation alive. But "his" family they had been, ever since, when he was a tiny, ailing boy, his father had married the gentle, ineffective Mary Grigson, with her long trail of soft, useless children. And when the influenza epidemic of 1919 carried off John Trent he had been left to be brought up as one of that clinging, grasping clan. He had got on in the world, made money, married money, but he had never got away from the "Grigsons." Save for his stepmother, to whom he grudgingly acknowledged that he owed his start in life, how he loathed them all! But "his" family they remained, expecting to be treated with brotherly affection, demanding his presence at family reunions, especially at Christmas-time.

At Christmas-time we hope to meet . . .

He put down his paper unread and stared forlornly out of the carriage window. It was at Christmas-time, four years before, that the whole thing started—at his stepmother's Christmas Eve party, just such a boring family function as the one he would have to attend in a few days' time. There had been some silly games to amuse the children—Blind Man's Buff and Musical Chairs—and in the course of them his wallet must have slipped fom his pocket. He discovered the loss next morning, went round to the house and retrieved it. But when it came into his hands again there was one item missing from its contents. Just one. A letter, quite short and explicit, signed in a name that had about then become fairly notorious in connection with an unsavoury enquiry into certain large-scale dealings in government securities. How he could have been fool enough to keep it a moment longer than was necessary! . . . but it was no good going back on that.

And then the messages from Leech had begun. Leech had the letter. Leech considered it his duty to send it to the principal of Trent's firm, who was also Trent's father-in-law. But, meanwhile, Leech was a trifle short of money, and for a small consideration . . . So it had begun, and so, year in and year out, it had gone on.

He had been so sure that it was James! That seedy, unsuccessful stock-jobber, with his gambling debts and his inordinate thirst for whisky, had seemed the very stuff of which blackmailers are made. But he had got rid of James last February, and here was Leech again, hungrier than ever. Trent shifted uneasily in his seat. "Got rid of him" was hardly the right way to put it. One must be fair to oneself. He had merely assisted James to get rid of his worthless self. He had done no more than ask James to dinner at his club, fill him up with whisky, and leave him to drive home on a foggy night with the roads treacherous with frost. There had been an unfortunate incident on the Kingston bypass, and that was the end of James—and, incidentally, of two perfect strangers who had happened to be on the road at the same time. Forget it! The point was that the dinner—and the whisky—had been a dead loss. He would not make the same mistake again. This Christmas Eve he intended to make sure who his persecutor was. Once he knew, there would be no half measures.

Revelation came at him midway through Mrs. John Trent's party—at the very moment, in fact, when the presents were being distributed from the Christmas tree, when the room was bathed in the soft radiance of coloured candles and noisy with the "Oohs!" and "Aahs!" of excited children and with the rustle of hastily unfolded paper parcels. It was so simple, and so unexpected, that he could have laughed aloud. Appropriately enough, it was his own contribution to the party that was responsible. For some time past it had been his unwritten duty, as the prosperous member of the family, to present his stepmother with some delicacy to help out the straitened resources of her house in providing a feast worthy of the occasion. This year, his gift had taken the form of half a dozen bottles of champagne—part of a consignment which he suspected of being corked. That champagne, acting on a head unused to anything stronger than lemonade, was enough to loosen Bessie's tongue for one fatal instant.

Bessie! Of all people, faded, spinsterish Bessie! Bessie, with her woolwork and her charities—Bessie with her large, stupid, appealing eyes and her air of frustration, that put you in mind of a bud frosted just before it could come into flower! And yet, when you came to think of it, it was natural enough. Probably, of all the Grigson tribe, he disliked her the most. He felt for her all the loathing one must naturally feel for a person one has treated badly; and he had been simple enough to believe that she did not resent it.

She was just his own age, and from the moment that he had been introduced into the family had constituted herself his protector against the unkindness of his elder stepbrother. She had been, in her revoltingly sentimental phrase, his "own special sister." As they grew up, the roles were reversed, and she became his protégée, the admiring spectator of early struggles. Then it had become pretty clear that she and everybody else expected him to marry her. He had considered the idea quite seriously for some time. She was pretty enough in those days, and, as the phrase went, worshipped the ground he trod on. But he had had the good sense to see in time that he must look elsewhere if he wanted to make his way in the world. His engagement to Hilda had been a blow to Bessie. Her old-maidish look and her absorption in good works dated from then. But she had been sweetly forgiving—to all appearances. Now, as he stood there under the mistletoe, with a ridiculous paper cap on his head, he marvelled how he could have been so easily deceived. As though, after all, anyone could have written that Christmas card but a woman!

Bessie was smiling at him still—smiling with the confidential air of the mildly tipsy, her upturned shiny nose glowing pink in the candle-light. She had assumed a slightly puzzled expression, as though trying to recollect what she had said. Timothy smiled back and raised his glass to her. He was stone-cold sober, and he could remind her of her words when the occasion arose.

"My present for you, Timothy, is in the post. You'll get it tomorrow, I expect. I thought you'd like a change from those horrid Christmas cards!"

And the words had been accompanied with an unmistakable wink.

"Uncle Timothy!" One of James's bouncing girls jumped up at him and gave him a smacking kiss. He put her down with a grin and tickled her ribs as he did so. He suddenly felt lighthearted and on good terms with all the world—one woman excepted. He moved away from the mistletoe and strolled round the room, exchanging pleasantries with all the family. He could look them in the face now without a qualm. He clicked glasses with Roger, the prematurely aged, overworked GP. No need to worry now whether his money was going in that direction!

He slapped Peter on the back and endured patiently five minutes' confidential chat on the difficulties of the motor-car business in these days. To Marjorie, James's window, looking wan and ever so brave in her made-over black frock, he spoke just the right words of blended sympathy and cheer. He even found in his pockets some half-crowns for his great, hulking step-nephews. Then he was standing by his stepmother near the fireplace, whence she presided quietly over the noisy, cheerful scene, beaming gentle good nature from her faded blue eyes.

"A delightful evening," he said, and meant it.

"Thanks to you, Timothy, in great part," she replied. "You have always been so good to us."

Wonderful what a little doubtful champagne would do! He would have given a lot to see her face if he were to say: "I suppose you are not aware that your youngest daughter, who is just now pulling a cracker with that ugly little boy of Peter's, is blackmailing me and that I shortly intend to stop her mouth for good?"

He turned away. What a gang they all were! What a shabby, out-at-elbows gang! Not a decently cut suit or a well-turned-out woman among the lot of them! And he had imagined that his money had been going to support some of them! Why, they all simply reeked of honest poverty! He could see it now. Bessie explained everything. It was typical of her twisted mind to wring cash from him by threats and give it all away in charities.

"You have always been so good to us." Come to think of it, his stepmother was worth the whole of the rest put together. She must be hard put to it, keeping up Father's old house, with precious little coming in from her children. Perhaps one day, when his money was really his own again, he might see his way to do something for her . . . But there was a lot to do before he could indulge in extravagant fancies like that.

Hilda was coming across the room towards him. Her elegance made an agreeable contrast to the get-up of the Grigson women. She looked tired and rather bored, which was not unusual for her at parties at this house.

"Timothy," she murmured, "can't we get out of here? My head feels like a ton of bricks, and if I'm going to be fit for anything tomorrow morning——"

Timothy cut her short.

"You go home straight away, darling," he said. "I can see that it's high time you were in bed. Take the car. I can walk—it's a fine evening. Don't wait up for me."

"You're not coming? I thought you said——"

"No. I shall have to stay and see the party through. There's a little matter of family business I'd better dispose of while I have the chance."

Hilda looked at him in slightly amused surprise.

"Well, if you feel that way," she said. "You seem to be very devoted to your family all of a sudden. You'd better keep an eye on Bessie while you are about it. She's had about as much as she can carry."

Hilda was right. Bessie was decidedly merry. And Timothy continued to keep an eye on her. Thanks to his attentions, by the end of the evening, when Christmas Day had been seen in and the guests were fumbling for their wraps, she had reached a stage when she could barely stand. "Another glass," thought Timothy from the depths of his experience, "and she'll pass right out."

"I'll give you a lift home, Bessie," said Roger, looking at her with a professional eye. "We can just squeeze you in."

"Oh, nonsense, Roger!" Bessie giggled. "I can manage perfectly well. As if I couldn't walk as far as the end of the drive!"

"I'll look after her," said Timothy heartily. "I'm walking myself, and we can guide each other's wandering footsteps home. Where's your coat, Bessie? Are you sure you've got all your precious presents?"

He prolonged his leave-taking until all the rest had gone, then helped Bessie into her worn fur coat and stepped out of the house, supporting her with an affectionate right arm. It was all going to be too deliciously simple.

Bessie lived in the lodge of the old house. She preferred to be independent, and the arrangement suited everyone, especially since James after one of his reverses on the turf had brought his family to live with his mother to save expense. It suited Timothy admirably now. Tenderly he escorted her to the end of the drive, tenderly he assisted her to insert her latchkey in the door, tenderly he supported her into the little sitting-room that gave out of the hall.

There Bessie considerately saved him an enormous amount of trouble and a possibly unpleasant scene. As he put her down upon the sofa she finally succumbed to the champagne. Her eyes closed, her mouth opened and she lay like a log where he had placed her.

Timothy was genuinely relieved. He was prepared to go to any lengths to rid himself from the menace of blackmail, but if he could lay his hands on the damning letter without physical violence he would be well satisfied. It would be open to him to take it out of Bessie in other ways later on. He looked quickly round the room. He knew its contents by heart. It had hardly changed at all since the day when Bessie first furnished her own room when she left school. The same old battered desk stood in the corner, where from the earliest days she had kept her treasures. He flung it open, and a flood of bills, receipts, charitable appeals and yet more charitable appeals came cascading out. One after another, he went through the drawers with ever increasing urgency, but still failed to find what he sought. Finally he came upon a small inner drawer which resisted his attempts to open it. He tugged at it in vain, and then seized the poker from the fireplace and burst the flimsy lock by main force. Then he dragged the drawer from its place and settled himself to examine its contents.

It was crammed as full as it could hold with papers. At the very top was the programme of a May Week Ball for his last year at Cambridge. Then there were snapshots, press-cuttings—an account of his own wedding among them—and,

for the rest, piles of letters, all in his handwriting. The wretched woman seemed to have hoarded every scrap he had ever written to her. As he turned them over, some of the phrases he had used in them floated into this mind, and he began to apprehend for the first time what the depth of her resentment must have been when he threw her over.

But where the devil did she keep the only letter that mattered?

As he straightened himself from the desk he heard close behind him a hideous, choking sound. He spun round quickly. Bessie was standing behind him, her face a mask of horror. Her mouth was wide open in dismay. She drew a long shuddering breath. In another moment she was going to scream at the top of her voice . . .

Timothy's pent-up fury could be contained no longer. With all his force he drove his fist full into that gaping, foolish face. Bessie went down as though she had been shot and her head struck the leg of a table with the crack of a dry stick broken in two. She did not move again.

Although it was quiet enough in the room after that, he never heard his stepmother come in. Perhaps it was the sound of his own pulses drumming in his ears that had deafened him. He did not even know how long she had been there. Certainly it was long enough for her to take in everything that was to be seen there, for her voice, when she spoke, was perfectly under control.

"You have killed Bessie," she said. It was a calm statement of fact rather than an accusation.

He nodded, speechless.

"But you have not found the letter."

He shook his head.

"Didn't you understand what she told you this evening? The letter is in the post. It was her Christmas present to you. Poor, simple, loving Bessie!"

He stared at her, aghast.

"It was only just now that I found that it was missing from my jewel-case," she went on, still in the same flat, quiet voice. "I don't know how she found out about it, but love—even a crazy love like hers—gives people a strange insight sometimes."

He licked his dry lips.

"Then you were Leech?" he faltered.

"Of course. Who else? How otherwise do you think I could have kept the house open and my children out of debt on my income? No, Timothy, don't come any nearer. You are not going to commit two murders tonight. I don't think you have the nerve in any case, but to be on the safe side I have brought the little pistol your father gave me when he came out of the army in 1918. Sit down."

He found himself crouching on the sofa, looking helplessly up into her pitiless old face. The body that had been Bessie lay in between them.

"Bessie's heart was very weak," she said reflectively. "Roger had been worried about it for some time. If I have a word with him, I daresay he will see his way to issue a death certificate. It will, of course, be a little expensive. Shall we say a thousand pounds this year instead of five hundred? You would prefer that, Timothy, I dare say, to—the alternative?"

Once more Timothy nodded in silence.

"Very well. I shall speak to Roger in the morning—after you have returned me Bessie's Christmas present. I shall require that for future use. You can go now, Timothy."

THAT'S THE TICKET
Mary Higgins Clark

AFTER HER HUSBAND SUDDENLY DIED, MARY HIGGINS CLARK, a relatively young mother of five, arose at five o'clock every morning, placed her typewriter on the kitchen table, and began writing a book before getting her kids off to school. Her first suspense novel, *Where Are the Children?* (1975), was an original combination of the Gothic novel and its modern counterpart, the novel of romantic suspense, in which the emphasis was not on romance but on suspense that became almost unbearable as the heroine was inundated with one dire situation after another. Clark followed that formula in subsequent books to become the world's bestselling writer of suspense fiction. "That's the Ticket" was first published in *Mistletoe Mysteries*, edited by Charlotte MacLeod (New York, Mysterious Press, 1989).

That's the Ticket

MARY HIGGINS CLARK

IF WILMA BEAN HAD NOT BEEN IN Philadelphia visiting her sister, Dorothy, it never would have happened. Ernie, knowing that Wilma had watched the drawing on television, would have rushed home at midnight from his job as a security guard at the Do-Shop-Here Mall in Paramus, New Jersey, and they'd have celebrated together. *Two million dollars!* That was their share of the special Christmas lottery.

Instead, because Wilma was in Philadelphia paying a pre-Christmas visit to her sister, Dorothy, Ernie stopped at the Friendly Shamrock Watering Hole for a pop or two and then topped off the evening at the Harmony Bar six blocks from his home in Elmwood Park. There, nodding happily to Lou, the owner-bartender, Ernie ordered his third Seven and Seven of the evening, wrapped his plump sixty-year-old legs around the bar stool, and dreamily reflected on how he and Wilma would spend their newfound wealth.

It was then that his faded blue eyes fell upon Loretta Thistlebottom, who was perched on the corner stool against the wall, a stein of beer in one hand, a Marlboro in the other. Ernie thought Loretta was a very attractive woman. Tonight her brilliant blond hair curled on her shoulders in a pageboy, her pinkish lipstick complemented her large purple-accented green eyes, and her generous bosom rose and fell with sensuous regularity.

Ernie observed Loretta with almost impersonal admiration. It was well known that Loretta Thistlebottom's husband, Jimbo Potters, a beefy truck driver, was extremely proud of the fact that Loretta had been a dancer in her early days and was also extremely jealous of her. It was hinted he wasn't above knocking Loretta around if she got too friendly with other men.

However, since Lou the bartender was Jimbo's cousin, Jimbo didn't mind if Loretta sat around the bar the nights Jimbo was on a long-distance haul. After all, it was a neighborhood hangout. Plenty of wives came in with their husbands and as Loretta frequently commented, "Jimbo can't expect me to watch the tube by myself or go to Tupperware parties whenever he's carting garlic buds or bananas along Route 1. As a person born in the trunk to a prominent show business family, I need people around."

Her show business career was the subject of much of Loretta's conversation and tended to grow in importance as the years passed. That was also why even though she was legally Mrs. Jimbo Potters, Loretta still referred to herself as Thistlebottom, her stage name.

Now in the murky light shed by the Tiffany-type globe over the well-scarred bar, Ernie silently admired Loretta, reflecting that even though she had to be in her mid-fifties, she had kept her figure very, very well. However, he wasn't really concerned about her. The winning lottery ticket, which he had pinned to his undershirt, was warming the area around his heart. It was like having a glowing fire there. Two million dollars. That was one hundred thousand dollars a year less taxes for twenty years. They'd be collecting well into the twenty-first century. By then they might even be able to take a cook's tour to the moon.

Ernie tried to visualize the expression on Wilma's face when she heard the good news. Wilma's sister, Dorothy, didn't have a television and seldom listened to the radio, so down in Philadelphia Wilma wouldn't know that now she was wealthy. The minute he'd heard the good news on his portable radio, Ernie had been tempted to rush to the phone and call Wilma but immediately decided that that wouldn't be fun. Now Ernie smiled happily, his round face creasing into a merry pancake as he visualized Wilma's homecoming tomorrow. He'd pick her up at the train station at Newark. She'd ask him how close they'd come to winning. "Did we have two of the numbers? Three of the numbers?" He'd tell her they didn't even have one of the winning combination. Then when they got home, she'd find her stocking hung on the mantel, the way they used to do when they were first married. In those days Wilma had worn stockings and garters. Now she wore queen-sized pantyhose, so she'd have to dig down to the toe for the ticket. He'd say, "Just keep looking; wait till you see the surprise." He could just picture the way she'd scream and throw her arms around him.

Wilma had been a darn cute young girl when they were married forty years ago. She still had a pretty face and her hair, a soft white-blond, was naturally wavy. She wasn't a showgirl type like Loretta but she suited him just right. Sometimes she got a little cranky about the fact that he liked to bend the elbow with the boys now and then but for the most part, Wilma was A-okay. And boy, what a Christmas they'd have this year. Maybe he'd take her to Fred the Furrier and get her a mouton lamb or something.

Contemplating the pleasure it would be to manifest his generosity, Ernie ordered his fourth Seven and Seven. His attention was diverted by the fact that Loretta Thistlebottom was engaged in a strange ritual. Every minute or two, she laid the cigarette in her right hand in the ashtray, the stein of beer in her left hand on the bar, and vigorously scratched the palm, fingers, and back of her right hand with the long pointed fingernails of her left hand. Ernie observed that her right hand was inflamed, angry red and covered with small, mean-looking blisters.

It was getting late and people were starting to leave. The couple who had been sitting next to Ernie and at a right angle to Loretta departed. Loretta, noticing that Ernie was watching her, shrugged. "Poison ivy," she explained. "Would you believe poison ivy in December? That dumb sister of Jimbo decided she had a green thumb and made her poor jerk of a husband rig up a greenhouse off their kitchen. So what does she grow? Weeds and poison ivy. That takes real talent." Loretta shrugged and repossessed the stein of beer and her cigarette. "So how ye been, Ernie? Anything new in your life?"

Ernie was cautious. "Not much."

Loretta sighed. "Me neither. Same old stuff. Jimbo and me are saving to get out of here next year when he retires. Everyone tells me Fort Lauderdale is a real swinging place. Jimbo's getting piles from all these years driving the rig. I keep telling him how much money I could make as a waitress to help out but he don't want anyone flirting with me." Loretta scratched her hand against the bar and shook her head. "Can you imagine after twenty-five years, Jimbo still thinks every guy in the world wants me? I kind of love it but it can be a pain in the neck, too." Loretta sighed, a world-weary sigh. "Jimbo's the most passionate guy I ever knew and that's saying something. But as my mother used to say, a good roll in the sack is even better when there's a full wallet between the spring and mattress."

"Your mother said that?" Ernie was bemused at the practical wisdom. He began to sip his fourth Seagrams and Seven-Up.

Loretta nodded. "She was a million laughs but she told it straight. The heck with it. Maybe someday I'll win the lottery."

The temptation was too great. Ernie slipped

over the two empty bar stools as fast as his out-of-shape body would permit. "Too bad you don't have my luck," he whispered.

As Lou the bartender yelled, "Last call, folks," Ernie patted his massive chest in the spot directly over his heart.

"Like they say, Loretta, 'X marks the spot.' There were sixteen winnin' tickets in the special Christmas drawing. One of them is right here pinned to my underwear." Ernie realized that his tongue was beginning to feel pretty heavy. His voice sank into a furtive whisper. "*Two million dollars.* How about that?" He put his finger to his lips and winked.

Loretta dropped her cigarette and let it burn unnoticed on the long-suffering surface of the bar. "*You're kidding!*"

"I'm not kidding." Now it was a real effort to talk. "Wilma 'n me always bet the same number 1-9-4-7-5-2. 1947 'cause that was the year I got out of high school. 'Fifty-two, the year Wee Willie was born." His triumphant smile left no doubt to his sincerity. "Crazy thing is Wilma don't even know yet. She's visiting her sister, Dorothy, and won't get home till tomorrow."

Fumbling for his wallet, Ernie signaled for his check. Lou came over and watched as Ernie stood uncertainly on the suddenly tilting floor. "Ernie, wait around," Lou ordered. "You're bombed. I'll drive you home when I close up. You gotta leave your car here."

Insulted, Ernie started for the door. Lou was insinuating he was tanked. What a nerve. Ernie opened the door of the women's restroom and was in a stall before he realized his mistake.

Sliding off the bar stool, Loretta said hurriedly, "Lou, I'll drop him off. He only lives two blocks from me."

Lou's skinny forehead furrowed. "Jimbo might not like it."

"So don't tell him." They watched as Ernie lurched unsteadily out from the women's restroom. "For Pete sake, do you think he'll make a pass at me?" she asked scornfully.

Lou made a decision. "You're doing me a favor, Loretta. *But don't tell Jimbo.*"

Loretta let out her fulsome ha-ha bellow. "Do you think I want to risk my new caps? They won't be paid for for another year."

From somewhere behind him Ernie vaguely heard the din of voices and laughter. Suddenly he was feeling pretty rotten. The speckled pattern of the tile floor began to dance, causing a sickening whirl of dots to revolve before his eyes. He felt someone grasp his arm. "I'm gonna drop you off, Ernie." Through the roaring in his ears, Ernie recognized Loretta's voice.

"Damn nice of you, Loretta," he mumbled. "Guess I chelebrated too much." Vaguely he realized that Lou was saying something about having a Christmas drink on the house when he came back for his car.

In Loretta's aging Bonneville Pontiac he leaned his head back against the seat and closed his eyes. He was unaware that they had reached his driveway until he felt Loretta shaking him awake. "Gimme your key, Ernie. I'll help you in."

His arm around her shoulders, she steadied him along the walk. Ernie heard the scraping of the key in the lock, felt his feet moving through the living room down the brief length of the hallway.

"Which one?"

"Which one?" Ernie couldn't get his tongue to move.

"Which bedroom?" Loretta's voice sounded irritated. "Come on, Ernie, you're no feather to drag around. Oh, forget it. It has to be the other one. This one's full of those statues of birds your daughter makes. Cripes, you couldn't give them away as a door prize in a looney bin. No one's *that* nutty."

Ernie felt a flash of instinctive resentment at Loretta's putdown of his daughter, Wilma Jr., Wee Willie as he called her. Wee Willie had real talent. Someday she'd be a famous sculptor. She'd lived in New Mexico ever since she dropped out of school in '68 and supported herself working evenings as a waitress at McDonald's. Days she made pottery and sculpted birds.

Ernie felt himself being turned around and

pushed down. His knees buckled and he heard the familiar squeak of the boxspring. Sighing in gratitude, in one simultaneous movement, he stretched out and passed out.

Wilma Bean and her sister, Dorothy, had had a pleasant day. In small doses Wilma enjoyed being with Dorothy, who was sixty-three to Wilma's fifty-eight. The trouble was that Dorothy was very opinionated and highly critical of both Ernie and Wee Willie, and Wilma could take just so much of that. But she was sorry for Dorothy. Dorothy's husband had walked out on her ten years before and now was living high on the hog with his second wife, a karate instructor. Dorothy and her daughter-in-law did not get along very well. Dorothy still worked part-time as a claims adjuster in an insurance office and as she frequently told Wilma, "the phony claims don't get past me."

Very few people believed they were sisters. Dorothy was, as Ernie put it, like one side of eleven, just straight up and down with thin gray hair which she wore in a tight knot at the back of her head. Ernie always said she should have been cast as Carrie Nation; she'd have looked good with a hatchet in her hand. Wilma knew that Dorothy was still jealous that Wilma had been the pretty one and that even though she'd gotten heavy, her face hadn't wrinkled or even changed very much. But still, Wilma theorized, blood is thicker than water and a weekend in Philadelphia every four months or so and particularly around holiday time was always enjoyable.

The afternoon of the lottery drawing day, Dorothy picked Wilma up from the train station. They had a late lunch at Burger King, then drove around the neighborhood where Grace Kelly had been raised. They had both been her avid fans. After mutually agreeing that Prince Albert ought to marry, that Princess Caroline had certainly calmed down and was doing a fine job, and that Princess Stephanie should be slapped into a convent until she straightened out, they went to a movie, then back to Doro-

thy's apartment. She had cooked a chicken, and over dinner, late into the evening, they gossiped.

Dorothy complained to Wilma that her daughter-in-law had no idea how to raise a child and was too stubborn to accept even the most helpful suggestions.

"Well, at least you have grandchildren," Wilma sighed. "No wedding bells in sight for Wee Willie. She has her heart set on her sculpting career."

"What sculpting career?" Dorothy snapped.

"If we could just afford a good teacher," Wilma sighed, trying to ignore the dig.

"Ernie shouldn't encourage Willie," Dorothy said bluntly. "Tell him not to make such a fuss over that junk she sends home. Your place looks like a crazy man's version of a birdhouse. How is Ernie? I hope you're keeping him out of bars. Mark my words. He has the makings of an alcoholic. All those broken veins in his nose."

Wilma thought of the outsized Christmas boxes that had arrived from Wee Willie a few days ago. Marked *Do not open till Christmas*, they'd been accompanied by a note. "Ma, wait till you see these. I'm into peacocks and parrots." Wilma also thought of the staff Christmas party at the Do-Shop-Here Mall the other night when Ernie had gotten schnockered and pinched the bottom of one of the waitresses.

Knowing that Dorothy was right about Ernie's ability to lap up booze did not ease Wilma's resentment at having the truth pointed out to her. "Well, Ernie may get silly when he has a drop or two too much but you're wrong about Wee Willie. She has real talent and when my ship comes in I'll help her to prove it."

Dorothy helped herself to another cup of tea. "I suppose you're still wasting money on lottery tickets."

"Sure am," Wilma said cheerfully, fighting to retain her good nature. "Tonight's the special Christmas drawing. If I were home I'd be in front of the set praying."

"That combination of numbers you always pick is ridiculous! 1-9-4-7-5-2. I can understand a person using the year her child was born but the year Ernie graduated from high school? That's ridiculous."

Wilma had never told Dorothy that it had taken Ernie six years to get through high school and his family had had a block party to celebrate. "Best party I was ever at," he frequently told her, memory brightening his face. "Even the mayor came."

Anyhow, Wilma liked that combination of numbers. She was absolutely certain that someday they would win a lot of money for her and Ernie. After she said good night to Dorothy, and puffing with the effort made up the sofabed where she slept on her visits, she reflected that as Dorothy grew older she got crankier. She also talked your ear off and it was no wonder her daughter-in-law referred to her as "that miserable pain in the neck."

The next day Wilma got off the train in Newark at noon. Ernie was picking her up. As she walked to their meeting spot at the main entrance to the terminal she was alarmed to see Ben Gump, their next-door neighbor, there instead.

She rushed to Ben, her ample body tensed with fear. "Is anything wrong? Where's Ernie?"

Ben's wispy face broke into a reassuring smile. "No, everything's just fine, Wilma. Ernie woke up with a touch of flu or something. Asked me to come for you. Heck, I've got nothing to do 'cept watch the grass grow." Ben laughed heartily at the witticism that had become his trademark since his retirement.

"Flu," Wilma scoffed. "I'll bet."

Ernie was a reasonably quiet man and Wilma had looked forward to a restful drive home. At breakfast, Dorothy, knowing she was losing her captive audience, had talked nonstop, a waterfall of acid comments that had made Wilma's head throb.

To distance herself from Ben's snail-paced driving and long-winded stories, Wilma concentrated on the pleasurable excitement of looking in the paper the minute she arrived home and checking the lottery results. 1-9-4-7-5-2, 1-9-4-7-5-2, she chanted to herself. It was silly.

The drawing was over but even so she had a *good* feeling. Certainly Ernie would have phoned her if they'd won but even coming close, like getting three or four of the six numbers, made her know that their luck was changing.

She spotted the fact the car wasn't in the driveway and guessed the reason. It was probably parked at the Harmony Bar. She managed to get rid of Ben Gump at the door, thanking him profusely for picking her up but ignoring his broad hints that he sure could use a cup of coffee. Then Wilma went straight to the bedroom. As she'd expected, Ernie was in bed. The covers were pulled to the tip of his nose. One look told her he had a massive hangover. "When the cat's away the mouse will play." She sighed. "I hope your head feels like a balloon-sized rock."

In her annoyance, she knocked over the four-foot-high pelican that Wee Willie had sent for Thanksgiving and that was perched on a table just outside the bedroom door. As it clattered to the floor, it took with it the pottery vase, an early work of Wee Willie's, and the arrangement of plastic baby's breath and poinsettias Wilma had labored over in preparation for Christmas.

Sweeping up the broken vase, rearranging the flowers and restoring the pelican, now missing a section of one wing, to the tabletop stretched Wilma's patience to the breaking point.

But the thought of the magic moment of looking up to see how close they'd come to winning the lottery and maybe finding that this time they'd come *really* close restored her to her usual good temper. She made a cup of coffee and fixed cinnamon toast before she settled at the kitchen table and opened the paper.

Sixteen Lucky Winners Share Thirty-Two Million Dollar Prize, the headline read.

Sixteen lucky winners. Oh to be one of them. Wilma slid her hand over the winning combination. She'd read the numbers one digit at a time. It was more fun that way.

1-9-4-7-5

Wilma sucked in her breath. Her head was pounding. Was it possible? In an agony of suspense she removed her palm from the final number.

2

Her shriek and the sound of the kitchen chair toppling over caused Ernie to sit bolt upright in bed. Judgement Day was at hand.

Wilma rushed into the room, her face transfixed. "Ernie, why didn't you tell me? *Give me the ticket!*"

Ernie's head sunk down on his neck. His voice was a broken whisper. "I lost it."

Loretta had known it was inevitable. Even so, the sight of Wilma Bean marching up the snow-dusted cement walk followed by a reluctant, downcast Ernie did cause a moment of sheer panic. "Forget it," Loretta told herself. "They don't have a leg to stand on." She'd covered her tracks completely, she promised herself as Wilma and Ernie came up the steps to the porch between the two evergreens that Loretta had decked out with dozens of Christmas lights. She had her story straight. She had walked Ernie to the door of his home. Anyone knowing how jealous Big Jimbo was would understand that Loretta would not step beyond the threshold of another man's home when his wife wasn't present.

When Wilma asked about the ticket, Loretta would ask, "What ticket?" Ernie never *mentioned* a ticket to her. He was in no condition to talk about anything sensible. Ask Lou. Ernie was pie-eyed after a coupla drinks. He'd probably stopped somewhere else first.

Did Loretta buy a lottery ticket for the special Christmas drawing? Sure she bought some. Wanna see them? Every week when she thought of it, she'd pick up a few. Never in the same place. Maybe at the liquor store, the stationery store. You know just for luck. Always numbers she thought of off the top of her head.

Loretta scratched her right hand viciously. Damn poison ivy. She had the 1-9-4-7-5-2 winning ticket safely hidden in the sugar bowl of her best china. You had a year to claim your win-

nings. Just before the year was up, she'd "accidentally" come across it. Let Wilma and Ernie try to howl that it was theirs.

The bell rang. Loretta patted her bright gold hair, which she'd teased into the tossed salad look, straightened the shoulder pads of her brilliantly sequined sweater, and hurried to the closet-sized foyer. As she opened the door she willed her face to become a wreath of smiles not even minding that she was trying not to smile too much. Her face was starting to wrinkle, a genetic family problem. She constantly worried about the fact that by age sixty her mother's face had looked as though it could hold nine days of rain. "Wilma, Ernie, what a delightful surprise," she gushed. "Come in. Come in."

Loretta decided to ignore the fact that neither Wilma nor Ernie answered her, that neither bothered to brush the snow from their overshoes on the foyer mat that specifically invited guests to do that very thing, that they had no friendly holiday smiles to match her greeting.

Wilma declined the invitation to sit down, to have a cup of tea or a Bloody Mary. She made her case clear. Ernie had been holding a two-million-dollar lottery ticket. He'd told Loretta about it at the Harmony Bar. Loretta had driven him home from the Harmony, gotten him into his room. Ernie had passed out and the ticket was gone.

In 1945, before she became a full-time hoofer, Loretta had studied acting at the Sonny Tufts School for Thespians. Drawing on the long-ago experience, she earnestly and sincerely performed her well-practiced scenario for Wilma and Ernie. Ernie never breathed a word to her about a winning ticket. She only drove him home as a favor to him and to Lou. Lou couldn't leave and anyhow Lou's such a runt, he couldn't fight Ernie for the car keys. "At least you agreed to let me drive," Loretta said to Ernie indignantly. "I took my life in my hands just letting you snore your way home in my car." She turned to Wilma and woman-to-woman reminded her: "You know how jealous Jimbo is of me, silly man. You'd think I was sixteen. But no way do

I go into your house unless you're there, Wilma. Ernie, you got smashed real fast at the Harmony. Just ask Lou. Did you stop anywhere else first and maybe talk to someone about the ticket?"

Loretta congratulated herself as she watched the doubt and confusion on both their faces. A few minutes later they left. "I hope you find it. I'll say a prayer," she promised piously. She would not shake hands with them, explaining to Wilma about her dumb sister-in-law's greenhouse harvest of poison ivy. "Come have a Christmas drink with Jimbo and me," she urged. "He'll be home about four o'clock Christmas Eve."

At home, sitting glumly over a cup of tea, Wilma said, "She's lying. I know she's lying but who could prove it? Fifteen winners have shown up already. One missing and with a year to claim." Frustrated tears rolled unnoticed down Wilma's cheeks. "She'll let the whole world know she buys a ticket here, a ticket there. She'll do that for the next fifty-one weeks and then *bingo* she'll find the ticket she forgot she had."

Ernie watched his wife in abject silence. A weeping Wilma was an infrequent sight. Now as her face blotched and her nose began to run, he handed her his red bandana handkerchief. His sudden gesture caused a ceramic hummingbird to fall off the sideboard behind him. The beak of the hummingbird crumbled against the imitation marble tile in the breakfast nook of the kitchen and brought a fresh wail of grief from Wilma.

"My big hope was that Wee Willie could give up working nights at McDonald's and study and do her birds full-time," Wilma sobbed. "And now that dream is busted."

Just to be absolutely sure, they went to the Friendly Shamrock near the Do-Shop-Here Mall in Paramus. The evening bartender confirmed that Ernie had been there the night before just around midnight, had two maybe three drinks but never said boo to nobody. "Just sat there grinning like the cat who ate the canary."

After a dinner which neither of them touched Wilma carefully examined Ernie's undershirt, which still had the safety pin in place. "She didn't even bother to unpin it," Wilma said bitterly. "Just reached in and tore it off."

"Can we sue her?" Ernie suggested tentatively. The enormity of his stupidity kept building by the minute. Getting drunk. Talking his head off to Loretta.

Too tired to even answer, Wilma opened the suitcase she had not yet unpacked and reached for her flannel nightgown. "Sure we can sue her," she said sarcastically, "for having a fast brain when she's dealing with a wet brain. Now turn off the light, go to sleep, and quit that damn scratching. You're driving me crazy."

Ernie was tearing at his chest in the area around his heart. "Something itches," he complained.

A bell sounded in Wilma's head as she closed her eyes. She was so worn out she fell asleep almost immediately, but her dreams were filled with lottery tickets floating through the air like snowflakes. From time to time she was pulled awake by Ernie's restless movements. Usually Ernie slept like a hibernating bear.

Christmas Eve dawned gray and cheerless. Wilma dragged herself around the house, going through the motions of putting presents under the tree. The two boxes from Wee Willie. If they hadn't lost the winning ticket they could have phoned Wee Willie to come home for Christmas. Maybe she wouldn't have come. Wee Willie didn't like the middle-class trap of the suburban environment. In that case Ernie could have thrown up his job and they could have visited her in New Mexico soon. And Wilma could have bought the forty-inch television that had so awed her in Trader Horn's last week. Just think of seeing J. R. forty inches big.

Oh well. Spilt milk. No, spilt *booze*. Ernie had told her about his plans to put the lottery ticket in her pantyhose on the mantel of the fake fireplace if he hadn't lost it. Wilma tried not to dwell on the thrill of finding the ticket there.

She was not pleasant to Ernie, who was still hung over and had phoned in sick for the second day. She told him exactly where he could stuff his headache.

In mid-afternoon, Ernie went into the bedroom and closed the door. After a while, Wilma became alarmed and followed him. Ernie was sitting on the edge of the bed, his shirt off, plaintively scratching his chest. "I'm all right," he said, his face still covered with the hangdog expression that was beginning to seem permanent. "It's just I'm so damn itchy."

Only slightly relieved that Ernie had not found some way to commit suicide, Wilma asked irritably, "What are you so itchy about? It isn't time for your allergies to start. I hear enough about them all summer."

She looked closely at the inflamed skin. "For God's sake, that's poison ivy. Where did you manage to pick that up?"

Poison ivy.

They stared at each other.

Wilma grabbed Ernie's undershirt from the top of the dresser. She'd left it there, the safety pin still in it, the sliver of ticket a silent, hostile witness to his stupidity. "Put it on," she ordered.

"But . . ."

"Put it on!"

It was instantly evident that the poison ivy was centered in the exact spot where the ticket had been hidden.

"That lying hoofer." Wilma thrust out her jaw and straightened her shoulders. "She said that Big Jimbo was gonna be home around four, didn't she?"

"I think so."

"Good. Nothing like a reception committee."

At three-thirty they pulled in front of Loretta's house and parked. As they'd expected, Jimbo's sixteen-wheel rig was not yet there. "We'll sit here for a few minutes and make that crook nervous," Wilma decreed.

They watched as the vertical blinds in the front window of Loretta's house began to bob erratically. At three minutes of four, Ernie pointed a nervous hand. "There. At the light. That's Jimbo's truck."

"Let's go," Wilma told him.

Loretta opened the door, her face again wreathed in a smile. With grim satisfaction Wilma noticed that the smile was very, very nervous.

"Ernie. Wilma. How nice. You did come for a Christmas drink."

"I'll have my Christmas drink later," Wilma told her. "And it'll be to celebrate getting our ticket back. How's your poison ivy, Loretta?"

"Oh, starting to clear up. Wilma, I don't like the tone of your voice."

"That's a crying shame." Wilma walked past the sectional, which was upholstered in a red-and-black checkered pattern, went to the window, and pulled back the vertical blind. "Well, what do you know? Here's Big Jimbo. Guess you two lovebirds can't wait to get your hands on each other. Guess he'll be real mad when I tell him I'm suing you for heartburn because you've been fooling around with my husband."

"I've what?" Loretta's carefully applied purple-kisses lipstick deepened as her complexion faded to grayish white.

"You heard me. And I got proof. Ernie, take off your shirt. Show this husband-stealer your rash."

"Rash," Loretta moaned.

"Poison ivy just like yours. Started on his chest when you stuck your hand under his underwear to get the ticket. Go ahead. Deny it. Tell Jimbo you don't know nothing about a ticket, that you and Ernie were just having a go at a little hanky-panky."

"You're lying. Get out of here. Ernie, don't unbutton that shirt." Frantically Loretta grabbed Ernie's hands.

"My what a big man Jimbo is," Wilma said admiringly as he got out of the truck. She waved to him. "A real big man." She turned. "Take off your pants too, Ernie." Wilma dropped the vertical blind and hurried over to Loretta. "He's got the rash *down there*," she whispered.

"Oh, my God. I'll get it. I'll get it. Keep your pants on!" Loretta rushed to the junior-sized dining room and flung open the china closet that contained the remnants of her mother's china. With shaking fingers she reached for the sugar bowl. It dropped from her hands and smashed as she grabbed the lottery ticket. Jimbo's key was turning in the door as she jammed the ticket in Wilma's hand. "Now get out. And don't say nothing."

Wilma sat down on the red-and-black checkered couch. "It would look real funny to rush out. Ernie and I will join you and Big Jimbo in a Christmas drink."

The houses on their block were decorated with Santa Clauses on the roofs, angels on the lawn, and ropes of lights framing the outside of the windows. With a peaceful smile as they arrived home, Wilma remarked how real pretty the neighborhood was. Inside the house, she handed the lottery ticket to Ernie. "Put this in my stocking just the way you meant to."

Meekly he went into the bedroom and selected her favorite pantyhose, the white ones with rhinestones. She fished in his drawer and came out with one of his dress-up argyle socks, somewhat lumpy because Wilma wasn't much of a knitter but still his best. As they tacked the stockings to the mantel over the artificial fireplace, Ernie said, "Wilma, I don't have poison ivy," his voice sunk into a faint whisper, "down there."

"I'm sure you don't but it did the trick. Now just put the ticket in my stocking and I'll put your present in yours."

"You bought me a present? After all the trouble I caused? Oh, Wilma."

"I didn't buy it. I dug it out of the medicine cabinet and put a bow on it." Smiling happily, Wilma dropped a bottle of calamine lotion into Ernie's argyle sock.

DEATH ON THE AIR

Ngaio Marsh

ALTHOUGH SHE IS ONE OF THE TWENTIETH CENTURY'S greatest writers of pure detective stories, Ngaio Marsh's first love was the theater, especially the plays of her native New Zealand. Her first name (pronounced Nigh-o) is the Maori name for a local flower. All of her thirty-two novels feature Scotland Yard's Inspector Roderick Alleyn. Marsh was given the Grand Master Award by the Mystery Writers of America for lifetime achievement. Curiously, her autobiography, *Black Beech and Honeydew* (1965), barely mentions mystery fiction, though she devoted much of nearly a half century to writing it. "Death on the Air" was first published as "Murder at Christmas" in the December 1934 issue of *The Grand Magazine*.

Death on the Air

NGAIO MARSH

ON THE 25TH OF DECEMBER AT 7:30 A.M. Mr. Septimus Tonks was found dead beside his wireless set.

It was Emily Parks, an under-housemaid, who discovered him. She butted open the door and entered, carrying mop, duster, and carpet-sweeper. At that precise moment she was greatly startled by a voice that spoke out of the darkness.

"Good morning, everybody," said the voice in superbly inflected syllables, "and a Merry Christmas!"

Emily yelped, but not loudly, as she immediately realised what had happened. Mr. Tonks had omitted to turn off his wireless before going to bed. She drew back the curtains, revealing a kind of pale murk which was a London Christmas dawn, switched on the light, and saw Septimus.

He was seated in front of the radio. It was a small but expensive set, specially built for him. Septimus sat in an armchair, his back to Emily, his body tilted towards the radio.

His hands, the fingers curiously bunched, were on the ledge of the cabinet under the tuning and volume knobs. His chest rested against the shelf below and his head leaned on the front panel.

He looked rather as though he was listening intently to the interior secrets of the wireless. His head was bent so that Emily could see his bald top with its trail of oiled hairs. He did not move.

"Beg pardon, sir," gasped Emily. She was again greatly startled. Mr. Tonks's enthusiasm for radio had never before induced him to tune in at seven-thirty in the morning.

"Special Christmas service," the cultured voice was saying. Mr. Tonks sat very still. Emily, in common with the other servants, was terrified of her master. She did not know whether to go or to stay. She gazed wildly at Septimus and realised that he wore a dinner-jacket. The room was now filled with the clamour of pealing bells.

Emily opened her mouth as wide as it would go and screamed and screamed and screamed . . .

Chase, the butler, was the first to arrive. He was a pale, flabby man but authoritative. He said: "What's the meaning of this outrage?" and then saw Septimus. He went to the armchair, bent down, and looked into his master's face.

He did not lose his head, but said in a loud voice: "My Gawd!" And then to Emily: "Shut your face." By this vulgarism he betrayed his agitation. He seized Emily by the shoulders and thrust her towards the door, where they were met by Mr. Hislop, the secretary, in his dressing-gown. Mr. Hislop said: "Good heavens, Chase, what is the meaning——" and then his voice too was drowned in the clamour of bells and renewed screams.

Chase put his fat white hand over Emily's mouth.

"In the study if you please, sir. An accident.

Go to your room, will you, and stop that noise or I'll give you something to make you." This to Emily, who bolted down the hall, where she was received by the rest of the staff who had congregated there.

Chase returned to the study with Mr. Hislop and locked the door. They both looked down at the body of Septimus Tonks. The secretary was the first to speak.

"But—but—he's dead," said little Mr. Hislop.

"I suppose there can't be any doubt," whispered Chase.

"Look at the face. Any doubt! My God!"

Mr. Hislop put out a delicate hand towards the bent head and then drew it back. Chase, less fastidious, touched one of the hard wrists, gripped, and then lifted it. The body at once tipped backwards as if it was made of wood. One of the hands knocked against the butler's face. He sprang back with an oath.

There lay Septimus, his knees and his hands in the air, his terrible face turned up to the light. Chase pointed to the right hand. Two fingers and the thumb were slightly blackened.

Ding, dong, dang, ding.

"For God's sake stop those bells," cried Mr. Hislop. Chase turned off the wall switch. Into the sudden silence came the sound of the doorhandle being rattled and Guy Tonks's voice on the other side.

"Hislop! Mr. Hislop! Chase! What's the matter?"

"Just a moment, Mr. Guy." Chase looked at the secretary. "You go, sir."

So it was left to Mr. Hislop to break the news to the family. They listened to his stammering revelation in stupefied silence. It was not until Guy, the eldest of the three children, stood in the study that any practical suggestion was made.

"What has killed him?" asked Guy.

"It's extraordinary," burbled Hislop. "Extraordinary. He looks as if he'd been——"

"Galvanised," said Guy.

"We ought to send for a doctor," suggested Hislop timidly.

"Of course. Will you, Mr. Hislop? Dr. Meadows."

Hislop went to the telephone and Guy returned to his family. Dr. Meadows lived on the other side of the square and arrived in five minutes. He examined the body without moving it. He questioned Chase and Hislop. Chase was very voluble about the burns on the hand. He uttered the word "electrocution" over and over again.

"I had a cousin, sir, that was struck by lightning. As soon as I saw the hand——"

"Yes, yes," said Dr. Meadows. "So you said. I can see the burns for myself."

"Electrocution," repeated Chase. "There'll have to be an inquest."

Dr. Meadows snapped at him, summoned Emily, and then saw the rest of the family—Guy, Arthur, Phillipa, and their mother. They were clustered round a cold grate in the drawing-room. Phillipa was on her knees, trying to light the fire.

"What was it?" asked Arthur as soon as the doctor came in.

"Looks like electric shock. Guy, I'll have a word with you if you please. Phillipa, look after your mother, there's a good child. Coffee with a dash of brandy. Where are those damn maids? Come on, Guy."

Alone with Guy, he said they'd have to send for the police.

"The police!" Guy's dark face turned very pale. "Why? What's it got to do with them?"

"Nothing, as like as not, but they'll have to be notified. I can't give a certificate as things are. If it's electrocution, how did it happen?"

"But the police!" said Guy. "That's simply ghastly. Dr. Meadows, for God's sake couldn't you——?"

"No," said Dr. Meadows, "I couldn't. Sorry, Guy, but there it is."

"But can't we wait a moment? Look at him again. You haven't examined him properly."

"I don't want to move him, that's why. Pull yourself together, boy. Look here. I've got a pal in the CID—Alleyn. He's a gentleman and all that. He'll curse me like a fury, but he'll come if he's in London, and he'll make things easier for you. Go back to your mother. I'll ring Alleyn up."

That was how it came about that Chief Detective-Inspector Roderick Alleyn spent his Christmas Day in harness. As a matter of fact he was on duty, and as he pointed out to Dr. Meadows, would have had to turn out and visit his miserable Tonkses in any case. When he did arrive it was with his usual air of remote courtesy. He was accompanied by a tall, thick-set officer—Inspector Fox—and by the divisional police-surgeon. Dr. Meadows took them into the study. Alleyn, in his turn, looked at the horror that had been Septimus.

"Was he like this when he was found?"

"No. I understand he was leaning forward with his hands on the ledge of the cabinet. He must have slumped forward and been propped up by the chair arms and the cabinet."

"Who moved him?"

"Chase, the butler. He said he only meant to raise the arm. *Rigor* is well established."

Alleyn put his hand behind the rigid neck and pushed. The body fell forward into its original position.

"There you are, Curtis," said Alleyn to the divisional surgeon. He turned to Fox. "Get the camera man, will you, Fox?"

The photographer took four shots and departed. Alleyn marked the position of the hands and feet with chalk, made a careful plan of the room and turned to the doctors.

"Is it electrocution, do you think?"

"Looks like it," said Curtis. "Have to be a PM, of course."

"Of course. Still, look at the hands. Burns. Thumb and two fingers bunched together and exactly the distance between the two knobs apart. He'd been tuning his hurdy-gurdy."

"By gum," said Inspector Fox, speaking for the first time.

"D'you mean he got a lethal shock from his radio?" asked Dr. Meadows.

"I don't know. I merely conclude he had his hands on the knobs when he died."

"It was still going when the housemaid found him. Chase turned it off and got no shock."

"Yours, partner," said Alleyn, turning to Fox. Fox stooped down to the wall switch.

"Careful," said Alleyn.

"I've got rubber soles," said Fox, and switched it on. The radio hummed, gathered volume, and found itself.

"No-o-el, No-o-el," it roared. Fox cut it off and pulled out the wall plug.

"I'd like to have a look inside this set," he said.

"So you shall, old boy, so you shall," rejoined Alleyn. "Before you begin, I think we'd better move the body. Will you see to that, Meadows? Fox, get Bailey, will you? He's out in the car."

Curtis, Hislop, and Meadows carried Septimus Tonks into a spare downstairs room. It was a difficult and horrible business with that contorted body. Dr. Meadows came back alone, mopping his brow, to find Detective-Sergeant Bailey, a fingerprint expert, at work on the wireless cabinet.

"What's all this?" asked Dr. Meadows. "Do you want to find out if he'd been fooling round with the innards?"

"He," said Alleyn, "or—somebody else."

"Umph!" Dr. Meadows looked at the Inspector. "You agree with me, it seems. Do you suspect———?"

"Suspect? I'm the least suspicious man alive. I'm merely being tidy. Well, Bailey?"

"I've got a good one off the chair arm. That'll be the deceased's, won't it, sir?"

"No doubt. We'll check up later. What about the wireless?"

Fox, wearing a glove, pulled off the knob of the volume control.

"Seems to be OK," said Bailey. "It's a sweet bit of work. Not too bad at all, sir." He turned his torch into the back of the radio, undid a couple of screws underneath the set, lifted out the works.

"What's the little hole for?" asked Alleyn.

"What's that, sir?" said Fox.

"There's a hole bored through the panel above the knob. About an eighth of an inch in diameter. The rim of the knob hides it. One might easily miss it. Move your torch, Bailey. Yes. There, do you see?"

Fox bent down and uttered a bass growl. A fine needle of light came through the front of the radio.

"That's peculiar, sir," said Bailey from the other side. "I don't get the idea at all."

Alleyn pulled out the tuning knob.

"There's another one there," he murmured. "Yes. Nice clean little holes. Newly bored. Unusual, I take it?"

"Unusual's the word, sir," said Fox.

"Run away, Meadows," said Alleyn.

"Why the devil?" asked Dr. Meadows indignantly. "What are you driving at? Why shouldn't I be here?"

"You ought to be with the sorrowing relatives. Where's your corpseside manner?"

"I've settled them. What are you up to?"

"Who's being suspicious now?" asked Alleyn mildly. "You may stay for a moment. Tell me about the Tonkses. Who are they? What are they? What sort of a man was Septimus?"

"If you must know, he was a damned unpleasant sort of a man."

"Tell me about him."

Dr. Meadows sat down and lit a cigarette.

"He was a self-made bloke," he said, "as hard as nails and—well, coarse rather than vulgar."

"Like Dr. Johnson perhaps?"

"Not in the least. Don't interrupt. I've known him for twenty-five years. His wife was a neighbour of ours in Dorset. Isabel Foreston. I brought the children into this vale of tears and, by jove, in many ways it's been one for them. It's an extraordinary household. For the last ten years Isabel's condition has been the sort that sends these psycho-jokers dizzy with rapture. I'm only an out-of-date GP, and I'd just say she

is in an advanced stage of hysterical neurosis. Frightened into fits of her husband."

"I can't understand these holes," grumbled Fox to Bailey.

"Go on, Meadows," said Alleyn.

"I tackled Sep about her eighteen months ago. Told him the trouble was in her mind. He eyed me with a sort of grin on his face and said: 'I'm surprised to learn that my wife has enough mentality to——' But look here, Alleyn, I can't talk about my patients like this. What the devil am I thinking about."

"You know perfectly well it'll go no further unless——"

"Unless what?"

"Unless it has to. Do go on."

But Dr. Meadows hurriedly withdrew behind his professional rectitude. All he would say was that Mr. Tonks had suffered from high blood pressure and a weak heart, that Guy was in his father's city office, that Arthur had wanted to study art and had been told to read for law, and that Phillipa wanted to go on to the stage and had been told to do nothing of the sort.

"Bullied his children," commented Alleyn.

"Find out for yourself. I'm off." Dr. Meadows got as far as the door and came back.

"Look here," he said, "I'll tell you one thing. There was a row here last night. I'd asked Hislop, who's a sensible little beggar, to let me know if anything happened to upset Mrs. Sep. Upset her badly, you know. To be indiscreet again, I said he'd better let me know if Sep cut up rough, because Isabel and the young had had about as much of that as they could stand. He was drinking pretty heavily. Hislop rang me up at ten-twenty last night to say there'd been a hell of a row; Sep bullying Phips—Phillipa, you know; always call her Phips—in her room. He said Isabel—Mrs. Sep—had gone to bed. I'd had a big day and I didn't want to turn out. I told him to ring again in half an hour if things hadn't quieted down. I told him to keep out of Sep's way and stay in his own room, which is next to Phips's, and see if she was all right when Sep cleared out. Hislop was involved. I won't tell you how. The servants were all out. I said that if I didn't hear from him in half an hour I'd ring again and if there was no answer I'd know they were all in bed and quiet. I did ring, got no answer, and went to bed myself. That's all. I'm off. Curtis knows where to find me. You'll want me for the inquest, I suppose. Goodbye."

When he had gone Alleyn embarked on a systematic prowl round the room. Fox and Bailey were still deeply engrossed with the wireless.

"I don't see how the gentleman could have got a bump-off from the instrument," grumbled Fox. "These control knobs are quite in order. Everything's as it should be. Look here, sir."

He turned on the wall switch and tuned in. There was a prolonged humming.

". . . concludes the programme of Christmas carols," said the radio.

"A very nice tone," said Fox approvingly.

"Here's something, sir," announced Bailey suddenly.

"Found the sawdust, have you?" said Alleyn.

"Got it in one," said the startled Bailey.

Alleyn peered into the instrument, using the torch. He scooped up two tiny traces of sawdust from under the holes.

"Vantage number one," said Alleyn. He bent down to the wall plug. "Hullo! A two-way adapter. Serves the radio and the radiator. Thought they were illegal. This is a rum business. Let's have another look at those knobs."

He had his look. They were the usual wireless fitments, Bakelite knobs fitting snugly to the steel shafts that projected from the front panel.

"As you say," he murmured, "quite in order. Wait a bit." He produced a pocket lens and squinted at one of the shafts. "Ye-es. Do they ever wrap blotting-paper round these objects, Fox?"

"Blotting-paper!" ejaculated Fox. "They do not."

Alleyn scraped at both the shafts with his penknife, holding an envelope underneath. He rose, groaning, and crossed to the desk. "A corner torn off the bottom bit of blotch," he said presently. "No prints on the wireless, I think you said, Bailey?"

"That's right," agreed Bailey morosely.

"There'll be none, or too many, on the blotter, but try, Bailey, try," said Alleyn. He wandered about the room, his eyes on the floor; got as far as the window and stopped.

"Fox!" he said. "A clue. A very palpable clue."

"What is it?" asked Fox.

"The odd wisp of blotting-paper, no less." Alleyn's gaze travelled up the side of the window curtain. "Can I believe my eyes?"

He got a chair, stood on the seat, and with his gloved hand pulled the buttons from the ends of the curtain-rod.

"Look at this." He turned to the radio, detached the control knobs, and laid them beside the ones he had removed from the curtain-rod.

Ten minutes later Inspector Fox knocked on the drawing-room door and was admitted by Guy Tonks. Phillipa had got the fire going and the family was gathered round it. They looked as though they had not moved or spoken to one another for a long time.

It was Phillipa who spoke first to Fox. "Do you want one of us?"

"If you please, miss," said Fox. "Inspector Alleyn would like to see Mr. Guy Tonks for a moment, if convenient."

"I'll come," said Guy, and led the way to the study. At the door he paused. "Is he—my father—still———?"

"No, no, sir," said Fox comfortably. "It's all ship-shape in there again."

With a lift of his chin Guy opened the door and went in, followed by Fox. Alleyn was alone, seated at the desk. He rose to his feet.

"You want to speak to me?" asked Guy.

"Yes, if I may. This has all been a great shock to you, of course. Won't you sit down?"

Guy sat in the chair farthest away from the radio.

"What killed my father? Was it a stroke?"

"The doctors are not quite certain. There will have to be a post-mortem."

"Good God! And an inquest?"

"I'm afraid so."

"Horrible!" said Guy violently. "What do you think was the matter? Why the devil do these quacks have to be so mysterious? What killed him?"

"They think an electric shock."

"How did it happen?"

"We don't know. It looks as if he got it from the wireless."

"Surely that's impossible. I thought they were fool-proof."

"I believe they are, if left to themselves."

For a second undoubtedly Guy was startled. Then a look of relief came into his eyes. He seemed to relax all over.

"Of course," he said, "he was always monkeying about with it. What had he done?"

"Nothing."

"But you said—if it killed him he must have done something to it."

"If anyone interfered with the set it was put right afterwards."

Guy's lips parted but he did not speak. He had gone very white.

"So you see," said Alleyn, "your father could not have done anything."

"Then it was not the radio that killed him."

"That we hope will be determined by the post-mortem."

"I don't know anything about wireless," said Guy suddenly. "I don't understand. This doesn't seem to make sense. Nobody ever touched the thing except my father. He was most particular about it. Nobody went near the wireless."

"I see. He was an enthusiast?"

"Yes, it was his only enthusiasm except—except his business."

"One of my men is a bit of an expert," Alleyn said. "He says this is a remarkably good set. You are not an expert, you say. Is there anyone in the house who is?"

"My young brother was interested at one time. He's given it up. My father wouldn't allow another radio in the house."

"Perhaps he may be able to suggest something."

"But if the thing's all right now——"

"We've got to explore every possibility."

"You speak as if—as—if——"

"I speak as I am bound to speak before there has been an inquest," said Alleyn. "Had anyone a grudge against your father, Mr. Tonks?"

Up went Guy's chin again. He looked Alleyn squarely in the eyes.

"Almost everyone who knew him," said Guy.

"Is that an exaggeration?"

"No. You think he was murdered, don't you?"

Alleyn suddenly pointed to the desk beside him.

"Have you ever seen those before?" he asked abruptly. Guy stared at two black knobs that lay side by side on an ashtray.

"Those?" he said. "No. What are they?"

"I believe they are the agents of your father's death."

The study door opened and Arthur Tonks came in.

"Guy," he said, "what's happening? We can't stay cooped up together all day. I can't stand it. For God's sake what happened to him?"

"They think those things killed him," said Guy.

"Those?" For a split second Arthur's glance slewed to the curtain-rods. Then, with a characteristic flicker of his eyelids, he looked away again.

"What do you mean?" he asked Alleyn.

"Will you try one of those knobs on the shaft of the volume control?"

"But," said Arthur, "they're metal."

"It's disconnected," said Alleyn.

Arthur picked one of the knobs from the tray, turned to the radio, and fitted the knob over one of the exposed shafts.

"It's too loose," he said quickly, "it would fall off."

"Not if it was packed—with blotting-paper, for instance."

"Where did you find these things?" demanded Arthur.

"I think you recognised them, didn't you? I saw you glance at the curtain-rod."

"Of course I recognised them. I did a portrait of Phillipa against those curtains when—he—was away last year. I've painted the damn things."

"Look here," interrupted Guy, "exactly what are you driving at, Mr. Alleyn? If you mean to suggest that my brother——"

"I!" cried Arthur. "What's it got to do with me? Why should you suppose——"

"I found traces of blotting-paper on the shafts and inside the metal knobs," said Alleyn. "It suggested a substitution of the metal knobs for the Bakelite ones. It is remarkable, don't you think, that they should so closely resemble one another? If you examine them, of course, you find they are not identical. Still, the difference is scarcely perceptible."

Arthur did not answer this. He was still looking at the wireless.

"I've always wanted to have a look at this set," he said surprisingly.

"You are free to do so now," said Alleyn politely. "We have finished with it for the time being."

"Look here," said Arthur suddenly, "suppose metal knobs were substituted for Bakelite ones, it couldn't kill him. He wouldn't get a shock at all. Both the controls are grounded."

"Have you noticed those very small holes drilled through the panel?" asked Alleyn. "Should they be there, do you think?"

Arthur peered at the little steel shafts. "By God, he's right, Guy," he said. "That's how it was done."

"Inspector Fox," said Alleyn, "tells me those holes could be used for conducting wires and that a lead could be taken from the—the transformer, is it?—to one of the knobs."

"And the other connected to earth," said Fox. "It's a job for an expert. He could get three hundred volts or so that way."

"That's not good enough," said Arthur quickly; "there wouldn't be enough current to do any damage—only a few hundredths of an amp."

"I'm not an expert," said Alleyn, "but I'm sure you're right. Why were the holes drilled then? Do you imagine someone wanted to play a practical joke on your father?"

"A practical joke? On *him*?" Arthur gave an unpleasant screech of laughter. "Do you hear that, Guy?"

"Shut up," said Guy. "After all, he is dead."

"It seems almost too good to be true, doesn't it?"

"Don't be a bloody fool, Arthur. Pull yourself together. Can't you see what this means? They think he's been murdered."

"Murdered! They're wrong. None of us had the nerve for that, Mr. Inspector. Look at me. My hands are so shaky they told me I'd never be able to paint. That dates from when I was a kid and he shut me up in the cellars for a night. Look at me. Look at Guy. He's not so vulnerable, but he caved in like the rest of us. We were conditioned to surrender. Do you know——"

"Wait a moment," said Alleyn quietly. "Your brother is quite right, you know. You'd better think before you speak. This may be a case of homicide."

"Thank you, sir," said Guy quickly. "That's extraordinarily decent of you. Arthur's a bit above himself. It's a shock."

"The relief, you mean," said Arthur. "Don't be such an ass. I didn't kill him and they'll find it out soon enough. Nobody killed him. There must be some explanation."

"I suggest that you listen to me," said Alleyn. "I'm going to put several questions to both of you. You need not answer them, but it will be more sensible to do so. I understand no one but your father touched this radio. Did any of you ever come into this room while it was in use?"

"Not unless he wanted to vary the programme with a little bullying," said Arthur.

Alleyn turned to Guy, who was glaring at his brother.

"I want to know exactly what happened in this house last night. As far as the doctors can tell us, your father died not less than three and not more than eight hours before he was found. We must try to fix the time as accurately as possible."

"I saw him at about a quarter to nine," began Guy slowly. "I was going out to a supper-party at the Savoy and had come downstairs. He was crossing the hall from the drawing-room to his room."

"Did you see him after a quarter to nine, Mr. Arthur?"

"No. I heard him, though. He was working in here with Hislop. Hislop had asked to go away for Christmas. Quite enough. My father discovered some urgent correspondence. Really, Guy, you know, he was pathological. I'm sure Dr. Meadows thinks so."

"When did you hear him?" asked Alleyn.

"Some time after Guy had gone. I was working on a drawing in my room upstairs. It's above his. I heard him bawling at little Hislop. It must have been before ten o'clock, because I went out to a studio party at ten. I heard him bawling as I crossed the hall."

"And when," said Alleyn, "did you both return?"

"I came home at about twenty past twelve," said Guy immediately. "I can fix the time because we had gone on to Chez Carlo, and they had a midnight stunt there. We left immediately afterwards. I came home in a taxi. The radio was on full blast."

"You heard no voices?"

"None. Just the wireless."

"And you, Mr. Arthur?"

"Lord knows when I got in. After one. The house was in darkness. Not a sound."

"You had your own key?"

"Yes," said Guy. "Each of us has one. They're always left on a hook in the lobby. When I came in I noticed Arthur's was gone."

"What about the others? How did you know it was his?"

"Mother hasn't got one and Phips lost hers weeks ago. Anyway, I knew they were staying in and that it must be Arthur who was out."

"Thank you," said Arthur ironically.

"You didn't look in the study when you came in?" Alleyn asked him.

"Good Lord, no," said Arthur as if the sug-

gestion was fantastic. "I say," he said suddenly, "I suppose he was sitting here—dead. That's a queer thought." He laughed nervously. "Just sitting here, behind the door in the dark."

"How do you know it was in the dark?"

"What d'you mean? Of course it was. There was no light under the door."

"I see. Now do you two mind joining your mother again? Perhaps your sister will be kind enough to come in here for a moment. Fox, ask her, will you?"

Fox returned to the drawing-room with Guy and Arthur and remained there, blandly unconscious of any embarrassment his presence might cause the Tonkses. Bailey was already there, ostensibly examining the electric points.

Phillipa went to the study at once. Her first remark was characteristic. "Can I be of any help?" asked Phillipa.

"It's extremely nice of you to put it like that," said Alleyn. "I don't want to worry you for long. I'm sure this discovery has been a shock to you."

"Probably," said Phillipa. Alleyn glanced quickly at her. "I mean," she explained, "that I suppose I must be shocked but I can't feel anything much. I just want to get it all over as soon as possible. And then think. Please tell me what has happened."

Alleyn told her they believed her father had been electrocuted and that the circumstances were unusual and puzzling. He said nothing to suggest that the police suspected murder.

"I don't think I'll be much help," said Phillipa, "but go ahead."

"I want to try to discover who was the last person to see your father or speak to him."

"I should think very likely I was," said Phillipa composedly. "I had a row with him before I went to bed."

"What about?"

"I don't see that it matters."

Alleyn considered this. When he spoke again it was with deliberation.

"Look here," he said, "I think there is very little doubt that your father was killed by an electric shock from his wireless set. As far as I know the circumstances are unique. Radios are normally incapable of giving a lethal shock to anyone. We have examined the cabinet and are inclined to think that its internal arrangements were disturbed last night. Very radically disturbed. Your father may have experimented with it. If anything happened to interrupt or upset him, it is possible that in the excitement of the moment he made some dangerous readjustment."

"You don't believe that, do you?" asked Phillipa calmly.

"Since you ask me," said Alleyn, "no."

"I see," said Phillipa; "you think he was murdered, but you're not sure." She had gone very white, but she spoke crisply. "Naturally you want to find out about my row."

"About everything that happened last evening," amended Alleyn.

"What happened was this," said Phillipa; "I came into the hall some time after ten. I'd heard Arthur go out and had looked at the clock at five past. I ran into my father's secretary, Richard Hislop. He turned aside, but not before I saw . . . not quickly enough. I blurted out: 'You're crying.' We looked at each other. I asked him why he stood it. None of the other secretaries could. He said he had to. He's a widower with two children. There have been doctor's bills and things. I needn't tell you about his . . . about his damnable servitude to my father nor about the refinements of cruelty he'd had to put up with. I think my father was mad, really mad, I mean. Richard gabbled it all out to me higgledy-piggledy in a sort of horrified whisper. He's been here two years, but I'd never realised until that moment that we . . . that . . ." A faint flush came into her cheeks. "He's such a funny little man. Not at all the sort I've always thought . . . not good-looking or exciting or anything."

She stopped, looking bewildered.

"Yes?" said Alleyn.

"Well, you see—I suddenly realised I was in love with him. He realised it too. He said: 'Of course, it's quite hopeless, you know. Us, I mean. Laughable, almost.' Then I put my arms round his neck and kissed him. It was very odd, but it seemed quite natural. The point is my father came out of his room into the hall and saw us."

"That was bad luck," said Alleyn.

"Yes, it was. My father really seemed delighted. He almost licked his lips. Richard's efficiency had irritated my father for a long time. It was difficult to find excuses for being beastly to him. Now, of course . . . He ordered Richard to the study and me to my room. He followed me upstairs. Richard tried to come too, but I asked him not to. My father . . . I needn't tell you what he said. He put the worst possible construction on what he'd seen. He was absolutely foul, screaming at me like a madman. He was insane. Perhaps it was dt's. He drank terribly, you know. I dare say it's silly of me to tell you all this."

"No," said Alleyn.

"I can't feel anything at all. Not even relief. The boys are frankly relieved. I can't feel afraid either." She stared meditatively at Alleyn. "Innocent people needn't feel afraid, need they?"

"It's an axiom of police investigation," said Alleyn and wondered if indeed she was innocent.

"It just *can't* be murder," said Phillipa. "We were all too much afraid to kill him. I believe he'd win even if you murdered him. He'd hit back somehow." She put her hands to her eyes. "I'm all muddled."

"I think you are more upset than you realise. I'll be as quick as I can. Your father made this scene in your room. You say he screamed. Did anyone hear him?"

"Yes. Mummy did. She came in."

"What happened?"

"I said: 'Go away, darling, it's all right.' I didn't want her to be involved. He nearly killed her with the things he did. Sometimes he'd . . . we never knew what happened between them. It was all secret, like a door shutting quietly as you walk along a passage."

"Did she go away?"

"Not at once. He told her he'd found out that Richard and I were lovers. He said . . . it doesn't matter. I don't want to tell you. She was terrified.

He was stabbing at her in some way I couldn't understand. Then, quite suddenly, he told her to go to her own room. She went at once and he followed her. He locked me in. That's the last I saw of him, but I heard him go downstairs later."

"Were you locked in all night?"

"No. Richard Hislop's room is next to mine. He came up and spoke through the wall to me. He wanted to unlock the door, but I said better not in case—he—came back. Then, much later, Guy came home. As he passed my door I tapped on it. The key was in the lock and he turned it."

"Did you tell him what had happened?"

"Just that there'd been a row. He only stayed a moment."

"Can you hear the radio from your room?"

She seemed surprised.

"The wireless? Why, yes. Faintly."

"Did you hear it after your father returned to the study?"

"I don't remember."

"Think. While you lay awake all that long time until your brother came home?"

"I'll try. When he came out and found Richard and me, it was not going. They had been working, you see. No, I can't remember hearing it at all unless—wait a moment. Yes. After he had gone back to the study from mother's room I remember there was a loud crash of static. Very loud. Then I think it was quiet for some time. I fancy I heard it again later. Oh, I've remembered something else. After the static my bedside radiator went out. I suppose there was something wrong with the electric supply. That would account for both, wouldn't it? The heater went on again about ten minutes later."

"And did the radio begin again then, do you think?"

"I don't know. I'm very vague about that. It started again sometime before I went to sleep."

"Thank you very much indeed. I won't bother you any longer now."

"All right," said Phillipa calmly, and went away.

Alleyn sent for Chase and questioned him about the rest of the staff and about the discovery of the body. Emily was summoned and dealt with. When she departed, awestruck but complacent, Alleyn turned to the butler.

"Chase," he said, "had your master any peculiar habits?"

"Yes, sir."

"In regard to the wireless?"

"I beg pardon, sir. I thought you meant generally speaking."

"Well, then, generally speaking."

"If I may say so, sir, he was a mass of them."

"How long have you been with him?"

"Two months, sir, and due to leave at the end of this week."

"Oh. Why are you leaving?"

Chase produced the classic remark of his kind.

"There are some things," he said, "that flesh and blood will not stand, sir. One of them's being spoke to like Mr. Tonks spoke to his staff."

"Ah. His peculiar habits, in fact?"

"It's my opinion, sir, he was mad. Stark, staring."

"With regard to the radio. Did he tinker with it?"

"I can't say I've ever noticed, sir. I believe he knew quite a lot about wireless."

"When he tuned the thing, had he any particular method? Any characteristic attitude or gesture?"

"I don't think so, sir. I never noticed, and yet I've often come into the room when he was at it. I can seem to see him now, sir."

"Yes, yes," said Alleyn swiftly. "That's what we want. A clear mental picture. How was it now? Like this?"

In a moment he was across the room and seated in Septimus's chair. He swung round to the cabinet and raised his right hand to the tuning control.

"Like this?"

"No, sir," said Chase promptly, "that's not him at all. Both hands it should be."

"Ah." Up went Alleyn's left hand to the volume control. "More like this?"

"Yes, sir," said Chase slowly. "But there's something else and I can't recollect what it was.

Something he was always doing. It's in the back of my head. You know, sir. Just on the edge of my memory, as you might say."

"I know."

"It's a kind—something—to do with irritation," said Chase slowly.

"Irritation? His?"

"No. It's no good, sir. I can't get it."

"Perhaps later. Now look here, Chase, what happened to all of you last night? All the servants, I mean."

"We were all out, sir. It being Christmas Eve. The mistress sent for me yesterday morning. She said we could take the evening off as soon as I had taken in Mr. Tonks's grog-tray at nine o'clock. So we went," ended Chase simply.

"When?"

"The rest of the staff got away about nine. I left at ten past, sir, and returned about eleven-twenty. The others were back then, and all in bed. I went straight to bed myself, sir."

"You came in by a back door, I suppose?"

"Yes, sir. We've been talking it over. None of us noticed anything unusual."

"Can you hear the wireless in your part of the house?"

"No, sir."

"Well," said Alleyn, looking up from his notes, "that'll do, thank you."

Before Chase reached the door Fox came in.

"Beg pardon, sir," said Fox, "I just want to take a look at the *Radio Times* on the desk."

He bent over the paper, wetted a gigantic thumb, and turned a page.

"That's it, sir," shouted Chase suddenly. "That's what I tried to think of. That's what he was always doing."

"But what?"

"Licking his fingers, sir. It was a habit," said Chase. "That's what he always did when he sat down to the radio. I heard Mr. Hislop tell the doctor it nearly drove him demented, the way the master couldn't touch a thing without first licking his fingers."

"Quite so," said Alleyn. "In about ten minutes, ask Mr. Hislop if he will be good enough

to come in for a moment. That will be all, thank you, Chase."

"Well, sir," remarked Fox when Chase had gone, "if that's the case and what I think's right, it'd certainly make matters worse."

"Good heavens, Fox, what an elaborate remark. What does it mean?"

"If metal knobs were substituted for Bakelite ones and fine wires brought through those holes to make contact, then he'd get a bigger bump if he tuned in with *damp* fingers."

"Yes. And he always used both hands. Fox!"

"Sir."

"Approach the Tonkses again. You haven't left them alone, of course?"

"Bailey's in there making out he's interested in the light switches. He's found the main switchboard under the stairs. There's signs of a blown fuse having been fixed recently. In a cupboard underneath there are odd lengths of flex and so on. Same brand as this on the wireless and the heater."

"Ah, yes. Could the cord from the adapter to the radiator be brought into play?"

"By gum," said Fox, "you're right! That's how it was done, Chief. The heavier flex was cut away from the radiator and shoved through. There was a fire, so he wouldn't want the radiator and wouldn't notice."

"It might have been done that way, certainly, but there's little to prove it. Return to the bereaved Tonkses, my Fox, and ask prettily if any of them remember Septimus's peculiarities when tuning his wireless."

Fox met little Mr. Hislop at the door and left him alone with Alleyn. Phillipa had been right, reflected the Inspector, when she said Richard Hislop was not a noticeable man. He was nondescript. Grey eyes, drab hair; rather pale, rather short, rather insignificant; and yet last night there had flashed up between those two the realisation of love. Romantic but rum, thought Alleyn.

"Do sit down," he said. "I want you, if you will, to tell me what happened between you and Mr. Tonks last evening."

"What happened?"

"Yes. You all dined at eight, I understand. Then you and Mr. Tonks came in here?"

"Yes."

"What did you do?"

"He dictated several letters."

"Anything unusual take place?"

"Oh, no."

"Why did you quarrel?"

"Quarrel!" The quiet voice jumped a tone. "We did not quarrel, Mr. Alleyn."

"Perhaps that was the wrong word. What upset you?"

"Phillipa has told you?"

"Yes. She was wise to do so. What was the matter, Mr. Hislop?"

"Apart from the . . . what she told you . . . Mr. Tonks was a difficult man to please. I often irritated him. I did so last night."

"In what way?"

"In almost every way. He shouted at me. I was startled and nervous, clumsy with papers, and making mistakes. I wasn't well. I blundered and then . . . I . . . I broke down. I have always irritated him. My very mannerisms——"

"Had he no irritating mannerisms, himself?"

"He! My God!"

"What were they?"

"I can't think of anything in particular. It doesn't matter, does it?"

"Anything to do with the wireless, for instance?"

There was a short silence.

"No," said Hislop.

"Was the radio on in here last night, after dinner?"

"For a little while. Not after—after the incident in the hall. At least, I don't think so. I don't remember."

"What did you do after Miss Phillipa and her father had gone upstairs?"

"I followed and listened outside the door for a moment." He had gone very white and had backed away from the desk.

"And then?"

"I heard someone coming. I remembered Dr.

Meadows had told me to ring him up if there was one of the scenes. I returned here and rang him up. He told me to go to my room and listen. If things got any worse I was to telephone again. Otherwise I was to stay in my room. It is next to hers."

"And you did this?" He nodded. "Could you hear what Mr. Tonks said to her?"

"A—a good deal of it."

"What did you hear?"

"He insulted her. Mrs. Tonks was there. I was just thinking of ringing Dr. Meadows up again when she and Mr. Tonks came out and went along the passage. I stayed in my room."

"You did not try to speak to Miss Phillipa?"

"We spoke through the wall. She asked me not to ring Dr. Meadows, but to stay in my room. In a little while, perhaps it was as much as twenty minutes—I really don't know—I heard him come back and go downstairs. I again spoke to Phillipa. She implored me not to do anything and said that she herself would speak to Dr. Meadows in the morning. So I waited a little longer and then went to bed."

"And to sleep?"

"My God, no!"

"Did you hear the wireless again?"

"Yes. At least I heard static."

"Are you an expert on wireless?"

"No. I know the ordinary things. Nothing much."

"How did you come to take this job, Mr. Hislop?"

"I answered an advertisement."

"You are sure you don't remember any particular mannerism of Mr. Tonks's in connection with the radio?"

"No."

"And you can tell me no more about your interview in the study that led to the scene in the hall?"

"No."

"Will you please ask Mrs. Tonks if she will be kind enough to speak to me for a moment?"

"Certainly," said Hislop, and went away.

Septimus's wife came in looking like death.

Alleyn got her to sit down and asked her about her movements on the preceding evening. She said she was feeling unwell and dined in her room. She went to bed immediately afterwards. She heard Septimus yelling at Phillipa and went to Phillipa's room. Septimus accused Mr. Hislop and her daughter of "terrible things." She got as far as this and then broke down quietly. Alleyn was very gentle with her. After a little while he learned that Septimus had gone to her room with her and had continued to speak of "terrible things."

"What sort of things?" asked Alleyn.

"He was not responsible," said Isabel. "He did not know what he was saying. I think he had been drinking."

She thought he had remained with her for perhaps a quarter of an hour. Possibly longer. He left her abruptly and she heard him go along the passage, past Phillipa's door, and presumably downstairs. She had stayed awake for a long time. The wireless could not be heard from her room. Alleyn showed her the curtain knobs, but she seemed quite unable to take in their significance. He let her go, summoned Fox, and went over the whole case.

"What's your idea on the show?" he asked when he had finished.

"Well, sir," said Fox, in his stolid way, "on the face of it the young gentlemen have got alibis. We'll have to check them up, of course, and I don't see we can go much further until we have done so."

"For the moment," said Alleyn, "let us suppose Masters Guy and Arthur to be safely established behind cast-iron alibis. What then?"

"Then we've got the young lady, the old lady, the secretary, and the servants."

"Let us parade them. But first let us go over the wireless game. You'll have to watch me here. I gather that the only way in which the radio could be fixed to give Mr. Tonks his quietus is like this: Control knobs removed. Holes bored in front panel with fine drill. Metal knobs substituted and packed with blotting-paper to insulate them from metal shafts and make them stay put.

Heavier flex from adapter to radiator cut and the ends of the wires pushed through the drilled holes to make contact with the new knobs. Thus we have a positive and negative pole. Mr. Tonks bridges the gap, gets a mighty wallop as the current passes through him to the earth. The switchboard fuse is blown almost immediately. All this is rigged by murderer while Sep was upstairs bullying wife and daughter. Sep revisited study some time after ten-twenty. Whole thing was made ready between ten, when Arthur went out, and the time Sep returned—say, about ten-forty-five. The murderer reappeared, connected radiator with flex, removed wires, changed back knobs, and left the thing tuned in. Now I take it that the burst of static described by Phillipa and Hislop would be caused by the short-circuit that killed our Septimus?"

"That's right. It also affected all the heaters in the house. *Vide* Miss Tonks's radiator."

"Yes. He put all that right again. It would be a simple enough matter for anyone who knew how. He'd just have to fix the fuse on the main switchboard. How long do you say it would take to—what's the horrible word?—to recondition the whole show?"

"M'm," said Fox deeply. "At a guess, sir, fifteen minutes. He'd have to be nippy."

"Yes," agreed Alleyn. "He or she."

"I don't see a female making a success of it," grunted Fox. "Look here, Chief, you know what I'm thinking. Why did Mr. Hislop lie about deceased's habit of licking his thumbs? You say Hislop told you he remembered nothing and Chase says he overheard him saying the trick nearly drove him dippy."

"Exactly," said Alleyn. He was silent for so long that Fox felt moved to utter a discreet cough.

"Eh?" said Alleyn. "Yes, Fox, yes. It'll have to be done." He consulted the telephone directory and dialled a number.

"May I speak to Dr. Meadows? Oh, it's you, is it? Do you remember Mr. Hislop telling you that Septimus Tonks's trick of wetting his fingers nearly drove Hislop demented. Are you

there? You don't? Sure? All right. All right. Hislop rang up at ten-twenty, you said? And you
telephoned him? At eleven. Sure of the times? I
see. I'd be glad if you'd come round. Can you?
Well, do if you can."

He hung up the receiver.

"Get Chase again, will you, Fox?"

Chase, recalled, was most insistent that Mr.
Hislop had spoken about it to Dr. Meadows.

"It was when Mr. Hislop had flu, sir. I went
up with the doctor. Mr. Hislop had a high temperature and was talking very excited. He kept
on and on, saying the master had guessed his
ways had driven him crazy and that the master kept on purposely to aggravate. He said if it
went on much longer he'd . . . he didn't know
what he was talking about, sir, really."

"What did he say he'd do?"

"Well, sir, he said he'd—he'd do something
desperate to the master. But it was only his rambling, sir. I daresay he wouldn't remember anything about it."

"No," said Alleyn, "I daresay he wouldn't."
When Chase had gone he said to Fox: "Go and
find out about those boys and their alibis. See if
they can put you on to a quick means of checking up. Get Master Guy to corroborate Miss
Phillipa's statement that she was locked in her
room."

Fox had been gone for some time and Alleyn
was still busy with his notes when the study door
burst open and in came Dr. Meadows.

"Look here, my giddy sleuth-hound," he
shouted, "what's all this about Hislop? Who says
he disliked Sep's abominable habits?"

"Chase does. And don't bawl at me like that.
I'm worried."

"So am I, blast you. What are you driving
at? You can't imagine that . . . that poor little
broken-down hack is capable of electrocuting
anybody, let alone Sep?"

"I have no imagination," said Alleyn wearily.

"I wish to God I hadn't called you in. If the
wireless killed Sep, it was because he'd monkeyed with it."

"And put it right after it had killed him?"

Dr. Meadows stared at Alleyn in silence.

"Now," said Alleyn, "you've got to give me a
straight answer, Meadows. Did Hislop, while he
was semi-delirious, say that this habit of Tonks's
made him feel like murdering him?"

"I'd forgotten Chase was there," said Dr.
Meadows.

"Yes, you'd forgotten that."

"But even if he did talk wildly, Alleyn, what
of it? Damn it, you can't arrest a man on the
strength of a remark made in delirium."

"I don't propose to do so. Another motive has
come to light."

"You mean—Phips—last night?"

"Did he tell you about that?"

"She whispered something to me this morning. I'm very fond of Phips. My God, are you
sure of your grounds?"

"Yes," said Alleyn. "I'm sorry. I think you'd
better go, Meadows."

"Are you going to arrest him?"

"I have to do my job."

There was a long silence.

"Yes," said Dr. Meadows at last. "You have to
do your job. Goodbye, Alleyn."

Fox returned to say that Guy and Arthur had
never left their parties. He had got hold of two
of their friends. Guy and Mrs. Tonks confirmed
the story of the locked door.

"It's a process of elimination," said Fox. "It
must be the secretary. He fixed the radio while
deceased was upstairs. He must have dodged
back to whisper through the door to Miss Tonks.
I suppose he waited somewhere down here until
he heard deceased blow himself to blazes and
then put everything straight again, leaving the
radio turned on."

Alleyn was silent.

"What do we do now, sir?" asked Fox.

"I want to see the hook inside the front door
where they hang their keys."

Fox, looking dazed, followed his superior to
the little entrance hall.

"Yes, there they are," said Alleyn. He pointed
to a hook with two latch-keys hanging from it.
"You could scarcely miss them. Come on, Fox."

Back in the study they found Hislop with Bailey in attendance.

Hislop looked from one Yard man to another. "I want to know if it's murder."

"We think so," said Alleyn.

"I want you to realise that Phillipa—Miss Tonks—was locked in her room all last night."

"Until her brother came home and unlocked the door," said Alleyn.

"That was too late. He was dead by then."

"How do you know when he died?"

"It must have been when there was that crash of static."

"Mr. Hislop," said Alleyn, "why would you not tell me how much that trick of licking his fingers exasperated you?"

"But—how do you know? I never told anyone."

"You told Dr. Meadows when you were will."

"I don't remember." He stopped short. His lips trembled. Then, suddenly he began to speak.

"Very well. It's true. For two years he's tortured me. You see, he knew something about me. Two years ago when my wife was dying, I took money from the cash-box in that desk. I paid it back and thought he hadn't noticed. He knew all the time. From then on he had me where he wanted me. He used to sit there like a spider. I'd hand him a paper. He'd wet his thumbs with a clicking noise and a sort of complacent grimace. Click, click. Then he'd thumb the papers. He knew it drove me crazy. He'd look at me and then . . . click, click. And then he'd say something about the cash. He'd never quite accused me, just hinted. And I was impotent. You think I'm insane. I'm not. I could have murdered him. Often and often I've thought how I'd do it. Now you think I've done it. I haven't. There's the joke of it. I hadn't the pluck. And last night when Phillipa showed me she cared, it was like Heaven—unbelievable. For the first time since I've been here I *didn't* feel like killing him. And last night someone else *did*!"

He stood there trembling and vehement. Fox and Bailey, who had watched him with bewildered concern, turned to Alleyn. He was about to speak when Chase came in. "A note for you, sir," he said to Alleyn. "It came by hand."

Alleyn opened it and glanced at the first few words. He looked up.

"You may go, Mr. Hislop. Now I've got what I expected—what I fished for."

When Hislop had gone they read the letter.

Dear Alleyn,

Don't arrest Hislop. I did it. Let him go at once if you've arrested him and don't tell Phips you ever suspected him. I was in love with Isabel before she met Sep. I've tried to get her to divorce him, but she wouldn't because of the kids. Damned nonsense, but there's no time to discuss it now. I've got to be quick. He suspected us. He reduced her to a nervous wreck. I was afraid she'd go under altogether. I thought it all out. Some weeks ago I took Phips's key from the hook inside the front door. I had the tools and the flex and wire all ready. I knew where the main switchboard was and the cupboard. I meant to wait until they all went away at the New Year, but last night when Hislop rang me I made up my mind at once. He said the boys and servants were out and Phips locked in her room. I told him to stay in his room and to ring me up in half an hour if things hadn't quieted down. He didn't ring up. I did. No answer, so I knew Sep wasn't in his study.

I came round, let myself in, and listened. All quiet upstairs but the lamp still on in the study, so I knew he would come down again. He'd said he wanted to get the midnight broadcast from somewhere.

I locked myself in and got to work. When Sep was away last year, Arthur did one of his modern monstrosities of painting in the study. He talked about the knobs making good pattern. I noticed then that they were very like the ones on the radio and later on I tried one and saw that it would fit if I packed it up a bit. Well, I did the job just as you worked it out, and it only took twelve minutes. Then I went into the drawing-room and waited.

He came down from Isabel's room and evidently went straight to the radio. I hadn't thought it would make such a row, and half expected someone would come down. No one came. I went back, switched off the wireless, mended the fuse in the main switchboard, using my torch. Then I put everything right in the study.

There was no particular hurry. No one would come in while he was there and I got the radio going as soon as possible to suggest he was at it. I knew I'd be called in when they found him. My idea was to tell them he had died of a stroke. I'd been warning Isabel it might happen at any time. As soon as I saw the burned hand I knew that cat wouldn't jump. I'd have tried to get away with it if Chase hadn't gone round bleating about electrocution and burned fingers. Hislop saw the hand. I daren't do anything but report the case to the police, but I thought you'd never twig the knobs. One up to you.

I might have bluffed through if you hadn't suspected Hislop. Can't let you hang the blighter. I'm enclosing a note to Isabel, who won't forgive me, and an official one for you to use. You'll find me in my bedroom upstairs. I'm using cyanide. It's quick.

I'm sorry, Alleyn. I think you knew, didn't you? I've bungled the whole game, but if you will be a supersleuth . . . Goodbye.

Henry Meadows

THE THIRTEENTH DAY OF CHRISTMAS

Isaac Asimov

ISAAC ASIMOV'S BUSINESS CARD gave his name and the designation "Natural Resource," which may have been an understatement. Of his more than three hundred books, those for which he was most famous were his novels and stories of science fiction, notably *I, Robot* (1950) and the Foundation trilogy, but he also wrote factual books that made it possible for ordinary readers to learn about and better understand such diverse subjects as black holes, the Bible, John Milton, the French Revolution, and the limerick form, at which he was a master. He loved the short story form for mystery fiction and wrote scores of puzzles for the Black Widowers to solve. "The Thirteenth Day of Christmas" was first published in the July 1977 issue of *Ellery Queen's Mystery Magazine,* and first collected in *The Twelve Crimes of Christmas,* edited by Carol-Lynn Rossell Waugh, Martin Harry Greenberg, and Isaac Asimov (New York, Avon, 1981).

The Thirteenth Day of Christmas

ISAAC ASIMOV

THIS WAS ONE YEAR WHEN WE WERE glad Christmas Day was over.

It had been a grim Christmas Eve, and I was just as glad I don't stay awake listening for sleigh bells any more. After all, I'm about ready to get out of junior high. —But then, I kind of stayed awake listening for bombs.

We stayed up till midnight of Christmas Day, though, up till the last minute of it, Mom and I. Then Dad called and said, "Okay, it's over. Nothing's happened. I'll be home as soon as I can."

Mom and I danced around for a while as though Santa Claus had just come, and then, after about an hour, Dad came home and I went to bed and slept fine.

You see, it's special in our house. Dad's a detective on the force, and these days, with terrorists and bombings, it can get pretty hairy. So when, on December twentieth, warnings reached headquarters that there would be a Christmas Day bombing at the Soviet offices in the United Nations, it had to be taken seriously.

The entire force was put on the alert and the F.B.I. came in too. The Soviets had their own security, I guess, but none of it satisfied Dad.

The day before Christmas he said, "If someone is crazy enough to want to plant a bomb and if he's not too worried about getting caught afterwards, he's likely to be able to do it no matter what precautions we take."

Mom said, "I suppose there's no way of knowing who it is."

Dad shook his head. "Letters from newspapers pasted on paper. No fingerprints; only smudges. Common stuff we can't trace, and he said it would be the only warning, so we won't get anything else to work on. What can we do?"

Mom said, "Well, it must be someone who doesn't like the Russians, I guess."

Dad said, "That doesn't narrow it much. Of course, the Soviets say it's a Zionist threat, and we've got to keep an eye on the Jewish Defense League."

I said, "Gee, Dad, that doesn't make much sense. The Jewish people wouldn't pick Christmas Day to do it, would they? It doesn't mean anything to them, and it doesn't mean anything to the Soviet Union, either. They're officially atheist."

Dad said, "You can't reason that out to the Russians. Now, why don't you turn in, because tomorrow may be a bad day all round, Christmas or not."

Then he left, and he was out all Christmas Day, and it was pretty rotten. We didn't even open any presents, just sat listening to the radio, which was tuned to an all-day news station.

Then at midnight, when Dad called and said nothing had happened, we breathed again, but I still forgot to open my presents.

That didn't come till the morning of the

twenty-sixth. We made *that* day Christmas. Dad had a day off, and Mom baked the turkey a day late. It wasn't till after dinner that we talked about it again.

Mom said, "I suppose the person, whoever it was, couldn't find any way of planting the bomb once the Department drew the security strings tight."

Dad smiled, as though he appreciated Mom's loyalty. He said, "I don't think you can make security that tight, but what's the difference? There was no bomb. Maybe it was a bluff. After all, it did disrupt the city a bit and it gave the Soviet people at the United Nations some sleepless nights, I bet. That might have been almost as good for the bomber as letting the bomb go off."

I said, "If he couldn't do it on Christmas Day, maybe he'll do it another time. Maybe he just said Christmas to get everyone keyed up, and then, after they relax, he'll—"

Dad gave me one of his little pushes on the side of my head. "You're a cheerful one, Larry. No, I don't think so. Real bombers value the sense of power. When they say something is going to happen at a certain time, it's got to be that time or it's no fun for them."

I was still suspicious, but the days passed and there was no bombing, and the Department gradually got back to normal. The F.B.I. left, and even the Soviet people seemed to forget about it, according to Dad.

On January second the Christmas–New Year's vacation was over and I went back to school, and we started rehearsing our Christmas pageant. We didn't call it that, of course, because we're not supposed to have religious celebrations at school, what with the separation of church and state. We just made an elaborate show out of the song, "The Twelve Days of Christmas," which doesn't have any religion to it—just presents.

There were twelve of us kids, each one singing a particular line every time it came up and then coming in all together on the "partridge in a pear tree." I was number five, singing "Five gold rings" because I was still a boy soprano and I could hit that high note pretty nicely, if I do say so myself.

Some kids didn't know why Christmas had twelve days, but I explained that on the twelfth day after Christmas, which was January sixth, the Three Wise Men arrived with gifts for the Christ child. Naturally, it was on January sixth that we put on the show in the auditorium, with as many parents there as wanted to come.

Dad got a few hours off and was sitting in the audience with Mom. I could see him getting set to hear his son's clear high note for the last time because next year my voice changes or I know the reason why.

Did you ever get an idea in the middle of a stage show and have to continue, no matter what?

We were only on the second day, with its "two turtledoves," when I thought, "Oh, my, it's the *thirteenth* day of Christmas." The whole world was shaking around me and I couldn't do a thing but stay on the stage and sing about five gold rings.

I didn't think they'd ever get to those "twelve drummers drumming." It was like having itching powder on instead of underwear—I couldn't stand still. Then, when the last note was out, while they were still applauding, I broke away, went jumping down the steps from the platform and up the aisle, calling, "Dad!"

He looked startled, but I grabbed him, and I think I was babbling so fast that he could hardly understand.

I said, "Dad, Christmas isn't the same day everywhere. It could be one of the Soviet's own people. They're officially atheist, but maybe one of them is religious and he wants to place the bomb for that reason. Only he would be a member of the *Russian* Orthodox Church. They don't go by our calendar."

"What?" said Dad, looking as though he didn't understand a word I was saying.

"It's *so*, Dad. I read about it. The Russian

Orthodox Church is still on the Julian Calendar, which the West gave up for the Gregorian Calendar centuries ago. The Julian Calendar is thirteen days behind ours. The Russian Orthodox Christmas is on *their* December twenty-fifth, which is *our* January seventh. It's *tomorrow*."

He didn't believe me, just like that. He looked it up in the almanac, then he called up someone in the Department who was Russian Orthodox.

He was able to get the Department moving again. They talked to the Soviets, and once the Soviets stopped talking about Zionists and looked at themselves, they got the man. I don't know what they did with him, but there was no bombing on the thirteenth day of Christmas, either.

The Department wanted to give me a new bicycle for Christmas, but I turned it down. I told them I was just doing my duty.

THE CHRISTMAS KITTEN

Ed Gorman

DO NOT EXPECT a cavity-inducing, sweet story about a cute little kitten in the manner of Lilian Jackson Braun or Rita Mae Brown; that simply isn't the type of story the versatile and prolific Ed Gorman writes. While most of his work has been in the mystery genre, he has also written many other types of fiction, including horror (he was nominated for Bram Stoker Awards from the Horror Writers Association) and westerns (he won a Spur Award from the Western Writers of America). He also has been nominated for two Edgar Awards by the Mystery Writers of America, for Best Short Story for "Prisoners" in 1991 and (with others) Best Biographical/Critical Work for *The Fine Art of Murder* in 1994. He was also honored with MWA's Ellery Queen Award in 2003, given primarily for his mystery fiction, his long editorship of *Mystery Scene Magazine,* and his many anthologies. "The Christmas Kitten" was first published in the January 1997 issue of *Ellery Queen's Mystery Magazine.*

The Christmas Kitten

ED GORMAN

1.

"She in a good mood?" I said.

The lovely and elegant Pamela Forrest looked up at me as if I'd suggested that there really *was* a Santa Claus.

"Now why would she go and do a foolish thing like that, McCain?" She smiled.

"Oh, I guess because—"

"Because it's the Christmas season, and most people are in good moods?"

"Yeah, something like that."

"Well, not our Judge Whitney."

"At least she's consistent," I said.

I had been summoned, as usual, from my law practice, where I'd been working the phones, trying to get my few clients to pay their bills. I had a 1951 Ford ragtop to support. And dreams of taking the beautiful Pamela Forrest to see the Platters concert when they were in Des Moines next month.

"You thought any more about the Platters concert?" I said.

"Oh, McCain, now why'd you have to go and bring *that* up?"

"I just thought—"

"You know how much I love the Platters. But I really don't think it's a good idea for the two of us to go out again." She gave me a melancholy little smile. "Now I probably went and ruined your holidays and I'm sorry. You know I like you, Cody, it's just—Stew."

This was Christmas 1959 and I'd been trying since at least Christmas 1957 to get Pamela to go out with me. But we had a problem—while I loved Pamela, Pamela loved Stewart, and Stewart happened to be not only a former football star at the university but also the heir to the town's third biggest fortune.

Her intercom buzzed. "Is he out there pestering you again, Pamela?"

"No, Your Honor."

"Tell him to get his butt in here."

"Yes, Your Honor."

"And call my cousin John and tell him I'll be there around three this afternoon."

"Yes, Your Honor."

"And remind me to pick up my dry cleaning."

"Yes, Your Honor."

"And tell McCain to get his butt in here. Or did I already say that?"

"You already said that, Your Honor."

I bade goodbye to the lovely and elegant Pamela Forrest and went in to meet my master.

"You know what he did this time?" Judge Eleanor Whitney said three seconds after I crossed her threshold.

The "he" could only refer to one person in the town of Black River Falls, Iowa. And that would be our esteemed chief of police, Cliff Sykes, Jr., who has this terrible habit of arresting people for murders they didn't commit and giving Judge Whitney the pleasure of pointing out the error of his ways.

A little over a hundred years ago, Judge Whitney's family dragged a lot of money out here from the East and founded this town. They pretty much ran it until World War II, a catastrophic event that helped make Cliff Sykes, Sr., a rich and powerful man in the local wartime construction business. Sykes, Sr., used his money to put his own members on the town council, just the way the Whitneys had always done. He also started to bribe and coerce the rest of the town into doing things his way. Judge Whitney saw him as a crude outlander, of course. Where her family was conversant with Verdi, Vermeer, and Tolstoy, the Sykes family took as cultural icons Ma and Pa Kettle and Francis the Talking Mule, the same characters I go to see at the drive-in whenever possible.

Anyway, the one bit of town management the Sykes family couldn't get to was Judge Whitney's court. Every time Cliff Sykes, Jr., arrested somebody for murder, the judge called me up and put me to work. In addition to being an attorney, I'm taking extension courses in criminology. The judge thinks this qualifies me as her very own staff private investigator, so whenever she wants something looked into, she calls me. And I'm glad she does. She's my only source of steady income.

"He arrested my cousin John's son, Rick. Charged him with murdering his girlfriend. That stupid ass."

Now in a world of seventh-ton crime-solving geniuses, and lady owners of investigative firms who go two hundred pounds and are as bristly as barbed wire, Judge Eleanor Whitney is actually a small, trim, and very handsome woman. And she knows how to dress herself. Today she wore a brown suede blazer, a crisp button-down, white-collar shirt, and dark fitted slacks. Inside the open collar of the shirt was a green silk scarf that complemented the green of her eyes perfectly.

She was hiked on the edge of the desk, right next to an ample supply of rubber bands.

"Sit down, McCain."

"He didn't do it."

"I said sit down. You know I hate it when you stand."

I sat down.

"He didn't do it," I said.

"Exactly. He didn't do it."

"You know, one of these times you're bound to be wrong. I mean, just by the odds, Sykes is bound to be right."

Which is what I say every time she gives me an assignment.

"Well, he isn't right this time."

Which is what she says every time I say the thing about the odds.

"His girlfriend was Linda Palmer, I take it."

"Right."

"The one found in her apartment?"

She nodded.

"What's Sykes's evidence?"

"Three neighbors saw Rick running away from the apartment house the night before last."

She launched one of her rubber bands at me, thumb and forefinger style, like a pistol. She likes to see if I'll flinch when the rubber band comes within an eighth of an inch of my ear. I try never to give her that satisfaction.

"He examine Rick's car and clothes?"

"You mean fibers and blood, things like that?"

"Yeah."

She smirked. "You think Sykes would be smart enough to do something like that?"

"I guess you've got a point."

She stood up and started to pace.

You'll note that I am not permitted this luxury, standing and pacing, but for her it is fine. She is, after all, mistress of the universe.

"I just keep thinking of John. The poor guy. He's a very good man."

"I know."

"And it's going to be a pretty bleak Christmas without Rick there. I'll have to invite him out to the house."

Which was not an invitation *I* usually wanted. The judge kept a considerable number of rattlesnakes in glass cages on the first floor of her house. I was always waiting for one of them to get loose.

I stood up. "I'll get right on it." I couldn't recall ever seeing the judge in such a pensive mood. Usually, when she's going to war with Cliff Sykes, Jr., she's positively ecstatic.

But when her cousin was involved, and first cousin at that, I supposed even Judge Whitney—a woman who had buried three husbands, and who frequently golfed with President Eisenhower when he was in the Midwest, and who had been ogled by Khrushchev when he visited a nearby Iowa farm—I supposed even Judge Whitney had her melancholy moments.

She came back to her desk, perched on the edge of it, loaded up another rubber band, and shot it at me.

"Your nerves are getting better, McCain," she said. "You don't twitch as much as you used to."

"I'll take that as an example of your Christmas cheer," I said. "You noting that I don't twitch as much as I used to, I mean."

Then she glowered at me. "Nail his butt to the wall, McCain. My family's honor is at stake here. Rick's a hothead but he's not a killer. He cares too much about the family name to soil it that way."

Thus basking in the glow of Christmas spirit, not to mention a wee bit of patrician hubris, I took my leave of the handsome Judge Whitney.

2.

Red Ford ragtops can get a little cold around Christmas time. I had everything buttoned down but winter winds still whacked the car every few yards or so.

The city park was filled with snowmen and Christmas angels as Bing Crosby and Perry Como and Johnny Mathis sang holiday songs over the loudspeakers lining the merchant blocks. I could remember being a kid in the holiday concerts in the park. People stood there in the glow of Christmas-tree lights listening to us sing for a good hour. I always kept warm by staring at the girl I had a crush on that particular year. Even back then, I gravitated toward the ones who didn't want me. I guess that's why my favorite holiday song is "Blue Christmas" by Elvis. It's really depressing, which gives it a certain honesty for romantics like myself.

I pulled in the drive of Linda Palmer's apartment house. It was a box with two apartments up, two down. There was a gravel parking lot in the rear. The front door was hung with holly and a plastic bust of Santa Claus.

Inside, in the vestibule area with the mailboxes, I heard Patti Page singing a Christmas song, and I got sentimental about Pamela Forrest again. During one of the times that she'd given up on good old Stewart, she'd gone out with me a few times. The dates hadn't meant much to her, but I looked back on them as the halcyon period of my entire life, when giants walked the earth and you could cut off slices of sunbeams and sell them as gold.

"Hi," I said as soon as the music was turned down and the door opened up.

The young woman who answered the bell to the apartment opposite Linda Palmer's was cute in a dungaree-doll sort of way—ponytail and Pat Boone sweatshirt and jeans rolled up to mid calf. "Hi."

"My name's McCain."

"I'm Bobbi Thomas. Aren't you Judge Whitney's assistant?"

"Well, sort of."

"So you're here about—"

"Linda Palmer."

"Poor Linda," she said, and made a sad face. "It's scary living here now. I mean, if it can happen to Linda—"

She was about to finish her sentence when two things happened at once. A tiny calico kitten came charging out of her apartment between her legs, and a tall man in a gray uniform with DERBY CLEANERS sewn on his cap walked in and handed her a package wrapped in clear plastic. Inside was a shaggy gray throw rug and a shaggy white one and a shaggy fawn-colored one.

"Appreciate your business, miss," the DERBY man said, and left.

I mostly watched the kitten. She was a sweetie. She walked straight over to the door facing Bobbi's. The card in the slot still read LINDA PALMER.

"You mind picking her up and bringing her in? I just need to put this dry cleaning away."

Ten minutes later, the three of us sat in her living room. I say three because the kitten, who'd been introduced to me as Sophia, sat in my lap and sniffed my coffee cup whenever I raised it to drink. The apartment was small but nicely kept. The floors were oak and not spoiled by wall-to-wall carpeting. She took the throw rugs from the plastic dry-cleaning wrap and spread them in front of the fireplace.

"They get so dirty," she explained as she straightened the rugs, then walked over and sat down.

Then she nodded to the kitten. "We just found her downstairs in the laundry room one day. There's a small TV down there and Linda and I liked to sit down there and smoke cigarettes and drink Cokes and watch *Bandstand*. Do you think Dick Clark's a crook? My boyfriend does." She shrugged. "Ex boyfriend. We broke up." She tried again: "So do you think Dick Clark's a crook?"

A disc jockey named Alan Freed was in trouble with federal authorities for allegedly taking bribes to play certain songs on his radio show. Freed didn't have enough power to make a hit record and people felt he was being used as a scapegoat. On the other hand, Dick Clark *did* have the power to make or break a hit record (Lord, did he, with *American Bandstand* on ninety minutes several afternoons a week), but the feds had rather curiously avoided investigating him in any serious way.

"Could be," I said. "But I guess I'd rather talk about Linda."

She looked sad again. "I guess that's why I was talking about Dick Clark. So we wouldn't *have* to talk about Linda."

"I'm sorry."

She sighed. "I just have to get used to it, I guess." Then she looked at Sophia. "Isn't she sweet? We called her our Christmas kitten."

"She sure is."

"That's what I started to tell you. One day Linda and I were downstairs and there Sophia was. Just this little lost kitten. So we both sort of adopted her. We'd leave our doors open so Sophia could just wander back and forth between apartments. Sometimes she slept here, sometimes she slept over there." She raised her eyes from the kitten and looked at me. "He killed her."

"Rick?"

"Uh-huh."

"Why do you say that?"

"Why do I say that? Are you kidding? You should've seen the arguments they had."

"He ever hit her?"

"Not that I know of."

"He ever *threaten* her?"

"All the time."

"You know why?" I said.

"Because he was so jealous of her. He used to sit across the street at night and just watch her front window. He'd sit there for hours."

"Would she be in there at the time?"

"Oh, sure. He always claimed she had this big dating life on the side but she never did."

"Anything special happen lately between them?"

"You mean you don't know?"

"I guess not."

"She gave him back his engagement ring."

"And that—"

"He smashed out her bedroom window with his fist. This was in the middle of the night and he was really drunk. I called the police on him. Just because he's a Whitney doesn't mean he can break the rules anytime he feels like it."

I'd been going to ask her if she was from around here but the resentment in her voice about the Whitneys answered my question. The Whitneys had been the valley's most imperious family for a little more than a century now.

"Did the police come?"

"Sykes himself."

"And he did what?"

"Arrested him. Took him in." She gave me a significant look with her deep blue eyes. "He was relishing every minute, too. A Sykes arresting a Whitney, I mean. He was having a blast."

So then I asked her about the night of the murder. We spent twenty minutes on the subject but I didn't learn much. She'd been in her apartment all night watching TV and hadn't heard anything untoward. But when she got up to go to work in the morning and didn't hear Linda moving around in her apartment, she knocked, and, when there wasn't any answer, went in. Linda lay dead, the left side of her head smashed in, sprawled in a white bra and half-slip in front of the fireplace that was just like Bobbi's.

"Maybe I had my TV up too loud," Bobbi said. "I love westerns and it was *Gunsmoke* night. It was a good one, too. But I keep thinking that maybe if I hadn't played the TV so loud, I could've heard her—"

I shook my head. "Don't start doing that to yourself, Bobbi, or it'll never end. If only I'd done this, if only I'd done that. You did everything you could."

She sighed. "I guess you're right."

"Mind one more question?"

She shrugged and smiled. "You can see I've got a pretty busy social calendar."

"I want to try and take Rick out of the picture for a minute. Will you try?"

"You mean as a suspect?"

"Right."

"I'll try."

"All right. Now, who are three people who had something against Linda—or Rick?"

"Why Rick?"

"Because maybe the killer wanted to make it *look* as if Rick did it."

"Oh, I see." Then: "I'd have to say Gwen. Gwen Dawes. She was Rick's former girlfriend.

She always blamed Linda for taking him away. You know, they hadn't been going together all that long, Rick and Linda, I mean. Gwen would still kind of pick arguments with her when she'd see them in public places."

"Gwen ever come over here and pick an argument?"

"Once, I guess."

"Remember when?"

"Couple months ago, maybe."

"What happened?"

"Nothing much. She and a couple of girl-friends were pretty drunk, and they came up on the front porch and started writing things on the wall. It was juvenile stuff. Most of us graduated from high school two years ago but we're still all kids, if you see what I mean."

I wrote Gwen's name down and said, "Anybody else who bothered Linda?"

"Paul Walters, for sure."

"Paul Walters?"

"*Her* old boyfriend. He used to wait until Rick left at night and then he'd come over and pick a fight with her."

"Would she let him in?"

"Sometimes. Then there was Millie Styles. The wife of the man Linda worked for."

"Why didn't she like Linda?"

"She accused Linda of trying to steal her husband."

"Was she?"

"You had to know Linda."

"I see."

"She wasn't a rip or anything."

"Rip?"

"You know, whore."

"But she—"

"—could be very flirtatious."

"More than flirtatious?"

She shrugged. "Sometimes."

"Maybe with Mr. Styles?"

"Maybe. He's an awfully handsome guy. He looks like Fabian."

She wasn't kidding. They weren't very far out of high school.

That was when I felt a scratching on my chin

and I looked straight down into the eager, earnest, and heartbreakingly sweet face of Sophia.

"She likes to kiss noses the way Eskimos do," Bobbi said.

We kissed noses.

Then I set Sophia down and she promptly put a paw in my coffee cup.

"Sophia!" Bobbi said. "She's always putting her paw in wet things. She's obsessed, the little devil."

Sophia paid us no attention. Tail switching, she walked across the coffee table, her left front paw leaving coffee imprints on the surface.

I stood up. "I appreciate this, Bobbi."

"You can save yourself some work."

"How would I do that?"

"There's a skating party tonight. Everybody we've talked about is going to be there." She gave me another one of her significant looks. "Including me."

"Then I guess that's a pretty good reason to go, isn't it?" I said.

"Starts at six-thirty. It'll be very dark by then. You know how to skate?"

I smiled. "I wouldn't exactly call it skating."

"Then what would you call it?"

"Falling down is the term that comes to mind," I said.

3.

Rick Whitney was even harder to love than his aunt.

"When I get out of this place, I'm going to take that hillbilly and push him off Indian Cliff."

In the past five minutes, Rick Whitney, of the long blond locks and relentlessly arrogant blue-eyed good looks, had also threatened to shoot, stab, and set fire to our beloved chief of police, Cliff Sykes, Jr. As an attorney, I wouldn't advise any of my clients to express such thoughts, especially when they were in custody, being held for premeditated murder (or as my doctor friend Stan Greenbaum likes to say, "pre-medicated murder"). "Rick, we're not getting anywhere."

He turned on me again. He'd turned on me three or four times already, pushing his face at me, jabbing his finger at me.

"Do you know what it's like for a Whitney to be in jail? Why, if my grandfather were still alive, he'd come down here and shoot Sykes right on the spot."

"Rick?"

"What?"

"Sit down and shut up."

"You're telling me to shut up?"

"Uh-huh. And to sit down."

"I don't take orders from people like you."

I stood up. "Fine. Then I'll leave."

He started to say something nasty, but just then a cloud passed over the sun and the six cells on the second floor of the police station got darker.

He said, "I'll sit down."

"And shut up?"

It was a difficult moment for a Whitney. Humility is even tougher for them than having a tooth pulled. "And shut up."

So we sat down, him on the wobbly cot across from my wobbly cot, and we talked as two drunks three cells away pretended they weren't listening to us.

"A Mrs. Mawbry who lives across the street saw you running out to your car about eleven p.m. the night of the murder. Dr. Mattingly puts the time of death at right around that time."

"She's lying."

"You know better than that."

"They just hate me because I'm a Whitney."

It's not easy going through life being of a superior species, especially when all the little people hate you for it.

"You've got fifteen seconds," I said.

"For what?"

"To stop stalling and tell me the truth. You went to the apartment and found her dead, didn't you? And then you ran away."

I watched the faces of the two eavesdropping winos. It was either stay up here in the cells, or use the room downstairs that I was sure Cliff Sykes, Jr., had bugged.

"Ten seconds."

He sighed and said, "Yeah, I found her. But I didn't kill her."

"You sure of that?"

He looked startled. "What the hell's that supposed to mean?"

"It means were you drinking that evening, and did you have any sort of alcoholic blackout? You've been known to tip a few."

"I had a couple beers earlier. That was it. No alcoholic blackout."

"All right," I said. "Now tell me the rest of it."

"Wonder if the state'll pass that new law," Chief Cliff Sykes, Jr., said to me as I was leaving the police station by the back door.

"I didn't know that you kept up on the law, Cliff, Jr."

He hated it when I added the Jr. to his name, but since he was about to do a little picking on me, I decided to do a little picking on him. With too much Brylcreem—Cliff, Jr., apparently never heard the part of the jingle that goes "A little dab'll do ya"—and his wiry moustache, he looks like a bar rat all duded up for Saturday night. He wears a khaki uniform that Warner Brothers must have rejected for an Errol Flynn western. The epaulets alone must weigh twenty-five pounds each.

"Yep, next year they're goin' to start fryin' convicts instead of hanging them."

The past few years in Iowa, we'd been debating which was the more humane way to shuffle off this mortal coil. At least when the state decides to be the shuffler and make you the shufflee.

"And I'll bet you think that Rick Whitney is going to be one of the first to sit in the electric chair, right?"

He smiled his rat smile, sucked his toothpick a little deeper into his mouth. "You said it, I didn't."

There's a saying around town that money didn't change the Sykes family any—they're still the same mean, stupid, dishonest, and uncouth people they've always been.

"Well, I hate to spoil your fun, Cliff, Jr., but he's going to be out of here by tomorrow night."

He sucked on his toothpick some more. "You and what army is gonna take him out of here?"

"Won't take an army, Cliff, Jr., I'll just find the guilty party and Rick'll walk right out of here."

He shook his head. "He thinks his piss don't stink because he's a Whitney. This time he's wrong."

4.

The way I figure it, any idiot can learn to skate standing up. It takes a lot more creativity and perseverance to skate on your knees and your butt and your back.

I was putting on quite a show. Even five-year-olds were pointing at me and giggling. One of them had an adult face pasted on his tiny body. I wanted to give him the finger but I figured that probably wouldn't look quite right, me being twenty-six and an attorney and all.

Everything looked pretty tonight, gray smoke curling from the big log cabin where people hung out putting on skates and drinking hot cider and warming themselves in front of the fireplace. Christmas music played over the loudspeakers, and every few minutes you'd see a dog come skidding across the ice to meet up with its owners. Tots in snowsuits looking like Martians toddled across the ice in the wake of their parents.

The skaters seemed to come in four types: the competitive skaters who were just out tonight to hone their skills; the show-offs who kept holding their girlfriends over their heads; the lovers who were melting the ice with their scorching looks; and the junior-high kids who kept trying to knock everybody down accidentally. I guess I should add the seniors; they were the most fun to watch, all gray hair and dignity as they made their way across the ice arm in arm. They probably came here thirty or forty years ago when Model-Ts had lined the parking area, and when the music had been supplied by Rudy Vallee. They were elegant and touching to watch here on the skating rink tonight.

I stayed to the outside of the rink. I kept moving because it was at most ten above zero. Falling down kept me pretty warm, too.

I was just getting up from a spill when I saw a Levi'd leg—two Levi'd legs—standing behind me. My eyes followed the line of legs upwards and there she was. It was sort of like a dream, actually, a slightly painful one because I'd dreamt it so often and so uselessly.

There stood the beautiful and elegant Pamela Forrest. In her white woolen beret, red cable-knit sweater, and jeans, she was the embodiment of every silly and precious holiday feeling. She was even smiling.

"Well, I'm sure glad you're here," she said.

"You mean because you want to go out?"

"No, I mean because I'm glad there's somebody who's even a worse skater than I am."

"Oh," I said.

She put out a hand and helped me up. I brushed the flesh of her arm—and let my nostrils be filled with the scent of her perfume—and I got so weak momentarily I was afraid I was going to fall right back down.

"You have a date?"

I shook my head. "Still doing some work for Judge Whitney."

She gave my arm a squeeze. "Just between you and me, McCain, I hope you solve one of these cases yourself someday."

She was referring to the fact that in every case I'd worked on, Judge Whitney always seemed to solve it just as I was starting to figure out who the actual culprit was. I had a feeling, though, that this case I'd figure out all by my lonesome.

"I don't think I've ever seen Judge Whitney as upset as she was today," I said.

"I'm worried about her. This thing with Rick, I mean. It isn't just going up against the Sykes family this time. The family honor's at stake."

I looked at her. "You have a date?"

And then she looked sad, and I knew what her answer was going to be.

"Not exactly."

"Ah. But Stewart's going to be here."

"I think so. I'm told he comes here sometimes."

"Boy, you're just as pathetic as I am."

"Well, that's a nice thing to say."

"You can't have him any more than I can have you. But neither one of us can give it up, can we?"

I took her arm and we skated. We actually did a lot better as a team than we did individually. I was going to mention that to her but I figured she would think I was just being corny and coming on to her in my usual clumsy way. If only I were as slick as Elvis in those movies of his where he sings a couple of songs and beats the crap out of every bad guy in town, working in a few lip locks with nubile females in the interim.

I didn't recognize them at first. Their skating costumes, so dark and tight and severe, gave them the aspect of Russian ballet artists. People whispered at them as they soared past, and it was whispers they wanted.

David and Millie Styles were the town's "artistic fugitives," as one of the purpler of the paper's writers wrote once. Twice a year they ventured to New York to bring radical new items back to their interior decorating "salon," as they called it, and they usually brought back a lot of even more radical attitudes and poses. Millie had once been quoted in the paper as saying that we should have an "All Nude Day" twice a year in town; and David was always standing on the library steps waving copies of banned books in the air and demanding that they be returned to library shelves. The thing was, I agreed with the message, it was the messengers I didn't care for. They were wealthy, attractive dabblers who loved to outrage and shock. In a big city, nobody would've paid them any attention. Out here, they were celebrities.

"God, they look great, don't they?" Pamela said.

"If you like the style."

"Skin-tight, all-black skating outfits. Who else would've thought of something like that?"

"You look a lot better."

She favored me with a forehead kiss. "Oh God, McCain, I sure wish I could fall in love with you."

"I wish you could, too."

"But the heart has its own logic."

"That sounds familiar."

"*Peyton Place.*"

"That's right."

Peyton Place had swept through town two years ago like an army bent on destroying everything in its path. The fundamentalists not only tried to get it out of the library, they tried to ban its sale in paperback. The town literary lions, such as the Styleses, were strangely moot. They did not want to be seen defending something as plebeian as Grace Metalious's book. I was in a minority. I not only liked it, I thought it was a good book. A true one, as Hemingway often said.

On the far side of the rink, I saw David Styles skate away from his wife and head for the warming cabin.

She skated on alone.

"Excuse me. I'll be back," I said.

It took me two spills and three near-spills to reach Millie Styles.

"Evening," I said.

"Oh," she said, staring at me. "You." Apparently I looked like something her dog had just dragged in from the backyard. Something not quite dead yet.

"I wondered if we could talk."

"What in God's name would you and I have to talk about, McCain?"

"Why you killed Linda Palmer the other night."

She tried to slap me but fortunately I was going into one of my periodic dives so her slap missed me by half a foot.

I did reach out and grab her arm to steady myself, however.

"Leave me alone," she said.

"Did you find out that Linda and David were sleeping together?"

From the look in her eyes, I could see that she had. I kept thinking about what Bobbi Thomas had said, how Linda was flirtatious.

And for the first time, I felt something human for the striking if not quite pretty woman wearing too much makeup and way too many New York poses. Pain showed in her eyes. I actually felt a smidge of pity for her.

Her husband appeared magically. "Is something wrong?" Seeing the hurt in his wife's eyes, he had only scorn for me. He put a tender arm around her. "You get the hell out of here, McCain." He sounded almost paternal, he was so protective of her.

"And leave me alone," she said again, and skated away so quickly that there was no way I could possibly catch her.

Then Pamela was there again, sliding her arm through mine.

"You have to help me, McCain," she said.

"Help you what?"

"Help me look like I'm having a wonderful time."

Then I saw Stew McGinley, former college football star and idle rich boy, skating around the rink with his girlfriend, the relentlessly cheery and relentlessly gorgeous Cindy Parkhurst, who had been a cheerleader at State the same year Stew was All Big-Eight.

This was the eternal triangle: I was in love with Pamela; Pamela was in love with Stew; and Stew was in love with Cindy, who not only came from the same class—right below the Whitneys—but had even more money than Stew did, and not only that but had twice done the unthinkable. She'd broken up with Stew and started dating somebody else. This was something Stew wasn't used to. *He* was supposed to do the breaking up. Stew was hooked, he was.

They were both dressed in white costumes tonight, and looked as if they would soon be on *The Ed Sullivan Show* for no other reason than simply existing.

"I guess I don't know how to do that," I said.

"How to do what?"

"How to help you look like you're having a wonderful time."

"I'm going to say something and then you throw your head back and break out laughing." She looked at me. "Ready?"

"Ready."

She said something I couldn't hear and then I threw my head back and pantomimed laughing.

I had the sense that I actually did it pretty well—after watching all those Tony Curtis movies at the drive-in, I was bound to pick up at least a few pointers about acting—but the whole thing was moot because Stew and Cindy were gazing into each other's eyes and paying no attention to us whatsoever.

"There goes my Academy Award," I said.

We tried skating again, both of us wobbling and waffling along, when I saw Paul Walters standing by the warming house smoking a cigarette. He was apparently one of those guys who didn't skate but liked to come to the rink and look at all the participants so he could feel superior to them. A sissy sport, I could hear him thinking.

"I'll be back," I said.

By the time I got to the warming house, Paul Walters had been joined by Gwen Dawes. Just as Paul was the dead girl's old boyfriend, Gwen was the suspect's old girlfriend. Those little towns in Kentucky where sisters marry brothers had nothing on our own cozy little community.

Just as I reached them, Gwen, an appealing if slightly overweight redhead, pulled Paul's face down to hers and kissed him. He kissed her right back.

"Hi," I said, as they started to separate.

They both looked at me as if I had just dropped down from a UFO.

"Oh, you're Cody McCain," Walters said. He was tall, sinewy, and wore the official uniform of juvenile delinquents everywhere—leather jacket, jeans, engineering boots. He put his Elvis sneer on right after he brushed his teeth in the morning.

"Right. I wondered if we could maybe talk a little."

"'We'?" he said.

"Yeah. The three of us."

"About what?"

I looked around. I didn't want eavesdroppers.

"About Linda Palmer."

"My one night off a week and I have to put up with this crap," he said.

"She was a bitch," Gwen Dawes said.

"Hey, c'mon, she's dead," Walters said.

"Yeah, and that's just what she deserved, too."

"You wouldn't happened to have killed her, would you, Gwen?" I said.

"That's why he's here, Paul. He thinks we did it."

"Right now," I said, "I'd be more inclined to say *you* did it."

"He works for Whitney," Walters said. "I forgot that. He's some kind of investigator."

She said, "He's trying to prove that Rick didn't kill her. That's why he's here."

"You two can account for yourselves between the hours of ten and midnight the night of the murder?"

Gwen eased her arm around his waist. "I sure can. He was at my place."

I looked right at her. "He just said this was his only night off. Where do you work, Paul?"

Now that I'd caught them in a lie, he'd lost some of his poise.

"Over at the tire factory."

"You were there the night of the murder?"

"I was—sick."

I watched his face.

"Were you with Gwen?"

"No—I was just riding around."

"And maybe stopped over at Linda's the way you sometimes did?"

He looked at Gwen then back at me.

"No, I—I was just riding around."

He was as bad a liar as Gwen was.

"And I was home," Gwen said, "in case you're interested."

"Nobody with you?"

She gave Walters another squeeze.

"The only person I want with me is Paul."

She took his hand, held it tight. She was protecting him the way Mr. Styles had just protected Mrs. Styles. And as I watched her now, it gave me an idea about how I could smoke out the real killer. I wouldn't go directly for the killer—I'd go for the protector.

"Excuse us," Gwen said, and pushed past me, tugging Paul along in her wake.

I spent the next few minutes looking for Pamela. I finally found her sitting over in the empty bleachers that are used for speed-skating fans every Sunday when the ice is hard enough for competition.

"You okay?"

She looked up at me with those eyes and I nearly went over backwards. She has that effect on me, much as I sometimes wished she didn't.

"You know something, McCain?" she said.

"What?"

"There's a good chance that Stew is never going to change his mind and fall in love with me."

"And there's a good chance that *you're* never going to change *your* mind and fall in love with *me*."

"Oh, McCain," she said, and stood up, the whole lithe, elegant length of her. She slipped her arm in mine again and said, "Let's not talk anymore, all right? Let's just skate."

And skate we did.

5.

When I got home that night, I called Judge Whitney and told her everything I'd learned, from my meeting with Bobbi Thomas to meeting the two couples at the ice rink tonight.

As usual, she made me go over everything to the point that it got irritating. I pictured her on the other end of the phone, sitting there in her dressing gown and shooting rubber bands at an imaginary me across from her.

"Get some rest, McCain," she said. "You sound like you need it."

It was true. I was tired and I probably sounded tired. I tried watching TV. *Mike Hammer* was on at 10:30. I buy all the Mickey Spillane books as soon as they come out. I think Darren McGavin does a great job with Hammer. But tonight the show couldn't quite hold my interest.

I kept thinking about my plan—

What if I actually went through with it?

If the judge found out, she'd probably say it was corny, like something out of a Miss Marple movie. (The only mysteries the judge likes are by Rex Stout and Margery Allingham.)

But so what if it was corny—if it turned up the actual culprit?

I spent the next two hours sitting at my desk in my underwear typing up notes.

Some of them were too cute, some of them were too long, some of them didn't make a hell of a lot of sense.

Finally, I settled on:

If you really love you-know-who, then you'll meet me in Linda Palmer's apt. tonight at 9:00 o'clock.

A Friend

Then I addressed two envelopes, one to David Styles and one to Gwen Dawes, for delivery tomorrow.

I figured that they each suspected their mates of committing the murder, and therefore whoever showed up tomorrow night had to answer some hard questions.

It was going to feel good, to actually beat Judge Whitney to the solution of a murder. I mean, I don't have that big an ego, I really don't, but I'd worked on ten cases for her now, and she'd solved each one.

6.

I dropped off the notes in the proper mailboxes before going to work, then I spent the remainder of the day calling clients to remind them that they, ahem, owed me money. They had a lot of wonderful excuses for not paying me. Several of them could have great careers as science fiction novelists if they'd only give it half a chance.

I called Pamela three times, pretending I wanted to speak to Judge Whitney.

"She wrapped up court early this morning," Pamela told me on the second call. "Since then, she's been barricaded in her chambers. She sent me out the first time for lunch—a ham-and-cheese on rye with very hot mustard—and the second time for rubber bands. She ran out."

"Why doesn't she just pick them up off the floor?"

"She doesn't like to reuse them."

"Ah."

"Says it's not the same."

After work, I stopped by the A&W for a burger, fries, and root-beer float. Another well-balanced Cody McCain meal.

Dusk was purple and lingering and chill, clear pure Midwestern stars suddenly filling the sky.

Before breaking the seal and the lock on Linda Palmer's door, I went over and said hello to Bobbi Thomas.

She came to the door with the kitten in her arms. She wore a white sweater that I found it difficult to keep my eyes off of, and a pair of dark slacks.

"Oh, hi, Cody."

"Hi."

She raised one of the kitten's paws and waggled it at me. "She says 'hi' too."

"Hi, honey." I nodded to the door behind me. "Can I trust you?"

"Sure, Cody. What's up?"

"I'm going to break into Linda's apartment."

"You're kidding."

"You'll probably hear some noises—people in the hallway and stuff—but please don't call the police. All right?"

For the first time, she looked uncertain. "Couldn't we get in trouble?"

"I suppose."

"And aren't you an officer of the court or whatever you call it?"

"Yeah," I said guiltily.

"Then maybe you shouldn't—"

"I want to catch the killer, Bobbi, and this is the only way I'll do it."

"Well—" she started to say.

Her phone rang behind her. "I guess I'd better get that, Cody."

"Just don't call the police."

She looked at me a long moment. "Okay, Cody. I just hope we don't get into any trouble."

She took herself, her kitten, and her wonderful sweater back inside her apartment.

7.

I kind of felt like Alan Ladd.

I saw a great crime movie once where he was sitting in the shadowy apartment of the woman who'd betrayed him. You know how a scene like that works. There's this lonely wailing sax music and Alan is smoking one butt after another (no wonder he was so short, probably stunted his growth smoking back when he was in junior high or something), and you could just feel how terrible and empty and sad he felt.

Here I was sitting in an armchair, smoking one Pall Mall after another, and if I wasn't feeling quite terrible and empty, I was at least feeling sort of sorry for myself. It was way past time that I show the judge that I could figure out one of these cases for myself.

When the knock came, it startled me, and for the first time I felt self-conscious about what I was doing.

I'd tricked four people into coming here without having any proof that any of them had had anything to do with Linda Palmer's murder at all. What would happen when I opened the door and actually faced them?

I was about to find out.

Leaving the lights off, I walked over to the door, eased it open, and stared into the faces of David and Millie Styles. They both wore black—black turtlenecks; a black peacoat for him; a black suede car coat for her; and black slacks for both of them—and they both looked extremely unhappy.

"Come in and sit down," I said.

They exchanged disgusted looks and followed me into the apartment.

"Take a seat," I said.

"I just want to find out why you sent us that ridiculous note," David Styles said.

"If it's so ridiculous, why did you come here?" I said.

As he looked at his wife again, I heard a knock on the back door. I walked through the shadowy apartment—somehow, I felt that lights-out would be more conducive to the killer blubbering a confession—and peeked out through the curtains near the stove: Gwen and Paul, neither of them looking happy.

I unlocked the door and let them in.

Before I could say anything, Gwen glared at me. "I'll swear under oath that Paul was with me the whole time the night she was murdered."

Suspects in Order of Likelihood

1. Millie
2. Gwen
3. David
4. Paul

That was before Gwen had offered herself as an alibi. Now Paul went to number one, with her right behind.

I followed them into the living room, where the Styleses were still standing.

I went over to the fireplace and leaned on the mantel and said, "One of us in this room is a murderer."

Millie Styles snorted. "This is just like a Charlie Chan movie."

"I'm serious," I said.

"So am I," she said.

"Each of you had a good reason to kill Linda Palmer," I said.

"I didn't," David Styles said.

"Neither did I," said Paul.

I moved away from the mantel, starting to walk around the room, but never taking my eyes off them.

"You could save all of us a lot of time and trouble by just confessing," I said.

"Which one of us are you talking to?" Gwen said. "I can't see your eyes in the dark."

"I'm talking to the real killer," I said.

"Maybe you killed her," David Styles said, "and you're trying to frame one of us."

This was pretty much how it went for the next fifteen minutes, me getting closer and closer to the real killer, making him or her really sweat it out, while I continued to pace and throw out accusations.

I guess the thing that spoiled it was the blood-red splash of light in the front window, Cliff Sykes, Jr.'s, personal patrol car pulling up to the curb, and then Cliff Sykes, Jr., racing out of his car, gun drawn.

I heard him on the porch, I heard him in the hall, I heard him at the door across the hall.

Moments after the door opened, Bobbi Thomas wailed, "All right! I killed her! I killed her! I caught her sleeping with my boyfriend!"

I opened the door and looked out into the hall.

Judge Whitney stood next to Cliff Sykes, Jr., and said, "There's your killer, Sykes. Now you get down to that jail and let my nephew go!"

And with that, she turned and stalked out of the apartment house.

Then I noticed the Christmas kitten in Bobbi Thomas's arms. "What's gonna happen to the kitty if I go to prison?" she sobbed.

"Probably put her to sleep," the ever-sensitive Cliff Sykes, Jr., said.

At which point, Bobbi Thomas became semi-hysterical.

"I'll take her, Bobbi," I said, and reached over and picked up the kitten.

"Thanks," Bobbi said over her shoulder as Sykes led her out to his car.

Each of the people in Linda Palmer's apartment took a turn at glowering at me as he walked into the hall and out the front door.

"See you, Miss Marple," said David Styles.

"So long, Sherlock," smirked Gwen Dawes.

Her boyfriend said something that I can't repeat here.

And Millie Styles said, "Charlie Chan does it a lot better, McCain."

When Sophie (I'm an informal kind of guy, and Sophia is a very formal kind of name) and I got back to my little apartment over a store that Jesse James had actually shot up one time, we both got a surprise.

A Christmas tree stood in the corner resplendent with green and yellow and red lights, and long shining strands of silver icing, and a sweet little angel right at the very tip-top of the tree.

And next to the tree stood the beautiful and elegant Pamela Forrest, gorgeous in a red sweater and jeans. Now, in the Shell Scott novels I read, Pamela would be completely naked and beckoning to me with a curling, seductive finger.

But I was happy to see her just as she was.

"Judge Whitney was afraid you'd be kind of down about not solving the case, so she asked me to buy you a tree and set it up for you."

"Yeah," I said. "I didn't even have Bobbi on my list of suspects. How'd she figure it out anyway?"

Pamela immediately lifted Sophie from my arms and started doing Eskimo noses with her. "Well, first of all, she called the cleaners and asked if any of the rugs that Bobbi had had cleaned had had red stains on it—blood, in other words, meaning that she'd probably killed Linda in her apartment and then dragged her back across to Linda's apartment. The blood came from Sophia's paws most likely, when she walked on the white throw rug." She paused long enough to do some more Eskimo nosing. "Then second, Bobbi told you that she'd stayed home and watched *Gunsmoke*. But *Gunsmoke* had been preempted for a Christmas special and wasn't on that night. And third—" By now she was rocking Sophie in the cradle of her arm. "Third, she found out that the boyfriend that Bobbi had only mentioned briefly to you had fallen under Linda's spell. Bobbi came home and actually found them in bed together—he hadn't even been gentleman enough to take it across the hall to Linda's apartment." Then: "Gosh, McCain, this is one of the cutest little kittens I've ever seen."

"Makes me wish I was a kitten," I said. "Or Sherlock Holmes. She sure figured it out, didn't she?"

Pamela carried Sophie over to me and said, "I think your daddy needs a kiss, young lady."

And I have to admit, it was pretty nice at that moment, Pamela Forrest in my apartment for the very first time, and Sophie's sweet little sandpaper tongue giving me a lot of sweet little kitty kisses.

THE SANTA CLAUS CLUB

Julian Symons

MUCH LIKE HIS CLOSE FRIEND H. R. F. Keating, Julian Symons
was an outstanding scholar of mystery fiction as well as one of its foremost prac-
titioners. In addition to biographies of Edgar Allan Poe, Arthur Conan Doyle,
and a critical study of Dashiell Hammett, he wrote an excellent history of the
genre, *Bloody Murder* (1972, titled *Mortal Consequences* in the United States),
in which he also defined the genre as he thought it ought to be, insisting that it
move away from pure puzzle-solving to a greater reliance on psychological elements of crime. He has been honored with lifetime achievement awards from
the Mystery Writers of America, the (British) Crime Writers' Association, and
the Swedish Academy of Detection. "The Santa Claus Club" was first published
in the December 1960 issue of *Suspense;* it was first collected in *Francis Quarles
Investigates* (London, Panther, 1965).

The Santa Claus Club

JULIAN SYMONS

IT IS NOT OFTEN, IN REAL LIFE, that letters are written recording implacable hatred nursed over the years, or that private detectives are invited by peers to select dining clubs, or that murders occur at such dining clubs, or that they are solved on the spot by a process of deduction. The case of the Santa Claus Club provided an example of all these rarities.

The case began one day, a week before Christmas, when Francis Quarles went to see Lord Acrise. He was a rich man, Lord Acrise, and an important one, the chairman of this big building concern and director of that and the other insurance company, and consultant to the Government on half a dozen matters. He had been a harsh, intolerant man in his prime, and was still hard enough in his early seventies, Quarles guessed, as he looked at the beaky nose, jutting chin, and stony blue eyes.

They sat in the study of Acrise's house just off the Brompton Road.

"Just tell me what you think of these," Lord Acrise said.

These were three letters, badly typed on a machine with a worn ribbon. They were all signed with the name James Gliddon. The first two contained vague references to some wrong done to Gliddon by Acrise in the past. They were written in language that was wild but unmistakably threatening. *You have been a whited sepulchre for too long, but now your time has come . . . You don't know what I'm going to do, now I've come*

back, *but you won't be able to help wondering and worrying . . . The mills of God grind slowly, but they're going to grind you into little bits for what you've done to me.*

The third letter was more specific. *So the thief is going to play Santa Claus. That will be your last evening alive. I shall be there, Joe Acrise, and I shall watch with pleasure as you squirm in agony.*

Quarles looked at the envelopes. They were plain and cheap. The address was typed, and the word *Personal* was on top of each envelope.

"Who is James Gliddon?" he asked.

The stony eyes glared at him. "I'm told you're to be trusted. Gliddon was a school friend of mine. We grew up together in the slums of Nottingham. We started a building company together. It did well for a time, then went bust. There was a lot of money missing. Gliddon kept the books. He got five years for fraud."

"Have you heard from him since then? I see all these letters are recent."

"He's written half a dozen letters, I suppose, over the years. The last one came—oh, seven years ago, I should think. From the Argentine." Acrise stopped, then added abruptly, "Snewin tried to find him for me, but he'd disappeared."

"Snewin?"

"My secretary. Been with me twelve years."

He pressed a bell. An obsequious, fattish man, whose appearance somehow put Quarles in mind of an enormous mouse, scurried in.

"Snewin—did we keep any of those old letters from Gliddon?"

"No sir. You told me to destroy them."

"The last ones came from the Argentine, right?"

"From Buenos Aires, to be exact, sir."

Acrise nodded, and Snewin scurried out.

Quarles said, "Who else knows this story about Gliddon?"

"Just my wife."

"And what does this mean about you playing Santa Claus?"

"I'm this year's chairman of the Santa Claus Club. We hold our raffle and dinner next Monday."

Then Quarles remembered. The Santa Claus Club had been formed by ten rich men. Each year they met, every one of them dressed up as Santa Claus, and held a raffle. The members took it in turn to provide the prize that was raffled—it might be a case of Napoleon brandy, a modest cottage with some exclusive salmon fishing rights attached to it, or a Constable painting. Each Santa Claus bought one ticket for the raffle, at a cost of one thousand guineas. The total of ten thousand guineas was given to a Christmas charity. After the raffle the assembled Santa Clauses, each accompanied by one guest, ate a traditional English Christmas dinner.

The whole thing was a combination of various English characteristics: enjoyment of dressing up, a wish to help charities, and the desire also that the help given should not go unrecorded.

"I want you to find Gliddon," Lord Acrise said. "Don't mistake me, Mr. Quarles. I don't want to take action against him, I want to help him. I wasn't to blame, don't think I admit that, but it was hard that Jimmy Gliddon should go to jail. I'm a hard man, have been all my life, but I don't think my worst enemies would call me mean. Those who've helped me know that when I die they'll find they're not forgotten. Jimmy Gliddon must be an old man now. I'd like to set him up for the rest of his life."

"To find him by next Monday is a tall order," Quarles said. "But I'll try."

He was at the door when Acrise said, "By the way, I'd like you to be my guest at the Club dinner on Monday night . . ."

There were two ways of trying to find Gliddon: by investigation of his career after leaving prison, and through the typewritten letters. Quarles took the job of tracing the past, leaving the letters to his secretary, Molly Player.

From Scotland Yard he found out that Gliddon had spent nearly four years in prison, from 1913 to late 1916. He had joined a Nottinghamshire regiment when he came out, and the records of this regiment showed that he had been demobilised in August, 1919, with the rank of Sergeant. In 1923 he had been given a sentence of three years for an attempt to smuggle diamonds. Thereafter all trace of him in Britain vanished.

Quarles made some expensive telephone calls to Buenos Aires, where the letters had come from seven years earlier. He learned that Gliddon had lived in that city from a time just after the Second World War until 1955. He ran an import-export business, and was thought to have been living in other South American Republics during the war. His business was said to have been a cloak for smuggling, both of drugs and of suspected Nazis, whom he got out of Europe into the Argentine. In 1955 a newspaper had accused Gliddon of arranging the entry into the Argentine of a Nazi war criminal named Hermann Breit. Gliddon disappeared. A couple of weeks later a battered body was washed up just outside the city.

"It was identified as Señor Gliddon," the liquid voice said over the telephone. "But you know, Señor Quarles, in such matters the police are sometimes unhappy to close their files."

"There was still some doubt?"

"Yes. Not very much, perhaps. But in these cases there is often a measure of doubt."

Molly Player found out nothing useful about the paper and envelopes. They were of the sort that could be bought in a thousand stores and shops in London and elsewhere. She had no more luck with the typewriter.

Lord Acrise made no comment on Quarles's recital of failure. "See you on Monday evening, seven-thirty, black tie," he said, and barked with laughter. "Your host will be Santa Claus."

"I'd like to be there earlier."

"Good idea. Any time you like. You know where it is? Robert the Devil Restaurant . . ."

The Robert the Devil Restaurant is situated inconspicuously in Mayfair. It is not a restaurant in the ordinary sense of the word, for there is no public dining-room, but simply several private rooms accommodating any number of guests from two to thirty. Perhaps the food is not quite the best in London, but it is certainly the most expensive.

It was here that Quarles arrived at half-past six, a big, suave man, rather too conspicuously elegant perhaps in a midnight-blue dinner jacket. He talked to Albert, the *maître d'hotel*, whom he had known for some years, took an unobtrusive look at the waiters, went into and admired the sparkling kitchens.

Albert observed his activities with tolerant amusement.

"You are here on some sort of business, Mr. Quarles?"

"I am a guest, Albert. I am also a kind of bodyguard. Tell me, how many of your waiters have joined you in the past twelve months?"

"Perhaps half a dozen. They come, they go."

"Is there anybody at all on your staff—waiters, kitchen staff, anybody—who has joined you in the past year, and who is over sixty years old?"

"No. There is not such a one."

The first of the guests came just after a quarter-past seven. This was the brain surgeon Sir James Erdington, with a guest whom Quarles recognized as the Arctic explorer, Norman Endell. After that they came at intervals of a minute or two: a junior minister in the Government;

one of the three most important men in the motor industry; a general elevated to the peerage to celebrate his retirement; a theatrical producer named Roddy Davis, who had successfully combined commerce and culture.

As they arrived, the hosts went into a special robing room to put on their Santa Claus clothes, while the guests drank sherry.

At seven-twenty-five Snewin scurried in, gasped, "Excuse me, place names, got to put them out," and went into the dining-room. Through the open door Quarles glimpsed a large oval table, gleaming with silver, bright with roses.

After Snewin came Lord Acrise, jutting-nosed and fearsome-eyed. "Sorry to have kept you waiting," he barked, and asked conspiratorially, "Well?"

"No sign."

"False alarm. Lot of nonsense. Got to dress up now."

He went into the robing room with his box—each of the hosts had a similar box, labelled "Santa Claus"—and came out again bewigged, bearded, and robed. "Better get the business over, and then we can enjoy ourselves. You can tell 'em to come in," he said to Albert.

This referred to the photographers, who had been clustered outside, and now came into the room specially provided for holding the raffle. In the centre of the room was a table, and on the table stood this year's prize, two exquisite T'ang horses. On the other side of the table were ten chairs arranged in a semi-circle, and on these sat the Santa Clauses. Their guests stood inconspicuously at the side.

The raffle was conducted with the utmost seriousness. Each Santa Claus had a numbered slip. These slips were put into a tombola, and Acrise put in his hand and drew out one of them. Flash bulbs exploded.

"The number drawn is eight," Acrise announced, and Roddy Davis waved the counterfoil in his hand.

"Isn't that *wonderful*? It's my ticket." He went

over to the horses, picked up one. "I'm bound to say that they couldn't have gone to *anybody* who'd have appreciated them more."

Quarles, standing near the general, whose face was as red as his robe, heard him mutter something uncomplimentary. Charity, he reflected, was not universal, even in a gathering of Santa Clauses. Then there were more flashes, the photographers disappeared, and Quarles's views about the nature of charity were reinforced when, as they were about to go into the dining-room, Sir James Erdington said, "Forgotten something, haven't you, Acrise?"

With what seemed dangerous quietness Acrise answered, "Have I? I don't think so."

"It's customary for the Club and guests to sing 'Noel' before we go in to dinner."

"You didn't come to last year's dinner. It was agreed then that we should give it up. Carols after dinner, much better."

"I must say I thought that was just for last year, because we were late," Roddy Davis fluted.

"Suggest we put it to the vote," Erdington said sharply.

Half a dozen of the Santas now stood looking at each other with subdued hostility. Then suddenly the Arctic explorer, Endell, began to sing "Noel, Noel" in a rich bass. There was the faintest flicker of hesitation, and then the guests and their hosts joined in. The situation was saved.

At dinner Quarles found himself with Acrise on one side of him and Roddy Davis on the other. Endell sat at Acrise's other side, and beyond him was Erdington. Turtle soup was followed by grilled sole, and then three great turkeys were brought in. The helpings of turkey were enormous. With the soup they drank a light, dry sherry, with the sole Chassagne Montrachet, with the turkey an Aloxe Corton.

"And who are *you*?" Roddy Davis peered at Quarles's card and said, "Of course, I know your name."

"I am a criminologist." This sounded better, Quarles thought, than "private detective."

"I remember your monograph on criminal calligraphy. Quite fascinating."

So Davis *did* know who he was. It would be easy, Quarles thought, to underrate the intelligence of this man.

"These beards really do get in the way rather," Davis said. "But there, one must suffer for tradition. Have you known Acrise long?"

"Not very. I'm greatly privileged to be here."

Quarles had been watching, as closely as he could, the pouring of the wine, the serving of the food. He had seen nothing suspicious. Now, to get away from Davis's questions, he turned to his host.

"Damned awkward business before dinner," Acrise said. "Might have been, at least. Can't let well alone, Erdington."

He picked up his turkey leg, attacked it with Elizabethan gusto, wiped his mouth and fingers with his napkin. "Like this wine?"

"It's excellent."

"Chose it myself. They've got some good Burgundies here." Acrise's speech was slightly slurred, and it seemed to Quarles that he was rapidly getting drunk.

"Do you have any speeches?"

"No speeches. Just sing carols. But I've got a little surprise for 'em."

"What sort of surprise?"

"Very much in the spirit of Christmas, and a good joke too. But if I told you, it wouldn't be a surprise, would it?"

There was a general cry of pleasure as Albert himself brought in the great plum pudding, topped with holly and blazing with brandy.

"That's the most wonderful pudding I've ever seen in my life," Endell said. "Are we really going to eat it?"

"Of course," Acrise said irritably. He stood up, swaying a little, and picked up the knife beside the pudding.

"I don't like to be critical, but our Chairman is really not cutting the pudding very well," Roddy Davis whispered to Quarles. And indeed, it was more of a stab than a cut that Acrise made at the pudding. Albert took over, and cut it quickly and efficiently. Bowls of brandy butter were circulated.

Quarles leaned towards Acrise. "Are you all right?"

"Of course I'm all right."

The slurring was very noticeable now. Acrise ate no pudding, but he drank some more wine, and dabbed at his lips. When the pudding was finished, he got slowly to his feet again and toasted the Queen. Cigars were lighted. Acrise was not smoking. He whispered something to the waiter, who nodded and left the room. Acrise got up again, leaning heavily on the table.

"A little surprise," he said. "In the spirit of Christmas."

Quarles had thought that he was beyond being surprised by the activities of the Santa Claus Club, but he was astonished at the sight of the three figures who entered the room.

They were led by Snewin, somehow more mouselike than ever, wearing a long, white smock and a red nightcap with a tassel. He was followed by an older man dressed in a kind of grey sackcloth, with a face so white that it might have been covered in plaster of Paris. This man carried chains, which he shook. At the rear came a young-middle-aged lady who seemed to be completely hung with tinsel.

"I am Scrooge," said Snewin.

"I am Marley," wailed grey sackcloth, clanking his chains vigorously.

"And I," said the young-middle-aged lady, with abominable sprightliness, "am the ghost of Christmas past."

There was a ripple of laughter.

"We have come," said Snewin in a thin, mouse voice, "to perform for you our own interpretation of *A Christmas Carol* . . . Oh, sir, what's the matter?"

Lord Acrise stood up in his robes, tore off his wig, pulled at his beard, tried to say something. Then he clutched at the side of his chair and fell sideways, so that he leaned heavily against Endell and slipped slowly to the floor.

There ensued a minute of confused, important activity. Endell made some sort of exclamation and rose from his chair, slightly obstructing Quarles. Erdington was first beside the body, hold-

ing the wrist in his hand, listening for the heart. Then they were all crowding round. Snewin, at Quarles's left shoulder, was babbling something, and at his right were Roddy Davis and Endell.

"Stand back," Erdington snapped. He stayed on his knees for another few moments, looking curiously at Acrise's puffed, distorted face, bluish around the mouth. Then he stood up.

"He's dead."

There was a murmur of surprise and horror, and now they all drew back, as men do instinctively from the presence of death.

"Heart attack?" somebody said.

Quarles moved to his side. "I'm a private detective, Sir James. Lord Acrise feared an attempt on his life, and asked me to come along here."

"You seem to have done well so far," Erdington said drily.

"May I look at the body?"

"If you wish."

As Quarles bent down, he caught the smell of bitter almonds. "There's a smell like prussic acid, but the way he died precludes cyanide, I think. He seemed to become very drunk during dinner, and his speech was slurred. Does that suggest anything to you?"

"I'm a brain surgeon, not a physician." Erdington stared at the floor. "Nitro benzene?"

"That's what I thought. We shall have to notify the police."

Quarles went to the door and spoke to a disturbed Albert. Then he returned to the room and clapped his hands.

"Gentlemen. My name is Francis Quarles, and I am a private detective. Lord Acrise asked me to come here tonight because he had received a threat that this would be his last evening alive. The threat said, 'I shall be there, and I shall watch with pleasure as you squirm in agony.' Lord Acrise has been poisoned. It seems certain that the man who made the threat is in this room."

"Gliddon," a voice said. Snewin had divested himself of the white smock and red nightcap, and now appeared as his customary respectable self.

"Yes. This letter, and others he had received, were signed with the name of James Gliddon, a man who bore a grudge against Lord Acrise which went back nearly half a century. Gliddon became a professional smuggler and crook. He would now be in his late sixties."

"But dammit, man, this Gliddon's not here." That was the General, who took off his wig and beard. "Lot of tomfoolery."

In a shamefaced way the other members of the Santa Claus Club removed their facial trappings. Marley took off his chains and the lady discarded her cloak of tinsel.

Quarles said, "Isn't he here? But Lord Acrise is dead."

Snewin coughed. "Excuse me, sir, but would it be possible for my colleagues from our local dramatic society to retire?"

"Everybody must stay in this room until the police arrive," Quarles said grimly. "The problem, as you will all realize, is how the poison was administered. All of us ate the same food, drank the same wine. I sat next to Lord Acrise, and I watched as closely as possible to make sure of this. After dinner some of you smoked cigars or cigarettes, but not Lord Acrise."

"Just a moment." It was Roddy Davis who spoke. "This sounds fantastic, but wasn't it Sherlock Holmes who said that when you'd eliminated all other possibilities, even a fantastic one must be right? Supposing poison in powder form was put on to Acrise's food? Through the pepper pots, say . . ."

Erdington was shaking his head, but Quarles unscrewed both salt and pepper pots and tasted their contents. "Salt and pepper," he said briefly. "Hello, what's this."

"It's Acrise's napkin," Endell said. "What's remarkable about that?"

"It's a napkin, but not the one Acrise used. He wiped his mouth half a dozen times on his napkin, and wiped his greasy fingers on it too, when he'd gnawed a turkey bone. He must certainly have left grease marks on it. But look at this napkin."

He held it up, and they saw that it was spotless. Quarles said softly, "The murderer's mistake."

Quarles turned to Erdington. "Sir James and I agree that the poison used was probably nitro benzene. This is deadly as a liquid, but it is also poisonous as a vapour—isn't that so?"

Erdington nodded. "You'll remember the case of the unfortunate young man who used shoe polish containing nitro benzene on damp shoes, put them on and wore them, and was killed by the fumes."

"Yes. Somebody made sure that Lord Acrise had a napkin that had been soaked in nitro benzene but was dry enough to use. The same person substituted the proper napkin, the one belonging to the restaurant, after Acrise was dead."

"That means the napkin must still be here," Davis said.

"It does."

"Then I vote that we submit to a search!"

"That won't be necessary," Quarles said. "Only one person here fulfils all the qualifications of the murderer."

"James Gliddon?"

"No. Gliddon is almost certainly dead, as I found out when I made enquiries about him. But the murderer is somebody who knew about Acrise's relationship with Gliddon, and tried to be clever by writing those letters to lead us along a wrong track." He paused. "Then the murderer is somebody who had the opportunity of coming in here before dinner, and who knew exactly where Acrise would be sitting."

There was a dead silence in the room.

Quarles said, "He removed any possible suspicion from himself, as he thought, by being absent from the dinner table, but he arranged to come in afterwards to exchange the napkins. He probably put the poisoned napkin into the clothes he discarded. As for motive, long-standing hatred might be enough, but he is also somebody who knew that he would benefit handsomely when Acrise died . . . stop him, will you?"

But the General, with a tackle reminiscent of the days when he had been the best wing three-quarter in the country, had already brought to the floor Lord Acrise's secretary, Snewin.

A CLASSIC

Little Christmas

THE FLYING STARS
G. K. Chesterton

THE SECOND GREATEST ENGLISH DETECTIVE in all of literature, surpassed only by the inimitable Sherlock Holmes, is the gentle and kindly Father Brown. What separates him from most of his crime-fighting colleagues is his view that wrongdoers are souls in need of redemption rather than criminals to be brought to justice. Could there be a better detective to be at the center of a Christmas story? The rather ordinary-seeming Roman Catholic priest possesses a sharp, subtle, sensitive mind, with which he demonstrates a deep understanding of human nature in solving mysteries. "The Flying Stars" was first published in the May 20, 1911, issue of *Saturday Evening Post,* and subsequently published in the June 1911 issue of *Cassell's Magazine;* it was first collected in *The Innocence of Father Brown* (London, Cassell, 1911).

The Flying Stars

G. K. CHESTERTON

"THE MOST BEAUTIFUL CRIME I EVER committed," Flambeau would say in his highly moral old age, "was also, by a singular coincidence, my last. It was committed at Christmas. As an artist I had always attempted to provide crimes suitable to the special season or landscapes in which I found myself, choosing this or that terrace or garden for a catastrophe, as if for a statuary group. Thus squires should be swindled in long rooms panelled with oak; while Jews, on the other hand, should rather find themselves unexpectedly penniless among the lights and screens of the Café Riche. Thus, in England, if I wished to relieve a dean of his riches (which is not so easy as you might suppose), I wished to frame him, if I make myself clear, in the green lawns and grey towers of some cathedral town. Similarly, in France, when I had got money out of a rich and wicked peasant (which is almost impossible), it gratified me to get his indignant head relieved against a grey line of clipped poplars, and those solemn plains of Gaul over which broods the mighty spirit of Millet.

"Well, my last crime was a Christmas crime, a cheery, cosy, English middle-class crime; a crime of Charles Dickens. I did it in a good old middle-class house near Putney, a house with a crescent of carriage drive, a house with a stable by the side of it, a house with the name on the two outer gates, a house with a monkey tree. Enough, you know the species. I really think my imitation of Dickens's style was dexterous and literary. It seems almost a pity I repented the same evening."

Flambeau would then proceed to tell the story from the inside; and even from the inside it was odd. Seen from the outside it was perfectly incomprehensible, and it is from the outside that the stranger must study it. From this standpoint the drama may be said to have begun when the front doors of the house with the stable opened on the garden with the monkey tree, and a young girl came out with bread to feed the birds on the afternoon of Boxing Day. She had a pretty face, with brave brown eyes; but her figure was beyond conjecture, for she was so wrapped up in brown furs that it was hard to say which was hair and which was fur. But for the attractive face she might have been a small toddling bear.

The winter afternoon was reddening towards evening, and already a ruby light was rolled over the bloomless beds, filling them, as it were, with the ghosts of the dead roses. On one side of the house stood the stable, on the other an alley or cloister of laurels led to the larger garden behind. The young lady, having scattered bread for the birds (for the fourth or fifth time that day, because the dog ate it), passed unobtrusively down the lane of laurels and into a glimmering plantation of evergreens behind. Here she gave an exclamation of wonder, real or ritual, and looking up at the high garden wall above her, beheld it fantastically bestridden by a somewhat fantastic figure.

"Oh, don't jump, Mr. Crook," she called out in some alarm; "it's much too high."

The individual riding the party wall like an aerial horse was a tall, angular young man, with dark hair sticking up like a hair brush, intelligent and even distinguished lineaments, but a sallow and almost alien complexion. This showed the more plainly because he wore an aggressive red tie, the only part of his costume of which he seemed to take any care. Perhaps it was a symbol. He took no notice of the girl's alarmed adjuration, but leapt like a grasshopper to the ground beside her, where he might very well have broken his legs.

"I think I was meant to be a burglar," he said placidly, "and I have no doubt I should have been if I hadn't happened to be born in that nice house next door. I can't see any harm in it, anyhow."

"How can you say such things?" she remonstrated.

"Well," said the young man, "if you're born on the wrong side of the wall, I can't see that it's wrong to climb over it."

"I never know what you will say or do next," she said.

"I don't often know myself," replied Mr. Crook; "but then I am on the right side of the wall now."

"And which is the right side of the wall?" asked the young lady, smiling.

"Whichever side you are on," said the young man named Crook.

As they went together through the laurels towards the front garden a motor horn sounded thrice, coming nearer and nearer, and a car of splendid speed, great elegance, and a pale green colour swept up to the front doors like a bird and stood throbbing.

"Hullo, hullo!" said the young man with the red tie. "Here's somebody born on the right side, anyhow. I didn't know, Miss Adams, that your Santa Claus was so modern as this."

"Oh, that's my godfather, Sir Leopold Fischer. He always comes on Boxing Day."

Then, after an innocent pause, which unconsciously betrayed some lack of enthusiasm, Ruby Adams added:

"He is very kind."

John Crook, journalist, had heard of that eminent City magnate; and it was not his fault if the City magnate had not heard of him; for in certain articles in *The Clarion* or *The New Age* Sir Leopold had been dealt with austerely. But he said nothing and grimly watched the unloading of the motor-car, which was rather a long process. A large, neat chauffeur in green got out from the front, and a small, neat manservant in grey got out from the back, and between them they deposited Sir Leopold on the doorstep and began to unpack him, like some very carefully protected parcel. Rugs enough to stock a bazaar, furs of all the beasts of the forest, and scarves of all the colours of the rainbow were unwrapped one by one, till they revealed something resembling the human form; the form of a friendly, but foreign-looking old gentleman, with a grey goat-like beard and a beaming smile, who rubbed his big fur gloves together.

Long before this revelation was complete the two big doors of the porch had opened in the middle, and Colonel Adams (father of the furry young lady) had come out himself to invite his eminent guest inside. He was a tall, sunburnt, and very silent man, who wore a red smoking-cap like a fez, making him look like one of the English Sirdars or Pashas in Egypt. With him was his brother-in-law, lately come from Canada, a big and rather boisterous young gentleman-farmer, with a yellow beard, by name James Blount. With him also was the more insignificant figure of the priest from the neighbouring Roman Church; for the colonel's late wife had been a Catholic, and the children, as is common in such cases, had been trained to follow her. Everything seemed undistinguished about the priest, even down to his name, which was Brown; yet the colonel had always found something companionable about him, and frequently asked him to such family gatherings.

In the large entrance hall of the house there was ample room even for Sir Leopold and the removal of his wraps. Porch and vestibule, indeed, were unduly large in proportion to the house, and formed, as it were, a big room with the front door at one end, and the bottom of the staircase at the other. In front of the large hall fire, over which hung the colonel's sword, the process was completed and the company, including the saturnine Crook, presented to Sir Leopold Fischer. That venerable financier, however, still seemed struggling with portions of his well-lined attire, and at length produced from a very interior tail-coat pocket, a black oval case which he radiantly explained to be his Christmas present for his god-daughter. With an unaffected vain-glory that had something disarming about it he held out the case before them all; it flew open at a touch and half-blinded them. It was just as if a crystal fountain had spurted in their eyes. In a nest of orange velvet lay like three eggs, three white and vivid diamonds that seemed to set the very air on fire all round them. Fischer stood beaming benevolently and drinking deep of the astonishment and ecstasy of the girl, the grim admiration and gruff thanks of the colonel, the wonder of the whole group.

"I'll put 'em back now, my dear," said Fischer, returning the case to the tails of his coat. "I had to be careful of 'em coming down. They're the three great African diamonds called 'The Flying Stars,' because they've been stolen so often. All the big criminals are on the track; but even the rough men about in the streets and hotels could hardly have kept their hands off them. I might have lost them on the road here. It was quite possible."

"Quite natural, I should say," growled the man in the red tie. "I shouldn't blame 'em if they had taken 'em. When they ask for bread, and you don't even give them a stone, I think they might take the stone for themselves."

"I won't have you talking like that," cried the girl, who was in a curious glow. "You've only talked like that since you became a horrid what's-his-name. You know what I mean. What do you call a man who wants to embrace the chimney-sweep?"

"A saint," said Father Brown.

"I think," said Sir Leopold, with a supercilious smile, "that Ruby means a Socialist."

"A radical does not mean a man who lives on radishes," remarked Crook, with some impatience; "and a Conservative does not mean a man who preserves jam. Neither, I assure you, does a Socialist mean a man who desires a social evening with the chimney-sweep. A Socialist means a man who wants all the chimneys swept and all the chimney-sweeps paid for it."

"But who won't allow you," put in the priest in a low voice, "to own your own soot?"

Crook looked at him with an eye of interest and even respect. "Does one want to own soot?" he asked.

"One might," answered Brown, with speculation in his eye. "I've heard that gardeners use it. And I once made six children happy at Christmas when the conjuror didn't come, entirely with soot—applied externally."

"Oh, splendid," cried Ruby. "Oh, I wish you'd do it to this company."

The boisterous Canadian, Mr. Blount, was lifting his loud voice in applause, and the astonished financier his (in some considerable deprecation), when a knock sounded at the double front doors. The priest opened them, and they showed again the front garden of evergreens, monkey tree and all, now gathering gloom against a gorgeous violet sunset. The scene thus framed was so coloured and quaint, like a back scene in a play, that they forgot a moment the insignificant figure standing in the door. He was dusty-looking and in a frayed coat, evidently a common messenger. "Any of you gentlemen Mr. Blount?" he asked, and held forward a letter doubtfully. Mr. Blount started, and stopped in his shout of assent. Ripping up the envelope with evident astonishment he read it; his face clouded a little, and then cleared, and he turned to his brother-in-law and host.

"I'm sick at being such a nuisance, colonel," he said, with the cheery colonial conventions; "but would it upset you if an old acquaintance called on me here tonight on business? In point of fact it's Florian, that famous French acrobat and comic actor; I knew him years ago out West (he was a French-Canadian by birth), and he seems to have business for me, though I hardly guess what."

"Of course, of course," replied the colonel carelessly. "My dear chap, any friend of yours. No doubt he will prove an acquisition."

"He'll black his face, if that's what you mean," cried Blount, laughing. "I don't doubt he'd black everyone else's eyes. I don't care; I'm not refined. I like the jolly old pantomime where a man sits on his top hat."

"Not on mine, please," said Sir Leopold Fischer, with dignity.

"Well, well," observed Crook, airily, "don't let's quarrel. There are lower jokes than sitting on a top hat."

Dislike of the red-tied youth, born of his predatory opinions and evident intimacy with the pretty godchild, led Fischer to say, in his most sarcastic, magisterial manner: "No doubt you have found something much lower than sitting on a top hat. What is it, pray?"

"Letting a top hat sit on you, for instance," said the Socialist.

"Now, now, now," cried the Canadian farmer with his barbarian benevolence, "don't let's spoil a jolly evening. What I say is let's do something for the company tonight. Not blacking faces or sitting on hats, if you don't like those—but something of the sort. Why couldn't we have a proper old English pantomime—clown, columbine, and so on. I saw one when I left England at twelve years old, and it's blazed in my brain like a bonfire ever since. I came back to the old country only last year, and I find the thing's extinct. Nothing but a lot of snivelling fairy plays. I want a hot poker and a policeman made into sausages, and they give me princesses moralising by moonlight, Blue Birds, or something. Blue Beard's more in my line, and him I liked best when he turned into the pantaloon."

"I'm all for making a policeman into sausages," said John Crook. "It's a better defini-

tion of Socialism than some recently given. But surely the get-up would be too big a business."

"Not a scrap," cried Blount, quite carried away. "A harlequinade's the quickest thing we can do, for two reasons. First, one can gag to any degree; and, second, all the objects are household things—tables and trowel-horses and washing baskets, and things like that."

"That's true," admitted Crook, nodding eagerly and walking about. "But I'm afraid I can't have my policeman's uniform? Haven't killed a policeman lately."

Blount frowned thoughtfully a space, and then smote his thigh. "Yes, we can!" he cried. "I've got Florian's address here, and he knows every *costumier* in London. I'll 'phone him to bring a police dress when he comes." And he went bounding away to the telephone.

"Oh, it's glorious, godfather," cried Ruby, almost dancing. "I'll be columbine and you shall be pantaloon."

The millionaire held himself stiff with a sort of heathen solemnity. "I think, my dear," he said, "you must get someone else for pantaloon."

"I will be pantaloon, if you like," said Colonel Adams, taking his cigar out of his mouth, and speaking for the first and last time.

"You ought to have a statue," cried the Canadian, as he came back, radiant, from the telephone. "There, we are all fitted. Mr. Crook shall be clown; he's a journalist and knows all the oldest jokes. I can be harlequin, that only wants long legs and jumping about. My friend Florian 'phones he's bringing the police costume; he's changing on the way. We can act it in this very hall, the audience sitting on those broad stairs opposite, one row above another. These front doors can be the back scene, either open or shut. Shut, you see an English interior. Open, a moonlit garden. It all goes by magic." And snatching a chance piece of billiard chalk from his pocket, he ran it across the hall floor, half-way between the front door and the staircase, to mark the line of the footlights.

How even such a banquet of bosh was got ready in the time remained a riddle. But they went at it with that mixture of recklessness and industry that lives when youth is in a house; and youth was in that house that night, though not all may have isolated the two faces and hearts from which it flamed. As always happens, the invention grew wilder and wilder through the very tameness of the *bourgeois* conventions from which it had to create. The columbine looked charming in an outstanding skirt that strangely resembled the large lamp-shade in the drawing-room. The clown and pantaloon made themselves white with flour from the cook, and red with rouge from some other domestic, who remained (like all true Christian benefactors) anonymous. The harlequin, already clad in silver paper out of cigar boxes, was, with difficulty, prevented from smashing the old Victorian lustre chandeliers, that he might cover himself with resplendent crystals. In fact he would certainly have done so, had not Ruby unearthed some old pantomime paste jewels she had worn at a fancy dress party as the Queen of Diamonds. Indeed, her uncle, James Blount, was getting almost out of hand in his excitement; he was like a schoolboy. He put a paper donkey's head unexpectedly on Father Brown, who bore it patiently, and even found some private manner of moving his ears. He even essayed to put the paper donkey's tail to the coat-tails of Sir Leopold Fischer. This, however, was frowned down. "Uncle is too absurd," cried Ruby to Crook, round whose shoulders she had seriously placed a string of sausages. "Why is he so wild?"

"He is harlequin to your columbine," said Crook. "I am only the clown who makes the old jokes."

"I wish you were the harlequin," she said, and left the string of sausages swinging.

Father Brown, though he knew every detail done behind the scenes, and had even evoked applause by his transformation of a pillow into a pantomime baby, went round to the front and sat among the audience with all the solemn expectation of a child at his first matinée. The spectators were few, relations, one or two local friends, and the servants; Sir Leopold sat in the front seat, his full and still fur-collared figure largely obscuring the view of the little cleric behind him; but it has never been settled by artistic authorities whether the cleric lost much. The pantomime was utterly chaotic, yet not contemptible; there ran through it a rage of improvisation which came chiefly from Crook the clown. Commonly he was a clever man, and he was inspired tonight with a wild omniscience, a folly wiser than the world, that which comes to a young man who has seen for an instant a particular expression on a particular face. He was supposed to be the clown, but he was really almost everything else, the author (so far as there was an author), the prompter, the scene-painter, the scene-shifter, and, above all, the orchestra. At abrupt intervals in the outrageous performance he would hurl himself in full costume at the piano and bang out some popular music equally absurd and appropriate.

The climax of this, as of all else, was the moment when the two front doors at the back of the scene flew open, showing the lovely moonlit garden, but showing more prominently the famous professional guest; the great Florian, dressed up as a policeman. The clown at the piano played the constabulary chorus in the "Pirates of Penzance," but it was drowned in the deafening applause, for every gesture of the great comic actor was an admirable though restrained version of the carriage and manner of the police. The harlequin leapt upon him and hit him over the helmet; the pianist playing "Where did you get that hat?" he faced about in admirably simulated astonishment, and then the leaping harlequin hit him again (the pianist suggesting a few bars of "Then we had another one"). Then the harlequin rushed right into the arms of the policeman and fell on top of him, amid a roar of applause. Then it was that the strange actor gave that celebrated imitation of a dead man, of which the fame still lingers round Putney. It was almost impossible to believe that a living person could appear so limp.

The athletic harlequin swung him about like a sack or twisted or tossed him like an Indian club; all the time to the most maddeningly ludicrous tunes from the piano. When the harlequin heaved the comic constable heavily off the floor the clown played "I arise from dreams of thee." When he shuffled him across his back, "With my bundle on my shoulder," and when the harlequin finally let fall the policeman with a most convincing thud, the lunatic at the instrument struck into a jingling measure with some words which are still believed to have been, "I sent a letter to my love and on the way I dropped it."

At about this limit of mental anarchy Father Brown's view was obscured altogether; for the City magnate in front of him rose to his full height and thrust his hands savagely into all his pockets. Then he sat down nervously, still fumbling, and then stood up again. For an instant it seemed seriously likely that he would stride across the footlights; then he turned a glare at the clown playing the piano; and then he burst in silence out of the room.

The priest had only watched for a few more minutes the absurd but not inelegant dance of the amateur harlequin over his splendidly unconscious foe. With real though rude art, the harlequin danced slowly backwards out of the door into the garden, which was full of moonlight and stillness. The vamped dress of silver paper and paste, which had been too glaring in the footlights, looked more and more magical and silvery as it danced away under a brilliant moon. The audience was closing in with a cataract of applause, when Brown felt his arm abruptly touched, and he was asked in a whisper to come into the colonel's study.

He followed his summoner with increasing doubt, which was not dispelled by a solemn comicality in the scene of the study. There sat Colonel Adams, still unaffectedly dressed as a pantaloon, with the knobbed whalebone nodding above his brow, but with his poor old eyes sad enough to have sobered a Saturnalia. Sir Leopold Fischer was leaning against the mantelpiece and heaving with all the importance of panic.

"This is a very painful matter, Father Brown," said Adams. "The truth is, those diamonds we all saw this afternoon seem to have vanished from my friend's tail-coat pocket. And as you—"

"As I," supplemented Father Brown, with a broad grin, "was sitting just behind him—"

"Nothing of the sort shall be suggested," said Colonel Adams, with a firm look at Fischer, which rather implied that some such thing *had* been suggested. "I only ask you to give me the assistance that any gentleman might give."

"Which is turning out his pockets," said Father Brown, and proceeded to do so, displaying seven and sixpence, a return ticket, a small silver crucifix, a small breviary, and a stick of chocolate.

The colonel looked at him long, and then said, "Do you know, I should like to see the inside of your head more than the inside of your pockets. My daughter is one of your people, I know; well, she has lately—" and he stopped.

"She has lately," cried out old Fischer, "opened her father's house to a cut-throat Socialist, who says openly he would steal anything from a richer man. This is the end of it. Here is the richer man—and none the richer."

"If you want the inside of my head you can have it," said Brown rather wearily. "What it's worth you can say afterwards. But the first thing I find in that disused pocket is this: that men who mean to steal diamonds don't talk Socialism. They are more likely," he added demurely, "to denounce it."

Both the others shifted sharply and the priest went on:

"You see, we know these people, more or less. That Socialist would no more steal a diamond than a Pyramid. We ought to look at once to the one man we don't know. The fellow acting the policeman—Florian. Where is he exactly at this minute, I wonder."

The pantaloon sprang erect and strode out of the room. An interlude ensued, during which the millionaire stared at the priest, and the priest at his breviary; then the pantaloon returned and said, with *staccato* gravity, "The policeman is still lying on the stage. The curtain has gone up and down six times; he is still lying there."

Father Brown dropped his book and stood staring with a look of blank mental ruin. Very slowly a light began to creep in his grey eyes, and then he made the scarcely obvious answer.

"Please forgive me, colonel, but when did your wife die?"

"Wife!" replied the staring soldier, "she died this year two months. Her brother James arrived just a week too late to see her."

The little priest bounded like a rabbit shot. "Come on!" he cried in quite unusual excitement. "Come on! We've got to go and look at that policeman!"

They rushed on to the now curtained stage, breaking rudely past the columbine and clown (who seemed whispering quite contentedly), and Father Brown bent over the prostrate comic policeman.

"Chloroform," he said as he rose; "I only guessed it just now."

There was a startled stillness, and then the colonel said slowly, "Please say seriously what all this means."

Father Brown suddenly shouted with laughter, then stopped, and only struggled with it for instants during the rest of his speech. "Gentlemen," he gasped, "there's not much time to talk. I must run after the criminal. But this great French actor who played the policeman—this clever corpse the harlequin waltzed with and dandled and threw about—he was—" His voice again failed him, and he turned his back to run.

"He was?" called Fischer inquiringly.

"A real policeman," said Father Brown, and ran away into the dark.

There were hollows and bowers at the extreme end of that leafy garden, in which the laurels and other immortal shrubs showed against sapphire sky and silver moon, even in that midwinter, warm colours as of the south. The green gaiety of the waving laurels, the rich purple indigo of the night, the moon like a monstrous crystal, make an almost irresponsible romantic picture; and among the top branches of the garden trees a strange figure is climbing, who looks not so much romantic as impossible. He sparkles from head to heel, as if clad in ten million moons; the real moon catches him at every movement and sets a new inch of him on fire. But he swings, flashing and successful, from the short tree in this garden to the tall, rambling tree in the other, and only stops there because a shade has slid under the smaller tree and has unmistakably called up to him.

"Well, Flambeau," says the voice, "you really look like a Flying Star; but that always means a Falling Star at last."

The silver, sparkling figure above seems to lean forward in the laurels and, confident of escape, listens to the little figure below.

"You never did anything better, Flambeau. It was clever to come from Canada (with a Paris ticket, I suppose) just a week after Mrs. Adams died, when no one was in a mood to ask questions. It was cleverer to have marked down the Flying Stars and the very day of Fischer's coming. But there's no cleverness, but mere genius, in what followed. Stealing the stones, I suppose, was nothing to you. You could have done it by sleight of hand in a hundred other ways besides that pretence of putting a paper donkey's tail to Fischer's coat. But in the rest you eclipsed yourself."

The silvery figure among the green leaves seems to linger as if hypnotised, though his escape is easy behind him; he is staring at the man below.

"Oh, yes," says the man below, "I know all about it. I know you not only forced the pantomime, but put it to a double use. You were going to steal the stones quietly; news came by an accomplice that you were already suspected, and a capable police officer was coming to rout you up that very night. A common thief would have been thankful for the warning and fled; but you are a poet. You already had the clever notion of hiding the jewels in a blaze of false stage jewellery. Now, you saw that if the dress were a harlequin's the appearance of a policeman would be quite in keeping. The worthy officer started from Putney police station to find you, and walked into the queerest trap ever set in this world. When the front door opened he walked straight onto the stage of a Christmas pantomime, where he could be kicked, clubbed, stunned, and drugged by the dancing harlequin, amid roars of laughter from all the most respectable people in Putney. Oh, you will never do anything better. And now, by the way, you might give me back those diamonds."

The green branch on which the glittering figure swung, rustled as if in astonishment; but the voice went on:

"I want you to give them back, Flambeau, and I want you to give up this life. There is still youth and honour and humour in you; don't fancy they will last in that trade. Men may keep a sort of level of good, but no man has ever been able to keep on one level of evil. That road goes down and down. The kind man drinks and turns cruel; the frank man kills and lies about it. Many a man I've known started like you to be an honest outlaw, a merry robber of the rich, and ended stamped into slime. Maurice Blum started out as an anarchist of principle, a father of the poor; he ended a greasy spy and tale-bearer that both sides used and despised. Harry Burke started his free money movement sincerely enough; now he's sponging on a half-starved sister for endless brandies and sodas. Lord Amber went into wild society in a sort of chivalry; now he's paying blackmail to the lowest vultures in London. Captain Barillon was the great gentleman-apache before your time; he died in a madhouse, screaming with fear of the "narks" and receivers that had betrayed him and hunted him down. I know the woods look very free behind you, Flambeau; I know that in a flash you could melt into them like a monkey. But some day you will be an old grey monkey, Flambeau. You will sit up in your free forest cold at heart and close to death, and the tree-tops will be very bare."

Everything continued still, as if the small man below held the other in the tree in some long invisible leash; and he went on:

"Your downward steps have begun. You used to boast of doing nothing mean, but you are doing something mean tonight. You are leaving suspicion on an honest boy with a good deal against him already; you are separating him from the woman he loves and who loves him. But you will do meaner things than that before you die."

Three flashing diamonds fell from the tree to the turf. The small man stooped to pick them up, and when he looked up again the green cage of the tree was emptied of its silver bird.

The restoration of the gems (accidentally picked up by Father Brown, of all people) ended the evening in uproarious triumph; and Sir Leopold, in his height of good humour, even told the priest that though he himself had broader views, he could respect those whose creed required them to be cloistered and ignorant of this world.

CHRISTMAS PARTY

Rex Stout

WITH NERO WOLFE, Rex Stout created one of the handful of great-est detectives in the history of mystery fiction. The genius if slothful detective weighs one-seventh of a ton, hates to leave his brownstone on Manhattan's West Thirty-fifth Street, and takes most cases only because the bank account requires it, as his housekeeper Fritz points out. While Wolfe is exclusively cerebral, his full-time employee, Archie Goodwin, is a big, tough detective who handles all the rough stuff. The combination of Goodwin's hard-boiled persona and Wolfe's purely deductive methods is unique among the major figures in all of crime fic-tion. "Christmas Party" was first published in the January 4, 1957, issue of *Col-lier's Weekly* as "The Christmas-Party Murder"; it was first collected under its more familiar title in *And Four to Go* (New York, Viking, 1958).

Christmas Party

REX STOUT

I

"I'm sorry, sir," I said. I tried to sound sorry. "But I told you two days ago, Monday, that I had a date for Friday afternoon, and you said all right. So I'll drive you to Long Island Saturday or Sunday."

Nero Wolfe shook his head. "That won't do. Mr. Thompson's ship docks Friday morning, and he will be at Mr. Hewitt's place only until Saturday noon, when he leaves for New Orleans. As you know, he is the best hybridizer in England, and I am grateful to Mr. Hewitt for inviting me to spend a few hours with him. As I remember, the drive takes about an hour and a half, so we should leave at twelve-thirty."

I decided to count ten, and swiveled my chair, facing my desk, so as to have privacy for it. As usual when we have no important case going, we had been getting on each other's nerves for a week, and I admit I was a little touchy, but his taking it for granted like that was a little too much. When I had finished the count I turned my head, to where he was perched on his throne behind his desk, and darned if he hadn't gone back to his book, making it plain that he regarded it as settled. That was much too much. I swiveled my chair to confront him.

"I really am sorry," I said, not trying to sound sorry, "but I have to keep that date Friday afternoon. It's a Christmas party at the office of Kurt Bottweill—you remember him, we did a job for

him a few months ago, the stolen tapestries. You may not remember a member of his staff named Margot Dickey, but I do. I have been seeing her some, and I promised her I'd go to the party. We never have a Christmas office party here. As for going to Long Island, your idea that a car is a death trap if I'm not driving it is unsound. You can take a taxi, or hire a Baxter man, or get Saul Panzer to drive you."

Wolfe had lowered his book. "I hope to get some useful information from Mr. Thompson, and you will take notes."

"Not if I'm not there. Hewitt's secretary knows orchid terms as well as I do. So do you."

I admit those last three words were a bit strong, but he shouldn't have gone back to his book. His lips tightened. "Archie. How many times in the past year have I asked you to drive me somewhere?"

"If you call it asking, maybe eighteen or twenty."

"Not excessive, surely. If my feeling that you alone are to be trusted at the wheel of a car is an aberration, I have it. We will leave for Mr. Hewitt's place Friday at twelve-thirty."

So there we were. I took a breath, but I didn't need to count ten again. If he was to be taught a lesson, and he certainly needed one, luckily I had in my possession a document that would make it good. Reaching to my inside breast pocket, I took out a folded sheet of paper.

"I didn't intend," I told him, "to spring this

551

on you until tomorrow, or maybe even later, but I guess it will have to be now. Just as well, I suppose."

I left my chair, unfolded the paper, and handed it to him. He put his book down to take it, gave it a look, shot a glance at me, looked at the paper again, and let it drop on his desk.

He snorted. "Pfui. What flummery is this?"

"No flummery. As you see, it's a marriage license for Archie Goodwin and Margot Dickey. It cost me two bucks. I could be mushy about it, but I won't. I will only say that if I am hooked at last, it took an expert. She intends to spread the tidings at the Christmas office party, and of course I have to be there. When you announce you have caught a fish it helps to have the fish present in person. Frankly, I would prefer to drive you to Long Island, but it can't be done."

The effect was all I could have asked. He gazed at me through narrowed eyes long enough to count eleven, then picked up the document and gazed at it. He flicked it from him to the edge of the desk as if it were crawling with germs, and focused on me again.

"You are deranged," he said evenly and distinctly. "Sit down."

I nodded. "I suppose," I agreed, remaining upright, "it's a form of madness, but so what if I've got it? Like what Margot was reading to me the other night—some poet, I think it was some Greek—'O love, resistless in thy might, thou triumphest even—'"

"Shut up and sit down!"

"Yes, sir." I didn't move. "But we're not rushing it. We haven't set the date, and there'll be plenty of time to decide on adjustments. You may not want me here any more, but that's up to you. As far as I'm concerned, I would like to stay. My long association with you has had its flaws, but I would hate to end it. The pay is okay, especially if I get a raise the first of the year, which is a week from Monday. I have grown to regard this old brownstone as my home, although you own it and although there are two creaky boards in the floor of my room. I appreciate working for the greatest private detective in the free world,

no matter how eccentric he is. I appreciate being able to go up to the plant rooms whenever I feel like it and look at ten thousand orchids, especially the odontoglossums. I fully appreciate—"

"Sit down!"

"I'm too worked up to sit. I fully appreciate Fritz's cooking. I like the billiard table in the basement. I like West Thirty-fifth Street. I like the one-way glass panel in the front door. I like this rug I'm standing on. I like your favorite color, yellow. I have told Margot all this, and more, including the fact that you are allergic to women. We have discussed it, and we think it may be worth trying, say for a month, when we get back from the honeymoon. My room could be our bedroom, and the other room on that floor could be our living room. There are plenty of closets. We could eat with you, as I have been, or we could eat up there, as you prefer. If the trial works out, new furniture or redecorating would be up to us. She will keep her job with Kurt Bottweill, so she wouldn't be here during the day, and since he's an interior decorator we would get things wholesale. Of course we merely suggest this for your consideration. It's your house."

I picked up my marriage license, folded it, and returned it to my pocket.

His eyes had stayed narrow and his lips tight. "I don't believe it," he growled. "What about Miss Rowan?"

"We won't drag Miss Rowan into this," I said stiffly.

"What about the thousands of others you dally with?"

"Not thousands. Not even a thousand. I'll have to look up 'dally.' They'll get theirs, as Margot has got hers. As you see, I'm deranged only up to a point. I realize—"

"Sit down."

"No, sir. I know this will have to be discussed, but right now you're stirred up and it would be better to wait for a day or two, or maybe more. By Saturday the idea of a woman in the house may have you boiling even worse than you are now, or it may have cooled you down to a simmer. If the former, no discussion will be needed. If the latter, you may decide it's worth a try. I hope you do."

I turned and walked out.

In the hall I hesitated. I could have gone up to my room and phoned from there, but in his present state it was quite possible he would listen in from the desk, and the call I wanted to make was personal. So I got my hat and coat from the rack, let myself out, descended the stoop steps, walked to the drugstore on Ninth Avenue, found the booth unoccupied, and dialed a number. In a moment a musical little voice—more a chirp than a voice—was in my ear.

"Kurt Bottweill's studio, good morning."

"This is Archie Goodwin, Cherry. May I speak to Margot?"

"Why, certainly. Just a moment."

It was a fairly long moment. Then another voice. "Archie, darling!"

"Yes, my own. I've got it."

"I knew you could!"

"Sure, I can do anything. Not only that, you said up to a hundred bucks, and I thought I would have to part with twenty at least, but it only took five. And not only that, but it's on me, because I've already had my money's worth of fun out of it, and more. I'll tell you about it when I see you. Shall I send it up by messenger?"

"No, I don't think—I'd better come and get it. Where are you?"

"In a phone booth. I'd just as soon not go back to the office right now because Mr. Wolfe wants to be alone to boil, so how about the Tulip Bar at the Churchill in twenty minutes? I feel like buying you a drink."

"I feel like buying *you* a drink!"

She should, since I was treating her to a marriage license.

II

When, at three o'clock Friday afternoon, I wriggled out of the taxi at the curb in front of the four-story building in the East Sixties, it was snowing. If it kept up, New York might have an off-white Christmas.

During the two days that had passed since I got my money's worth from the marriage license, the atmosphere around Wolfe's place had not been very seasonable. If we had had a case going, frequent and sustained communication would have been unavoidable, but without one there was nothing that absolutely had to be said, and we said it. Our handling of that trying period showed our true natures. At table, for instance, I was polite and reserved, and spoke, when speaking seemed necessary, in low and cultured tones. When Wolfe spoke he either snapped or barked. Neither of us mentioned the state of bliss I was headed for, or the adjustments that would have to be made, or my Friday date with my fiancée, or his trip to Long Island. But he arranged it somehow, for precisely at twelve-thirty on Friday a black limousine drew up in front of the house, and Wolfe, with the brim of his old black hat turned down and the collar of his new gray overcoat turned up for the snow, descended the stoop, stood massively, the mountain of him, on the bottom step until the uniformed chauffeur had opened the door, and crossed the sidewalk and climbed in. I watched it from above, from a window of my room.

I admit I was relieved and felt better. He had unquestionably needed a lesson and I didn't regret giving him one, but if he had passed up a chance for an orchid powwow with the best hybridizer in England I would never have heard the last of it. I went down to the kitchen and ate lunch with Fritz, who was so upset by the atmosphere that he forgot to put the lemon juice in the soufflé. I wanted to console him by telling him that everything would be rosy by Christmas, only three days off, but of course that wouldn't do.

I had a notion to toss a coin to decide whether I would have a look at the new exhibit of dinosaurs at the Natural History Museum or go to the Bottweill party, but I was curious to know how Margot was making out with the license, and also how the other Bottweill personnel were making out with each other. It was surprising that they were still making out at all. Cherry Quon's position in the setup was apparently minor, since she functioned chiefly as a receptionist and phone-answerer, but I had seen her black eyes dart daggers at Margot Dickey, who should have been clear out of her reach. I had gathered that it was Margot who was mainly relied upon to wrangle prospective customers into the corral, that Bottweill himself put them under the spell, and that Alfred Kiernan's part was to make sure that before the spell wore off an order got signed on the dotted line.

Of course that wasn't all. The order had to be filled, and that was handled, under Bottweill's supervision, by Emil Hatch in the workshop. Also funds were required to buy the ingredients, and they were furnished by a specimen named Mrs. Perry Porter Jerome. Margot had told me that Mrs. Jerome would be at the party and would bring her son Leo, whom I had never met. According to Margot, Leo, who had no connection with the Bottweill business or any other business, devoted his time to two important activities: getting enough cash from his mother to keep going as a junior playboy, and stopping the flow of cash to Bottweill, or at least slowing it down.

It was quite a tangle, an interesting exhibit of bipeds alive and kicking, and, deciding it promised more entertainment than the dead dinosaurs, I took a taxi to the East Sixties.

The ground floor of the four-story building, formerly a de luxe double-width residence, was now a beauty shop. The second floor was a real-estate office. The third floor was Kurt Bottweill's workshop, and on top was his studio. From the vestibule I took the do-it-yourself elevator to the top, opened the door, and stepped out into the glossy gold-leaf elegance I had first seen some months back, when Bottweill had hired Wolfe to find out who had swiped some tapestries. On that first visit I had decided that the only big difference between chrome modern and Bottweill gold-leaf modern was the color, and I still thought so. Not even skin deep; just a two-

hundred-thousandth of an inch deep. But on the panels and racks and furniture frames it gave the big skylighted studio quite a tone, and the rugs and drapes and pictures, all modern, joined in. It would have been a fine den for a blind millionaire.

"Archie!" a voice called. "Come and help us sample!"

It was Margot Dickey. In a far corner was a gold-leaf bar, some eight feet long, and she was at it on a gold-leaf stool. Cherry Quon and Alfred Kiernan were with her, also on stools, and behind the bar was Santa Claus, pouring from a champagne bottle. It was certainly a modern touch to have Santa Claus tend bar, but there was nothing modern about his costume. He was strictly traditional, cut, color, size, mask, and all, excepting that the hand grasping the champagne bottle wore a white glove. I assumed, crossing to them over the thick rugs, that that was a touch of Bottweill elegance, and didn't learn until later how wrong I was.

They gave me the season's greetings, and Santa Claus poured a glass of bubbles for me. No gold leaf on the glass. I was glad I had come. To drink champagne with a blonde at one elbow and a brunette at the other gives a man a sense of well-being, and those two were fine specimens—the tall, slender Margot relaxed, all curves, on the stool, and little slant-eyed black-eyed Cherry Quon, who came only up to my collar when standing, sitting with her spine as straight as a plumb line, yet not stiff. I thought Cherry worthy of notice not only as a statuette, though she was highly decorative, but as a possible source of new light on human relations. Margot had told me that her father was half Chinese and half Indian—not American Indian—and her mother was Dutch.

I said that apparently I had come too early, but Alfred Kiernan said no, the others were around and would be in shortly. He added that it was a pleasant surprise to see me, as it was just a little family gathering and he hadn't known others had been invited. Kiernan, whose title was business manager, had not liked a certain step I had taken when I was hunting the tapestries, and he still didn't, but an Irishman at a Christmas party likes everybody. My impression was that he really was pleased, so I was too. Margot said she had invited me, and Kiernan patted her on the arm and said that if she hadn't he would. About my age and fully as handsome, he was the kind who can pat the arm of a queen or a president's wife without making eyebrows go up.

He said we needed another sample and turned to the bartender. "Mr. Claus, we'll try the Veuve Clicquot." To us: "Just like Kurt to provide different brands. No monotony for Kurt." To the bartender: "May I call you by your first name, Santy?"

"Certainly, sir," Santa Claus told him from behind the mask in a thin falsetto that didn't match his size. As he stooped and came up with a bottle a door at the left opened and two men entered. One of them, Emil Hatch, I had met before. When briefing Wolfe on the tapestries and telling us about his staff, Bottweill had called Margot Dickey his contact woman, Cherry Quon his handy girl, and Emil Hatch his pet wizard, and when I met Hatch I found that he both looked the part and acted it. He wasn't much taller than Cherry Quon and skinny, and something had either pushed his left shoulder down or his right shoulder up, making him lop-sided, and he had a sour face, a sour voice, and a sour taste.

When the stranger was named to me as Leo Jerome, that placed him. I was acquainted with his mother, Mrs. Perry Porter Jerome. She was a widow and an angel—that is, Kurt Bottweill's angel. During the investigation she had talked as if the tapestries belonged to her, but that might have only been her manners, of which she had plenty. I could have made guesses about her personal relations with Bottweill, but hadn't bothered. I have enough to do to handle my own personal relations without wasting my brain power on other people's. As for her son Leo, he must have got his physique from his father—tall, bony, big-eared and long-armed. He was probably approaching thirty, below Kiernan but above Margot and Cherry.

When he shoved in between Cherry and me, giving me his back, and Emil Hatch had something to tell Kiernan, sour no doubt, I touched Margot's elbow and she slid off the stool and let herself be steered across to a divan which had been covered with designs by Euclid in six or seven colors. We stood looking down at it.

"Mighty pretty," I said, "but nothing like as pretty as you. If only that license were real! I can get a real one for two dollars. What do you say?"

"*You!*" she said scornfully. "You wouldn't marry Miss Universe if she came on her knees with a billion dollars."

"I dare her to try it. Did it work?"

"Perfect. Simply perfect."

"Then you're ditching me?"

"Yes, Archie darling. But I'll be a sister to you."

"I've got a sister. I want the license back for a souvenir, and anyway I don't want it kicking around. I could be hooked for forgery. You can mail it to me, once my own."

"No, I can't. He tore it up."

"The hell he did. Where are the pieces?"

"Gone. He put them in his wastebasket. Will you come to the wedding?"

"What wastebasket where?"

"The gold one by his desk in his office. Last evening after dinner. Will you come to the wedding?"

"I will not. My heart is bleeding. So will Mr. Wolfe's—and by the way, I'd better get out of here. I'm not going to stand around and sulk."

"You won't have to. He won't know I've told you, and anyway, you wouldn't be expected—Here he comes!"

She darted off to the bar and I headed that way. Through the door on the left appeared Mrs. Perry Porter Jerome, all of her, plump and plushy, with folds of mink trying to keep up as she breezed in. As she approached, those on stools left them and got onto their feet, but that courtesy could have been as much for her companion as for her. She was the angel, but Kurt Bottweill was the boss. He stopped five paces short of the bar, extended his arms as far as they would go, and sang out, "Merry Christmas, all my blessings! Merry merry merry!"

I still hadn't labeled him. My first impression, months ago, had been that he was one of them, but that had been wrong. He was a man all right, but the question was what kind. About average in height, round but not pudgy, maybe forty-two or -three, his fine black hair slicked back so that he looked balder than he was, he was nothing great to look at, but he had something, not only for women but for men too. Wolfe had once invited him to stay for dinner, and they had talked about the scrolls from the Dead Sea. I had seen him twice at baseball games. His label would have to wait.

As I joined them at the bar, where Santa Claus was pouring Mumms Cordon Rouge, Bottweill squinted at me a moment and then grinned. "Goodwin! You here? Good! Edith, your pet sleuth!"

Mrs. Perry Porter Jerome, reaching for a glass, stopped her hand to look at me. "Who asked you?" she demanded, then went on, with no room for a reply, "Cherry, I suppose. Cherry *is* a blessing. Leo, quit tugging at me. Very well, take it. It's warm in here." She let her son pull her coat off, then reached for a glass. By the time Leo got back from depositing the mink on the divan we all had glasses, and when he had his we raised them, and our eyes went to Bottweill.

His eyes flashed around. "There are times," he said, "when love takes over. There are times—"

"Wait a minute," Alfred Kiernan cut in. "You enjoy it too. You don't like this stuff."

"I can stand a sip, Al."

"But you won't enjoy it. Wait." Kiernan put his glass on the bar and marched to the door on the left and on out. In five seconds he was back, with a bottle in his hand, and as he rejoined us and asked Santa Claus for a glass I saw the Pernod label. He pulled the cork, which had been pulled before, filled the glass halfway, and held it out to Bottweill. "There," he said. "That will make it unanimous."

"Thanks, Al." Bottweill took it. "My secret public vice." He raised the glass. "I repeat, there are times when love takes over. (Santa Claus, where is yours? but I suppose you can't drink through that mask.) There are times when all the little demons disappear down their ratholes, and ugliness itself takes on the shape of beauty; when the darkest corner is touched by light; when the coldest heart feels the glow of warmth; when the trumpet call of good will and good cheer drowns out all the Babel of mean little noises. This is such a time. Merry Christmas! Merry merry merry!"

I was ready to touch glasses, but both the angel and the boss steered theirs to their lips, so I and the others followed suit. I thought Bottweill's eloquence deserved more than a sip, so I took a healthy gulp, and from the corner of my eye I saw that he was doing likewise with the Pernod. As I lowered the glass my eyes went to Mrs. Jerome, as she spoke.

"That was lovely," she declared. "Simply lovely. I must write it down and have it printed. That part about the trumpet call—*Kurt!* What is it? *Kurt!*"

He had dropped the glass and was clutching his throat with both hands. As I moved he turned loose of his throat, thrust his arms out, and let out a yell. I think he yelled, *"Merry!"* but I wasn't really listening. Others started for him too, but my reflexes were better trained for emergencies than any of theirs, so I got him first. As I got my arms around him he started choking and gurgling, and a spasm went over him from head to foot that nearly loosened my grip. They were making noises, but no screams, and someone was clawing at my arm. As I was telling them to get back and give me room, he was suddenly a dead weight, and I almost went down with him and might have if Kiernan hadn't grabbed his arm.

I called, "Get a doctor!" and Cherry ran to a table where there was a gold-leaf phone. Kiernan and I let Bottweill down on the rug. He was out, breathing fast and hard, but as I was straightening his head his breathing slowed down and foam showed on his lips. Mrs. Jerome was commanding us, "Do something, do something!"

There was nothing to do and I knew it. While I was holding on to him I had got a whiff of his breath, and now, kneeling, I leaned over to get my nose an inch from his, and I knew that smell, and it takes a big dose to hit that quick and hard. Kiernan was loosening Bottweill's tie and collar. Cherry Quon called to us that she had tried a doctor and couldn't get him and was trying another. Margot was squatting at Bottweill's feet, taking his shoes off, and I could have told her she might as well let him die with his boots on but didn't. I had two fingers on his wrist and my other hand inside his shirt, and could feel him going.

When I could feel nothing I abandoned the chest and wrist, took his hand, which was a fist, straightened the middle finger, and pressed its nail with my thumbtip until it was white. When I removed my thumb the nail stayed white. Dropping the hand, I yanked a little cluster of fibers from the rug, told Kiernan not to move, placed the fibers against Bottweill's nostrils, fastened my eyes on them, and held my breath for thirty seconds. The fibers didn't move.

I stood up and spoke. "His heart has stopped and he's not breathing. If a doctor came within three minutes and washed out his stomach with chemicals he wouldn't have with him, there might be one chance in a thousand. As it is—"

"Can't you *do* something?" Mrs. Jerome squawked.

"Not for him, no. I'm not an officer of the law, but I'm a licensed detective, and I'm supposed to know how to act in these circumstances, and I'll get it if I don't follow the rules. Of course—"

"*Do something!*" Mrs. Jerome squawked.

Kiernan's voice came from behind me. "He's dead."

I didn't turn to ask what test he had used. "Of course," I told them, "his drink was poisoned. Until the police come no one will touch anything, especially the bottle of Pernod, and no one will leave this room. You will—"

I stopped dead. Then I demanded, "Where is Santa Claus?"

Their heads turned to look at the bar. No bartender. On the chance that it had been too much for him, I pushed between Leo Jerome and Emil Hatch to step to the end of the bar, but he wasn't on the floor either.

I wheeled. "Did anyone see him go?"

They hadn't. Hatch said, "He didn't take the elevator. I'm sure he didn't. He must have—" He started off.

I blocked him. "You stay here. I'll take a look. Kiernan, phone the police. Spring seven-three-one-hundred."

I made for the door on the left and passed through, pulling it shut as I went, and was in Bottweill's office, which I had seen before. It was one-fourth the size of the studio, and much more subdued, but was by no means squalid. I crossed to the far end, saw through the glass panel that Bottweill's private elevator wasn't there, and pressed the button. A clank and a whirr came from inside the shaft, and it was coming. When it was up and had jolted to a stop I opened the door, and there on the floor was Santa Claus, but only the outside of him. He had molted. Jacket, breeches, mask, wig . . . I didn't check to see if it was all there, because I had another errand and not much time for it.

Propping the elevator door open with a chair, I went and circled around Bottweill's big gold-leaf desk to his gold-leaf wastebasket. It was one-third full. Bending, I started to paw, decided that was inefficient, picked it up and dumped it, and began tossing things back in one by one. Some of the items were torn pieces of paper, but none of them came from a marriage license. When I had finished I stayed down a moment, squatting, wondering if I had hurried too much and possibly missed it, and I might have gone through it again if I hadn't heard a faint noise from the studio that sounded like the elevator door opening. I went to the door to the studio and opened it, and as I crossed the sill two uniformed cops were deciding whether to give their first glance to the dead or the living.

* * *

III

Three hours later we were seated, more or less in a group, and my old friend and foe, Sergeant Purley Stebbins of Homicide, stood surveying us, his square jaw jutting and his big burly frame erect.

He spoke. "Mr. Kiernan and Mr. Hatch will be taken to the District Attorney's office for further questioning. The rest of you can go for the present, but you will keep yourselves available at the addresses you have given. Before you go I want to ask you again, here together, about the man who was here as Santa Claus. You have all claimed you know nothing about him. Do you still claim that?"

It was twenty minutes to seven. Some two dozen city employees—medical examiner, photographer, fingerprinters, meat-basket bearers, the whole kaboodle—had finished the on-the-scene routine, including private interviews with the eyewitnesses. I had made the highest score, having had sessions with Stebbins, a precinct man, and Inspector Cramer, who had departed around five o'clock to organize the hunt for Santa Claus.

"I'm not objecting," Kiernan told Stebbins, "to going to the District Attorney's office. I'm not objecting to anything. But we've told you all we can, I know I have. It seems to me your job is to find him."

"Do you mean to say," Mrs. Jerome demanded, "that no one knows anything at all about him?"

"So they say," Purley told her. "No one even knew there was going to be a Santa Claus, so they say. He was brought to this room by Bottweill, about a quarter to three, from his office. The idea is that Bottweill himself had arranged for him, and he came up in the private elevator and put on the costume in Bottweill's office. You may as well know there is some corroboration of that. We have found out where the costume came from—Burleson's on Forty-sixth Street. Bottweill phoned them yesterday afternoon and ordered it sent here, marked personal. Miss

Quon admits receiving the package and taking it to Bottweill in his office."

For a cop, you never just state a fact, or report it or declare it or say it. You admit it.

"We are also," Purley admitted, "covering agencies which might have supplied a man to act Santa Claus, but that's a big order. If Bottweill got a man through an agency there's no telling what he got. If it was a man with a record, when he saw trouble coming he beat it. With everybody's attention on Bottweill, he sneaked out, got his clothes, whatever he had taken off, in Bottweill's office, and went down in the elevator he had come up in. He shed the costume on the way down and after he was down, and left it in the elevator. If that was it, if he was just a man Bottweill hired, he wouldn't have had any reason to kill him—and besides, he wouldn't have known that Bottweill's only drink was Pernod, and he wouldn't have known where the poison was."

"Also," Emil Hatch said, sourer than ever, "if he was just hired for the job he was a damn fool to sneak out. He might have known he'd be found. So he wasn't just hired. He was someone who knew Bottweill, and knew about the Pernod and the poison, and had some good reason for wanting to kill him. You're wasting your time on the agencies."

Stebbins lifted his heavy broad shoulders and dropped them. "We waste most of our time, Mr. Hatch. Maybe he was too scared to think. I just want you to understand that if we find him and that's how Bottweill got him, it's going to be hard to believe that he put poison in that bottle, but somebody did. I want you to understand that so you'll understand why you are all to be available at the addresses you have given. Don't make any mistake about that."

"Do you mean," Mrs. Jerome demanded, "that we are under suspicion? That *I* and *my son* are under suspicion?"

Purley opened his mouth and shut it again. With that kind he always had trouble with his impulses. He wanted to say, "You're goddam right you are." He did say, "I mean we're going to find that Santa Claus, and when we do we'll see. If we can't see him for it we'll have to look further, and we'll expect all of you to help us. I'm taking it for granted you'll all want to help. Don't you want to, Mrs. Jerome?"

"I would help if I could, but I know nothing about it. I only know that my very dear friend is dead, and I don't intend to be abused and threatened. What about the poison?"

"You know about it. You have been questioned about it."

"I know I have, but what about it?"

"It must have been apparent from the questions. The medical examiner thinks it was cyanide and expects the autopsy to verify it. Emil Hatch uses potassium cyanide in his work with metals and plating, and there is a large jar of it on a cupboard shelf in the workshop one floor below, and there is a stair from Bottweill's office to the workroom. Anyone who knew that, and who also knew that Bottweill kept a case of Pernod in a cabinet in his office, and an open bottle of it in a drawer of his desk, couldn't have asked for a better setup. Four of you have admitted knowing both of those things. Three of you—Mrs. Jerome, Leo Jerome, and Archie Goodwin—admit they knew about the Pernod but deny they knew about the potassium cyanide. That will—"

"That's not true! She did know about it!"

Mrs. Perry Porter Jerome's hand shot out across her son's knees and slapped Cherry Quon's cheek or mouth or both. Her son grabbed her arm. Alfred Kiernan sprang to his feet, and for a second I thought he was going to sock Mrs. Jerome, and he did too, and possibly would have if Margot Dickey hadn't jerked at his coattail. Cherry put her hand to her face but, except for that, didn't move.

"Sit down," Stebbins told Kiernan. "Take it easy. Miss Quon, you say that Mrs. Jerome knew about the potassium cyanide?"

"Of course she did." Cherry's chirp was pitched lower than normal, but it was still a chirp. "In the workshop one day I heard Mr. Hatch telling her how he used it and how careful he had to be."

"Mr. Hatch? Do you verify—"

"Nonsense," Mrs. Jerome snapped. "What if he did? Perhaps he did. I had forgotten all about it. I told you I won't tolerate this abuse!"

Purley eyed her. "Look here, Mrs. Jerome. When we find that Santa Claus, if it was someone who knew Bottweill and had a motive, that may settle it. If not, it won't help anyone to talk about abuse, and that includes you. So far as I know now, only one of you has told us a lie. You. That's on the record. I'm telling you, and all of you, lies only make it harder for you, but sometimes they make it easier for us. I'll leave it at that for now. Mr. Kiernan and Mr. Hatch, these men"—he aimed a thumb over his shoulder at two dicks standing back of him—"will take you downtown. The rest of you can go, but remember what I said. Goodwin, I want to see you."

He had already seen me, but I wouldn't make a point of it. Kiernan, however, had a point to make, and made it: he had to leave last so he could lock up. It was so arranged. The three women, Leo Jerome, and Stebbins and I took the elevator down, leaving the two dicks with Kiernan and Hatch. Down the sidewalk, as they headed in different directions, I could see no sign of tails taking after them. It was still snowing, a fine prospect for Christmas and the street cleaners. There were two police cars at the curb, and Purley went to one and opened the door and motioned to me to get in.

I objected. "If I'm invited downtown too I'm willing to oblige, but I'm going to eat first. I damn near starved to death there once."

"You're not wanted downtown, not right now. Get in out of the snow."

I did so, and slid across under the wheel to make room for him. He needs room. He joined me and pulled the door shut.

"If we're going to sit here," I suggested, "we might as well be rolling. Don't bother to cross town, just drop me at Thirty-fifth."

He objected. "I don't like to drive and talk. Or listen. What were you doing there today?"

"I've told you. Having fun. Three kinds of champagne. Miss Dickey invited me."

"I'm giving you another chance. You were the only outsider there. Why? You're nothing special to Miss Dickey. She was going to marry Bottweill. Why?"

"Ask her."

"We have asked her. She says there was no particular reason, she knew Bottweill liked you, and they've regarded you as one of them since you found some tapestries for them. She stuttered around about it. What I say, any time I find you anywhere near a murder, I want to know. I'm giving you another chance."

So she hadn't mentioned the marriage license. Good for her. I would rather have eaten all the snow that had fallen since noon than explain that damn license to Sergeant Stebbins or Inspector Cramer. That was why I had gone through the wastebasket. "Thanks for the chance," I told him, "but I can't use it. I've told you everything I saw and heard there today." That put me in a class with Mrs. Jerome, since I had left out my little talk with Margot. "I've told you all I know about those people. Lay off and go find your murderer."

"I know you, Goodwin."

"Yeah, you've even called me Archie. I treasure that memory."

"I know you." His head was turned on his bull neck, and our eyes were meeting. "Do you expect me to believe that guy got out of that room and away without you knowing it?"

"Nuts. I was kneeling on the floor, watching a man die, and they were around us. Anyway, you're just talking to hear yourself. You don't think I was accessory to the murder or to the murderer's escape."

"I didn't say I did. Even if he was wearing gloves—and what for if not to leave no prints?—I don't say he was the murderer. But if you knew who he was and didn't want him involved in it and let him get away, and if you let us wear out our ankles looking for him, what about that?"

"That would be bad. If I asked my advice I would be against it."

"Goddam it," he barked, "do you know who he is?"

"No."

"Did you or Wolfe have anything to do with getting him there?"

"No."

"All right, pile out. They'll be wanting you downtown."

"I hope not tonight. I'm tired." I opened the door. "You have my address." I stepped out into the snow, and he started the engine and rolled off.

It should have been a good hour for an empty taxi, but in a Christmas-season snowstorm it took me ten minutes to find one. When it pulled up in front of the old brownstone on West Thirty-fifth Street it was eight minutes to eight.

As usual in my absence, the chain-bolt was on, and I had to ring for Fritz to let me in. I asked him if Wolfe was back, and he said yes, he was at dinner. As I put my hat on the shelf and my coat on a hanger I asked if there was any left for me, and he said plenty, and moved aside for me to precede him down the hall to the door of the dining room. Fritz has fine manners.

Wolfe, in his oversized chair at the end of the table, told me good evening, not snapping or barking. I returned it, got seated at my place, picked up my napkin, and apologized for being late. Fritz came, from the kitchen, with a warm plate, a platter of braised boned ducklings, and a dish of potatoes baked with mushrooms and cheese. I took enough. Wolfe asked if it was still snowing and I said yes. After a good mouthful had been disposed of, I spoke.

"As you know, I approve of your rule not to discuss business during a meal, but I've got something on my chest and it's not business. It's personal."

He grunted. "The death of Mr. Bottweill was reported on the radio at seven o'clock. You were there."

"Yeah. I was there. I was kneeling by him while he died." I replenished my mouth. Damn the radio. I hadn't intended to mention the murder until I had dealt with the main issue from my standpoint. When there was room enough for my tongue to work I went on, "I'll report on that in full if you want it, but I doubt if there's a job in it. Mrs. Perry Porter Jerome is the only suspect with enough jack to pay your fee, and she has already notified Purley Stebbins that she won't be abused. Besides, when they find Santa Claus that may settle it. What I want to report on happened before Bottweill died. That marriage license I showed you is for the birds. Miss Dickey has called it off. I am out two bucks. She told me she had decided to marry Bottweill."

He was sopping a crust in the sauce on his plate. "Indeed," he said.

"Yes, sir. It was a jolt, but I would have recovered, in time. Then ten minutes later Bottweill was dead. Where does that leave me? Sitting around up there through the routine, I considered it. Perhaps I could get her back now, but no thank you. That license has been destroyed. I get another one, another two bucks, and then she tells me she has decided to marry Joe Doakes. I'm going to forget her. I'm going to blot her out."

I resumed on the duckling. Wolfe was busy chewing. When he could he said, "For me, of course, this is satisfactory."

"I know it is. Do you want to hear about Bottweill?"

"After dinner."

"Okay. How did you make out with Thompson?"

But that didn't appeal to him as a dinner topic either. In fact, nothing did. Usually he likes table talk, about anything from refrigerators to Republicans, but apparently the trip to Long Island and back, with all its dangers, had tired him out. It suited me all right, since I had had a noisy afternoon too and could stand a little silence. When we had both done well with the duckling and potatoes and salad and baked pears and cheese and coffee, he pushed back his chair.

"There's a book," he said, "that I want to look at. It's up in your room—*Here and Now*, by Herbert Block. Will you bring it down, please?"

Though it meant climbing two flights with a full stomach, I was glad to oblige, out of appreciation for his calm acceptance of my announce-

ment of my shattered hopes. He could have been very vocal. So I mounted the stairs cheerfully, went to my room, and crossed to the shelves where I keep a few books. There were only a couple of dozen of them, and I knew where each one was, but *Here and Now* wasn't there. Where it should have been was a gap. I looked around, saw a book on the dresser, and stepped to it. It was *Here and Now*, and lying on top of it was a pair of white cotton gloves.

I gawked.

IV

I would like to say that I caught on immediately, the second I spotted them, but I didn't. I had picked them up and looked them over, and put one of them on and taken it off again, before I fully realized that there was only one possible explanation. Having realized it, instantly there was a traffic jam inside my skull, horns blowing, brakes squealing, head-on collisions. To deal with it I went to a chair and sat. It took me maybe a minute to reach my first clear conclusion.

He had taken this method of telling me he was Santa Claus, instead of just telling me, because he wanted me to think it over on my own before we talked it over together.

Why did he want me to think it over on my own? That took a little longer, but with the traffic under control I found my way through to the only acceptable answer. He had decided to give up his trip to see Thompson, and instead to arrange with Bottweill to attend the Christmas party disguised as Santa Claus, because the idea of a woman living in his house—or of the only alternative, my leaving—had made him absolutely desperate, and he had to see for himself. He had to see Margot and me together, and to talk with her if possible. If he found out that the marriage license was a hoax he would have me by the tail; he could tell me he would be delighted to welcome my bride and watch me wriggle out. If he found that I really meant it he would know what he was up against and go on from there. The point was this, that he had shown what he really thought of me. He had shown that rather than lose me he would do something that he wouldn't have done for any fee anybody could name. He would rather have gone without beer for a week than admit it, but now he was a fugitive from justice in a murder case and needed me. So he had to let me know, but he wanted it understood that that aspect of the matter was not to be mentioned. The assumption would be that he had gone to Bottweill's instead of Long Island because he loved to dress up like Santa Claus and tend bar.

A cell in my brain tried to get the right of way for the question, considering this development, how big a raise should I get after New Year's? but I waved it to the curb.

I thought over other aspects. He had worn the gloves so I couldn't recognize his hands. Where did he get them? What time had he got to Bottweill's and who had seen him? Did Fritz know where he was going? How had he got back home? But after a little of that I realized that he hadn't sent me up to my room to ask myself questions he could answer, so I went back to considering whether there was anything else he wanted me to think over alone. Deciding there wasn't, after chewing it thoroughly, I got *Here and Now* and the gloves from the dresser, went to the stairs and descended, and entered the office.

From behind his desk, he glared at me as I crossed over.

"Here it is," I said, and handed him the book. "And much obliged for the gloves." I held them up, one in each hand, dangling them from thumb and fingertip.

"It is no occasion for clowning," he growled.

"It sure isn't." I dropped the gloves on my desk, whirled my chair, and sat. "Where do we start? Do you want to know what happened after you left?"

"The details can wait. First where we stand. Was Mr. Cramer there?"

"Yes. Certainly."

"Did he get anywhere?"

"No. He probably won't until he finds Santa Claus. Until they find Santa Claus they won't dig very hard at the others. The longer it takes to find him the surer they'll be he's it. Three things about him: nobody knows who he was, he beat it, and he wore gloves. A thousand men are looking for him. You were right to wear the gloves, I would have recognized your hands, but where did you get them?"

"At a store on Ninth Avenue. Confound it, I didn't know a man was going to be murdered!"

"I know you didn't. May I ask some questions?"

He scowled. I took it for yes. "When did you phone Bottweill to arrange it?"

"At two-thirty yesterday afternoon. You had gone to the bank."

"Have you any reason to think he told anyone about it?"

"No. He said he wouldn't."

"I know he got the costume, so that's okay. When you left here today at twelve-thirty did you go straight to Bottweill's?"

"No. I left at that hour because you and Fritz expected me to. I stopped to buy the gloves, and met him at Rusterman's, and we had lunch. From there we took a cab to his place, arriving shortly after two o'clock, and took his private elevator up to his office. Immediately upon entering his office, he got a bottle of Pernod from a drawer of his desk, said he always had a little after lunch, and invited me to join him. I declined. He poured a liberal portion in a glass, about two ounces, drank it in two gulps, and returned the bottle to the drawer."

"My God." I whistled. "The cops would like to know *that*."

"No doubt. The costume was there in a box. There is a dressing room at the rear of his office, with a bathroom—"

"I know. I've used it."

"I took the costume there and put it on. He had ordered the largest size, but it was a squeeze and it took a while. I was in there half an hour or more. When I re-entered the office it was empty, but soon Bottweill came, up the stairs from the workshop, and helped me with the mask and wig. They had barely been adjusted when Emil Hatch and Mrs. Jerome and her son appeared, also coming up the stairs from the workshop. I left, going to the studio, and found Miss Quon and Miss Dickey and Mr. Kiernan there."

"And before long I was there. Then no one saw you unmasked. When did you put the gloves on?"

"The last thing. Just before I entered the studio."

"Then you may have left prints. I know, you didn't know there was going to be a murder. You left your clothes in the dressing room? Are you sure you got everything when you left?"

"Yes. I am not a complete ass."

I let that by. "Why didn't you leave the gloves in the elevator with the costume?"

"Because they hadn't come with it, and I thought it better to take them."

"That private elevator is at the rear of the hall downstairs. Did anyone see you leaving it or passing through the hall?"

"No. The hall was empty."

"How did you get home? Taxi?"

"No. Fritz didn't expect me until six or later. I walked to the public library, spent some two hours there, and then took a cab."

I pursed my lips and shook my head to indicate sympathy. That was his longest and hardest tramp since Montenegro. Over a mile. Fighting his way through the blizzard, in terror of the law on his tail. But all the return I got for my look of sympathy was a scowl, so I let loose. I laughed. I put my head back and let it come. I had wanted to ever since I had learned he was Santa Claus, but had been too busy thinking. It was bottled up in me, and I let it out, good. I was about to taper off to a cackle when he exploded.

"Confound it," he bellowed, "marry and be damned!"

That was dangerous. That attitude could easily get us onto the aspect he had sent me up to my room to think over alone, and if we got started on that anything could happen. It called for tact.

"I beg your pardon," I said. "Something caught in my throat. Do you want to describe the situation, or do you want me to?"

"I would like to hear you try," he said grimly.

"Yes, sir. I suspect that the only thing to do is to phone Inspector Cramer right now and invite him to come and have a chat, and when he comes open the bag. That will—"

"No. I will not do that."

"Then, next best, I go to him and spill it there. Of course—"

"No." He meant every word of it.

"Okay, I'll describe it. They'll mark time on the others until they find Santa Claus. They've got to find him. If he left any prints they'll compare them with every file they've got, and sooner or later they'll get to yours. They'll cover all the stores for sales of white cotton gloves to men. They'll trace Bottweill's movements and learn that he lunched with you at Rusterman's, and you left together, and they'll trace you to Bottweill's place. Of course your going there won't prove you were Santa Claus, you might talk your way out of that, and it will account for your prints if they find some, but what about the gloves? They'll trace that sale if you give them time, and with a description of the buyer they'll find Santa Claus. You're sunk."

I had never seen his face blacker.

"If you sit tight till they find him," I argued, "it will be quite a nuisance. Cramer has been itching for years to lock you up, and any judge would commit you as a material witness who had run out. Whereas if you call Cramer now, and I mean now, and invite him to come and have some beer, while it will still be a nuisance, it will be bearable. Of course he'll want to know why you went there and played Santa Claus, but you can tell him anything you please. Tell him you bet me a hundred bucks, or what the hell, make it a grand, that you could be in a room with me for ten minutes and I wouldn't recognize you. I'll be glad to cooperate."

I leaned forward. "Another thing. If you wait till they find you, you won't dare tell them that Bottweill took a drink from that bottle shortly after two o'clock and it didn't hurt him. If you told about that after they dug you up, they could book you for withholding evidence, and they probably would, and make it stick. If you get Cramer here now and tell him he'll appreciate it, though naturally he won't say so. He's probably at his office. Shall I ring him?"

"No. I will not confess that performance to Mr. Cramer. I will not unfold the morning paper to a disclosure of that outlandish masquerade."

"Then you're going to sit and read *Here and Now* until they come with a warrant?"

"No. That would be fatuous." He took in air through his mouth, as far down as it would go, and let it out through his nose. "I'm going to find the murderer and present him to Mr. Cramer. There's nothing else."

"Oh. You are."

"Yes."

"You might have said so and saved my breath, instead of letting me spout."

"I wanted to see if your appraisal of the situation agreed with mine. It does."

"That's fine. Then you also know that we may have two weeks and we may have two minutes. At this very second some expert may be phoning Homicide to say that he has found fingerprints that match on the card of Wolfe, Nero—"

The phone rang, and I jerked around as if someone had stuck a needle in me. Maybe we wouldn't have even two minutes. My hand wasn't trembling as I lifted the receiver, I hope. Wolfe seldom lifts his until I have found out who it is, but that time he did.

"Nero Wolfe's office, Archie Goodwin speaking."

"This is the District Attorney's office, Mr. Goodwin. Regarding the murder of Kurt Bottweill. We would like you to be here at ten o'clock tomorrow morning."

"All right. Sure."

"At ten o'clock sharp, please."

"I'll be there."

We hung up. Wolfe sighed. I sighed.

"Well," I said, "I've already told them six times that I know absolutely nothing about Santa Claus, so they may not ask me again. If they do, it will be interesting to compare my voice when I'm lying with when I'm telling the truth."

He grunted. "Now. I want a complete report of what happened there after I left, but first I want background. In your intimate association with Miss Dickey you must have learned things about those people. What?"

"Not much." I cleared my throat. "I guess I'll have to explain something. My association with Miss Dickey was not intimate." I stopped. It wasn't easy.

"Choose your own adjective. I meant no innuendo."

"It's not a question of adjectives. Miss Dickey is a good dancer, exceptionally good, and for the past couple of months I have been taking her here and there, some six or eight times altogether. Monday evening at the Flamingo Club she asked me to do her a favor. She said Bottweill was giving her a runaround, that he had been going to marry her for a year but kept stalling, and she wanted to do something. She said Cherry Quon was making a play for him, and she didn't intend to let Cherry take the rail. She asked me to get a marriage-license blank and fill it out for her and me and give it to her. She would show it to Bottweill and tell him now or never. It struck me as a good deed with no risk involved, and, as I say, she is a good dancer. Tuesday afternoon I got a blank, no matter how, and that evening, up in my room, I filled in, including a fancy signature."

Wolfe made a noise.

"That's all," I said, "except that I want to make it clear that I had no intention of showing it to you. I did that on the spur of the moment when you picked up your book. Your memory is as good as mine. Also, to close it up, no doubt you noticed that today just before Bottweill and Mrs. Jerome joined the party Margot and I stepped aside for a little chat. She told me the license did the trick. Her words were, 'Perfect, simply perfect.' She said that last evening, in his office, he tore the license up and put the pieces in his wastebasket. That's okay, the cops didn't find them. I looked before they came, and the pieces weren't there."

His mouth was working, but he didn't open it. He didn't dare. He would have liked to tear into me, to tell me that my insufferable flummery had got him into this awful mess, but if he did so he would be dragging in the aspect he didn't want mentioned. He saw that in time, and saw that I saw it. His mouth worked, but that was all. Finally he spoke.

"Then you are not on intimate terms with Miss Dickey."

"No, sir."

"Even so, she must have spoken of that establishment and those people."

"Some, yes."

"And one of them killed Bottweill. The poison was put in the bottle between two-ten, when I saw him take a drink, and three-thirty when Kiernan went and got the bottle. No one came up in the private elevator during the half-hour or more I was in the dressing room. I was getting into that costume and gave no heed to footsteps or other sounds in the office, but the elevator shaft adjoins the dressing room, and I would have heard it. It is a strong probability that the opportunity was even narrower, that the poison was put in the bottle while I was in the dressing room, since three of them were in the office with Bottweill when I left. It must be assumed that one of those three, or one of the three in the studio, had grasped an earlier opportunity. What about them?"

"Not much. Mostly from Monday evening, when Margot was talking about Bottweill. So it's all hearsay, from her. Mrs. Jerome has put half a million in the business—probably you should divide that by two at least—and thinks she owns him. Or thought. She was jealous of Margot and Cherry. As for Leo, if his mother was dishing out the dough he expected to inherit to a guy who was trying to corner the world's supply of gold leaf, and possibly might also marry him, and if he knew about the jar of poison in the workshop, he might have been tempted. Kiernan, I don't know, but from a re-

mark Margot made and from the way he looked at Cherry this afternoon, I suspect he would like to mix some Irish with her Chinese and Indian and Dutch, and if he thought Bottweill had him stymied he might have been tempted too. So much for hearsay."

"Mr. Hatch?"

"Nothing on him from Margot, but, dealing with him during the tapestry job, I wouldn't have been surprised if he had wiped out the whole bunch on general principles. His heart pumps acid instead of blood. He's a creative artist, he told me so. He practically told me that he was responsible for the success of that enterprise but got no credit. He didn't tell me that he regarded Bottweill as a phony and a fourflusher, but he did. You may remember that I told you he had a persecution complex and you told me to stop using other people's jargon."

"That's four of them. Miss Dickey?"

I raised my brows. "I got her a license to marry, not to kill. If she was lying when she said it worked, she's almost as good a liar as she is a dancer. Maybe she is. If it didn't work she might have been tempted too."

"And Miss Quon?"

"She's half Oriental. I'm not up on Orientals, but I understand they slant their eyes to keep you guessing. That's what makes them inscrutable. If I had to be poisoned by one of that bunch I would want it to be her. Except for what Margot told me—"

The doorbell rang. That was worse than the phone. If they had hit on Santa Claus's trail and it led to Nero Wolfe, Cramer was much more apt to come than to call. Wolfe and I exchanged glances. Looking at my wristwatch and seeing 10:08, I arose, went to the hall and flipped the switch for the stoop light, and took a look through the one-way glass panel of the front door. I have good eyes, but the figure was muffled in a heavy coat with a hood, so I stepped halfway to the door to make sure. Then I returned to the office and told Wolfe, "Cherry Quon. Alone."

He frowned. "I wanted—" He cut it off. "Very well. Bring her in."

V

As I have said, Cherry was highly decorative, and she went fine with the red leather chair at the end of Wolfe's desk. It would have held three of her. She had let me take her coat in the hall and still had on the neat little woolen number she had worn at the party. It wasn't exactly yellow, but there was yellow in it. I would have called it off-gold, and it and the red chair and the tea tint of her smooth little carved face would have made a very nice kodachrome.

She sat on the edge, her spine straight and her hands together in her lap. "I was afraid to telephone," she said, "because you might tell me not to come. So I just came. Will you forgive me?"

Wolfe grunted. No commitment. She smiled at him, a friendly smile, or so I thought. After all, she was half Oriental.

"I must get myself together," she chirped. "I'm nervous because it's so exciting to be here." She turned her head. "There's the glove, and the bookshelves, and the safe, and the couch, and of course Archie Goodwin. And you. You behind your desk in your enormous chair! Oh, I know this place! I have read about you so much— everything there is, I think. It's exciting to be here, actually here in this chair, and see you. Of course I saw you this afternoon, but that wasn't the same thing, you could have been anybody in that silly Santa Claus costume. I wanted to pull your whiskers."

She laughed, a friendly little tinkle like a bell.

I think I looked bewildered. That was my idea, after it had got through my ears to the switchboard inside and been routed. I was too busy handling my face to look at Wolfe, but he was probably even busier, since she was looking straight at him. I moved my eyes to him when he spoke.

"If I understand you, Miss Quon, I'm at a loss. If you think you saw me this afternoon in a Santa Claus costume, you're mistaken."

"Oh, I'm sorry!" she exclaimed. "Then you haven't told them?"

"My dear madam." His voice sharpened. "If you must talk in riddles, talk to Mr. Goodwin. He enjoys them."

"But I *am* sorry, Mr. Wolfe. I should have explained first how I know. This morning at breakfast Kurt told me you had phoned him and arranged to appear at the party as Santa Claus, and this afternoon I asked him if you had come and he said you had and you were putting on the costume. That's how I know. But you haven't told the police? Then it's a good thing I haven't told them either, isn't it?"

"This is interesting," Wolfe said coldly. "What do you expect to accomplish by this fantastic folderol?"

She shook her pretty little head. "You, with so much sense. You must see that it's no use. If I tell them, even if they don't like to believe me they will investigate. I know they can't investigate as well as you can, but surely they will find something."

He shut his eyes, tightened his lips, and leaned back in his chair. I kept mine open, on her. She weighed about a hundred and two. I could carry her under one arm with my other hand clamped on her mouth. Putting her in the spare room upstairs wouldn't do, since she could open a window and scream, but there was a cubbyhole in the basement, next to Fritz's room, with an old couch in it. Or, as an alternative, I could get a gun from my desk drawer and shoot her. Probably no one knew she had come here.

Wolfe opened his eyes and straightened up. "Very well. It is still fantastic, but I concede that you could create an unpleasant situation by taking that yarn to the police. I don't suppose you came here merely to tell me that you intend to. What do you intend?"

"I think we understand each other," she chirped.

"I understand only that you want something. What?"

"You are so direct," she complained. "So very abrupt, that I must have said something wrong. But I do want something. You see, since the police think it was the man who acted Santa

Claus and ran away, they may not get on the right track until it's too late. You wouldn't want that, would you?"

No reply.

"I wouldn't want it," she said, and her hands on her lap curled into little fists. "I wouldn't want whoever killed Kurt to get away, no matter who it was, but you see, I know who killed him. I have told the police, but they won't listen until they find Santa Claus, or if they listen they think I'm just a jealous cat, and besides, I'm an Oriental and their ideas of Orientals are very primitive. I was going to make them listen by telling them who Santa Claus was, but I know how they feel about you from what I've read, and I was afraid they would try to prove it was you who killed Kurt, and of course it could have been you, and you did run away, and they still wouldn't listen to me when I told them who did kill him."

She stopped for breath. Wolfe inquired, "Who did?"

She nodded. "I'll tell you. Margot Dickey and Kurt were having an affair. A few months ago Kurt began on me, and it was hard for me because I—I—" She frowned for a word, and found one. "I had a feeling for him. I had a strong feeling. But you see, I am a virgin, and I wouldn't give in to him. I don't know what I would have done if I hadn't known he was having an affair with Margot, but I did know, and I told him the first man I slept with would be my husband. He said he was willing to give up Margot, but even if he did he couldn't marry me on account of Mrs. Jerome, because she would stop backing him with her money. I don't know what he was to Mrs. Jerome, but I know what she was to him."

Her hands opened and closed again to be fists. "That went on and on, but Kurt had a feeling for me too. Last night late, it was after midnight, he phoned me that he had broken with Margot for good and he wanted to marry me. He wanted to come and see me, but I told him I was in bed and we would see each other in the morning. He said that would be at the studio

with other people there, so finally I said I would go to his apartment for breakfast, and I did, this morning. But I am still a virgin, Mr. Wolfe."

He was focused on her with half-closed eyes. "That is your privilege, madam."

"Oh," she said. "Is it a privilege? It was there, at breakfast, that he told me about you, your arranging to be Santa Claus. When I got to the studio I was surprised to see Margot there, and how friendly she was. That was part of her plan, to be friendly and cheerful with everyone. She has told the police that Kurt was going to marry her, that they decided last night to get married next week. Christmas week. I am a Christian."

Wolfe stirred in his chair. "Have we reached the point? Did Miss Dickey kill Mr. Bottweill?"

"Yes. Of course she did."

"Have you told the police that?"

"Yes. I didn't tell them all I have told you, but enough."

"With evidence?"

"No. I have no evidence."

"Then you're vulnerable to an action for slander."

She opened her fists and turned her palms up. "Does that matter? When I know I'm right? When I *know* it? But she was so clever, the way she did it, that there can't be any evidence. Everybody there today knew about the poison, and they all had a chance to put it in the bottle. They can never prove she did it. They can't even prove she is lying when she says Kurt was going to marry her, because he is dead. She acted today the way she would have acted if that had been true. But it has got to be proved somehow. There has got to be evidence to prove it."

"And you want me to get it?"

She let that pass. "What I was thinking, Mr. Wolfe, you are vulnerable too. There will always be the danger that the police will find out who Santa Claus was, and if they find it was you and you didn't tell them—"

"I haven't conceded that," Wolfe snapped.

"Then we'll just say there will always be the danger that I'll tell them what Kurt told me, and you did concede that that would be unpleasant.

So it would be better if the evidence proved who killed Kurt and also proved who Santa Claus was. Wouldn't it?"

"Go on."

"So I thought how easy it would be for you to get the evidence. You have men who do things for you, who would do anything for you, and one of them can say that you asked him to go there and be Santa Claus, and he did. Of course it couldn't be Mr. Goodwin, since he was at the party, and it would have to be a man they couldn't prove was somewhere else. He can say that while he was in the dressing room putting on the costume he heard someone in the office and peeked out to see who it was, and he saw Margot Dickey get the bottle from the desk drawer and put something in it and put the bottle back in the drawer, and go out. That must have been when she did it, because Kurt always took a drink of Pernod when he came back from lunch."

Wolfe was rubbing his lip with a fingertip. "I see," he muttered.

She wasn't through. "He can say," she went on, "that he ran away because he was frightened and wanted to tell you about it first. I don't think they would do anything to him if he went to them tomorrow morning and told them all about it, would they? Just like me. I don't think they would do anything to me if I went to them tomorrow morning and told them I had remembered that Kurt told me that you were going to be Santa Claus, and this afternoon he told me you were in the dressing room putting on the costume. That would be the same kind of thing, wouldn't it?"

Her little carved mouth thinned and widened with a smile. "That's what I want," she chirped. "Did I say it so you understand it?"

"You did indeed," Wolfe assured her. "You put it admirably."

"Would it be better, instead of him going to tell them, for you to have Inspector Cramer come here, and you tell him? You could have the man here. You see, I know how you do things, from all I have read."

"That might be better," he allowed. His tone was dry but not hostile. I could see a muscle twitching beneath his right ear, but she couldn't. "I suppose, Miss Quon, it is futile to advance the possibility that one of the others killed him, and if so it would be a pity—"

"Excuse me. I interrupt." The chirp was still a chirp, but it had hard steel in it. "I know she killed him."

"I don't. And even if I bow to your conviction, before I could undertake the stratagem you propose I would have to make sure there are no facts that would scuttle it. It won't take me long. You'll hear from me tomorrow. I'll want—"

She interrupted again. "I can't wait longer than tomorrow morning to tell them what Kurt told me."

"Pfui. You can and will. The moment you disclose that, you no longer have a whip to dangle at me. You will hear from me tomorrow. Now I want to think. Archie?"

I left my chair. She looked up at me and back at Wolfe. For some seconds she sat, considering, inscrutable of course, then stood up.

"It was very exciting to be here," she said, the steel gone, "to see you here. You must forgive me for not phoning. I hope it will be early tomorrow." She turned and headed for the door, and I followed.

After I had helped her on with her hooded coat, and let her out, and watched her picking her way down the seven steps, I shut the door, put the chain-bolt on, returned to the office, and told Wolfe, "It has stopped snowing. Who do you think will be best for it, Saul or Fred or Orrie or Bill?"

"Sit down," he growled. "You see through women. Well?"

"Not that one. I pass. I wouldn't bet a dime on her one way or the other. Would you?"

"No. She is probably a liar and possibly a murderer. Sit down. I must have everything that happened there today after I left. Every word and gesture."

I sat and gave it to him. Including the question period, it took an hour and thirty-five minutes. It was after one o'clock when he pushed his chair back, levered his bulk upright, told me good night, and went up to bed.

VI

At half past two the following afternoon, Saturday, I sat in a room in a building on Leonard Street, the room where I had once swiped an assistant district attorney's lunch. There would be no need for me to repeat the performance, since I had just come back from Ost's restaurant, where I had put away a plateful of pig's knuckles and sauerkraut.

As far as I knew, there had not only been no steps to frame Margot for murder; there had been no steps at all. Since Wolfe is up in the plant rooms every morning from nine to eleven, and since he breakfasts from a tray up in his room, and since I was expected downtown at ten o'clock, I had buzzed him on the house phone a little before nine to ask for instructions and had been told that he had none. Downtown Assistant DA Farrell, after letting me wait in the anteroom for an hour, had spent two hours with me, together with a stenographer and a dick who had been on the scene Friday afternoon, going back and forth and zigzag, not only over what I had already reported, but also over my previous association with the Bottweill personnel. He only asked me once if I knew anything about Santa Claus, so I only had to lie once, if you don't count my omitting any mention of the marriage license. When he called a recess and told me to come back at two-thirty, on my way to Ost's for the pig's knuckles I phoned Wolfe to tell him I didn't know when I would be home, and again he had no instructions. I said I doubted if Cherry Quon would wait until after New Year's to spill the beans, and he said he did too and hung up.

When I was ushered back into Farrell's office at two-thirty he was alone—no stenographer and no dick. He asked me if I had had a good lunch, and even waited for me to answer, handed me some typewritten sheets, and leaned back in his chair.

"Read it over," he said, "and see if you want to sign it."

His tone seemed to imply that I might not, so I went over it carefully, five full pages. Finding no editorial revisions to object to, I pulled my chair forward to a corner of his desk, put the statement on the desk top, and got my pen from my pocket.

"Wait a minute," Farrell said. "You're not a bad guy even if you are cocky, and why not give you a break? That says specifically that you have reported everything you did there yesterday afternoon."

"Yeah, I've read it. So?"

"So who put your fingerprints on some of the pieces of paper in Bottweill's wastebasket?"

"I'll be damned," I said. "I forgot to put gloves on."

"All right, you're cocky. I already know that." His eyes were pinning me. "You must have gone through that wastebasket, every item, when you went to Bottweill's office ostensibly to look for Santa Claus, and you hadn't just forgotten it. You don't forget things. So you have deliberately left it out. I want to know why, and I want to know what you took from that wastebasket and what you did with it."

I grinned at him. "I am also damned because I thought I knew how thorough they are and apparently I didn't. I wouldn't have supposed they went so far as to dust the contents of a wastebasket when there was nothing to connect them, but I see I was wrong, and I hate to be wrong." I shrugged. "Well, we learn something new every day." I screwed the statement around to position, signed it at the bottom of the last page, slid it across to him, and folded the carbon copy and put it in my pocket.

"I'll write it in if you insist," I told him, "but I doubt if it's worth the trouble. Santa Claus had run, Kiernan was calling the police, and I guess I was a little rattled. I must have looked around for something that might give me a line on Santa Claus, and my eye lit on the wastebasket, and I went through it. I haven't mentioned it because it wasn't very bright, and I like people to think

I'm bright, especially cops. There's your why. As for what I took, the answer is nothing. I dumped the wastebasket, put everything back in, and took nothing. Do you want me to write that in?"

"No. I want to discuss it. I know you *are* bright. And you weren't rattled. You don't rattle. I want to know the real reason you went through the wastebasket, what you were after, whether you got it, and what you did with it."

It cost me more than an hour, twenty minutes of which were spent in the office of the District Attorney himself, with Farrell and another assistant present. At one point it looked as if they were going to hold me as a material witness, but that takes a warrant, the Christmas weekend had started, and there was nothing to show that I monkeyed with anything that could be evidence, so finally they shooed me out, after I had handwritten an insert in my statement. It was too bad keeping such important public servants sitting there while I copied the insert on my carbon, but I like to do things right.

By the time I got home it was ten minutes past four, and of course Wolfe wasn't in the office, since his afternoon session up in the plant rooms is from four to six. There was no note on my desk from him, so apparently there were still no instructions, but there was information on it. My desk ashtray, which is mostly for decoration since I seldom smoke—a gift, not to Wolfe but to me, from a former client—is a jade bowl six inches across. It was there in its place, and in it were stubs from Pharaoh cigarettes.

Saul Panzer smokes Pharoahs, Egyptians. I suppose a few other people do too, but the chance that one of them had been sitting at my desk while I was gone was too slim to bother with. And not only had Saul been there, but Wolfe wanted me to know it, since one of the eight million things he will not tolerate in the office is ashtrays with remains. He will actually walk clear to the bathroom himself to empty one.

So steps were being taken, after all. What steps? Saul, a free lance and the best operative anywhere around, asks and gets sixty bucks a day, and is worth twice that. Wolfe had not called him in for any routine errand, and of course the idea that he had undertaken to sell him on doubling for Santa Claus never entered my head. Framing someone for murder, even a woman who might be guilty, was not in his bag of tricks. I got at the house phone and buzzed the plant rooms, and after a wait had Wolfe's voice in my ear.

"Yes, Fritz?"

"Not Fritz. Me. I'm back. Nothing urgent to report. They found my prints on stuff in the wastebasket, but I escaped without loss of blood. Is it all right for me to empty my ashtray?"

"Yes. Please do so."

"Then what do I do?"

"I'll tell you at six o'clock. Possibly earlier."

He hung up. I went to the safe and looked in the cash drawer to see if Saul had been supplied with generous funds, but the cash was as I had last seen it and there was no entry in the book. I emptied the ashtray. I went to the kitchen, where I found Fritz pouring a mixture into a bowl of pork tenderloin, and said I hoped Saul had enjoyed his lunch, and Fritz said he hadn't stayed for lunch. So steps must have been begun right after I left in the morning. I went back to the office, read over the carbon copy of my statement before filing it, and passed the time by thinking up eight different steps that Saul might have been assigned, but none of them struck me as promising. A little after five the phone rang and I answered. It was Saul. He said he was glad to know I was back home safe, and I said I was too.

"Just a message for Mr. Wolfe," he said. "Tell him everything is set, no snags."

"That's all?"

"Right. I'll be seeing you."

I cradled the receiver, sat a moment to consider whether to go up to the plant rooms or use the house phone, decided the latter would do, and pulled it to me and pushed the button. When Wolfe's voice came it was peevish; he hates to be disturbed up there.

"Yes?"

"Saul called and said to tell you everything

is set, no snags. Congratulations. Am I in the way?"

"Oddly enough, no. Have chairs in place for visitors; ten should be enough. Four or five will come shortly after six o'clock; I hope not more. Others will come later."

"Refreshments?"

"Liquids, of course. Nothing else."

"Anything else for me?"

"No."

He was gone. Before going to the front room for chairs, and to the kitchen for supplies, I took time out to ask myself whether I had the slightest notion what kind of charade he was cooking up this time. I hadn't.

VII

It was four. They all arrived between six-fifteen and six-twenty—first Mrs. Perry Porter Jerome and her son Leo, then Cherry Quon, and last Emil Hatch. Mrs. Jerome copped the red leather chair, but I moved her, mink and all, to one of the yellow ones when Cherry came. I was willing to concede that Cherry might be headed for a very different kind of chair, wired for power, but even so, I thought she rated that background and Mrs. Jerome didn't. By six-thirty, when I left them to cross the hall to the dining room, not a word had passed among them.

In the dining room Wolfe had just finished a bottle of beer. "Okay," I told him, "it's six-thirty-one. Only four. Kiernan and Margot Dickey haven't shown."

"Satisfactory." He arose. "Have they demanded information?"

"Two of them have, Hatch and Mrs. Jerome. I told them it will come from you, as instructed. That was easy, since I have none."

He headed for the office, and I followed. Though they didn't know, except Cherry, that he had poured champagne for them the day before, introductions weren't necessary because they had all met him during the tapestry hunt. After circling around Cherry in the red leather

chair, he stood behind his desk to ask them how they did, then sat.

"I don't thank you for coming," he said, "because you came in your own interest, not mine. I sent—"

"I came," Hatch cut in, sourer than ever, "to find out what you're up to."

"You will," Wolfe assured him. "I sent each of you an identical message, saying that Mr. Goodwin has certain information which he feels he must give the police not later than tonight, but I have persuaded him to let me discuss it with you first. Before I—"

"I didn't know others would be here," Mrs. Jerome blurted, glaring at Cherry.

"Neither did I," Hatch said, glaring at Mrs. Jerome.

Wolfe ignored it. "The message I sent Miss Quon was somewhat different, but that need not concern you. Before I tell you what Mr. Goodwin's information is, I need a few facts from you. For instance, I understand that any of you—including Miss Dickey and Mr. Kiernan, who will probably join us later—could have found an opportunity to put the poison in the bottle. Do any of you challenge that?"

Cherry, Mrs. Jerome, and Leo all spoke at once. Hatch merely looked sour.

Wolfe showed them a palm. "If you please. I point no finger of accusation at any of you. I merely say that none of you, including Miss Dickey and Mr. Kiernan, can prove that you had no opportunity. Can you?"

"Nuts." Leo Jerome was disgusted. "It was that guy playing Santa Claus. Of course it was. I was with Bottweill and my mother all the time, first in the workshop and then in his office. I can prove *that*."

"But Bottweill is dead," Wolfe reminded him, "and your mother is your mother. Did you go up to the office a little before them, or did your mother go up a little before you and Bottweill did? Is there acceptable proof that you didn't? The others have the same problem. Miss Quon?"

There was no danger of Cherry's spoiling

it. Wolfe had told me what he had told her on the phone: that he had made a plan which he thought she would find satisfactory, and if she came at a quarter past six she would see it work. She had kept her eyes fixed on him ever since he entered. Now she chirped, "If you mean I can't prove I wasn't in the office alone yesterday, no, I can't."

"Mr. Hatch?"

"I didn't come here to prove anything. I told you what I came for. What information has Goodwin got?"

"We'll get to that. A few more facts first. Mrs. Jerome, when did you learn that Bottweill had decided to marry Miss Quon?"

Leo shouted, "No!" but his mother was too busy staring at Wolfe to hear him. "What?" she croaked. Then she found her voice. "Kurt marry *her*? That little strumpet?"

Cherry didn't move a muscle, her eyes still on Wolfe.

"This is wonderful!" Leo said. "This is marvelous!"

"Not so damn wonderful," Emil Hatch declared. "I get the idea, Wolfe. Goodwin hasn't got any information, and neither have you. Why you wanted to get us together and start us clawing at each other, I don't see that, I don't know why you're interested, but maybe I'll find out if I give you a hand. This crowd has produced as fine a collection of venom as you could find. Maybe we all put poison in the bottle and that's why it was such a big dose. If it's true that Kurt had decided to marry Cherry, and Al Kiernan knew it, that would have done it. Al would have killed a hundred Kurts if it would get him Cherry. If Mrs. Jerome knew it, I would think she would have gone for Cherry instead of Kurt, but maybe she figured there would soon be another one and she might as well settle it for good. As for Leo, I think he rather liked Kurt, but what can you expect? Kurt was milking mamma of the pile Leo hoped to get some day, and I suspect that the pile is not all it's supposed to be. Actually—"

He stopped, and I left my chair. Leo was on his way up, obviously with the intention of plug-ging the creative artist. I moved to head him off, and at the same instant I gave him a shove and his mother jerked at his coattail. That not only halted him but nearly upset him, and with my other hand I steered him back onto his chair and then stood beside him.

Hatch inquired, "Shall I go on?"

"By all means," Wolfe said.

"Actually, though, Cherry would seem to be the most likely. She has the best brain of the lot and by far the strongest will. But I understand that while she says Kurt was going to marry her, Margot claims that he was going to marry *her*. Of course that complicates it, and anyway Margot would be my second choice. Margot has more than her share of the kind of pride that is only skin deep and therefore can't stand a scratch. If Kurt did decide to marry Cherry and told Margot so, he was even a bigger imbecile than I thought he was. Which brings us to me. I am in a class by myself. I despise all of them. If I had decided to take to poison I would have put it in the champagne as well as the Pernod, and I would have drunk vodka, which I prefer—and by the way, on that table is a bottle with the Korbeloff vodka label. I haven't had a taste of Korbeloff for fifteen years. Is it real?"

"It is. Archie?"

Serving liquid refreshment to a group of invited guests can be a pleasant chore, but it wasn't that time. When I asked Mrs. Jerome to name it she only glowered at me, but by the time I had filled Cherry's order for scotch and soda, and supplied Hatch with a liberal dose of Korbeloff, no dilution, and Leo had said he would take bourbon and water, his mother muttered that she would have that too. As I was pouring the bourbon I wondered where we would go from there. It looked as if the time had come for Wolfe to pass on the information which I felt I must give the police without delay, which made it difficult because I didn't have any. That had been fine for a bait to get them there, but what now? I suppose Wolfe would have held them somehow, but he didn't have to. He had rung for beer, and Fritz had brought it and was putting the tray on his desk when the doorbell rang. I handed Leo his bourbon and water and went to the hall. Out on the stoop, with his big round face nearly touching the glass, was Inspector Cramer of Homicide.

Wolfe had told me enough, before the company came, to give me a general idea of the program, so the sight of Cramer, just Cramer, was a letdown. But as I went down the hall other figures appeared, none of them strangers, and that looked better. In fact it looked fine. I swung the door wide and in they came—Cramer, then Saul Panzer, then Margot Dickey, then Alfred Kiernan, and, bringing up the rear, Sergeant Purley Stebbins. By the time I had the door closed and bolted they had their coats off, including Cramer, and it was also fine to see that he expected to stay a while. Ordinarily, once in, he marches down the hall and into the office without ceremony, but that time he waved the others ahead, including me, and he and Stebbins came last, herding us in. Crossing the sill, I stepped aside for the pleasure of seeing his face when his eyes lit on those already there and the empty chairs waiting. Undoubtedly he had expected to find Wolfe alone, reading a book. He came in two paces, glared around, fastened the glare on Wolfe, and barked, "What's all this?"

"I was expecting you," Wolfe said politely. "Miss Quon, if you don't mind moving, Mr. Cramer likes that chair. Good evening, Miss Dickey. Mr. Kiernan, Mr. Stebbins. If you will all be seated—"

"Panzer!" Cramer barked. Saul, who had started for a chair in the rear, stopped and turned.

"I'm running this," Cramer declared. "Panzer, you're under arrest and you'll stay with Stebbins and keep your mouth shut. I don't want—"

"No," Wolfe said sharply. "If he's under arrest take him out of here. You are not running this, not in my house. If you have warrants for anyone present, or have taken them by lawful police power, take them and leave these premises. Would you bulldoze me, Mr. Cramer? You should know better."

That was the point, Cramer did know him. There was the stage, all set. There were Mrs. Jerome and Leo and Cherry and Emil Hatch, and the empty chairs, and above all, there was the fact that he had been expected. He wouldn't have taken Wolfe's word for that; he wouldn't have taken Wolfe's word for anything; but whenever he appeared on our stoop *not* expected I always left the chain-bolt on until he stated his business and I had reported to Wolfe. And if he had been expected there was no telling what Wolfe had ready to spring. So Cramer gave up the bark and merely growled, "I want to talk with you."

"Certainly." Wolfe indicated the red leather chair, which Cherry had vacated. "Be seated."

"Not here. Alone."

Wolfe shook his head. "It would be a waste of time. This way is better and quicker. You know quite well, sir, it was a mistake to barge in here and roar at me that you are running my house. Either go, with whomever you can lawfully take, or sit down while I tell you who killed Kurt Bottweill." Wolfe wiggled a finger. "Your chair."

Cramer's round red face had been redder than normal from the outside cold, and now was redder still. He glanced around, compressed his lips until he didn't have any, and went to the red leather chair and sat.

VIII

Wolfe sent his eyes around as I circled to my desk. Saul had got to a chair in the rear after all, but Stebbins had too and was at his elbow. Margot had passed in front of the Jeromes and Emil Hatch to get to the chair at the end nearest me, and Cherry and Al Kiernan were at the other end, a little back of the others. Hatch had finished his Korbeloff and put the glass on the floor, but Cherry and the Jeromes were hanging on to their tall ones.

Wolfe's eyes came to rest on Cramer and he spoke. "I must confess that I stretched it a little. I can't tell you, at the moment, who killed Bottweill; I have only a supposition; but soon I can, and will. First some facts for you. I assume you know that for the past two months Mr. Goodwin has been seeing something of Miss Dickey. He says she dances well."

"Yeah." Cramer's voice came over sandpaper of the roughest grit. "You can save that for later. I want to know if you sent Panzer to meet—"

Wolfe cut him off. "You will. I'm headed for that. But you may prefer this firsthand. Archie, if you please. What Miss Dickey asked you to do last Monday evening, and what happened."

I cleared my throat. "We were dancing at the Flamingo Club. She said Bottweill had been telling her for a year that he would marry her next week, but next week never came, and she was going to have a showdown with him. She asked me to get a blank marriage license and fill it out for her and me and give it to her, and she would show it to Bottweill and tell him now or never. I got the blank on Tuesday, and filled it in, and Wednesday I gave it to her."

I stopped. Wolfe prompted me. "And yesterday afternoon?"

"She told me that the license trick had worked perfectly. That was about a minute before Bottweill entered the studio. I said in my statement to the District Attorney that she told me Bottweill was going to marry her, but I didn't mention the license. It was immaterial."

"Did she tell you what had happened to the license?"

So we were emptying the bag. I nodded. "She said Bottweill had torn it up and put the pieces in the wastebasket by the desk in his office. The night before. Thursday evening."

"And what did you do when you went to the office after Bottweill had died?"

"I dumped the wastebasket and put the stuff back in it, piece by piece. No part of the license was there."

"You made sure of that?"

"Yes."

Wolfe left me and asked Cramer, "Any questions?"

"No. He lied in his statement. I'll attend to that later. What I want—"

Margot Dickey blurted, "Then Cherry took it!" She craned her neck to see across the others. "You took it, you slut!"

"I did not." The steel was in Cherry's chirp again. Her eyes didn't leave Wolfe, and she told him, "I'm not going to wait any longer—"

"Miss Quon!" he snapped. "I'm doing this." He turned to Cramer. "Now another fact. Yesterday I had a luncheon appointment with Mr. Bottweill at Rusterman's restaurant. He had once dined at my table and wished to reciprocate. Shortly before I left to keep the appointment he phoned to ask me to do him a favor. He said he was extremely busy and might be a few minutes late, and he needed a pair of white cotton gloves, medium size, for a man, and would I stop at some shop on the way and get them. It struck me as a peculiar request, but he was a peculiar man. Since Mr. Goodwin had chores to do, and I will not ride in taxicabs if there is any alternative, I had engaged a car at Baxter's, and the chauffeur recommended a shop on Eighth Avenue between Thirty-ninth and Fortieth Streets. We stopped there and I bought the gloves."

Cramer's eyes were such narrow slits that none of the blue-gray showed. He wasn't buying any part of it, which was unjustified, since some of it was true.

Wolfe went on. "At the lunch table I gave the gloves to Mr. Bottweill, and he explained, somewhat vaguely, what he wanted them for. I gathered that he had taken pity on some vagabond he had seen on a park bench, and had hired him to serve refreshments at his office party, costumed as Santa Claus, and he had decided that the only way to make his hands presentable was to have him wear gloves. You shake your head, Mr. Cramer?"

"You're damn right I do. You would have reported that. No reason on earth not to. Go ahead and finish."

"I'll finish this first. I didn't report it because

I thought you would find the murderer without it. It was practically certain that the vagabond had merely skedaddled out of fright, since he couldn't possibly have known of the jar of poison in the workshop, not to mention other considerations. And as you know, I have a strong aversion to involvement in matters where I have no concern or interest. You can of course check this—with the staff at Rusterman's, my presence there with Mr. Bottweill, and with the chauffeur, my conferring with him about the gloves and our stopping at the shop to buy them."

"You're reporting it now."

"I am indeed." Wolfe was unruffled. "Because I understood from Mr. Goodwin that you were extending and intensifying your search for the man who was there as Santa Claus, and with your army and your resources it probably wouldn't take you long when the holiday had ended to learn where the gloves were bought and get a description of the man who bought them. My physique is not unique, but it is—uncommon, and the only question was how long it would take you to get to me, and then I would be under inquisition. Obviously I had to report the episode to you and suffer your rebuke for not reporting it earlier, but I wanted to make it as tolerable as possible. I had one big advantage: I knew that the man who acted as Santa Claus was almost certainly not the murderer, and I decided to use it. I needed first to have a talk with one of those people, and I did so, with Miss Quon, who came here last evening."

"Why Miss Quon?"

Wolfe turned a hand over. "When I have finished you can decide whether such details are important. With her I discussed her associates at that place and their relationships, and I became satisfied that Bottweill had in fact decided to marry her. That was all. You can also decide later whether it is worthwhile to ask her to corroborate that, and I have no doubt she will."

He was looking at Cherry, of course, for any sign of danger. She had started to blurt it out once, and might again. But, meeting his gaze, she didn't move a muscle.

Wolfe returned to Cramer. "This morning I acted. Mr. Goodwin was absent, at the District Attorney's office, so I called in Mr. Panzer. After spending an hour with me here he went to do some errands. The first one was to learn whether Bottweill's wastebasket had been emptied since his conversation with Miss Dickey in his office Thursday evening. As you know, Mr. Panzer is highly competent. Through Miss Quon he got the name and address of the cleaning woman, found her and talked with her, and was told that the wastebasket had been emptied at about six o'clock Thursday afternoon and not since then. Meanwhile I—"

"Cherry took it—the pieces," Margot said.

Wolfe ignored her. "Meanwhile I was phoning everyone concerned—Mrs. Jerome and her son, Miss Dickey, Miss Quon, Mr. Hatch, and Mr. Kiernan—and inviting them to come here for a conference at six-fifteen. I told them that Mr. Goodwin had information which he intended to give the police, which was not true, and that I thought it best to discuss it first with them."

"I told you so," Hatch muttered.

Wolfe ignored him too. "Mr. Panzer's second errand, or series of errands, was the delivery of some messages. He had written them in longhand, at my dictation here this morning, on plain sheets of paper, and had addressed plain envelopes. They were identical and ran as follows:

When I was there yesterday putting on my costume I saw you through a crack in the door and I saw what you did. Do you want me to tell the cops? Be at Grand Central information booth upper level at 6:30 today. I'll come up to you and say "Saint Nick."

"By god," Cramer said, "you admit it."

Wolfe nodded. "I proclaim it. The messages were signed 'Santa Claus.' Mr. Panzer accompanied the messenger who took them to the persons I have named, and made sure they were delivered. They were not so much shots at random as they may appear. If one of those people had killed Bottweill it was likely that the poison had been put in the bottle while the vagabond was donning the Santa Claus costume; Miss Quon had told me, as no doubt she has told you, that Bottweill invariably took a drink of Pernod when he returned from lunch; and, since the appearance of Santa Claus at the party had been a surprise to all of them, and none of them knew who he was, it was highly probable that the murderer would believe he had been observed and would be irresistibly impelled to meet the writer of the message. So it was a reasonable assumption that one of the shots would reach its target. The question was, which one?"

Wolfe stopped to pour beer. He did pour it, but I suspected that what he really stopped for was to offer an opening for comment or protest. No one had any, not even Cramer. They all just sat and gazed at him. I was thinking that he had neatly skipped one detail: that the message from Santa Claus had not gone to Cherry Quon. She knew too much about him.

Wolfe put the bottle down and turned to go on to Cramer. "There was the possibility, of course, that more than one of them would go to you with the message, but even if you decided, because it had been sent to more than one, that it was some hoax, you would want to know who perpetrated it, and you would send one of them to the rendezvous under surveillance. Any one or more, excepting the murderer, might go to you, or none might; and surely only the murderer would go to the rendezvous without first consulting you. So if one of those six people was guilty, and if it had been possible for Santa Claus to observe him, disclosure seemed next to certain. Saul, you may now report. What happened? You were in the vicinity of the information booth shortly before six-thirty?"

Necks were twisted for a view of Saul Panzer. He nodded. "Yes, sir. At six-twenty. Within three minutes I had recognized three Homicide men scattered around in different spots. I

don't know if they recognized me or not. At six twenty-eight I saw Alfred Kiernan walk up near the booth and stand there, about ten feet away from it. I was just about to go and speak to him when I saw Margot Dickey coming up from the Forty-second Street side. She approached to within thirty feet of the booth and stood looking around. Following your instructions in case more than one of them appeared and Miss Dickey was one of them, I went to her and said, 'Saint Nick.' She said, 'Who are you and what do you want?' I said, 'Excuse me, I'll be right back,' and went over to Alfred Kiernan and said to him, 'Saint Nick.' As soon as I said that he raised a hand to his ear, and then here they came, the three I had recognized and two more, and then Inspector Cramer and Sergeant Stebbins. I was afraid Miss Dickey would run, and she did start to, but they had seen me speak to her, and two of them stopped her and had her."

Saul halted because of an interruption. Purley Stebbins, seated next to him, got up and stepped over to Margot Dickey and stood there behind her chair. To me it seemed unnecessary, since I was sitting not much more than arm's length from her and might have been trusted to grab her if she tried to start anything, but Purley is never very considerate of other people's feelings, especially mine.

Saul resumed, "Naturally it was Miss Dickey I was interested in, since they had moved in on a signal from Kiernan. But they had her, so that was okay. They took us to a room back of the parcel room and started in on me, and I followed your instructions. I told them I would answer no questions, would say nothing whatever, except in the presence of Nero Wolfe, because I was acting under your orders. When they saw I meant it they took us out to two police cars and brought us here. Anything else?"

"No," Wolfe told him. "Satisfactory." He turned to Cramer. "I assume Mr. Panzer is correct in concluding that Mr. Kiernan gave your men a signal. So Mr. Kiernan had gone to you with the message?"

"Yes." Cramer had taken a cigar from his pocket and was squeezing it in his hand. He does that sometimes when he would like to squeeze Wolfe's throat instead. "So had three of the others—Mrs. Jerome, her son, and Hatch."

"But Miss Dickey hadn't?"

"No. Neither had Miss Quon."

"Miss Quon was probably reluctant, understandably. She told me last evening that the police's ideas of Orientals are very primitive. As for Miss Dickey, I may say that I am not surprised. For a reason that does not concern you, I am even a little gratified. I have told you that she told Mr. Goodwin that Bottweill had torn up the marriage license and put the pieces in his wastebasket, and they weren't there when Mr. Goodwin looked for them, and the wastebasket hadn't been emptied since early Thursday evening. It was difficult to conceive a reason for anyone to fish around in the wastebasket to remove those pieces, so presumably Miss Dickey lied; and if she lied about the license, the rest of what she told Mr. Goodwin was under suspicion."

Wolfe upturned a palm. "Why would she tell him that Bottweill was going to marry her if it wasn't true? Surely a stupid thing to do, since he would inevitably learn the truth. But it wasn't so stupid if she knew that Bottweill would soon die; indeed it was far from stupid if she had already put the poison in the bottle; it would purge her of motive, or at least help. It was a fair surmise that at their meeting in his office Thursday evening Bottweill had told her, not that he would marry her, but that he had decided to marry Miss Quon, and she decided to kill him and proceeded to do so. And it must be admitted that she would probably never have been exposed but for the complications injected by Santa Claus and my resulting intervention. Have you any comment, Miss Dickey?"

Cramer left his chair, commanding her, "Don't answer! I'm running this now," but she spoke.

"Cherry took those pieces from the wastebasket! She did it! She killed him!" She started

up, but Purley had her arm and Cramer told her, moving for her, "She didn't go there to meet a blackmailer, and you did. Look in her bag, Purley. I'll watch her."

IX

Cherry Quon was back in red in the red leather chair. The others had gone, and she and Wolfe and I were alone. They hadn't put cuffs on Margot Dickey, but Purley had kept hold of her arm as they crossed the threshold, with Cramer right behind. Saul Panzer, no longer in custody, had gone along by request. Mrs. Jerome and Leo had been the first to leave. Kiernan had asked Cherry if he could take her home, but Wolfe had said no, he wanted to speak with her privately, and Kiernan and Hatch had left together, which showed a fine Christmas spirit, since Hatch had made no exceptions when he said he despised all of them.

Cherry was on the edge of the chair, spine straight, hands together in her lap. "You didn't do it the way I said," she chirped, without steel.

"No," Wolfe agreed, "but I did it." He was curt. "You ignored one complication, the possibility that you had killed Bottweill yourself. I didn't, I assure you. I couldn't very well send you one of the notes from Santa Claus, under the circumstances; but if those notes had flushed no prey, if none of them had gone to the rendezvous without first notifying the police, I would have assumed that you were guilty and would have proceeded to expose you. How, I don't know; I let that wait on the event; and now that Miss Dickey has taken the bait and betrayed herself it doesn't matter."

Her eyes had widened. "You really thought I might have killed Kurt?"

"Certainly. A woman capable of trying to blackmail me to manufacture evidence of murder would be capable of anything. And, speaking of evidence, while there can be no certainty about a jury's decision when a personable young woman is on trial for murder, now that Miss Dickey is manifestly guilty you may be sure that Mr. Cramer will dig up all he can get, and there should be enough. That brings me to the point I wanted to speak about. In the quest for evidence you will all be questioned, exhaustively and repeatedly. It will—"

"We wouldn't," Cherry put in, "if you had done it the way I said. That would have been proof."

"I preferred my way." Wolfe, having a point to make, was controlling himself. "It will be an ordeal for you. They will question you at length about your talk with Bottweill yesterday morning at breakfast, wanting to know all that he said about his meeting with Miss Dickey in his office Thursday evening, and under the pressure of inquisition you might inadvertently let something slip regarding what he told you about Santa Claus. If you do they will certainly follow it up. I strongly advise you to avoid making such a slip. Even if they believe you, the identity of Santa Claus is no longer important, since they have the murderer, and if they come to me with such a tale I'll have no great difficulty dealing with it."

He turned a hand over. "And in the end they probably won't believe you. They'll think you invented it for some cunning and obscure purpose—as you say, you are an Oriental—and all you would get for it would be more questions. They might even suspect that you were somehow involved in the murder itself. They are quite capable of unreasonable suspicions. So I suggest these considerations as much on your behalf as on mine. I think you will be wise to forget about Santa Claus."

She was eying him, straight and steady. "I like to be wise," she said.

"I'm sure you do, Miss Quon."

"I still think you should have done it my way, but it's done now. Is that all?"

He nodded. "That's all."

She looked at me, and it took a second for me to realize that she was smiling at me. I thought it wouldn't hurt to smile back, and did. She left the chair and came to me, extending a hand, and I arose and took it. She looked up at me.

"I would like to shake hands with Mr. Wolfe, but I know he doesn't like to shake hands. You know, Mr. Goodwin, it must be a very great pleasure to work for a man as clever as Mr. Wolfe. So extremely clever. It has been very exciting to be here. Now I say good-by."

She turned and went.

THE RAFFLES RELICS

E. W. Hornung

THE GREATEST GENTLEMAN JEWEL THIEF in all of mystery
fiction is A. J. Raffles, the fearless burglar who mainly stole to help others who
found themselves in desperate situations. He was accompanied in most cases
by his utterly loyal sidekick, Bunny Manders. The stories are the mirror image
of the Sherlock Holmes stories written by Arthur Conan Doyle, who was Hornung's brother-in-law, and it has been noted in various sources that Hornung
wrote about a crook and his faithful partner to tweak the humor-challenged
Doyle. This is the next-to-last Raffles story that Hornung wrote and there is not
much of Christmas in it, but the character is so iconic that he deserved a place in
this (or any) collection. "The Raffles Relics" was first collected in *A Thief in the
Night* (London, Chatto & Windus, 1905).

The Raffles Relics

E. W. HORNUNG

IT WAS IN ONE OF THE MAGAZINES for December, 1899, that an article appeared which afforded our minds a brief respite from the then consuming excitement of the war in South Africa. These were the days when Raffles really had white hair, and when he and I were nearing the end of our surreptitious second innings, as professional cracksmen of the deadliest dye. Piccadilly and the Albany knew us no more. But we still operated, as the spirit tempted us, from our latest and most idyllic base, on the borders of Ham Common. Recreation was our greatest want; and though we had both descended to the humble bicycle, a lot of reading was forced upon us in the winter evenings. Thus the war came as a boon to us both. It not only provided us with an honest interest in life, but gave point and zest to innumerable spins across Richmond Park, to the nearest paper-shop; and it was from such an expedition that I returned with inflammatory matter unconnected with the war. The magazine was one of those that are read (and sold) by the million; the article was rudely illustrated on every other page. Its subject was the so-called Black Museum at Scotland Yard; and from the catchpenny text we first learnt that the gruesome show was now enriched by a special and elaborate exhibit known as the Raffles Relics.

"Bunny," said Raffles, "this is fame at last! It is no longer notoriety; it lifts one out of the ruck of robbers, into the society of the big brass gods, whose little delinquencies are written in water

by the finger of time. The Napoleon Relics we know, the Nelson Relics we've heard about, and here are mine!"

"Which I wish to goodness we could see," I added longingly. Next moment I was sorry I had spoken. Raffles was looking at me across the magazine. There was a smile on his lips that I knew too well, a light in his eyes that I had kindled.

"What an excellent idea!" he exclaimed quite softly, as though working it out already in his brain.

"I didn't mean it for one," I answered, "and no more do you."

"Certainly I do," said Raffles. "I was never more serious in my life."

"You would march into Scotland Yard in broad daylight?"

"In broad limelight," he answered, studying the magazine again, "to set eyes on my own once more. Why, here they all are, Bunny—you never told me there was an illustration. That's the chest you took to your bank with me inside, and those must be my own rope-ladder and things on top. They reproduce so badly in the twopenny magazines that it's impossible to swear to them. There's nothing for it but a visit of inspection."

"Then you can pay it alone," said I grimly. "You may have altered, but they'd know me at a glance."

"By all means, Bunny, if you'll get me the pass."

"A pass!" I cried triumphantly. "Of course we should have to get one, and of course that puts an end to the whole idea. Who on earth would give a pass for this show, of all others, to an old prisoner like me?"

Raffles addressed himself to the reading of the magazine with a shrug that showed some temper.

"The fellow who wrote this article got one," said he shortly. "He got it from his editor, and you could get one from yours if you tried. But pray don't try, Bunny: it would be too terrible for you to risk a moment's embarrassment to gratify a mere whim of mine. And if I went instead of you, and got spotted, which is so likely with this head of hair, and the general belief in my demise, the consequences to you would be too awful to contemplate! Don't contemplate them, my dear fellow. And do let me read my magazine."

Need I add that I set about the rash endeavour without further expostulation? I was used to such ebullitions from the altered Raffles of these later days, and I could well understand them. All the inconvenience of the new conditions fell on him. I had purged my known offences by imprisonment, whereas Raffles was merely supposed to have escaped punishment in death. The result was that I could rush in where Raffles feared to tread, and was his plenipotentiary in all honest dealings with the outer world. It could not but gall him to be so dependent upon me, and it was for me to minimise the humiliation by scrupulously avoiding the least semblance of an abuse of that power which I now had over him. Accordingly, though with much misgiving, I did his ticklish behest in Fleet Street, where, despite my past, I was already making a certain lowly footing for myself. Success followed, as it will when one longs to fail; and one fine evening I returned to Ham Common with a card from the Convict Supervision Office, New Scotland Yard, which I treasure to this day. I am surprised to see that it was undated, and might still "Admit Bearer to see the Museum," to say nothing of the bearer's friends, since my editor's name "and party" is scrawled beneath the legend.

"But he doesn't want to come," as I explained to Raffles. "And it means that we can both go, if we both like."

Raffles looked at me with a wry smile; he was in good enough humour now.

"It would be rather dangerous, Bunny. If they spotted you, they might think of me."

"But you say they'll never know you now."

"I don't believe they will. I don't believe there's the slightest risk; but we shall soon see. I've set my heart on seeing, Bunny, but there's no earthly reason why I should drag you into it."

"You do that when you present this card," I pointed out. "I shall hear of it fast enough, if anything happens."

"Then you may as well be there to see the fun?"

"It will make no difference if the worst comes to the worst."

"And the ticket is for a party, isn't it?"

"It is."

"It might even look peculiar if only one person made use of it?"

"It might."

"Then we're both going, Bunny! And I give you my word," cried Raffles, "that no real harm shall come of it. But you mustn't ask to see the Relics, and you mustn't take too much interest in them when you do see them. Leave the questioning to me: it really will be a chance of finding out whether they've any suspicion of one's resurrection at Scotland Yard. And I think I can promise you a certain amount of fun, old fellow, as some little compensation for your pangs and fears."

The early afternoon was mild and hazy, and unlike winter but for the prematurely low sun struggling through the haze, as Raffles and I emerged from the nether regions at Westminster Bridge, and stood for one moment to admire the infirm silhouettes of Abbey and Houses in flat grey against a golden mist. Raffles murmured of Whistler and of Arthur Severn, and threw away a good Sullivan because the smoke would curl between him and the picture. It is perhaps the picture that I can now see clearest of all the set scenes of our lawless life. But at the time I was filled with gloomy speculation as to whether Raffles would keep his promise of providing an entirely harmless entertainment for my benefit at the Black Museum.

We entered the forbidding precincts; we looked relentless officers in the face, and they almost yawned in ours as they directed us through swing-doors and up stone stairs. There was something even sinister in the casual character of our reception. We had an arctic landing to ourselves for several minutes, which Raffles spent in an instinctive survey of the premises, while I cooled my heels before the portrait of a late Commissioner.

"Dear old gentleman!" exclaimed Raffles, joining me. "I have met him at dinner, and discussed my own case with him, in the old days. But we can't know too little about ourselves in the Black Museum, Bunny. I remember going to the old place in Whitehall, years ago, and being shown round by one of the tip-top 'tecs. And this may be another."

But even I could see at a glance that there was nothing of the detective and everything of the clerk about the very young man who had joined us at last upon the landing. His collar was the tallest I have ever seen, and his face was as pallid as his collar. He carried a loose key, with which he unlocked a door a little way along the passage, and so ushered us into that dreadful repository which perhaps has fewer visitors than any other of equal interest in the world. The place was cold as the inviolate vault; blinds had to be drawn up, and glass cases uncovered, before we could see a thing except the row of murderers' death-masks—the placid faces with the swollen necks—that stood out on their shelves to give us ghostly greeting.

"This fellow isn't formidable," whispered Raffles, as the blinds went up; "still, we can't be too careful. My little lot are round the corner, in the sort of recess; don't look till we come to them in their turn."

So we began at the beginning, with the glass case nearest the door; and in a moment I discov-ered that I knew far more about its contents than our pallid guide. He had some enthusiasm, but the most inaccurate smattering of his subject. He mixed up the first murderer with quite the wrong murder, and capped his mistake in the next breath with an intolerable libel on the very pearl of our particular tribe.

"This revawlver," he began, "belonged to the celebrited burgular, Chawles Peace. These are his spectacles, that's his jemmy, and this here knife's the one that Chawley killed the policeman with."

Now, I like accuracy for its own sake, strive after it myself, and am sometimes guilty of forcing it upon others. So this was more than I could pass.

"That's not quite right," I put in, mildly. "He never made use of the knife."

The young clerk twisted his head in its vase of starch.

"Chawley Peace killed two policemen," said he.

"No, he didn't; only one of them was a policeman; and he never killed anybody with a knife."

The clerk took the correction like a lamb. I could not have refrained from making it, to save my skin. But Raffles rewarded me with as vicious a little kick as he could administer unobserved.

"Who was Charles Peace?" he inquired, with the bland effrontery of any judge upon the bench.

The clerk's reply came pat and unexpected.

"The greatest burgular we ever had," said he, "till good old Raffles knocked him out!"

"The greatest of the pre-Raffleites," the master murmured, as we passed on to the safer memorials of mere murder. There were misshapen bullets and stained knives that had taken human life; there were lithe, lean ropes which had retaliated after the live letter of the Mosaic law. There was one bristling broadside of revolvers under the longest shelf of closed eyes and swollen throats. There were festoons of rope-ladders—none so ingenious as ours—and then at last there was something that the clerk knew all about. It was a small tin cigarette-box, and the name upon the gaudy wrapper was not the name of Sullivan. Yet Raffles and I knew even more about this exhibit than the clerk.

"There, now," said our guide, "you'll never guess the history of that! I'll give you twenty guesses, and the twentieth will be no nearer than the first."

"I'm sure of it, my good fellow," rejoined Raffles, a discreet twinkle in his eye. "Tell us about it, to save time."

And he opened, as he spoke, his own old twenty-five tin of purely popular cigarettes; there were a few in it still, but between the cigarettes were jammed lumps of sugar wadded with cotton-wool. I saw Raffles weighing the lot in his hand with subtle satisfaction. But the clerk saw merely the mystification which he desired to create.

"I thought that'd beat you, sir," said he. "It was an American dodge. Two smart Yankees got a jeweller to take a lot of stuff to a private room at Kellner's, where they were dining, for them to choose from. When it came to paying, there was some bother about a remittance; but they soon made that all right, for they were far too clever to suggest taking away what they'd chosen but couldn't pay for. No; all they wanted was that what they'd chosen might be locked up in the safe and considered theirs until their money came for them to pay for it. All they asked was to seal the stuff up in something; the jeweller was to take it away and not meddle with it, nor yet break the seals, for a week or two. It seemed a fair enough thing, now, didn't it, sir?"

"Eminently fair," said Raffles, sententiously.

"So the jeweller thought," crowed the clerk. "You see, it wasn't as if the Yanks had chosen out the half of what he'd brought on appro; they'd gone slow on purpose, and they'd paid for all they could on the nail, just for a blind. Well, I suppose you can guess what happened in the end? The jeweller never heard of those Americans again; and these few cigarettes and lumps of sugar were all he found."

"Duplicate boxes!" I cried, perhaps a thought too promptly.

"Duplicate boxes!" murmured Raffles, as profoundly impressed as a second Mr. Pickwick.

"Duplicate boxes!" echoed the triumphant clerk. "Artful beggars, these Americans, sir! You've got to crawss the 'Erring Pond to learn a trick worth one o' that!"

"I suppose so," assented the grave gentleman with the silver hair. "Unless," he added, as if suddenly inspired, "unless it was that man Raffles."

"It couldn't 've bin," jerked the clerk from his conning-tower of a collar. "He'd gone to Davy Jones long before."

"Are you sure?" asked Raffles. "Was his body ever found?"

"Found and buried," replied our imaginative friend. "Maltar, I think it was; or it may have been Giberaltar. I forget which."

"Besides," I put in, rather annoyed at all this wilful work, yet not indisposed to make a late contribution—"besides, Raffles would never have smoked those cigarettes. There was only one brand for him. It was—let me see——"

"Sullivan!" cried the clerk, right for once. "It's all a matter of 'abit," he went on, as he replaced the twenty-five tin box with the vulgar wrapper. "I tried them once, and I didn't like 'em myself. It's all a question of taste. Now, if you want a good smoke, *ana* cheaper, give me a Golden Gem at quarter of the price."

"What we really do want," remarked Raffles mildly, "is to see something else as clever as that last."

"Then come this way," said the clerk, and led us into a recess almost monopolised by the iron-clamped chest of thrilling memory, now a mere platform for the collection of mysterious objects under a dust-sheet on the lid. "These," he continued, unveiling them with an air, "are the Raffles Relics; taken from his rooms in the Albany after his death and burial, and the most complete set we've got. That's his centre-bit, and this is the bottle of rock-oil he's supposed to have kept dipping it in to prevent making a noise. Here's the revawlver he used when he shot at the gentleman on the roof down Horsham way; it was afterwards taken from him on the P & O boat before he jumped overboard."

I could not help saying I understood that Raffles had never shot at anybody. I was standing with my back to the nearest window, my hat jammed over my brows and my overcoat collar up to my ears.

"That's the only time we know about," the clerk admitted; "and it couldn't be brought 'ome, or his precious pal would have got more than he did. This empty cawtridge is the one he 'id the Emperor's pearl in, on the Peninsular and Orient. These gimlets and wedges were what he used for fixin' doors. This is his rope-ladder, with the telescope walking-stick he used to hook it up with; he's said to have 'ad it with him the night he dined with the Earl of Thornaby, and robbed the house before dinner. That's his life-preserver; but no one can make out what this little thick velvet bag's for, with the two holes and the elawstic round each. Perhaps you can give a guess, sir?"

Raffles had taken up the bag that he had invented for the noiseless filing of keys. Now he handled it as though it were a tobacco-pouch, putting in finger and thumb, and shrugging over the puzzle with a delicious face; nevertheless, he showed me a few grains of steel-filing as the result of his investigations, and murmured in my ear, "These sweet police!" I, for my part, could not but examine the life-preserver with which I had once smitten Raffles himself to the ground; actually there was his blood upon it still; and seeing my horror, the clerk plunged into a characteristically garbled version of that incident also. It happened to have come to light among others at the Old Bailey, and perhaps had its share in promoting the quality of mercy which had undoubtedly been exercised on my behalf. But the present recital was unduly trying, and Raffles created a noble diversion by calling attention to an early photograph of himself, which may still hang on the wall over the historic chest, but which I had carefully ignored. It shows him in flannels, after some great feat upon the tented field. I am afraid there is a Sullivan between his

lips, a look of lazy insolence in the half-shut eyes. I have since possessed myself of a copy, and it is not Raffles at his best; but the features are clean-cut and regular; and I often wish that I had lent it to the artistic gentlemen who have battered the statue out of all likeness to the man.

"You wouldn't think it of him, would you?" quoth the clerk. "It makes you understand how no one ever did think it of him at the time."

The youth was looking full at Raffles, with the watery eyes of unsuspecting innocence. I itched to emulate the fine bravado of my friend.

"You said he had a pal," I observed, sinking deeper into the collar of my coat. "Haven't you got a photograph of him?"

The pale clerk gave such a sickly smile, I could have smacked some blood into his pasty face.

"You mean Bunny?" said the familiar fellow. "No, sir, he'd be out of place; we've only room for real criminals here. Bunny was neither one thing nor the other. He could follow Raffles, but that's all he could do. He was no good on his own. Even when he put up the low-down job of robbing his old 'ome, it's believed he hadn't the 'eart to take the stuff away, and Raffles had to break in a second time for it. No, sir, we don't bother our heads about Bunny; we shall never hear no more of 'im. He was a harmless sort of rotter, if you awsk me."

I had not asked him, and I was almost foaming under the respirator that I was making of my overcoat collar. I only hoped that Raffles would say something—and he did.

"The only case I remember anything about," he remarked, tapping the clamped chest with his umbrella, "was this; and that time, at all events, the man outside must have had quite as much to do as the one inside. May I ask what you keep in it?"

"Nothing, sir."

"I imagined more relics inside. Hadn't he some dodge of getting in and out without opening the lid?"

"Of putting his head out, you mean," returned the clerk, whose knowledge of Raffles and his Relics was really most comprehensive on the whole. He moved some of the minor memorials, and with his penknife raised the trapdoor in the lid.

"Only a skylight," remarked Raffles, deliciously unimpressed.

"Why, what else did you expect?" asked the clerk, letting the trapdoor down again, and looking sorry that he had taken so much trouble.

"A back door, at least!" replied Raffles, with such a sly look at me that I had to turn aside to smile. It was the last time I smiled that day.

The door had opened as I turned, and an unmistakable detective had entered with two more sightseers like ourselves. He wore the hard round hat and the dark thick overcoat which one knows at a glance as the uniform of his grade; and for one awful moment his steely eye was upon us in a flash of cold inquiry. Then the clerk emerged from the recess devoted to the Raffles Relics, and the alarming interloper conducted his party to the window opposite the door.

"Inspector Druce," the clerk informed us in impressive whispers, "who had the Chalk Farm case in hand. He'd be the man for Raffles, if Raffles was alive today!"

"I'm sure he would," was the grave reply. "I should be very sorry to have a man like that after me. But what a run there seems to be upon your Black Museum!"

"There isn't really, sir," whispered the clerk. "We sometimes go weeks on end without having regular visitors like you two gentlemen. I think those are friends of the Inspector's, come to see the Chalk Farm photographs that helped to hang his man. We've a lot of interesting photographs, sir, if you like to have a look at them."

"If it won't take long," said Raffles, pulling out his watch; and as the clerk left our side for an instant, he gripped my arm. "This is a bit too hot," he whispered, "but we mustn't cut and run like rabbits. That might be fatal. Hide your face in the photographs, and leave everything to me. I'll have a train to catch as soon as ever I dare."

I obeyed without a word, and with the less uneasiness as I had time to consider the situation. It even struck me that Raffles was for once inclined to exaggerate the undeniable risk that we ran by remaining in the same room with an officer whom both he and I knew only too well by name and repute. Raffles, after all, had aged and altered out of knowledge; but he had not lost the nerve that was equal to a far more direct encounter than was at all likely to be forced upon us. On the other hand, it was most improbable that a distinguished detective would know by sight an obscure delinquent like myself; besides, this one had come to the front since my day. Yet a risk it was, and I certainly did not smile as I bent over the album of horrors produced by our guide. I could still take an interest in the dreadful photographs of murderous and murdered men; they appealed to the morbid element in my nature; and it was doubtless with degenerate unction that I called Raffles's attention to a certain scene of notorious slaughter. There was no response. I looked round. There was no Raffles to respond. We had all three been examining the photographs at one of the windows; at another the three newcomers were similarly engrossed; and without one word, or a single sound, Raffles had decamped behind all our backs.

Fortunately the clerk was himself very busy gloating over the horrors of the album; before he looked round I had hidden my astonishment, but not my wrath, of which I had the instinctive sense to make no secret.

"My friend's the most impatient man on earth!" I exclaimed. "He said he was going to catch a train, and now he's gone without a word!"

"I never heard him," said the clerk, looking puzzled.

"No more did I; but he did touch me on the shoulder," I lied, "and say something or other. I was too deep in this beastly book to pay much attention. He must have meant that he was off. Well, let him be off! I mean to see all that's to be seen."

And in my nervous anxiety to allay any suspicions aroused by my companion's extraordinary behaviour, I outstayed even the eminent detective and his friends, saw them examine the Raffles Relics, heard them discuss me under my own nose, and at last was alone with the anaemic clerk. I put my hand in my pocket, and measured him with a sidelong eye. The tipping system is nothing less than a minor bane of my existence. Not that one is a grudging giver, but simply because in so many cases it is so hard to know whom to tip and what to tip him. I know what it is to be the parting guest who has not parted freely enough, and that not from stinginess but the want of a fine instinct on the point. I made no mistake, however, in the case of the clerk, who accepted my pieces of silver without demur, and expressed a hope of seeing the article which I had assured him I was about to write. He has had some years to wait for it, but I flatter myself that these belated pages will occasion more interest than offence if they ever do meet those watery eyes.

Twilight was falling when I reached the street; the sky behind St. Stephen's had flushed and blackened like an angry face; the lamps were lit, and under every one I was unreasonable enough to look for Raffles. Then I made foolishly sure that I should find him hanging about the station, and hung thereabouts myself until one Richmond train had gone without me. In the end I walked over the bridge to Waterloo, and took the first train to Teddington instead. That made a shorter walk of it, but I had to grope my way through a white fog from the river to Ham Common, and it was the hour of our cosy dinner when I reached our place of retirement. There was only a flicker of firelight on the blinds: I was the first to return after all. It was nearly four hours since Raffles had stolen away from my side in the ominous precincts of Scotland Yard. Where could he be? Our landlady wrung her hands over him; she had cooked a dinner after her favourite's heart, and I let it spoil before making one of the most melancholy meals of my life.

Up to midnight there was no sign of him; but long before this time I had reassured our landlady with a voice and face that must have given my words the lie. I told her that Mr. Ralph (as she used to call him) had said something about going to the theatre; that I thought he had given up the idea, but I must have been mistaken, and should certainly sit up for him. The attentive soul brought in a plate of sandwiches before she retired; and I prepared to make a night of it in a chair by the sitting-room fire. Darkness and bed I could not face in my anxiety. In a way I felt as though duty and loyalty called me out into the winter's night: and yet whither should I turn to look for Raffles? I could think of but one place, and to seek him there would be to destroy myself without aiding him. It was my growing conviction that he had been recognised when leaving Scotland Yard, and either taken then and there, or else hunted into some new place of hiding. It would all be in the morning papers; and it was all his own fault. He had thrust his head into the lion's mouth, and the lion's jaws had snapped. Had he managed to withdraw his head in time?

There was a bottle at my elbow, and that night I say deliberately that it was not my enemy but my friend. It procured me at last some surcease from my suspense. I fell fast asleep in my chair before the fire. The lamp was still burning, and the fire red, when I awoke; but I sat very stiff in the iron clutch of a wintry morning. Suddenly I slewed round in my chair. And there was Raffles in a chair behind me, with the door open behind him, quietly taking off his boots.

"Sorry to wake you, Bunny," said he. "I thought I was behaving like a mouse; but after a three hours' tramp one's feet are all heels."

I did not get up and fall upon his neck. I sat back in my chair and blinked with bitterness upon his selfish insensibility. He should not know what I had been through on his account.

"Walk out from town?" I inquired, as indifferently as though he were in the habit of doing so.

"From Scotland Yard," he answered, stretching himself before the fire in his stocking soles.

"Scotland Yard!" I echoed. "Then I was right; that's where you were all the time. And yet you managed to escape!"

I had risen excitedly in my turn.

"Of course I did," replied Raffles. "I never thought there would be much difficulty about that, but there was even less than I anticipated. I did once find myself on one side of a sort of counter, and an officer dozing at his desk at the other side. I thought it safest to wake him up and make inquiries about a mythical purse left in a phantom hansom outside the Carlton. And the way the fellow fired me out of that was another credit to the Metropolitan Police: it's only in the savage countries that they would have troubled to ask how one had got in."

"And how did you?" I asked. "And in the Lord's name, Raffles, when and why?"

Raffles looked down on me under raised eyebrows, as he stood with his coat-tails to the dying fire.

"How and when, Bunny, you know as well as I do," said he, cryptically. "And at last you shall hear the honest why and wherefore. I had more reasons for going to Scotland Yard, my dear fellow, than I had the face to tell you at the time."

"I don't care why you went there," I cried. "I want to know why you stayed, or went back, or whatever it was you may have done. I thought they had got you, and you had given them the slip?"

Raffles smiled as he shook his head.

"No, no, Bunny, I prolonged the visit, as I paid it, of my own accord. As for my reasons, they are far too many for me to tell you them all; they rather weighed upon me as I walked out; but you'll see them for yourself if you turn round."

I was standing with my back to the chair in which I had been asleep; behind the chair was the round lodging-house table; and there, reposing on the cloth with the whisky and sandwiches, was the whole collection of Raffles Relics which had occupied the lid of the silver-chest in the Black Museum at Scotland Yard! The chest alone was missing. There was the revolver that I had only once heard fired, and there the blood-stained life-preserver, brace-and-bit, bottle of rock-oil, velvet bag, rope-ladder, walking-stick, gimlets, wedges, and even the empty cartridge-case which had once concealed the gift of a civilised monarch to a potentate of colour.

"I was a real Father Christmas," said Raffles, "when I arrived. It's a pity you weren't awake to appreciate the scene. It was more edifying than the one I found. You never caught *me* asleep in my chair, Bunny!"

He thought I had merely fallen asleep in my chair. He could not see that I had been sitting up for him all night long. The hint of a temperance homily, on top of all I had borne, and from Raffles of all mortal men, tried my temper to its last limit; but a flash of late enlightenment enabled me just to keep it.

"Where did you hide?" I asked grimly.

"At the Yard itself."

"So I gather; but whereabouts at the Yard?"

"Can you ask, Bunny?"

"I am asking."

"It's where I once hid before."

"You don't mean in the chest?"

"I do."

Our eyes met for a minute.

"You may have ended up there," I conceded. "But where did you go first, when you slipped out behind my back, and how the devil did you know where to go?"

"I never did slip out," said Raffles, "behind your back. I slipped in."

"Into the chest?"

"Exactly."

I burst out laughing in his face.

"My dear fellow, I saw all these things on the lid just afterwards. Not one of them was moved. I watched that detective show them to his friends."

"And I heard him."

"But not from the inside of the chest!"

"From the inside of the chest, Bunny. Don't look like that—it's foolish. Try to recall a few words that went before, between the idiot in the collar and me. Don't you remember my asking him if there was anything in the chest?"

"Yes."

"One had to be sure it was empty, you see.

Then I asked if there was a back door to the chest as well as a skylight."

"I remember."

"I suppose you thought all that meant nothing?"

"I didn't look for a meaning."

"You wouldn't; it would never occur to you that I might want to find out whether anybody at the Yard had found out that there *was* something precisely in the nature of a side door—it isn't a back door—to that chest. Well, there is one; there was one soon after I took the chest back from your rooms to mine, in the good old days. You push one of the handles down—which no one ever does—and the whole of that end opens like the front of a doll's house. I saw that was what I ought to have done at first; it's so much simpler than the trap at the top, and one likes to get a thing perfect for its own sake. Besides, the trick had not been spotted at the bank, and I thought I might bring it off again some day; meanwhile, in one's bedroom, with lots of things on top, what a port in a sudden squall!"

I asked why I had never heard of the improvement before, not so much at the time it was made, but in these later days, when there were fewer secrets between us, and this one could avail him no more. But I did not put the question out of pique. I put it out of sheer obstinate incredulity. And Raffles looked at me without replying, until I read the explanation in his look.

"I see," I said. "You used to get into it to hide from me!"

"My dear Bunny, I am not always a very genial man," he answered; "but when you let me have a key of your rooms, I could not very well refuse you one of mine, although I picked your pocket of it in the end. I will only say that when I had no wish to see you, Bunny, I must have been quite unfit for human society, and it was the act of a friend to deny you mine. I don't think it happened more than once or twice. You can afford to forgive a fellow after all these years!"

"That, yes," I replied, bitterly; "but not this, Raffles."

"Why not? I really hadn't made up my mind

to do what I did. I had merely thought of it. It was that smart officer in the same room that made me do it without thinking twice."

"And we never even heard you!" I murmured, in a voice of involuntary admiration which vexed me with myself. "But we might just as well!" I was as quick to add in my former tone.

"Why, Bunny?"

"We shall be traced in no time through our ticket of admission."

"Did they collect it?"

"No; but you heard how very few are issued."

"Exactly. They sometimes go weeks on end without a regular visitor. It was I who extracted that piece of information, Bunny, and I did nothing rash until I had. Don't you see that with any luck it will be two or three weeks before they are likely to discover their loss?"

I was beginning to see.

"And then, pray, how are they going to bring it home to us? Why should they even suspect us, Bunny? I left early; that's all I did. You took my departure admirably; you couldn't have said more or less if I had coached you myself. I relied on you, Bunny, and you never more completely justified my confidence. The sad thing is that you have ceased to rely on me. Do you really think that I would leave the place in such a state that the first person who came in with a duster would see that there had been a robbery?"

I denied the thought with all energy, though it perished only as I spoke.

"Have you forgotten the duster that was over these things, Bunny? Have you forgotten all the other revolvers and life-preservers that there were to choose from? I chose most carefully, and I replaced my relics with a mixed assortment of other people's which really look just as well. The rope-ladder that now supplants mine is, of course, no patch upon it, but coiled up on the chest it really looks much the same. To be sure, there was no second velvet bag; but I replaced my stick with another quite like it, and I even found an empty cartridge to understudy the setting of the Polynesian pearl. You see the sort of fellow they have to show people round: do you think he's the kind to see the difference next time, or to connect it with us if he does? One left much the same things lying much as he left them, under a dust-sheet which is only taken off for the benefit of the curious, who often don't turn up for weeks on end."

I admitted that we might be safe for three or four weeks. Raffles held out his hand.

"Then let us be friends about it, Bunny, and smoke the cigarette of Sullivan and peace! A lot may happen in three or four weeks; and what should you say if this turned out to be the last as well as the least of all my crimes? I must own that it seems to me their natural and fitting end, though I might have stopped more characteristically than with a mere crime of sentiment. No, I make no promises, Bunny; now I have got these things, I may be unable to resist using them once more. But with this war one gets all the excitement one requires—and rather more than usual may happen in three or four weeks!"

Was he thinking even then of volunteering for the Front? Had he already set his heart on the one chance of some atonement for his life— nay, on the very death he was to die? I never knew, and shall never know. Yet his words were strangely prophetic, even to the three or four weeks in which those events happened that imperilled the fabric of our Empire, and rallied her sons from the four winds to fight beneath her banner on the veldt. It all seems very ancient history now. But I remember nothing better or more vividly than the last words of Raffles upon his last crime, unless it be the pressure of his hand as he said them, or the rather sad twinkle in his tired eyes.

THE PRICE OF LIGHT

Ellis Peters

THE VERSATILE EDITH MARY PARGETER, under the name
Ellis Peters, had been writing historical novels, general fiction, and translat-
ing works from Czech to English for more than four decades before she created her most famous and beloved protagonist, Brother Cadfael, a Benedictine
monk who worked in twelfth-century Shropshire. Pargeter first tried her hand
at writing a mystery in 1951, when she published *Fallen Into the Pit* under her
pseudonym. As she had been publishing straight fiction under her real name for
so many years, she decided to use a pseudonym for her mysteries and chose Ellis Peters, retaining her initials and using her brother's first name. That novel,
and many others, featured the adventures of the Felse family, in which various
members took center stage in different books. The first Brother Cadfael novel,
A Morbid Taste for Bones, appeared twenty-six years after her debut as a mystery
writer. "The Price of Light" was first published in *Winter's Crimes #11* (London, Gollancz, 1979).

The Price of Light

ELLIS PETERS

HAMO FITZHAMON OF LIDYATE HELD two fat manors in the north-eastern corner of the county, towards the border of Cheshire. Though a gross feeder, a heavy drinker, a self-indulgent lecher, a harsh landlord and a brutal master, he had reached the age of sixty in the best of health, and it came as a salutary shock to him when he was at last taken with a mild seizure, and for the first time in his life saw the next world yawning before him, and woke to the uneasy consciousness that it might see fit to treat him somewhat more austerely than this world had done. Though he repented none of them, he was aware of a whole register of acts in his past which heaven might construe as heavy sins. It began to seem to him a prudent precaution to acquire merit for his soul as quickly as possible. Also as cheaply, for he was a grasping and possessive man. A judicious gift to some holy house should secure the welfare of his soul. There was no need to go so far as endowing an abbey, or a new church of his own. The Benedictine abbey of Shrewsbury could put up a powerful assault of prayers on his behalf in return for a much more modest gift.

The thought of alms to the poor, however ostentatiously bestowed in the first place, did not recommend itself. Whatever was given would be soon consumed and forgotten, and a rag-tag of beggarly blessings from the indigent could carry very little weight, besides failing to confer a lasting lustre upon himself. No, he wanted some-thing that would continue in daily use and daily respectful notice, a permanent reminder of his munificence and piety. He took his time about making his decision, and when he was satisfied of the best value he could get for the least expenditure, he sent his law-man to Shrewsbury to confer with abbot and prior, and conclude with due ceremony and many witnesses the charter that conveyed to the custodian of the altar of St. Mary, within the abbey church, one of his free tenant farmers, the rent to provide light for Our Lady's altar throughout the year. He promised also, for the proper displaying of his charity, the gift of a pair of fine silver candlesticks, which he himself would bring and see installed on the altar at the coming Christmas feast.

Abbot Heribert, who after a long life of repeated disillusionments still contrived to think the best of everybody, was moved to tears by this penitential generosity. Prior Robert, himself an aristocrat, refrained, out of Norman solidarity, from casting doubt upon Hamo's motive, but he elevated his eyebrows, all the same. Brother Cadfael, who knew only the public reputation of the donor, and was sceptical enough to suspend judgement until he encountered the source, said nothing, and waited to observe and decide for himself. Not that he expected much; he had been in the world fifty-five years, and learned to temper all his expectations, bad or good.

It was with mild and detached interest that he observed the arrival of the party from Lidyate, on the morning of Christmas Eve. A hard, cold Christmas it was proving to be, that year of 1135, all bitter black frost and grudging snow, thin and sharp as whips before a withering east wind. The weather had been vicious all the year, and the harvest a disaster. In the villages people shivered and starved, and Brother Oswald the almoner fretted and grieved the more that the alms he had to distribute were not enough to keep all those bodies and souls together. The sight of a cavalcade of three good riding horses, ridden by travellers richly wrapped up from the cold, and followed by two pack-ponies, brought all the wretched petitioners crowding and crying, holding out hands blue with frost. All they got out of it was a single perfunctory handful of small coin, and when they hampered his movements FitzHamon used his whip as a matter of course to clear the way. Rumour, thought Brother Cadfael, pausing on his way to the infirmary with his daily medicines for the sick, had probably not done Hamo FitzHamon any injustice.

Dismounting in the great court, the knight of Lidyate was seen to be a big, over-fleshed, top-heavy man with bushy hair and beard and eyebrows, all grey-streaked from their former black, and stiff and bristling as wire. He might well have been a very handsome man before indulgence purpled his face and pocked his skin and sank his sharp black eyes deep into flabby sacks of flesh. He looked more than his age, but still a man to be reckoned with.

The second horse carried his lady, pillion behind a groom. A small figure she made, even swathed almost to invisibility in her woollens and furs, and she rode snuggled comfortably against the groom's broad back, her arms hugging him round the waist. And a very well-looking young fellow he was, this groom, a strapping lad barely twenty years old, with round, ruddy cheeks and merry, guileless eyes, long in the legs, wide in the shoulders, everything a country youth should be, and attentive to his duties into the bargain, for he was down from the saddle in one lithe leap, and reaching up to take the lady by the waist, every bit as heartily as she

had been clasping him a moment before, and lift her lightly down. Small, gloved hands rested on his shoulders a brief moment longer than was necessary. His respectful support of her continued until she was safe on the ground and sure of her footing; perhaps a few seconds more. Hamo FitzHamon was occupied with Prior Robert's ceremonious welcome, and the attentions of the hospitaller, who had made the best rooms of the guest-hall ready for him.

The third horse also carried two people, but the woman on the pillion did not wait for anyone to help her down, but slid quickly to the ground and hurried to help her mistress off with the great outer cloak in which she had travelled. A quiet, submissive young woman, perhaps in her middle twenties, perhaps older, in drab homespun, her hair hidden away under a coarse linen wimple. Her face was thin and pale, her skin dazzlingly fair, and her eyes, reserved and weary, were of a pale, clear blue, a fierce colour that ill suited their humility and resignation.

Lifting the heavy folds from her lady's shoulders, the maid showed a head the taller of the two, but drab indeed beside the bright little bird that emerged from the cloak. Lady FitzHamon came forth graciously smiling on the world in scarlet and brown, like a robin; and just as confidently. She had dark hair braided about a small, shapely head, soft, full cheeks flushed rosy by the chill air, and large dark eyes assured of their charm and power. She could not possibly have been more than thirty, probably not so much. FitzHamon had a grown son somewhere, with children of his own, and waiting, some said with little patience, for his inheritance. This girl must be a second or a third wife, a good deal younger than her stepson, and a beauty, at that. Hamo was secure enough and important enough to keep himself supplied with wives as he wore them out. This one must have cost him dear, for she had not the air of a poor but pretty relative sold for a profitable alliance, rather she looked as if she knew her own status very well indeed, and meant to have it acknowledged. She would look well presiding over the high table at Lidyate, certainly, which was probably the main consideration.

The groom behind whom the maid had ridden was an older man, lean and wiry, with a face like the bole of a knotty oak. By the sardonic patience of his eyes he had been in close and relatively favoured attendance on FitzHamon for many years, knew the best and the worst his moods could do, and was sure of his own ability to ride the storms. Without a word he set about unloading the pack-horses, and followed his lord to the guest-hall, while the young man took FitzHamon's bridle, and led the horses away to the stables.

Cadfael watched the two women cross to the doorway, the lady springy as a young hind, with bright eyes taking in everything around her, the tall maid keeping always a pace behind, with long steps curbed to keep her distance. Even thus, frustrated like a mewed hawk, she had a graceful gait. Almost certainly of villein stock, like the two grooms. Cadfael had long practice in distinguishing the free from the unfree. Not that the free had any easy life, often they were worse off than the villeins of their neighbourhood; there were plenty of free men, this Christmas, gaunt and hungry, forced to hold out begging hands among the throng round the gatehouse. Freedom, the first ambition of every man, still could not fill the bellies of wives and children in a bad season.

FitzHamon and his party appeared at Vespers in full glory, to see the candlesticks reverently installed upon the altar in the Lady Chapel. Abbot, prior and brothers had no difficulty in sufficiently admiring the gift, for they were indeed things of beauty, two fluted stems ending in the twin cups of flowering lilies. Even the veins of the leaves showed delicate and perfect as in the living plant. Brother Oswald the almoner, himself a skilled silversmith when he had time to exercise his craft, stood gazing at the new embellishments of the altar with a face and mind curiously torn between rapture and regret, and ventured to delay the donor for a moment, as he was being ushered away to sup with Abbot Heribert in his lodging.

"My lord, these are of truly noble workmanship. I have some knowledge of precious metals, and of the most notable craftsmen in these parts, but I never saw any work so true to the plant as this. A country-man's eye is here, but the hand of a court craftsman. May we know who made them?"

FitzHamon's marred face curdled into deeper purple, as if an unpardonable shadow had been cast upon his hour of self-congratulation. He said brusquely: "I commissioned them from a fellow in my own service. You would not know his name—a villein born, but he had some skill." And with that he swept on, avoiding further question, and wife and men-servants and maid trailed after him. Only the older groom, who seemed less in awe of his lord than anyone, perhaps by reason of having so often presided over the ceremony of carrying him dead-drunk to his bed, turned back for a moment to pluck at Brother Oswald's sleeve, and advise him in a confidential whisper: "You'll find him short to question on that head. The silversmith—Alard, his name was—cut and ran from his service last Christmas, and for all they hunted him as far as London, where the signs pointed, he's never been found. I'd let that matter lie, if I were you."

And with that he trotted away after his master, and left several thoughtful faces staring after him.

"Not a man to part willingly with any property of his," mused Brother Cadfael, "metal or man, but for a price, and a steep price at that."

"Brother, be ashamed!" reproved Brother Jerome at his elbow. "Has he not parted with these very treasures from pure charity?"

Cadfael refrained from elaborating on the profit FitzHamon expected for his benevolence. It was never worth arguing with Jerome, who in any case knew as well as anyone that the silver lilies and the rent of one farm were no free gift. But Brother Oswald said grievingly: "I wish he had directed his charity better. Surely these are beautiful things, a delight to the eyes, but well sold, they could have provided money enough to buy the means of keeping my poorest petitioners alive through the winter, some of whom will surely die for the want of them."

Brother Jerome was scandalised. "Has he not given them to Our Lady herself?" he lamented indignantly. "Beware of the sin of those apostles who cried out with the same complaint against the woman who brought the pot of spikenard, and poured it over the Saviour's feet. Remember Our Lord's reproof to them, that they should let her alone, for she had done well!"

"Our Lord was acknowledging a well-meant impulse of devotion," said Brother Oswald with spirit. "He did not say it was well advised! 'She hath done what she could' is what he said. He never said that with a little thought she might not have done better. What use would it have been to wound the giver, after the thing was done? Spilled oil of spikenard could hardly be recovered."

His eyes dwelt with love and compunction upon the silver lilies, with their tall stems of wax and flame. For these remained, and to divert them to other use was still possible, or would have been possible if the donor had been a more approachable man. He had, after all, a right to dispose as he wished of his own property.

"It is sin," admonished Jerome sanctimoniously, "even to covet for other use, however worthy, that which has been given to Our Lady. The very thought is sin."

"If Our Lady could make her own will known," said Brother Cadfael drily, "we might learn which is the graver sin, and which the more acceptable sacrifice."

"Could any price be too high for the lighting of this holy altar?" demanded Jerome.

It was a good question, Cadfael thought, as they went to supper in the refectory. Ask Brother Jordan, for instance, the value of light. Jordan was old and frail, and gradually going blind. As yet he could distinguish shapes, but like shadows in a dream, though he knew his way about cloisters and precincts so well that his gathering darkness was no hindrance to his freedom of movement. But as every day the twilight closed in on him by a shade, so did his profound love

of light grow daily more devoted, until he had forsaken other duties, and taken upon himself to tend all the lamps and candles on both altars, for the sake of being always irradiated by light, and sacred light, at that. As soon as Compline was over, this evening, he would be busy devoutly trimming the wicks of candle and lamp, to have the steady flames smokeless and immaculate for the Matins of Christmas Day. Doubtful if he would go to his bed at all until Matins and Lauds were over. The very old need little sleep, and sleep is itself a kind of darkness. But what Jordan treasured was the flame of light, and not the vessel holding it; and would not those splendid two-pound candles shine upon him just as well from plain wooden sconces?

Cadfael was in the warming-house with the rest of the brothers, about a quarter of an hour before Compline, when a lay brother from the guest-hall came enquiring for him.

"The lady asks if you'll speak with her. She's complaining of a bad head, and that she'll never be able to sleep. Brother Hospitaller recommended her to you for a remedy."

Cadfael went with him without comment, but with some curiosity, for at Vespers the Lady FitzHamon had looked in blooming health and sparkling spirits. Nor did she seem greatly changed when he met her in the hall, though she was still swathed in the cloak she had worn to cross the great court to and from the abbot's house, and had the hood so drawn that it shadowed her face. The silent maid hovered at her shoulder.

"You are Brother Cadfael? They tell me you are expert in herbs and medicines, and can certainly help me. I came early back from the lord abbot's supper, with such a headache, and have told my lord that I shall go early to bed. But I have such disturbed sleep, and with this pain how shall I be able to rest? Can you give me some draught that will ease me? They say you have a perfect apothecarium in your herb garden, and all your own work, growing, gathering, drying, brewing and all. There must be something there that can soothe pain and bring deep sleep."

Well, thought Cadfael, small blame to her if she sometimes sought a means to ward off her old husband's rough attentions for a night, especially for a festival night when he was likely to have drunk heavily. Nor was it Cadfael's business to question whether the petitioner really needed his remedies. A guest might ask for whatever the house afforded.

"I have a syrup of my own making," he said, "which may do you good service. I'll bring you a vial of it from my workshop store."

"May I come with you? I should like to see your workshop." She had forgotten to sound frail and tired, the voice could have been a curious child's. "As I already am cloaked and shod," she said winningly. "We just returned from the lord abbot's table."

"But should you not go in from the cold, madam? Though the snow's swept here in the court, it lies on some of the garden paths."

"A few minutes in the fresh air will help me," she said, "before trying to sleep. And it cannot be far."

It was not far. Once away from the subdued lights of the buildings they were aware of the stars, snapping like sparks from a cold fire, in a clear black sky just engendering a few tattered snow-clouds in the east. In the garden, between the pleached hedges, it seemed almost warm, as though the sleeping trees breathed tempered air as well as cutting off the bleak wind. The silence was profound. The herb garden was walled, and the wooden hut where Cadfael brewed and stored his medicines was sheltered from the worst of the cold. Once inside, and a small lamp kindled, Lady FitzHamon forgot her invalid role in wonder and delight, looking round her with bright, inquisitive eyes. The maid, submissive and still, scarcely turned her head, but her eyes ranged from left to right, and a faint colour touched life into her cheeks. The many faint, sweet scents made her nostrils quiver, and her lips curve just perceptibly with pleasure.

Curious as a cat, the lady probed into every sack and jar and box, peered at mortars and bottles, and asked a hundred questions in a breath.

"And this is rosemary, these little dried needles? And in this great sack—is it grain?" She plunged her hands wrist-deep inside the neck of it, and the hut was filled with sweetness. "Lavender? Such a great harvest of it? Do you, then, prepare perfumes for us women?"

"Lavender has other good properties," said Cadfael. He was filling a small vial with a clear syrup he made from eastern poppies, a legacy of his crusading years. "It is helpful for all disorders that trouble the head and spirit, and its scent is calming. I'll give you a little pillow filled with that and other herbs, that shall help to bring you sleep. But this draught will ensure it. You may take all that I give you here, and get no harm, only a good night's rest."

She had been playing inquisitively with a pile of small clay dishes he kept by his work-bench, rough dishes in which the fine seeds sifted from fruiting plants could be spread to dry out; but she came at once to gaze eagerly at the modest vial he presented to her. "Is it enough? It takes much to give me sleep."

"This," he assured her patiently, "would bring sleep to a strong man. But it will not harm even a delicate lady like you."

She took it in her hand with a small, sleek smile of satisfaction. "Then I thank you indeed! I will make a gift—shall I?—to your almoner in requital. Elfgiva, you bring the little pillow. I shall breathe it all night long. It should sweeten dreams."

So her name was Elfgiva. A Norse name. She had Norse eyes, as he had already noted, blue as ice, and pale, fine skin worn finer and whiter by weariness. All this time she had noted everything that passed, motionless, and never said word. Was she older, or younger, than her lady? There was no guessing. The one was so clamant, and the other so still.

He put out his lamp and closed the door, and led them back to the great court just in time to take leave of them and still be prompt for Compline. Clearly the lady had no intention of attending. As for the lord, he was just being helped away from the abbot's lodging, his grooms supporting him one on either side, though as yet he was not gravely drunk. They headed for the guest-hall at an easy roll. No doubt only the hour of Compline had concluded the drawn-out supper, probably to the abbot's considerable relief. He was no drinker, and could have very little in common with Hamo FitzHamon. Apart, of course, from a deep devotion to the altar of St. Mary.

The lady and her maid had already vanished within the guest-hall. The younger groom carried in his free hand a large jug, full, to judge by the way he held it. The young wife could drain her draught and clutch her herbal pillow with confidence; the drinking was not yet at an end, and her sleep would be solitary and untroubled. Brother Cadfael went to Compline mildly sad, and obscurely comforted.

Only when service was ended, and the brothers on the way to their beds, did he remember that he had left his flask of poppy syrup unstoppered. Not that it would come to any harm in the frosty night, but his sense of fitness drove him to go and remedy the omission before he slept.

His sandalled feet, muffled in strips of woollen cloth for warmth and safety on the frozen paths, made his coming quite silent, and he was already reaching out a hand to the latch of the door, but not yet touching, when he was brought up short and still by the murmur of voices within. Soft, whispering, dreamy voices that made sounds less and more than speech, caresses rather than words, though once at least words surfaced for a moment. A man's voice, young, wary, saying: "But how if he *does* . . . ?" And a woman's soft, suppressed laughter: "He'll sleep till morning, never fear!" And her words were suddenly hushed with kissing, and her laughter became huge, ecstatic sighs; the young man's breath heaving triumphantly, but still, a moment later, the note of fear again, half-enjoyed: "Still, you know him, he *may* . . ." And she, soothing: "Not for an hour, at least . . . then we'll go . . . it will grow cold here . . ."

That, at any rate, was true; small fear of them

wishing to sleep out the night here, even two close-wrapped in one cloak on the bench-bed against the wooden wall. Brother Cadfael withdrew very circumspectly from the herb garden, and made his way back in chastened thought towards the dortoir. Now he knew who had swallowed that draught of his, and it was not the lady. In the pitcher of wine the young groom had been carrying? Enough for a strong man, even if he had not been drunk already. Meantime, no doubt, the body-servant was left to put his lord to bed, somewhere apart from the chamber where the lady lay supposedly nursing her indisposition and sleeping the sleep of the innocent. Ah, well, it was no business of Cadfael's, nor had he any intention of getting involved. He did not feel particularly censorious. Doubtful if she ever had any choice about marrying Hamo; and with this handsome boy for ever about them, to point the contrast . . . A brief experience of genuine passion, echoing old loves, pricked sharply through the years of his vocation. At least he knew what he was condoning. And who could help feeling some admiration for her opportunist daring, the quick wit that had procured the means, the alert eye that had seized on the most remote and adequate shelter available?

Cadfael went to bed, and slept without dreams, and rose at the Matin bell, some minutes before midnight. The procession of the brothers wound its way down the night stairs into the church, and into the soft, full glow of the lights before St. Mary's altar.

Withdrawn reverently some yards from the step of the altar, old Brother Jordan, who should long ago have been in his cell with the rest, knelt upright with clasped hands and ecstatic face, in which the great, veiled eyes stared full into the light he loved. When Prior Robert exclaimed in concern at finding him there on the stones, and laid a hand on his shoulder, he started as if out of a trance, and lifted to them a countenance itself all light.

"Oh, brothers, I have been so blessed! I have lived through a wonder . . . Praise God that ever it was granted to me! But bear with me, for I am forbidden to speak of it to any, for three days. On the third day from today I may speak . . . !"

"Look, brothers!" wailed Jerome suddenly, pointing. "Look at the altar!"

Every man present, except Jordan, who still serenely prayed and smiled, turned to gape where Jerome pointed. The tall candles stood secured by drops of their own wax in two small clay dishes, such as Cadfael used for sorting seeds. The two silver lilies were gone from the place of honour.

Through loss, disorder, consternation, and suspicion, Prior Robert would still hold fast to the order of the day. Let Hamo FitzHamon sleep in happy ignorance till morning, still Matins and Lauds must be properly celebrated. Christmas was larger than all the giving and losing of silverware. Grimly he saw the services of the church observed, and despatched the brethren back to their beds until Prime, to sleep or lie wakeful and fearful, as they might. Nor would he allow any pestering of Brother Jerome by others, though possibly he did try in private to extort something more satisfactory from the old man. Clearly the theft, whether he knew anything about it or not, troubled Jordan not at all. To everything he said only: "I am enjoined to silence until midnight of the third day." And when they asked by whom? he smiled seraphically, and was silent.

It was Robert himself who broke the news to Hamo FitzHamon, in the morning, before Mass. The uproar, though vicious, was somewhat tempered by the after-effects of Cadfael's poppy draught, which dulled the edges of energy, if not of malice. His body-servant, the older groom Sweyn, was keeping well back out of reach, even with Robert still present, and the lady sat somewhat apart, too, as though still frail and possibly a little out of temper. She exclaimed dutifully, and apparently sincerely, at the outrage done to her husband, and echoed his demand that the thief should be hunted down, and the candle-sticks recovered. Prior Robert was just as zealous in the matter. No effort should be spared to regain the princely gift, of that they could be sure. He had already made certain of various circumstances which should limit the hunt. There had been a brief fall of snow after Compline, just enough to lay down a clean film of white on the ground. No single footprint had as yet marked this pure layer. He had only to look for himself at the paths leading from both parish doors of the church to see that no one had left by that way. The porter would swear that no one had passed the gatehouse; and on the one side of the abbey grounds not walled, the Meole brook was full and frozen, but the snow on both sides of it was virgin. Within the enclave, of course, tracks and cross-tracks were trodden out everywhere; but no one had left the enclave since Compline, when the candlesticks were still in their place.

"So the miscreant is still within the walls?" said Hamo, glinting vengefully. "So much the better! Then his booty is still here within, too, and if we have to turn all your abode doors out of dortoirs, we'll find it! It, and him!"

"We will search everywhere," agreed Robert, "and question every man. We are as deeply offended as your lordship at this blasphemous crime. You may yourself oversee the search, if you will."

So all that Christmas Day, alongside the solemn rejoicings in the church, an angry hunt raged about the precincts in full cry. It was not difficult for all the monks to account for their time to the last minute, their routine being so ordered that brother inevitably extricated brother from suspicion; and such as had special duties that took them out of the general view, like Cadfael in his visit to the herb garden, had all witnesses to vouch for them. The lay brothers ranged more freely, but tended to work in pairs, at least. The servants and the few guests protested their innocence, and if they had not, all of them, others willing to prove it, neither could Hamo prove the contrary. When it came to his own two grooms, there were several witnesses to testify that Sweyn had returned to his bed in the lofts of the stables as soon as he had put his lord to bed, and certainly empty-handed; and Sweyn, as Cadfael noted with interest, swore unblinkingly that young Madoc, who had come in an hour after him, had none the less returned with him, and spent that hour, at Sweyn's order, tending one of the pack-ponies, which showed signs of a cough, and that otherwise they had been together throughout.

A villein instinctively closing ranks with his kind against his lord? wondered Cadfael. Or does Sweyn know very well where that young man was last night, or at least what he was about, and is he intent on protecting him from a worse vengeance? No wonder Madoc looked a shade less merry and ruddy than usual this morning, though on the whole he kept his countenance very well, and refrained from even looking at the lady, while her tone to him was cool, sharp, and distant.

Cadfael left them hard at it again after the miserable meal they made of dinner, and went into the church alone. While they were feverishly searching every corner for the candlesticks he had forborne from taking part, but now they were elsewhere he might find something of interest there. He would not be looking for anything so obvious as two large silver candlesticks. He made obeisance at the altar, and mounted the step to look closely at the burning candles. No one had paid any attention to the modest containers that had been substituted for Hamo's gift, and just as well, in the circumstances, that Cadfael's workshop was very little visited, or these little clay pots might have been recognised as coming from there. He moulded and baked them himself as he wanted them. He had no intention of condoning theft, but neither did he relish the idea of any creature, however sinful, falling into Hamo FitzHamon's mercies.

Something long and fine, a thread of silver-gold, was caught and coiled in the wax at the base of one candle. Carefully he detached candle from holder, and unlaced from it a long, pale hair; to make sure of retaining it, he broke off the

imprisoning disc of wax with it, and then hoisted and turned the candle to see if anything else was to be found under it. One tiny oval dot showed; with a fingernail he extracted a single seed of lavender. Left in the dish from beforetime? He thought not. The stacked pots were all empty. No, this had been brought here in the fold of a sleeve, most probably, and shaken out while the candle was being transferred.

The lady had plunged both hands with pleasure into the sack of lavender, and moved freely about his workshop investigating everything. It would have been easy to take two of these dishes unseen, and wrap them in a fold of her cloak. Even more plausible, she might have delegated the task to young Madoc, when they crept away from their assignation. Supposing, say, they had reached the desperate point of planning flight together, and needed funds to set them on their way to some safe refuge . . . yes, there were possibilities. In the meantime, the grain of lavender had given Cadfael another idea. And there was, of course, that long, fine hair, pale as flax, but brighter. The boy was fair. But so fair?

He went out through the frozen garden to his herbarium, shut himself securely into his workshop, and opened the sack of lavender, plunging both arms to the elbow and groping through the chill, smooth sweetness that parted and slid like grain. They were there, well down, his fingers traced the shape first of one, then a second. He sat down to consider what must be done.

Finding the lost valuables did not identify the thief. He could produce and restore them at once, but FitzHamon would certainly pursue the hunt vindictively until he found the culprit; and Cadfael had seen enough of him to know that it might cost life and all before this complainant was satisfied. He needed to know more before he would hand over any man to be done to death. Better not leave the things here, however. He doubted if they would ransack his hut, but they might. He rolled the candlesticks in a piece of sacking, and thrust them into the centre of the pleached hedge where it was thickest. The meagre, frozen snow had dropped with the brief sun. His arm went in to the shoulder, and when he withdrew it, the twigs sprang back and covered all, holding the package securely. Whoever had first hidden it would surely come by night to reclaim it, and show a human face at last.

It was well that he had moved it, for the searchers, driven by an increasingly angry Hamo, reached his hut before Vespers, examined everything within it, while he stood by to prevent actual damage to his medicines, and went away satisfied that what they were seeking was not there. They had not, in fact, been very thorough about the sack of lavender, the candlesticks might well have escaped notice even if he had left them there. It did not occur to anyone to tear the hedges apart, luckily. When they were gone, to probe all the fodder and grain in the barns, Cadfael restored the silver to its original place. Let the bait lie safe in the trap until the quarry came to claim it, as he surely would, once relieved of the fear that the hunters might find it first.

Cadfael kept watch that night. He had no difficulty in absenting himself from the dortoir, once everyone was in bed and asleep. His cell was by the night stairs, and the prior slept at the far end of the long room, and slept deeply. And bitter though the night air was, the sheltered hut was barely colder than his cell, and he kept blankets there for swathing some of his jars and bottles against frost. He took his little box with tinder and flint, and hid himself in the corner behind the door. It might be a wasted vigil; the thief, having survived one day, might think it politic to venture yet another before removing his spoils.

But it was not wasted. He reckoned it might be as late as ten o'clock when he heard a light hand at the door. Two hours before the bell would sound for Matins, almost two hours since the household had retired. Even the guest-hall should be silent and asleep by now; the hour was carefully chosen. Cadfael held his breath, and waited. The door swung open, a shadow stole past him, light steps felt their way unerringly to where the sack of lavender was propped against the wall. Equally silently Cadfael swung the door to again, and set his back against it. Only then did he strike a spark, and hold the blown flame to the wick of his little lamp.

She did not start or cry out, or try to rush past him and escape into the night. The attempt would not have succeeded, and she had had long practice in enduring what could not be cured. She stood facing him as the small flame steadied and burned taller, her face shadowed by the hood of her cloak, the candlesticks clasped possessively to her breast.

"Elfgiva!" said Brother Cadfael gently. And then: "Are you here for yourself, or for your mistress?" But he thought he knew the answer already. That frivolous young wife would never really leave her rich husband and easy life, however tedious and unpleasant Hamo's attentions might be, to risk everything with her penniless villein lover. She would only keep him to enjoy in secret whenever she felt it safe. Even when the old man died she would submit to marriage at an overlord's will to another equally distasteful. She was not the stuff of which heroines and adventurers are made. This was another kind of woman.

Cadfael went close, and lifted a hand gently to put back the hood from her head. She was tall, a hand's-breadth taller than he, and erect as one of the lilies she clasped. The net that had covered her hair was drawn off with the hood, and a great flood of silver-gold streamed about her in the dim light, framing the pale face and startling blue eyes. Norse hair! The Danes had left their seed as far south as Cheshire, and planted this tall flower among them. She was no longer plain, tired and resigned. In this dim but loving light she shone in austere beauty. Just so must Brother Jordan's veiled eyes have seen her.

"Now I see!" said Cadfael. "You came into the Lady Chapel, and shone upon our half-blind brother's darkness as you shine here. You are the visitation that brought him awe and bliss, and enjoined silence upon him for three days."

The voice he had scarcely heard speak a word until then, a voice level, low and beautiful, said:

"I made no claim to be what I am not. It was he who mistook me. I did not refuse the gift."

"I understand. You had not thought to find anyone there, he took you by surprise as you took him. He took you for Our Lady herself, disposing as she saw fit of what had been given her. And you made him promise you three days' grace." The lady had plunged her hands into the sack, yes, but Elfgiva had carried the pillow, and a grain or two had filtered through the muslin to betray her.

"Yes," she said, watching him with unwavering blue eyes.

"So in the end you had nothing against him making known how the candlesticks were stolen." It was not an accusation, he was pursuing his way to understanding.

But at once she said clearly: "I did not steal them. I took them. I will restore them—to their owner."

"Then you don't claim they are yours?"

"No," she said, "they are not mine. But neither are they FitzHamon's."

"Do you tell me," said Cadfael mildly, "that there has been no theft at all?"

"Oh, yes," said Elfgiva, and her pallor burned into a fierce brightness, and her voice vibrated like a harp-string. "Yes, there has been a theft, and a vile, cruel theft, too, but not here, not now. The theft was a year ago, when FitzHamon received these candlesticks from Alard who made them, his villein, like me. Do you know what the promised price was for these? Manumission for Alard, and marriage with me, what we had begged of him three years and more. Even in villeinage we would have married and been thankful. But he promised freedom! Free man makes free wife, and I was promised, too. But when he got the fine works he wanted, then he refused the promised price. He laughed! I saw, I heard him! He kicked Alard away from him like a dog. So what was his due, and denied him, Alard took. He ran! On St. Stephen's Day he ran!"

"And left you behind?" said Cadfael gently.

"What chance had he to take me? Or even to bid me farewell? He was thrust out to manual labour on FitzHamon's other manor. When his chance came, he took it and fled. I was not sad! I rejoiced! Whether I live or die, whether he remembers or forgets me, he is free. No, but in two days more he will be free. For a year and a day he will have been working for his living in his own craft, in a charter borough, and after that he cannot be haled back into servitude, even if they find him."

"I do not think," said Brother Cadfael, "that he will have forgotten you! Now I see why our brother may speak after three days. It will be too late then to try to reclaim a runaway serf. And you hold that these exquisite things you are cradling belong by right to Alard who made them?"

"Surely," she said, "seeing he never was paid for them, they are still his."

"And you are setting out tonight to take them to him. Yes! As I heard it, they had some cause to pursue him towards London . . . indeed, into London, though they never found him. Have you had better word of him? *From* him?"

The pale face smiled. "Neither he nor I can read or write. And whom should he trust to carry word until his time is complete, and he is free? No, never any word."

"But Shrewsbury is also a charter borough, where the unfree may work their way to freedom in a year and a day. And sensible boroughs encourage the coming of good craftsmen, and will go far to hide and protect them. I know! So you think he may be here. And the trail towards London a false trail. True, why should he run so far, when there's help so near? But, daughter, what if you do not find him in Shrewsbury?"

"Then I will look for him elsewhere until I do. I can live as a runaway, too, I have skills, I can make my own way until I do get word of him. Shrewsbury can as well make room for a good seamstress as for a man's gifts, and someone in the silversmith's craft will know where to find a brother so talented as Alard. I shall find him!"

"And when you do? Oh, child, have you looked beyond that?"

"To the very end," said Elfgiva firmly. "If I find him and he no longer wants me, no longer thinks of me, if he is married and has put me out of his mind, then I will deliver him these things that belong to him, to do with as he pleases, and go my own way and make my own life as best I may without him. And wish well to him as long as I live."

Oh, no, small fear, she would not be easily forgotten, not in a year, not in many years. "And if he is utterly glad of you, and loves you still?"

"Then," she said, gravely smiling, "if he is of the same mind as I, I have made a vow to Our Lady, who lent me her semblance in the old man's eyes, that we will sell these candle-sticks where they may fetch their proper price, and that price shall be delivered to your almoner to feed the hungry. And that will be our gift, Alard's and mine, though no one will ever know it."

"Our Lady will know it," said Cadfael, "and so shall I. Now, how were you planning to get out of this enclave and into Shrewsbury? Both our gates and the town gates are closed until morning."

She lifted eloquent shoulders. "The parish doors are not barred. And even if I leave tracks, will it matter, provided I find a safe hiding-place inside the town?"

"And wait in the cold of the night? You would freeze before morning. No, let me think. We can do better for you than that."

Her lips shaped: *We?* in silence, wonder-ing, but quick to understand. She did not ques-tion his decisions, as he had not questioned hers. He thought he would long remember the slow, deepening smile, the glow of warmth mantling her cheeks. "You believe me!" she said.

"Every word! Here, give me the candlesticks, let me wrap them, and do you put up your hair again in net and hood. We've had no fresh snow since morning, the path to the parish door is well trodden, no one will know your tracks among the many. And, girl, when you come to the town end of the bridge there's a little house off to the left, under the wall, close to the town gate. Knock there and ask for shelter over the night till the gates open, and say that Brother Cadfael sent

you. They know me, I doctored their son when he was sick. They'll give you a warm corner and a place to lie, for kindness' sake, and ask no ques-tions, and answer none from others, either. And likely they'll know where to find the silversmiths of the town, to set you on your way."

She bound up her pale, bright hair and cov-ered her head, wrapping the cloak about her, and was again the maidservant in homespun. She obeyed without question his every word, moved silently at his back round the great court by way of the shadows, halting when he halted, and so he brought her to the church, and let her out by the parish door into the public street, still a good hour before Matins. At the last moment she said, close at his shoulder within the half-open door. "I shall be grateful always. Some day I shall send you word."

"No need for words," said Brother Cadfael, "if you send me the sign I shall be waiting for. Go now, quickly, there's not a soul stirring."

She was gone, lightly and silently, flitting past the abbey gatehouse like a tall shadow, towards the bridge and the town. Cadfael closed the door softly, and went back up the night stairs to the dortoir, too late to sleep, but in good time to rise at the sound of the bell, and return in procession to celebrate Matins.

There was, of course, the resultant uproar to face next morning, and he could not afford to avoid it, there was too much at stake. Lady FitzHamon naturally expected her maid to be in attendance as soon as she opened her eyes, and raised a petulant outcry when there was no submissive shadow waiting to dress her and do her hair. Calling failed to summon and search to find Elfgiva, but it was an hour or more before it dawned on the lady that she had lost her ac-complished maid for good. Furiously she made her own toilet, unassisted, and raged out to com-plain to her husband, who had risen before her, and was waiting for her to accompany him to Mass. At her angry declaration that Elfgiva was nowhere to be found, and must have run away during the night, he first scoffed, for why should a sane girl take herself off into a killing frost when she had warmth and shelter and enough to eat where she was? Then he made the inevitable connection, and let out a roar of rage.

"Gone, is she? And my candlesticks gone with her, I dare swear! So it was *she*! The foul little thief! But I'll have her yet, I'll drag her back, she shall not live to enjoy her ill-gotten gains. . . ."

It seemed likely that the lady would heartily endorse all this; her mouth was already open to echo him when Brother Cadfael, brushing her sleeve close as the agitated brothers ringed the pair, contrived to shake a few grains of lavender on to her wrist. Her mouth closed abruptly. She gazed at the tiny things for the briefest instant before she shook them off, she flashed an even briefer glance at Brother Cadfael, caught his eye, and heard in a rapid whisper: "Madam, softly!—proof of the maid's innocence is also proof of the mistress's."

She was by no means a stupid woman. A second quick glance confirmed what she had already grasped, that there was one man here who had a weapon to hold over her at least as deadly as any she could use against Elfgiva. She was also a woman of decision, and wasted no time in bitterness once her course was chosen. The tone in which she addressed her lord was almost as sharp as that in which she had complained of Elfgiva's desertion.

"She your thief, indeed! That's folly, as you should very well know. The girl is an ungrateful fool to leave me, but a thief she never has been, and certainly is not this time. She can't possibly have taken the candlesticks, you know well enough when they vanished, and you know I was not well that night, and went early to bed. She was with me until long after Brother Prior discovered the theft. I asked her to stay with me until you came to bed. *As you never did!*" she ended tartly. "You may remember!"

Hamo probably remembered very little of that night; certainly he was in no position to gainsay what his wife so roundly declared. He took out a little of his ill-temper on her, but she was not so much in awe of him that she dared

not reply in kind. Of course she was certain of what she said! *She* had not drunk herself stupid at the lord abbot's table, she had been nursing a bad head of another kind, and even with Brother Cadfael's remedies she had not slept until after midnight, and Elfgiva had then been still beside her. Let him hunt a runaway maidservant, by all means, the thankless hussy, but never call her a thief, for she was none.

Hunt her he did, though with less energy now it seemed clear he would not recapture his property with her. He sent his grooms and half the lay servants off in both directions to enquire if anyone had seen a solitary girl in a hurry; they were kept at it all day, but they returned empty-handed.

The party from Lidyate, less one member, left for home next day. Lady FitzHamon rode demurely behind young Madoc, her cheek against his broad shoulders; she even gave Brother Cadfael the flicker of a conspiratorial smile as the cavalcade rode out of the gates, and detached one arm from round Madoc's waist to wave as they reached the roadway. So Hamo was not present to hear when Brother Jordan, at last released from his vow, told how Our Lady had appeared to him in a vision of light, fair as an angel, and taken away with her the candlesticks that were hers to take and do with as she would, and how she had spoken to him, and enjoined on him his three days of silence. And if there were some among the listeners who wondered whether the fair woman had not been a more corporeal being, no one had the heart to say so to Jordan, whose vision was comfort and consolation for the fading of the light.

That was at Matins, at midnight of the day of St. Stephen's. Among the scattering of alms handed in at the gatehouse next morning for the beggars, there was a little basket that weighed surprisingly heavily. The porter could not remember who had brought it, taking it to be some offerings of food or old clothing, like all the rest; but when it was opened it sent Brother Oswald, almost incoherent with joy and wonder, running to Abbot Heribert to report what seemed to be a miracle. For the basket was full of gold coin, to the value of more than a hundred marks. Well used, it would ease all the worst needs of his poorest petitioners, until the weather relented.

"Surely," said Brother Oswald devoutly, "Our Lady has made her own will known. Is not this the sign we have hoped for?"

Certainly it was for Cadfael, and earlier than he had dared to hope for it. He had the message that needed no words. She had found him, and been welcomed with joy. Since midnight Alard the silversmith had been a free man, and free man makes free wife. Presented with such a woman as Elfgiva, he could give as gladly as she, for what was gold, what was silver, by comparison?

H. R. F. Keating

THE MOST POPULAR CHARACTER CREATED BY H. R. F. KEATING
was Inspector Ganesh Ghote of the Bombay Criminal Investigation Division,
a protagonist he invented in an effort to find an American publisher. It is the
same type of convoluted notion that Keating brought to his humorous novels,
in which strange events befall odd people in peculiar situations. In addition to
winning numerous awards for mystery fiction, Keating was also acknowledged
as a great scholar of crime fiction, being the reviewer for *The Times* (London) for
fifteen years and the author of books about Agatha Christie, Sherlock Holmes,
and many others. "A Present for Santa Sahib" was first collected in *Inspector
Ghote, His Life and Crimes* (London, Hutchinson, 1989).

A Present for Santa Sahib

H. R. F. KEATING

INSPECTOR GHOTE PUT A HAND TO his hip pocket and made sure it was firmly buttoned up. Ahead of him, where he stood in the entrance doorway to one of Bombay's biggest department stores, the crowds were dense just two days before the festival of Christmas. It was not only the Christians who celebrated the day by buying presents and good things to eat in the huge cosmopolitan city. People of every religion were always happy to share in the high days and holidays in each other's calendars. When Hindus honoured Bombay's favourite god, elephant-headed Ganesh, by taking huge statues of him to be immersed in the sea, Moslems, Parsis, and Christians delighted to join the enormous throngs watching them go by. Everyone had a day off too, and enjoyed it to the full for the Moslem Idd holiday.

But the crowds that gathered in the days before any such celebration brought always trouble as well as joy, Ghote thought to himself with a sigh. When people came in their thousands to buy sweets and fireworks for Diwali or to acquire stocks of coloured powders to throw and squirt in the springtime excitement of Holi, they made a very nice golden opportunity for the pickpockets.

He had, in fact, caught a glimpse just as he had entered the shop of a certain Ram Prasad, a well-known jackal stalking easy prey if ever there was. It equally had been the sight of the fellow, spotting him himself and turning rapidly back, that had made him check that his wallet was secure. It would look altogether bad if an Inspector of Crime Branch had to go back minus one wallet and empty-handed to the wife who had as usual commissioned him to buy a present for her Christian friend, Mrs. D'Cruz, in return for the one they had received at Diwali.

And he had another little obligation, too, on this trip to the store. Not only was there a gift to get for Mrs. D'Cruz but there was a visit to pay to Santa Claus as he sat—voluminously wrapped in shiny red coat, a silky red cap trimmed in fluffy white on his head, puffy cottonwool beard descending from his chin, sack of presents tucked away beside him—in his special place in the store.

Ghote was not actually going to line up with the children waiting to be given, in exchange for a rupee surreptitiously handed over by a hovering mother, a bar of chocolate or a packet of sweets from the big sack. Santa was an old friend who merited a word or two of greeting. Or, if not exactly a friend, he was at least someone known for a good long time.

In fact Santa—his actual name was Moti Popatkar—was a small-fry con-man. There was no getting past that. For all save the ten days each year leading up to Christmas, he made a dubious living from a variety of minor anti-social activities. There was the fine story he had for any British holidaymaker he happened upon—his English was unusually good, fruit of a mission

school education long ago—about how he had
been batman to an Army officer still living in
retirement in India and how he needed just the
rail fare to go back and look after Colonel Sahib
again. Or he would offer himself as a guide to
any lone European tourist he could spot, and
sooner or later cajole them into buying him po-
tent country liquor at some illicit drinking den.

It was at one such that Ghote had first met
him. A visiting German businessman had complained to the police that, on top of being persuaded into handing over to his guide a much
bigger tip than he had meant to give, he had also
been induced to fork out some fifty rupees for
drinks at a place tucked away inside a rabbit-
warren building in Nagandas Master Road
called the Beauty Bar.

There was not much that could be done about
the complaint, but since the businessman had
had a letter of introduction to a junior Minister
in the State Government, Ghote had been detailed to investigate. He had dutifully gone along
to the Beauty Bar, which proved to be very much
as he had expected, a single room with a shabby
counter in one corner, its walls painted blue
and peeling, half a dozen plastic-topped tables
set about. Where sat a handful of men, white-
capped office messengers, a khaki-uniformed
postman delaying on his round, a red-turbaned
ear-cleaner with his little aluminium case beside
him, an itinerant coldwaterman who had left
his barrel pushcart outside. All hunched over
smeary glasses of clear fluid.

But one of the drinkers seemed to answer to
the description the German businessman had
given of his guide. And, at the first sharp question, the fellow had cheerfully admitted that he
was Moti Popatkar and that, yes, he had brought
a German visitor to the place the day before.

"Exciting for him, no?" he had said. "Seeing
one damn fine Indian den of vice?"

Ghote had looked at the peeling walls, at a
boy lackadaisically swiping at one of the table
tops with a sodden heap of darkly grey cloth, at
the two pictures hanging askew opposite him,
one of an English maiden from some time in the

past showing most of her breasts, the other of
the late Mrs. Gandhi looking severe.

"Well, do not let me be catching you bringing
any visitor from foreign to such a fourth class
place again," he said.

"Oh, Inspectorji, I would not. In nine–ten
days only I would be Santa Claus."

So then it had come out what job Moti Popatkar had every year in the run-up to Christmas.

"And I am keeping same," he had ended up.
"When I was first beginning, too many years
past, the son of Owner, who is himself Ownerji
now, was very much liking me when his mother
was bringing him to tell his wishings to old
Santa. So now Manager Sahib cannot be giving
me one boot, however much he is wanting."

There had been then something in Moti
Popatkar's cheerful disregard of the proper
respect due to a police inspector, even of the
cringing most of his like would have adopted
before any policewalla, that had appealed to a
side of Ghote which he generally felt he ought
to keep well hidden. He felt a trickle of liking for this fellow, however much he knew he
should disapprove of anyone who led visitors to
India into such disgraceful places, and however
wrong it seemed that such a good-for-nothing
should wear the robe, even for a short period,
of a figure who was after all a Christian saint,
to be revered equally with Hindu holy man or
Muslim pir.

So, visiting Santa's store a few days later to
get Mrs. D'Cruz her present, he had gone out of
his way to have a look at Moti Popatkar, happy-
go-lucky specimen of Bombay's riff-raffs, im-
personating Santa Claus, Christian holy man of
bygone days.

There had been a lull in the stream of children coming to collect chocolate bars and
breathily whisper wishes into Santa's spreading
cottonwool beard at the time, so he had stayed to
chat with the red-robed fellow for a few minutes.
And every successive year since he had found
himself doing the same thing, for all that he still
felt he ought to disapprove of the man behind
the soft white whiskers. The truth was he some-

how liked his irresponsible impudent approach to life and to his present task in particular.

Only last year Father Christmas had had a particularly comical tale to tell.

"Oh, Inspectorji, you have nearly seen me in much, much trouble."

"How is that, you Number One scallywag?"

Moti Popatkar grinned through his big white beard, already looking slightly grimy.

"Well, you know, Inspector, I am half the time making the *baba log* believe they will be getting what for they are wishing, and half the time also I am taking one damn fine good look at the mothers, if they are being in any way pretty. Well, just only ten minutes past, a real beauty was coming, Anglo-Indian, short skirt an' all. Jolly spicy. And—oh, forgive, forgive God above—I was so much distracted I was giving her little girl not just only one bar of chocolate but a half-kilo cake of same. And then—then who should come jumping out from behind but Manager Sahib himself? What for are you giving away so much of Store property, he is demanding and denouncing. Then—oh, Inspector, I am a wicked, wicked fellow. You know what I am saying?"

"No?"

"I am saying, quick only as one flash of lightning, 'But, Manager sahib, that little girl has come with her governess. She is grand-daughter of multi-millionaire Tata, you are knowing.'"

Ghote had laughed aloud. He could not help himself. Besides, the Manager, whom he had once had dealings with, was a very self-satisfied individual.

"But then, Inspectorji, what is Manager sahib saying to me?"

"Well, tell."

"He is saying, 'Damn fool, you should have given whole kilo cake.'"

And Ghote had felt then his Christmas was all the merrier. Mrs. D'Cruz had got a better present than usual, too.

So now he decided to pay his visit to Santa Claus before he went present-buying. But when he came to the raised platform on which Father

Christmas was installed, his fat sack of little gifts on the floor beside him, he found the scene was by no means one of goodwill to all men.

Moti Popatkar was sitting in state as usual on his throne-like chair, his bright red shiny robe as ever gathered round him, his floppy red hat with the white trimming on his head. But he was not bending forward to catch the spit-laden whisperings of the children. Nor was he rocking back and issuing some Ho, ho, hos. Instead he was looking decidedly shifty under his cottonwool beard, and in front of him there was standing the Store Manager, both enraged and triumphant.

A lady dressed in a silk sari that must have cost several thousand rupees was standing just behind the Manager holding the hand of a little girl, evidently her daughter, plainly bewildered and on the verge of tears.

"You are hearing what this lady is stating," the Manager was shouting as Ghote came up. "When she was bringing this sweet little girl to visit Santa Claus there was in her handbag one note-case containing many, many hundred-rupee notes. But, just after leaving you, she was noticing the handbag itself was wide open and she was shutting same—click—and then when she was wanting to pay for purchase made at Knick-knacks and Assorted counter, what was she finding? That note-case had gone."

Instinctively, Ghote felt at his hip again. But *thik hai*, no *pocket-maar* had been light-fingered with his wallet.

"But, no, Manager sahib. No, no. I was not taking any note-case. Honest to God, no."

Yet Moti Popatkar's protestations had about them—there could be no doubting it—a ring of desperation.

"I am going to search you, here and now only," the Manager stormed.

"No!"

"Yes, I am saying."

And the Manager darted a hand into each of the big, sagging pockets of the shiny red robe one after the other. Only to withdraw from the second holding nothing more incriminating than a fluff-covered *paan* which Santa Claus had

had no opportunity to pop into his mouth and chew.

"Open up robe," the Manager demanded.

Ghote stood watching, a feeling of grey sadness creeping over him, as Moti Popatkar, now dulled into apathy, allowed Santa's robe to be tugged open and eager fingers to dip into shirt pocket and trouser pockets beneath.

But they found nothing more in the way of evidence than the fluff-fuzzed *paan* already brought to light.

The Manager, furiously baffled, took a step back. Moti Popatkar behind his spreading white beard—distinctly pulled apart during the search—had still not regained anything of his customary good spirits.

The Manager turned to offer explanations to the complaining customer.

Ghote gave a deep sigh.

"Look into Santa's sack, Manager sahib," he said.

"Ah! Yes. Yes, yes."

The big sack was jerked wide. The Manager plunged to his knees.

"Wait," Ghote shouted suddenly.

The Manager turned and looked up.

"You should let a police officer handle this," Ghote said.

He stepped up on to the platform and knelt in his turn beside the gaping sack. Then, very carefully, he felt about inside it, easing his fingers past bars of chocolate, little bags of sweets.

At last he rose to his feet.

Between the tip of the forefinger of his right hand and its thumb he was holding a crocodile-skin note-case frothed at the rim with big blue one-hundred rupee notes.

"Mine," exclaimed the watching lady customer.

Beside her, her daughter burst into tears.

"Inspector," the Manager said, "kindly charge-sheet this fellow."

"Well, Manager sahib," Ghote replied, "I am thinking I should not do that until I have evidences. Fingerprint evidences."

"But . . . but we have caught him red-handed only."

"Are you sure, Manager sahib? Were you actually observing this Santa placing the note-case inside his sack? And, more, did you not observe his manner when you were accusing? He was not at all his usual chirpy self. Now, if he was thinking that by hiding himself this note-case in his sack he would altogether trick you because you would not look there, I am believing he would have found something cheeky to be saying. It was because he was not that I was suddenly realising what must have happened."

"And what was that, Inspector?" the rich customer demanded.

"Oh, madam, you could not be knowing, but just only as I was entering this store I was catching sight of one Ram Prasad, notorious pickpocket. And he also was catching sight of myself, and *ek dum* he was turning round and making his way more into the store. It was soon after, I am thinking, that he was dropping the note-case he had already lifted from your open handbag into this sack. This Santa must have spotted him doing that, but been unable to prevent, and Ram Prasad will have had the intention of removing his loot when he had seen that I myself had left the store. I do not have much of doubt that it will be his fingerprints, which we have had ten–twelve years upon the file, that will be found on his very nice shiny crocodile-skin surface."

And it was then that, behind the bedraggled cottonwool of his beard, Santa sahib gave a wide, wide smile.

"Ho, ho, ho," he chuckled.

THE CHRISTMAS TRAIN
Will Scott

LARGELY FORGOTTEN TODAY, Will Scott wrote more than two thousand stories in his career, beginning with short humorous tales for various British periodicals before turning to crime. Among his most interesting characters are the oddly named Giglamps, a combination hobo, detective, and rogue; Disher, an egregiously fat and pompous detective who once (and maybe more than once!) said, "It is the most boring thing in all the world, of course, but I am always right"; and Jeremiah Jones, also known as the Laughing Crook, who, in a long series of stories, consistently gets the better of Scotland Yard Inspector Beecham. "The Christmas Train" was first published in the December 23, 1933, issue of *Passing Show*.

The Christmas Train

WILL SCOTT

"YOU'RE SURE OF YOUR FACTS, MAXWELL?" Mr. Jeremiah Jones inquired.

"Positive, sir," replied the sober Maxwell. "Mr. Hadlow Cribb landed this morning at Southampton. He has the jewels with him. Forty thousand pounds' worth. The trouble is, you can't get that lot through the Customs without somebody getting to know. And I got to know. It cost a bit!"

"Luxuries," reflected Mr. Jones, with a grin, "are always expensive. But go on."

"Mr. Hadlow Cribb leaves Liverpool Street tonight for his country home at Friars Topliss where he intends to spend Christmas," Maxwell proceeded. "The jewels, of course, go with him. The train is due out at fourteen minutes past six."

"Four hours," murmured Mr. Jones, with a glance at his watch. "Busy train. It won't be too easy. Still, nothing ventured, nothing gained. I wish I'd had a little experience of this kind of work."

"I ought to add," Maxwell resumed, "that Mr. Hadlow Cribb was accompanied up from Southampton by Marks."

"Marks?" Mr. Jeremiah Jones's eyebrows lifted quickly. "The new fellow in Beecham's office?"

"Exactly," said Maxwell with a sigh.

"Scotland Yard protection! No, it isn't going to be too easy," Mr. Jones repeated. "Can you get word to Dawlish?" he added as he reached for the telephone.

"Dawlish?"

Mr. Jones nodded.

"You mean—as it were—put him wise?"

"Very wise, in a tactful way."

"I might," said Maxwell doubtfully.

"Aren't you sure?"

"I'm positive," said Maxwell.

"Right. Then go and do it. Meet me here at five-thirty. Have everything ready—most important—mind you've got a bag that's as near as blow it to the one Mr. Hadlow Cribb will carry his jewels in."

"It shall be done," Maxwell promised. And away he went.

Mr. Jones unhooked the receiver.

"That Scotland Yard?" he was saying presently. "Inspector Beecham? Say Mr. Jones—an old friend!"

A minute passed and then a sly smile spread across Mr. Jones's cheerful face.

"That you, Beecham? How are you? Merry Christmas! Well, why not? Peace on earth, goodwill to all men, and that kind of thing.

"Listen, Beecham, my own—I've a Christmas box for you. You remember I promised you, if I could get it, the—er—inside dope, as it's called—crude expression, I know, but it *is* called that, isn't it? I thought you'd know . . . My dear fellow, I *am* getting on with it; do let me finish . . .

"About that hold-up at Clapham the other week, when the girl was knocked out. You know how I hate brutality. I mean, he could have drugged her quite as easily, couldn't he? . . . But I'm telling you! I've got your man, address and everything.

"Listen, I shall be in the Baltic at four . . . No, no, Beecham, dear, I'd much rather see you personally . . . It's your face. It brightens my day. Baltic at four. Better write it down. You're *so* forgetful!"

After which Mr. Jones, with a happy chuckle, hooked the receiver, went to Liverpool Street, bought a couple of first-class train tickets, and proceeded to his accustomed corner in the dim saloon of the Baltic Hotel, off Piccadilly.

Promptly at four o'clock the stolid face of Detective-Inspector Beecham of Scotland Yard appeared in sight, and the Scotland Yard man took a seat beside Mr. Jones without a word.

"Compliments of the season!" said the latter brightly.

Beecham grunted.

"Cheer up!" Mr. Jones beamed.

"You owe me some information," Beecham reminded him.

"I have it here," said Mr. Jones, producing a pocket-book, which he placed on the table.

"When I say *owe* I mean owe," Beecham added. "Don't imagine you're paying off a debt. You're merely paying off arrears. You've slipped through my fingers so often that I take this without hesitation. I've a right to it. But it wipes nothing off. If I can get you tomorrow, I'll get you!"

"Why not tonight?" Mr. Jones smiled.

"The first chance I get," Beecham growled.

Mr. Jones pulled a slip of paper from his pocket-book and began to unfold it. If he heard the suppressed gasp at his side he took no notice of it. He proceeded to unfold the little slip. But it wasn't the slip that had caused the Scotland Yard man to gasp. It was the sight of the two railway tickets. First class. To Friars Topliss.

"Here's the address," said Mr. Jones, passing the slip to the detective. "You'll find your man there. You'll find the evidence too. And he richly deserves what's coming to him. You can tell him

I said so, if you like, when you explain I obtained the information against him and so did your job for you."

"Anything else?" asked Beecham.

"Nothing," said Mr. Jones, "unless you'll let me call the waiter again, so that we can toast each other in the true festive——"

"I'll be going," said Beecham curtly as he rose.

"You have a heart of stone, dear Beecham," sighed Mr. Jones. "And yet, on Christmas Eve, when you see your stocking and the chimney shaft—who knows?"

But Detective-Inspector Beecham was already on his way to the door—and Scotland Yard.

Back in his office the big man rang a bell and summoned his new assistant Marks to his side.

"Ah, Marks," he said crisply. "About Mr. Hadlow Cribb. He's being accompanied tonight on the train?"

"I'm going myself, sir," said Marks.

"You needn't trouble," Beecham grunted.

"Not trouble, sir?"

"*I'm* going, myself!"

And as Beecham pecked the end off a big cigar he almost smiled his self-satisfaction.

The six-fourteen out of Liverpool Street faced the snow before it started. The snow blew in through the open end of the great building, covering the front of the engine and the sides of the passengers and the friends who were seeing them off. It was agreed by the majority that the weather was seasonable, but the vote was unanimous that the journey was certain to be long and uncomfortable.

In the laughing, grumbling, cheerful, and anxious holiday crowds a small greyish man passed unnoticed. The cheerful ones were too cheerful to take the slightest interest in a figure so small and grey; the anxious ones too anxious. He passed through to the train as though he and the inconspicuous black bag he carried did not in fact exist, and when he sank wheezily into the corner of a first-class compartment that compartment still seemed empty.

Whereas everybody, cheerful or anxious, had at least one glance to spare for the tall and handsome Mr. Jeremiah Jones, who, with the grave and dignified Maxwell at his heels, strode along the platform with an assurance which implied that if he had not bought the station at least he had a ten-day option upon it.

But since nobody had noticed the first greyish man, nobody noticed now that the inconspicuous black bag which Maxwell carried in the wake of Mr. Jones was the very twin brother of the inconspicuous black bag which the greyish man had carried a few moments before.

Except, that is, just one eager watcher with a black half-moon moustache, who now moved out of the obscurity of a dark corner and passed through the barrier not twenty feet behind Mr. Jones and Maxwell.

Mr. Jones and Maxwell passed the first-class compartment in which the greyish Mr. Hadlow Cribb sat with his forty thousand pounds' worth of jewels, walked on until they were beyond the dining car and then selected a first-class compartment of their own.

But the eagerly watchful Detective-Inspector Beecham had a few quiet words with the guard at the other end of the train and sank back into obscurity once more, this time in the shadows of the guard's van.

The train moved out of the station and Detective-Inspector Beecham moved out of the guard's van together. The train moved out into the unfriendliness of the winter night, but Beecham moved out into the comparative cosiness of the corridor. This he traversed as far as the second coach where, having satisfied himself that Mr. Hadlow Cribb was still alone and his shabby case unmolested, he took up his stand round the angle of the passage at the end of the coach and watched.

Mile succeeded mile, minute succeeded minute. Detective-Inspector Beecham began to grow restless. The corridor windows were coated with snow. There was nothing to see and as little

to do. Cheerful Christmasy shouts reached his ears from the ends of the train. He began to feel out of it. He began to feel bored. He shook himself and set out to walk the length of the train.

He passed through the dining car. He passed through two coaches beyond the dining car—satisfied that neither Mr. Jones nor Maxwell had seen him do so—before he pulled up, again round the angle of a passage at the end of a coach.

Again he had perforce to play a waiting game. Again he began to feel out of it and bored. But at last, about an hour out of Liverpool Street he was pleased to hear a door slide down the corridor and thrilled to see that the two men who came out of the first-class compartment and made off in the direction of the rear of the train were Mr. Jones and Maxwell. And Maxwell carried the second shabby little bag.

"Ah!" said Beecham softly to himself.

He let them get round the angle at the end of the coach; then he followed. He followed them through the next coach. He gave them three-quarters of a minute, then he plunged into the dining car prepared for the interesting bit in the rear section of the train.

But there he stopped.

And there Mr. Jones stopped, too. Stopped ordering turkey and Christmas pudding to stare up at Detective-Inspector Beecham and exclaim:

"Why, look who's here! Who could have thought it? Maxwell—wish the gentleman a Merry Christmas!"

"A Merry Christmas to you, sir," said Maxwell, with a respectful dip of the head to the detective.

"Sit down and join us," Mr. Jones invited. "After all, it only comes once a year and you can mutter 'Without prejudice' under your breath as you drink my beer. Or shall it be port?"

Beecham sank wearily into the comfortable chair opposite the pair of them.

"I—" He stopped.

"Yes, dear fellow?" Mr. Jones prompted.

"Nothing," the detective mumbled.

"Don't tell me you're going away for Christmas," said Mr. Jones. "I understand you don't believe in such tosh. Or am I wrong? Does that hard face of yours hide a heart that weeps after three glasses of rum punch and the sight of a holly berry?"

"The point is where are *you* going?" Beecham demanded.

"I don't see that's the point at all," Mr. Jones smiled. "Waiter—or should it be steward? I travel so little—bring my friend Detective-Inspector Beecham, of Scotland Yard, turkey and plum pudding and all things seasonable to eat and drink. Beecham, I don't think you know the steward, do you? The steward—Detective-Inspector Beecham. Of Scotland Yard, you know. My very good friend."

The attendant departed smiling, while the detective, with a neck going steadily pinker, attempted the futility of looking out of the window.

"When I want to advertise . . ." he said fiercely.

"You never will," Mr. Jones assured him. "Too well known to need it. Too deeply established in the affections of the multitude to require such a cheap device. Advertise? You? When you have to civilization will have perished. What about the skating prospects for the holidays? I'd like your opinion."

"What I'm never sure about," said Beecham, turning a fierce glare on Mr. Jones, "is whether you're a crafty fool or just a fool."

"Shall we say a lucky fool?" suggested Mr. Jones.

"Luck, yes!" snapped Beecham.

"That shows," said Mr. Jones, "how little you know me. You must get to know me better. Call round some time. Second Thursdays, you know. Tea. *And* cakes."

To give the grim old man of Scotland Yard his due he almost enjoyed the turkey and plum pudding and the port that followed.

Despite his company he would have enjoyed the unusual even entirely had it not been for the business which found him there. As it was he said little. Nor did he do more than listen oc-

casionally to the ceaseless flow of light-hearted chatter which poured from the lips of Mr. Jones.

He gave himself up to a waiting game and tried to calculate the number of miles that had pounded themselves out under the wheels of the train.

Mr. Jones glanced at his watch.

"Eight o'clock? The snow's keeping us back. We were due in at Friars Topliss at five minutes to, surely?"

Beecham looked up at the mention of Friars Topliss, but still he said nothing. Mr. Jones offered a cigar, which was refused, and then lit one himself.

Ten minutes later the train began to slow down.

"Now where are we?" said Mr. Jones.

All down the dining car there was much rubbing of steamed windows, which answered no questions. An attendant, laden with Christmas fare on a tray passed quickly.

"Tell me, steward, where are we?" Mr. Jones inquired.

"Running into Etching Vale, sir," replied the attendant. "Friars Topliss in twenty-five minutes."

"Thank you," said Mr. Jones, and turned to Maxwell.

"This is where we get off," he said. "Got everything, Maxwell?"

"Everything, sir," Maxwell answered.

"Don't forget the bag."

Maxwell stopped and picked up the shabby bag.

"Here it is, sir."

Mr. Jones rose. Maxwell rose too. Beecham stared, dissatisfied with he knew not what.

Maxwell helped Mr. Jones into his big overcoat, pulled on his own and waited. Mr. Jones pulled his hat down over his ears and turned up the collar of his coat.

The train stopped.

"Well, good-bye, Beecham, dear fellow," Mr. Jones said breezily. "And, if I don't see you before, a Happy New Year."

And out to the snow-covered platform he

went, with Maxwell and the shabby little bag after him.

Beecham blinked. That little bag . . . Was it possible? Even before Hadlow Cribb reached the train? Or, by some trick, while he, Beecham, had been waiting his chance in the guard's van?

"Crafty, but I wonder if he's *really* a fool?" he thought solemnly.

The driving wind covered Mr. Jones and the faithful Maxwell with snow in the twinkling of an eye. They dashed across the bleak platform of Etching Vale to the shelter of the station wall. And under this shelter they hurried to the barriers. Here Mr. Jones offered two tickets.

The collector peered at the tickets in the doubtful lamplight.

"Pardon, sir," he said, "but this is Etching Vale."

"Remarkable how you can tell, with all this snow on it," remarked Mr. Jones.

"These tickets are for Friars Topliss, sir," said the collector.

"I know," said Mr. Jones, "but I've changed my mind. I thought I'd get off here. It sort of called to me."

"Not allowed to break the journey, sir," the collector reminded him. "I'm afraid you'll have to pay again."

Mr. Jones thrust a note into the collector's hand.

"Take it out of that," he said, "and buy your wife something for Christmas out of the balance."

"No wife, sir," the collector grinned.

"Soon will have," Mr. Jones assured him, "with such charm as yours."

He passed out into the snow-covered station square of Little Etching Vale, the soft footfalls of Maxwell on his left and, as he soon realized, other soft footfalls on his right. He turned and there once more was the stolid figure of Detective-Inspector Beecham.

"Not again!" he exclaimed. "But, my dear Beecham, I thought you were going on?"

"I thought you might be, too," said Beecham.

"I changed my mind," Mr. Jones informed him.

"I changed my mind," retorted Beecham.

"A costly process, I found it," said Mr. Jones.

"I didn't!" said Beecham.

"Oh, well, of course, you're known to the police," said Mr. Jones, "which makes a difference!"

He smiled and waited, but Beecham waited too.

"Where now?" he asked.

"Where would you like to go?" said Beecham.

"You don't mean, do you, that the drinks are now on you?" said Mr. Jones. "But Beecham, my own, this is too touching! Very well—there's a decent-looking, old-fashioned hostel over there. Shall we?"

"Anywhere," growled Beecham.

They crossed the square to the old-fashioned hostel where, to Mr. Jones's surprise, the Scotland Yard man immediately booked a private room and ordered the drinks to be sent up there.

"If you'll join me," he said to Mr. Jones.

"Delighted," Mr. Jones agreed. "Does Maxwell remain in the weather and hold the horses' heads?"

"There'll be room for the three of us upstairs," said Beecham.

"What could be better?" said Mr. Jones.

And upstairs they went, with a waiter and tray to follow them.

"Cosy," remarked Mr. Jones, when the waiter had left them and closed the door. "Shall you be staying here long?"

"About as long as it will take me to go through that little bag of yours," Beecham answered.

"Beecham!" Mr. Jones gasped. "I don't understand you."

"You will," said Beecham. "I always thought you'd be too clever. You let me see your train tickets this afternoon. After that, I just had to take this trip with you. Hand over the bag."

"You know, Beecham, my sweet," said Mr. Jones, "really I don't think you have the right."

"I can soon get that," said Beecham. "Please

yourself, if you want to waste time. You'll waste it in my presence, that's all."

Mr. Jones sighed.

"Maxwell," he said, "nobody trusts us. It's a suspicious world. Pass the little bag to the gentleman."

Maxwell passed the little bag to the gentleman, and the gentleman, frowning, promptly dragged it open. Out fell pyjamas, combs, and toothbrushes. Nothing else. Beecham clicked his teeth and looked up.

"Pockets, probably?" he said.

"No friendliness at all," observed Mr. Jones with a fresh sigh. "Your pockets, Maxwell."

Maxwell emptied his pockets. Mr. Jones emptied his. The detective's complexion darkened. He turned once more to the little bag, fumbled inside it, threw it on the floor. His hands passed swiftly, but certainly, down the attire of the other two men; then, with a muttered exclamation, he picked up a telephone that stood on a corner table.

"Friars Topliss police, quick!" he shouted.

"You might tell me, sweet Beecham," Mr. Jones put in, "what *is* on your mind."

But Beecham didn't. He sat glaring at the instrument in front of his nose until there was a faint tinkle.

"Yes?" he roared. "This is Detective-Inspector Beecham of Scotland Yard. Is the six-fourteen from Liverpool Street—what? Good Lord! Battered up? But I saw him—the jewels? Gone! I'll come along!"

He dropped the receiver and spun round.

"Without having the faintest idea as to what is on your mind," said Mr. Jones, "I think you must admit that I never batter them up. I may have many failings, but *never* that."

"I don't exactly know where you come into this," snapped Beecham, "but bear this in mind. I'll land you."

"I doubt it." Mr. Jones smiled. "You'd like to, I fear, but it's such a disappointing world."

Beecham strode to the door.

"Say good-bye to the gentleman, Maxwell," said Mr. Jones.

And Maxwell said good-bye to the gentleman.

"Dapper" Dawlish, expert but unlikeable, let himself into his Baker Street flat and snapped on the lights. He was satisfied with himself and the world in general. Or, at least, he was until he snapped on the lights.

Then he found himself looking down the barrel of an automatic, and he changed his opinion of the world at once.

"Good evening," said Mr. Jones. "Or morning. Or what is it? Travelling about the world in a snowstorm makes one lose one's sense of time."

"Who are you?" snarled Dawlish.

"Doesn't matter in the least," said Mr. Jones.

"What do you want?"

"The jewels you stole from Mr. Hadlow Cribb on the Friars Topliss train," said Mr. Jones. "And I want them now. I've been waiting two hours without a fire. I'm depressed. And when I'm depressed I'm nasty. That bulge in your right pocket, I believe. Come on! One—two——"

Which was where "Dapper" Dawlish threw in.

"I'm hanged if I see how you knew," he grumbled.

"But, of course, I knew," said Mr. Jones. "It was I who had you put wise this afternoon that the stuff would be on the train."

"You?"

"Mind, you wouldn't have stood an earthly chance if I hadn't been on the train to take their attention away," Mr. Jones added. "They watched dear old Cribb and you'd never have got near him. Brains, my lad. That's what gets you to the top.

"Mind, *I couldn't* have got the things. I'm too popular with the C.I.D. They won't let me out of their sight. Which is why I sometimes have to leave the labouring to others. Which reminds me."

He opened the parcel of gems, separated one from the rest, and tossed it on the table.

"The labourer is worthy of his hire," he said, with a smile. "You'd have got two—or even three—if you hadn't battered him up. Battering-up is a thing I detest. Or, at least, I've always thought so. I may change my mind one day. Even this day. Try following me and see! Good-bye, Mr.—Dawlish the name is, I believe. Charmed to have met you. And a Merry Christmas."

MARKHEIM

Robert Louis Stevenson

IT MAY BE DIFFICULT TO REMEMBER that Robert Louis Stevenson, one of the greatest adventure story authors of all time with such classics as *Treasure Island* (1883), *Prince Otto* (1885), *Kidnapped* (1886), and *The Black Arrow* (1888) to his credit, also wrote the beloved volume of poems for young readers, *A Child's Garden of Verses* (1885). He frequently wrote of mystery and crime, most famously *The Strange Case of Dr. Jekyll and Mr. Hyde* (1886), a macabre allegory once described as the only crime story in which the solution is more terrifying than the problem. The classic murder story "Markheim" was first published in *The Broken Shaft* (London, Unwin, 1885).

Markheim

ROBERT LOUIS STEVENSON

"YES," SAID THE DEALER, "OUR windfalls are of various kinds. Some customers are ignorant, and then I touch a dividend on my superior knowledge. Some are dishonest," and here he held up the candle, so that the light fell strongly on his visitor; "and in that case," he continued, "I profit by my virtue."

Markheim had but just entered from the daylight streets, and his eyes had not yet grown familiar with the mingled shine and darkness in the shop. At these pointed words, and before the near presence of the flame, he blinked painfully and looked aside.

The dealer chuckled. "You come to me on Christmas Day," he resumed, "when you know that I am alone in my house, put up my shutters, and make a point of refusing business. Well, you will have to pay for that; you will have to pay for my loss of time, when I should be balancing my books; you will have to pay, besides, for a kind of manner that I remark in you today very strongly. I am the essence of discretion, and ask no awkward questions; but when a customer cannot look me in the eye, he has to pay for it."

The dealer once more chuckled; and then, changing to his usual business voice, though still with a note of irony, "You can give, as usual, a clear account of how you came into the possession of the object?" he continued. "Still your uncle's cabinet? A remarkable collector, sir!"

And the little pale, round-shouldered dealer stood almost on tip-toe, looking over the top of his gold spectacles, and nodding his head with every mark of disbelief. Markheim returned his gaze with one of infinite pity, and a touch of horror.

"This time," said he, "you are in error. I have not come to sell, but to buy. I have no curios to dispose of; my uncle's cabinet is bare to the wainscot; even were it still intact, I have done well on the Stock Exchange, and should more likely add to it than otherwise, and my errand to-day is simplicity itself. I seek a Christmas present for a lady," he continued, waxing more fluent as he struck into the speech he had prepared; "and certainly I owe you every excuse for thus disturbing you upon so small a matter. But the thing was neglected yesterday; I must produce my little compliment at dinner; and, as you very well know, a rich marriage is not a thing to be neglected."

There followed a pause, during which the dealer seemed to weigh this statement incredulously. The ticking of many clocks among the curious lumber of the shop, and the faint rushing of the cabs in a near thoroughfare, filled up the interval of silence.

"Well, sir," said the dealer, "be it so. You are an old customer after all; and if, as you say, you have the chance of a good marriage, far be it from me to be an obstacle. Here is a nice thing for a lady now," he went on, "this hand glass—fifteenth century, warranted; comes from a good collection, too; but I reserve the name, in the interests of my customer, who was just like your-self, my dear sir, the nephew and sole heir of a remarkable collector."

The dealer, while he thus ran on in his dry and biting voice, had stopped to take the object from its place; and, as he had done so, a shock had passed through Markheim, a start both of hand and foot, a sudden leap of many tumultu-ous passions to the face. It passed as swiftly as it came, and left no trace beyond a certain trem-bling of the hand that now received the glass.

"A glass," he said hoarsely, and then paused, and repeated it more clearly. "A glass? For Christmas? Surely not?"

"And why not?" cried the dealer. "Why not a glass?"

Markheim was looking upon him with an indefinable expression. "You ask me why not?" he said. "Why, look here—look in it—look at yourself! Do you like to see it? No! nor—nor any man."

The little man had jumped back when Markheim had so suddenly confronted him with the mirror; but now, perceiving there was noth-ing worse on hand, he chuckled. "Your future lady, sir, must be pretty hard-favoured," said he.

"I ask you," said Markheim, "for a Christmas present, and you give me this—this damned re-minder of years, and sins and follies—this hand-conscience? Did you mean it? Had you a thought in your mind? Tell me. It will be better for you if you do. Come, tell me about yourself. I hazard a guess now, that you are in secret a very charitable man?"

The dealer looked closely at his companion. It was very odd, Markheim did not appear to be laughing; there was something in his face like an eager sparkle of hope, but nothing of mirth.

"What are you driving at?" the dealer asked.

"Not charitable?" returned the other gloom-ily. "Not charitable; not pious; not scrupulous; unloving, unbeloved; a hand to get money, a safe to keep it. Is that all? Dear God, man, is that all?"

"I will tell you what it is," began the dealer, with some sharpness, and then broke off again into a chuckle. "But I see this is a love match of yours, and you have been drinking the lady's health."

"Ah!" cried Markheim, with a strange curi-osity. "Ah, have you been in love? Tell me about that."

"I," cried the dealer. "I in love! I never had the time, nor have I the time to-day for all this nonsense. Will you take the glass?"

"Where is the hurry?" returned Markheim. "It is very pleasant to stand here talking; and life is so short and insecure that I would not hurry away from any pleasure—no, not even from so mild a one as this. We should rather cling, cling to what little we can get, like a man at a cliff's edge. Every second is a cliff, if you think upon it—a cliff a mile high—high enough, if we fall, to dash us out of every feature of humanity. Hence it is best to talk pleasantly. Let us talk of each other: why should we wear this mask? Let us be confidential. Who knows, we might be-come friends?"

"I have just one word to say to you," said the dealer. "Either make your purchase, or walk out of my shop!"

"True, true," said Markheim. "Enough fool-ing. To business. Show me something else."

The dealer stooped once more, this time to replace the glass upon the shelf, his thin blond hair falling over his eyes as he did so. Markheim moved a little nearer, with one hand in the pocket of his greatcoat; he drew himself up and filled his lungs; at the same time many different emotions were depicted together on his face—terror, horror, and resolve, fascination and a physical repulsion; and through a haggard lift of his upper lip, his teeth looked out.

"This, perhaps, may suit," observed the dealer: and then, as he began to re-arise, Markheim bounded from behind upon his vic-tim. The long, skewerlike dagger flashed and fell. The dealer struggled like a hen, striking his temple on the shelf, and then tumbled on the floor in a heap.

Time had some score of small voices in that shop, some stately and slow as was becoming to their great age; others garrulous and hurried. All these told out the seconds in an intricate chorus of tickings. Then the passage of a lad's feet, heavily running on the pavement, broke in upon these smaller voices and startled Markheim into the consciousness of his surroundings.

He looked about him awfully. The candle stood on the counter, its flame solemnly wagging in a draught; and by that inconsiderable movement, the whole room was filled with noiseless bustle and kept heaving like a sea: the tall shadows nodding, the gross blots of darkness swelling and dwindling as with respiration, the faces of the portraits and the china gods changing and wavering like images in water. The inner door stood ajar, and peered into that leaguer of shadows with a long slit of daylight like a pointing finger.

From these fear-stricken rovings, Markheim's eyes returned to the body of his victim, where it lay both humped and sprawling, incredibly small and strangely meaner than in life. In these poor, miserly clothes, in that ungainly attitude, the dealer lay like so much sawdust. Markheim had feared to see it, and, lo! it was nothing. And yet, as he gazed, this bundle of old clothes and pool of blood began to find eloquent voices. There it must lie; there was none to work the cunning hinges or direct the miracle of locomotion—there it must lie till it was found. Found! ay, and then? Then would this dead flesh lift up a cry that would ring over England, and fill the world with the echoes of pursuit. Ay, dead or not, this was still the enemy.

"Time was that when the brains were out," he thought; and the first word struck into his mind. Time, now that the deed was accomplished—time, which had closed for the victim, had become instant and momentous for the slayer.

The thought was yet in his mind, when, first one and then another, with every variety of pace and voice—one deep as the bell from a cathedral turret, another ringing on its treble notes the prelude of a waltz—the clocks began to strike the hour of three in the afternoon.

The sudden outbreak of so many tongues in that dumb chamber staggered him. He began to bestir himself, going to and fro with the candle, beleaguered by moving shadows, and startled to the soul by chance reflections. In many rich mirrors, some of home designs, some from Venice or Amsterdam, he saw his face repeated and repeated, as it were an army of spies; his own eyes met and detected him; and the sound of his own steps, lightly as they fell, vexed the surrounding quiet.

And still, as he continued to fill his pockets, his mind accused him with a sickening iteration, of the thousand faults of his design. He should have chosen a more quiet hour; he should have prepared an alibi; he should not have used a knife; he should have been more cautious, and only bound and gagged the dealer, and not killed him; he should have been more bold, and killed the servant also; he should have done all things otherwise—poignant regrets, weary, incessant toiling of the mind to change what was unchangeable, to plan what was now useless, to be the architect of the irrevocable past.

Meanwhile, and behind all this activity, brute terrors, like the scurrying of rats in a deserted attic, filled the more remote chambers of his brain with riot; the hand of the constable would fall heavy on his shoulder, and his nerves would jerk like a hooked fish; or he beheld, in galloping defile, the dock, the prison, the gallows, and the black coffin.

Terror of the people in the street sat down before his mind like a besieging army. It was impossible, he thought, but that some rumour of the struggle must have reached their ears and set on edge their curiosity; and now, in all the neighbouring houses, he divined them sitting motionless and with uplifted ear—solitary people, condemned to spend Christmas dwelling alone on memories of the past, and now startlingly recalled from that tender exercise; happy family parties, struck into silence round the table, the mother still with raised finger: every degree and age and humour, but all, by their own hearths, prying and hearkening and weaving the rope that was to hang him.

Sometimes it seemed to him he could not move too softly; the clink of the tall Bohemian goblets rang out loudly like a bell; and alarmed by the bigness of the ticking, he was tempted to stop the clocks. And then, again, with a swift transition of his terrors, the very silence of the place appeared a source of peril, and a thing to strike and freeze the passer-by; and he would step more boldly, and bustle aloud among the contents of the shop, and imitate, with elaborate bravado, the movements of a busy man at ease in his own house.

But he was now so pulled about by different alarms that, while one portion of his mind was still alert and cunning, another trembled on the brink of lunacy. One hallucination in particular took a strong hold on his credulity. The neighbour hearkening with white face beside his window, the passer-by arrested by a horrible surmise on the pavement—these could at worst suspect, they could not know; through the brick walls and shuttered windows only sounds could penetrate.

But here, within the house, was he alone? He knew he was; he had watched the servant set forth sweet-hearting, in her poor best, "out for the day" written in every ribbon and smile. Yes, he was alone, of course; and yet, in the bulk of empty house above him, he could surely hear a stir of delicate footing—he was surely conscious, inexplicably conscious of some presence. Ay, surely; to every room and corner of the house his imagination followed it; and now it was a faceless thing, and yet had eyes to see with; and again it was a shadow of himself; and yet again behold the image of the dead dealer, reinspired with cunning and hatred.

At times, with a strong effort, he would glance at the open door which still seemed to repel his eyes. The house was tall, the skylight small and dirty, the day blind with fog; and the light that filtered down to the ground story was exceedingly faint, and showed dimly on the threshold of the shop. And yet, in that strip of doubtful brightness, did there not hang wavering a shadow?

Suddenly, from the street outside, a very jovial gentleman began to beat with a staff on the shop-door, accompanying his blows with shouts and railleries in which the dealer was continually called upon by name. Markheim, smitten into ice, glanced at the dead man. But no! he lay quite still; he was fled away far beyond earshot of these blows and shoutings; he was sunk beneath seas of silence; and his name, which would once have caught his notice above the howling of a storm, had become an empty sound. And presently the jovial gentleman desisted from his knocking and departed.

Here was a broad hint to hurry what remained to be done, to get forth from this accusing neighbourhood, to plunge into a bath of London multitudes, and to reach, on the other side of day, that haven of safety and apparent innocence—his bed. One visitor had come; at any moment another might follow and be more obstinate. To have done the deed, and yet not to reap the profit, would be too abhorrent a failure. The money, that was now Markheim's concern; and as a means to that, the keys.

He glanced over his shoulder at the open door, where the shadow was still lingering and shivering; and with no conscious repugnance of the mind, yet with a tremor of the belly, he drew near the body of his victim. The human character had quite departed. Like a suit half-stuffed with bran, the limbs lay scattered, the trunk doubled, on the floor; and yet the thing repelled him. Although so dingy and inconsiderable to the eye, he feared it might have more significance to the touch.

He took the body by the shoulders, and turned it on its back. It was strangely light and supple, and the limbs, as if they had been broken, fell into the oddest postures. The face was robbed of all expression; but it was as pale as wax, and shockingly smeared with blood about one temple. That was, for Markheim, the one displeasing circumstance. It carried him back, upon the instant, to a certain fair-day in a fishers' village: a gray day, a piping wind, a crowd upon the street, the blare of the brasses, the booming of drums, the nasal voice of a ballad singer; and a boy going to and fro, buried over head in the crowd and divided between interest and fear, until, coming out upon the chief place of concourse, he beheld a booth and a great screen with pictures, dismally designed, garishly coloured: Brownrigg with her apprentice; the Mannings with their murdered guest; Weare in the death-grip of Thurtell; and a score besides of famous crimes.

The thing was as clear as an illusion; he was once again that little boy; he was looking once again, and with the same sense of physical revolt, at these vile pictures; he was still stunned by the thumping of the drums. A bar of that day's music returned upon his memory; and at that, for the first time, a qualm came over him, a breath of nausea, a sudden weakness of the joints, which he must instantly resist and conquer.

He judged it more prudent to confront than to flee from these considerations; looking the more hardily in the dead face, bending his mind to realise the nature and greatness of his crime. So little a while ago that face had moved with every change of sentiment, that pale mouth had spoken, that body had been on fire with governable energies; and now, by his act, that piece of life had been arrested, as the horologist, with interjected finger, arrests the beating of the clock. So he reasoned in vain; he could rise to no more remorseful consciousness; the same heart which had shuddered before the painted effigies of crime, looked on its reality unmoved. At best, he felt a gleam of pity for one who had been endowed in vain with all those faculties that can make the world a garden of enchantment, one who had never lived and who was now dead. But of penitence, no, not a tremor.

With that, shaking himself clear of these considerations, he found the keys and advanced towards the open door of the shop. Outside, it had begun to rain smartly; and the sound of the shower upon the roof had banished silence. Like some dripping cavern, the chambers of the house were haunted by an incessant echoing, which filled the ear and mingled with the ticking of the clocks. And, as Markheim approached the door, he seemed to hear, in answer to his own cautious tread, the steps of another foot withdrawing up the stair. The shadow still palpitated loosely on the threshold. He threw a ton's weight of resolve upon his muscles, and drew back the door.

The faint, foggy daylight glimmered dimly on the bare floor and stairs; on the bright suit of armour posted, halberd in hand, upon the landing; and on the dark wood-carvings, and framed pictures that hung against the yellow panels of the wainscot. So loud was the beating of the rain through all the house that, in Markheim's ears, it began to be distinguished into many different sounds. Footsteps and sighs, the tread of regiments marching in the distance, the chink of money in the counting, and the creaking of doors held stealthily ajar, appeared to mingle with the patter of the drops upon the cupola and the gushing of the water in the pipes.

The sense that he was not alone grew upon him to the verge of madness. On every side he was haunted and begirt by presences. He heard them moving in the upper chambers; from the shop, he heard the dead man getting to his legs; and as he began with a great effort to mount the stairs, feet fled quietly before him and followed stealthily behind. If he were but deaf, he thought, how tranquilly he would possess his soul! And then again, and hearkening with ever fresh attention, he blessed himself for that unresting sense which held the outposts and stood a trusty sentinel upon his life. His head turned continually on his neck; his eyes, which seemed starting from their orbits, scouted on every side, and on every side were half-rewarded as with the tail of something nameless vanishing. The four-and-twenty steps to the first floor were four-and-twenty agonies.

On that first story, the doors stood ajar, three of them like three ambushes, shaking his nerves like the throats of cannon. He could never again, he felt, be sufficiently immured and fortified from men's observing eyes; he longed to be home, girt in by walls, buried among bedclothes, and invisible to all but God. And at that thought he wondered a little, recollecting tales of other murderers and the fear they were said to entertain of heavenly avengers. It was not so, at least, with him. He feared the laws of nature, lest, in their callous and immutable procedure, they should preserve some damning evidence of his crime. He feared tenfold more, with a slavish, superstitious terror, some scission in the continuity of man's experience, some wilful illegality of nature. He played a game of skill, depending on the rules, calculating consequence from cause; and what if nature, as the defeated tyrant overthrew the chessboard, should break the mould of their succession?

The like had befallen Napoleon (so writers said) when the winter changed the time of its appearance. The like might befall Markheim: the solid walls might become transparent and reveal his doings like those of bees in a glass hive; the stout planks might yield under his foot like quicksands and detain him in their clutch; ay, and there were soberer accidents that might destroy him: if, for instance, the house should fall and imprison him beside the body of his victim; or the house next door should fly on fire, and the firemen invade him from all sides. These things he feared; and, in a sense, these things might be called the hands of God reached forth against sin. But about God Himself he was at ease; his act was doubtless exceptional, but so were his excuses, which God knew; it was there, and not among men, that he felt sure of justice.

When he had got safe into the drawing-room, and shut the door behind him, he was aware of a respite from alarms. The room was quite dismantled, uncarpeted besides, and strewn with packing cases and incongruous furniture; several great pier-glasses, in which he beheld himself at various angles, like an actor on a stage; many pictures, framed and unframed, standing with their faces to the wall, a fine Sheraton sideboard, a cabinet of marquetry, and a great old bed, with tapestry hangings. The windows opened to the floors; but by great good fortune the lower part of the shutters had been closed, and this concealed him from the neighbours. Here, then, Markheim drew in a packing case before the cabinet, and began to search among the keys.

It was a long business, for there were many; and it was irksome, besides; for after all there might be nothing in the cabinet, and time was on the wing. But the closeness of the occupation sobered him. With the tail of his eye he saw the door—even glanced at it from time to time directly, like a besieged commander pleased to verify the good estate of his defences. But in truth he was at peace. The rain falling in the street sounded natural and pleasant. Presently, on the other side, the notes of a piano were wakened to the music of a hymn, and the voices of many children took up the air and words. How stately, how comfortable was the melody! How fresh the youthful voices!

Markheim gave ear to it smilingly, as he sorted out the keys; and his mind was thronged with answerable ideas and images; church-going children and the pealing of the high organ; children afield, bathers by the brookside, ramblers on the brambly common, kite-flyers in the windy and cloud-navigated sky; and then, at another cadence of the hymn, back again to church, and the somnolence of summer Sundays, and the high genteel voice of the parson (which he smiled a little to recall) and the painted Jacobean tombs, and the dim lettering of the Ten Commandments in the chancel.

And as he sat thus, at once busy and absent, he was startled to his feet. A flash of ice, a flash of fire, a bursting gush of blood, went over him, and then he stood transfixed and thrilling. A step mounted the stair slowly and steadily and presently a hand was laid upon the knob, and the lock clicked, and the door opened.

Fear held Markheim in a vice. What to expect he knew not, whether the dead man walking, or the official ministers of human justice, or some chance witness blindly stumbling in to consign him to the gallows. But when a face thrust into the aperture, glanced round the room, looked at him, nodded and smiled as if in friendly recognition, and then withdrew again, and the door closed behind it, his fear broke loose from his control in a hoarse cry. At the sound of this the visitant returned.

"Did you call me?" he asked pleasantly, and with that he entered the room and closed the door behind him.

Markheim stood and gazed at him with all his eyes. Perhaps there was a film upon his sight, but the outlines of the newcomer seemed to change and waver like those of the idols in the wavering candlelight of the shop; and at times he thought he knew him; and at times he thought he bore a likeness to himself; and always, like a lump of living terror, there lay in his bosom the conviction that this thing was not of the earth and not of God.

And yet the creature had a strange air of the commonplace, as he stood looking on Markheim with a smile; and when he added: "You are looking for the money, I believe?" it was in the tones of everyday politeness.

Markheim made no answer.

"I should warn you," resumed the other, "that the maid has left her sweetheart earlier than usual and will soon be here. If Mr. Markheim be found in this house, I need not describe to him the consequences."

"You know me?" cried the murderer.

The visitor smiled. "You have long been a favourite of mine," he said; "and I have long observed and often sought to help you."

"What are you?" cried Markheim; "the devil?"

"What I may be," returned the other, "cannot affect the service I propose to render you."

"It can," cried Markheim; "it does! Be helped by you? No, never; not by you! You do not know me yet; thank God, you do not know me!"

"I know you," replied the visitant, with a sort of kind severity or rather firmness. "I know you to the soul."

"Know me!" cried Markheim. "Who can do so? My life is but a travesty and slander on myself. I have lived to belie my nature. All men

do, all men are better than this disguise that grows about and stifles them. You see each dragged away by life, like one whom bravos have seized and muffled in a cloak. If they had their own control—if you could see their faces, they would be altogether different, they would shine out for heroes and saints! I am worse than most; myself is more overlaid; my excuse is known to men and God. But, had I the time, I could disclose myself."

"To me?" inquired the visitant.

"To you before all," returned the murderer. "I supposed you were intelligent. I thought—since you exist—you could prove a reader of the heart. And yet you would propose to judge me by my acts! I was born and I have lived in a land of giants; giants have dragged me by the wrists since I was born out of my mother—the giants of circumstance. And you would judge me by my acts! But can you not look within? Can you not see within me the clear writing of conscience, never blurred by any willful sophistry, although too often disregarded? Can you not read me for a thing that surely must be common as humanity—the unwilling sinner?"

"All this is very feelingly expressed," was the reply, "but it regards me not. These points of consistency are beyond my province, and I care not in the least by what compulsion you may have been dragged away, so as you are but carried in the right direction. But time flies; the servant delays, looking in the faces of the crowd and at the pictures on the hoardings, but still she keeps moving nearer; and remember, it is as if the gallows itself was striding towards you through the Christmas streets! Shall I help you; I, who know all? Shall I tell you where to find the money?"

"For what price?" asked Markheim.

"I offer you the service for a Christmas gift," returned the other.

Markheim could not refrain from smiling with a kind of bitter triumph. "No," said he, "I will take nothing at your hands; if I were dying of thirst, and it was your hand that put the pitcher to my lips, I should find the courage to refuse. It may be credulous, but I will do nothing to commit myself to evil."

"I have no objection to a deathbed repentance," observed the visitant.

"Because you disbelieve their efficacy!" Markheim cried.

"I do not say so," returned the other; "but I look on these things from a different side, and when the life is done my interest falls. The man has lived to serve me, to spread black looks under colour of religion, or to sow tares in the wheat-field, as you do, in a course of weak compliance with desire. Now that he draws so near to his deliverance, he can add but one act of service—to repent, to die smiling, and thus to build up in confidence and hope the more timorous of my surviving followers. I am not so hard a master. Try me. Accept my help. Please yourself in life as you have done hitherto; please yourself more amply, spread your elbows at the board; and when the night begins to fall and the curtains to be drawn, I tell you, for your greater comfort, that you will find it even easy to compound your quarrel with your conscience, and to make a truckling peace with God. I came but now from such a deathbed, and the room was full of sincere mourners, listening to the man's last words; and when I looked into that face, which had been set as a flint against mercy, I found it smiling with hope."

"And do you, then, suppose me such a creature?" asked Markheim. "Do you think I have no more generous aspirations than to sin, and sin, and sin, and, at the last, sneak into heaven? My heart rises at the thought. Is this, then, your experience of mankind? Or is it because you find me with red hands that you presume such baseness? And is this crime of murder indeed so impious as to dry up the very springs of good?"

"Murder is to me no special category," replied the other. "All sins are murder, even as all life is war. I behold your race, like starving mariners on a raft, plucking crusts out of the hands of famine and feeding on each other's lives. I follow sins beyond the moment of their acting; I find in all that the last consequence is death; and to my eyes, the pretty maid who thwarts her mother with such taking graces on a question of a ball, drips no less visibly with human gore than such a murderer as yourself. Do I say that I follow sins? I follow virtues also; they differ not by the thickness of a nail, they are both scythes for the reaping angel of Death. Evil, for which I live, consists not in action but in character. The bad man is dear to me; not the bad act, whose fruits, if we could follow them far enough down the hurtling cataract of the ages, might yet be found more blessed than those of the rarest virtues. And it is not because you have killed a dealer, but because you are Markheim, that I offer to forward your escape."

"I will lay my heart open to you," answered Markheim. "This crime on which you find me is my last. On my way to it I have learned many lessons; itself is a lesson, a momentous lesson. Hitherto I have been driven with revolt to what I would not; I was a bond-slave to poverty, driven and scourged. There are robust virtues that can stand in these temptations; mine are not so: I had a thirst of pleasure. But to-day, and out of this deed, I pluck both warning and riches—both the power and a fresh resolve to be myself. I become in all things a free actor in the world; I begin to see myself all changed, hands the agents of good, this heart at peace. Something comes over me out of the past; something of what I have dreamed on Sabbath evenings to the sound of the church organ, of what I forecast when I shed tears over noble books, or talked, an innocent child, with my mother. There lies my life; I have wandered a few years, but now I see once more my city of destination."

"You are to use this money on the Stock Exchange, I think?" remarked the visitor; "and there, if I mistake not, you have already lost some thousands?"

"Ah," said Markheim, "but this time I have a sure thing."

"This time, again, you will lose," replied the visitor quietly.

"Ah, but I keep back the half!" cried Markheim.

"That also you will lose," said the other.

The sweat started upon Markheim's brow. "Well, then, what matter?" he exclaimed. "Say it be lost, say I am plunged again in poverty, shall one part of me, and that the worst, continue until the end to override the better? Evil and good run strong in me, haling me both ways. I do not love the one thing, I love all. I can conceive great deeds, renunciations, martyrdoms; and though I be fallen to such a crime as murder, pity is no stranger to my thoughts. I pity the poor; who knows their trials better than myself? I pity and help them; I prize love, I love honest laughter; there is no good thing nor true thing on earth but I love it from my heart. And are my vices only to direct my life, and my virtues without effect, like some passive lumber of the mind? Not so; good, also, is a spring of acts."

But the visitant raised his finger. "For six-and-thirty years that you have been in this world," said he, "through many changes of fortune and varieties of humour, I have watched you steadily fall. Fifteen years ago you would have started at a theft. Three years back you would have blanched at the name of murder. Is there any crime, is there any cruelty or meanness, from which you still recoil?—five years from now I shall detect you in the fact! Downward, downward, lies your way; nor can anything but death avail to stop you."

"It is true," Markheim said huskily, "I have in some degree complied with evil. But it is so with all; the very saints, in the mere exercise of living, grow less dainty, and take on the tone of their surroundings."

"I will propound to you one simple question," said the other; "and as you answer, I shall read to you your moral horoscope. You have grown in many things more lax; possibly you do right to be so; and at any account, it is the same with all men. But granting that, are you in any one particular, however trifling, more difficult to please with your own conduct, or do you go in all things with a looser rein?"

"In any one?" repeated Markheim, with an anguish of consideration. "No," he added, with despair, "in none! I have gone down in all."

"Then," said the visitor, "content yourself with what you are, for you will never change; and the words of your part on this stage are irrevocably written down."

Markheim stood for a long while silent, and indeed it was the visitor who first broke the silence. "That being so," he said, "shall I show you the money?"

"And grace?" cried Markheim.

"Have you not tried it?" returned the other. "Two or three years ago did I not see you on the platform of revival meetings, and was not your voice the loudest in the hymn?"

"It is true," said Markheim; "and I see clearly what remains for me by way of duty. I thank you for these lessons from my soul; my eyes are opened, and I behold myself at last for what I am."

At this moment, the sharp note of the doorbell rang through the house; and the visitant, as though this were some concerted signal for which he had been waiting, changed at once in his demeanour.

"The maid!" he cried. "She has returned, as I forewarned you, and there is now before you one more difficult passage. Her master, you must say, is ill; you must let her in, with an assured but rather serious countenance—no smiles, no overacting, and I promise you success! Once the girl within, and the door closed, the same dexterity that has already rid you of the dealer will relieve you of this last danger in your path. Thenceforward you have the whole evening—the whole night, if needful—to ransack the treasures of the house and to make good your safety. This is help that comes to you with the mask of danger. Up!" he cried; "up, friend; your life hangs trembling in the scales: up, and act!"

Markheim steadily regarded his counsellor. "If I be condemned to evil acts," he said, "there is still one door of freedom open—I can cease from action. If my life be an ill thing, I can lay it down. Though I be, as you say truly, at the beck of every small temptation, I can yet, by one decisive gesture, place myself beyond the reach of all. My love of good is damned to barrenness; it may, and let it be! But I have still my hatred of evil; and from that, to your galling disappointment, you shall see that I can draw both energy and courage."

The features of the visitor began to undergo a wonderful and lovely change: they brightened and softened with a tender triumph, and, even as they brightened, faded and dislimned. But Markheim did not pause to watch or understand the transformation. He opened the door and went downstairs very slowly, thinking to himself. His past went soberly before him; he beheld it as it was, ugly and strenuous like a dream, random as chance-medley—a scene of defeat. Life, as he thus reviewed it, tempted him no longer; but on the farther side he perceived a quiet haven for his bark.

He paused in the passage, and looked into the shop, where the candle still burned by the dead body. It was strangely silent. Thoughts of the dealer swarmed into his mind, as he stood gazing. And then the bell once more broke out into impatient clamour.

He confronted the maid upon the threshold with something like a smile.

"You had better go for the police," said he. "I have killed your master."

A CHAPARRAL CHRISTMAS GIFT

O. Henry

TIMES CHANGE, AND SO DOES PUBLIC TASTE, it seems. William Sidney Porter, under the pseudonym of O. Henry, wrote more than six hundred short stories that once were as critically acclaimed as they were popular. Often undervalued today because of their sentimentality, many nonetheless remain iconic and familiar, notably such classics as "The Gift of the Magi," "The Furnished Room," "A Retrieved Reformation" (better known for its several stage and film versions as *Alias Jimmy Valentine*) and "The Ransom of Red Chief." *The O. Henry Memorial Award Prize Stories*, a prestigious annual anthology of the year's best short stories, has been published since 1919. "A Chaparral Christmas Gift" was one of O. Henry's earliest stories, written while he was in prison. It was first published in the December 1903 issue of *Ainslee's;* it was first collected in *Whirligigs* (New York, Doubleday, Page, 1910).

A Chaparral Christmas Gift

O. HENRY

THE ORIGINAL CAUSE OF THE TROUBLE was about twenty years in growing. At the end of that time it was worth it.

Had you lived anywhere within fifty miles of Sundown Ranch you would have heard of it. It possessed a quantity of jet-black hair, a pair of extremely frank, deep-brown eyes and a laugh that rippled across the prairie like the sound of a hidden brook. The name of it was Rosita McMullen; and she was the daughter of old man McMullen of the Sundown Sheep Ranch.

There came riding on red roan steeds—or, to be more explicit, on a paint and a flea-bitten sorrel—two wooers. One was Madison Lane, and the other was the Frio Kid. But at that time they did not call him the Frio Kid, for he had not earned the honours of special nomenclature. His name was simply Johnny McRoy.

It must not be supposed that these two were the sum of the agreeable Rosita's admirers. The bronchos of a dozen others champed their bits at the long hitching rack of the Sundown Ranch. Many were the sheeps'-eyes that were cast in those savannas that did not belong to the flocks of Dan McMullen. But of all the cavaliers, Madison Lane and Johnny McRoy galloped far ahead, wherefore they are to be chronicled.

Madison Lane, a young cattleman from the Nueces country, won the race. He and Rosita were married one Christmas day. Armed, hilarious, vociferous, magnanimous, the cowmen and the sheepmen, laying aside their hereditary hatred, joined forces to celebrate the occasion.

Sundown Ranch was sonorous with the cracking of jokes and six-shooters, the shine of buckles and bright eyes, the outspoken congratulations of the herders of kine.

But while the wedding feast was at its liveliest there descended upon it Johnny McRoy, bitten by jealousy, like one possessed.

"I'll give you a Christmas present," he yelled, shrilly, at the door, with his .45 in his hand. Even then he had some reputation as an offhand shot.

His first bullet cut a neat underbit in Madison Lane's right ear. The barrel of his gun moved an inch. The next shot would have been the bride's had not Carson, a sheepman, possessed a mind with triggers somewhat well oiled and in repair. The guns of the wedding party had been hung, in their belts, upon nails in the wall when they sat at table, as a concession to good taste. But Carson, with great promptness, hurled his plate of roast venison and frijoles at McRoy, spoiling his aim. The second bullet, then, only shattered the white petals of a Spanish dagger flower suspended two feet above Rosita's head.

The guests spurned their chairs and jumped for their weapons. It was considered an improper act to shoot the bride and groom at a wedding. In about six seconds there were twenty or so bullets due to be whizzing in the direction of Mr. McRoy.

"I'll shoot better next time," yelled Johnny; "and there'll be a next time." He backed rapidly out the door.

Carson, the sheepman, spurred on to attempt further exploits by the success of his plate-throwing, was first to reach the door. McRoy's bullet from the darkness laid him low.

The cattlemen then swept out upon him, calling for vengeance, for, while the slaughter of a sheepman has not always lacked condonement, it was a decided misdemeanour in this instance. Carson was innocent; he was no accomplice at the matrimonial proceedings; nor had any one heard him quote the line "Christmas comes but once a year" to the guests.

But the sortie failed in its vengeance. McRoy was on his horse and away, shouting back curses and threats as he galloped into the concealing chaparral.

That night was the birthnight of the Frio Kid. He became the "bad man" of that portion of the State. The rejection of his suit by Miss McMullen turned him to a dangerous man. When officers went after him for the shooting of Carson, he killed two of them, and entered upon the life of an outlaw. He became a marvellous shot with either hand. He would turn up in towns and settlements, raise a quarrel at the slightest opportunity, pick off his man and laugh at the officers of the law. He was so cool, so deadly, so rapid, so inhumanly blood-thirsty that none but faint attempts were ever made to capture him. When he was at last shot and killed by a little one-armed Mexican who was nearly dead himself from fright, the Frio Kid had the deaths of eighteen men on his head. About half of these were killed in fair duels depending upon the quickness of the draw. The other half were men whom he assassinated from absolute wantonness and cruelty.

Many tales are told along the border of his impudent courage and daring. But he was not one of the breed of desperadoes who have seasons of generosity and even of softness. They say he never had mercy on the object of his anger. Yet at this and every Christmastide it is well to give each one credit, if it can be done, for whatever speck of good he may have possessed. If the Frio Kid ever did a kindly act or felt a throb of generosity in his heart it was once at such a time and season, and this is the way it happened.

One who has been crossed in love should never breathe the odour from the blossoms of the ratama tree. It stirs the memory to a dangerous degree.

One December in the Frio country there was a ratama tree in full bloom, for the winter had been as warm as springtime. That way rode the Frio Kid and his satellite and co-murderer, Mexican Frank. The kid reined in his mustang, and sat in his saddle, thoughtful and grim, with dangerously narrowing eyes. The rich, sweet scent touched him somewhere beneath his ice and iron.

"I don't know what I've been thinking about, Mex," he remarked in his usual mild drawl, "to have forgot all about a Christmas present I got to give. I'm going to ride over to-morrow night and shoot Madison Lane in his own house. He got my girl—Rosita would have had me if he hadn't cut into the game. I wonder why I happened to overlook it up to now?"

"Aw, shucks, Kid," said Mexican, "don't talk foolishness. You know you can't get within a mile of Mad Lane's house to-morrow night. I see old man Allen day before yesterday, and he says Mad is going to have Christmas doings at his house. You remember how you shot up the festivities when Mad was married, and about the threats you made? Don't you suppose Mad Lane'll kind of keep his eye open for a certain Mr. Kid? You plumb make me tired, Kid, with such remarks."

"I'm going," repeated the Frio Kid, without heat, "to go to Madison Lane's Christmas doings, and kill him. I ought to have done it a long time ago. Why, Mex, just two weeks ago I dreamed me and Rosita was married instead of her and him; and we was living in a house, and I could see her smiling at me, and—oh! h——l, Mex, he got her; and I'll get him—yes, sir, on

Christmas Eve he got her, and then's when I'll get him."

"There's other ways of committing suicide," advised Mexican. "Why don't you go and surrender to the sheriff?"

"I'll get him," said the Kid.

Christmas Eve fell as balmy as April. Perhaps there was a hint of faraway frostiness in the air, but it tingled like seltzer, perfumed faintly with late prairie blossoms and the mesquite grass.

When night came the five or six rooms of the ranch-house were brightly lit. In one room was a Christmas tree, for the Lanes had a boy of three, and a dozen or more guests were expected from the nearer ranches.

At nightfall Madison Lane called aside Jim Belcher and three other cowboys employed on his ranch.

"Now, boys," said Lane, "keep your eyes open. Walk around the house and watch the road well. All of you know the 'Frio Kid,' as they call him now, and if you see him, open fire on him without asking any questions. I'm not afraid of his coming around, but Rosita is. She's been afraid he'd come in on us every Christmas since we were married."

The guests had arrived in buckboards and on horseback, and were making themselves comfortable inside.

The evening went along pleasantly. The guests enjoyed and praised Rosita's excellent supper, and afterward the men scattered in groups about the rooms or on the broad "gallery," smoking and chatting.

The Christmas tree, of course, delighted the youngsters, and above all were they pleased when Santa Claus himself in magnificent white beard and furs appeared and began to distribute the toys.

"It's my papa," announced Billy Sampson, aged six. "I've seen him wear 'em before."

Berkly, a sheepman, an old friend of Lane, stopped Rosita as she was passing by him on the gallery, where he was sitting smoking.

"Well, Mrs. Lane," said he, "I suppose by this Christmas you've gotten over being afraid of

that fellow McRoy, haven't you? Madison and I have talked about it, you know."

"Very nearly," said Rosita, smiling, "but I am still nervous sometimes. I shall never forget that awful time when he came so near to killing us."

"He's the most cold-hearted villain in the world," said Berkly. "The citizens all along the border ought to turn out and hunt him down like a wolf."

"He has committed awful crimes," said Rosita, "but—I—don't—know. I think there is a spot of good somewhere in everybody. He was not always bad—that I know."

Rosita turned into the hallway between the rooms. Santa Claus, in muffling whiskers and furs, was just coming through.

"I heard what you said through the window, Mrs. Lane," he said. "I was just going down in my pocket for a Christmas present for your husband. But I've left one for you, instead. It's in the room to your right."

"Oh, thank you, kind Santa Claus," said Rosita, brightly.

Rosita went into the room, while Santa Claus stepped into the cooler air of the yard.

She found no one in the room but Madison.

"Where is my present that Santa said he left for me in here?" she asked.

"Haven't seen anything in the way of a present," said her husband, laughing, "unless he could have meant me."

The next day Gabriel Radd, the foreman of the X O Ranch, dropped into the post-office at Loma Alta.

"Well, the Frio Kid's got his dose of lead at last," he remarked to the postmaster.

"That so? How'd it happen?"

"One of old Sanchez's Mexican sheep herders did it!—think of it! the Frio Kid killed by a sheep herder! The Greaser saw him riding along past his camp about twelve o'clock last night, and was so skeered that he up with a Winchester and let him have it. Funniest part of it was that the Kid was dressed all up with white Angora-skin whiskers and a regular Santy Claus rig-out from head to foot. Think of the Frio Kid playing Santy!"

THE CHOPHAM AFFAIR

Edgar Wallace

IT HAS BEEN REPORTED FREQUENTLY — and it may even be true—that, during the height of his popularity in the 1920s, Edgar Wallace, the most successful thriller writer who ever lived, was the author of one of every four books sold in England. He self-published his first mystery, *The Four Just Men*, in 1905. It was a financial disaster, but he went on to produce one hundred seventy-three books, seventeen plays, countless short stories, and the original scenario for the first *King Kong* motion picture. "The Chopham Affair" was first collected in the author's short story collection, *The Woman from the East* (London, Hutchinson, 1934).

The Chopham Affair

EDGAR WALLACE

LAWYERS WHO WRITE BOOKS ARE NOT, as a rule, popular with their confrères, but Archibald Lenton, the most brilliant of prosecuting attorneys, was an exception. He kept a case-book and published extracts from time to time. He has not published his theories on the Chopham affair, though I believe he formulated one. I present him with the facts of the case and the truth about Alphonse or Alphonso Riebiera.

This was a man who had a way with women, especially women who had not graduated in the more worldly school of experience. He described himself as a Spaniard, though his passport was issued by a South American republic. Sometimes he presented visiting cards which were inscribed "Le Marquis de Riebiera," but that was only on very special occasions.

He was young, with an olive complexion, faultless features, and showed his two rows of dazzling white teeth when he smiled. He found it convenient to change his appearance. For example: when he was a hired dancer attached to the personnel of an Egyptian hotel he wore little side whiskers which, oddly enough, exaggerated his youthfulness; in the casino at Enghien, where by some means he secured the position of croupier, he was decorated with a little black moustache. Staid, sober, and unimaginative spectators of his many adventures were irritably amazed that women said anything to him, but then it is notoriously difficult for any man, even

an unimaginative man, to discover attractive qualities in successful lovers.

And yet the most unlikely women came under his spell and had to regret it. There arrived a time when he became a patron of the gambling establishments where he had been the most humble and the least trusted of servants, when he lived royally in hotels where he once was hired at so many piastre per dance. Diamonds came to his spotless shirt-front, pretty manicurists tended his nails and received fees larger than his one-time dancing partners had slipped shyly into his hand.

There are certain gross men who play interminable dominoes in the cheaper cafés that abound on the unfashionable side of the Seine, who are amazing news centres. They know how the oddest people live, and they were very plain-spoken when they discussed Alphonse. They could tell you, though heaven knows how the information came to them, of fat registered letters that came to him in his flat in the Boulevard Haussman. Registered letters stuffed with money, and despairing letters that said in effect (and in various languages): "I can send you no more—this is the last." But they did send more.

Alphonse had developed a well-organized business. He would leave for London, or Rome, or Amsterdam, or Vienna, or even Athens, arriving at his destination by sleeping-car, drive to the best hotel, hire a luxurious suite—and telephone. Usually the unhappy lady met him by appointment, tearful, hysterically furious, bitter, insulting, but always remunerative.

For when Alphonse read extracts from the letters they had sent to him in the day of the Great Glamour and told them what their husbands' income was almost to a pound, lira, franc, or guelder, they reconsidered their decision to tell their husbands everything, and Alphonse went back to Paris with his allowance.

This was his method with the bigger game; sometimes he announced his coming visit with a letter discreetly worded, which made personal application unnecessary. He was not very much afraid of husbands or brothers; the philosophy which had germinated from his experience made him contemptuous of human nature. He believed that most people were cowards and lived in fear of their lives, and greater fear of their regulations. He carried two silver-plated revolvers, one in each hip-pocket. They had prettily damascened barrels and ivory handles carved in the likeness of nymphs. He bought them in Cairo from a man who smuggled cocaine from Vienna.

Alphonse had some twenty "clients" on his books, and added to them as opportunity arose. Of the twenty, five were gold mines (he thought of them as such), the remainder were silver mines.

There was a silver mine living in England, a very lovely, rather sad-looking girl, who was happily married, except when she thought of Alphonse. She loved her husband and hated herself and hated Alphonse intensely and impotently. Having a fortune of her own she could pay—therefore she paid.

Then in a fit of desperate revolt she wrote saying: "This is the last, etc." Alphonse was amused. He waited until September when the next allowance was due, and it did not come. Nor in October, nor November. In December he wrote to her; he did not wish to go to England in December, for England is very gloomy and foggy, and it was so much nicer in Egypt; but business was business.

His letter reached its address when the woman to whom it was addressed was on a visit to her aunt in Long Island. She had been born an American. Alphonse had not written in answer to her letter; she had sailed for New York feeling safe.

Her husband, whose initial was the same as his wife's, opened the letter by accident and read it through very carefully. He was no fool. He did not regard the wife he wooed as an outcast; what happened before his marriage was her business—what happened now was his.

And he understood these wild dreams of her, and her wild, uncontrollable weeping for no reason at all, and he knew what the future held for her.

He went to Paris and made enquiries: he sought the company of the gross men who play dominoes, and heard much that was interesting.

Alphonse arrived in London and telephoned from a call-box. Madam was not at home. A typewritten letter came to him, making an appointment for the Wednesday. It was the usual rendezvous, the hour specified, an injunction to secrecy. The affair ran normally.

He passed his time pleasantly in the days of waiting. Bought a new Spanza car of the latest model, arranged for its transportation to Paris and, in the meantime, amused himself by driving it.

At the appointed hour he arrived, knocked at the door of the house and was admitted. . . .

Riebiera, green of face, shaking at the knees, surrendered his two ornamented pistols without a fight. . . .

At eight o'clock on Christmas morning Superintendent Oakington was called from his warm bed by telephone and was told the news.

A milkman driving across Chopham Common had seen a car standing a little off the road. It was apparently a new car, and must have been standing in its position all night. There were three inches of snow on its roof, beneath the body of the car the bracken was green.

An arresting sight even for a milkman who, at seven o'clock on a wintry morning, had no other thought than to supply the needs of his customers as quickly as possible and return at the earliest moment to his own home and the festivities and feastings proper to the day.

He got out of the Ford he was driving and stamped through the snow. He saw a man lying face downwards, and in his grey hand a silver-barrelled revolver. He was dead. And then the startled milkman saw the second man. His face was invisible: it lay under a thick mask of snow that made his pinched features grotesque and hideous.

The milkman ran back to his car and drove toward a police-station.

Mr. Oakington was on the spot within an hour of being called. There were a dozen policemen grouped around the car and the shapes in the snow; the reporters, thank God, had not arrived.

Late in the afternoon the superintendent put a call through to one man who might help in a moment of profound bewilderment.

Archibald Lenton was the most promising of Treasury Juniors that the Bar had known for years. The Common Law Bar lifts its delicate nose at lawyers who are interested in criminal cases to the exclusion of other practice. But Archie Lenton survived the unspoken disapproval of his brethren and, concentrating on this unsavoury aspect of jurisprudence, was both a successful advocate and an authority on certain types of crime, for he had written a textbook which was accepted as authoritative.

An hour later he was in the superintendent's room at Scotland Yard, listening to the story.

"We've identified both men. One is a foreigner, a man from the Argentine, so far as I can discover from his passport, named Alphonse or Alphonso Riebiera. He lives in Paris, and has been in this country for about a week."

"Well off?"

"Very, I should say. We found about two hundred pounds in his pocket. He was staying at the Nederland Hotel, and bought a car for twelve hundred pounds only last Friday, paying cash. That is the car we found near the body. I've been

on the 'phone to Paris, and he is suspected there of being a blackmailer. The police have searched and sealed his flat, but found no documents of any kind. He is evidently the sort of man who keeps his business under his hat."

"He was shot, you say? How many times?"

"Once, through the head. The other man was killed in exactly the same way. There was a trace of blood in the car, but nothing else."

Mr. Lenton jotted down a note on a pad of paper.

"Who was the other man?" he asked.

"That's the queerest thing of all—an old acquaintance of yours."

"Mine? Who on earth——?"

"Do you remember a fellow you defended on a murder charge—Joe Stackett?"

"At Exeter, good lord, yes! Was that the man?"

"We've identified him from his fingerprints. As a matter of fact, we were after Joe—he's an expert car thief who only came out of prison last week; he got away with a car yesterday morning, but abandoned it after a chase and slipped through the fingers of the Flying Squad. Last night he pinched an old car from a second-hand dealer and was spotted and chased. We found the car abandoned in Tooting. He was never seen again until he was picked up on the Chopham Common."

Archie Lenton leant back in his chair and stared thoughtfully at the ceiling.

"He stole the Spanza—the owner jumped on the running-board and there was a fight"—he began, but the superintendent shook his head.

"Where did he get his gun? English criminals do not carry guns. And they weren't ordinary revolvers. Silver-plated, ivory butts carved with girls' figures—both identical. There were fifty pounds in Joe's pocket; they are consecutive numbers to those found in Riebiera's pocket-book. If he'd stolen them he'd have taken the lot. Joe wouldn't stop at murder, you know that, Mr. Lenton. He killed that old woman in Exeter, although he was acquitted. Riebiera must have given him the fifty——"

A telephone bell rang; the superintendent drew the instrument toward him and listened. After ten minutes of a conversation which was confined, so far as Oakington was concerned, to a dozen brief questions, he put down the receiver.

"One of my officers has traced the movements of the car; it was seen standing outside 'Greenlawns,' a house in Tooting. It was there at nine forty-five and was seen by a postman. If you feel like spending Christmas night doing a little bit of detective work, we'll go down and see the place."

They arrived half an hour later at a house in a very respectable neighbourhood. The two detectives who waited their coming had obtained the keys, but had not gone inside. The house was for sale and was standing empty. It was the property of two old maiden ladies who had placed the premises in an agent's hands when they had moved into the country.

The appearance of the car before an empty house had aroused the interest of the postman. He had seen no lights in the windows, and decided that the machine was owned by one of the guests at the next door house.

Oakington opened the door and switched on the light. Strangely enough, the old ladies had not had the current disconnected, though they were notoriously mean. The passage was bare, except for a pair of bead curtains which hung from an arched support to the ceiling.

The front room drew blank. It was in one of the back rooms on the ground floor that they found evidence of the crime. There was blood on the bare planks of the floor and in the grate a litter of ashes.

"Somebody has burnt paper—I smelt it when I came into the room," said Lenton.

He knelt before the grate and lifted a handful of fine ashes carefully.

"And these have been stirred up until there isn't an ash big enough to hold a word," he said.

He examined the blood-prints and made a careful scrutiny of the walls. The window was covered with a shutter.

"That kept the light from getting in," he said, "and the sound of the shot getting out. There is nothing else here."

The detective-sergeant who was inspecting the other rooms returned with the news that a kitchen window had been forced. There was one muddy print on the kitchen table which was under the window, and a rough attempt had been made to obliterate this. Behind the house was a large garden and behind that an allotment. It would be easy to reach and enter the house without exciting attention.

"But if Stackett was being chased by the police why should he come here?" he asked.

"His car was found abandoned not more than two hundred yards from here," explained Oakington. "He may have entered the house in the hope of finding something valuable, and have been surprised by Riebiera."

Archie Lenton laughed softly.

"I can give you a better theory than that," he said, and for the greater part of the night he wrote carefully and convincingly, reconstructing the crime, giving the most minute details.

That account is still preserved at Scotland Yard, and there are many highly placed officials who swear by it.

And yet something altogether different happened on the night of that 24th of December. . . .

The streets were greasy, the car-lines abominably so. Stackett's mean little car slithered and skidded alarmingly. He had been in a bad temper when he started out on his hungry quest; he grew sour and savage with the evening passing on with nothing to show for his discomfort.

The suburban high street was crowded too; street cars moved at a crawl, their bells clanging pathetically; street vendors had their stalls jammed end to end on either side of the thoroughfare; stalls green and red with holly wreaths and untidy bunches of mistletoe; there were butcher stalls, raucous auctioneers holding masses of raw beef and roaring their offers;

vegetable stalls; stalls piled high with plates and cups and saucers and gaudy dishes and glassware, shining in the rays of the powerful acetylene lamps. . . .

The car skidded. There was a crash and a scream. Breaking crockery has an alarming sound. . . . A yell from the stall owner; Stackett straightened his machine and darted between a tramcar and a trolley. . . .

"Hi, you!"

He twisted his wheel, almost knocked down the policeman who came to intercept him, and swung into a dark side street, his foot clamped on the accelerator. He turned to the right and the left, to the right again. Here was a long suburban road; houses monotonously alike on either side, terribly dreary brick blocks where men and women and children lived, were born, paid rent, and died. A mile further on he passed the gateway of the cemetery where they found the rest which was their supreme reward for living at all.

The police whistle had followed him for less than a quarter of a mile. He had passed a policeman running toward the sound—anyway, flatties never worried Stackett. Some of his ill humour passed in the amusement which the sight of the running copper brought.

Bringing the noisy little car to a standstill by the side of the road, he got down, and, relighting the cigarette he had so carefully extinguished, he gazed glumly at the stained and battered mudguard which was shivering and shaking under the pulsations of the engine. . . .

Through that same greasy street came a motorcyclist, muffled to the chin, his goggles dangling about his neck. He pulled up his shining wheel near the policeman on point duty and, supporting his balance with one foot in the muddy road, asked questions.

"Yes, sergeant," said the policeman. "I saw him. He went down there. As a matter of fact, I was going to pinch him for driving to the common danger, but he hopped it."

"That's Joe Stackett," nodded Sergeant Kenton of the C.I.D. "A thin-faced man with a pointed nose?"

The point-duty policeman had not seen the face behind the wind-screen, but he had seen the car, and that he described accurately.

"Stolen from Elmer's garage. At least, Elmer will say so, but he probably provided it. Dumped stuff. Which way did you say?"

The policeman indicated, and the sergeant kicked his engine to life and went chug-chugging down the dark street.

He missed Mr. Stackett by a piece of bad luck—bad luck for everybody, including Mr. Stackett, who was at the beginning of his amazing adventure.

Switching off the engine, he had continued on foot. About fifty yards away was the wide opening of a road superior in class to any he had traversed. Even the dreariest suburb has its West End, and here were villas standing on their own acres—very sedate villas, with porches and porch lamps in wrought-iron and oddly coloured glass, and shaven lawns, and rose gardens swathed in matting, and no two villas were alike. At the far end he saw a red light, and his heart leapt with joy. Christmas—it was to be Christmas after all, with good food and lashings of drink and other manifestations of happiness and comfort peculiarly attractive to Joe Stackett.

It looked like a car worth knocking off, even in the darkness. He saw somebody near the machine and stopped. It was difficult to tell in the gloom whether the person near the car had got in or had come out. He listened. There came to him neither the slam of the driver's door nor the whine of the self-starter. He came a little closer, walked boldly on, his restless eyes moving left and right for danger. All the houses were occupied. Bright lights illuminated the casement cloth which covered the windows. He heard the sound of revelry and two gramophones playing dance tunes. But his eyes always came back to the polished limousine at the door of the end house. There was no light there. It was completely dark, from the gabled attic to the ground floor.

He quickened his pace. It was a Spanza. His heart leapt at the recognition. For a Spanza is a car for which there is a ready sale. You can get as much as a hundred pounds for a new one. They are popular amongst Eurasians and wealthy Hindus. Binky Jones, who was the best car fence in London, would pay him cash, not less than sixty. In a week's time that car would be crated and on its way to India, there to be resold at a handsome profit.

The driver's door was wide open. He heard the soft purr of the engine. He slid into the driver's seat, closed the door noiselessly, and almost without as much as a whine the Spanza moved on.

It was a new one, brand new. . . . A hundred at least.

Gathering speed, he passed to the end of the road, came to a wide common and skirted it. Presently he was in another shopping street, but he knew too much to turn back toward London. He would take the open country for it, work round through Esher and come into London by the Portsmouth Road. The art of car-stealing is to move as quickly as possible from the police division where the machine is stolen and may be instantly reported, to a "foreign" division which will not know of the theft until hours after.

There might be all sorts of extra pickings. There was a big luggage trunk behind and possibly a few knick-knacks in the body of the car itself. At a suitable moment he would make a leisurely search. At the moment he headed for Epsom, turning back to hit the Kingston by-pass. Sleet fell—snow and rain together. He set the screen-wiper working and began to hum a little tune. The Kingston by-pass was deserted. It was too unpleasant a night for much traffic.

Mr. Stackett was debating what would be the best place to make his search when he felt an unpleasant draught behind him. He had noticed there was a sliding window separating the interior of the car from the driver's seat, which had possibly worked loose. He put up his hand to push it close.

"Drive on, don't turn round or I'll blow your head off!"

Involuntarily he half turned to see the gaping muzzle of an automatic, and in his agitation put his foot on the brake. The car skidded from one side of the road to the other, half turned and recovered.

"Drive on, I am telling you," said a metallic voice. "When you reach the Portsmouth Road turn and bear toward Weybridge. If you attempt to stop I will shoot you. Is that clear?"

Joe Stackett's teeth were chattering. He could not articulate the "yes." All that he could do was to nod. He went on nodding for half a mile before he realized what he was doing.

No further word came from the interior of the car until they passed the race-course; then unexpectedly the voice gave a new direction:

"Turn left toward Leatherhead."

The driver obeyed.

They came to a stretch of common. Stackett, who knew the country well, realized the complete isolation of the spot.

"Slow down, pull in to the left. . . . There is no dip there. You can switch on your lights."

The car slid and bumped over the uneven ground, the wheels crunched through beds of bracken. . . .

"Stop."

The door behind him opened. The man got out. He jerked open the driver's door.

"Step down," he said. "Turn out your lights first. Have you got a gun?"

"Gun? Why the hell should I have a gun?" stammered the car thief.

He was focused all the time in a ring of light from a very bright electric torch which the passenger had turned upon him.

"You are an act of Providence."

Stackett could not see the face of the speaker. He saw only the gun in the hand, for the stranger kept this well in the light.

"Look inside the car."

Stackett looked and almost collapsed. There was a figure huddled in one corner of the seat— the figure of a man. He saw something else—a bicycle jammed into the car, one wheel touching the roof, the other on the floor. He saw the man's white face. . . . Dead! A slim, rather short man, with dark hair and a dark moustache, a foreigner. There was a little red hole in his temple.

"Pull him out," commanded the voice sharply.

Stackett shrank back, but a powerful hand pushed him toward the car.

"Pull him out!"

With his face moist with cold perspiration, the car thief obeyed; put his hands under the armpits of the inanimate figure, dragged him out and laid him on the bracken.

"He's dead," he whimpered.

"Completely," said the other.

Suddenly he switched off his electric torch. Far away came a gleam of light on the road, coming swiftly toward them. It was a car moving towards Esher. It passed.

"I saw you coming just after I had got the body into the car. There wasn't time to get back to the house. I'd hoped you were just an ordinary pedestrian. When I saw you get into the car I guessed pretty well your vocation. What is your name?"

"Joseph Stackett."

"Stackett?"

The light flashed on his face again. "How wonderful! Do you remember the Exeter Assizes? The old woman you killed with a hammer? I defended you!"

Joe's eyes were wide open. He stared past the light at the dim grey thing that was a face.

"Mr. Lenton?" he said hoarsely. "Good God, sir!"

"You murdered her in cold blood for a few paltry shillings, and you would have been dead now, Stackett, if I hadn't found a flaw in the evidence. You expected to die, didn't you? You remember how we used to talk in Exeter Gaol about the trap that would not work when they tried to hang a murderer, and the ghoulish satisfaction you had that you would stand on the same trap?"

Joe Stackett grinned uncomfortably.

"And I meant it, sir," he said, "but you can't try a man twice——"

Then his eyes dropped to the figure at his feet, the dapper little man with a black moustache, with a red hole in his temple.

Lenton leant over the dead man, took out a pocket-case from the inside of the jacket and at his leisure detached ten notes.

"Put these in your pocket."

He obeyed, wondering what service would be required of him, wondered more why the pocket-book with its precious notes was returned to the dead man's pocket.

Lenton looked back along the road. Snow was falling now, real snow. It came down in small particles, falling so thickly that it seemed that a fog lay on the land.

"You fit into this perfectly . . . a man unfit to live. There is fate in this meeting."

"I don't know what you mean by fate."

Joe Stackett grew bold: he had to deal with a lawyer and a gentleman who, in a criminal sense, was his inferior. The money obviously had been given to him to keep his mouth shut.

"What have you been doing, Mr. Lenton? That's bad, ain't it? This fellow's dead and——"

He must have seen the pencil of flame that came from the other's hand. He could have felt nothing, for he was dead before he sprawled over the body on the ground.

Mr. Archibald Lenton examined the revolver by the light of his lamp, opened the breech and closed it again. Stooping, he laid it near the hand of the little man with the black moustache and, lifting the body of Joe Stackett, he dragged it toward the car and let it drop. Bending down, he clasped the still warm hands about the butt of another pistol. Then, at his leisure, he took the bicycle from the interior of the car and carried it back to the road. It was already white and fine snow was falling in sheets.

Mr. Lenton went on and reached his home two hours later, when the bells of the local Anglo-Catholic church were ringing musically.

There was a cable waiting for him from his wife:

A Happy Christmas to you, darling.

He was ridiculously pleased that she had remembered to send the wire—he was very fond of his wife.

A CHRISTMAS TRAGEDY

Agatha Christie

IT WILL SURPRISE NO ONE TO SAY that Agatha Christie is the most popular writer of detective fiction who ever lived (her sales in all languages are reported to have surpassed four billion copies). Her remarkably proficient first book, *The Mysterious Affair at Styles* (1920), is generally and rightfully given credit as the landmark volume that initiated what has been called the Golden Age of mystery fiction. This era, bracketed by the two World Wars, saw the rise of the fair play puzzle story and the series detective, whether an official member of the police department, a private detective, or an amateur sleuth, and it was Christie who towered above all others, outselling, outproducing, and outliving the rest. "A Christmas Tragedy" was first collected in *The Thirteen Problems* (London, Collins, 1932).

A Christmas Tragedy

AGATHA CHRISTIE

"I HAVE A COMPLAINT TO MAKE," said Sir Henry Clithering.

His eyes twinkled gently as he looked round at the assembled company. Colonel Bantry, his legs stretched out, was frowning at the mantelpiece as though it were a delinquent soldier on parade, his wife was surreptitiously glancing at a catalogue of bulbs which had come by the late post, Dr. Lloyd was gazing with frank admiration at Jane Helier, and that beautiful young actress herself was thoughtfully regarding her pink polished nails. Only that elderly spinster lady, Miss Marple, was sitting bolt upright, and her faded blue eyes met Sir Henry's with an answering twinkle.

"A complaint?" she murmured.

"A very serious complaint. We are a company of six, three representatives of each sex, and I protest on behalf of the down-trodden males. We have had three stories told tonight—and told by the three men! I protest that the ladies have not done their fair share."

"Oh!" said Mrs. Bantry with indignation. "I'm sure we have. We've listened with the most intelligent appreciation. We've displayed the true womanly attitude—not wishing to thrust ourselves into the limelight!"

"It's an excellent excuse," said Sir Henry; "but it won't do. And there's a very good precedent in the Arabian Nights! So, forward, Scheherazade."

"Meaning me?" said Mrs. Bantry. "But I don't know anything to tell. I've never been surrounded by blood or mystery."

"I don't absolutely insist upon blood," said Sir Henry. "But I'm sure one of you three ladies has got a pet mystery. Come now, Miss Marple—the 'Curious Coincidence of the Charwoman' or the 'Mystery of the Mothers' Meeting.' Don't disappoint me in St. Mary Mead."

Miss Marple shook her head.

"Nothing that would interest you, Sir Henry. We have our little mysteries, of course—there was that gill of picked shrimps that disappeared so incomprehensibly; but that wouldn't interest you because it all turned out to be so trivial, though throwing a considerable light on human nature."

"You have taught me to dote on human nature," said Sir Henry solemnly.

"What about you, Miss Helier?" asked Colonel Bantry. "You must have had some interesting experiences."

"Yes, indeed," said Dr. Lloyd.

"Me?" said Jane. "You mean—you want me to tell you something that happened to me?"

"Or to one of your friends," amended Sir Henry.

"Oh!" said Jane vaguely. "I don't think anything has ever happened to me—I mean not that kind of thing. Flowers, of course, and queer messages—but that's just men, isn't it? I don't think"—she paused and appeared lost in thought.

"I see we shall have to have that epic of the shrimps," said Sir Henry. "Now then, Miss Marple."

"You're so fond of your joke, Sir Henry. The shrimps are only nonsense; but now I come to think of it, I *do* remember one incident—at least not exactly an incident, something very much more serious—a tragedy. And I was, in a way, mixed up in it; and for what I did, I have never had any regrets—no, no regrets at all. But it didn't happen in St. Mary Mead."

"That disappoints me," said Sir Henry. "But I will endeavour to bear up. I knew we should not rely upon you in vain."

He settled himself in the attitude of a listener. Miss Marple grew slightly pink.

"I hope I shall be able to tell it properly," she said anxiously. "I fear I am very inclined to become *rambling*. One wanders from the point—altogether without knowing that one is doing so. And it is so hard to remember each fact in its proper order. You must all bear with me if I tell my story badly. It happened a very long time ago now.

"As I say it was not connected with St. Mary Mead. As a matter of fact, it had to do with a Hydro—"

"Do you mean a seaplane?" asked Jane with wide eyes.

"You wouldn't know, dear," said Mrs. Bantry, and explained. Her husband added his quota:

"Beastly places—absolutely beastly! Got to get up early and drink filthy-tasting water. Lot of old women sitting about. Ill-natured tittle tattle. God, when I think—"

"Now, Arthur," said Mrs. Bantry placidly. "You know it did you all the good in the world."

"Lot of old women sitting round talking scandal," grunted Colonel Bantry.

"That, I am afraid, is true," said Miss Marple. "I myself—"

"My dear Miss Marple," cried the colonel, horrified. "I didn't mean for one moment—"

With pink cheeks and a little gesture of the hand, Miss Marple stopped him.

"But it is *true*, Colonel Bantry. Only I should like to say this. Let me recollect my thoughts. Yes. Talking scandal, as you say—well it *is* done a good deal. And people are very down on it—especially young people. My nephew, who writes books—and very clever ones, I believe—has said some most *scathing* things about taking people's characters away without any kind of proof—and how wicked it is, and all that. But what I say is that none of these young people ever stop to *think*. They really don't examine the facts. Surely the whole crux of the matter is this. *How often is tittle tattle*, as you call it, *true*! And I think if, as I say, they really examined the facts they would find that it was true nine times out of ten! That's really just what makes people so annoyed about it."

"The inspired guess," said Sir Henry.

"No, not that, not that at all! It's really a matter of practice and experience. An Egyptologist, so I've heard, if you show him one of those curious little beetles, can tell you by the look and the feel of the thing what date BC it is, or if it's a Birmingham imitation. And he can't always give a definite rule for doing so. He just *knows*. His life has been spent handling such things.

"And that's what I'm trying to say (very badly, I know). What my nephew calls 'superfluous women' have a lot of time on their hands, and their chief interest is usually *people*. And so, you see, they get to be what one might call *experts*. Now young people nowadays—they talk very freely about things that weren't mentioned in my young days, but on the other hand their minds are terribly innocent. They believe in everyone and everything. And if one tries to warn them, ever so gently, they tell one that one has a Victorian mind—and that, they say, is like a *sink*."

"After all," said Sir Henry, "what is wrong with a *sink*?"

"Exactly," said Miss Marple eagerly. "It's the most necessary thing in any house; but, of course, not romantic. Now I must confess that I have my *feelings*, like everyone else, and I have sometimes been cruelly hurt by unthinking remarks. I know gentlemen are not interested in domestic matters, but I must just mention my maid Ethel—a very good-looking girl and obliging in every way. Now I realized as soon as I saw her that she was the same type as Annie Webb and poor Mrs. Bruitt's girl. If the opportunity arose *mine and thine* would mean nothing to her. So I let her go at the month and I gave her a written reference saying she was honest and sober, but privately I warned old Mrs. Edwards against taking her; and my nephew, Raymond, was exceedingly angry and said he had never heard of anything so wicked—yes, *wicked*. Well, she went to Lady Ashton, whom I felt no obligation to warn—and what happened? All the lace cut off her underclothes and two diamond brooches taken—and the girl departed in the middle of the night and never heard of since!"

Miss Marple paused, drew a long breath, and then went on.

"You'll be saying this has nothing to do with what went on at Keston Spa Hydro—but it has in a way. It explains why I felt no doubt in my mind the first moment I saw the Sanders together that he meant to do away with her."

"Eh?" said Sir Henry, leaning forward.

Miss Marple turned a placid face to him.

"As I say, Sir Henry, I felt no doubt in my own mind. Mr. Sanders was a big, good-looking, florid-faced man, very hearty in his manner and popular with all. And nobody could have been pleasanter to his wife than he was. But I knew! He meant to make away with her."

"My dear Miss Marple—"

"Yes, I know. That's what my nephew Raymond West, would say. He'd tell me I hadn't a shadow of proof. But I remember Walter Hones, who kept the Green Man. Walking home with his wife one night she fell into the river—and *he* collected the insurance money! And one or two other people that are walking about scot free to this day—one indeed in our own class of life. Went to Switzerland for a summer holiday climbing with his wife. I warned her not to go—the poor dear didn't get angry with me as she might have done—she only laughed. It seemed to her funny that a queer old thing like me

should say such things about her Harry. Well, well, there was an accident—and Harry is married to another woman now. But what could I *do?* I *knew,* but there was no proof."

"Oh! Miss Marple," cried Mrs. Bantry. "You don't really mean—"

"My dear, these things are very common—very common indeed. And gentlemen are especially tempted, being so much the stronger. So easy if a thing looks like an accident. As I say, I knew at once with the Sanders. It was on a tram. It was full inside and I had had to go on top. We all three got up to get off and Mr. Sanders lost his balance and fell right against his wife, sending her headfirst down the stairs. Fortunately the conductor was a very strong young man and caught her."

"But surely that must have been an accident."

"Of course it was an accident—nothing could have looked more accidental. But Mr. Sanders had been in the Merchant Service, so he told me, and a man who can keep his balance on a nasty tilting boat doesn't lose it on top of a tram if an old woman like me doesn't. Don't tell me!"

"At any rate we can take it that you made up your mind, Miss Marple," said Sir Henry. "Made it up then and there."

The old lady nodded.

"I was sure enough, and another incident in crossing the street not long afterwards made me surer still. Now I ask you, what could I do, Sir Henry? Here was a nice contented happy little married woman shortly going to be murdered."

"My dear lady, you take my breath away."

"That's because, like most people nowadays, you won't face facts. You prefer to think such a thing couldn't be. But it was so, and I knew it. But one is so sadly handicapped! I couldn't, for instance, go to the police. And to warn the young woman would, I could see, be useless. She was devoted to the man. I just made it my business to find out as much as I could about them. One has a lot of opportunities doing one's needlework round the fire. Mrs. Sanders (Gladys, her name was) was only too willing to talk. It seems they had not been married very long. Her husband had some property that was coming to him, but for the moment they were very badly off. In fact, they were living on her little income. One has heard that tale before. She bemoaned the fact that she could not touch the capital. It seems that somebody had had some sense somewhere! But the money was hers to will away—I found that out. And she and her husband had made wills in favour of each other directly after their marriage. Very touching. Of course, when Jack's affairs came right—That was the burden all day long, and in the meantime they were very hard up indeed—actually had a room on the top floor, all among the servants—and so dangerous in case of fire, though, as it happened, there was a fire escape just outside their window. I inquired carefully if there was a balcony—dangerous things, balconies. One push—you know!

"I made her promise not to go out on the balcony; I said I'd had a dream. That impressed her—one can do a lot with superstition sometimes. She was a fair girl, rather washed-out complexion, and an untidy roll of hair on her neck. Very credulous. She repeated what I had said to her husband, and I noticed him looking at me in a curious way once or twice. *He* wasn't credulous; and he knew I'd been on that tram.

"But I was very worried—terribly worried—because I couldn't see how to circumvent him. I could prevent anything happening at the Hydro, just by saying a few words to show him I suspected. But that only meant his putting off his plan till later. No, I began to believe that the only policy was a bold one—somehow or other to lay a trap for him. If I could induce him to attempt her life in a way of my own choosing—well, then he would be unmasked, and she would be forced to face the truth however much of a shock it was to her."

"You take my breath away," said Dr. Lloyd. "What conceivable plan could you adopt?"

"I'd have found one—never fear," said Miss Marple. "But the man was too clever for me. He didn't wait. He thought I might suspect, and

so he struck before I could be sure. He knew I would suspect an accident. So he made it murder."

A little gasp went round the circle. Miss Marple nodded and set her lips grimly together.

"I'm afraid I've put that rather abruptly. I must try and tell you exactly what occurred. I've always felt very bitterly about it—it seems to me that I ought, somehow, to have prevented it. But doubtless Providence knew best. I did what I could at all events.

"There was what I can only describe as a curiously eerie feeling in the air. There seemed to be something weighing on us all. A feeling of misfortune. To begin with, there was George, the hall porter. Had been there for years and knew everybody. Bronchitis and pneumonia, and passed away on the fourth day. Terribly sad. A real blow to everybody. And four days before Christmas too. And then one of the housemaids—such a nice girl—a septic finger, actually died in twenty-four hours.

"I was in the drawing room with Miss Trollope and old Mrs. Carpenter, and Mrs. Carpenter was being positively ghoulish—relishing it all, you know.

"'Mark my words,' she said. '*This isn't the end.* You know the saying? *Never two without three.* I've proved it true time and again. There'll be another death. Not a doubt of it. And we shan't have long to wait. *Never two without three.*'

"As she said the last words, nodding her head and clicking her knitting needles, I just chanced to look up and there was Mr. Sanders standing in the doorway. Just for a minute he was off guard, and I saw the look in his face as plain as plain. I shall believe till my dying day that it was that ghoulish Mrs. Carpenter's words that put the whole thing into his head. I saw his mind working.

"He came forward into the room smiling in his genial way.

"'Any Christmas shopping I can do for you ladies?' he asked. 'I'm going down to Keston presently.'

"He stayed a minute or two, laughing and

talking, and then went out. As I tell you I was troubled, and I said straight away:

"'Where's Mrs. Sanders? Does anyone know?'

"Mrs. Trollope said she'd gone out to some friends of hers, the Mortimers, to play Bridge, and that eased my mind for the moment. But I was still very worried and most uncertain as to what to do. About half an hour later I went up to my room. I met Dr. Coles, my doctor, there, coming down the stairs as I was going up, and as I happened to want to consult him about my rheumatism, I took him into my room with me then and there. He mentioned to me then (in confidence, he said) about the death of the poor girl Mary. The manager didn't want the news to get about, he said, so would I keep it to myself. Of course I didn't tell him that we'd all been discussing nothing else for the last hour—ever since the poor girl breathed her last. These things are always known at once, and a man of his experience should know that well enough; but Dr. Coles always was a simple unsuspicious fellow who believed what he wanted to believe and that's just what alarmed me a minute later. He said as he was leaving that Sanders had asked him to have a look at his wife. It seemed she'd been seedy of late—indigestion, etc.

"Now that very self-same day Gladys Sanders had said to me that she'd got a wonderful digestion and was thankful for it.

"You see? All my suspicions of that man came back a hundredfold. He was preparing the way—for what? Dr. Coles left before I could make up my mind whether to speak to him or not—though really if I had spoken I shouldn't have known what to say. As I came out of my room, the man himself—Sanders—came down the stairs from the floor above. He was dressed to go out and he asked me again if he could do anything for me in town. It was all I could do to be civil to the man! I went straight into the lounge and ordered tea. It was just on half-past five, I remember.

"Now I'm very anxious to put clearly what happened next. I was still in the lounge at a quarter to seven when Mr. Sanders came in. There were two gentlemen with him and all three of them were inclined to be a little on the lively side. Mr. Sanders left his two friends and came right over to where I was sitting with Miss Trollope. He explained that he wanted our advice about a Christmas present he was giving his wife. It was an evening bag.

"'And you see, ladies,' he said. 'I'm only a rough sailor-man. What do I know about such things? I've had three sent to me on approval and I want an expert opinion on them.'

"We said, of course, that we would be delighted to help him, and he asked if we'd mind coming upstairs, as his wife might come in any minute if he brought the things down. So we went up with him. I shall never forget what happened next—I can feel my little fingers tingling now.

"Mr. Sanders opened the door of the bedroom and switched on the light. I don't know which of us saw it first . . .

"Mrs. Sanders was lying on the floor, face downwards—dead.

"I got to her first. I knelt down and took her hand and felt for the pulse, but it was useless, the arm itself was cold and stiff. Just by her head was a stocking filled with sand—the weapon she had been struck down with. Miss Trollope, silly creature, was moaning and moaning by the door and holding her head. Sanders gave a great cry of 'My wife, my wife,' and rushed to her. I stopped him touching her. You see, I was sure at the moment that he had done it, and there might have been something that he wanted to take away or hide.

"'Nothing must be touched,' I said. 'Pull yourself together, Mr. Sanders. Miss Trollope, please go down and fetch the manager.'

"I stayed there, kneeling by the body. I wasn't going to leave Sanders alone with it. And yet I was forced to admit that if the man was acting, he was acting marvellously. He looked dazed and bewildered and scared out of his wits.

"The manager was with us in no time. He made a quick inspection of the room then turned us all out and locked the door, the key of which he took. Then he went off and telephoned to the police. It seemed a positive age before they came (we learnt afterwards that the line was out of order). The manager had to send a messenger to the police station, and the Hydro is right out of the town, up on the edge of the moor; and Mrs. Carpenter tried us all very severely. She was so pleased at her prophecy of 'Never two without three' coming true so quickly. Sanders, I hear, wandered out into the grounds, clutching his head and groaning and displaying every sign of grief.

"However, the police came at last. They went upstairs with the manager and Mr. Sanders. Later, they sent down for me. I went up. The inspector was there, sitting at a table writing. He was an intelligent-looking man and I liked him.

"'Miss Jane Marple?' he said.

"'Yes.'

"'I understand, Madam, that you were present when the body of the deceased was found?'

"I said I was and I described exactly what had occurred. I think it was a relief to the poor man to find someone who could answer his questions coherently, having previously had to deal with Sanders and Emily Trollope, who, I gather, was completely demoralized—she would be, the silly creature! I remember my dear mother teaching me that a gentlewoman should always be able to control herself in public, however much she may give way in private."

"An admirable maxim," said Sir Henry gravely.

"When I had finished the inspector said:

"'Thank you, Madam. Now I'm afraid I must ask you just to look at the body once more. Is that exactly the position in which it was lying when you entered the room? It hasn't been moved in any way?'

"I explained that I had prevented Mr. Sanders from doing so, and the inspector nodded approval.

"'The gentleman seems terribly upset,' he remarked.

"'He seems so—yes,' I replied.

"I don't think I put any special emphasis on the 'seems,' but the inspector looked at me rather keenly.

"'So we can take it that the body is exactly as it was when found?' he said.

"'Except for the hat, yes,' I replied.

"The inspector looked up sharply.

"'What do you mean—the hat?'

"I explained that the hat had been on poor Gladys's head, whereas now it was lying beside her. I thought, of course, that the police had done this. The inspector, however, denied it emphatically. Nothing had, as yet, been moved or touched. He stood looking down at that poor prone figure with a puzzled frown. Gladys was dressed in her outdoor clothes—a big dark-red tweed coat with a grey fur collar. The hat, a cheap affair of red felt, lay just by her head.

"The inspector stood for some minutes in silence, frowning to himself. Then an idea struck him.

"'Can you, by any chance, remember, Madam, whether there were ear-rings in the ears, or whether the deceased habitually wore ear-rings?'

"Now fortunately I am in the habit of observing closely. I remembered that there had been a glint of pearls just below the hat brim, though I had paid no particular notice to it at the time. I was able to answer his first question in the affirmative.

"'Then that settles it. The lady's jewel case was rifled—not that she had anything much of value, I understand—and the rings were taken from her fingers. The murderer must have forgotten the ear-rings, and come back for them after the murder was discovered. A cool customer! Or perhaps—' He stared round the room and said slowly. 'He may have been concealed here in this room—all the time.'

"But I negatived that idea. I myself, I explained, had looked under the bed. And the manager had opened the doors of the wardrobe. There was nowhere else where a man could hide. It is true the hat cupboard was locked in the middle of the wardrobe, but as that was only a shallow affair with shelves, no one could have been concealed there.

"The inspector nodded his head slowly whilst I explained all this.

"'I'll take your word for it, Madam,' he said. 'In that case, as I said before, he must have come back. A very cool customer.'

"'But the manager locked the door and took the key!'

"'That's nothing. The balcony and the fire escape—that's the way the thief came. Why, as likely as not, you actually disturbed him at work. He slips out of the window, and when you've all gone, back he comes and goes on with his business.'

"'You are sure,' I said, 'that there *was* a thief?'

"He said dryly:

"'Well, it looks like it, doesn't it?'

"But something in his tone satisfied me. I felt that he wouldn't take Mr. Sanders in the rôle of the bereaved widower too seriously.

"You see, I admit it frankly, I was absolutely under the opinion of what I believe our neighbours, the French, call the *idée fixe*. I knew that that man, Sanders, intended his wife to die. What I didn't allow for was that strange and fantastic thing, coincidence. My views about Mr. Sanders were—I was sure of it—absolutely right and *true*. The man was a scoundrel. But although his hypocritical assumptions of grief didn't deceive me for a minute, I do remember feeling at the time that his *surprise* and *bewilderment* were marvellously well done. They seemed absolutely *natural*—if you know what I mean. I must admit that after my conversation with the inspector, a curious feeling of doubt crept over me. Because if Sanders had done this dreadful thing, I couldn't imagine any conceivable reason why he should creep back by means of the fire escape and take the ear-rings from his wife's ears. It wouldn't have been a *sensible* thing to do, and Sanders was such a very sensible man—that's just why I always felt he was so dangerous."

Miss Marple looked round at her audience.

"You see, perhaps, what I am coming to? It is, so often, the unexpected that happens in this world. I was so *sure,* and that, I think, was what blinded me. The result came as a shock to me. *For it was proved, beyond any possible doubt, that Mr. Sanders could not possibly have committed the crime . . .*"

A surprised gasp came from Mrs. Bantry. Miss Marple turned to her.

"I know, my dear, that isn't what you expected when I began this story. It wasn't what I expected either. But facts are facts, and if one is proved to be wrong, one must just be humble about it and start again. That Mr. Sanders was a murderer at heart I knew—and nothing ever occurred to upset that firm conviction of mine.

"And now, I expect, you would like to hear the actual facts themselves. Mrs. Sanders, as you know, spent the afternoon playing bridge with some friends, the Mortimers. She left them at about a quarter past six. From her friends' house to the Hydro was about a quarter of an hour's walk—less if one hurried. She must have come in then, about six-thirty. No one saw her come in, so she must have entered by the side door and hurried straight up to her room. There she changed (the fawn coat and skirt she wore to the bridge party were hanging up in the cupboard) and was evidently preparing to go out again, when the blow fell. Quite possibly, they say, she never even knew who struck her. The sandbag, I understand, is a very efficient weapon. That looks as though the attackers were concealed in the room, possibly in one of the big wardrobe cupboards—the one she didn't open.

"Now as to the movements of Mr. Sanders. He went out, as I have said, at about five-thirty—or a little after. He did some shopping at a couple of shops and at about six o'clock he entered the Grand Spa Hotel where he encountered two friends—the same with whom he returned to the Hydro later. They played billiards and, I gather, had a good many whiskies and sodas together. These two men (Hitchcock and Spender, their names were) were actually with him the whole time from six o'clock onwards. They walked back to the Hydro with him and he only left them to come across to me and Miss Trollope. That, as I told you, was about a quarter to seven—at which time his wife must have been already dead.

"I must tell you that I talked myself to these two friends of his. I did not like them. They were neither pleasant nor gentlemanly men, but I was quite certain of one thing, that they were speaking the absolute truth when they said that Sanders had been the whole time in their company.

"There was just one other little point that came up. It seems that while bridge was going on Mrs. Sanders was called to the telephone. A Mr. Littleworth wanted to speak to her. She seemed both excited and pleased about something—and incidentally made one or two bad mistakes. She left rather earlier than they had expected her to do.

"Mr. Sanders was asked whether he knew the name of Littleworth as being one of his wife's friends, but he declared he had never heard of anyone of that name. And to me that seems borne out by his wife's attitude—she too, did not seem to know the name of Littleworth. Nevertheless she came back from the telephone smiling and blushing, so it looks as though whoever it was did not give his real name, and that in itself has a suspicious aspect, does it not?

"Anyway, that is the problem that was left. The burglar story, which seems unlikely—or the alternative theory that Mrs. Sanders was preparing to go out and meet somebody. Did that somebody come to her room by means of the fire escape? Was there a quarrel? Or did he treacherously attack her?"

Miss Marple stopped.

"Well?" said Sir Henry. "What is the answer?"

"I wondered if any of you could guess."

"I'm never good at guessing," said Mrs. Bantry. "It seems a pity that Sanders had such a wonderful alibi; but if it satisfied you it must have been all right."

Jane Helier moved her beautiful head and asked a question.

"Why," she said, "was the hat cupboard locked?"

"How very clever of you, my dear," said Miss Marple, beaming. "That's just what I wondered myself. Though the explanation was quite simple. In it were a pair of embroidered slippers and some pocket handkerchiefs that the poor girl was embroidering for her husband for Christmas. That's why she locked the cupboard. The key was found in her handbag."

"Oh!" said Jane. "Then it isn't very interesting after all."

"Oh! but it is," said Miss Marple. "It's just the one really interesting thing—the thing that made all the murderer's plans go wrong."

Everyone stared at the old lady.

"I didn't see it myself for two days," said Miss Marple. "I puzzled and puzzled—and then suddenly there it was, all clear. I went to the inspector and asked him to try something and he did."

"What did you ask him to try?"

"*I asked him to fit that hat on the poor girl's head*—and of course he couldn't. It wouldn't go on. *It wasn't her hat, you see.*"

Mrs. Bantry stared.

"But it was on her head to begin with?"

"Not on *her* head—"

Miss Marple stopped a moment to let her words sink in, and then went on.

"We took it for granted that it was poor Gladys's body there; but we never looked at the face. She was face downwards, remember, and the hat hid everything."

"But she *was* killed?"

"Yes, later. At the moment that we were telephoning to the police, Gladys Sanders was alive and well."

"You mean it was someone pretending to be her? But surely when you touched her—"

"It was a dead body, right enough," said Miss Marple gravely.

"But, dash it all," said Colonel Bantry, "you can't get hold of dead bodies right and left. What did they do with the—the first corpse afterwards?"

"He put it back," said Miss Marple. "It was a wicked idea—but a very clever one. It was our talk in the drawing room that put it into his head. The body of poor Mary, the housemaid—why not use it? Remember, the Sanders' room was up amongst the servants' quarters. Mary's room was two doors off. The undertakers wouldn't come till after dark—he counted on that. He carried the body along the balcony (it was dark at five), dressed it in one of his wife's dresses and her big red coat. And then he found the hat cupboard locked! There was only one thing to be done, he fetched one of the poor girl's own hats. No one would notice. He put the sandbag down beside her. Then he went off to establish his alibi.

"He telephoned to his wife—calling himself Mr. Littleworth. I don't know what he said to her—she was a credulous girl, as I said just now. But he got her to leave the bridge party early and not to go back to the Hydro, and arranged with her to meet him in the grounds of the Hydro near the fire escape at seven o'clock. He probably told her he had some surprise for her.

"He returns to the Hydro with his friends and arranges that Miss Trollope and I shall discover the crime with him. He even pretends to turn the body over—and I stop him! Then the police are sent for, and he staggers out into the grounds.

"Nobody asked him for an alibi *after* the crime. He meets his wife, takes her up the fire escape, they enter their room. Perhaps he has already told her some story about the body. She stoops over it, and he picks up his sandbag and strikes . . . Oh, dear! it makes me sick to think of, even now! Then quickly he strips off her coat and skirt, hangs them up, and dresses her in the clothes from the other body.

"*But the hat won't go on*. Mary's head is shingled—Gladys Sanders, as I say, had a great bun of hair. He is forced to leave it beside the body and hope no one will notice. Then he carries poor Mary's body back to her own room and arranges it decorously once more."

"It seems incredible," said Dr. Lloyd. "The risks he took. The police might have arrived too soon."

"You remember the line was out of order," said Miss Marple. "That was a piece of *his* work. He couldn't afford to have the police on the spot too soon. When they did come, they spent some time in the manager's office before going up to the bedroom. That was the weakest point—the chance that someone might notice the difference between a body that had been dead two hours and one that had been dead just over half an hour; but he counted on the fact that the people who first discovered the crime would have no expert knowledge."

Dr. Lloyd nodded.

"The crime would be supposed to have been committed about a quarter to seven or thereabouts, I suppose," he said. "It was actually committed at seven or a few minutes later. When the police surgeon examined the body it would be about half-past seven at earliest. He couldn't possibly tell."

"I am the person who should have known," said Miss Marple. "I felt the poor girl's hand and it was icy cold. Yet a short time later the inspector spoke as though the murder must have been committed just before we arrived—and I saw nothing!"

"I think you saw a good deal, Miss Marple," said Sir Henry. "The case was before my time. I don't even remember hearing of it. What happened?"

"Sanders was hanged," said Miss Marple crisply. "And a good job too. I have never regretted my part in bringing that man to justice. I've no patience with modern humanitarian scruples about capital punishment."

Her stern face softened.

"But I have often reproached myself bitterly with failing to save the life of that poor girl. But who would have listened to an old woman jumping to conclusions? Well, well—who knows? Perhaps it was better for her to die while life was still happy than it would have been for her to live on, unhappy and disillusioned, in a world that would have seemed suddenly horrible. She loved that scoundrel and trusted him. She never found him out."

"Well, then," said Jane Helier, "she was all right. Quite all right. I wish—" she stopped.

Miss Marple looked at the famous, the beautiful, the successful Jane Helier and nodded her head gently.

"I see, my dear," she said very gently. "I see."

Permissions Acknowledgments

THE BLACK LIZARD BIG BOOK OF PULPS
The Best Crime Stories from the Pulps During Their Golden Age—
The '20s, '30s, & '40s

Weighing in at over a thousand pages, containing more than fifty stories and two novels, this book is big, baby, bigger and more powerful than a freight train—a bullet couldn't pass through it. Here are the best stories and every major writer who ever appeared in celebrated pulps like *Black Mask, Dime Detective, Detective Fiction Weekly*, and more. These are the classic tales that created the genre and gave birth to hard-hitting detectives who smoke criminals like cheap cigars; sultry dames whose looks are as lethal as a dagger to the chest; and gin-soaked hideouts where conversations are just preludes to murder. This is crime fiction at its gritty best.

Crime Fiction

THE BLACK LIZARD BIG BOOK OF
BLACK MASK STORIES

The Greatest Crime Fiction from
the Legendary Magazine

An unstoppable anthology of crime stories culled from *Black Mask*, the magazine where the first hard-boiled detective story, which was written by Carroll John Daly, appeared. It was the slum in which Dashiell Hammett, Raymond Chandler, Horace McCoy, Cornell Woolrich, and John D. MacDonald all got their start. It was the home of stories with titles like "Murder *Is* Bad Luck," "Ten Carats of Lead," "Diamonds Mean Death," and "Drop Dead Twice." Also here is *The Maltese Falcon* as it originally appeared in the magazine. Crime writing gets no better than this.

Crime Fiction

THE BIG BOOK OF ADVENTURE STORIES

The Most Daring, Dangerous, and Death-Defying Collection of Adventure Tales
Ever Captured in One Mammoth Volume

Everyone loves adventure, and Otto Penzler has collected the best adventure stories of all time into one awe-inspiring volume. With stories by Jack London, O. Henry, H. Rider Haggard, Alistair MacLean, Talbot Mundy, Cornell Woolrich, and many others, this wide-reaching and fascinating volume contains some of the best characters from the most thrilling adventure tales, including The Cisco Kid; Sheena, Queen of the Jungle; Bulldog Drummond; Tarzan; The Scarlet Pimpernel; Conan the Barbarian; Hopalong Cassidy; King Kong; Zorro; and The Spider. Divided into sections that embody the greatest themes of the genre—Sword & Sorcery; Megalomania Rules; Man vs. Nature; Island Paradise; Sand and Sun; Something Feels Funny; Go West, Young Man; Future Shock; I Spy; Yellow Peril; In Darkest Africa—it is destined to be the greatest collection of adventure stories ever compiled.

Fiction

THE VAMPIRE ARCHIVES

The Most Complete Volume of Vampire Tales
Ever Published

The Vampire Archives is the biggest, hungriest, undeadliest collection of vampire stories, as well as the most comprehensive bibliography of vampire fiction ever assembled.
Whether imagined by Bram Stoker or Anne Rice, vampires are part of the human lexicon
and as old as blood itself. They are your neighbors, your friends, and they are always
lurking. Now Otto Penzler has compiled the darkest, the scariest, and by far the most evil
collection of vampire stories ever. With more than eighty stories, including the works of
Stephen King and D. H. Lawrence alongside Lord Byron and Tanith Lee, not to mention
Edgar Allan Poe and Harlan Ellison, it will drive a stake through the heart of any other
collection out there.

Fiction

ZOMBIES! ZOMBIES! ZOMBIES!

The legendary editor of *The Vampire Archives* now brings us *Zombies! Zombies!
Zombies!*, an unstoppable anthology of the living dead. These superstars of horror
are everywhere, storming the world of print and visual media. Their endless march
will never be stopped. It's the Zombie Zeitgeist! Now, with his wide sweep of knowledge and keen eye for great storytelling, Otto Penzler offers a remarkable catalog of
zombie literature. From world-renowned authors like Stephen King, Joe R. Lans-
dale, Robert McCammon, Robert E. Howard, and Richard Matheson to the writer
who started it all, W. B. Seabrook, *Zombies! Zombies! Zombies!* is the darkest, the
living-deadliest, scariest, and—dare we say—tasteful collection of the wandering zombie
horde ever assembled. Its relentless pages will devour horror fans from coast to coast.

Fiction

ALSO AVAILABLE:

Agents of Treachery

The Big Book of Ghost Stories

BLOODSUCKERS: *The Vampire Archives, Volume 1*

FANGS: *The Vampire Archives, Volume 2*

COFFINS: *The Vampire Archives, Volume 3*

VINTAGE CRIME/BLACK LIZARD
Available wherever books are sold.
www.weeklylizard.com
www.vintagebooks.com